SILVIA MORENO-GARCIA

SIGNAL TO NOISE

SOLARIS

First published 2015 by Solaris
an imprint of Rebellion Publishing Ltd,
Riverside House, Osney Mead,
Oxford, OX2 0ES, UK

www.solarisbooks.com

UK ISBN: 978-1-78108-298-0
US ISBN: 978-1-78108-299-7

10 9 8 7 6 5 4 3 2 1

A CIP catalogue record for this book is available from the
British Library.

Designed & typeset by Rebellion Publishing

Printed in the US

SIGNAL TO NOISE

Mexico City, 2009

MECHE FOLDED THE magazine and finally decided to look out the window. The Federal District lay below, a great beast with no beginning and no end, towers and buildings rising and dotting the valley. The roads were twisted snakes criss-crossing its surface, the cars tiny ants racing to their anthill. Twenty million people all gathered together—smashed against each other in the subway, crammed into the buses—with the Angel of Independence saluting them from above its pedestal.

It was eighteen years since she'd seen the city. Twenty since she'd last seen her father.

Now he was dead.

He had been pickling his liver for three decades and smoking since he turned twelve, but she'd thought him immortal.

Meche rubbed the bridge of her nose.

She didn't even have a black dress. She knew her dad would have said to wear whatever the hell she wanted: dead is dead. But her mother would expect black. The whole nine days of mourning. The food they'd feed the guests. The nightly prayers.

If it had been up to Meche she would have cremated him and tossed his ashes in the Gulf of California, like he wanted. But her mother had insisted on the casket, the funeral, the prayers to follow.

She collected her bags and pulled the luggage, trying to find the familiar face among the sea of strangers.

"Meche!"

Her cousin Jimena stepped forward, giving her a big hug and

a kiss on each cheek. Jimena's hair was dyed a fake-looking red. She wore a lot more makeup than Meche remembered. Jimena's lipstick was so dark it looked purple and Meche could feel the greasy traces of it on her face.

"Girl, how was your trip?"

"Alright," Meche said, rubbing off the smudges of lipstick with her hand. "I thought my mom was picking me up."

"She's too busy. Your dad didn't make any arrangements."

"Ah."

That sounded like him. Inconsiderate until the end. He was probably chuckling from beyond the grave thinking of how, even in death, he could screw everyone over. Because that was her father.

Jimena's car was very small and there were plush toys sitting on the back seat of it. A Garfield was stuck on a window, grinning. It had been there since the 80s.

Jimena turned the key and the car sputtered into life. Meche could not see a CD player. Just the old cassette deck.

"I heard you're working with computers now," Jimena said. "Do you build them?"

Her cousin switched on the radio and ear-cringing pop music filled the car. Clearly Jimena's taste had not improved with time.

"I do software programming."

"Well, you sure had the brains for it. We were all drinking beer on the weekends and you were doing your math homework. You were such a nerd."

"I remember."

"Do you make much money? You must if you can fly your mom over to Oslo for Christmas every year."

"The benefits of being a nerd," Meche said with a shrug.

"Do you remember what you used to wear? Oh, my God. I remember that dress you had on at Tita's party."

"I remember you were hot," Meche shot back.

Jimena did not seem to catch the pointed use of the past tense and smiled, very proud of herself. "Yes. Absolutely. Hey, do you remember..."

Meche looked at the little kid juggling balls while the traffic light glowed red. The yellow and red balls flew up and down in the air.

He took a bow, then walked by the cars, cap in hand. Meche rolled down the window and gave him a bill.

Jimena frowned.

"You shouldn't do that," Jimena told her.

"What?"

"Give money to the street kids."

She shouldn't be in Mexico City either, breathing the sticky, grey air of the city and filling her lungs with pollution, but she was.

Jimena took out a pack of cigarettes, pulled one out and lit it.

Meche disliked smoke and smokers. They reminded her of her father. It had never mattered that he made his living through his voice and that cigarettes could—would—one day ruin it. He never quit. He chain-smoked and he even did it inside the radio studio, even though it was forbidden.

"Do you want one?"

"No," Meche said sternly. She rolled the window down.

It wasn't any better with the window rolled down, but it was a symbolic gesture. She pulled out her music player and picked a playlist, pressing the earbuds into place.

"I'm going to close my eyes," she told Jimena.

She did and pumped the volume up, listening to Nina Simone. Don't Let Me Be Misunderstood. The Animals covered it and Santa Esmeralda made it famous, but Nina sang it like it was nobody's business. Powerful blues and a voice that just punched you in the gut.

She let Nina sing to her, watching the city fly by. The old neighbourhood began revealing itself. Buildings had come down. The pharmacy had been replaced by condos. The bakery was gone, in its place a bank. The park seemed intact, still shitty and desolate, with its concrete benches and its sad trees. The teenagers used to make out there, by the bushes, but not Meche.

The cantina remained and she turned her head to stare at the men standing by the entrance, almost expecting her father to be there, waving back to her after drinking a dozen *reposados*.

Jimena touched her shoulder and Meche took out the earbuds.

"I said you'll never believe who I saw the other day."

Meche did not know and frankly did not care, but she understood she should bite her tongue and try to be congenial.

"Who?" she asked.

"Okay. Tall. Dark hair. He used to play with you when you were a kid."

"I have no idea."

"You're not even trying!"

Meche was not in the mood for trying. The drawers of her memory were shut tight, and with good reason. She had hated the neighbourhood and everyone living in it. If she'd had a can of gasoline when she was about fifteen, she would have organized the biggest bonfire and laughed like Nero while it burned.

She had promised herself nothing would drag her back to that ugly web of streets and peeling paint, stray dogs and factory workers leaning against the walls of the corner store, back to the circle of hell from which she had escaped.

"I'll give you another clue," Jimena said. "He used to draw on his shoes with markers."

Meche had grown to become a person of a certain composure. Things took place inside her head and heart, but she did not let people take a peek, preferring to show them only the smallest ripples of herself. Jimena's words, however, had the capacity to make her forget about her cool exterior and she turned her head whip-quick, staring at Jimena with wide eyes.

"Sebastian?"

"That's the one," Jimena said chuckling.

"I figured he moved."

God, she didn't want to see him again. If he was living with his mother she would probably run into him.

"He did. But his mom's been sick and he's come back; been looking over her."

"She still lives in the area?"

"Same apartment."

Three blocks from Meche. Past the *tortilleria*. Fourth floor. Blue curtains with sunflowers. Knock three times. That was the code.

"He has a fancy car. He got hot," Jimena said.

Meche laughed.

"No, really. He was such a dweeb. Who would have thought?"

He had never been ugly, but Jimena wouldn't have noticed back then. His skin had been too dark, his hair too black, for Jimena to fancy him. Like all the girls in the neighbourhood, Meche included, Jimena would have gone for the blond, hazel-eyed Constantino.

"I was the dweeb," Meche muttered. "He was the freak."

"I always figured you two would end up together," Jimena said.

"In a parallel universe where I didn't want to rip out his asshole, maybe."

"I never got that. You guys were sewn together at the hip and one day you just stopped talking."

"Childhood friendships don't last."

Jimena laughed loudly, her painted mouth open wide.

"He used to have that stupid motorcycle and you guys used to ride it all around the block. Oh, my God, it was so old! It used to make so much noise! It was falling apart and you'd jump on it together and think you were so cool!"

They had been cool. Sebastian had been gangly and greasy-haired, Meche as developed as an eleven-year old boy with pimples dotting her face. They'd both dressed in atrocious clothes and the company they kept—sickly, chubby little Daniela, with the stash of Twinkies and Chocotorros under her bed—didn't help.

But they *had* been cool. For a little while. When magic was real.

And she had cared the world for him.

And he'd said, once, "Let's run away." On the old motorcycle, of all things. Like it would even make it to the outskirts of the city, never mind to the highway. "Let's just run away from this fucking place, this fucking city, this fucking everything."

And Meche, staring at the maps on his wall.

The map of France and the map of Spain. The Arctic circle.

Because they were going to take over the world.

Together.

Fucking Sebastian. Fucking, fucking Sebastian.

Daniela, too.

No, childhood friendships will never last. No friendship will ever last.

"You know, I don't remember that," Meche said, lying with a flat voice. "I don't remember any of that."

"Really?"

"I remember you looked like a marshmallow in your *quinceañera* dress."

"Oh, well. It was a while back."

Meche put her earbuds back in and pressed play, hoping that was the last bit of chatter she would have to endure. She tried to stare ahead and focus on Nina's voice, but despite her attempt not to look, she craned her head and glanced at Sebastian's building as they drove past it.

She wanted to know if the curtains were blue.

They were green.

This made her feel relieved. Like the building was saying, "Hey Meche, it's not 1988. You are here. In the present. Relax."

There was movement by the curtain and, for a moment, Meche thought Sebastian was about to pop up, in the window, and she'd be looking straight at him. The prospect of seeing him there, framed by the old window, caused her to panic, as though it wasn't just some guy she'd known as a teenager, but the damn shark from *Jaws*.

Nobody looked out the window and Meche let out her breath slowly.

Three blocks later Jimena parked the car. Meche pulled her luggage from the trunk while Jimena looked for the keys to the building, which were sitting somewhere in the abysmal depths of her huge purse. After a small eternity, Jimena pulled out her key chain and pushed the heavy front door open.

Meche dragged her bags into the hallway, stopping to glance at the statue of the Virgin of Guadalupe sitting on its niche with the plastic flowers and the bare light bulb.

The long, dark hallway led towards a wide staircase. Meche rested a hand on the bannister. This building looked the same. The changes that had dotted the neighbourhood had not reached inside. Stepping up would mean stepping into a replica of her past. She was afraid of bumping into the ghost of her dad and slipping into bitter memories.

But hadn't she done that already?

Jimena went past her, up the steps and turned to look at her.

"What?"

"Nothing," Meche said, hauling her suitcase.

What the hell. She was here.

Mexico City, 1988

MECHE DID NOT do sports. She resented the uniform they had to wear each Tuesday and Thursday: short white shorts and white shirt. As though they were trapped in the 1950s. Had no one heard of pants and sweatshirts in the intervening decades? Besides, she had no desire to chase after a ball, like an eager puppy.

As a result, Meche tried to spend as much time as she could evading gym class. When she was forced to participate in some group activity, she stood at the back, listened to her Walkman. Her classmates knew not to pass her the ball. A tacit understanding— Meche was invisible—took place.

When the students gathered in the central patio of the school and put up the nets Meche grabbed a cassette and began listening to Serú Girán singing Canción de Alicia en el País, about the dictatorship in Argentina. She had reached the part where the walruses have vanished when a ball hit her smack in the face.

Meche pressed her hands against her nose and heard the unmistakable, loud laughter of Teofilo spreading across the play yard.

Squinting, feeling her face tingling with pain, Meche stared at the boy.

Meche had a lot of little hates nestled in her heart, but she reserved the biggest for Teofilo, the bully of the class. He was tall, fat and liked to slap the asses of all the girls in his class. When he tried to slap Meche's ass, she told him to go to hell and he had made it his mission that fall to get back at her.

One day she found her Math book had been defaced with a big

red marker. The pages had been marked with UGLY WHORE. Someone stole her sweater and dumped it in a puddle. She earned herself a new nickname: Unibrow. Meche had no proof this was the work of Teofilo, but she knew. The evidence was in his smug grin.

She knew perfectly well that Teofilo had done this on purpose and she knew perfectly well there was nothing she could do to get back at him.

"Are you alright?" Daniela asked.

Meche nodded. "Yeah."

Meche wiped her mouth with the back of her hand. She tasted copper and rage.

MECHE SLAMMED THE door to her room and fell back on the bed, the cool compress pressed against her face. She tried for serenity because there was no benefit in reliving the whole episode. But her stomach was an ugly black pit which had to be filled with something.

She filled it with music.

Meche put her dad's copy of The Doors' debut album on the portable record player. The cymbals clanged and Break on Through bounced against the walls as she stared at the ceiling thinking about Teofilo. Thinking how much she hated him. Thinking how much she wished she could hurt him.

But really, what could she do?

Meche could not appeal to a higher power. She could not seek assistance from the teachers or her parents or the other kids.

Meche didn't have anything except the record sleeves strewn around her bed as she pictured that big bully.

Teofilo had to be stopped.

In a corner of her room, the thumb-tacked poster of Jim Morrison agreed.

So she played the record and she tried to believe. Tried to hold on to that slim thread of hope that something was going to happen soon. Something good. Because, damn it, something *had* to happen.

Jim Morrison yelled "break on through" and she pictured Teofilo breaking, shattering like a piece of glass. She imagined her foot slamming on his arm and the arm crumbling like a sugar cookie.

When the song finished playing she got up, moved the tone-arm and began playing it again. She turned the volume up and the room vibrated. She felt very tired all of a sudden, as though this great weight had descended upon her, crushing her chest. Meche closed her eyes.

MONDAY. HOMEWORK DONE. Heavy textbooks stuffed inside the backpack. White socks—which looked yellow—on. Meche kissed her grandma goodbye—her mother had already left for the pharmacy, her dad was sleeping after a late night of drinking—and headed to school.

She took a short cut instead of her usual route because she did not feel like talking to Sebastian. She did not feel like talking to anyone. There was still a bitterness in her stomach and she felt like nursing her wounds alone, to the tune of her cassettes. She was tired and irritated, dark circles around her eyes a quiet testimony to her unpleasant weekend.

So she walked to school by herself, feet shuffling slowly towards their destination.

Around eleven, she encountered Teofilo on the school's main staircase. She was coming down and he was going up.

He didn't see her. He was busy chatting with his friends. Meche felt like slamming his head against the wall and beating him senseless. She gripped her Walkman and flipped the cassette.

And then, just then, Teofilo slipped. There was no reason why he should slip: no obstacle, nothing at all. But his feet stumbled, as if hitting an invisible barrier. It was just as she had been picturing it all weekend: he simply tumbled down the stairs. Bam! Slipped, fell at a weird angle and suddenly he was splayed on the floor, whining like a baby. A big asshole like that, just bawling his eyes out.

She watched him, crumpled at the bottom of the stairs, his notebooks lying all around him on the floor, and realized he had broken his arm.

His friends tried to help him up.

Meche stomped over one of the open notebooks, leaving her footprint upon Teofilo's homework.

She chuckled. A few minutes later as she was walking to Arts and Crafts, she realized it had not been a coincidence. It couldn't be a coincidence.

It was the record's fault.

MECHE RUSHED DOWN the hallway, her notebook pressed against her chest. She went into the bathroom and leaned close to a mirror, staring at her reflection, trying to see if there was a visible change. Did magic change you?

The mirror was old and had a thin crack near the bottom. It reflected the pea-green sink which matched the tiles. It revealed a teenager, long hair neatly pulled back in a ponytail and smeared in place with a generous amount of lemon juice and hair gel. It showed her slightly rumpled navy school uniform with the gold buttons. It did not, however, provide proof of any great psychic or magical powers.

She had not sprouted an extra finger or changed her eye colour. She was Meche. The same Meche who had walked the one dozen blocks between home and school that morning, plaid skirt hitting her below the knee, an egg *torta* tucked in her knapsack for lunch, three yellow pencils and a blue pen tucked in a pencil case.

Meche stared at her reflection for a long time, ignoring the bell which indicated a change of classes.

Three girls walked into the bathroom, chatting and giggling together. Isadora Galván and her two hierophants. They gave her a weird look, like it was some bizarre occurrence to run into her even though they were all in the same grade. School girls went to the bathroom in packs. Meche only had Daniela and Sebastian, and she couldn't giggle outside the stalls while Sebastian peed, so her pack was immediately nonexistent.

Which reminded her that she needed to find Daniela.

She walked out and headed to the second floor, trying to poke her head through the window and see if Daniela was in Typing.

Daniela was sitting at the other end of the room. The machines went ding-ding clang-clang as the girls bent over the keys. Old Miss Viridiana sat half-asleep behind her desk, her hands folded over her tummy.

Meche waved to her. Daniela did not see her.

"Dani. Psst."

Daniela was busy looking at what she was typing.

Meche ripped a piece of paper from her notebook, balled it up and tossed it at Daniela. It hit her on the head. Daniela turned around.

"Hey," Meche said.

Daniela moved towards the window, glancing at Miss Viridiana to make sure she was still half-asleep.

"Why aren't you in class?" she asked.

"Teofilo just broke his arm."

"How?"

"He fell down the stairs."

"Is he with the nurse? Is he alright?"

"Who cares?" Meche said. "I think I just discovered something cool."

"What?"

"Magic."

Real magic, the kind grandmother talked about. Her father did not believe grandma's wild tales of shape-changing witches and amulets which could heal the sick. Meche, however, was fascinated by this stuff.

"Are you and Sebastian talking about weird stuff again?" Daniela asked, wrinkling her nose.

"No. This doesn't have anything to do with that."

"I don't like it when you talk about that devil-worshipper."

"Oh, my god, Aleister Crowley was not a devil-worshipper."

"Mercedes Vega."

Shit. Meche turned, trying to don her most innocent expression.

Principal Estrada was a thin, unpleasant woman. She dyed her hair blonde and wore a grey, buttoned up sweater every day of the week. She enjoyed patrolling the hallways, ordering the girls who had folded their skirt in order to show more leg to pull the skirts down, ordering others to wipe the lipstick from their faces, telling the boys to tuck their shirts and cut their hair. When she couldn't catch you committing an infraction, she'd make one up. Like, "Don't stare at me so oddly, Vega," or, "Why are you walking funny, Vega?"

Sebastian called her Frankenstrada behind her back and she did kind of have a resemblance to Boris Karloff, what with the square-shaped head and the general stiffness.

Estrada glared at Meche, her thin eyebrows arched with contempt.

"What class are you supposed to be in?"

"Arts and Crafts."

"And why aren't you in Arts and Crafts?"

"I had to pee."

"What, do you have the bladder of a two-year-old? You were hanging out by the bathrooms an hour ago."

Meche did not understand how Estrada knew the comings and goings of all students but she did. And, indeed, Meche had been hanging out by the bathrooms just an hour ago.

"Get yourself to your classroom this instant."

"Yes, Miss Estrada," she muttered.

It was not like anything exciting was going to happen in Arts and Crafts. They were supposedly making papier-mâché sculptures that week—*alebrijes*, bizarre creatures from Mexican folklore, part bird, part lizard and part whatever you wanted—but Professor Ortega liked to drone on about Art and quickly lost his train of thought, which meant they did precious few crafts. At least it wasn't Home Economy.

Meche went down the stairs, crossing the patio. Like any decent Mexican school, Queen Victoria had an interior square where the students could gather for recess. Most of the classrooms were located on the north side of this square in a structure that resembled a big box of Kleenex with holes, which some idiot with a desire to create prisons had built in the 70s. To the east there were the great metal double-doors which allowed access to the school and Don Fermin— the school guard who made sure nobody left the premises—sleeping on his stool. There was really very little need for Fermin. If any students wanted to escape the school they could follow the wall towards the west side and climb it at an angle hidden by a clump of trees, which passed as their version of nature among the cement.

Also to the west was another, smaller gate which connected the junior high and high school to the primary school.

To the south was what had once been the original Queen Victoria in the 1940s: a great, old Mexican house, three stories high. It had housed an all-girls contingent before mixed education became fashionable among the middle class. Now it was where the school's offices sat. This was also where the Arts and English classes took place.

Meche trotted up the stairs and slipped in the back, sitting next to Sebastian. He was drawing a skull on his desk, carefully decorating the teeth with his black marker. The teacher had begun to talk about form and meaning, which meant they could whisper in peace for at least another fifteen minutes.

"I thought you weren't coming."

"Did I miss something?"

"No," Sebastian said, snorting.

"I had a close encounter with Frankenstrada," Meche said. "She thinks I shouldn't pee."

"How are you supposed to do that?"

"I don't know. Carry a bottle around with me and just go in there?"

"She told me I have to cut my hair again this morning or she'll cut it for me."

Sebastian had a pseudo-punk aesthetic going and he liked to style his black hair with an obscene amount of hairspray. It was still pretty tame compared to what real, hardcore punks did with their hair, but then again the Queen Victoria didn't smile too kindly on any of that stuff so you really couldn't try a mohawk. Plus, punk was a bit lame.

Rich Mexican kids who could visit the USA and England imported this wild aesthetic, but it was all show and no substance. Sure, some good bands had emerged from that primordial ooze, like Atoxxxico and Ritmo Peligroso, but Meche was pretty tired of the studded belts and bracelets, patches, and junk which supposedly went with being punk.

The only reason why Meche could stomach Sebastian was because he was pseudo-punk. He knew, or cared, little about punk music or punk culture in general. But he liked sci-fi and horror movies and had watched *Mad Max* obsessively, to the point of using a couple of old car tires to build himself what he termed a "rubber exo-skeleton" on top of his leather jacket. For him it was the aesthetic thrill of the whole thing.

"You should get a tattoo and really piss her off," she said.

"Sure. Then I'll get kicked out by my mom."

Meche leaned her chin against the back of her hand and looked at Sebastian's skull with its wide grin.

"Hey, can you come to my place after school? I want to show you something."

"It's meatball dinner."

"So go home later and have the meatballs."

"They'll be cold. Plus, my brother will eat them all if I don't show up." Sebastian paused. "What's your grandma making for dinner?"

"I dunno. Green beans with egg."

"Gross."

"Come on, what are you going to do all afternoon by yourself? Homework?"

"Read and draw," he muttered.

"Come on over. Dani's coming."

Meche had not even told Daniela she was invited, but she assumed Daniela would tag along. Dani was as different from Sebastian as night was from day, always dressed in pink, her Barbies still lined up on her shelves, an Easy-Bake oven in her room—even though the three of them were fifteen—and a predilection for soap operas. She liked listening to Lucerito, which made Meche want to barf, and thought Luis Miguel was the hottest man in the world, which was a double-barf. As far as Meche was concerned the only way she would listen to Ahora te Puedes Marchar was if someone tied her hands and feet with duct tape, then pushed a rag into her mouth to drown her screams.

But hey, Daniela was a good listener and of the three friends she was the one with the most money, which meant a chance to have free tickets to the movie theatre and loads of pop courtesy of her father, the accountant of a small furniture store.

"Mmm," said Sebastian. "You're not going to play *boleros*, are you? That shit's so *old*."

Meche punched him on the arm and he turned to stare at her with his usual stiff, offended face.

"You're talking about Agustin Lara, you idiot. One of the greatest Mexican songwriters of all time."

"You know, I really do want to have meatballs. Why don't you come over to my place?"

"My mom doesn't like me going over to your place."

Meche's mom had this over-developed fear of teenage pregnancies, courtesy of too many articles in too many ladies' magazines. It was a bit hard to get pregnant when Meche had never even been kissed, let alone had a boyfriend, but Meche's mother considered every boy in a twenty-block radius to be a danger to her daughter. As if anyone would try and date her.

"Fine," Sebastian said. "I'll come."

Meche tried to grab the marker Sebastian was using, but he slapped her hand away and hunched over, busy with his drawing. She sighed, unrolled the headphones and pressed play on the Walkman.

The tape rolled and Black Sabbath sang about children of tomorrow and revolution while she tapped her fingers against the desk, waiting for the bell to ring.

"SO WHAT YOU'RE saying essentially is that you've gone nuts."

Sebastian lay on the floor of Meche's room, drawing in his notebook. He had traded the skulls for stars and was busy creating a night sky.

"Why is it so nuts to believe in magic? My grandmother says there are witches and in the countryside you can see them fly at nights in the shape of balls of fire."

"Your grandma is a really good cook, but no offence, I wouldn't take her stories at face value."

"Why not?" Meche asked, sitting down in front of Sebastian. "You're the one who told me about spiritism and mediums and shit in the nineteenth century."

"I believe in ghosts," ventured Daniela, raising her hand weakly.

"See?" Meche said. "She believes."

"Okay. So how about we play Teenage Idol. Do I get to become Emanuel tomorrow and sing at a bunch of concerts?" Sebastian asked.

"Why don't we find out?"

"You're serious."

Meche stared at Sebastian. He ripped out the page from his notebook, balled it and threw it in her wastebasket.

"Why shouldn't music have power? My dad says it's the most powerful thing in the world. Nietzsche says that without music, life would be a mistake."

"Don't quote me Nietzsche. I showed you Nietzsche," Sebastian said in an offended tone.

"Why can't music be magic? Aren't spells just words you repeat? And what are songs? Lyrics that play over and over again. The words are like a formula."

All around Meche's room posters of band members and enlarged album covers looked down at them. Freddie Mercury leaned back on stage, Pedro Infante played the guitar. In a corner the Beatles were ready to ride the Yellow Submarine. Stacks of records were piled along Meche's floor, cassettes poked out from a couple of boxes.

"Okay, how about backmasking?" said Meche. "Doesn't Aleister Crowley suggest that adepts should listen to records reversed?"

"Yes," said Sebastian. "But that doesn't..."

"And all these people flipping out because they think Led Zeppelin's Stairway to Heaven has a Satanic message?"

"So we should play records backwards? Do a Satanic ceremony?"

"Guys, I just want to remind you I have to be home by seven," Daniela said. "I'm also not allowed to do any Satanic stuff."

Sebastian and Meche looked at their friend. Daniela blinked and went back to working on the personality test culled from a teen magazine she was completing.

"Not a Satanic ceremony. You're always talking about this stuff. Crowley? Rasputin had to be killed three times?"

"Because I like to read lots of weird shit. But I don't want to go around brewing poisons and stuff. People already think I'm odd, I don't want to give them any extra ammunition," Sebastian muttered.

Sebastian began drawing on the side of his tennis shoes. More stars in black marker.

Meche wanted to hit them both on the back of the head. They didn't get it! She expected it from Daniela because Daniela got about

10 percent of what went on in the world, but Sebastian? Sebastian loved this stuff. They had become friends four years before because Meche had been listening to Alan Parsons Project's *Tales of Mystery and Imagination* and she didn't get the references. So she decided to ask the only person in her class who might have the answer. At first Sebastian had been offended she didn't know Edgar Allan Poe, but she had been equally offended he didn't know Alan Parsons Project because they sang Games People Play from *The Turn of a Friendly Card* which, in her opinion, was a very nice concept album. Not the best, but nice. The best was an easy pick. Most people would probably say the concept album of all time was *The Dark Side Of The Moon*, but Meche preferred The Kinks' *Arthur (Or the Decline and Fall of the British Empire)*. Her parents had met thanks to that album.

"Aren't you curious to see if it works?" Meche asked.

Sebastian capped his marker and stuffed it back in his pocket.

"It'll never work," he said with finality. "I have to go. I have a couple of hours bagging groceries tonight. Later."

Meche scowled as Sebastian stepped out of her room. Great. The big ninny was not going to play ball. Daniela, looking pained, patted Meche on the knee.

"Cheer up. Why don't we go to my house and bake some cupcakes?"

"The stuff you make in the Easy-Bake oven tastes like ass," Meche muttered.

MECHE COPIED THE linear equations neatly into her notebook. She was good at math.

Daniela wasn't. Sebastian sucked even more.

Most students thought math was boring, but math was the foundation for so many things, including music. Music of the stars and all, and hadn't Kepler…

Meche held her pencil, suspended over the page. She looked at the book again, at the black letters and numbers against the white pages.

Equations. Letters are not letters in equations. They stand for numbers and if you balance them right, you'll find the right number. What if it was the same for music? Songs stand for something, don't they? They have a symbolic value. So if you were to somehow balance them… ugh, she was getting herself all into knots.

She heard the door opening and looked up. Her father shuffled in, taking off his coat and putting it on a peg.

"Hey, Meche," he said, patting her head as he walked by. "Doing homework?"

"Math," she said.

"What did you eat today?"

"Grandma made green beans. Should I heat them up?"

"Don't bother. I'll have some cookies."

He sat down, poured himself a glass of milk and opened a box of animal crackers. Meche's dad and her mom had married young and sometimes he still looked like half a kid himself when he sat hunched over a glass of milk, his shoulder-length hair pulled back.

He was the coolest grownup Meche knew. She wanted to be like him when she grew up.

"Does mom have another late shift at the pharmacy?" her dad asked.

"All week," Meche said, shrugging.

"I don't remember her telling me."

"She did."

"Your grandmother in bed yet?"

"An hour ago."

Her dad ate a cracker and lit a cigarette, nodding absentmindedly.

"What did you play today?"

"Oh, let me see," he said. "Miguel Bosé. A bit of Sabina. A bit of everything."

Ever since Meche had been born her dad had worked as a DJ. He had originally intended to study veterinary medicine but had never cared for the career, which he had been more or less forced into by his family. He eventually dropped it altogether and went to work at a record store, where he'd met Meche's mom. The radio station was where he was most comfortable. The microphone was his natural prop. Without it he seemed unreal.

He cut a cracker in half and dipped it in the milk.

"Do you believe in magic?"

"What's your grandma been telling you?" he asked. "I hope you're not believing any of her kooky stories about putting saints upside down so you can get a boyfriend."

"No. I mean like serious magic."

"Nothing serious about magic. Just superstitions."

"What about music?"

"What about it?"

"I don't know," Meche muttered, looking at her equations.

"Cracker?"

Meche nodded, taking a cracker shaped like a lion.

Her dad closed the box and took the glass to the kitchen, leaving it in the sink. Then he grabbed his jacket.

"I'm going out."

He didn't have to say he'd be at the bar. Weekdays it was at the bar. Weekends it was the pool hall. Sometimes, when he stayed out too late, her mom had her go pull him out. Meche felt humiliated when this happened.

Her mother was out late tonight, so maybe Meche wouldn't have to put on the sweater and head there. It wasn't far. It was just… annoying.

She wished he'd come home early. Otherwise her parents might fight. Again.

"Be careful," she said.

"Yup. Finish your homework, alright? Don't skim on the reading. You can't read, you can't do shit. No matter how good you are at adding numbers."

"I'm going to work with computers, dad," she reminded him.

She had decided this two years before when her parents finally bought her a Commodore 64. She had learned how to program little games on it and thought she could make a go at it as a real career when she grew up.

"You still need to read."

"Yes, captain."

"Arrr. Don't stay up late."

Meche raised her hand, saluting her dad. She watched him put on his old leather jacket and step out.

She dropped her hand and chewed on her pencil, starring at the numbers.

*　　*　　*

IT WAS A rainy morning. Meche jumped and tiptoed around puddles to the rhythm of Soda Stereo. She shook her head and snapped her fingers.

A hand grasped her shoulder and she frowned, turning around. Sebastian Soto, lanky and dour, just like every morning of the week, stood with an umbrella under his arm. He was the tallest kid in her class and when he stood like that, grimly looking down at her, Meche had to agree with the kids that teased him: he did resemble Lurch from afar.

"Hey," he said. "I was thinking about what you said yesterday."

"And?"

"I don't know. Maybe we should give it a try."

"For real? When?"

"How about now?"

"School day."

"So?"

"Oh my God, you just want to skip the chemistry test."

"Maybe. But do you really want to go to school?"

"Nope."

Sebastian rocked back and forth on his shoes, which, against school regulations, he had painted with faint traces of whiteout spelling out THE RAVEN. Meche pulled up her left sock, with the broken elastic.

"Daniela will be pissed if we skip out without inviting her."

"Yeah, but her mom drives her to school. Tough luck. I'm heading to the factory. Are you coming?"

"I studied for the test."

"Why bother when you can cheat?"

Meche rolled her eyes and held on to the straps of her backpack. On the one hand she was annoyed at Sebastian for trying to miss the test. On the other hand this might be a good chance to convince him about the music and spells. He was halfway there already. She could tell. He had the same expression as he did when they had done that Ouija session. Daniela had freaked out because she had recently seen a movie about demon-possessed people, and she swore she'd never speak to them again because they were morbid and freaky, but she came back to roost with them all the same. What else could she do? It was not like any of them had much of a social circle.

"Fine," Meche said.

Sebastian led the way, purposely sinking into the puddles and splashing her.

Wanker.

Meche put her headphones on again and the cassette player told her about a voyeur staring through the window.

She followed Sebastian until they reached the abandoned pantyhose factory. Most of the windows were covered with wooden boards, but Sebastian ducked and went in through a large opening, obviously knowing what to do.

Meche leaned down.

She had never liked the pantyhose factory. The little kids enjoyed playing tag there and the older ones came to drink beer and make out, but it had always seemed so sad and grey.

She shoved her backpack in and then crawled in herself, emerging into one of the cavernous factory rooms. It was dark and she was glad when Sebastian took out a flashlight, even if he did shine it in her face.

"Let's go up," he said, handing her the flashlight.

They rushed up the stairs, their feet clattering upon the metal and making the building echo with their footsteps.

They went into a large room with scattered furniture: a table, some chairs piled in a corner. Someone—probably not the original factory workers—had dragged a lumpy, red couch into the middle of the room.

There were more windows on the second floor and fewer of these were boarded, so there was significantly more light, even though dirt had accumulated upon the panes, blurring the view. Meche walked up to the circular window on the east wall and wiped it with the sleeves of her too-large sweater, which she had inherited from her older cousin Jimena.

The neighbourhood looked different when seen like this, so diffused.

"You've been coming here a lot?" she asked.

"Not often."

Sebastian tossed his umbrella on the floor and threw himself on the couch, propping his feet up.

"So now you believe me about the magic?"

"I think you are cr-aaaa-zy," he said. "But what the hell. Life can't get any crappier, can it?"

"Was your dad home last night?" Meche asked, frowning.

Sebastian's dad wasn't living with them, but he came around periodically to collect money and beat the kids. For old time's sake.

"It's got nothing to do with him," Sebastian said, meaning it probably had everything to do with him.

She shoved his feet away and sat on the couch. Sebastian had the backpack pressed against his chest and was staring at the ceiling.

"What's it got to do with?" she asked.

"I don't know. I just wish it was all different. You know?"

"Yeah."

Meche scratched her leg and sat quietly, thinking about all the things she would change if she could. She'd get rid of the pimples. She'd get nice, new clothes. Not Jimena's hand-me-downs. Her mother would yell less. She'd go out on a date with Constantino.

"How do we do it?"

"I don't know," Meche said. "I haven't thought about it too much. I mean, we need a turntable and lots of records, I guess. We have to figure out the formula."

"So you're saying you have no idea?" he asked flatly.

"I have some idea," Meche said, feeling offended. "It's just going to take some experimenting. I need to do more research. I wonder if there are any books I can use at the school library…"

"Aha."

"We need to convince Daniela. I figure we need three people."

"Why three?"

"Because it's the first lucky prime number."

Sebastian looked at her blankly, as though she had just spoken in Dutch. She sighed.

"Stuff always comes in threes. Like there are three notes in a triad, which is your basic chord. Or the holy trinity."

"'Double, double toil and trouble; Fire burn, and caldron bubble'," he said.

"What?" Meche asked. She had no idea what he was talking about.

"Macbeth's witches," Sebastian said, frowning. "Hey, I'm not a girl. Does that matter?"

"I don't think it does. You can be a warlock, can't you?"

"I suppose. We don't have to wear capes, do we? I don't think I'd look good in one."

She felt like telling him that, yeah, they most definitely had to use capes and pointy hats, and then watching what face he made at that, but Meche decided to spare him the unnecessary cruelty.

"No."

"Good. Do you have any food? I didn't eat breakfast."

He never ate breakfast. He also tended to eat Meche or Daniela's lunch. Meche's, usually, because Daniela was less generous with her food allocations. Meche figured that if half a cheese and ham sandwich was what it took to convince Sebastian to join her cause, it would be a small price.

She took out her battered tin lunchbox and scooped the sandwich, giving him half. Sebastian munched on it and grabbed her thermos without even asking for permission, taking a big gulp.

"What are Macbeth witches?" she asked, punching one of the lumpy cushions and putting it behind her head.

"I really can't believe you are like half-illiterate."

"I'm not half-illiterate."

"You are clueless when it comes to books. Rodriguez is so going to fail you in Spanish and World Literature."

"You are going to fail all the sciences, so who's talking?"

"Blah blah," he said, opening and closing his left hand. "That's what remedials were made for."

"What are Macbeth witches?"

"*Macbeth* is a play by Shakespeare," Sebastian said, grabbing the sandwich crumbs that were left and stuffing them into his mouth. "It's about this guy who meets with these three witches and they prophesize that he'll be king. So he begins to think about it all the time and then ends up killing the guy in charge and becomes king. It's a tragedy."

"It doesn't sound too tragic to become king."

"Obviously things don't go as planned. You should read that book I gave you."

Meche had read some of the books Sebastian had given her. Correction. Probably some of the *only* books she read were the ones he gave her, but she hadn't read this particular one because she was still a little pissed off that he'd only given her a book for her birthday instead of the album she had wanted. Getting Shakespeare's sonnets and complete works for your fifteenth birthday was like getting a sweater from your mom for Christmas: bullshit.

"I'm working on it," she said. "Slowly working on it."

"Illiterate."

"Ass," she said tossing her backpack at his face.

Sebastian dodged it and shrugged. "Better an ass than to be illiterate."

"I can't hear you," Meche said, sliding to the floor and pressing the play button on her Walkman.

"What are you listening to?" Sebastian said, sliding down next to her.

Meche pulled out her extra pair of headphone and plugged it into one of the jacks. Sebastian put on the headphones. Meche pressed the rewind button. They tilted their head backs and Soda Stereo began to sing Persiana Americana from the very beginning.

MECHE TIPTOED INTO the apartment, trying to sneak into her bedroom. She was half an hour early and needed to hide for a bit. Grandmother Dolores was in the kitchen, humming. She spent most of her time there, looking after a boiling pot or frying onions and chillis, always on her feet and always ready to make a meal. She'd been a maid for many years before old age made her unemployable. Cooking had been her favourite task during that time.

"Meche, did you skip school today?"

Meche stopped in her tracks and cursed inwardly. Mama Dolores had an internal lie detector, so there was no sense in trying to fool her.

"Yeah."

"You shouldn't miss classes. Come, sit down. You can peel some potatoes. I'm making *picadillo* the way your mom likes it."

"What's the point? Mom and dad both eat outside."

"Well, maybe one day your mother will come home early."

Meche walked into the kitchen, dumping her backpack on one of the two plastic chairs and sitting at the table. She grabbed a peeler and began slicing the skins off the potatoes.

Mama Dolores turned on the little radio sitting next to the narrow kitchen windows and Pedro Infante began singing Amorcito Corazón while the old woman hummed and poured some oil into a frying pan. She swished the onions to the tune of the love song.

"Mama Dolores, can you tell me something and tell me the truth?"

"What, baby?"

"Were there really witches in your town?"

"Of course there were. They'd fly off at nights in the shape of great balls of fire, nestling in the trees and cackling."

"And they did magic and it worked?"

"It did. They cast all sorts of spells."

"If they were so powerful why didn't they leave the town and become billionaires?"

"Oh, magic is more complex than that. You have to give as much as you take. There's a price to everything."

"What about music? Could there be magic in music?"

"There's magic everywhere, if you look carefully," her grandmother said. "The trouble is wanting it enough, and holding on to it."

Meche slanted the peeler, slowly stripping the potato.

"What if magic…"

"Magic will break your heart, Meche," Mama Dolores said very seriously.

Meche frowned.

MECHE'S MOTHER, NATALIA, was good looking. When angered, however, she resembled the Medusa in one of Meche's story books. Except she still had to grow some snakes on her head. Any day now, Meche thought those would begin to sprout.

"Okay, Meche," Natalia said, from behind the pharmacy counter. "How come I got a call from school today to ask if you were sick?"

"I don't know," Meche said. "I'm just here because I need money for the tortillas and grandma doesn't have any."

"I left money on top of the refrigerator."

"It's not there."

"Your goddamn father," her mother muttered. "Did he take it?"

"I don't know."

Meche rested her chin against the glass counter and shrugged. If she had known it was going to be such a big deal to get the pesos she needed, she would have borrowed them from someone. This was Spanish Inquisition stuff.

"Wait three minutes," her mother said as she headed to the back of the pharmacy.

Meche eyed the arcade machine sitting in a corner, right by the little children's coin-operated horse and the scale that would tell you your weight and fortune. She could play a game. Or just get the hell out of the pharmacy before her mother started asking too many questions.

"Here," her mother said, coming out from behind the counter and opening her change purse, handing her two bills. "Buy the tortillas and give the rest of the money to your grandmother."

"Alright."

"Meche, if I find out that you and Sebastian Soto are skipping classes, I'm going to beat you black and blue."

"I wasn't skipping nothing," Meche said, though she was impressed by her mother's psychic skills.

VICENTE VEGA STILL had most of his hair, only a small—though increasing—gut, and a great quantity of his charm. He had, however, misplaced his common sense and his optimism as he stumbled through the streets of Mexico City. Thirty-eight—not too old, not really young—he went through life like a zombie navigating a closed course, from home to the radio cabin and from the cabin to the cantina.

On Mondays he had the seafood soup. Tuesdays the stuffed chilli. Wednesdays he fought with his wife. The weekends were for playing pool and dominoes. He drank every day.

He remembered being young once, being happy. He remembered marrying a pretty young woman he had adored and somehow stumbling into a cold, distant stranger in bed one morning. He had been his parents' pride and joy, now a sore disappointment, their eyes turned to his younger brother who had done as he was told and—his mother reminded him every time he spoke to her—had made something of himself. His brother was a *licenciado* and he had a big house and two nice cars, wearing good suits which threatened to explode as he moved his corpulent form around the office. At heart, his brother was still the same tricky, devious bastard he'd always been, but he played in bigger leagues now. He had set his sights squarely on the Mexican dream: lots of money and lots of women.

Vicente, always unable to understand these simplistic desires, never one to lust after lots of money or numerous broads, had looked for that elusive something else in life. Meaning. Answers that were not printed in triplicate or faxed to the office. Beauty. But life, being the bitch that she was, had denied Vicente what he asked for, had rewarded him only with ugliness and pessimism, had sunk his dreams low.

Music. He loved music. Playing it, writing songs. He'd quit veterinary school and gone to work at the record shop and then he had got the part-time stint as a DJ because—and here he could quote more than a few people—he had the most amazing voice. But that golden voice was false gold and when the demands of parenthood, of making money and getting by intruded on the band, he quit the musician bit and went full-on onto radio.

He thought this would make Natalia happy. Natalia, however, was never happy, accumulating little hates and grudges, cataloguing them by date and carefully filing them so she could pull them out later and toss them in his face.

Only Meche loved him.

She'd been born like him, Meche. Not just the looks—the shape of the eyes, the firm mouth—but his temper and his proclivities.

If he hadn't had Meche, Vicente might have gone to live at the bar forever, installed himself in a corner and drunk himself under the table. If he shuffled his feet home every night and stumbled out of bed in the mornings, it was because of his daughter.

Vicente went up the steps, trudging back into the apartment. After hanging his jacket he went towards the stereo, running his hands over the turntable. He carefully selected a record, plugged in his headphones and sat on the floor, listening to The Beatles playing in the dark as he smoked a cigarette.

He was almost done with one side of the recording when the door opened and the clatter of heels announced the presence of his wife. She turned on the lights and glanced at him.

She didn't say anything. Her heels just moved away, towards the bedroom, with a soft sort of indifference which mirrored his own.

Mexico City, 2009

THE APARTMENT HAD shrunk or had been bigger in her memory. She walked in slowly, feeling like an intruder even though she had grown up here. At some point her mother had taken down the old wallpaper and now the interior was painted in soft, institutional beiges.

Meche looked at the photos sitting all around: Natalia as a baby, Natalia as a child, Natalia at the beach. Photos of her mother's second husband, Lorenzo. Almost like an afterthought, Natalia and Meche, her teenaged face staring at the camera.

"Mercedes," her mother said as she drifted into the living room and gave her a hug. "Little Meche."

"Hey, mom," she muttered.

"How was your flight?"

"Good. Fine."

"I have had the most awful time getting *tamales*," her mother said, wrapping an arm around her shoulders.

"*Tamales?*"

"For the *novena*," Jimena said helpfully.

"I really wished we didn't have to do a *novena*," Meche said.

"There's no way around it," her mother said. "God knows your father can use all the prayers he can get."

"Dad didn't believe in this stuff."

"I talked to the baker and we are going to have canapés for the first night," Jimena said. "He agreed to a discount, seeing as it was us."

"Good," Natalia said, patting her niece's hand. "Meche, you are going to have to go through your father's things."

Meche had barely entered the apartment and had just sat down. She looked up at her mother, surprised.

"What?"

"Well, I certainly won't have the time. I would ask Lorenzo, but it doesn't seem right to have him going through your father's clothes. And you know how he was. It's probably a mess. But some of the records are bound to be valuable."

Valuable.

"Maybe you can play some at the party," her mother said. "I have no idea what we are going to do for music."

"You want me to go to dad's apartment and see if he had records that are worth any money?"

"Ay, don't take it like that," Jimena said. "You want a coffee?"

Norwegians drank a lot of coffee; strong and black. Meche had never taken to this custom, but she had developed a tea addiction after her year in London.

"No."

"You might as well sort it out and take whatever you want," her mother said. "Whatever he had, he left it all to you. Nothing for me."

There was a pointed bitterness to her words. Meche's father had failed her so many times and Meche got that—because dumping your family one fine day will certainly create a few grudges. And yet… the asshole was gone. No need to auction off his goods. As far as Meche was concerned, she thought they should stuff all his possessions in cardboard boxes and give them to charity. She wasn't going to go on eBay and see if someone paid a dollar for a dusty LP. But if her mother insisted, Meche would make an effort.

"I told Meche Sebastian Soto is hanging around the neighbourhood," Jimena said. "You sure you don't want a coffee?"

"Nope."

"Yes, that nice boy."

"You never liked him," Meche said.

Meche's mother chuckled and sat next to her, patting her leg. Her hair was a burnished brown. It matched the furniture. Jimena slipped out, probably to the kitchen for that coffee she yearned for.

"I did like him."

Sebastian's new car sure must be something to cause such a tremendous change of opinion in the women in Meche's family.

"Where's Lorenzo?" she asked.

"Trying to fix the paperwork and arrange the burial," her mother said, lifting her hands in the air.

"Maybe I'll go to father's apartment tomorrow," Meche muttered. "Before the funeral."

At least in her father's apartment she'd be alone. She didn't think she could stomach her mother and her cousin at this time.

VICENTE VEGA'S APARTMENT was smack in downtown Mexico City, in an old building which must have been quite something two hundred years before, but which was now nothing more than a tired ruin, perched at the end of an alley, waiting in the shadows. It was cold and damp as Meche walked up the stairs and when she actually opened the door to the apartment and stepped in she realized the apartment itself was even colder.

She locked the door and looked around. The first thing she noticed was a tiny kitchen that had no right to call itself a kitchen, dirty dishes piled high. She started by washing them because it was too depressing to stare at the dregs inside coffee cups and the stains of old spaghetti. Once she was done, she stood in the living room, which also served as the dining room, looking at the piles of old LPs her father had accumulated. They were sitting on shelves, but also spilled onto the floor, peeking from beneath the sofas, drowning the side table, resting upon the battered TV set.

She went to the room which served as an office, but really was nothing more than another space used to pile boxes with records, mountains of sleeves and vinyl. In a corner, forlorn, sat her father's typewriter. When his music career failed, he had tried—and never succeeded in—writing a compendium of the history of Latin American rock-and-roll. Now that she thought about it, her father had never succeeded at anything, except maybe in finding the bottom of a bottle of tequila.

She stepped into his bedroom and discovered the same chaotic mass of records, though her father, perhaps in an effort to escape the clutter that reigned in the other parts of the apartment, had cleared a section of the wall and pinned up a large poster depicting palm trees and a sunset. The thick curtains also had a lively pattern of palm trees, this time with flamingos, so kitsch it made her wonder if it was really her father who had rented this apartment.

She remembered when she had been younger and her dad had told her he planned to spend the end of his days on a beach, watching the waves come in.

He never made it to the seaside, though he did spend several years in Guadalajara before returning to Mexico City.

His kidneys had failed him. That's what had done him in. Not the booze. The liver put up a good fight. It was the kidneys which gave up. Her mother had told her he was on dialysis, but Meche hadn't phoned him.

Meche took a look in the bathroom. The medicine cabinet was cluttered with pills and expired medications. His glasses sat on the water tank of the toilet.

She walked back to the bedroom, sat on the sagging bed and wondered what it would be like to wake every morning to the old picture of the beach, feet shuffling upon the cold floor. Dying and knowing you were dying.

On the floor, by the bed, half-hidden under a sweater, was the portable turntable. Meche moved the sweater away and looked at it, hesitantly.

Was it the same one? It seemed to be the same walnut case. The one Meche used to have in her room could play full-size LPs, so chances were it *was* the same one.

Meche grabbed it, put it on her knees and found the sticker on the side. The little heart which Daniela had left there.

That was it. But it just looked so... ordinary and worn now. No magic to it.

Would it still work?

She reached towards a stack of records on the bedside table and picked the first one off the top. The Beach Boys.

The needle went down. Good Vibrations began to play. She flipped the record sleeve around, looking at the image of the five young men. It had been released in 1966. That would have made her father... what... sixteen when it came out?

Meche opened the bedside drawer and found a stack of unpaid bills. There were some loose pages, stained with coffee smudges: notes for his glorious book. A matchbook. Tucked beneath the matchbook, like a postscript, a postcard from Puerto Vallarta. Meche looked at the remittance address but it had never been sent. It was an old Puerto Vallarta, Puerto Vallarta from the seventies, just left there to moulder in the drawer.

She closed the drawer and The Beach Boys finished their song, the needle lifted from the record and the apartment was silent.

Meche sighed and started going through the records, making three piles: throw away, sell and keep. She placed each record in the right pile, trying to maintain the keep pile as low as she could.

The silence was depressing. She could see why her father had kept the turntable by the bed, to liven his nights and mornings. She looked for another Beach Boys record, maybe *Summer Days (And Summer Nights!!)*, but it was not to be found. She settled on *Hotel California* by The Eagles—which was not quite the same thing at all—and pulled apart the curtains to see what the view was like.

But there was no view. The windows showed the grey façade of another building. She dropped the curtains and the flamingos returned, masking the greyness, cheerfully frolicking in a land of palm trees.

She remembered that she was now almost the same age her father had been when he had left them.

Mexico City, 1988

IT'S NOT THAT Meche hated school, because she didn't. She just hated the people at school, all them crawling around with their petty thoughts and their annoying habits. A few were outright assholes, like Teofilo. Others merely bumped into you on the stairs, giggled when you walked by, talked under their breath.

There were some—few and far between—who made it worth attending. Daniela and Sebastian, of course. But also Constantino. Especially Constantino Dominguez. She looked at him across the courtyard as she sat with her friends, eating her sandwich.

Sebastian had once dubbed Constantino the King of the Clones because his friends were always intent on copying his mannerisms and clothes. Sebastian also called him Floro Tinoco on account of the comic book character from *La Familia Burron*, swearing that Constantino was equally stupid and also built like a tractor. Meche only knew what all the other fifteen-year-old girls knew: Constantino had dirty-blond hair and hazel eyes, and when he smiled, he showed off perfectly straight, white teeth.

Today Constantino was standing next to Isadora Galván, a very common occurrence. They were not an item anymore, but hung out together in the way that the beautiful and popular will gravitate to each other. You could regularly find them in the Pit—which was an empty lot two blocks from school where the smokers liked to gather—and at other high school landmarks.

Isadora was certainly pretty, in a way which Meche could never expect to achieve. She had reddish-brown hair and it curled just the right amount around her shoulders. Her skin was very pale and this alone had earned her the lead in more than one school play while Meche and Daniela had to carry heavy props and scenery backstage.

Meche would have given anything to be like Isadora for a single day.

Maybe she could. If the magic worked.

"I think we should do the spell tonight," she told Daniela and Sebastian.

They didn't answer. Sebastian was also looking at Isadora, his eyes fixed on her long legs and her very short skirt. That kind of skirt looked sloppy and unflattering when Meche wore it, but on Isadora it was positively lovely. She supposed Isadora could wear a garbage bag and look amazing.

Daniela, for her part, was busy writing in her diary. Well, writing was an exaggeration. She just drew lots of little hearts with arrows going through them.

Meche snatched the diary away and hit Sebastian on the back of the head with it.

The boy looked at her, irritated.

"What?"

"I said we should do the spell tonight."

"I can't go out tonight," Daniela said.

"Who are you kidding, you can never go out," Meche muttered.

"No, I mean it."

"Then we'll go to your place."

"Okay," Daniel said demurely. "Can I have my notebook back, please?"

Meche looked at the diary and tapped her finger against the page.

"This is what we need," she told Sebastian.

"My diary?" Daniela asked.

"No, dummy. A place where we write down what we do. A *grimoire*."

"What's a gri-moy-re?" Daniela asked.

"You should pay more attention when we watch horror movies," Meche admonished her. "It's like a recipe book for witches. We've got to have one. If we're going to do this right."

"There's really no point in explaining it to her right now when she's so distracted," Sebastian said. "We'll do it later."

Daniela pouted, but Sebastian was right. Daniela was always going off on a tangent, dreaming away, getting distracted. The only thing Daniela's brain was able to retain was the cheesy dialogue from those romance novels she borrowed from her sister.

Sebastian extended a hand towards Meche's juice box. She frowned, but gave it to him in the end. Sebastian was constantly broke, this despite his attempts to earn a few extra pesos by bagging groceries at the supermarket, a job, which, by the way, he was getting too old for: everyone preferred very young baggers and he was reaching the end of his career as a bag boy.

Sebastian sipped the juice, his eyes fixed on Isadora again. Isadora, probably feeling the weight of his gaze, turned her head and looked in their direction.

Sebastian immediately dropped his head, staring at the juice box between his hands. Meche smirked and jabbed him on the ribs.

LITERATURE WAS LIKE having needles pushed under her eyelids. Meche could not understand or even remotely pay attention to what was happening on the blackboard; she rested her head against the desk and tried to add numbers in her head, repeat lyrics of songs. She wondered what she would eat that afternoon.

Daniela, however, was in love with the teacher and she sat all perky and straight next to Meche, with a docile smile on her face, nodding periodically while Rodriguez—the youngest of the faculty, but no prize pie in the looks department—strolled by, babbling on about Cervantes. Windmills. Some Spanish asshole who was nuts and a fat guy on a donkey.

"What are we going to wish for?" Sebastian asked.

He wasn't taking notes either, but he didn't have to take notes. Sebastian knew all this stuff. He liked it. Hell, he had read *Moby Dick* which was as thick as a damned brick. You could maim someone with that book.

"I'm not sure," Meche said. "Something big. What do you want to wish for?"

"I'm making a list."

"God, won't he shut up," Meche whispered.

"Then he couldn't listen to himself."

Meche smirked.

"What is amusing you today, Mercedes?"

She hated it when people called her by her full name. She'd told Rodriguez this, but he refused to ever use her nickname. Meche did not reply, staring down at her book and pretending she was reading.

"No, really. I'm interested. Because you two lovebirds have been whispering for about half an hour."

The class erupted into laughter at the word 'lovebirds,' making Meche blush with mortification.

"Maybe Sebastian Soto is not such a fag," someone yelled from the back of the room.

Rodriguez let them chuckle, then gave her a twisted smile. "Extra homework for you. Stay at the end of class."

"Can hardly wait," she whispered.

MECHE GRABBED HER backpack and shuffled to the front of the class, stopping before Rodriguez's desk. She could see Daniela standing outside the door, waiting for her.

The teacher raised his eyes and nodded at her.

"You were disruptive today. Again."

"Sorry, Mr. Rodriguez."

"You know, I can't really tell if you do it on purpose, Mercedes," he said, lacing his hands together, trying to look stern although his incipient moustache made him more comical than scary. "Is it just the sugar from all those cereals coursing through your body?"

"My brain is stuck from shooting glue," she said.

Rodriguez did not get the Ramones reference. He just raised an eyebrow at her.

"It's a song," she explained, fearing he'd take it seriously and call the principal.

"That's your problem, Mercedes. Your head is filled with songs. If you spent less time watching music videos and more time doing your readings, you wouldn't be failing my class."

He shuffled a stack of papers and put them in a folder.

"You need to do some extra work."

"Professor…"

"No, you do," he said. "I can help you if you need it. I tutor after school."

"I've got a tutor," she said, thinking of Sebastian. He knew books. He could help her.

"I think you could benefit from my…"

"Yeah, where's the assignment?" she asked, pissed off and just wanting to get out of the classroom.

He handed her a piece of paper. Meche stuffed it in her sweater pocket and walked out. Daniela peeked her head inside and saw her heading towards the door. She smiled at the teacher then looked at Meche.

"What did he say?"

THE NEIGHBOURHOOD WHERE they lived was cut by a large avenue, dividing it into two starkly different halves. To the west, the buildings and houses became progressively nicer, the cars newer, the people better dressed. To the east there were no houses. Just numerous apartment buildings sandwiched together. These turned uglier, rattier and more dangerous the more you moved in that direction. In the east side people built tin-houses in the alleys and streets. Gang members could dismantle a car in five minutes flat and beat you for your lunch money.

Sebastian was the one who lived closest to the east, just a mere two blocks from the large avenue and the division between lower middle-class and outright poverty. Meche was situated three blocks further to the west. Although three blocks might not seem like much, it gave her a surer social footing at school.

Daniela lived closest to the west, not in an apartment, but in a house with a high wall covered with a purple bougainvillea. Her father was an accountant for a furniture chain and his wealth manifested conspicuously—without taste—all through this house in the form of Tiffany lamps, shiny tables and a plaster replica of the Venus de Milo greeting you when you entered the home. Daniela's house, like her father, was big and ostentatious. The jolly, obese man had a wife as round as he was and three daughters, all quiet and polite, educated in archaic manners and ways right out of the 1940s. Daniela's father believed in the sanctity of virginity and the role of the woman as wife and mother. He thought men who wore earrings were fags and those with long hair hippies or anarchists. He was, however, unable to manifest any ill-will towards them, or towards almost anyone, convinced that God would sort them out in his due time.

He was a harmless, dull fellow of few ideas and few complaints, who liked nothing more than to drink a few beers, eat large portions of spicy *birria* and coddle his daughters. None of the three was more coddled than Daniela, the youngest daughter and also the one with lupus—twin conditions which ensured she was guarded as carefully as a princess in a fairy tale.

Daniela was picked up and dropped off at school even though she was located closer to the Queen Victoria than her two friends. She was not to play sports of any kind for if she suffered the most minor bruise, her skin would turn an ugly shade of purple and there was always the danger of a scrape turning into a mountain of turmoil. She was not permitted any boyfriends, though this was not an issue because in addition to her childish ways—no doubt rooted in the babying imposed on her by her parents—Daniela was a moon-faced, limpid girl. Her greatest assets were her breasts which had started swelling at the tender age of eleven, turning into two rather large embarrassments, causing Daniela to walk everywhere looking a little hunched.

In fact, Daniela and Meche made quite a pair when they were side by side. Meche, thin and flat as a board, pimpled, dark of complexion and intentions, standing always very straight. Daniela, dwarfing Meche with her greater height, chubby and pale, shy and slumped, with short frizzy hair of a vaguely reddish hue which she had inherited from a Scottish ancestor who had stumbled into Mexico some eighty years before.

Daniela liked watching soap operas and reading romance novels. She painted her room pink and kept all her Barbies on shelves. She was, in short, the polar opposite of Meche and loved her friend precisely because of this.

Sometimes, though, Daniela had to admit Meche scared her. Early on in their friendship she had been warned by some of the other girls at school that Meche was odd, different, perhaps slightly crazy. However, beggars can't be choosers and Daniela did not have many friends. Plus, Meche's energy attracted Daniela, even if this same intensity made her step quietly back at times.

Meche had a way of roping you in with her words, of convincing you to do the unthinkable. One minute you were firmly telling yourself that you would never play with a Ouija board, the next you were gathered in the bathroom, the board sitting on top of the toilet lid, while Meche urged you on before the principal came and busted you all.

Daniela, never one to put up much resistance, constantly fell under the sway of Meche's stronger personality, always the handmaiden to the queen.

Like that day.

She had told Meche there would be no spell casting in her home, but Meche informed Daniela that they couldn't do it in her apartment because her mother was around and they couldn't do it in Sebastian's apartment because he shared a room with his brother, and Daniela was the one who had an empty house on Thursdays because her mother and her sisters went grocery shopping that day during the afternoon. It all made perfect sense, see? Before Daniela knew it she had said "yes."

Meche arrived with Sebastian, placed the portable record player on the floor, flipped the case open, and was riffling through the records she had brought inside a tattered, nylon market bag.

Daniela wrung her hands, hoping her mother and siblings would not burst in any time soon and that this whole witchcraft thing did not involve anything gross. Once, when she was little, Daniela's mother had taken her to an old healer for a *limpia*. The woman had rubbed an egg and a lemon all over her body, then made her drink this bitter brew, telling her it would heal her. It hadn't. Daniela still had lupus and her mother still would not let her play sports for fear of lacerations.

"What are you doing?" Daniela asked eventually, because standing there and staring at her two friends was starting to bore her.

"We are picking spell music," Meche said.

"What spell are we doing?"

"Something about success."

"Okay, why don't we use the Iggy Pop song?" Sebastian asked, holding up a record.

"Too obvious," Meche said.

"What? We get points for being cryptic?" Sebastian said.

"You don't just go out there and blurt it out," Meche replied.

"Why not?"

"Because it would be too easy."

"Easy is good."

"My mother will be back soon," Daniela muttered.

Sebastian and Meche turned towards her, eyebrows arched, with that look that meant, *Daniela, you don't get it*. It was a very common look.

"Fine," Sebastian said. "David Bowie. We play Fame and call it even."

"That's about two degrees less lame," Meche said.

"David Bowie is lame?"

"No, using that song is lame. There's like zero effort."

"Oh, okay. So let's go with this guy we've never heard of," Sebastian said, holding up another record, "because that's not lame."

"Without Robert Johnson you wouldn't have Elvis, no Beatles, no…"

"The lyrics you showed me don't say a single thing about success."

"They don't have to. He's standing at the crossroads because he's about to sell his soul to the devil."

"I don't want to do any devil songs," Daniela said. "I don't want to give birth to a baby with hooves who throws his mom down a staircase."

"That's like a fucked up version of *Rosemary's Baby* crossed with *The Omen*," Meche said.

"No devil songs."

"Daniela, wouldn't you prefer to play a David Bowie song?" Sebastian asked.

Meche's eyes said 'absolutely not,' but Daniela could not side with her this time. She bobbed her head timidly.

"Yes," she said.

"That is not fair," Meche said.

"There's three of us and we just out-voted you," Sebastian said, smugly sliding the record from its sleeve.

He lifted the needle. There was the faint scratch against the vinyl and then the song began to play.

"Okay, now we hold hands and dance around it," Meche said.

"Really," Sebastian replied dryly.

"Yes. That's what witches do. They dance around the fire. Only we don't have a fire, so we'll dance around the record player."

Sebastian rolled his eyes. Meche pinched his arm. They joined hands, clumsily turning around, like children playing Doña Blanca, only they weren't little kids and this was not a game at recess.

"Ugh, your palms are sweaty," Sebastian said, drawing away from Daniela.

"Don't break the circle," Meche told him.

"How about I spin in my place?" he asked, wiping his hands against his trousers.

"Seriously," Meche muttered, but she didn't ask them to hold hands again.

They did spin. They whirled. At first, it seemed silly and Daniela thought she was going to get dizzy and throw up. But the more they did it, the longer the seconds stretched, the more it seemed to make sense. Daniela felt very warm, like there was fire blooming from the pit of her stomach, stretching up her chest and stinging her mouth. Their fingers brushed as they turned.

She watched as Meche spun. Her friend's gaze was fixed on a distant point, her body turning but her eyes always returning to that distant something. Sebastian, similarly, seemed to have locked his eyes on something. Daniela closed her eyes and licked her lips; her cheeks burned.

She didn't feel dizzy from the movement. Not really. But there was something dizzying, hypnotic about the music, and she was reminded of a documentary they'd shown at school in which some monks were dancing, their skirts flaring around them.

Fame, fame, fame.

Daniela's head lolled to the side and she snapped her eyes open.

Something seemed to lift from them, quickly leaving the room, cooling her skin. She blinked. She shivered, suddenly afraid because she had almost touched *something* that didn't seem like another of Meche's games.

Meche lifted the needle and they stood around the player in silence, nobody daring to be the first one to speak.

Finally, Sebastian found his voice.

"Did it work?" he asked. "Do you feel different?"

Daniela flexed her hands. Meche moved towards the white, wooden vanity with the pink necklaces strewn around its surface. She leaned forward, a hand against the mirror.

"Not really," she said.

"Me neither," Daniela added.

"But something happened," Meche said.

Neither Sebastian nor Daniela answered her. Daniela stared at her hands, at the ugly, bitten nails. She could not stop chewing them. Sometimes she even hurt herself and this alarmed her mother greatly because every little scrape could become a life or death matter.

Daniela heard the front door opening, her mother and her sisters' voices heralding their arrival. Whatever uncertain power still remained in the room now definitely dissipated with the intrusion of the women.

Meche began gathering her records, putting them back in her bag.

"A SIX PAGE essay on Cervantes and his connection with modern realist literature," she told him as they walked home.

She was wearing a heavy, green jacket which made her look like a bag lady. He'd told her that one time and Meche had punched him, but it was true. It was a formless sack. Meche resembled a very large, very green jellyfish from behind. She drowned in that jacket, but then again she seemed to drown in all her clothes. Only the fingertips peeking out from the sleeves, the neck erased by folds of clothing. Beneath the jacket she tended to wear oversized t-shirts with names like Iron Maiden, Queen and The Who emblazoned on them.

"He must be very mad at you."

"It's a scam. He wanted me to take this tutoring session with him.

All he wants is to make extra money."

"You could use some tutoring."

"Not with Rodriguez. He is such a dick."

Sebastian was carrying the portable record player, Meche had the bag. They walked down the narrow streets, side by side. It seemed to Sebastian they were always walking, going from or to school, going to the market together, stopping at the store to buy a soft drink. Except, that was, when he took the motorcycle out for a spin.

The motorcycle had belonged to his older brother, but his brother had given up on it. He'd called it a piece of crap and left it to rot. Sebastian tried to get it going again, and it sputtered to life now and then, though it was an unreliable creature. He liked riding it, when he could, because he thought the leather jacket he had found at the *tianguis*—used, Sebastian could never buy new stuff—coupled with the sunglasses made him look more masculine.

The boys called him Sebastian Soto el Joto and Sebastian Puto, and sometimes, to be creative and not rhyme, Sebastian Pansy. No matter what the nickname was, the crude conclusion was always the same: he was gay. Sebastian was straight, but accuracy did not have much say when it came to these things. Marking him as effeminate was just a way to toss him into the pile of the undesirables, to mock his everything, to serve as an excuse for their rudeness.

He remembered one time when Constantino caught him looking at Isadora and snapped, "What are you looking at, faggot?" Sebastian had wanted to beat the crap out of him, to paint the pavement red with the guy's blood.

Sebastian wondered if the magic would fix this. If he might grow more muscled, leaving his scrawniness behind. Maybe Isadora would look at him if he looked tougher, if he had nicer clothes, new sneakers. Sneakers that weren't painted with a black marker.

They stopped by the bakery and stared at the confectionery for the Day of the Dead: the little candy skulls glittering in the twilight, the sugar looking like tiny diamonds. He liked this time of year. The end of October, the appearance of the orange and yellow flowers, the *papel picado* and the colourful skeletons which heralded the arrival of the festival, and with it, the end of the rainy season and the beginning of the cold months of the year.

"Is your grandma going to bake bread for the Day of the Dead?" he asked.

"Yeah. Next week."

"Can I come and eat some?"

"Sure."

Meche entered the shop and bought two pieces of sweet bread. Sebastian didn't have any money. One more reason why he walked everywhere. She gave him one of the breads and they sat on the steps of a nearby building, eating and watching the few people go by as it got dark and the street lights bloomed into life.

"Do you think it'll all be different in the morning?" he asked.

"You still do not believe me?" she asked.

He licked some cream which was spilling from the bread onto his hand and shrugged, not wanting to look too excited by the whole idea. Not wanting this too badly, although he did.

"I'm not sure."

"Fine."

"Hey, don't get mad."

"I'm not mad."

He sat back, his head against the door of the building. Meche, in turn, rested her head against his shoulder. For others, it might have been an intimate gesture. Maybe it was, but not in the way most people might think. Meche and Sebastian were used to each other, comfortable in their proximity. They folded and kept their dreams in the same drawer, spun fantasies side by side, lived in the easy harmony of youth which did not know the need for tall walls and sturdy defenses.

Sebastian popped the last bit of bread into his mouth and chewed it slowly. The sweet potato seller pushed his cart in front of them, the hiss of steam announcing his arrival, his voice slicing the night.

"*Camotes*! I sell *camotes*!"

The man paused and glanced in their direction, but his small, black eyes did not seem to see them. They skipped over Sebastian and Meche as he moved away, the wheels of the cart turning, the steam rising towards the night sky.

Though he was not particularly musical, Sebastian thought of a song. Duncan Dhu, singing En Algún Lugar, and for a reason he did not understand he had this image of Meche stepping onto a plane. He put an arm around Meche's shoulders, holding her tight.

MECHE WOKE UP the next morning with the giddy excitement of a child heading to open her Christmas presents. She brushed her teeth, combed her hair, rolled up the sleeves of her sweater and put on her shoes. Then she bounced towards school, eager to meet up with Sebastian.

He was waiting for her at the street corner and they walked together, as they usually did, quiet and filled with hope.

Hope began to disintegrate around noon when it became obvious that nothing had changed for them. They were still the same losers as the day before, still sitting in the same corner of the schoolyard, still looking forlorn at the more popular, more beautiful, more-everything kids. When the bell signalling the end of the day rang, Meche could barely contain herself. Jaw locked tightly, she hurried back home.

"Hey," she heard Sebastian say, but didn't slow down to let him catch up with her and she dashed home, hands tight around the straps of her backpack.

They had failed.

She stomped up the steps towards her apartment, rushing into her bedroom and tossing the backpack on the floor. Meche put on a record and listened to Frank Sinatra promising to fly her to the moon. Tears threatened to leak from her eyes so she rubbed them. She hated crying. Hated feeling weak.

Meche sniffled and cleaned her nose with the back of her hand.

She had seriously thought it would work. She had pinned her heart on a stupid record, like a modern-day Jack showing off his beans.

Of course it would never work.

They would always be the same.

Life would always be this dull shade.

Meche turned her head and looked out the window, at the fragment of mocking grey sky. Birds sometimes dropped dead in Mexico City. That's how polluted the city was. Because of the overwhelming smog, you couldn't even hope for a glimpse of its snow-capped volcanoes.

Meche draped a blanket around her shoulders and went to sleep.

She did not bother changing out of her uniform and into her regular clothes.

When she woke up it was dark and there was the smell of food wafting into her room. Meche walked towards the kitchen and found her grandmother busy, humming over a pot. She smiled at Meche.

"I'm making chicken soup today," she said. "It has the potatoes and carrots all nicely chopped, the way you like them."

"Thank you," she muttered.

Meche's grandmother filled a chipped bowl with soup and Meche began to eat. The warm food soothed her belly and she slowly started feeling better. Her grandmother poured her a glass of lemonade. Meche sipped it, holding the glass with both hands.

"Are you getting sick, Meche?"

She shook her head.

"Okay."

Grandmother was quiet. She didn't push or ask questions. But her silences pulled the truth out of you anyway, made you speak despite the desire to remain silent. So Meche spoke, her hands sliding against the cool glass.

"Mama Dolores, what did you mean when you said magic will break your heart?"

"You're still going on about that?" she asked, placing a bunch of tortillas wrapped in a warm cloth by Meche's plate.

Meche peeled open the wrapping and pulled out a tortilla, dipping it in the broth.

"Maybe."

"Magic gets you what you want, but it doesn't solve your problems."

"That doesn't make any sense."

"It does," Mama Dolores pulled out a chair, sitting next to Meche. "There was a man in my town who wanted to get married but he could not find himself a bride. He went to a witch and asked her for a charm. Something that would get him a wife."

"Did it work?"

"It did. He was married within a month's time."

"Then it did solve his problems."

Mama Dolores cut a lemon in half and carefully sprinkled a bit of sugar on it.

"No. Because one year later she ran away with another man."

"That's a bad story."

"Blame the magic, not the story."

Mama Dolores bit into her lemon.

"But you also told me witches fly through the night, they turn into animals, they put curses on you—"

"True. They do all that."

"But then?"

"Nothing, that. But a man may turn into a coyote as many times as he wants and may steal chickens from the farm, but the chickens won't be his and they will still be stolen. And the coyote will still be nothing but a large, ugly dog."

Meche sighed, staring into the contents of her bowl of soup. She didn't understand what her grandmother meant.

"If I was a witch—"

"Ugh, it's pouring outside. You could not believe the rain," Meche's mother said, shaking her umbrella out as she entered.

Even soaked and with her mascara running, she looked very beautiful. Meche's mother had once held aspirations to become an actress, make it big in the movies or maybe a soap. Natalia certainly had the looks. She only lacked the talent. She had given up on her dreams several years before and had gone to work at a department store. Now it was the pharmacy, where she worked as a cashier and part-time model: her photos adorned some of the flyers advertising the pharmacy. This was not as much an achievement as a form of charity because the owner of the pharmacy, Don Fernando, was Natalia's godfather.

"What did you make?" Natalia asked.

"Chicken soup," Meche's grandmother said.

"Did you take off the skin from my piece of chicken? You know I can't eat chicken with the skin on."

"Yes, yes."

"I don't want a lot of rice in my bowl. No potatoes either."

"You have to have one potato."

"It's too starchy. Is it warm? I have to go back to the drugstore for the rest of my shift. Leona is sick again this week."

Natalia sat across from Meche. Meche looked at her mother,

waiting for her to say something to her. Eventually, possibly because Meche just kept staring at her, Natalia spoke.

"How was school?"

"Alright."

"Do you have a lot of homework?"

"Some."

There was a systematic indifference to Natalia's voice. It was a chore doing this, playing the mother-daughter bond. Meche saw her fret in discomfort. Normally she would have simply stepped away, back to her room, and let her mother eat in peace. She did not feel charitable that evening, so she stayed put.

"I saw you walking with that boy yesterday."

"Sebastian?"

"Yes."

Meche did not remember if they had gone by the drugstore. Possibly. Their path had zigzagged through the whole neighbourhood as they chased stars which could not be seen in the night sky, hearts filled with promise. A promise which now lay squashed beneath the soles of their feet.

"You say his name like you don't know him," Meche muttered.

"Meche, he's here all the time. Or you're somewhere with him. You act like you are Siamese twins. It's not healthy."

"Daniela is also with us."

"Yes, that chubby little girl is also not a good role model. Plus, I don't want you catching something from her."

"You can't catch lupus."

"Well, I don't know about that."

"It's not scientifically possible," Meche said.

"Never mind. Meche, running around the block with a boy was OK when you were a little girl. You're fifteen now."

"And?"

Mama Dolores held up the cloth with the tortillas, but Natalia shook her head.

"I don't eat tortillas, you know that."

Mama Dolores set the tortillas down. Meche grabbed the saltshaker and began salting her broth. Her mother shook her head.

"Salt will bloat you."

"It needs salt."

"Too much salt is not good for you."

Meche kept slowly salting her soup, even though she knew now it would be *too* salty. She felt like making a point.

"What I'm trying to say—and perhaps I'm failing to express myself clearly here, Meche—is that it doesn't look right to be with a boy so much."

"It doesn't look right to whom?"

"Well, Catalina Coronado was telling me she saw you going into the abandoned factory with him the other morning."

Of course. Catalina Coronado. The neighbourhood gossip, with her sharp, hawk-eyed gaze and her forked tongue. Ready to spill bad news at a moment's notice and spit venom in your face. She had probably relished the opportunity to tattle on Meche.

"When did she tell you that?"

"She was at the drugstore today, buying some cough drops, and she told me she happened to see you. Meche, you do know what teenagers do in that factory, don't you?"

They had sex, drank booze, and smoked dope. Meche, feigning stupidity, stared at her mother.

"No, please tell me what they do."

Natalia did not reply. She stirred her soup with her spoon, carefully inspecting each chunk of vegetable, each scrap of chicken.

"Please, tell me," Meche insisted.

"You are not a child."

"No, I'm not. I don't understand why that means I can't hang out with Sebastian like I always do. Because Catalina Coronado doesn't like him?"

"Sebastian's brother just got his girlfriend pregnant and I do not want a similar surprise, alright?"

Meche did not know that. How had her mother found out? She supposed that was one of the benefits of working at the drugstore, all the little crumbs of information that fell into your lap. But it didn't matter. His brother had nothing to do with her.

"He's my best friend," Meche said. "Grandma, can I finish my food later? I think I am coming down with a cold."

Meche drifted towards the doorway. She glanced back at her

mother. Natalia rolled out a magazine, already busy looking at the '10 Beauty Tips of the Week' and the 'Most Flattering Skirts of the Season.' Meche returned to her room and the company of her records.

SEBASTIAN TRIED TO catch up with Meche. She lost him at an intersection, disappearing behind a row of food stands. He did not understand what was wrong with her, why she had not waited for him.

He gave up on finding his friend and continued on his way home, observing the sky and wondering if it would start raining before he got to his apartment. Too late he noticed Isadora and her friends hanging out near a little corner store, drinking soda pop, and immediately felt the desire to dash in the opposite direction. However, they had already seen him, and completely turning around would be too conspicuous. He forced himself to keep on walking, eyes straight ahead.

He already knew what was coming.

The boys immediately perked up when they saw him, the girls looked at him curiously.

"Look! It's the faggot! What ya'up to, faggot?" one of them asked.

Sebastian wished he had a Walkman like Meche. Then he might have put on the headphones and completely ignored their taunts, protected by the music. He did not have a Walkman, so he had to listen to the insults.

"Do you thinks he fucks men or he lets them fuck him up the ass?"

"I think he lets them fuck him."

"He's going to get butt cancer."

Sebastian jammed his hands into his trousers, his chin up, shoulders tense. He was taller than the whole lot, but there were four boys and he was alone. He wouldn't put it past them to try and hit him. They hadn't done it before, limiting themselves to tossing garbage in his direction—empty bottles of Frutsi, and on one memorable occasion a whole hotdog—but you never knew. They might feel adventurous that afternoon.

"He's so gay."

Sebastian walked by, his eyes flitting over Isadora. For a brief moment, Isadora looked back at him, seeming a little pained. Like she was sorry he had to endure this treatment. Then she looked away and he looked away too. Before he reached the corner, Sebastian felt something hit him in the back. The raucous laughter of the boys was now joined by a chorus of giggling girls. Was Isadora laughing, too? He did not dare to look back. He turned the corner.

When Sebastian arrived home, the whole apartment was pitch black. He flicked on the lights and wandered into the kitchen, looking for something to eat. His mother did not have the time nor the inclination to cook and his brother, Romualdo—who was supposed to cook for himself and Sebastian—had barely done so when he was in high school. Now that he was in university, he did not bother.

Sebastian cut a piece of cheese and rolled it into a slice of ham. He ate standing up in the kitchen, glancing at the dirty dishes piling up in the sink. Those were also his brother's responsibility, while Sebastian was in charge of the laundry. Unlike most Mexican families who could pay a maid— they came cheap in this country— no matter how lowly their social class, Sebastian's mother could not afford any help. Sebastian and Romualdo were supposed to divide all the chores equally, solving this issue, but Romualdo, full of misplaced machismo, refused to do girls' chores. Washing dishes was beneath him. In a few days, their mother would scream at Romualdo and force him to scrub the pots but until then they would sit there, ignored.

The cat meowed at Sebastian and he checked its dish. He filled it with cat food, then cleaned the water dish and filled it too. This was supposed to also be his brother's responsibility, but if it were not for Sebastian the cat would starve.

Sebastian went to his bedroom. It was a small apartment and a small bedroom, and he had to share it with Romualdo. His brother's side of the room was plastered with posters of women, some in bikinis, some completely naked; stacks of magazines full of girlie pictures, bare flesh spread all over the bed. Sebastian's side was papered with maps and pictures of Europe, many of which had come from his grandfather, who had lived in Barcelona until his late teens. Europe. That's where Sebastian was going to go one day, to write great stories in a Parisian café. Or, perhaps, he'd venture to Italy, where he could order an espresso and pretend he was in a Fellini movie, which grandpa had loved. He didn't have girlie magazines. Instead, Sebastian's books were all neatly sitting on a shelf. *The Ambassadors*, *One Hundred Years of Solitude*, *Hopscotch*.

He supposed that's why the boys at school said he was gay. Because he didn't have big-tittie posters. Because he spent all his spare time reading. Because he drew stars on his tennis shoes with a black marker. Sebastian would have loved to have been normal. He realized his predilection for novels instead of soccer had distanced him from his father, even before the old man and his mother divorced, but he could not help it.

Or maybe his father hated him because he was a measured, quiet little bag boy, packing groceries three afternoons a week, saying "yes miss" and "no miss", his sneakers squeaking over the floor as he moved to put the plastic bags in the shopping cart. He certainly knew that the boys and girls at school made fun of him because of that, giggling whenever they were in the checkout line with their parents; lofty because they didn't have to scramble for a few pesos, stretch their hands like urchins, make their money from tips in dirty change. He was a *cerillo*, a nothing, a thin kid wearing a black vest and a tie as he packed and packed groceries and dreamed of Europe.

Sebastian lay on his bed and stretched his arms, staring at the ceiling, the acid memory of the taunts the boys had yelled at him still fresh, still ringing in his ears. He felt his muscles relaxing in the pleasant darkness, his eyelids fluttering close to sleep.

Romualdo walked in and turned on the light. He was tall, just like Sebastian, but his brother seemed better proportioned, better looking, better prepared overall. He gave Sebastian an indifferent glance.

"I need to phone Margarita, asshole."

That was his girlfriend. She was pretty and nice enough, but Sebastian didn't like it when she came around because Romualdo kicked him out of the bedroom so he could have sex with her. Sebastian then had to wander around the block or take a ride on the motorcycle, and sometimes he really didn't want to go out but there was no reasoning with Romualdo.

Or, just like now, Romualdo would phone Margarita and that also meant Sebastian needed to step out because he wanted some privacy. Funny how Romualdo had the right to privacy, but Sebastian didn't have the right to anything.

"Phone her."

"Go to the living room."

Sebastian grabbed his backpack and shuffled out of the room. Romualdo closed the door.

Sebastian tried to read, then gave up and turned on the television. He rested his chin against the arm of the couch and watched a Timbiriche music video. They were singing Tu Y Yo Somos Uno Mismo. The lyrics and the images were incredibly corny: a man and a woman running together on the beach, a tear slipping down the woman's cheek, the kiss and the catchy, pop tune. Meche would have hated it.

But Sebastian wanted it. He wanted that corny, fabricated music video universe in which a couple could pop up from under the waves, water dripping from their bodies, embracing each other.

He had nothing of that. Just the book in his lap, the ratty couch and the cat which now drifted next to him, rubbing against his leg.

He supposed he never would, now that Meche's spell had failed.

Sebastian turned off the TV set.

Mexico City, 2009

IT WASN'T THAT Meche hated Lorenzo. She just had never taken to him. After her parents' divorce, her mother's swift remarriage had left her a little breathless and Meche had never felt quite at home after he moved in. It wasn't anything that he did or said, but she knew she was an intruder whenever she visited. Two brief Christmas vacations in Mexico City had convinced Meche there was no reason for her to ever set foot in that apartment again. The third Christmas, when she asked if her mother could fly to Monterrey instead, Lorenzo happily paid for the plane ticket. After graduation, when she secured a job in Europe, Lorenzo had also been instrumental in soothing any fears of distances and dangers. Meche knew that, as far as Lorenzo was concerned, the less he saw of Natalia's taciturn daughter, the better.

"Did you make much progress today?" Lorenzo asked, trying to make polite conversation.

"My father had a lot of things," she said. "It's hard going through all of it."

"How many records did he have?" Jimena asked, grabbing another piece of sweet bread from the centre basket.

"Thousands."

"Is that all he had?"

The question was crass, but then again so was Jimena with her bright red nails and her bright red smile. Since when had she become so cozy with her mother? Meche supposed it was to be expected. Natalia had a tendency to replace people. First her father, now Meche. She didn't blame her on the part about Vicente. Natalia had taken too long to divorce him. It should have happened years before.

Meche shook her head.

"He didn't collect CDs, only vinyl."

Meche knew Jimena had not been wondering about records. She was asking if he had anything valuable. Meche doubted he did, but discussing the amount of pesos they might make from the sale of her father's collection was very inappropriate.

"What will you do with them?"

"Ship some back to Oslo," Meche said, shrugging. "Throw away the rest. I can't carry too many things but I could buy a suitcase and pack it with the ones I want to keep. I might also take the typewriter and his manuscript."

"The manuscript," Natalia said, as she shook her head. "He was always going to finish it next summer."

Her mother smiled, gently, and for once in a long time Meche thought she glimpsed a certain tenderness towards the old man. She sounded almost fond of him.

"Ay, we need to serve the coffee. Where's my head?" Natalia asked, blinking and heading towards the kitchen. "Everyone is having coffee, right?"

"I'd like some tea with milk, please," Meche said.

In Norway Meche drank her tea from a glass, with lots of milk, a custom acquired after living in London. An unusual gesture now in Mexico where she might be expected to ask for *atole* or coffee.

"We're out of milk," Lorenzo told her.

"I can go buy some."

"I'll go," Lorenzo said.

"No. I'll just head to the corner store."

Jimena and Lorenzo looked at her, doubtful. Meche chuckled. She knew they were worried about her. She had not cried during the funeral. She just stood under her umbrella, eyeing the casket with scepticism, thinking that Vicente Vega would have been shocked and outraged by the whole spectacle. He certainly would have said a few words about the cross sitting atop him, considering he had been a staunch atheist.

"It's still in the same place, right?"

"Sure," Lorenzo said.

"Then I'll be right back."

Stepping out into the street was a blessing. The apartment felt stuffy and her family were very noisy. Of course, Meche was accustomed to living by herself, not having cousins and aunts rolling in and out of an apartment in preparation for her father's prayers, which began that night with a late mass and finger foods after going to church. Nine nights of prayer, to ensure the dead man's soul would reach his final destination. Nine whole nights she had to remain here. Meche had already tried talking about the necessity of flying back to Europe, but her mother had blocked any plans of an early flight.

Meche walked into the corner store, which was not really at the corner but that was what everyone called them in Mexico. It wasn't really a proper store either, but the first floor of someone's house, arranged to store foods and beverages, with the owners living on the top. In her time, the owner had been Don Chemo, the surly old man who always looked carefully at the kids, making sure they didn't steal candy.

The little store looked exactly as it had when she was a teenager. She was sure that even some of the ads on the walls behind the counter were the same, though the attendant behind the counter had changed. He did, however, bear an uncanny resemblance to Don Chemo. Meche wondered if this could be his grandson who would have been an annoying little kindergartener the last time she'd seen him.

Meche found the milk and riffled through the store, looking at the candy and chips. They had the regular tamarind Pelón Pelo Rico and a sour lime flavour she had never seen before, peanuts dipped in chilli, and chocolate Carlos V.

Meche took out a bill and placed it on the counter. Don Chemo's grandson—he had to be, he had the same disposition—gave her her change and slowly placed the things she had bought in a plastic bag.

As soon as Meche stepped out it began to rain. A light drizzle which made her smile.

She loved the rain.

Meche reached into her pocket and turned on her iPod, picking a song from the playlist. For the sake of nostalgia she settled on Miguel Bosé. Nena, which was from '86. The writhing of the handsome

Bosé and a blonde woman in white all along the floor had sent her mother into a bizarre state of agitation the first time it aired on TV. Natalia had quickly changed the channel and railed against music videos, which exposed youth to so many nasty images.

But Meche liked Nena. There was something real about it. Not like some of the other videos which contaminated the airwaves. Certainly better than the chirpings of Thalía or—dear God— Lucerito. When Bosé sang about an impossible woman with an insatiable mouth and they fought—and rolled around the floor—it seemed gritty and true. A fucked up relationship, but fascinating all the same.

Meche raised her head. The street was empty except for someone standing on the other side, holding an umbrella.

Meche looked down at her iPod again, pumping up the volume so she could hear nothing but the deep voice of Bosé.

When she looked up again the person with the umbrella was still in the same place.

It was a guy in a business suit and a long, black raincoat; a matching umbrella with a nice wooden handle.

He was staring at her.

It took longer than it should have for Meche to recognize him. But then she saw the resemblance. The very tall, thin frame—though now it was not cadaveric, he was lean without seeming unhealthily skinny—was the first thing to trigger her memory. Then the other pieces were all pulled together. Very black hair, cropped short in a fashionable style. A stern mouth which had grown sterner. A carefully trimmed goatee which had never been there before. The dark, dark eyes which resembled a pair of pebbles.

Sebastian Soto, in the flesh.

He looked so different. Only the eyes had remained the same.

She wondered what she must look like now, her long hair—it had reached her waist—cut short in a boyish style, the thick eyebrows plucked, her clothes actually fitting her.

He looked at her and Meche wanted to laugh. Not a good laugh. A bitter, angry laugh. She had been so fearful of meeting Sebastian again and she had found him, smack across the street.

Meche held the plastic bag with her purchases in one hand and jammed the other hand in the pocket of her jeans, tilting her head a little, daring him to cross the street and say hello.

He just looked at her, though by now she was sure he had identified her, and stood his ground. His gaze did not waver but he did not make any effort to move her way, wave hello or open his mouth.

Like two duelists at noon, about to draw their guns, they stood on their respective sides of the street. Finally he snapped, looking away from her and continuing along the path he had been following, keeping to his side. Meche also turned away, walking in the opposite direction.

The rain did not seem pleasant anymore. The dirty puddles reflected the street lights and the trash strewn on the ground was beginning to clog the drain. Later, the whole street would ooze and the water level would rise.

Mexico City was sinking. A city slowly descending into the muck from where it had come. The Spaniards had drained its Venice-like canals and filled them with earth, creating shaky foundations for their churches. Centuries later, their descendants paid for their folly with constant inundations which threatened to turn the whole metropolis into the lake it had been when the Aztecs made their way there. A fetid sea of sewage swamped the sidewalks every year.

In Mexico City everything returns. The rains and the past and everything in between.

Meche, upset by her encounter with Sebastian, gave in and went by the house owned by Daniela's parents. They were happy to supply their daughter's number.

Mexico City, 1988

IT WAS ANOTHER one of those days; it was always one of those days with Natalia. She flogged him with her tongue, excoriated him for real and imaginary flaws, drew blood. This time the fight had been over cigarettes. They were a needless expense. He should quit smoking. Not because of his health, no. Natalia could care less if he died of cancer. Her concern was the money. They could save so many pesos if he would only stop smoking.

"You could stop doing your nails," he countered. "They're more expensive than my half pack a day."

"I do my nails because of my job."

"What job? You work at the pharmacy."

"It's customer service."

"It's bullshit. You do your nails because you want to, so don't come telling me it's because of some demanding job."

"I could get an audition."

"But you won't," he said.

She slapped him. He left afterwards, didn't even try the chicken soup that was supposed to be his dinner, and went to eat at the *cantina* instead.

There he nursed his glass and his feelings, hunched over a table. Eventually some of the regulars arrived and he joined a game of dominoes, trying to find meaning in the black-and-white pieces, like a man trying to read the Tarot cards.

Where had he gone wrong? Where had his road forked towards defeat? Somehow, at some point, he had become a loser. Maybe he'd always been one but had been unable to recognize it in his youth.

Vicente smoked his cheap cigarettes. Cigarettes which were staining his once pristine teeth, turning them an ugly yellow. But did it matter? He had been a decent looking chap but that was gone. He had the same face, but it was lined with discomfort and misery. It was not the face of a music idol.

As for Natalia... Natalia had changed. Each year her eyes narrowed more, fixed more sternly on his shoulders. Each year, he knew she found the leather jackets shabbier, the long hair more off-putting, the little tricks he did to charm people—like recite the year when any song had come on the air—more stale. Each year she measured him and found him more and more wanting.

How different from when they had first met at the record store, when Natalia had wandered in looking for a present for the boyfriend she had at the time. Her taste in music did not run very deep and Vicente had spent a good hour chatting to her about this and that band, the benefits of a certain record over another, finally settling on *Arthur (Or the Decline and Fall of the British Empire)* as his recommendation for a birthday present. When he gave Natalia her change he wrote his number on the back of a bill.

"Let's go out sometime," he said.

"I told you I have a boyfriend," she said.

"It's not going to last."

It didn't and one month later she was back at the store, trying to exchange the record for another one, although, truth be told, she just wanted to see him.

He had charm aplenty in those days. He wrote letters to Natalia every day and quickly won her heart. Maybe he still had charm, but Natalia had ceased to be impressed by it. She didn't want him to compose songs for her and she certainly didn't want to read his eternal compendium on Latin American music.

Vicente smoked and drank. Around midnight Meche popped in. She'd been sent to get him from the *cantina* since she was ten years old. Vicente knew the routine, he said goodbye to his friends, put out his cigarette and nodded to his daughter, following her outside.

She was stuffed into her oversized green jacket, carrying her Walkman.

"What are you listening to?" he asked. He always asked her. It made her happy when he asked.

"Dylan. All Along the Watchtower."

"Depressing."

"Well, you know," Meche muttered, kicking a can of soda down the sidewalk. "Happiness is in short supply."

She passed it to him and Vicente kicked it for a little bit, then passed it to her and paused to light a cigarette. Meche looked at him with eyes that were his own. Large and sad and painted with the same seeds of misery he carried in his own gut.

"Then you steal it."

Meche frowned, confused. "What do you mean?"

"If happiness doesn't come to you, then you take it. Any way you can," he said.

He thought of the ocean. He had wanted to live by the beach but Natalia had been opposed to that. What would they do there? His fantasies of building a hut, of combing the sand for treasure, of running barefoot with nothing but a single change of clothes and a guitar, pounding on the typewriter by candlelight, did not impress her.

Maybe he could still do it. Maybe he could have his ocean and the sound of the waves heavy in his ears as he went to sleep.

Steal it if you can't get it...

"Yeah," Meche said, nodding.

MECHE NEVER LIKED dragging her father back home. She thought her mother sent her to punish him, to humiliate him. It seemed petty to her. Especially that night. She had told her mother she did not feel like going out, too busy nursing her disappointment, but her mother had shoved Meche into her jacket and pushed her out the door.

Her father had to go to work the next day, her mother said. She'd better bring him before it got too late.

Later, as Meche and her dad sat in the kitchen, dipping animal crackers in a glass of milk, she thought about what he'd said about happiness.

Steal it if you must.

Meche was willing. But that bitch, happiness, wasn't being very cooperative.

Why had the spell failed?

She looked at the box of crackers with its colourful picture of a lion tamer and a lion jumping through a hoop.

She sighed, wishing magic was more like something she could understand. More like math.

Equations, she could get. Computer languages, she could get.

Mysticism, apparently, not.

Meche paused, the lion-shaped cracker hovering before her mouth.

Wait.

When you type a computer command, you don't just type *any* random phrase. You have to be specific.

If you are, the desired result occurs.

"Holy mother," Meche whispered.

She ate her cracker.

SEBASTIAN AND DANIELA looked around the room, carefully inspecting their surroundings. It had taken Meche a couple of days to fix it up, but the place no longer looked like an abandoned factory room: it looked frankly awesome. She had swept the floor and put up posters of several bands. Cut-outs from magazines and some record sleeves were fashioned into large collages. There were all the big names: The Beatles, Elvis Presley, Pedro Infante, Toña la Negra. Newer, younger ones too.

She had cleaned the old couch as best she could. She brought some blankets so they could sit on the floor. There was also a little coffee table with candles on top: the factory had no electricity.

Meche sat in the centre of the room, by the portable record player, smiling.

"What do you think?" she asked.

"It's nice," Sebastian said.

"We are not supposed to be here," Daniela reminded them.

"I bought a lock," Meche said, showing it to them, "so we can close up and others can't get in when we're not here."

"Um... why?" Daniela asked.

"Because this is going to be our base of operations. You see, I didn't get it. Not last time. We need the right environment. You know, just like with a computer program. Plus, we went too big. We need to focus on something smaller. We have to be specific."

"Oh, not the spell thing again," Daniela said.

"Yes, the spell thing again," Meche said. "I've got a notebook that is going to be our *grimoire* and I've got the records. Now we focus, we are specific and we experiment until we get it right."

They didn't say anything. Daniela just looked down at her pink and white tennis shoes. Sebastian slid his hands into his pockets.

"What do you say?"

"I'm up for it," Sebastian said.

Daniela seemed surprised by that. She bobbed her head, imitating Sebastian. "Sure."

"Okay, we have to focus on one thing," Meche said. "A single thing. What do you want to do? Something we can fix?"

"My motorcycle is busted again," Sebastian said with a shrug.

"Motorcycle," Meche said, "that's good. Now, let's find the right music."

She knelt on the floor, going through the piles of records she had dragged to the factory. Her friends also sat down. They began looking into her cardboard boxes, pulling records out.

"Subete a Mi Moto," Daniela said, holding up the Menudo record.

"Don't be too obvious," Meche said.

"Flans!" Daniela said excitedly.

"No."

"Lucerito!"

"It's not phone-in-the radio-station-for-your-favourite-song."

"Aw, but I like Lucerito."

Meche rolled her eyes. Of course Daniela would like Lucerito, the most saccharine, inane teenager singer on the market. And Flans... why not stab each other in the ears now?

"Cindy Lauper?" Daniela asked hopefully.

Meche was willing to grant her that, but what Cindy Lauper song were they supposed to use?

"Duncan Dhu," Sebastian said.

Meche looked up at him as he offered her the record.

"En Algún Lugar," he whispered.

Meche grabbed the record and felt a tiny, electric charge running up her arm. Like static electricity. It almost... felt warm. As though it had been resting on top of a stove.

Weird.

Meche lowered it carefully, holding the needle between her fingers. Sebastian stared at her.

She let the needle drop.

The record hissed, like steam escaping a kettle.

The guitar split the silence, and then the beat began.

The three of them stood up.

This time they did not spin around. Instead they joined hands and stepped close around the portable record player, their heads almost touching as they looked down at the record, seeing it turn.

Meche did not feel anything. Not at first. Just Daniela's sweaty hands, Sebastian's steady grip.

And then it was... something she couldn't identify. Just this warmth, the same warmth which had permeated the vinyl now stretching up her fingers, making her arms tingle. Her body felt a bit numb yet there was this odd current churning through her blood, swimming up her veins.

It felt like the time she had sipped some clandestine tequila. That had stung her mouth and this stung her body. Not very pleasant, but also not painful.

The beat rose and fell and the singers spoke of running away, of a rider who does not turn his head, leaving with the wind, the hoofs of his horse sinking into a dusty road.

Meche could see the road, painted red, lonely, and the rider reaching the bend of the road, the evening sun staining the sky red.

Meche tasted dust. She closed her eyes and opened them again.

She was standing by the road and when the rider swept by, she extended her hand and he pulled her onto his horse. They were galloping towards the horizon.

Meche opened her mouth; heat that had been accumulating inside escaped. It rose like a golden streamer, drifting like smoke, touching the ceiling. Golden tendrils also escaped from Sebastian and Daniela, coiling together.

The three of them looked up, amazed.

"What is that?" Daniela asked.

"Magic," Meche whispered.

The golden streamers coalesced into a ball and the ball grew larger, then began to collapse and dissolve, bits of it floating away until there was nothing left.

"Is that it?" Sebastian asked, sounding disappointed.

As if punctuating his words, several dirty glass panels shattered. Daniela yelped. Meche laughed.

"Let's see if it worked!" she yelled and rushed out of the room, leaving the record spinning.

They stomped downstairs and made it to the street, heading straight for Sebastian's building. When they reached it they were all out of breath. Meche slid down against the doors to his building while Sebastian fumbled for his keys. He kept the motorcycle inside, on the first floor, beneath the stairs.

"Go check it out," she said.

He nodded, turned the key and stepped inside. Meche, too exhausted to move, just waited. Daniela half-collapsed next to her, her hair in her eyes.

Sebastian walked the motorcycle out. Meche straightened up, carefully watching him as he straddled it and placed the key in the ignition.

The motorcycle coughed, sputtered and did not move.

Meche bit her lip.

Sebastian tried again and this time it worked. The old, banged-up machine roared into life. Meche jumped, clapping.

Sebastian was beaming. Daniela seemed in shock.

"Fucking yes!" Meche said jumping up and down.

"Get on," Sebastian said.

Meche turned to look at Daniela and Daniela nodded. "Go ahead. I want to rest."

Meche hurried towards him, quickly throwing her leg over. She scooted close to Sebastian, holding on to his jacket.

He twisted the grip, applied the throttle, and they sped away, turning the corner. She leaned forward along with him and they zoomed past the corner store, then the pharmacy, the small video store, the *tortilleria*.

At some point her hair band snapped and Meche's hair streamed freely down her shoulders. She laughed.

"It works!" she yelled.

"Of course it works!" he yelled back.

At the stoplight, she squeezed Sebastian tight and stared at the cars as they crossed the junction in front of them. Catalina Coronado looked at them, with a disapproving glare, as she crossed the street. Meche chuckled.

She didn't care if Catalina told her mother she had been riding around on Sebastian's bike. They had power. Real power.

Things were never going to be the same again.

Mexico City, 2009

MECHE SAT IN the restaurant, looking at her cup of tea, absently folding and refolding her napkin.

"Baby, baby what are you going to do when you grow up?" asked Miguel Mateos in her ear, singing like it was the 80s again and he was pushing the cause of "rock in your language"—Spanish-language music to compete with the imports introduced by MTV.

"Meche, is that you?"

Meche looked up and tugged out the earbuds.

Daniela was pleasantly plump. She had traded her pink sneakers and pink shirts for black shoes in a ballerina style and a white peasant shirt. She looked warm and sweet, similar to the Daniela she had known.

"Yeah," Meche said extending her hand.

Daniela hugged her, planting a kiss on her cheek. A typical Mexican greeting, though it startled Meche a bit, unused to such a personal hello.

"It's so good to see you," Daniela said, pulling out a chair.

"Do you want something?" Meche asked.

"Just a latte."

Meche motioned to the server and the woman took their order.

Daniela looked at Meche expectantly, a big smile on her face.

"So, is Norway cold? What am I saying, of course it's cold."

"It's fine," Meche said. "I've been there for four years now."

"Where were you before that?"

"Spain. The United Kingdom. Wherever there's work. You'd be surprised. Software development is actually quite big in Romania."

"Well, that's awesome."

Daniela's smile faltered a little.

"I heard your dad had passed away."

"Who told you?"

"Sebastian."

"How would he know?"

"When something happens in the neighbourhood people know. He knows."

"So you still talk to him?"

"Oh, maybe once a year," Daniela said with a shrug. "He's been living in Tijuana for a long time now so we don't see much of each other. He only moved back this spring."

"I saw him yesterday," Meche said, taking a sip of tea.

"Yeah? What did he say?"

"Nothing. I just saw him standing across the street."

"You didn't say hi?"

"He didn't say hi either."

Daniela's coffee arrived. She opened three little packets of sugar and poured them in.

"Are you still angry at him?"

"What do you think?"

"You always could hold a grudge."

"Bingo," Meche said winking and pointing a finger at Daniela.

Daniela sighed, resting her elbows on the table, holding her cup carefully.

"I guess you've forgiven me?"

"You were not the major issue," Meche said, "although you played your part."

"Meche, we couldn't keep on forever. Casting spells, playing with people..."

"Why not?"

"It wasn't right."

"That's not why we stopped, though."

"Maybe it was a bit of why we stopped. A lot. Because you—"

Meche shook her head, tossing her tea bag onto a napkin and folding it all into a ball.

"We stopped because Sebastian broke the circle and convinced you to abandon it, to boot. He betrayed me. Fucked my life."

"He didn't..."

"He didn't?"

"Meche, Sebastian adored you."

Meche leaned back, an unpleasant smirk on her face. Adored her? Right. He had a funny way of showing it. A funny way of being her best friend.

"Look, I guessed you were still on good terms with him. That's why I wanted to talk to you. I don't want him showing for my father's *novena*. I know it may seem the polite thing to do, but I don't want him in my mother's apartment. I'm pretty sure Jimena invited him, but I'm against it. He should stay away."

"Meche, that's not right."

"It is what it is."

"Are you going to tell me to stay out of your apartment too?"

Meche shrugged, her face cold. She didn't care if Daniela came, but she wasn't going to encourage it either.

"That's mean, Meche," Daniela said. "We both knew your dad."

"Well, he's dead. He won't miss you."

Daniela chuckled, looking down at her hands.

"Here I thought you were trying to reconnect."

"I'm a bitch like that. See, I wouldn't want someone hexing me or my mom. Old habits."

"We wouldn't hex you."

"Liar," Meche whispered. "Just tell him to stay out of the apartment."

"I brought something for you," Daniela said, reaching for her large purse and pulling out a fat manila envelope. "Don't worry. It's not hexed."

She set the envelope in the middle of the table. Meche glanced at it but made no attempt to look inside.

"You know, Meche, I always thought you were the smartest of us. You were always so sharp. But now I realize you've always been half-blind, and not nearly as sharp as you think."

"What do you mean?" Meche asked.

"You need to let it go. My regards to your mother."

Daniela slipped away. Meche drank her tea slowly, taking her time. When she was done she opened the envelope and looked inside. It was Meche's notebook. Her old *grimoire*. There were also lots of photographs. Daniela's *quinceañera* party and Daniela looking like a bottle of Pepto-Bismol in her gigantic dress. Meche leaning against a wall, headphones on, staring at the camera as if she was daring someone to take a snapshot. Ah, Constantino and Isadora's group. Sebastian's motorcycle. And...

... Sebastian and Meche. It was a series of photos taken inside a booth. They were making faces in the first two frames, their tongues sticking out. By the third one they had settled down and were looking at the camera with a smile. The fourth one showed them looking at each other. In that last bit of black-and-white film, their expressions were inscrutable.

Meche stuffed the photos back inside the envelope.

Mexico City, 1988

SHE RECOGNIZED THE notes of power in the air. She could see them the same way one can see a spider's web when a shaft of light hits it at the right angle.

Meche's web of power.

Dolores clicked her needles together and smiled, remembering her own days of spells.

She didn't think about magic very much anymore. That was part of her childhood, when Dolores and her sisters stitched spells with their needles. Spells to make the clouds release a gentle drizzle upon their heads. Spells to catch the eye of the boys in town. All those spells which were now gone, erased the same way a slate is erased with a warm cloth. But the memory of the feeling, of the magic… ah, that was still there.

Where had she put her old thimble? It had been made of porcelain and carefully painted by her eldest sister. Dolores hadn't looked at her object of power in ages. She wondered whether it still had any strength in it.

"Grandma! I'm home!" Meche yelled, and she heard the front door bang shut, then the quick patter of feet across the hallway.

It was no more than a few seconds before a record started playing. Dolores smiled and kept knitting.

HE WAS WATCHING his classmates across the schoolyard, eating their lunch. Isadora was leaning down to talk to Constantino and he was laughing.

Now that the Day of the Dead had passed, November marked the real festivity of the season: Isadora's birthday party. Each year she threw a birthday bash and each year Sebastian did not attend. It was not that he was not invited: everybody was. He never dared to show up.

He kept thinking about attending, wearing brand new sneakers, his hair combed back, looking like a rock star.

"What are we going to wish for next?" Daniela asked.

"Isadora's birthday party," Sebastian said before Meche could open her mouth.

The girls blinked and looked at each other, then back at him.

"We should go, at least for a little bit. Go in style. Make them notice us."

Daniela shrugged. Meche sipped her bottle of apple juice and began peeling its label off with careful fingers.

"It's not a bad idea," Meche said. "All the cool kids will be there."

"We could be just as cool as them. Couldn't we?" Daniela asked.

"If I had Constantino's money I'm sure I could look cool too," Sebastian replied.

"So are we wishing for money?" Daniela asked.

"Yeah," Sebastian said. "Enough dough to buy new outfits. What do you say, Meche? You girls could get your hair done. Makeup. The whole nine yards."

"Makeup is not going to cover my pimples," Meche said.

"So we wish away the pimples," Sebastian said.

Daniela giggled. "Can I wish for a different eye colour? Just for the weekend?"

"Sure," Sebastian said.

"We can't be wishing too much, too often," Meche warned them.

"Why not?" Daniela asked.

"'Cause I felt tired after what we did. Didn't you feel it? I slept like a rock."

"Me too," Daniela said "Why would it work like that?"

"I dunno."

Sebastian watched as Isadora moved away from her group, heading towards the school's little general store. Sebastian had no business near the store: he could not afford the drinks or sandwiches they sold there.

But he had the wild desire to talk to Isadora, to open his mouth and regale her with a sentence for once in his life. He was still high from the motorcycle trip with Meche and he felt this day he might actually do it.

"Okay, no wishing too often, got it," Sebastian said hastily. "I'll be back."

He walked quickly, moving in the same direction Isadora had gone. He stood behind her in line, with nothing more than one peso in his pocket. When she glanced at him, Sebastian nodded and smiled.

She gave him this weird look, like she was a little surprised to see him standing behind her, but did not speak to him.

Sebastian waited in line, his hands deep in his pockets, trying to keep calm.

"So... umm... your birthday's this Saturday, right?"

"Yes," Isadora said.

"What kind of presents are you hoping for?"

"I don't know. I like jewellery."

Constantino's father owned a jewellery store. For a moment Sebastian saw his opportunities dwindle, but then he remembered he could buy anything they wanted. They had magic now. He could look for a nice, golden bracelet for Isadora. Or a little chain. Something pretty, which she might wear often.

"Cool."

"Are you going to come?" she asked.

"Maybe," he said.

"Your friends too?" She lifted her chin, looking in Meche and Daniela's direction.

Sebastian nodded. "All right. I'll see you then."

The line moved, Isadora bought a soft drink and stepped aside. Sebastian looked at the candy and junk food for sale, trying to figure out what he could buy.

WHEN HE WALKED by the Pit that afternoon, Sebastian saw Isadora, Constantino and some other students standing there, smoking and chatting.

Isadora held her cigarette with two fingers and she smiled, just a tiny smile.

He felt like waving and smiling back, but Constantino turned his head and saw him. Sebastian continued on his way, eyes fixed straight ahead.

"YOU KNOW WHAT it's like? It's like reverse engineering."

"What's reverse engineering?" Sebastian asked.

"Umm... it's when you lack the software specifications so you poke around the program interface trying to find the solution. That's what we are doing with magic."

Meche grabbed another record, looking at it critically. They had tried four different albums and none of them had produced the same magic effect as last time. Meche had been sure all they had to do was focus and be specific, but apparently that was not enough.

"I don't understand," Sebastian said.

"Okay, like the TU-4."

"The what?"

"During World War II the Russians didn't have a strategic bomber like the US and they wanted one. But they couldn't figure out how to build it. Then a few B-29 bombers had to make emergency landings in Russia and the Russians looked at them, figured how they were made and made their own bombers. It's like... like building a puzzle without the instructions. Figuring it backwards. Something like that."

"You mean it's like taking a stab in the dark," Sebastian said.

"An *educated* stab."

"How'd you learn about World War II?"

"That time they punished me and I had to spend a whole month during recess in the library. I had to read the encyclopedia and write a report on Russia during World War II."

"Who'd know," he said with a smirk.

"What?"

"You can read."

Meche punched his arm and Sebastian chuckled.

"I still don't understand what we are doing," Daniela said, holding up a bunch of record sleeves in her hands.

"We don't know either," Sebastian said.

"Oh."

Daniela blinked, then looked at her records. They had been at this for more than an hour and he sensed that soon enough Daniela would ask to go home. If they were going to figure how to cast a spell a second time around, they had to do it quick.

"Okay, let's try Money's Too Tight To Mention," Sebastian said. He was out of other ideas.

They crowded around the portable record player, holding hands tight, just like last time. The little beat began and then the chorus, "We're talking 'bout money, money!" But nothing happened. The room remained cold and still.

"Ugh," Meche said, falling back against the floor. "What's wrong? We've done obvious songs, not so obvious songs…"

"We can try Material Girl again," Sebastian suggested.

That had been the first song they'd attempted to use. A second try might not amount to anything, but Sebastian did not know what else to pick. Meche rubbed her hands against her eyes.

"Okay," Daniela said, sounding chipper. "Let me find it one more time."

Sebastian sat down next to Meche, bumping his sneaker against hers.

"Hey, we have time to get it right," he said. "We'll wish for the money, wish for the—"

"I so wanted to get a decent dress that's not like two sizes too big," Meche muttered. "And maybe get rid of the pimples… somehow."

"They're not *that* bad," he said, trying to be kind, though they were bad. Meche often had pimples all around her mouth and smack in the middle of her forehead. She tried to hide them with her bangs, but it didn't help. "Just fucking hormones."

"Gee, Doctor Soto, you think?"

"Don't be annoying."

Meche bumped his shoe back and turned to look at him, frowning. She looked very solemn, but a grin was about to break through, shattering her sour expression.

"Ouch!"

Sebastian raised his head. "What's up, Dani?"

"It's hot!"

"What's hot?" Meche muttered, taking a long pause after each word.

"The record."

That was about the weirdest thing he'd ever heard.

"Records are not hot," Sebastian said.

"Wait," Meche said, sitting up at once. "Hot?"

"Yeah."

"Which one?"

Daniela looked at the floor, at a record sleeve next to her foot. Meche scrambled forward and lifted it very carefully.

"Dead or Alive."

"You Spin Me Round (Like a Record)," Meche said. "Sebastian, touch it."

"Alright," he said.

He didn't expect it to really burn him, but as soon as he touched it Sebastian felt like he was handling a potato that had been pulled out of a boiling pot of water. He thrust it back into Meche's hands and she set it down on the floor.

"What's that?" Sebastian asked.

"I don't know," Meche muttered.

She knelt down, took the record out of the sleeve. Her fingers hovered above the shiny, black vinyl surface, very carefully.

"It's very warm. It's like… there's electricity here."

"There can't be."

Meche pressed her index finger against the record and a little blue spark actually shot up. She laughed. Daniela pressed both hands against her mouth. Sebastian just raised an eyebrow.

"You know what this means, right?" she told them. "It's not just any record. Some of them have power and some of them don't. Look, feel it."

Sebastian and Daniela both knelt down. He carefully touched the edge of the record. Another blue spark shot up.

"You think?" Sebastian asked.

"Look for other records which feel warm," Meche said.

Daniela began to go through one of the cardboard boxes. Sebastian grabbed another box, his fingers dancing over the sleeves, pulling some out, leaving others in its place. Nothing, nothing... and then bingo. A sleeve that itched his palm. He pulled out a single. It felt like a warm tortilla, just wrapped in a cloth.

"Hey," he said. "This one's the same."

"What is it?"

"Billy Idol," Sebastian said. "Dancing With Myself. Touch it."

Meche extended her hand, carefully setting it against the sleeve. She nodded very slightly.

"I feel it."

"It's... is it beating? Can you feel it?"

It was very weird. A sensation similar to the one you might get if you pressed your palm against your chest, over your heart. A little thumping.

Meche frowned. "I don't feel the beating."

"This is the one, Meche," Sebastian said. "The one for our money spell."

"Are you sure?"

"Oh, yeah."

"Then put it on. Daniela, are you ready?"

"Yes."

They gathered close to the record player, hands joined. The music began and Sebastian slowly moved his foot. Just a little bit, heel lifting and falling. Lifting and falling. Meche and Daniela's feet followed his lead, raising and falling and then Billy screamed and he grabbed Daniela and they began to dance.

Daniela was a terrible dancer but she moved quite easily now, and despite her ridiculous pink dress she could have danced in Billy Idol's music video. Sebastian felt a jolt of electricity when their palms touched and they laughed, jumped back and forward.

He turned around and grabbed Meche's hand. He spun her, one, two, three times. Her long skirt, reaching beneath the knee, flared up, showing her legs for an instant, her knee-high stockings with the loose elastic pooling down by her ankles.

He spun her again and Meche stepped forward, her palms pressing against his chest for a moment.

Golden tendrils spilled from her fingers, curling up in the air. Sebastian raised his left arm and another golden tendril rose from his hand. He glanced at Daniela and she pointed at them, a gold ribbon extending and touching the two ribbons hovering near the ceiling. They knotted themselves together.

The room glowed golden for a second, as though a small sun had installed itself over their heads. Then little flecks of gold began to fall like snow. Their little sun was chipping away into nothingness.

The needle lifted itself and Sebastian brushed his hair from his face.

"We are going to tear the town up," he muttered.

"What?" Meche said.

"We're going to tear the town up, baby!" he yelled, grabbing Meche by the waist and lifting her up.

"Yeah, baby!"

Daniela giggled, jumping up and down. "How much money will we get? How will we get it?"

"Treasure. Hidden in some distant location and we'll need a shovel to dig it out," he told them, still holding Meche up. "Aye, aye, Jim Hawkins."

"Jim, who?"

"Really, Meche?" he said, putting her down. "You don't even open my birthday presents, do you?"

"Not if I have to read them."

"You suck."

"Sticks and stones, Sebastian Soto," she said, standing on her tiptoes and jamming her finger against the hollow of his throat. "Let's find that cash and spend it."

They rushed down the stairs together, trying to see who made it out of the factory first.

Mexico City, 2009

MECHE FOUND THE old boxes where her mom said they would be and pulled them open. There were ancient textbooks there, old toys. A video game she had not played in years and years. Meche scooped them all out and set them on the floor.

She found Sebastian's books at the bottom. *Treasure Island*. Shakespeare's complete works. *El Lazarillo de Tormes*. Sebastian had definitely been an optimist, thinking one day she might develop a taste for reading.

The smallest of all the books was the last one he had ever given her: Auden.

She opened it to the first page and looked at the inscription, the letters crisp and very straight. Sebastian's handwriting.

Suppose the lions all get up and go,
And all the brooks and soldiers run away?
Will Time say nothing but I told you so?
—Always and always your best friend. Sebos.

"Always and always," she muttered.

Meche lifted the book and a picture fell out. She thought it might be another snapshot of her with Daniela and Sebastian. But the Polaroid was of her father, holding her as a toddler. He was helping her take an uncertain step.

Her mother had gotten rid of many of the photos of her dad. Meche disposed of the ones she had with indifference. This Polaroid had escaped the culling.

There had been no photos of Vicente in his apartment. Meche had only been able to picture him tenuously, like a jumble of half-remembered features. This picture brought his features into the light, sharpened him, made him real.

And damn it, she looked a lot like her father. She'd forgotten that.

Meche wandered into the kitchen and put the kettle on the stove. She would have to go to her dad's apartment again. There were so many things to sort out and another night of food and prayer to look forward to.

"Are you hungry?" her mother asked, wandering into the kitchen and opening the refrigerator.

"I'm fine."

"You haven't had breakfast."

"I never have breakfast."

"That's not good for you. I'll make you some eggs."

"Ma…"

"Just two eggs."

Meche knew it was futile to fight back. She sat down at the kitchen table. The kettle whistled and her mother poured the boiling water into a cup, then handed it to her along with a little box full of tea bags.

"Did you ever feel sorry for dad?"

"Sorry about what?"

"In general."

"Your father made his choices. No, I didn't feel sorry for him."

Her mother turned her back on her, her attention on the eggs she was frying. She grabbed a spatula and flipped them over.

"I have no idea what he was up to these last few years," Meche said.

"The same thing as always. Pretending to write. The bar. Smoking like a train. The last few times he came over…"

"He'd come over?" Meche asked, quite shocked at that.

Her mother turned off the stove and plated the eggs. She set them down before Meche and handed her a fork.

"In the last couple of years. Not a lot. He wanted to know how you were doing. I showed him some of the pictures you sent me, of the Northern Lights. 'Too cold,' he told me."

Natalia sat down across from Meche, holding a glass of orange juice between her hands. Meche really did not want to eat, but she took a tiny bite.

"He wanted to write to you. I gave him your e-mail..."

"Why would you do that?" Meche asked.

She had told Natalia not to give her personal information to her father. He'd had it before and they had few, sparse conversations over the years, generally on Christmas and her birthday. When she lived in London he phoned one night, teary and drunk, talking about music. An incoherent babble of self-pity, of "Let me explain a few things to you about myself," and all of it mixed with lyrics from songs. A mess. She told her mother not to give her phone number to him again and changed the number.

"He was dying, Meche," Natalia said, palms up. "What else was I supposed to do? He said he was going to write to you from an internet café. I guess he didn't."

"Nope."

Meche added a couple of spoons of sugar to her tea, stirring it slowly.

"Do you miss him?" her mother asked.

"My father?" Meche asked. "How could I miss someone I hadn't seen for half my life before he died?"

"Because you look like you miss him."

MECHE CONTINUED CATALOGUING her father's albums. Around noon, she realized she should have eaten the eggs instead of just taking a bite. Her father's cupboards were barren, the kitchen minimally stocked. Above the sink she found a big box of animal crackers. There was also powdered milk.

She thought of eating the crackers, but the memories of her father and a younger Meche enjoying them with a glass of milk made her pause. She grabbed her jacket and walked two blocks away, to a narrow Chinese café. She asked for tea, but this being a Mexican-Chinese café, there was none. She settled for café-au-lait and fresh bread rolls, watching the woman half-asleep behind the cash register; thinking that this café could be right from the 1980s, so old and worn it looked.

Meche grabbed her earbuds and pressed play, but despite the cheery assurances of Elvis Presley the world seemed dim and grey. She paid, went back to her father's apartment, and found it dimmer and greyer than the café.

She did not feel like sorting his records. She was tired of looking at album covers and decided to put some of his other things in boxes. The typewriter, to begin with.

It was impossible to believe a man would continue to use a typewriter well into this decade, but he had. It was a heavy beast, many keys worn with the passage of time. Meche set it in the box, then began to gather his manuscript pages. There was, literally, a pile of them and many more scattered all over the house.

While looking for more pages, she found a dozen shoeboxes under the bed. Each box was packed with tiny little notebooks, inscribed with her father's spidery handwriting. Most of the notebooks contained songs. Songs he'd written. A few things for the book, but it was mostly his songs and his random thoughts.

Meche had never seen any of her father's songs. She knew he'd written them and she knew he'd stopped. But he hadn't stopped. There were notebooks from the 70s, but others were labelled from the 80s and 90s, and as recently as a few months before. She pulled out a bunch of yellowed letters and discovered these were the love letters he had written to her mother years before, when he was courting her. He had written lyrics in the margins.

Secretly, under his bed, Vicente Vega had collected decades worth of lyrics and of his life.

Meche grabbed one notebook from 1973 and opened it, turning the pages curiously, looking at the careful, small letters, the tiny script with almost no spaces in between words.

Natalia and I agreed that if we have a boy, she'll pick the name, and if it's a girl, I get to pick. I know we are going to have a girl. I know she will have my eyes. I have been thinking of a proper name for her. There are many pretty names from songs which she could have. At first I thought maybe Emily because of the song For Emily, Whenever I May Find Her, but then I changed my mind. I thought about Julia because of The Beatles' song from The White

Album. *Then I figured maybe I should name her after a singer instead of a song, and oh boy, anyone who knows me knows my first choice was Janice. But yesterday I was listening to Mercedes Sosa singing Gracias a la Vida by Violeta Parra and I think I will call her Mercedes Violeta, in honour of two great Latin American writers. Life has not given me many things, but it will give me the most important thing I can ever have: my very own Mercedes.*

Meche looked around the house and found the record she was looking for easily. It had been in the stack next to her father's bed: Mercedes Sosa singing Gracias a la Vida. She put the record on and sat on the floor in her father's bedroom, looking at the painted palm trees.

Meche took out the picture of her in her father's arms and she wondered about this man she did not know, this stranger who had passed away and left nothing but papers, records and songs.

Mexico City, 1988

SEBASTIAN AND MECHE were both sitting on the floor and leaning over the book, carefully absorbing every word. Daniela, meanwhile, sulked in a corner. She had videotaped some episodes of *El Extraño Retorno de Diana Salazar*—the soap opera starring Lucía Méndez about a woman from 16th century colonial Mexico with psychic powers who reincarnates in modern Mexico—and had intended to watch them that afternoon. Meche had invented a mathematics study session, pulled her out of her home and dragged her to the factory. What they were studying was magic and Daniela was not willing to help with their research, preferring to sit on the couch and immerse herself in a bodice ripper with a sexy pirate on the cover.

"But here, what about this part?" Sebastian asked. "An amulet. An object of power."

"What does it mean?"

"Like witches with wands. Only not that stupid, I guess."

"Art-ha-me," Meche said, turning the page of the book. "Dani, aren't you even going to look at it?"

"Not if it has demons in it."

Sebastian had found a used book about witchcraft with plenty of extracts from *The Key of Solomon*. It mentioned a bevy of demons and the garish cover with a bug-eyed woman had scared Daniela away. She insisted she was not going to read it, study it or anything of the sort.

"It's not Hollywood demons," Meche said.

Daniela shook her head and Meche rolled her eyes.

"Okay, so objects of power. We can't be carrying staffs around Mexico City. What can we keep to be our object?"

"I don't know," Sebastian said with a shrug. "Couldn't we keep whatever we want? Whatever matters to us?"

"That's fine with me. We should keep it a secret. Never tell anyone. Not even each other."

"Why would we keep secrets from each other?" Sebastian asked, frowning.

"Ugh. Don't you listen when you speak out loud? Didn't you just tell us about Merlin and that chick Vivi?"

"Vivien."

"That one. She figured Merlin's weakness, tricked him and made him sleep forever."

"But we wouldn't trick each other."

"Yeah, but it feels kind of personal."

"Fine."

"I'll write this thing about objects of power in the *grimoire*," Meche said taking her pen and opening the notebook. "Did you hear about objects of power?"

"I heard," Daniela said.

Meche began writing, neatly labelling the entry with the date and a heading. Sebastian stretched his feet and reached for the large bag of chips Meche had brought. There were also a couple of sodas and some chocolate. He munched the chips loudly and wondered what object he might pick. A book. Would that be too obvious? Where would he put it? He shared his room with Romualdo and that didn't leave many chances for privacy. There was a loose tile in the kitchen which could be loosened a bit more. Or perhaps he should just tuck it at the back of his closet. Under the bed.

"We still don't have the money," Sebastian reminded Meche.

She held the pen between her teeth and nodded.

"Maybe it takes longer to take effect when it's cash," Daniela suggested.

"Well, we're going to need it if we want to buy new clothes and stuff," Sebastian said. "Are your parents even going to let you go, Dani?"

"Yeah. My mom thinks it'll be good if I go. As long as I'm back early, by ten. She can pick us up and drop us off."

"Wanna hitch a ride with Dani?" Sebastian asked.

"I want to stay late," Meche said. "Can't we take a cab?"

Sebastian considered his reduced finances. Bagging groceries was not a lucrative operation and a *cerillo* had no regular wage or contract, just the tips he could gather. On top of that, it was near the end of the month and that meant money was short. He didn't have cash to splurge on a cab and since their spell hadn't actually worked yet, he was reluctant to promise a taxi, even if they split it.

"We can take my motorcycle or the bus," he proposed.

"I don't want to mess my hair and clothes on the bus," Meche said.

"We could walk…"

"All the way to Isadora's house?"

Sebastian did not want to sound like he was cheap. He hated putting his situation into words, so he simply sat on the couch, picking up a couple of records and examining them, hoping Meche might drop the point for now.

Meche went back to her *grimoire*. After a while she sighed and sat between Daniela and Sebastian.

"Rodriguez is so going to fail me," she said.

"Why?" Daniela asked.

"Because he's a freak. Didn't you see him in class today, 'Miss Vega, can you tell us one of the important symbols in *Anna Karenina* and then he kept drilling me and drilling me, like it was the Spanish Inquisition. I did the reading and he still told me he's giving me a bad mark."

"I'm not doing too great either," Daniela said.

"What are you talking about? You always get an 8."

"Yeah, but my dad doesn't like me getting anything but 10s," Daniela said. "And I'm seriously studying hard."

"Isadora is passing with flying colours," Meche said. "Maybe I need to flash my panties at the creep more often."

Sebastian gave Meche an irritated, sideways glance, his jaw growing tense at the mention of the girl he liked.

"She does not flash her panties at anyone."

"Oh, hoho. With that short skirt?" Meche said, snorting. "She flashes plenty. And her squeaky little voice. 'Mr. Rodriguez, I don't understand why Anna Karenina throws herself in front of the train.'

Newsflash: because it's fucking foreshadowed like pages before. Even *I* got that."

"If you're going to be a bitch why don't you do it alone?" Sebastian said, grabbing his backpack.

"Where are you going?" Meche asked.

"I've got a shift at the supermarket."

"At *six*?"

"Yeah, I think I'll leave early."

"Ugh, Sebos, don't be a dick."

"Bye," he muttered.

NINE O'CLOCK and two more hours until he could take off his vest and roll into bed. Sebastian bagged groceries robotically, tossing onions and avocados and potatoes together, stretching out his hand and waiting for the clock to advance another minute.

He felt the headphones pressing against his ears as Meche stood behind him, standing on her tiptoes. He turned around and raised an eyebrow at her.

"What?"

"You said you wanted to borrow my Walkman so you could listen to music at work tonight," she said.

"You didn't have to…"

"It's got The Who on there. Which is probably like giving pearls to a pig, but knock yourself out with it."

Sebastian shook his head. Even when Meche was trying to apologize in her own Meche-way, she had a way of insulting you once again. And yet, looking down at the girl with her oversized green jacket, the sleeves covering her fingers, the collar of her shirt sticking out at an odd angle, he thought she was the only person who ever got him.

"You shouldn't talk shit about other people," he said.

"That's what they do. What do you think they say about us?"

"Yeah, well. We've got to be the better persons and all. I suppose."

"Says who?"

"I dunno. But I don't like gossipy people."

Meche snorted, shuffling her feet.

"Fine. I won't talk crap about Isadora if you don't want me to."

"Thanks."

Meche saluted, a mock-serious expression on her face. She stepped back and started walking away.

"Thanks. I'll get it back to you later," he called after her.

Sebastian pressed Play and the drums began to roll as The Who proclaimed this was their generation. Sebastian bagged his groceries to the rhythm, bobbing his head up and down.

WALKING HOME THAT night Sebastian decided to cut his way through the neglected, concrete wasteland of the park. It was arranged in the shape of a large rectangle with four paths leading to the centre, where the hobos and the hoodlums tended to gather. Sad trees and ugly bushes looked at the large cement benches. The northeast corner was an impromptu waste disposal facility: people who missed or did not care to wait for the morning garbage truck dumped their supermarket plastic bags filled with garbage there, attracting many stray dogs looking for a meal.

As he walked by a cement bench he noticed a wallet on the ground and picked it up. It had no identifications inside, only bills. Lots of bills. Sebastian looked around, checked nobody was watching him, and tucked it in his trousers.

THREE TIMES A week Vicente Vega stopped by a little travel agency and met with Azucena Bernal for an hour of sex. He could not say it had started innocently but he had never intended for it to become what it had become. Unlike many other Mexican men—fixated with the idea of being macho, with a desire for a *casa chica*, for a mistress and its ensuing complications—Vicente had never seriously considered establishing ties with another woman.

Yet there he was, with Azucena. Three times a week and just as many phone calls when they did not meet. They were into the fourth week of their relationship and it showed no signs of stopping or ceasing in intensity. Meanwhile, Natalia stared at him across the table at nights, ate him alive with her words, piled indifference and scorn upon his shoulders. Azucena, as plain as his wife was beautiful, was sweeter, more understanding, did not yell at him demanding he turn off the reading light or ask him to explain why he was still working on that worthless book. Vicente was seriously considering moving out. If he had a little money he would definitely do it. They could move to Puerto Vallarta and he would play his records until late at night with no one to tell him to turn the music down.

Vicente looked at the brochures he'd picked from Azucena's office: beaches, happy couples holding hands. And he, still young, not yet old, trapped in the middle of his life with a woman who resented him, growing greyer and fatter by the day. To escape… to start anew…

If only he could finish his book. Vicente had thought that by now he'd have it all edited and proofed. Then he could sell it. He might not make a fortune, but enough to ditch Natalia.

Natalia who had never allowed him to go to Puerto Vallarta because the sun was bad for her skin even when, back then, her father had agreed to pay for the trip. Instead, they went to Cuernavaca on their honeymoon and Natalia spent the money her dad had reserved for the trip on a new wardrobe. When her father passed away, leaving Natalia a bit of money, she refused to take a vacation in Cancún. She had bought herself a new car—not *their* car, because he was not allowed to drive it—and some jewellery.

There was still enough money left from that time to go on vacation—at least a little one, at least Puerto Vallarta—but it was all in the family savings fund. Money which one day would go to Meche for university. Not a penny could be touched. Vicente didn't have a say in the matter. Vicente didn't have a say in anything.

Smoking his cigarettes in a corner of the apartment and nursing real and imaginary wounds with a few drinks, Vicente felt himself growing old.

"I DON'T KNOW," he told his wife that night.

"You're never going to finish that book."

Vicente smiled and lit his cigarette.

"At the very least you should see about a promotion. Announcers don't make shit. You should be a show producer."

"I like being on air."

"Announcers are becoming obsolete."

"How are the acting classes going?" he asked, throwing the ball at her.

For the past year his wife had been taking acting classes at a little school downtown. He had seen the coach and could almost vouch she was also having an affair, but he wasn't about to hurl stones. If it kept her off his case, he was frankly okay with it.

"Fine," Natalia said, looking sour.

Vicente smiled. She had never been able to act her way out of a paper bag. At least Vicente could play an instrument, write songs, write a book (though it remained unfinished, remained an eternal work in progress). Perhaps that was where the animosity was first born. A bitter jealousy over his superior artistic talent. Talent which didn't amount to much, but it was better than nothing, and that was what Natalia had: nothing. Not a splinter of artistic ability.

"Mmm," Vicente said. "I'm going to listen to some music before going to bed."

"Turn off the lights when you are done. You are always wasting power and then the bill comes very high."

"I'll turn them off."

HE SAT IN the dark, listening to The Temptations and smoking.

He thought about what anchored him to this city, to this apartment, to this chair and found very little, the thread of his existence stretched thin.

Vicente saw himself exiting in the middle of the night, grabbing his leather jacket and his old guitar, and simply getting on a bus and heading to nowhere. He pictured himself as a shadow melting into shadows and disappearing.

He closed his eyes.

Vicente opened them when he heard voices. Male and female. Young.

"I found it in the park, just laying there. It's full of money."

"How much is in there?"

It was Meche talking to the tall boy, the one she was always with:

Sebastian. He didn't know what they were discussing. He checked his watch and saw it was late, stood up to remind them Sebastian should be home by now and promptly sat back down. Their voices sounded so content and happy. He remembered sounding like that.

He let them drone on until he heard the door close and Meche shuffle towards her room.

He thought what he might do if he was that young again, of opportunities lost and moments which pass you by.

MECHE LOOKED INTO the mirror, critically analyzing the neon yellow skirt. This was foreign territory. Her regular daywear included jeans, t-shirts and the occasional jacket, sleeves rolled up, with a pair of really heavy, masculine boots. There was no money for the latest fashions so she made do with leftovers from her older cousin or opted for cheap, unfashionable items. Meche looked positively... dainty in this outfit.

"Are you sure girls wear this stuff?" she asked Daniela.

"Look," Daniela said, handing her one of the teen magazines tucked in her backpack.

She matched the girl in the picture. But Meche didn't look like her—she was far less attractive. Meche felt like she was a cheap copy sold in La Lagunilla. This despite that they were shopping at a nice store because the money spell had come through in the shape of the wallet from the park, its contents promptly plundered. Finally, they could shop in Polanco. Sadly, nothing seemed to fit Meche properly.

"I like it. Do you like mine?" Daniela asked.

Meche glanced at her friend's outfit. It was predictably pink and purple. Daniela resembled a large meringue, but Meche supposed it *did* look like the stuff the girls in the magazine were wearing.

"I guess it's alright," Meche said. She leaned towards the mirror, zeroing on the zits around her mouth, and sighed. "I need to fix my skin."

"You should put on a nice avocado mask before going to bed."

"I need a major intervention, not an avocado mask. How can so many pimples appear every damn day? It's like they know I want to go to a party."

"It's no big deal."

"You say that because you don't look like me," Meche muttered.

"Do you want to see what Sebastian is wearing?" Daniela asked.

"Okay."

The girls stepped out of their changing room and knocked at one of the other doors.

"Seboooos," Meche said.

"What?" came the gruff answer.

"Show us."

"No."

"Sebos…"

"No!"

Meche tried jumping to get a look over the door, but could not reach high enough. Over the stores' speakers What I Like About You began to play and Meche began knocking on the door to the rhythm of the music.

"Come oooon."

"Fine!"

He opened the door unexpectedly, making Meche stumble back. He glared at both girls, crossing his arms over his chest. Sebastian—he of the minimalist, all-black attires—looked like he had stepped out of an episode of *Miami Vice* and was going to give Don Johnson a run for his money. He was wearing a bubblegum-pink t-shirt, a white jacket with wide lapels and loafers *sans* socks.

Meche couldn't help it. She just laughed. This caused Sebastian to immediately retreat into the changing room.

"I'm sorry," Meche said, following inside and laughing. "I'm sorry."

"I knew I shouldn't follow Daniela's stupid advice," Sebastian muttered, taking off the jacket and putting it back on the hanger.

"It's not bad."

"Yeah. Your reaction proved it."

"Daniela, come here," Meche said.

"What?" Daniela asked, poking her head in.

"Do you like it?" Meche asked, her thumb pointing at Sebastian.

"I think he looks nice."

"See? You look nice."

"I'll change into something else. The trousers are too damn tight," he muttered.

"I can ask for a bigger size," Daniela said, happily scampering off in her pink and purple tutu-like dress.

Meche looked at the shirts and jackets Sebastian had piled on a chair, raising a skeptical eyebrow at a pastel-coloured tie.

"That skirt is short," Sebastian said.

"It seems to be the purpose of mini-skirts," Meche replied.

"Yeah, but you hate skirts."

"I know."

"I can see your ass."

Meche resisted the impulse to pull the hem down, but she did give Sebastian a pronounced, irritated look.

"The point of this whole thing is to look cool," she said. "You know, unlike we regularly do."

"I think you shouldn't confuse 'cool' with 'mildly obscene.'"

"Thanks, Grandpa Smurf."

"No... I mean, it's... disturbing," he concluded.

Meche didn't even know what to say to that. She opted for nothing and went back to her own changing room. She picked a pair of neon green leggings and sighed.

THE GIRLS WANTED to get haircuts. That's when Sebastian pulled the brakes. He was willing to go shopping for new clothes, he was even willing to show them the clothes he picked, but he was not going to the hairdresser with them.

Daniela looked crestfallen. She had brought numerous cut-outs from magazines showing various hairstyles she thought would look good on him. Sebastian's longish hair, however, was going to remain exactly as it was.

As the girls wandered towards the hair stylist, Sebastian quietly made his way to a jewelry shop. He stopped before the displays, peering down at the sparkling diamonds and the flash of gold until he spotted a gold heart on a chain. He took out the wallet and counted the remaining bills.

* * *

"UGH... I DON'T feel very well," Daniela said.

"That's because you drank the milkshake too fast," Meche said. "Brain freeze. When are you going to learn?"

"I suppose..."

Meche saw Sebastian's spidery hand reach towards her plate, plucking a fry, dipping it in ketchup and throwing it in his mouth. She retaliated by reaching for his burger and giving it a big bite, then opening her mouth and showing him the food.

"Gross," he said.

"Gwa," Meche said, turning to Daniela and also showing her the food.

Daniela did not react. She blinked in confusion. Meche shrugged, closed her mouth and chewed.

"I want to go see a movie," Meche said. "We should buy a big bucket of popcorn."

"No more food," Daniela muttered.

"A shocking development," Meche said, pointing a fry at Daniela. "Do you want to watch a movie?"

"I want to go home," Daniela said.

"Don't be a spoilsport. Sebos, what do you want to do?"

"Finish my food."

"After you finish your food?"

"Why don't we go to the arcade?"

"How much money do we have left?"

Sebastian pulled out a bill and placed it on the table. Meche nodded thoughtfully. They'd get more bang out of their buck if they went to play at the machine in the pharmacy near home because it was cheaper, but that meant Meche might bump into her mom. Plus, there were only two machines and the little kids around the block tended to get on them pretty early in the afternoon. The arcade wouldn't have these issues but it was more expensive.

"I think the arcade's a good idea. Dani, you want to come?" Meche asked.

"No. I think I want to have a nap."

"Alright," Meche said. "Suit yourself."

* * *

AFTER THEY FINISHED their hamburgers, Sebastian and Meche saw Daniela home. They dumped their purchases at Meche's house before rushing off to Arcadeland, the arcade closest to their home. It had over twenty machines and two bored, young attendants who sold tokens and exchanged tickets for tiny plastic bracelets and other assorted crap. In a corner of the joint, there was a stand selling stale pizza and pop.

Sebastian and Meche ignored the bad food and bought a bunch of tokens, dumping them into the machines of their choice. For Sebastian, that was Pac-Man. For Meche, it was something which involved shooting.

Eventually they both got behind the steering wheel and competed in several driving games. The pixelated car did the Monaco circuit, animated girls in bikinis holding up signs saying 'Number 1' and 'Race On!' while some muffled music—Meche thought it might well be Eurythmics—pumped through the arcade.

"Win, win, win!" Meche yelled.

"Let's try the air hockey table."

Meche knew Sebastian wanted to play air hockey because he could easily beat her and rub it in her face, paying her back for her previous wins at the racing machine, but she felt like being a good sport and followed him.

They both stopped in their tracks once they were near the table: Constantino and some of the other boys were gathered around it.

Sometimes, when Meche looked at Constantino, she could almost feel her brain flying through her skull and exiting her body. Coherent thought escaped her and she was left with a terrible longing.

This was one such moment. The lights and sounds of the arcade seemed to dim, leaving only Constantino, standing by the table, looking down, a lazy smile on his lips. She had the urge to extend her hand, touch his shoulder or brush her fingers through his hair. To hold a minuscule part of him, just for a few seconds. To cup the sound of his laughter against her ear.

The boys, taking note of them, looked at Meche and Sebastian and grinned. One of the boys chuckled and someone—she did not know who—must have said something funny because they all started laughing.

Meche and Sebastian moved away, back to a corner of the arcade and she threw a coin into a slot, her fingers trembling as she gripped the joystick.

The sugar-high she had been on had emptied out and she felt herself crashing down, her stomach heaving and turning with the unpleasant taste of sadness.

Would they also laugh at them at Isadora's party, when they wore their new clothes? If they did, they could curse them, make their teeth fall out; the benefit of becoming teenage witches.

From now on, Sebastian, Daniela and Meche were the ones with the upper hand. Which is why she had a hard time understanding why obstinate tears were prickling her eyes.

No crying. Ever. That was her motto.

Sebastian leaned down, rested his chin against her shoulder and whispered into her ear.

"It's fine," he said.

She turned her head by a small fraction and tried to smile.

Meche looked back at the arcade machine. Sebastian also threw a coin into the slot and pressed the start button.

Now that she paid attention, Meche was pretty sure Eurythmics was what they were listening to. It sounded like Here Comes the Rain Again.

PEOPLE WHO HAVE never spent time inside a radio cabin cannot understand the appeal of that small enclosed space, its turntable and its microphone. Behind insulated walls and tape reels hides a spark, a magic, you can't find anywhere else.

Music.

Vicente sat in the cabin, closed his eyes and the world spun away.

Television, movies—they can't compare to radio. To the music over airwaves. It's like a portal to another world.

He was needing other worlds more and more these days. Things at home were nastier than ever and the book was going nowhere.

Vicente smoked his cigarette and opened his notebook, re-reading his notes from yesterday. He had his great ideas, all scribbled tight, but when it came time to type them out he seemed to lose his rhythm. The brilliant sentence turned limp and stale. The turn of phrase was dull.

Maybe his wife was right. Maybe he was never going to finish the book. It would be just like his musical career: down the drain and away.

He quietly pulled out the hip flask he had taken to carrying inside his coat's pocket and saw his face, distorted against the metal, before taking a sip.

Animal fetuses of different kinds sat in jars filled with formaldehyde. They floated in the yellow substance and seemed to stare at the students. There was a big vat with whale ambergris in a corner, which you could supposedly use to make perfumes. A large poster of the periodic table was pinned to the back wall. The blackboard was filled with symbols of a vague, alchemical cast.

Everyone was supposed to have a chemistry partner during lab work, but Meche, Daniela and Sebastian worked as a trio. Miss Costa already had enough trouble trying to enforce the necessity of lab coats and safety procedures, so she let them have their way.

But Daniela was missing today.

"Remember to put on your goggles," the teacher said in a monotonous drone.

Sebastian placed the stirring bar in the large beaker and began pouring the potassium iodate.

"You think she's had another episode?" Meche asked.

Daniela was often sick and they knew the drill. They'd bring her candy, sit by her bed, maybe even take turns reading one of those horrid romance novels to her—Sebastian often read parts of *Flowers in the Attic* or *Corazón Salvaje*, which took much aplomb on his part—then pat her hand and she'd be back in class in a day or two.

"Maybe she just caught a cold or has an upset stomach," Sebastian said. "It could be nothing."

"We should go see her, after school."

Isadora laughed. Sebastian raised his head and looked in her direction. Their pretty classmate was playfully sitting next to Constantino, in a position which was strategically hiking her skirt up. Meche thought Sebastian was going to turn into jelly and collapse upon the floor, foaming from the mouth. She wondered if she shouldn't finish the chemistry demonstration for fear he would blow them up.

"Turn on the stirring plate," Sebastian said, checking his notes.

"Stirring plate," Meche muttered.

"I need the hydrogen peroxide."

Meche passed him the diluted solution. They watched as the solution in the beaker turned amber and then a deep shade of blue.

Isadora was laughing again, chirping about some inanity or other. She spoke too loudly and she did it to get the attention of the class. Judging by Sebastian's reaction, it had the intended effect.

"Well then, that's a chemical oscillator reaction," Meche said, carefully writing in her notebook. "You know, chemistry is a lot like magic."

"Huh?" Sebastian asked.

She would have blamed his blank stare on the fumes, but Meche knew better.

"Well, chemistry was started by alchemists. All of them with their formulas and books and secrecy. I think they were a lot like us."

"I suppose so."

"Except we are not looking for the philosopher's stone."

"The what?"

"You know, the substance that turns lead into gold."

"Maybe we are. In a way," Sebastian said.

Meche glanced at Isadora and she thought she wouldn't have Sebastian, not even if he was plated in gold. Sebastian was stupid.

Then Meche remembered Constantino and realized she was as dumb as her friend.

THEY WOULD HAVE taken the motorcycle, but Sebastian was out of gas and didn't have money to fill the tank. So they walked instead. He did not mind. It meant they would spend more time together.

"Are you going to need help with your literature homework again?" he asked.

"Why? You need help with math again?"

"Even trade," he said. "My lit for your math, as usual."

"Throw in a bar of chocolate and it's a deal."

"I'm not throwing in a bar of nothing."

"Blah."

"Stay and watch TV with me. That's your extra payment."

Meche made a face, like it would be such a chore to sit with him and watch two hours of whatever stupid programming was on, but he knew that was exactly what she wanted to do. They could make cheese sandwiches and grill them on the stove. As far as Sebastian was concerned, that was his definition of happy.

By the time they reached Daniela's house they had decided Meche would purchase the Cheetos, seeing as Sebastian was in the gutter money-wise. Sebastian would make the sandwiches and they would fix themselves some lemonade.

They agreed to stay with Daniela for an hour before setting off together. They regularly brought Daniela her homework when she was not feeling well and they did not expect anything but the usual "hello" and "come in." But when Daniela's dad opened the door he looked very tired and he had this sad, sad look on his face.

"Can we see Daniela?" Meche asked.

"Daniela is in the hospital," her father said, shaking his head.

Daniela's lupus flared up now and then. Last summer she had spent a whole month in bed. When Daniela was sick, little purple bruises appeared all over her body and her face. She got tired and had to stay inside because sunlight made her sicker. Her mom was always afraid she'd get a kidney infection and die.

"Is she really sick?" Meche asked. "Can we go see her?"

"She has a fever... she has Macrophage Activation Syndrome. Her body is attacking itself. She needs to rest."

The long words floated in the air, stinging their ears. Meche did not say a word, twisting the cuffs of her sweater. Sebastian took the reins and spoke.

"We're very sorry. Can you tell her we came by?"

"I will."

Meche and Sebastian looked at each other. They walked quietly back home, kicking an empty juice bottle. After a few blocks, Meche looked up at Sebastian.

"But she can't be sick. We are going to the party together next week. Her dad even gave her permission to go, which is a major win," Meche said.

"Yeah, but she's really bad," Sebastian muttered. "She might have to stay in bed for several days."

"We need to help her. We have to cast a spell."

"Just the two of us?" Sebastian asked.

"We don't have much of a choice. Come on, hurry."

She ran towards the factory and he ran behind her.

GETTING MONEY THANKS to a spell was one thing, but Sebastian was not sure they could actually cure Daniela. He did not dare to air his doubts to Meche. She seemed very determined to find a solution and he let her keep her hopes up.

"I feel something here," Meche said, showing him a record.

"Elvis Presley," Sebastian said. "What song?"

"Jailhouse Rock."

"Okay."

Meche put the record in place. Presley's voice boomed across the factory. *Dun dum. Dun dum.*

Meche tiptoed around in an imitation of Elvis Presley, hips swinging to the beat of the music. Though Sebastian knew nothing about the dance moves of this time period, and though he had rarely laid eyes on Elvis on the TV, his feet seemed to know the necessary moves. It all felt really fine, all the pieces coming together, and there was that flare of energy that rose from some deep place inside him, rose and became a golden thread, a vapour which reached the ceiling and dissipated. But this time, unlike the previous ones, he felt a stabbing pain in his stomach, as though someone had kicked him.

Sebastian groaned and hugged himself. He saw Meche bending down, also touching her midsection.

"Ouch," he muttered. "What is that?"

Suddenly the room seemed to grow too cold, even for autumn and even for an abandoned factory. It was as though someone had opened a refrigerator door. Sebastian felt tired. He licked his lips and sat down.

"Man, it's like I just ran a marathon."

"It's so... odd."

"What's happening?"

"I don't know," Meche said. "When I did that first spell by myself I slept for a long time and it was also very cold. But it hasn't happened again."

"Maybe it's easier when we are all together," Sebastian said. "Maybe we shouldn't ever cast spells by ourselves."

"Maybe that's the whole point of the Witches' Sabbath," Meche said. "We are stronger together. Like a bunch of batteries in a remote control."

She crossed her arms over her chest, teeth chattering.

"Come," Sebastian said. "You can have my jacket."

"I don't want your jacket. I have my jacket."

"I don't want it," he said, taking it off.

Meche hesitated. Then she sat down next to him, the jacket around her shoulders. She still shivered.

Sebastian's eyelids felt like they were made of lead. His muscles ached.

"I need to rest," Sebastian whispered.

He lay flat against the hard floor and though it was uncomfortable, he was too exhausted to care.

"You're going to fall asleep here?" Meche asked.

"I can't reach the door."

"Okay."

She lay next to him. The floor felt as cold as a block of ice. The only source of warmth was Meche's body, curled up against him, as she hummed a tune he didn't know. Sebastian rested his chin upon her head and closed his eyes.

He had this dream about a woman who was looking at him. She was standing on the other side of the street, and the sight of her made him very nervous, half-afraid. Her hair was short, her eyes dark and cold. Slowly he recognized her as Meche. An older version of Meche. He tried to open his mouth and say hello, but she walked away and he said nothing.

When Sebastian woke up it was dark. The factory looked spooky when it was shrouded by shadows like this. Light trickled through some of the window panes, creating puddles here and there. He looked down at Meche and for a moment he was afraid she had changed, that she changed into that strange woman with the short hair. But it was still his Meche, still a teenager, still the girl with the very long dark hair and the resolute mouth.

He stared at her, wondering if one day she might become that other Meche who did not seem to know him.

Meche opened her eyes slowly and stretched her arms.

"What time is it?" she asked.

Sebastian checked his cheap plastic wristwatch. "Past seven."

"Ugh, we better head home."

"So why are witches always in groups?"

"Is it time to talk about spells again?" her grandmother asked.

Meche had Miguel Bosé's Aire Soy on the record player and a glass of milk with her. She sat next to her grandmother, watching her as she knit.

"Yeah," Meche said.

"A circle is the most perfect shape, isn't it? A witches' circle uses this perfect arrangement. It is wholeness, persons joining and connecting."

Meche thought about records being essentially circles. Power harnessed into the right shape.

"But you can have lone witches?"

"You can. If they are powerful enough."

"Did you know any lone witches?"

"Well, one hears a lot of things in a small town."

"What did you hear?"

"I heard there was a girl in town who could talk to the stones."

"That's useful," Meche snorted.

"It was. Every stone has a story. Imagine speaking to the stones in a house and learning the secrets of the people who live there."

Meche decided that was actually a useful skill. She wondered if what they were doing with the records was something similar. Like listening to what the records were really saying while regular people could only hear the songs.

"Did you ever try to cast a spell?"

Her grandmother did not reply.

DANIELA WOKE UP feeling... odd. Not bad, as she had been feeling all day, but odd. The pain was gone but its absence was strange. She touched her lips, pressed a hand against her forehead. The skin felt cool. No trace of a fever.

This had never happened before. Curious, she tiptoed into the bathroom, careful to not wake up the girl sharing the hospital room with her. She looked at herself in the mirror. Her skin was normal. No telltale marks, no 'butterfly' rash across her cheeks. Daniela looked whole and healthy, as though she had not had a bad flare up.

Impossible. And yet theirs was now a world full of impossibilities.

Daniela smiled.

"IT'S AWESOME!" DANIELA said. "It looks great!"

"Duh. Did you doubt it would?" Meche said.

Meche and Sebastian had strung streamers around the room. Balloons dotted the floor and were taped to the walls. There was a big sign that said 'Welcome back Dani.' They had even baked a cake and frosted it pink.

"That's not all. Sebos, are you ready?"

"Yep."

"Okay, sit down," Meche said.

Daniela sat on the couch and smiled, her hands in her lap.

Sebastian started the music. It was an old song. Volare. Meche and Sebastian hummed together and when the singer said, "Volare, wohoo hohohho," they moved their arms and two of the balloons bounced in their direction.

Daniela gasped. Meche pointed at a balloon and it flew through the air, towards her. Sebastian made a wide sweeping motion and a whole cluster of balloons ripped themselves from the walls and bounced around him, like a wave of colours.

Meche and Sebastian lowered their hands and the balloons gently settled to the floor.

Daniela stood up and clapped, feeling giddy.

"How did you ever learn to do that?" she asked.

"Oh, we figured it out by accident when we were putting up the decorations," Meche said.

"Can you teach me?"

"Sure. It'll be better with you," Meche said. "Sebastian and I get a bit tired if it's just the two of us."

"It's like running for several blocks and getting a charley horse," Sebastian explained.

"I so want to do it!" Daniela said, rushing to their side.

"Okay," Meche said. "First you focus on what you're going to move."

MECHE WAITED WITH Daniela at the coffee shop for her sister to pick her up. They had foamy coffees and shared a large cookie. Daniela seemed very perky and she chatted noisily, her hands fluttering up and down.

Meche smiled and checked the notes in her *grimoire*.

"Hey, that's Constantino across the street," Daniela said.

Meche turned her head. It was. He was walking with Isadora. Meche sighed, leaning back and brushing the hair off her face.

"She's got every boy in school running after her. Man, can't I get just a little bit of that?" Meche muttered.

"Not every boy," Daniela said, probably trying to perk her up.

"Sebastian thinks she's hot."

"Yeah?"

"He practically drools over her."

"She's pretty."

"I want someone to drool over me."

"Well... maybe someone will. At the party."

Meche nodded, but with little enthusiasm. Wasn't there magic that could make you irresistible? Something to spellbind another person? There had to be. The trick was in finding it.

THEY WALKED INTO the party around nine, glancing around the house with curiosity. The floors had been waxed and Meche walked slowly because she was wearing heels and was afraid of falling down. She glanced at a large mirror by the entrance, making sure her lipstick looked fine. She'd borrowed the makeup from her cousin and painted her nails with a bright pink nail polish Jimena insisted was all the rage. Meche looked different, odd—but wasn't that the point of it? To transform into someone else entirely.

Meche followed the sound of the music, her heels carefully clicking against the floor.

"Man, Isadora's dad must be loaded," Daniela said.

That was something coming from Daniela. Meche had to agree. The house was not only huge, but there were uniformed waiters walking around with trays in their hands. One of them offered them tiny little sausages and Meche took one, nodding. Sebastian grabbed three, tossing them in his mouth in quick succession.

Meche looked at the heavy furniture, the large windows, the air of opulence drifting from every corner of the room. Ugliness had no place there. Real taste, however, seemed to have escaped Isadora. The sweet, candy pop sound of Timbiriche—the mark of a limited, mundane imagination—threatened to give Meche a headache, but she decided to stand firm, smile, and try to have a good time.

"Let's get a drink," she said to her friends.

They drifted around. Meche had the distinct feeling that everyone was staring at them. She had not, in the end, picked the mini-skirt, instead donning tight stirrup pants in a light yellow and a long-sleeve shirt with a very wide black belt.

Sebastian had opted for the *Miami Vice* look, but with a more subdued baby blue t-shirt under his jacket. Daniela, having no qualms about her wardrobe, went for a metallic pink dress and a black, studded bolero jacket.

When Meche finally found something to drink it turned out to be beer. She handed one to Sebastian and another to Daniela. Daniela took a sip and made a face.

"Can't we have a soda?" Daniela asked.

"Do you see anyone else drinking soda?" Meche asked.

Daniela looked around and shook her head.

"Drink your beer," Meche ordered.

"Shouldn't we find Isadora?" Sebastian asked.

"What for?" Meche said.

"It's her birthday party."

"We're not here because of her."

"It's rude not to say hi."

Meche shrugged. Constantino was across the room, next to a window, hanging out with a circle of classmates. Damn it. Meche had copious makeup and hair gel, and was hoping she'd be able to get a chance to talk to him in all her finery. She positioned herself strategically, next to the hallway which led to the washrooms.

"I'm going to find her," Sebastian said.

"Good luck," Meche said, dismissively because—as far as she was concerned—Isadora mattered squat.

Daniela bobbed her head up and down and smiled. "What do we do now?" she asked.

"Hang out."

"Do you want to dance?"

Meche considered her high heels, the possibility of slipping and falling on her ass. She shook her head. Nope.

Daniela looked a little crestfallen. Meche did not have time to baby her, so she simply sipped her beer and tried to strike a pose, ready to chat with Constantino when he happened to walk by.

SEBASTIAN FOUND ISADORA in the kitchen. She was trying to drag a large box towards the table.

"Hey, let me help you," he said, cheerfully grabbing the box and hauling it onto the table.

"Thanks," she said.

"No problem."

Sebastian opened the box and found more beer bottles inside. He smiled.

"You must be making Tecate rich."

"Well, it's Saturday."

"That it is," he said.

Sebastian wiped his hands against his jacket and nodded. He had nothing else to say and felt his mouth clamming shut.

The heart necklace, he thought. *I should give it to her.*

"Well, you came," she said, plucking a bottle. "Bye."

Sebastian was going to say something witty, but he couldn't string the right words together. Isadora turned around and walked away, leaving him by himself.

He looked down at the floor, furious with himself. He felt the little necklace tucked in his jacket and knew he was a coward and a fool.

Sebastian grabbed a bottle and drank it quick.

CONSTANTINO WAS STILL chatting with his friends, apparently glued to his spot. Meche had been standing very straight but after a while she began to tire and sat on a chair next to Daniela.

He had to walk by eventually. Unless he was planning on peeing in the bushes.

Meche leaned forward, resting her chin against her knuckles.

She had pictured it all before coming to the party: he'd walk by, notice her beautiful outfit, her improved appearance, and immediately start talking with her. She did not expect to be sitting in the same spot after one hour with no Constantino, exactly like the loser she'd always been.

DANIELA TRIED TO be a good sport. She tried to chat with Meche. But she was so stiff, so unpleasant. She gave up and decided enough was enough. Daniela placed her little pink purse on the chair she had been sitting on and headed towards the centre of the room.

"Where are you going?" Meche asked.

"I'm going to dance."

"By yourself?"

"If I have to."

Meche opened her mouth, probably to protest, but Daniela did not want to hear it. She had come for the party and she was not going to go unless she had one good dance. At first she danced by herself, but eventually a couple of classmates joined her and the three of them began joining in with the song's chorus.

* * *

MECHE LOOKED AT the clock. Nine thirty. An hour and a half and Constantino had not even moved close to her. It was impossible for her to approach him, not when he was shielded by all his friends. When he finally did move, he was intercepted by Isadora.

Meche watched them as they spoke. Isadora seemed upset. She was shaking her head and making little motions with her hands.

Sebastian plopped himself next to her, in the chair Daniela had been occupying, long limbs spreading carelessly.

"What's up?" he asked.

"Nothing," she muttered.

He nodded, lifted his beer and before it touched his lips, he frowned.

"Is that Daniela over there?"

"Yeah."

"Dancing."

"Yeah."

"Ha! Good for her."

The swirl of bodies—more people kept arriving—made it difficult to see if Constantino was still at his place by the window. Had he moved? Had he gone somewhere else? Was he still talking to Isadora? Meche began to panic.

"Do you want to dance?"

"My shoes hurt."

"You could take them off."

"I'm not taking them off."

Sebastian took a swig. He offered her his bottle. Meche had not touched her own beer. It was still sitting beneath her chair. She shoved his hand back and the beer spilled all over her new pants.

Meche shot up, horrified.

"You ruined them!"

Sebastian stood up too.

"I'll get a napkin," he said.

Meche did not reply. She rushed towards the bathroom, locking the door behind her. She grabbed a towel and tried to clean the pants; the stain was bad. It looked like she had peed herself. Her lips, under the glare of the light bulbs, looked a horrid crimson. Meche hurled the towel into the sink.

She leaned against the door, feeling the beat of the happy music outside, and winced.

Meche slid out, crossing her arms and walking across the room, evading Sebastian and sneaking outside, into Isadora's walled garden. She stepped away until the ridiculous pop music was nothing but a faint whisper behind her.

Meche closed her eyes and took off her shoes, just like Sebastian had suggested, holding them in her left hand and staring up at the moon.

"You're not having fun?"

Meche glanced to her left and saw Constantino leaning against the ivy-encrusted wall. His cigarette glowed faintly in the dark.

"Not a lot," she admitted.

"You don't like the food."

"The music," she said. "And you?"

"I'm just having a smoke."

Meche nodded, licking her lips. Surprise had overridden her nervousness but now as the seconds dragged by she tried to recall the dialogue she had rehearsed. But she had not rehearsed any dialogue. She had thought he'd be struck by her looks, would ask her to dance, and they'd place their arms around each other, swaying gently to the music. A good song. Not something stupid and corny.

Alas, there was no decent soundtrack playing and Meche clasped her hands together behind her back.

"What don't you like about the music?"

"It's trite."

"What would you play if you could?"

"It would be Jimmy Fontana singing Il Mondo."

"Wanna see if they have it?" he asked, tossing his cigarette butt on the ground.

"Okay."

Meche followed Constantino back into the house and he guided her towards the sound system and the big shelving unit with lots of records.

"Do you see it?"

It's not going to be here, Meche thought.

But she forced herself to think the opposite. To think it *would* be there. That all she had to do was reach forward and her hands would alight upon the right record. Meche closed her eyes and pulled a record sleeve…

… and it was Jimmy Fontana.

"Il Mondo," she whispered.

Meche lifted the lid from the record player, lifted the needle.

She felt all the heads in the room turning, surprised by the sudden interruption. Meche placed the record in its place, lowered the needle.

And Jimmy began to sing in Italian.

There was a collective groan from the crowd, but slowly they began to shuffle their feet. Slowly the teenage boys slid their hands around their partner's waists, slowly the girls began to follow the boys' lead. Slowly they stepped left and right. Sway. Rise. Fall.

Ask me to dance, she thought and she willed it just like she'd willed the record, feeling that it could, *would* happen.

"You want to dance?" Constantino asked.

Meche nodded. She put one hand on his shoulder and clasped the other. Forward, step to the side, and then a step to close the feet together. She realized, as she glanced down, that she had not put her high heels on again, had misplaced them at some point, and was dancing barefoot.

Constantino glanced down, chuckling at the sight of her bare toes. A good-natured chuckle matched with a good-natured smile.

She looked up at Constantino and smiled back at him.

As she turned, Meche saw Sebastian, standing by himself, holding a napkin in his hand. He stared at her.

No smile adorned his face.

THERE WAS NO reason for Sebastian to be upset. But he was upset. On Monday, when they walked together to school, he did not speak a word to her. He failed to appear during recess and after school he walked back alone.

Meche did not understand what was going on in his head. She did not care to find out either but Daniela—quiet Daniela, who seemed to know very little of what happened around her, but who in this case seemed to know much—said he was hurting.

"He tried talking to Isadora at the party and she rebuffed him," Daniela said. "And then you danced with Constantino."

Ah, so that was that. He was jealous of her. Jealous because Meche had achieved what Sebastian could not: the attention of the object of her desire, followed on Monday by the briefest of nods, the briefest of affirmations proving that she now existed, that he knew her, remembered their stunted chat.

If Sebastian had been too tongue-tied, too stupid, to achieve similar results with Isadora, then Meche was not to blame for his lack of success. Meche decided to have a chat with him. Around six p.m. she went to his apartment building and sneaked inside when she saw a lady come out.

Sebastian's elevator was perpetually broken, ever since she had been eleven and first walked into his building. Meche walked up the six flights of stairs, humming to herself, and knocked loudly—three times, as was their practice.

"I know you're there!" she yelled.

The door opened and he looked down at her, all in black and all gloomy depression.

"What do you want?"

"I'm seeing what you are up to."

"I'm doing my homework. You should be doing the same."

"Uy, so serious."

He moved towards the kitchen. Meche closed the door and followed him. Sebastian filled a bowl with Choco Krispis and poured himself some milk, then turned around to look at her.

"What crawled up your butt?" Meche asked, tilting her head a little and smiling at him.

"You know, Meche? You think you're cute when you behave like this, but you are annoying and bratty."

"Good, because I wasn't trying to be cute. Why are you angry at me?"

"*A pastar fang!*" he cried, setting the bowl down on the counter, then stomping towards his room.

"Did you just insult me in Catalán?" Meche asked, scoffing, because Sebastian had picked a few choice words from his grandfather, the yellow, weathered gentleman of Barcelona.

"Ah!"

Meche was more energized than angry at his welcome, so she simply followed him, right into his room, chuckling and shaking her head.

"You *are* jealous," she said. "You just can't take the fact that I got what I wanted and you didn't. It's not my fault Isadora dissed you."

"Rub it in, won't you?"

"Loser."

Sebastian was picking his sneakers from his bedroom floor. He promptly dropped them and hurried towards Meche. She was leaning against the door frame, her arms crossed, smug and confident. Sebastian stretched up his whole, tall, bony length and glared down at her and for the first time in her life Meche felt much smaller than her friend. Meche tilted her head up, staring back into Sebastian's eyes, her teeth bared in a harsh smile.

"What?" she asked.

Sebastian leaned down and she thought he was going to bark another insult at her. Maybe in Catalán, maybe in Spanish.

He opened his mouth and said... nothing. Sebastian stomped away as quickly as he had come, falling onto his bed and pulling the cover around his shoulders.

"Just go," he said.

Normally, that wouldn't be enough to shoo Meche out. But there was a new intonation in his voice that afternoon. It prickled Meche's skin and made her step back, confused, and she left without another word, not bothering to close the front door behind her.

ROMUALDO ARRIVED AROUND eight. Sebastian was still in bed. He had not moved an inch, curled up under the covers, staring at the wall and feeling like there was a piece of lead in his stomach.

"Are you sick, asshole?" Romualdo asked, his usual, cheery hello.

"No," Sebastian asked.

"The front door was open."

"Nobody would come in to steal."

"It doesn't matter. Get up and go to the living room. I need to phone Margarita."

"Why don't you use the pay phone down at the corner, asshole?"

Romualdo punched him in the ribs, hard. Sebastian sat up, rubbing his side and glared at his brother.

"What?" Romualdo asked. "Wanna fight?"

Romualdo was a lot stronger and beefier than Sebastian. Any fight would end with Sebastian bleeding. For a moment, though, he considered it. Then it all seemed like such a bother. Sebastian shook his head, too worn to bother with his brother.

"No. Excuse me, my cereal must be getting all soggy."

Sebastian walked past his brother and headed into the kitchen. It was beyond soggy. He threw the cereal down the drain and poured himself a fresh bowl.

"So what did you fight with Meche about?"

"How'd you know that?" Sebastian asked, his spoon frozen in mid-air.

Romualdo laughed. "Oh, come on. You're having chick trouble. And the only chick who ever hangs around with your sorry self is Meche. Or maybe Daniela. And I know Daniela wouldn't rile you up like this. So what's going on with you two?"

"Like I'd tell you."

"Fine," Romualdo said, lifting his hands in the air.

Sebastian rolled his eyes, he thrust the spoon into his mouth and spoke while chewing at the same time. "I dunno. She irritated me. Sometimes Meche thinks she's so much better than me. It's like she rubs it in my face. She can be such a major bitch."

"Then stop being friends with her."

"Well... it doesn't mean I hate her," Sebastian said carefully. "It's just we've been talking about this magic... um... music and magic thing and it all kind of started with this spell—"

"You are so funny."

"What?"

"Look, you are fucked up in the head. Meche is too. You're just both really weird."

"Thanks," Sebastian said dryly.

"It's true. I was never like you and you're definitely not like other kids. But it's okay because Meche gets you. I don't know why or how, but she totally does get you. And that's a good thing. Most people, they'll never understand you. So, after you deal with this hormonal attack or whatever it is you're having, make up."

"Yeah," Sebastian said, running a hand through his hair.

He stirred his cereal and smiled a bit, then glanced at his brother, feeling contrite.

"I'm sorry. You should phone Margarita."

"Ah, it's okay," Romualdo said. "I already know what she's going to say."

"Is she… is she really pregnant?"

"Yeah."

"What are you going to do?"

"I have no idea."

They stood in silence, nodding. Sebastian felt, for a brief moment, like he was actually close to his brother.

"Did you really fix my old motorcycle?" Romualdo asked. "Mom told me you were out riding it the other day."

"I did."

"How?"

"Magic," Sebastian said taking another spoonful of cereal.

DANIELA WAS DREAMING of an adventure in the South Seas. A ship. Pirates. Marooned on an island. She imagined herself in a flowing 19th century dress, a parasol between her hands, the blinding sun scorching the sky. White sand dunes and a man approaching from afar, his shirt open to his waist. Mr. Rodriguez in the role of the hero.

"Maybe I should just ignore it. I don't have to apologize. Do I?" Meche asked.

Daniela sighed. Meche had been going on about Sebastian all morning. She did not like it when they fought because Daniela often ended up in the middle, a courier between two upset parties. But she was not willing to play mediator this time. Besides, Meche was cutting into her daydreaming.

"I don't know," she said.

The bell rang. Meche grabbed her books. Mr. Rodriguez raised his voice, trying to be heard over the drone of teenage voices and the shuffling of feet.

"Remember. I have two tutoring spots left in the afternoons," he said.

Daniela and Meche hurried to the bathroom. They had chemistry lab next and that meant they had to change into their lab coats before climbing the narrow steps to the classroom. If the coat was not spotless Miss Costa would deduct points from their lab work. Meche, as usual, had neither washed nor ironed her coat, and was trying to quickly clean a ketchup stain which had landed smack on the front of the coat.

"I was thinking of taking some tutoring sessions with Rodriguez," Daniela said, checking her hair in the mirror to make sure her bangs were still stiff with hair spray.

"Man, I hate Rodriguez. He smiles too much."

"There's nothing wrong with being friendly."

"It's annoying. Okay, what's good for cleaning ketchup stains?"

"I don't know. Bleach?"

"Ugh!"

"You asked."

Meche tossed the coat in the sink and pressed both hands on each side of it, staring into the mirror.

"I hate Sebastian."

"Meche..."

"He's being unfair!"

"He's hurt. The girl he likes doesn't give a crap about him and then you are all mean to him."

"I didn't think he *really* wanted to dance," Meche protested.

"Oh, I don't think it's the dance that's bothering him... he told me you went to see him and called him a loser."

"What a tattletale! That's why he can't get a girlfriend."

Meche opened the faucet, pumped some soap onto the coat, and began scrubbing it vigorously.

"I'm not apologizing," Meche said firmly.

That was the thing about Meche and Sebastian. Both were too proud and too damn stubborn to simply make up.

Meche put on the coat, which was soaking wet. Instead of a red stain she now had a pink stain. It still looked terrible.

"I wonder if I can turn it inside out?" she muttered.

"I think Costa's going to deduct points no matter what you do. We've got to go or we'll be late."

"Fine. Worst day ever," Meche muttered. "Constantino didn't even look at me today. It's like he noticed me once and now I'm back to being invisible."

"You're not invisible," Daniela said.

Meche said something about boys, but Daniela was already flying away into her daydream. Pirates and South Seas and a dashing admiral saving her life.

THREE KNOCKS. MECHE, of course. Sebastian could ignore her. But he knew how persistent she could be. If she was back after what happened two days before, that meant she was back with a vengeance. He opened the door a crack.

"We need to talk," Meche said. "And spare me the dirty look."

"We do?" Sebastian said, raising an arm and resting it against the door frame.

"Don't..."

"No, *you* don't," he replied.

"You are such a baby," Meche whispered and held out a piece of paper. "Here. Take it."

Sebastian looked at the paper warily. She kept waving it in front of his face so he grabbed and unfolded it. It was a rail map of Europe. He looked carefully at the jumble of colours, the red and yellow and blue lines, and back at Meche.

"It's for the wall. For your collection," she said.

Sebastian was quiet. Meche sighed.

"I'm trying to apologize to you," she whispered.

He did not budge. It had come to this. She had to use her trump card. Meche didn't want to. He could tell.

She gave in.

"My object of power is the Duncan Dhu record," she told him. "The one we played that time in the factory. I selected it after we were done. I keep it my room in a box with some toys."

"You're not lying?"

"What do you think?"

Sebastian opened the door wider, letting her in. Meche walked in and they looked at each other.

"Um… I'm sorry too," he admitted. "I made a big deal out of nothing. Do you want… I can put the map up right now and we can go for a ride afterwards."

"Sure."

Sebastian made his way around a mound of dirty clothes Romualdo had piled up near the entrance to their room. He found the box with the thumbtacks and put the map right above the one of France, where he could look at them before going to sleep at night.

"It's really awesome. Thanks," he told her.

"Sure."

"I'm going to spend a whole year in Europe after high school. I'll travel all the countries and see all the major cities. All the way up north, so I can see the midnight sun."

He knew he'd talked about this a million times before, but he liked to hear himself say it. It sounded more real when there was somebody listening to him. Like it could really happen; that these were not the ramblings of a kid. He had the guidebooks; he had the maps; all he needed was a bit of money.

"Cool."

"You should come with me," he said.

Meche sat on the floor of his bedroom, stretching her legs and smiling.

"All the way to Europe?"

"All the way. We can run away together."

"I think we tried that three years ago."

"We went to Coyoacán without permission. Daniela forced us to turn back and kept bawling her eyes out because she was afraid her dad would find out she had skipped class."

"It was pretty silly."

"No, but we should do it. This time for real."

"What the hell would I do in Europe?"

"What wouldn't you do?" he said, sliding down next to her. "It's not like we've got it super amazing here in Mexico City."

Really, what was there for them? For him? This miserable apartment. The school where nobody liked him. Isadora, who didn't even know he existed. The accumulated tedium of hundreds of days piling on top of each other.

"Yeah, but going looking for the midnight sun sounds…"

"… crazier than casting spells with records?" he asked. "I don't think so."

"It sounds cold."

"We'll buy parkas. Blankets. What do people wear in Norway?"

"Bear furs, probably. What do people eat in Norway?"

"Bears."

Sebastian laid down on the floor, his hands behind his head. Meche also lay back, her hands folded over her chest.

"People don't eat bears," Meche said.

"They do. But you shouldn't eat polar bear liver."

"Why not?"

"It'll make you sick. Too much vitamin A."

"You're making it up."

"I am not. I read it somewhere."

"There's a song by Ella Fitzgerald called Midnight Sun," Meche said.

"Everything is a song with you."

"At least it's not bear meat."

Sebastian felt himself getting sleepy. This was their usual banter. This was their usual selves. He could relax now. He could be happy. The pain gnawing him all day long would subside.

"How does the song go?"

"Mmm… let me see," Meche said. "There's a meadow in December, ice and oh darling… something about lips close by. People kissing basically…"

Meche coughed.

"Of course, she sings it much better than I do," she concluded.

"You'll have to play it for me sometime."

"But jazz is boooring," she said, imitating him.

Sebastian let out a loud *hmpf* and turned his head to look at her. They were side by side, but Meche's legs were pointed in the opposite direction and she was tapping her foot to the beat of an imaginary tune. Probably Fitzgerald's song. She was staring at the ceiling.

He pictured Meche walking down a long hallway, towards an airplane. She was ahead of him by a long stretch. With every step he took the distance between them seemed to grow until Meche was just a tiny little smudge against a bright opening. Then she was gone.

"Can I ask you something?" he said.

"What?"

"Something serious."

"Then definitely not."

Meche glanced at him. When he didn't laugh, she turned her body completely towards him, leaning against her elbow and looking down at him.

"What?"

"Promise you'll never leave."

"Leave where?"

"Anywhere," he said. "Without me, that is."

"Gee. Should we stitch our sides together like artificial Siamese twins? Hey, isn't there an episode of the *Twilight Zone* where that happens? Or is that the one of the guy with two heads?"

"I'm not kidding."

Sebastian sat and looked down at her sternly. Meche looked like she was about to laugh. But then she nodded instead of chuckling.

"Alright."

"Never go."

"I won't."

Sebastian hugged her and did not understand why he suddenly felt so sad. He closed his eyes.

"You're lying."

"I'm not."

He thought he could hear the chords of a song. Fitzgerald's song as he imagined it without his ever having heard it. Slow and lovely and somewhat painful.

"There is a *Twilight Zone* episode called Midnight Sun," he said as he stood up, offering Meche his hand.

"What's it about?"

"Earth has moved from its orbit and is heading into the Sun. Everyone will be cooked alive."

"Creepy."

He pulled her up and Meche smiled.

"Let's go for a ride," he said.

They trotted downstairs and grabbed the motorcycle. Meche jumped behind him and placed her hands on his shoulders, then rested them on his waist.

"Ready?" he asked.

"Yep."

They roared away together, through the darkened streets of the city.

Mexico City, 2009

JIMENA HAD A placid smile on her face. A smile Meche knew well. The smile said *I know something you don't*. Meche drank a cup of *atole* and ate a piece of *tamal*, trying to ignore the smile. It had never boded well in her youth and she did not think it could bode well now. There were sweet *tamales* and salty ones, some filled with chicken and others with pineapple. There were even *tamales chiapanecos*, wrapped in a banana leaf and stuffed with pork.

All this business of eating and praying was having a narcotic effect on Meche. When her mother came to her side and spoke she did not hear her. On a shelf, a photograph of her father looking younger than he had ever been presided over the dinner. He stared at Meche with a sad, startled expression.

"Huh?" she asked.

"Are you going to put on another record?" her mother said again.

Meche realized the turntable had gone quiet. Meche nodded. That was her job: keep the music going. Jimena was in charge of the food, her mother, the greeting of people, her stepfather seemed to be managing the distribution of the *atole* and the soft drinks. All Meche had to do was keep some soft, pleasant music playing. She had decided she could not stomach CDs. Her father would have hated that. So she had hooked up the old turntable.

Meche picked a collection of jazz songs. She started with Stormy Weather.

She mouthed the lyrics to the song and felt comforted by the familiar tune, the trumpet and the piano and Billie's voice.

"Hey, Meche, come here."

Meche raised her head and saw Jimena motioning to her, by the kitchen door.

"What?" she asked, wondering if she was going to have to distribute *tamales*. She didn't want to. Meche was happy standing in her corner, blending in with the curtains and avoiding chatting with her relatives and former neighbours.

Jimena gestured more emphatically and Meche hurried to her side.

"What?" she muttered.

"Here she is," Jimena said brightly. "Meche, your buddy is here."

Jimena was grinning from ear to ear. Sebastian stood next to her, looking very sober, a cup of *atole* in his hands; well-dressed and well-groomed.

"Hi," he said, stretching out his hand.

Meche shook it stiffly.

"Hello."

"I've come to pay my respects to your mother," he said, like a perfect gentleman.

"I can find her for you," Meche offered.

"Oh, I'll find her," Jimena said. "I need to get this tray out, anyway. I'll be back. Don't you move."

Jimena flashed a wide smile to Sebastian and shoved Meche, carrying her large tray with the *tamales*. Some things never changed. Jimena was still able to flirt with anything that had a pulse.

Sebastian looked at his cup.

"I thought I saw you the other night but I wasn't sure it was you."

"Then it probably was me," Meche said.

"I would have said hi—"

"No worries," Meche said brusquely. "Didn't Daniela talk to you?"

"She phoned me promptly yesterday."

"Then you still like being a dick."

Sebastian looked up at her, lifting the corners of his mouth into a wry, small smile.

"Daniela's coming tomorrow. We're long past being teenagers and we're not afraid of you. We have a right to say hi to your mom and pay our respects."

"And I have every right to ignore you. Eat up, it's all free."

Meche pivoted on her heels, slowly walking out of the kitchen.

"Cry Me a River."

"Excuse me?" she said, turning around and placing her hands on her hips.

"That's what's playing. Ella Fitzgerald is singing Cry Me A River."

Meche realized he was right. The previous song had finished and Cry Me had started to play.

"Did you become a jazz fan at some point?" she asked, with that easy, snide tone she liked to employ with him from years and years back.

"No. But I do know my Ella."

"Congratulations. Should I give you a medal?"

Sebastian chuckled. "Daniela was right. You're exactly the same."

Meche walked away.

"DID YOU KNOW he was coming?" Meche asked her cousin.

They were tidying up the apartment. Moving empty glasses to the kitchen, tossing any garbage which had found its way onto the floor into a bin, and trying to implement a degree of order. Meche had positioned herself behind the sink, dutifully scrubbing dishes, while Jimena brought her more dirty cups.

"No," Jimena said.

"Are you sure?"

"I said no. What's wrong? He's cute, isn't he? Why, if I could get my hands…"

"Aren't you married?" Meche asked sharply.

"That doesn't stop me from looking at the menu," Jimena said with a shrug. "What about you? You're single, no?"

Meche's last serious relationship had taken place two years before and lasted eight months. She knew it caused her mother much anxiety to know she remained unmarried and childless. In Natalia's eyes, Meche was a spinster, doomed to a life of unhappiness. She viewed her as dangerously contaminated by foreign traits. Marriage and motherhood were a woman's ways. Anything else was an aberration stemming from too many imported shows. If Meche chanced to remind her mother that she herself had divorced her husband and was therefore not exactly a paragon of Catholic virtues, Natalia would deny any wrongdoing. Comically, Natalia had even asked Meche—in a quiet little voice—if she was a lesbian.

"I am single," Meche said to her cousin. "I am also uninterested in Sebastian Soto."

"And I thought you'd be glad to see him."

"I haven't talked to him since I was a teenager. Why would I be glad to see him now?"

"Well, seeing as you did like him back then…"

"I also painted my nails neon green one time. It doesn't mean I'm rushing to buy puke-coloured nail polish this instant," Meche muttered.

"Uh, you know who was hot?" Jimena asked. "That C kid… um, Constantino Dominguez."

"Yeah."

"He's married now. He's fat and married and balding," Jimena said. "He's got three kids and they're all damn ugly. Who would have thought?"

"Does he still live around here?"

"No. I saw him at the mall a couple of times when I was working in a pet shop. He chatted with me for a little bit. At first I didn't recognize him, but then when he began talking I remembered. Constantino Dominguez."

"Do you remember a girl named Isadora?" Meche asked. "She was in my grade, so maybe you didn't know her."

"In the Queen? Before you went away?"

"Yeah. She was pretty. Skinny, tallish."

Jimena snapped her fingers. "I remember her! She was Sebastian's girlfriend, wasn't she?"

"I wouldn't know," Meche said.

But Meche did know. Even though Meche did not speak a word to Sebastian after the spring of 1989, even though she moved to a different city that same summer, she was aware of it. It was hard not to be aware of it when she lived three blocks from him. Three blocks and three knocks. But those blocks stretched miles long, separated them as though they were oceans, and she did not take the path which led to his apartment building after that time at the factory.

That time…

"Well, she married him."

"Isadora is married to Sebastian?"

"He's not married," Jimena said. "Weren't you paying attention? I said he's single."

"Yeah, but…"

"They got married right out of high school. We all thought she was pregnant. It's the same thing as with his brother, we thought, but no. It lasted maybe a year. Was it two? It wasn't long. They divorced, she moved back in with her parents and he ended up moving away. You know, he was living in Monterrey in 1998. I thought for sure you guys had met up then."

"I wasn't living in Monterrey in 1998," Meche said. "I had already moved to Europe."

"Oh, well. Then you missed each other."

"Probably."

Meche squeezed some more liquid soap onto her sponge.

"He's in marketing now," Jimena said.

"I didn't ask," Meche replied.

"You were wondering about it," Jimena said with all the aplomb of the neighbourhood gossip. "Same as you're wondering if he's seeing someone: I don't think so."

"Man, your mental powers suck, Kalimán," Meche said.

"Well, then what are you thinking?" Jimena asked, giving Meche a little bump with her hip.

Meche frowned, looking at the murky, soapy water and the cup she was washing.

"I'm thinking about music," she said.

Mexico City, 1988

DECEMBER BROUGHT THE Nativity play. Sebastian, Meche and Daniela had non-speaking roles, playing shepherds. Isadora, Constantino and their friends were the angels and the demons in the *pastorela*, as befitted their station.

Meche sat with her friends at the back of the room and watched her classmates rehearse their lines, her eyes fixed on Constantino. The handsome boy had not talked to her again. The party, the dance, remained a freak occurrence. Had the magic driven him to her? Had it been something else? She did not know.

Meche could not spin fantasies in her head like Daniela; she could not feed on phantom lovers. She wanted Constantino and she wanted him now. What to do? A love spell? Would the others agree to perform it with her? Meche felt too ashamed to tell them about it. She could imagine the face Sebastian would make. He would laugh. But there seemed no other way.

Meche rested her elbows against her knees and leaned forward.

"Is your grandma going to bake a *rosca de reyes*?" Sebastian asked.

Food. A primary topic for Sebastian.

"Yeah."

"Nice. When is she making it? I'll come over."

"I don't know."

"You can also buy a slice at the posada in two weeks," Daniela reminded him, lowering her romance novel for a moment.

The posada was part of the play. Or, rather, the play came before the posada. After the performance was finished, the students and their families were ushered out into the school courtyard, where food stands offered typical Mexican Christmas foods and treats: mandarins, *tejocotes*, sugar canes, *tamales*, *tostadas*. Punch made with guava. Chocolate and *atole* to stay warm. There was a Nativity complete with life-sized figures of Joseph, Mary, the baby Jesus and the three kings. A piñata dangled from a rope, ready for the students to smash it to pieces and collect some of the candy. People bought tickets for a raffle and purchased holiday knick knacks made by the mothers of some of the students. The more intrepid students found this a perfect time to make out in the washrooms, marking a yearly tradition.

"Why would I buy it when I can eat it for free?" Sebastian asked.

"She's not even a good actress," Meche said, raising a hand and pointing at Isadora.

Despite the simple dialogue required, the pretty girl was wooden. She did not even seem able to stand still and look credible, though Meche had to admit the white robes she was wearing fitted her well.

"Like you'd do better," Sebastian said.

"I might," Meche muttered. "Only we'll never know, will we?"

Isadora placed a hand on Constantino—he was a devil, though he had not cared to don his costume for this rehearsal, only the horns—and whispered something in his ear. Meche felt her gut churn.

"You always have to complain, don't you?" Sebastian said.

"Yeah, and you always have to defend her," Meche replied.

"Don't fight," Daniela said.

"Look, the school posada is going to blow. Let's go to my cousin Jimena's place after the play. She'll have a real posada. What do you say?"

"Are we invited?" Daniela asked.

"You are if you bring your own booze."

"Will she have *rosca de reyes* and *tejocote*?" Sebastian asked.

"How should I know?" Meche said feeling irritated. "There will be *something* to eat."

"I don't know," Sebastian said.

"Fine. Go to the school posada and make googly eyes at Isadora. Like that's more fun. I'm going home. It's not like we're even needed at this stupid rehearsal."

Meche grabbed her things and hurried outside.

She put on her headphones; Edith Piaf was singing about a life in pink. She wasn't even sure why she was angry. Lately Sebastian's interest in Isadora just rubbed her the wrong way. Like it was a bit, well… it was frankly insulting that he liked such a simpleton. Because, let's face it, Isadora was a bit of a simpleton and for all of Sebastian's intellectual talk about "Oh my God, how come you've never read that book," it didn't seem to trouble him that the only thing Isadora read was the daily horoscope and the graffiti in the lavatories.

When Meche arrived in her apartment she waved a weak "hello" to her grandmother, who was knitting in the living room, and headed for the kitchen, pulling out the milk from the fridge. She dunked animal crackers in the glass, listening to more music in French because it was the day for that kind of thing.

Her father walked in and patted her head.

"What's up, Meche?"

"Hey," she muttered.

He sat down across from her, pouring himself a glass of milk and grabbing a few crackers.

"What are you listening to?"

"Eh," Meche said sliding the headphones off and shrugging.

She ran her hands over the plastic table mats with ugly yellow flowers on them.

"What's the most powerful love song of all time?" she asked him, scratching one of the flowers.

Meche thought the most romantic album cover of all time was *The Freewheelin*, which showed a very young Dylan walking arm-in-arm with his then-girlfriend. There was something about the composition, the street, the sky, the smiles, which made her think falling in love should be like that snapshot.

"Mmm. Good question," her father said, rubbing his chin. "Well, it would have to be A Whiter Shade of Pale."

"Procol Harum?" Meche said with a frown. "It doesn't talk about love."

"It doesn't have to. Are you alright, Meche?"

"Yeah. Just tired," she said, smiling.

"Okay. I have to write for a bit. Do you want to listen to some Rolling Stones later?"

"Sure."

"Okay."

Her father gave her another pat on the head and grabbed his glass, taking it with him. Meche wandered back into the living room and sat next to Grandmother Dolores, resting her head against her shoulder.

"Can you tell me another story about witches?" she asked, grabbing the ball of yarn and putting it on her lap.

Grandmother Dolores nodded, her needles clicking.

"There was a girl in my village who once fell in love with a *nahual*. He came to her house one night, in the shape of a fox to steal some chickens and she..."

Meche closed her eyes and listened to her grandmother, her voice transporting her from the little apartment to other lands.

IN ADDITION TO his job bagging groceries, Sebastian had picked up a seasonal gig at the mall wrapping gifts. It paid more than his supermarket gig but he had to wear a ridiculous plastic crown which was meant to identify him as one of the Three Kings.

But he needed the money, even if he looked like a dork.

He planned to use the money to buy small gifts for his family, Daniela and Meche. Sebastian had considered returning the necklace he had bought Isadora for her birthday and using the cash for something else, but he decided to keep it. Maybe one day he could give it to her. Maybe he could give it to another girl. He wished he had a girlfriend like all the other boys.

It didn't even have to be an amazingly beautiful girlfriend like Isadora. It could just be a regular girl. Someone to talk to, hold hands with, kiss, make out with. He envied the easy confidence of his peers. They could go up to girls and ask for their numbers. Sebastian had tried asking a girl—a fellow grocery bagger—out but she just stared at him like he had said an insult. Afterwards Sebastian stopped even thinking of asking anyone out. It seemed like a futile enterprise.

Sebastian cut wrapping paper and folded it, his long fingers carefully taping the sides.

He decided to think about something else. Meche's Christmas present. He usually bought her books, which she invariably hated, but he tended to complement those with mix tapes, which she liked. He was thinking of buying her a book of Auden's poetry and he could make a mix tape of songs from the 60s because Meche liked that time period.

He pasted bows and cut more wrapping paper. Once in a while he looked down at the list of songs he had written on a little piece of paper and struck one out.

"I didn't know you worked here."

He looked up. Isadora was carrying a couple of boxes in her arms. She set them down on his counter. Sebastian felt terribly embarrassed to be caught looking like such a fool, wrapping gifts for a few pesos an hour.

"Just 'til Epiphany," he said. "Those two?"

"Yes."

Sebastian tried to cut the paper as quickly as he could, his fingers flying over the boxes.

"Are you excited about the play tomorrow?" she asked.

"Not really."

"Me neither. It's always the same deal every year. The posada might be fun," she said with a little shrug.

"I am not staying for the posada after it."

"No?"

"There's a party at Jimena Estrada's house later. Do you know her?"

"I don't think so."

"My friend Meche thinks the school posada is kind of lame so we're going to Jimena's posada. You're... ah... welcome to join us."

Isadora did not say anything. Sebastian regretted his attempt at small talk. He should have just kept his stupid mouth shut. Like Isadora would care what he did in his free time.

"Well, here you go," he said, putting two red bows on the packages and handing them back to her.

"Thanks."

"Bye," he said cutting more little pieces of tape and readying himself for the next client.

"I'm sorry if I was rude to you at my birthday party."

Sebastian looked up at her, shocked to hear her say that.

"You weren't really rude," he said.

"No, I was. You were just trying to be friendly. It's just, Constantino was being annoying... ugh, anyway, you're always nice to everyone."

"I don't try to be nice."

"That's why you are."

She grabbed her presents and paused for a moment.

"Where is that posada? I might go."

"Do you have a piece of paper? I can write it down for you."

"I don't have paper."

"Give me your arm."

Isadora put down her packages and he grabbed her arm, carefully writing the address with blue ink.

"Thanks," she said.

"Cool."

He watched her walk away and smiled.

SEBASTIAN DID NOT listen to a single line during the performance. He stood in his place at the back of the stage with Meche and Daniela, simply staring at Isadora and willing the performance to end so they could all escape to Jimena's apartment.

After the show, they decided to go home and change. Sebastian said he would pick Meche up. He was late because he'd taken special care in choosing his clothes. He wore a nice black shirt and jeans and had combed his hair back with a lot of gel.

He jumped on his motorcycle to pick up Meche. She climbed behind him and they sang The Fishes in the River at the top of their lungs. Sebastian had never understood the significance of a song which talked about fishes drinking river water while the baby Jesus was being born, but it was one of the few Christmas songs he knew from beginning to end, so he was happy to sing it.

When they reached her apartment, Jimena greeted them with a

loud, festive hug, planting a kiss on each of their cheeks. She was dressed in nearly nothing, belly bared, and tottered on high heels. Pretty much what you'd expect from Jimena.

"I brought beer," Meche said.

"Put in the kitchen, girl," Jimena said. "Your little friend is here."

"Who?" Sebastian asked, perking up.

"Dani."

"Oh."

They dropped the beer in the kitchen and Sebastian served himself fortified punch with a big piece of cinnamon. Meche carried two little plastic cups in her hands, giving one to Daniela, who had found a place near the sound system.

"Hey," she said. "Where were you? I've been waiting for ever."

"I dunno. He took forever," Meche said, giving Daniela a little cup.

"Thanks. My mom said I could only stay 'til nine, so I can't be here for long."

"Aw. That's like nothing at all."

"You know how she is. She's afraid I'm going to have a relapse."

"You just want to go home and watch your soaps."

They pulled up a couple of chairs and sat with Daniela, drinking their punch until it was time for her to leave; then they walked her downstairs and waited for her dad to arrive. They waved goodbye when Daniela got in the car.

"Man, Jimena sure poured a lot of booze in that punch this year."

"Yup," Sebastian said.

"We should have some more," Meche snapped her fingers. "Oh, Jimena gave me money to buy more ice. Wanna go with me?"

"Okay."

"Race you to the store."

Sebastian was ready to chase after Meche but then he saw Isadora and Constantino approaching. She was wearing a very nice red coat with large brass buttons. Her hair was pulled back in a ponytail and she was smiling at him.

"Hi," she said. "I brought Constantino with me. I hope that's okay."

"That's fine," Sebastian said.

"Third floor?"

"Yeah."

"We're going to buy ice," Meche said sharply.

"See you inside," Sebastian added.

Meche and Sebastian walked briskly, hands in their pockets.

"You invited her to my cousin's posada?" she asked.

"The whole neighbourhood is invited to your cousin's posada."

"Yeah, but you didn't even ask."

"Sorry."

Meche shook her head, walking to the corner store and back in a regal silence which spoke volumes. Sebastian felt bad briefly, but once they reached the door of the apartment he was actually pissed at Meche for being so selfish. She made it worse by pulling away from him and going to stand next to Jimena, like he did not exist. Sebastian put the ice in the kitchen, mixed a couple of rum and Cokes, and went in search of Isadora.

She was sitting by herself, looking out the window and smoking a cigarette.

"Um... I didn't know what you wanted, so I brought this," he said, handing her the cup.

"Thanks," she said, placing it on the window sill and smiling again. "That's very thoughtful of you."

"No problem. Where's Constantino?"

"Somewhere," Isadora said with a little huff. "I wanted to come alone but when he heard I was heading here he insisted on coming. Sorry about that. I didn't want him here."

"I thought you were friends," Sebastian said.

"We are," Isadora said, looking at her nails.

Isadora and Constantino had gone out for six months but broke up before the school year started. From what Sebastian understood, Constantino had dumped Isadora to go out with Miroslava, one of Isadora's friends. Sebastian thought this was pretty stupid because Miroslava wasn't half as pretty as Isadora.

"I think he's just jealous that you invited me," she said. "He's silly like that."

"He doesn't have anything to be jealous about," Sebastian paused. "Are you guys together again?"

"No," Isadora said.

"Sorry. I shouldn't have asked that. I mean, who am I?"

"No, it's okay," she replied. "Everyone thinks Constantino is so great but he's not that awesome."

"I guess."

"Sorry. I know he's a bit of a dick with you."

"I guess it's a night for 'sorries.'"

Isadora finished her cigarette and flicked the butt out the window, giving him a half-smile.

"You know, I don't think I've ever spoken more than half a dozen words with you," she said. "Why's that?"

"We orbit around different suns, I suppose."

It was the type of corny line that Meche would have rolled her eyes at—no sense in discussing suns, stars, moons and similes with her—but Isadora did not seem to mind.

"I kind of like that," she said and the smile grew.

He decided, right then and there, to mail the golden heart on the chain to her and to hell with the consequences.

MECHE HAD BEEN surveying the room from Jimena's side, studying the crowd and keeping an eye on Isadora and Sebastian. When the girl started giggling she'd had enough. Meche rolled her eyes and rolled herself into the kitchen, pouring herself an obscene amount of punch and drinking it in one long gulp. She poured herself another and walked out, holding her drink, and saw that Isadora and Sebastian were still talking.

"I think your boyfriend is making a pass at Isadora," Constantino said.

He was by himself, eyes fixed on their beautiful classmate.

"He's my buddy," she said. "Not my boyfriend."

"Honest mistake."

"I think your girlfriend wants to make out with my buddy."

"She's not my girlfriend."

"Honest mistake," Meche replied as she finished her drink. "Thirsty?"

"Yep."

"Let's get you a refill."

They went to the kitchen and Meche filled their cups. Constantino leaned against the refrigerator, drumming his fingers against its side. Meche sat on one of the kitchen counters, swinging her legs and thinking thoughts as deep and dark as black holes.

"Why did you dance with me the other night?" she asked him.

"What? Did I need a permit?"

"I'm curious."

"I felt like I should."

Meche chuckled. "You want to go out and see what they're up to?"

"Yes."

"You still have a thing for her?"

He did not admit it, but didn't need to and she got why he'd danced with her at the party—to piss Isadora off.

"Don't let me hold you back," she said, jumping off the counter.

They moved towards the living room. Constantino flew to Isadora like an arrow, installing himself by her side. Meche watched as Sebastian pulled away, slowly drifting from them as Constantino wrapped an arm around the girl, beginning what looked like a very animated conversation.

Sebastian looked in Meche's direction. Their eyes locked together.

Meche felt a bitter knot in her stomach. It was not the product of the cheap alcohol in the punch; Jimena's apartment was too crowded, the noise too much. Beneath the buzz of the conversations played Total Eclipse of the Heart. She could not make out the words, barely could hear the music, just felt the beat. She wanted pain and loneliness and everyone to stop talking and Sebastian and no one, all at the same time. Meche grabbed her jacket and headed downstairs.

She did not expect Sebastian to follow her, but he did.

"Hey, what's up?" he asked.

"I'm getting more ice," she said and hoped he'd leave it at that.

"I'll help you."

"No!"

"I'll get my jacket."

"I said no!"

She rushed down the steps and hurried out into the street. When she heard him behind her she ran. She rushed towards her home, turned a corner and bumped into a mound of garbage, tripped over something and fell.

She felt the glass cutting her hand and looked down to see she had sliced her palm with a dirty beer bottle. Meche groaned.

"Are you alright?" Sebastian asked.

He looked concerned. His anxiety irritated her. Meche stood up, wiping her hand against her jeans and nodding.

"I'm drunk," she announced. "That's all."

"You shouldn't be walking by yourself like this."

"Shouldn't you be back at the posada? You've left your guest all alone."

"Fuck that, I'm taking you home."

"I have two legs and can walk it."

"I'm not letting you go without me."

Meche was going to tell him to fuck himself but then a wave of nausea hit her and she turned around, vomiting all over the sidewalk. The bitter taste in her mouth seemed like a fine coda for the night and she promised herself she would wish for a different life come morning.

"Here, it's alright," he said.

Sebastian brushed the hair out from her face and offered her a tissue. Meche dabbed it against her mouth and smiled.

"You're so thoughtful," she said. "I fucking hate that."

"I hate you too, Meche."

Meche laughed. Sebastian joined in. He curled his fingers around her shoulder.

"Come on," he said. "Let's get you home."

"What about your motorcycle?"

"I'll pick it up tomorrow. Right now we are going to walk back to your place, where I'll give you a big glass of water and tuck you in."

"And will you sing Ne me quitte pas to me?" she asked, the words slurred together.

She liked that song. She liked how Jacques sang it and the line about beads of rain from faraway countries.

"What?"

"Jacques Brel. You don't know *anything*."

"Not about music."

She looked down, at his sneakers with all the inked drawings and words.

RELEASED FROM THE chains of school, winter break holding its arms wide open, Daniela and Meche dedicated their days to watching TV together and—in a smaller measure—Christmas shopping. This was the third record store they had hit that morning. Daniela was starting to get tired and she still did not know what Meche was trying to accomplish.

"I found it," Daniela said. "Procol Harum, right?"

"Right," Meche said.

Meche grabbed the record, touched it carefully and dismissed it.

"No. It's not right," Meche said, shaking her head.

"What's wrong with it? It's the record you wanted."

"Yes. But it needs to be very powerful."

"It feels warm."

"Warm. Not hot. I know there's a copy of that record somewhere and it's searing hot."

"What do you plan to do with it when you find it?"

"A love spell."

"Really?" Daniela asked, eyes wide. "Who do you want to fall in love with you?"

"Same guy I've always wanted. Constantino."

"I heard he was getting cozy with Isadora at Jimena's posada."

"Funny, I thought Sebastian was getting cozy with Isadora. It must have been after we left."

"Sebastian and Isadora? Really?"

"Tell me about it. It's mildly disgusting."

"Why?"

"*Obviously* she's just teasing him."

"You don't think she likes him?"

Meche looked at Daniela with a *really?* expression. Daniela put the record back.

They drifted around the store and Daniela pulled out one of Luis

Miguel's records, smiling at the blond, attractive young man. She ran her fingers over his photograph.

"Maybe I could wish to be swept off my feet by Luis Miguel."

"That's not very realistic," Meche replied.

"Magic doesn't have to be realistic. Does it?"

"I wouldn't push it too far."

"Then maybe a kiss from Mr. Rodriguez."

"Eww. He's our teacher and like a billion years older than us."

"Mr. Rochester was older than Jayne Eyre."

Daniela wished life were more like books. Well, not all books, but at least the books she read. Caridad Bravo Adams was her favourite author, though she also appreciated the work of Danielle Steel and Barbara Cartland. Her fantasies were embroidered with details from a multitude of novels, but they all concluded with a handsome man, a wedding, a kiss and a picture-perfect happy ending. All she wanted was a little tiny taste of that.

"Wouldn't it be wonderful if life were like the novels?" she said. "Then Constantino could be the handsome general who saves you from a band of robbers. Mr. Rodriguez could be a dashing pirate who kidnaps me for a ransom but ends up falling in love with me. Sebastian could even be the daring young man who wins over a princess."

"No way."

"I'm going to buy this," Daniela decided, grabbing the Luis Miguel record.

"Just promise you won't play it when I'm around."

"Awww. Hey, do you want me to make cupcakes in my Easy-Bake oven?"

SEBASTIAN AND MECHE sat together atop a table in the courtyard of the mall, right by the Nutrisa store, and ate frozen yogurt. Sebastian was spending all his spare time wrapping gifts for a mob of crazy shoppers, who thrust packages and bills in his face, asked for red or green bows, all demanding it be done in five minutes. If she wanted to hang out with him she had to do it during his lunch break.

Daniela was off to Mazatlán for a week, to spend Christmas by the sea with all the assorted uncles and cousins who lived there. This left Meche to her own devices, with Sebastian as her only companion. Her strategy was to hunt around the record shops in the morning, visit him for lunch, then head home to listen to whatever she had bought while she played on the computer.

That day she was carrying a Queen album under her arm after another failed attempt to find the perfect copy of A Whiter Shade of Pale. She was beginning to think the record was her own white whale, and although Sebastian might be proud to know she had internalized some of his knowledge about *Moby Dick*, she would much rather find the damn thing.

"Do you really have to head back?" Meche asked.

"Yeah. I have another four hours, maybe six if I pick up some extra time."

"You're working like all day long."

"I'm making money."

"Bo-ring."

"That's because you have money."

"I only have my allowance and that ain't much."

"More than I have. It's just a couple more days."

"No, after Christmas comes Epiphany," Meche reminded him. "You'll be wrapping presents 'til January and we won't get to do anything."

"Well, that's the way it is."

"We could cast a spell to get some more money."

"Just the two of us? I thought that wasn't a good idea."

Well, that was the official rule. Not that Meche wasn't ready to bend the rules a bit, though she wasn't sure she should tell Sebastian that.

"Do you want to come over and play a video game later? Daniela lent me her Nintendo and we can rent a game at Chaplin's," he suggested.

"My mom doesn't like me going to your place."

"Do you want her to phone my brother? He's around today."

"I don't know."

Meche finished her frozen yoghurt and jumped down from the table, tossing the plastic container and the spoon in the garbage can.

Sebastian also tossed his away and they headed back towards the gift wrapping station.

Meche eyed an instant photo booth with interest.

"Do you have coins?" she asked him.

"What for?"

Meche did not bother answering, she grabbed Sebastian by the wrist and pulled him into the photo booth, swinging aside a tattered red curtain. The compartment was small and long-limbed Sebastian barely managed to fold himself in, Meche squeezing next to him.

She lifted her palm and he handed her a few coins. Meche threw them into the slot and waited.

The first flash went off with Meche sticking her tongue out. The second was much of the same, her hand lifting behind Sebastian's head to make a pair of horns. Flash a third time and she smiled sweetly.

"Last one," Sebastian said.

Meche turned to look at him and Sebastian picked that moment to also turn his head and look at her.

Time slowed down. The seconds crawled, lazily, and she looked at Sebastian and Sebastian looked at her for what was maybe two, three months. A whole season passed in his gaze and her heart—which she knew should beat at 60-100 per minute, knowledge gleaned from her science textbook—beat maybe once or twice.

The walls of the booth, which had imprisoned them in its narrow space, drifted away further and further and the roof melted, all of which caused Meche to panic.

Then the flash went off, bathing them with its white light, illuminating every corner of the booth and making Meche gasp in surprise.

The light faded, the walls crept back together and Meche's heart regained its usual healthy rate, time suddenly returning to its normal course.

"Let's look at the pictures," she said, hastily exiting the booth.

Sebastian remained inside, behind the tattered red curtain, while Meche leaned down near the little opening which was supposed to spit out the photos. She tapped her foot impatiently, wishing the photos would just develop.

Sebastian stepped out of the booth just at the moment the photos appeared. He opened his mouth and she held the photos for him to see.

"They came out okay," she said.

"Yeah," Sebastian muttered.

"I'll pay you back the money... um, I'm going home now."

"Alright. Are you coming over for the video game?"

Meche just wanted to get home fast, so she nodded and stepped back, stuffing the photos in her back pocket.

"I'll meet you at Chaplin's around six!" he yelled.

CHAPLIN'S HAD A big, ugly sign outside which showed a silhouette of the famous comedian raising his hat. The store's full name was Chaplin's Movie Emporium, but nobody called it that. It rented videos in Betamax and a small selection of video games. Videocentro was bigger, but they charged more for rentals and it was further away. Plus, the clerk at Chaplin's usually threw in a free bag of microwaveable popcorn. The clerk was only a couple of years older than they were and he was dating Jimena, which explained the added bonus.

"So are we going with *Castlevania*?" Sebastian asked.

Meche was looking over the videos, not paying much attention to him. She wore her heavy, green jacket and her matching green sneakers. Every once in a while she bit her lower lip, like when she didn't know an exam question.

She didn't look very happy to be at the video store and Sebastian wondered what was up with that.

"*Castlevania* is fine."

Sebastian paid, feeling a bit glad that he could do this. He grabbed the game and the popcorn and they walked back to his apartment.

The elevator did not work so they trudged up the stairs. Inside it was as dirty as usual even though Romualdo had promised to clean up when they had spoken during breakfast. Sebastian sighed.

"Romu!" he yelled.

No answer. Sebastian put the keys on a hook by the door.

"He's probably gone to buy something for dinner. Do you want some juice?"

"I'm fine."

They sat on the couch in front of the banged-up television set. Sebastian plugged in the Nintendo and pushed in the game, grabbing a controller. Meche sat at the edge of the couch, the heavy jacket firmly buttoned up to her neck.

"Do you have a cold?" he asked.

"No," Meche said.

"You look pale."

"I'm just tired."

"You don't have to play with me if you don't want to."

"I'm here, am I not?"

"Okay."

Meche took off her jacket and tossed it on the back of the sofa. She was wearing one of her oversized t-shirts. It said 'Blondie' with big, pink letters on a black background. Sebastian thought she looked very small in it, like she was about to be swallowed by the shirt.

"What?" Meche asked testily.

"Nothing."

"Just push play."

He did, guessing that Simon Belmont might be the solution for whatever weirdness was happening that day. Because he did feel weird. In the phone booth there had been this uncomfortable moment when he had looked at Meche and she had looked back at him, and it didn't feel like looking at Meche. Hell, he looked at Meche every day of the week and he knew exactly what she looked like, but when the flash went off he thought, for a second, that he didn't know her. It was... bizarre.

A few levels later Romualdo still had not showed up but at least Meche seemed more relaxed. She pressed the buttons on the controller, trying to manipulate Belmont's whip, then handed it to Sebastian when she got killed.

"Your turn."

"Can I ask you something?" she said, as he grabbed the controller.

"What?"

"Do you really like Isadora?"

"What do you mean?"

"Just that."

Sebastian frowned. "Are you going to tell me she's a ditz?"

"No. I'm just asking."

"She's cute."

"Yeah, so is Cindy Crawford."

"Cindy Crawford doesn't go to the same school I go to."

"So it's convenience?"

"It's… ah… well, you like Constantino, no?"

"Don't you sometimes think we're chasing after mirages?"

"What's so awesome about reality?" he asked, turning and looking at her.

"It's what we have."

"We have magic."

"I'm getting the feeling that doesn't work as often as we expected."

Meche leaned back and rubbed her eyes, shrugging. The music on the video game played loudly, the rhythmic electronic beats repeating themselves. Sebastian pressed the pause button.

"What do you mean?"

"I've been looking for this stupid Procol Harum record for the past few days so I can cast a love spell… have Constantino fall in love with me."

"What? You think if you play a song from that band he'll go nutty and start making out with you in a flash?"

Meche blushed, looking down, as though she were trying to find out if the lettering on her t-shirt was still there.

"Would that be so bad?" she asked. "I was also thinking maybe a glamour spell…"

"A what?"

"Something to make me look pretty."

"Meche, you *are* pretty."

Meche raised her head, her eyes dark and cold. "I'm not and I don't like it when you lie to make me feel better," she said flatly.

"I'm not a liar."

Meche said nothing, though skepticism danced in her eyes. Fine. Maybe he was trying to be nice; was that such a big crime? When had a kindness become a slap in the face? The truth was it would take some spell for Constantino to pick Meche over Isadora, but he didn't want to say it outright.

"I'm polite."

She was getting ready to come back at him with a quick, witty jab and Sebastian found himself holding his breath, waiting. Before Meche could speak and needle him with some cynical line from a song, he leaned down and in a sudden case of insanity—maybe because he felt bad about her, maybe because he felt bad about himself, maybe because Constantino was never going to pick her but Isadora was not going to pick him either—kissed her.

Meche opened her mouth, no doubt to insult him, but all this did was deepen the kiss.

Sebastian knew he probably wasn't doing it right because the only time he had kissed another girl before had been in sixth grade, when he'd been invited to a dreadful game of Spin the Bottle and ended up locking lips with a classmate who seemed utterly grossed out by the fact that it was Sebastian instead of the boy sitting next to him.

Meche's sharp intake of breath made him pause and he drew back, just staring at her in utter confusion.

Meche looked like she had been run over by a truck, her eyes all big and wide.

"I'm sorry," he said. "I didn't mean it." He paused and added, "Are we cool?"

"Jesus," Meche said, reaching behind the couch and grabbing her jacket.

"Meche..."

"My backpack. Where is it?"

She looked around the couch, finding the backpack on the floor and quickly zipping it closed.

"Why are you mad?"

"Because you're right. You didn't mean it," she said.

Sebastian raised his hands, unable to articulate a proper response. She slammed the door shut on her way out.

MECHE DID NOT understand. The room was dark, the apartment was quiet. She had her Walkman by the pillow, the cassette tape turning, playing Leonard Cohen. This was a quick recipe for sleep but sleep did not come.

She got up and brushed past her poster of The Police, her hands dancing over her records, the familiar shapes of the action figures sitting on the shelves.

She peeked out the window and tried to find the moon but she did not see it and sat back on her bed, wondering if Sebastian was also awake.

Meche did not understand what happened. Had Sebastian gone mad? Why had he done a thing like that? And then, he had been sorry... obviously.

She pressed a finger against her lips and opened the window.

VICENTE SAT LISTENING to his wife and his daughter. It was like tuning into one of the old radio dramas on XEW. All it lacked was the appropriate, tear-jerker music. He wasn't in the mood for dramas and every word was like a nail into his skull. He wanted to tell them to fight outside.

"What did I say?"

"I don't know," Meche replied, ignoring Natalia and opening the refrigerator door.

"I said I don't want you to spend so much time with that boy. Catalina Coronado saw you together."

"Oh my God. Is that woman with the Federal Police or something? Can I go work on my computer now?"

"It's not funny. Catalina happens to be a good friend—"

"She's a nosy bitch," Vicente said, folding his newspaper. "Go work."

Meche huffed and stomped towards her room. Natalia gifted him with one of her deadly stares.

"Thank you. Now she'll never get the point."

"The point being, what?" Vicente asked.

He was playing a record by Joaquín Sabina and did not want to get into an argument, but Natalia's tone and the way she was shaking her head at him irked him to the core.

"If she keeps hanging out with teenage boys she'll wind up sleeping with them."

"Don't teenagers generally sleep with each other? Or are we selling her off to some feudal lord?"

"Watch her get pregnant."

"Get her condoms, for God's sake. You work at a pharmacy."

"She'll pick the wrong kid and ruin her life."

Natalia didn't say "just like me," but she did not have to. Vicente burst out laughing. He could not help it.

"You are useless," Natalia muttered.

Vicente just kept laughing. He clutched the record's liner notes and sank into his chair, feeling all the misery of his marriage dripping down his shoulders and pooling at his feet.

SEBASTIAN FELT LIKE he was reading a map which had all the street names erased. Lost, confused and surprised, he replayed the events of the night with Meche in his head. He had offended her, he understood that much. He also understood he must fix it.

Sebastian could think of only one way to make amends with Meche. He walked the three blocks from his building to her apartment, listening to the sound of fireworks going off in the streets.

He pressed her buzzer, was given access and climbed the stairs, taking care to light the sparkler before he reached her door.

"Happy New Year!" he said, waving the sparkler before her face.

Meche rested her head against the door frame. "It's not New Year's yet."

"Well, it will be in two hours."

"I'm supposed to be putting away the ham."

"You had ham?" Sebastian asked.

"What do you want?"

"I want to take you for a ride around the block."

"I want to put away the ham."

"Look, I'm sorry if I offended you."

"You didn't... ugh," Meche slid out and closed the door, resting her back against it. "You didn't offend me. But it's not nice... look, I don't like being the leftover turkey sandwich you feel obliged to eat after Christmas."

"You're not a sandwich. Come on."

"Do you *really* think I'm pretty?"

No, he thought. That was his natural reaction. A box he had long ticked off.

But he looked at her and she *was* kind of pretty. Not like Isadora, not like the other girls. When you looked at Meche the first impression was that she was going to punch you in the face; she was made of such strong angles. However, if you looked long enough there was a delicate softness beneath her which manifested in the very long neck, the graceful fingers which were meant to play instruments, the petite frame. She was a knot of contradictions and these, thrown together, created an interesting composition. When she grew up, he thought, people would see it more clearly.

"Yeah," he said faintly and then growing more self-assured, he nodded. "Yeah, you are."

Meche smiled a little. She turned her face and tried to cover it by pretending to cough, but he saw her smile and it made him smile too.

"Can you go with me for a ride?"

"Yes," she said.

They rushed downstairs, the sparkler still in his hands.

HALF AN HOUR later Sebastian parked the bike in front of Meche's building. He searched in his pockets and found the cassette he had neatly labelled that morning.

"I made a mix-tape for you, for Epiphany. I also got you a book, but I can give you that tomorrow."

"Books," Meche muttered, opening the cassette and reading the song list. "Forever Young."

"It's like a soundtrack for us. The soundtrack of our lives."

"And Alphaville will be singing on our soundtrack?"

"Among others."

She reached for her Walkman—always tucked inside her jacket, always there—and put the cassette inside, pressing play. She put on the headphones and nodded, tapping her foot.

Meche reached up and hugged him. For three minutes he danced with her to music he could not hear, a song which rang only in her ears.

*   *   *

TWO DAYS LATER Meche pinned the pictures from the photo booth against the factory wall, right beside the cover of Dylan's *The Freewheelin*.

It was a declaration of some sort, although she did not understand what she was declaring. Just that she needed to tell Sebastian something and since she could not write it down she tried putting it the only way she could: in shorthand.

Mexico City, 2009

MECHE WOKE UP early and stopped at the corner store to buy a small bag of peanuts. The shopkeeper stared at her, just like his grandfather had, as though she were a kid trying to steal merchandise. Of course, she *had* stolen merchandise back in the day but it was not like she was going to run out without paying now that she was a grown woman. Meche placed the money on the counter, the shopkeeper counted every coin and then handed her a receipt, still frowning.

Meche hopped on a bus. It was safer than taking a taxi and she didn't mind being squeezed into a tight corner. But she was lucky: the bus was half empty and she had a chance to sit in the back, listening to her music.

Meche kept an optimistic outlook for the first couple of hours as she classified records and moved around her father's apartment. It looked completely doable. She could tidy everything up in a day. Another hour later and Meche had despaired. Reality kicked in. It was impossible to go through all of her father's stuff in just a few hours. He had too much crap and frankly, she was tired of the whole thing, bled dry and exhausted as she tossed another record onto a pile and tried to remember what was the purpose of this. Meche lay down on the floor, in the middle of the living room, knowing she should make herself some coffee because she needed it. Maybe she also needed an injection of sugar.

Someone knocked three times and for a moment she had a sense of displacement, because that knock should have come at her mother's apartment, like it always did when Daniela or Sebastian visited.

Meche opened the door and he was there, wearing a long, dark coat and looking very proper with a tie and all.

"Can I come in?" Sebastian asked.

"How did you find me?"

"Daniela and I paid a visit to your mom this morning. We gave her our condolences and chatted for a bit. She suggested I come over because you need to lug some heavy boxes."

"Aren't you the thoughtful, kind moving man?"

"I didn't mean to upset you the other night."

"Nah, of course not," she said, smiling with her sharpest smile.

"We just wanted to pay our condolences."

"And help me carry boxes."

"Heavy ones."

Meche opened the door wide, banging the wall in the process. She spread her arms open.

"Hey, walk right in. I mean, what the fuck, you're already here. Might as well be useful."

Meche should have offered to put his coat away. She didn't and hoped it got wrinkled. She headed to the kitchen and filled the kettle with hot water. He didn't follow her into the kitchen and she was grateful for that because as soon as she stood in front of the stove she felt the desire to yell and break into a fit of giggles, all at the same time. Meche stared at the kettle, crossing her arms, wondering if she shouldn't have told him to get out of the building.

Shoulda, woulda.

The kettle screamed and Meche poured two cups of tea.

Tea, after all.

Habits die hard.

She headed into the living room and placed his cup on top of a Bee Gees record, sitting herself on the floor because the couch was buried beneath piles of records. Sebastian grabbed the cup and also sat on the floor, carefully folding his long legs. He'd always been more legs than anything. This thin scarecrow of a boy.

"How many records do you think your dad had?" he asked.

"Thousands," Meche said, tired of the question. "It'll take forever to go through it all but I only have until next week."

"Are you leaving after the *novena* is over?"

"As soon as I can book the flight."

"To Oslo?"

"That's home," Meche said, sipping her tea. There was no milk and no sugar and she made a face when she tasted the chamomile.

"Your dad was always nice to us. Daniela and me... we just felt we should visit."

"He's dead. Saying a couple of prayers is not going to get him out of hell and it's not earning you brownie points."

"All the same, Daniela and I would like to pray with your family tonight or tomorrow."

"With my mother and my cousin," Meche said. "I don't pray. My father was an atheist. He would be offended if I started with the Hail Marys. Hey, maybe I should pray after all."

Meche smiled and took a big gulp of tea, downing the hot drink. She would get something else later. Maybe some food.

"What did you have for breakfast?" Sebastian asked, as if reading her mind.

"I don't have breakfast."

"That's not good for you."

"Says who?"

"Let's go have lunch. I can put those boxes in my car later."

"Don't you have stuff to do?"

"Yes—I have lunch with you."

He sounded like when they were teenagers and he wanted to skip school. And she knew he'd won this round already, probably from the moment she opened the door.

Meche thought of tossing the remains of her tea in his face, watch it stain his nice, crisp shirt and equally nice tie. But she was tired and she was hungry, and the desire for a fight was already dying back to a simmer.

"You're buying," she said.

EVEN THOUGH JIMENA had gushed about Sebastian's new wheels, Meche didn't really like the car. Frankly, she missed the motorcycle. It had been a piece of crap, ugly, worn and unreliable, but she liked sitting behind Sebastian, twining her arms around his waist and riding around the block on it.

Meche flicked on the stereo and Lena Horne started singing Stormy Weather. Meche raised her eyebrows and scoffed.

"Are you trying to impress me?" she asked.

"I like jazz."

"What would you know about jazz?"

"Quite a bit, actually. I started with Fitzgerald."

"Like I suggested."

"Yeah."

"Who wrote Stormy Weather?"

"Are you testing me, Meche?"

"Answer the question."

"Harold Arlen and Ted Koehler. Ethel Waters first sang it at The Cotton Club."

He gave her a smug sideways glance and Meche felt like pinching him. Where the hell was the restaurant? She was starting to get impatient and shifted in her seat, wiggling her toes inside her shoes. Traffic in Mexico City. Dear God. It was murder. They should have walked somewhere nearby instead of jumping in his fancy vehicle.

"Well, if you really like jazz you should take some of my dad's records. You play vinyl, right?"

"I don't, no."

"Then you're not a real aficionado," she said, feeling like she had the upper hand again. "You can't compare an MP3 to vinyl."

"I don't like vinyl."

"You shouldn't believe the crap they say about sound fidelity and CDs. Vinyl is not inferior to your digital files."

He glanced at her, looking very sombre all of a sudden.

"I don't play vinyl because it reminds me of you."

Meche frowned and stared at the stereo.

SHE DECIDED TO pay herself back for all those lunches Sebastian had eaten. All those free meals he had stolen, the pieces of sandwich he had pinched away, the times he sipped from her bottle, the popcorn he grabbed from her bag. A big freeloader, that's what he had been, but now he had shiny, fancy shoes and she bet there was a nice, fat wallet to go with them. She ordered the most expensive item on the menu—steak—and added a cocktail for good measure. A double, because she needed it.

The restaurant was very stylish, but the tablecloths were too white and the chairs too stiff. She was used to eating her meals by the computer or at a little café around the corner from her apartment.

Meche leaned both elbows against the table and took out her iPod, looking at the playlist. Force of habit. She listened to music when she ate. Well, she listened to music all the time. When she coded and when she went for a jog. Music was there, the constant in her life.

"You always have dark circles under your eyes?" Sebastian asked.

"It depends on the project."

"Were you working on a big project?"

"Yeah. Now I'm here. Unfortunately."

Meche shook her head and attacked her steak, cutting off a piece and chewing on it with gusto.

"I didn't think I'd ever see you again," he said.

"Yeah, me too. It kind of spoils the thing. I was trying very hard to keep that enemy-mine thing going but I don't know if Mothra ever had lunch with Godzilla."

He smiled and it reminded her of the goofy smile of his youth. Goofy but charming because it was so dumb. But there was a dusting of grey in his hair, faint but marking the passage of time and the long stretch between the teenager and the man was she was eating with.

"You're still funny."

"I'm a fucking riot," Meche said. "So?"

"I don't know. I thought about contacting you before but I didn't think enough time had passed."

"For me to forget?"

"For you to remember."

Meche lifted her fork and looked at the piece of meat sticking from it.

"Remember, what exactly?"

"How we used to be friends."

"Two decades ago. Before," Meche made a little circular motion with the fork, "the whole stabbing in the back thingy."

"We had fun times."

"We were teenagers. Scoring enough coins to play at the arcade for an hour was the crowning achievement of the year. What do you want me to do? Get all teary-eyed and tell you I've missed you?"

"I'm not sure how you remember it, but I remember that the world used to stop spinning when we were hanging out and it felt like everything was possible."

"Magic," Meche said. "Magic was possible."

"Not magic. Not spells. Before the magic. We got each other."

"And then?"

"And then I don't know," he said. "I wanted to see you again."

Meche put her fork down. The steak looked kind of bloody and not so appetizing anymore. She grabbed the glass of water and took a sip.

"There's nothing to see."

"I know you hold grudges. Hell, you like to hold them."

"Compartmentalizing works. You build systems like that."

Sebastian sat back. He tilted his head just as she remembered he used to, like he was taking a mental pause to process something.

"You're really going to hate me forever?"

"Forever is a very irrational concept. Let's just leave it at a very long time. Can I order dessert? I need more tea and some sort of pastry."

Meche waved to the server, not caring if it was a crude way to get his attention.

"I can believe that," he said.

"Catching on, are you?"

"Well, holding grudges was your forte."

"It does wonders for the complexion." Meche looked at the server. "I'll need a strawberry tart and some tea with milk."

"What movie are we watching tomorrow?"

Meche looked at him with an *are-you-fucking-insane* look in her eyes. He looked back at her with an innocent smile.

"A what?"

"I owe you a movie. 1989. I promised we'd go out and we never did."

Ah, yeah. *That* night.

"Um, it's okay? You can do your own thing and I'll do mine," Meche said.

"We can go to the latest show."

"You really think I'll go with you," she said flatly.

"What was my forte?"

"I don't know," Meche said with a shrug.

"I was stubborn. I gave you eight books for presents even though you said you did not want another book."

"I'm still pissed about that."

"How does *The Ambassadors* end?"

"Not a clue," Meche said. "I never read it."

She was lying and he knew she was lying. She had actually spent a whole weekend trying to find that same book the first time she went to Paris, just because she thought she ought to read it in the damn city where it took place. But she was not going to prove his point.

"I like comic books and albums from the 60s," she said.

"And Jacques Brel."

Ah, touché. He remembered that.

The server put the tart and tea before Meche. She poured a bit of milk into the cup and smirked.

"You can just take them and drop them off at my mom's place."

She shoved the box aside with her foot.

"I can drive you back to your mom's place."

"I'm not leaving right now."

"I could wait."

"Aren't you going to get in trouble at your job?" she asked. "You've been with me for two hours."

Not that she cared what his job thought. She just wanted him out of the apartment. When she was with him she had the bizarre sensation that ants were running up and down her arms. It was terribly irritating.

"I'm not a surgeon. People are not going to die if I show up late. It's marketing."

"Oh, yeah. Marketing," Meche said, folding the flaps of another box. "What do you do, like peddle potato chips and shit?"

"I'm a Creative Director. I oversee the copy chief, the art director, and—"

"Wasn't that what I just said? Peddle and shit."

He looked amused as he sat on the floor of her father's living room. Like he was having a really good time though she had said nothing nice to him all morning long.

"What do you do in Oslo?"

"I'm a coding monkey. Didn't I say that?"

If she had not told him, then she was sure her mother had.

"When you're not coding."

"I don't know. I watch TV. I take care of Svend."

"Is that your boyfriend?"

"It's a very big fern. I have several ferns but I only baptized one because if you name more than one inanimate object you're heading into crazy cat lady territory."

"That's the rule?"

"Yeah."

He smiled and she felt herself smiling back, which was not what she had been going for. Unfortunately, Sebastian had a way of disarming her. He'd had it when they were kids and he still had it now. Even though she knew she shouldn't allow herself to be disarmed, that such behaviour led to shameful ruin, she was smiling.

"As much as I'd love to have a long chat about Pteridophyta, I really need some time to work and you're distracting me."

"Just how distracting am I?" he asked scooting closer.

Meche slammed a record against his chest, her eyebrows knitted together.

"Just carry these downstairs and get out, will you?"

He grabbed the boxes looking mightily amused, like that time when he had all the answers to the Spanish Literature quiz and she got none, so she sat at her desk in a panic while Sebastian smirked at her. Later she threw a piece of sandwich at the back of his head, but she didn't have a sandwich at the moment.

"Don't forget I'm taking you to the movies."

"Go back to planet deluded," she muttered.

She closed the door behind him and plucked a record sleeve from a pile.

"What do you think, Steve Perry?" she asked, smirking at the single—it was Oh Sherrie—and then tossing it to the floor because she realised she was talking to an inanimate object.

Mexico City, 1989

THE FIRST DAY back in class was usually a quiet, lazy progression of hours which everyone—teachers included—took easy. They were all recovering from the festivities. It was not a day for great happenings. But this year something very big did happen.

It took place right after English class. Sebastian, Meche and Daniela were sitting in their usual configuration.

Isadora Galván walked over towards them and in plain sight of about half a dozen other students, paused before Sebastian's desk.

"Thank you for the nice Christmas present," she said. "I'm wearing it today."

"You're... ah... welcome," Sebastian said.

"A bunch of us are going to the movies tonight. Do you want to come?"

"Yeah. Sure."

"Good. Let's talk after school."

Just like that Isadora bounced away, short skirt swaying, dazzling smile lighting the classroom. Gone and gone, leaving half a dozen students—as well as Meche and Daniela—completely stunned.

"Did I miss something while I was away?" Daniela asked.

"I'd say we both did."

"I bought her a necklace," Sebastian replied.

Meche's voice was caramel-coated razors. "Gee, purchasing affection."

"What do you know about it?"

"She just invited you to make Constantino jealous," Meche said.

Daniela noticed how Sebastian twitched at that, as though he'd been zapped with a small taser. His eyes fixed on Meche and Meche rolled her eyes in turn.

"We need to change into the lab coats for chemistry. I have to wash mine again. I spilled something on it," Meche said.

Daniela and Meche headed to the bathrooms. Meche grabbed the coat and placed it in the sink, rubbing it quickly.

"Do you think he'll really go out with them tonight?" Daniela asked.

"What am I? A mind-reader?"

"I'm just asking."

"Ugh," Meche said. "Hey, how do you get rid of an avocado stain?"

"Beats me. When were you eating avocado?"

Meche put on the coat and looked in the mirror, brushing the hair away from her face.

"I don't remember. Did you have a nice time in Mazatlán?"

"It was real nice. I wish we could have stayed longer."

"Tell me about it," Meche muttered. "How the hell does Rodriguez go about giving us an assignment during winter break? What am I saying, you don't have anything to worry about. You'll be doing the tutoring thing with him and he'll give you an A just so you keep paying him."

"I don't know," Daniela said. "It might not be so easy. We have our first session Friday and he's already given me reading material."

"I hate his little beady eyes."

"He does not have little beady eyes."

"Does too."

They walked out of the bathroom and went up the stairs, following the flow of students moving at the sound of the bell.

"Did you have fun with Sebastian while I was away?" Daniela asked.

"It was alright," Meche said, giving Daniela a sideways glance. "He..."

Meche trailed off and Daniela waited patiently for her to complete her sentence.

"Yeah?"

"Oh, nothing. Something dumb."

*   *   *

SEBASTIAN WATCHED THE screen without watching it, his eyes out of focus, and when they stepped into the lobby he could not have said what movie had been screened.

"We're going to the washroom," Isadora told the boys.

She walked away, followed by the other girls. Sebastian stood a bit to the side, not really engaging the boys in the group. Constantino and the other three clones glanced in his direction, smirked and talked amongst themselves.

It was to be expected. But then Constantino motioned to him and Sebastian walked towards them, shuffling forward, his shoulders hunched; a lumbering giant.

"Yeah?" he asked.

"We're glad you could make it tonight," Constantino said.

Sebastian nodded, a bit surprised by that.

"I'm glad too."

"But don't make a habit out of it."

"What do you mean?"

"I mean we don't want you going out with Isadora again."

"We or you?" Sebastian asked, surprising himself with the boldness lurking in his voice.

The boys glanced at each other, then back at him. Constantino's lips curled into a smile.

"What's your friend's name?"

"What friend?" Sebastian asked cautiously.

"The one who likes music. She wears her headphones all the time."

"Meche."

"Yeah. She's a good dancer. She's got good moves."

Sebastian recalled the night at Isadora's party, when he'd seen Meche twirling in Constantino's arms and the sick feeling in his gut. He said nothing.

"If you fuck with my girl, I'll fuck with yours," Constantino said. "I'll give it to her up the ass."

Sebastian stood straight, unfolded to his full length and glared down at Constantino, his fingers pressing against his throat, making the shorter boy gasp with shock because Sebastian had never before put up a fight. The others must have also been in shock because they did not interfere.

"Never, ever try that," he whispered. "Or I'll cut off your dick."

He released Constantino and stepped back. The boys, normally itching to pile insults on him, seemed to have lost their will and looked dully at him. Constantino straightened up, his handsome face ugly with anger.

"I'll teach you a lesson some other time."

"Try it," Sebastian said.

He thought how they might fare if he cast a spell. Maybe Constantino could contract a nasty disease. These dark thoughts must have been reflected in his eyes for the boys looked away and Constantino pressed his lips tightly together and did not speak again.

The girls returned. Isadora smiled at him and Sebastian smiled back. There was some talk of going for a bite and Sebastian, tight on finances as usual, looked at his watch and pretended he was expected for supper back at home.

"I should go," Sebastian told her. "But thanks for the invitation."

"Maybe we can go out some other time," she said.

"Yes."

The boys glared at him. Sebastian walked out of the movie theatre.

GRANDMOTHER'S NEEDLES CLICKED together as she knitted, fingers steady, always knowing what movement would follow. Practice, she'd told Meche. All it takes is a little practice.

Maybe it was the same with magic. Meche thought they were getting better but there was still the need for practice.

They should have been in the factory that evening. But Sebastian was out with Isadora and her friends.

Meche glanced at the clock. The little hand had scarcely moved.

She sighed and looked at her homework. She had finished the math problems ages ago and was now stuck on some short story readings. The words seemed to jump and dance before her eyes. She could not concentrate.

"Can you tell me the story of the girl in the well, grandmother?" she asked.

"Aren't you working?"

"I'm tired."

"There once was a little girl who lived deep in a well. The *chaneques* had taken her when she was little, stolen her from her mother and placed her deep in the middle of the forest, inside a well—"

The phone rang and Meche rushed to pick it up, breathlessly holding the receiver.

"Yes?"

"Hey, Meche," her father said.

Oh. She thought it might have been Sebastian. He would tell her the evening had been crap and they would laugh together about it.

"I'm going to be home late tonight. I've got some business over here."

"Do I leave your plate out?"

"Just put it in the refrigerator. Thanks, sweetheart."

"Okay. Night."

Meche went to the kitchen and put some *picadillo* on a dish, then began covering it with plastic. Her mother walked in and glanced at her.

"Dad's coming late."

Her mother did not say anything. She dropped her glass in the sink and walked out, but Meche could see it in her eyes: she was angry. Dad was probably at the bar, getting drunk. She hoped she was not going to be sent out to find him. But, as was regularly the case, an hour later she was putting on her green jacket and gnashing her teeth.

She poked her head into the bar and looked around. Her father was not playing dominoes and he was not chatting with the regulars. He was not there.

Meche walked back home and poured herself a glass of milk before going to bed. Her mother, nestling a cup of coffee between her hands, was reading a magazine.

"He wouldn't come," Meche lied, though she did not know why she did.

Her mother turned a page and nodded.

* * *

VICENTE LAY IN the arms of his mistress and thought of his wife. It was the worst time possible to be doing this, but he could not get Natalia out of his mind.

He needed to leave her. He was tired of sneaking around. He was just plain tired. When he woke up in the morning he saw a middle-aged man with grey hair and a forlorn expression in the mirror. He hated that man. He hated himself.

But there were some practical things to consider. Their daughter, for one. And, though it might sound crass, there was the issue of the money.

Vicente had none. His desire to move to Puerto Vallarta, to live by the beach and spend his days watching sunsets, drowned in the reality of his scant possibilities.

He wished he was fifteen, even ten years younger than he currently was. He wished he had never met nor married his wife. Then he didn't wish that because that would mean Meche would not exist.

Azucena had told him about a business venture of a cousin of hers, something guaranteed to bring in dough. Vicente imagined himself rich, with a house in el Pedregal and a brand new sports car. Meche could live with them. She'd like it there. He'd buy her nice clothes and take her to eat out every night of the week.

"What is it that your cousin does, again?" he asked Azucena.

Mexico City, 2009

MECHE BOUGHT PISTACHIOS and a Coke at the corner store. Catalina Coronado was there too, buying eggs. The old woman stood gossiping and Meche had to wait ten minutes as the gnarled witch informed the shopkeeper of the movements of everyone in the colonia. Finally, Meche was able to pay, dumping her coins on the counter. Then it was onto the bus, headphones on, until she reached her father's apartment.

The apartment seemed to be getting more depressing every day and Meche was sure the flamingoes were growing anemic. Their ugly, faded, pink bodies blurred into one large pink blob when she stared at the curtains for too long. If she stared at the records the faces on the covers also blurred and changed, becoming faces of people she had known. Becoming her father.

KEEP MOVING. KEEP going. Keep running. Go through another pile of records, toss another box in a corner. Repeat.

Three more nights of prayer and then it was over.

She switched to her father's papers, cramming pages from his book into a box, slamming the typewriter on the top. She emptied the bedside table and found his diary for the current year.

March's entry. Written with his tight handwriting, filling every centimetre on the page.

I am planning on visiting Meche next year in Norway. She doesn't know it yet. I have decided to save enough money for the plane ticket and go in the summer. I want to see Meche before I die.

Meche went into the kitchen and searched the cabinets for her father's booze. But there was none. The old drunkard was disappointing her: he wouldn't even share his liquor.

Meche laughed. She opened the front door, determined to leave for Oslo right that instant. Determined to escape the dark, dingy apartment, the singers plastered on the covers of an army of records, the notebooks crammed with his life. She was going to die if she didn't get some air.

But back home there would be the food, the prayers, the people, the conversations and her father's picture in a silver frame set high upon a shelf for everyone to see.

She hurried back to the bedroom, lay on the bed and turned up the volume on the iPod, searching for a recent song. Something fresh. Meche closed her eyes.

When she woke up there was a tall, dark shadow in the doorway, blocking the light which filtered from the living room.

"Sebos?" she asked, her mouth dry.

She must be dreaming of him, like she did in Europe, during the long winter nights when he used to come into her room and sit quietly at the foot of her bed. The ghost of a boy who had not died.

"Nobody calls me Sebos anymore," he said and when he stepped forward she saw it was not the young Sebastian who had haunted her. It was the older one. The real one.

"What are you doing here?"

"I went to your home for the *novena* and nobody knew where you were. I thought you might still be here. We had a movie to watch."

"How did you get in?" she asked, wondering if he still had some magic tricks under his sleeve. Turning into mist and slipping under the door maybe.

"You left the door open."

How prosaic. Meche shook her head, still groggy. She pulled out the earbuds, stuffing them in her pocket.

"Is the praying over?"

"Yes."

"Good."

"What are you doing?"

"I was taking a nap until you interrupted me."

"No, I mean what are you *doing*," he asked, the inflexion falling on the last word.

He sat on the bed and she sat up so that she was level with him.

"Thinking," she said.

"I had a hard time when my dad died."

"When did he die?"

"A couple of years ago."

"You hated him," Meche said. "He used to beat you up."

"He did. But he also did nice things. He made toys for me. Little things of wire and tin. I try to remember the good things."

"Then you're a better person than I," she muttered, folding her legs into a lotus position.

"When did you get so sad?"

"Oh, please," Meche said. "Am I crying?"

"No. Then?"

"When I was seven years old I fell down and I said, 'I'm not going to cry about this.' And I didn't. I've stayed true to that. Waterworks don't work for me, all that stupid melodrama…"

"You didn't cry because you wanted to show your dad you were brave," Sebastian said turning his head and looking at her. "You told me that story. I remember."

"Great. So what? Should I start weeping all over your shirt and you can wipe my tears with that God-damn nasty tie you're wearing?" she asked, jamming a finger against one of the buttons on his shirt. Poking his chest. "You get your kicks like that these days?"

"I can go if you want."

"You do that," she said and grabbed the notebook she had been reading before. She tossed it at him, hitting him on the face.

It made her incredibly happy. If only she could pelt him with about two dozen other notebooks. Seized by a desire for destruction, Meche grabbed a bunch of records and flipped them at him. Sebastian evaded them this time, ducking. She kept throwing them, like Frisbees.

"Look! Take On Me. Now that's a classic. And here, La Puerta de Alcalá.' 'Look at her, look at her, seeing time pass. The door of

Alcala.' It was a big hit back in 1985. Oh, look at this one?" Meche showed him the sleeve. "Mi Unicornio Azul by Silvio Rodriguez. My dad liked that song a lot."

Meche buried her face in the pillow.

She felt Sebastian's fingers on her shoulder; tried to shove him away and failed, then lay still and blinked.

"I hate this city," she told the pillow, because she wouldn't tell him.

Sebastian's hand just rested there as it had so many times before: comforting her after the news of a bad grade; the nasty words some classmate spoke at school; even the time when she got so many zits she promised she'd never leave the apartment again and Sebastian had arrived, luring her out with the promise of the arcade.

A phone rang. His cell. The hand left her.

"Yes. Mom? Yeah."

He walked towards the doorway and Meche rolled over, grabbing the blanket and wrapping herself into it. She was not cold in Oslo but this apartment packed the cold of too many winters in its heart.

Sebastian returned and sat next to her.

"Jimena said your mom is sick."

"Cancer. Romualdo and I take turns looking after her. That's why I'm back in the city. The chemo has worked. I'm betting she lives to a hundred."

She thought of her own father, shuffling alone through his apartment in his slippers with no one to watch over him. Nothing but the songs for company.

"You're going to go visit her now?"

"No. I can stay."

"I'm not asking you to stay," Meche said looking over her shoulder.

"You think I'd leave just like that?"

Well, you did once before, she thought. Well, technically she'd left. But only after he completely abandoned her by the curbside.

"I don't know you," she muttered. To the pillow, again. "You're a stranger."

He turned her around and Meche frowned as she looked into eyes which were exactly the same as she remembered them. But the rest wasn't. And this man... she had never ridden down the boulevard on this man's motorcycle, never scrawled idly in his books, never listened to vinyl records in an old pantyhose factory with him.

And that was that. You don't get to rewind your life like a tape and splice it back together, pretending it never knotted and tore, when it did and you know it did.

Didn't he get that?

They'd never be friends again. Never care like they cared, never dance like they danced. Time had sucked the marrow out of her and they were both too old.

He stretched his arms and pulled Meche forward, resting his chin upon her head.

"I know," he said.

Meche squeezed her eyes shut and let him hold her for a good, long time. They'd lain like that on the factory floor, Sebastian wrapping his arms around her as they fell asleep.

"I can't see you again," she said. Her voice sounded dinted and strained.

"Why not?"

"Compartments. Plus, it's not as if I like you."

Sebastian laughed lightly.

"Then pretend to like me for a couple more days."

"Why?"

"Because you'll be gone after that."

Oslo, with the little apartment. The shelves and the books—yes, she had bought them. She even had *The Ambassadors*, damn it—and the vinyl records proudly displayed on the walls instead of photographs of her family. Yellow walls and little white dishes as she sipped her tea and looked out the window, facing north. For half a second she wished he could see the place right now.

Meche shifted and slipped from his embrace. She looked down at him as she stood beside the bed and she shook her head, just the slightest movement.

She headed to the living room, pushed her hands deep in her pockets, brushing a pile of records on her way and making it tumble onto the floor. The front door was two paces away.

The keys.

Meche sighed, heading back towards the living room and bumping into Sebastian, who was standing there, leaning on the doorframe, looking down at her.

Sebastian stretched out a hand, pulling her closer and pressing his forehead against hers.

She felt completely lost and tried to shove him back, gently. He didn't budge, instead pressing a kiss against her cheek.

"Second movement," he said.

He kissed her mouth. Meche shook her head and looked away, staring at the shadows. She stood like that for a long time.

Coda, she thought. *You mean a coda.* She slid her hands up, touched the stubble of his jaw. It was odd, the texture of his skin beneath her fingers. Meche closed her eyes and kissed him harder than he had kissed her, wrapping her arms loosely around his neck.

He smiled against her mouth and she wished he was not so damn *pleased* with himself. Then she smiled too, only a little.

Mexico City, 1989

MID-JANUARY VICENTE Vega withdrew all the savings from their bank account. He was investing them in the business venture of Azucena's cousin. By the end of January, Azucena and the venture had vanished. Natalia found out at the end of February.

Vicente grabbed two suitcases and left on the last day of the month.

FEBRUARY WAS AN explosion of pink and red at Daniela's house. Valentine's Day approached with its excuse for her to indulge in craft-making on a grand scale. She went downtown and bought all kinds of supplies: silicone for the hot glue gun, fabric, shiny paper, bits of lace. She made Valentines for all her family—including the extended cousins in Mazatlán— and for all her classmates, even though they did not give her any Valentines. Then she began working on Sebastian's birthday gift: he was turning sixteen.

Sebastian had been born the morning before Valentine's Day and this gave Daniela the perfect excuse to put her talents to use for a gift which was part birthday present and part homage to this holiday. Her creations were all pink and sparkly, hideous and kitsch, best viewed from afar or not viewed at all. Sebastian, not wanting to hurt his friend's feelings, accepted each with a smile, posed for a picture with Daniela holding the gift and stuck it somewhere on a shelf.

This year she was working on something which seemed to be a cross between an elephant and a zebra, a creature capable of giving Dali nightmares.

Sebastian observed her from the couch, wrapped in a warm blanket while Meche fumed.

"I thought we were going to practise some spells."

"I'm here, ain't I?" Sebastian said.

"I thought we were taking a break," Daniela said, pressing sequins against the head of the deformed elephant.

"That was half an hour ago," Meche said.

Daniela shrugged and Meche turned to Sebastian. It was cold in the factory with the broken panes letting in sharp winter air. He felt quite comfortable snuggled underneath the blanket, but he relented and walked towards Meche. Daniela, noticing it was now two against one, gave in.

They did not need to dance or hold hands anymore, though they sometimes did. For the past two weeks they had been working on something called a glamour, or as Meche pronounced it— gla-mur. She'd found out about it from a book of fairy tales she pilfered from the school library and was determined to make it work, although the results, so far, were far from perfect. There had been a creepy moment last week when they made Daniela's eyes apparently vanish and she walked around as though she was a mole-person.

"Why don't we try to imitate a whole person?" Meche asked.

"We can't get eye colour right, let alone the eyes. Why bother with a whole person?" Sebastian asked.

"I have a feeling it might be easier."

Magic happened like that for them: in feelings and hunches and surprise insights which came in the middle of the night.

"Okay," Daniela said. "Who will we imitate? A movie star?"

"Can I see one of your magazines?" Meche asked.

Daniela grabbed her purse and pulled out one of her teen magazines. Meche thumbed through it, finally ripping out a page and holding it up.

"This one," she said.

Her choice was a pretty girl wearing a black leotard. Her hair was in a ponytail. Sebastian looked carefully at the photo, trying to memorize her face, her expression.

"Who are we focusing on?" Sebastian asked.

"How about Daniela?"

"Fine."

Meche fiddled with a record. A song began to play. Take On Me. Sebastian tapped his foot, picturing Daniela as the girl. Erasing Daniela and sketching a whole new face on her, a whole new body. Clothes stitched themselves together, hair changed colour and grew, Daniela gained height and the contours of her body were reshaped. The final result was a good approximation but though it looked like an accurate copy of the picture, it also looked a bit glossy, perfect and two-dimensional; too much like the picture in a way, their imaginations producing a young woman whose skin had the rubbery quality of a mannequin.

Daniela walked around the room. It was like she had become a large Barbie doll, taking extremely long steps with her new slender legs. Then the outlines of Daniela's body seemed to fizzle—like one image had been superimposed upon another. Streams of colour cascaded down Daniela's shoulders, tumbling down; the threads of the illusion came apart, golden dust drifting towards the floor and disappearing as soon as it touched the ground.

The three of them sat down in unison. That had been interesting but not exactly what Sebastian had imagined.

"We need to keep working on it," Meche said.

"It's almost four," Daniela said, putting the crafts she had been working on back in her big market bag. "I need to go to my tutoring session."

"Really?" Meche said. "It's Saturday."

"Yeah, it doesn't matter," Daniela said. "I'm paying for it. We can meet tomorrow."

"Can we come by your house around noon?"

"Sure." Daniela rubbed her eyes and yawned. "My mom will make us lunch. Anyway, my sister's picking me up. I better go."

"Bye."

Daniela waved a happy, cheerful goodbye and clomped down the stairs. Meche locked the door behind her and looked at the picture from the magazine, biting her lower lip.

"Maybe we need to look at a moving picture instead of a still image," Meche ventured.

"What are you getting me for my birthday?" Sebastian asked, flopping onto the couch and grabbing hold of the blanket again.

"You'll have more than enough with Daniela's awesome birthday present. Did you see all that glitter?"

"I did."

"I think she mistakes you for a five-year-old girl," Meche said.

"She means well."

"Of course she does."

"Come here," he said. "I want to show you something."

Meche sat down next to him, propping her legs over the arm of the couch and resting her back against his arm.

"What?"

He cracked open his copy of *The Ambassadors* and pulled out a cut-out from a magazine.

"I got it the other day. It's from a *National Geographic*. The Northern Lights."

"Cool."

"We have to go to the North Cape to see them."

Meche handed back the clipping. She grabbed the blanket and pulled it over herself so that they were both covered. Things were back to normal between them—the December incident vanished—except when they weren't; moments like this when Sebastian felt there was a little splinter in both of their brains.

He opened his mouth to ask Meche something. The trouble was he wasn't sure what question he wanted to ask.

Sebastian sighed.

DANIELA'S SISTER DROPPED her off in front of Mr. Rodriguez's place and told her she'd be back in a couple of hours. Daniela rang the bell and hummed as she waited for him to come down the stairs and let her in.

Her teacher had told her she was progressing well with her essays and Daniela felt proud of herself. She was not a brilliant student, rather average in her achievements, and it felt good to know she could shine at something.

Mr. Rodriguez let her into his apartment and smiled.

"Hi," he said. "How are you doing today, Daniela?"

"I'm good," she said, peeling off her sweater and putting it in the entrance closet, before following Mr. Rodriguez inside.

He had a little apartment with potted plants by the windows. The living room/dining room combo contained numerous shelves crammed with books. Photographs of a girlfriend Daniela had yet to meet adorned one shelf. The furniture was all a bit worn but it all looked rather chic and effortless.

Daniela sat at the dining room table and took out her notebook and her books, piling them all neatly.

"Do you want a soda? Some water?"

"No, sir. I'm fine."

The living room had a view of the kitchen and she watched as Mr. Rodriguez poured himself a glass of water. Daniela opened her notebook.

"I finished the assignment you gave me."

"What did you think of the book?"

"I thought it was fun."

"*Wuthering Heights* was fun?"

"Well… yeah?" Daniela said cautiously.

She realized she should have said dramatic, moving, romantic—any of those words. Fun was such a stupid choice.

"Here," he said, setting a glass before her. "I figure you might get thirsty."

"Thanks," she said, though she didn't need it at all.

"You were saying it's fun?"

"Yes. I mean, I finished it quickly and it wasn't hard at all. I wrote my impressions on it, like you asked."

Mr. Rodriguez stood next to her, leaning down to look at her notes. Sometimes, when Daniela stood in line at the supermarket, boys brushed by her, touching the side of her breasts. Meche would not allow anyone to cop a feel, but Daniela just tried to ignore it. It didn't happen too frequently, anyway, and she tried to tell herself the boys did not mean it, that it was an accident.

When she felt Mr. Rodriguez's hand brush against the side of her breast Daniela stiffened and stared at her notebook, figuring he hadn't meant it.

"What did you think about Heathcliff?"

Daniela's tongue clicked. Yes. Just an accident. "He's a complex character. You'd think he'd be the hero, but he acts like the bad guy sometimes…"

There. She felt it again. Large fingers brushing against her breast.

Daniela looked down. She scooted a bit to the right, reaching towards a book, moving away a little from him.

"… there is a part where…"

The fingers again, though this time they rested on her thigh.

Daniela's eyes went round. She swallowed.

"Mr. Rodriguez, you're making me uncomfortable," she muttered.

"I'm sorry."

The hand tugged at the hem of her purple peasant skirt.

"I'm going home," she said and stood up.

Mr. Rodriguez smiled at her and it was such an innocent smile that for a split second Daniela thought maybe she had imagined it, that her overactive imagination was mixing a plot from one of her books with real life.

"Look here, I know how you look at me," Mr. Rodriguez said. "Let's not be a baby about it."

The shock of his words numbed Daniela and she sat in her chair, motionless, an overstuffed doll. Mr. Rodriguez's hand returned to her thigh.

"Look, I'm doing you a favour."

The books she read did not contain scenes like this; they offered no solutions and no maps through this forest. Daniela tried to think, tried to move from the chair and was only able to utter a weak, "Please stop, sir."

He reached for her shirt, about to take it off, and Daniela raised a leg and kneed him in the balls. He howled in pain, bending down. Daniela pushed him away and rushed towards the door.

For a few panicky seconds she thought the doorknob would not turn, but the door swung open easily and she rushed out like a scared rabbit, running faster than she thought possible. Two blocks from his place she tripped and skinned her knees, but she got up again and ran and ran until she was out of breath.

* * *

"SHE'S STILL IN bed," Daniela's sister said.

"But it's noon," Meche said. "She told us to come at noon. Is she sick again? Can we see her?"

"Well... you can try. I took her breakfast up today and she wouldn't even open the door. She says she has a cold."

"We were supposed to have lunch together," Sebastian explained.

"Yeah, I know. Maybe she'll come down if you talk to her. She's been acting weird since yesterday."

"Alright," Meche said.

They went up the stairs to Daniela's room. Her door had a colorful sign bordered with flowers which read 'Daniela.' Meche knocked three times and waited.

"What?"

"Hey, it's us," Meche said. "We're here for lunch."

"Go away."

Meche frowned and glanced at Sebastian. When Daniela was sick, she liked having them around. They read to her or played board games. She enjoyed the company and, in fact, felt sad when they didn't show up.

"Stop kidding and let us in."

"I'm not kidding. I don't want to talk to you."

"Come on. We're not going to go. What's up with you?"

"If I tell you... you can't tell anyone else."

"Who are we going to tell?" Meche said. "Open up."

Daniela unlocked the door. Meche and Sebastian walked in. The curtains were drawn. Daniela, in her pyjamas, looked tired and her eyes were red from crying. She shuffled back into bed, pulling the covers up to her chin.

"Hey, what's up with you?" Meche asked. "Did you catch a bug?"

"No," Daniela muttered.

Meche frowned. She sat at the edge of Daniela's bed.

"What's wrong?" she asked very seriously.

Daniela covered her face with her hands and shook her head. "It's embarrassing..."

"We won't laugh. Right, Sebos?"

"No, promise," Sebastian said.

"He grabbed my boob."

Sebastian looked at Meche, eyes wide. She turned towards Daniela.

"Who did?" Meche asked.

Daniela kept her hands over her eyes. She pursed her lips.

"Who?" Meche demanded. "Tell us or we'll find out."

"Rodriguez," Daniela whispered.

Meche knew it! She just knew he was an asshole. There was something unpleasant and oily about him. She wanted to wring his neck like a chicken.

"What?" Sebastian asked.

"He also touched my leg. He said he was doing me a favour."

Meche grabbed her by the shoulders, pulling her up. "Did he rape you?"

"No! But he would have... I ran out and... and tomorrow I'm going to have to see him in school. I can't. I just can't."

"No, you're never going to have to see him again because he's going to get his ass fired," Meche said. "Frankenstrada is going to kick him out on the spot."

"Yeah... yeah," Sebastian agreed. "He won't teach again."

"I don't want to tell the principal."

"We'll go with you," Meche said. "We'll tell her together."

"What if she doesn't believe me?"

"She's got to."

Daniela uncovered her face. She nodded weakly. Meche sat with her and held her hand.

"It'll be fine."

THEY SHOWED UP promptly at Principal Estrada's office on Monday morning, asking for a brief meeting and were admitted into her office. Estrada sat behind her massive desk, photographs of former students decorating the walls, the history and pride of the institution reflected through the decades. She listened to them, hands clasped in front of her, and sat very still as Daniela spoke.

Once Daniela had finished she placed her hands upon the desk.

"That's quite a story," she said.

"It's true," Meche said. "Mr. Rodriguez is a creep."

"Mr. Rodriguez has been with us for five years. He performs very well on his evaluations and has never given us a cause for concern."

"Well, there's a cause here," Meche replied.

"Look, I understand," the principal said.

Meche sighed with relief.

"It's hard being a kid these days. All that sex in music videos on the television. There is very little sense of decency left. It's terribly confusing."

"What does that have to do with Daniela?" Sebastian asked.

Principal Estrada gave Daniela a kind, motherly look.

"Look, I talked to Professor Rodriguez already—"

"You did?" Daniela mumbled.

"Yes. Yesterday. He told me you tried to kiss him. He was terribly ashamed about the whole thing."

"It's the other way around," Meche said. "He was trying to touch her boob."

Principal Estrada rose, circling the desk and standing next to Daniela. She stared down at the girl. Daniela lowered her head, as if she were trying to look at something stuck to the floor.

"Did he really try to touch you?"

Daniela did not answer. Meche saw how she gripped the arms of the chair she was sitting in.

"Can I leave?" Daniela asked.

"I asked you a question."

"No. Can I go now?"

"Yes. That goes for the three of you."

Daniela rushed out of the office. Sebastian hurried after her. Meche stopped at the door, looking back at Principal Estrada.

Estrada sat back behind her desk, tidying her papers and utterly ignoring her.

"WAIT," MECHE SAID, running after them and catching up as they exited into the courtyard. "We can't leave it at that."

"We are going to leave it at that," Daniela whispered. "She doesn't care."

"She doesn't care, but we do," Meche said. "We have to do something."

"Like what?!" Daniela turned around, clutching her books against her chest. "What can we do?"

"Everything," Meche said. "That's what magic is for."

"What kind of spell are you talking about?" Sebastian asked.

"Something to teach him a lesson, so he'll never bug Daniela or any other girl again."

Daniela and Sebastian looked at each other nervously. Daniela stared down at her shoes, biting her lower lip.

"Black magic?"

"Oh, black magic is the shit they say in movies," Meche said with a chuckle. "Magic is magic."

"It's not the same to ask for money as it is to hurt a man," Sebastian said, feeling terribly uncomfortable with the whole conversation.

"Like I don't know it?"

"No, I don't think you do."

Meche's eyes narrowed. She grabbed Sebastian's arm, digging her nails into his skin. Like when they played Where Did the Eagle Land. Only not really, because there was this glimmer in her eye which he did not like. Sebastian brushed her hand off.

"Rodriguez must pay," Meche said.

"Maybe," Sebastian said. "But magic it's not the way to do it."

"Can we even do it?" Daniela asked.

"Oh, yeah," Meche said. "I'm sure we can."

DANIELA SAT IN the front seat, nervously touching the steering wheel and staring at Meche through the rear-view mirror.

"I don't know if I can do this," Daniela said. "I don't have a permit yet. This is not even my car. If my sister finds out…"

"Shhh. I'll be quick."

"Yeah, I don't know about this either," Sebastian said. "You're making an awful lot of assumptions here."

"We practised."

"Um, barely."

Meche handed him the portable record player, placing the record on top of it.

"It'll be fine."

"Why don't you let me go?" Sebastian asked. "I can do it."

"Nope. I can do this and I can do it better than either of you can."

"How do you know that?"

"Because I know," Meche said.

Meche jumped out of the car before he could say anything else. Sebastian stretched his head out the window. She went around the corner and rang the interphone.

"Yeah?" Mr. Rodriguez's voice came through the speaker.

"Hi, Mr. Rodriguez? It's Meche. I'm here for the tutoring session."

"Oh, alright. Come on in."

The door opened and Meche slipped into the building. She reached the end of a hallway and had hardly knocked when Rodriguez swung the door open, letting her in.

"You're early," he said.

"I caught a ride."

"Good. Come in."

Meche followed him, hands in the pockets of her heavy jacket. She eyed the living room carefully, looking at all the books and the photographs sitting on a shelf. She glanced out a window and saw Daniela's car below. Meche checked her watch. Three more minutes.

"Do you want something to drink? Soda? A glass of water?"

"Water is fine."

Rodriguez went to the kitchen, filling a glass for her. He handed it to Meche and she took a tiny sip, nodding.

"Mr. Rodriguez, you know I'm friends with Daniela, don't you?"

"I'm aware of that."

"Friends tell each other things, Mr. Rodriguez."

He raised a hand, scratching the back of his head and smiling. "I'm not sure what you're talking about."

"I think you are."

The man's eyes narrowed and the smile grew a little crooked. "Are you going to start making accusations against me?"

"Oh, they're not accusations. It's the truth. Ten."

"What?"

Meche turned her wrist, looking at the watch. Tick tick tick it went, marking each passing second.

"Eight."

"What are you going on about?"

"Just counting down. Four."

Meche paused.

"To what?"

"Candyman. Siouxsie and the Banshees," she said.

The little minute hand reached the mark and Meche dropped the glass. It shattered on the nice, oiled floor of Mr. Rodriguez's apartment. He stared at the puddle and Meche shrugged, making an exaggerated pout.

"Oops. Clumsy me."

"What are you... maybe you better leave."

"So fast? You don't want to make a pass at me? Try to rub your dirty crotch against my side?"

"Hey," Rodriguez said, stepping towards her and wagging an angry finger at her.

Meche raised a hand and a book flew through the air, hitting him on the head. Rodriguez stumbled, touching his head and looking up in surprise.

"Now how did that happen?" Meche wondered out loud. "Oh, yeah, it went a bit like this!"

She extended her other hand and a thick dictionary whacked him on the back. Rodriguez turned around, surprised.

"What is happening?"

Meche looked at her nails, flicking a finger, and a third book bounced against his leg.

"Magic," she said.

She couldn't hear the music but she could feel it outside, swimming up and stretching up her arms.

Rodriguez rushed towards her, perhaps thinking he could overpower her. Meche raised the glass shards from the floor, sending them flying into his face like darts. He fell on his knees and began to roll on the floor, crying like a little baby. Meche pressed a foot against his ribcage and looked down at him, feeling rather numb at the sight of his pained face and the blood.

"If we ever see you again, we'll make it *really* hurt," she said. "And if you ever touch another girl we'll make you cut off your balls and eat them. Believe me, we can."

She gave him a kick, for good measure, and slammed the door when she left. The whole building crackled with the power. When she leaned down next to the car, her hand rested against the hood and a little spark of electricity shot through her fingers.

Meche felt like she had just drunk a whole bottle of tequila. She opened the back door and collapsed next to Sebastian.

MECHE SQUINTED. SEBASTIAN was smoothing her hair. She could feel his long fingers and the familiar smell of him that was... him.

"Mmm," she muttered, smacking her lips.

"How's it going?" he asked. "You've been out for ten minutes."

"Great," she said, feeling groggy. "I guess telekinesis takes its toll, huh?"

"Maybe it's 'cause we weren't in the room with you."

"You were very near, though."

"I don't know the rules of this," Sebastian said with a chuckle.

"Meche, you sure you're okay?" Daniela asked.

"Yup."

Meche sat up. Saw they were in motion already. Good. She rested her head against Sebastian's shoulder, frowning.

"Are you guys hungry? I need to eat something."

"Famished," Sebastian agreed.

"How about *birria* tacos?" Daniela asked.

"Where?"

"By the subway station," Sebastian said. "Take a left."

THEY DRANK JARRITOS, lifted tacos with expert fingers while holding little plastic blue plates and elbowed their space around the crowded stand. Meche spoke.

"What are we going to do to Frankenstrada?"

Sebastian wasn't sure he had heard her right with all the people around her, so he shook his head. "What?"

"What are we going to do about Frankenstrada?" she repeated.

"Meaning?"

"We have to punish her too. We can't let her go on her merry way, can we?"

Neither Sebastian nor Daniela spoke. He grabbed a napkin, carefully cleaning his greasy fingers and wiping his lips. Daniela sucked on a lemon and looked down.

"Really? You pussies!" Meche said dismissively.

"Hey, I didn't *enjoy* doing what we did to Rodriguez and I don't want to do it again," Sebastian said.

"Liar," Meche said. "You liked the power as much as I did."

He recalled the rush of power as the music played, the intensity of it coursing through his veins. The taste of raw anger in his mouth, pleasant and sickly sweet. But despite this, he had not enjoyed it. It was not something he would choose again.

"I did not."

"Then maybe you are not a real warlock. Just some second-rate impostor."

It stung to be called an impostor and her tone of voice made it even more painful. Sebastian snatched his Jarrito and sipped it, biting down on the straw.

"I didn't like it either," Daniela ventured weakly. "It was scary."

"It was fucking awesome," Meche said, chuckling.

"No, it was not," Sebastian muttered.

"Okay. Then it wasn't. For you. Whatever. She didn't lift a finger against that pervert. Do you want to let her get away with it? Doesn't that deserve some sort of punishment? I say it does."

"Well, it's three of us," Sebastian replied. "And I vote we let her be."

"Daniela, what do you think? Aren't you still mad at Frankenstrada?"

"I am still mad," Daniela whispered, her thin lips barely opening and letting the words out.

"Then should we punish her?"

"You don't have to do what she says," Sebastian said, reaching towards Daniela.

Meche pressed a hand against his chest, pushing him back. Not shoving. Her fingers just gently pressed against his shirt, the slightest of contacts and yet it had a very clear, sharp meaning. A defiance. It made him pause in his trajectory.

Meche, strong-willed, most often than not led the pack. He didn't like the way she looked at him right now, eyebrow quirked, blocking his path.

"So?" Meche asked, turning her head, addressing Daniela with dark, piercing eyes.

"I do want to punish her a little," Daniela said.

"Good," Meche said, picking up her soft drink and taking a long sip.

"I'm full," Sebastian said, putting down his plastic plate.

"WHY ARE YOU being a hard-ass?" Meche asked him. "I'm not."

They were standing at the bottom of the stairs to her apartment. She had her arms crossed and looked rather smug, lips slightly curved into a smile. He hated it, hated her, when she got like this.

"You think you're better than us," he said.

"Oh?"

"At magic."

"Maybe a tad," she said with a shrug. "I figured out the whole spell thing, didn't I?"

"At life."

"What are you—"

"I just want you to know, I don't agree with what you are making us do."

"I'm not making you do anything. We took a vote. You lost."

"You can't push Daniela around all the time."

"Loser."

"You think I'm joking?"

"Blah, I'm bored," Meche said, climbing up a couple of steps.

He grabbed her by the wrist, giving her a strong yank. Meche stumbled down, bending against him.

She still stood two steps above him but she had almost lost her balance and was holding on to the collar of his jacket for support. He raised an arm, resting it against her back, holding her in place.

"One day, if you're not careful, all your bullshit is going to bite you in the ass," he whispered.

"Really, mister?" Meche asked, tipping her head at him. "You don't scare me. I can hex the life out of you if I want to."

"Yeah? Let me step back so you can hit your face against the ground," he said.

"Try it," she said, her hand inching up and resting against the back of his neck for leverage.

Though they had played and teased each other in a myriad of ways, this didn't seem like their regular games. He felt an ache—dull and uncomfortable—which made him wince.

Sebastian grabbed her by the waist and deposited her on the ground.

"Coward," she said.

She scared him, the way her eyes gleamed. There was something ugly and much too cold in her, and it made him want to run off. But, as usual, when he took two steps back with Meche he wanted to take three forward. That was her most distressing form of sorcery, the hold she had on them.

On him.

"I'll see you tomorrow at school," he said.

ON MONDAYS THE students assembled in the courtyard for the salute to the flag. The national anthem played, five students marched with the flag and everyone raised their left hand, resting it against their chest. Sometimes the principal said a few words, before everyone shuffled off to class.

That Monday the students marched, the flag went by, the national anthem finished playing.

Sebastian, Meche and Dolores stood at the back of their group and watched as a teacher went to the microphone and briefly talked about an upcoming event.

Principal Estrada took her place, ready to dismiss them, grabbing the microphone.

She opened her mouth and croaked loudly.

The students giggled.

The principal, looking rather surprised, opened her mouth again.

The croak was louder. The giggles multiplied.

A third time and everyone broke down in laughter.

The principle doubled over and began vomiting, a sticky, dark substance. *Ewws* mingled with the laughter as principal Estrada bent down on her knees and continued to vomit. Finally she finished and rose on wobbly legs, stumbling into the school offices.

"Children, children," said the physical education teacher. "Head to your classes. Now..."

Meche, leaning against the wall, grinned in satisfaction and began whistling a merry tune.

"ARE YOU GOING to give me grief just like Sebastian?" Meche asked her.

"No. I just said it was a bit extreme," Daniela said.

"Why shouldn't we be extreme?"

"You really have no fear, do you?"

"Fear of what?"

"Of what we are doing."

"Why should I?"

"Because it's dangerous."

God, how was it dangerous? It wasn't like there was a magic police force waiting to give them a ticket. Nobody could suspect them. Nothing bad would happen to them. Plus, she didn't feel any guilt over the whole thing.

Power was meant to be wielded.

Meche snorted. "Dangerous for anyone who stands in our way."

Daniela looked at her, shaking her head while Meche shrugged.

"Look, Estrada deserved it," Meche said. "She crossed us one too many times and she got what was coming for her. She's lucky we didn't break her damn back."

"Gee, I hope you never get mad at me."

Meche draped her arm over the shoulders of a cardboard cut-out of David Bowie and eyed the records at the back of the store. It was a wash out. There was no Whiter Shade of Pale in the store and no records with any significant power. This seemed to be the case with most stores which offered new merchandise. Meche had found records with power at used shops, making her guess the power might be related to the previous owner or persons they had come into contact with; a patina that somehow impregnated the vinyl, like thumb prints upon the surface. This was a conjecture she had scribbled in her *grimoire*, but it made sense. And wasn't most of everything pertaining to the world of magic a conjecture, anyway?

"What are you getting Sebastian?" Daniela asked, giving up the fight.

"I was thinking a Tom Waits album, but then I decided on a movie," Meche said, her hands drifting over the records, flicking through album covers.

"Like a date?"

"Not like a date," Meche frowned. "Why would you think I'd go out with him on a date?"

"Oh... No-nothing. It just crossed my mind. It's all."

"I'm done here," Meche said, tossing the record back in its bin.

"He's going out with Isadora again."

Meche raised an eyebrow at that. "How do you know?"

"He told me. They're going out on Sunday."

"Sunday we're supposed to practice! And why didn't he tell me? This is the kind of thing we need to vote on. He can't just run off..."

"Maybe because you would have asked to vote on it?"

"Ugh," Meche said and bit her lower lip.

It wasn't that she wanted Sebastian to practise every day, but this magic thing required some discipline. They were improving at the glamour and although they had triumphed over Rodriguez and Estrada, both spells had worn them down. The one they had cast on Estrada, especially. Meche's body had ached so afterwards she ate a whole roasted chicken on the way home from the factory, famished and exhausted by the experience. But she could feel they were getting better. They needed to practise their powers, to explore the limits of their sorcery. To attempt bigger things. What else might they accomplish, the three of them?

But they would get squat if Sebastian went out on Sundays with Isadora. Of all the girls! Sure, Isadora was hot but that was about it. Meche felt slightly insulted that her best friend would go for the rich ditz. There was a vague, distant possibility, that Sebastian might actually get it on with the girl and ditch Meche and Daniela for full-time pursuit of his wet dream. With the circle broken, Meche was not sure she could make magic. Not to its full potential.

Maybe she needed to study alone, to see if she could cast hexes and spells without the others. She'd cast a hex by herself the first time, after all.

"Let's head out," Meche said.

DOLORES FOUND THE thimble in the back of her clothes drawer, packed along with old postcards, a pressed flower and pictures of her sisters. She smiled at the picture of the girls in their white summer dresses with the hair tied in pigtails. Finally, she took out the thimble and pressed it against her ear. She couldn't hear anything but the faintest of whispers. Magic is for children, for the young.

"Grandma, do you want me to make the rice today?"

Dolores blinked and raised her head. Meche was standing at the doorway. Meche had already changed out of her uniform and into her day clothes. Dolores had spent half the afternoon daydreaming and had not even realized her granddaughter was home.

"The rice," Dolores said. "Yes. I've got to boil the rice."

She stood up and the thimble tumbled from her hands, landing on the floor. Meche scooped it up. She frowned.

"Feels warm," she muttered. Meche raised her eyes and stared at her. "Is this—"

"An antique. From days past."

"But—"

"Days past, my girl. Stories I've forgotten."

Meche nodded and handed her the thimble. Dolores placed it in the front pocket of her apron and rubbed her hands together.

"Now, we need to make rice, don't we?"

SEBASTIAN KNEW HE was a beggar at a banquet, invited only out of pity or as a joke. A new amusement. Perhaps he was an annoyance, simply meant to piss off Constantino, but he still appreciated the chance to go out with Isadora and her friends a second time.

Well, he could do without the friends. The boys hated him and the girls ignored him, but Isadora was what mattered and she listened to him chatter, smiled at a joke and even shared a bag of popcorn with him.

When it was time to part ways, she kissed him on the cheek and he practically sprinted all the way back home. He lay on his bed, lacing his fingers behind his head and wondered if Isadora actually liked him, if maybe, just maybe...

... the phone rang loudly. He tried to ignore it, but it kept ringing and he finally picked it up, pressing the receiver against his ear.

"Yes?"

"What took you so long?"

Meche. Sebastian closed his eyes. "I was sleeping."

"So you didn't go out tonight then?"

"I went out," he said.

"Oh."

Was that disappointment, annoyance or regular variety Meche? He straightened up, tugging at the phone cord.

"What do you want?"

"I wanted to say Happy Birthday. But maybe you're too busy wanking in the bathroom, so good—"

"Yeah, if I was wanking you already ruined it."

"Gross."

"You brought it up."

"You confirmed it."

Sebastian smiled, turning and looking at the wall with his maps and pictures of Europe. He pressed a thumb against Paris, which was a red dot surrounded by smaller black dots.

"Meche, do you ever..."

His finger slid up the wall, following a river and he did not even know what to ask, the words were all smudged inside his head.

"Thanks for phoning."

"I'll see you tomorrow."

MECHE WAS ON the computer when the screaming started. She hated it when they screamed. If only parents could tear each other to pieces in silence, like civilized people. She turned up the volume on her Walkman until Mecano's Perdido en mi Habitación was as loud as it could be.

It was not loud enough.

Meche decided to make a run for Daniela's house. Daniela would bake her cupcakes which tasted like ass, but it was better than the constant shouts streaming through the walls.

Meche put on her jacket, grabbed the backpack and found her father also preparing to leave. He was pulling two suitcases down the hallway.

"What's up?" she asked, placing her hands in her pockets.

He smiled faintly at her.

"Meche, I've got to move out."

"What?"

Her parents fought. Like, a lot. But Meche could not picture them separated. What, was this temporary? When was he coming back?

"Dad—"

"I'll give you my address, when I have it. You can come and visit. I'm going to be moving to Puerto Vallarta next year and you can come with me for the summer. It'll be awesome."

"Puerto Vallarta?"

"Yeah. It's all part of the plan. The taxi is going to leave if I don't get downstairs."

He grabbed the suitcases and kept on walking. Meche followed him in shock. When they reached the door he turned around and gave her a hug.

"You be good, alright?"

"Dad?" Meche said, watching him head towards the staircase. "Daddy?"

"Get inside!"

Meche turned around. Her mother's eyes were narrowed, her face was as hard as rock; no signs of weakness.

"He's really going?"

"We are getting a divorce."

"Why?"

"You don't need to hear the reasons. Get inside."

* * *

SHE MANAGED TO avoid Sebastian for a good number of days, but Friday, when Meche was crossing the street, she felt hands wrap around her waist and Sebastian lifted her, spinning her around.

"Put me down, please?" she demanded.

"Are you going to skip school with me today?" he asked.

"No."

He set her down with a frown.

"Why not?"

Meche looked at her sweater's cuffs, pulling at a little thread and shrugging.

"I don't feel like it."

"I've got a bag of chips and several cans of soda."

"Oh my God, it's my teenage dream," she said, squealing with mock enthusiasm.

"Well, I dunno. You've been mopey all week."

"So an overdose of salt and carbonated beverages will cure me?"

"It's all I've got. Oh, and a record from Hombres G. What do you say?"

She wanted to wallow in private. Plus, if she kept skipping school the principal was going to phone her mom. But then... it might be fun. Meche weighed the negatives against the chance to get a sugar high and ended up sighing.

"Okay."

MECHE AND SEBASTIAN were hanging out in the factory. They lay on the floor, their feet resting against the wall and little bits of potato chips littering the space around them. The sky was purple like a bruise. They would have to light candles if they wanted to remain into the evening.

"My parents are getting a divorce."

Sebastian put down the book he had been reading and turned his head to look at her.

"I didn't know. When did this happen?"

"Few days ago. Just took his clothes and left."

"Why didn't you tell me sooner?" he asked.

"Because if I told you, you'd tell Daniela and then Daniela would bake cupcakes to make me feel better. And if I told her, she'd tell you and we'd end up having a heartfelt discussion about it. Which is totally not what I want. I mean, I don't even know why they're getting divorced."

"But is it serious? Maybe they're just having a fight."

"My mom changed the lock to our apartment so my dad can't get back in."

He stretched a hand and caught a stray chip which had fallen on his shirt, popping it into his mouth.

"What does your dad say?"

"He called yesterday to give me his temporary address and to say he's seeing about a new job in Puerto Vallarta."

"You think he'll get it?"

"I don't know."

Sebastian found another chip, trapped in the cuff of his shirt and held it up, staring at it. He was glad when his parents divorced. Their separation ended his father's beatings, but Meche's dad did not beat her and he was always nice to Sebastian when he went by the apartment.

"The worst part is my mom is getting totally overbearing. Like we couldn't meet at my place today because then she'd flip out."

"Why?" Sebastian asked, frowning.

"Because she's nuts. She has this fixation; thinks you're my 'secret' boyfriend. Right now, she'd probably imagine we are totally making out. It's gross."

Sebastian frowned. "I'm gross?"

"No, you dummy. My mother's bizarre nightmares about teenagers making out are gross."

Sebastian tucked an arm behind his head, deep in thought.

"So what you're saying is making out with me would *not* be gross?"

Meche turned her head and raised an eyebrow at him, with that *come-again-asshole* look she sometimes sported when a random construction worker yelled an inappropriate comment at her.

"Do I need to answer that one?"

"Yeah. Bad question."

*   *   *

EIGHT O'CLOCK and all hell was about to break loose. Since Vicente had moved out, Meche's mother had apparently decided she would quarrel with Meche in what Meche could only imagine was supposed to be a display of motherly concern. It smelled more like bullshit than love.

"You think I'm stupid."

"Is that a rhetorical question?"

Meche's mother looked like her head was about to start spinning like the girl in *The Exorcist*. In Meche's experience backing down would be an admission of guilt. She was not going to be bullied into the guilty square. It was not the 17th century and she was tired of getting the Inquisition treatment.

"You skipped school again and you standing here, a complete liar, in front of me."

Meche crossed her arms and glanced over her mother's shoulder, at the face of Sting on the wall.

"What were you doing?"

"I wasn't doing anything."

"Out with Sebastian Soto again?"

"Oh my God," Meche muttered under her breath.

"Do you two have to meet every single day? You go to school together. Then you spend every moment outside school together. What is going on?"

"Nothing!" Meche yelled. "God, is your life so boring you have to invent this drama to keep you entertained? No wonder dad dumped you!"

The slap came as a bit of a surprise. This was a new level of theatrics. Meche rubbed her cheek, knitting her eyebrows together angrily.

Her mother gave her a long, cold stare and slammed her bedroom door shut. Meche put on the headphones and gritted her teeth.

SEBASTIAN DID NOT understand how Principal Estrada knew they had been behind the public humiliation levied upon her during the school assembly, but she knew. That killer instinct which helped her pounce on teenagers trying to smoke in the bathrooms must have also prepared her to recognize the undeniable stench of a hex. Whatever it was, she was onto them and a confrontation was imminent.

Just after recess on Friday, when Sebastian, Daniela and Meche were preparing to drag their feet to Biology class, Estrada appeared, blocking their way, just like the robot in the bad B-movie from the 50s he had been watching on the TV the night before.

"Mr. Soto, I've had enough of that hair of yours. You are getting a haircut."

"Yeah," he said. "Over the weekend. I promise."

"No, Mr. Soto," the principal said. "Right now."

Estrada grabbed him by the arm and pulled him towards the office. Meche raised her voice in protest.

"You can't do that."

"Watch yourself, Miss Vega, unless you want to be in detention for the rest of the school year."

Estrada walked with quick steps, her heels clicking upon the pavement and down the hallway towards her offices. She told him to sit down and Sebastian just stared at the woman.

"You'd like to be expelled, Mr. Soto?"

He could imagine his mother's face if that happened. She'd have one son who had impregnated his girlfriend and was dropping out of university, plus another one kicked out of school. It would be too terrible to bear. If his father found out… well, that would be an epic beating. Just because his dad didn't live with them anymore didn't mean he wouldn't make a special guest appearance to kick the crap out of Sebastian.

Between the humiliation of the haircut and the dicey outcome at home, he picked humiliation and sat still as Estrada took out a pair of scissors and unceremoniously chopped off his long hair.

"Now people can see your face," Estrada said. Like she'd done him a favour.

Sebastian saw his faint reflection in a glass display case and quietly disagreed.

He hurried out of the principal's office, only to hear Daniela and Meche calling for him. He ignored them and hurried towards the west wall. There he climbed one of the trees, stood on the wall and lowered himself onto the other side.

Sebastian held on to the straps of his backpack and began walking, head down.

"Hey!"

He did not bother looking back nor did he quicken his pace and soon Meche was at his side, brushing leaves from her uniform and glancing at him.

"What are you doing?" she asked. "We've got Bio."

"I don't. I'm going home."

"It doesn't look so bad," she said, sounding like she was about to laugh.

Sebastian stopped. He looked down at her, wanting to kick her.

"Really?" he said. "Because I have the feeling it looks like a donkey chomped on my head."

Meche sighed and stepped on his toes, then stood on her tiptoes in order to reach him. Her fingers brushed his hair.

"You're still cute."

"I think 'still' and 'cute' are incompatible in that sentence."

"Then you're such an ugly motherfucker that no one will notice the difference, so stop crying like a baby," she said, her hand slipping down and away.

Sebastian caught it and frowned.

"You're serious?"

"The baby part or the motherfucker?"

"The cute."

"Not if you're going to get weird about that. Can you let go?"

"Sure."

He released her hand. Meche stepped down and pulled at her sweater's sleeves, hiking them up. Then she took out her Walkman, tugging at the headphones and he spoke quickly, before she could shield herself with songs.

"Thanks. I never thought you thought... I'm... like, okay looking."

"Gee, should I fax you a notice about it? Forget it," she said, looking uncomfortable.

Sebastian nodded. Later, in the factory, Meche played music and he sat on the floor by the couch, one knee drawn up. He watched her as she grabbed some albums, read the liner notes and stood by the record player.

Sebastian pulled himself up and hovered by Meche, feigning an interest in the record she was examining.

"What... which one is this?" he asked.

"Sarah Vaughan. Body and Soul. It's jazz."

"Doesn't ring a bell."

"It never rings a bell for you," she said, chuckling. "Look, you'll know this one. It's Nat King Cole."

Meche knelt down and placed the record on the turntable, dropping the needle. The man's voice was spectacular and it seemed to tickle something in his brain.

"Isn't it from a TV commercial?"

"It's Unforgettable," she said, rolling her eyes. "The day you learn anything about jazz I'll know you've lost it."

"Maybe I will one day. To keep up with you," he said kneeling next to her.

"Start with Fitzgerald."

"Who?"

"Ella Fitzgerald. And then maybe Louis Armstrong. Thelonious Monk. Chet Baker. There are like dozens and dozens of people—"

"It's romantic. This song."

"It was written by Irving Gordon. The arrangement is by Nelson Riddle... you have no idea who I'm talking about."

"No."

"I can put something else on."

"I like it," he whispered.

Nevertheless, she heard him, her head turning slightly towards him. Meche's hands were resting on her lap and he stretched his fingers to clutch one of them. Meche let him hold it for maybe a second before she scooted forward and pulled the needle up.

"I don't think it's a day for Mr. Cole," she said very seriously.

VICENTE VEGA HAD fucked up again. With the profits from his investment, Vicente had planned to quit his job at the radio station and dedicate himself full-time to his book, which was bound to become a bestseller once he could find the right publisher.

Now he was back to square one. In truth, he had never even left square one.

He smoked his cigarette and sat in the bar, nursing a double scotch, with his notebook in front of him. He'd been writing song lyrics but they wouldn't come right, so he'd decided to have one drink. That had turned into two and now he was on the sixth.

A couple more and he'd be ready to shuffle back to his apartment. A couple more and he could start smiling at the songs playing inside the joint. A couple more and he could whistle a tune as he walked out.

It was going to be better. One day. Soon.

Mexico City, 2009

MECHE BLINKED AND raised her hand. Sunlight slipped through the curtains, sneaking through her parted fingers as she shielded her face. She turned around and frowned. It was a narrow bed and long-limbed Sebastian was taking up most of the space.

She slipped on her t-shirt, running quickly towards the kitchen. She decided to make tea.

The kettle whistled and Meche poured the hot water into a cup. She sat on the counter and tilted her head, looking at the cheap calendar on the wall, the kind one gets from a grocer every year. It read May 2009 and had a sappy picture of puppies. Her father had forgotten to change the month—or had not been bothered enough to do it.

What would Mr. Vega have said about this development? He would have laughed, no doubt. Her father had a sick sense of humour and he would have found some pleasure in her embarrassment. He might even have pointed out that they shared a genetic code and thus a proclivity to make really bad choices; to fuck people they shouldn't fuck, and fuck themselves into a corner.

She had always considered herself a bit more level-headed, at least since she'd grown up.

Turns out she was wrong.

"Awesome," Meche muttered.

She wish she had music. Her iPod was in the bedroom but she was reluctant to fetch it. She decided to think about songs, go over lyrics in her head. Love Will Tear Us Apart was the first thing she could conjure. No, not *that*. Jazz, that old friend, would do. Sebastian interrupted her before she had even reached the third line of "How High The Moon."

"You always get up so early?"

Meche did not look at him, finding the puppies a good focal point.

"I usually get up around noon," she said. "I code at nights and wake up late."

"And then you don't have breakfast."

"Breakfast in Norway is pickled beets and sweet pickles and *Gammelost*. Maybe *fårepølse*. I've never been able to get into it."

He stood in front of her, shirtless, and Meche blushed even though she was far too old to be blushing.

"I can't believe how short your hair is," he said, raising a hand to touch it.

"I'm sorry, this is too weird," she said, jumping down from the counter and evading his touch.

"What?"

"I've never seen you naked."

"You have now."

"That is not... yeah, that's why it's weird. We never had a *thing*. It wasn't like that."

"Of course not. I was too dumb. I barely even kissed you that one time."

"Sorry. I can't talk without my trousers," Meche said. "It's freaking me out."

She marched back into the bedroom and scooped up her jeans, buttoning them and wondering if she shouldn't have just run out of the apartment when she woke up. It might have avoided this very awkward conversation.

"Shoes," she whispered, looking under the bed. Where the hell had they gone? "Okay, yeah, explain that to me."

Meche knelt next to the bed and set her hands upon the sheets, frowning and looking in Sebastian's direction.

"Why are you suddenly developing this bizarre passion for me?" she asked. "You were not even into me."

Sebastian lay on the bed and placed his hands behind his head, looking at the ceiling.

"You think so?"

"Absolutely. I mean, you had a thing for Isadora Galván."

"I did."

Meche tilted her head and smirked. "So is this like a stamp collection or something? Diddle all your ex-classmates and you get a prize?"

"No. I didn't understand back then, what you meant to me. I assumed I could find the same easy feeling with many other people. But time passed, people passed and it was never quite the same. Then the other day I was walking to my mom's place and I saw you across the street. It all just... hit me. I haven't been able to stop feeling... I've felt things I haven't felt in ages. It's all because of you. I was so alive when I was with you. It was like... like it even hurt."

"Sounds like a book I read," she said. "It was shelved under 'sappy.'"

"You didn't feel like that about me?"

He looked at her with dark, steady eyes. Meche had to avert her gaze, sitting cautiously onto the mattress.

She remembered being a teenager, being near Sebastian, very clearly. It had been thrilling. Every single morning, walking at his side to school, their shoes dipping into puddles, their easy smiles and the easier banter. Oh, she had been so in love with him and not in the 'sappy' way. Not the crush a teenager has for a handsome boy, like Constantino. She loved him absolutely and if she never kissed him then—*really* kissed him, not whatever microsecond of a kiss they had shared—never made him her lover, it was because they had already touched more deeply than any youthful caress.

"Maybe. It was a while ago."

"How long have you waited for someone?"

"Oh come on, you got married," Meche said, flipping on her stomach and pressing her chin against the back of her hand. "You probably had two dozen girlfriends after that. You weren't waiting for nothing."

"I have been waiting for something, always without knowing it."

He peered at her from beneath thick eyebrows and Meche half-smiled because maybe—just maybe, this was no admission—she had walked the streets of Paris once-upon-a-time expecting to stumble onto *somebody*. Maybe she sat by the river and read her map and wondered if *someone* would turn a corner and appear there.

"God, the way you talk," she said, trying to rub the half-smile off her face. "You didn't spew those lines when we were young."

He'd seen it though, recognized her mirth, and was now giving her a sly look.

"An improvement or a drawback?"

"Did you ever visit Europe?" she asked, changing the topic because she would have liked him even if he couldn't string two words together and she wasn't about to tell him that.

"No," he said. "Something always got in the way."

"Even though you could afford it by now?"

"Maybe I was afraid I wouldn't find you. Or I would and it would be different."

She chuckled and he shifted, looking down at her.

"What's funny?"

"I have no idea," Meche said.

There was a scar on his left hand which had not been there before, a long gash which went up his arm.

"What happened?"

"Car accident," he said. "Three years ago."

Meche stretched out a hand, touching his brow, a tiny little line there.

"And that one?"

"Someone cracked a bottle open on my head."

"Really?"

"It was a wild 1999."

He stretched his hand down her leg and tugged at the denim, exposing her tattoo. It was a sentence, circling the ankle.

"'A kingdom for a stage, princes to act,'" he read. "Someone finally read Shakespeare."

Just so I could come back at you when you called me illiterate, she thought and that sounded too much like admitting he'd had some huge influence on her life. Which was not the case. Not really.

"Drunk in Amsterdam, 2000. It seemed like a good idea at the time. At least it's not a Looney Tunes character or some Chinese character I can't read." She glanced at him. "No tattoos?"

"No tattoos and no piercings."

"What kind of damn punk were you?" she asked moving closer to him and he shifted a bit too, closing the gap between them.

"A very low-key punk."

"Your shirts look expensive."

"Some are. Still with the t-shirts?"

"Can't wean myself off them," she said looking down at the one she was wearing. Abba. "My defense is it's vintage-chic."

"That's not chic. They do fit better than they used to though."

"Yeah, well, bras help."

"Do you keep a bag-lady jacket in your closet?" he asked.

"That was an awesome jacket," she said.

"No. It was god-awful."

"You drew on your shoes."

"I still doodle. Not on my shoes. You should come to my place and look at some of my drawings."

Meche scoffed. "That's such a cheap come-on."

"I can try something better."

Meche touched his clavicle, curious. It just looked so sharp and chiseled. He was still very thin, although now there was some strength. Sebastian caught her hand and held it, kissing her lightly.

"I think you're lovely," he said.

"That's still a cheap come-on."

"It's true."

Meche lapsed into silence, pondering, glancing at the palm trees and the flamingoes on the curtains.

"I have a lot of organizing," she said. "I assume you have that job you need to show up for. Mr. Creative Director."

"Not until nine."

"What time is it?"

"Six. Do you want to have breakfast with me? Even though you don't do breakfast?"

No, she thought. *What's the point of that?*

"I should shower," she said, which was not exactly what she had been intending to say.

"Ah," he said, kissing her shoulder. "Not yet."

*   *   *

MECHE LOOKED AT the grapefruit, sinking her spoon into it, toying with the pulpy interior and wondering at what point she had lost her mind and whether she was going to get it back soon.

Breakfast with Sebastian Soto. Not only that, breakfast with Sebastian Soto after she'd had sex with him. Twice. As if to make a point that mistakes were better performed in pairs.

In for a pound, she thought.

"Time?" she asked, twisting his hand, trying to get a look at his wristwatch.

"We have time enough."

"You said you had work later."

"I'll worry about work."

He caught her fingers, turned her hand up to look at her palm and smiled.

"It's good to have you back," he said.

The smile stabbed her hard. Meche wished she could slink under the table and stay there for about a decade.

"Hey, since we missed the movie we could go to listen to some live music. Jazz in Coyoacán. It's a small joint. Well, it's really a house and they can only fit like twenty people, but it's good."

She had a vague idea of what a jazz club with Sebastian would look like, a pleasant, blurry sort of image, as seen through a black and white lens. Like the cover of a really nice record. Now who was being sappy?

Meche shook her head.

"I'm flying to Oslo in a few days," she reminded him. "I'd also like to point out this doesn't negate my previous opinion of you."

"You still hate me," he said, digging into his green *chilaquiles* with gusto. "You still hold a grudge against me."

"Essentially, yes."

"Even though you had sex with me."

God, who cared? Meche tossed three sugar cubes into her cup of tea and raised her shoulders slowly.

"Please. It's not some secret promise. We don't have to be," she raised her fingers, turning them into imaginary quotes marks, "'really, really in love to go all the way.' Last time I checked we weren't exactly blushing virgins. We're grownups and grownups do stupid things."

She drew some pleasure from his expression, as though she'd just doused him with a bucket of cold water. He'd started this. It was his fault. What had he expected, anyway?

"Thank you," he said tersely, "for classifying me as a stupid thing."

"Are you going to get majorly offended?"

"No, I'm not going to get," he raised his hands, now making the imaginary quote marks for himself, "'majorly offended.'"

Meche added another sugar cube for good measure and took a sip, then scooped out some grapefruit.

"This is exactly why I didn't want to talk to you. I knew you'd be all melodramatic."

"Me? Melodramatic?"

"What do you call this? 'How long have you waited for someone?' *Pfff*. I make one mistake fuck and I've got damn Romeo at my doorstep."

"Forget it."

He grabbed his fork, busied himself with the *chilaquiles*. Suddenly, he put the fork down and took out his wallet, pulling out several bills and placing them neatly under his glass.

"Here. That should cover it," he said.

"What? You're leaving?"

"Yes. Phone my cell if you want to see me again. If you don't, I'll just be majorly offended at my place, alright?"

Meche scoffed and crossed her arms. "I don't have your cellphone number."

"Then you are going to have to work for it," he said.

Sebastian leaned down next to her chair, to speak into her ear.

"I'm in love with you. There. Should have said it twenty years ago. Your move."

She watched him walk away and she had a feeling like when they made a house of cards one time and Meche pulled one card and the whole thing came tumbling down.

Meche plunged the spoon into the heart of the grapefruit and pushed her plate away. This was just... insane.

"I hate breakfast," she told the grapefruit.

*   *   *

"WHAT'S UP WITH you?" her mother asked.

Meche was laying on the couch, listening to Wild is the Wind. She shrugged.

"Nothing," she said, her voice clipped.

"It looks like something."

"I'm overdosing on Nina Simone."

"Your dad used to do that."

Meche rubbed her eyes. She turned her head. Her mother was still standing in the living room, holding a cup, as though she were expecting to continue the conversation.

"Why didn't you like him?"

"Who?"

"Sebastian. When we were kids, you were always all over his case. And don't say you liked him. That's a lie."

Her mother smiled, setting her cup on the coffee table. She nodded.

"You loved him too much."

Meche looked at her in surprise. She didn't say anything, tucking her chin down and frowning.

"You love somebody that much, one day it all unravels and... it's just bad. Here, I made tea."

"Mom, you don't have to keep making stuff for me all day long."

"That's what I'm supposed to do. I'm your mother."

"Yeah, yeah," Meche said, reaching for the cup and taking a little sip. "It has no sugar."

"It won't kill you to have a cup without sugar."

"I like sugar. I should go back to dad's apartment and finish with the boxes. I'm practically done."

"Finish your tea."

Her mother got up and moved towards the kitchen.

Meche stretched her legs and listened to the music. Nina Simone sang Where Can I Go Without You.

Mexico City, 1989

Isadora chewed her nails. It was a bad habit she could not kick. He thought it was cute. It made her flawed and consequently human.

"I think you chew your nails in class because you smoke. It's a compensation mechanism."

She offered him a drag, but he declined. She smiled a little.

"Have you been reading our biology textbook or something?"

"Something," he said.

"Why is it that you don't smoke but you agree to come here with me?" she asked.

"You asked."

Three times. She had asked him three times that month and he had agreed. Normally he walked after school with Meche but he had made an exception for Isadora and walked her to the Pit instead. He didn't know why she asked and he didn't really want to know because most likely it was pity or sick amusement.

"Would you like to go to the movies with me tonight?" she asked.

"Sure. What time are you guys getting there?"

"I was thinking we might go alone."

They had never been together without her friends. He wondered what could possibly inspire her to go out with him by herself as though... as though it were a date.

"Hey, Isa."

Sebastian turned his head. Constantino, along with some of the other boys, was standing on the sidewalk, giving him a very ugly look.

"You coming with us or not?" Constantino asked.

"Gotta go," Isadora said. "Meet me at seven?"

"That works."

"Alright."

"Isa, what the hell? Get your ass here!"

"Coming," Isadora said, dropping the cigarette and stepping on it with the heel of her shoe.

She hurried off with them and Sebastian stood alone, in the middle of the empty lot, heart hammering in his chest.

ISADORA'S DRIVER DROPPED her off right on time in front of the movie theatre. Sebastian watched as she crossed the street, short purple skirt, matching purse and tall boots, looking so very beautiful. There was no reason why she should be hanging out with him. No reason at all. It was a mistake. Pretty girls never looked at him. Hell, no girls looked at him. He was swarthy, which was enough to put off most of his classmates who hungered for the paler boys. He was too tall and odd. When he spoke the words came out wrong.

He watched the movie and ate his popcorn and tried hard to have a good time, but something was off. When the movie was over and they were standing outside, waiting for Isadora's cab to arrive, he dared to speak up.

"Why are you asking me to hang out with you?"

Isadora clutched her purse with both hands and looked down.

"Well, well. So you did go out after all."

Constantino. Sebastian turned around. The boy was there with his buddies in tow, all five of them dressed exactly the same: sweaters tied around the shoulders, polo shirts, even the same haircut.

"Hi," Isadora said. "I thought you weren't in the mood for the movies."

"I wasn't. I just wanted to see if you'd be with him," Constantino pointed a finger at Sebastian. "Why are you sniffing around my girlfriend? Do you have a death wish?"

"I'm not sniffing around anything," Sebastian said. "Besides, she's not your girlfriend."

"Fuck you."

Sebastian dodged Constantino's punch and managed to land one of his own, right in the middle of the bastard's face. Big mistake. This infuriated Constantino, who began yelling obscenities, telling his friends to get him, kick the crap out of him, teach him a lesson. Sebastian had heard that tune before. He did what any rational person would do in this situation—he ran.

He managed to sprint for several blocks before someone tackled him to the ground, flipped him around and punched him in the stomach, making Sebastian gag. Another punch, this one to the ribs. Then it was all kicks. Sebastian rolled, tried to find purchase on a wall and pull himself up, but he was summarily beaten with something—it might have been an empty beer bottle—and stumbled down again, next to a lamp post. He touched the back of his head. It felt damp and he was dizzy.

"Stop it!" Isadora yelled.

She had followed them. Sebastian felt even worse now, knowing she was witnessing the whole spectacle. There was nothing like a good beating with a side of humiliation.

"Please, stop! No more!"

Nobody listened to her. The boys laughed and continued kicking him. Sebastian raised his hands trying to shield his face. He swallowed blood.

The boys paused and Sebastian was able to stand up. He did not know if they were done with him or if they had just paused for a breather. He was not about to find out. Sebastian limped away.

He heard them when he turned the corner, coming his way. Ready for more fun.

A street musician was playing the guitar nearby. Sebastian concentrated on the melody, his eyes fixed on the hands plucking the strings and he changed his face, his shape. Glamour—just like they'd been practising.

When the boys ran by they saw a stooped, old man resting next to a wall and ignored him. A few seconds later, Sebastian sighed and the tattered illusion he had constructed shattered.

He slid down to the ground, curled up on the sidewalk. People who walked by him took him for a drunk or a street kid.

A couple of hours later, Sebastian opened his eyes, got unsteadily to his feet and began walking home.

*　　*　　*

Meche sat with her grandmother, sorting scraps of yarn into balls. Her grandmother did not believe in wasting anything and the collected little bits of yarn would be used for new projects.

The needles clicked and Meche set the balls from largest to smallest, then arranged them by colour. She'd done this since she was a child and it was kind of fun, especially if she could play some good music in the background and get her grandmother to tell stories.

"Some witches can cut their chests with sharp blades and will not bleed. Others can summon invisible spirits. And then there are those who can fascinate animals with their gaze."

"I'd prefer to fascinate people with my gaze," Meche replied.

"You might be able to do that too," her grandmother said.

Meche placed the balls of yarn in a big bowl and set it down on the floor.

"Grandma, did you ever cast a spell?"

"You keep asking that."

"I want to know."

"I might have tried, once or twice."

"Did it work?"

"It was such a long time ago."

"What did you try?"

"I tried to be invisible."

"How did you do it?"

"That would be telling, wouldn't it?"

"Please."

"Alright. I knitted a blanket, dark as night, and wore it around me. It made me... disappear. Of course, I wouldn't be able to do that anymore." She paused to look at the cover she was knitting. "My eyes are not what they used to be. Anyway, magic is for the young."

"Maybe you could try again," Meche said. "I could help you."

"You don't like to knit."

"I *would* knit a magic blanket."

"The only problem is I don't stitch spells anymore."

"Why not?"

"I hurt people, once."

"Did they deserve to be hurt?"

Grandmother touched Meche's chin. "Don't they always, when you're a girl?"

Meche thought some people deserved a taste of their own medicine and she didn't see why anyone would stop using spells when they could be so much fun. Why let go of the power? She sure as hell wouldn't.

"Oh, come on. Show me one spell."

Her grandmother smiled and set her needles down. "I'm tired, Meche."

She stood up, stumbling. Meche helped steady her.

"Are you alright, grandma?"

"I'm tired," she said, patting Meche's shoulder. "I'm just tired."

SEBASTIAN STUMBLED INTO his apartment. His body ached something awful and the coppery taste of blood lingered in his mouth.

The door to his bedroom was closed. By the noises filtering out, his brother was with a girl. He wanted to get out of the dirty, stained clothes he was wearing. Sebastian knocked, pressing his forehead against the door.

"Go away," came Romualdo's reply.

"I need to come in."

"Go the fuck away."

Something snapped in Sebastian. Furious, he kicked the door and it slammed open. A naked girl he didn't know squealed, pulling the covers over herself. Romualdo glared at him.

"What the hell?! What are you doing, barging in…"

Sebastian pulled a duffel bag from under his bed and dumped some clothes in it. When Romualdo stalked towards him, Sebastian stretched up his whole length—which was considerable—and looked his brother in the eye. Romualdo took two steps back and Sebastian returned to the duffel bag, tossing in two books and zipping it closed.

He stopped to look at himself in the bathroom mirror. His left eye was very bruised. It would be purple, swollen, awful in the morning. Caked blood dirtied his collar. He opened the faucet and drank from it, spitting out blood. He washed his face and his hands, took off the soiled clothes and looked at the bruises on his chest.

He changed into dark jeans and a dark shirt, put on a clean jacket and hurried out the door. He strapped the bag to the motorcycle and went to the corner, tossing a couple of coins into the payphone.

Meche answered at the fifth ring.

"Yes?"

"Meche, be downstairs."

"You're coming over? Now? It's nearly midnight."

"Be there."

He hung up and by the time he parked his bike across the street from her building, Meche was standing outside, arms crossed and wearing a large grey sweater. She looked annoyed, but as he walked closer her expression changed.

"What happened to you?" she asked. "Did you have an accident?"

"Constantino and his friends beat me up."

"Why?"

"Because I went out with Isadora tonight."

"What the hell? What are you going to do?"

He knew what he wanted. No trouble coming up with a picture. It was black on white, very simple.

"Get on the bike. We're going."

"My mom's not going to let me go for a ride at this time of the night, I—"

"No, I mean go as in *go*."

"What?"

"Run away with me."

MECHE TRIED TO process the four words properly, but they were too daunting. *Run away with me.*

"Let's go to Europe together," he said. "Let's see the Arctic circle."

"Okay, unless you have a super-duper motorcycle that can float all the way to…"

"That's not what I mean."

"What do you mean? You're freaking me out."

Sebastian leaned down, grabbing her hands between his and pulling her up, so she had to stand on her tiptoes to look at his face.

"I hate this place. I hate this neighbourhood. I hate the kids here. I hate the school. I hate the view from my apartment window. You hate it too. What are we waiting for? Let's run away together."

Meche had never seriously considered running away. That's the kind of stuff people did in the movies, like joining the circus. It didn't happen in real life. Meche didn't want to go. She didn't like high school much but there was her dad, mom, grandma. The records and the computer sitting in the living room. Daniela. Her room with the posters of several bands and the narrow bed. She feared abandoning all that.

"Sebastian, that's silly," she whispered.

"Meche, you said you'd never leave me."

"Come on."

His hands clutched her own together and he pulled her forward, her knuckles brushing his chest.

"Come with me."

Meche wondered what was his plan was. Would they just get off in some other city when they ran out of gas? Then, what? What were two teenagers supposed to do to survive? Beg for a coin, wash car windows at the stoplight, sell bubble gum to the drivers? Meche had seen street kids. She didn't hold any wild dreams that somehow they'd make it to Paris whole, get a garret with a view of the Seine and Sebastian could be a bohemian writer while Meche coded some awesome bit of software which made them millionaires. That was the kind of shit to be found in one of Daniela's novels. Shit which never happens because when teenagers run away they end up living in some abandoned hovel which smells of piss, prostituting themselves to make ends meet.

"We can cast a spell. We can get the money. We can do it."

Meche opened her mouth. His face had the kind of need she had never seen in another human being and there was a hunger there she did not understand.

She was fifteen. The intensity of him, of this moment, caught her unprepared. She felt that if she went with Sebastian he'd steal a deep part of her. She would change and she feared this. She feared him, feared what it might mean.

"I am—"

"No," she said jumping back. "No way."

Sebastian didn't believe her. For a long minute he smiled, confident, believing she was just joking. She would laugh soon and tell him of course she was going. His smile died as she backed away, towards the entrance of the building.

He walked back to his motorcycle and jumped on it before turning to look at her.

The look he gave her turned Meche to stone. His face was splintered with pain. He looked ahead and Meche raised her hands, thinking of stopping him, thinking—

Too late. The motorcycle sped away and she walked back into her building.

SEBASTIAN STOOD OUTSIDE his apartment building, counting the beats of his heart.

How stupid of him. Idiotic. To think he would do something as silly, and Meche, that she might—

He leaned over the motorcycle, thinking he was about to cry.

"Sebastian?"

He looked up and saw Isadora stepping out of a car, pressing her hands against her mouth. Her driver gave him an indifferent glance, as though he were a stain on the ground.

"I'm so sorry about what happened," she said.

"What are you doing here?" he muttered.

"I was very worried."

"I'm alright."

Isadora walked to his side, squeezing his arm. "He's a brute," she whispered. "Oh, I truly am sorry."

"No broken bones," he said, wincing. "Just bruises."

"I should get you to a doctor."

"I'm fine. Really. I just need some sleep."

They were both quiet.

Her hand rose and settled on his cheek. She kissed him there and Sebastian couldn't help smiling, despite everything.

"You're very brave," she said. "Again, I'm sorry. I'll see you at school, alright?"

"Sure."

She slipped back into the car and waved at him.

The car rolled away and Sebastian stood in the middle of the street, hands in his pockets. He waited there for about ten minutes thinking perhaps Meche might come around.

She did not.

Sebastian took a deep breath and saw the moon hiding, skittish behind a cloud. He shook his head and decided to call it a night, erasing the faint path she had traced in his mind.

TWO DAYS LATER she offered him revenge with the same casual tone a vendor at the *tianguis* might offer to discount you a bunch of rotting bananas.

He had not talked to her about the incident. Her refusal stung, the look on her face had torn him apart. There were so many things he wanted to tell her and knew very well he shouldn't. So he kept his mouth shut.

"We should hex the guys who beat you," Meche said, licking a chilli lollipop. "Make them pay for what happened."

It was a cheap trick to buy his sympathy or a blatant misinterpretation of his emotions. Either way, it showed she did not understand him at all.

"Why?"

"They deserve it."

"It wouldn't fix anything."

"Well, we could at least heal your wounds."

"The exterior ones don't matter."

"You are so lame sometimes."

"Most of the times," he corrected her.

"Why, if some boys beat you to a bloody pulp, wouldn't you beat them back? Why—"

"Because they don't matter," he snapped at her.

"You're a pussy."

"Yeah, and I'm gay too, no? 'Sebastian Soto, el Joto', right? Thanks. Many thanks."

Meche gave her lollipop a final lick and tossed it away, raising a petulant eyebrow at him. No doubt she thought herself very smart, very talented, because of the spells. Superior to him in every way because he was a coward who wouldn't respond to fire with fire.

"If life offers you something, you should take it," she said. "Life's offering you a chance to get even."

"Take it, huh?"

"Yeah."

"I'll remember next time."

He'd show her one day... yeah.

They did not say anything else the rest of the way home.

Mexico City, 2009

SOMEWHERE BETWEEN THREE and four a.m. Meche rose from her bed and walked across the room, staring at a wall where there used to be a poster of The Police. It had come down many years before but the wall still bore its outline, the marks of yellowed tape showing where it had been.

This, she thought, *is the real meaning of a haunting.*

She grabbed her father's manuscript and went into the kitchen. She made tea and put her earbuds in, idly turning the pages as she took little sips. She ought to read it. Ought to go through the whole thing and yet—

She kept getting distracted.

Around nine in the morning she phoned Daniela.

"Hey," Meche said. "Today is the last night of the *novena*. I was wondering if you're coming over."

"You've had a change of heart?"

"I'm leaving soon. I'd like to say goodbye to you."

"Sure. I'll be there."

"Um… Sebastian can come too."

"Do you want to see him?"

Meche ran a finger down the page, frowning. Yes. No. Both.

"Just tell him it'll be okay if he comes over."

"I can give you his phone number. You can phone him yourself."

"No, it's fine. I have some stuff to do now. See you."

Meche pressed her forehead against the table, slowly straightening up.

*   *   *

GENTRIFICATION HAD SWEPT through the *colonia* but it had left the factory intact. There was a sign announcing the upcoming construction of an apartment building in its place, but the factory still stood for now. Still ruinous, the outside now sprayed with all kinds of graffiti.

Meche looked at it, looming over her like a strange stone idol. Their usual entry point had been half-heartedly boarded up, and she pulled the plywood apart easily. She slid in, dragging the portable record player with her.

The interior of the factory—definitely no designer's wet dream in her younger days—had become even more of an eyesore. Rusted pipes, peeling walls, debris, bits of glass, all these were familiar sights, but twenty years had made the decay more prominent.

Meche climbed the stairs, creating echoes as she moved.

The door to their room was open.

Meche paused before it, holding her breath, and walked in.

It was empty. Disappointment hit her like a wave. She did not know what she had expected to find, but it wasn't there.

Someone had stolen the couch and the tables. All the posters—the great musical collage she had created—had been taken away.

She moved towards the circular window and looked outside. The neighborhood had changed, but the light filtering through the window still had the same spectral quality and the view was hazy, as though the city were shrouded in mist.

Meche put the record player down in the centre of the room and walked back towards the door, closing it. She smirked, realizing that one poster had been left in place, taped onto the back of the door: Jim Morrison.

Meche took out the bottle of Coke and the records. She took a sip of the sugary soft drink, smacked her lips and placed Time After Time on the player, hesitating before letting the needle touch the vinyl.

She pulled out her dad's manuscript and began reading the whole thing. Twenty years too late but better late than never.

THE AIR SMELLED of rain and thunder. Meche had no umbrella. She eyed the clouds with a quirked eyebrow, wondering if they were plotting to unleash a storm upon her. Her father's restless spirit might be preparing to teach her a lesson. But if he had not haunted his apartment, he probably wouldn't bother with the cemetery.

Meche looked at the grave marker and the wilting flowers.

"Here you are," she muttered. "You left your apartment and your life a mess, you know that?"

Meche turned her head and looked at the rows of tombstones, feeling a bit uncomfortable. She did not know exactly what she was doing there, with a record and a bunch of flowers under her arm. Maybe she was there because he *hadn't* haunted his old place. Stumbling onto his semi-transparent figure might have connected the dots floating in her head. Her father's book, his letters and records had taught her only one thing: she hadn't known him very well. Hell, she'd had done such a good job of forgetting him, she scarcely remembered him.

"I was looking in the mirror the other day and I realized I look a lot like you. I think I *am* a lot like you. Which is very unsettling, to say the least.

"I've missed you. And... I'm in a bit of a pickle right now. It's not the kind of stuff I can talk about with mom or Jimena, so, I suppose I'll tell you."

Meche smiled, her mouth trembling.

"There's something incredibly stupid I want to do. The problem is... well, it's stupid. I can imagine what you'd say about that, "Hey, just do it!" But it's not that easy. What if..."

Meche trailed off. She cringed and shook her head.

"Anyway, I've... I've brought you something. Here are some flowers," she said, putting the bouquet down. "And this is for you."

She placed the record next to the flowers.

"Gracias a la Vida," she said. "You never told me how you came up with my name. I should have figured it out."

Meche leaned down, touching the gravestone with the tip of her fingers.

"Bye, dad."

Mexico City, 1989

"I'M SO SORRY," Isadora said.

They were back at the Pit. They had not exchanged a word in a couple of weeks, but she'd approached him after school that afternoon and he had followed her there.

Sebastian pushed an empty glass bottle with his foot. Back and forth. Back and forth until he gave it a good kick and it went rattling into some bushes.

"It wasn't your fault."

"But it was. I... I've been asking you to hang out with me to piss Constantino off. It started at my birthday party. We were fighting and then he went to dance with your friend and I thought I'd get back at him by going to that posada, and then I've just..."

"Kept it up," Sebastian said helpfully.

"Yeah," Isadora admitted. "He says he wants to get back together with me but he goes after all these other girls... I just wanted to make him jealous. Give him a taste of his own medicine."

"So are you?"

"Am I what?" Isadora asked.

"Getting back together with him."

Isadora pulled out a cigarette and her lighter. She shook her head as she lit the cigarette.

"I'm not sure."

"Pardon me if I say he's an asshole."

"I know," Isadora muttered. "I know."

"I suppose this means I won't see much of you anymore."

Isadora did not answer. Sebastian slid his hands into his pockets.

Of course. What else could he have expected?

"I shouldn't have asked you to go with me," Isadora said.

"It wasn't your fault. You couldn't know."

"I still feel awful."

"Water under the bridge," he said. "I'd still like to show you the factory sometime."

"The what?"

"It's a place where we hang out. It's no big deal if you don't want to go. Or you, know, speak to me again."

Sebastian bit his lip and stepped forward.

"If... if you still feel like talking to me and if you feel like it, maybe you can take a ride with me some time and we can go there. We've made it nice inside and... um... it's just a good place. A safe place."

"You're very nice."

"But?"

"But what?"

"There has to be a but."

Isadora chuckled. "There is no but."

SEBASTIAN AND MECHE sat in her dining room, doing their homework. The stereo played Botellita de Jerez as they scratched their answers across the notebook. He tapped his foot to the music. Fast, fast, fast.

"You know what the problem is?" she asked.

Sebastian paused mid-equation and looked at Meche.

"We're trying to copy people we don't know."

"What are you talking about?"

"The glamour."

Sebastian, caught off-guard, simply blinked at her. Meche sighed.

"I'm talking about the spells. I think we are failing because we are picking people out of magazines instead of real people."

"I thought we were doing homework."

"Do you think the Mulata de Cordoba went, 'Oh, it's homework time now, I can't think about spells?'"

"The Mulata lived in a time when there was no homework," Sebastian replied. "Besides, she was caught by the Spanish Inquisition.

Have you actually been reading history books?"

"Myths and legends," Meche corrected him. "I'm reading everything I can about magic. Someone needs to be the research and development arm of this corporation. Anyway, what we need is to copy a real person. Once we've mastered that we can probably try some sympathetic magic, steal a bit of hair and all."

"Hair? OK, Jesus, can I finish this homework before we start talking about this stuff? It's due tomorrow."

"Okay, look. I've been toying with something," Meche said.

She stood up, found a record and put it on. Sebastian was not familiar with the song. Something smooth and jazzy. The singer crooned, "I'm a fool to want you," and Meche sat down again.

She reached across the table and placed a hand on top of his own, then placed the other against her face, covering her features. She slid her fingers down revealing a pair of eyes, a nose, a mouth—a face that was not her own.

It was a crude copy, to be sure. It looked like a rubber mask and it did not resemble Isadora as much as caricaturize her, but there was some clear effort and talent put into it.

"Make it go away," he said.

"Wait," Meche said, her hand upon his own, concentrating.

The mask seemed to grow snugger. It fit better. It lost most of its rubbery quality and the skin now had pores. The eyes were the right colour instead of an unusual, artificial shade. Eyelashes grew where there had been none and the lips moistened.

She was close now. Very close.

Isadora smiled.

Sebastian jumped up in his seat.

"Stop it," he said.

"It's good, isn't it? I think we can do much better."

"Stop."

She shrugged and shook her head. Isadora's face chipped and cracked and fell, revealing Meche's real features.

"Why did you do that?" he asked. "Why did you have to imitate her?"

"Why not?"

"You are cruel," he said.

He gathered his notebook, his pencils and pens. Meche watched as he tossed the stuff in his bag.

"You're going?" she asked.

"Yes, I'm going," he said. "You think I should stay and let you torture me a little longer?"

"I thought you'd appreciate it. Maybe laugh."

"It's not funny."'

"Aw. Come on. You're not in loooove with her are you?" Meche asked in her patented mocking tone.

Sebastian did not bother answering. Any answer he gave would be the subject of much snickering. He did not have the stomach for Meche's japes that afternoon.

"You're not serious about her, are you?" Meche asked dryly.

"What does it matter?" he replied.

"I'm just asking."

"She's nice, alright?"

Sebastian zipped his bag closed.

"You go with her to the movies a lot."

"We've gone a few times. And the last time was a disaster."

"You don't ask me and Daniela to the movies anymore."

"Do you want to go see a movie with me? Damn it, I'll take you next weekend."

"Forget it."

"No, I mean it. You wanted to look at some records, no? We'll watch a movie after that, you and me."

"I'm not your fucking charity case. Piss off."

She headed to her room, abandoning him in the middle of the dining room. Sebastian cursed in Catalán and followed her.

It was always like this with Meche. She was like a cat, sometimes purring and letting herself be petted, the next showing her claws and biting your hand. She could never, ever, make it easy for anyone. Sebastian did not understand why everything had to be a battlefield with her, but it was.

"I didn't say you were. What's your problem?" he asked, holding the door when she tried to slam it shut.

Meche sat on her bed, crossing her arms and staring at a poster of Blondie.

"If you have better things to do, go and do them," she said.

"I have nothing better to do," he replied.

"Yeah, well it seems—"

He sat next to Meche and held her hand. They laced their fingers together and looked at the poster.

"Movie, then?" he asked.

"Records Saturday. Movie Sunday."

"Fine."

"Fine."

"You annoy me."

"Same."

Meche rested her chin against his shoulder with a sigh.

MECHE DID NOT know what to think about Sebastian lately. She watched him as they rode the subway, on the way to the record store where they would meet Daniela, and thought he was turning into a stranger. He was just not himself. With Isadora this and Isadora that. He never seemed interested in the magic anymore and he sure as hell did not seem interested in spending time with them as much as he did before. He was drifting away from her.

You did this, said a nagging little voice inside Meche's head. *You hurt him and it's not the same.*

Well, she couldn't possibly have run away with him. That would have been idiotic. Who did that kind of thing?

Clearly he did. And clearly she was too chicken to follow him.

She did not want to think about it and, so, pumped up the Walkman's volume, drowning her thoughts with the voice of Joan Manuel Serrat, singing about a man who falls in love with a store mannequin.

They arrived at quarter to eleven, a little after they had agreed. Daniela was already there and greeted them with a big smile, a Timbiriche album under her arm, constant reminder of her lack of musical taste.

It was a small store. The walls were adorned with albums and the ceiling was plastered with posters advertising a number of music acts. The back wall was dominated by a huge, floor-to-ceiling image of Jimi Hendrix.

While Sebastian and Daniela riffled through the cassettes and records at the front, she felt herself drawn to the back, as though she were following an invisible trail.

"Hey Meche, what do you say…"

She ignored Daniela. Meche walked with sure footsteps. Her hands tingled, growing warmer. When she reached the back of the store they were sweating. She drifted towards the third bin to the left. Her fingers danced over the record sleeves, brushing them aside until she touched one which burned like a coal.

She held it up, her mouth opening a little.

Her hands trembled. It was A Whiter Shade of Pale.

"Hey, you found it!" Daniela chirped behind her, looking over her shoulder.

"Found what?" Sebastian asked.

Meche pressed the record against her chest.

Nothing, she was going to say.

"The record for the spell," Daniela said.

Meche closed her eyes, mouthing a curse. Daniela! She couldn't keep her mouth shut.

"What?"

"Just an experiment I'm running. I mentioned it before."

Meche turned around and faked a bored look at Sebastian, trying to downplay the importance of her discovery.

"Like?" Sebastian asked cautiously.

"I think I can use this record to cast a special spell. Of course, it's far-fetched, but—"

"Let me see."

His finger fell upon the record sleeve. Meche pulled it back, frowning.

"What? I can't look at it?"

"*Look* at it all you want," Meche said, holding it up, "just don't get your dirty fingers on it. I'm going to pay for this."

MECHE WALKED TOWARDS the cash register. Sebastian watched her with narrowed eyes, irritated by her secrecy. What the hell? Now he couldn't even touch the records?

"What does she want it for?" Sebastian asked gruffly.

Daniela shrugged. "Um... just a spell. Like she said."

"Yeah. For what?"

"She... I don't think I'm supposed to say."

"Spit it out. I'll find out eventually."

Daniela started chewing on a strand of hair, a sure sign she was about to buckle.

"I think it's a love spell for Constantino," she blurted.

Constantino. She wanted him to fall in love with her. He remembered Meche mentioning something about love spells back in December but he didn't believe she'd *seriously* pursue this, especially if it meant she was going for Constantino. The same Constantino who had beaten the hell out of Sebastian with the assistance of his clones. That piece of shit. Sebastian felt offended. He felt hurt. He felt fucking angry.

Meche marched back towards them, a plastic bag dangling from her fingers.

"I'm ready to go," she said.

"I NEED TO borrow the record," he said.

"No," Meche replied.

The subway was crowded and there was no place to sit down. Meche and Sebastian occupied a narrow space between a street vendor carrying a huge bag packed with salted nuts and a mother with a small child. They were barely inches apart, sweating and uncomfortable. Three more stations to go and it seemed like it might take forever.

"Why not?" Sebastian asked.

"Because it's mine."

"Are you going to use it to get that asshole to pay attention to you?"

Meche chuckled. She lifted a lofty eyebrow. Her words were pure venom.

"Let me guess: you are going to try to get into that ditzy little thing's pants?"

"She's not a ditz."

"And I'm Madonna."

"I'm asking, as a favour—"

"And I'm saying no."

The look she gave him was the exact same look she might use on a grubby beggar asking for a coin. It made his blood boil, to be viewed with such contempt. As though Meche were the queen and he was a serf, a nothing she could jostle around when it pleased her.

"It's a very shitty thing to say, you realize that?"

"The record is mine."

"Yeah, but—"

"You wouldn't be able to use it. You suck as a warlock."

"Yeah? I'm part of the circle, so whatever—"

"Not for long, I'll bet." She shoved him aside, his back colliding with the back of the street vendor. "Don't stand so close to me. You're sweaty and disgusting."

Gingerly, she pulled out her headphones and put them on, switching on her Walkman. Though the subway car was packed to the brim, he felt absolutely alone.

SEBASTIAN SLAMMED HIS backpack against the bed. He slammed it again and again until he finally understood the futility of this and tossed it away. He slid onto the bed, seething.

Meche was full of shit. She was a bad friend. Hell, she'd always been a bad friend but he had not really cared until now. Why couldn't she lend him the record? She thought he wouldn't be able to use it properly. She was the real witch and he was just a two-bit imitation.

And the way she talked to him! And the way she had looked at him, shoved him away.

Well, he would show her.

He wanted her to know she was not everything to him, that he was more than her tributary.

"HEY DAD," SHE said.

"Hey, sweetheart. How are you doing?"

"I'm great. How are things?"

"Pretty good. I've got a place, a little apartment. As soon as I've fixed it up you can come and visit."

Her father's voice had always soothed Meche. It was rich and vibrant and pleasant. As she pressed the receiver against her ear she felt comforted just by the tone of his voice.

"So then... you won't be coming back home soon?"

"I don't think so, no."

"But you still care about mom."

Meche bit her lip and waited. He sighed and did not speak.

"Meche, your mom and I have a lot of problems."

"It could get better," she said.

Now that she had the record it would, for sure.

"I wish it would."

Meche closed her eyes, picturing them as they had been a few years before, when she was a small child. When they loved each other.

"Dad, could you come by tomorrow? Maybe take me out to dinner?"

"Well... alright," he said.

"And can I play some music for you?"

"I don't know, Meche..."

"Please?"

"Alright."

They talked for a few more minutes. When Meche hung up she felt giddy with excitement. She went to her room, pulled out the record and stroked her fingers across the sleeve, feeling its warmth. This was her secret weapon. This represented her parents' hearts and they would be back together again, as they should be.

Magic could fix anything.

Meche thought about Sebastian. That thought made her curl her fingers and sigh, all the mirth vanishing. She'd been mean to him. Lately she did not know any other way to deal with him. She wanted to be nice. She really did. But things always went wrong and she was just so angry... and he made her want to scream some times. He was so difficult.

She shouldn't have said that about the circle, but she really felt it was going to end soon. He was going to call it quits. He wanted to spend his time chasing after Isadora. Daniela and Meche would be left to their own devices.

Meche tried to picture the world without Sebastian. She erased him and pictured a vast, white expanse which seemed to her like snow.

Meche lay back on her bed and pressed the record against her face, closing her eyes.

SEBASTIAN DID NOT know how this was supposed to work. He had only cast a spell on his own once, and that had been an unexpected event. He did not know if he could manage it again. But he wanted to try. At the very least, he would give Meche a good scare.

Sebastian knocked and Meche's grandmother opened the door, smiling at him.

"Meche's not in, Sebastian," she said. "She's out doing the grocery shopping with her mom."

Sebastian already knew this. Sunday morning was always grocery day for Meche and her mom. Sebastian feigned surprise.

"She was going to lend me some records."

This was not an unusual occurrence and Meche's grandmother nodded.

"Do you want to look for them?"

"Sure," Sebastian said with a smile.

As soon as he was in Meche's room he began pulling at drawers, rifling through her shelves. He found A Whiter Shade of Pale fast enough, resting in a box filled with old toys. He also found the Duncan Dhu record right next to it.

Sebastian frowned. He had not planned on taking Meche's object of power but now that he had it in his hands he thought it might not be a bad idea. If Meche got mad at him, he could tell her to cool it or he would scratch the damn thing. Well... at least he'd let her think he would scratch it.

Satisfied, Sebastian grabbed the records, thanked her grandmother and hurried downstairs.

Isadora was waiting for him next to the motorcycle. She smiled when he came out.

"I'm ready now," he said. "Let's go."

*   *   *

He parked the motorcycle in the alley behind the factory and sneaked in first before helping Isadora through. She looked at the abandoned building skeptically, her eyes darting across the dusty floors.

"It's over here," he said, grabbing her hand and guiding her up the stairs.

He unlocked the door and ushered her in with a sweeping motion. Isadora walked in slowly and her mouth curved into a smile as she saw the posters, the images of singers from magazines, the little coffee table with the candles on it.

"You did this?"

"My friends did," he said, not wanting to take all the credit. "We come here to listen to music. Do you... would you mind if I play some records?"

"Sure," Isadora said, as she sat on the couch.

Meche dragged the bag full of vegetables into the kitchen, humming as she shoved the tomatoes into the refrigerator.

"Meche, your friend came looking for you," her grandmother said.

"Who came?"

"Sebastian."

Sebastian was supposed to take her to the movies that afternoon, but not until three. Meche frowned, her spine tingling with an unpleasant hunch.

"What did he want?"

"He came to borrow a few records. I told him to bring them back when he's done with them."

Meche's hands stilled. She slammed the refrigerator drawer shut and hurried to her room. She pulled the cardboard box from inside her closet and immediately saw which records were missing.

"Asshole!" she yelled, giving the box a good kick.

She curled her right hand into a fist.

She should have been more careful. She should have suspected this. Fortunately, Meche had a good idea of where he might be.

* * *

SEBASTIAN HAD PLAYED a couple of songs by Mecano and one by Simple Minds before his fingers grazed the Procol Harum record. He swallowed, not knowing what to do.

"Maybe you could put on something to dance to?" Isadora suggested.

"What kind of music?" he said, raising his head and looking at her.

"Your pick."

A spectral light filtered through the old window panes, filling the room with an odd glow. He grabbed the record, set it down and lifted the needle. There was a tiny little hiccup as the needle slid across the vinyl surface and then the song began.

"It's slow music," he muttered. "We don't have to dance to it. I can put something el—"

"It sounds nice."

Isadora stood up. Despite his greater height, he felt very small as he took her hand, trying not to shake. Such moments did not happen in reality. They were reserved for movies and books. Any minute now he would wake up; it would turn out he was daydreaming again.

Sebastian placed his hands against Isadora's waist, carefully moving his feet to the rhythm of the music. Twice he looked down to make sure he was taking the right steps, but then he began to relax, and even smiled broadly at Isadora as he pulled her closer to him.

"What?' she asked, smiling back.

"I think I'd like to kiss you," he admitted.

Her hands crept up and wrapped around his neck.

"You think?"

"I'm sure."

"Why don't you?"

"I'm not sure if it's the right moment."

"It's right," she whispered as she pulled him down.

When their lips touched it was as though a circuit had been closed and the power which surged in him when he cast spells now manifested once more, except it was different this time. It did not flow out of him, but seemed to flow through him and he was all of a sudden giddy, intoxicated, brimming and drowning in a sea of pleasure.

It lasted for a small eternity and then he lazily opened his eyes only to see Meche standing at the door.

As SHE HURRIED up the factory's stairs, she heard it. First faintly, then growing stronger as she climbed. The door was not locked and she pushed it a little way open, looking through the crack.

Sebastian was dancing with Isadora. They were very close together, her arms wrapped around his neck as they swayed to the melody of A Whiter Shade of Pale, the lovely, haunting organ pipes echoing through the room.

Sebastian's hands were resting on the girl's waist and he was moving very slowly.

When the singer sang "and although my eyes were open," Isadora reached up and pulled him down for a kiss.

Sebastian closed his eyes, his fingers fluttering up and molding around the beautiful girl's face.

Meche felt her heart grinding to a slow halt, like a broken clock. She smiled, though it was the grimace of despair.

Sebastian raised his head and opened his eyes just in that instant, locking with her own gaze.

Meche stepped back as he opened his mouth. Perhaps he intended to speak, but whether it was to Isadora or to her, she did not know.

Meche, who had prepared an abundance of insults for this occasion, suddenly found herself without a voice. Every syllable stuck to the roof of her mouth. She could not produce a single sound. Even worse, she felt tears gathering in her eyes.

She would not cry; not in front of him. She'd rather die than let him see her tears.

Meche closed the door, very gently, very quietly and hurried down the steps.

Once she was outside she surveyed the sky, trying to blink the tears away and managing only to sniffle. She wiped her nose with the back of her jacket.

A couple of hours later she returned to the factory. They were gone by then.

A Whiter Shade of Pale had been left on the turntable, like the remnant of a shipwreck upon the sand. Meche touched the record, but it felt cold. There was no warmth in it. She played it and heard only ordinary music. There was no magic in the recording. She looked at the sleeve, looked inside it, shook it, desperate to find a crumb of power but the power was gone. Her father was coming over in an hour and the record was useless.

Desperate, she looked for her object of power, thinking perhaps it might fix the problem. It might furnish the useless record with new magic. But Sebastian had taken the Duncan Dhu record with him.

Meche unpinned the photographs taken inside the photo booth and stomped on them.

SEBASTIAN WAITED FOR Meche, knowing she'd show up that night. She had to. He read for an hour, then shifted to the couch and watched some television, zipping through the channels.

He felt nervous. Like maybe he had overdone it. He'd wanted to best Meche, but as the minute hand dragged itself around the face of the clock, he felt he'd made a mistake.

He remembered dancing with Isadora, the kiss. He smiled. But then he also remembered the look on Meche's face. He'd only seen it for a couple of seconds, but her eyes had seemed so pained.

He should apologize. Make it up to her.

Then he frowned, thinking about all her little cruel comments, her coldness when he'd needed her, the indifference which sometimes punctuated their exchanges.

Let her be angry. At least for a little while.

At nine o'clock the knocks came. Three in a row.

He smiled when he opened the door, feeling smug and content, savouring the acid expression on her face, the ways her eyes lit up with righteous fury.

"Hey," he said. "How you doing?"

He expected Meche to launch into a long, angry tirade. To stomp and yell and use barbed words which would sting, lacerate the soul.

He was not prepared for the cold, long stare she gave him and the very hard slap that followed.

Sebastian blinked, aghast, and rubbed his cheek, too stunned by this greeting to even speak. She had punched him in the arm before, in jest, but never this.

Meche shoved him away and marched into his apartment.

"Where's my object of power?" she asked.

She headed into his bedroom and began tearing his maps from the walls, ripping the postcards and tossing the sheets from his bed.

"Hey!" he yelled as she opened the doors of his armoire and pulled out his shirts, throwing them on the floor.

"Where do you have it?"

"It's not here and I am not giving it back to you tonight."

"When are you going to give it back, asshole?"

"When I damn feel like it!"

She turned around, shoulders raised, and walked away.

"Come back here!" he yelled.

"Go to hell," came the reply.

He chased her down the stairs, furiously stomping on every step.

"You're jealous, isn't that right? That's what this is about. You're jealous of me."

"Like I'd be jealous of you!"

"Well, you are."

"You knew I needed that record," she told him, stopping on the second landing and turning around, slamming him against the wall even though he was much bigger than her. "You knew it and you stole it!"

"I borrowed it."

"You are a thief!"

"Didn't you say to take what I wanted? When life offers you something, grab it. I've grabbed it, alright."

"How did you dare, to go into my house, into my room…"

"You wouldn't lend it to me! You were being selfish! Now you're angry because I used it, because I have the girl and you don't have the guy."

"What goddamn guy?" she asked.

"Constantino! Which other guy would it be?"

"You thought I was going to play that record to get together with Constantino?"

He grabbed her by the shoulders, gripping her tight and flipping her around so that she was now against the wall, his fingers digging into her flesh.

"Who else?" he muttered.

Meche let out a low laugh which startled him. Confusion, doubt, flashed across his face.

"I wanted to play that record for my parents. So they'd get back together."

His hands grew slack and she brushed them off her.

"I didn't know."

"Of course not. You're too busy being selfish."

"You can have it back. The record—"

"—I tried it. It has no power left."

"What do you mean?" he asked.

"You drained it! You took it all for yourself and for her! Are you in love now, Sebastian?" she asked, pushing him back so that his back hit the bannister. "Does your heart beat a little faster?"

"I didn't know records could be drained."

"Doesn't matter now, does it? Pat yourself on the back. You have the girl of your dreams and I have nothing."

"Don't exaggerate. Look, Meche—"

"You're going to regret this," she whispered.

He closed his eyes for a second, feeling like they were standing at the edge of a cliff and were about to fall.

"Can we pause and rewind?"

"No."

She shoved him away, her elbow hitting his ribs, and then she was gone.

Twin desires, to seek her forgiveness and to ignore her, warred with each other. His pride was hurt by the angry slap. He did not want to acknowledge he had done any wrong. To do so would be to admit she had been right and, once again, his pride would be stomped over.

He would talk to her later. Give her a day or two to cool down. Seek Daniela's intercession if necessary.

But why the hell did he feel like they'd already hit the ground and shattered?

DANIELA WRUNG HER hands and pushed the cupcake moulds into the Easy-Bake oven, trying to focus on her cooking. But Meche would not stop. She had been going on about it for nearly an hour and Daniela knew this was not a storm which would subside. This was a hurricane, gaining speed, preparing to rip the ground apart. Daniela did not know what to do. She did not know how to stop it. She felt that with every passing minute she was being engulfed by Meche's nervous energy, dragged along, small satellite that she was.

"I said, will you help me hex him?"

There. The question. Point-blank. Daniela squeezed her eyes shut.

"I need to finish baking."

"Quit playing silly games," Meche said, crouching down and looking straight at Daniela's face. "Are you going to help me or not?"

"What you want to do… it's mean," Daniela whispered.

"You think what he did to me is right? You think stealing is nice?"

"No."

"And ruining my parents' marriage?"

"No."

"And getting together with her, with Isadora, that is nice? How many times has she made fun of us at recess and suddenly she's all over him? And he likes it?"

"I know, it's just—"

"It'll only be a little tumble from the motorcycle. A few scrapes. He can take it."

Daniela shook her head and closed the oven door. She set the timer and rubbed her hands against her skirt.

"He'll ache for a couple of days and then he will be fine."

"You should talk to him," Daniela said. "You should talk it out."

"I'll talk to him after we are even."

"Why not talk to him *now*?"

"There is nothing to talk about."

Meche stood up and walked to the other side of the room, standing before Daniela's shelves and looking at her dolls and toys.

She grabbed a stuffed bunny and squeezed it between her hands. It was pointless, once Meche had boiled herself up to this state, to expect her to cool down. Daniela knew it. There had been other fights, other times when she had been called on to act as conspirator and ally of one of her friends—mostly Meche. However, this time it felt different. More dangerous. It was not a childish prank, not about cutting holes into Sebastian's t-shirt. This was about inflicting actual physical pain.

"I thought you cared about Sebastian. Loved him. When you love someone—"

"What?"

Meche's quick turn of the head and the way she spit out the words, as though she had just swallowed sour milk, made Daniela realize she had misspoken. She blinked and scrambled to correct herself.

"I... I meant..."

"What did you say?" Meche asked, frowning.

"Nothing. I... we can cast the hex," Daniela said, wishing only to avert Meche's wrath, to make those dark eyes turn away from her.

Her acceptance had the expected effect. Meche smiled, looking smug, and tossed the bunny away.

"We should head to the factory," she said.

Every crack on the pavement spoke words of warning to Daniela as she rushed behind Meche, towards the old, abandoned building. But there was nothing to do now. She was a coward and would obey, bend the knee. She always did.

"Are you ready?" she asked.

"Meche, you can't," Daniela whispered.

The factory was cold. Shadows gathered at the corners of the window. The distant moon turned its face away from them, hiding behind a cloud.

Meche knew they shouldn't do it. She could feel it in every fibre of her being, feel it from the tips of her toes to the top of her head, but she did not care. She would have her revenge. She would have her hex.

"It's Sebastian."

"I know exactly who he is," Meche said.

She held the needle above the groove. There was only one song for such a spell, only one song for this kind of hex and she had known it from the moment her hand had found the record—guided by some unknown force, just like it had been guided in the record shop to find A Whiter Shade of Pale—waiting on the third bin to the left, near the Jimi Hendrix poster.

It was *In the Court of the Crimson King*. Recorded in 1969, it was the debut album by the British rock group King Crimson. Although it contained five tracks she knew which one she needed. Side two. Fifth song.

It was a track to bring down houses and topple monarchs and surely it would teach a lesson to a teenage boy. A lesson he would not be likely to forget.

The music began to play. Daniela and Meche held hands tight as the building groaned, reverberating to the sound of Greg Lake's voice.

DANIELA WANTED TO pull her hand away, but Meche dug her nails into her palm and Daniela stopped fretting.

She was scared. The windows were tinkling, the glass straining in the frames and Meche's hand felt like it was a hot iron poker. When she looked at Meche's face, her eyes looked darker and older.

Shadows seemed to cloak Meche. She was robed in darkness. And the power in her burned, making Daniela wince.

SEVERAL BLOCKS AWAY Sebastian turned a corner as he had done many times before. But this time something felt wrong. Invisible hands seemed to hover on top of his own hands, invisible fingers making the motorcycle speed up, howl and screech and rush down hill.

He knew the hands.

This was Meche's doing. She was trying to scare him.

"Screw you!" he yelled.

He didn't know if she could hear him, but she hoped his defiance reached her.

The pressure of the hands increased, he swerved and almost lost control of the bike.

A cold bead of sweat dripped down his forehead and he was suddenly afraid. He realized she was not playing. It was not a prank.

"Mercedes!" he yelled.

The car hit him right at that instant and sent him flying through the air, tumbling over the pavement.

DOLORES WAS HALF-asleep on the couch, her hands resting over a ball of yarn, when she felt the tugging. The web of magic drifting through their apartment shivered and moaned. She opened her eyes slowly, specks of darkness dancing before her eyes.

And she knew what was happening all of a sudden. Meche was casting a new spell. A very dark spell.

A spell of death.

Dolores stood up and shuffled towards her bedroom without bothering to put on her slippers. She opened a drawer and pulled out her thimble. She looked at her sisters in the photograph and wished they were still around. Lone witches are never much good. Maybe if the others were still alive they could have taught Meche the way Dolores couldn't. Because Dolores had never been the head witch. Just a minor echo for her eldest sister. Always half-afraid of the spells and now unable to even remember most of them. They'd poured out of her one summer, long, long ago.

But perhaps there was one last spell she might remember.

Dolores put on the thimble. She took needle and thread and began stitching a handkerchief. Sweat beaded her forehead as she worked. The needle rose and fell, dipping until she tied a knot and cut it with her scissors.

There was a hiss, like steam escaping a kettle. Dolores winced as the thimble burned her finger.

She felt Meche's death spell eroding and decaying, bits of it falling to the floor. The thimble also slid from her finger, shattering, bits of white dust scattered all around her.

Dolores closed her eyes and sighed.

*   *   *

DANIELA SAT ON the couch, heart beating fast, and stared at Meche. Meche was on the floor wrapped in a blanket, a cushion behind her head, eyes closed and humming. Daniela could barely breathe but Meche seemed to be making a quick recovery.

Watching her from her position on the couch, Daniela knew her friend was dangerous. She felt the same horror she might feel at discovering a scorpion in her shoe and though she was exhausted, hungry and in desperate need for a nap, she pulled her knapsack over her shoulder.

"I should go," she said.

"Go," Meche said, eyes closed.

Daniela walked out quietly, looking over her shoulder before she closed the door.

MECHE WALKED HOME listening to los Fabulosos Cadillacs sing Mi Novia se Cayó en un Pozo Ciego. She felt festive, moving to the rhythm of the trumpets, bobbing her head and smiling. By the time she stepped into the apartment she was dancing.

"Hey, mom," she said, noticing that the kitchen light was on.

She poked her head in the kitchen. Her mother's eyes looked raw and red.

"Where were you?" she asked.

"I was hanging out with Daniela," Meche said. "What's up? Is this about Sebos?"

"Sebastian?" her mother said. "No."

Odd. Because Meche thought maybe Sebastian's mother had already called to give them the bad news: that her son had a little traffic accident, that he'd broken his leg and Meche could feign innocence. Buy flowers. Take them to the hospital. The joy of his pain would be like a candy, melting in her mouth. Perhaps he would think twice about messing with her again. He thought himself a warlock? Fine. She was a witch.

"Then what's with you?"

"Your grandmother had a stroke. I just came to pick some clothes for her, some things—"

"She didn't have a stroke," Meche said.

"She did have a stroke. This evening."

"But she couldn't have."

"Meche, I need to go to the hospital," her mother said, rubbing her eyes and reaching for her purse. "I have to get a cab and get back there."

"Can I go?"

"All you'd be doing is waiting."

"I can wait."

Her mother nodded and they hurried down the stairs.

The telephone began to ring when they shut the door, a lonesome and sad cry.

Sebastian held the receiver and leaned back, trying to find a comfortable position on the couch. He had bruised his knee, had scrapes here and there, a sprained ankle and a broken wrist.

"You are an idiot," Romualdo said. "How come you were driving so fast? Don't you watch where you are going?"

Sebastian pressed the plastic bag filled with ice and wrapped with an old towel against his leg, watching the bruises with a certain detachment, as though this had happened to someone else. It felt like it had happened to someone else. Like he was a character in a video game, controlled by another player.

Meche.

The phone rang and rang.

Answer, he thought, gritting his teeth. *Answer me. Tell me it was an accident, a game; you didn't mean it. Tell me now.*

"You know what's going to happen, right? Mom is going to take away the bike. Not only that, she's going to blame it on me for giving it to you in the first place. She's going to say I did this. That's bullshit."

The phone seemed to pulsate between his hands, like a heart. Sebastian squeezed it, tried to find purchase on its surface, slick with his sweat.

Meche...

He needed her now. There. If she answered now, this might be forgiven. But she wasn't answering. She was hiding from him.

He could see her in his mind, savouring her victory, her eyes indifferent to his pain. Indifferent to him.

He hung up and hung his head while Romualdo brought him another cushion and yelled and ranted.

MECHE WOKE UP feeling very cold, her eyes fluttering open. She had a vague, unpleasant sensation, like the one you might get when you crush an insect and rub your palm against your trousers, trying to wipe it away.

She thought of the hex she had cast with Daniela and for the first time that night seriously wondered if Sebastian was alright. The hospital's clock read one a.m. and she considered, for a few seconds, daring to phone Sebastian.

Then she feared what he would say if she did phone and woke him up. His anger would still be so raw.

Even worse, she feared if he did not answer. What if she had really hurt him? What if he did not lift the phone and speak? What would she do then?

Meche took off her jacket and rolled it into a makeshift pillow, laying down on the plastic hospital chairs, staring at the white walls of the hallway.

She knew herself—wicked and cruel, the way true witches are, as in the stories grandmother told her. She knew herself and curled up into a tight ball, flipping on the Walkman and listening to Starship sing We Built This City, which was corny and sappy. But she needed corny and sappy.

"I'm going to make it all better," she promised herself. "I can fix this."

DANIELA HEARD IT from Catalina Coronado, who was faster than a telex: Sebastian Soto had an accident, ended up at the hospital and was sent home with a cast. She asked her sister to drive her to his apartment, a box of chocolates on her lap. Romualdo opened the door and let her in. Daniela shuffled her feet and bent her head as she walked inside.

"Hi, Sebastian."

"Hi," he said.

He was sitting in the living room, wrapped in a blanket, watching television. She noticed the cast on his left hand and the bruises on his face, blooming an ugly purple.

Daniela handed him the chocolates.

"Thanks," he said, placing them at his side.

"How are you feeling?"

"Eh. Between this and the beating I'm developing a higher threshold for pain."

"You know we did it, right?"

"I figured as much."

Daniela placed her hands behind her back and stared at the scratched wooden floor.

"I'm sorry," Daniela said.

Sebastian pressed the mute button on the TV remote. He sighed.

"Where is Meche?"

"I'm not sure."

Sebastian drummed his fingers against the couch's arm and shook his head. He did not look good and Daniela could tell it was not just as a result of the accident.

"Well, she has talent," he muttered. "I could feel her hands over mine as the motorcycle swerved left and right."

"Yeah, she has loads of talent. That's probably not a good thing."

Sebastian did not say anything. He was looking at the numbers on the remote control, rubbing a thumb across the buttons.

"She scared me. When we cast that spell on you… my God, there is something dark inside her. Magic only makes that darkness stronger."

"What are you saying?"

"You know."

Sebastian put the remote on top of the box of chocolates and knitted his long fingers together, flexing them slowly.

"She's the real witch among us," he said. "Meche doesn't need a circle. At least, not for long. Whatever it is you're supposed to have, she has it."

Daniela had known it for a while. They were backup singers to the real star. Hearing Sebastian say it, however, made it tangible.

"That's it. That's what frightens me."

"You shouldn't be frightened. Meche is not mad at you."

"But you? What if—"

"I have her object of power. Besides, I don't think she would hurt me once more."

"How do you know?"

"Because it's Meche and Meche I know."

Daniela did not think that was quite enough, but what else could she say? She brushed the hair from her face. Her lips trembled a little as she spoke.

"I am so sorry, Sebastian. I really am. I helped do this to you."

"It'll be okay. I'll be fine."

She hugged him and Sebastian patted her back.

MECHE AND HER mother were sitting in the kitchen, eating in silence. Meche dipped her animal crackers in milk while her mother sipped her coffee.

"Your grandmother is going to have to go to Monterrey," her mother said, all of a sudden.

"Since when?" Meche asked.

This was the first she had heard of this. Had she missed some important family meeting or was she supposed to divine tea leaves in order to be up to date? Really, what the hell.

"I talked to your aunt about it. We had a long conversation. Your grandmother is going to need a lot of care."

"She could get better."

"She had a stroke," her mother said. "She can't walk and she can't talk. She can barely eat mush."

"I noticed," Meche said dryly.

"Your aunt is a nurse. Plus, she has more money than we do. A bigger place. Your grandmother needs more care than I can give her."

"You're just going to pack her off 'cause she's sick."

"There's nothing I can do about it."

"Don't I get a vote in this?"

Her mother did not reply. She looked at her coffee cup, long nails tapping the ceramic mug.

"Awesome," Meche said, pushing her chair back and scraping the floor in the process.

"I NEED TO talk to you," Meche said, cornering her outside the bathroom stalls.

Daniela had been evading her all day long. A clumsy effort at best because Daniela did not know the meaning of subtle. She waddled through school like a great, big goose, a panicked look on her face.

"I don't want to talk," Daniela whispered.

"Listen: I need your help."

"To do what?"

"My grandmother had a stroke. She's not well. I want to heal her. I think we might need Sebastian for this."

Daniela moved towards the sinks, slowly opening a faucet and rubbing her hands with liquid soap.

"Sebastian is at home, resting. He's in a cast. I don't think he'd be up for it and frankly I don't think he'll be talking to you until you do some serious apologizing."

"Apologize?" Meche scoffed.

"Didn't you hear me? He's in a cast."

Daniela closed the faucet. The paper towel dispenser was empty, so she rubbed her hands against her skirt.

"I heard you fine. I'm not apologizing. He got what was coming to him."

"Then don't expect him to help you."

Meche was tired, nervous and more than a little irritated. She squeezed Daniela's arm and gave her a sharp, intense look.

"Convince him to help. Tell him to come by the factory and bring my Duncan Dhu record."

"No way," Daniela said. "I've done enough already. I won't goad him into it."

"I don't care what you want," Meche said. "He will be back in our circle, ready to offer his assistance or *you* will be the next one hexed."

"You wouldn't do that," Daniela said.

"Try me. I think you'll find I'm becoming very good at this sort of thing."

Daniela's eyes went round and glassy like marbles. She was really scared. Meche felt bad for a few seconds. She shoved the feeling aside. She needed Sebastian and Daniela. At the very least, she wanted her damn record back. If it took a bit of pushing around, so be it.

Daniela wriggled free of her grasp and took a couple of steps back.

"Okay. I'll talk to him."

"Today?" Meche asked.

"Today," Daniela said.

"Remind him he still has something that belongs to me. He better bring it to the factory."

SEBASTIAN DID NOT reply. He was staring at the big glass full of milk and chocolate powder, observing the beads of moisture rolling down the sides, trying not to think. Trying to ignore it.

"And then?" Daniela asked.

"I won't help her."

"She'll hurt us," Daniela muttered.

Sebastian did not want to believe it. Meche was many things, but would she really force them to obey her?

She could have killed you, he thought. *She's Meche but she's also something else now.*

Sebastian sipped his milk. They sat in the darkened dining room and he listened to the clock tick, measuring the minutes.

"It's time we did something about this magic circle," he said. "But not what she expects."

"What, then?"

"Tell her I'll be at the factory Friday evening."

"You'll do what she wants?"

"No," Sebastian said, shaking his head. "I won't do anything of the sort."

This day was supposed to come, he thought. He remembered his vision of Meche heading towards an airplane. He'd *known*, long before, that he'd lose her, but he couldn't escape this melody.

* * *

THE HOSPITAL SMELLED like disinfectant. It wasn't like the smell when grandma cleaned the clothes at home or washed the floors. It was more powerful and unpleasant. Then there was the cold. Meche had to keep her sweater buttoned up, otherwise her arms would get goosebump.

She didn't like the hospital and she liked the hospital room even less. Grandma shared it with another two women and all that separated her from the next bed was a thin curtain. Meche had to sit very close to the bed in an uncomfortable, old chair.

"Do you know what I did today?" Meche asked and paused to wait for a reply even though her grandmother could not answer.

She had washed her grandmother's hair in a little basin and was carefully combing it with a plastic, wide-tooth comb.

"I made *picadillo*. I didn't boil the potatoes long enough so they were a little hard."

Meche set the comb down and looked at her grandmother's face.

"You're going to get better," she said, smiling. "That's a promise."

MECHE WAS RE-READING their *grimoire*, pausing to scribble little annotations on the margin of the page. She checked her watch. They were late. Were they even coming? It would be a cruel joke to leave her waiting. But this might be Sebastian's way of getting back at her.

Night was falling so she lit the candles around the room to keep herself distracted. Two dozen stubs of wax. She looked out the circular window and pressed her cheek against the glass.

With a sigh she struck another match and lit the rest of the candles on top of the coffee table.

The door opened. Daniela and Sebastian walked in, sweeping their flashlights in a wide arc. They dropped their backpacks by the door. When Sebastian moved into the light Meche felt her arrogant smile fade a bit. He had a cast on his hand, like Daniela said, and when he walked he limped a bit. There was a cut across his forehead.

He looked at her, eyes sharp and unpleasant.

She looked back, chin raised.

"Hi," he said. "I'm here. Like you wanted."

"Good." Meche knelt down to open the portable record player.

"You needn't bother, I'm not casting any spells with you."

Meche raised her head and looked at him with a frown. She brushed the top of the record player with her right hand.

"What do you mean?"

"I've come to tell you I'm done with your little circle."

"So am I," Daniela said.

Meche did not mean to laugh, but she did anyway. Their determined yet frightened expressions were just too hilarious.

"Oh come on," she said. "You don't mean that."

"Yes we do," Daniela said.

"Did he put you up to this?" Meche asked, pointing at Sebastian.

"No. I'm tired of having you boss me around. This magic... this is not fun anymore. It's nasty and I want to be done with it."

"Do you want to be done with me, too?" she asked Sebastian.

He glanced away and shook his head, smiling at her. Why, yes, of course. Now he had Isadora.

"I can't believe you," he said. "I can't believe your absolute selfishness."

"My selfishness?" she asked. "I want to heal my grandmother. Is that selfish?"

"Everything is about you, Meche. This circle was never about us. We were just your assistants, here to help get what you wanted. You did not even ask what we wanted."

"I asked what you wanted. And you have what you want, anyway," Meche said, remembering the little dance with Isadora. "So now give me what I need."

"Your circle is no more. You might as well get over it."

"Is that so?" Meche said. She glanced at Sebastian, then at Daniela. "You really want to piss me off?"

"We are not afraid of you," Sebastian said.

"Good," Meche said. "Remember that later."

She opened the record player and the needle pressed down on the record. It was Strange Days by The Doors. It had a certain kick to it, a certain pick-me-up that had electrified Meche the first time she had grabbed the record, tickling something inside her head.

She snapped her fingers and narrowed her eyes. She did not need them. A couple of losers to weigh her down. She could do this by herself. She'd show them magic.

Meche snapped her fingers again and the candle flames jumped up, grew brighter as though they were being fanned by an invisible hand.

"Bubble, bubble, hu?" she told Sebastian. "Circles are for weaklings."

She snapped her fingers again and the light of the candles grew even brighter, imbuing everything with a golden glow. Daniela and Sebastian stared at her.

She'd started by casting spells alone and it seemed she would finish casting them by herself. They could both go to hell.

The song grew and so did her magic. Meche made the candles drip rivers of wax upon the floor, long white tendrils reaching towards Daniela and Sebastian.

"My Duncan Dhu record. I want it."

"You're scaring me," Daniela said, stepping back, closer to the wall.

Meche shrugged. Always such a little baby, Daniela. The wax snaked around them, drawing secret patterns upon the floor.

"You're scaring me," Daniela squeaked, the flashlight trembling in her hands, the beam of light bouncing up and down.

"Stop it," Sebastian said. "She's frightened."

"Oh, come on," Meche said rolling her eyes. "I'll make it stop when you give me my record."

"Enough of this," Sebastian said.

"I'm scared!" Daniela wailed.

"Enough!"

Sebastian screamed. The scream made her jump back, staggered by the ferocity of it. Sebastian reached for his backpack and pulled out a record.

Meche could not see from where she was standing because Sebastian was half in shadows. Instead, she felt it, like a great, beating heart crouched in the corner of the room.

For a moment she smiled, feeling her object of power so close to her, almost back in her arms...

... and then he snapped the Duncan Dhu record in two. It made a sound like bones breaking .

She screamed as an invisible fissure traveled up her feet, up her legs and through her chest until it reached her chest. There came the sensation of being ripped apart. Her heart was squeezed ferociously and she could not breathe...

... and then breath returned to her in a shocked gasp.

The candles all went out at the same time, plunging the room into darkness.

Meche dropped down, crouching by the record player.

Her trembling hands touched the needle, quieting the music.

The whole factory was silent.

Sebastian stepped forward, his flashlight pointed at her.

"Are you alright?"

"It's gone," she whispered. "The magic."

Meche looked at him and could not stop the tears streaming down her cheeks.

He stretched out a hand towards her. Meche slapped it away. She closed the record player and grabbed it in one hand, hurrying down the stairs and holding on to the bannister with the other.

"Meche, you can't see!" he yelled.

He was right. It was very dark. But it did not matter. Blindly she stepped down and in darkness found the way out, bursting onto the street with the record player clutched against her chest.

She ran home, her feet pounding the pavement, jumping from puddle of light to puddle of light.

When she reached the apartment she pulled her suitcase from under the bed and filled it with some clothes. She latched it and hurried to the door, bumping against her mother in the living room.

"Meche," she said. "What are you doing?"

"I'm leaving," Meche said. "I'm getting out of this place and going to live with dad."

"Meche, you are not going anywhere."

She had to. She could not stay. Humiliation, rage, despair, that was the only thing which could grow between these walls, on that whole street.

"Dad will be glad to have me over."

"Your father can't take care of you," her mother said, tugging at the suitcase.

Meche pulled it back.

"Why not? He's my dad."

"Because he drinks. Because he's never able to do anything right."

"Oh, bullshit."

"Watch your mouth."

"You don't even like me! And I don't like you!"

"He stole our money!" her mother roared and tugged at the suitcase hard enough to pull it free from Meche's grasp.

Meche huffed, pressing a hand against her chest. "What do you mean?"

"Our savings, Meche. He stole our savings and spent them on that woman."

"He did not," Meche said, feeling offended. "The savings fund is for me. For university and for—"

"I barely have enough money to put food on the table. Your grandmother is going to end up in Monterrey because I can't support both of you. I am not making this up. I am—"

"You are nuts!"

Meche rushed out, carrying the record player under her arm. She heard her mother screaming after her, but she ran down the stairs fast as she could and out onto the street.

HER DAD SMILED, though his smile was a little creased at the edges.

"Meche. How's it going?" he asked. "Um... were you coming to visit today?"

"No," she said and set the record player by the entrance, looking around the apartment.

It was very small and there were lots of boxes. He had not unpacked most of his things, it seemed. Meche sat down on a little blue couch and her father took an old rattan chair across from her. There was a ratty coffee table in between them and she noticed an ashtray filled to the brim and a glass with some dregs at the bottom. It smelled like whiskey. Her father grabbed the glass.

"I should take this to the sink. Do you want a soda?" he said. "I've got soda in the refrigerator. I don't have food. I'm eating out. I do have potato chips."

Meche took off her green jacket and placed it on her knees.

"It's cool. I don't really—"

"They're good chips," he said.

Her father wandered into the kitchen, pulling out glasses, filling a little bowl with chips.

"Dad, is it okay if I come stay with you?" she asked, trying to sound casual. Like it wasn't a big deal. Because it probably wasn't.

He poked his head out of the kitchen.

"For the weekend?" he asked, rubbing the stubble on his cheek. "I'm busy this weekend."

"No, for good."

"Aw, Meche... seriously?"

Meche nodded. He leaned forward, clasping his hands together. His smile wavered.

"That's probably not a great idea."

"Why not?"

"This place is very small."

"You said you were trying to get a bigger place. And next year you're moving to Puerto Vallarta, anyway. So it almost doesn't matter at all."

He placed the glasses and the soda on the coffee table. He went back to the kitchen and returned with the bowl of chips.

"Yes, but it's a bit difficult right now with the current situation," he said. "And the Puerto Vallarta thing is a little messy. I've sent my demo tape. I did. A couple of weeks ago. As soon as they play it they're going to love my voice. But, of course, these things take time. The whole hiring process is so silly these days. Human resources department this and fill that form and... it's best if you stay with your mom."

Meche felt like she had swallowed a mouthful of bleach.

"You said I could go with you one day," she said. "We'll live in Puerto Vallarta and get nice tans all year long."

"Things are a bit weird right now, Meche. But we will absolutely go to Puerto Vallarta and I'll finish my book there. It's going to be fun. You'll see."

"Dad, I can't stay with mom."

"You can't stay here either, sweetheart."

Her father took out a cigarette and lit it, raising it to his lips.

"Did you steal money from mom?"

He smiled a jovial smile. "What?"

"Did you steal from her?"

"Stealing is an exaggeration."

"Our savings," Meche said, through gritted teeth. "Did you take them?"

Her father's smile, which was always so big, folded and disappeared. He nodded and took a drag.

"Yeah. I did."

"Awesome," Meche said, standing up.

"Meche, you don't get it—"

"No dad, *you* don't get it."

She put on her jacket and zipped it up in one quick motion.

"You're a fucking disgrace," she said. "I can't believe you'd steal from us."

"Hey," Vicente said, spitting the cigarette from his mouth. "Hey, you watch that mouth!"

"I'm not watching anything! You're a lousy father."

"Yeah, too bad," he said with a sneer.

"Good thing I figured it out."

"You don't have to come back 'round here if you feel like that, Meche!"

Meche opened the door. She eyed the portable record player sitting on the floor and gave it a good kick. After all, it didn't matter anymore. Very little did.

"Bye, dad."

WHEN SHE CAME home, her mother was waiting for her in the kitchen, looking at her cup of coffee. Meche rested her hands on the chair and sighed. Her mother stared at Meche. Neither one spoke for what seemed an aeon.

"You think it's so simple, don't you," her mother said finally, "Life. It's very hard, Meche. I do what I can."

"I know."

"When you were a baby you cried a lot. Nothing could calm you down. You bawled and bawled. But when your dad put on a record and held you, you'd quiet down. It was like magic. I tried putting on records and holding you, but it wasn't the music. You knew it was him. And you knew when it was me. I can't be him."

"I don't want you to be him."

Meche found a stray crumb and rolled it between her fingers.

"Mom, I just... I want to go away. I can't stay here."

"Where would you go?"

"Monterrey. With grandma. I'd help take care of her."

"Your school?

"There are schools in Monterrey."

Her mother shook her head and chuckled, resting her elbows on the table. "You want to get away from me so badly?"

"No," Meche said. "But I do want to go somewhere else. This is not my place."

"We all think that when we are fifteen."

"It really isn't. And I'll phone. I'll be here during vacation."

"What kind of mother would I be if I send you to live with your aunt?"

"Mom," Meche said extending her hand. "You know I love you. But I can't live with you. You know that, don't you?"

Her mother grabbed her hand and shook her head.

VICENTE VEGA LEANED down and picked up the portable record player, setting it on the counter. He opened it, pressed a button and saw the platter was not spinning. It could be fixed. He'd work on it in the morning. For now, he needed a drink. Vicente grabbed a glass and poured himself some whiskey. He was out of ice and it was warm and unpleasant, but he drank it and lit a cigarette.

He walked back to the living room and patted one of the boxes filled with records, opening it and pulling out the *danzón* of *danzónes*: Danzon 2 by Arturo Marquez.

The slow rhythm of the *danzón*—music fit only for prostitutes in the early 20th century— soothed him

He turned off the lights, sitting in the dark.

*   *   *

LOVE DIES IN different ways. For most, it is a slow, agonizing death. Meche, however, cut her love the same way the executioner might chop a head: with a single, accurate swing.

She never saw her father after that day.

She did not speak to Daniela and Sebastian either.

Mexico City, 2009

MECHE'S MOTHER WAS boiling hibiscus flowers for the *jamaica* water and the whole apartment had a sweet, pleasant smell.

"Your cousin was looking for you," her mother said, wiping her hands against her apron. "She wanted to know if you need a ride to the airport tomorrow."

"I could use a ride from Jimena. But I'm leaving early. I don't know if she wants to get up at four a.m."

"You can ask."

"Sure."

She leaned over her mother's shoulder to look at the big, boiling pot of water. The water was blooming into a nice shade of red.

"You know, *jamaica* water is essentially tea, but cooled down."

"I know that," Meche said.

"You should take a few bags of it and make it at home."

Meche nodded. Her mother stirred the pot with a wooden spoon.

"I'm getting rid of most of dad's records."

"Are you sure?"

"Yeah," she said firmly and paused before speaking again. "I read his book."

"Was it any good?"

"It was. A bit jumbled. It needs some editing... but it was good."

It felt odd admitting it. And it was sad. Sad to know her dad could have done something else with his life. He'd wasted away in that little apartment, with his notes and his records, so close to finishing his big project and yet so far.

"I salvaged something for you. Wait a second."

Meche returned to the kitchen with a small box and set it on the table. Her mother peeked inside.

"What's this?" she asked, pulling out an envelope.

"Dad was obsessive about keeping everything he wrote. These are letters he sent to you. Remember?"

"Letters?"

"Yeah. When he was trying to get you to go out with him."

"Oh, my," her mother whispered, unfolding one. "I remember. I didn't know he kept them."

"I thought you might want them."

"I do."

Her mother pulled out another letter and shook her head, chuckling.

"He could write, couldn't he? He wrote on anything. Bits of napkins and the backs of receipts. That was Vicente."

Her mother put the letters back in the box. She closed the lid and looked at Meche.

"I wish you could have talked to him before he died," her mother said.

"Whenever we talked he was drunk and sad," Meche said. "But I wish I'd talked to him."

"Well, are you going to need help packing? Do you need—"

"I could use a hug."

Meche placed a hand on her mother's shoulder. Her mother smiled.

ASSORTED EMPANADAS CONSTITUTED the dish for the last day of the *novena*. There were spicy tuna ones and sweet ones filled with pineapple jam.

Meche played tangos. Her father said tango was a music for mending or breaking hearts. Rhythms for close embraces and invitations to dance telegraphed with the eyes and a tilt of the head.

She saw Daniela and waved to her. The woman approached her, a broad smile painting her face.

"Hey," Meche said. "How... um... how's your day been?"

"Long. I've been up since six and have not stopped. Two kids and a full-time job," she said. "They're six and ten."

"Seriously? You have a ten-year old child? That's impossible."

"Not that impossible. It's been a while."

"No kidding. What do you do for a living?"

"I'm a cook."

"That seems strangely appropriate."

"Well, I did go crazy with that Easy-Bake oven."

"Sebos ate everything you made. Even when it sucked."

"My cooking has improved."

Meche smiled. She felt strangely sheepish, her hands dipping into her pockets as she looked down.

"You're wondering if he's coming after all," Daniela said.

Meche opened her mouth to protest, raising her hand.

"Don't deny it."

"How do you—"

"It's all over your face."

Meche huffed. Daniela placed a hand on her shoulder, squeezing it a little.

"He's coming. He's probably delayed by traffic."

"Has he been talking to you?" Meche asked, wondering if he had spilled the beans about their tryst. Now that would be embarrassing.

"No more than a few words. But it doesn't take a genius to figure it out. I mean, I figured it out, even back then."

"What?"

"That you were head-over-heels in love with him. I told you so. But you wouldn't listen."

Meche opened her mouth and then shut up when she saw Sebastian entering the apartment. He nodded at her and waded his way through the crowded living room, evading Jimena and her tray of *empanadas*.

"I'll let you talk," Daniela said, moving aside.

"Hey, wait," Meche said.

"I don't think you need me to translate for you."

"Well…" Meche said, grabbing her arm. "Thanks. I don't think I ever said thanks to you."

"For what?" Daniela asked.

She thought about all the times Daniela had put up with her, showing kindness when Meche was a bundle of irritated nerves and impatience. Smiling at her when Meche made a sour face. Listening patiently when Meche ranted. Meche had just accepted all of this as fact, never questioning Daniela's devotion.

"For everything."

Daniela smiled, drifting towards the other end of the room.

"Hi."

Sebastian was holding his jacket under his arm and he looked very formal, though he carried a backpack on his right shoulder. She still could not quite square his current self with his former self.

"Just got off work?" she asked.

"Yep. I came right over."

Meche nodded. She wished she had a plate of *empanadas*, a glass of water, something to keep her hands from fluttering nervously in front of her face. She placed her hands behind her back as a last resort.

"You could have asked me to come yourself, you know," he said.

"I never do," Meche said, thinking about poor Daniela, who had served as her messenger on more than one occasion. "Bad habit of mine."

Meche glanced down, softly moving one foot to the rhythm of Carlos Gardel's "Volver." In a baritone Carlos told her the stars mockingly look on and in their indifference observe the return of an old lover. She shuffled her feet to each word. Impatient. Annoyed. Tense. He just looked at her, which didn't help.

"I wasn't trying to insult you at the restaurant," she muttered.

"Of course you were."

"I did, but I wasn't *trying*," Meche said. "It just came out all wrong. I'm not exactly a perfect orator."

"I noticed. I think the first time we ever spoke you called me 'horse-faced weirdo.'"

"It was just horse-face," she muttered. "I called you weirdo the next time we talked."

"Yeah, and I still befriended you."

"That good old masochism."

"Well, you made a very compelling case for yourself: you told me I could eat from your bag of potato chips. How's a guy going to resist a gal offering him chips?"

Meche laughed. She felt like slapping his arm, like she might have done when they were younger. Then she sobered.

Sebastian was quiet, as though he were waiting for her to say something. When she did not, he finally spoke.

"I brought you something."

Sebastian unzipped the backpack and took out a mangled, old box. Meche frowned.

"What is this?" she asked.

"Open it."

She took the lid off and saw his old sneakers with all the inked doodles.

"This is my object of power," he said. "I'm giving it to you."

The room seemed to suddenly go... muffled. As though someone had pressed a pillow against the speakers, drowning out the sound. Only that wasn't possible. The emptiness in her ears was a bizarre auditory hallucination.

She stood in that silence staring at Sebastian, not knowing what to say.

"I'm... what do you want me to do with them?" she asked, and hated the hesitation in her voice. Like she'd swallowed peanut butter and it was sticking to the roof of her mouth.

"Do what you want with them. I also have this," he said and he showed her a record sleeve.

Duncan Dhu. *El Grito del Tiempo*. Track one: En Algún Lugar.

Meche put the box down and grabbed the sleeve. She took out the record and immediately saw the cracks running down its surface.

"I glued it back together years ago."

"You can't glue it back together," she whispered. "It can't be fixed. You can't undo..."

"I know we can't undo anything. I know that," he said sternly. "I'm not asking for that."

"What are you asking, then?"

He brushed her cheek with his thumb and smiled the faintest smile.

"Don't leave me behind this time."

Meche clutched the record and frowned. She had thought about it, but it was an entry under 'idiot things that occur to me.' Only an idiot would think about starting something with someone they hadn't spoken to in years, someone who was a total stranger.

Especially when she had somewhere to be. The little apartment in Oslo with her ferns, her computer... her entire life.

"Oh, whatever for... it's ridiculous," she said, shaking her head and coughing because something had lodged in her throat.

"Yeah. I'm pretty sure it is."

"I didn't... I mean, I didn't want you here for... that. I wanted to tell you something. I'm sorry. I shouldn't have cast that spell on you. I should have been kinder. I should have understood you better."

Sebastian slid his hands in his pockets and he shook his head. He looked sad and embarrassed and irritated, and it made her want to pinch him because she wasn't faring any better. And... damn it.

"You're giving me the brush off, again," he said.

"I'm apologizing."

"It still feels like a brush off."

"You don't want to be hanging out with me," she said, smiling. "I'm bad for your health."

He managed to smile back, the corners of his lips rising a little. He shook his head, a chuckle escaping his throat, though it sounded dull and forced.

"Of course you are. You are terrible for me. Not that I ever gave a damn. Not that I'd start giving a damn now."

"Please don't use that tone."

"What tone?"

That sad, defeated tone. Like she had just stabbed his hand with a fork. Like she had just run over his favourite puppy. Like she was this awful person. She wasn't. Not when you looked at it all rationally.

"I didn't want to leave without saying goodbye," she muttered, ignoring the question. "You know, like a thief."

"Maybe you should have," he said. "It's better than saying 'Let's pretend nothing happened.'"

"When did I say that?"

"Wasn't that coming next?"

Meche bit her lip. It wasn't exactly what she was thinking, but it wasn't far off. It sounded perfectly reasonable in her head. Now he made it seem like an insult. It was all very disjointed and unpleasant.

"I bet you wish you never spoke to me again."

"Not really," she muttered.

"Oh, come on. Well, don't worry. *I* wish I hadn't seen you again."

That kind of hurt. It shouldn't, but it did.

He pinched the bridge of his nose and sighed.

"No, I didn't mean that," he said. "I… um… thanks, I guess. For the honesty and all."

"I fly out tomorrow. Thanks for the record."

She thought about giving him a final hug but it was already weird enough between them. Besides, if she hugged him, she'd have to kiss him on the cheek and that was just… not right.

Meche stepped back, raised her right hand, signaling 'bye.' He raised both hands as if he were surrendering.

She turned around and headed towards her bedroom. The tango was over. A new song was playing.

Mexico City, 2009

MECHE LOOKED AT the plane tickets, checking her row for the third time. The problem with flying these days was that you had to be at the airport three hours before your flight left to get through the security checkpoints. That meant you couldn't just dash onto your plane, sit down in your seat and be on your way. No. You had to wait at a coffee stand and ask if they had tea. Only they did not have the tea you wanted, which only served to increase the impatience quotient.

And the music. She did not even want to mention the airport music. Some banal, tiresome selection of soft rock hits which had her stuffing her earbuds into her ears as soon as the first song started playing.

Meche tapped the little circular table with her nails and wished she could board a train and be home in two hours, like in Europe. Everything was two hours away by rail there.

She looked at her iPod, pressing the arrow button. It was stuffed to the gills with songs and she couldn't find the one she was looking for. Who would have thought that in the years since she had left Mexico she had never once bothered to purchase a single album by Duncan Dhu?

Meche took out the earbuds.

MECHE STOPPED BEFORE the door and knocked three times in quick succession. The lock turned and Sebastian stood there, looking at her suspiciously, like she had just sneaked into his building to smuggle a bomb.

"Mercedes," he said.

It was probably the first and only time in his life that he had used her real name as opposed to the nickname. Nobody, ever, called her Mercedes. Least of all him, spitting her name out like it was a kick to the gut.

She wondered if he was going to slam the door in her face and start yelling in Catalán.

"I need to give these back to you," she said, handing him the box with the shoes. "They are yours."

"I gave them—"

"They don't belong to me," she said. "I can't take them."

Sebastian cleared his throat rather loudly but did not attempt to dissuade her. He grabbed the box and set it aside, on a small table sitting by the door.

"I thought you were flying out today," he said. His gaze was not on her face but instead had fixed on some point over her shoulder.

"I was, but then the weirdest thing happened."

"What, exactly?"

"Do you know the distance between Oslo and Mexico City?" she asked him.

Sebastian frowned. He turned his face a couple of millimeters, then looked down at her fully, though with caution.

"About 9,200 kilometres. I've measured it on a map. Bad habit."

"That's quite a few kilometres."

"Yeah."

Meche looked down, nodding and shuffling a step closer to him.

"I looked it up when I was at the airport."

"And then you decided to return my shoes and tell me that factoid?"

"You are not going to make this easy on me, are you?" she said, crossing her arms.

Sebastian leaned against the door frame, all tall and smirking. He rubbed a finger against the wooden door frame, as though he were checking that the varnish was intact.

"No," he said, staring at her. "Why should I?"

"I'd appreciate the favour."

"I'd appreciate the speech, thank you."

"I'm not giving you a speech," she said. "It's not one of your books."

Besides, she was bad with words. They came out all crooked and deformed and sounded just plain wrong. Numbers and music: those she could work with.

"Mix-tapes are outdated so I decided to just make a playlist for you. Kind of like you did before when you gave me that soundtrack. You know, this is a sort of... I'm afraid it's a..."

"Present?" he finished for her.

"Something like that," she said, extending the iPod towards him.

"Love letter."

Meche said nothing to that, rolling her eyes. But he waited and she recalled how he was extremely stubborn and patient. They could probably stand there, at the doorway, for an entire decade and he would not budge until she'd spelled it out.

"Take the iPod."

"I don't know. You're missing three words."

"You know I—"

Meche sputtered a word that was not a word. More like a string of consonants without a single vowel in between them.

"Just fucking take it," she said.

Meche waved the iPod and the earbuds before him. Sebastian put them on. He pushed the play button. He clicked it again, looked at the LCD display and shook his head.

"I don't hear anything."

"It's empty."

He looked at her in confusion.

"We need to make a new soundtrack. Together," Meche said with a shrug.

"Together as in I—"

"*Jeg elsker deg*," she said, feeling breathless when she spoke, like she'd been running for a long time.

"Meaning?"

"They're words, alright? It counts. I'll buy you a Norwegian dictionary."

Sebastian smiled very slowly and pulled the earbuds away, stuffing them in his pockets.

"And what will be the first song?" he asked.

"I figure Absolute Beginners, though if you don't like Bowie—"

She was going to suggest a whole swathe of songs. Somewhere Only We Know by Keane if he wanted to go recent and even Coldplay's Swallowed in the Sea and the Goo Goo Dolls with Iris if he wanted to be cliché and had never watched *Wings of Desire*. Though if he mentioned I Can't Fight This Feeling Anymore she was going to just stomp away. There were some things she would not accept.

Not even for him.

"Bowie will do," Sebastian said, interrupting her with a kiss.

She twined her fingers into his hair and smiled against his lips.

"Want to see the Northern Lights this weekend?" she asked.

"Sure. It's about time."

Mexico City, 1984

A GIRL SITS outside her apartment building, headphones on, listening to her music. She has a bag of potato chips, a bottle of soda and her idle thoughts. She'll do her homework later. For now, as the sun rolls down, she simply taps her foot to the rhythm of the music and listens to one of her dad's tapes. It's Boston singing More Than a Feeling. She sips her soda.

A man walks a dog. The seller of *camotes* pushes his cart. Kids kick a soccer ball down the street.

The girl scratches her leg. She's awkward and dressed in clothes a size too large. Her hair falls loose below her shoulders.

A boy walks on the other side of the street and glances at her. Something clicks in her brain and she thinks this is the new kid. The weirdo who lugs all those books around. She saw him with a book called *Tales of Mystery & Imagination* and she wants to ask him how it connects with Alan Parsons Project because she doesn't understand that album.

A BOY DRAGS the market bag with him trying to remember the things he's supposed to get. A kilo of tortillas. On the way back, two litres of milk and a box of detergent. He repeats them in his head as he walks—Tortillas. Milk. Detergent.

He shuffles his feet. He's a tall kid. He's skinny and dark, his long fingers curling around the plastic handle of the bag.

There's a girl his age sitting on the bottom step of an apartment building, listening to music.

The boy keeps to himself and walks with his head down, but he raises his eyes to look at her because she looks kind of funny with those big headphones on her ears.

She stares right at him. The look is like having a pin inserted into his chest. He stumbles, shifts, switches the bag from one hand to the other.

"Hey, horse-face!" she yells.

He blinks.

She takes off her headphones and points at him.

"Yeah, you. Do you like music?"

"No, sorry," he says, shrugging.

"That's too bad."

He should have said 'yes'. Maybe she would have played with him if he did. He can't make friends. He always botches it.

"Do you like potato chips?"

"I like chips," he says.

"What ya' doing over there then?"

He crosses the street and sits next to her, setting his bag on the ground. He forgets he had to run errands for his mother.

SHE OFFERS HIM her chips and he takes a few.

"I'm Sebastian," he says.

"I'm Meche."

"Hi."

"Hi."

He grins at her with ease even though things like this—smiling, chatting, being friendly—are never easy for him. It feels easy now.

She smiles back. It's not her usual drill. She's a scowler. Even though she's just about to hit puberty she can already tell being a teenager is going to be a load of crap. She smiles brightly for him because she feels bright, like someone just lit a match.

THEY SIT TOGETHER and watch the world go by.

Deep down they know one fine morning they'll run away together to a place where the sun shines at midnight.

INFORMATION TECHNOLOGY LAW

Efallai nad yw'r wybodaeth
sydd yn y rhifyn hwn yn
adlewyrchu
DEDDFWRIAETH
BRESENNOL

Information contained within
this edition may not be
CURRENT LAW

Information Technology Law

Eighth Edition

Ian J. Lloyd

*Senior Specialist, HSU, National Research University,
Russian Federation and Visiting Professor,
Open University of Tanzania*

UNIVERSITY PRESS

Great Clarendon Street, Oxford, OX2 6DP,
United Kingdom

Oxford University Press is a department of the University of Oxford.
It furthers the University's objective of excellence in research, scholarship,
and education by publishing worldwide. Oxford is a registered trade mark of
Oxford University Press in the UK and in certain other countries

Published in the United States of America by Oxford University Press
198 Madison Avenue, New York, NY 10016, United States of America

British Library Cataloguing in Publication Data
Data available

Library of Congress Control Number: 2017934658

ISBN 978–0–19–878755–6

Printed in Great Britain by
Bell & Bain Ltd., Glasgow

Preface

I naively used to think that writing new editions of a book would become easier over time. The pace of change in the IT Law field is frightening. Topics that were seen as important five years ago have faded into obsolescence to be replaced by other issues. Matters are even more difficult this time around with the multiple uncertainties concerning the impact of the Brexit vote on the shape of IT law in the United Kingdom.

Blame for the many faults and failings of the work lie with me. Things would be worse without the help of many friends. It remains a notable feature of IT law that it is populated by nice people and, in all cases, I am acknowledging the help of friends rather than mere colleagues. I've known and worked with Steve Saxby for (too) many years and we established together an LLM course at Southampton, to which I contributed whilst living 500 miles away in Glasgow. I could not bear to be separated from my beloved Celtic whilst Steve owns a number of season tickets at Southampton FC. There are things that are much more important than Law. I also work with and greatly appreciate the advice and friendship of David Mellor, the Honorary President of the United Kingdom Telecommunications Academy. It is perhaps not the best-known of organisations but it, and David in particular, do great work in providing education in the sector to students in developing countries. Christopher Millard and Richard Susskind are also friends of long standing. Richard goes from strength to strength and is undoubtedly the world's leading authority on the impact of IT on the legal profession. Christopher has followed a slightly different career path. From being a partner in major city law firms he has switched very successfully to academic life at the Centre for Commercial Law Studies in Queen Mary University. I'd like to thank also Tom Randall, commissioning editor at OUP for his help and understanding during the production process—including tolerating my request that the colours on the book should reflect the away strip of a certain football team.

Last, but certainly not least, a few words for people who are more than friends. Moira, who I was lucky enough to marry; I love you very much. Love also to our sons, Thomas and James. Aged thirteen and ten, you may not have helped much with the academic content of the book (although James is far more skilled at Nintendo games than I am), but life would be so much poorer without you. Any worthwhile elements of this book are dedicated to Moira, Thomas, and James with all my love.

Ian Lloyd
2017

New to this Edition

Key revisions to the 8th edition include:

- the Investigatory Powers Act and the scope of the legislation
- the rise of online fraud and the Computer Misuse Act
- discussion of Regulation (EU) 2016/679 and the Directive (EU) 2016/680 on the protection of personal data
- discussion of the unprecedented loss of personal data by Yahoo
- commentary on the misuse of personal information and the European Commission's regulation of digital operators, such as Google and Facebook
- clarification on determining adequacy in protection of data transfer in relation to *Schrems v Data Protection Commissioner Case 362/14*
- new legislation addressing unwarranted dissemination of sexual images and revenge pornography
- revised and updated chapters on patent law
- updated coverage of copy protection and digital rights management
- discussion of the Consumer Rights Act 2015 in relation to digital products and content
- coverage of governance and regulation of the Internet

Outline Contents

Detailed Contents

PART II Computer-Related Crime

PART IV E-Commerce

List of Tables and Figures

Late Developments

One of the most frustrating elements of writing in a field such as information technology law is that any text inevitably becomes dated before it can be published. It might be helpful for the reader to give an indication of the publication schedule and constraints under which this work has been prepared. The basic text was delivered to the publisher (amazingly more or less on schedule) at the start of October 2016. From that point there are various production stages, copy-editing to ensure that the use of headings and structure is consistent and proof reading which provides the opportunity to catch basic mistakes. There is the well-known story of one of the early printed versions of the Bible where the proof reader failed to notice the omission of the word not, with the consequence that readers were advised that "Thou shalt commit adultery"[1]. That remains a nightmare scenario at proof stage but perhaps the more important point is that for valid reasons publishers advise against making substantial changes at the final proof stages. It is perhaps a strange analogy to draw in respect of a book on IT Law that the text was effectively carved in tablets of stone in Autumn 2016. This section has been delivered at the last possible moment and seeks to highlight a number of issues that have arisen since the main body of the text was finalised.

The past year has been a difficult one for legal commentators and the IT field is perhaps especially problematic. Much of the legal landscape has been predicated on the UK's membership of the European Union. That is, of course, likely to change. What is less clear is what the legal implications will be. This is the case at a general level, but there are a number of IT-specific issues that cause me concern – if not at the level of sleepless nights!

The changing legal landscape adds to the difficulties involved in seeking to keep a work as up to date as possible. This section of the book will attempt to achieve two goals. First it will offer some comments on possible legal consequences arising from Brexit. Second, and more in line with previous editions, it will seek to outline some new issues that have emerged subsequent to the main text being finalised.

Brexit and IT Law

In some respects, this section could be encapsulated in two words: "Who knows?" However, in attempting to answer this short question, a number of rather complex issues arise. The first concerns the ongoing status of existing laws. In many cases, EU legislation has been incorporated into domestic law under the authority of the European Community Act 1972. There has been much discussion of the "Great Repeal Bill" that will sweep away this legal authority for the application of EU Law in the United Kingdom. In fact, the name is something of a misnomer. The European Community Act is a very short measure. As enacted, it had 12 sections, some of which have subsequently been repealed. By statutory standards its repeal would be a fairly straightforward task. The complicating factor is, of course, that the many hundreds of pieces of secondary legislation made under its auspices will lose their legal justification.

---

[1] See <https://www.theguardian.com/books/2015/oct/21/rare-sinners-bible-on-sale-bonhams-auction>

There is perhaps a (worrying) precedent. Around the turn of the century, major efforts were made, largely at a EU level, to encourage the use of digital signatures and to remove legal barriers to their validity. In the UK at the time it was estimated that there were several hundred statutes that imposed requirements of signature that were predicated upon the use of a traditional form of signature. One approach that was adopted in other jurisdictions (including Ireland) was to introduce a simple piece of legislation providing for the universal acceptance of electronic signatures. The UK government decided that it would be necessary to consider each piece of legislation on an individual basis. The complexity of the task was significantly greater than anticipated.

There may well be areas where domestic reform could be desirable and reasonably feasible. In spite of constant EU references to the single market, the conceptual differences between common and civil law notions of copyright have always proved difficult to resolve. Linguistic issues constitute a more significant barrier to the establishment of a single digital market than any regulatory ones data flows.

Patent law does raise different issues and consideration is given in the text to the notion of the unitary patent that will cover all EU states. There have been suggestions from the UK Government that it will ratify the necessary agreements before Brexit. This would certainly be beneficial to the UK, but is perhaps questionable whether it might be seen in the same way in the other Member States. Although much has been written and spoken about the consequences of Brexit, much, at least in the UK media attention has focused on this country's aspirations. Politics, it is sometimes said, is the art of the possible. To give one example of the issues that may lie in wait, it has been suggested that the United Kingdom will ratify the agreements relating to the establishment of the EU Unitary Patent. As the name suggests (and discussed in more detail in this book) this system provides for the establishment of a single patent award to apply in all of the EU's Member States. A major selling point of the new system is that applications may be submitted in one of three languages (English, French or German) thereby reducing significantly the translation costs traditionally associated with the patent process. There are strong arguments in favour of using English as a language of availability – not leas because the single country that generates the largest number of applications under the current EPO system is the United States – and mainly use the English language. It has been said that politics encapsulates the art of the possible, Usage of these dark elements may be necessary if new regimes are to work.

The Role of Judges

Traditionally in the UK, great deference has been paid to Acts of Parliament. Statutory instruments have been afforded only slightly less deference. One of the features of EU membership has been the extent to which the Court of Justice has been willing to challenge the validity of legislative instruments. Reference is made to a number of such decisions in the body of the text. Since this was written we have had the decision of the Court of Justice in the joined cases of *Tele2 Sverige AB (C203/15)* v *Post-och telestyrelsen, and Secretary of State for the Home Department (C698/15)* v *Tom Watson, Peter Brice, Geoffrey Lewis*[2]. The litigation was concerned with the legitimacy of domestic legislation in Sweden and the United Kingdom in the area of data retention. As discussed in more detail, the legitimacy of such legislation has been contentious over a period of years. In

---

[2] http://www.bailii.org/eu/cases/EUECJ/2016/C20315.html

the case of the UK, the proceedings related to a ruling by the High Court in July 2015 that the Data Retention and Investigatory Powers Act 2014 was unlawful. This measure was itself introduced following a decision of the European Court in the case of *Digital Rights Ireland* v *Minister for Communications, Marine and Natural Resources, Minister for Justice, Equality and Law Reform, Commissioner of the Garda Síochána*[3] that the data retention regime established under European Directives was unlawful as constituting a disproportionate response to the threats posed by digital communications. Following the High Court ruling, the UK government lodged an appeal that resulted in the Court of Appeal seeking a preliminary ruling from the European Court. Its key conclusions were to the effect that:

> Article 15(1) of Directive 2002/58/EC of the European Parliament and of the Council of 12 July 2002 concerning the processing of personal data and the protection of privacy in the electronic communications sector (Directive on privacy and electronic communications), as amended by Directive 2009/136/EC of the European Parliament and of the Council of 25 November 2009, read in the light of Articles 7, 8 and 11 and Article 52(1) of the Charter of Fundamental Rights of the European Union, must be interpreted as precluding national legislation which, for the purpose of fighting crime, provides for general and indiscriminate retention of all traffic and location data of all subscribers and registered users relating to all means of electronic communication.

> 2. Article 15(1) of Directive 2002/58, as amended by Directive 2009/136, read in the light of Articles 7, 8 and 11 and Article 52(1) of the Charter of Fundamental Rights, must be interpreted as precluding national legislation governing the protection and security of traffic and location data and, in particular, access of the competent national authorities to the retained data, where the objective pursued by that access, in the context of fighting crime, is not restricted solely to fighting serious crime, where access is not subject to prior review by a court or an independent administrative authority, and where there is no requirement that the data concerned should be retained within the European Union.

At the time of writing, we await the ruling of the Court of Appeal, although the advice of the European Court seems fairly unequivocal. In one sense the enactment of the Investigatory Powers Act 2016 renders the particular litigation otiose. The key issue is perhaps to question what may happen in the future? It is arguable that in the light of the European Court's words, a similar conclusion could be applied in relation to the 2016 Act. At a practical level, it should be noted that legal proceedings in respect of the 2014 Act have now been running for almost three years with no definitive end in prospect. It has been indicated that the two year exit procedures triggered under Article 50 of the Treaty will begin to run from March 2017. This would make any EU reference effectively of no relevance, but what is not clear is how the domestic Courts will approach the situation. Will there be a continued willingness to consider challenges to the validity of legislation or a reversion to more deferential days?

The General Data Protection Regulation

Of the many areas of uncertainty that affect this book, the Data Protection Regulation (and also the associated proposals for EU reform in the electronic communications sector) constitutes a major issue. The Regulation was adopted in 2016. It is a rather unusual form

---

[3] http://www.bailii.org/eu/cases/EUECJ/2009/C30106.html

of legislation. The traditional notion is that a Regulation becomes law in the Member States without the need for domestic legislation. This is not quite what the Regulation provides for. Whilst it contains some general principles regarding acceptable data processing in relation to enforcement and procedural issues, it continues to rely on nationally-implemented legislation. Whether or to what extent that may happen in the United Kingdom is an – as yet – unanswered question. Comments from the Information Commissioner[4] appear to suggest that domestic reform will occur although the legislative work schedule may become a rather heavy one and historically data protection has been a rather low priority in domestic terms.

The Resurrection of the Digital Economy Act?

It was announced in January 2017 that a number of major ISPs, including BT, Virgin Media, TalkTalk, and Sky, had agreed to begin sending emails to customers whose accounts had been associated with the unlawful downloading of copyright protected materials[5]. This was a significant element in the controversial Digital Economy Act but one that has not to date come into operation. The Act envisaged that sanctions, possibly extending to the denial of Internet access, might be imposed upon users who were identified as multiple offenders. The new procedures are significantly weakened in that there is no provision for the imposition of sanctions in the event that a user continues infringing activities. Even in the event that one ISP should deny access to a customer, there is a wide range of service providers that a user could turn to.

Robots as Legally Responsible Entities?

Recent months have seen considerable attention paid to the role of artificial intelligence and the possible legal liabilities that may arise in the event that the operation of robotic devices causes injury to an individual. A case that received extensive publicity concerned the involvement of a driver-less car in a fatal accident. A report approved by the Legal Affairs Committee of the European Parliament in January 2017[6] entitled "European Civil Law Rules in Robotics" posed the question:

> Have we already reached the point where we need to devise a legislative instrument on robotics and artificial intelligence? The classic line of thinking is that legislating becomes necessary once a societal or technological change calls for an adequate legal framework. Once each home and business has an autonomous robot, society will change dramatically. People will work, cooperate, interact, have fun, live, and perhaps even fall in love, with highly sophisticated machines. Society will need to reconsider humanity's place in the face of these technologies. The presence of robots will give rise to unresolved questions and issues. The split between past and future societal models will be such that we cannot expect to take the emergence of information technology, the Internet or mobile phones as a starting point for reflection.

[4] https://ico.org.uk/about-the-ico/news-and-events/news-and-blogs/2017/01/gdpr-and-accountability/
[5] See <http://www.bbc.co.uk/news/technology-38583357>
[6] See http://www.europarl.europa.eu/RegData/etudes/STUD/2016/571379/IPOL_STU(2016)571379_EN.pdf entitled "European Civil Law Rules in Robotics"

Although the report is lacking in concrete suggestions, there seems no doubt that this is an area where important policy decisions will need to be made. One scenario that has been discussed[7] is whether a self-driving vehicle should be programmed to emphasise protection for its passengers in the event of a situation of danger or whether the interests of third parties should dominate.

Ian Lloyd
February 2017

[7] See, e.g., https://www.theguardian.com/science/2016/jun/23/will-your-driverless-car-be-willing-to-kill-you-to-save-the-lives-of-others.

Table of Cases

Table of Statutes

Austria

France

Table of Statutory Instruments

Table of European Legislation

Decisions

Recommendations

Table of Conventions and Other Enactments

PART I

Privacy, Anonymity, and Data Protection

INTRODUCTION

In 2013 extensive publicity was given to disclosures by Edward Snowden concerning the extent to which the United States' National Security Agency (NSA) and the United Kingdom's Government Communications Headquarters (GCHQ) conducted what is referred to as bulk surveillance of electronic communications. These disclosures followed closely upon others disseminated by the organisation, Wikileaks. The controversy continues to reverberate and the Investigatory Powers Bill that we will consider in detail at a later stage represents the most recent attempt to establish a new legal regime.[1]

Although much of the public attention has concerned the activities of the NSA, in some respects, the activities of GCHQ were potentially more intrusive. Largely for historical reasons (the United Kingdom was the world's leading maritime power when international telecommunications networks were established in the nineteenth century), many of the underwater cables which form the backbone of the global communications network were laid by British companies using British ships and pass through the United Kingdom's territory. GCHQ, it appears, has extensive capabilities to monitor traffic carried over these cables. Even today most Internet traffic is routed via cable rather than satellite as the former technology enables faster transmission speeds. We can see this in our everyday lives. OFCOM research published in 2015 indicated that the average fixed line broadband speed was 22.8 Mbits/s. Mobile broadband speeds are significantly lower although the increased penetration of 4G technology has introduced significant improvements. OFCOM estimated that average 4G mobile connections speeds in April 2015 were 14.7 MBs. This compares with estimates of speeds of 5.9 MBs that might typically be achieved using 3G technology.

Returning to the issue of bulk surveillance, the *Guardian* and other media sources have reported that:

> The [Snowden] documents reveal that by last year GCHQ was handling 600m 'telephone events' each day, had tapped more than 200 fibre-optic cables and was able to process data from at least 46 of them at a time.

---

[1] See also the Bulk Powers Review published in 2016 by the Independent Reviewer of Terrorism Legislation. Available from <https://www.terrorismlegislationreviewer.independent.gov.uk/wp-content/uploads/2016/08/Bulk-Powers-Review-final-report.pdf>.

Each of the cables carries data at a rate of 10 gigabits per second, so the tapped cables had the capacity, in theory, to deliver more than 21 petabytes a day—equivalent to sending all the information in all the books in the British Library 192 times every 24 hours.[2]

It also reported that the intelligence agency is seeking to develop the ability to 'exploit any phone, anywhere, any time'.[3]

It is not, of course only the activities of national security agencies that have attracted attention over the past couple of years. We also had the Leveson Inquiry into phone hacking by or on behalf of elements of the media. In autumn 2013 the House of Commons Home Affairs Select Committee engaged in a public dispute with the Serious Organised Crime Agency (SOCA) over delays in publishing details of the identity of businesses and individuals identified during the course of an Inquiry, Operation Millipede, into the hacking activities of a number of private investigators. A number of solicitors' firms have been reported to use such services. One is reported as commenting that it had used a private investigator to track down an individual who had embezzled £20 million from their client. In part this was necessary, it was argued:

> Solicitors who used private investigators said they were forced to because police cuts had resulted in fewer dedicated anti-fraud teams.
>
> They claimed the police often said clients would have to use the civil courts to track down money taken through fraud, fuelling the market in potential illegal data access by private investigators.[4]

This is a topic of current controversy with police tending to refer allegations of online fraud to the organisation, 'Action Fraud' which has very limited power to take action to investigate cases. Its website states that:

> When you report a fraud to Action Fraud, you are given a police crime reference number and your case will be referred on to the National Fraud Intelligence Bureau (NFIB), which is run by the police service.
>
> In some cases the police and other law enforcement agencies may want to contact you for further details, so it's important that you provide your correct contact details and keep any relevant information about the fraud.
>
> Although the police cannot investigate every report individually, the information you provide will aid them. The police use your information to build up intelligence about fraud, which includes who is committing what fraud and against whom. This contributes to making the UK a more hostile place for fraudsters to operate in and helps to keep other potential victims safe.[5]

Linking to another topic covered in this book, the criticism is frequently made that police forces are unwilling to investigate cases of debit or credit card fraud reported by individuals. Home Office Guidance to police forces indicates that:

> Account holders attempting to report cheque, plastic card or online bank account fraud offences at police stations will be asked in the first instance if they have been specifically told to do so by their Financial Institution. If they have, they will be referred to the Action Fraud contact centre. If they have not, they will be told to contact their Financial Institution who will deal with the account holder. It is not necessary to record a crime related incident.[6]

---

[2] <http://www.theguardian.com/uk/2013/jun/21/gchq-cables-secret-world-communications-nsa>.

[3] <https://www.theguardian.com/uk-news/2013/aug/01/nsa-paid-gchq-spying-edward-snowden>.

[4] <http://www.bbc.co.uk/news/uk-politics-23493112>.

[5] <http://www.actionfraud.police.uk/report-a-fraud/what-we-do-with-your-information<http://www.gov.uk/government/uploads/system/uploads/attachment_data/file/210800/count-fraud-april-2013.pdf>.

[6] <http://www.actionfraud.police.uk/report-a-fraud/what-we-do-with-your-information<http://www.gov.uk/government/uploads/system/uploads/attachment_data/file/210800/count-fraud-april-2013.pdf>.

The emergence of privacy

Recent years have seen the acceptance of privacy rights by the UK courts, albeit using established legal notions such as the doctrine of breach of confidence rather than establishing a specific right to privacy. The area is fraught with legal and practical difficulties and I must admit that I have never managed to develop an overall theory that strikes me as satisfactory. The seminal article, 'The Right to Privacy' by Warren and Brandeis is one of the most frequently quoted legal publications. As it has been developed in the United States it has been linked closely to physical property; essentially adopting the notion that 'an Englishman's home is his castle'. Individuals can seek protection in their private property but lose it when they move into the public domain.

The UK and European approach to privacy protection is rather broader but it is fair to say that most of our cases have also involved some degree of interference with private space. Again, the essence of most of the cases has been that personal or private information is being put into the public domain. We will look a little later at the case of *Douglas v Hello!* where unauthorised photos taken at the wedding of the actors Michael Douglas and Catherine Zeta Jones were published. In essence the case was about money as much as reputation. The couple had entered into an exclusive contract (worth $1.55 million) with another magazine for the publication of wedding photos. This perhaps illustrates one of the problems of privacy. Nobody offered me a million pounds for my wedding photos! Most of our lives are of no interest to anyone outside our closest family and friends.

Another fact limiting the extent to which the law can protect privacy—at least in the Warren and Brandeis sense—is that we live much of our lives in public. It is not feasible for me to walk down a city street and expect everyone else to avert their gaze. It may be that the nature of attention may raise legal issues. The civil and criminal offence of harassment, for example, may be committed by a person whose behaviour is likely to upset another person. In most cases, however, we have no direct remedy from the attentions of others. In addition to direct human observation, our actions are frequently recorded on surveillance cameras. It has been estimated that the United Kingdom has some 14 million surveillance cameras: approximately one for every four inhabitants. The accuracy of the figures has been challenged but it does seem clear that there are more cameras per head of population in the United Kingdom than in any other state. We now have a Surveillance Camera Commissioner[7] who has developed and promulgated a code of conduct regarding the use of this technology.[8]

A more recent development has been in the field of automated image recognition. This technology is very widely used within the road system. Cameras, both fixed and mobile, capture the registration numbers of passing vehicles. Around 30 million images are captured each day encompassing the car number plate and the front seat passengers in the car. The move to abolish the system of car licensing discs was enabled in large part by the tracking potential offered by this system. There are about 35 million cars on the road in the United Kingdom. As can be seen from the figures, most will be captured by an APR camera every day and the data will be automatically checked against the licensing database. There are certainly concerns that the level of licence evasion has increased following the elimination of physical tax discs but the level of surveillance of the vast majority of innocent motorists has been identified as a cause of concern by the Information Commissioner[9] who has promulgated a code of practice regarding the use of surveillance cameras. APR data is retained for two years with its database containing some 2 billion items.

---

[7] <https://www.gov.uk/government/organisations/surveillance-camera-commissioner>.
[8] <https://www.gov.uk/government/publications/surveillance-camera-code-of-practice>.
[9] See <https://ico.org.uk/media/for-organisations/documents/1542/cctv-code-of-practice.pdf>.

Although systems of facial image recognition have been trialled, their effectiveness has yet to be established.[10] Google and Facebook are currently the subject of legal actions in the United States regarding their image recognition systems that classify photographs held on their systems by reference to the people whose images are recorded.[11] Apple announced the introduction of a similar system in 2016. Again legal issues may arise.[12] To date legal actions regarding individual identification seem to have been confined to the United States but there must be a significant query as to whether such processing would be considered fair under European data protection legislation. In 2012, the Article 29 Working Party which has a membership of data protection commissioners from EU countries issued an Opinion on the topic,[13] although the technology has moved on from that time.

To date in our increasingly urbanised society we have enjoyed a considerable degree of anonymity. Again, of course, different factors may apply to celebrities. Other people may see my actions but they will not know who I am and, human memory being what it is, recollection will soon fade.

It is tempting to suggest that anonymity is no longer what it was, but that is perhaps misleading and indeed some people would suggest that too much anonymity is a bad thing. In previous generations people tended to live in small, close-knit communities. Every act would be seen and commented on by family, friends, and neighbours. Today, there is generally a culture of indifference to the lives of those around us, something which is frequently the subject of media comment when, for example, it is discovered that someone has been lying dead in their house for months without anyone noticing. Anonymity, however, in respect of public transactions is diminishing. It was reported as 'far' back as 2010 that the volume of transactions involving credit or debit cards exceeded those using cash. In many situations today—for example purchasing petrol late at night—it may be difficult to pay by cash. Garages may well take the view that it is unsafe for the company and its staff for potentially large amounts of cash to be held on their premises.

Paying by debit or credit card links an individual with a transaction in a way that is not possible with cash. It is not just credit and debit cards of course. Millions of people hold retail 'loyalty cards'. These link the holder to purchases linked to the card. The same applies to transport cards such as London Transport's Oyster card. The system retains a record of all journeys made using a card for eight weeks with data being retained in anonymised format for an indefinite period. One of the issues that is arising with improvements in processing power is whether supposedly anonymous data might be re-linked to an identifiable individual?

Oyster card data has proved a valuable investigative tool for police forces in the investigation of crime. It is reported that more than 6,200 requests (around seventeen a day) were made by the Metropolitan Police in 2011.[14] The figure has increased steadily since 2008 and the current figures may well be higher. It is quite common to see evidence led in criminal cases that an accused person's Oyster card was recorded at an underground station in the locale of

---

[10] For an interesting article on the technology and links to further material on privacy implications see <http://www.theatlantic.com/technology/archive/2015/07/how-good-facial-recognition-technology-government-regulation/397289/>.

[11] <http://www.theverge.com/2016/6/16/11934456/apple-google-facial-recognition-photos-privacy-faceprint>.

[12] See <http://www.theverge.com/2016/6/16/11934456/apple-google-facial-recognition-photos-privacy-faceprint/in/11687401>.

[13] <http://ec.europa.eu/justice/data-protection/article-29/documentation/opinion-recommendation/files/2012/wp192_en.pdf>.

[14] <http://www.macworld.co.uk/news/apple/oyster-card-accounts-regularly-accessed-police-tfl-admits-3336685/>.

Table 1.1 Number of authorisations and notices for communications data between 2012 and 2014

Year	Authorisations and notices	Urgent oral authorisations and notices
2014	517,236	55,346
2013	514,608	42,293
2012	570,135	39,092

a crime at around the time the offence was committed. At a wider level as we will discuss later, the Regulation of Investigatory Powers Act 2000 empowers law enforcement and other public authorities to seek access to communications data. This power has been extensively used as can be seen in Table 1.1, published by the Interception of Communications Commissioner.[15]

By way of comparison, 2,795 requests were made for authorisation to intercept the content of communications—the traditional notion of telephone tapping. One reason for this is certainly the procedures and controls relating to the acquisition of communications data—data relating to the time destination and duration of calls together with location data in the case of calls originating or terminating on mobile phones are much less stringent than those applying to interception of content. It appears that one of the reasons why GCHQ was a welcome participant in some of the NSA's activities is that UK law relating to acquisition of communications data is less restrictive than its US equivalent.

It is difficult to know how to approach such issues. Few would argue that law enforcement agencies should not be allowed to use new technologies, especially as terrorists and criminals are reported to be avid users. Fingerprints perhaps provide a good illustration and, perhaps more contentious, the use of DNA data. What is perhaps different in information-based tactics is that a trawl for data will inevitably involve intrusions into the lives of large numbers of completely innocent people. There is also, perhaps, a debatable linkage between data and individuals. The temptation is to assume that because my Oyster card indicated I was at a particular underground station at a particular time, that I was with it. Possibly, but all we can really know is that the card was at the location. I may have lent it to a friend.

We (almost) all spend a significant portion of our lives online, whether it be using social networking sites, engaging in e-commerce, or searching the Internet. It is reported that more people in the age range 18–24 rely on social media as their main source of news than more traditional media such as newspapers or broadcast media.[16] Few actions on the Internet go unrecorded and although many sites such as Facebook allow users to select the extent to which their content is available to other persons, default settings often allow unrestricted access and relatively few people take the time to change these.

An old saying is that 'knowledge is power'. Today we tend to say that 'information is power' and that is certainly true. There is a critical distinction between the concepts of knowledge and information. In this book I am trying to transfer my knowledge of information technology law. Knowledge transfer is not an easy task and can seldom, if ever, be completely successful. I will explain some concepts poorly, may well be wrong in some areas, and readers will also misunderstand the meaning of some passages. The words in the book constitute information and the transfer will be a complete success. Every reader will have the same information that I

---

[15] <http://www.iocco-uk.info/sections.asp?sectionID=12&type=top>.
[16] <http://www.digitalnewsreport.org/>.

put into the book. We do perhaps rely too much on information as a substitute for knowledge. My Internet browser groans under the weight of hundreds of bookmarked pages. I have the information but must confess that I have not read, let alone understood, many of the pages. An uncritical acceptance of recorded information can be a dangerous thing but more and more decisions that can impact significantly on our lives are made on this basis.

Can the law help to protect us? A lot of emphasis has been put on the enactment of special-ised statutes referred to in Europe as data protection laws, and elsewhere as privacy protection. We will discuss the scope of these laws extensively in this Part but one of the major problems that law faces is in trying to find an approach that will ensure its core values of stability and predictability in the context of technologies that are developing with incredible speed. To give a simple example, at the time when the UK government was beginning to think about legisla-tion in the 1970s a White Paper, 'Computers and Privacy' was published that was able to give the very precise figure that there were 13,263 computers installed in the country in 1975.

Defining what is a computer is not a simple task. Mobile phones, especially smart phones, which the telecoms regulator OFCOM currently estimates make up more than 60 per cent of the UK market, would undoubtedly fall into this category. In some respects they may seem innocuous devices, at least so far as individual privacy is concerned, but it has been estimated that if a modern smart phone could be transmitted backwards in time to 1985, it would then have been the most powerful computing device on earth. Staying in the twenty-first century, there are somewhere in the region of 150 million computing devices in the United Kingdom. In less than forty years, the number of computers has increased by a factor of 11,300.

One of the pioneers in the field of what was then called Computer Law was Alan Westin. He wrote in the 1970s to the effect that 'you do not find computers on street corners or in free nature, you find them in big powerful organisations'. How times have changed! It is unusual to stand at a street corner and not be surrounded by people texting on their mobile phones; the majority of customers in coffee shops seem to be using the free wi-fi to browse the Internet or catch up with emails. It is a requirement of data protection law in the United Kingdom that anyone who processes personal data on a computer has to notify the Information Commis-sioner of the nature and extent of their activities—and pay an annual fee of £35 for the privi-lege. At a guesstimate, some 40 million people should be notifying. At the latest count, 400,000 notifications had been made. Failure to notify constitutes a criminal offence.

We also have increasing amounts of computing power incorporated into the most mundane physical objects and one of the developing concepts is that of machine-to-machine com-munications. My fridge may be able to tell that it is running low on bottles of white wine and place an order with a supermarket for an online delivery. In another context it is reported that:

> The European Commission has adopted two proposals to ensure that, by October 2015, cars will automatically call emergency services in case of a serious crash. The 'eCall' system automatically dials 112—Europe's single emergency number—in the event of a serious accident. It communi-cates the vehicle's location to emergency services, even if the driver is unconscious or unable to make a phone call. It is estimated that it could save up to 2500 lives a year.[17]

One of the key concepts in data protection law is the notion of data controllers: persons or enti-ties who control the nature and extent of processing. With social networking, cloud computing, and the more general concept of Web 2.0 which involves much more user-generated content, it is difficult to determine who is the data controller.

---

[17] <http://www.eubusiness.com/topics/transport/e-call>.

Conclusions

One comment seems very appropriate to this Part and, indeed, to almost every section of the book. Old legal models are broken but it is not clear what should replace them. In less than fifty years we have moved from a situation where computers were scarce devices with limited processing power to today's reality of an all-pervasive technology. It is reported that the first telegraph message sent using the (now obsolete) Morse code was 'What hath God wrought?' What, indeed, is the Internet and what will it become? These questions will recur constantly in the book but in this opening Part we will focus on its impact on our private lives.

1

Privacy, technology, and surveillance

INTRODUCTION

In 2004 Richard Thomas, then the Information Commissioner for the United Kingdom,[18] warned against the dangers of the country 'sleepwalking into a surveillance society'.[19] This theme was developed in a report published by his office in 2006 entitled *A Surveillance Society*.[20] In the foreword to the report he went further claiming that 'we are in fact waking up to a surveillance society that is already all automatically around us'.

Smoke and mirrors—from echelon to prism

> Imagine a global spying network that can eavesdrop on every single phone call, fax or e-mail, anywhere on the planet.
> It sounds like science fiction, but it's true.[21]

The summer and autumn of 2013 saw a plethora of media postings concerning revelations about the US government's systems for obtaining access to communications data. The passage quoted above would seem to fit well into these but actually comes from 1999 and relates to the disclosure of a massive surveillance operation, known as project ECHELON which allegedly allowed the US security agencies (and also those from the United Kingdom and a number of other countries) to monitor the content of all email traffic over the Internet. For anyone interested, the footnote below provides a link to a report on ECHELON produced by a European Parliamentary Committee.[22] In the world of espionage and national security, little seems to change. There are always more questions than answers.

In summer 2013 we learned much about two surveillance programmes apparently operated by the United States' NSA and the Federal Bureau of Investigation (FBI). Under the first, the authorities have apparently been granted a secret court order requiring the major US telecommunications company Verizon (which offers fixed-line and mobile telecommunications services as well as broadband Internet access) to transmit on an ongoing basis a wide range of data concerning its users' communications to the NSA and the FBI.[23] In the United Kingdom (and the EU more generally) we are not strangers to the

---

[18] The status and role of the Information Commissioner will be discussed more extensively in subsequent chapters. Essentially, the Commissioner is charged with enforcement of the United Kingdom's data protection (and freedom of information) legislation. Again, this will be considered more fully in later chapters.

[19] <http://news.bbc.co.uk/1/hi/uk_politics/6260153.stm>.

[20] <http://www.ico.gov.uk/upload/documents/library/data_protection/practical_application/surveillance_society_full_report_2006.pdf>.

[21] <http://news.bbc.co.uk/1/hi/503224.stm>.

[22] <http://www.europarl.europa.eu/sides/getDoc.do?pubRef=-//EP//NONSGML+REPORT+A5–2001 –0264+0+DOC+PDF+V0//EN&language=EN>.

[23] <http://www.guardian.co.uk/world/interactive/2013/jun/06/verizon-telephone-data-court-order>.

notion that communications providers should be required to retain communications data and, under specified circumstances and procedures, transfer it to law enforcement agencies (and indeed to a range of public authorities). The transfer of communications data is authorised under the Regulation of Investigatory Powers Act 2000 and is supervised by the Interception Commissioner. In his report published in September 2016[24] he indicated that, during the reporting year, the security services (GCHQ, MI5, and MI6) submitted just over 43,100 requests for communications data. Police forces and other public authorities submitted some 717,000 requests for communications data (the vast majority of these requests came from police forces.[25]) Local authorities who have been criticised in the past for misuse of their powers under the legislation submitted a 'mere' 975 requests.

This may seem a substantial figure but to put it into some international perspective, Verizon have nearly 145 million customers, data on all of whom is required to be submitted on an ongoing basis to the NSA and FBI. It is not known whether other US communications companies (in particular AT&T which is similar in size to Verizon) have been served with similar court orders but there are suggestions that these networks have been very willing to cooperate with law enforcement.[26] In theory the requirement to obtain a court order is stricter than the UK procedure which requires only approval by a senior member of staff within the public authority. The fact that proceedings are secret and the fact that the US Verizon order became known only through a leak does not inspire confidence.

The second element of US practice that was exposed by the whistleblower Edward Snowden, concerned NSA access to content-related data held by a range of Internet-related companies such as Google, Apple, and Facebook. This data is clearly much more sensitive than the communications data discussed above. As with all aspects of the story there is uncertainty over even basic issues. The claim is that the NSA enjoyed direct access to servers. This has been vehemently denied by a number of the companies involved. A Google statement asserted that:

> Google cares deeply about the security of our users' data. We disclose user data to government in accordance with the law, and we review all such requests carefully. From time to time, people allege that we have created a government 'back door' into our systems, but Google does not have a back door for the government to access private user data.[27]

Google publishes on a regular basis a so-called 'Transparency Report'.[28] This provides data on the number of requests it receives from governments around the world for access to data on the browsing history of individuals. This does not, however, give details of how many requests from the US authorities relate to national security concerns. A number of other Internet companies have produced similar statistics although, again, with very limited data about the proportion of national security requests.[29]

The Investigatory Powers Bill and Act

The Regulation of Investigatory Powers Act was enacted in 2000 essentially as a reaction to the perceived deficiencies of existing laws relating to the interception of communications in the emerging era of mobile phones. The measure was controversial at the time of its

---

[24] Available from <http://www.iocco-uk.info/docs/56850%20HC%20255%20ICCO%20Web%20only.pdf>.
[25] <http://www.intelligencecommissioners.com/docs/0496.pdf>.
[26] <http://online.wsj.com/article_email/SB10001424127887324049504578543800240266368-lMyQjAxMTAzMDEwMzExNDMyWj.html>.
[27] <http://www.guardian.co.uk/world/2013/jun/06/us-tech-giants-nsa-data>.
[28] <http://www.google.com/transparencyreport/>.
[29] <http://www.guardian.co.uk/technology/2013/jun/17/apple-reveals-us-surveillance-requests>.

enactment and that has remained the case. At one level—and largely outside the scope of the present work—concerns have been voiced regarding what has been seen as extensive use of physical surveillance techniques by local authorities in cases such as fly tipping and the attempt by a parent to get a child admitted to a school on the basis of a false claim of residence in a particular locality. Reprehensible conduct, perhaps, but maybe not sufficiently bad to be placed at a significant level on the spectrum of criminal activity.

A further criticism of the legislation takes a different direction with the argument that in the communications field it has become out of date and of limited effectiveness. What is probably the best known 'over the top' communications service, SKPYE began its operations in 2003, three years after the interception law was enacted. The technologies involved in such activities—involving the separation of communications into small packages that potentially will be sent to their destination by a myriad of routes and reassembled only at the end point, means that the traditional notion of telephone tapping involving listening in to telephone calls in real time in the course of their transmission has become infeasible. A range of other factors have also come into play, including the widespread use of encryption technology either by individual users or through features incorporated in smart phones and applications such as messaging services.[30] Reference should also be made to the expansion of cloud computing services that allow users to share information without making use of what might be regarded as traditional forms of communications. The sharing of links on a cloud service allows access to data without actually sending the data to the recipient. The topic of data retention has also become of increasing significance and will be discussed further. We might also take account of the seemingly increasing use of bulk interception of communications data conducted by national security agencies. At the moment in the United Kingdom, this is authorised under section 94 of the Telecommunications Act 1984 although in a manner that is very obscure in its nature. Headed 'Directions in the Interest of National Security etc', the section provides that:

(1) The Secretary of State may, after consultation with a person to whom this section applies, give to that person such directions of a general character as appear to the Secretary of State to be necessary in the interests of national security or relations with the government of a country or territory outside the United Kingdom.

(2) If it appears to the Secretary of State to be necessary to do so in the interests of national security or relations with the government of a country or territory outside the United Kingdom, he may, after consultation with a person to whom this section applies, give to that person a direction requiring him (according to the circumstances of the case) to do, or not to do, a particular thing specified in the direction.

In general, legislation has developed in a rather unstructured manner, as have arrangements for the oversight of the exercise of powers conferred by the law. There is a Parliamentary Committee on Interception and Surveillance[31] and an Independent Reviewer of Terrorism[32] as well as an Interception of Communications Commissioner[33] and the Information Commissioner[34] whose remit extends over the wider field of data protection legislation. Divide and rule has long been an element of government strategy although one of the key elements in the new legislation is the appointment of an Investigatory Commissioner who will take on the duties performed by the existing agencies.

---

[30] Reference might be made to the recent controversy (and legal proceedings) between Apple and the US law enforcement agencies concerning access to the contents of messages stored on an iPhone belonging to an individual involved in a multiple killing.

[31] <http://isc.independent.gov.uk/>.

[32] <https://terrorismlegislationreviewer.independent.gov.uk/category/reports/>.

[33] <http://www.iocco-uk.info/>.

[34] <https://ico.org.uk/>.

In 2013 proposals were tabled by the then government for reform of the law but these were withdrawn following opposition from its then coalition partners. They have now been reintroduced in the Investigatory Powers Bill which was initially presented to Parliament in November 2015 in draft form. A definitive Bill was tabled in March 2016 and the measure received Royal Assent in November 2016. For further discussion of the Act see the 'Latest Developments' section at the start of the book.

As an opening comment it might be noted that the new measure is significantly larger than its precursor. The 2000 Act accounted for 113 pages on the statute book whilst the new measure weighs in more than double the size at 257 pages. Even allowing for consolidation of provisions across a range of statutes, this does represent a significant increase in terms of size and also of the complexity of the legislation.

Scope of the legislation

As indicated, the Bill covers a wide range of forms of activity. Key provisions relate to the issuance of warrants relating to the:

- Interception of communications (telephone tapping and seeking access to the content of sites accessed on the Internet or of email communications)
- Access to communications and location data
- Bulk interception warrants.

There are also further provisions relating to

- Data retention requirements
- The use of technologies that are designed to interfere with the operation of communications technologies such as mobile phones.

Some of these elements represent updating of existing law whilst others, principally concerned with the disruption of telecommunications and provisions for bulk interception, do mark a new development in the field.

Interception of communications

The ability to intercept communications has been a long-standing interest of governments. Initially this applied to postal communications and has extended into the era of electronic communications. In many respects, the monitoring of individual communications is a rather blunt weapon. A range of human rights instruments such as the European Convention on Human Rights (ECHR) place considerable emphasis on the right of individuals to engage in communications without the risk that they are being monitored by the state. Article 6 is one of the best known provisions in the Convention and states that:

1. Everyone has the right to respect for his private and family life, his home and his correspondence.
2. There shall be no interference by a public authority with the exercise of this right except such as is in accordance with the law and is necessary in a democratic society in the interests of national security, public safety or the economic wellbeing of the country, for the prevention of disorder or crime, for the protection of health or morals, or for the protection of the rights and freedoms of others.

As always, the sting is in the detail and the provisions in paragraph 2 of the Article are of key importance. Historically in the United Kingdom (as in many other countries) telecommunications services were provided by the state and interception of communications was largely a matter for inter-departmental understanding. Such a *laissez faire* approach was declared to be incompatible with the requirements of the ECHR in the case of *Malone v United Kingdom*.[35] In this case the informal inter-departmental agreements that had operated in the country were declared to be incompatible with the Convention's requirements that interception should be 'in accordance with the law'. The Interception of Communications Act 1985 provided an initial response to this ruling and the Regulation of Investigatory Powers Act 2000 took legislative matters a stage further. There does, however, remain uncertainty as to whether UK law complies with the other requirement of the Convention that interception should be 'necessary' in the context of the specific justifications identified. This adjective has been problematic for the United Kingdom in a number of contexts with governments mistakenly tending to equate the concept of necessity with that of desirability or utility.

A key feature of all the legislative instruments referred to is that interception of communications is unlawful unless it is appropriately authorised. This leads on to the further question what forms of authorisation are required. Developments in telecommunications technology have made the question significantly more complex. In previous eras we would talk about interception of communications in terms of telephone tapping or the surreptitious opening and reading of postal communications. In the era of mobile phones and the Internet a much wider range of information is potentially available. In some respects the contents of communications are less significant than the identification of who is talking to whom, from where and at what times. In a significant number of criminal cases, information relating to Google searches forms a significant element of the prosecution's evidence.[36]

If interception is unlawful unless authorised, consideration needs to be given to the issue of oversight, that is, who is to be empowered to authorise interception? Here the policy decision has tended to relate to whether responsibility should lie with a police officer, a government minister, or a member of the judiciary. As with many questions there is no simple or single answer. As indicated earlier, the concept of interception has become more complex.

The Bill contains extensive provisions in this regard. A request to intercept the contents of communications to and from identified individuals is required to be made to a Secretary of State. If approved by this government minister (and the requirement is that it should be personally approved) it requires also to be approved by a Judicial Commissioner who will be a senior member of the judiciary. In the event of conflict between these parties, a further appeal may be made to the Investigatory Powers Commissioner, a new appointment established under the legislation who will replace the trio of existing agencies identified above.

Location and communications data

In the era of land-line (fixed) telephones, location was not an issue of any real significance. A phone would be used where it was installed and that location would be a matter of record. Mobile phones have changed the situation dramatically and location data provides a source of data that can be of considerable value to law enforcement agencies. Location data, that is emitted whenever a mobile phone is switched on, can track its movements to a considerable degree of accuracy—in urban areas to within a few metres. At a simple level, apps used on smart phones allow users to track the location of their friends with their consent. Apps are also widely available that allow for more surreptitious monitoring although the legality of these is highly debatable.

As well as location data we have the concept of communications data. This is a controversial topic that has relevance both to telephone usage and to Internet access and which

---

[35] <http://www.worldlii.org/eu/cases/ECHR/1984/10.html>.
[36] See, eg, the case reported at < http://www.valuewalk.com/2014/08/florida-man-asks-siri-how-to-dispose-of-a-dead-body/> and also <http://www.bbc.co.uk/news/uk-england-bristol-15368208>.

applies in relation to both fixed and mobile phones. The definition of communications data and its relationship with that of content data is complex with the Act providing that:

'Communications data', in relation to a telecommunications operator, telecommunications service or telecommunication system, means entity data or events data—

> (a) which is (or is to be or is capable of being) held or obtained by, or on behalf of, a telecommunications operator and—
>
> > (i) is about an entity to which a telecommunications service is provided and relates to the provision of the service,
> >
> > (ii) is comprised in, included as part of, attached to or logically associated with a communication (whether by the sender or otherwise) for the purposes of a telecommunication system by means of which the communication is being or may be transmitted, or
> >
> > (iii) does not fall within sub-paragraph (i) or (ii) but does relate to the use of a telecommunications service or a telecommunication system,
>
> (b) which is available directly from a telecommunication system and falls within sub-paragraph (i), (ii) or (iii) of paragraph (a), or 5
>
> (c) which—
>
> > (i) is (or is to be or is capable of being) held or obtained by, or on behalf of, a telecommunications operator,
> >
> > (ii) is about the architecture of a telecommunication system, and
> >
> > (iii) is not about a specific person,
>
> but does not include the content of a communication.

The Act continues to provide that

> (6) The content of a communication is the elements of the communication, and any data attached to or logically associated with the communication, which reveal anything of what might reasonably be expected to be the meaning of the communication but—
>
> > (a) anything in the context of web browsing which identifies the telecommunications service concerned is not content, and
> >
> > (b) any meaning arising from the fact of the communication or from any data relating to the transmission of the communication is to be disregarded.

In the context of traditional voice based telecommunications, this is a relatively straightforward distinction. Communications data encompasses the numbers called and calling and the time and duration of the calls but does not extend to the words exchanged. Matters become more complex when we consider data relating to Internet access. An example might see a device associated with a particular IP address accessing a website associated with another IP address. The mere fact of access to a website will constitute communications data but depending on the scale of the site might indicate also the contents that have been accessed. There has been considerable debate on how substantial the level of detail relating to Internet access might be before it extends beyond communications data. In some respects the distinction is more important at the procedural rather than the practical level. Law enforcement agencies have long been able to seek access to the contents of communications but this has required to approval of a judge whereas approval for access to location and communications data can be given by a senior police officer. As indicated above, these powers have been used very extensively.

A controversial aspect of UK law relating to interception of communications is that evidence obtained as a result of lawful interception of communications is not admissible or usable in the course of legal proceedings. The Act provides that:

> No evidence may be adduced, question asked, assertion or disclosure made or other thing done in, for the purposes of or in connection with any legal proceedings or Inquiries Act proceedings which (in any manner)—
>
> (a) discloses, in circumstances from which its origin in interception-related conduct may be inferred, any of the content of an intercepted 35 communication or any related communications data, or
>
> (b) tends to suggest that any interception-related conduct has or may have occurred or may be going to occur.

Essentially, evidence obtained through the interception of communications may not be relied on (or questioned) directly in the course of criminal proceedings. The rationale behind this policy is explained clearly in a 2009 report, 'Intercept as Evidence'[37] presented to Parliament by the Home Office. This explained that:

> Sensitive intercept material, techniques and capabilities must be protected to avoid terrorists and other serious criminals evading detection and frustrating the investigation of their activities. Most targets have a rudimentary understanding of interception capabilities based on observation of police work and court proceedings, but it will be very imprecise. If terrorists and other criminals develop a more accurate understanding of the techniques and capabilities deployed against them, the task of protecting the public and national security will be considerably harder.

In 2014, the Information Tribunal—the major body responsible for determining the legitimacy of requests by individuals or organisations for access to official information under freedom of information legislation—ruled that a request for access to the legal advice underpinning this report should be made available.[38] To date this does not appear to have happened and the Bill largely continues existing practice in the area. Subject to some exceptions laid down in Schedule 3, it is provided that:

> (1) No evidence may be adduced, question asked, assertion or disclosure made or other thing done in, for the purposes of or in connection with any legal proceedings or Inquiries Act proceedings which (in any manner)—
>
> (a) discloses, in circumstances from which its origin in interception-related conduct may be inferred—
>
> (i) any content of an intercepted communication, or
>
> (ii) any secondary data obtained from a communication, or
>
> (b) tends to suggest that any interception-related conduct has or may have occurred or may be going to occur.

Any person breaching this provision is declared to be guilty of a criminal offence that may be punished by a term of imprisonment of twelve months.

Interference with communications

Whilst much of the legislative focus is intended to ensure that defects in equipment design or manufacture do not inadvertently cause interference with other equipment, a further

---

[37] <https://www.gov.uk/government/uploads/system/uploads/attachment_data/file/228715/7760.pdf>.

[38] <http://www.informationtribunal.gov.uk/DBFiles/Decision/i1690/Bingham%20Centre%20 EA.2014.0097%20%20Final%209Dec15.pdf>.

aspect concerns the use of technologies specifically designed to restrict or prevent mobile phone use. Such technologies might be attractive to, for example, theatres or train operating companies wishing to prevent mobile phone use that might interrupt performances or to enforce noise restrictions in 'quiet coaches'. Especially within the context of what is often referred to as cyber-warfare, attention is being paid to the value of being able to disrupt electronic communications.[39] It has also been reported that:

> Thousands of people in the UK are using 'GPS jammers' that plug into car cigarette lighters and can stop tracking systems used to detect stolen cars, monitor vehicle use or stop drivers working overlong hours, according to new findings from experts.[40]

Guidance issued by OFCOM[41] has indicated that use of any such devices is likely to constitute a contravention of the Wireless Telegraphy Act 2006. This provides in section 8 that it is unlawful to use wireless telegraphy devices except in accordance with authorisations given by OFCOM and that these may only be given where devices are not likely to 'involve undue interference with wireless telegraphy'.[42] In addition to this specific provision, OFCOM has commented that the use of jamming devices is unlikely to meet the requirements of the Electromagnetic Compatibility Directive[43] as they are likely to cause interference with items of wireless equipment other than mobile phones and have effect in areas other than those in which they are intended to be effective.

One exception currently applies to the general prohibition in the form of the Prisons (Interference with Wireless Telegraphy) Act 2012. This provides that the Secretary of State may authorise prison governors (or the heads of similar institutions) to 'interfere with wireless telegraphy' inside the institution with the aim of preventing or detecting the use within those premises of any 'device capable of transmitting or receiving images, sounds or information by electronic communications (including a mobile telephone)'.[44] The intention is to allow prison authorities legally to take steps to block mobile phone reception and thereby the use by inmates of mobile phones within the premises.

The Investigatory Powers Act takes matters rather further. It extends the range of institutions where jamming will be permitted to encompass psychiatric hospitals and immigration detention centres.

Bulk interception and acquisition orders

The concept of bulk interception orders is one of the most controversial aspects of the legislative proposals. It is essentially linked to the capability of intelligence agencies to intercept and filter massive amounts of communications data and was very much at the heart of the allegations made by the US whistleblower, Edward Snowden. The major UK security agency active in this area is the Government Communications Headquarters (GCHQ) which historically has worked closely with US security agencies such as the National Security Agency (NSA). A review of existing UK practice was commissioned by the government from the Royal United Services Institute for Defence and Security Studies and published in 2015.[45] This indicated that there was no evidence of abuse on the part of security services but

---

[39] See, eg, <http://www.ibtimes.co.uk/uk-special-forces-target-isis-communications-black-ops-electronic-warfare-1560137>. This describes how British aircrews attempted to jam ISIS communications, effectively by transmitting signals on the frequencies typically used and preventing their use.

[40] <http://www.guardian.co.uk/technology/2013/feb/13/gps-jammers-uk-roads-risks>.

[41] <http://stakeholders.ofcom.org.uk/enforcement/spectrum-enforcement/jammers/>.

[42] Wireless Telegraphy Act 2006, s. 8(5).

[43] Directive EC89/336 as amended.

[44] Prisons (Interference with Wireless Telegraphy) Act 2012, s. 1.

[45] <https://rusi.org/sites/default/files/20150714_whr_2–15_a_democratic_licence_to_operate.pdf>.

that the legal regulatory regime should be clarified. It was arguable that the conduct could be legitimised under a range of existing legal provisions—in particular section 20 of the Regulation of Investigatory Powers Act, but that these should be brought together and specific reference made to forms of conduct.

Bulk interception orders may be sought only in respect of international communications. The explanatory notes to the Investigatory Powers Act[46] explain that:

> A bulk warrant is sought for the interception of communications. The primary objective of the warrant is to obtain the communications of persons believed to be outside the UK, which are likely to be of national security interest and may be selected for examination subsequently. Due to the nature of internet-based communications, it is inevitable that some communications between persons in the UK will also be intercepted. In order to select for examination the content of those communications, a targeted examination warrant must be sought. This will need to be authorised personally by the Secretary of State and approved by a judicial commissioner.

Effectively, under the authorisation of a bulk interception warrant, security agencies will be able to collect large amounts of communications and filter out communications from outside the United Kingdom that appear likely to be of relevance to their work. These can be subjected to more detailed analysis but communications to and from the United Kingdom may only be scrutinised under the terms of a specific or targeted warrant.

Public and private surveillance

There is no doubt that communications data can be a valuable investigative tool for crime detection. In evidence before the Committee the Director General of the then Serious and Organised Crime Agency indicated that it was used in 'around 95 per cent' of their investigations. It is very common for information about Internet activity to be led in criminal cases. What we are seeing increasingly—especially as telecommunications networks and services are located squarely in the private sector—is that distinctions between public and private surveillance are becoming blurred. Surveillance systems such as Prism could not operate without the involvement and cooperation, whether voluntary or under legal compulsion, of private companies.

In 2012, the *Daily Telegraph* reported on a murder trial in which the female victim had vanished from her home with her body being found several weeks later. At the trial of the accused, a Dutch engineer named Tabak, prosecution evidence was led on the following lines:

> Lyndsey Farmery, an internet use analyst who assisted police with the investigation, took the jury through Tabak's online activity in the days after killing 25-year-old Miss Yeates.
>
> Web records from work and personal laptops show he researched the Wikipedia page for murder and maximum sentence for manslaughter, she said.
>
> While regularly checking the Avon and Somerset police website and a local news site, the Dutch engineer was also checking body decomposition rates.
>
> Days after killing Miss Yeates at her Clifton flat on December 17, Tabak watched a time-lapse video of a body decomposing, Bristol Crown Court heard.
>
> Tabak—who denies murder but admits manslaughter—also went on Google to look up the definition of sexual assault.[47]

---

[46] <http://www.publications.parliament.uk/pa/bills/cbill/2016–2017/0002/en/17002en06.htm>.

[47] <http://www.telegraph.co.uk/news/uknews/crime/8836161/Vincent-Tabak-researched-unsolved-murders-after-killing-Joanna-Yeates.html>.

In any matter relating to criminal investigations and even concerning issues of national security, there has to be a balance between the legitimate need for secrecy and public accountability. The key issue is perhaps proportionality. We live very large parts of our existence online. Data from the Office of Communications indicates that 86 per cent of UK households have Internet access. It further indicates that in 2016 the average UK consumer now sends fifty texts per week—a figure that has more than doubled in four years—with over 101 billion SMS messages sent in 2015–16, although the popularity of this form of communication is diminishing as instant messaging (IM) services have come to dominate the market. It was estimated in 2014 that 160 billion IMs were sent and it is likely that this figure has increased in subsequent years.[48] OFCOM also calculates that:

> [W]e are spending more time on media and communications than on sleeping. The average UK adult uses media and communications services for 8 hours 45 minutes, and sleeps for 8 hours 18 minutes.[49]

Almost another ninety minutes per week is spent accessing social networking sites and email, or using a smart phone to access the Internet, while for the first time ever fewer phone calls are being made on both fixed and mobile phones than in the previous year. In all these situations we disseminate data that can readily be accessed, stored, and processed. There is increasing use of mobile devices with the OFCOM report indicating that a majority of people now use these devices as their primary means of accessing the Internet. These devices, of course generate location data allowing their movements to be tracked often to within a few metres. Readers of this book who use features such as Apple's 'Find My Friends' (or its Android equivalent) on their smart phone will be aware how precise location data can be. An alternative example you might consider would be a system such as Google maps that give detailed route guidance to pedestrians. Reference has been made above to the activities of national security agencies in the United Kingdom and the United States in this respect and legal implications will be considered in more detail later.

Bulk collection and processing of email is not limited to national security agencies. In 2014 Google admitted that it engaged in analysis of its customers' Gmail messages for advertising purposes.[50] In 2016 the instant messaging service WhatsApp announced a change to its privacy policy that would allow it to share data with its patent company, Facebook, to allow the latter to send 'targeted' adverts to users.[51] The conformity of this change with data protection law is perhaps questionable.[52]

To finish this introductory section on a lighter note, but one that does perhaps make the point about proportionality, I recall an intellectual exercise intended to identify the best way to reduce casualties in road accidents. We can all think of suggestions, invariably involving additional or improved safety features in cars. The winning suggestion was rather different. Prohibit seat belts and air bags. Instead make it mandatory to have a sharp spike fitted on the steering wheel pointing directly at the driver's heart. I'm sure it would cut the number of accidents but . . .

---

[48] <http://stakeholders.ofcom.org.uk/market-data-research/market-data/communications-market-reports/>.

[49] <http://www.digitaldayresearch.co.uk>.

[50] See <https://www.theguardian.com/technology/2014/apr/15/gmail-scans-all-emails-new-google-terms-clarify>.

[51] <http://www.bbc.co.uk/news/technology-37184651>.

[52] <https://ico.org.uk/about-the-ico/news-and-events/news-and-blogs/2016/08/statement-on-changes-to-whatsapp-and-facebook-s-handling-of-personal-data/>.

Forms of surveillance

In 1971, Alan Westin in his seminal work, *Information Technology in a Democracy*,[53] identified three forms of surveillance that might be conducted by public authorities:

- physical
- psychological
- data.

Physical surveillance, as the name suggests, involves the act of watching or listening to the actions of an individual. Such surveillance, even making use of technology, has tended to be an expensive undertaking capable of being applied only to a limited number of individuals. In investigations subsequent to the 7 July 2005 bombings in London, it emerged that at least one of the bombers had come to the notice of the security services but had not been placed under surveillance. An intelligence source was reported as suggesting that MI5 considered that at the time of the London bombings in 2005, there were in the region of 800 Al Qaeda suspects, a figure which subsequently rose by a further 200. Whilst the security services tried to keep as many people under surveillance as possible, this was an extremely labour-intensive process, with the source suggesting that keeping a person under surveillance for twenty-four hours a day would require a team of between twenty and forty watchers. At the lower estimate, this would require MI5 to have 20,000 operatives. At the time in question, the total staff to cover all aspects of its work was in the region of 2,000[54] although in November 2015, the then Chancellor announced very extensive extensions to the staffing resources of the agencies.[55] Obviously—and as illustrated by the failure to monitor the actual bombers more closely—only a small proportion of identified suspects could be subjected to physical surveillance.

Examples of *psychological surveillance* include forms of interrogation or the use of personality tests, as favoured by some employers. Once again, logistical and cost constraints have served to limit the use of these techniques. The end-product of any form of surveillance is data or information.

With both physical and psychological surveillance, an active role is played by the watcher. *Data surveillance* involves a different, more passive approach. Every action by an individual reveals something about the person. Very few actions do not involve individuals in giving out a measure of information about themselves. This may occur directly, for example, in filling out a form, or indirectly, as when goods or services are purchased. The essence of data surveillance lies in the collection and retention of these items of information.

With the ability to digitise any form of information, boundaries between the various forms of surveillance are disappearing with the application of information technology linking surveillance techniques into a near seamless web of surveillance. Developments in data processing suggest that the distinction between informational and physical privacy is becoming more and more flimsy. The reach of systems of physical surveillance has been increased enormously by the involvement of the computer to digitise and process the information received.

---

[53] Unir Microfilms Int., 1971.

[54] <http://thescotsman.scotsman.com/londonbombings/MI5-spied-on-only-one.5282797.jp>. The Intelligence and Security Committee made the same point in their report on the bombings (available from <http://www.cabinetoffice.gov.uk/publications/reports/intelligence/isc_7july_report.pdf>) although the precise numbers cited here were omitted for reasons of national security.

[55] <http://www.telegraph.co.uk/news/politics/11984575/George-Osborne-announces-1000-extra-intelligence-staff-to-tackle-threat-of-Isil.html>.

Today, the critical distinction between forms of surveillance is perhaps between direct and targeted surveillance of particular individuals and the more general, all pervasive surveillance which permeates all our lives without being specifically directed at any particular purpose. As George Orwell wrote in his famous novel, *1984*:

> There was of course no way of knowing whether you were being watched at any given moment. How often, or on what system, the Thought Police plugged in on any individual wire was guesswork. It was even conceivable that they watched everybody all the time, but at any rate they could plug in your wire whenever they wanted to. You have to live—did live, from habit that became instinct—in the assumption that every sound you made was overheard, and, except in darkness, every movement scrutinized.

This certainly has echoes of much of the debate about current surveillance. When we are directly and personally the subject of scrutiny, there may well be the sense that our privacy is being infringed—and this chapter will continue to consider the extent to which rights of privacy are accepted and protected in the United Kingdom. In other cases, the issue is perhaps more that we are losing the ability to transact anonymously. In our information-based society, extensive details concerning the most trivial actions undertaken are recorded. In the context of e-commerce, an online bookshop will know, at least once customers have bought goods or accepted the presence of cookies on their computers, the title of every book which is examined and the nature of catalogue searches made. This can be linked to name and address details.

Perhaps the most noticeable and extensive surveillance tool is the closed-circuit television camera (CCTV). It is a rare high street or even shop which does not have one or more cameras. The estimate is frequently cited that there are in the region of 14.2 million CCTVs in the United Kingdom. With a population approaching 60 million, that equates to roughly one camera for every fourteen inhabitants of the country. Two million motorists are fined each year as a result of being caught by speed cameras. In general, it is estimated that the average person can expect to be 'caught' on camera around 300 times a day.[56]

Traditionally, CCTV systems have relied upon images being viewed and assessed by human operators. In at least some instances this is no longer the case. A nationwide system of automatic number plate recognition (ANPR) cameras is being installed on the United Kingdom's roads. Around 10 million number plates are recorded each day with a total of some 7 billion records stored[57] and compared against records maintained by the Driver and Vehicle Licensing Agency (DVLA) and motor insurance companies to identify vehicles which are not taxed or insured. The system also links with police databases to flag the appearance of any vehicle recorded as being of interest to the police.[58]

Within the physical environment, trials are being conducted with image-recognition systems linked to CCTV cameras,[59] which can monitor the movements of specific individuals. It has been reported[60] that the Metropolitan Police trialled such systems at the Notting Hill Carnival in 2016 in order to identify individuals who might be on record as potential troublemakers.

---

[56] <http://news.bbc.co.uk/1/hi/uk/6108496.stm>.

[57] <http://www.npia.police.uk/en/10505.htm>.

[58] Details of the system and its possible uses are given in a document, 'ANPR Strategy for the Police Service 2005–8', produced by the Association of Chief Police Officers and available from <http://www.acpo.police.uk/asp/policies/Data/anpr_strat_2005–08_march05_12x04x05.doc>.

[59] As was reported in *The Independent*, 12 January 2004, more than 4 million CCTV cameras are in use in the United Kingdom. At a ratio of one camera to fifteen people, this, it is claimed, makes the United Kingdom the 'most-watched nation in the world'.

[60] <http://www.independent.co.uk/news/uk/home-news/notting-hill-carnival-2016-police-security-crime-dates-a7213836.html>.

Surveillance devices in the workplace allow employers to monitor the activities and efficiency of individuals. At a potentially extreme level, the US Patent Office published an application from Microsoft for a system which will monitor an employee's heart rate, body temperature, blood pressure, and movement. It is claimed that the system will automatically detect signs of stress or illness.[61] Even the Internet and World Wide Web (WWW), which are often touted as the last refuge of individualism, might equally accurately be described as a surveillance system par excellence. An individual browsing the Web leaves electronic trails wherever he or she passes. A software program can transmit a tracer known as a 'cookie'[62] from a website to the user's computer. Cookies can take a variety of forms and may retain details relating to the user's actions, either for the duration of a visit to a site or for a specified and potentially unlimited period of time.[63]

In terms of goods themselves, the ubiquitous barcode which facilitates identification of the product and its price at the checkout may be replaced by radio frequency identification tags (RFID). These are essentially a form of microchip capable of transmitting information, both prior to and after the point of sale. This would, for example, enable the movement of the object to be tracked, both in the store and also externally. One possibility which has been canvassed is that future generations of banknotes will have RFID tags embedded in them in order to enable movements of cash to be tracked with a view to countering money laundering. In respect of motor cars, the European Commission has launched a programme designed to specify standards for electronic vehicle identification (EVI). The programme, it is stated, aims to develop:

> an *electronic, unique identifier for motor vehicles*, which would enable a wealth of applications, many of them of crucial importance for the public authorities to combat congestion, unsafe traffic behaviour and vehicle crime on the European roads. It is clear that such an identifier as well as the communication means to remotely read it should be standardised and *interoperable* all over Europe.[64]

In the United Kingdom, it has been reported in a similar context that plans are being drawn up to fit all cars with a microchip which will monitor driving behaviour and automatically report a range of traffic offences, including speeding, road tax evasion, and illegal parking.[65]

Examples of thickening information threads and trails are legion. Barely ten years ago, the only records compiled by UK telephone companies regarding telephone usage concerned the number of units of charge (an amalgam of the time of day when a call is made, its duration, and its identification as local, long distance, or international). Today, it is near universal practice to present users with itemised bills. These may provide considerable assistance to the person (or company) responsible for paying the bill in monitoring and controlling usage but also provide useful marketing information to the service provider, as well as raising issues concerning the privacy of other persons who might make use of the facility. Recent research conducted on behalf of BT illustrates well the issues involved. It is reported that 15,000 calls an hour are made from work phones to sex or chat telephone lines.[66] With mobile phones, even more data is recorded, with location data enabling the

---

[61] <https://www.techdirt.com/articles/20071228/021905.shtml>.

[62] For information about the nature of these devices see <http://www.cookiecentral.com/faq.htm>.

[63] A Report on Privacy on the Internet has been prepared for the European Commission Working Party on Data Protection and gives some interesting insights into the topic. The report is available from <http://ec.europa.eu/justice/policies/privacy/docs/wpdocs/2000/wp37en.pdf>.

[64] <http://www.publications.parliament.uk/pa/cm200304/cmselect/cmtran/319/319we45.htm> (emphasis in original).

[65] See <http://www.heraldscotland.com/news/home-news/death-driver-broke-limit-80-times.25756959> for an interesting example of the use to which this technology might be put.

[66] Cited on Ceefax (an electronic information service broadcast by the BBC), 21 July 2003.

movements of the phone to be tracked with ever greater precision. Again, the widespread use of cash-dispensing machines allows the withdrawals of bank customers to be tracked on a real-time basis, both nationally and internationally.

Surveillance and the law

Concern at the privacy implications of information technology usage was famously expressed by Lord Hoffmann when delivering his judgment in the House of Lords in the case of *R v Brown*:

> My Lords, one of the less welcome consequences of the information technology revolution has been the ease with which it has become possible to invade the privacy of the individual. No longer is it necessary to peep through keyholes or listen under the eaves. Instead, more reliable information can be obtained in greater comfort and safety by using the concealed surveillance camera, the telephoto lens, the hidden microphone and the telephone bug. No longer is it necessary to open letters, pry into files or conduct elaborate inquiries to discover the intimate details of a person's business or financial affairs, his health, family, leisure interests or dealings with central or local government. Vast amounts of information about everyone are stored on computers, capable of instant transmission anywhere in the world and accessible at the touch of a keyboard. The right to keep oneself to oneself, to tell other people that certain things are none of their business, is under technological threat.[67]

The potential dangers were further considered by Lord Browne-Wilkinson VC in *Marcel v Metropolitan Police Commissioner*.[68] Documents belonging to the plaintiff had been seized by the police in the course of a criminal investigation. Civil proceedings were also current in respect of the same incident, and a subpoena was served on behalf of one of the parties to this litigation seeking disclosure of some of these documents. Holding that the subpoena should be set aside, the judge expressed concern that:

> if the information obtained by the police, the Inland Revenue, the social security offices, the health service and other agencies were to be gathered together in one file, the freedom of the individual would be gravely at risk. The dossier of private information is the badge of the totalitarian state.[69]

As indicated in the above passage, an appropriate balance between privacy—classically expressed in terms of the right to be left alone—and surveillance—representing the wish to discover information about another—is difficult to define. Although initially appearing as opposites, privacy and surveillance are linked almost as if they were conjoined twins.

Whilst it would be an unusual person who placed no value upon privacy, significant difficulties have to be overcome in the attempt to give the concept concrete legal meaning. First, it is undoubtedly the case that different people and societies have widely varying interpretations as to which matters are private and which reasonably belong in the public arena. Millions of (mainly) younger people place details of their lives on social networking websites such as 'MySpace'[70] or 'Facebook'.[71] In many cases, the level of detail exposed

---

[67] [1996] 1 All ER 545 at 555–6.
[68] [1992] Ch 225.
[69] [1992] Ch 225 at 240. This quotation is also of considerable relevance to the emerging practice of data matching, which is considered more fully later.
[70] <http://www.myspace.com/>.
[71] <http://www.facebook.com/>.

appears excessive to those of an older generation.[72] Celebrities may court and value a greater degree of attention than the average person would find tolerable although, as cases such as *Campbell v MGN*[73] and *Douglas v Hello!*[74] illustrate, even celebrities draw distinctions between public and private life. Those living in close-knit communities may accept that their every action will be known to and commented upon by others. City-dwellers may expect much more in the way of freedom from observation but this may carry with it the spectre of the lack of interest and concern.

At a societal level, the United Kingdom is noted for attaching great value to privacy in respect of dealings with the tax system. In Sweden, by way of contrast, information about tax returns is a matter of public record. This is reported to have produced problems for the authorities at the time when the pop group Abba was at the height of its fame. Many thousands of fans discovered that they could readily and cheaply obtain copies of their idols' tax returns (which included a photograph). Dealing with the demand for copies is claimed to have brought the system close to meltdown. Even in the age of freedom of information legislation, it is difficult to envisage such a scenario being acceptable to the average British citizen. As perhaps an anecdote, however, whilst traditional forms of publication of financial information caused little stir, the emergence of a website, 'Ratsit.se', pushed even Swedish notions of openness to their limits when it started publishing financial details obtained from the national tax authority on its website, from where they could be accessed by anyone free of charge. The service proved popular, with about 50,000 searches being made each day. Many, it appears, were made by individuals curious to know details about their friends and neighbours. Whilst most might have hesitated to make a personal visit or request to the tax authorities for the data, the anonymity associated with web searches proved attractive. Numerous complaints were made to the Swedish data protection authorities. The tax authorities indicated to the website owners that, whilst Swedish freedom of information law obliged them to supply anyone with tax data, it did not require that it be supplied in electronic form. Provision of the data in this form would have involved a massive and disproportionate amount of work to convert paper documents into electronic form. Faced with this prospect, the site was re-organised. From June 2007, access could be obtained only upon payment of a fee and, in line with the principles applying in respect of Swedish credit reference agencies, the subject would be informed of the fact that a request had been made and of the identity of the requesting party.

Whilst surveillance is often seen as involving the surreptitious and unwelcome collection of personal data, this is not always the case. Although individuals may claim to value privacy, they frequently appear to do little to protect themselves. Millions of individuals have applied for supermarket 'loyalty cards'. Such cards provide an invaluable point of linkage between details of individual transactions and the more generic stock management computer systems which have long been a feature of retail life. The seller now knows not only what has been bought but also who has bought it, when, in conjunction with what other products, and what form of payment has been tendered. Analysis of the information will reveal much about the individual's habits and lifestyle which may be used as the basis for direct marketing, targeted at the individual customer.[75] Again, many thousands of individuals respond to lifestyle questionnaires which may be delivered either as a mailshot or accompanying a magazine. In return for the chance to win what are often low-value prizes, respondents freely disclose all manner of items of personal information.

---

[72] See, eg, <http://nymag.com/news/features/27341/>.
[73] [2005] UKHL 61.
[74] [2007] UKHL 21.
[75] For an excellent collection of links to materials on this topic see <http://www.nocards.org/>.

Privacy issues

The classical legal definition of privacy is attributed to a US judge, Judge Cooley, who opined that it consists of 'the right to be left alone'. A considerable number of other definitions have been formulated over the years. A number of these were cited in the *Report of the Committee on Privacy*.[76] The essential component, at least for the purposes of the present book, may be stated in terms that an individual has the right to control the extent to which personal information is disseminated to other people.

This notion, which is often referred to as involving 'informational privacy', has two main components. The first concerns the right to live life free from the attentions of others, effectively to avoid being watched. This is perhaps the essence of privacy as a human condition or state. Once a third party has information, the second element comes into play, with the individual seeking to control the use to which that information is put and, in particular, its range of dissemination.

The post-Second World War expansion of rights to privacy

Notions of a right to privacy have formed a feature of many domestic laws for decades and even centuries. Generally, however, rights to privacy would be rooted in a number of other legal concepts. In the United States, for example, the right of privacy has been seen as emerging from a range of constitutionally guaranteed protections. As was stated by Mr Justice Douglas in the case of *Griswold v Connecticut*:

> Various guarantees create zones of privacy. The right of association contained in the penumbra of the First Amendment is one, as we have seen. The Third Amendment in its prohibition against the quartering of soldiers 'in any house' in time of peace without the consent of the owner is another facet of that privacy. The Fourth Amendment explicitly affirms the 'right of the people to be secure in their persons, houses, papers, and effects, against unreasonable searches and seizures.' The Fifth Amendment in its Self-Incrimination Clause enables the citizen to create a zone of privacy which government may not force him to surrender to his detriment. The Ninth Amendment provides: 'The enumeration in the Constitution, of certain rights, shall not be construed to deny or disparage others retained by the people.'[77]

This expansive basis for the right to privacy has resulted in the doctrine being held applicable to an extensive range of situations, including forming the basis of the seminal Supreme Court ruling in the case of *Roe v Wade*,[78] which established a constitutional right to abortion.

In the aftermath of the Second World War, the concept of human rights began to be recognised at an international level. In 1948, the General Assembly of the United Nations adopted the Universal Declaration of Human Rights. This proclaimed in Article 12 that:

> No one shall be subjected to arbitrary interference with his privacy, family, home or correspondence, nor to attacks upon his honour and reputation. Everyone has the right to the protection of the law against such interference or attacks.

Although influential, the Universal Declaration has no binding legal force. Such a legal instrument was not long delayed. In 1949, the Council of Europe was established by international treaty. Its stated goals include the negotiation of agreements with the aim

---

[76] (1972) Cmnd 5012.
[77] (1965) 381 United States 479 at 484.
[78] 410 United States 113.

of securing 'the maintenance and further realisation of human rights and fundamental freedoms'.[79] One of the first actions undertaken within the Council was the negotiation of the Convention for the 'Protection of Fundamental Rights and Fundamental Freedoms' (European Convention on Human Rights, hereafter, 'the Convention'). The Convention was opened for signature in November 1950 and entered into force in September 1953. As its Preamble states, the signatory states reaffirmed:

> their profound belief in those fundamental freedoms which are the foundation of justice and peace in the world and are best maintained on the one hand by an effective political democracy and on the other by a common understanding and observance of the human rights upon which they depend . . .

Of the many rights conferred by the Convention, Article 8 is of particular relevance in the present context. This provides that:

1. Everyone has the right to respect for his private and family life, his home, and his correspondence.

2. There shall be no interference by a public authority with the exercise of this right except such as is in accordance with the law and is necessary in a democratic society in the interests of national security, public safety or the economic well-being of the country, for the prevention of disorder or crime, for the protection of health or morals, or for the protection of the rights and freedoms of others.

Although the second paragraph of Article 8 is couched in terms relating to interference by public authority, the jurisprudence of the European Court of Human Rights has established that the obligation imposed upon Member States is to ensure that private and family life is protected by law against intrusions by any person or agency, whether within the public or the private sector. In the case of *Hatton v United Kingdom*,[80] the Court referred to the existence of 'a positive duty on the State to take reasonable and appropriate measures to secure the applicants' rights under Article 8 § 1 of the Convention'.

The term, 'private life', is not defined further in the Convention. As with the US concept of privacy, the term has been broadly interpreted by the European Court of Human Rights, which was established to supervise the state's compliance with the Convention's requirements. In one important respect, the Convention right goes beyond the US notion of privacy. In the United States, a critical distinction exists between activities taking place on private property and those in public (or semi-public) places. The European notion of private life is less tied to physical objects, and may protect individuals in respect of their activities in the public arena. In the case of *Halford v United Kingdom*,[81] the European Court of Human Rights held that the protection of Article 8 extended to telephone conversations made by the applicant from her office phone. When her employers monitored the calls in the course of disciplinary proceedings against the applicant, the Court ruled that there had been a breach of Article 8.

The case of *Copland v United Kingdom*[82] is also of considerable significance. Here, the applicant was employed at a college in Wales. The college's Deputy Principal formed a suspicion about her relationship with another individual and believed that the applicant was misusing college facilities for personal purposes. Although there was no direct monitoring of the content of calls, the communications records of both outgoing and incoming telephone calls were analysed. Monitoring and analysis extended also to Internet usage in

---

[79] Statute of Council of Europe, Art. 1.
[80] (Application No. 36022/97) (2003) 15 BHRC 259.
[81] 1997, 3 BHRC 31.
[82] [2007] ECHR 62617/00.

the form of the locations of the websites viewed, together with the dates and duration of browsing activities. Details of the addresses of email messages were subjected to a similar process.[83] Arguing that there had been no breach of the applicant's rights under Article 8, the UK government claimed that:

> Although there had been some monitoring of the applicant's telephone calls, e-mails and internet usage prior to November 1999, this did not extend to the interception of telephone calls or the analysis of the content of websites visited by her. The monitoring thus amounted to nothing more than the analysis of automatically generated information to determine whether College facilities had been used for personal purposes which, of itself, did not constitute a failure to respect private life or correspondence.[84]

This contention was rejected by the Court which, referring to its previous decision in *Halford*, held that email messages should be regarded in the same manner as telephone calls. Although in this case there was no monitoring of the content of either telephone calls or emails, the data recorded, it was held, constituted an 'integral element of the communications'.[85] In the absence of any warning having been given to the applicant of the possibility of monitoring, the conduct constituted a breach of Article 8.

In addition to expanding the scope of private life beyond the limits of private property, the jurisprudence of the European Court of Human Rights has shown that the enforcement of the right to respect for private life imposes positive obligations encompassing the grant of access to at least some forms of personal data. In the case of *Gaskin v United Kingdom*,[86] the complainant, whose childhood had been spent in the care of Liverpool City Council, sought access in adulthood to a wide range of social work and medical records compiled during these years. At the time the request was made, the Data Protection Act 1984 provided a right of subject access only in respect of data held in electronic format. Although the Council took significant steps to assist the complainant—in particular by seeking the consent of all those responsible for creating records to their disclosure—access was denied, except where positive consent had been obtained.[87] Recognising that the grant of access to records containing personal data was an integral part of the requirements of Article 8, the Court held that the United Kingdom was in breach of its obligations by failing to establish an appropriate mechanism for determining the extent to which access should be granted.

As demonstrated in *Gaskin*,[88] although the breadth of Article 8 rights offers benefits for individuals, it also suffers from an inevitable lack of precision, especially in situations where conflict arises between competing claims. Building on the general principles, a trend emerged within Western Europe during the last third of the twentieth century for the introduction of data protection laws concerned specifically with the issues arising from the processing of personal data. One of the major concerns was that the capability of the computer to store, process, and disseminate information posed significant threats to the individual's ability to control the extent to which personal information was disseminated and the uses to which it might be put.

A linkage has frequently been drawn between the general right to privacy and the notion of informational privacy. This is clearly seen, both in the Council of Europe Convention on the Automated Processing of Personal Data and, more recently and extensively, in the

---

[83]   At the time that the activities occurred (around 1998–9), UK law made no provision regarding such conduct. The Telecommunications (Lawful Business Practice) Regulations 2000 made under the authority of the Regulation of Investigatory Powers Act 2000 would now apply to this form of activity.

[84]   para. 32.   [85]   para. 43.

[86]   (1990) 12 EHRR 36.

[87]   In some cases, consent was refused but in a majority of cases, the original author either could not be traced or failed to respond to the request. Effectively, silence was regarded as constituting refusal.

[88]   *Gaskin v United Kingdom* (1990) 12 EHRR 36.

text of the EC Directive on the Protection of Individuals with Regard to the Processing of Personal Data and on the Free Movement of Such Data,[89] which makes no fewer than fourteen references to the noun 'privacy'. Article 1 of the Directive is explicit:

> In accordance with this Directive, Member States shall protect the fundamental rights and freedoms of natural persons, and in particular their right to privacy with respect to the processing of personal data.

The scope of these measures will be discussed in more detail in the following chapters.

Privacy and surveillance

One of the main ways in which privacy can be threatened is by the act of placing an individual under surveillance. Surveillance can take a variety of forms. Physical surveillance is as old-established as society. At an official level, it might involve placing individuals suspected of criminal conduct under surveillance, whilst at the private level, reference can be made to the nosy neighbour looking at life through the corner of a set of lace curtains. In some instances, the success of surveillance may depend on its existence being unknown to its target. In other cases, the fact that conduct may be watched is itself used as an instrument for social control. As George Orwell described in his novel *1984*, the mere fact that people were aware that their activities might be subject to monitoring by the authorities would cause them to modify their behaviour, regardless of whether they were being watched or not.

There is no doubt that the world we inhabit today has changed and is changing at considerable speed. As well as being a commodity in its own right, data is the motor and fuel which drives the information society. A database with no data is a poor creature indeed and with the development of more and more sophisticated search-engine technologies, the value of a database lies increasingly in the amount of data held rather than the thought which lies behind the selection and organisation of material. The Internet and its use in academic life provides a very apposite example. There is no doubt that it provides teachers and students with access to a massively increased range of data. An author trying to track down a missing citation need often only submit a few words to a search engine such as 'Google' in order to be presented with the answer in seconds. More, however, does not always mean better. Excessive use of electronic resources will cause traditional research skills to atrophy, the availability of one hundred electronic articles saying the same thing adds little to the reader's understanding of a topic—even making the charitable assumption that the articles are accurate in what they say. The tendency is to seek to find the answer before one has understood the question.

Similar issues arise in the wider world. Information is replacing knowledge and the change in terminology also indicates reliance on a more mechanistic- and statistical-based view of the world. An example can be seen in the increasing use of DNA technology for crime-detection purposes. In the United Kingdom, aided by a policy of taking and retaining samples from everyone charged and convicted of even the most minor offence, the national police DNA database now contains over 2 million entries. This tool, as with most forms of scientific evidence, is based upon calculations of probability. Recent high-profile cases in the United Kingdom have shown up some of the failings of such an approach and, in particular, that technology is only as effective as those using it. The consequences for those wrongly identified and convicted on the basis of the misunderstanding of statistics has been profound and, on occasion, tragic.

---

[89] Directive 95/46/EC, OJ 1995 L 281/31 (the Data Protection Directive).

Although we may question the efficacy of some of the models, there is no doubt that the underlying principles of data protection matter more today than ever before. With developments in data processing and other forms of technology, there is the potential for every movement we make to be tracked and recorded. There is a well-established tradition of providing for necessary exceptions from the strict application of data protection principles in the context of national security and crime prevention and detection. These have been applied in the context of specific investigations and with the attempt made to secure a reasonable balance between the interests of the state and of individuals. With a move towards reliance upon databases, whether of DNA samples or other forms of information, there has been a significant shift in the nature of policing, from the attempt to find evidence linking an individual with an offence, to one where an individual is sought whose profile fits that of a suspected offender. In many cases, such an approach is justified but, as will be discussed in the final section of this chapter, the perceived and accepted need to defeat terrorism is leading to the removal of some data protection safeguards, with little being put in place to replace these. As with all aspects of design, unless components are included at an early stage, it is more difficult and expensive to incorporate them at a later stage.

Many of the recorded instances of the misuse of information have occurred, not as part of the original design, but as a by-product of the fact that the information is available. The story has been told of how the elaborate population registers maintained by the Dutch authorities prior to the Second World War (no doubt with the best possible motives) were used by the invading Germans to facilitate the deportation of thousands of people.[90] In this case, as in any similar case, it is clear that it was not the information per se that harmed individuals, but rather the use that was made of it. In this sense, information is a tool, but a very flexible tool; and whenever personal information is stored, the subject is to some extent 'a hostage to fortune'. Information which is freely supplied today, and which reflects no discredit in the existing social climate, may be looked upon very differently should circumstances change. It may, of course, be questioned how far any legal safeguards may be effective in the situation of an external invasion or unconstitutional usurpation of power. In discussions on this point in Sweden it has been suggested that:

> Under a threat of occupation there may be reason to remove or destroy computer installations and various registers in order to prevent the installations or important information from falling into enemy hands. An enemy may, for example, wish to acquire population registers and other records which can assist his war effort. There may be reason to revise the plans as to which data processing systems should be destroyed or removed in a war situation.[91]

Whilst such plans and procedures might appear to afford protection against the possibility of outside intervention, it must be recognised that, in the past, the use of personal information as a weapon against individuals has not been the exclusive province of totalitarian states. Again, during the Second World War, the US government used information supposedly supplied in confidence during the Census to track down and intern citizens of Japanese ancestry.[92] More recently, it has been reported that the US Selective Service system

---

[90] F. W. Hondius, *Emerging Data Protection in Europe* (Amsterdam, 1975). See also Victor Mayer-Schünberger, *Delete: The Virtue of Forgetting in a Digital Age* (Princeton, 2009). This states fairly precise figures and comments:

Because of the information contained in the comprehensive Registry, the Nazis were able to identify, deport and murder a much higher percentage (73 percent) of the Dutch Jewish population than in Belgium (40 percent) or France (25 percent), or any other European nation.

Obviously, all sorts of factors would have affected the scale of Nazi atrocities in different countries but as so often, history is trying to warn us.

[91] *Transnational Data Report*, 1(5) (1978), p. 17.

[92] W. Petersen, *Japanese Americans* (New York, 1971).

purchased a list of 167,000 names of boys who had responded to a promotion organised by a chain of ice-cream parlours offering a free ice cream on the occasion of their eighteenth birthday. This list of names, addresses, and dates of birth was used in order to track down those who had failed to register for military service.[93] Such practices illustrate, first, the ubiquitous nature of personal information and, second, that no clear dividing line can be drawn between public- and private-sector users, as information obtained within one sector may well be transferred to the other.

At a slightly less serious level, it was reported in the United Kingdom that information supplied in the course of the 1971 Census describing the previous occupations of respondents was passed on to health authorities, who used it to contact retired nurses with a view to discovering why they left the profession and to encourage them to consider returning to work.[94] Whilst it may be argued that no harm was caused to the individuals concerned by the use to which this information was put, it provides further evidence of the ubiquitous nature of information, and of the ease with which information supplied for one purpose can be put to another use.

Conclusions

Seven decades ago, the world was recovering from the trauma of global conflict. The negotiation of the Universal Declaration and the European Convention on Human Rights was regarded as a major legislative component of the road to recovery. The enhancement of individual rights was seen as the best response to the trauma of global terror. Today, the view appears to be that rights need to be restricted in order to defeat terror. Whilst it may, of course, be argued that a closer parallel is with the enactment of emergency legislation in time of war, the present situation is perhaps more akin to the image portrayed in George Orwell's novel *1984*, where a condition of perpetual and undeclared war existed between three power blocs, with shifting alliances and battles generally fought far from home but used as justification for repressive domestic policies.

Few issues in the field admit of easy answers. Any attempt to strike a balance between competing interests is difficult, especially in a fast-changing environment. Most would agree that law enforcement agencies should be provided with the best possible tools to enable them to perform their vital tasks. Data can constitute an extremely valuable investigative tool but the whole premise of data protection legislation over the decades has been that the potential for misuse is considerable. At least within a UK context, the main problem is perhaps a lack of awareness. If data were nuclear particles or perhaps even genetically modified foodstuffs, people would be aware of and respectful of the dangers involved in their use and transportation. The danger today is that data flows are invisible and when society becomes aware of the potential for misuse, it may be too late to put this technological genie back in the bottle.

---

[93] *Transnational Data Report*, 10(4) (1987), p. 25.
[94] D. Madgwick and T. Smythe, *The Invasion of Privacy* (London, 1974).

2

The emergence of data protection

INTRODUCTION

As discussed in the previous chapter, a range of concerns about the potential use and misuse of computers spawned a widespread call for legislative intervention. Although similar issues were faced by most countries, there has not been a uniform legal response. Two main areas of divergence can be identified. Within Europe, as will be discussed in this and the following chapters, omnibus data protection legislation has been the norm, covering all aspects of processing of personal data. In the United States and perhaps the majority of countries in the world, a more sectoral approach has been the preferred option, with a range of statutes being enacted to regulate specific forms of information handling, often referred to as privacy protection laws.

In substantive terms, there is little difference between the privacy and data protection models. Both tend, for example, to establish requirements that processing be fair and lawful and provide for data subjects to obtain access to information relating to them. The major area of divergence occurs at the level of enforcement. The European data protection model is based on the premise that there should be dedicated agencies, ready and able to act to secure the interests of individuals. This is very different from the approach adopted in the United States. In support of the European approach, one leading authority, Professor Spiros Simitis, former Data Protection Commissioner for the German state of Hesse, suggested that:

> data protection presupposes . . . the establishment of an independent control authority. Experience confirms what was already stated in the earliest debates: It is not enough to trace a mandatory framework for data processing. The legislator must also secure the monitoring of the processing conditions . . . Even if the data subject is entrusted with a series of rights he remains an outsider, deprived of the necessary information permitting him to analyze and evaluate the activities of the various public and private agencies.[1]

By way of contrast, it has been that suggested that the approach favoured in the United States:

> [is] designed to put the individual in the centre of the action, to let him have a large voice in decisions as to what information will be collected, used and disseminated about him. The Europeans take a paternalistic approach choosing to vest enforcement in bureaucracy.[2]

Both techniques have points in their favour. There is no doubt that supervisory agencies are better placed than individuals to take an overview of the legitimacy of processing activities that may impact on millions of people. However, the agencies have to straddle—sometimes uncomfortably—a wide range of roles ranging from consumer ombudsman, through law enforcer, to acting as advocate for legislative change. This has been notable in the United Kingdom in recent years, with the Information Commissioner seeking to play a role as a

---

[1] S. Simitis, 'Reviewing Privacy in an Information Society', *University of Pennsylvania Law Rev*, 135(3) (March, 1987), pp. 707–46.

[2] L. Hummer, 'Transnational Data Regulation: The Realities', *Online Conferences* (1979).

protagonist in the ongoing debate as to the future development of the law in fields such as identity cards and data sharing, where the interests of law enforcement potentially clash with informational privacy.[3]

The purpose of this chapter is to chart the historical development of data protection legislation at both an international level and in the specific context of the United Kingdom.

The development of data protection laws

The first legislative initiatives in the field occurred at the national level with the German state of Hesse adopting the world's first data protection statute in 1970 and Sweden adopting its Data Protection Act in 1973. The fact that data protection laws were pioneered in these two countries may not be entirely a matter of coincidence, and also illustrates what might be classed as the positive and negative aspects of the system. In the case of Germany, there had been experience of the misuse of data by totalitarian governments, both under the Nazis and also looking eastward at the time to the Communist regime in what was then East Germany. In seeking to place limits on the ability of public and private sector bodies to process personal data, the law can be seen as acting primarily in a defensive manner. The Swedish situation was rather different. Here, there was no history of totalitarianism, but, as referred to in the previous chapter, a more than two-centuries long tradition of freedom of information, under which almost any item of information held by public bodies was considered to be in the public domain. By conferring rights on individuals to access information held on any computer, data protection could be seen as extending some of the concepts of freedom of information into the private sector. Historically, neither experiences of tyranny nor of openness have featured strongly in the United Kingdom and it is perhaps not surprising that data protection has sometimes seemed to be a peripheral, rootless branch of law. It may be that with the recent Snowden revelations, things may be changing.

International data protection initiatives

From the emergence of the electric telegraph in the nineteenth century, international data transfers have played a major role. Although the first data protection laws were enacted on a national basis, even before this, pressure had been exerted for international action in the field.

In the data protection context, two—perhaps contradictory—concerns prompted international action. There were fears that national laws, which tended to have strong controls over the export of data, might have a protectionist effect. Conversely, fears were expressed by states that had adopted data protection legislation that national laws and policies could be circumvented through organisations sending data abroad for processing in countries (now referred to as data havens) which imposed few controls over their processing activities.

At another level, the 1970s also marked the period where developments in computers and communications technology rendered feasible a massive expansion in multinational organisations. Although these had existed for many years, they tended to be restricted to activities such as car production, where assembly plants in different companies operated largely as independent fiefdoms. Although standardisation has occurred, thirty years ago a Ford motor car produced in a German factory would be significantly different to its French

---

[3] As a personal anecdote, I raised an issue with the Information Commissioners Office in 2010 and received an automated reply indicating that it was taking the office seven weeks to acknowledge (let alone start to deal with) complaints. Given that data controllers are required by law to respond to subject access requests within forty days, this did seem a rather strange situation.

or UK equivalent and even more so with respect to the output from US plants. For good or ill, the year 1971 marked the opening of the first McDonald's fast food outlet in Europe.[4] The essence of this and similar businesses in the service sector is uniformity of product and identity across the globe. Such activities required the application of computer systems able to communicate across national boundaries. Beyond fast food, we have seen also the development of global legal and accountancy firms.

It was quickly recognised that international solutions were required in order to reconcile the interests of individual privacy with commercial interests. It was accepted that impossible burdens could be placed upon multinational enterprises should they be required to comply with differing standards in every country in which they acquired, stored, processed, or even transferred data. This remains a problematic issue, with companies such as Google advocating global data/privacy protection standards in order to simplify their task of complying with laws on a global basis.[5]

From the late 1960s, a range of international agencies have been active in the field of data and privacy protection. At the initial stages, the most prominent actors were the Council of Europe and the Organisation for Economic Co-operation and Development (OECD). The following sections will consider the major activities carried out under the auspices of these organisations. Brief attention will also be paid to work conducted under the auspices of the United Nations (UN). During the 1990s, much of the focus—at least so far as relates to the impact upon the United Kingdom—switched to work within the EU and the slow progress towards the adoption of the Data Protection Directive.[6] From May 2018, the Directive will be replaced by the 2016 Data Protection Regulation although it is unclear what the impact of this will be for the United Kingdom following the referendum vote to leave the European Union.

The Council of Europe

As far back as 1968, the Parliamentary Assembly of the Council of Europe requested the Committee of Ministers to consider the extent to which the provisions of the European Convention on Human Rights (ECHR) safeguarded the individual against the abuse of modern technology.[7]

Whilst identifying the dangers of computer abuse, the Assembly's report also drew attention to a paradox which remains largely unresolved to this day. Data protection seeks to give an individual a greater measure of control over personal information and to place controls over the dissemination of this information. Essentially this relates to the provisions of Article 8 of the ECHR stating that 'Everyone has the right to respect for his private and family life, his home and his correspondence.' This provision frequently conflicts with Article 10 which states that: '[e]veryone has the right to freedom of expression. This shall include freedom to hold opinions and to receive and impart information and ideas . . .'.

Essentially Article 8 has been seen as protecting individual privacy and the right to be left alone, whilst Article 10 has tended to be invoked by the media as justifying investigative journalism. The conflict is well illustrated in cases such as *Campbell v Mirror Group Newspapers*[8] and *Douglas v Hello!*,[9] where celebrities clashed with newspapers and

---

[4] In Zaandam near Amsterdam in the Netherlands.

[5] See, eg, <http://news.bbc.co.uk/1/hi/technology/6994776.stm>.   [6] Directive 95/46/EC.

[7] The linkage between data protection and notions of fundamental human rights remains significant with the recent European Charter of Fundamental Rights adopted in 2007 (but not applicable in the United Kingdom) providing in Art. 8 that 'Everyone has the right to the protection of personal data concerning him or her'.

[8] [2004] UKHL 22 on appeal from [2002] EWCA Civ 1373 and [2002] EWHC 499 (QB).

[9] [2007] UKHL 21 on appeal from [2005] EWCA Civ 106 and [2005] EWCA Civ 595, [2005] EWCA Civ 861.

magazines over the publication of photographs and stories about them. In both cases, the disputes went to the House of Lords, which delivered judgment for the complainants by slender 3:2 majorities.

Acting upon the Assembly's report, two separate resolutions were adopted by the Committee of Ministers, dealing with the private and the public sectors. The differences between the two sets of recommendations are comparatively minor, and for both sectors it was recommended that national laws should ensure that legislation requires that personal data be obtained fairly, and be accurate and up to date, relevant, and not excessive nor retained for longer than is necessary. The recommendations also provided for controls over the range of disclosure of data, the grant of subject access, and the application of procedures to allow any errors in data to be corrected.[10]

To a very considerable extent, these principles remain at the heart of data protection laws to this day. In some respects, given that consistency is a quality much respected in law, this is a benefit. If consideration is given, however, to developments in computer technology in the three decades since the original recommendations, problems may be identified. The recommendations, and most subsequent data protection law, are based on the notion of a single controller with a single computer holding data. This bears little resemblance to today's networked environment. In particular, reactive controls may not be sufficient. Once inaccurate data has found its way onto the Internet, the damage can never be undone.

The initial Council of Europe resolutions did not attempt to prescribe the means by which Member States should give effect to the principles contained therein. As more and more European countries enacted data protection legislation, so too did the problems resulting from the international trade of information—frequently referred to as transborder data flows—become more acute. In an effort to minimise restrictions on the free flow of information, and in the hope of preventing major discrepancies between the national data protection laws, the Council of Europe moved beyond its earlier recommendations to sponsor the Convention for the Protection of Individuals with Regard to the Automatic Processing of Personal Data (hereafter, 'the Convention'). The Convention was opened for signature in January 1981 and was to enter into force when it was ratified by five Member States of the Council of Europe. This did not occur until October 1985. The Convention has been amended by an additional protocol, 'regarding supervisory agencies and transborder data flows', which was opened for signature in October 2001 and entered into force in July 2004. At the time of writing, forty-two countries have ratified the Convention and twenty-eight have adopted an additional protocol which strengthens the original provisions in the areas of transborder data flow. In common with many Council of Europe instruments, the Convention is open for signature by countries who are not members of the Council of Europe and, to date, Mauritius, Senegal, and Uruguay have ratified it.[11] The United States participated in preliminary discussions regarding the Convention but ultimately decided not to participate.[12] In the course of a meeting of the Committee of Experts charged with drafting the text of the Convention, the US observer contrasted the sectoral approach adopted in that country with the omnibus data protection legislation envisaged under the Convention, and concluded that:

> the draft convention appears to regulate a function, that is, it appears to regulate automated or electronic data processing and what the automated data processing industry may do with records about individuals. To our mind the draft convention is, in essence, a scheme for the regulation of computer communications technology as it may be applied to personal data

[10] Resolution (73) 22.
[11] A list of all ratifications can be found at <http://www.coe.int/en/web/conventions/full-list/-/conventions/treaty/108/signatures?p_auth=tzrssbMq>.
[12] By contrast, the United States has ratified the Council of Europe Convention on Cybercrime (discussed in Chapter 10).

record-keeping. The establishment and exercise of individual rights and the privacy of the individual seem to be treated in a secondary fashion. I would note particularly that the word 'privacy' is rarely mentioned in the Convention and is not included in its title.[13]

Such criticism is perhaps unfounded. The Convention, as with much of the Council of Europe's work, is deeply rooted in the human rights context, specifically in the ECHR, whilst as noted earlier in this section, Article 8 of the European Union's Charter of Fundamental Rights provides that 'Everyone has the right to the protection of personal data concerning him or her.' Within Europe there is thus a strong linkage between notions of privacy and data protection.

In its Preamble, the Convention reaffirms the Council of Europe's commitment to freedom of information regardless of frontiers, and proceeds to prohibit the erection of national barriers to information flow on the pretext of protecting individual privacy.[14] This prohibition extends, however, only where the information is to be transferred to another signatory state. Impliedly, therefore, the Convention permits the imposition of sanctions against any non-signatory state, especially one whose domestic law contains inadequate provision regulating the computerised processing of personal data.[15] A recalcitrant state could effectively be placed in data quarantine. The standards required of domestic laws are laid down in Chapter 2 of the Convention, and its requirements will be considered in detail when considering the substantive aspects of data protection.

In addition to the Convention itself, the Council of Europe has adopted a substantial number of recommendations concerning the interpretation and application of the Convention principles in particular sectors, and in processing for the purposes of particular forms of activity such as might be carried out by police authorities or insurance companies.[16] Following an eight-year period of inactivity, a further recommendation on processing for the purposes of profiling was adopted in 2010.

The Organisation for Economic Co-operation and Development

At much the same time as the Council of Europe began its work in the field of data protection, the topic also appeared on the agenda of the Organisation for Economic Co-operation and Development (OECD). The OECD was established by international convention in 1960 and, as its title suggests, is primarily concerned with facilitating cooperation between Member States in order to promote economic development. This might be contrasted with the Council of Europe's emphasis on human rights. Unlike some other international organisations, the OECD is something of a Members' Club, with states wishing to join being required to satisfy the existing members as to their suitability. The OECD currently has thirty-five full members almost exclusively from the developed world, and cooperative agreements are in force with about seventy developing countries,[17] ensuring that the organisation's influence extends far beyond its formal membership. A Council consisting of representatives of all the Member States is 'the body from which all acts of the organization derive.'[18]

The OECD's work in what it has tended to refer to as the privacy protection field began in 1969 when a group of experts was appointed to analyse 'different aspects of the privacy issue,

---

[13] Text of US Department of State telegram, quoted in *Transnational Data Report*, 1(7) (1978), p. 22.

[14] Art. 12(2).

[15] The additional protocol referred to earlier was drafted to bring the Convention into line with the EU's Data Protection Directive. It provides that data may be transferred to an external state only if that state guarantees an adequate level of protection. These issues will be considered in more detail in Chapter 8.

[16] The text of all these instruments can be obtained from <http://www.coe.int/t/dghl/standardsetting/dataprotection/Legal_instruments_en.asp>.

[17] <http://www.oecd.org/pages/0_3417_en_36734052_36761800_1_1_1_1_1_00.html>.

[18] Art. 7.

e.g. in relation to digital information, public administration, transborder data flows, and policy implications in general'.[19] A further group was established in 1978 under Mr Justice Kirby, then Chairman of the Australian Law Commission. The US representatives also played a prominent role in the group's activities and the resulting product in the form of a Recommendation to Member States Concerning Guidelines on the Protection of Privacy and Transborder Data Flows was endorsed by the OECD Council in September 1980.

It was part of the group's remit that its 'work was to be carried out in close cooperation with the Council of Europe and the European Community'.[20] Although covering much the same ground as the Convention, the Guidelines can perhaps be seen as a common law-based approach to the issues, as opposed to the Convention which was drafted very much in line with the civil law tradition. It has been suggested that:

> In the final result, although substantially similar in core principles, the Convention and the Guidelines could be analogised, albeit in a rough fashion, to the civil and common law approaches, respectively. Common law systems proceed pragmatically, formulating the rules of legal behaviour as they acquire experience, while the civil law tradition tends to rely upon codification of rules in advance of action.[21]

Again, whilst the Convention is a legally binding instrument, the Guidelines, as the terminology indicates, have no legal force.

A further Declaration on Transborder Data Flows was adopted by the OECD in April 1985. This made reference to the fact that:

> Flows of computerised data and information are an important consequence of technological advances and are playing an increasing role in national economies. With the growing economic interdependence of Member countries, these flows acquire an international dimension.

It also indicated its signatories' intention to:

1. *Promote* access to data and information and related services, and avoid the creation of unjustified barriers to the international exchange of data and information.

2. *Seek* transparency in regulations and policies relating to information, computer and communications services affecting transborder data flows.

3. *Develop* common approaches for dealing with issues related to transborder data flows and, when appropriate, develop harmonised solutions.

4. *Consider* possible implications for other countries when dealing with issues related to transborder data flows.

It is clear from these objectives that commercial and trading interests provide at least as significant a force for action as do concerns for individual rights. Although the Declaration commits its member countries to conduct further work relating to specific types of transborder data flows, especially those accompanying international trade, marketed computer services, and computerised information services and intra-corporate data flows, no further measures have been adopted.

In addition to its work in producing legal texts, the OECD has also sponsored the development of what is referred to as a privacy generator. This online package is intended to be used by website developers and others to incorporate procedures and safeguards to ensure that sites operate in conformity with the principles laid down in the Guidelines.[22]

---

[19] <http://www.oecd.org/document/18/0_3343_en_2649_34255_1815186_1_1_1_1_00.html>.

[20] <http://www.oecd.org/document/18/0_3343_en_2649_34255_1815186_1_1_1_1_00.html>.

[21] Cited in L. Kirsch, *Legal Issues of European Integration* (Amsterdam, 1982), 21 at 45.

[22] <http://www.oecd.org/document/39/0_2340_en_2649_34255_28863271_1_1_1_1_00.html>.

The Asia-Pacific Privacy Charter initiative

At a less formal level than within Europe, significant work has been carried out by a range of countries in the Asia-Pacific region (including the United States) who have established the Asia-Pacific Privacy Charter Council. Hosted at the Cyberspace Law and Policy Centre of the University of New South Wales, the Council is described as a 'regional expert group' which aims to:

> develop independent standards for privacy protection in the region in order to influence the enactment of privacy laws in the region, and the adoption of regional privacy agreements, in accordance with those standards.[23]

The Council's work draws heavily on the APEC Privacy Framework drawn up by the Asia-Pacific Economic Cooperation (APEC) organisation, the Preamble to which recognises the need for APEC economies to provide adequate protection for personal data in order to give individuals the confidence necessary to participate in electronic commerce, behaviour which almost of necessity requires the transfer of significant amounts of personal data.[24] Although still at a relatively early stage of development, the work provides further recognition of the global nature of privacy issues and the relationship between the development of e-commerce and the effective protection of individuals' data.

The United Nations

On 20 February 1990, the United Nations' Economic and Social Council agreed to the Guidelines Concerning Computerised Personal Data Files.[25] These identify ten principles which, it is stated, represent the 'minimum guarantees that should be provided in national legislation'. The principles follow what might be regarded as the standard model, but there are two features of these Guidelines which justify mention at this point. First, they make provision for the application of the principles by international agencies,[26] bodies which might fall outside of national laws. Secondly, the UN Guidelines provide the option for the extension of the principles, both to manual files and to files held concerning legal persons.[27] In line with the Convention's approach, the UN Guidelines envisage the establishment of a supervisory agency providing that:

> the law of every country shall designate the authority which, in accordance with its domestic legal system, is to be responsible for supervising observance of the principles set forth above. This authority shall offer guarantees of impartiality, independence vis-à-vis persons or agencies responsible for processing and establishing data, and technical competence. In the event of violation of the provisions of the national law implementing the aforementioned principles, criminal or other penalties should be envisaged together with the appropriate individual remedies.[28]

Recent years have seen attempts made to involve the UN more deeply in the data protection field. At the 2009 meeting of data and privacy protection commissioners, a proposal was endorsed encouraging the adoption of:

> 'International Standards for the Protection of Privacy and Personal Data', allowing the development of a universal, binding legal document, which must be backed by the most extensive institutional and social consensus via the participation of the authorities and institutions

---

[23] <http://www.bakercyberlawcentre.org/appcc/members.htm>.
[24] <http://www.bakercyberlawcentre.org/ipp/apec_privacy_framework/index.html>.
[25] Available from <http://www.unhcr.org/refworld/publisher_UNGA_THEMGUIDE_3ddcafaac_0.html>.
[26] Part B.   [27] para. 10.   [28] para. 8.

guaranteeing data protection and privacy and representatives of both public and private entities and organisations.[29]

In February 2010 the UN rapporteur on human rights made a call for the establishment of global privacy standards.[30] It is unclear when, or if, such an activity might be undertaken. The meeting of data and privacy protection commissioners, as the name implies, is dominated by representatives from countries which endorse the European model of protection with the establishment of dedicated supervisory authorities. As has been discussed, belief in the efficacy of this approach is not shared in other jurisdictions. There is also a gulf between countries which view data protection as essentially rooted in notions of human rights and those which see data protection as having an economic basis. In part this is based on notions of international data flows but at an internal level there is also often the belief that e-commerce and other online activities will flourish only if individuals have confidence that their data will not be misused.

The development of data protection legislation in the United Kingdom

As with many inventions, the United Kingdom can claim credit for some pioneering developments in the field of data protection, failing to develop these, and subsequently having to act in response to external pressures. As early as 1969, a Data Surveillance Bill was introduced in the House of Commons by Kenneth Baker MP. If matters had been different, the United Kingdom would have been the first country to adopt a data protection law but, in common with most private members' initiatives, this failed to make significant progress. In the following parliamentary session, a further private member's Bill was introduced by Brian Walden MP. This sought to establish a statutory right to privacy. In an approach that has not changed significantly over the past decades, ministers (of all political persuasions) expressed reluctance to establish what would necessarily be a rather vague right. An agreement was made with the Bill's sponsor that in return for its withdrawal, the government would establish the Committee on Privacy, chaired by Sir Kenneth Younger.[31]

In its report, the Committee devoted a chapter to the implications of the computer. After receiving evidence as to the nature and scale of processing activities, it concluded that '[w]e cannot on the evidence before us conclude that the computer as used in the private sector is at present a threat to privacy'.[32] Despite this, the Committee identified the computer's ability to store and process large amounts of personal information, to develop personal profiles, and to allow remote access to databases as factors causing legitimate public concern.

The Committee's report was published in July 1972. Its contents and recommendations were debated in the House of Commons one year later, in July 1973. Speaking in this debate, the Home Secretary studiously avoided expressing any views on the Younger proposals on computers, but announced the publication for later that year, of a White Paper describing computer practices in the public sector and outlining the government's response to the Committee on Privacy's recommendations.[33] In fact, setting a precedent which was to become depressingly familiar, the White Paper, entitled *Computers and Privacy*, was not published until some two and a half years later, in December 1975.[34] As indicated, the

---

[29] <http://www.privacyconference2009.org/home/index-iden-idweb.html>.
[30] <http://www.theregister.co.uk/2010/01/20/un_terror/>.
[31] Cmnd 5012, 1972.   [32] Cmnd 5012, para. 619.
[33] 859 HC Official Report (5th series), col. 1956, 13 July 1973.
[34] Cmnd 6353.

White Paper's coverage extended into the public sector, with a supplement detailing the extent of government computer usage. It indicated that there were some 10,000 computers in the private sector and 13,000 in the public. Times have changed!

Whilst the White Paper reiterated the finding that there was little concrete evidence of computer abuse, its conclusion was rather different. The potential dangers were considered so substantial that:

> In the Government's view the time has come when those who use computers to handle personal information can no longer remain the sole judges of whether their own systems adequately safeguard privacy.[35]

Accordingly, it was announced that a Data Protection Committee was to be established, with a remit to make detailed recommendations as to the scope and extent of data protection legislation and as to the form of supervisory mechanism which should be introduced.

The Committee on Data Protection

With hindsight, the publication of the 1975 White Paper can be seen as marking a high-water point in governmental enthusiasm for the concept of data protection. This enthusiasm was certainly matched by that of the Data Protection Committee, which, under the chairmanship of Sir Norman Lindop, presented its voluminous report in June 1978.[36] Although dated in technological terms, his remains the most comprehensive and detailed survey of the impact of data processing activities upon the rights and liberties of the individual conducted in the United Kingdom.

The Lindop Committee's report was published towards the end of 1978. In early 1979, a general election saw a change of government, with the arrival of a Conservative Party pledged to reduce bureaucracy. Proposals to establish a new supervisory agency were not received with acclamation. International developments were to bring about a change of mind. During the 1970s, the lack of data protection law could be seen as a factor which would make the United Kingdom attractive to companies wishing to establish a European data processing centre. Unlike the situation in other countries, no formal or procedural requirements would limit the nature of the processing which could be conducted. As communications technologies increasingly facilitated the international transfer of data, the possibility that national controls might be evaded was not lost on countries possessing data protection laws and with the adoption of the Council of Europe Convention, the possibility of data sanctions being imposed against the United Kingdom became more significant. More extensive controls over the export of personal data were introduced. In commending the first Data Protection Bill to the House of Commons, the then Home Secretary commented that it was designed 'to meet public concern, to bring us into step with Europe and to protect our international, commercial and trading interests'.[37] Whilst undoubtedly civil libertarian concerns are fundamental to the concept of data protection—and indeed the 2009 Charter on Fundamental Rights and Freedoms (subject to a UK opt-out) affords data protection the status of a fundamental human right—it is significant that in 1982 these represented only one out of five interests identified and that, at least numerically, commercial and trading factors assumed greater significance. In a manner akin to a stereotype of the British Establishment's way of proceeding, a significant catalyst for action was a letter sent to *The Times* newspaper by a number of leading industrialists lamenting the fact that the lack of data protection legislation was beginning to impact adversely upon overseas trade

---

[35] Cmnd 6353, para. 30.
[36] Cmnd 7341.
[37] HC Official Report (6th series), col. 562, 11 April 1983.

by causing the United Kingdom to be regarded as an 'offshore data haven'. The clear conclusion was that data protection legislation was needed in the nation's commercial interest.[38]

Commercial concerns and lobbying succeeded where civil libertarian concerns had failed, and, in March 1981, the Home Secretary announced that: 'The Government has decided in principle to introduce legislation for this purpose when an opportunity occurs.'[39]

Following a further round of consultations, a further White Paper was published in April 1982.[40] By this time, the Lindop Report was reduced to the status of 'very helpful background information'. A Bill based on the provisions of the White Paper was introduced in the House of Lords in November 1982. It successfully passed through that House, but fell at the committee stage in the House of Commons when Parliament was dissolved prior to the 1983 general election. An amended Bill was speedily introduced by the incoming government, receiving the Royal Assent on 12 July of the Orwellian year, 1984.

The Data Protection Act 1984

Given that the Data Protection Act 1984 was replaced in its entirety by the Data Protection Act 1998, detailed consideration of its contents is unnecessary. Many of its provisions do, of course, remain applicable under the current regime and decisions made by the courts and the Data Protection Tribunal, which was established as an appellate body, continue to be cited as valid precedent. A few general comments concerning the 1984 Act and a brief assessment of its impact may be helpful in providing initial comment on the impact and relevance of data protection within a UK context.

As indicated earlier, the legislation was not introduced out of any genuine enthusiasm by the (Conservative) government of the day. Time after time, *Hansard* reports comments from ministers to the effect that the legislation was being introduced for commercial reasons in order to enable the United Kingdom to ratify the Council of Europe Convention. This was to be done at the most minimal level. On every occasion where the Convention prescribed minimal standards but left the way open for signatories to provide additional protection in national legislation, the UK Data Protection Act 1984 remained conspicuously silent. Moving ahead some fifteen years to the introduction of the Data Protection Act 1998, *Hansard* reports that the debates are replete with comments from (Labour) ministers to the effect that the legislation was being introduced reluctantly in order to comply at a minimal level with European requirements, this time in the form of European Directive 95/46. It is tempting to suggest that the Conservative ministers of the 1980s could have succeeded in an action alleging breach of copyright in their speeches.

Lack of governmental commitment has been a factor which bedevils data protection to this day. A decision that the concept should not impose any financial burdens on the taxpayer led to the introduction of an outdated and bureaucratic system of registration, whereby anyone involved in processing personal data was obliged to register details of their activities and pay a fee. Failure to do so constituted (and remains) a criminal offence. It is likely that any person who owns a mobile phone is legally required to register (now notify) details of the use to which they put the device. Beyond providing the supervisory agency's only significant source of revenue, it is difficult to identify any significant benefits arising from the concept. The financial straitjacket imposed in the Data Protection Act 1984 continues under the Data Protection Act 1998 (although the Commissioner's functions in respect of the Freedom of Information Act are publicly funded), with the consequence that, whilst terminology changes from registration to notification and, more recently, there

---

[38] *The Times*, 3 March 1980.
[39] HC Official Report (6th series), col. 161, 19 March 1981.
[40] Cmnd 8539.

has been the introduction of a two-tiered scale of notification fees with larger users being required to pay higher fees than their smaller counterparts, the requirement to pay what is effectively a tax associated with computer ownership remains.

The European Data Protection Directive and the Data Protection Act 1998

Until the early 1990s, the EU had played a peripheral role in the data protection arena. This could be ascribed to two main causes. First, the limited nature of the legislative competencies conferred by the establishing treaties gave rise to doubts as to whether, and to what extent, the EU was empowered to act in this field. Although the increasing importance of information as a commodity within the Single Market has provided a basis for European action, the exclusion of matters coming within the ambit of national security and, to a partial extent criminal and taxation policy, has served to limit the scope of the EU's intervention.

A second factor influencing work in this field had been a reluctance on the part of the Commission to duplicate work being conducted under the auspices of the Council of Europe and in 1981, the Commission addressed a Recommendation to Member States that they sign and ratify the Convention.[41] By 1990, the Convention had been signed by all the Member States, but ratified only by six.[42] As will be described, the Convention establishes minimal standards but affords considerable discretion to signatories. A number of Member States, such as Germany and Sweden, had enacted laws which were considerably in advance of the Convention's minimum standards, whilst others, such as the United Kingdom, had openly indicated an intention to do the bare minimum necessary to satisfy obligations under that instrument. By 1990, Commission concern at the effect that discrepancies in the Member States' laws and regulations might have on inter-community trade resulted in proposals being brought forward for a Directive on the Protection of Individuals with Regard to the Processing of Personal Data and on the Free Movement of Such Data.[43] The EU legislation, it was stated, would 'give substance to and amplify'[44] the provisions of the Convention. The objective of the proposal was stated to be to harmonise the data protection laws of the Member States at a 'high level'.[45] This approach was necessary because the Directive was adopted under the authority of Article 100a of the Treaty of Rome. This provides that the Community's law-making bodies may:

> adopt the measures for the approximation of the provisions laid down by law, regulation or administrative action in Member States which have as their object the establishing and functioning of the internal market.

Reliance upon Article 100a has the further significant consequence that any harmonising measures introduced under its authority have to secure 'a high level of protection'. Effectively, therefore, the Directive has to secure a level of protection equivalent to the highest currently available in the Member States. It is unclear how effective the Directive has been in this regard, with complaints being aired from countries such as Germany that implementation might dilute their existing regimes, especially in respect of transborder data flows. For the United Kingdom, implementation of the Directive required significant

---

[41] OJ 1981 L 246/31.
[42] Denmark, France, Germany, Luxembourg, Spain, and the United Kingdom.
[43] OJ 1990 C 277/03.
[44] OJ 1990 C 277/03, para. 22.
[45] OJ 1990 C 277/03, Preamble, para. 7.

change to the Data Protection Act 1984, as well as its expansion. A Consultation Paper was published by the Home Office in March 1996, seeking views on the implementation of the Directive and indicating a preference for a minimalist approach to law reform:

> Over-elaborate data protection threatens competitiveness, and does not necessarily bring additional benefits for individuals. *It follows that the Government intends to go no further in implementing the Directive than is absolutely necessary to satisfy the United Kingdom's obligations in European law. It will consider whether any additional changes to the current data protection regime are needed so as to ensure that it does not go beyond what is required by the Directive and the Council of Europe Convention.*[46]

The Commission's proposal for a general Directive in the area of data protection was accompanied by a further proposal for a Directive 'Concerning the Protection of Personal Data and Privacy in the Context of Public Digital Telecommunications Networks'.[47] Following a five-year journey through the EU's legislative process,[48] the Data Protection Directive was adopted on 24 October 1995,[49] with a requirement that it be implemented within the Member States by 24 October 1998. The Telecoms Directive—which for a while appeared to have been dropped from the legislative agenda—resurfaced, to be adopted in December 1997.[50] It also required to be implemented by October 1998. The Telecoms Data Protection Directive proved to be a somewhat short-lived measure. In conjunction with a much broader reform of the European telecommunications regulatory regime, the Directive was replaced in 2002 by the Directive 'Concerning the Processing of Personal Data and the Protection of Privacy in the Electronic Communications Sector'.[51] This was required to be implemented in the Member States by 31 October 2003. Once again, aspects of the Directive proved short-lived with the adoption of Directive 2009/136/E, generally referred to as the 'Citizens' Rights Directive' in November 2009. This Directive required to be implemented in the Member States by May 2011. The provisions of these sector-specific measures will be discussed in more detail in Chapter 7.

In January 1998 the Data Protection Bill was introduced in the House of Lords. Its progress through Parliament was relatively uncontroversial, with only one division being required throughout its parliamentary passage.[52] The major feature of the Bill's progress was the very large number of amendments tabled by the government—more than 200 in total. The Act received the Royal Assent on 16 July, although its entry into force was delayed pending the drafting of what proved to be seventeen items of secondary legislation and it was not until 1 March 2000 that the new legislation entered into force. In its failure timeously to implement the Data Protection Directive,[53] the United Kingdom was joined by a majority of the Member States. Legal action was raised by the Commission against Denmark, France, Germany, Ireland, Luxembourg, and the Netherlands, alleging a continuing failure to implement the Directive, although in the case of every state except Luxembourg, the belated implementation of the Directive resulted in the legal proceedings being abandoned.[54]

---

[46] para. 1.2 (emphasis in original).

[47] OJ 1990 C 277/12.

[48] A timescale that has essentially been repeated with the new Data Protection Regulation.

[49] Directive 95/46/EC, OJ 1995 L 281/31.

[50] Directive 97/66/EC Concerning the Protection of Personal Data and Privacy in the Context of Public Digital Telecommunications Networks, OJ 1998 L 24.

[51] Directive 2002/58/EC, OJ 2002 L 201/37 (Privacy and Electronic Communications Directive).

[52] This was in relation to proposals in the Bill to provide ministers with wide-ranging powers to exempt processing activities from the subject access provisions. The House of Lords voted to remove these powers from the Bill. A more closely defined provision was introduced in the House of Commons.

[53] Directive 95/46/EC.

[54] For current information on the status of implementation, see <http://ec.europa.eu/justice/policies/privacy/lawreport/index_en.htm#firstreport>.

The Data Protection Act 1998

As an initial comment, it may be noted that the Data Protection Act 1998 is considerably larger than the 1984 legislation. The Data Protection Act 1984 has forty-three sections and six Schedules; the 1998 statute has seventy-five sections and sixteen Schedules. To an extent greater than its 1984 precursor, the Act provides only a framework, with significant matters remaining to be determined by statutory instruments. Although this approach will allow easier modification and updating of the legislation than was possible with the 1984 Act, significant issues relating to the identification of those data controllers who may be exempted from the notification requirement are not covered in the Act.

Given that the Data Protection Act 1998 is intended to implement a European Directive,[55] account has to be taken of the provisions of the latter. In *Campbell v MGN Ltd*,[56] Lord Phillips of Worth Matravers MR stated that:

> In interpreting the Act it is appropriate to look to the Directive for assistance. The Act should, if possible, be interpreted in a manner that is consistent with the Directive. Furthermore, because the Act has, in large measure, adopted the wording of the Directive, it is not appropriate to look for the precision in the use of language that is usually to be expected from the parliamentary draftsman. A purposive approach to making sense of the provisions is called for.

The European Court of Justice has also held in *Österreichischer Rundfunk*[57] that at least some of the provisions of the Directive are sufficiently precise to be relied upon directly by individuals within the Member States.

Within the United Kingdom, from its earliest days, data protection has been seen as a somewhat isolated measure. Things have not changed significantly although in its report on the press, the Leveson Inquiry devoted considerable attention to the role of data protection law. Its conclusions will be referred to throughout Part I of this book, but at the outset we may note its opening comments:

> 1.2 The UK data protection regime suffers from an unenviable reputation, perhaps not wholly merited, but nevertheless important to understand at the outset. To say that it is little known or understood by the public, regarded as a regulatory inconvenience in the business world, and viewed as marginal and technical among legal practitioners (including by our higher courts), might be regarded as a little unfair by the more well-informed, but is perhaps not so far from the truth. And yet the subject-matter of the data protection regime, how personal information about individuals is acquired, used and traded for business purposes, could hardly be more fundamental to issues of personal integrity, particularly in a world of ever- accelerating information technology capability, nor, on the face of it, more central to the concerns of this Inquiry.[58]

Essentially, although data protection is vitally important to us all, few recognise the fact and it is perhaps a fair criticism that it has become mired in bureaucracy and to an extent has lost sight of its core principles. The Data Protection Act 1998 should be seen as one of a trilogy of measures operating in the same general field. The Human Rights Act 1998 incorporates the ECHR into domestic law. The provisions of Articles 8 and 10 are of particular relevance to data protection. Article 8 provides that 'everyone has the right to respect for

---

[55] Directive 95/46/EC.
[56] [2002] EWCA Civ 1373, [2003] QB 633 at [96].
[57] Joined Cases C-465/00, C-138/01, and C-139/01 [2003] ECR I-4989.
[58] Lord Justice Leveson, *An Inquiry into the Culture, Practices and Ethics of the Press*, 4 vols. (London, 2012), III, Pt H.

his private and family life, his home and his correspondence'. Any interference with such rights by a public authority must be sanctioned by law and be:

> necessary in a democratic society in the interests of national security, public safety or the economic well being of the country, for the prevention of disorder or crime, for the protection of health or morals, or for the protection of the rights and freedoms of others.[59]

In its jurisprudence, the European Court of Human Rights has interpreted Article 8 liberally to include rights of access to personal data. Indeed, following the decision of the court in the case of *Gaskin v United Kingdom*,[60] changes were required to be made to statutory provisions relating to subject access.

Perhaps the most controversial aspect of the interface between the Human Rights Act 1998 and the Data Protection Act 1998 concerns the activities of the media.

A further area where the Data Protection Act 1998 has to relate with other measures is connected with the introduction of freedom of information legislation. A White Paper, *Your Right to Know*, was published in December 1997,[61] and a Bill was introduced in Parliament in 1999, receiving Royal Assent in 2000 but not entering into force until January 2005.[62] There is a clear overlap between the two concepts and the Information Commissioner has responsibility in respect of both statutes. In other countries which have freedom of information legislation, it has been estimated that some 80 per cent of requests relate to the inquirer's own personal data. In respect of this issue, freedom of information legislation may well supplement rights under the Data Protection Act 1998 by extending these to a wider range of manual records, but, with proposals for significant variations in access rights and exceptions thereto, the prospect arises of what the House of Commons Select Committee on Public Administration described as a 'confusing and messy patchwork of different provisions under which one may obtain access to one's own file'.[63] Even more significantly, however, there will be the potential for conflict between the aims and objectives of the statutes where personal data relates to a party other than the inquirer.[64] Here, whilst freedom of information may give priority to openness and accessibility, data protection seeks to protect individual privacy and confidentiality.

In many respects, it might have been desirable had reform of the Data Protection Act proceeded in parallel with the freedom of information legislation. The Select Committee, whilst welcoming the prospect of freedom of information legislation, commented critically on the possibility for overlap and conflict between the two systems. It is perhaps ironic that whilst the prospect of the European Directives adopted was used to justify much-needed reform of the UK system during the first half of the 1990s, the desire to comply with the timetable for its implementation resulted in the 1998 Act being brought forward in isolation rather than as part of a comprehensive and coherent strategy governing access to information. To compound the irony, of course, the delay in formulating necessary items of secondary legislation meant that the United Kingdom ultimately failed to meet the European deadline.

New directions for data protection?

For a number of years the European Commission sought to promote a new data protection regime to replace the aging Directive 95/46. Two main concerns were identified; first that given the increasing use and importance of the Internet and the sophisticated

---

[59] Art. 10(2).   [60] (1990) 12 EHRR 36.   [61] Cm. 3818.
[62] Separate legislation applies within Scotland.
[63] *Third Report from the Select Committee on Public Administration* (HC Paper 398/1 (1997–8)), para. 17.
[64] See the discussion of the case of *Common Services Agency v Scottish Information Commissioner* in Chapter 3 and more recently the case of *Edem v The Information Commissioner and Financial Services Authority* [2014] EWCA 92.

nature of IT systems, strengthening of the protection afforded to individuals was required. The second factor was the concern that the level of protection currently provided in the Member States varied significantly. As well as impacting on the level of protection, divergences between national legislative approaches were also seen as creating difficulties for multinational companies who may have been required to comply with up to twenty-seven different regulatory regimes. The view was taken that the Directive should be replaced by a more prescriptive Regulation. The end product was 'Regulation (EU) 2016/679 of the European Parliament and of the Council of 27 April 2016 on the protection of natural persons with regard to the processing of personal data and on the free movement of such data'.[65] The Regulation is accompanied by 'Directive (EU) 2016/680 of the European Parliament and of the Council of 27 April 2016 on the protection of natural persons with regard to the processing of personal data by competent authorities for the purposes of the prevention, investigation, detection or prosecution of criminal offences or the execution of criminal penalties, and on the free movement of such data'.[66]

Both instruments were adopted in May 2016. In the case of the Regulation, this will come into direct effect in May 2018. For the Directive, the requirement is that its provisions should be implemented by the Member States, in the same month (with a few days' difference in the timescale). The extent to which they will impact on the UK process is unclear at a legal level given the proposed withdrawal from the EU.

Although it does seem that attitudes are changing in some respects, the United Kingdom, and especially its legislature, has historically had a somewhat ambivalent attitude towards these topics. Certainly in recent years the notion of accepting a legal right to privacy as part of the law in the United Kingdom has derived in large part from the provisions of the ECHR which was adopted under the auspices of the Council of Europe rather than the EU and is enshrined in domestic law by the Human Rights Act of 1998. As such it will not be directly affected by Brexit although there have been suggestions that the United Kingdom will replace the Human Rights Act with a more domestically oriented Bill of Rights and effectively eschew the jurisdiction of the European Court of Human Rights, which has become something of a bête noire for a number of politicians.

As well as currently implementing the EU Data Protection Directive, the United Kingdom is a signatory to the Council of Europe Convention 108 on the Automated Processing of Personal Data. Once again, Brexit will not of itself change this situation and there seems no great political pressure to change this. After a good many years of internal discussion, the EU adopted its new data protection Regulation in May 2016. The Regulation will enter into force in all the Member States in May 2018—less than the two-year period for exit negotiations envisaged once the United Kingdom invokes Article 50. The Regulation will require significant changes and extensions to current data protection law, introducing concepts such as mandatory breach notification whereby organisations whose compilations of personal data are compromised—perhaps by hackers—are required to notify all the individuals involved of the occurrence and give advice as to steps that might be taken to minimise the risk of damage.

In itself, compliance with the Regulation may not be a major problem—at a cynical level the United Kingdom could ignore its terms, safe in the knowledge that it will have left the EU well before any legal proceedings against it could be brought before the European Court of Justice. In practice, matters may not be so simple. Assuming the United Kingdom

---

[65] OJ 2016 L119/1.
[66] OJ 2016 L119/89.

remains party to the Council of Europe Convention, it will benefit from its provisions relating to transborder data flows. Article 12 provides that:

1. The following provisions shall apply to the transfer across national borders, by whatever medium, of personal data undergoing automatic processing or collected with a view to their being automatically processed.

2. A Party shall not, for the sole purpose of the protection of privacy, prohibit or subject to special authorisation transborder flows of personal data going to the territory of another Party.

3. Nevertheless, each Party shall be entitled to derogate from the provisions of paragraph 2:

   a insofar as its legislation includes specific regulations for certain categories of personal data or of automated personal data files, because of the nature of those data or those files, except where the regulations of the other Party provide an equivalent protection;

   b when the transfer is made from its territory to the territory of a non-Contracting State through the intermediary of the territory of another Party, in order to avoid such transfers resulting in circumvention of the legislation of the Party referred to at the beginning of this paragraph.

Article 12(3)(a) creates a potential problem here. There is no doubt that the provisions of the EU Regulation go beyond those of the Convention (although there are discussions ongoing within the Council of Europe to upgrade the Convention to bring it in line with the Regulation's requirements) and the determination whether a non-Member State provides an equivalent level of protection may be a complex one.

The Regulation provides that:

2. When assessing the adequacy of the level of protection, the Commission shall, in particular, take account of the following elements:

   (a) the rule of law, respect for human rights and fundamental freedoms, relevant legislation, both general and sectoral, including concerning public security, defence, national security and criminal law and the access of public authorities to personal data, as well as the implementation of such legislation, data protection rules, professional rules and security measures, including rules for the onward transfer of personal data to another third country or international organisation which are complied with in that country or international organisation, case-law, as well as effective and enforceable data subject rights and effective administrative and judicial redress for the data subjects whose personal data are being transferred;

   (b) the existence and effective functioning of one or more independent supervisory authorities in the third country or to which an international organisation is subject, with responsibility for ensuring and enforcing compliance with the data protection rules, including adequate enforcement powers, for assisting and advising the data subjects in exercising their rights and for cooperation with the supervisory authorities of the Member States; and

   (c) the international commitments the third country or international organisation concerned has entered into, or other obligations arising from legally binding conventions or instruments as well as from its participation in multilateral or regional systems, in particular in relation to the protection of personal data.

3. The Commission, after assessing the adequacy of the level of protection, may decide, by means of implementing act, that a third country, a territory or one or more specified sectors within a third country, or an international organisation ensures an adequate

level of protection within the meaning of paragraph 2 of this Article. The implementing act shall provide for a mechanism for a periodic review, at least every four years, which shall take into account all relevant developments in the third country or international organisation. The implementing act shall specify its territorial and sectoral application and, where applicable, identify the supervisory authority or authorities referred to in point (b) of paragraph 2 of this Article. The implementing act shall be adopted in accordance with the examination procedure referred to in Article 93(2).

The potential pitfalls for the United Kingdom are clear especially if, as indicated above, there should be any movement away from the European Convention on Human Rights. Short of significant reform to domestic legislation along the lines laid down in the Regulation, it is difficult to see that the United Kingdom could satisfy the EU requirements of adequacy.

Alternative approaches are available, and an obvious model is the Privacy Shield Agreement[67] negotiated between the EU and the United States following the striking down of the 'Safe Harbor' Agreement by the Court of Justice. It has, however, taken a period of years to conclude this agreement, even given what appears to have been an increasing level of goodwill between the European and US administrations and the political will to conclude an agreement. There remains, however, the prospect of a challenge to the validity of the Privacy Shield Agreement before the Court of Justice and it would be a brave lawyer who would dismiss the possibility that such an action would succeed given previous case law on the point.

There are also provisions in the EU Data Protection Regulation sanctioning the use of model contractual clauses and providing legislative authority for the adoption of Binding Corporate Rules as mechanisms to ensure that an adequate level of protection will be achieved. Although useful in the case of limited transfers, these are unlikely to fully meet the needs of the UK's financial services sector. Take-up has been limited and the list[68] given in Table 2.1 identifies the companies that currently meet EU requirements.

Some of the names on the list are quite familiar, but two points can perhaps be made. First, the number of companies that have sought approval for binding corporate rules is limited. There is no mention of the concept in the current data protection Directive but it does feature in the new Regulation, something that may encourage usage. It is, however, likely to remain a somewhat niche activity. Second, perusal of the list above shows that the United Kingdom has been one of the countries most involved in the field. A company wishing to adopt binding corporate rules has to secure approval from a nominated national supervisory agency. The fate of the companies that have currently nominated the Information Commissioner's Office for this role is unclear.

Plus ça change?

Many of the key definitions survive unchanged from the original Directive. In some respects this is not a surprise but the emergence of cloud computing has raised some novel and serious issues regarding the applicability of the concepts of data controller and processor and it is unfortunate that the opportunity has not been taken to address the issue.

There is a potentially significant change in the definition of consent. The UK approach has traditionally been to accept that the use of 'opt out' approaches is a valid means of securing and evidencing consent. The Regulation takes a different approach stating that the

---

[67]   See <http://europa.eu/rapid/press-release_IP-16–2461_en.htm>.

[68]   <http://ec.europa.eu/justice/data-protection/international-transfers/binding-corporate-rules/bcr_cooperation/index_en.htm>.

Table 2.1 List of companies for which the EU BCR cooperation procedure is closed © European Union, 1995–2016

Compay (*sic*) name	Lead authority
ABN AMRO Bank N.V.	Dutch DPA
Astra Zeneca plc	ICO (UK)
Accenture	ICO (UK)
Airbus (Controller)	CNIL (FR)
Akastor ASA (Controller)	Norwegian DPA
Aker Solutions ASA (Controller)	Norwegian DPA
Akzo Nobel N.V. (Controller)	Dutch DPA
Align Technologies B.V. (Controller and Processor)	Dutch DPA
American Express	ICO (UK)
ArcelorMittal Group	Luxemburg
Atmel	ICO (UK)
Atos (Controller and Processor)	CNIL (FR)
AXA	CNIL (FR)
Axa Private Equity	CNIL (FR)
BakerCorp International Holdings Inc. (Controller)	Dutch DPA
BMC Software (Controller and Processor)	CNIL (FR)
BMW	DPA of Bavaria (Germany)
BP	ICO (UK)
Bristol Myers Squibb	CNIL (FR)
CA plc	ICO (UK)
Capgemini (Controller and Processor)	CNIL (FR)
Cardinal Health, Inc.	IDPC (MT)
Care Fusion	ICO (UK)
Cargill, Inc.	ICO (UK)
Citigroup	ICO (UK)
CMA-CGM	CNIL (FR)
Continental Group	DPA of Lower Saxony (Germany)
Corning (Controller)	CNIL (FR)
D.E. Master Blenders 1753 ('DEMB') ex Sara Lee International B.V. (indirect subsidiary of Sara Lee Corporation)	Dutch DPA
Deutsche Post DHL	BfDI, Germany
Deutsche Telekom	BfDI, Germany
DSM	Dutch DPA
e-Bay	Luxemburg
ENGIE (ex GDF SUEZ; Controller)	CNIL (FR)
Ernst & Young	ICO (UK)
First Data Corporation (Controller and Processor)	ICO (UK)
Fluor Corporation Inc.	ICO (UK)

(Continued)

Table 2.1 List of companies for which the EU BCR cooperation procedure is closed © European Union, 1995–2016 (*continued*)

Compay (*sic*) name	Lead authority
Flextronics International Ltd	ICO (UK)
General Electric (GE)	CNIL (FR)
Giesecke & Devrient	DPA of Bavaria (Germany)
GlaxoSmithKline plc	ICO (UK)
Hermès	CNIL (FR)
HP Enterprise (Controller)	CNIL (FR)
HP Inc. (ex Hewlett Packard; Controller)	CNIL (FR)
Hyatt	ICO (UK)
IMS Health Incorporated	ICO (UK)
ING Bank N.V.	Dutch DPA
Intel Corporation	Ireland
International SOS	CNIL (FR)
Johnson Controls	Belgian DPA
JPMC	ICO (UK)
Koninklijke DSM N.V. and affiliated companies	Dutch DPA
LeasePlan Corporation N.V. (Controller)	Dutch DPA
Legrand (Controller)	CNIL (FR)
Linkbynet (Controller and Processor)	CNIL (FR)
Linklaters	ICO (UK)
LVMH	CNIL (FR)
Maersk Group	Danish DPA
Merck Sharp & Dohme (MSD)	Belgian DPA
Michelin	CNIL (FR)
Motorola Mobility LLC	ICO (UK)
Motorola Solutions, Inc.	ICO (UK)
NetApp Inc. (Controller)	Dutch DPA
NOVARTIS	CNIL (FR)
Novo Nordisk A/S	Danish DPA
Nutreco N.V.(Controller)	Dutch DPA
Osram	DPA of Bavaria (Germany)
OVH	CNIL (FR)
Rabobank Nederland	Dutch DPA
Rockwool	Danish DPA
Royal Philips Electronics	Dutch DPA
Safran	CNIL (FR)
Salesforce (Processor)	CNIL (FR)
Sanofi Aventis	CNIL (FR)
Schlumberger Ltd	Dutch DPA

Table 2.1 List of companies for which the EU BCR cooperation procedure is closed © European Union, 1995–2016 (*continued*)

Compay (*sic*) name	Lead authority
Schneider Electric	CNIL (FR)
Shell International B.V.	Dutch DPA
Siemens Group	DPA of Bavaria (Germany)
Simon-Kucher & Partners	DPA of North Rhine-Westphalia (Germany)
Société Générale	CNIL (FR)
Sopra HR Software (ex HR Access; Controller and Processor)	CNIL (FR)
Spencer Stuart	ICO (UK)
Starwood Hotels and Resorts (Controller)	Belgian DPA
TMF Group B.V. (Controller and Processor)	Dutch DPA
Total	CNIL (FR)
UCB (Controller)	Belgian DPA

data subject's 'consent' means any freely given specific, informed, and explicit indication of his or her wishes by which the data subject, either by a statement or by a clear affirmative action, signifies agreement to personal data relating to them being processed.

It is further provided that '[c]onsent shall not provide a legal basis for the processing, where there is a significant imbalance between the position of the data subject and the controller'. It is difficult to see how this can be implemented but the effect could be devastating for many data controllers. A passenger seeking to book a railway ticket online is in a weak position compared with the train provider. The choice is between accepting the conditions of carriage or finding another mode of transport. It is normal practice for websites to 'offer' to send further promotional mailings if the traveller consents. It seems that this will no longer be possible. This seems draconian, especially given that if there was real evidence of abuse of a dominant position, there could be a challenge on the ground that consent was not freely given. Many consumers might actually value being notified of future offers.

A further change to the notion of consent relates to the processing of data relating to children under the age of 13. In such cases it is provided that processing 'shall only be lawful if and to the extent that consent is given or authorised by the child's parent or custodian'. It is difficult to see what problem this provision is seeking to overcome and again the consequences may be undesirable. If a child should be injured and taken to hospital it would appear that it would be unlawful for the hospital to take any X-rays without parental consent. Whilst consent might be desirable, the consequences could be serious in the case of an emergency and where the parent cannot be contacted.

Likewise, perhaps, the data protection principles have remained largely unchanged since the earliest days of data protection legislation. They can fairly be analogised to religious notions such as the Ten Commandments (or mother's apple pie). Few might disagree with the concepts but the devil is always in the detail.

The headline change proposed in the Regulation is that there should be an explicit right to be forgotten—to block access to data held about oneself. This has, of course been the subject of litigation and debate under the Directive with the European Court's ruling in the case of *Google v Spain* being particularly significant. These points are discussed in more detail below.

Article 17 is headed 'Right to be forgotten and to erasure'. The first part of this is abject nonsense. Just as a computer cannot be deceived, so it cannot forget. Even placed in a human context, no law can compel forgetfulness—although human frailty may be more effective.

There is no doubt that the emergence of social networking sites has lured many users into placing sensitive aspects of their lives into a public or semi-public domain. It does seem clear beyond doubt that this data may be used in ways which would not have been conceived of or approved by the individual. Article 17 goes on at some length:

The data subject shall have the right to obtain from the controller the erasure of personal data relating to them and the abstention from further dissemination of such data, especially in relation to personal data which are made available by the data subject while he or she was a child, where one of the following grounds applies:

(a) the data are no longer necessary in relation to the purposes for which they were collected or otherwise processed;

(b) the data subject withdraws consent on which the processing is based according to point (a) of Article 6(1), or when the storage period consented to has expired, and where there is no other legal ground for the processing of the data;

(c) the data subject objects to the processing of personal data pursuant to Article 19;

(d) the processing of the data does not comply with this Regulation for other reasons.

Whilst certainly well meaning, it is difficult to see what this provision will accomplish that could not have been attained under existing provisions. It has always been the case, for example, that data must be processed fairly and that it must not be retained for longer than is necessary for the controller's legitimate purposes.

There have long been questions as to whether an individual is aware of the implications of their online conduct but the reality is that once data is put into the public domain it cannot be retrieved. It does appear that responsible social networking sites have made efforts to inform users and, within their possibilities of control, accede to requests that data be deleted. It is hard to see this provision as anything other than an attempt at headline grabbing which takes advantage of vulnerable elements of society. However, it is wrong to give a headline promise of legislative support that is not worth the paper it is written on.

One of the most impressive legal documents of recent times has been the Hargreaves Report on the digital economy. Covering issues such as the value of software patents and the losses caused by copyright piracy it makes the point again and again that what is needed is an evidence-based approach. In some respects it seems the Commission is falling into the trap of making proposals without evidence. There are certainly tales of individuals being denied employment because a potential employer has viewed their social networking postings. A recent survey has suggested that 69 per cent of employers have denied an applicant a job on the basis of such a search. That is the bad news. On the other side of the coin, 68 per cent of employers have indicated that they have offered a job because they have been impressed by online postings. A bigger problem perhaps is the malicious dissemination of personal data. Reference might be made to the recent English case of *AMP v Persons Unknown*.[69] This relates to the sad, but perhaps increasingly common situation (again discussed further below) where a teenage girl had used her mobile phone to take intimate photographs of herself. They were intended to be sent to her boyfriend (itself often a source of problems) but the phone was stolen and an unknown person posted copies on the Internet. In this case, the courts issued orders compelling any ISPs who can be identified to take steps to block access to the pictures and ordering that the anonymity of the complainant be preserved. It appears, however, that in order to serve a similar order in the United States on Google, US law requires that the identity of the complainant be disclosed.

---

[69] [2011] EWHC 3454 (TCC).

Data portability

Linked in some respects to the deletion of data is the issue of portability. The draft Regulation proposes that:

> The data subject shall have the right, where personal data are processed by electronic means and in a structured and commonly used format, to obtain from the controller a copy of data undergoing processing in an electronic and structured format which is commonly used and allows for further use by the data subject.

Concerns have been expressed that data subjects might effectively be locked into online services, perhaps in particular social networking (or blogging) sites because of the investment in time and effort expended in creating their profiles. It is not clear, however, to what extent competing sites operate in ways that are sufficiently interoperable to make the right of significant value.

Data security breaches

The imposition of requirements to notify supervisory authorities and data subjects of security breaches which may have implications for data subjects was introduced in the Directive on Privacy in Electronic Communications. It is now proposed to extend it to the more general field of data protection with the Regulation providing that:

> In the case of a personal data breach, the controller shall without undue delay and, where feasible, not later than 24 hours after having become aware of it, notify the personal data breach to the supervisory authority.

When the personal data breach is likely to adversely affect the protection of the personal data or privacy of the data subject, the controller shall, after giving the required notification, communicate the personal data breach to the data subject without undue delay.

The question of undue delay is not elaborated upon. In an era of 24/7 online businesses there might perhaps be a query over whether supervisory authorities are in a position to respond to notifications received between 5pm on Friday and 9am on Mondays.[70]

It is perhaps strange that the formula for notifying data subjects is less extensive than that for notifying the supervisory authority. Certainly it can be accepted that it is easier to notify one person then perhaps several millions but it is hard to see what constructive purpose is served by such a notification. One of the criticisms made of breach notification requirements (which have been commonplace in the United States for several years) is that the number of notifications required is too great so that there is the danger of notifications of potentially serious breaches being disregarded following a number of trivial notifications. In the event of a potentially serious breach—perhaps involving details of credit cards or bank accounts—there seems no reason why controllers should not be subject to the same twenty-four-hour rule. Many businesses manage to send marketing communications on a daily basis to millions of subjects so there is no valid reason why they should not be as quick to send breach notifications on a similar timescale.

Data protection officers

The notion of in-house supervisory officials has been an established feature of the German data protection scheme. Although it is sanctioned in the Data Protection Act 1988, it does

---

[70] See, eg, the report at <http://www.telegraph.co.uk/personal-banking/current-accounts/i-rang-to-report-a-6900-scam-but-tsb-said-its-fraud-team-was-bus/> suggesting that banks fraud departments are closed after 5pm and during the weekends.

not appear to have been adopted to any significant extent within the United Kingdom. The Regulation provides for what will be a significant change. Every public authority or private sector undertaking employing more than 250 persons will have to appoint a data protection officer:

> The controller or processor shall designate the data protection officer on the basis of professional qualities and, in particular, expert knowledge of data protection law and practices and ability to fulfil the tasks referred to in Article 37. The necessary level of expert knowledge shall be determined in particular according to the data processing carried out and the protection required for the personal data processed by the controller or the processor.
>
> The controller or the processor shall ensure that any other professional duties of the data protection officer are compatible with the person's tasks and duties as data protection officer and do not result in a conflict of interests.

The tasks of the data protection officer are stated to be to inform the data controller of the extent of its obligations under the Regulation and to monitor its compliance with its requirements. A data protection officer (who may be an employee of the data controller or an independent sub-contractor—possibly a lucrative new source of work for IT lawyers?) is to be appointed on a fixed term contract of at least two years' duration. Within this period the data protection officer may be dismissed only for a failure to fulfil data protection obligations.

Any legislative move to increase awareness amongst data controllers and their staff as to data protection issues is to be welcomed. In some respects, however, the approach demonstrates some of the weaknesses of the new approach. It specifies that there is to be a data protection officer and what their prime duties are to be. However, it does not indicate how extensive requirements may be. Is it to be a full-time job or a part-time (how part-time?) position? If part-time and the position is held by an employee, what is to happen if the person is considered to be guilty of misconduct in other aspects of their work sufficient to justify dismissal? Much more detail is required. In this provision, as with a number of the other Articles, the Regulation provides that the Commission is to have power to make supplementary provisions. These will not, however, have legal effect.

Data protection by design and by default

Considerable work has been carried out by the United Kingdom's Information Commissioner under the general heading of privacy by design. The basic premise is that it is easier and better to take data protection factors into consideration at the earliest stage of designing IT systems than to seek to attempt to include them at a later stage. The Regulation endorses this approach providing that:

1. Having regard to the state of the art and the cost of implementation, the controller shall, both at the time of the determination of the means for processing and at the time of the processing itself, implement appropriate technical and organizational measures and procedures in such a way that the processing will meet the requirements of this Regulation and ensure the protection of the rights of the data subject.

2. The controller shall implement mechanisms for ensuring that, by default, only those personal data are processed which are necessary for each specific purpose of the processing and are especially not collected or retained beyond the minimum necessary for those purposes, both in terms of the amount of the data and the time of their storage. In particular, those mechanisms shall ensure that by default personal data are not made accessible to an indefinite number of individuals.

Such an approach could create difficulties for many websites. The word 'necessary' has featured prominently in many instruments in the field of human rights. It sets a high threshold for data collection. An e-commerce website sending goods to consumers through a postal system will not *need*, for example, details of phone numbers. The same will apply with systems such as airline booking systems. Very often these give customers the option of giving a mobile phone number so that they can be advised of any schedule alterations by SMS. It might be argued that this should be classed as a distinct form of processing, but what is a well-meaning attempt to protect individuals could all too easily turn into a bureaucratic nightmare.

Subject rights

In many respects what has been considered above is intended to protect the interests of data subjects. It has also been a feature of data protection laws that subjects should have the right to object to certain forms of processing The Regulation provides that:

> The data subject shall have the right to object, on grounds relating to their particular situation, at any time to the processing of personal data which is based on points (d), (e) and (f) of Article 6(1), unless the controller demonstrates compelling legitimate grounds for the processing which override the interests or fundamental rights and freedoms of the data subject.

This is a significant and very welcome change from the current legislation which provides that, except in the case of processing with a view to direct marketing and a few other limited situations, a data subject can object to processing only if he or she can demonstrate that the processing is unlawful (as implemented in the United Kingdom the requirement is to show that the processing would cause substantial and unwarranted damage or distress). It seems entirely appropriate to reverse the burden of proof and after many paragraphs of criticising aspects of the new Regulation, three cheers are in order.

Supervisory authorities

In some respects the provisions regarding the status, powers, and duties of supervisory authorities appear to be based on those contained in the Electronic Communications Privacy Directive. There may well be implications for the UK regime and it is perhaps here where it becomes difficult to identify the basis for a Regulation.

> Each Member State shall provide that one or more public authorities are responsible for monitoring the application of this Regulation and for contributing to its consistent application throughout the Union, in order to protect the fundamental rights and freedoms of natural persons in relation to the processing of their personal data and to facilitate the free flow of personal data within the Union. For these purposes, the supervisory authorities shall co-operate with each other and the Commission.

The Regulation states that supervisory authorities are to be given 'complete independence' and in particular provides that:

> Each Member State shall ensure that the supervisory authority is provided with the adequate human, technical and financial resources, premises and infrastructure necessary for the effective performance of its duties and powers, including those to be carried out in the context of mutual assistance, co-operation and participation with the European Data Protection Board.

Throughout, the terminology of the Regulation appears consistent only with the notion that the supervisory authority should be a multi-membered authority; something which has been recommended by the United Kingdom's former Information Commissioner but which has not been adopted as government policy.

In terms of the powers to be afforded to supervisory authorities, the draft Regulation provides that there should be a general auditing power:

> Each supervisory authority shall have the investigative power to obtain from the controller or the processor:
>
> access to all personal data and to all information necessary for the performance of its duties;
>
> access to any of its premises, including to any data processing equipment and means, where there are reasonable grounds for presuming that an activity in violation of this Regulation is being carried out there.

Such a power has long been sought by the United Kingdom's Information Commissioner.

One further element of the Regulation may have significant implications for data protection in the United Kingdom. At present, the Information Commissioner's office is funded almost entirely through fees paid by data controllers upon notification. The Regulation proposes that responsibility for maintaining the data associated with notification should lie with the data controller and that this should only be supplied to the supervisory authority on specific request. There does not appear to be any possibility of the authority charging fees and it appears that significant change will be required to the United Kingdom's funding mechanism. Given that the section of the Information Commissioner's office which is responsible for the freedom of information legislation is funded directly by the Exchequer, it would seem logical to treat data protection in the same way.

Transborder data flows

The attempt to regulate transborder data flows was one of the most controversial aspects of the data protection Directive. With its headline of 'you shall not transfer personal data outside the European Economic Area unless there is a guarantee of an adequate level of protection' the legislation offered so many hostages to fortune.

There is remarkably little change in the headline provisions of the Regulation. Given the small number of findings of adequacy which have been made in the nineteen years Directive 95/46 has been in force, it might be questioned whether it serves as a particularly useful rule. Assuming (perhaps a big assumption) that transfers are lawful, there are so many other mechanisms which can be used to confer legitimacy. The notion of adequacy if a complex one and certainly as interpreted by the Commission would not seem to provide a basis which would secure sufficient global acceptance to form part of any wider privacy protection instrument.

Binding corporate rules

The concept of binding corporate rules has emerged through the Article 29 Working Party this year as a potential mechanism for evidencing an adequate level of protection in the case of transborder data flows. The concept has been applied without any specific statutory provision, something which the Regulation proposes to rectify, although without changing significantly anything in the system as it has been applied.

The European Data Protection Board–and consistency

Since the implementation of Directive 95/46, the Article 29 Working Party has provided a forum for national data protection supervisors to meet and publish opinions and guidance on a wide range of data protection related issues. The Regulation provides that it should be replaced by a European Data Protection Board. The membership will be essentially the same but the intention appears to be that it should operate on a more formal basis with the general duty to 'ensure the consistent application of this Regulation'.

The Data Protection Board's powers are however limited and legal authority to ensure the consistent operation of the Regulation lies with the Commission. The Regulation establishes a general obligation for supervisory authorities to 'cooperate with each other and with the Commission'. In respect of a range of issues, principally relating to the regulation of transborder data flows, any national proposals are required to be notified to the Commission which, after consulting the European Data Protection Board, may approve the proposal, require modifications, or require that it be withdrawn.

Conclusions

The Regulation has been the subject of internal discussion within the Commission and consultation with external parties for a number of years. My initial impression might be summed up by the old aphorism 'the elephant has laboured and given birth to a mouse'.

Few would deny that there have been problems with the implementation of Directive 95/46. These were perhaps inevitable. At the time of its adoption two countries in particular raised concerns. Germany feared that the Directive was too weak and might weaken its own strong data protection regime. The United Kingdom, which abstained in the final vote in the Council, complained that it went too far. Given the normal problems that arise concerning national implementation of a Directive, problems were perhaps inevitable.

Although it does seem to me that there is now greater awareness of the value of data protection in the United Kingdom than was the case in the 1990s, the core problems do remain. The decision to proceed on the basis of a Regulation may overcome some of the problems of inconsistency although the political road to implementation may be a long and tortuous one. Some of the headline elements of the draft Regulation, such as the right to be forgotten, are stronger on style than on substance. It is probably politically inconceivable that a single European Data Protection Supervisory Authority would be acceptable to all the Member States, but in its absence it is unclear how consistency of application will be achieved in practice.

Perhaps the main cause for concern is how reluctant the Regulation is to accept that the computer world has moved on from the 1970s. In previous eras, it was important to know what data was physically held by a data controller. Today the key question is 'what data can be accessed'? Networks and data sharing agreements have transformed the data processing world but this is not reflected in the Regulation. It still reads like a twentieth-century piece of legislation. Individuals certainly need more rights but there is also need for a workable regime for data controllers.

As a final point, and perhaps as important as any, we are faced every day with evidence that the Internet operates on a global basis. National borders have not disappeared and we also continually see evidence of nation-states trying to flex their muscles in respect of particular activities. As is perhaps emerging in the field of computer crime, there is a need for the establishment of wide consensus. It is not clear that the Regulation will assist in this endeavour. Fortress Europe may have some appeal but history tells us that medieval fortresses which were largely resistant to bows and arrows crumbled before the cannon. It is unfortunate that part of the effort which has obviously gone into drafting the new proposals was not diverted to seeking a basis for a wider Convention which might better protect the interests of EU citizens, at least in the medium term.

3

The scope of data protection

INTRODUCTION

Dictionaries seldom make compulsive reading, but in the law an appreciation of basic concepts is key to the understanding of a topic. Prior to considering substantive aspects of data protection, this chapter will consider in some detail the core terms that define the scope of data protection legislation. A number of definitions are closely linked to form a knot almost Gordian in its complexity. Any attempt to describe and analyse them is hindered by the fact that appreciation of the scope of one term presupposes to some extent understanding of others. In the absence of a sufficiently sharp sword, the following précis may serve as an introduction. The italicised terms will be subjected to more detailed analysis in the remainder of the chapter:

> Data protection legislation applies where *personal data* (including *sensitive personal data*) relating to an *identifiable individual* (*data subject*) is subjected to certain forms of *processing*. The nature and extent of the processing will be determined by a *data controller*, although the actual processing may be carried out by a *data processor* operating under an outsourcing or similar contract with the data controller.

The apparent simplicity of the terms is unfortunately misleading and there has been extensive debate and uncertainty, both as to the scope of the concepts per se and as to the extent to which the United Kingdom's legislation adequately implements the provisions of the Directive. Decisions of the courts also have to be taken into account, with leading authorities being the decisions of the English Court of Appeal in *Durant v Financial Services Authority*[1] and *Edem v Information Commissioner*[2] and the House of Lords in the case of *Common Service Agency v Scottish Information Commissioner*,[3] and the judgment of the European Court of Justice in the case of *Bodil Lindqvist*.[4]

The concept of personal data

The Data Protection Directive defines personal data in relatively simple terms as 'any information relating to an identified or identifiable natural person (data subject)'.[5] The Data Protection Act's approach is rather more complicated and analysis of its scope needs to proceed through a number of steps. The legislation initially states that it applies to 'data which, relate to a living individual'.[6] The Act contains an additional element, providing that the term extends 'to any expression of opinion about the individual and any indication of the intentions of the data controller or any other person in respect of the individual'. This represents in large part an unfortunate legacy from the original Act of 1984 which

---

[1] [2003] EWCA Civ 1746.   [2] [2003] EWCA Civ 92.   [3] [2008] UKHL 47.   [4] C101/01.
[5] Art. 2(a).   [6] s. 1(1).

made a widely criticised distinction between statements of opinion—which were classed as personal data—and statements of the data controller's intentions towards the data subject—which were not. The argument put forward by the government of the day was that statements of intention were personal to the data controller rather than to the subject. This is certainly arguable, but the point applies with equal if not greater validity with regard to statements of opinion. Even the then Data Protection Registrar was moved to comment to the effect that he found the distinction unclear and the provision in the Data Protection Act 1998 should perhaps be seen as a measure to remove what had generally been considered an unsatisfactory distinction, rather than a deliberate effort to depart from the requirements of the Directive.

There are, however, significant questions as to whether the Act's provisions fully meet the requirements of the Directive. One perhaps peripheral issue is whether the legislation should apply to data relating to deceased individuals. The Directive, it will be recalled, applies in respect of data relating to a 'natural person'. It is arguable that this state continues after the individual's death. A minority of Member States have, indeed, chosen to extend their national laws to this category of data. Even accepting the validity of the United Kingdom's interpretation of the concept of a 'natural person' as a living individual, there may be circumstances in which data concerning a deceased person may also have implications for living individuals and therefore come within the scope of the legislation. Certain diseases such as haemophilia are hereditary in nature. The son of a woman suffering from the disease in its active form will always inherit the condition. Data indicating the mother's condition will therefore convey information about the medical condition of any male children.

Again, some EU Member States apply at least elements of the legislation to data relating to legal persons. The United Kingdom does not, although it should be noted that legal persons do acquire some protection under the provisions of the communications-specific Directive on Universal Service and Users' Rights Relating to Electronic Communications Networks and Services.[7] The provisions of this Directive and its implementation in the United Kingdom will be discussed in Chapter 7.

Although in its early stages data protection law tended to apply almost exclusively to textual information, developments in technology mean that almost any form of recorded information is likely to come within the ambit of the legislation. In the event that an individual interacts with an automated telephone service by speaking a series of numbers or words to allow a call to be directed to the appropriate department, those recorded words will class as personal data. Again, CCTV or similar camera systems generally fall within the scope of the legislation in respect of the video images recorded. The Information Commissioner has published guidance regarding the application of the Data Protection Act in respect of such data.

Much attention is paid today to the collection and use of biometric data in situations such as the issuance of passports and visas. Although the term does not have a precise definition, it is generally regarded as encompassing two categories of data. The first relates to the physiological characteristic relating to aspects of physical identity. This category would include items such as fingerprints and, perhaps relating to more advanced forms of technology, face and iris recognition. A second category of biometric data relates to what are referred to as behavioural characteristics. As the name suggests, this concerns the manner in which a person acts. A simple and long-established example would relate to the manner in which a person signs his or her name. More technologically advanced versions relate to the use of software to monitor the manner in which a particular individual

---

[7] Directive 2009/136/EC, OJ 2009 L 337/11.

uses a computer keyboard in terms of the speed, accuracy, and force with which keys are depressed.

Biometric data, which forms a cornerstone of modern passports, is clearly an aspect of personal data. Data may be objective or subjective and, indeed, true or false. In an Opinion on the concept of personal data,[8] the Article 29 Working Party suggested that:

> As a result of a neuro-psychiatric test conducted on a girl in the context of a court proceeding about her custody, a drawing made by her representing her family is submitted. The drawing provides information about the girl's mood and what she feels about different members of her family. As such, it could be considered as being 'personal data'. The drawing will indeed reveal information relating to the child (her state of health from a psychiatric point of view) and also about e.g. her father's or mother's behaviour. As a result, the parents in that case may be able to exert their right of access on this specific piece of information.

As indicated in the above example, personal data may relate to more than one person, a topic which will be considered in more detail later.

Sensitive personal data

Any piece of information, however insignificant, might be classed as personal data. The extent to which certain forms of data can be classed as especially sensitive and deserving of special protection has long been a contentious issue. During the passage of the Data Protection Act 1984, the attempt to identify sensitive data was compared, somewhat scornfully, by government ministers with the quest for the unicorn. Both were considered mythical creatures. In the case of personal data, the context in which data was held or used was considered far more important than the data itself. A list of names and addresses, for example, would not normally be considered sensitive, but this view might change if it referred to the movements of prominent persons and was in the hands of a terrorist organisation. Whilst this view is not without merit, it does seek to transform the exceptional into the norm. Almost invariably, however, data protection statutes have recognised that there are certain categories of information which would generally be regarded as possessing a degree of sensitivity and the processing of which should be subjected to more stringent controls than would generally be applicable.

The Data Protection Act provides for special treatment for data relating to:

   (a) the racial or ethnic origin of the data subject;

   (b) his political opinions;

   (c) his religious beliefs or other beliefs of a similar nature;

   (d) whether he is a member of a trade union;

   (e) his physical or mental health or condition;

   (f) his sexual life;

   (g) the commission or alleged commission by him of any offence; or

   (h) any proceedings for any offence committed or alleged to have been committed by him, the disposal of such proceedings, or the sentence of the court in such proceedings.[9]

With the exception of substituting the term 'other beliefs of a similar nature' for the Directive's 'philosophical beliefs', the Act's terminology mirrors that of the Directive.

---

[8] Available from <http://ec.europa.eu/justice_home/fsj/privacy/docs/wpdocs/2007/wp136_en.pdf>.

[9] s. 2.

Table 3.1 Attitudes towards sensitivity of types of data

	Percentage
Financial data	88.0
Health information	72.0
Personal contact details	68.0
Sexual life information	67.0
Biometric information	63.0
Genetic information	63.0
Criminal records	58.0
Clickstream data	43.0
Political opinions	42.0
Education qualification	42.0
Data concerning race or ethnic origin	41.0
Employment history	41.0
Membership of political party/organisation	38.0
Religious or philosophical beliefs	37.0
Trade-union membership	33.0

This definition is rather broad and undoubtedly reflects diverse attitudes towards issues across the Member States of the European Union. Research conducted for the Information Commissioner in 2006[10] sought views on the extent to which respondents regarded specific types of information as being sensitive. The results are set out in Table 3.1. Interestingly, financial data, which attracted the highest response rate, is not included in the statutory list of sensitive data.

In addition to covering a wide range of categories of information, the scope of particular categories has been broadly interpreted by the courts. In *Bodil Lindqvist*,[11] the European Court of Justice was asked to give a preliminary ruling in response to a number of questions posed by the Swedish courts. Mrs Lindqvist had been convicted of breaches of the Swedish data protection law in respect of her work as a catechist in the Swedish Lutheran Church and preparation of a number of *www* pages which contained information about Mrs Lindqvist and eighteen of her parish colleagues, including brief details of the nature of their work and hobbies. It appears that much of the information was presented in what was intended to be a light-hearted manner. One particular item of information which was the cause of specific investigation was the indication that a named person had injured her foot and as a consequence was able to work only on a part-time basis. Data concerning the subject's health life? Mrs Lindqvist was prosecuted by the Swedish authorities on a number of charges, including one of processing sensitive personal data without having secured authorisation from the data protection authorities. The European Court of Justice was asked to rule on the question of whether the reference to the foot injury of Mrs Lindqvist's colleague constituted sensitive data relating to health. The court's reply was succinct and emphatic:

> In the light of the purpose of the Directive, the expression data concerning health used in Article 8(1) thereof must be given a wide interpretation so as to include information concerning all aspects, both physical and mental, of the health of an individual.

---

[10] *2006 Annual Tracking Report*, available from <http://www.ico.gov.uk/upload/documents/library/corporate/research_and_reports/2006_annual_tracking_report_individuals_final.pdf>.

[11] Case 101/01, [2004] QB 1014.

In some respects, the decision in *Bodil Lindqvist* illustrates the difficulties surrounding the concept of sensitive data. Once included in a list of sensitive data, it is almost impossible to say that a reference to illness or injury is not included, but as indicated earlier, context is perhaps more important than content. A reference to the fact that an athlete was unable to compete in a race because of a broken leg, for example, does not seem to be possessed of a sufficient degree of sensitivity to justify the imposition of additional controls.

Personal data relating to the data subject

In *Bodil Lindqvist*, there was no doubt that the information about the foot injury related to the individual concerned. In other cases the situation may be more complex. In the example of the child's drawing cited earlier, the data contained might relate in varying degrees to the child and to other family members. Neither the Directive nor the Act provides any definition of when data relates to an individual and this has been a rather contentious issue. The point was discussed extensively in the case of *Durant v Financial Services Authority*,[12] and more recently has been considered in an Opinion of the Article 29 Working Party and in Guidance produced by the United Kingdom's Information Commissioner together with the decision of the House of Lords in the case of *Common Services Agency v Scottish Information Commissioner*,[13] and most recently the decision of the Court of Appeal in *Edem v The Information Commissioner and Financial Services Authority*.[14]

In *Durant*, the appellant had been involved in a protracted dispute with Barclays Bank. This had resulted in unsuccessful litigation in 1993 and a continuing course of complaints to the then industry regulatory body, the Financial Services Authority (FSA). The present case arose from a request from the appellant for access to a range of records under the ambit of the subject access provisions of the Data Protection Act 1998. Although some information was supplied, access to other records was provided only in partial form through the concealment or redaction of information which it was considered related to third parties. Other records were withheld on the grounds either that the information contained therein did not constitute personal data relating to the appellant, or—as will be discussed later, in the case of a number of records which were maintained in manual filing systems—that the system was not covered by the Data Protection Act.

Although there was no doubt that much, if not all, of the data in question had been generated following complaints from the appellant, the critical issue was whether it related to him. Counsel for Durant argued that the term 'relate to' should be interpreted broadly to encompass any data which might be generated following a search of a database made by reference to an individual's name. Thus, for example, a document describing the action which had been taken in response to a complaint from the appellant would be classed as personal data by virtue merely of the fact that his name would appear within the text. Counsel for the respondent advocated a more restrictive approach, making reference to the *Shorter Oxford English Dictionary*, which contained two definitions of the term, a broad reference to having 'some connection with, be connected to' and a also more restrictive notion that there should be reference to or concern with a subject, 'implying, in this context, a more or less direct connection with an individual'.

This more restrictive interpretation was adopted by the Court of Appeal. The purpose of the subject access provisions in the legislation was, it was stated, to enable the data subject to verify that processing did not infringe his or her rights of privacy and to exercise any available remedies in the event this was considered not to be the case. The purpose of the

---

[12] [2003] EWCA Civ 1746.   [13] [2008] UKHL 47.   [14] [2014] EWCA Civ 92.

legislation was not, it was held, to give an automatic right of access to information purely by virtue of the fact that he might be named in a record or have some interest in the matters covered. In particular, it was stated, subject access was not intended

> to assist him, for example, to obtain discovery of documents that may assist him in litigation or complaints against third parties.

Giving effect to this interpretation it was held that the mere fact that a search of a computer's contents by reference to a data subject's name revealed a number of documents did not mean that these documents necessarily constituted personal data relating to the subject. A more sophisticated analysis was required:

> It seems to me that there are two notions that may be of assistance. The first is whether the information is biographical in a significant sense, that is, going beyond the recording of the putative data subject's involvement in a matter or an event that has no personal connotations, a life event in respect of which his privacy could not be said to be compromised. The second is one of focus. The information should have the putative data subject as its focus rather than some other person with whom he may have been involved or some transaction or event in which he may have figured or have had an interest, for example, as in this case, an investigation into some other person's or body's conduct that he may have instigated. In short, it is information that affects his privacy, whether in his personal or family life, business or professional capacity.[15]

This approach adopts, it is suggested, an overly restrictive view of the rationale of data protection laws. Whilst determining the legality of data processing and correcting errors certainly constitute important elements, equally important is the ability to become aware of what data is held. Much of the Data Protection Directive[16] and the Data Protection Act 1998's requirements relating to the factors legitimising data processing stress the importance of the data subject being aware of what is happening with regard to personal data. As was stated by the German Constitutional Court in the 1980s:

> The possibilities of inspection and of gaining influence have increased to a degree hitherto unknown and may influence the individual's behaviour by the psychological pressure exerted by public interest . . . if someone cannot predict with sufficient certainty which information about himself in certain areas is known to his social milieu, and cannot estimate sufficiently the knowledge of parties to whom communication may possibly be made, he is crucially inhibited in his freedom to plan or to decide freely and without being subject to any pressure/influence.[17]

These factors support the adoption of an expansive definition of the scope of personal data. In a case such as *Durant*, it may well be that personal data in the form of an individual's name or other identifying data makes a peripheral appearance in a record. Rather than arguing that the appearance of the data does not come within the scope of the Act, it might be preferable to focus upon the extent of the information which might be supplied. Whilst the court was clearly concerned that the data protection legislation was being invoked in the present case in the attempt to obtain discovery of documents and data that could not be obtained through other legal channels, it might have been preferable to have laid greater stress on the limited nature of the information which would be classed as personal data.

The Information Commissioner has subsequently noted that 'the Court of Appeal was widely understood to have adopted a rather narrower interpretation of personal data . . .

---

[15] *Durant v Financial Services Authority* [2003] EWCA Civ 1746 at paras. 27–8.
[16] Directive 95/46/EC.
[17] 'The Census Decision', *Human Rights Law Journal* 5 (1984), p. 94.

than most practitioners and experts had followed previously.[18] The Article 29 Working Party's Opinion provides extensive guidance when data relates to an individual. Referring to its previous work in relation to radio frequency identification (RFID) chip technology, it affirms that 'data relates to an individual if it refers to the identity, characteristics or behaviour of an individual or if such information is used to determine or influence the way in which that person is treated or evaluated'.[19]

The Opinion identifies three elements which may indicate that data relates to a particular individual. These are referred to as content, purpose, and result elements. The distinction between the elements may be complex on occasion but the Working Party stresses that only one element needs to be present in order to justify a finding that data relates to a particular individual. The content element will be satisfied when information relates unequivocally to an individual. A medical or personnel record, for example, will fall within this category. The purpose element applies when the data is intended to be used to determine the manner in which an individual is treated. Data may, for example, be recorded by an employer of the websites accessed from workplace computers. The purpose may be to take disciplinary action against employees who violate Internet usage policies. Finally, a result element applies when the use of data, even though not collected originally for that purpose, is likely to have even a minor impact upon an individual's rights and interests. Guidance produced by the United Kingdom's Information Commissioner emphasises similar criteria, suggesting that:

> Data which identifies an individual, even without a name associated with it, may be personal data where it is processed to learn or record something about that individual, or where the processing of that information has an impact upon that individual.

Subsequently, issues of the definition of personal data came before the House of Lords in the case of *Common Services Agency v Scottish Information Commissioner*.[20] The case revolved around what is a complex and sometimes difficult relationship between two statutes that are concerned with rather different aspects of information policy. A key tenet of data protection law—and one which is seldom far from the news today—is that information supplied for one purpose should be kept securely and used only for that purpose. The basic element of the Freedom of Information Act, which was enacted in the year 2000, is that information held by public bodies should be disclosed to anyone upon request.

As has been noted, the Data Protection Act was rushed into force in an ultimately unsuccessful attempt to meet the implementation deadline for the European Data Protection Directive. With hindsight, it might have been preferable to have delayed another year and introduced the two statutes co-terminously (or even to have combined them in a single Information Policy Act).

This case was concerned with a request submitted to the appellant agency, a Health Board, under the terms of the Freedom of Information (Scotland) Act 2002[21] for the provision of information relating to instances of childhood cancer within the locality of a nuclear power station. Under the terms of the 2002 Act a range of exceptions apply regarding the types of information which may be supplied and, in particular, it is stated that

---

[18] Data Protection Technical Guidance, 'Determining What Is Personal Data'. Published by the Office of the Information Commissioner, Wilmslow. Available from <http://ico.org.uk/for_organisations/guidance_index/~/media/documents/library/Data_Protection/Detailed_specialist_guides/PERSONAL_DATA_FLOWCHART_V1_WITH_PREFACE001.ashx>.

[19] Working Party Document No. WP 105: 'Working Document on Data Protection Issues Related to RFID Technology', adopted on 19 January 2005, p. 8.   [20] [2008] UKHL 47.

[21] The Scottish legislation is equivalent in all relevant respects to the Freedom of Information Act 2000 applying in England and Wales.

personal data is not to be disclosed where this would be in contravention of any of the data protection principles.[22] Relying on this provision the appellant refused to disclose information. The Scottish Information Commissioner ruled that such a blanket refusal was unlawful. Although the raw data identifying individual patients was undoubtedly personal data, disclosure would not be in breach of the data protection principles were to it be processed using a procedure known as 'barnardisation' which would modify statistical elements so that no individual could be identified. The appellant was ordered to conduct such a process. The Commissioner's ruling was upheld by the highest Scottish court, the Court of Session.[23] Applying the approach of the Court of Appeal in *Durant v Financial Services Authority*[24] that 'mere mention of the data subject in a document held by a data controller does not necessarily amount to personal data',[25] the Lord President ruled that:

> Although the underlying information concerns important biographical events of the children involved, by the stage of the compilation of the barnardised table that information has become not only statistical but perturbed to minimise the risk of identification of any individual child. It is no longer, in respect of any child, 'biographical in a significant sense'. The focus has, in my view, also moved away from the individual children to the incidence of disease in particular wards in particular years. The rights to privacy of the individual children are not infringed by the disclosure of the barnardised data.[26]

A further appeal was made to the House of Lords where, delivering the leading judgment, Lord Hope gave detailed consideration to the scope of the definition of personal data—and also of sensitive personal data. In respect of the former he indicated that the Court of Appeal decision in *Durant* should be distinguished as it related to the operation of the subject information provisions rather than the definition of personal data per se. The answer to that issue, he held, 'must be found in the wording of section 1(1) (of the Data Protection Act 1998) read in the light of Council Directive 95/46/EC'.[27] The Act refers to the possibility that an individual might be identified from data 'and other information which is in the possession of the data controller'. As the appellant had the means to recreate data identifying individuals, the barnardised data remained personal data.

Turning to the question whether the data could be disclosed in conformity with the provisions of the Act, Lord Hope cited the provisions of Recital 26 of the Directive to the effect that when data was truly anonymous 'the principles of protection shall not apply to data'. Section 1(1) it was held, gave effect to this provision.

As noted previously, Recital 26 of the Directive states that in making decisions as to whether an individual can be identified 'account should be taken of all the means likely reasonably to be used either by the controller or by any other person to identify the said person'. The appellant clearly had the means to match data to named individuals but the issue in this respect was whether a third party receiving the barnardised data would be able to re-engineer it. The Scottish Information Commissioner, it was held, should have considered more fully this issue and, accordingly, the case was remitted for him to make findings of fact in this respect. Ultimately, the Commissioner issued a further ruling[28] holding that he was not satisfied that anonymity could be guaranteed and on this basis the freedom of access request was denied.

In some respects the decision in *Common Services Agency* might be seen to have limited the application of *Durant* although the rather opaque way in which it has been done cannot eliminate all scope for confusion. What appears to be the effect of Lord Hope's dicta is that any element of data relating to an individual will be classed as personal data.

---

[22] s. 38.   [23] [2006] CSIH 58.   [24] [2003] EWCA Civ 1746.   [25] para. 28.

[26] para. 23.   [27] para. 20.

[28] Available from <http://www.itspublicknowledge.info/applicationsanddecisions/Decisions/2005/200500298.asp>.

There will remain the issue of when data relates to a subject who is applying for subject access—a topic that will be considered in more detail in Chapter 6.

Issues of identification

The premise underlying data protection legislation is that the processing of data relating to individuals constitutes a threat to the subject's rights and freedoms. If an individual cannot be identified from the manner in which data is collected, processed, or used, there can be no significant threat to privacy and no justification for the application of legislative controls. The Data Protection Directive provides that:

> an identifiable person is one who can be identified directly or indirectly, in particular by reference to an identification number or to one or more factors specific to his physical, psychological, mental, economic, cultural or social identity.[29]

Also relevant are the provisions of Recital 26 to the Directive. This states that:

> Whereas the principles of protection must apply to any information concerning an identified or identifiable person; whereas, to determine whether a person is identifiable, account should be taken of all the means likely reasonably to be used either by the controller or by any other person to identify the said person.

The United Kingdom's Data Protection Act 1998 provides that personal data:

> means data which relates to a living individual who can be identified—
>
> (a) from those data; or
>
> (b) from those data and other information which is in the possession of, or is likely to come into the possession of, the data controller.

It will be recognised that the Directive and the Act differ in that the Act restricts its application to information which is or is likely to come into the possession of the data controller. The Directive's application is open-ended, applying whenever anyone might be able to identify an individual. A recent example might illustrate a difference between the two approaches. In 2006, AOL (America Online), one of the early operators in the ISP field placed on the Internet data relating to search requests made by millions of its subscribers. Although no names were published, in at least some cases it proved possible to identify individuals following analysis of their search history. One case concerned a user allocated the identifying number 4417749. This user had conducted searches on a range of topics, including medical conditions relating to humans and animals, landscape gardening, persons with a particular surname (Arnold), and house sales in a particular area of the United States. Taking this data, researchers focused on a particular individual, Thelma Arnold, who, when read a list of the searches, confirmed that they had been made by her.[30]

Under the UK approach, it is likely that the data would not have been considered personal data at the point it was compiled by AOL because that organisation would not have possessed the necessary additional information to identify users.[31] Under the Directive's

---

[29] Directive 95/46/EC, Art. 2(a).

[30] <http://www.iht.com/articles/2006/08/09/business/aol.php>.

[31] Given that AOL operates on a subscription service it may be that the company would have possessed the necessary data. The example might be more accurate in the event that it applied to an organisation such as Google, which does not require users to give their names. Indeed, one of the reasons why Google refused to comply with a US government request for access to search data was because of concerns that individuals might be identified. See <http://news.bbc.co.uk/1/hi/technology/4630694.stm>.

criteria, the material would probably have been classed as personal data, as AOL would have been required to consider the possibility that third parties could perform the task of identification. It is likely that if its disclosure and decoding were to be carried out in the United Kingdom (or any other state of the European Economic Area (EEA)) the person identifying individuals would be classed as a data controller in his or her own right and subject to the same obligations to comply with data protection law. Matters would be much less satisfactory were the decoder to be located outside of the EEA and, of course, dissemination of information via the Internet is global in its nature.

The AOL example undoubtedly represents an extreme case but the issue of identifiability may frequently be an issue. Once again, the Article 29 Opinion on the concept of personal data identifies a wide range of potential situations and provides extensive guidance. Linking data to a name is an obvious form of identification, although especially in the case of a common name such as Smith or McDonald this may not be sufficient. Use of an identification number may aid identification. In other cases, an individual may be identifiable indirectly. The example might be posited of a CCTV operator instructing an undercover police officer to detain the person wearing a Glasgow Rangers' football shirt and carrying a can of lager sitting slumped in the doorway of 27 Hoops Street, Glasgow. No name is given but the individual would be readily identifiable to the police officer. Again, Internet Service Providers (ISPs) and possibly employers may maintain records of Internet use associated with particular computers and from these to the individuals behind the computers. Identification may not always be possible; the Working Party posits the example of computers used in an Internet café, but stresses that so long as identification is possible in some cases, all processing will be covered by the legislation.

The concept of processing

Much of what has been said to date is predicated on the notion that data is processed. It is now appropriate to consider what forms of activity can be classed as constituting processing. The Directive provides that processing includes:

> any operation or set of operations which is performed upon personal data, whether or not by automatic means, such as collection, recording, organization, storage, adaptation or alteration, retrieval, consultation, use, disclosure by transmission, dissemination or otherwise making available, alignment or combination, blocking, erasure or destruction.[32]

The Act's definition differs slightly in terminology, largely because of the need to make separate provision for the treatment of non-automated or manual processing. It provides that:

> 'processing', in relation to information or data, means obtaining, recording or holding the information or data or carrying out any operation or set of operations on the information or data, including—

> (a) organisation, adaptation or alteration of the information or data;

> (b) retrieval, consultation or use of the information or data;

> (c) disclosure of the information or data by transmission, dissemination or otherwise making available; or

> (d) alignment, combination, blocking, erasure or destruction of the information or data.[33]

---

[32] Art. 2(b).   [33] s. 1(1).

Linked to this is a definition of the word data:

(a) is being processed by means of equipment operating automatically in response to instructions given for that purpose;

(b) is recorded with the intention that it should be processed by means of such equipment; or

(c) is recorded as part of a relevant filing system or with the intention that it should form part of a relevant filing system.[34]

The term 'relevant filing system' is designed to extend the legislation to certain forms of manual filing systems and will be considered separately in the next section. It will be noted that the scope of the definition is extremely broad. It might be suggested, with little element of exaggeration, that whilst the act of dreaming about data will not constitute processing, any further activities will bring a party within the scope of the legislation.

Although not yet at issue before a UK court, the question of what acts constitute processing was raised before the European Court in *Bodil Lindqvist*.[35] An initial issue concerned the question of whether the mention of a person on a web page constituted processing of personal data as defined in the Data Protection Directive.[36] Two issues arose in this context: first, whether the data on Mrs Lindqvist's web page included personal data. The court's reply was unequivocal:

The term undoubtedly covers the name of a person in conjunction with his telephone coordinates or information about his working conditions or hobbies.[37]

Equally clear and unsurprising was the court's determination that processing had taken place. The Swedish government argued for a broad approach, suggesting that 'as soon as personal data are processed by computer, whether using a word-processing programme or in order to put them on an Internet page, they have been the subject of processing'. Although counsel for Mrs Lindqvist argued that something more was needed beyond compilation of what was effectively a word-processed document and that only meta tags and other technical means used to assist with the compilation of indexes and retrieval of information would suffice, the Court agreed with the Swedish government's submission:

According to the definition in Article 2(b) of Directive 95/46, the term processing of such data used in Article 3(1) covers any operation or set of operations which is performed upon personal data, whether or not by automatic means.[38]

Although all forms of processing are potentially covered by the Data Protection Directive,[39] the most stringent controls apply in the case of processing by automatic means. It is arguable that any use of a computer to create a document comes within the scope of this criterion, as there is no direct physical link between the author pressing a key and a letter or symbol appearing on the screen. The act of loading a page onto a web server involves a number of operations, some at least of which are performed automatically.

Non-automated filing systems

Under the Data Protection Act 1984, access was strictly limited to data which had been the subject of some form of automated processing. The Data Protection Directive[40] required

---

[34] s. 1(1).   [35] Case 101/01, [2004] QB 1014.   [36] Directive 95/46/EC.
[37] Case 101/01, [2004] QB 1014, para. 24.   [38]Case 101/01, para. 25.   [39] Directive 95/46/EC.
[40] Directive 95/46/EC.

an extension to certain forms of manual records. Article 2 of the Directive provides that its scope is to extend to any 'personal data filing system' defined in terms of:

any structured set of personal data which are accessible according to specific criteria, whether centralised, decentralised or dispersed on a functional or geographical basis.

By omitting any reference to automated processing the effect is clearly to encompass manual record-keeping systems. Whilst every automated system is covered by the legislation, reflecting the ease with which modern retrieval systems can perform full text searches of vast collections of data in accordance with criteria determined by a user, not every manual system is to be included. Recital 15 of the Data Protection Directive[41] explains that:

Whereas the processing of such data is covered by this Directive only if it is automated or if the data processed are contained or are intended to be contained in a filing system structured according to specific criteria relating to individuals, so as to permit easy access to the personal data in question; . . .

Recital 27 continues the story:

Whereas the protection of individuals must apply as much to automatic processing of data as to manual processing; whereas the scope of this protection must not in effect depend on the techniques used, otherwise this would create a serious risk of circumvention; whereas nonetheless, as regards manual processing, this Directive covers only filing systems, not unstructured files; whereas, in particular, the content of a filing system must be structured according to specific criteria relating to individuals allowing easy access to the personal data; whereas, in line with the definition in Article 2(c), the different criteria for determining the constituents of a structured set of personal data, and different criteria governing access to such a set, may be laid down by each Member State; whereas files or sets of files as well as their cover pages, which are not structured according to specific criteria, shall under no circumstances fall within the scope of the Directive.

This provision clearly leaves considerable scope for Member States to determine the extent to which manual records should be brought within the scope of their implementing legislation. As indicated earlier, the Data Protection Act 1998 utilises the concept of a 'relevant filing system' as the vehicle for this endeavour. The statutory definition is somewhat complex, in large part because the legislation seeks to co-exist with a range of earlier statutes which had provided for a right of access to certain medical, educational, social work, and credit reference files. In its essential element, however, it provides that:

'relevant filing system' means any set of information relating to individuals to the extent that, although the information is not processed by means of equipment operating automatically in response to instructions given for that purpose, the set is structured, either by reference to individuals or by reference to criteria relating to individuals, in such a way that specific information relating to a particular individual is readily accessible.[42]

The extension to some forms of manual records has been the cause of considerable controversy, largely concerning the potential costs to organisations of complying with requests for subject access. It should be noted, however, that the Consumer Credit Act 1974 and the Access to Health Records Act 1990 have long provided for access to credit and medical records, irrespective of the format in which these are stored. More recently, the Freedom of

---

[41] Directive 95/46/EC.   [42] s. 1(1).

Information Act 2000 has provided very extensive rights of access to public sector information and as the Information Commissioner has commented:

> Experience elsewhere indicates that in practice, in many cases, information provided in response to Freedom of Information requests will relate to the individual making the request.[43]

In determining what manual records will be covered, the question of when information should be considered 'readily accessible' is of critical importance. In the discussion of the extent of the provision in Parliament, it was suggested that it would not be sufficient that information about an individual should be located in a single place, for example, a manila folder containing all of an employee's work records. In order for the records to be covered, it would additionally be required that the information within the folder should be held in a structured format so that individual items might readily be extracted. Speaking during the Bill's report stage in the House of Lords, Lord Williams stated that:

> Our intentions are clear. We do not wish the definition to apply to miscellaneous collections of paper about individuals, even if the collections are assembled in files with the individual's name or other unique identifier on the front, if specific data about the individual cannot be readily extracted from that collection. An example might be a personnel file with my name on the front. Let us assume that the file contains every piece of paper or other document about me which the personnel section has collected over the course of my career and those papers are held in the file in date order with no means of readily identifying specific information about me except by looking at every document. The Government's clear intention is that such files should not be caught.[44]

The then Data Protection Registrar, however, commented that:

> It has . . . been put to us that 'particular information' refers to information of a very specific nature. On this analysis information held in a file relating to an immigration application would arguably be covered as all the information in the file will, or should, be directly pertinent to that application. However, it has been argued that information held in a normal personnel file will not be 'particular information' as there will be a range of information concerning such matters as sickness absence, performance, pay, next of kin. We find this distinction unconvincing. The range of information in a personnel file may be wide because there is a wide range of information relevant to an individual's employment. Nevertheless, the information is 'particular' in that it is all information held for, and relevant to, employment.[45]

Some answers (but at least as many questions) to the issues raised can be found in the Court of Appeal decision in *Durant v Financial Services Authority*.[46] In addition to the issue discussed earlier of whether data is classed as personal in its nature, the court gave extensive consideration to the appellant's claim for access to a range of manual records. As described in the judgment, these took a variety of forms and demonstrated differing levels of structure and organisation. In some cases, documents were located in a folder under Mr Michael Durant's name but in other instances the name on the file was that of the bank against which complaints had been made—whether by Mr Durant or by other persons. It was accepted by the FSA that all of these files contained some information which related to the appellant. The degree and level of identification varied, with some files identifying him

---

[43] Data Protection Registrar. Our Answers. Response to the Consultation Paper on the EC Data Protection Directive 1998, para. 3.8.

[44] 587 HL Official Report (5th series), col. 467, 16 March 1998.   [45] Briefing Note, 29 January 1998.

[46] [2003] EWCA Civ 1746.

'by reference to specific dividers within the file'. Files also contained a range of documents, including copies of telephone attendance notes and

> a report of forensic examination of documents, transcripts of judgments, handwritten notes, internal memoranda, correspondence with Barclays Bank, correspondence with other individuals and correspondence between the FSA and him.[47]

Again taking account of the issue of whether data might be regarded as personal, the court considered the extent to which the records in question could be considered to constitute a relevant file. Reference was made once more to the Act's intention being to protect the privacy of the data subject rather than that of documents. As has been described, it would be a relatively simple task to identify documents but a more complex one to determine whether a document constituted personal data. Consideration was given to the magnitude of the task which a data controller might be faced with in seeking to respond to a request for subject access. The responsibility for the task, it was held, would often fall on administrators who might not have a specialised knowledge of the subject area or documents involved. In order for the extent of access to be manageable, the obligations could only be applied in respect of manual systems

> that enable identification of relevant information with a minimum of time and costs, through clear referencing mechanisms within any filing system potentially containing personal data the subject of a request for information. Anything less, which, for example, requires the searcher to leaf through files to see what and whether information qualifying as personal data of the person who has made the request is to be found there, would bear no resemblance to a computerised search.[48]

It is not clear whether this conclusion is necessarily supported by the reality of modern databases. A Google-type search, for example across an organisation's electronic filing systems, might identify a large number of documents in which an applicant's name appeared—as indeed was at issue in the *Durant* case. Whilst certainly there could be no obligation on a data controller to read, or request an administrator to read, every piece of paper in the organisation, the level of structure and organisation required seems excessive.

It is often stated that hard cases make bad laws. It may also be the case that bad cases make hard laws. There is no doubt that the judges in *Durant* were extremely wary of what was regarded as an attempt to invoke the provisions of the Data Protection Act 1998 for purposes beyond those envisaged by the legislature. It might be noted that in many cases, data of the kind sought by Durant could have been obtained under the Freedom of Information Act 2000, although this legislation was not in force at the time his litigation commenced. Given that the FSA had identified the material relating to Durant's case in the context of the data protection proceedings, it might be difficult to refuse any future freedom of information request on the basis that the information would be excessively difficult to collect. Perhaps the most intractable problem facing the courts in a case such as this is that there is the clear signal, not least from the Data Protection Directive,[49] that the legislation is concerned with the protection of the right to privacy, yet, as discussed extensively elsewhere, this remains something which is not explicitly protected in the United Kingdom. The content of the right to privacy has long evaded precise definition. The classic formulation, however, refers to the right 'to be left alone', whilst references to the concept of informational privacy lay stress on the more proactive ability to control the storage and dissemination of personal data. If the right to exercise at least a measure of control over the collection and use of personal data is to have any meaning, knowledge of the nature and

---

[47] para. 17.   [48] para. 45.   [49] Directive 95/46/EC.

extent of the information which is held must be a necessary concomitant. In adopting a restrictive view of the scope of relevant filing systems, the court in *Durant* pays insufficient regard to the concept of informational privacy.

Data protection actors

Data controllers

Data controllers are subject to the most extensive forms of control under the Data Protection Act and Directive. The Directive provides that:

> 'controller' shall mean the natural or legal person, public authority, agency or any other body which alone or jointly with others determines the purposes and means of the processing of personal data; where the purposes and means of processing are determined by national or Community laws or regulations, the controller or the specific criteria for his nomination may be designated by national or Community law.[50]

The Data Protection Act provides that a party will be classed as a data controller when it:

> (either alone or jointly or in common with other persons) determines the purposes for which and the manner in which personal data are, or are to be, processed.[51]

In the case where data are processed only for purposes required by statute, for example the compilation of an electoral roll, the agency charged with conducting the work will be classed as the data controller.

The key element of the above definitions relates, with the exception of the performance of statutory functions, to the ability to determine the nature and extent of the processing which is to be carried out. It is quite possible for persons to be classed as data controllers even though they do not own a computer. An example might concern the owner of a small business who records details of transactions on pieces of paper which are stored in the archetypal shoebox. Once a year, the shoebox may be collected by an accountant, who transfers the data to a computer in order to prepare a set of accounts. Assuming that some of the data in the accounts relate to individual creditors and debtors, all the criteria necessary for the application of the legislation will be satisfied and, doubtless much to their surprise, the business person will be classed as a data controller. In such a situation, the accountant will also be so regarded, the Divisional Court confirming in *Data Protection Registrar v Griffin*,[52] a case brought under the Data Protection Act 1984, that anyone who processed data on behalf of clients would be regarded as a data user (now controller) when he or she possessed any control or discretion concerning the manner in which the processing was carried out.

A similar result is predicted in the Recitals to the Data Protection Directive:

> where a message containing personal data is transmitted by means of a telecommunications or electronic mail service, the sole purpose of which is the transmission of such messages, the controller in respect of the personal data contained in the message will normally be considered to be the person from whom the message originates, rather than the person offering the transmission services; whereas, nevertheless, those offering such services will normally be considered controllers in respect of the processing of the additional personal data necessary for the operation of the service.[53]

---

[50] Art. 2(d).   [51] s. 1(1).   [52] *The Times*, 5 March 1993.   [53] Directive 95/46/EC, Recital 41.

Data processors

As in the example given above, some data controllers may seek to have processing carried out on their behalf by a third party. This was perhaps more prevalent in the early days of computing than is the case today, although one aspect which remains significant is where undertakings make arrangements as part of a disaster recovery plan, to obtain access to external processing facilities in the event of some interruption to service. Mirroring once again the terminology of the Data Protection Directive,[54] the Data Protection Act 1998 utilises the term 'data processor' which encompasses:

> any person (other than an employee of the data controller) who processes the data on behalf of the data controller.[55]

The phrase in brackets was included to avoid the possibility that employees engaged in processing in the course of their employment might be regarded as data processors. Given the expanded definition of processing adopted in the 1998 Act, it will be the case that any other person who collects data for the controller—perhaps by conducting market research surveys using pen and paper—will be classed as a processor.

Although a wide range of persons may be classed as data processors, the requirements imposed on them are limited. Data processors will not be subject to the notification requirements,[56] whilst, in respect of the requirement to maintain appropriate security (now found in the seventh principle), the onus is placed upon the data controller for whom processing is conducted. The controller is responsible for selecting a processor who can provide satisfactory guarantees regarding security.[57] A written contract must also be entered into obliging the processor to act only on instructions from the controller in respect of the processing carried out, and also to comply with the requirements of the seventh principle.[58] Further, it is only the data controller who may be liable to compensate data subjects for losses arising from processing.[59]

Data subjects

A data subject is 'an individual who is the subject of personal data'.[60] It would be a unique individual who is not to be classed as a data subject—many times over. In contrast to the situation with data controllers and processors, where the focus is very much on the obligations imposed under the legislation, for data subjects, the purpose of the statute is to confer rights. The most important right for data subjects is undoubtedly that of obtaining access to data held by controllers and of securing the correction of any errors contained therein.

Jurisdictional issues

The Data Protection Act 1984 'applies to all data users who control the contents and use of personal data from within the United Kingdom'.[61] In part, this approach was necessary in order to comply with the Council of Europe's provisions regarding mutual assistance. In the situation where data is processed in the United Kingdom relating to, for example, French or German data subjects, the Data Protection Act will apply, with the main issue being the identification of the data user. The question of whether an undertaking can be considered

---

[54] Directive 95/46/EC.   [55] s. 1(1).
[56] s. 17, which provides for notification, refers only to this obligation being imposed upon data controllers.
[57] Sch. 1, Pt 2, para. 11.   [58] Sch. 1, Pt 2, para. 12.   [59] s. 13.
[60] s. 1(1). The Data Protection Act 1984, s. 1(4) contains the equivalent provision.   [61] s. 39.

resident in the United Kingdom is one which arises in a number of contexts and which may produce different results. As the Commissioner has commented, a company could be regarded as resident in the United Kingdom for the purpose of the Data Protection Act but not for taxation purposes. In the event that the company is not considered resident, it may be that it will be represented in the United Kingdom by a 'servant or agent' who will be classed as a data user for this purpose. It may also be the case that the undertaking which carries out the processing may be regarded as a computer bureau for the purpose of the legislation.

Similar problems arise when data relating to UK data subjects is processed abroad. In many instances, the data will remain under the legal control of the United Kingdom-based user, who will therefore be subject to the legislation. The view has been taken by the Commissioner that jurisdiction will be claimed even where all aspects of the processing are carried out abroad but where it is intended that the data will be used in the United Kingdom—regardless of the form in which it is imported. The correctness of this interpretation has not been tested before the courts or the Information Tribunal.

In the Data Protection Directive,[62] it is provided that EU Member States are to apply national laws where processing 'is carried out in the context of the activities of an establishment of the controller on the territory of the Member State'. Such a formulation may lead to extraterritorial application of national laws. Article 28(6) provides further that:

> Each supervisory authority is competent, whatever the national law applying to the processing in question, to exercise, on the territory of its own Member State, the powers conferred on it (to investigate suspected violations of the law and to intervene by legal or administrative measures to terminate breaches). Each authority may be requested to exercise its powers by an authority of another Member State.

There is potential for overlapping jurisdiction in the situation where multinational undertakings process personal data in a variety of Member States. In its Consultation Paper, the Home Office asserted that:

> While some of the provisions relating to geographical extent are clear enough, others are obscure and potentially ambiguous. There is, therefore, the potential for inconsistent approaches being adopted in different Member States. The danger is that this could make it possible for the national law of more than one Member State to apply to a single processing operation, or for no Member State's law so to apply.[63]

The multiple jurisdiction situation would appear to be an inevitable consequence of the free movement of data within the EU. Given that a major purpose of the Data Protection Directive[64] is to harmonise the laws of the Member States, such a result should not be excessively burdensome for data users and, indeed, corresponds to the UK Commissioner's interpretation of the existing situation under domestic law. It is difficult to envisage that a reasonable interpretation of the Directive's terms could produce a situation where no national law applied. In implementing the Directive's provisions, the Data Protection Act 1998 will apply where:

(a) the data controller is established in the United Kingdom and the data are processed in the context of that establishment; or

(b) the data controller is established neither in the United Kingdom nor in any other EEA state but uses equipment in the United Kingdom for processing the data otherwise than for the purposes of transit through the United Kingdom.[65]

---

[62] Directive 95/46/EC.
[63] *Data Protection: The Government's Proposals* (1997), para. 2.27.
[64] Directive 95/46/EC.
[65] s. 5(1).

An example of the latter situation might be where equipment forming part of a computer network, perhaps involving an ISP, is located in the United Kingdom but managed from the United States.

The question of establishment is defined more precisely than under the Data Protection Act 1984. The criteria adopted are that the controller satisfies one of the following criteria:

1. The controller is an individual who is ordinarily resident in the United Kingdom.

2. The controller is a body incorporated under United Kingdom law.

3. The controller is a partnership or unincorporated association subject to United Kingdom law.

4. The controller is a person maintaining an office, branch agency, or regular practice in the United Kingdom.[66]

For multinational companies, it is the case that they will be regarded as being established in every country in which they operate. The geographical location of any data processing operation will not be relevant. A company established, for example, in France, Germany, and the United Kingdom will need to comply with the national laws of each of these states. The effect will be that the Information Commissioner would be obliged to assist any inquiries made by the German supervisory authority regarding processing relating to German citizens carried out in the United Kingdom and to apply German law in determining the legality of this processing. The Data Protection Act 1998 provides that an Order may be made by the Secretary of State relating to the manner in which these functions might be exercised.[67]

Conclusions

Given the expanded nature of some of its basic definitions, there is little doubt that the Data Protection Act 1998 governs a greater range of activities than was the case under the Data Protection Act 1984. In addition to legal changes, developments in technology, such as permitting the automatic identification of individuals whose images are captured on video camera or, indeed, car number-plates, will mean that many of these forms of surveillance will also be governed by the legislation. The scope of the legislation has begun to be examined by the courts. In *Bodil Lindqvist*,[68] the European Court adopted an expansive view of the scope of the legislation. In *Durant v Financial Services Authority*,[69] the Court of Appeal took a rather more restrictive approach. It may well be that further decisions of the European Court will be necessary in order to provide a comprehensive and consistent approach to the scope of the Data Protection Directive[70] across the EU Member States.

It is clearly the task of the courts to apply legislative provisions at issue before them. The courts have perhaps been ill-served by the legislature, which has promulgated laws that are rather imprecise. In *Campbell v MGN*,[71] Lord Phillips of Worth Matravers MR said:

In interpreting the Act it is appropriate to look to the Directive [Data Protection Directive][72] for assistance. The Act [Data Protection Act 1998] should, if possible, be interpreted in a

---

[66] Data Protection Act 1998, s. 5(3).

[67] s. 51(3). The Data Protection (Functions of Designated Authority) Order 2000, SI 2000/186, makes provisions for the Commissioner to cooperate with, and seek the cooperation of, other Member State supervisory authorities in such matters. This provision is discussed in more detail in Chapter 6.

[68] Case 101/01, [2004] QB 1014.   [69] [2003] EWCA Civ 1746.   [70] Directive 95/46/EC.

[71] [2002] EWCA Civ 1373, [2003] QB 633.   [72] Directive 95/46/EC.

manner that is consistent with the Directive. Furthermore, because the Act has, in large measure, adopted the wording of the Directive, it is not appropriate to look for the precision in the use of language that is usually to be expected from the parliamentary draftsman. A purposive approach to making sense of the provisions is called for.[73]

Even the most purposive form of interpretation cannot and should not provide an excuse for unfettered judicial decision-making. Beyond issues of ambiguity and lack of precision in the drafting of the legislation, the Directive and the Act are to a considerable extent surviving dinosaurs from the age when computers were free-standing machines, used almost exclusively by businesses and large organisations but with limited networking capabilities. The world has moved on and, whilst the European Court was undoubtedly correct in determining that the development of a web page constituted processing as defined in the legislation, it is difficult to see that this, and a myriad of other pages maintained by individuals effectively by way of a hobby, constitute a sufficiently serious threat to the rights and freedoms of other individuals to justify the imposition of criminal sanctions. As will be discussed in Chapter 6, the legislation does not apply where processing is for social or domestic purposes. The problem, which arises also in the context of copyright infringement, is that what used to be clear-cut distinctions, not least in terms of the scale of activities possible, are no longer applicable. The old models are broken but the form of their replacements has yet to be resolved in a satisfactory manner.

---

[73] [2002] EWCA Civ 1373, [2003] QB 633 at [96].

4

Supervisory agencies

INTRODUCTION

The establishment of a dedicated supervisory agency has become a defining element of the European approach towards data protection. Much publicity continues to be given to the actions (or inactions) of supervisory agencies in respect of activities such as Google's collection of personal data in the course of its 'Street View' development activities, and, more recently, major losses of personal data held by organisations such as Yahoo.[1] This case, which has been reported as constituting the single biggest data loss in history, involving details of around 500 million users, raises a number of important questions. First, and linking to topics raised elsewhere in the book, there has been the suggestion that the hacking attack was state sponsored and, second, is the fact that the hack occurred in 2014 but was only admitted to by the company in 2016. The incident has certainly attracted the attention and, indeed the ire, of data protection authorities in Europe (and elsewhere).[2]

The Council of Europe Data Protection Convention made only minimal provision for the appointment of supervisory agencies. The Data Protection Directive is more expansive.[3] It specifies in Recital 62 that the establishment of independent supervisory authorities is 'an essential component of the protection of individuals with regard to the processing of personal data', and requires under Article 28 that:

> Each Member State shall provide that one or more public authorities are responsible for monitoring the application within its territory of the provisions adopted by the Member States pursuant to this Directive. These authorities shall act with complete independence in exercising the functions entrusted to them.

In all bar one of the European Union States, a single agency has been established. The exception is in Germany which, because of the federal nature of its constitution, has around twenty supervisory agencies working in the field of data protection.

In addition to national supervisory agencies, the Treaty of Amsterdam—which made significant changes to the treaties establishing the EU—provided that an independent supervisory agency was to be established in respect of the data processing activities of the European institutions. Acting on this, Regulation 45/2001 'on the protection of individuals with regard to the processing of personal data by the Community institutions and bodies and on the free movement of such data'[4] was adopted, entering into force at the end of January 2001. The

---

[1] The incident has been widely reported. See, eg, <http://www.bbc.com/news/world-us-canada-37447016> regarding the response of the UK's Information Commissioner.

[2] See, eg, < https://ico.org.uk/about-the-ico/news-and-events/news-and-blogs/2016/09/information-commissioner-s-response-to-yahoo-data-breach/>.

[3] The general data protection Regulation requires that further powers be granted to data protection authorities. These are discussed further below.

[4] OJ 2001 L 8/1.

Regulation provides for the appointment of a European Data Protection Supervisor[5] and contains provisions, broadly equivalent in scope to those contained in the current Data Protection and Electronic Communications Privacy Directives, which will apply to processing carried out by the European institutions. A further two years were to elapse before Decision 2004/55[6] announced the appointment of Peter Hustinx as the first Supervisor for a five-year term of office. Mr Hustinx's appointment was continued for a second term in 2009,[7] and in 2014 Mr Giovanni Buttarelli was appointed[8] to the position, again with a five-year term of office.

Forms of supervisory agencies

Presupposing the existence of a supervisory agency, one of the key issues for law-makers concerns the form that this body should take. Many options are available but the key choice lies perhaps between the appointment of a single regulator, albeit supported by what may be a substantial staff, or vesting authority in a multi-membered commission or authority. The relative merits of single and multiple regulators have been ventilated in many other areas. A single regulator may be able to bring a more focused and consistent approach to regulation, although much will obviously depend upon the personality and abilities of the post holder. Experience within the United Kingdom would suggest that each Information Commissioner has brought his or her own approach to the post. With a collegiate body there is more potential for internal dissent, but it is also likely that a wider range of interests and expertise may be represented, with the consequence that decisions, when reached, may carry greater weight.

In part, the choice of whether to appoint a single regulator or a commission is influenced by national traditions. Historically, the United Kingdom has favoured the appointment of a single official. Examples include the Information Commissioner, the Director General of Fair Trading, and the regulators for the privatised gas, electricity, and railway industries. More recently, however, the Communications Act 2003 provided for the establishment of the Office of Communications (OFCOM) as a multi-membered regulatory body to take over the functions of five individual regulators in the media and telecommunications sector. In 2008 the *Data Sharing Review*,[9] produced by the Information Commissioner and Dr Mark Walport, the Director of the Wellcome Trust, canvassed the notion that a multi-membered authority might be established. Posing the question whether the existing institutional arrangement was the most appropriate, the report commented: 'We have come to the firm conclusion that it is not.'[10] It does not appear, however, that any legislative changes are likely to follow although speaking in 2008, the then Information Commissioner commented that:

> The post is perhaps somewhat anachronistic in some respects as a sole Commissioner. Most of the former Directors General in other areas of regulation were converted to Boards or Commissions some years ago. I would not wish to call myself a dinosaur—indeed there are others who are sole practitioners like myself, such as the Parliamentary Ombudsman—but I do recognise that we are perhaps an unusual species these days.[11]

[5] Art. 1.
[6] OJ 2004 L 012/47.
[7] See <https://secure.edps.europa.eu/EDPSWEB/edps/EDPS>.
[8] Decision 2014/886/EU.
[9] Available from <http://www.connectingforhealth.nhs.uk/systemsandservices/infogov/links/datasharingreview.pdf>.
[10] para. 8.71.
[11] <http://www.ico.gov.uk/upload/documents/library/freedom_of_information/notices/cri_lecture_jan08.pdf>.

The issue of the optimal form of supervisory agency was considered in some detail in the Leveson Report on Press Standards. Acting in the specific context of media activities it concluded:

> The evidence before the Inquiry suggested that the constitution of the ICO as a corporation sole may, in at least some of these dimensions, have risked its ability to discharge effectively its functions in relation to the press. Unresolved questions must remain, for example, as to whether:
>
> (a) the informal approach adopted by the ICO to its regulatory functions (partly a matter, perhaps, of presiding over a regime struggling for a profile, also possibly a matter of personal leadership style) has contributed to a reluctance to bring issues to a head through the use of regulatory powers, and has allowed inaction to be an unremarked default within its own structure;
>
> (b) the tendencies of Information Commissioners to see themselves as having a major, even dominant, outward-facing role with a political or campaigning dimension has been at the expense of their ability to provide clear, engaged, understood and accountable leadership in the decisions made within their office, to the detriment of the quality of those decisions, and has posed some risk to the regulatory reputation of the ICO, including in relation to its quasi-judicial functions; and
>
> (c) its current constitution leaves the ICO with insufficient strength to match major business sectors with power and influence, such as the press.

In large part, any changes to the nature of the Information Commissioner's role have been put on hold pending the adoption of the European Data Protection Regulation. The danger of 'regulatory capture' is one that has been widely recognised across a range of sectors and there is no doubt that any agency—whatever its composition—has to make choices whether to work with or in possible conflict with those it is seeking to regulate. The Leveson report recites evidence from the then Information Commissioner:

> 1.27 . . . Mr Thomas recalled a conversation within the office around 2007 along the lines:
>
> 'Thank God we didn't take the journalists to court. They'd have gone all the way to Strasbourg.' In other words, they would have challenged any action we would have taken, we would have gone right to Strasbourg, the Court of Human Rights, Article 10 issues coming in. We'd seen all the material being thrown at us during What Price Privacy? and the Bill.'
>
> 1.28 There was a gut instinct that litigation against the press would present the Information Commissioner's office (ICO) with enormous difficulties. These were evidently perceived to be difficulties over and above the normal litigation issues of accessing and deploying evidence, navigating the law, and the overall strengths and weaknesses of the case.[12]

Key functions of supervisory agencies

In addition to requiring the establishment of an independent agency or agencies, the Data Protection Directive also prescribes the basic powers to be vested in these agencies. These agencies, it is provided, are to be afforded:

- investigative powers, such as powers of access to data forming the subject-matter of processing operations and powers to collect all the information necessary for the performance of its supervisory duties;

---

[12] Lord Justice Leveson, *An Inquiry into the Culture, Practices and Ethics of the Press*, 4 vols. (London, 2012), III, Pt H.

- effective powers of intervention, such as, for example, that of delivering opinions before processing operations are carried out, in accordance with Article 20, and ensuring appropriate publication of such opinions, of ordering the blocking, erasure, or destruction of data, of imposing a temporary or definitive ban on processing, of warning or admonishing the controller, or that of referring the matter to national parliaments or other political institutions;

- the power to engage in legal proceedings where the national provisions adopted pursuant to this Directive have been violated or to bring these violations to the attention of the judicial authorities.[13]

It is further provided that:

> Each supervisory authority shall hear claims lodged by any person, or by an association representing that person, concerning the protection of his rights and freedoms in regard to the processing of personal data. The person concerned shall be informed of the outcome of the claim.[14]

The United Kingdom's implementation of these requirements continues to be a matter of controversy with the European Commission issuing a 'reasoned opinion'[15] in July 2010 alleging that a failure to grant the Information Commissioner adequate powers to audit compliance with the legislation meant that the country was in breach of its obligation to implement the Directive. To date, the issue remains unresolved.

The Information Commissioner and the Information Tribunal

Under the Data Protection Act 1984, the office of Data Protection Registrar was created. In addition to the Registrar, the Act provided for the establishment of a Data Protection Tribunal to hear appeals by data users (or computer bureaux) against decisions taken by the Registrar.

In 1996 the then Registrar, Elizabeth France, indicated concern that the title of Registrar placed undue emphasis on one (perceived as rather bureaucratic) aspect of her role and suggested that with the introduction of a new Data Protection Act there should be a change in nomenclature so that the office should be described as Privacy Protection Commissioner. The UK government and legislature has traditionally been wary of making specific references to privacy—and still more to rights thereto. The notion of a Privacy Commissioner was rejected but the 1998 Act established the office of Data Protection Commissioner. With the enactment of the Freedom of Information Act 2000, the Commissioner also became responsible for the operation of that legislation. Recognising this fact, there has been a further change in the nomenclature to Information Commissioner.[16] At the same time, the Data Protection Tribunal was renamed as the Information Tribunal, reflecting additional responsibilities placed on it under the Freedom of Information Act. The Information Tribunal is now subsumed into the General Regulatory Chamber that is referred to as the First Tier Tribunal system.[17,18] Appeals against decisions by this body lie to the Upper Tribunal.[19]

The Data Protection Act 1998 specifies the terms and conditions under which the Commissioner is to be appointed. This is to be for a fixed term, not exceeding five years. Within this period, the Commissioner might be removed from office only following a

---

[13] Art. 28(3).   [14] Art. 28(4).

[15] Service of such a notice is potentially a precursor to the commencement of formal proceedings before the European Court of Justice.

[16] Introduced by s. 18 of the Freedom of Information Act 2000.

[17] <https://www.gov.uk/courts-tribunals/first-tier-tribunal-general-regulatory-chamber>.

[18] <https://www.gov.uk/guidance/information-rights-appeal-against-the-commissioners-decision>.

[19] For details of the Tribunal system see <https://www.gov.uk/government/organisations/hm-courts-and-tribunals-service/about>.

resolution passed by both Houses of Parliament, a status equivalent to that of High Court judges. One change made from the 1984 Act is the provision that a Commissioner may only serve for two terms, save where special circumstances make a continuation of appointment 'desirable in the public interest'.[20] Under the 1984 Act, there was no limit on the number of terms which could be served. Concern has been expressed in the past that a government's role in deciding whether to continue an appointment might deter the supervisory agency from investigating public sector data processing. Although the matter is not likely to be of significance in the near future, it might be considered unfortunate that the default has effectively been switched from the assumption that the Commissioner might continue in the post for more than two terms, to the assumption that this will not be the case.

Logistically, the ICO is a substantial organisation. Separate offices, each headed by an Assistant Commissioner have been established for Scotland, Wales, and Northern Ireland. The Commissioner's annual report for 2016[21] indicated that around 400 staff were employed although there is no breakdown between staff responsible for data protection and those working in relation to the Freedom of Information Act. Inevitably, the operation of such a substantial organisation requires considerable resources and the 2016 report indicates expenditure of around £23 million. The issue of how the supervisory agency's work should be funded has been at the core of many of the debates about the format of the legislation. Although the Data Protection Act 1998 makes provision for public funds to be used to meet the Commissioner's expenses, it has been the practice that the office should be largely self-financing. This decision drives many others concerning the scope of the Act and the obligations imposed upon data users. The only significant source of income for the Commissioner comes from the fees payable by data controllers in connection with the Act's notification procedures. In 2015 these raised some £18 million.[22] Clearly, maximisation of the numbers of those classed as data controllers will have a similar effect upon the income of the Commissioner, whilst any significant reduction in the numbers of those liable to register would have significant implications, either for the financial burdens imposed on those remaining subject to a registration requirement or for the Commissioner's income stream. This again has been a matter where changes have been made with the introduction from 2010 of a two-tier system of fees with larger users being required to pay significantly more by way of notification fees.

Initially, this chapter will focus on the establishment and maintenance of the Data Protection Register and the obligations imposed on data controllers to register details of their activities. Attention will then be paid to the investigative and enforcement powers conferred on the Commissioner, before concluding with an account of the remaining powers and duties imposed on the Commissioner.

Procedural requirements for data controllers

A feature of many of the early data protection statutes was the imposition of a system of licensing of data users. Although terminology in the field is somewhat inconsistent, the procedure might be analogised to the obtaining of a licence for the possession of a gun or the driving of a motor vehicle, with the onus being placed on the applicant to demonstrate fitness to receive the award. With the massive increase in the number of computers since the 1970s, the impossibility of exercising effective control in this manner has been widely

---

[20] Data Protection Act 1998, Sch. 5, para. 2.

[21] <https://ico.org.uk/media/about-the-ico/documents/1624517/annual-report-2015–16.pdf>.

[22] Some £4.25 million was paid directly by government in respect of the Commissioner's activities under the Freedom of Information Act. There has been significant publicity regarding the monetary penalty notices (fines) served by the Information Commissioner on organisations that are considered to have breached the Data Protection Act. These payments are received by the Treasury rather than the Information Commissioner.

recognised. An initial step, which was implemented in the Data Protection Act 1984, saw the introduction of a system of registration of data users. Registration continues to require those wishing to process personal data to seek authorisation and retains qualitative criteria, but switches the onus to the supervisory agency to indicate the cause of an application being rejected. In the fourteen years that the registration system operated, very few applications were formally refused. Thirty-two applications were refused in the year 1994–5, thirty-one in 1995–6, and none in subsequent years.[23] Even at the 'higher' levels, this translated into a refusal rate of one in every 2,650 applications.

From registration to notification

The effectiveness of the registration process adopted in the Data Protection Act 1984 was criticised from the outset. More recent statutes, such as the German Data Protection Act of 1990, moved away from the requirements of universal registration by exempting large numbers of data controllers from any procedural requirements. Even where users remain subject to a requirement to record details of their processing, systems of declaration or notification have been adopted. Notification, as the terminology suggests, involves the controller giving information about the nature of processing activities but does not give the supervisory agency any power of rejection—although concerns about the activities notified might serve to trigger further enforcement actions. The Data Protection Directive follows this model. It initially provides that:

> Member States shall provide that the controller or his representative, if any, must notify the supervisory agency . . . before carrying out [processing of personal data].[24]

Having established the principle of notification, the Data Protection Directive[25] continues to provide that simplification or exemption from this requirement may be offered:

> for categories of processing operations which are unlikely, taking account of the data to be processed, to affect adversely the rights and freedoms of data subjects.

This was subject to conditions being imposed on the kinds of data to be processed, the persons to whom it is to be disclosed, and the length of time the data are to be stored. A range of other possible exemptions are identified in the Directive, some of which are adopted in the Data Protection Act 1998.[26]

Implementing the Directive, the Data Protection Act 1998 imposes a general requirement to notify details of processing:

> Subject to the following provisions of this section, personal data must not be processed unless an entry in respect of the data controller is included in the Register maintained by the Commissioner.[27]

Exemptions from the requirement to notify

Under the Data Protection Act 1984, the list of categories of exempt processing was defined exhaustively in the statute.[28] The 1998 Act adopted a more flexible approach providing that:

> If it appears to the Secretary of State that processing of a particular description is unlikely to prejudice the rights and freedoms of data subjects, notification regulations may provide [for exemption from the requirement to notify].[29]

---

[23] *Fifteenth Report of the Data Protection Registrar* (1999), ch. 5.
[24] Directive 95/46/EC, Art. 18(1).   [25] Directive 95/46/EC.   [26] Art. 18(2).   [27] s. 17(1).
[28] ss. 32 and 33.   [29] s. 17(3).

In initial consultation exercises concerning the extent of exemptions, the then Registrar advocated that extensive use should be made of this provision in order to exclude 'potentially hundreds of thousands of data controllers from notification'. Subsequently, this position changed, in large part because of perceived difficulties in defining the proper scope of any exemptions but perhaps mainly for financial reasons. The fees obtained from those submitting applications for notification constitute virtually the only source of income for the Commissioner. The Data Protection Act 1998 provides that, in fixing the level of fees, 'the Secretary of State shall have regard to the desirability of securing that the fees payable to the Commissioner are sufficient to offset the costs of running the Commissioner and Tribunal's statutory activities'.[30] A significant reduction in the level of those required to notify would inevitably increase the level of fees for those remaining subject to the requirement.

The scope of the exemptions

In the event, the Data Protection (Notification and Notification Fees) Regulations 2000[31] (the 'Notification Regulations') provide for a limited number of data controllers to be exempted from the notification requirement. The exemptions can be placed in two categories, the first relating to particular forms of processing and the second to specific categories of data controller. Especially in respect of the first category, it should be noted that whilst some forms of processing need not be notified, in the (likely) event that a controller engages in additional and notifiable forms of processing, a choice will be given, either to notify everything or to include an indication in the Register entry to the effect that:

This data controller also processes personal data which is exempt from Notification.

The purpose of this is to put data subjects on notice that the entry on the Register will not give a complete picture of the controller's activities.

The Notification Regulations[32] provide for exemption in respect of three forms of processing, involving what has been referred to by the Commissioner as 'core business activities'.[33] It is stressed, however, that the conditions attached to the exemptions are likely to ensure that they will apply only to small businesses. In addition to the purpose-related exemptions, a further exemption applies in respect of certain forms of processing conducted by non-profit-making organisations.

Staff administration

Although the concept of staff administration sounds relatively broad, the scope of the exemption is much more narrowly circumscribed. The activity of staff administration is defined as involving the purposes of:

Appointments or removals, pay, discipline, superannuation, work management or other personnel matters.[34]

Data held may relate to past, present, or potential employees, or to 'any person, the processing of whose personal data is necessary for the exempt purposes'. This latter category might

---

[30] s. 26(2). It was indicated in Parliament that the cumulative deficit on the Registrar's activities since 1986 is some £4.5 million. The Act further provides that account may be taken of the amount of any outstanding deficit when fixing fees. The Act contains a further provision allowing different levels of fees to be charged to different categories of controller (s. 26(1)).

[31] SI 2000/188.   [32] SI 2000/188.

[33] *Notification Exemptions: A Self Assessment Guide*, available from <http://www.dpr.gov.uk/notify/self/index.html>.   [34] SI 2000/188, Sch., para. 2.

include, for example, the processing of data relating to the partner of an employee who will be entitled to pension or other benefits in the event of the employee's death. The data may consist of names, addresses, and other identifiers, as well as information relating to:

(i) qualifications, work experience, or pay

(ii) other matters, the processing of which is necessary for the exempt purposes.

Two further requirements will also need to be satisfied for an exemption to be available. First, the data must not be disclosed to third parties, except with the consent of the data subject, or where this is necessary for the exempt purposes. An example within the latter category would concern the transfer of data to HM Revenue & Customs for the purpose of operating the system of PAYE. Secondly, the data must not be retained for longer than is necessary for the exempt purposes. In most cases, this might be taken to mean that data may not be retained once an employee has left employment.[35]

The word 'necessary' has been quoted on several occasions in the previous paragraphs and is used extensively throughout the provisions relating to exemption. A *Concise Oxford Dictionary* definition of the adjective 'necessary' refers to concepts such as:

Unavoidable, indispensable, enforced, that which cannot be left out or done without.

The restrictions imposed by these definitions should be borne in mind when considering all of the exemptions. An employer might, quite reasonably, seek to maintain a record of employees' next of kin. This will be of obvious benefit (perhaps not least to the employee) in the event of an accident or illness occurring at work. It is more arguable, however, whether the holding of such data is essential for staff administration purposes.

Advertising, marketing, and public relations

This exemption applies when processing is:

For the purpose of advertising or marketing the data controller's business, activity, goods or services and promoting public relations in respect of that business or activity or those goods or services.[36]

Whilst the purpose is broad, the exemption is subject to limitations largely similar to those described in relation to the nature of the data that may be processed, the range of disclosure, and period of retention. The exemption applies only in respect of the marketing of the controller's own goods or services.

Accounts and records

This exemption is couched in terms very similar to those applying under the Data Protection Act 1984. Exemption is offered in respect of processing conducted:

for the purposes of keeping accounts relating to any business or other activity carried on by the data controller, or deciding whether to accept any person as a customer or supplier, or keeping records of purchases, sales or other transactions for the purpose of ensuring that the requisite payments and deliveries are made or services provided by or to the data controller in respect of those transactions, or for the purpose of making financial or management forecasts to assist him in the conduct of any such business or activity.[37]

---

[35] SI 2000/188, Sch., para. 2(d).
[36] SI 2000/188, Sch., para. 3(a).
[37] SI 2000/188, Sch., para. 4(1)(a).

Data must be limited to personal identifiers, together with information about the financial standing of the data subject and any other information necessary to conduct the exempt processing.

The exemption is somewhat broader than that previously provided for under the Data Protection Act 1984, but, once again, the requirement to show that data must necessarily be processed will constitute a significant limitation.

Non-profit-making organisations

Under the Data Protection Act 1984, exemption was offered in respect of the activities of 'unincorporated members clubs'. This proved to be a difficult concept to define and the Notification Regulations provide for exemption for non-profit-making organisations. The concept is undoubtedly broader than that applying under the 1984 Act but, as with the other exceptions discussed above, only a limited range of activities will be covered. Processing is exempt insofar as it:

(a) is carried out by a data controller which is a body or association which is not established or conducted for profit; and

(b) is for the purposes of establishing or maintaining membership of or support for the body or association, or providing or administering activities for individuals who are either members of the body or association or have regular contact with it.[38]

The data processed may relate only to limited categories of individuals, principally present, past, or prospective members of the organisation and be limited to identifiers, together with such information as is necessary for the purposes of the organisation, for example data relating to subscription records. In common with the other exemptions, the data may be disclosed to third parties only with the consent of the data subject or where this is necessary for the exempt purpose.

Independent data protection supervisors

Under German data protection law, it is common practice for data controllers to appoint 'in-house' data protection supervisors. Provided that such supervisors possess sufficient independence, this will exempt the controller from the requirement to notify the Federal Data Protection Commissioner. The Data Protection Directive also sanctions the adoption of such an approach,[39] and the Data Protection Act 1998 provides that the Secretary of State may make an order enabling controllers to appoint a data protection supervisor who will 'monitor in an independent manner the data controller's compliance' with the legislation. Any order will also specify the extent to which such action will exempt the controller from the notification requirement.[40]

In debate on this provision, the UK government pointed out that when such an option had been outlined in the consultation exercise preceding the introduction of the legislation, it had received some expressions of interest but little active support. It was indicated that, given the workload involved in implementing the new legislation, the making of any enabling regulations would not be seen as a priority issue.[41] Sixteen years later, we await any enabling regulations. In a paper published in 2007, *Sharing*

---

[38] SI 2000/188, Sch., para. 5.
[39] Directive 95/46/EC, Art. 18(2).
[40] s. 23.
[41] HC Official Report, SC D (Data Protection Bill), cols. 165–6, 19 May 1998.

Personal Information—A New Approach, the ICO indicated that a code of practice would be developed which would make provision for in-house data protection supervisors.[42] A draft code was published in August 2007 which made no reference to this possibility.[43] Quite apart from the notification aspect, it does appear that the appointment of internal data protection supervisors might be a practical way of providing reassurance to the public that data protection interests will be taken fully into account in the development of data sharing.

Information to be supplied on notification

The Data Protection Act 1998 specifies the information which must be supplied to the Commissioner.[44] Referred to as the 'registrable particulars', this encompasses:

- the controller's name and address together with that of any nominated representative;
- a description of the personal data to be processed and the categories of data subject to whom it relates;
- a description of the purposes for which the data will be processed;
- a description of the intended recipients or categories of recipient of the data;
- in the event any additional processing is being carried out under the terms of an exemption from the notification requirement, a statement to this effect; and
- details of any countries outside the EEA to which it is intended that the data may be transferred. Controllers have the option either of specifying particular countries or indicating that 'worldwide' transfers are envisaged.[45]

The above information will be made publicly available in the form of the Data Protection Register.

In addition to the information which will appear on the Register, controllers are required to provide:

a general description of measures to be taken for the purpose of complying with the seventh data protection principle.[46]

The seventh principle relates to the requirement to maintain appropriate data security measures. The Commissioner has identified four matters which need to be addressed:

- a statement of information security policy
- control of physical security (restrictions on access to sites and equipment)
- controls on access to information (anti-hacking measures such as the use of passwords and encryption)
- a business continuity plan (disaster recovery).

Specific reference to and endorsement of is made to BS 7799, the British Standard on Information Security Management, and to the certification scheme 'c:cure' associated

---

[42] <http://www.ico.gov.uk/upload/documents/library/data_protection/detailed_specialist_guides/pinfo-framework.pdf>.

[43] <http://www.ico.gov.uk/upload/documents/library/data_protection/practical_application/ico_information_sharing_framework_draft_1008.pdf>.

[44] s. 16(1).

[45] Notification Handbook, available from <http://ico.org.uk/for_organisations/guidance_index/~/media/documents/library/Data_Protection/Detailed_specialist_guides/notification_handbook_final.ashx>.

[46] s. 18(2)(b).

with it.[47] It should be stressed that this information—which might be of use to potential hackers—will not appear on the publicly accessible register.

Preliminary assessments

In most cases, once notification of processing is submitted, processing operations may commence. Certain forms of processing may, however, be subject to additional controls. The Data Protection Directive obliges Member States to:

> [d]etermine the processing operations likely to present specific risks to the rights and free-doms of data subjects and shall check that these processing operations are examined prior to the start thereof.[48]

As implemented in the Data Protection Act 1998, regulatory power is conferred on the Secretary of State to determine categories of processing, referred to as 'assessable processing', which appear particularly likely:

    (a) to cause substantial damage or substantial distress to data subjects, or

    (b) otherwise significantly to prejudice the rights and freedoms of data subjects.[49]

To date, no order has been made specifying the form of processing which will be subject to preliminary assessment. It has been indicated that few forms of processing will be covered by such regulations. In Parliament, specific reference was made to activities involving data matching, genetic data, and private investigations.[50]

Where processing comes within the ambit of such regulations, the controller may not commence activities until an assessment of its compliance with the data protection principles has been made by the Commissioner. The timetable for the Commissioner to act is a tight one. When receiving notification from any data controller, the Commissioner is to consider whether any of the processing activities described involve assessable processing[51] and, if so, whether the processing is likely to comply with the requirements of the statute. Such notice is to be given within ten days from receipt of the notification. The Commissioner is then required to give notice of his or her opinion to the controller within twenty-eight days from the date of receipt of notification, which period might, in special circumstances, be extended by a further fourteen days.[52] Processing must not be carried on during this period. In the event the Commissioner's assessment is that the processing would be unacceptable, there would not appear to be any mechanism to prevent the controller continuing with the plans, although it might be expected that an enforcement notice would be served in short order should this occur.

The Data Protection Register

The Data Protection Act requires the Commissioner to:

    (a) provide facilities for making the information contained in the entries in the Register available for inspection (in visible and legible form) by members of the public at all reasonable hours and free of charge and

---

[47] Data Protection Commissioner, *Notification Handbook* (London, 2000), para. 3.2.3, available from <http://www.ico.gov.uk/upload/documents/library/data_protection/detailed_specialist_guides/notification_handbook_final.pdf>.

[48] Directive 95/46/EC, Art. 20.   [49] s. 22(1).

[50] HC Official Report, SC D (Data Protection Bill), cols. 160–1, 19 May 1998.

[51] Data Protection Act 1998, s. 18(2).   [52] Data Protection Act 1998, s. 18(3).

(b) provide such other facilities for making the information contained in those entries available to the public free of charge as he considers appropriate.

Continuing the practice established under the 1984 Act, the Register can be accessed over the Internet.[53]

It is unclear, however, how useful the information contained on the Register may be to the average data subject. The Register currently holds more than 400,000 entries.[54] In one respect, the size of the Register makes browsing a daunting task for data subjects. The Register can only be searched by reference to the name of a data controller or a registration number. Unless a subject knows that an organisation is likely to hold information about them, the Register will be of very little assistance in a quest to discover who might hold personal information. If a data subject knows of an organisation there may be little need to consult the Register, other perhaps than to confirm contact details for making a request for a copy of the information held.

Although the figure of 400,000 entries may seem large, it is perhaps the case that after more than twenty years of data protection legislation, many data controllers have failed to comply with the notification requirements. On a point of comparison, Jersey, which has a population of around 87,000 and a data protection law almost identical to that applying in the United Kingdom, has around 3,500 entries on its Data Protection Register. A similar ratio of entries to population would give the United Kingdom a register with almost 2.5 million entries. It is relevant to note that the heavy dependence of Jersey's economy on the financial services sector, with its voracious appetite for personal data, may result in a proportionately higher number of data controllers; nonetheless, it does appear that non-notification is a fact of data protection life in the United Kingdom. As indicated, failure to notify does constitute a criminal offence although very few prosecutions have been brought on this basis. In April 2013 an estate agent was convicted of this offence and fined £300 (the maximum penalty for the offence is a fine of £5,000). This followed a campaign by the ICO to increase the number of agents registering under the Act and three separate individual contacts with the particular individual.[55]

Enforcement of the legislation

Having established a Register of those processing personal data, the ongoing task for the supervisory agency is to seek to ensure that controllers remain within the scope of their entries on the Register and that in general, processing complies with the substantive requirements of the legislation. The nature of these requirements, principally in the form of the data protection principles, will be considered in Chapter 5. Failures on the part of controllers may constitute an offence and will also expose them to a range of sanctions made available to the Commissioner.

Powers of entry and inspection

Section 50 of and Schedule 9 to the Data Protection Act 1998 provide that the Commissioner may approach a circuit judge (or in Scotland, a sheriff) seeking a warrant to enter and search any premises. The warrant will be granted if the judge is satisfied that a data controller is in

[53] <http://www.ico.gov.uk/ESDWebPages/search.asp>.
[54] <https://ico.org.uk/for-organisations/register/>.
[55] <http://www.ico.org.uk/news/latest_news/2013/ico-praises-estate-agents-commitment-to-data-protection-as-rogue-company-boss-prosecuted-08042013>.

breach of one or more of the principles or has committed an offence under the Act, and that evidence to that effect is to be found at the address specified. The warrant will empower the Commissioner or his or her staff to:

> [i]nspect, examine, operate and test any equipment found there which is intended to be used for the processing of personal data and to inspect or seize any document or other material found there.[56]

Procedures for the award of the warrant are similar to those found in the Data Protection Act 1984, although one significant loophole has been closed. Under the earlier Act, if the Registrar had sought entry to premises and had been granted admission only for the occupier to refuse to cooperate further with inquiries, it was not subsequently possible in England to obtain a search warrant. The Data Protection Act 1998 now provides that a warrant may be sought in the situation where:

> Although entry to the premises was granted, the occupier unreasonably refused to comply with a request by the Commissioner or any of the Commissioner's officers or staff to [perform any of the acts which might be permitted in the execution of a search warrant].[57]

Apart from delaying action, there will be little benefit to a data controller in exercising evasionary tactics of the kind identified.

Information notices

Although the Data Protection Act 1984 empowered the Registrar to seek and execute search warrants in the event a breach of the principles was suspected,[58] that statute conferred no general investigative power and placed data users under no obligation to cooperate with any inquiries made by the Registrar. The Data Protection Act 1998 stops short of providing a general investigative power, but confers a new power on the Commissioner to serve an 'information notice', requiring the supply within a specified time of specified information relating to the matter under investigation.[59] An appeal against service of an information notice will lie to the Information Tribunal and, save in exceptional circumstances, this act will suspend the operation of the notice.[60] Failure to comply with an information notice will constitute an offence, as will the reckless or intentional provision of false information in response to an information notice.[61]

An information notice may be served either on the Commissioner's own initiative, when he or she considers that information is reasonably required in order to determine 'whether the data controller has complied or is complying with the data protection principles',[62] or following a complaint from a data subject. In this latter respect, the Data Protection Act 1998 provides that any person may contact the Commissioner seeking an assessment whether it is likely that personal data has been or is being processed lawfully.[63] The Commissioner is obliged to consider the request and determine an appropriate response taking into account, inter alia, whether the data subject could have obtained the information by means of a request for subject access.[64]

Although the information notice does constitute a new weapon in the Commissioner's armoury, it may be queried as to how useful the power will be in practice. The notice may be served when the Commissioner reasonably requires information to determine whether the principles are being observed, rather than the requirement for service of an enforcement notice that the Commissioner be satisfied that a breach has occurred. Beyond this,

---

[56] Sch. 9, para. 1(3).   [57] Sch. 9, para. 2(1)(b)(ii).
[58] s. 16.   [59] s. 43(1).   [60] s. 43(4)–(5).
[61] s. 47.   [62] s. 43(1).   [63] s. 42(1).   [64] s. 42(7).

however, the appeal procedures are identical. Whilst it may be expected that many control-lers will be happy to respond to an information notice in order to clarify what might be a misunderstanding of the nature of their processing activities, the possibility for appeals may persuade less-scrupulous controllers to prevaricate in their response. Even if the Information Tribunal ultimately upholds the information notice and the Commissioner obtains information indicating that a breach of the principles has occurred, no action can be taken until an enforcement notice, with its own appeal procedures, has been served.

Enforcement notices

The Data Protection Act 1998 retains the 1984 Act's concept of enforcement notices.[65] Under these, the Commissioner may serve notice on data controllers where he or she is satisfied that a breach of one or more of the data protection principles has occurred. The notice will identify the act or omission complained of and specify the steps that require to be taken to put matters right. Failure to comply with an enforcement notice constitutes an offence.[66] As with all other forms of notice served by the Commissioner, the recipient data controller may appeal to the Information Tribunal. Save in exceptional circumstances, the lodging of an appeal will suspend the operation of the notice.

Experience under the Data Protection Act 1984 indicated that a period of years might elapse between the initial moves to serve an enforcement notice and the completion of appeal proceedings. Little can be done to speed up the process itself, but one of the prob-lems identified under the previous regime was that the passage of time might render all or part of the terms of an enforcement notice of dubious relevance. The Data Protection Act 1998 establishes a more flexible approach, providing that the Commissioner may, if he or she considers that all of its provisions need not be complied with in order to ensure compli-ance with the principles, vary or cancel an enforcement notice.[67] The recipient controller may also make a written request to the Commissioner for variation or cancellation on the ground that a change of circumstances means that compliance with its terms is not neces-sary to secure compliance with the principles.[68] In order to avoid the possibility of a double appeal, such a request may only be made after the time available for submitting an appeal to the Tribunal has elapsed.

Undertakings

Although the concept does not have any statutory recognition, the Commissioner has placed considerable reliance upon obtaining formal undertakings from organisations whose processing activities it is considered might contravene the data protection legislation. Breach of an undertaking may well serve as a trigger for more formal enforcement proceedings.

Audits

Linked in many respects to the making of assessments of processing is the concept that the Information Commissioner should be able to conduct an audit of an organisation's processing activities. Under the present legislation, as was stated earlier, the Commissioner may act only with the consent of the controller or where there is evidence of breach suf-ficient to justify service of an information notice. It is perhaps doubtful whether this

---

[65] s. 40.
[66] s. 47.
[67] s. 41(1).
[68] s. 41(2).

approach complies with the provisions of the Data Protection Directive, which requires that national supervisory agencies be granted:

> investigative powers such as powers of access to data forming the subject-matter of processing operations and powers to collect all the information necessary for the performance of its supervisory duties.[69]

For a number of years, successive Commissioners have lobbied to be granted audit powers. In evidence before the House of Commons Justice Committee in December 2007,[70] the Commissioner lamented what he described as a 'bizarre situation' where, unlike almost all other national data protection authorities and, indeed, many other UK regulatory authorities such as those concerned with health and safety and the financial services sector, the Information Commissioner had no general power of audit.

Some developments have taken place in the aftermath of the loss of child benefit data, with the Prime Minister announcing that the Information Commissioner would be enabled to perform spot checks on public sector controllers. This was sanctioned as a matter of administrative direction rather than as a legal requirement, but more general audit powers were conferred on the Commissioner by section 173 of the Coroners and Justice Act 2009. This adds a new section 41A to the Data Protection Act and provides that the Commissioner may conduct an audit of public sector data controllers following service of an 'assessment notice' requiring the recipient to facilitate access by the Commissioner's staff to specified premises to inspect any documents held there and to observe data processing activities. The procedures relating to service of a notice and the conduct of an audit are laid down in a code of practice[71] published by the Commissioner in July 2010. The Commissioner still does not, however, have any specific audit powers in respect of private sector data controllers, except in respect of activities in the electronic communications sector which fall under the auspices of the Privacy and Electronic Communications Regulations 2011.[72] The Data Protection Act does, however, provide in section 51(7) that the Commissioner may, with the consent of the relevant data controller conduct an assessment of processing 'for the following of good practice and shall inform the data controller of the results of the assessment'. Some effort has been put into conducting consensual audits of private sector processing. The Commissioner's annual report for 2013 notes that:

> During the year we conducted 58 audits of data controllers, a 38% increase on last year. In line with ICO priority areas these have included a significant number of local authorities and criminal justice organisations such as police forces and probation trusts. We also followed up on 35 completed audits to ensure that recommendations made have been implemented, a 66% increase on the number conducted last year.
>
> We completed the first full year of our advisory visit programme, aimed at assisting and educating smaller organisations such as charitable and voluntary sector services. We undertook 78 advisory visits which is a 30% increase on the originally projected numbers.[73]

Monetary penalties

A criticism that might be made against all of the Commissioner's powers described in this chapter is that they might amount to little more than an admonishment to 'go away

---

[69] Art. 28.

[70] *Protection of Personal Data*, First Report of Session 2007–8, 17 December 2007.

[71] Available from <http://www.ico.gov.uk/upload/documents/library/corporate/detailed_specialist_guides/assessment_notices_code_of_practice.pdf>.

[72] SI 2011/1208. These regulations are discussed in more detail in Chapter 7.

[73] At p. 16 of the report.

and sin no more'. Certainly service of an enforcement notice or the publicity associated with a requirement on a senior manager in a company to proffer a formal undertaking to improve processing standards might have damaging consequences but the Information Commissioner's powers had been contrasted unfavourably with those available to other supervisory agencies. Contrast was particularly made with the powers of the Financial Services Authority (perhaps wrongly in the light of recent developments in that sector). In June 2010, for example, the Nationwide Building Society was fined almost £1 million for failing to maintain adequate security measures in respect of personal data. The case originated with reports of the theft of a laptop from the home of a member of staff. Perhaps the most expensive laptop in history!

The Data Protection (Monetary Penalties) Order 2010 gives the Information Commissioner power for the first time to impose financial penalties upon data controllers. The maximum amount of the penalty is £500,000. This is certainly significantly lower than the amounts imposed by the Financial Services (now Conduct) Authority although many of the cases of data misuse investigated by the Information Commissioner have concerned public sector organisations and it may be queried what useful purpose is served by imposing a penalty (the proceeds of which will go to the government) on an organisation within the public sector? The figures involved continue to be substantial with the Commissioner's 2016 report indicating that penalties of £2 million were imposed on those organisations found to have committed serious breaches of the Data Protection Act and Privacy and Electronic Communications Regulations. The majority of the penalties have related to breaches of the requirement to keep data securely but one penalty was imposed in 2013 on the Prudential Insurance Company in respect of its unfair processing. As the Commissioner's 2013 report notes:

> Prudential was issued with a penalty of £50,000 after consistently mixing up two customers' accounts, resulting in tens of thousands of pounds ending up in the wrong account.[74]

General duties of the Information Commissioner

Disseminating information

The remaining powers of the Commissioner follow in large part those established under the Data Protection Act 1984. The Commissioner is to disseminate information giving guidance about good practice under the Data Protection Act 1998.[75] Good practice is defined as:

> Such practice in the processing of personal data as appears to the Commissioner to be desirable having regard to the interests of data subjects and others and includes (but is not limited to) compliance with the requirements of this Act.[76]

Under the 1984 Act, a wide range of material was published, perhaps most notably the series of Guidelines giving information about the Registrar's interpretation of the legislation. Members of the Registrar's office were also frequent speakers at conferences. It is likely that these activities will continue. The 1998 Act does give a new power to the Commissioner to levy fees for any matters concerned with the exercise of her powers.[77] It was indicated in Parliament that income from publications and presentations might account for 10 per cent of the Commissioner's income.[78]

---

[74] At p. 32 of the report.   [75] s. 51(1).
[76] s. 51(9).   [77] s. 51(8).
[78] HC Official Report, SC D (Data Protection Bill), col. 253, 2 June 1998.

Codes of practice

Provision relating to codes of practice was inserted into the Data Protection Act 1984 at a late stage during its parliamentary passage by a somewhat reluctant government, which pointed to the nebulous legal status of these documents. Under the 1984 regime, the Registrar's role is limited to encouraging 'trade associations or other bodies' to prepare and disseminate codes of practice.[79] The decision of the Data Protection Tribunal in the case of *Innovations (Mail Order) Ltd v Data Protection Registrar*[80] lends support to this view. Here, the Tribunal held that the appellant was in breach of the data protection principle relating to the fair obtaining of data, even though its conduct complied with a relevant industry code of practice.

In spite of doubts concerning their legal status, a considerable number of codes were adopted under the Data Protection Act 1984. The Data Protection Directive also envisages a substantial role for both national and Community codes, providing that:

1. The Member States and the Commission shall encourage the drawing up of codes of conduct intended to contribute to the proper implementation of the national provisions adopted by the Member States pursuant to this Directive, taking account of the specific features of the various sectors.

2. Member States shall make provision for trade associations and other bodies representing other categories of controllers which have drawn up draft national codes or which have the intention of amending or extending existing national codes to be able to submit them to the opinion of the national authority.

3. Member States shall make provision for this authority to ascertain, among other things, whether the drafts submitted to it are in accordance with the national provisions adopted pursuant to this directive. If it sees fit, the authority shall seek the views of data subjects or their representatives.

4. Draft Community codes, and amendments or extensions to existing Community codes, may be submitted to the Working Party referred to in Article 29. This Working Party shall determine, among other things, whether the drafts submitted to it are in accordance with the national provisions adopted pursuant to this Directive. If it sees fit, the authority shall seek the views of data subjects or their representatives. The Commission may ensure appropriate publicity for the codes which have been approved by the Working Party.[81]

The major novelty for the United Kingdom is the provision in the Directive that supervisory agencies should take a view on the conformity of a draft code with statutory requirements. This comes close to giving an unelected agency law-making powers—a practice which has been traditionally resisted in the United Kingdom.

The Data Protection Act 1998 establishes two roles for the Commissioner in respect of codes of practice. Acting either on his or her own initiative or under the direction of the Secretary of State, and after consulting with relevant trade associations and representatives of data subjects, the Commissioner may 'prepare and disseminate codes of practice for guidance as to good practice'.[82] Any code of practice prepared following directions from the Secretary of State is to be laid before Parliament, either in its own right or as part of another report by the Commissioner to Parliament.[83]

---

[79] s. 36(4).
[80] Case DA/92 31/49/1.
[81] Directive 95/46/EC, Art. 27.
[82] s. 51(3).
[83] s. 52(3).

As with the procedure under the Data Protection Act 1984, the Commissioner is also under a duty to encourage the adoption and dissemination of codes by relevant trade associations. Additionally, however, it is provided that:

> where any trade association submits a code of practice to him for his consideration, consider the code and, after such consultation with data subjects or persons representing data subjects as appears to him to be appropriate, notify the trade association whether in his opinion the code promotes the following of good practice.[84]

In many respects, this provision formalises practice under the 1984 Act, where many of the codes adopted contain a foreword from the Registrar indicating her views on the appropriateness of the code.

International cooperation

As was the case under the Data Protection Act 1984, the Commissioner is the UK agency responsible for liaison with other data protection agencies under the auspices of the Council of Europe Convention.[85] The Commissioner is also responsible for working with the various Committees and Working Parties established at EU level[86] by the Data Protection Directive.[87] Such bodies have a particularly important role to play in determining whether third countries provide an adequate level of protection for personal data. The Commissioner is charged with the duty of disseminating information about any such findings and seeking to implement these within the United Kingdom.[88]

The Data Protection Directive[89] also contains provisions requiring national supervisory agencies to cooperate with each other. In particular, '[e]ach authority may be requested to exercise its powers by an authority of another Member State'. The Data Protection Act 1998 provides that the Secretary of State may make an order relating to such tasks and specifying, in particular, the approach to be taken when a request for assistance relates to processing which is exempt under the UK legislation but is included in the national law of the requesting state.[90] The Data Protection (International Co-operation) Order 2000[91] makes appropriate provision. Article 5 applies in the situation where processing is taking place in the United Kingdom but where the provisions of section 5 would normally exclude jurisdiction—principally where the controller is not established in the United Kingdom. Where the processing is subject to the jurisdiction of a supervisory authority from another Member State, the Commissioner may, in responding to a request for assistance from that authority, act as if the processing were subject to the 1998 Act. Article 6 of the Order provides that the Commissioner may make a similar request for assistance to another supervisory authority in respect of processing subject to UK jurisdiction which is being carried out in another Member State.

Professional secrecy

In addition to providing that powers be conferred on supervisory agencies, the Data Protection Directive also requires that:

> Member States shall provide that members and staff of the supervisory authority, even after their employment has ended, are to be subject to a duty of professional secrecy with regard to confidential information to which they have access.[92]

---

[84] Data Protection Act 1998, s. 51(4)(b).
[85] The Data Protection (Functions of Designated Authority) Order 2000, SI 2000/186.
[86] Data Protection Act 1998, s. 54(1).   [87] Directive 95/46/EC.
[88] Data Protection Act 1998, s. 51(6).   [89] Directive 95/46/EC.
[90] s. 54(2).   [91] SI 2000/190.   [92] Directive 95/46/EC, Art. 28(7).

The Data Protection Act 1998's interpretation of this provision was the cause of a degree of controversy, and, indeed, was criticised by the then Commissioner as likely to impede the effective performance of her duties. It is provided that an offence will be committed where information obtained in the course of employment and relating to an 'identified or identifiable individuals or business' is disclosed by past or present Commissioners or members of staff without lawful authority.[93] The term 'lawful authority' is defined as requiring the consent of the individual or the availability of statutory authority, necessity for the performance of functions under the Act, compliance with Community obligations, or in the course of legal proceedings. Finally, and most significantly, it is provided that 'having regard to the rights and freedoms or legitimate interests of any person, the disclosure is necessary in the public interest'.[94]

Although it is clearly reasonable that confidential information relating to a data controller should not be disclosed, the effect of this provision might be, for example, to prevent the Commissioner from publicising the fact that data controllers have been served with enforcement notices. It was indicated in Parliament that the government has 'found it difficult to get the provision right' and that the issue might be revisited in the context of freedom of information legislation.[95] The format finally adopted is less restrictive than that originally proposed, which would have empowered disclosure only when 'necessary for reasons of substantial public interest', but it remains unclear how extensively it might be interpreted. One possible compromise was suggested in Parliament, that notification regulations may require controllers to include information regarding enforcement notices (or other notices) as part of their entry on the Register.[96]

Appellate bodies

As originally established, the Information Tribunal was a dedicated body responsible for hearing appeals under the Data Protection and Freedom of Information Acts. It now serves as a division, on Information Rights, of the general Regulatory Chamber. The Tribunal's membership consists of a Chairman and a number of Deputy Chairmen.[97] These appointees are to be barristers, advocates, or solicitors of at least seven years' standing.[98] Additionally, a number of other members may be appointed by the Secretary of State representing the interests of data users and of data subjects.[99] A panel of three members will be convened to hear particular appeals.

Under the Data Protection Act 1984, the Tribunal's sole function was to hear appeals brought by data users (or computer bureaux) against decisions by the Registrar adverse to their interests. The only notable change introduced by the Data Protection Act 1998 is that in very limited cases concerned with the application of the exemption for data processed for national security purposes, a data subject will, for the first time, have the right to bring a case before the Tribunal.[100] The procedures to be followed before the Tribunal are specified in detail in the Data Protection Tribunal (Enforcement Appeals) Rules 2000.[101] More specialised rules are prescribed for proceedings involving national security. Here, the provisions of the Data Protection Tribunal (National Security Appeals) Rules 2000[102] will apply. The Tribunal may uphold the Registrar's original ruling, reverse it, or, where the Registrar's

---

[93] s. 59(1).   [94] s. 59(2).
[95] 316 HC Official Report (6th series), cols. 603–4, 2 July 1998.
[96] 316 HC Official Report (6th series), col. 602, 2 July 1998.
[97] The number of deputy chairmen is to be determined at the discretion of the Lord Chancellor.
[98] s. 3(4).   [99] s. 3(5).   [100] s. 28.   [101] SI 2000/189.
[102] SI 2000/206.

act involves the exercise of a discretion, substitute its own ruling.[103] First-tier decisions may be appealed on a point of law to the Upper Tribunal and, with consent to the Court of Appeal (or Court of Session).[104]

Other supervisory agencies

Although not part of the formal data protection structure, brief reference should be made to the fact that many data controllers may be subject to other forms of regulation and that a failure to comply with data protection requirements may result in sanctions being imposed by these regulators. Perhaps the best example can be taken from the financial services regulator where, as stated above, the responsible regulator, has imposed very substantial penalties on organisations in respect of security breaches. In 2007 a fine of £1.26 million was imposed on the insurance company Norwich Union Life for a failure to maintain adequate security in respect of customers' personal data. As the Financial Services (now the Financial Conduct) Authority's press release stated, weaknesses in Norwich Union's systems allowed fraudsters to access the data and commit instances of identity fraud. In addition to accessing confidential data, the criminals were also able to request the surrender of seventy-four insurance policies and receive payments totalling some £3.3 million. Previously, a fine of almost £1 million was imposed on the Nationwide Building Society following the loss of personal data as a consequence of the theft of a laptop computer from a Nationwide employee's home.

Although the penalties might not be as substantial, it might be expected that other regulators such as those in the medical and legal fields would adopt a similar approach in respect of unduly lax data processing practices.

Conclusions

We live in interesting data protection times and the role of supervisory agencies has become contentious. It is perhaps significant how extensive were the data protection considerations in the report of the Leveson Inquiry and, indeed, how trenchant were some of the criticisms made of the current UK regime. Certainly the model of a single Commissioner places great reliance on the individual appointed but as important is the level of resources available to the agency. In an era of austerity, this is always likely to be a difficult issue but the almost total reliance for income on fees from a largely discredited notification regime must be a cause for concern. It may be appropriate to conclude this chapter with a personal anecdote which does, however, indicate some of the resource problems. I submitted a data protection subject access request to my local council. As will be described in Chapter 6, access requests are by law to be complied with within forty days. Forty days came and went and then a reply from the Council. The schools are on holiday and we can't access data until they get back. A bit, perhaps very, strange. I may have missed something, but don't think any exemption exists from the forty-day period relating to councils responding to access requests refers to school holidays.

I pointed this out and received no response. The Information Commissioner has an online form allowing data subjects to make complaints. I submitted and received an automated reply on 13 August indicating that someone would get in touch with me. A month later and still no response from the council. Perhaps, I thought hopefully, a phone call to the

---

[103] s. 14(3)–(4).　　　[104] s. 14(5).

Information Commissioner. One of the phone numbers given in their email did not work. A second one did, and I spoke to a very pleasant person who confirmed that my complaint had been received, but that the office was busy and had to deal with complaints in the order they were received. At that time (13 September) they were starting to deal with complaints received at the beginning of August. It would take another fortnight before my submission was read.

At one level it concerns me that a major local authority should feel that they can ignore the legislation although this does not appear to be an isolated incident. My main concern is different. Data controllers, as I have said, are supposed to respond to access requests within forty days. At a relatively rough calculation, the ICO is taking sixty days to read complaints, even before possibly taking any action on them. As the old saying goes, '*Quis custodiet ipsos custodes*?' Who will guard the guardians?

5

The data protection principles

INTRODUCTION

Whilst we have seen significant changes in procedural aspects of data protection over the past thirty years, the formulation of general statements of acceptable processing practice has been a feature of data protection legislation from the earliest days. Article 6 of the Data Protection Directive prescribes five 'principles relating to data quality', requiring Member States to ensure that personal data is:

(a) processed fairly and lawfully;

(b) collected for specified, explicit and legitimate purposes and not further processed in a way incompatible with those purposes;

(c) adequate, relevant and not excessive in relation to the purposes for which they are collected and/or further processed;

(d) accurate and where necessary, kept up to date; every reasonable step must be taken to ensure that data which are inaccurate or incomplete, having regard to the purposes for which they were collected or for which they are further processed, are erased or rectified; and

(e) kept in a form which permits identification of data subjects for no longer than is necessary for the purposes for which the data were collected or for which they are further processed.

Adding a degree of inflation, the Data Protection Act 1998 provides a set of eight data protection principles with Schedule 1 requiring that:

1. Personal data shall be processed fairly and lawfully and, in particular, shall not be processed unless—

    (a) at least one of the conditions in Schedule 2 is met; and

    (b) in the case of sensitive personal data, at least one of the conditions in Schedule 3 is also met.

2. Personal data shall be obtained only for one or more specified and lawful purposes, and shall not be further processed in any manner incompatible with that purpose or those purposes.

3. Personal data shall be adequate, relevant and not excessive in relation to the purpose or purposes for which they are processed.

4. Personal data shall be accurate and, where necessary, kept up to date.

5. Personal data processed for any purpose or purposes shall not be kept for longer than is necessary for that purpose or those purposes.

6. Personal data shall be processed in accordance with the rights of data subjects under this Act.

7. Appropriate technical and organisational measures shall be taken against unauthorised or unlawful processing of personal data and against accidental loss or destruction of, or damage to, personal data.

8. Personal data shall not be transferred to a country or territory outside the European Economic Area unless that country or territory ensures an adequate level of protection for the rights and freedoms of data subjects in relation to the processing of personal data.[1]

The scope of the UK principles is broader than those adopted under Article 6 but the additional topics covered, namely the rights of data subjects, the maintenance of adequate security, and controls over transborder data flows, are dealt with elsewhere in the Directive. On this occasion differences in terminology do not appear to indicate any distinctions of substance.

The data protection principles span the whole continuum of data processing, from the stage when data is first acquired, perhaps using pen and paper, to the time when it is permanently and irretrievably destroyed. A formula frequently used to justify data protection legislation is to the effect that there should be no processing whose very existence is a secret. More expansively, the principles seek to ensure that data subjects are aware who processes data about them and for what purposes; they should feel confident that it will be kept in secure conditions and that they will be able to verify the accuracy and relevance of the data held.

As with all general statements, almost all of the principles require expansion in the context of particular forms of activity. Detailed guidance concerning the application of the principles can be taken from a variety of sources. No fewer than four Schedules to the Data Protection Act 1998 expand upon the interpretation of the principles. This has prompted an expression of concern from the Commission as possibly restricting the scope of the provisions beyond the level required by the Directive.[2] Provisions in the body of the statute make additional provisions, often in the form of providing exceptions from or restrictions to their applications giving priority to other interests, for example, the prevention or detection of crime. As with other statutes, further guidance on issues of interpretation comes from decisions of the courts and the Information Tribunal. Finally, a significant role is envisaged for sector-specific codes of practice, with the 1998 Act providing for these to receive an enhanced legal status compared with their 1984 forbears.

For the purposes of the present work, the sixth and the eighth principles dealing with the rights of the data subject and controls over transborder data flows, respectively, will be considered separately. Focusing on the remaining six principles, this chapter will consider to what extent and under what conditions a data controller may lawfully process personal data. Use may take a variety of forms and will include disclosure of data to a third party. Finally, this chapter will consider the operation of the seventh data protection principle, requiring that users adopt appropriate security measures.

Fair and lawful processing

Both Act and Directive require that data be processed 'fairly and lawfully'. This is undoubtedly the key component of the data protection principles and it might be argued that the majority of the remaining principles merely provide specific illustrations as to what might be considered fair processing. Under the Data Protection Act, the first principle imposes three cumulative obligations on data controllers. They are required to process data:

- fairly
- lawfully
- in accordance with at least one of the specific Schedule 2 or 3 conditions.

[1] Sch. 1.
[2] Analysis and impact study on the implementation of Directive 95/46 in Member States, available from <http://ec.europa.eu/justice_home/fsj/privacy/lawreport/index_en.htm>.

Failure in any respect may place the controller in breach of the legislation. Processing might be fair and lawful but if it does not come within one of the Schedule 2 or 3 conditions, it will be in breach of the Data Protection Act. Again, as will be described further in the context of fair processing, it may be lawful but considered to be unfair.

In some respects the determination whether processing is lawful will be one of the simpler aspects of the legislation. Particular reference should be made to the provisions of Schedules 2 and 3. Schedule 2 applies in respect of the processing of what might be classed as 'normal' data whilst Schedule 3 applies in respect of the processing of sensitive personal data. The provisions of these schedules will be discussed in more detail later but, essentially, compliance with their provisions or with the requirements of any other statute will render processing lawful. Whether it is also fair raises more complex issues.

Fair processing

The notion of fair processing is key to the legislation although, as with its application in other areas of the law, it is difficult to provide precise definitions. Two aspects of fair processing are of particular relevance. First, reference is made in the legislation to some specific requirements with regard to the manner in which information is obtained; and, secondly, a number of actions brought by the Commissioner and decisions of the Information Tribunal illustrate how the concept may be applied in respect of particular forms of processing.

In Part II of Schedule 1 to the Data Protection Act, guidance is given concerning the interpretation of a number of the data protection principles. In respect of the act of obtaining information it is provided that:

> regard shall be had to the method by which it was obtained, including in particular whether any person from whom it was obtained was deceived or misled as to the purpose or purposes for which it is to be held, used or disclosed.[3]

Surreptitious and deceptive collection of personal data, perhaps in the form of taking a photograph, would contravene this requirement but would also be likely to constitute a breach of the data subject's rights under Article 8 of the European Convention on Human Rights (ECHR) and be classed as unlawful. Again seeking information under the guise of market research when it will actually be used to attempt to sell items will constitute unfair processing.

It is not enough that the data subject is not misled as to the purpose for which the data is to be used. In order for processing to be fair it is necessary that specific information be given to the data subject about the purposes for which processing will be carried out. Two situations are specified in the Act and the Directive, the first applying where the data is collected directly from the data subject, perhaps through the completion of a form, and the second where data is obtained from some other source.

Information obtained from the data subject

Where data is obtained from the data subject, it is provided that information as to the purpose for which it is sought must be given to or 'made readily available' to the data subject. This formulation differs from that used in the Directive, which requires that information be provided to the subject 'except where he already has it.'[4] It is not clear whether the United

---

[3] Sch. 1, Pt II, para. 1.
[4] Art. 10.

Kingdom's approach fully implements the Directive. If a website, for example, provides a prominent link to its data protection policy giving the necessary details, it could be argued that the information is 'readily available', but unless and until the data subject follows the link it cannot be argued that 'he already has it'.

In terms of the information required to be presented to the data subject, the Act requires details as to the identity of the controller (or that of a nominated representative for cases where the controller is not established in the EEA)[5] and also the purposes for which the data are intended to be used, and any intended recipients of the data. The subject must also be supplied with such:

> further information which is necessary, having regard to the specific circumstances in which the data are or are to be processed, to enable processing in respect of the data subject to be fair.[6]

The extent of this requirement is not defined further in the Act. The Data Protection Directive, however, states that subjects must also be informed whether providing answers to any questions is voluntary or compulsory and as to the possible consequences of a failure to reply.[7] This can be seen in operation on many websites such as airline reservation systems where certain details are marked, typically with an asterisk, as being compulsory. A refusal, for example, to give details of name and address will result in a booking being refused. The supply of other pieces of information such as a contact telephone number may be optional. The Directive specifies also that notice must also be given of the right of subject access.

The Act does not indicate when the information is required to be given to the data subject. In a case brought under the 1984 legislation, *Innovations (Mail Order) v Data Protection Registrar*,[8] the Data Protection Tribunal ruled that the requirements must be met at the time the data was collected from the data subject. The Commissioner has expressed the view that the same approach would be followed under the 1998 Act.[9]

Information not obtained from the data subject

In many instances, information about a data subject may be obtained from a source other than the individual himself. An example might be in the situation where a medical practitioner compiles an assessment of a patient's medical condition and passes this on to a third party, such as a potential employer. In such a situation the Act provides for notification—similar in scope and extent to that described above—to be given to the data subject by the third party.[10] Detailed, and somewhat complex, provision is made for the time at which notification is to be given:

> If the data is processed by the recipient data controller, notification must be made at that time.
>
> If data is disclosed to a third party, notification must be given at that time.
>
> If it is subsequently determined that data is unlikely to be disclosed, notification must be made at that time.
>
> In any other situation, notification must be given within a reasonable period.[11]

---

[5] s. 5(2). [6] Sch. 1, Pt II, para. 2(3).

[7] Directive 95/46/EC, Art. 10(c).

[8] Case DA/92, available from <http://www.informationtribunal.gov.uk/DBFiles/Decision/i163/innovations.pdf>.

[9] *Legal Guidance*, para. 3.1.7.7, available at <http://www.ico.gov.uk/upload/documents/library/data_protection/detailed_specialist_guides/data_protection_act_legal_guidance.pdf>.

[10] Sch. 1, Pt 2, para. 2(1)(b).

[11] Sch. 1, Pt 2, para. 2(2).

Given the fact that the statutory definition of processing includes the acts of 'obtaining, recording or holding'[12] the data, it is difficult to envisage how any time other than that at which the data is obtained would constitute the moment at which notification may be required.

In some cases, it might be that data concerning particular subjects makes only a peripheral and individually insignificant appearance in a collection of data. An example might be the individual voters listed in the edited version of the Electoral Register, which may be purchased by a data controller. The Act provides that notification need not be given where it would involve a 'disproportionate effort'.[13] No definition is given as to what might constitute 'disproportionate effort'. The Information Commissioner has expressed the view that this will be a question of fact to be determined in each individual case. A balancing act will require to be performed between the costs and workload implications for the controller and the possible prejudicial effect of the data for the interests of the subject. One specific factor identified as being of relevance would be the extent to which the subject may already know about the processing of the personal data. In the example given at the beginning of this section concerning a medical examination, although the issue of disproportionate effect may not arise, the data subject would be likely to be well aware that the results of his medical examination would be forwarded to the potential employer as part of the process of determining whether an offer of employment would be made.

Unfair processing subsequent to obtaining data

In many instances processing of data in the possession of the data controller will be assessed by reference to some of the other data protection principles. Data, for example, must not be retained for longer than is necessary. Other changes to the nature of processing may be more subtle and might be challenged on the ground of fairness. An example of the operation of this concept can be seen in the enforcement notice served by the Commissioner in August 2006 against the operators of a website company B4U.com. The website promoted itself as providing facilities for tracking the location of individuals using the Electoral Roll. As the enforcement notice[14] states:

> This website offers 'people searching' facilities and claims to contain 'over 45 million records from the United Kingdom Electoral Roll'. The website further claims that those records are 'from the 2001 roll'. These search facilities are offered free of charge and require no subscription or registration. Users need only enter the surname and rough location of the person they wish to trace for the system to return a list of electoral register entries that match the search criteria.[15]

Use of the Electoral Roll for commercial and other non-voting purposes had long been a cause of controversy. It is perhaps the nearest document in the United Kingdom to a definitive list of the names and addresses of every adult in a particular constituency. Under the terms of the Representation of the People (Amendment) Regulations 1990,[16] electoral registration officers were obliged to supply copies of the register for their area upon request. Prior to the introduction of these regulations, the officers were required to supply copies of the register only where these were readily available. The consequence was a massive increase in the usage

---

[12] s. 1(1).
[13] Sch. 1, Pt 2, para. 3(2)(a).
[14] Available from <http://www.ico.gov.uk/upload/documents/library/corporate/notices/b4u_enforcement_notice_130706.pdf>.
[15] para. 3.
[16] SI 1990/520.

of data from the Electoral Rolls for direct marketing and similar purposes. Following the report of a working group, the Home Secretary reported to Parliament concerns that:

> As the law stands, anyone may buy a copy of the electoral register for any purpose. The Home Office and electoral administrators receive more complaints about that than any other subject. People are unhappy about the large amount of unsolicited mail—junk mail—from companies that have obtained their details from the electoral register.
>
> Perhaps more worryingly, the advent of powerful CD-ROMs compiled from the electoral register, which allow for searching by name, means for example that abusive spouses can trace their former partners with considerable ease using a single CD-Rom. People who feel threatened in that way may simply not dare to register.[17]

The conclusion drawn was that commercial and other non-electoral uses of the registers should be restricted. Section 9 of the Representation of the People Act 2000 provided for regulations to be made to establish two versions of the Electoral Register. As implemented in the Representation of the People (England and Wales) (Amendment) Regulations 2001,[18] voters are given information regarding the purposes for which data contained in the register might be used and given the opportunity to opt out of having their data disclosed. Registration officers will then be charged with producing two registers. The full register will contain details of all persons eligible to vote, which will be restricted to electoral purposes and a number of closely defined applications. Although this is available for public consultation it is provided in Regulation 6 that:

> A person who inspects the full register and makes a copy of it or records any particulars included in it otherwise than by means of hand-written notes shall be guilty of an offence.

An edited copy excluding the details of those who have opted out will also be produced, which may be supplied[19] and used for commercial purposes.[20]

By 2005 it appears that around 30 per cent of voters had exercised their right to opt out of the commercially available Electoral Register. Such a level would clearly diminish the value of the resource. The data held on the B4U.com website was taken from the 2001 Electoral Roll, the last created before the 2002 Regulations. The use to which the data was put was lawful under the law as it stood at the time that the Electoral Roll was drawn up. However, the Information Commissioner determined that the use of the data in 2006 constituted unfair processing. The enforcement notice concluded that:

1. The Commissioner considers that it is inherently unfair for individuals to be compelled to provide personal information on penalty of a criminal conviction only for that information to be subsequently disclosed to commercial organisations without any express restrictions on its use.

2. Given that individuals now have a right to request that they are excluded from the edited register, it is unfair to undermine the express wishes of those who have exercised that right and the 2002 Regulations by continuing to make the relevant data available on the data controller's website.

3. The Commissioner considers that the processing of the relevant data by the data controller is unfair given that a significant proportion of the individuals whose details are contained in the relevant data will have subsequently exercised their right not to have those details included in the edited electoral register.

---

[17] Official Report (HoC), 30 November 1999, col. 168.

[18] SI 2001/341. Equivalent provisions are made for Scotland by SI 2001/497.

[19] When supplied in electronic format, the charge will be £20 plus an additional £1.50 for each 1,000 names on the register (Reg. 110).

[20] s. 9.

Accordingly, the website owner was ordered to cease making the data available on its website.[21]

The case may be seen as a borderline one and it is perhaps unfortunate that the Information Tribunal was not called upon to deliver a determination. If the data had been ten years old, could processing still be classed as unfair? Or twenty years old? Original census data is released after one hundred years so we might assume that this would be legitimate also in respect of the Electoral Register. The difficulty that is perhaps inherent in the notion of fair processing is that, whilst equity would suggest that controllers should be able to assess whether their processing will comply with the requirements of the legislation at least in this area, it is submitted the state of the law is insufficiently precise.

Although Electoral Registers may represent the most extensive record of their kind, similar issues have arisen with other forms of records which are required to be made available to the public. Concern has been expressed on a number of occasions at the use made of lists of company shareholders, particularly in the case of privatised undertakings which might have several hundred thousand shareholders. It may be argued that the purpose of making details of shareholders publicly available is to allow identification of the owners of a limited liability company. Use of this information for the purposes of compiling mailing lists for direct marketing purposes raises different issues, although it is difficult to see how prohibitions might be enforced against the use of publicly available information for such purposes.

The credit reference agency cases

A further aspect of the fair processing requirement was at issue in a number of cases brought before the Data Protection Tribunal under the provisions of the 1984 Act. At issue was the conduct of the then four leading credit reference agencies: CCN, Credit and Data Marketing Services, Equifax, and Infolink, each of which was the recipient of an enforcement notice served by the Registrar.

Although the details of their operations vary, each of the credit reference agencies referred to above holds an extensive collection of data culled from public sources such as the Electoral Register, postcode data as made available by the Post Office, and also data relating to judgments handed down by the courts in civil disputes.

In addition to publicly available information, each agency holds information supplied by its subscribers reporting instances of bad debts and also maintains records of searches made. An indication of the scale of the agencies' operations can be taken from the Data Protection Tribunal's judgments which indicate that the Infolink agency conducted some 30 million searches per year.

The information held by the credit reference agencies and extracted in connection with a particular application for credit might be used in a variety of ways. The established method of operation would be for the agency to supply the information generated to its client, the potential creditor, leaving the determination whether to extend credit facilities entirely to the recipient. All of the credit reference agencies involved in the Tribunal actions operated on this basis. In a number of cases, the agencies also offered more extensive facilities. Instead of supplying a client with raw data, the client's own acceptance criteria might be applied. These might operate at a fairly simple level so as, for example, to reject all applicants who were not home owners. If searches revealed this fact, a recommendation that the application be rejected would be transmitted to the client.

---

[21] When checked in September 2007, the site posted a notice claiming that its systems were being upgraded and providing a link to a 'sister site' selling electrical goods.

The critical point concerning the agencies' operations, and the aspect to which exception was taken by the Registrar, is that in all cases, searches were conducted by reference to an address rather than a name. Although at first the practice might seem illogical, it was based upon a number of supposedly objective factors. Names constitute a rather inefficient means of identification. A glance at any telephone directory will show that most surnames appear more than once. Even full names are unlikely to be unique and most recipients of 'junk mail' will be aware of the many and various permutations of names and initials that may appear on envelopes. By contrast, addresses tend to be represented in a reasonably static format and, especially with the use of postcodes, the possibility of duplication is limited. However, the consequence of processing by reference to address would inevitably be that a search resulting from an application for credit by one individual, would retrieve information about previous residents at the address given and as to members of family or others who shared the address with the applicant.

The extraction of third-party data in making decisions about an individual applicant was considered by the Registrar to constitute unfair processing of personal data and, as such, contravened the first data protection principle. After discussions with the credit industry failed to provide an acceptable solution, enforcement notices were served on the four major agencies in August 1990. The terms of these notices were virtually identical, requiring the recipients to ensure that:

> personal data relating to the financial status of individuals ceases to be processed by reference to the current or previous address or addresses of the subject of the search whereby there is extracted in addition to information about the subject of the search any information about any other individual who has been recorded as residing at any time at the same or similar current or previous address as the subject of the search.[22]

Appeals were lodged by all the agencies with the Data Protection Tribunal which considered evidence submitted on behalf of the appellant, arguing that depriving them of third-party information would render their operations less effective. The consequence would be either an increase in bad debts or the denial of credit to persons who might otherwise have been accepted. It might even be that certain creditors would cease to operate in the consumer field.

The Tribunal accepted that the operation of credit reference agencies provided benefits but held that the prime purpose of the legislation was to protect the rights of the individual. Whilst the interests of the credit industry should not be ignored, primacy must be given to the interests of the individual applicant. On this basis it was considered:

> unfair for a credit reference agency, requested by its customers to supply information by reference to a named individual, so to program the extraction of information as to search for information about all persons associated with a given address or addresses notwithstanding that they may have no links with the individual [who is] the subject of the inquiry or may have no financial relationship with that individual.[23]

It was also argued that much of the information held—for example, judgments from county courts—was public information. It was in the public interest that such data should be readily available. Whilst not disputing this argument, the Tribunal pointed out that they were concerned with a much narrower issue: whether the extraction of this information in connection with a search relating to an unconnected individual could be considered fair. The answer to this must be in the negative.

---

[22] para. 18.
[23] <http://www.informationtribunal.gov.uk/DBFiles/Decision/i233/infolink.pdf> at para. 53.

The key ground of objection in the credit reference case was that decisions about individuals were being made other than on the basis of information about them. A person might, for example, be denied credit because of a debt incurred by a previous occupant of the property. There are, however, cases where account may be taken of factors other than those relating to the individual. A more recent case concerned with the issue of fair processing is *Johnson v Medical Defence Union.*[24] The case centred upon whether the use of a risk assessment policy by the Medical Defence Union could be considered unfair. The claimant applied to the defendant for renewal of his professional liability insurance and was refused. The reason given was that the risk assessment processes took account of the volume of incidents reported involving a particular member and it was an integral element that limited regard was had for the outcome of such cases. The claimant had reported a number of disputes with patients although none had made a formal complaint or brought legal proceedings against him. The view was taken that if a doctor had a significant history of complaints brought against him in the past, this would be a reliable indicator that the trend would continue, regardless of whether the previous complaints had proved to be unfounded. The prediction would be that the Medical Defence Union would be required to incur continuing expenditure in representing the doctor in the future.

Although there was disagreement between the judges on whether processing had taken place, a point discussed in more detail in Chapter 6, there was unanimity on the issue of fairness. At trial, Mr Justice Rimer concluded that:

> there is in principle nothing relevantly unfair about the MDU's risk assessment policy or about the way in which it processed information in applying that policy . . . the policy is directed at risk management—at preserving the MDU funds against a risk of claims, and the incurring of costs, *in the future*. The MDU experience is that a risk of that nature cannot be measured simply by awaiting the happening of a statistically significant number of occurrences that do in fact cause a drain on its funds.[25]

Such a situation could be distinguished from that applying in the credit reference agency cases, where there was only the most tenuous statistical correlation between data about a third party and the likelihood that an applicant would default on a credit agreement. In the present case:

> it is not open to this court to hold that the MDU's risk assessment policy was unfair; . . . and that its operation involved . . . no unfair processing for the purposes of the first data protection principle.[26]

This conclusion was unanimously upheld by the Court of Appeal. It may be noted that had the risk assessment processes been carried out completely automatically the complainant would have had the right to object under the provisions of section 12 of the Act. This will be discussed in more detail in the next chapter. By providing for some degree of human intervention, the Medical Defence Union processes fell outside the scope of section 12 and, although the result may have been perceived as unfair by one data subject, the evidence presented to the court satisfied it that the process was based upon rational criteria and sought to produce results which were fair to the totality of the data subjects who made up the membership of the Medical Defence Union, and were also compatible with its legitimate and necessary goal of managing its level of exposure to risk.

---

[24] [2007] EWCA Civ 262.
[25] [2006] EWHC 321 (Ch) at para. 122.
[26] [2006] EWHC 321 (Ch) at para. 124.

Requirements for processing to be lawful

As with the requirement of fairness, neither the Act nor the Directive provides any defini-tion of when conduct will be lawful. In the decision of the House of Lords in *R v R*, a case concerned with marital rape, the concept of unlawful conduct was defined by Lord Keith as relating to 'something which is contrary to some law or enactment or is done without law-ful justification or excuse'.[27] In *Legal Guidance on the Act*,[28] the Information Commissioner indicated that:

> This means that a data controller must comply with all relevant rules of law whether derived from statute or common law, relating to the purpose and ways in which the data controller processes personal data.

A number of particular areas were identified as being of particular relevance:

(a) confidentiality arising from the relationship of the data controller with the data subject;

(b) the ultra vires rule and the rule relating to the excess of delegated powers, under which the data controller may only act within the limits of its legal powers;

(c) legitimate expectation—that is, the expectation of the individual as to how the data controller will use the information relating to him; and

(d) Article 8 of the ECHR (the right to respect for private and family life, home, and correspondence).

Many of these topics are dealt with in the Data Protection Act itself, although, again, there is evidence of collision between concepts of fairness and lawfulness.

Specific factors legitimising processing

In addition to imposing a general requirement that data be processed fairly and lawfully, the Act places the onus on the data controller to evidence specific justification for processing. In the case of general data, processing will be permitted only where the controller can dem-onstrate compliance with one of a list of conditions laid down in Schedule 2. For sensitive data, Schedule 3 provides a more restrictive set of qualifying conditions. In both Schedules, the list of legitimising factors begins with the notion of subject consent.

Subject consent

It is a fundamental tenet of contract law that silence cannot constitute acceptance of an offer. Silence, however, can take a variety of forms. Many supermarket transactions may be carried out without the exchange of a single word, let alone one possessing legal sig-nificance. Silence coupled with conduct indicating a wish to contract can establish a valid contract.

Over the years, there has been extensive debate on how a data subject may validly give consent to the processing of personal data. Anyone who has entered into almost any form of mail order or online transaction will be familiar with the basic techniques which are used. Typically, as was described in the context of the *Innovations* and *Linguaphone* Tribunal cases discussed later in this section, a note of the data controller's processing

---

[27] [1992] 1 AC 599.

[28] Available from <http://www.ico.gov.uk/upload/documents/library/data_protection/detailed_special-ist_guides/data_protection_act_legal_guidance.pdf>.

intentions will be given on an order form or similar document. Under what is referred to as an 'opt-out' procedure, the data subject will be told that the specified forms of processing will take place unless notice of objection is received. This would normally require that the subject places a mark in an 'opt-out' box. The alternative approach, referred to as 'opting in', is again to give notice of the desired forms of processing but also to ask the data subject to indicate that they are content for this to take place. Typically, data controllers have sought to maximise the use of the former technique, as it is well accepted that this will also maximise the number of persons whose data may be processed. In many cases, data subjects may not read the notice or may be unaware of the full implications of what is being proposed. A typical formulation might be along the lines, 'We would like to share your data with other carefully selected companies whose goods or services we consider may be of interest to you.' A rough translation might be along the lines, 'We will sell your details to anyone who pays us money'! Whilst data subject apathy may help controllers on an opt-out basis, the reverse will be the case where subjects are asked to opt in.

Schedule 2 to the Data Protection Act 1998 provides that processing will be lawful when 'the data subject has given his consent to the processing'. Schedule 3 requires that the subject gives 'explicit consent'. Neither phrase is defined in the Act. The Data Protection Directive is a little more helpful, providing that:

> the data subject's consent shall mean any freely given specific and informed indication of his wishes by which the data subject signifies his agreement to personal data relating to him being processed.[29]

In the context of consent to the processing of data, the Directive requires that consent be given unambiguously. This term is not defined. As interpreted in the United Kingdom, it is generally seen as being compatible with either an opt-out or opt-in approach, with the basic requirement being that the data subject is able readily to give an indication of his wishes. Albeit in a different context, the Article 29 Working Party appears to suggest that an opt-in approach may be needed. In an 'Opinion on unsolicited communications for marketing purposes'[30] it considered the requirement in the Privacy and Electronic Communications Directive that prior consent be obtained before commercial emails are sent to data subjects. It concluded that:

> Implied consent to receive such mails is not compatible with the definition of consent of Directive 95/46/EC and in particular with the requirement of consent being the indication of someone's wishes, including where this would be done 'unless opposition is made' (opt-out). Similarly, pre-ticked boxes, e.g., on websites are not compatible with the definition of the Directive either.

At least pending any court decision either in the United Kingdom or before the European Court of Justice, it appears that an 'opt-out' approach will be accepted in the United Kingdom. A key criterion in determining the acceptability of the technique concerns the clarity of the notification. In *Linguaphone Institute v Data Protection Registrar*,[31] a case brought before the Tribunal under the 1984 Act, the appellant included in its advertisements a notice to the effect that:

> (Please) tick here if you do not wish Linguaphone to make your details available to other companies who may wish to mail you offers of goods or services.

---

[29] Directive 95/46/EC, Art. 2(h).

[30] Opinion 5/2004, available from <http://ec.europa.eu/justice_home/fsj/privacy/docs/wpdocs/2004/wp90_en.pdf>.

[31] Case DA/94 31/49/1.

In holding that there was a breach of the data protection principles, the Tribunal expressed concern that:

> the opt-out box appears in minute print at the bottom of the order form. In the Tribunal's view the position, size of print and wording of the opt-out box does not amount to a sufficient indication that the company intends or may wish to hold, use or disclose that personal data provided at the time of enquiry for the purpose of trading in personal data.

Beyond giving information to the data subject, the controller must afford a reasonable opportunity for the subject to express consent (or the lack of it). This was at issue in another case brought before the Data Protection Tribunal under the 1984 Act, *Innovations v Data Protection Registrar*.[32] In this case, the appellant was in the business of mail order sales. Custom was solicited in a variety of ways, including the distribution of catalogues and the placing of advertisements in various media, including newspapers, radio, and television. The appellant's catalogues gave customers notice of use of their data for broking purposes and its order forms offered customers the opportunity to exclude this. Some adverts, especially those appearing on radio or television, did not make mention of the possibility, and in the event that catalogue orders were placed by telephone, no mention would be made of this secondary purpose. An acknowledgement of an order would, however, be sent and this would convey the message:

> For your information. As a service to our customers we occasionally make our customer lists available to carefully screened companies whose products or services we feel may interest you. If you do not wish to receive such mailings please send an exact copy of your address label to . . .

The Registrar took the view that notification of the intended use came too late in the contractual process and served an enforcement notice alleging a breach of the first data protection principle, which, as formulated under the 1984 Act, required that data be obtained fairly and lawfully.

A number of arguments were put forward by the applicant as justifying their practices. It was suggested that, at the time of placing an order, customers would be concerned primarily with obtaining the goods and that a notice along the lines referred to above would have limited impact. Where orders were made by telephone, giving specific notice would increase the length of the call, thereby increasing costs for both the supplier and the customer. It was also pointed out that the details would not be used for list-broking purposes until thirty days from the date the acknowledgement order was sent. This, it was suggested, allowed ample time for the customer to opt out. It was also pointed out that the appellant's practices were in conformity with an industry code of practice and the Council of Europe's Recommendation on the protection of personal data used for the purposes of direct marketing.[33]

Notwithstanding these factors, the Tribunal upheld the Registrar's ruling. Although codes of practice and recommendations might constitute useful guidance, the task for the Tribunal was to interpret the law. Use of the data for list-broking purposes, it was held, was not a purpose which would be obvious to the data subjects involved. Fair obtaining required that the subject be told of the non-obvious purpose before the data was obtained. Whilst a later notification might 'be a commendable way of providing a further warning', it could not stand by itself. Where prior notification might not be practicable, the Tribunal ruled that 'the obligation to obtain the data subject's positive consent for the non-obvious use of their data falls upon the data user'.[34]

---

[32] *Innovations (Mail Order) Ltd v Data Protection Registrar*, Case DA/92 31/49/1.
[33] Recommendation 85/20.
[34] para. 31.

Duration of consent

Consent is not a permanent condition. It is open to a data subject to withdraw consent at any time. This point is not specified directly in either the Data Protection Act or the Directive. Article 9 of the Directive on Privacy and Electronic Communications,[35] which refers specifically to the processing of personal data in the electronic communications sector,[36] provides that:

> Users or subscribers shall be given the possibility to withdraw their consent for the processing of location data other than traffic data at any time.

There is no doubt that whilst the withdrawal of consent cannot have retrospective effect, it would serve to render unlawful any future processing which is dependent upon this head of authority.

Other factors legitimising processing

Although the concept of consent has been a high-profile aspect of the new regime, it constitutes only one of a number of grounds, capable of legitimising processing. For both general and sensitive data, a range of grounds are specified which may allow processing to take place without the subject's consent being obtained.[37]

General data

Necessity for concluding or performing a contract with the data subject

Processing may lawfully take place when this is necessary, either for entering into or performing a contract with the subject. Some stress should be placed on the adjective 'necessary'. This frequently appears in instruments such as the European Convention on Human Rights, and the jurisprudence of the ECHR—which has been approved by the European Court of Justice—has adopted an interpretation requiring that the practice in question be close to essential for the specified purpose.[38] Clearly, information about a data subject's income may be necessary for a lender to determine whether to grant a loan and information as to address will be vital for a mail order sale, but controllers should take care not to require more information than is strictly necessary for the purpose.

Necessity for the controller to comply with a legal obligation

Similar comments apply to this requirement. A controller may, for example, require information to ensure that credit facilities are not extended to those under the age of eighteen. It would be reasonable for such a controller to require applicants to give an indication that they are over eighteen years of age.

Necessity to protect the vital interests of the data subject

It is easy to envisage situations where the interests of the data subject may require that data be processed in situations where it is not practicable to obtain consent. The limitation to the subject's 'vital interests' might mean, in practice, that the data is likely to be of a kind considered sensitive. The Information Commissioner has indicated support for

---

[35] Directive 2002/58/EC, OJ 2002 L 201/37.
[36] The provisions of this Directive are discussed in Chapter 7.
[37] As will be discussed later, a data subject has the right to object to processing in limited circumstances.
[38] See, eg, the case of *Barthold v Germany* (1985) 7 EHRR 383.

this view. The only significant exception might be in respect of information relating to a data subject's financial affairs. As was noted earlier, public opinion surveys conducted for the Commissioner indicate that protection of financial data was ranked higher by most respondents than the protection of many of the categories of data designated as sensitive. Processing designed to guard against the dangers of identity theft, for example, might be seen as coming within the scope of this provision, although, as will be discussed later, the first data protection principle does not apply where processing is conducted in connection with the prevention or detection of crime and where compliance with the principle would prejudice the attainment of those purposes.[39]

Necessity for the administration of justice, etc

Data may be processed lawfully when this is necessary for a range of specified public sector purposes. In addition to the administration of justice, processing may be carried out when necessary for the exercise of statutory functions, for example in compiling registers of data controllers, in the exercise of governmental functions, or any other functions of a public nature exercised in the public interest. This might include, for example, the operation of systems of educational scholarships.

Legitimate interests of the controller

This final justification for processing is perhaps the most extensive. It sanctions processing where this is:

> necessary for the purposes of legitimate interests pursued by the data controller or by the third party or parties to whom the data are disclosed, except where the processing is unwarranted in any particular case by reason of prejudice to the rights and freedoms or legitimate interests of data subjects.[40]

It is provided that regulations may be made to specify the circumstances in which this provision may or may not be applied.[41] To date, no regulations have been made.

Although many situations might be identified in which it will be useful for a data controller to hold information, the restrictions associated with the adjective 'necessary' must constantly be borne in mind. It would, for example, be useful for an employer to record details of employees' next of kin in the event of accident or illness at work. This would not, however, be essential for the normal purposes of employment.

It should be noted that although all processing activities must come under the scope of a Schedule 2 condition, it is not required that it is always the same condition. In the example given above, the legitimate interest processing may be supplemented by subject consent. In the example cited, it might be assumed that it would be a reasonably straightforward matter to obtain the details from an employee at the stage employment commences under the consent heading (although it might well be the next of kin who should be consenting). Even if consent is not forthcoming, the matter can be handled in a relatively simple manner by, for example, inserting a note to the effect that contact details have been refused. Matters become more complicated when a controller has to overcome an initial failure to seek consent by subsequent actions. The likelihood is that only a small percentage of subjects will respond to a request for retrospective consent, with the low response rate being due as much to indifference as to opposition. As with many aspects of the law, prevention is much easier than cure.

---

[39] s. 29.
[40] Sch. 2, para. 6(a).
[41] Sch. 2, para. 6(b).

Factors legitimising the processing of sensitive data

Schedule 3 of the Data Protection Act contains a series of conditions legitimising the processing of sensitive data. These are generally similar in scope to the Schedule 2 conditions but associated conditions are stricter. As with Schedule 2, a controller needs to comply with only one condition.

Explicit subject consent

As with general data, the first ground specified as legitimising processing of sensitive personal data is the fact that the subject has given consent. In this case, the requirement is that consent be 'explicit'. Although the term is not defined in either Act or Directive the *Concise Oxford Dictionary* definition refers to it being:

> not implied merely but distinctly; plain in language; outspoken; clear; unreserved.

Although the definition is perhaps not incompatible with an opt-out approach to consent, more may be required of the data controller to ensure that the subject is aware of what is proposed to be done with the data. The Information Commissioner has suggested that:

> The consent of the data subject should be absolutely clear. In appropriate cases it should cover the specific detail of the processing, the particular type of data to be processed (or even the specific information), the purposes of the processing and any special aspects of the processing which may affect the individual, for example disclosures which may be made of the data.[42]

It is difficult to conceive of many circumstances in which anything other than opt-in consent would be considered valid where sensitive personal data is concerned.

Beyond the grant of explicit consent to the processing, the Act provides for a range of other grounds legitimising processing. This list has been supplemented by a number of items of secondary legislation.

Employment-related processing

> The processing is necessary for the purposes of exercising or performing any right or obligation which is conferred or imposed by law on the data controller in connection with employment.[43]

It is further provided that the Secretary of State may either exclude the application of this provision in certain cases or impose additional conditions. It may be noted that, in respect of the processing of employment-related data, the Data Protection Directive requires the provision of 'adequate safeguards'.[44] Unless it can be assumed that existing employment law provides adequate safeguards for the data subject, UK law will not comply with the Directive unless and until the regulations are made.

Vital interests

> Processing is necessary to protect the vital interests of the data subject or of another person where the data subject is incapable of giving consent or where the controller cannot reasonably be expected to obtain consent.[45]

---

[42] *Legal Guidance*, a. 3.1.5.
[43] Data Protection Act 1998, Sch. 3, para. 2.
[44] Directive 95/46/EC, Art. 8(2)(b).
[45] Data Protection Act 1998, Sch. 3, para. 3(a).

Examples of such situations might be where medical data relating to the subject requires to be processed in order to treat the subject who is unconscious in hospital. Again, processing may be justified where the subject is a carrier of an infectious disease and where the data is needed to provide treatment to a third party. It is further provided that processing may take place when this is:

> necessary to protect the vital interests of a third party and the subject unreasonably with-holds consent.[46]

This situation may well be similar to that discussed above, but with the distinction that the subject has been identified by the controller. An example might be where the subject suffers from an infectious disease but refuses to consent to the disclosure of a list of persons who might have come into contact with the subject and who might require to be contacted to receive treatment.

Processing by specified bodies

> The processing is carried out in the course of legitimate activities by a non-profit-making body or association existing for political, philosophical, religious or trade union purposes. In such cases, appropriate safeguards must be provided for the rights and freedoms of data subjects, the data must relate only to members of the association or those in regular contact with it and does not involve disclosure of the data to third parties without the consent of the data subject.[47]

Given the extension of the definition of processing to include the collection of data, this definition may have some unanticipated consequences. It was conceded in Parliament that political canvassing would be covered if the intention were to transfer returns onto a computer system. A similar situation would apply where religious organisations sought to obtain converts through door-to-door visits. For political data, it was indicated that special regulations would be made.[48]

Information in the public domain

> The information contained in the personal data has been made public as a result of steps deliberately taken by the data subject.[49]

It is significant to note in this context that it will not suffice that the information has come into the public domain; this must have occurred through the deliberate actions of the subject. There is clearly a relationship between this provision and the statutory provisions discussed later relating to the activities of the media.

Legal proceedings and the administration of justice

> The processing is necessary for the purpose of or in connection with legal proceedings (including prospective proceedings), for obtaining legal advice or to establish, exercise or defend legal rights.[50]

This provision was criticised in Parliament as being excessively broad. Certainly, the provision relating to 'prospective proceedings' appears somewhat opaque.

---

[46] Sch. 3, para. 3(b).
[47] Data Protection Act 1998, Sch. 3, para. 4.
[48] 315 HC Official Report (6th series), col. 613, 2 July 1998.
[49] Data Protection Act 1998, Sch. 3, para. 5.
[50] Data Protection Act 1998, Sch. 3, para. 6.

The processing is necessary for the administration of justice, for the exercise of statutory or governmental functions. Once again, the Secretary of State may exclude the application of this provision in certain situations or require that additional conditions be satisfied.[51]

An obvious example of such a situation would be the maintenance of criminal records. It may be noted that the Data Protection Directive provides that 'a complete register of criminal convictions may be kept only under the control of official authority'.[52]

Processing for medical purposes

The processing is necessary for medical purposes and is undertaken by a health professional or by a person owing an equivalent duty of confidentiality.[53]

The term 'medical purposes' is defined broadly to include 'preventative medicine, medical diagnosis, medical research, the provision of care and treatment and the management of healthcare services'.[54] It should be stressed that in this case, as with all the exceptions described in the present section, the effect is essentially to free the controller from the requirement to seek explicit consent to processing. The processing must be carried out in accordance with the data protection principles and other requirements of the Act.

Ethnic monitoring

The processing relates to data indicating racial or ethnic origin but is carried out in order to monitor compliance with equal opportunities legislation. Appropriate safeguards must also be taken for the rights and freedoms of data subjects.[55]

Once again, it is provided that the Secretary of State may define more precisely the activities coming within the scope of this provision. Care will certainly require to be taken to ensure that information supplied for this purpose, for example by an applicant for employment, is used only for monitoring purposes and retained, at least in a form which can identify the subject, for no longer than is necessary.

Order of the Secretary of State

The processing occurs in circumstances specified by the Secretary of State.[56]

This provision confers a wide-ranging power on the Secretary of State to extend the range of exemptions. The Data Protection Directive requires that additional exemptions must be justified by 'reasons of substantial public interest',[57] and must be notified to the Commission.[58]

The regulatory power has been exercised with the making of the Data Protection (Processing of Sensitive Personal Data) Order 2000.[59] This provides no fewer than ten additional grounds justifying the processing of sensitive personal data.

---

51 Data Protection Act 1998, Sch. 3, para. 7.
52 Directive 95/46/EC, Art. 8(5).
53 Data Protection Act 1998, Sch. 3, para. 8.
54 Directive 95/46/EC, Art. 8(5).
55 Data Protection Act 1998, Sch. 3, para. 9.
56 Data Protection Act 1998, Sch. 3, para. 10.
57 Directive 95/46/EC, Art. 8(4).
58 Directive 95/46/EC, Art. 8(6).
59 SI 2000/417.

The first two grounds relate to processing for the purposes 'of the prevention or detection of any unlawful act' and the discharge of any functions intended to secure the public against:

(i)   dishonesty, malpractice, or other seriously improper conduct by, or the unfitness or incompetence of, any person, or

(ii) mismanagement in the administration of, or failures in services provided by any body or association.

In all cases, it is a requirement that the processing must necessarily be carried out without the explicit consent of the data subject.

A third ground might be seen as a form of whistleblower's charter. It legitimises the disclosure of data relating to crime, dishonesty, or seriously improper conduct or mismanagement when this is with a view to the publication of the information and where the party making the disclosure reasonably believes that the publication will be in the public interest.

Processing may be carried out without explicit subject consent when this is in the public interest in connection with the provision of counselling, support, or other services. The exemption here is not an open-ended one, with the controller being required to demonstrate that it is impracticable, unreasonable, or undesirable to seek to obtain subject consent.

With developments in DNA research and increased awareness of the role of genetic factors in influencing life expectancy, data of this kind is of potential value to insurance companies. A person applying for insurance cover might be required to supply details relating to the health of parents, grandparents, or siblings. In the event that these persons remain alive, the processing of this data might contravene the requirements of the Data Protection Act 1998. The regulations legitimise this form of processing subject to three conditions: that it is not reasonable to obtain explicit consent; that the controller does not have actual knowledge that consent has been withheld; and that the processing is not used as the basis for decisions which will affect the data subjects concerned.

Processing for insurance purposes also benefits from a further transitional exemption covering activities which were underway prior to the commencement of the Data Protection Act 1998. Under the previous regime, the need for consent was less strict and it is provided that, save where there is actual knowledge that the data subject does not consent to processing, this may continue when it is necessary for the purpose and where it is not reasonable to expect the controller to seek explicit consent (or where the processing must necessarily be conducted without consent).

Two further exemptions serve to permit the continuance of activities which are generally considered desirable but which might otherwise contravene the data protection principles. Many employers may, whether required by law or otherwise, seek to process information to monitor the operation of policies relating to equal opportunities with the view to promoting such equality. It is provided that processing may take place where this is not used to support decisions affecting a particular subject and where the processing is not likely to cause substantial damage or distress to the data subject or to any other person.

Political data

One matter which attracted considerable discussion when the Data Protection Act 1998 was before Parliament was the realisation that the restrictions on the processing of sensitive data would serve to restrict the ability of political parties to conduct activities such as the canvassing of voters where this would involve maintaining a record of likely voting intentions. The regulations seek to avoid this prospect by providing that information relating to political opinions may be processed by persons or organisations registered under the Registration of Political Parties Act 1998 to the extent that this is not likely to cause substantial damage or distress. It is further provided that data subjects may give written notice that their personal data is not to be processed for such purpose. The Data Protection (Processing of Sensitive Personal Data) (Elected Representatives) Order 2002[60] makes further provisions regarding the use of such data by elected representatives.

A further exemption applies where data is processed for research purposes. This will apply where the processing is in the substantial public interest, for example as part of a medical research project; will not result in action being taken with regard to the particular data subject without explicit consent; and is not likely to cause substantial damage or distress.

The final exemption is the shortest of all, but carries significant implications. Sensitive data may be processed where this is:

> necessary for the exercise of any functions conferred on a constable by any rule of law.[61]

Given the extensive powers conferred on constables under the common law, this provision might serve to justify many forms of processing.

Exceptions to the application of the first data protection principle for law enforcement and revenue-gathering purposes

A significant exception to the operation of the first data protection principle applies where data is acquired for the purposes of the prevention or detection of crime, the apprehension or prosecution of offenders, or the assessment or collection of any tax or duty and where compliance with the principle would be prejudicial to the attainment of the purpose in question.

The rationale behind the exception lies in the recognition that law enforcement agencies might reasonably acquire information in ways which might normally be regarded as unfair, for example as the result of overhearing—or even eavesdropping on—a conversation. It might, however, be considered unfortunate that the Commissioner should not be given the power to define the concept of fairness in the light of the particular situation of the user involved rather than by providing a near-complete exception from the requirement to act fairly. It may also be noted that the restriction upon the Commissioner's ability to act exists even where the data has been acquired unlawfully, although here it may be difficult to sustain the argument that observance of the law would prejudice the prevention or detection of crime, the apprehension or prosecution of offenders, or the assessment or collection of any tax or duty.

The second data protection principle—purpose limitation

The second data protection principle requires that:

> Personal data shall be obtained only for one or more specified and lawful purposes and shall not be processed further in any manner incompatible with that purpose or those purposes.[62]

Given the breadth of the definition of processing—which refers specifically to the obtaining of data—it is difficult to identify a real need for the second data protection principle. In

---

[60] SI 2002/2905.
[61] Data Protection Act 1998, Sch. 3, para. 10.
[62] Sch. 1, para. 2.

interpreting the second principle, the Act provides that the purposes for which data is to be processed may be specified either by the giving of notice to the data subject (as discussed in the context of the first principle) or in the notification made to the Commissioner. It is to be noted, however, that notification by itself will not satisfy the requirements of the first data protection principle.

The more significant element of the second principle concerns what might be regarded as ongoing processing activities. Data may be obtained for one purpose with due notification given to the data subject but changes in circumstance or technical developments may make other forms of activity attractive to the controller. The Commissioner has indicated that a strict view will be taken in determining whether any future forms of processing—whether carried out by the controller or by a third party to whom the data are disclosed—are compatible with those originally notified to the Commissioner or to the data subject.[63]

A further aspect of unlawful obtaining has been much in the news recently with massive publicity about the behaviour of certain sections of the media in seeking to hack into computers and mobile phones of newsworthy people. The behaviour may also be carried out for other commercial purposes. A trio of private investigators were fined sums of up to £10,000[64] for obtaining unauthorised access to mobile phone data of individuals involved in the dispute between Tottenham Hotspur and West Ham football clubs over which should be given tenancy of the former London Olympic stadium.

In the situation where the investigator obtained direct access to data held on a computer, it would be likely that an offence would be committed under the Computer Misuse Act 1990. In many instances, however, the information would be obtained, either through bribing an employee of the data user or by misleading the user as to identity and entitlement to access the data. In these situations, the investigator would not normally be guilty of any offence. To remedy this situation, section 55 of the Data Protection Act 1998 provides that an offence will be committed by a person who 'knowingly or recklessly, without the consent of the data controller' seeks to obtain or disclose personal data or procure its disclosure to a third party. An exception is provided where the data is obtained in connection with the prevention or detection of crime or in pursuance of a court order. A further offence is committed by a person who sells or offers to sell data obtained in contravention of this provision. Both convictions are punishable by a fine of up to £5,000 in the magistrates' court and to a potentially unlimited amount in the Crown Court.

In spite of the prohibition, there is extensive evidence that the trade in unlawfully acquired personal information is continuing. Taking action against those involved in the practice was identified as a priority in the Information Commissioner's Regulatory Strategy published in 2005 and between 2002 and 2007 twenty-eight prosecutions were brought, with a maximum fine of £4,200 being imposed in a case in 2006. This figure was made up of fourteen fines of £300 each, imposed in respect of a number of offences, and the Commissioner expressed disappointment at the generally low level of punishments imposed by the courts.[65] A report published by the Information Commissioner in May 2006 entitled *What Price Privacy?* provides extensive evidence of the techniques and tactics used. Based on information obtained in the course of one investigation into the activities of one private investigator, the report presents a list of the sums charged for obtaining items of personal data; these included £17.50 for checking addresses on the Electoral Roll, £65–£75 for obtaining an ex-directory telephone number, £500 for a criminal records check, and £750 for obtaining data relating to a mobile telephone

---

[63] *Legal Guidance*, para. 3.2.
[64] The case is reported at <http://www.bbc.co.uk/news/uk-england-london-25468278>.
[65] Foreword in *What Price Privacy?*

account. As stated in a follow-up report, *What Price Privacy Now?*[66] published in December 2006:

> Suppliers use two main methods to obtain the information they want: through corruption, or more usually by some form of deception, generally known as 'blagging'. Blaggers pretend to be someone they are not in order to wheedle out the information they are seeking. They are prepared to make several telephone calls to get it. Each call they make takes them a little further towards their goal: obtaining information illegally which they then sell for a specified price.[67]

The Information Commissioner argued for an extension of the penalties provided for the offence to include a maximum term of imprisonment of six months on conviction in the magistrates' court and two years before the Crown Court. Following a consultation exercise conducted by the Department of Constitutional Affairs in the second half of 2006, it was announced in February 2007 that the government had decided to accept the Commissioner's proposals and that legislation to this end would be brought forward when parliamentary time permitted. Section 77 of the Criminal Justice and Immigration Act gives power to the Secretary of State to alter the penalties for breach of section 55. To date this power has not been exercised.

The third data protection principle—relevance

The third data protection principle requires that data shall be 'adequate, relevant and not excessive in relation to the purpose or purposes for which they are processed'. The Data Protection Directive[68] uses the same term. No further interpretation is provided in either instrument. The principle is, however, identically worded to one found in the Data Protection Act 1984. This was at issue before the Data Protection Tribunal in the course of proceedings brought against a number of community charge registration officers.[69]

The community charge or 'poll tax' proved one of the most controversial forms of taxation introduced in recent times. Although much of the publicity generated concerned its financial aspects, the implementation of the requirement that registers be established of those liable to pay the tax attracted the attention of the Data Protection Registrar, who took issue with the processing proposals indicated by a number of local authorities: Harrow Borough Council,[70] Runnymede Borough Council,[71] Rhondda Borough Council,[72] and South Northamptonshire District Council.[73] Ultimately, registration was refused on the basis that the Registrar was satisfied that the applicants were likely to contravene the fourth data protection principle. Appeals against these decisions were brought before the Data Protection Tribunal.

Under the terms of the Local Government Finance Act 1988, charging authorities were required to compile and maintain a Community Charge Register.[74] It was specifically

---

[66] Available from <http://www.ico.gov.uk/upload/documents/library/corporate/research_and_reports/what_price_privacy_now.pdf>.

[67] At p. 5 of the report.

[68] Directive 95/46/EC.

[69] The officers involved represented Runnymede Borough Council, South Northamptonshire District Council, Harrow Borough Council, and Rhondda Borough Council.

[70] Case DA/90 24/49/5.

[71] Case DA/90 24/49/3.

[72] Case DA/90 24/49/2.

[73] Case DA/90 24/49/4.

[74] s. 6.

provided that the register should include details of the name and address of every person liable to pay the community charge, which was payable by everyone over the age of eighteen. In some cases, local authorities, including Rhondda Borough Council, requested the date of birth of every member of the household, regardless of whether they were over eighteen or not. Dates of birth are clearly items of personal data.

Objecting to this form of processing the Data Protection Registrar, although accepting that a record would need to be held of those who would reach the age of eighteen and become liable to pay the charge during the course of a tax year, took the view that the date of birth was irrelevant in the case of those who were already of an age to pay the tax. The appellant argued that many inhabitants of the Rhondda shared surnames and forenames. The addition of a note of date of birth would limit the possibility that an individual might escape inclusion on the register because his or her identity was confused with some other person of the same name. It was also argued that the inclusion of the information would assist the Registration Officer in the efficient performance of his or her duties.

These arguments were rejected by the Tribunal. It heard evidence that, nationally, fewer than 1 per cent of households contained persons who shared the same surname and forename. Although it accepted that the figure might be higher in the Rhondda, it did not consider that this justified the appellant's actions. The Tribunal concluded that:

> We find that the information the appellant wishes to hold on database concerning individuals exceeds substantially the minimum amount of information which is required in order for him to fulfil the purpose for which he has sought registration . . . to fulfil his duty to compile and maintain the Community Charges Register.

Similar issues were involved in the case of the other councils. Each of the appellants held, or proposed to hold, details of the type of property occupied by each subject. Again, information of this type would be classed as personal data and the Registrar raised objection on the ground that its inclusion was, or would be likely to constitute, a breach of the fourth data protection principle. In the case of Harrow and Runnymede Borough Councils, action took the form of a refusal to accept an application for registration. In the case of South Northamptonshire District Council, whose application for registration had previously been accepted, an enforcement notice was served.

In terms of the status of the information relating to type of property, the Tribunal held that whilst there might be justification for holding some information additional to that required under the Local Government Finance Act 1988, the wish to record details of type of property in every case was excessive. The Tribunal endorsed the advice given to data users by the Registrar,[75] to the effect that they should seek to identify the minimum amount of personal data which is required in order to enable them to fulfil their purpose. Where additional data might be required in certain cases, these should again be identified and the further information sought or held only in those cases.

More recently, the application of the third (and also the fifth principle requiring that data not be kept for longer than is necessary) data protection principles was at issue before the Information Tribunal in the case of *The Chief Constables of West Yorkshire, South Yorkshire and North Wales Police and the Information Commissioner*.[76] This case started a long-running dispute between the Information Commissioner and police authorities regarding the latter's policies in respect of the retention of data relating to three individuals' criminal convictions. In each case, records were maintained of criminal convictions: in one

---

[75] Information Commissioner's Office, Guideline Booklet No. 4, *The Data Protection Principles* (Wilmslow, 1998).

[76] Available from <http://www.informationtribunal.gov.uk/DBFiles/Decision/i204/north_wales_police.pdf>.

case, a single offence dating back to 1979; in the second, five offences relating to the taking of motor vehicles, the last conviction also being in 1979; and in the case of the third data subject, five offences ending with a conviction for theft in 1969. In each case, the primary cause for complaint was not that the information had been retained by the police but that it had been disclosed for purposes unconnected with the operation of the criminal record system. In one case this was in connection with the investigation of a complaint made by the data subject in respect of the conduct of a police officer; in another disclosure was made to the US immigration authorities in respect of a visa application and, in the third, to an employer in connection with an application for employment. Following the receipt of complaints from the data subjects, the Information Commissioner exercised his powers under section 42 of the Act to conduct an assessment of the legitimacy of the processing of the personal data. After extensive correspondence with the police authorities in question, the Commissioner served each with an enforcement notice alleging breaches of the third and fifth data protection principles. The authorities appealed to the Information Tribunal.

In all the cases, data had been retained on the police national computers and it was accepted that it was held in accordance with the latest version of 'Weeding Rules', which had been the subject of discussion, if not agreement, between the Information Commissioner (and his predecessors) and the Association of Chief Police Officers. In essence, these provide for details of relatively minor offences to be retained for thirty years and more serious offences for a period of one hundred years—a period designed to ensure that the data is retained for the lifetime of the offender. It was accepted by the Tribunal that:

> the Weeding Rules in their present form and edition demonstrate that there is some incontestable value in retaining conviction data dependent largely upon the nature of the offence. The Weeding Rules represent a considered exchange between the parties, i.e. the Commissioner on the one hand and ACPO on the other which has in the result forged some form of generalised understanding that after a given data, certain offences should be removed from the PNC. However, the Tribunal finds equally that the Weeding Rules do not and could not conceivably represent an unqualified and rigid code.[77]

The Tribunal drew a distinction between retention and disclosure of the data. Accepting the benefit for policing purposes of retention of data, even at the level of maintaining links to fingerprint and DNA samples, it amended the Commissioner's ruling to require that within six months the appellants:

> procure that the Conviction Data relating to (the complainant data subjects) currently held on the PNC database be retained on the PNC subject to the retention rules of any current ACPO Code of Practice or any equivalent thereof and not be open to inspection other than by the data controller or by any other data controller who is or represents a chief officer of police.[78]

The Commissioner returned to the question of the conformity of police data retention in the later case of *Chief Constable of Humberside Police and Ors v Information Commissioner*. This marked the first occasion in which a decision of the Information Tribunal[79] was the subject of an appeal to the Court of Appeal.[80]

The *South Yorkshire* case had focused in large part on issues concerned with the disclosure of data for purposes other than those concerned with core policing activities. These were again at issue in the *Humberside* litigation but the prime focus was on the retention of data on the Police National Computer itself.

---

[77] para. 206.

[78] para. 218.

[79] Available from <http://www.informationtribunal.gov.uk/Public/search.aspx>.

[80] [2009] EWCA Civ 1079.

Following a series of complaints from data subjects, the Commissioner served enforce-ment notices on five police forces, each relating to records relating to one individual and requiring removal of the data from the Police National Computer. As discussed in rela-tion to the *South Yorkshire* case, access to data might be restricted although at issue in most of the present cases was an act of disclosure to other statutory agencies, generally in connection with the system of extended disclosure certificates introduced under the Police Act 1997. Any person seeking to work with vulnerable individuals such as children is required to obtain such a certificate which will detail any criminal convictions or formal reprimands received by the individual.

In four of the cases forming the basis of the enforcement notices the individuals con-cerned had been convicted of relatively minor criminal offences some time in the past. One subject, referred to as HP, is perhaps typical. He had been convicted on two counts of shoplifting in 1984 when aged sixteen. No further convictions were recorded against him. The conviction details were listed on an enhanced disclosure certificate which he was required to obtain twenty-two years later when seeking a position with a local authority as a care officer.

Three of the other cases were broadly similar but in the final case a thirteen-year old girl (referred to as SP) had been accused of assault. She had accepted a formal reprimand but was assured that details would be deleted from the Police National Computer when she reached the age of eighteen if she had not committed any further criminal offences. By the time of her eighteenth birthday, police policy had changed and the details were retained, again to appear on an enhanced disclosure certificate obtained in connection with an appli-cation for employment as a care worker. In this case the enforcement notice alleged also a breach of the first data protection principle, that the retention of the data in breach of undertakings given constituted unfair processing.

The Tribunal received statistical evidence indicating that where individuals had such long periods without being convicted of any offences, the likelihood of them being con-victed in the future was effectively the same as that of a person with no previous criminal conviction. The Tribunal agreed with the Commissioner that the continued presence of the data on the Police National Computer offered no significant operational benefits to the police and upheld the enforcement notice. The police forces concerned appealed against the Tribunal decision and were successful before the Court of Appeal which was highly critical both of the Commissioner's original decision to serve the enforce-ment notices and of the Tribunal's decision to uphold them. Delivering the leading judg-ment, Lord Justice Waller quoted the evidence given to the Bichard Inquiry by the then Information Commissioner. This was set up in the wake of a case in which a school caretaker had murdered two young girls. Subsequently evidence came to light that the caretaker was known to other police forces in connection with inappropriate conduct towards girls but that this information had not been passed on to the force in whose area the murders took place. Responding to suggestions by some police authorities that the requirements of data protection legislation had prevented the sharing of informa-tion, the then Information Commissioner gave evidence to the Inquiry in the following terms:

> Police judgements about operational needs will not be lightly interfered with by the Information Commissioner. His office 'cannot and should not substitute [their] judgement for that of experienced practitioners'. His office will give considerable latitude to the police in their decision making. If a reasonable and rational basis exists for a decision, 'that should be the end of the story'.[81]

---

[81] para. 4.45.2.

The same principle, Lord Justice Waller held, should apply in the present case, 'If the police say rationally and reasonably that convictions, however old or minor, have a value in the work they do that should, in effect, be the end of the matter.'

Accordingly, the enforcement notices were quashed on this point. The case of SP and the alleged unfair processing did divide the court but by a majority it was held that the processing had not been unfair. The retention of her data was as a result of a general change in policing policy and was not directed specifically at her.

The fourth data protection principle—adequacy and timeousness

The fourth data protection principle requires that: 'personal data shall be accurate and, where necessary, kept up to date'. Data is defined as being inaccurate when it is 'incorrect or misleading as to any matter of fact'.[82] In the event that personal data is inaccurate, a data subject may be entitled to seek its rectification and, in certain cases, compensation for any resultant damage or distress.[83]

Rather like beauty, accuracy may frequently lie in the eye of the beholder. Although many instances are reported of inaccurate data (eg, it has been suggested that data on the Police National Computer was subject to an 86 per cent error rate),[84] the question of whether data is accurate will not always be susceptible of a straightforward answer. In cases where data relates simply to an issue of fact, objective verification may be possible. A record reading 'Joe Bloggs is 75' will be inaccurate if Joe Bloggs is aged only twenty-five. In some cases, however, a record may repeat information supplied by a third party. The statement may be in the format: 'Fred Smith informs us that Joe Bloggs has defaulted on three loan agreements.' If it is assumed that Joe Bloggs is in reality a person of the utmost financial probity, can it be said that the statement is false? In determining this issue, the fourth data protection principle is interpreted as follows:

> The fourth principle is not to be regarded as being contravened by reason of any inaccuracy in personal data which accurately record information obtained by the data controller from the data subject or a third party in a case where—
>
> (a) having regard to the purpose or purposes for which the data were obtained and further processed, the data controller has taken reasonable steps to ensure the accuracy of the data; and
>
> (b) if the data subject has notified the data controller of the data subject's view that the data are inaccurate, the data indicate that fact.[85]

These requirements are cumulative.

The second element of this principle requires that necessary updating of information shall be carried out. The Data Protection Act 1998 does not expand on this requirement, but it would appear that the question of whether updating is required will be dependent upon the nature of the data and the purpose to which it will be put. If the data is merely a record of a transaction between the data user and the data subject, no updating would be either necessary or justified. Where the information is being used as the basis for continuing decisions and

[82] Data Protection Act 1998, s. 70(2).
[83] Data Protection Act 1998, ss. 13–14.
[84] 'Errors Rife in Police Data Files', *Computer Weekly*, 27 April 2000, p. 5.
[85] Data Protection Act 1998, Sch. 1, Pt II, para. 7. These provisions are substantially similar to those applying to the data subject's claim to compensation for, or rectification of, inaccurate data.

actions, regular updating may be essential. Thus, where information is to be used for assessing an employee's suitability for promotion, an indication of periods of absence would require to be supplemented by any explanations which might subsequently have been provided.

The fifth data protection principle—duration of record-keeping

The issue of data retention is highly contentious and is discussed in more detail elsewhere in this book. Within the general data protection context the key requirement as laid down in the fifth data protection principle is that data should be retained for no longer than is necessary for the purpose for which it is held by the data controller. The Data Protection Directive contains an equivalent provision.[86] Neither instrument provides further interpretative guidance.

In some cases, data users will be under a legal obligation to retain data for a specified period of time, for example solicitor–client data. In more general terms, there would appear justification for retaining data until the expiry of any limitation period for possible legal action. Beyond situations where specific legal rules or regulations may apply, matters may be more difficult to define. It may also be the case that the nature of processing may change. An example might be taken from university or college exam marks. Whilst a student is at the institution it is clear that records of performance will require to be retained in order to determine the level of any degree awarded. Once a student has graduated, the justification for retaining data on this basis disappears. A past student seeking a reference perhaps twenty years in the future might be disappointed if a reply was in terms 'we do not hold any records'. As with so many aspects of the legislation, difficult decisions may require to be made by a data controller.

The seventh data protection principle—data security

Data security is a topic of major concern today. The media is replete with tales of identity fraud and there are major concerns about the use of botnets to effectively hijack personal computers and put them to criminal use. This chapter has previously considered also attempts to obtain illicit access to personal data held by a controller. Under the terms of the seventh data protection principle data controllers and the operators of computer bureaux are obliged to ensure that:

Appropriate technical and organisational measures shall be taken against unauthorised or unlawful processing of personal data and against accidental loss or destruction of, or damage to, personal data.

Additionally, controllers will be responsible for ensuring that any data processors contracted by them comply with the requirements of the principle.

The comparable requirement in the Data Protection Directive is that, taking account of the state of the art and making an assessment of costs and risks involved:

the controller must implement appropriate technical and organizational measures to protect personal data against accidental or unlawful destruction or accidental loss, alteration, unauthorized disclosure or access, in particular where the processing involves the transmission of data over a network.[87]

---

[86] Directive 95/46/EC, Art. 6(1)(e).
[87] Directive 95/46/EC, Art. 17(1).

In determining whether security measures are appropriate, account has to be taken both of technical measures—for example, whether passwords are required to access data—and also of the level or training provided to employees and associated control mechanisms. Almost all of the monetary penalties imposed by the Information Commissioner in recent years have related to a breach of the data security principle. A few examples taken from the Information Commissioner's website might illustrate the scope of the provision.

4. . . . A thief reached in through an open window and stole his briefcase from a seat in the car. The briefcase contained an external hard drive, some documents and approximately £3,600 in cash.

5. The external hard drive was protected by an 11-character (letters and numbers) password, but it was unencrypted. It contained a complete copy of the data controller's customer database including the details of approximately 250 clients such as their name, address, contact number, date of birth, nationality, passport number, proof of address (utility bills and bank statements) and proof of identity (passports and driving licences).[88]

A penalty of £5,000 was imposed on the data controller. There have been a number of similar cases where laptop computers or memory sticks have been lost whilst in the custody of employees and in general it may be commented that technological developments have permitted storage capabilities that would previously have been the preserve of major mainframe computers to be held in tiny—and, from personal experience, very easily lost—memory sticks. In other cases penalties have been more severe. The consumer electronics company Sony were penalised to the extent of £250,000 after hackers were able to access its customer database.

Codes of practice

One of the most notable features of the data protection principles is their generality. Given the range of applications across which they have to be applied and the multitude of users subjected to regulation, it is difficult to envisage any other approach. In a considerable number of sectors, codes of practice have been adopted by trade associations seeking to give sector-specific guidance as to the interpretation of the principles. One of the major legal issues concerns the status and respect that should be afforded to such codes. It cannot be the case that data controllers can define the scope of their obligations or even that a party such as the Information Commissioner should be able to exercise what would effectively be law-making powers.

The Data Protection Directive envisages a substantial role for codes of practice to operate at both a national and a Community level. The Directive's Recitals state that:

Member States and the Commission in their respective spheres of competence, must encourage the trade associations and other representative organizations concerned to draw up codes of conduct so as to facilitate the operation of this Directive, taking account of the specific circumstances of the processing carried out in certain sectors, and respecting the national provisions adopted for its implementation.[89]

Article 27 of the Directive[90] provides that draft codes are to be submitted to the national supervisory authority, which is to ascertain 'whether the drafts submitted to it are in

---

[88] <http://ico.org.uk/enforcement/~/media/documents/library/Data_Protection/Notices/jala-transport-limited-monetary-penalty-notice.pdf>.

[89] Directive 95/46/EC, Recital 61.

[90] Directive 95/46/EC.

accordance with the national provisions adopted pursuant to this Directive'. Such a development would also go at least part of the way to meeting the suggestion of the Registrar in his 1989 review of the working of the legislation that upon receipt of the Registrar's endorsement, the provisions of a code should have a status equivalent to the Highway Code—namely, that although breach of its provisions would not itself constitute an offence, this could be taken into account in determining whether any provision of the legislation had been violated.

Conclusions

As was indicated at the beginning of this chapter, the adoption of general statements of acceptable processing practices has been a feature of data (and privacy) protection legislation from the earliest days. In some respects this is non-contentious. Few would challenge the statement that data must should processed lawfully or fairly. Like other general precepts, however, context is vitally important and few principles can be absolute. Even a seemingly absolute religious commandment such as 'thou shalt not kill' raises issues in contexts such as self-defence and the notion of 'justified war'. In the data protection context, obtaining data following some form of surveillance which might generally be considered unfair might be regarded differently if it is for the purpose of preventing a terrorist attack.

At the level of general principles there can be little to object to or criticise in the underlying principles. As always, the devil is in the detail and in some important respects there may be a need to update the definition of concepts in order to better meet the needs of modern data processing realities.

Specific areas where there may be need for more explicit legislative provision might include the requirements imposed on data controllers to inform subjects of the uses to which data might be put. In the case of social networking sites, for example, this could include clear statements of privacy options and the positive and negative implications of choices which might be made by subjects. Provision might also be made regarding the default settings associated with such sites and data processing in general. It could, for example, be provided that a minimal range of access to or dissemination of data should be provided unless and until subjects make an informed choice to extend these.

6

Individual rights and remedies

INTRODUCTION

Previous chapters have focused on the obligations imposed upon data controllers to ensure that processing complies with the data protection principles. The role of ensuring compliance with these requirements is largely one for supervisory agencies and indeed, as shown by incidents such as the 'inadvertent' collection of personal data by Google in the course of its Street View programme, there are significant limits to the extent to which individuals might take effective legal action against parties suspected of infringing data protection legislation. This, indeed, has been one of the major arguments advanced to justify the establishment of data protection authorities. The Google example does perhaps cast some doubt on the validity of the approach with the response of European data protection authorities perhaps falling to be described as vacillating and confusing.

In other instances, however, the individual data subject may take centre stage and in this chapter consideration will be given to the rights that are specifically conferred upon data subjects and to the remedies which may be available in the event of any breach.

The Data Protection Act 1998 provides in the sixth data protection principle that 'Personal data shall be processed in accordance with the rights of data subjects under this Act.' Part II of the Act is entitled 'Rights of Data Subjects and Others' and provides for rights of access, the right to receive certain items of information, and rights either total or qualified to object to certain forms of processing of their personal data.

Subject access and information rights

The concept of subject access is the aspect of data protection which may impact most directly on individuals. The Data Protection Directive requires that:

Member States shall guarantee every data subject the right to obtain from the controller:

(a) without constraint at reasonable intervals and without excessive delay or expense:

- confirmation as to whether or not data relating to him are being processed and information at least as to the purposes of the processing, the categories of data concerned, and the recipients or categories of recipients to whom the data are disclosed,

- communication to him in an intelligible form of the data undergoing processing and of any available information as to their source,

- knowledge of the logic involved in any automatic processing of data concerning him at least in the case of the automated decisions referred to in Article 15 (1).

In implementing this provision, the Act requires that a data controller respond to requests which are made in writing,[1] which contain sufficient information to allow for identification of the data subject and which enclose any fee required by the controller.[2] A maximum fee of £10 may be required before the controller responds to an access request.[3] In terms of the information which is to be provided, it is now stated that:

Subject to the following provisions of this Section and to Sections 8 and 9, an individual is entitled—

(a) to be informed by any data controller whether personal data of which that individual is the data subject are being processed by or on behalf of that data controller;

(b) if that is the case, to be given by the data controller a description of—

(i) the personal data of which that individual is the data subject;

(ii) the purposes for which they are being or are to be processed; and

(iii) the recipients or classes of recipients to whom they are or may be disclosed;

(c) to have communicated to him in an intelligible form—

(i) the information constituting any personal data of which that individual is the data subject; and

(ii) any information available to the data controller as to the source of those data.

(d) where the processing by automatic means of personal data of which that individual is the data subject for the purpose of evaluating matters relating to him such as, for example, his performance at work, his creditworthiness, his reliability or his conduct, has constituted or is likely to constitute the sole basis for any decision significantly affecting him, to be informed by the data controller of the logic involved in that decision-taking.[4]

A request in respect of one of the items of information referred to above is to be taken as extending to most of the other items.[5] A request to be informed, therefore, whether personal data is held is to be taken as extending to a request for the information itself and for the further information specified relating to purposes, etc. The provision relating to information regarding the logic of processing is treated somewhat differently. The extent of the information to be supplied under this heading was the subject of considerable debate in the House of Lords, where concerns were expressed that the controller might be required to supply information which constituted valuable intellectual property.[6] It is provided that the obligation is not to extend to any information which 'constitutes a trade secret' (section 8(5)), but, as was pointed out in Parliament, this concept is an ill-defined one. The Data Protection (Subject Access) (Fees and Miscellaneous Provisions) Regulations 2000 provide that specific request must be made for receipt of this information.[7]

The traditional approach towards subject access has been to require that a written copy of data be supplied. The Act imposes the requirement that the copy be supplied in

---

[1] s. 64 of the Act provides in respect of the access procedures and a variety of other procedures under the Act that the requirement for writing may be satisfied where a notice is transmitted by electronic means, received in legible form, and is capable of being used for subsequent reference. An email message would seem to satisfy these requirements.   [2] s. 7.   [3] The Data Protection (Subject Access) (Fees and Miscellaneous Provisions) Regulations 2000, SI 2000/191, Reg. 3.   [4] s. 7(2).   [5] s. 7(2), implemented by the Data Subject (Subject Access) (Fees and Miscellaneous Provisions) Regulations 2000, SI 2000/191.   [6] 586 HL Official Report (5th series), cols. CWH 43–5, 23 February 1998.

[7] SI 2000/191, Reg. 2. Rather strangely, it is also provided that a request for information about the logic employed in processing will not automatically be taken as extending to the other items of information in s. 7.

'intelligible form'.[8] With developments in processing technology, it is possible that data may take the form of audio or video clips, and although the provision of written copies may be expected to remain the norm, expansion of the definition is clearly desirable. In terms of the material to be provided, it was stated by the Court of Appeal in *Durant v Financial Services Authority* that:

> The intention of the Directive, faithfully reproduced in the Act [Data Protection Act 1998], is to enable an individual to obtain from a data controller's filing system, whether computerised or manual, his personal data, that is, information about himself. It is not an entitlement to be provided with original or copy documents as such, but, as Section 7(1)(c)(i) and 8(2) provide, with information constituting personal data in intelligible and permanent form. This may be in documentary form prepared for the purpose and/or where it is convenient in the form of copies of original documents.[9]

It is further provided that, although the copy of the information is normally to be provided in permanent form, this requirement may be waived with the consent of the subject or in a case where the supply of such a copy would be either impossible or involve a disproportionate effort.[10] No indication is given of what might constitute a disproportionate effort but the Commissioner has indicated that decisions will have to be made in the light of the circumstances of each case. A significant factor will be the cost implications to the controller of responding to the request. The information supplied must be that which was held at the time the access request was received, except where any subsequent changes 'would have been made regardless of the receipt of the request'.[11]

The concept of subject access was pioneered in the United Kingdom by the Consumer Credit Act 1974, which provided that individuals should be entitled to obtain a copy of information held by a credit reference agency.[12] The 1974 Act's procedures were unaffected by the original Data Protection Act of 1984. Given that the credit sector has historically generated the largest number of complaints to the Commissioner by data subjects, the retention of two separate regimes was considered unsupportable and the 1998 legislation incorporates the provisions for access to data held by credit reference agencies. Provision is made for different fee levels to be fixed by the Secretary of State, and the Data Protection (Subject Access) (Fees and Miscellaneous Provisions) Regulations 2000[13] provides that a fee of £2 will be payable in respect of access to such records.[14] One issue concerning the change did cause discussion in Parliament.[15] Under the 1974 Act, a modified access procedure applies where the subject is a business person.[16] Effectively, this limits the amount of information supplied so that, for example, the applicant would not receive information about adverse credit reports which had been provided by bankers or suppliers. Where the business constitutes a sole trader or partnership, the general access provisions of the Data Protection Act 1998 will replace the specialised provisions. Concern was expressed that the consequence might be that third parties would be reluctant to supply such information in the knowledge that it could be obtained, with the consequence being that small businesses might find it more difficult to obtain credit. Whilst giving an undertaking to keep the matter under review, the government indicated that it was not convinced that the concerns were justified, and a proposal to amend the Bill to retain the current procedures was rejected.[17]

---

[8] s. 7(1)(c).   [9] [2003] EWCA Civ 1746 at [26].   [10] s. 8(2).

[11] s. 8(6).   [12] s. 158.

[13] SI 2000/191.   [14] Reg. 4.

[15] s. 9.   [16] s. 160.

[17] 316 HC Official Report (6th series), cols. 578–9, 2 July 1998.

Access timetable

Valid requests for access must be satisfied within forty days.[18] Where data is held by a credit reference agency, the current shorter time limit of seven days is to apply.[19] The information supplied must generally be that held at the date of receipt of the access request. Account may be taken, however, of any amendments or deletions made subsequently where these would have been made 'regardless of the receipt of the request'.[20] Having satisfied an access request from a data subject, a controller is not obliged to comply with a subsequent identical or similar request until a reasonable interval has elapsed.[21] In making his or her determination, account is to be taken of the nature of the data, the purpose of the processing, and the frequency with which amendments are made.

Exceptions to the subject access provisions

In certain situations, the individual's interest in obtaining access to personal data has to be restricted, either in the subject's own interests or as a result of giving priority to other competing claims. Access to medical data provides an example of the first situation, where it is provided that an access request may be refused where it is considered that this might be prejudicial to the enquiring subject's physical or mental health, whilst restrictions on access to data held for the purpose of crime prevention or detection illustrate how the subject's desire to know what information is held might reasonably be subjugated to the requirements of the data controller or those of society at large.

The Data Protection Directive provides that Member States may provide for exemptions from subject access when this constitutes a necessary measure to safeguard:

(a) national security;

(b) defence;

(c) public security;

(d) the prevention, investigation, detection, and prosecution of criminal offences, or of breaches of ethics for regulated professions;

(e) an important economic or financial interest of a Member State or of the EU, including monetary, budgetary, and taxation matters;

(f) a monitoring, inspection, or regulatory function connected, even occasionally, with the exercise of official authority in cases referred to in (c), (d), and (e); or

(g) the protection of the data subject or of the rights and freedoms of others.[22]

In respect of the various provisions to be discussed, a variety of approaches exist. Where data is held for national security purposes, total exemption is offered from all aspects of the legislation. In the case of data held for historical, research, or statistical purposes, the exemption relates only to subject access and the related supply of information relating to source, processing purpose, and intended disclosures as defined in section 7 of the Data Protection Act 1998. In other cases, however, the exemption is stated as applying also in respect of the requirements of the first data protection principle relating to the fair and lawful processing of personal data. Although in many cases, the application of the exemption is limited to instances where it is necessary to avoid prejudicing the purpose for which the

---

[18] Data Protection Act 1998, s. 7(10).   [19] Data Protection (Subject Access) (Fees and Miscellaneous Provisions) Regulations 2000, SI 2000/191, Reg. 4.   [20] Data Protection Act 1998, s. 8(6).
[21] s. 8(3).   [22] Directive 95/46/EC, Art. 13(1).

data is being processed, its linkage with subject access does mean that provisions which purport to protect data subjects may, in reality, work to their disadvantage.

Prior to considering the circumstances under which a user may legally deny a subject's access request, mention should be made of a problem that may arise whenever the user determines that all or part of a request for access falls within the scope of an exception. Under the Data Protection Act 1998's definitions, personal data is classed as data to which the subject is entitled to have access. Where an exception is properly relied upon, it may be accepted that it is as undesirable from the user's standpoint to inform the subject that they hold data which they are not willing to disclose as it would be to divulge the information. In the event that a subject suspects that personal data has not been supplied pursuant to a request for access, action may be raised before the courts.[23] An alternative course of action will be to make a complaint to the Commissioner. In the event the Commissioner takes action, the onus will be on the user to justify their action. However, dependent upon the circumstances and the nature of the data, it may be that a subject who receives the reply that no relevant personal data is held may accept this at face value and will make no attempt to pursue the matter before the courts or with the Commissioner.

Third-party data

In some cases, as has been discussed earlier, the linkage of data relating to a third party with mention of a data subject may lead to the conclusion that a record does not constitute personal data relating to the data subject. In other cases, there can be no doubt that a record does constitute personal data but that this relates to more than one individual. It may be that data relates to some form of joint activity: transactions, for example, in connection with the operation of a joint bank account. In this situation, where one subject submits an access request, there is unlikely to be a serious issue concerning the identity of the other subject or subjects, but there may be a case for deleting items of data such as cheque or cash-machine withdrawals made under the signature or against the PIN of the other account holder. In a second situation, the data may relate to the enquiring subject but emanate from a third party. An example might see a social work record recounting an allegation from a named third party that a subject is behaving in a violent manner to other persons. The record could state that 'Fred Smith has reported that Joe Bloggs is mistreating his wife and children'. There is clearly personal data about Joe Bloggs here and it may be desirable to allow the subject to see and possibly refute the allegation of violence. The record also contains personal data relating to Fred Smith as the source of the data. It is likely to be extremely unwelcome to this person if the fact of his report is disclosed to Joe Bloggs. How the balance is to be struck has been a continuing cause of difficulty.

Under the Data Protection Act 1984, a data user was under no obligation to supply information relating to a third party—including the fact that the third party had been the source of information relating to the data subject. No obligation, however, was imposed on the data user to inquire whether the third party would be willing for the information to be transmitted to the subject.[24] A significant change to the extent of access rights required came as a consequence of the decision of the European Court of Human Rights in the case of *Gaskin v United Kingdom*.[25] The applicant in this case had spent much of his childhood in local authority care. In adulthood, he claimed that he had been the subject of ill-treatment and instituted legal proceedings against the local authority. As part of these proceedings,

---

[23] Data Protection Act 1998, s. 7(9).
[24] s. 21(4)(a).
[25] (1990) 12 EHRR 36.

he sought discovery of all documents held by the authority relating to his case. Many of the documents had been compiled by third parties, such as doctors and social workers. Acting in excess of the statutory obligations imposed upon them, the authority contacted the third parties, seeking their approval to disclosure. Whilst the majority agreed to disclosure of the data, a number of parties refused consent and the authority took the view that this was determinative of the issue. Under UK law as it stood this was undoubtedly the case, but proceedings were raised before the European Court of Human Rights alleging that the failure of the UK legislation to provide the applicant with a right of access to the data constituted a breach of its obligations under Article 8 of the European Convention on Human Rights (ECHR) requiring respect for private and family life. The European Court of Human Rights held that, whilst the applicant did not have an unqualified right of access to data, the failure to provide an independent review in the event that a third party refused consent constituted a breach of his rights:

> The Court considers . . . that under such a system the interests of the individual seeking access to records relating to his private and family life must be secured when a contributor to the records either is not available or improperly refuses consent. Such a system is only in conformity with the principle of proportionality if it provides that an independent authority finally decides whether access has to be granted in cases where a contributor fails to answer or withholds consent. No such procedure was available to the applicant in the present case.[26]

In seeking to bring UK law into conformity with the ECHR, the Data Protection Act 1998 now provides that:

> Where a data controller cannot comply with the request (for information) without disclosing information relating to another individual who can be identified from that information, he is not obliged to comply with the request unless—

> (a) the other individual has consented to the disclosure of the information to the person making the request, or

> (b) it is reasonable in all the circumstances to comply with the request without the consent of the other individual.[27]

In determining whether it is reasonable for a controller to provide access without the third party's consent the Act provides that account is to be taken in particular of:

> (a) any duty of confidentiality owed to the other individual,

> (b) any steps taken by the data controller with a view to seeking the consent of the other individual,

> (c) whether the other individual is capable of giving consent, and

> (d) any express refusal of consent by the other individual.[28]

It is further provided that 'reference to information relating to another individual includes a reference to information identifying that individual as the source of the information sought by the request'. The provision, however, 'is not to be construed as excusing a data controller from communicating so much of the information sought by the request as can be communicated without disclosing the identity of the other individual concerned, whether by the omission of names or other identifying particulars or otherwise.'[29]

The application of these provisions was at issue in the case of *Durant v Financial Services Authority*.[30] The background to this case has been described earlier under 'Subject access

---

[26] (1990) 12 EHRR 36 at 50.   [27] s. 7(4).   [28] s. 7(6).   [29] s. 7(5).
[30] [2003] EWCA Civ 1746.

and information rights'. Although some information was supplied, access to other records was provided only in partial form through the concealment or redaction of information which it was considered related to a third party who was an employee of the defendant. The complainant sought access to the names of this person. It appears that the data controller sought the views of the individual who 'had understandably withheld his or her consent because Mr Durant had abused him or her over the telephone'.

One issue which does not appear to have been discussed before the court concerned the status of the individual who it appears was an employee of the Financial Services Authority. This was a significant factor in the later case of *Edem v The Information Commissioner and The Financial Services Authority*.[31] The Data Protection Act provides that the term 'third party' does not include any person 'authorised to process data for the data controller'.[32] Employees would undoubtedly fall into this category,[33] although the court in *Durant* made extensive reference to data relating to third parties. However, section 7(5)–(6) refers to data relating to 'another individual' and does not use the term 'third party'. Although, as discussed previously, there may be a question of whether the identity of an employee dealing with a data subject forms part of that subject's personal data, it would appear a strange result if a data controller could reject or respond only in part to an access request on the ground that data related to a member of staff.

Although in this particular case, the data controller had sought consent for disclosure of the data, the court continued to give guidance as to the nature of the consideration that the statute required to be given by a data controller when faced with such an access request. The general criterion, it was stated, was 'whether it is reasonable to *comply* with the request for information notwithstanding that it may disclose information about another, not whether it is reasonable to *refuse* to comply'. The distinction, it was stated:

> may be of importance, depending on who is challenging the data controller's decision, to the meaning of 'reasonable' in this context and to the court's role in examining it. The circumstances going to the reasonableness of such a decision, as I have just noted, include, but are not confined to, those set out in Section 7(6) [of the Data Protection Act 1998], and none of them is determinative. It is important to note that Section 7(4) leaves the data controller with a choice whether to seek consent; it does not oblige him to do so before deciding whether to disclose the personal data sought or, by redaction, to disclose only part of it. However, whether he has sought such consent and, if he has done so, it has been refused, are among the circumstances mentioned in the non-exhaustive list in Section 7(6) going to the reasonableness of any decision under Section 7(4)(b) to disclose, without consent.[34]

It is difficult to conceive of many situations where a data controller should decline to seek the third party's consent and then refuse an access request on the ground that the data would identify a third party. Such a result would conflict sharply with the principles laid down in *Gaskin*. In the event that the third party—as in the present case—was asked to consent, refused, and the controller determined not to disclose the data to the enquiring data subject, the courts, it was held, should be reluctant to routinely:

> 'second-guess' decisions of data controllers, who may be employees of bodies large or small, public or private or be self-employed. To so interpret the legislation would encourage litigation and appellate challenge by way of full rehearing on the merits and, in that manner, impose disproportionate burdens on them and their employers in their discharge of their many responsibilities under the Act [Data Protection Act 1998].

---

[31] [2014] EWCA Civ 92.
[32] s. 70(1).   [33] Information Commissioner's Office, *Legal Guidance*.
[34] para. 56.

The judgment continued to observe that:

> the right to privacy and other legitimate interests of individuals identified in or identifiable from a data subject's personal data are highly relevant to, but not determinative of, the issue of reasonableness of a decision whether to disclose personal data containing information about someone else where that person's consent has not been sought. The data controller and, if necessary, a court on an application under Section 7(9), should also be entitled to ask what, if any, legitimate interest the data subject has in disclosure of the identity of another individual named in or identifiable from personal data to which he is otherwise entitled . . .
>
> . . . Much will depend, on the one hand, on the criticality of the third party information forming part of the data subject's personal data to the legitimate protection of his privacy, and, on the other, to the existence or otherwise of any obligation of confidence to the third party or any other sensitivity of the third party disclosure sought. Where the third party is a recipient or one of a class of recipients who might act on the data to the data subject's disadvantage . . . his right to protect his privacy may weigh heavily and obligations of confidence to the third party(ies) may be non-existent or of less weight. Equally, where the third party is the source of the information, the data subject may have a strong case for his identification if he needs to take action to correct some damaging inaccuracy, though here countervailing considerations of an obligation of confidentiality to the source or some other sensitivity may have to be weighed in the balance.[35]

A final issue concerns the question of when a third party is to be considered identifiable. A controller is obliged to supply as much information as is possible without disclosing the third party's identity. In particular, it is stated, this might involve the omission of names or other identifying particulars. Account is to be taken of:

> any information which in the reasonable belief of the data controller, is likely to be in, or to come into, the possession of the data subject making the request.[36]

In the *Durant* case, this task was relatively straightforward. The data subject did not know the identity of the employee he had been dealing with and a motive behind the access request was to obtain this information. This requirement may cause some difficulties for data controllers. In a case such as *Gaskin*,[37] for example, it may be a very difficult task for a data controller to assess whether the enquiring data subject would have, after the passage of many years, any recollection of the identity of particular doctors or social workers who had been responsible for submitting reports.

National security

Under the Data Protection Act 1984, information held for the purpose of national security was totally exempted from the legislation.[38] Given the increasing involvement of national security agencies such as MI5 in crime-related functions, such as operations against suspected drug dealers, the division between national security and criminal functions is frequently blurred. This has led the Registrar to express concern that exemptions have been claimed on an organisational rather than a task-related basis.[39] Although no changes were required to the 1984 Act in this regard, national security falling outwith the ambit of Community law-making competence, the Data Protection Act 1998 does contain significant new provisions. As under the 1984 Act, a certificate may be issued by a minister of the Crown indicating that personal data is held for the purpose of national security.[40]

---

[35] para. 66.   [36] Data Protection Act 1998, s. 7(5).
[37] *Gaskin v United Kingdom* (1990) 12 EHRR 36.
[38] s. 27.   [39] See, eg, *Sunday Times*, 1 February 1998.   [40] s. 28(2).

Under the 1984 Act, such a certificate was not open to challenge. It is now provided, how-ever, that it may be challenged before the Information Tribunal by any person 'directly affected'. This may include a data subject who for the first and only time is given a right to initiate proceedings before the Tribunal. Applying 'the principles applied by the court on an application for judicial review', the Tribunal may quash the certificate if it considers that the minister did not have 'reasonable grounds' for issuing it.[41] Detailed provisions for the procedures to be followed in the Tribunal are now found in the Information Tribunal (National Security Appeals) Rules 2005.[42]

With the introduction of the new right of appeal, a number of cases were brought before the Information Tribunal. In the first case, *Norman Baker v Secretary of State for the Home Department*,[43] the claimant, a Liberal Democrat MP, had sought access to records which he believed were held about him by the security services. This prompted a response:

> Under the Data Protection Act 1998 the Security Service intends to notify the Data Protection Commissioner that it processes data for three purposes. These are: staff admin-istration, building security CCTV and commercial agreements. The Security Service has checked its records and holds no data about you in any of these categories.

> Any other personal data held by the Security Service is exempt from the notification and subject access provisions of the Data Protection Act 1998 on the ground that such exemp-tion is required for the purpose of safeguarding national security, as provided for in Section 28(1) of the Act. Thus, if it were to be the case that the Service held any data regarding you other than for the purposes set out in paragraph 2 above, the Data Protection Act would not confer a right of access. There is therefore no data to which you are entitled to have access under the Act, but you should not assume from this letter that any such data is held about you.

> I would point out that a right of appeal exists under Section 28 of the Act. The Section provides that the exemption described above can be confirmed by a certificate signed by a Minister of the Crown who is a member of the Cabinet, or by the Attorney General. A certificate relating to the work of the Security Service was signed by the Home Secretary on 22 July. Any person directly affected by the issuing of the certificate may appeal . . .[44]

Such an appeal was brought and provided the opportunity for the first sitting of the National Security Appeals Panel of the Information Tribunal. The appellant argued before the Tribunal that he had been given information that the security services had collected information in connection with his past activities in support of an ecological group. Although his involvement with the organisation had now ceased, he indicated that he had been informed that the file remained in existence.

The Tribunal reviewed the certificate which had been issued by the Secretary of State. This, it was stated, 'can fairly be described as a blanket exemption for 'any personal data that is processed by the Security Service' in the performance of its statutory functions':[45]

> By exempting the Security Service from the duty under Section 7(1)(a) of the Act [Data Protection Act 1998] to inform the individual making the request whether or not his per-sonal data are being processed, the Certificate authorises the non-committal reply which was given to Mr Baker. This means that both the Certificate and the response gave effect to the policy which is known colloquially as 'neither confirm nor deny' and by the acronym 'NCND'. We have no doubt that they were intended to do so.[46]

---

[41] s. 28(5).
[42] SI 2005/13.   [43] [2001] UKHRR 1275.
[44] [2001] UKHRR 1275 at [14].   [45] [2001] UKHRR 1275 at [25].
[46] [2001] UKHRR 1275 at [30].

The certificate at issue in the present case was typical of all certificates issued in response to requests for access under the Data Protection Act 1998. The case for applying this policy was that a reply indicating that information was held but was not being made available to an applicant could of itself compromise the national security interests for which the information had been collected.

Although such a policy raises major issues relating to access to national security data, the issue before the Tribunal was a more limited one, namely to determine whether the Secretary of State had acted reasonably in formulating a certificate which left the decision of whether and to what extent a request for access should be granted entirely to the security services. As was stated:

> if the NCND response is permitted in all cases then the practical result is that the Service is not obliged to consider each request on its individual merits. That follows if the NCND reply is invariably justified, and we were furnished with no evidence that individual consideration is given to the possible consequences of making a positive response to every request.[47]

The question for the Tribunal was whether such a blanket policy was acceptable or whether the legislation imposed an obligation to give consideration to the individual circumstances of each application.

Discussion of whether the Secretary of State had reasonable grounds for issuing the certificate focused on the question of whether his action constituted a proportionate response to the need to balance the interests of individual rights and state security. After reviewing the principles appropriate to an action for judicial review, the Tribunal recognised that different situations called for different approaches:

> Where the context is national security judges and tribunals should supervise with the lightest touch appropriate; there is no area (foreign affairs apart) where judges have traditionally deferred more to the executive view than that of national security; and for good and sufficient reason. They have no special expertise; and the material upon which they can make decisions is perforce limited. That the touch should be the lightest in comparative terms does not, of course, assist in weighing up how light that should be in absolute terms.[48]

Even on this basis, however, the Tribunal was of the view that the certificate should be quashed. A blanket exemption, as provided for by the certificate, was wider than was necessary to preserve national security. It was clear from the evidence that there were cases where information held by the security services could be disclosed without prejudicing national security and no evidence that the task of sifting these cases from others where the established 'neither confirm nor deny' response was given would impose unreasonable burdens upon the security service. The decision in the *Baker* case[49] was not concerned in any respect with the merits of a decision that access should not be granted. It provides authority for the proposition that each request must be considered on its merits.

In two further cases brought before the National Security Appeals Panel, *Hitchens v Secretary of State for the Home Department* and *Gosling v Secretary of State for the Home Department*,[50] the attempt was made to challenge the merits of decisions to refuse to supply information which the appellants believed was held by the security services concerning their past activities. In the former case, the period covered was some thirty years previously when the claimant, who was to become a somewhat right-wing newspaper columnist, was a member of an extreme Marxist group at York University. Whilst he accepted that the

---

[47] [2001] UKHRR 1275 at [32].

[48] [2001] UKHRR 1275 at [76].   [49] [2001] UKHRR 1275.

[50] The transcript of these decisions can be obtained from the Department of Constitutional Affairs website at <http://www.dca.gov.uk/foi/inftrib.htm>.

security services would have been justified to take an interest in his youthful activities he argued:

> My aim is purely to know what, if anything, is in these records, mainly because I feel I am entitled to know the details of such records as a matter of natural justice. Since I am no longer a revolutionary Marxist, and the politics of this country have been utterly trans-formed in the intervening period, and it is most unlikely that any individual mentioned in these files still holds a sensitive position of any kind, I can see no argument for withhold-ing these files from me. I would, if asked, be quite happy to co-operate with the Security Service to ensure that no sensitive information was accidentally disclosed. Their response, however, is simple blank refusal . . . covered by the meaningless and hard-to-justify claim that this is 'safeguarding national security'. I think the Security Service needs to do better than this to justify secrecy over files almost 30 years old concerning my own youthful follies and their attempts to monitor them.

Following the panel's decision in *Baker*, the format of the ministerial certificate had been amended to make it incumbent upon the security service to give individual consideration to each request for access. The focus of argument in this case was on the merits of the indi-vidual decision. Here, the Panel was referred to the Investigatory Powers Tribunal, which was established under section 65 of the Regulation of Investigatory Powers Act 2000 to deal with a wide range of complaints that may be made about the exercise of powers under the Act. This tribunal, it was held, had jurisdiction to deal with complaints of the kind brought by the appellant. Furthermore:

> we believe that the Investigatory Powers Tribunal is the body best placed to determine any specific complaint that the Service has applied the provisos to the certificate in a manner that is manifestly unjustified. That Tribunal is presided over by a distinguished senior judge and has the appropriate expertise to investigate a complaint of this nature.[51]

On this basis, the appeal was rejected.

Whilst it is encouraging that another method of appeal should be available to individu-als, the result appears indicative of a somewhat confused and confusing approach towards information policy. Whilst it may well be the case that the structure of the Investigatory Powers Tribunal makes it better equipped to deal with arguments on the merits of a partic-ular access request, the question arises as to what is the continuing function of the National Security Appeals Panel. Having quashed the first version of the ministerial certificate in *Baker*, the terms of the revised version were accepted in *Hitchens*. Short of further changes in format, it is difficult to identify any circumstances in which an appeal to the panel would serve any useful purpose.

Data held for policing and revenue-gathering purposes

The Data Protection Act 1998 provides an exception from the subject access provisions where personal data is processed in connection with:

  (a) the prevention or detection of crime,

  (b) the apprehension or prosecution of offenders, or

  (c) the collection or assessment of any tax or duty

to the extent that the grant of access would be prejudicial to the attainment of the purpose in question.[52]

---

[51] [2001] UKHRR 1275 at [56].   [52] s. 29(1).

The determination of whether access would be prejudicial to any of the above purposes requires to be made in the context of an individual request for access. In the event that a denial of access is challenged before the Commissioner, the onus will be on the data user to demonstrate a likelihood of prejudice in the circumstances of the particular case. The criteria to be invoked were discussed before the High Court in *Lord v Secretary of State*,[53] an action in which a prisoner was seeking access to reports produced in the course of a prison review to determine whether his status should be reduced from that of a high-risk (category A) inmate. For the authorities it was argued, inter alia, that disclosure would be likely to prejudice the interests of crime prevention. Considering the approach to be adopted, Mr Justice Mumby commented:

> I accept that 'likely' in Section 29(1) does not mean more probable than not. But on the other hand, it must connote a significantly greater degree of probability than merely 'more than fanciful'. A 'real risk' is not enough. I cannot accept that the important rights intended to be conferred by Section 7 are intended to be set at nought by something which measures up only to the minimal requirement of being real, tangible or identifiable rather than merely fanciful. Something much more significant and weighty than that is required. After all, the Directive, to which I must have regard in interpreting Section 29(1), permits restrictions on the data subject's right of access to information about himself only (to quote the language of Recital (43)) 'in so far as they are *necessary* to safeguard' or (to quote the language of Article 13(1)) 'constitute a *necessary* measure to safeguard' the prevention and detection of crime [emphasis added]. The test of necessity is a strict one . . . In my judgment 'likely' in Section 29(1) connotes a degree of probability where there is a very significant and weighty chance of prejudice to the identified public interests. The degree of risk must be such that there 'may very well' be prejudice to those interests, even if the risk falls short of being more probable than not.[54]

Consideration was also given to the extent to which the decision of whether data should be disclosed should be made solely by reference to the circumstances of the particular applicant, whilst recognising that this does not mean that one can simply ignore the consequential effect that disclosure in the particular case may have on others.[55]

It was held that a blanket policy of non-disclosure failed to satisfy the test and an order was made that the data should be released to the claimant.

A further exception operates at a higher level of generality. This provides that subject access will not be permitted where personal data is processed by a government department, local authority, or other authority administering housing benefit or council tax benefit as part of a system of risk assessment relating to the assessment of collection of tax or duty, the prevention or detection of crime, or the apprehension or prosecution of offenders and:

> where the offence concerned involves any unlawful claim for payment out of, or any unlawful application of, public funds

and reliance on exemption is required in the interests of the operation of the system.[56]

By referring to the operation of the system, the provision obviates the need to show that allowing a particular data subject access would have prejudicial effects. It was explained on behalf of the government that the provision was intended primarily to benefit the Inland Revenue. An example might be that:

> the Inland Revenue's recently introduced self-assessment system uses a range of indicators to identify individual tax returns which justify further inquiries. Subsection 4 will allow an exemption to be made for withholding this critical risk assessment information from data

---

[53] [2003] EWHC 2073 (Admin).   [54] paras. 99–100.   [55] para. 122.
[56] Data Protection Act 1998, s. 29(4).

subjects. If it was not withheld, tax experts, if not the individuals concerned, could soon start to compare cases and deduce the revenue's criteria for further inquiry.[57]

It is to be noted that the exemption relates only to the subject access provision and not to the requirements of the first data protection principle that data be obtained and processed fairly and lawfully.

Health data

The Data Protection Act 1984 established the general principle that access should be provided to medical and social work data. The Access to Personal Files Act 1987 and Access to Health Records Act 1990 extended these rights to manual files with procedures which are now gathered under the umbrella of the Data Protection Act 1998. The 1998 Act confers power on the Secretary of State to make regulations exempting or modifying the subject information provisions in respect of health data.[58] Such an approach is envisaged by the Data Protection Directive which states in Recital 42:

> Member States may, in the interest of the data subject or so as to protect the rights and freedoms of others, restrict rights of access and information; whereas they may, for example, specify that access to medical data may be obtained only through a health professional.

Article 11 provides that measures may be taken to 'restrict the scope' of access rights on a range of grounds including 'the protection of the data subject or of the rights and freedoms of others'. The UK legislation perhaps stretches the concept of 'restrict' to its limits by providing for access to be excluded. The Data Protection (Subject Access Modification) (Health) Order 2000[59] provides for exemption when, in the opinion of a relevant health professional, the grant of access would 'cause serious harm to the physical or mental health or condition of the data subject or any other person'.

In cases where the data controller concerned is not a health professional, any decision to grant or refuse access may be made only after consultation with an 'appropriate health professional'. This term is defined as:

(a) the health professional who is currently or was most recently responsible for the clinical care of the data subject in connection with the matters to which the information which is the subject of the request relates; or

(b) where there is more than one such health professional, the health professional who is the most suitable to advise on the matters to which the information which is the subject of the request relates.[60]

A request for access may not be denied on the ground that disclosure would identify a health professional as being responsible for the compilation of a record, except where it can be shown that serious harm is likely to be caused to the physical or mental health or condition of the health professional. This is perhaps likely to apply only in the situation where there are grounds for suspecting that the data subject might be liable to attack or harass the health professional identified.

Special provision is made for the situation where access is sought, typically by a parent or guardian, on behalf of a child or a person suffering some mental incapacity. In such a case, it is provided that data is exempted from the access rights where it has been:

---

[57] 586 HL Official Report (5th series), col. 505, 16 March 1998.
[58] s. 30(1).
[59] SI 2000/413.
[60] SI 2000/413, Art. 2.

(a) provided by the data subject in the expectation that it would not be disclosed to the person making the request;

(b) obtained as a result of any examination or investigation to which the data subject consented in the expectation that the information would not be disclosed; or

(c) which the data subject has expressly indicated should not be so disclosed.[61]

By providing that access may be denied only to the extent that this would cause 'serious harm' to the health of the data subject, the Order[62] must be seen as establishing a strong presumption in favour of access. Whilst recognising that circumstances—particularly those connected with psychiatric illness—may exist in which the supply of a copy of a medical record may not be in the best interests of the patient, it may be doubted whether the procedures adopted under the Order are, in themselves, likely to prove any less harmful. In common with the situations arising under other exemptions, a health professional may respond to a request for access with the statement that no relevant personal data is held. To an extent perhaps greater than with the other exceptions, the data subject is likely to be aware of the fact that data is held. The failure to supply data may well be a source of distress in itself, whilst discovery of the fact that the data has been withheld for fear that access would cause serious harm to the patient's health would, in itself, appear inimical to his or her health interests.

Education and social work data

The basic format of the exemptions in respect of these categories of data is similar to that applying to health records. The relevant statutory instruments are the Data Protection (Subject Access Modification) (Education) Order 2000[63] and the Data Protection (Subject Access Modification) (Social Work) Order 2000.[64] In both cases, access may be denied in situations where its grant 'would be likely to cause serious harm to the physical or mental health or condition of the data subject or any other person'. Unlike the situation with health records, however, there is no requirement that the decision of whether to grant or refuse access should be made by a person possessing appropriate qualifications.

In both sectors, it is provided that a request for access may not be refused on the basis that the data would identify a third party where this would refer to an employee of the data controller responsible for producing a record in the course of employment, again subject to an exception where it can be shown that the grant of access would be likely to result in serious harm to the individuals concerned.

In the case of both categories of records—but especially in the case of educational records—there is a possibility that access may be sought by a third party acting on behalf of a data subject. In addition to the general ground for refusing access, it is provided in the case of educational records that access may be denied in respect of information indicating that the child is, or may be, at risk of child abuse and where the grant of access would not be in the best interests of the child. In respect of social work records, the criteria are identical to those described earlier concerning health data.

Regulatory activity

A broad range of statutory agencies engaged in regulatory tasks are provided with exemptions from the subject information provisions to the extent that compliance with these would prejudice the attainment of their purpose.[65] A number of agencies are specifically

---

[61] SI 2000/413, Art. 5(3).   [62] SI 2000/413.
[63] SI 2000/414.   [64] SI 2000/415.   [65] s. 31.

identified in the Data Protection Act 1998, namely the Parliamentary, Health Service, Local Government, and Northern Irish Assembly, and Complaints Ombudsmen. Exemption is also offered to the Director General of Fair Trading (whose functions have now been transferred to a range of other departments) in respect of the discharge of functions in the fields of consumer protection and competition policy. In addition to named agencies, exemption is also offered to those performing 'relevant functions' which are designed to protect against specified risks. The term 'relevant functions' is defined to encompass functions conferred by statute, performed by the Crown, ministers, or government departments, or 'any other function' which is of a 'public nature and is exercised in the public interest'. The activities involved relate to protection against loss due to 'dishonesty, malpractice or other seriously improper conduct' within the financial services, corporate, and professional sectors, or through the conduct of discharged or undischarged bankrupts. Also exempted are functions concerned with the supervision of charities and the protection of health and safety, both for workers and for third parties who might be affected by particular activities.

Research, history, and statistics

Exemption for data of this description continues the approach adopted in the Data Protection Act 1984. Where data is 'not processed to support measures or decisions with regard to particular individuals', and where the processing is not likely to cause substantial damage or distress to any data subject, exemption is offered from the subject access provisions subject to the further condition that the results of processing are not made available in a form permitting identification of data subjects.[66]

Information required to be made available to the public

In many instances, personal data will be contained in some document which is made available to the public. An example would be the Electoral Roll, copies of which may be supplied in electronic format. In the situation where the data made available is the only data held concerning the data subject, there would be little value for the subject in exercising a right of access. Such an exemption previously applied under the Data Protection Act 1984 and continues under the Data Protection Act 1998, however, again, with the additional benefit to the data controller that there will be exemption from the first data protection principle.[67]

Miscellaneous exceptions

Schedule 7 to the Data Protection Act 1998 contains a substantial list of additional exceptions, which list may be supplemented by regulations made by the Secretary of State.[68] As described in the following paragraphs, the extent of the individual exemptions varies, ranging from the application of modified access procedures, through to exemption from access, and to exemption from the fair processing requirement.

Confidential references

In many cases under the Data Protection Act 1984, such references would have been excluded from scrutiny under provisions referring to the processing of data purely in order to create the text of a document (the word-processing exemption).[69] This exemption is not retained in the Data Protection Act 1998 and the expanded definition of processing in the 1998 Act will bring such documents within its scope. It is provided that the subject access

---

[66] s. 33.   [67] s. 34.   [68] s. 38(1).   [69] s. 1(8).

provisions will not apply to references given in connection with the data subject's education, employment, or appointment to any office, as well as to the provision of any services by the data subject.[70]

Armed forces

The subject information provisions will not apply where their application would be likely to prejudice the combat effectiveness of the armed forces.[71] This is a new provision and it is difficult to identify situations in which it is likely to apply.

Judicial appointments and honours

Under the Data Protection Act 1984, information held for the first of these purposes was exempted from the subject access provisions.[72] The Data Protection Act 1998 extends the scope of the exemption to data processed in connection with the 'conferring by the Crown of any honour'. Such data is exempt from the subject information provisions, regardless of any issue of prejudice.[73]

Crown employment and Crown and ministerial appointments

Regulatory power is conferred on the Secretary of State to exempt data processed for the purpose of assessing a person's suitability for specified appointments. The Data Protection (Crown Appointments) Order 2000[74] provides that this is to apply in respect of the appointment of senior religious figures in the Church of England and a range of other dignitaries, including the Poet Laureate and the Astronomer Royal.

Management forecasts

Personal data processed for this (undefined) purpose benefits from an exemption to the subject information provisions, where compliance would prejudice the attainment of the purpose.[75] Under the Data Protection Act 1984, a data user was not required to give access to information indicating intentions held towards the data subject. This exemption no longer applies but such information might frequently be held in records maintained for career-planning purposes and these may benefit from this provision.

Corporate finance

Extensive provisions are made for exemptions under this heading. The exemption will apply to data processed by 'relevant persons' concerned with the underwriting of share issues or the provision of advice on capital structure, industrial strategy, and acquisitions and mergers, and will apply when the application of the subject information provisions could affect the price of any shares or other instruments. In the situation where this criterion is not satisfied, it is further provided that exemption may be granted 'for the purpose of safeguarding an important economic or financial interest of the United Kingdom'. It is provided that the Secretary of State may specify in more detail the circumstances and situations in which this latter exemption is to apply and this power is exercised in the Data Protection (Corporate Finance Exception) Order 2000.[76] This specifies that account is to be taken of the 'inevitable prejudicial effect' on:

(a) the orderly functioning of financial markets, or

(b) the efficient allocation of capital within the economy,

---

[70] Sch. 7, para. 1.   [71] Data Protection Act 1998, Sch. 7, para. 2.   [72] s. 31.   [73] Sch. 7, para. 3.
[74] SI 2000/416.   [75] Data Protection Act 1998, Sch. 7, para. 4.   [76] SI 2000/184.

through granting access to data which might affect the decision of any person on whether or how to act within the financial markets or in respect of the conduct of any business activity.

Negotiations

Data processed in relation to negotiations between the controller and subject which records the intentions of the controller are exempt from the subject information provisions where compliance with these would be likely to prejudice those negotiations.[77] An example of such a situation might concern data relating to an employer's business strategy in a situation where an employee who has been identified as critical to the success of the business is seeking to negotiate a pay rise.

Examination marks and examination scripts

The Data Protection Act 1984 made special provision allowing examination authorities to delay responding to requests for access beyond the normal forty-day period.[78] This was considered necessary for large-scale examinations, such as the GCSE, where a period of months might elapse between examination and publication of the results. This approach is continued in the Data Protection Act 1998.[79] One point which should be noted is that where an examination authority relies upon the extended time limits upon receipt of an access request, its response must provide information as to the data held at the time of receipt of the request, at the time the request is complied with, and any further data which was held at any intervening stage. An enquiring subject will, therefore, receive details of any changes made to exam marks during the various stages of the assessment process.

A novel exemption from the subject access provision relates to the materials produced by students during the examination process.[80] Under the Data Protection Act 1984, it is unlikely that these would have been covered by the legislation. With the extension to some forms of manual records and the deletion of the text-processing exemption, the Data Protection Act 1998 may well govern such materials.

Information about human embryos

The Data Protection Act 1998 provides an exemption from the subject information provisions in respect of information indicating that an individual was born following IVF treatment. The Data Protection Act 1984 made a similar provision with regard to the subject access right.[81] An alternative access procedure involving prior counselling is, however, provided under the Human Fertilisation and Embryology Act 1990.[82] These provisions are continued by the Data Protection (Miscellaneous Subject Access Exemptions) Order 2000.[83]

Legal professional privilege

Data is exempt from the subject information provisions where it consists of information in respect of which a claim to legal professional privilege (or client–lawyer confidentiality in Scotland) could be maintained in legal proceedings.[84] This provision replaces an equivalent exemption under the Data Protection Act 1984,[85] but once again with an extension from subject access to the subject information provisions.

---

[77] Data Protection Act 1998, Sch. 7, para. 7.   [78] s. 35.   [79] Sch. 7, para. 8.
[80] Sch. 7, para. 9.   [81] s. 35A.
[82] s. 31.   [83] SI 2000/419.
[84] Data Protection Act 1998, Sch. 7, para. 10.
[85] s. 31(2).

Self-incrimination

Data controllers need not supply information in response to a request for access when the provision of the information would indicate that an offence might have been committed (other than under the Data Protection Act 1998), thereby exposing them to the risk of criminal prosecution. Any information supplied pursuant to a request for access is not admissible in any proceedings for an offence under the 1998 Act.[86]

Matters arising subsequent to an access request

Denial of access

If the subject's request is not satisfied, an action seeking access may be raised before the court. Here, it is provided that the court may order the grant of access, except where it considers that it would be unreasonable to do so 'because of the frequency with which the applicant has made requests to the data user . . . or for any other reason'.[87] Use of the word 'may' in the statute implies that the court possesses a measure of discretion on whether to order the grant of access. This point was raised in the case of *Durant v Financial Services Authority*. At first instance, it was indicated by the judge that, even if he were to accept that the claimant had a right of access to the personal data in question, he would not have made an order to this effect for three reasons:

> First, I cannot see that the information could be of any practical value to the appellant. Secondly, the purpose of the legislation . . . is to ensure that records of an inaccurate nature are not kept about an individual. A citizen needs to know what the record says in order to have an opportunity of remedying an error or false information. In this case the appellant seeks disclosure not to correct an error but to fuel a separate collateral argument that he has either with Barclays Bank or with the FSA, litigation which is in any event doomed to failure. [Thirdly,] I am entirely satisfied on the facts of the case that the FSA have acted at all times in good faith, and indeed there has been no suggestion to the contrary from the appellant; his argument is with Barclays Bank, not with the FSA.[88]

Assuming that a £10 access fee would cover the costs incurred by most users in satisfying access requests, it may be doubted whether this provision will be utilised to any extent. It has also been suggested, however, that a campaign of mass access requests might be used as a part of an industrial or other campaign directed against a data user. In the field of local government, for example, a spokesman for one authority has suggested that a concerted campaign causing several thousands of applications to arrive simultaneously would create major problems in complying with the legislation's time limits.[89]

On behalf of the claimant, it was argued that the Data Protection Directive requires that Member States 'guarantee' the right of access and that the exercise of any discretion to refuse access would apply only where it was considered that one of the exemptions described earlier applies. The Court of Appeal disagreed with Lord Justice Auld, holding that the discretion conferred by section 7(9) was 'general and untrammelled'. It was added, however, that:

> as a corollary to my comment in paragraph 66 on the subject of reasonableness of disclosure of information about a third party under Section 7(4)(b), that it might be difficult for a court to conclude under that provision that it was reasonable to comply with a data subject's

---

[86] Sch. 7, para. 11.
[87] Data Protection Act 1998, s. 21(8).
[88] [2003] EWCA Civ 1746 at para. 69.
[89] *Glasgow Herald*, 28 December 1987.

request so as to disclose such information, yet exercise its discretion under Section 7(9) against ordering compliance with that aspect of the data subject's request.[90]

Rectification of inaccurate data

Data will be considered inaccurate if it is false or misleading as to any matter of fact. In such an event, the data subject may request the court to order the controller to 'rectify, block, erase or destroy'[91] the data in question.[92] These remedies may also be invoked when the data controller has acted in such a fashion as would give the subject an entitlement to claim compensation under the Data Protection Act 1998. Additionally, the controller may be ordered to amend any statement of opinion which appears to be based on the inaccurate data. Where data constitutes an accurate transcription of information received from a third party, the court may make one of the above orders. Alternatively, it may permit the data to be retained but be supplemented by a further statement of the true facts as determined by the court.[93] Where the court determines that data is inaccurate and requires that it be rectified, blocked, erased, or destroyed, it may, where this is considered reasonably practical, order that the controller notify details of the changes to any third party to whom the data has previously been disclosed.[94] Such a remedy may provide a valuable audit trail, allowing the detrimental consequences of inaccurate data to be minimised.

Compensation

Under the Data Protection Act 1984, data subjects were entitled to claim compensation for damage and distress resulting from inaccuracy in data or from its unauthorised destruction or disclosure. These rights were seldom utilised,[95] the requirement in particular to demonstrate both damage and distress proving a substantial hurdle.

The Data Protection Act 1998 adopts a more extensive approach in terms of the basis for liability. Compensation may be claimed in respect of losses caused through any breach of the legislation. Except, however, in the situation where a claim arises as a result of the processing of data for media purposes (the 'special purposes'), the 1998 Act retains the requirement that damage be demonstrated as a prerequisite to any claim alleging distress. In all cases, the controller will have a defence if it can be shown that reasonable care was taken to avoid the breach.

Although the claim was ultimately rejected, consideration was given by the court of first instance in the case of *Johnson v Medical Defence Union*.[96] The background to the case has been described in Chapter 5. Essentially, the complainant alleged that his personal data had been subject to unfair processing and that this had caused him some pecuniary damage and also distress and damage to his professional reputation.

Considerable discussion took place on the issue of whether the Act fully implements the provisions of the Data Protection Directive which requires in Article 23 that:

1. Member States shall provide that any person who has suffered 'damage as a result of an unlawful processing operation or of an act incompatible with the national

---

[90] para. 74.   [91] The distinction between erasure and destruction of the data may relate to the nature of the storage medium involved. Manual files may well be destroyed through burning or shredding. With computer records, the concept of erasure is more relevant, given that data may only be completely destroyed following complete reformatting of the storage device.   [92] s. 14(1).   [93] s. 14(2).   [94] s. 14(3).
[95] The *Fourteenth Report of the Data Protection Registrar* (1998) cites one case where a credit reference agency wrongly registered adverse data against the complainant. The mistake continued for some considerable time and the report indicates that, following the Registrar's intervention, 'a substantial ex gratia payment was made' (p. 88).   [96] [2006] EWHC 321 (Ch).

provisions adopted pursuant to this Directive' is entitled to receive compensation from the controller for the damage suffered.

The Directive, it was suggested, used the term 'damage' as encompassing any form of damage, whether pecuniary in nature or not. Evidence was presented to the court indicating that the status of implementation of this provision across the EEA was unclear. Some states provided compensation awards limited to pecuniary damage, whilst others took a more liberal approach. Whilst not commenting on the proper interpretation of the Directive, the conclusion was reached that section 13(1) provided an entitlement to compensation only for pecuniary damage. This heading excluded any compensation for general damage to reputation. After examining and rejecting a range of headings of expenditure, the only item potentially accepted by the court related to a sum of £10.50 spent paying for breakfast for a Medical Defence Union official who the complainant had been asked to meet. This small sum could have served as the trigger to a more substantial claim for distress under the provisions of section 13(2), although it was noted that:

> I also consider, however, that any compensation under that head must be exclusively in respect of any distress associated with the damage for which recovery is in principle recoverable under Section 13(1). In particular, having concluded that Mr Johnson is not entitled to recover general compensation under Section 13(1) for his claimed loss of professional reputation, I would regard it as inconsistent to permit the recovery under Section 13(2)(a) of compensation in respect of the distress claimed to be suffered by reason of Mr Johnson's perception that the non-renewal of his membership had damaged his reputation.[97]

In respect of other forms of distress, the main claim was to the effect that the complainant had been left without insurance cover for a period of some two months following termination of his MDU membership and that this had caused him anxiety and distress. It was indicated that had the substantive elements of the complainant's case been upheld, compensation of £5,000 might have been awarded. The size of this figure was criticised before the Court of Appeal,[98] although given that the complainant's case had failed, it 'would be an undue use of judicial time to reason the matter out'.[99]

Misuse of personal information

Recent media reports have suggested that moves are afoot within the European Commission to establish a more structured form of regulation of digital operators such as Google and Facebook.[100] There is also the ongoing issue between the Commission and Google concerning the possible abuse by the latter of a dominant position in the market for search engines. Issues concerning responsibilities and liabilities of global Internet Service Providers (ISPs) seem likely to be a prominent feature in the legal landscape for the coming years. The recent decision of the English Court of Appeal in the case of *Google v Vidal-Hall and Others*,[101] gives an indication of the kind of issues that may arise.

Cookies have been a prominent and controversial aspect of the Internet for a number of years. The key issue in this case was the claim that Google had used these to track the Internet activities of users of Apple's Safari browser in breach of its stated privacy policy and without having obtained their express consent to this. The information identifying the browser used (browser generated information (BGI)) would then be passed on to advertisers.

---

[97] para. 236.   [98] [2007] EWCA Civ 262.   [99] para. 77.
[100] See <http://www.theguardian.com/technology/2015/apr/27/digital-regulator-europe-google-facebook-amazon-apple>.   [101] [2015] EWCA Civ 311.

The claimants alleged that Google's conduct constituted the tort (delict) of misuse of personal information and or breach of confidence. It was additionally argued that it constituted a breach of the Data Protection Act 1998. Significantly in this last respect, the claimants sought damages for distress even though it was conceded that they had not suffered any form of pecuniary loss.

Critical to the issue was the question whether the English courts had jurisdiction to try the case, given that Google is registered in the state of Delaware. Reference might be made to the decision of the Court of Session in the case of *Clark v Trip Advisor LLC*,[102] where the court declined to hear an action seeking to compel the peer review company to disclose the identity of a number of its reviewers who had allegedly posted defamatory reviews of the claimant's hotel business. The court's rationale was that any such action should have been brought before the US courts in line with the standard conditions of use laid down by Trip Advisor. In the case of Google, its terms of use include provision that:

> The Terms, and your relationship with Google under the Terms, shall be governed by the laws of the State of California without regard to its conflict of laws provisions. You and Google agree to submit to the exclusive jurisdiction of the courts located within the county of Santa Clara, California to resolve any legal matter arising from the Terms. Notwithstanding this, you agree that Google shall still be allowed to apply for injunctive remedies (or an equivalent type of urgent legal relief) in any jurisdiction.[103]

To an extent greater than had occurred in the Trip Advisor case, the Court of Appeal focused attention not on contractual issues—which seem relatively clear cut—but on the issue of non-contractual liability under the law of tort (delict) and also liability for breach of statutory obligations under the Data Protection Act 1998. In such cases, English law provides for jurisdiction to be claimed if 'in all the circumstances, England was clearly or distinctly the appropriate forum for the trial of the dispute'. It held that proceedings could be brought against Google before the English courts alleging that the company had committed the tort of misuse of personal information.

The Court considered also the extent of the remedies that might be available to a claimant for breach of the Data Protection Act 1998. As enacted this required that a claimant show evidence of some form of financial loss before and award of compensation for distress might be awarded. The Court of Appeal held that this requirement was not compatible with the provisions of the EU Data Protection Directive and held that it should be removed from the UK legislation.

The English courts have over centuries evolved notions of what forms of conduct might give rise to tortious liability. Debates concerning the extent of individual rights of privacy have featured prominently in recent years and were central to the present case. In many respects the issues illustrate a tension between the judiciary and the legislature. The Human Rights Act 2000 requires, mirroring the terms of the ECHR, respect for private life. Parliament has consistently refused to define what this somewhat nebulous phrase might mean and a consequence has been that the courts have been left to seek to give effect to the Human Rights Act by adapting established notions—chiefly breach of confidence—to promote the notion that there is a right of privacy under English law. A difficulty with the notion of breach of confidence is that it is closely connected with the notion of a contractual or quasi-contractual obligation. This would clearly be an obstacle to the English courts claiming jurisdiction against Google on the ground of non-contractual (tortious) liability.

---

[102] [2014] CSOH 20.
[103] <https://www.google.co.uk/chrome/browser/privacy/eula_text.html> at clause 19.7.

The Court quoted with approval observations made by Lord Nicholls in the case of *Douglas v. Hello!*[104]

> As the law has developed breach of confidence, or misuse of confidential information, now covers two distinct causes of action, protecting two different interests: privacy, and secret ('confidential') information. It is important to keep these two distinct. In some cases information may qualify for protection both on grounds of privacy and confidentiality. In other instances information may be in the public domain, and not qualify for protection as confidential, and yet qualify for protection on the grounds of privacy. Privacy can be invaded by further publication of information or photographs already disclosed to the public. Conversely, and obviously, a trade secret may be protected as confidential information.[105]

In some respects, the issues are rather artificial. In domestic terms the distinction between a tort and a contract may be of limited importance but in international disputes the matter is of much greater importance. As the Court concluded:

> [M]isuse of private information should now be recognised as a tort for the purposes of service out the jurisdiction. This does not create a new cause of action. In our view, it simply gives the correct legal label to one that already exists. We are conscious of the fact that there may be broader implications from our conclusions, for example as to remedies, limitation and vicarious liability, but these were not the subject of submissions, and such points will need to be considered as and when they arise.[106]

This is a significant finding. As indicated above, there is increasing concern at the activities of global companies such as Google and the extent to which they might effectively be regulated. What the Court of Appeal ruling means is that there can be potential liability in countries whose citizens are impacted by the activities of companies such as Google.

The Data Protection Act provides in section 13 that

> An individual who suffers damage by reason of any contravention by a data controller of any of the requirements of this Act is entitled to compensation from the data controller for that damage.

> (2) An individual who suffers distress by reason of any contravention by a data controller of any of the requirements of this Act is entitled to compensation from the data controller for that distress if— (a) the individual also suffers damage by reason of the contravention, . . .

This formulation differs from the provisions of the EU Data Protection Directive which requires in its Article 23 that:

> Member States shall provide that any person who has suffered damage as a result of an unlawful processing operation or of any act incompatible with the national provisions adopted pursuant to this Directive is entitled to receive compensation from the controller for the damage suffered.[107]

Under the traditional UK approach, the concept of 'damage' is equated to some form of quantifiable financial loss, whereas 'distress' relates to the less quantifiable notion of emotional upset. The linkage of the two terms has been interpreted in a number of cases as requiring that financial loss be demonstrated before there could be any award of compensation for distress. In some respects the distinction is an artificial one. In the case of *Halliday v Creation Consumer Finance*,[108] for example, the Court of Appeal assessed pecuniary loss at a notional sum of £1 and used this to trigger an award for distress amounting to £750. In cases such as the present, however, no element of pecuniary loss could reasonably be identified.

---

[104] [2008] 1 AC 1.   [105] para. 255.   [106] para. 51.   [107] Art. 23.   [108] [2013] EWCA Civ.

This is perhaps a rather artificial approach and the court in the present case took a rather more radical approach. Accepting that there is a requirement where possible to interpret UK legislation in conformity with the provisions of European Directives, it held that:

> [A]rticle 23 of the Directive must be given its natural and wide meaning so as to include both material and non-material damage. In reaching this conclusion, we have regard to the aim of the Directive as evidenced by the recitals in the preamble and article 1.

> Since what the Directive purports to protect is privacy rather than economic rights, it would be strange if the Directive could not compensate those individuals whose data privacy had been invaded by a data controller so as to cause them emotional distress (but not pecuniary damage). It is the distressing invasion of privacy which must be taken to be the primary form of damage (commonly referred to in the European context as 'moral damage') and the data subject should have an effective remedy in respect of that damage.[109]

A literal interpretation of Section 13 of the Data Protection Act, it was conceded must make an element of pecuniary loss a prerequisite for a claim for compensation for distress. Such an interpretation would mean that the United Kingdom had failed to meet its obligation to implement the Directive into domestic law. In further considering the issue, reference was made to the previous decision of the Court of Appeal in the case of *Benkharbouche and Janah v Embassy of Sudan and Others*.[110] This case concerned a claim by an employee of the embassy that its wages were in breach of minimum wage legislation. The embassy relied on the terms of the State Immunity Act 1978 which essentially provides that foreign embassies are not to be subject to the jurisdiction of the UK courts. Considering a number of items of EU law relating to the field, the court held that it would disapply the provisions of the 1978 Act where these conflicted with measures such as the EU Charter of Fundamental Rights. Its conclusions were summarised by the present court in the following terms:

> [W]here there is a breach of a right afforded under EU law, article 47 of the Charter is engaged; (ii) the right to an effective remedy for breach of EU law rights provided for by article 47 embodies a general principle of EU law; (iii) (subject to exceptions which have no application in the present case) that general principle has horizontal effect; (iv) in so far as a provision of national law conflicts with the requirement for an effective remedy in article 47, the domestic courts can and must disapply the conflicting provision; and (v) the only exception to (iv) is that the court may be required to apply a conflicting domestic provision where the court would otherwise have to redesign the fabric of the legislative scheme.[111]

In the case of Section 13 of the Data Protection Act there was no evidence that Parliament had not made a deliberate choice as to the approach adopted. Disapplying the provisions of section 13(2) of the UK Data Protection Act, it was held, would not involve a fundamental redesign of the legislation and the court concluded:

> What is required in order to make section 13(2) compatible with EU law is the disapplication of section 13(2), no more and no less. The consequence of this would be that compensation would be recoverable under section 13(1) for *any* damage suffered as a result of a contravention by a data controller of any of the requirements of the DPA. No legislative choices have to be made by the court.[112]

This is a very significant decision in two respects: The case provides a basis for global entities such as Google to be called to account for their activities before national courts. Whether that is a good or a bad thing is perhaps open to debate, but there is something uncomfortable about situations such as Trip Advisor referred to at the start of this section where contractual terms—which most users will never read—can operate to make

---

[109] para. 77.   [110] [2015] EWCA Civ 33.   [111] para. 98.   [112] para. 105.

litigation practically difficult, and possibly prohibitively expensive. Also evident, perhaps, is the problem that currently exists in Europe of multiple data protection regimes and enforcement mechanisms.

At a domestic level, the case is also important in curing one of the (many) defects in the UK's Data Protection Act. The Act was brought forward by a reluctant government seeking to do the bare minimum necessary to implement the EU Directive. In some respects it fails to achieve this limited objective and the limitation on rights of compensation has been a significant example. Few instances of data misuse may have direct financial consequences for the data subject but the potential for emotional upset is all too clear. Removal of the artificial distinction between damage and distress is to be welcomed. The legislation was described in the well-known case of *Campbell v MGN*[113] as 'a thicket' and as 'certainly a cumbersome and inelegant piece of legislation'. It is hard to disagree. Possibly a future Data Protection Regulation will bring a greater measure of clarity to the area but this may be to exalt hope over expectation.

Although the case is important it must be kept in mind that we are at an early stage of legal proceedings. What has been decided is that Google can be sued before the English courts. It is by no means certain that it will ultimately be held liable. One important issue that was discussed but left open by the Court of Appeal, is whether the data collected by Google, referred to as 'browser generated information (BGI)' should be classed as personal data? If this question should be decided in the negative, the substantive action will be doomed to failure.

Other subject rights

Right to request an assessment of processing

Section 42 of the Data Protection Act provides that anyone directly affected by processing—typically the data subject—may request the Information Commissioner to conduct an assessment of the processing in order to determine whether it is being conducted in conformity with the requirements of the legislation. It is the practice of the Information Commissioner to treat any complaint received from a data subject as a request under section 42. The complainant is to be informed of the result of the assessment and of any action which has been taken.

Right to resist enforced subject access

The situation whereby access rights imprison rather than empower the data subject has long been the subject of criticism, not least by the Data Protection Registrar. Devising an appropriate method of control has proved more difficult. The major difficulty facing any attempt to control the practice is the imbalance of power typically existing in such situations. If the subject is seeking employment, for example, a request that the information be supplied may carry as much weight as a demand. The initial drafts of the Data Protection Directive provided that data subjects should be entitled:

> to refuse any demand by a third party that he should exercise his right of access in order to communicate the data in question to that third party.

In the final text, the Directive contained the somewhat enigmatic provision that data subjects should be guaranteed the right to exercise access 'without constraint'.[114] Other

---

[113] [2003] QB 633 at [72].   [114] Directive 95/46/EC, Art. 11(a).

language versions of the Directive make it clearer that the provision is intended to apply to enforced access, the German text, for example, requiring that access be provided *frei und ungehindert*.

Although the government indicated the intention to act against enforced subject access from the earliest stages of the Data Protection Act 1998's parliamentary passage, finding an appropriate form of prohibition proved a difficult task. A variety of possibilities were considered. Subject access might, for example, be provided only in person rather than in writing. This would, of course, have made a dramatic change to the whole system of subject access and would have caused great inconvenience in the event, for example, that a data subject was located in Glasgow and the data controller in London. An alternative suggestion was that all access requests should be filtered through the Commissioner. Again, practical constraints might make this solution unworkable. Ultimately, however, it was determined that the only feasible approach was to make the practice criminal. The prohibitions apply, however, only in respect of certain forms of records—criminal records, prison records, and Department of Work and Pensions records—and in respect of a limited range of situations. A person must not require the provision of information obtained following a request for access (a relevant record) in connection with the recruitment or continued employment of the data subject or with any contract under which the subject is to provide services. Similarly, when the person is concerned with the provision of goods, facilities, or services to members of the public, it is prohibited to require the production of any relevant records as a condition for the provision of such goods, facilities, or services.[115] It is further provided that any contractual terms will be void insofar as they purport to require the production of any medical information obtained pursuant to an access request.[116] Although it is provided that these categories may be extended by statutory instrument,[117] it may be queried whether the provisions comply fully with the Data Protection Directive's requirements.[118]

In this, as in other areas, the provisions of the Data Protection Act 1998 will not operate in isolation. Under the provisions of the Police Act 1997, new arrangements were made for providing access to criminal records. Three categories of access were created. A basic certificate may be sought by any applicant which will reveal details of any convictions which are not spent under the Rehabilitation of Offenders Act 1974. A more extensive 'criminal record certificate', adding details of spent convictions, will be issued upon the joint application of the individual and an organisation which is exempted from the provisions of the 1974 Act. This will include professional organisations, such as the Law Society, in respect of its role in determining whether individuals might be considered suitable for admission to the profession. The most extensive certificate, the 'enhanced criminal record certificate', will include police intelligence data and details of acquittals, and will be reserved for situations where an individual is seeking to work with children or vulnerable adults (or other sensitive positions, such as those related to gambling or judicial appointments).

Given the large numbers of requests for access relating to criminal records, there will clearly be a close relationship between the access provisions of the Police Act 1997 and those of the Data Protection Act 1998. It was stated in Parliament that the provisions of the Data Protection Act 1998 would not be implemented before those of the Police Act 1997. In his *Annual Report for 2003*, the Information Commissioner noted:

> Whilst we are keen that Section 56 should be brought into effect as soon as possible there appear to be two obstacles. Firstly, there is the question of Northern Ireland. Although the Criminal Records Bureau (CRB) has been established for England and Wales and a similar arrangement is in place in Scotland, as far as we are aware there are no plans to introduce

---

[115] s. 56.   [116] s. 57.   [117] s. 56(8).
[118] Directive 95/46/EC, Art. 11(a).

a comparable system in Northern Ireland. Secondly, it appears likely that as a result of an independent review of the Criminal Record Bureau's strategies and operations the launch of basic disclosures in England and Wales is to be postponed indefinitely. It therefore seems that the day on which the relevant sections of the Police Act 1997 are all in force across the whole of the United Kingdom might never arrive.[119]

It was suggested that the government might bring section 56 into force, even though the prescribed condition had not been met. This was not done until 2015 and the adoption of the Data Protection (Commencement Number 4) Order.[120] As was recognised in the Information Tribunal decision of the *Chief Constables of West Yorkshire, South Yorkshire, and North Wales Police, and the Information Commissioner*,[121] 'the overwhelming majority of the 200,000-odd police subject access requests per year are currently enforced'.[122] Foreign embassies are major 'beneficiaries' of enforced subject access and it was recognised that even the bringing into force of section 56 might have little practical effect, as embassies are not subject to national law.

Right to object to data processing

Direct marketing

It is a little-known fact that those persons who purchase black-ash furniture are twenty times more likely to respond to a fashion promotion than those whose tastes are less exotic. Such nuggets of information may constitute interesting trivia to most people, but to those engaged in the retail industry they can represent the path to fortune. Direct marketing is one of the fastest-growing sectors of the economy. Although it tends to be referred to under the epithet of 'junk mail', each item delivered represents a not inconsiderable investment on the part of the sender. In many instances, retailers will possess information linking an individual to a purchase and may use this in order to attempt to stimulate further sales. The purchaser of a motor vehicle, for example, is likely to receive a communication from the seller around the anniversary of the purchase in the hope that the buyer might be considering buying a new model. The increasing use of store-based credit cards coupled with the utilisation of laser-scanning cash points provides retailers with detailed information about their customers and their purchases. There are few technical barriers in the way of processing data so as to be able to 'talk to every customer in his or her own life style terms'.[123] It has been suggested, for example, that 'intelligent shopping trolleys' might guide customers towards promotions which analysis of their previous purchases suggests might prove alluring.[124] Assuming that the data users involved have registered the fact that they intend to process personal data for sales and marketing purposes, the only legal barrier to such techniques might come from a determination that such processing is unfair.

The use of personal data for purposes of direct marketing has been the cause of some recent controversy. Reference has previously been made to the *Innovations* case[125] and the data protection implications of list broking. Additionally, however, organisations are seeking to exploit their customer databases by entering into agreements to provide mailings on behalf of other companies. This may take a variety of forms. Analysis of, for example, purchases made with a credit card may indicate that an individual frequently stays in hotels.

[119] *Annual Report and Accounts 2003*, p. 37.   [120] SI 2015/312.

[121] <http://www.informationtribunal.gov.uk/DBFiles/Decision/i204/north_wales_police.pdf>.

[122] para. 82.

[123] Roger Hymas, GE Capital Executive Director, quoted in *Financial Times*, 4 April 1991.

[124] *Financial Times*, 4 April 1991.

[125] *Innovations (Mail Order) Ltd v Data Protection Registrar* Case DA/92 31/49/1 (see Chapter 4).

The credit card company may then enter into an agreement with a hotel chain to include a promotional leaflet with its statement of account. In this example, no personal data will be transferred between the companies. In a guidance note relating to direct marketing,[126] the Registrar has indicated that in certain circumstances use of financial data for such purposes might constitute a breach of confidence.[127] More recently, action has been taken against a number of utilities engaging in the practice of cross-selling, with enforcement notices being served against a number of utilities which sent offers of other products and services to their customers. Significantly, the fact that the utilities offered customers the opportunity to opt out of these offers was not considered sufficient, the Registrar arguing that an opt-in system should apply.[128]

Treatment of data obtained and used for the purposes of direct marketing constituted one of the most controversial aspects of the Data Protection Directive.[129] As originally drafted, the legislation would have imposed strict obligations on data controllers to inform subjects whenever data was to be used for such a purpose. The proposals were weakened in subsequent drafts and, as enacted, the Directive offers Member States a choice of control regimes. It may be provided that data subjects be given the right to object to a controller's intention to process or to disclose data for the purposes of direct marketing. No fees are to be charged in this event.[130] It is arguable that this reflects current UK practice, especially after the decisions of the Data Protection Tribunal in the *Innovations* and *Linguaphone* cases.[131] As an alternative, the Directive provides that controllers might be required to give specific notice to data subjects before data is used by or on behalf of third parties for direct marketing purposes.[132] This is coupled with the requirement that steps be taken to inform data subjects of their rights.

The Data Protection Act 1998 adopts the second of these options, providing that:

> An individual is entitled at any time by notice in writing to a data controller to require the data controller at the end of such period as is reasonable in the circumstances to cease, or not to begin, processing for the purposes of direct marketing personal data of which he is the data subject.[133]

Other forms of processing

In the case of direct marketing data, the subject's wishes are absolute. With other forms of processing, the subject may serve notice requiring the cessation of processing on the basis that this is likely to cause substantial and unwarranted damage or distress. This right will not apply:

- where the subject has previously consented to the processing;
- where the processing is necessary to conclude or perform a contract with the data subject;
- where it is necessary to comply with any legal obligation on the data controller; or
- where the processing is necessary to protect the vital interests of the data subject.[134]

---

[126] *Direct Marketing* Information Commissioner's Office. Available from <http://ico.org.uk/~/media/documents/library/Privacy_and_electronic/Practical_application/direct-marketing-guidance.pdf>.

[127] paras. 81–8.

[128] *Thirteenth Report of the Data Protection Registrar* (1997), pp. 26–7.

[129] Directive 95/46/EC.

[130] Art. 14(b).

[131] *Innovations (Mail Order) Ltd v Data Protection Registrar* Case DA/92 31/49/1; *Linguaphone Institute v Data Protection Registrar* Case DA/94 31/49/1.

[132] Art. 14(b).   [133] s. 11(1).   [134] Data Protection Act 1998, s. 10(1).

The Secretary of State may specify other situations in which the right to object is to be withdrawn.[135] Upon receipt of such a notice, the controller must respond in writing within twenty-one days, either indicating that the subject's request will be granted or giving reasons why or to what extent this should not be the case.[136] A negative response may be appealed to the courts, which may make such order for ensuring compliance as it thinks fit.[137]

Whilst the principle that the data subject should be entitled to exercise control over the situations in which personal data is processed must be welcomed, the requirement that 'substantial and unwarranted damage or distress' be demonstrated, coupled with the exceptions described earlier, may remove much of the value from the provision. It may be noted that the Data Protection Directive, in providing for the right to object, states that this is to be based on 'compelling legitimate grounds'.[138] Whilst this term is not defined in the legislation, it does seem rather less demanding criteria than those adopted in the Data Protection Act 1998.

Automated decision-making

Increasingly, the results of data processing may trigger further actions affecting the data subject with minimal intervention from any human agency. A trivial example may be taken from the operation of automated cash-dispensing machines. A customer may approach a machine at midnight, insert a bank card, enter a personal identifier number (PIN), and request a sum of money. Details of the customer's account will be checked with the bank's computer system and if the customer is sufficiently in funds, cash will be dispensed. If the customer is not in funds, no money will be issued. There will be no human involvement at any stage of the transaction. In other instances, it is possible that human agents may be reduced to little more than a cipher. An example might be seen in the operation of systems of credit scoring. Here, an applicant for credit is required to fill in a form giving information about matters such as marital status, employment, and housing status, etc. Points are allocated depending on the answers. A married person, for example, may be awarded one point, a single person two, and a divorced person three. The pointage values are based upon an assessment of the risk of default. Each creditor may establish a predetermined acceptance level. If a customer's total falls below this, the application will be rejected.

The operation of credit scoring has been criticised by the Director General of Fair Trading on the basis of perceived unfairness to persons whose profile may not fit the automated model yet whose credit history may be flawless, and the recommendation has been made that those operating the technique should build in an appeals procedure. A similar approach is adopted in the Data Protection Directive which, drawing on provisions in the French Data Protection Act, provides that individuals must be granted the right:

> not to be subject to a decision which produces legal effects concerning him or significantly affects him and which is based solely on automated processing of data intended to evaluate certain personal aspects relating to him, such as his performance at work, creditworthiness, reliability, conduct, etc.[139]

Inevitably, this general statement is subject to exceptions, the Directive continuing to provide that automated decisions are permissible in the course of entering into or performing a contract, so long as the outcome is favourable to the subject or provision is made to safeguard 'legitimate interests'. An appeals procedure such as that referred to earlier, allowing the subject to present additional information, would appear to meet this requirement. It is further provided that other automated decisions may be sanctioned by law, so long as this also contains safeguards for the subject's legitimate interests.

[135] s. 10(2). [136] s. 10(3).
[137] s. 10(4). [138] Directive 95/46/EC, Art. 14. [139] Directive 95/46/EC, Art. 15.

Although there might be debate about how significant any element of human interven-tion in a decision-making process is required to be, most applications should pose few intractable problems in that a delay in implementing a decision will not cause significant problems for either data controller or subject. The cash-dispensing example cited at the beginning of this section may be a more difficult issue. In the event a customer is denied funds late at night, there seems little doubt that the statutory criteria will be satisfied. It may be doubted whether there is any realistic prospect of providing an immediate right of appeal. In Lord Denning's memorable phrase from *Thornton v Shoe Lane Parking*,[140] the customer 'may protest to the machine, even swear at it; but it will remain unmoved'.

Conclusions

Under the Data Protection Act 1984, the right of access to data, coupled with rights to require the correction of inaccurate data and very restricted rights to compensation, con-stituted the major innovation from the standpoint of data subjects. By moving to what are described as 'subject information rights', the Data Protection Act 1998 does confer new entitlements on data subjects. The right to object to data processing and to resist attempts to compel the exercise of access rights also constitute significant advances. That said, what the opening paragraphs of a section confer is often removed by the exceptions and qualifi-cations which tend to litter subsequent paragraphs. It would not be practicable or desirable to permit a data subject an absolute right to require that data not be processed, otherwise an individual with a long history of bad debts could require that a credit reference agency expunge all records from its files. Nevertheless, the statutory provision appears somewhat mean-spirited. Much the same can be said of the provisions relating to enforced subject access. Certainly, it must be admitted that it will be very difficult to stamp out such prac-tices. In many cases, such as the making of an application for employment, the imbalance in power between an employing data controller and applicant data subject will be such that a mere expression of desire might be sufficient to make the subject feel compelled to com-ply. Undoubtedly, the data subject is in a stronger position under the Data Protection Act 1998 than has hitherto been the case. The criticism may be that the level of improvement has not been more pronounced.

---

[140] [1971] 1 All ER 686.

7

Sectoral aspects of data protection

INTRODUCTION

The application of data protection principles to particular sectors of activity can be a difficult task. Notions of fairness, as has already been discussed in earlier chapters, are highly context-dependent. This chapter will consider two topics concerned with the application of data protection principles within the media and electronic communications sectors. In both areas, the operation of data protection principles has been contentious. Data protection issues are principally concerned with the application of what might be regarded as 'traditional' data protection principles in the context of activities where different priorities might legitimately be identified. In some respects media processing might be compared with law enforcement agencies. Digging out the truth about the unsavoury activities of powerful elements in society might well require the use of tactics and techniques that would be regarded as unfair in more general contexts.

With the increasing importance of the electronic communications sector—epitomised by the fact that there are now more mobile phones in use in the United Kingdom than there are people[1]—more and more data processing activities are being conducted over some communications network. Apart, of course, from the growth of mobile phone usage for voice and text communications, we have seen the massive increase in Internet access and usage. We all live more and more (and increasingly sensitive) aspects of our lives in an online environment. From the 1990s the need has been identified to develop sector-specific interpretations of general data protection laws.

Data protection and the media

The application of data protection provisions in respect of media activities raises a number of complex issues. As illustrated by the Leveson Inquiry, at the stage of gathering information with a view to publication, investigative journalism in particular may involve the use of tactics and techniques which would normally be stigmatised as unfair (if not unlawful). The Information Commissioner's report *What Price Privacy?*[2] contains extensive information regarding the techniques used by journalists—often assisted by private investigators—to obtain access to information. At a perhaps extreme end of the scale, a journalist and a private investigator were jailed in 2007 after pleading guilty to intercepting voicemail messages belonging to members of the royal family.[3] Debate continues as to whether this was an isolated example or whether the practice is more entrenched in at least some

---

[1] In its Communications Market Report for 2013—available at http://media.ofcom.org.uk/facts/, OFCOM estimated that there were 82.7 million mobile phone subscriptions active in the United Kingdom.

[2] Available from <http://www.ico.org.uk/~/media/documents/library/Corporate/Research_and_reports/WHAT_PRICE_PRIVACY.pdf>.

[3] See <http://news.bbc.co.uk/1/hi/6301243.stm>.

areas of the media and this was, of course, at the centre of the Leveson Inquiry and the ongoing debate about the appropriate form of regulation of press conduct.[4] At almost the other end of the publication spectrum in terms of time, many newspapers and journals now maintain copies of issues in electronic format. These will certainly come within the scope of the Data Protection Act 1998, under whose general provisions a subject would be entitled to require the rectification of any errors, coupled with a reformulation of any resultant statements of opinion. Whilst generally desirable, the rewriting of documents which claim to represent data as published on a certain date calls to mind the operation of George Orwell's Ministry of Truth. This latter topic will be considered in more detail in the context of actions for defamation.

The Recitals to the Data Protection Directive[5] recognise the conflicts inherent in the area, stating that:

> Whereas the processing of personal data for purposes of journalism or for purposes of literary or artistic expression, in particular in the audiovisual field, should qualify for exemption from the requirements of certain provisions of this Directive in so far as this is necessary to reconcile the fundamental rights of individuals with freedom of information and notably the right to receive and impart information, as guaranteed in particular in Article 10 of the European Convention for the Protection of Human Rights and Fundamental Freedoms.[6]

The Recitals continue to suggest that national laws should provide for alternative measures—such as the submission of reports to the supervisory agency—to ensure that data subjects' rights are not abused. In terms of the articles, themselves, the Directive is somewhat imprecise. Article 9 states that:

> Member States shall provide for exemptions or derogations from the provisions of this Chapter, Chapter IV and Chapter VI for the processing of personal data carried out solely for journalistic purposes or the purpose of artistic or literary expression only if they are necessary to reconcile the right to privacy with the rules governing freedom of expression.

It is clear that this formula empowers rather than requires Member States to act, but for the United Kingdom, the decision was taken to include special provisions for these activities, described as the 'special purposes' in the Data Protection Act 1998.

Scope of the provisions

Section 3 of the Data Protection Act 1998 defines the concept of 'special purposes'. It is provided that these relate to the processing of personal data:

(a) for the purposes of journalism,

(b) artistic purposes, and

(c) literary purposes.

It was stressed in Parliament that no qualitative criteria would be applied to determine whether a work could be classed as artistic, journalistic, or literary. Although much of the debate in Parliament focused on the activities of the media, this definition recognises that literary and artistic works also raise issues of freedom of expression. The prime purpose of the Act's exceptional provisions is to place limits on the ability of data subjects to invoke

---

[4] See the report of the House of Commons' Culture, Media and Sports Committee on *Press Standards, Privacy and Libel* (February 2010). The report is available from <http://www.publications.parliament.uk/pa/cm/cmcumeds.htm>.

[5] Directive 95/46/EC.   [6] Recital 37.

statutory rights to impede publication of a work. Similar restrictions are placed upon the powers of the Information Commissioner, with modified provisions for the service of information and enforcement notices. Once the work is in the public domain, the provisions of the general law will apply, including the law of defamation, although, as indicated in Chapter 6, the 1998 Act does provide new rights of compensation for distress caused as a result of processing carried out in connection with one of the special purposes.

Activities covered

The Data Protection Act 1998 applies a three-stage test to determine whether processing for a special purpose should benefit from exemption. Personal data must be subject to processing:

(a) ... with a view to the publication by any person of any journalistic, literary or artistic material;

(b) the data controller reasonably believes that, having regard in particular to the special importance of the public interest in freedom of expression, publication would be in the public interest; and

(c) the data controller reasonably believes that, in all the circumstances, compliance with (statutory provisions) is incompatible with the special purposes.[7]

It was suggested in Parliament that:

> We have deliberately placed on the face of the Bill, I believe for the first time in an Act of Parliament in this country, that the public interest is not the narrow question of whether this is a public interest story in itself but that it relates to the wider public interest, which is an infinitely subtle and more complicated concept.[8]

In determining whether belief that publication is in the public interest might be considered reasonable, it is provided that account is to be taken of any relevant code of practice. Power is conferred on the Secretary of State to designate codes which are to be taken into account in this way. The Data Protection (Designated Codes of Practice) Order 2000[9] lists five codes:

- the Code on Fairness and Privacy issued by the Broadcasting Standards Commission in 1998 under the terms of the Broadcasting Act 1996

- the ITC Programme Code issued by the Independent Television Commission in 1998 under the terms of the Broadcasting Act 1990

- the Press Complaints Commission's Code of Practice published in 1997

- the Producers' Guidelines issued by the British Broadcasting Corporation in 1996

- the Programme Code issued by the Radio Authority in 1998 under the terms of the Broadcasting Act 1990.

Citation of codes in this manner is a novel feature of the Data Protection Act. It may additionally be noted that whilst three of the codes have some form of statutory basis, the remaining two have no such backing.

In respect of the section 32 provisions, the Leveson report has recommended changes to require publishers to demonstrate that the processing of personal data is 'necessary for publication, rather than simply being in fact undertaken with a view to publication' and

---

[7] s. 32(1).   [8] 585 HL Official Report (5th series), col. 442, 2 February 1998.   [9] SI 2000/418.

also that they have reasonable grounds to believe that the publication would be or is in the public interest. Such an assessment should be conducted without the need for a balancing act between individual rights to privacy and those relating to freedom to publish.

Scope of the exemption

Section 31 of the Data Protection Act defines a range of provisions which will not apply where processing is carried out for the special purposes. With the exception of the seventh principle relating to data security, the data protection principles will not operate; neither will the subject access provisions nor those enabling a data subject to object to data being processed. Also excluded are the provisions of section 12, relating to subject rights in respect of automated decision-making, and the general provisions of section 14, relating to the subject's rights to compensation. These latter provisions are substituted, however, by special and more extensive rights.

These exceptions are wide-ranging. One consequence will be that even the unlawful obtaining of personal data will not expose the controller to action under the Data Protection Act—although other criminal sanctions, such as a charge of theft, may be imposed in respect of the offending conduct.

Procedural aspects

The question of whether processing is covered by one of the special purpose exemptions is likely to arise in the course of legal proceedings. In this regard, it is provided that proceedings must be stayed when the data controller claims, or it appears to the court, that the data are being processed for a special purpose and:

> With a view to publication by any person of any journalistic, literary or artistic material which, at the time twenty-four hours immediately before the relevant time, had not previously been published by the data controller.[10]

The relevant time will be the moment at which the controller makes the claim for protection or the court determines that the processing is for a special purpose.

It will be recognised that there is no requirement that the controller's claim that processing is covered by the special purpose should have any merit. As discussed later, procedures for the lifting of such a stay are complex, and the Commissioner has criticised the situation whereby an unscrupulous party could delay proceedings for a period of months, if not years, with little justification.[11]

Once a court has determined that procedures should be stayed, the focus of attention switches to the Commissioner, who will be required to make a written determination as to whether the processing is being conducted only in connection with one of the special purposes or with a view to the publication of material not previously published by the data controller.[12] In obtaining evidence necessary to reach such a view, the Commissioner may require to exercise powers conferred under the legislation to serve a special information notice. Service of such notice may itself be the subject of an appeal to the Information Tribunal. If the Commissioner determines that the processing is not exempt, this finding may itself be appealed to the Tribunal. It will only be when appeal procedures have been exhausted that the determination will come into effect and the court will be in a position to lift the stay.

---

[10] Data Protection Act 1998, s. 32(4).
[11] Briefing Note, 'Media Exceptions', 16 February 1998.
[12] Data Protection Act 1998, s. 45.

The application of the Data Protection Act's provisions relating to media processing was at issue in the case of *Campbell v Mirror Group Newspapers Ltd.* Finding in favour of the claimant in the High Court,[13] Moreland J held that information relating to her drug addiction was sensitive personal data, that the defendant had failed to show that its processing of the data conformed with any of the provisions of Schedule 3 setting out conditions for the lawful processing of personal data or with the Press Complaints Commission code of practice, an instrument which had been designated by the Secretary of State under section 32. In respect of the defence provided by section 32 it was held that, whilst this would operate in order to prevent a claimant from stopping publication, its benefit ceased at this point and did not confer any form of immunity in respect of a subsequent action for damages on the basis that the unfair or unlawful processing had caused distress to the data subject. Damages of £3,500 were awarded in respect both of the contravention of the Data Protection Act 1998 and of the claimant's claim that the publication constituted a breach of confidence.

The judge's findings in respect of the Data Protection Act were overturned by the Court of Appeal.[14] Delivering the judgment of the court, Lord Phillips MR was critical of the structure of the Data Protection Act 1998. Echoing the views of Moreland J, who described the interpretative task as akin to 'weaving his way through a thicket', the Act was described as 'a cumbersome and inelegant piece of legislation'.[15]

Before the Court of Appeal, the appellant did not seek to argue that its processing of Ms Campbell's personal data complied with the requirements of Schedule 3 to the Data Protection Act—as was stated, 'much of their argument was founded on the submission that it was virtually impossible for journalists to comply with the requirements of the Act'[16]—but argued that the effect of the section 32 defence was to confer immunity in respect of any action for damages made subsequent to publication. It was argued for the appellant that the result of the High Court's ruling would be that:

> Without the consent of the data subject, a newspaper would hardly ever be entitled to publish any of the information categorised as sensitive without running the risk of having to pay compensation. Indeed, it would be difficult to establish that the conditions for processing any personal information were satisfied. If this were correct, it would follow that the Data Protection Act had created a law of privacy and achieved a fundamental enhancement of Article 8 rights, at the expense of Article 10 rights, extending into all areas of media activity, to the extent that the Act was incompatible with the Human Rights Convention.[17]

Analysing the provisions of the section 32 defence, the Court of Appeal first focused on subsections (4) and (5). These were described as procedural measures designed to provide for the stay of proceedings brought against a publisher until after publication and there was no dispute that 'the purpose of these provisions is to prevent the restriction of freedom of expression that might otherwise result from gagging injunctions'.[18]

The court continued to examine the provisions of section 32(1)–(3) which, it was stated:

> on their face, provide widespread exemption from the duty to comply with the provisions that impose substantive obligations upon the data controller, subject only to the simple conditions that the data controller reasonably believes (i) that publication would be in the

---

[13] [2002] EWHC 499 (QB), [2002] All ER (D) 448 (Mar).

[14] *Campbell v Mirror Group Newspapers Ltd* [2002] EWCA Civ 1373, [2003] QB 633.

[15] [2002] EWCA Civ 1373, [2003] QB 633 at [72].

[16] *Campbell v Mirror Group Newspapers Ltd* [2002] EWCA Civ 1373, [2003] QB 633 at [74].

[17] [2002] EWCA Civ 1373 at [92].

[18] *Campbell v Mirror Group Newspapers Ltd* [2002] EWCA Civ 1373, [2003] QB 633 at [117].

public interest and (ii) that compliance with each of the provisions is incompatible with the special purpose—in this case journalism.[19]

It was concluded that:

> If these provisions apply only up to the moment of publication it is impossible to see what purpose they serve, for the data controller will be able to obtain a stay of any proceedings under the provisions of Subsections (4) and (5) without the need to demonstrate compliance with the conditions to which the exemption in Subsections (1) to (3) is subject.[20]
>
> ... For these reasons we have reached the conclusion that, giving the ... provisions of the Subsections their natural meaning and the only meaning that makes sense of them, they apply both before and after publication.[21]

Support for this approach was taken from the comments of the responsible government minister as recorded in the *Hansard* report of the debate of the second reading of the Bill. Here it was indicated that:

> Following the meetings to which I referred, we have included in the Bill an exemption which I believe meets the legitimate expectations and requirements of those engaged in journalism, artistic and literacy [*sic*] activity. The key provision is Clause 31. This ensures that provided that certain criteria are met, before publication—I stress 'before'—there can be no challenge on data protection grounds to the processing of personal data for the special purposes. The criteria are broadly that the processing is done solely for the special purposes; and that it is done with a view to the publication of unpublished material. Thereafter, there is provision for exemption from the key provisions where the media can show that publication was intended; and that they reasonably believe both that publication would be in the public interest and that compliance with the bill would have been incompatible with the special purposes.[22]

Although it was indicated that the court, mindful of the dicta of Lord Hoffmann in *Robinson v Secretary of State for Northern Ireland* that reference to *Hansard* should be a matter of 'last resort',[23] did not base its decision on this passage, it may be queried whether the comments do fully support the interpretation that the section 32 defence applies totally, pre- and post-publication. As indicated by the court, the section 32 defence is indeed a measure in two parts. Subsections (4) and (5) provide a very straightforward method of protection against gagging orders. Subsections (1)–(3), it is submitted, should swing into action only after publication. In conformity with the Data Protection Directive's strictures that:

> Member States shall provide for exemptions or derogations from the provisions of this Chapter, Chapter IV and Chapter VI for the processing of personal data carried out solely for journalistic purposes or the purpose of artistic or literary expression only if they are necessary to reconcile the right to privacy with the rules governing freedom of expression.[24]

The use of the words 'only' and 'necessary' must indicate both that exemptions may be provided only when and to the extent strictly necessary to reconcile the competing rights. This may involve allowing publication to take place but cannot, it is submitted, justify a removal of rights to compensation (and rectification) after the event. As was stated by the Article 29 Working Party:

> The Directive[25] requires a balance to be struck between two fundamental freedoms. In order to evaluate whether limitations of the rights and obligations flowing from the Directive are

---

[19] At [118].   [20] [2002] EWCA Civ 1373 at [118].   [21] [2002] EWCA Civ 1373 at [121].
[22] 585 HL Official Report (5th series), col. 442, 2 February 1998.
[23] [2002] UKHL 32, [2002] All ER (D) 364 (Jul) at [40].   [24] Directive 95/46/EC, Art. 9.
[25] 95/46/EC.

proportionate to the aim of protecting freedom of expression particular attention should be paid to the specific guarantees enjoyed by the individuals in relation to the Media. Limits to the right of access and rectification prior to publication could be proportionate only in so far as individuals enjoy the right to reply or obtain rectification of false information after publication.

Individuals are in any case entitled to adequate forms of redress in case of violation of their rights.[26]

The basis for the individual's claim to compensation is laid down in section 13 of the Act. This provides that compensation is payable for distress caused as a result of processing for the special purposes which is conducted in breach of any of the Act's provisions. It is further provided that:

In proceedings brought against a person for breach of this Section it is a defence to prove that he had taken such care as in all the circumstances was reasonably required to comply with the requirement concerned.

Perhaps more significantly, the Data Protection (Processing of Sensitive Personal Data) Order 2000,[27] adds to the Schedule 3 list of factors legitimising processing of sensitive personal data in the situation whereby:

(1) The disclosure of personal data—

    (a)   is in the substantial public interest;

    (b)   is in connection with—

        (i)   the commission by any person of any unlawful act (whether alleged or established),

        (ii)   dishonesty, malpractice, or other seriously improper conduct by, or the unfitness or incompetence of, any person (whether alleged or established), or

        (iii) mismanagement in the administration of, or failures in services provided by, any body or association (whether alleged or established);

    (c)   is for the special purposes as defined in Section 3 of the Act; and

    (d)   is made with a view to the publication of those data by any person and the data controller reasonably believes that such publication would be in the public interest.[28]

Whilst not conferring immunity upon data controllers, this provision does provide a defence in situations where disclosure can be justified in the public interest.

Special information notices

A modified form of information notice applies where data is being processed for a special purpose. Acting either in response to a request from a data subject for an assessment of whether data is being processed in accordance with the principles,[29] or where there are reasonable grounds for suspecting that a data controller has wrongfully claimed the benefit of the special purpose—for example, to refuse a request for access—the Commissioner may serve a 'special information notice'.[30] The notice will require that the controller supply

---

[26] Recommendation 1/97, 'Data Protection Law and the Media'.   [27] SI 2000/417.
[28] Sch., para. 3.   [29] s. 42.   [30] s. 44.

the Commissioner with specified information to enable the Commissioner to determine whether the processing is being conducted for a special purpose or with a view to publication of new information. The notice must indicate the ground upon which the Commissioner is making the request and give notice of the controller's rights of appeal. The notice will not come into effect until the expiry of the twenty-eight-day period allowed for the lodging of appeals.[31] In cases of urgency, it is provided that the notice may require that information be supplied within seven days.[32]

Having received the information required, the Commissioner will make the determination referred to above as to whether processing is being conducted only for the special purposes. If the determination is that this is not the case, the Commissioner may serve the normal form of information notice seeking information to be supplied allowing a determination whether processing is lawful.[33]

Enforcement notices

Whether following service of an enforcement notice or otherwise, a determination by the Commissioner that processing is unlawful may be followed by service of an enforcement notice. Once again, different procedures apply in relation to the special purposes. An enforcement notice may only be served with the leave of the court.[34] Leave will only be granted if the court is satisfied that 'the Commissioner has reason to suspect a contravention of the data protection principles which is of substantial public importance', and that 'except where the case is one of urgency', notice has been given to the controller of the Commissioner's intention to apply for leave.[35]

Individual rights and remedies

As discussed in Chapter 6, the Data Protection Act 1998 gives extended rights to data subjects to institute proceedings before the courts seeking compensation for damage and distress resulting from a breach of any of the Act's requirements.[36] In the case of processing for the special purposes, damages may be awarded for distress without the need for any related damage. The data subject may also bring action in the normal manner seeking rectification, blocking, or erasure of inaccurate data.[37] The question of whether and to what extent such remedies are provided is at the discretion of the court, and it may be assumed that account will be taken of the requirements of the special purposes so that, for example, the court will not order the alteration of the contents of a database containing the contents of stories which have been published in a newspaper. Even where a story contains errors, a notice of correction appended to the file would appear a more appropriate course of action.

Granting of assistance by the Commissioner

Section 53 of the Data Protection Act 1998 confers a new power on the Commissioner to provide assistance following an application from a party to proceedings relating to the special purposes.[38] This will include all the forms of proceeding described earlier, with the assistance taking the form of a contribution towards the costs of legal advice and

---

[31] The Information Tribunal (Enforcement Appeals) Rules 2005, SI 2005/14, r. 5.   [32] s. 44(6).
[33] s. 46(3).   [34] s. 46(1).   [35] s. 46(2).   [36] s. 13(1).   [37] s. 14.   [38] s. 53(1).

representation and with indemnification against any award of costs to the other party.[39] The criterion for the award of such assistance is that the Commissioner is of the opinion that 'the case involves a matter of substantial public importance'.[40] The Commissioner's decision of whether or not to grant support must be transmitted to the applicant as soon as practicable. If the Commissioner decides not to grant assistance, reasoned notification to this effect must be given.[41]

Data protection in the electronic communications sector

In the early days of the telephone, all calls were connected by human operators. In order to bill customers accurately, the operator would record when the call was connected, the number to which it was made, and when the call terminated. It was not unknown for operators to listen to the conversation itself and indeed the motivation for the invention of the world's first automated telephone exchange by a funeral director from Kansas named Alvin Strowger, is reported to have lain in his discovery that the wife of a competitor who was employed as a telephone operator was monitoring his calls in order to redirect business to her husband.[42]

Automated dialling took time to be adopted—it was not until 1979 that the United Kingdom's last staffed exchanges were shut down—but the initial system of subscriber trunk dialling (STD) established what might be regarded as a 'golden age' of communications privacy. Calls were connected without human intervention, and while each telephone line had its own meter located in the telephone exchange, the operation of these was analogous to electricity and gas meters in that they merely recorded the number of units of connection time consumed. If, for whatever reason, the authorities wished to be able to identify details of the time and duration of specific calls, a special device referred to as a 'call logger' needed to be attached to an individual line.

From the 1980s the telephone network began to switch from analogue to digital technology, with the last analogue exchanges being closed on 11 March 1998.[43] While the use of digital technology has brought considerable benefits in terms of quality, reliability, and the range of services offered, an inevitable by-product is that increased amounts of data are collected about users. A simple example can be seen with the introduction of systems of itemised billing, where customers are presented with a bill describing, at least for long-distance calls, details of time, duration, and the cost of individual calls.[44]

With the emergence of mobile networks, even more data concerning user behaviour is generated and retained. Whenever it is switched on, every mobile phone transmits a signal every few minutes. All base stations of that network within range respond and through

---

[39] Sch. 10.　　　[40] s. 53(2).　　　[41] s. 53(3)–(4).

[42] Although the first Automatic Switching was rather crude, the first patents were registered by Connolly, Connolly, and McTighe (US Patent No. 222458, 9 December 1879 and British Patent No. 4114, 13 December 1879). In 1891 Strowger patented a two-motion selector (US Patent No. 447918). This system was adopted by the British Post Office and was in service for almost 100 years although it remained policy until the 1950s that all calls of more than fifteen miles should be made via an operator rather than dialled directly, J. Atkinson *Telephony*, II: *Automatic Exchanges* (London, 1950).

[43] The last analogue exchanges served Leigh on Sea and Selby and were converted to digital on 11 March 1998.

[44] Itemised billing provides a good example of the regulatory conflicts which frequently apply in the electronic communications sector. It provides information which may be valuable to the account holder to enable the accuracy of a bill to be checked but may also disclose information about calls made by other members of the account holder's household with potentially adverse implications for their communications privacy. These issues are discussed in Chapter 7.

the use of triangulation techniques the location of phones can be identified. In geographical terms, the degree of accuracy with which a particular handset can be located will depend on the number of base stations which are in range. Typically, in an urban area, a 3G phone can be placed within a range of 15 metres.[45] As well as usage for network purposes, applications such as 'Find my Friends' available on many smartphones allow individuals to track the location of family and friends, perhaps to arrange to meet a nearby friend for a coffee. Less happily, data from such systems have featured in a number of divorce cases.

This data, referred to in the legislation as 'location data', can be retained almost indefinitely and governments are increasingly taking powers to require that it be retained for periods of years against the eventuality that access may be sought in connection with criminal or national security investigations.

In quantitative and qualitative terms the most extensive source of communications data is the Internet. Every transmission, whether in the form of sending an email or the accessing and browsing of websites, gives out information about the individual user. Details of every web page viewed can be recorded by the site owner and linked to the Internet Protocol (IP) address from which the communication originated.[46] In the context, for example, of an e-commerce site, the data recorded is analogous to that which might be obtained by a physical retailer who follows a customer around the store noting not only what goods are purchased but any others that are looked at during the course of the visit. An important and contentious aspect of this involves the use by websites of what are referred to as cookies. The simple and seemingly innocuous term can encompass a wide range of forms of activity. The Article 29 Working Party established under the European Data Protection Directive has produced an Opinion on the legitimacy of cookies. This identifies a range of possibilities:

> Cookies are often categorized according to the following characteristics:
>
> 1) Whether they are 'session cookies' or 'persistent cookies'.
> 2) Whether they are 'third party cookies' or not.
>
> A 'session cookie' is a cookie that is automatically deleted when the user closes his browser, while a 'persistent cookie' is a cookie that remains stored in the user's terminal device until it reaches a defined expiration date (which can be minutes, days or several years in the future).[47]

Third-party cookies can be experienced frequently when accessing an Internet site associated with, for example, a newspaper where advertisements may be presented (under contract with the site owner) by a third party based on previous visits to other sites. A user who has previously been looking at sites concerned with holiday accommodation may find, when visiting an online news site, banner advertisements for such a facility.

---

[45] A number of systems allow individuals to track the location of mobile phones. Although a voluntary code of practice drawn up by the Mobile Broadband Group (available from <http://www.mobilebroadbandgroup.com/documents/UKCoP_location_servs_210706v_pub_clean.pdf>) seeks to protect individuals against the risk of third parties being able to access their location data, concerns have been expressed how effective the safeguards are. See <http://news.bbc.co.uk/1/hi/programmes/click_online/4747142.stm>.

[46] Two forms of IP addresses exist. Static addresses are typically allocated to specific fixed-line connections. An individual accessing the Internet from home will have a dedicated IP address linked to that location. Mobile networks operate on a different basis. A pool of addresses exists and one will be allocated to a particular connection from any individual user. If a particular user connects to the Internet on ten occasions, it is likely that each session will be allocated a different IP address.

[47] Opinion 04/2012 on Cookie Consent Exemption.

A further area of controversy relates to the handling of email and text messages. Although often regarded by users as akin to voice communications in terms of speed and informality, unlike telephone conversations these electronic communications do not exist only in real time. While any third party wishing to monitor a telephone conversation must do so while the conversation is being conducted, copies of emails and text messages will be made at various stages of the transmission process and may be recovered with relative ease days, months, or even years after their transmission. Especially when, as is increasingly the case, messages are sent from a mobile phone or similar device, location data will also be captured.

The above activities raise specific data protection issues, while other forms of behaviour relating to the use of communication networks fall more naturally into the wider topic of personal privacy. The increasing number of unsolicited calls received by many consumers is frequently seen as an infringement of domestic privacy. Similar considerations apply with faxes and emails and, as will be discussed later, the legislative provisions seeking to regulate the use of these have been highly controversial.

The development of sector-specific legislation

Although all aspects of communications networks are regulated under the general provisions of data protection law, almost from the inception of the general regime the EU identified a need for a more specialised form of regulation, to 'particularise and complement'[48] the general data protection Directive adopted in 1995.[49] The provisions of the general Directive were therefore supplemented by more specific provisions in the form of the Directive of 15 December 1997 'concerning the processing of personal data and the protection of privacy in the telecommunications sector'.[50] This Directive was implemented in the United Kingdom by the Telecommunications (Data Protection and Privacy) (Direct Marketing) Regulations 1998 and the Telecommunications (Data Protection and Privacy) Regulations 1999.[51]

It is testimony to the pace of developments in the sector (and perhaps also of the slow pace of the initial legislative process) that less than two years after the Directive's adoption the 1999 Communications Review commented that:

> The terminology used in the Telecoms Data Protection Directive, which was proposed in 1990, is appropriate for traditional fixed telephony services but less so for new services which have now become available and affordable for a wide public. This creates ambiguities and has led in practice to divergence in national transposition of the Directive. To ensure a consistent application of data protection principles to public telecommunications services and network throughout the EU, the Commission proposes to update and clarify the Directive taking account of technological developments converging markets.

A point which comes out strongly throughout the document is that data relating to communications have become both more extensive and more valuable. It is important that the optimal use should be made of valuable resources but there are increasingly conflicts between the interests of service providers and their users. The establishment of effective legal controls and safeguards was therefore seen as a matter of importance and Directive 2002/58/EC[52] concerning the processing of personal data and the protection of privacy in the electronic communications sector (Directive on Privacy and Electronic Communications) constituted one of the five Directives that made up the 2002 regulatory

---

[48] Art. 1(2).   [49] Directive 95/46/EC, OJ 1995 L281/31.
[50] Directive 97/66/EC, OJ 1998 L24/01.   [51] SI 1999/2093.   [52] OJ 2002 L201/37.

package. The Directive was implemented in the United Kingdom by the Privacy and Electronic Communications (EC Directive) Regulations 2003.[53]

As so often in the sector, technology and practice soon outpaced aspects of the legislative provisions. The development of data retention legislation in response to terrorist attacks in cities such as London and Madrid tilted the balance between respect for individual privacy and the requirements of law enforcement agencies. Legislation has been adopted, at both UK and EU levels, requiring communications providers to retain communications and location data for up to two years in the interests of law enforcement.

Further changes to the European legislation were adopted in 2009 with the European Directive 2009/136 on universal service and users rights (the 'Citizens' Rights Directive')[54] making a number of significant changes to the 2002 Directive. These were implemented in the United Kingdom by the Privacy and Electronic Communications (EC Directive) (Amendment) Regulations 2011.[55] A particularly contentious element of the legislation concerned its provisions regarding the use of cookies. The Directive's provisions in this regard have been widely criticised as being extremely unclear and, although the provisions formally came into effect in May 2011, the Information Commissioner issued guidance to the effect that he would not seek actively to enforce the legislation save in the case of blatant and deliberate infringements for a further year. There do not appear to have been any enforcement actions in recent years. Essentially the legislation can be regarded as misconceived. Very many websites—including the Information Commissioner's own—rely upon their use to provide access to their full functions.

The Privacy and Electronic Communications Directive and Regulations

The Privacy and Electronic Communications Directive's proclaimed aim is to harmonise:

> national provisions required to ensure an equivalent level of protection of fundamental rights and freedoms, and in particular the right to privacy and confidentiality, with respect to the processing of personal data in the electronic communication sector and to ensure the free movement of such data and of electronic communication equipment and services in the Community.[56]

As was also the case in respect of the earlier Telecommunications Data Protection Directive, the 2002 measure's stated aim is to 'particularise and complement' the provisions of the general Data Protection Directive.[57] It also expands the scope of this measure in one important respect by providing at least some rights for legal as well as private persons.[58]

The scope of the Communications Data Privacy Directive[59] is defined in Article 3(1) as extending to:

> the processing of personal data in connection with the provision of publicly available electronic communications services in public communications networks in the Community.

In the context of communications-related activities, it may be assumed that individuals will often be identifiable by reference to telephone numbers or email addresses, matched to lists of subscribers maintained by network providers or ISPs. IP addresses[60] allocated to identifiable users will also be classed as personal data. It is difficult to conceive of any

---

[53] SI 2003/2426.   [54] OJ 2009, L337/11.   [55] SI 2011/1208.
[56] Art. 1(1) as amended.   [57] Art. 1(2).   [58] Art. 1(2).   [59] Directive 2002/58/EC.
[60] IP addresses provide the mechanism by which the source and destination of email traffic can be identified and are key to the functioning of the Internet.

communications-related activity which will not involve processing and, save perhaps in the situation where a payphone is used (with, as is increasingly rare, payment made in cash), will not be carried out by reference to an identifiable individual.

Obligations imposed on network and service providers

The Directive and Regulations impose a range of obligations upon network and also service providers in respect of a range of aspects of electronic communications services.

Security and confidentiality

The first substantive obligation imposed is that the provider of a public communication network or service must 'take appropriate technical and organisational measures' to ensure the security of the network and any messages transmitted over it.[61] The 2011 Regulations expand the requirement providing that:

The measures . . . shall at least—

(a) ensure that personal data can be accessed only by authorised personnel for legally authorized purposes;

(b) protect personal data stored or transmitted against accidental or unlawful destruction, accidental loss or alteration, and unauthorised or unlawful storage, processing, access or disclosure; and

(c) ensure the implementation of a security policy with respect to the processing of personal data.

The most obvious and well-publicised risk will be that of an unauthorised person obtaining access to data being transmitted. Beyond interception of voice traffic, perhaps the most significant and certainly the most high-profile risks associated with modern communications are those associated with the Internet, with concerns frequently being raised about the security of personal and financial data transmitted in the course of an e-commerce transaction. The obligations imposed upon service providers are twofold. First, appropriate security measures must be put in place to protect data[62] and, secondly, customers must be warned of the risks involved and advised about self-help measures such as encryption which may be used and of the likely costs of such measures.[63]

While the Directive's provisions regarding data security are addressed to network and service operators, obligations are imposed upon governments to ensure that legal sanctions may be imposed against those who breach the confidentiality of communications. Legal prohibitions are to be imposed against 'listening, tapping, storage or other kinds of interception or surveillance of communications' other than any measures which are necessary in connection with the transmission of data. Exceptions are sanctioned in cases where interception is necessary in the interests of national security, law enforcement, and 'the unauthorised use of electronic communications systems'.[64] It is also permissible to record commercial communications where this is 'carried out in the course of lawful business practice for the purpose of providing evidence of a commercial transaction'.

For the United Kingdom, the provisions of the Telecommunications (Lawful Business Practice) (Interception of Communications) Regulations[65] are relevant in this situation. Made under the auspices of the Regulation of Investigatory Powers Act 2000, these provide legal authority for the monitoring or recording of a wide range of electronic and voice communications. Examples would include recording of telephone calls received by businesses

---

[61] Art. 5 and Reg. 5.   [62] Reg. 5(1).   [63] Reg. 5(3).   [64] Art. 15(1).   [65] SI 2000/2699.

and the monitoring of employees' telephone and email communications by employers to determine compliance with policies regarding usage of these facilities.

Although the Regulations[66] and Directive[67] do provide legal authority for substantial forms of monitoring, it should be recalled that the general Data Protection Act's requirement is that processing should be both fair and lawful. While employer-directed monitoring of the kind described above may well satisfy the second requirement, the Information Commissioner has suggested that processing carried out without giving proper notice to the individuals affected might well be considered unfair.

Breach notification

While prevention is normally the best form of cure, lapses in security can occur and one of the key issues for data protection legislation is how these should be dealt with. The Citizens' Rights Directive introduces a provision which is new to European legislation but which, under the title 'breach notification', has been used in some areas of processing in the United States for some time.[68] The draft European Data Protection Regulation (which it is envisaged will be adopted in 2014 and will replace the current Directive and the Data Protection Act 1998) allows for the introduction of such provisions into general data protection legislation but pending its (possible) adoption the Citizens' Rights Directive marks its only legislative appearance within the EU.

The Directive contains the term 'personal data breach' which is defined as:

> a breach of security leading to the accidental or unlawful destruction, loss, alteration, unauthorised disclosure of, or access to, personal data transmitted, stored or otherwise processed in connection with the provision of a publicly available electronic communications service.[69]

In the event a breach occurs, the service provider involved is to notify the appropriate national supervisory authority and, where the breach is likely to affect adversely individual users,[70] to inform those concerned directly. The supervisory authority may independently require a provider to make notification. As implemented in the 2011 Regulations it is provided that:

(2) If a personal data breach occurs, the service provider shall, without undue delay, notify that breach to the Information Commissioner.

(3) Subject to paragraph (6), if a personal data breach is likely to adversely affect the personal data or privacy of a subscriber or user, the service provider shall also, without undue delay, notify that breach to the subscriber or user concerned.

(4) The notification referred to in paragraph (2) shall contain at least a description of—

   (a) the nature of the breach;

   (b) the consequences of the breach; and

   (c) the measures taken or proposed to be taken by the provider to address the breach.

---

[66] SI 2000/2699.   [67] Directive 2002/58/EC.
[68] For useful information on developments in the United States, see <http://www.csoonline.com/article/221322/cso-disclosure-series-data-breach-notification-laws-state-by-state>.
[69] Art. 2(c) adding a new para. (h) to Art. 2 of the 2002 Directive.
[70] The obligation to notify individuals will not arise if the data has been stored in a form in which it will be unintelligible to unauthorised parties—effectively that it has been encrypted using a strong form of protection.

(5) The notification referred to [sic] the paragraph (3) shall contain at least—

   (a) a description of the nature of the breach;

   (b) information about contact points within the service provider's organisation from which more information may be obtained; and

   (c) recommendations of measures to allow the subscriber to mitigate the possible adverse impacts of the breach.

(6) The notification referred to in paragraph (3) is not required if the service provider has demonstrated, to the satisfaction of the Information Commissioner that—

   (a) it has implemented appropriate technological protection measures which render the data unintelligible to any person who is not authorised to access it,[71] and

   (b) that those measures were applied to the data concerned in that breach.

Cookies

As indicated previously, cookies are frequently used by Internet sites. In the case, for example, of a website, they may be used to identify the fact that a particular machine (and often by inference a particular individual) has accessed the site previously and may be used to customise the pages presented according to previous activities. Typically, an e-commerce site may present a user with a list of recommended buys based on an analysis of that person's purchasing history.

Such practices may be welcomed in many instances. Cookies may also be used to relieve a user of the need to supply full details of name, address, and credit cards whenever making a purchase from a website. There are however, also implications for the privacy and anonymity of Internet users. The Citizens' Rights Directive provides that:

(1) Member States shall ensure the confidentiality of communications and the related traffic data by means of a public communications network and publicly available electronic communications services, through national legislation. In particular, they shall prohibit listening, tapping, storage or other kinds of interception or surveillance of communications and the related traffic data by persons other than users, without the consent of the users concerned, except when legally authorised to do so in accordance with Article 15(1). This paragraph shall not prevent technical storage which is necessary for the conveyance of a communication without prejudice to the principle of confidentiality.

. . .

(3) Member States shall ensure that the storing of information, or the gaining of access to information already stored, in the terminal equipment of a subscriber or user is only allowed on condition that the subscriber or user concerned has given his or her consent, having been provided with clear and comprehensive information, in accordance with Directive 95/46/EC, inter alia about the purposes of the processing. This shall not prevent any technical storage or access for the sole purpose of carrying out the transmission of a communication over an electronic communications network, or as strictly necessary in order for the provider of an information society service explicitly requested by the subscriber or user to provide the service.

---

[71] Typically, this might require that the data has been encrypted in a manner which makes it highly unlikely that any third party will be able to access the contents.

This formulation raises a number of issues and points of uncertainty. There has been a long-standing and largely unresolved issue between the UK government and the European Commission concerning the manner in which user consent to online actions should be obtained. The key question is whether consent needs to be obtained expressly (often referred to as 'opt in') or whether it may be implied from the fact that the user, having been provided with information about intended activities, has not exercised an opportunity to object ('opt out').

In the context of cookies, there are issues and controversies about how explicit the level of notification need be. A common formulation used by website owners is along the lines of 'we use cookies to enhance your browsing experience'. A rather vague formulation! Another issue relates to the extent to which a user may legitimately be put into a situation where the choice is between accepting cookies or eschewing access to the website. The United Kingdom's Information Commissioner's website informs users, for example, that if they do not accept cookies, they will not be able to access all the features of the site. The Directive provides that cookies are legitimate when they 'are strictly necessary in order for the provider of an information society service explicitly requested by the subscriber or user to provide the service'. This is a stringent requirement and one of the major issues is how it should be applied in relation to what might be referred to as 'legacy' websites—those developed before the adoption of the 2009 Directive. For a good many years, cookies have been used because they are helpful (not least to website owners) rather than because they are 'strictly necessary'.

The Directive's provisions have been implemented in the United Kingdom by the Privacy and Electronic Communications (EC Directive) (Amendment) Regulations 2011.[72] This inserts amendments to Regulation 6 of the 2003 Regulations to provide that:

(1) Subject to paragraph (4), a person shall not [store or] gain access to information stored, in the terminal equipment of a subscriber or user unless the requirements of paragraph (2) are met.

(2) The requirements are that the subscriber or user of that terminal equipment—

(a)   is provided with clear and comprehensive information about the purposes of the storage of, or access to, that information; and

[(b)   has given his or her consent].

(3) Where an electronic communications network is used by the same person to store or access information in the terminal equipment of a subscriber or user on more than one occasion, it is sufficient for the purposes of this regulation that the requirements of paragraph (2) are met in respect of the initial use.

[(3A) For the purposes of paragraph (2), consent may be signified by a subscriber who amends or sets controls on the internet browser which the subscriber uses or by using another application or program to signify consent.]

(4) Paragraph (1) shall not apply to the technical storage of, or access to, information—

(a)   for the sole purpose of carrying out . . . the transmission of a communication over an electronic communications network; or

(b)   where such storage or access is strictly necessary for the provision of an information society service requested by the subscriber or user.

---

[72] SI 2011/1208.

The Information Commissioner has published an extensive guidance note on the operation of the new provisions.[73] The major problem area, it suggests, is to modify existing systems to cope with the new requirements:

> Implementing these rules requires considerable work in the short term but compliance will get significantly easier with time. The initial effort is where the challenge lies—auditing of cookies, resolving problems with reliance on cookies built into existing systems and websites, making sure the information provided to users is clear and putting in place specific measures to obtain consent. This work takes place in the context of limited consumer awareness and understanding of what cookies do. In time a number of factors are likely to make compliance much more straightforward. New sites and systems and upgrades to existing systems can be designed to facilitate compliance with the rules, those operating websites will be more aware about how they choose to use cookies and enhanced browser options will increasingly allow websites to rely on browser settings to help to satisfy themselves they have consent to set cookies.[74]

While the Commissioner indicates that obtaining explicit consent to the use of cookies from users would secure 'regulatory certainty' the guidance note states:

> Early reporting on the new rule led some to believe that an explicit, opt-in style consent would be required for every cookie each time it was set. The Information Commissioner's guidance made it clear that although an explicit opt-in mechanism might provide regulatory certainty it was not the only means of gaining consent. In some circumstances those seeking consent might consider implied consent as an option that was perhaps more practical than the explicit opt-in model.
> . . . consent (whether it is implied or express) has to be a freely given, specific and informed indication of the individual's wishes. For implied consent to work there has to be some action taken by the consenting individual from which their consent can be inferred. This might for example be visiting a website, moving from one page to another or clicking on a particular button. The key point, however, is that when taking this action the individual has to have a reasonable understanding that by doing so they are agreeing to cookies being set.[75]

One approach that is widely used is to display a message on the opening screen of a website indicating that cookies are being used, giving a general description of their purpose and indicating that if the user proceeds to use the site further, consent to their use will be assumed.

Traffic and location data

The term 'traffic data' encompasses any data processed in connection with the transmission of signals over a communication network. It will include data relating to the point of origin of a communication, its destination, and the duration of the communication. In the case of a fixed-line telephone, the point of origin will be obvious. With mobile communications, as has been referred to previously, the location of the user may constantly be changing. Data transmitted periodically from the mobile phone will allow the network to remain aware of the phone's location. This is clearly necessary in order to be able to make and receive calls but the retention and processing of location data raises serious issues for the individual's right to privacy.

---

[73] Available at <http://www.ico.gov.uk/for_organisations/privacy_and_electronic_communications/the_guide/cookies.aspx>.

[74] pp. 3–4.   [75] pp. 6–7.

Undoubtedly reflecting its origins in the era when mobile phones constituted a niche rather than a mass market, the Telecoms Data Protection Directive[76] referred only to traffic data and provided that it might be processed subsequent to a communication only for billing purposes, or—with the consent of the customer—limited items of data might be processed by the telecommunications service provider for marketing purposes.[77]

The term traffic data was not defined in the Telecoms Data Protection Directive.[78] The Communications Data Privacy Directive, however, provides that it is to consist of 'any data processed for the purpose of the conveyance of a communication on an electronic communications network or for the billing thereof'.[79] This will encompass both data relating to use of a telephone and any data which might be processed by an Internet Service Provider (ISP) concerned with Internet usage.

The Directive retains the basic prohibition against processing but extends the range of permissible uses. Article 6 provides that:

> For the purpose of marketing electronic communications services or for the provision of value added services, the provider of a publicly available electronic communications service may process the (traffic) data . . . to the extent and for the duration necessary for such services or marketing, if the subscriber or user to whom the data relate has given his or her prior consent. Users or subscribers shall be given the possibility to withdraw their consent for the processing of traffic data at any time.[80]

'Value added services' are defined as communication services requiring the processing of data 'beyond what is necessary for the transmission of a communication or the billing thereof'.[81] This would include services such as the downloading of ringtones for mobile phones or the provision of information services. User consent is required and must be given on the same basis as that needed in the Data Protection Directive, which demands a 'freely given, specific and informed indication of his wishes by which the data subject signifies his agreement to personal data relating to him being processed'.[82] The key requirement is that the subject be informed of the uses proposed. In this eventuality, it is acceptable for the processing to take place, unless the subject actively indicates objection (opting out). Consent can be withdrawn at any time.

Additionally, the Communications Data Privacy Directive makes provision for the handling of location data, defined as:

> any data processed in an electronic communications network, indicating the geographic position of the terminal equipment of a user of a publicly available electronic communications service.[83]

Beyond use for the purpose of network operation, location data may be processed only when it is rendered anonymous or, with user consent, for the provision of a value added service. Information must be provided to the user of the type of data which will be processed, the purposes for which it will be used, the duration of any further use, and whether this will involve a transfer to third parties.

Although this provision may seem at first glance to provide considerable assistance to users, it is likely that the information may be provided in a relatively lengthy and complex

---

[76] Directive 97/66/EC.
[77] The Annex to the Directive contained a list of the types of data which might be processed. This included data relating to the volume of calls but not the destination or duration of individual calls.
[78] Directive 97/66/EC.   [79] Directive 2002/58/EC, Art. 2(b).
[80] Art. 6(3) as amended by the Citizens' Rights Directive, Art. 2.
[81] Art. 6(3) as amended by the Citizens' Rights Directive, Art. 2.
[82] Art. 6(3) as amended by the Citizens' Rights Directive, Art. 2.
[83] Art. 6(3) as amended by the Citizens' Rights Directive, Art. 2.

list of standard conditions associated with provision of the overall communications service. Admittedly, prior to the implementation of the Communications Data Privacy Directive, one of the major mobile networks used a clause empowering them to:

> [c]ontact you or allow carefully selected third parties to contact you with information about products and services by post, telephone, mobile text message or email (subject to any pref-erences expressed by you).

Given that the processing of data will take place in real time and be associated with the movements and location of the user, the processing might be considered rather more sensi-tive than is the case where traffic data is used for marketing purposes. It is perhaps unfor-tunate that the requirement is not that the provider seek a positive indication of consent (opt in).

In addition to providing users with the right to opt out of such uses of their data, the Communications Data Privacy Directive requires that users must be given the possibility 'of temporarily refusing the processing of such data for each connection to the network or for each transmission of a communication'.[84] It is likely that this right could be exercised in a manner similar to that currently applying in relation to the use of systems of 'caller id', where prefixing a number with 141 will prevent details of the caller's number being made available to the recipient.

Data retention

Significant inroads on the level of protection conferred by the Communications Data Privacy Directive came with the inclusion at a late stage in the legislative process of the acceptance by the European Parliament of an amendment permitting Member States to 'adopt legislative measures providing for the retention of data for a limited period justified on the grounds laid down in this paragraph'.[85] The grounds referred to include the safe-guarding of 'national security, defence, public security, and the prevention, investigation, detection and prosecution of criminal offences or of unauthorised use of the electronic communication system'.

In the United Kingdom, the provisions of the Regulation of Investigatory Powers Act 2000 empower a senior police officer to require a communications provider to disclose any communications data in its possession where this is considered necessary in the interests of national security, the prevention or detection of crime, or a number of other situations.[86] The term 'communications data' is defined broadly to include traffic and location data, although as was stated by the Home Office:

> It is important to identify what communications data does include but equally important to be clear about what it does *not* include. The term communications data in the Act does not include the content of any communication.[87]

The procedures to be followed in requesting or requiring disclosure are laid down in a Code of Practice on the Acquisition and Disclosure of Communications Data, which was brought into force by the Regulation of Investigatory Powers (Acquisition and Disclosure of Communications Data: Code of Practice) Order 2007.[88]

The Regulation of Investigatory Powers Act 2000 did not require that providers retain data, although data protection concerns had been expressed that mobile phone operators

---

[84] Art. 6(3) as amended by the Citizens' Rights Directive, Art. 9(2).
[85] Art. 6(3) as amended by the Citizens' Rights Directive, Art. 15.   [86] s. 22.
[87] Consultation Paper on a Code of Practice for Voluntary Retention of Communications Data, March 2003.   [88] SI 2007/2197.

were retaining data for a period of months, and in some cases years. The conformity of this practice with the requirements of the Data Protection Act 1998, that 'Personal data processed for any purpose or purposes shall not be kept for longer than is necessary for that purpose or those purposes',[89] had been doubted. The passage of the Anti-Terrorism, Crime and Security Act 2001 provided a legal basis for the retention of data. The Act conferred power on the Secretary of State to draw up a code of practice, specifying periods of time during which communications providers would be required to retain communications data.[90] Although the Secretary of State is granted legislative power, it was envisaged that a voluntary code would be agreed between the government and the communications industry.

Initial proposals by the government for the establishment of a code of practice received heavy criticism, both in terms of the period of time within which data might be required to be retained and in terms of the range of government agencies which might be granted access to this data. An initial draft code was withdrawn in July 2002, and a further draft was published in September 2003[91] and entered into force on 5 December 2003, pursuant to the provisions of the Retention of Communications Data (Code of Practice) Order 2003.[92] The code provides authority for the retention of communications data in the interests of national security or the detection or prevention of crime for periods after the business case for retention might have expired up to a maximum period of twelve months.

Compliance with the 2003 code was voluntary. This situation changed upon the implementation of the European Directive 'on the retention of data generated or processed in connection with the provision of publicly available electronic communications services or of public communications networks'[93] (the Data Retention Directive). This Directive, which was introduced in the aftermath of the Madrid and London bombings in 2004 and 2005 respectively, amends the provisions of Directive 2002/58 concerned with privacy in electronic communications networks. Recital 9 to the Directive explains:

> Because retention of data has proved to be such a necessary and effective investigative tool for law enforcement in several Member States, and in particular concerning serious matters such as organised crime and terrorism, it is necessary to ensure that retained data are made available to law enforcement authorities for a certain period, subject to the conditions provided for in this Directive.

Article 5 of the Directive specifies a very wide range of items of communications data relating to the source and destination of telephone calls, emails, and Internet access.

The periods for which items of data are to be retained are to be specified by Member States within the range of six months to two years. The Directive was implemented in the United Kingdom by the Data Protection (EC Directive) Regulations 2007,[94] which entered into force on 1 October 2007. Initially these Regulations did not require retention of Internet data but The Data Retention (EC Directive) Regulations 2009 provided for this. Rather than the voluntary retention scheme applying under the Code, Regulation 5 requires that data must be retained relating to:

> (a) the telephone number from which the telephone call was made and the name and address of the subscriber and registered user of that telephone;

---

[89] Sch. 1, fifth data protection principle.   [90] s. 102.

[91] Available from <http://www.opsi.gov.uk/si/si2003/draft/5b.pdf>.   [92] SI 2003/3175.

[93] Directive 2006/24/EC, OJ 2006 No. L105/54.

[94] SI 2007/2199. These regulations were replaced by the Electronic Communications (EC Directive) Regulations 2009 S1 2009/859. The 2007 Regulations had applied only to the telephone sector but the 2009 Regulations extend the scope of the retention requirements to Internet and email traffic.

(b) the telephone number dialled and, in cases involving supplementary services such as call forwarding or call transfer, any telephone number to which the call is forwarded or transferred, and the name and address of the subscriber and registered user of such telephone;

(c) the date and time of the start and end of the call; and

(d) the telephone service used.

Additional information is required to be retained in respect of mobile calls:

(a) the International Mobile Subscriber Identity (IMSI) and the International Mobile Equipment Identity (IMEI) of the telephone from which a telephone call is made;

(b) the IMSI and the IMEI of the telephone dialled;

(c) in the case of pre-paid anonymous services, the date and time of the initial activation of the service and the cell ID from which the service was activated;

(d) the cell ID at the start of the communication; and

(e) data identifying the geographic location of cells by reference to their cell ID.

In respect of Internet and email communications, the key retention requirements relate to:

11.–(1) The user ID allocated.

(2) The user ID and telephone number allocated to the communication entering the public telephone network.

(3) The name and address of the subscriber or registered user to whom an IP address, user ID or telephone number was allocated at the time of the communication.

Data is also required to be retained relating to the destination of any communications and as to the date and time at which communications were made. In all cases the data must be retained for a period of twelve months.[95]

Data retention is not a cost-free activity. Capital and running costs have been estimated at around £46 million over an eight-year period.[96] Under the Regulations, the government is empowered rather than obliged to compensate providers for the costs involved.[97] It has been suggested that payments of £18.5 million have been made to date to cover a five-year period.[98]

Itemised billing

The issue of itemised billing is rather less contentious than that of data retention but does serve to illustrate some of the changes which have occurred in the communications sector over the past decade and also some potential conflicts between rights to privacy and to information.

The initial provision of the Communications Data Privacy Directive may appear somewhat strange. Subscribers, it is provided, 'will have the right to receive non-itemised bills'.[99] While few people may want to exercise the option, the rationale lies perhaps in the fact that it has become very much the norm for individuals to receive itemised bills and indeed the Universal Service Directive provides for the right of users to receive itemised bills.[100] In this situation, given that the Directive is seeking to provide for exceptions, the logical approach is to assume the provision of itemised bills and confer a right to refuse these.

---

[95] The Electronic Communications (EC Directive) Regulations 2009 S1 2009/859, Reg. 5.

[96] <http://webarchive.nationalarchives.gov.uk/20100418065544/http://www.homeoffice.gov.uk/documents/cons-2008-transposition-dir/index.html>.   [97] Reg. 11.

[98] <http://www.out-law.com/page-9350>.

[99] Directive 2002/58/EC, Art. 7.   [100] See para. 9–032.

While it is almost inevitably the case that the person responsible for a communications bill would be interested in information regarding the calls made, other persons may have different preferences. The Communications Data Privacy Directive uses two terms—'subscriber' and 'user'. The term 'subscriber' is not defined in the Directive,[101] although it appears that it must refer to the party who has contracted for the provision of services. Perhaps rather inconsistently, the Directive does provide a definition of the term 'user' as 'any natural person using a publicly available electronic communications service, for private or business purposes, without necessarily having subscribed to this service'.[102]

In a household, it will be common for one member to be classed as the subscriber but for other family members to use the equipment. While the subscriber may wish to be able to analyse what calls have been made, the latter may have an interest in maintaining the privacy of their communications. In many cases it may be accepted that the wishes and interests of the subscriber should prevail, but there may be instances, for example where calls have been made to counselling or support agencies, perhaps arising from the behaviour of the subscriber towards the user. The Communications Data Privacy Directive requires that national implementing measures should seek to reconcile the interests of the parties involved 'by ensuring that sufficient alternative privacy enhancing methods of communications or payments are available to such users and subscribers'.[103]

Even by the general standards of EU Directives, this formulation is opaque. In the United Kingdom, there are some 750,000 payphones and it might be argued that this provides sufficient access to telecommunications for users who do not want details of their calls made available to third-party subscribers. The Recitals to the Communications Data Privacy Directive also recommend that Member States:

> encourage the development of electronic communication service options such as alternative payment facilities which allow anonymous or strictly private access to publicly available electronic communications services, for example calling cards and facilities for payment by credit card.[104]

A further possibility canvassed is that itemised bills may delete 'a certain number of digits' from the lists of called numbers. This might well prove useful in the situation, for example, that calls are made to a medical or emotional support helpline. Again, however, it is difficult to see why such an option would be attractive to subscribers and in the event that only certain numbers were censored, the presence of these might in itself be a cause for suspicion. One reasonable option, however, would appear to be to ensure that calls made to Freephone numbers (0800) should not appear on bills. These are frequently provided by support agencies. Given that such calls do not involve any cost implications for the subscriber, the balance of interests may be seen as lying with potential users.

Directory information

When the 1997 Directive was adopted, virtually the only form of communications directories were telephone directories published by major telecommunications operators. In the past fifteen years, there has been a massive increase in the number of telephones in use due to the continuing growth in the mobile market. Tens of millions of individuals have also acquired email addresses as this form of electronic communication has expanded,

---

[101] The Telecoms Data Protection Directive (Directive 97/66/EC) did define the term as 'any natural or legal person who or which is party to a contract with the provider of publicly available telecommunications services for the supply of such services' (Art. 2).

[102] Directive 2002/58/EC, Art. 2.   [103] Directive 2002/58/EC, Art. 7(2).

[104] Directive 2002/58/EC, Recital 33.

to the extent that the volume of email communications dwarfs that carried by the postal networks. Beyond an increase in the range of materials which might be contained in communications directories there has been a similar growth in the level of sophistication of directory services. Increasingly provided in electronic form, directories may include facilities such as reverse searching. While a traditional directory can be searched only in the manner structured by the compiler, typically by alphabetical order, an electronic directory might, for example, allow a user to enter a telephone number and be presented with the name and physical and email address of the person to whom it has been allocated.

The Telecoms Data Protection Directive provided that the information contained in public directories should be limited to that necessary to identify particular customers, that there should be a right to require that details be withheld from the directory, and also that customers should be able to indicate:

> that his or her personal data may not be used for the purpose of direct marketing, to have his or her address omitted in part and not to have a reference revealing his or her sex, where this is applicable linguistically.[105]

The first element of this requirement was met through the establishment of the telephone preference service, which enabled customers to indicate their wish not to receive calls for marketing purposes.[106] Under the Telecommunications (Data Protection and Privacy) Regulations 1999,[107] it is provided that marketing-related communications must not be made to a telephone number which appears on a list maintained by the Director General of Telecommunications of subscribers who have indicated objection to this practice.[108] Breach of this requirement will constitute a contravention of the Data Protection Act 1998 and may entitle the subscriber to compensation for any damage caused. To date, it does not appear that any party has obtained compensation for burnt meals caused by unwarranted interruptions by telephone marketers. In 1999, the Director entered into a contract with the Telephone Preference Service for the compilation and maintenance of the list. Effect was given to the remaining requirements of the Directive by the Telecommunications (Data Protection and Privacy) Regulations 1999.[109] Over 1 million subscribers have now registered with the service.

The Communications Data Privacy Directive adopts a somewhat different approach. Subscribers are to be informed of the nature and purposes of the information which will be made available in a public directory or directory information service and 'of any further usage possibilities based on search functions embedded in electronic versions of the directory'. This information must be supplied prior to publication of the directory.[110] Having been informed of the purposes envisaged, subscribers are to have the right to require that their details be removed in whole or in part. No charge is to be made for this or for compliance with the subscriber's request that errors be corrected.

Especially with electronic directories, it is possible that third parties may seek to copy significant amounts of information and use these for their own purposes. The body of the Communications Data Privacy Directive makes no provision in this respect, although the Recitals indicate that:

> Where the data may be transmitted to one or more third parties, the subscriber should be informed of this possibility and of the recipient or the categories of possible recipients. Any transmission should be subject to the condition that the data may not be used for other purposes than those for which they were collected. If the party collecting the data from the subscriber or any third party to whom the data have been transmitted wishes to use the data

---

[105] Directive 97/66/EC, Art. 11.   [106] <http://www.tpsonline.org.uk/tpsr/html/default.asp>.
[107] SI 1999/2093.   [108] Reg. 9.   [109] SI 1999/2093.   [110] Directive 2002/58/EC, Art. 12.

for an additional purpose, the renewed consent of the subscriber is to be obtained either by the initial party collecting the data or by the third party to whom the data have been transmitted.[111]

Although not a direct legal requirement, the Telecommunications Directory Information Fair Processing Code, drawn up by the then Data Protection Registrar in 1998, is likely to be very relevant. This provides, inter alia, that controllers should take steps to prevent information being misused. Bulk copying might be inhibited by technical measures designed to limit the number of records which can be accessed and copied by a single search. It is also suggested that encryption techniques might be used and, perhaps now outdated, that there should be no online interface to directories. Encryption of data might also be used to prevent reverse searching.

Although not legally binding, a failure to comply with the Code may be regarded as constituting unfair processing under the Data Protection Act 1998 and result in the service of an enforcement notice by the Information Commissioner. Under the Telecommunications (Open Network Provision) (Voice Telephony) Regulations,[112] an undertaking required BT (effectively), when providing directory information to a third party, to obtain an undertaking that the recipient would comply with the Code. Any breach of the undertaking would render the third party's processing unfair. A similar effect is now provided by condition 22 of the General Conditions of Entitlement. This provides that every communications provider is obliged to supply details of its subscribers to any other provider upon reasonable request. This obligation is expressly stated to be 'subject to the requirements of relevant data protection legislation'.

Calling and connected line identification

Systems of calling line identification, often referred to as 'caller id', allow a user to identify the number from which a call originates prior to answering the call. A related system allows a user to discover details of the last call made to the telephone by dialling 1471. As with itemised billing, the systems offer major benefits to individuals, not least as a means of deterring the making of hoax or malicious calls, but there may also be reason why a party making a call may not wish details to be available to a called party. At a trivial level, a person may not wish their partner to be aware that rather than a call originating from their office where work demands are requiring a late departure, it is coming from a local pub. Again, following the break-up of a relationship, one party may wish to contact the other but not to allow the possibility of the call being returned or—especially in an era of reverse searchable directories—to allow their physical location to be discovered. Caller id is also used extensively for commercial purposes. Some companies use systems linked to a database of customers so that the caller's identity is known at the time the call is answered. Many taxi companies use such systems to simplify the task of dispatching vehicles and also to provide some check against the making of hoax calls. Less desirable, perhaps, is the situation where a company 'captures' phone numbers from persons calling to inquire about goods or services and uses these for subsequent marketing activities.[113] The situation may therefore arise where subscribers may wish to know who is calling them but, at least in certain situations, may not want their telephone number to be made available to the party they are calling.

---

[111] Directive 2002/58/EC, Recital 39.

[112] SI 1998/1580.

[113] Such processing may, of course, be considered unfair under the provisions of the Data Protection Act 1998.

As well as presenting the called party with information about the origin of a call, the same technology—referred to in this case as connected line information—allows the caller to see the actual number at which the call is answered. Although in the majority of cases this will be the number which was dialled, it may also be the case that calls are forwarded to another number. While in the vast majority of cases the practice will be unobjectionable, there may be situations where the called party is reluctant for this to happen. Out-of-hours calls to a doctor's surgery may be forwarded to the physician's home number, and there may be reluctance to allow patients to know this number.

In respect of caller id, the Communications Data Privacy Directive requires that subscribers and users be presented with a range of options. Users are to be offered the option, free of charge, of blocking the presentation of the number from which they are making a call. In the United Kingdom, this is normally accomplished by prefixing '141' to the telephone number called. Users should also be offered the option of blocking the display of information on a permanent basis, although a charge may be levied for this.[114]

While callers will be entitled to block presentation of their identity, the Communications Data Privacy Directive sets the scene for what might almost be regarded as a battle of the systems by providing that subscribers are to be offered the option to reject incoming calls where the caller has chosen to prevent display of his or her number.[115] One limitation of this approach is that identification details may be withheld either by the deliberate act of the caller or—as typically happens in a work environment—because outgoing calls will be routed through a central switchboard. Even though each instrument may have its own number which can be dialled directly by callers from outside the premises, the identification details will be stripped out in respect of outgoing calls.

In exceptional cases, it may be provided that attempts by callers to conceal details of the number from which a communication originates can be overridden. This may take place on a temporary basis in the event that a subscriber requests the assistance of the service provider in tracing the origin of malicious or nuisance calls and permanently in respect of lines used by the emergency services.[116]

Broadly similar provisions apply in respect of connected line identification. Here, subscribers must be offered the possibility 'using a simple means and free of charge of preventing the presentation of the connected line information'.[117]

Unsolicited communications

For many people, receipt of unsolicited commercial communications, whether by post, telephone, fax, or email, is a major cause of annoyance. BT estimated in 2005 that almost half of domestic phone users chose to remove their details from telephone directories. A high proportion, it is suggested, do so in order to minimise the numbers of unsolicited marketing calls.[118] Proposals in 2009[119] by a directory enquiry service, '118 800' to establish a directory of mobile numbers attracted significant objections and implementation of the facility was temporarily suspended. More than three years later, the service is still not available. As indicated, very considerable numbers of people have signed up to the telephone and fax preference service. Currently, much publicity is given to the use of the Internet for unsolicited or junk emails, generally referred to as spam; one respected source estimates

---

[114] Directive 2002/58/EC, Art. 8(1).
[115] Directive 2002/58/EC, Art. 8(2). BT currently charges £3.33 per month for use of this facility.
[116] Directive 2002/58/EC, Art. 10.
[117] Directive 2002/58/EC, Art. 8(4).
[118] Directory Information <http://www.oftel.gov.uk/publications/1995_98/consumer/dqchap.htm>.
[119] <http://news.bbc.co.uk/1/hi/programmes/working_lunch/8091621.stm>.

that 92 per cent of all Internet-based emails are spam.[120] According to a recent Harris poll, 80 per cent of Internet users claimed to be 'very annoyed' about spam with 74 per cent of those surveyed favouring a legal ban.[121]

A further tactic, which was the subject of an enforcement notice served by the Information Commissioner in the United Kingdom, concerns the use of automated calling systems. With these, numbers are dialled automatically and when the call is answered, a recorded message is played to the recipient. Beyond any nuisance value, these systems have been implicated in at least one fatality in Canada, where a fire broke out in a property just at the moment an automated call was received. Although the householder attempted to terminate the call so that the emergency services might be summoned, the message continued to be transmitted with the result that the user was unable to make an outgoing call. In the case of *Scottish National Party v Information Commissioner,*[122] the political party in question had made use of automated systems during the course of the 2005 general election campaign. It appears that it was not alone in making use of the technology but was perhaps less careful than others in consulting the registers of those who had opted out of receiving unsolicited marketing calls and the Commissioner served an enforcement notice requiring it to desist from what he considered to be processing in breach of the Privacy and Electronic Communications Regulations. On appeal to the Information Tribunal, the Scottish National Party argued principally that as a political party, its communications did not fall into the category of 'marketing'. The Tribunal disagreed and upheld the enforcement notice. Marketing, it was held, was concerned with seeking to influence the way people acted and the fact that in the present case there was no commercial motive was of no relevance. The Scottish National Party was seeking to persuade people to vote for it in preference to other political parties and this, it was held, was no different in principle from one manufacturer or retailer seeking to persuade consumers to deal with them rather than a competitor.

A similar 'opt-in' approach was adopted in respect of the use of fax machines for the purposes of unsolicited marketing. The rationale for treating fax transmissions more restrictively than voice communications was an economic one. While receipt of a telephone call does not have any cost implications for the subscriber, paper and ink will need to be used to print out the contents of a fax. This was undoubtedly a more significant consideration in 1990 when the Telecoms Data Protection Directive was initially drafted, as at that time fax machines had to use special and very expensive paper and, given the developments in technology, it is perhaps surprising that it should have continued.

Perhaps unsurprisingly, the original Telecoms Data Protection Directive[123] made no reference to email. Both with the growth in Internet usage and with the expansion in the scope of the legislation, inclusion of provisions concerning email has been a major and contentious feature of the new legislation. As originally introduced, the explanatory memorandum accompanying the draft Communications Data Privacy Directive indicated that:

> Four Member States already have bans on unsolicited commercial e-mail and another is about to adopt one. In most of the other Member States opt-out systems exist. From an internal market perspective, this is not satisfactory. Direct marketers in opt-in countries may not target e-mail addresses within their own country but they can still continue to send unsolicited commercial e-mail to countries with an opt-out system. Moreover, since e-mail

---

[120] <http://www.symantec.com/connect/blogs/spam-and-phishing-landscape-september-2010>.
[121] <http://news.zdnet.co.uk/story/0,t269-s2128193,00.html>.
[122] Case number EA/2005/0021. Available via <http://www.informationtribunal.gov.uk/Public/search.aspx>.
[123] Case number EA/2005/0021. Available via <http://www.informationtribunal.gov.uk/Public/search.aspx>.

addresses very often give no indication of the country of residence of the recipients, a system of divergent regimes within the internal market is unworkable in practice. A harmonised opt-in approach solves this problem.

Accordingly, a prohibition was proposed except in respect of individuals who had indicated the wish to receive commercial emails. This approach was highly controversial and in October 2001 the European Parliament voted in favour of an 'opt-out' system. In December 2001, however, the Council voted to reinstate the opt-in approach and the Communications Data Privacy Directive was finally adopted with this format, the Directive providing that the sending of 'electronic mail for the purposes of direct marketing may only be allowed in respect of subscribers who have given their prior consent'.[124]

Although the term 'prior consent' might appear compatible with the use of an opt-out approach where failure on the part of a user to indicate a preference would equate to consent, the Recitals make reference to the need to ensure that the 'prior explicit consent of the recipients is obtained before such communications are addressed to them'.[125] Use of the adjective 'explicit' clearly imposes a heavier burden upon persons wishing to send emails.

The Communications Data Privacy Directive provides for one situation where commercial emails can be sent without prior consent. This applies where there has been a previous commercial relationship between the parties and:

> a natural or legal person obtains from its customers their electronic contact details for electronic mail, in the context of the sale of a product or a service—the same natural or legal person may use these electronic contact details for direct marketing of its own similar products or services provided that customers clearly and distinctly are given the opportunity to object, free of charge and in an easy manner, to such use of electronic contact details when they are collected and on the occasion of each message in case the customer has not initially refused such use.[126]

Use of a hypertext link in the emails allowing recipients to 'click here to unsubscribe from mailings' would suffice to meet with this requirement.

Even where consent has been given to the transmission of commercial emails or where the email is sent to a previous customer, the Directive imposes a final requirement that commercial emails should be clearly identifiable as such and that they should always use a valid return address.[127] In many cases, it may be obvious from the heading of the email that its subject is commercial. A trawl through the author's mailbox reveals subjects such as:

> Need a NEW Computer? No Credit—No Problem
>
> Earn $75/hr with Your Own Home Based Business Processing
>
> Sample the weight loss patch—on us!

Nothing more need be done in these situations. Other spammers, perhaps aware that messages with obviously commercial headings may be deleted unread, make use of headings such as:

> Please get back to me
>
> Re your enquiry
>
> Hello

---

[124] Directive 2002/58/EC, Art. 13(1).   [125] Directive 2002/58/EC, Recital 40.
[126] Directive 2002/58/EC, Art. 13(2).
[127] Directive 2002/58/EC, Art. 13(4). Many spammers attempt to conceal the genuine address from which the message is sent to avoid possible action by the ISP involved, which may well have an anti-spam condition in its contract of supply.

Headers such as this are now unlawful under the Communications Data Privacy Directive.

While well-meaning, it is uncertain how effective the Directive's approach will be. A very considerable percentage of commercial email originates from the United States or from other countries outside the EU. Unless and until these legal systems adopt a similar approach, there will be little that can practically be done to bring proceedings against spammers. Even within the EU, given the ease with which persons can set up email accounts, the task of tracking down offenders will be a difficult one.

Conclusions

Those using communications services justifiably have an expectation that the privacy of their communications will be respected. There are, of course, significant issues concerned with the intrinsic security of certain forms of communication. Transmitting an email has been seen as analogous, for example, with using a postcard to send a communication by post. Although the Communications Data Privacy Directive[128] is relevant in respect of these issues, perhaps its most important role relates to the use of traffic data generated as a consequence of the use of networks. Although subject to the inevitable exceptions in the interests of national security and law enforcement, these will provide a reasonable degree of protection.

Undoubtedly, the most publicised provisions in the Communications Data Privacy Directive[129] are those dealing with the processing of junk mail and other forms of unsolicited commercial communications. While likely to be welcomed by the majority of users, it may be questioned as to how effective the prohibition against unsolicited email communications is likely to be. Although estimates as to the costs incurred by industry in dealing with email spam are legion,[130] it is doubtful whether these stand serious comparison with losses due to improper or wasteful use of other resources, such as telephones, stationery, or even heating and lighting. It is difficult to justify the adoption of an opt-in approach for this specific sector while other forms of unsolicited communication using media such as the mail or telephone can continue to operate on an opt-out basis.

---

[128] Directive 2002/58/EC.   [129] Directive 2002/58/EC.

[130] One estimate puts the global cost at $9 billion per year: see <http://news.bbc.co.uk/1/hi/technology/2983157.stm>.

8

Transborder data flows

INTRODUCTION

For centuries governments have sought to control channels of communication both internally and also, perhaps more extensively, in respect of transfers to and from other countries. Historically, arrangements for the transfer of messages between states relied upon bilateral treaties and the very real possibility of inspecting messages at the point that they crossed national borders. The emergence of the electric telegraph, well described as the 'Victorian Internet',[1] brought massive changes. For the first time, a communications network was being created which could transmit messages almost instantaneously and almost irrespective of distance.

Direct international transfers using the telegraph required interconnection between national telegraph networks, something which many governments were initially reluctant to permit. National security concerns are not a twenty-first century phenomenon and the 1850s and 1860s, when telegraph technology was developing at speed, was a period of considerable political and social upheaval across the continent of Europe.

After a number of failed initiatives the International Telegraph Union (ITU) (now the International Telecommunications Union) was established in 1865. It is testimony to the international nature of electronic communications that the ITU is classed as the world's first international governmental organisation, with its establishment preceding by a decade the Universal Postal Union which plays a similar harmonising role in respect of postal traffic. The ITU provided a set of rules relating to the international transfer of telegraph messages and required that governments allowed free passage to messages which complied with those rules.

In keeping with history's tendency to repeat itself, as the computer developed and became linked to communication networks, concerns at the implications of transborder data flows have evolved, paralleling the development of national data protection statutes. Typically, the fear is expressed that an absence of control may result in the evasion of national controls. As has been stated:

> [P]rotective provisions will be undermined if there are no restrictions on the removal of data to other jurisdictions for processing or storage. Just as money tends to gravitate towards tax havens, so sensitive personal data will be transferred to countries with the most lax, or no data protection standards. There is thus a possibility that some jurisdictions will become 'data havens' or 'data sanctuaries' for the processing or 'data vaults' for the storage of sensitive information.[2]

---

[1] See the book of that name by Tom Standage (London, 1998).

[2] C. Millard, *Legal Protection of Computer Programs and Data* (London, 1985), p. 211. It has been suggested (see <http://www.telegraph.co.uk/technology/2016/07/16/britain-could-become-data-haven-after-brexit-technology-group-sa/>) that the United Kingdom could become a data haven following departure from the European Union. Whether this would be a desirable or, indeed, effective approach is perhaps debatable.

Controls over transborder data flows have been a feature of almost all national data protection statutes, with restrictions being justified on the basis of safeguarding the position of individuals. In the pioneering Swedish Data Act of 1973, it was provided that personal data might be transferred abroad only with the prior consent of the Swedish Data Inspection Board. Section 11 of the law provided that:

> If there is reason to assume that personal data will be used for automatic data processing abroad, the data may be disclosed only after permission from the Data Inspection Board. Such permission may be given only if it may be assumed that the disclosure of the data will not involve undue encroachment upon personal privacy.

As concern at the impact of national controls over telegraphic and then voice traffic led to the establishment of the ITU, so international initiatives have sought to establish what are effectively free-trade zones in respect of personal data. In 1980, the Organisation for Economic Co-operation and Development (OECD) adopted 'Guidelines on the Protection of Privacy and Transborder Flows of Personal Data'. These Guidelines were supplemented by a Declaration on Transborder Data Flows, adopted in 1995, which declared its signatories' intention to 'avoid the creation of unjustified barriers to the international exchange of data and information'. As discussed, the Council of Europe Convention on the Automated Processing of Personal Data was the first legally binding international instrument. The Convention states that:

> A Party shall not, for the sole purpose of the protection of privacy, prohibit or subject to special authorisation transborder flows of personal data going to the territory of another Party.[3]

As in other areas of the topic, there is inevitable tension between competing interests: the desirability of encouraging free communications and the desire to ensure that data protection laws are not circumvented.

Regulating transborder data flows

The Council of Europe Convention was shaped by the experiences and practices of the Western European states which have adopted data protection legislation in the late 1970s and early 1980s. Such legislation has three major features: first, it applies to all sectors of automated data processing; secondly, it contains substantive provisions regulating the forms of processing which can take place and the rights and remedies available to individuals; and, finally, it provides for the establishment of some form of supervisory agency. As indicated earlier, a different approach has prevailed in other countries, notably the United States.

Initially, the discrepancies in approach between Europe and the rest of the world were of limited practical significance. The Council of Europe Convention, as originally adopted,[4] makes no explicit reference to the imposition of controls over data to non-signatory states. Although some states such as Sweden required some form of prior approval, others, such as the United Kingdom, provided only that the supervisory agency might block a transfer if it was satisfied that this was likely to result in a contravention of the data protection principles. In the decade and a half that the 1984 legislation was in force, this power was

---

[3] Art. 12(2).
[4] An additional protocol was adopted in 2001 and entered into force in 2004 effectively restating the provisions of the European Data Protection Directive with regard to controls over transborder data flows.

invoked only once.[5] The Data Protection Directive adopts a different and significantly more rigorous approach. Although recognising that:

cross-border flows of personal data are necessary to the expansion of international trade; whereas the protection of individuals guaranteed in the Community by this Directive does not stand in the way of transfers of personal data to third countries which ensure an adequate level of protection; whereas the adequacy of the level of protection afforded by a third country must be assessed in the light of all the circumstances surrounding the transfer operation or set of transfer operations.

Article 25 of the Directive lays down as a basic principle the requirement that:

The Member States shall provide that the transfer to a third country of personal data which are undergoing processing or are intended for processing after transfer may take place only if, without prejudice to compliance with the national provisions adopted pursuant to the other provisions of this Directive, the third country in question ensures an adequate level of protection.

Effect is given to this provision by the Data Protection Act 1998's eighth data protection principle which provides that:

Personal data shall not be transferred to a country or territory outside the European Economic Area unless that country or territory ensures an adequate level of protection for the rights and freedoms of data subjects in relation to the processing of personal data.

By including the matter in the principles, it follows that any breach, or anticipated breach, can be responded to by service of an enforcement notice prohibiting the transfer. The need, therefore, for an additional transfer prohibition notice disappeared. Controllers intending to transfer personal data outside the EEA are required to indicate this fact in their notification. If transfer to ten or fewer countries is envisaged the names of these countries must be notified; where more extensive transfers are planned notification should be given that transfers may take place on a 'worldwide' basis.[6]

Procedures for determining adequacy

The uniform application of the Data Protection Directive would clearly be threatened if the decision on whether third countries offered an adequate level of protection was to be made by each Member State. It is provided, therefore, that the Member States and the Commission are to inform each other of any cases where they feel that a third country does not provide an adequate level of protection.[7] In practice, general decisions regarding formal findings of adequacy will be made at a Community level with a key role being played by the Article 29 Working Party. Article 29 of the Directive provides specifically that the Working Party is to give the Commission an opinion on the level of protection in the Community and in third countries.

---

[5] A transfer prohibition notice was served in 1990, requiring the cessation of the transfer of personal data in the form of names and addresses to a variety of US organisations bearing such titles as the 'Astrology Society of America', 'Lourdes Water Cross Incorporated', and 'Win With Palmer Incorporated'. These companies, which had been involved in the promotion of horoscopes, religious trinkets, and other products in the United Kingdom, were the subject of investigations by the US postal authorities, alleging wire fraud and a variety of other unsavoury trading practices.

[6] Notification Handbook, available from <http://www.ico.gov.uk/upload/documents/library/data_protection/detailed_specialist_guides/notification_handbook_final.pdf>.

[7] Art. 25(3).

The Directive provides further that should the Working Party determine that a third country does not provide an adequate level of protection, a report is to be made to a committee established under its Article 31.[8] Consisting of representatives of the Member States and chaired by the Commission, the Committee will consider a proposal from the Commission for action on the basis of the Working Party's findings and deliver an opinion. The Commission may then adopt legal measures. If these are in accord with the Committee's opinion, the measures will take immediate effect. If there is any variation, application will be deferred for three months, within which time the Council of Ministers may adopt a different decision. Member States are obliged to take any measures necessary to prevent data transfers to the country involved.[9]

To date, no country has been specifically identified as failing to provide an adequate level of protection. Given the reference in the Directive to the role of 'sectoral rules', 'professional rules and security measures', it is perhaps unlikely that there will ever be 'black listings' affecting all data processing activities in a particular jurisdiction. More significantly, the Directive also provides for the procedures described above to be used to identify countries which do provide an adequate level of protection[10] and there has been extensive activity in this respect.

Defining adequacy

Although, as will be discussed later, a range of exemptions are provided, determination as to whether a third country provides an adequate level of protection is a key issue and effectively opens the way for data transfers to and from that country. Given different approaches globally to issues of data or privacy protection, it is obviously essential to establish a mechanism through which decisions as to adequacy can be made. A first attempt to define criteria was made in the Article 29 Working Party's Working Paper 4, 'First Orientations on Transfers of Personal Data to Third Countries—Possible Ways Forward in Assessing Adequacy', published in 1987.[11] The ideas raised in this document were presented in an expanded form in Working Paper 12, 'Transfers of Personal Data to Third Countries: Applying Articles 25 and 26 of the EU Data Protection Directive', which was published in July 1998,[12] and remains the most significant document in the field. In terms of the general approach, it is suggested that:

> Using directive 95/46/EC as a starting point, and bearing in mind the provisions of other international data protection texts, it should be possible to arrive at a 'core' of data protection 'content' principles and 'procedural/enforcement' requirements, compliance with which could be seen as a minimum requirement for protection to be considered adequate.

In terms of substantive legal requirements, the Working Party identifies five core principles which reflect very closely the provisions of the Data Protection Directive:

1) the purpose limitation principle—data should be processed for a specific purpose and subsequently used or further communicated only insofar as this is not incompatible with the purpose of the transfer . . .

2) the data quality and proportionality principle—data should be accurate and, where necessary, kept up to date. The data should be adequate, relevant and not excessive in relation to the purposes for which they are transferred or further processed.

3) the transparency principle—individuals should be provided with information as to the purpose of the processing and the identity of the data controller in the third country, and other information insofar as this is necessary to ensure fairness . . .

---

[8] Directive 95/46/EC.   [9] Art. 25(4).   [10] Art. 25(6).
[11] Available from <http://ec.europa.eu/justice_home/fsj/privacy/docs/wpdocs/1997/wp4_en.pdf>.
[12] Available from <http://ec.europa.eu/justice_home/fsj/privacy/docs/wpdocs/1998/wp12_en.pdf>.

4) the security principle—technical and organisational security measures should be taken by the data controller that are appropriate to the risks presented by the processing. Any person acting under the authority of the data controller, including a processor, must not process data except on instructions from the controller.

5) the rights of access, rectification, and opposition—the data subject should have a right to obtain a copy of all data relating to him/her that are processed, and a right to rectification of those data where they are shown to be inaccurate. In certain situations he/she should also be able to object to the processing of the data relating to him/her . . .

6) restrictions on onward transfers—further transfers of the personal data by the recipient of the original data transfer should be permitted only where the second recipient (i.e. the recipient of the onward transfer) is also subject to rules affording an adequate level of protection.[13]

In terms of procedural requirements, the key requirements are that the agencies established in the third country should be in a position:

1) To deliver a good level of compliance with the rules.

2) To provide support and help to individual data subjects in the exercise of their rights.

3) To provide appropriate redress to the injured party where rules are not complied with.[14]

Activity in determining adequacy

To date, the Article 29 Working Party has published opinions indicating that an adequate level of protection is provided under the regimes operating in Andorra, Argentina, Canada, the Faeroe Islands, Guernsey, the Isle of Man, Israel, Jersey, New Zealand, Switzerland, and Eastern Uruguay. The Hungarian regime was also accepted as being adequate, although Hungary's subsequent membership of the European Union has made this finding otiose as the adequacy procedures apply only to transfers to or from non-Member States. A further opinion indicated that the regime in Australia did not provide a sufficient level of protection to justify a finding of adequacy. Commission decisions[15] subsequently gave legal effect to the Working Party's positive findings in respect of all these countries.

Issues of adequacy were considered by the Court of Justice of the European Union in the case of *Maximillian Schrems v Data Protection Commissioner*.[16,17] The case was primarily concerned with a complaint regarding the adequacy of the, so called, 'Safe Harbor' agreement entered into between the EU and the United States. These aspects will be considered in more detail below. There are also some interesting rulings regarding the meaning of the term 'adequate'. It ruled that:

The word 'adequate' in Article 25(6) of Directive 95/46 admittedly signifies that a third country cannot be required to ensure a level of protection identical to that guaranteed in the EU legal order. However, as the Advocate General has observed in point 141 of his Opinion, the term 'adequate level of protection' must be understood as requiring the third country in

---

[13] p. 5.   [14] p. 7.
[15] <http://ec.europa.eu/justice/data-protection/document/international-transfers/adequacy/index_en.htm>.
[16] Case 362/14.
[17] For an update on the case before the Irish courts see <https://www.dataprotection.ie/docs/28-9-2016-Explanatory-memo-on-litigation-involving-Facebook-and-Maximilian-Schrems/1598.htm>

fact to ensure, by reason of its domestic law or its international commitments, a level of protection of fundamental rights and freedoms that is essentially equivalent to that guaranteed within the European Union by virtue of Directive 95/46.[18]

Essentially adequacy is defined in terms of equivalence and a major factor identified by the court related to the existence of an effective supervisory agency.

It is clear from the above listing that only a small proportion of the world's near 200 states are included in the list. A majority of the countries receiving a finding of adequacy have close legal and political links with Member States and the data protection laws in Guernsey, Jersey, and the Isle of Man are effectively identical in scope to the United Kingdom's Data Protection Act 1998. In other cases, decisions and recommendations have been more finely balanced. Initially, it appeared that the Article 29 Working Party adopted a strict approach, effectively equating adequacy with equivalence. It does not appear that many dictionaries would support such a definition and more recent findings have been more tolerant of differences in approach. In respect of the law in Jersey, for example, the Working Party concluded:

> While there may be some doubt that Jersey Law would fully meet the requirements imposed upon the Member States by the Data Protection Directive, the Working Party recalls, though, that adequacy does not mean complete equivalence with the level of protection set by the Directive. Some concerns exist in the areas of definitions of personal data and other concepts; transparency; and powers of the Commissioner but, after taking into account the explanations and assurances given by the Jersey Authorities the Working Party does not consider that these are significant in relation to the protection provided for personal data transferred from EU member states to Jersey.[19]

Warning signals for the United Kingdom might be identified in this somewhat lukewarm acceptance. In its most recent report, concerning the adequacy of the law in Uruguay, the Working Party, after describing in some details relevant legal and procedural safeguards, contents itself with a simple statement that it considers the Uruguay provisions to be adequate.

Given its mistrust of the value of supervisory agencies, it is unlikely that the US law would ever be considered to provide an adequate level of protection. Clearly, however, data transfers between Europe and the United States are of massive economic significance and it was recognised from the early days of the Directive that mechanisms would have to be established to facilitate lawful data transfers across the Atlantic. The so-called 'Safe Harbor' agreement represents one significant step in this direction.

The 'Safe Harbor' agreement and the Privacy Shield

Reference has been made previously to differences in approach between the United States and the EU concerning the mechanisms best suited to protect individual privacy. The difference in terminology between data and privacy protection illustrates some of the key issues. Following the adoption of the Data Protection Directive, discussions took place between the Commission and the US Department of Commerce with a view to devising mechanisms to avoid the prospect of a transatlantic data war. The result was agreement on a set of conditions, generally referred to as the 'Safe Harbor' principles, observance of which by US-based companies would be accepted by the Commission as ensuring conformity with European data protection requirements.

Safe Harbor was contentious from its inception. Throughout the negotiations between the Commission and the Department of Commerce, the Article 29 Working Party issued

---

[18] para. 75.   [19] p. 11.

a number of documents concerned with the proposed agreement.[20] These demonstrated a significantly greater degree of scepticism concerning the effectiveness of enforcement mechanisms than was exhibited by the Commission. In Opinion 7/99, published in December 1999, the Working Party indicated the view that the then proposals did not constitute a satisfactory basis for action. Referring to previous reports, it stated that:

> The Working Party notes that some progress has been made but deplores that most of the comments made in its previous position papers do not seem to be addressed in the latest version of the US documents. The Working Party therefore confirms its general concerns.

In spite of the Working Party's concerns, the Safe Harbor provisions were approved by a Commission Decision [21]

The Safe Harbor principles basically encapsulate the contents of the Data Protection Directive's[22] principles relating to data quality. They require that notice must be given of the fact that data is held and the purposes for which it will be processed, and relevant 'opt-out' opportunities must be given where it is intended that data will be used or disclosed for purposes other than envisaged or notified at the time of collection. Requirements relating to data security and integrity must also be accepted, as must the principle of subject access.[23] Supplementing the principles are a set of fifteen Frequently Asked Questions (FAQs), which provide detailed guidance on the interpretation of a range of issues, such as the scope of the concept of sensitive data and the manner in which subject access should be provided.

The principles are very much compatible with the contents of the OECD Guidelines. Given the extensive involvement of the United States in the work of this organisation, it is not surprising that discussions with the EU on the principles themselves did not prove particularly contentious. Most of the difficulty centred on the issue of enforcement. As has been discussed, the United States has tended to reject the concept of specialised supervisory agencies, which is integral to the European data protection model. In respect of enforcement, the Directive states that:

> Effective privacy protection must include mechanisms for assuring compliance with the principles, recourse for individuals to whom the data relate affected by non-compliance with the principles, and consequences for the organization when the principles are not followed. At a minimum, such mechanisms must include (a) readily available and affordable independent recourse mechanisms by which each individual's complaints and disputes are investigated and resolved by reference to the principles and damages awarded where the applicable law or private sector initiatives so provide; (b) follow up procedures for verifying that the attestations and assertions businesses make about their privacy practices are true and that privacy practices have been implemented as presented; and (c) obligations to remedy problems arising out of failure to comply with the principles by organizations announcing their adherence to them and consequences for such organizations. Sanctions must be sufficiently rigorous to ensure compliance by organizations.

The Safe Harbor FAQs indicate that points (a) and (c) in this paragraph may be satisfied by the organisation indicating a willingness to cooperate with European Data Protection Authorities. Under the terms of FAQ 5, a Data Protection Panel was established as an 'informal grouping' of seven European data protection authorities (including the United Kingdom's Information Commissioner),[24] which would provide advice to US organisations

---

[20] See Documents WP15, WP19, WP21, and WP23.
[21] Decision 2000/520/EC OJ 2000 L 215/7.   [22] Directive 95/46/EC.
[23] Copies of the Safe Harbor documents, together with much useful background material can be found on the US Department of Commerce website at <http://www.export.gov/safeharbor/>.
[24] <http://circa.europa.eu/Public/irc/secureida/safeharbor/home>.

('harborites') concerning the operation of the scheme and investigate and seek to resolve disputes between European data subjects and such organisations.

In accordance with the establishing Commission decision,[25] the operation of the Safe Harbor arrangements were to be closely monitored by the Commission. A first report was published in 2002 and a second in 2004. Both reports identified similar strengths and weaknesses in the functioning of the system. The 2002 report commented that:

> Compared with the situation before it was available, the framework is providing a simplifying effect for those exporting personal data to organisations in the Safe Harbour and reduces uncertainty for US organisations interested in importing data from the EU by identifying a standard that corresponds to the adequate protection required by the [Data Protection] Directive.[26]

Concerns were expressed in both reports, supported by a research report produced under contract to the Commission, that a number of organisations which had signed up to the principles did not have or did not publish privacy policies in conformity with its requirements. Concern was also expressed at the lack of enforcement action by the Federal Trade Commission (FTC) and also at the fact that not a single case had been referred to the European Union's Data Protection Panel. It was also noted that around 30 per cent of harborites were engaging in the transfer of human resource data concerning employees and that this form of processing was outside the remit of the FTC. It was also noted that, although the FTC claimed that the breach of undertakings regarding privacy policies would be actionable, this had not been affirmed by the courts.

Take up of Safe Harbor was limited, with only around 3,000 US companies signing up to its terms. Comparison cannot be exact as many small and medium-sized companies will not look to make international transfers but reference might be made to the fact that the United Kingdom has around 400,000 notifications (and France 700,000) although a number of major companies such as Microsoft, Intel, Hewlett-Packard, and Procter & Gamble joined Safe Harbor.

As matters transpired, Safe Harbor was perhaps to prove to have been an inappropriate term. Reference was made above to the case of *Schrems v Data Protection Commissioner*.[27] The key element of the case was the claim that the Safe Harbor agreement was unlawful because it did not ensure compliance with the adequacy requirements of Directive 95/46. The case was initiated before the Irish courts and referred to the European Court for a preliminary ruling. The basis for the action was a complaint the Facebook transferred information relating to EU citizens to servers sited in the United States and that this did not guarantee an adequate level of protection for the data. Facebook had signed up to the Safe Harbor agreement.[28] Although not directly related to the case, it does seem that the Snowden revelations regarding the extent of surveillance conducted by US espionage agencies was a major factor behind the ruling. The Court's finding was clear although perhaps also avoiding discussion of some of the key issues. It ruled:

> However, the Commission did not state, in Decision 2000/520, that the United States in fact 'ensures' an adequate level of protection by reason of its domestic law or its international commitments.
>
> Consequently, without there being any need to examine the content of the safe harbour principles, it is to be concluded that Article 1 of Decision 2000/520 fails to comply with the

---

[25] 520/2000/EC of 26 July 2000.   [26] Directive 95/46/EC.

[27] Case 362/14.

[28] <https://safeharbor.export.gov/list.aspx>.

requirements laid down in Article 25(6) of Directive 95/46, read in the light of the Charter, and that it is accordingly invalid.[29]

As discussed throughout this chapter there are alternative justifications available for transborder data flows. A comment from Facebook noted that:

> This case is not about Facebook. The Advocate General himself said that Facebook has done nothing wrong.
>
> What is at issue is one of the mechanisms that European law provides to enable essential transatlantic data flows.
>
> Facebook, like many thousands of European companies, relies on a number of the methods prescribed by EU law to legally transfer data to the US from Europe, aside from Safe Harbor.
>
> It is imperative that EU and US governments ensure that they continue to provide reliable methods for lawful data transfers and resolve any issues relating to national security.[30]

It is not inappropriate to describe the Court's ruling as having a seismic effect, albeit perhaps more at the political than the legal level. As indicated above, take up of Safe Harbor had been limited and companies such as Facebook were well able to seek alternative solutions. Some of these will be discussed below. The notion of a trans-Atlantic data war made for far better headlines and, perhaps fortunately, it has also been the case that there has been a rapprochement between Europe and the United States concerning many of the issues involved. Following further negotiations, a new transborder framework—the Privacy Shield—was agreed between the authorities in July 2016.[31] It remains unclear how effective this agreement will be. As described in a Press Release published by the European Commission:

> The EU–U.S. Privacy Shield is based on the following principles:
>
> - **Strong obligations on companies handling data:** under the new arrangement, the U.S. Department of Commerce will conduct **regular updates and reviews** of participating companies, to ensure that companies follow the rules they submitted themselves to. If companies do not comply in practice they face sanctions and removal from the list. The tightening of conditions for the **onward transfers** of data to third parties will guarantee the same level of protection in case of a transfer from a Privacy Shield company.
>
> - **Clear safeguards and transparency obligations on U.S. government access:** The **U.S. has given the EU assurance** that the access of public authorities for law enforcement and national security is subject to clear limitations, safeguards and oversight mechanisms. Everyone in the EU will, also for the first time, benefit from **redress mechanisms** in this area. The U.S. has ruled out indiscriminate mass surveillance on personal data transferred to the U.S. under the EU–U.S. Privacy Shield arrangement. The Office of the Director of National Intelligence further clarified that bulk collection of data could only be used under specific preconditions and needs to be as targeted and focused as possible. It details the safeguards in place for the use of data under such exceptional circumstances. The U.S. Secretary of State has established a **redress possibility** in the area of national intelligence for Europeans through an **Ombudsperson mechanism** within the Department of State.
>
> - **Effective protection of individual rights:** Any citizen who considers that their data has been misused under the Privacy Shield scheme will benefit from several accessible and affordable dispute resolution mechanisms. Ideally, the complaint

---

[29] At paras. 97–8.

[30] <http://uk.businessinsider.com/facebook-safe-harbor-response-ecj-max-schrems-2015–10>.

[31] Formal endorsement of the agreement can be found in the Commission Decision C (2016) 4176 final.

will be resolved **by the company** itself; or **free of charge Alternative Dispute resolution** (ADR) solutions will be offered. Individuals **can also go to their national Data Protection Authorities, who will work with the Federal Trade Commission to ensure that complaints by EU citizens are investigated and resolved**. If a case is not resolved by any of the other means, as a last resort there will be an **arbitration** mechanism. Redress possibility in the area of national security for EU citizens will be handled by an **Ombudsperson** independent from the U.S. intelligence services.

- **Annual joint review mechanism:** the mechanism will monitor the functioning of the Privacy Shield, including the commitments and assurance as regards access to data for law enforcement and national security purposes. The European Commission and the U.S. Department of Commerce will conduct the review and associate national intelligence experts from the U.S. and European Data Protection Authorities. The Commission will draw on all other sources of information available and will issue a public report to the European Parliament and the Council.[32]

On the basis of past precedent, there can be no guarantee that the new agreement will survive a challenge before the Court of Justice of the European Union. A change of presidential regime in the United States may also impact on it.

Consequences of a finding of adequacy

In the event a finding of adequacy is made, the Member States must allow transfers to the third country concerned.[33] The laws of a number of Member States continues to require, however, that prior permission must be sought from the data protection authorities, an approach which has been criticised by the Commission on the grounds of inconsistency

> with Chapter IV of the Directive, which aims at guaranteeing both adequate protection and flows of personal data to third countries without unnecessary burdens. Notifications to national supervisory authorities may be required under Article 19, but notifications cannot be turned into de facto authorisations in those cases where the transfer to a third country is clearly permitted either in all cases or in the situation where the law of recipient country does not guarantee an adequate level of protection.[34]

Of the thirty states which are members of the European Economic Area, fifteen—Austria, Bulgaria, Cyprus, Estonia, France, Greece, Iceland, Latvia, Lichtenstein, Lithuania, Malta, the Netherlands, Romania, Slovenia, and Spain—require some degree of prior notification.[35] The controls vary significantly in extent. In some States such as Austria, it is provided that prior permission must be sought from the data protection authorities for all data flows outwith the EEA.[36] In other countries, there may be a requirement to notify the supervisory authority, whilst in others, such as the United Kingdom, there are no procedural requirements to notify the Information Commissioner.

---

[32] <http://europa.eu/rapid/press-release_IP-16-2461_en.htm>.

[33] Art. 25(6).

[34] As defined by the Commission of the European Communities and discussed more extensively later.

[35] Commission Staff Working Document SEC (2006) 95. Available from <http://ec.europa.eu/justice/policies/privacy/docs/modelcontracts/sec_2006_95_en.pdf>.

[36] s. 13 of the Federal Act Concerning the Processing of Personal Data.

The discrepancy between national approaches has been the cause of criticism of national laws by the European Commission, which has argued that this results in 'an inability to audit compliance with the principles relating to transborder data flows':[37]

> An overly lax attitude in some Member States—in addition to being in contravention of the Directive—risks weakening protection in the EU as a whole, because with the free movement guaranteed by the Directive, data flows are likely to switch to the 'least burdensome' point of export. An overly strict approach, on the other hand, would fail to respect the legitimate needs of international trade and the reality of global telecommunications networks and risks creating a gap between law and practice which is damaging for the credibility of the Directive and for Community law in general.

It has been commented further that:

> it would appear that pending such a formal determination, individual controllers can make this assessment for themselves, and can therefore decide to transfer data to third countries with regard to which there is no formal domestic or European finding of adequacy, if they have come to the conclusion that the country in question ensures an adequate level of protection.[38]

This certainly appears to be an accurate portrait of the system operating in the United Kingdom.

The SWIFT case

The activities of financial services companies (and transportation companies) are excluded from the remit of the FTC. A very major issue arose between Europe and the United States in the course of 2006, involving the activity of the Society for Worldwide Interbank Financial Telecommunications (SWIFT). SWIFT is a Belgian-based cooperative which processes financial messages for nearly 8,000 financial institutions around the world. SWIFT processes around 2.5 billion messages every year, some two-thirds of which are related to transactions involving parties located in Europe. It has two operating centres, one in Europe and one in the United States, which act as mirror sites for each other. Copies of all messages are retained for 124 days.

Around June 2006, media reports indicated that SWIFT had been providing substantial amounts of data to US authorities for terrorism investigation purposes since 2001. This data was supplied under the terms of sixty-four administrative subpoenas served on SWIFT in the intervening years in connection with the Treasury's Terrorist Financing Tracking Program (TFTP). When the fact of the transfers came to light, great concerns were expressed within the EU institutions and the Article 29 Working Party launched an immediate investigation. The Working Party's report was published in November 2006,[39] and concluded that the transfers had placed SWIFT and the financial institutions making up its membership in major and continuing breach of its obligations under the Data Protection Directive and the Belgian data protection law to which its operations were subject. As was stated:

> the hidden, systematic, massive and long-term transfer of personal data by SWIFT to the UST in a confidential, non-transparent and systematic manner for years without effective

---

[37] Commission Staff Working Document SEC (2006) 95. Available from <http://ec.europa.eu/justice/policies/privacy/docs/modelcontracts/sec_2006_95_en.pdf>.

[38] Analysis and impact study on the implementation of Directive EC 95/46 in Member States, available from <http://ec.europa.eu/justice_home/fsj/privacy/docs/lawreport/consultation/technical-annex_en.pdf>.

[39] Opinion 10/2006 'On the Processing of Personal Data by the Society for Worldwide Interbank Financial Telecommunication (SWIFT)', available from <http://ec.europa.eu/justice_home/fsj/privacy/docs/wpdocs/2006/wp128_en.pdf>.

legal grounds and without the possibility of independent control by public data protection supervisory authorities constitutes a violation of fundamental European principles as regards data protection and is not in accordance with Belgian and European law. An existing international framework is already available with regard to the fight against terrorism. The possibilities already offered there should be exploited while ensuring the required level of protection of fundamental rights.

Following negotiations between the Commission and the US Department of the Treasury, the United States offered a number of undertakings regarding the controls which would be imposed over the use of any data obtained from SWIFT.[40] These included the statements that:

> The program contains multiple, overlapping layers of governmental and independent controls to ensure that the data, which are limited in nature, are searched only for counterterrorism purposes and that all data are maintained in a secure environment and properly handled.
>
> . . .
>
> The SWIFT data are maintained in a secure physical environment, stored separately from any other data, and the computer systems have high-level intrusion controls and other protections to limit access to the data solely as described herein. No copies of SWIFT data are made, other than for disaster recovery back-up purposes. Access to the data and the computer equipment are limited to persons with appropriate security clearances. Even among such persons, access to the SWIFT data is on a read-only basis and is limited through the TFTP on a strict need-to-know basis to analysts dedicated to the investigation of terrorism and to persons involved in the technical support, management, and oversight of the TFTP.

In order to allay European concerns it was suggested that:

> As a sign of our commitment and partnership in combating global terrorism, an eminent European person will be appointed to confirm that the program is implemented consistent with these Representations for the purpose of verifying the protection of EU-originating personal data. In particular, the eminent person will monitor that processes for deletion of non-extracted data have been carried out.

Subsequently, steps were taken to put the agreement on a more formal basis and negotiations took place between the US and European authorities. Following these, a draft agreement was approved by the Council of Ministers although significantly a number of States, including Germany and Austria which have perhaps the strongest domestic data protection legislation, abstained. The German minister was quoted as saying of the decision, 'a not completely-satisfying agreement in this field of data exchange combating terrorism is—in the interest of European and also German data protection—better than no agreement'.

The European Parliament, however, disagreed and flexing newly acquired muscles to reject agreements of this nature, it did so in February 2010 largely, it would appear, based on concerns about the lack of data protection provisions in the agreement. Following additional negotiations a further agreement was submitted to Parliament and approved in July 2010. Significantly, although not perhaps surprisingly, the Article 29 Working Party indicated continuing concerns. The Article 29 Working Party is essentially concerned with the purity of data protection law whilst more politically oriented institutions within the European Union do have to take wider issues into account. The final agreement makes provision for the transfer of data to the United States in connection with its 'Terrorist Finance Tracking' programme. Although the agreement is stated to operate for a five-year term, the intention

---

[40] OJ 2007 C166/18.

appears to be that a European programme, equivalent to the US tracking programme will be established and that this will enable data transfers to be applied on a 'push'—namely, initiated by the European authorities or supplied in response to a specific request—rather than the current 'pull' basis where data will be collected by the US authorities with the terms of the agreement operating to control the use which may be made of the data.

Air passenger data

The handling of data relating to airline passengers was included in the Safe Harbor agreement and provides a basis for the transfer of passenger information for the purposes of transportation.[41] It has subsequently been the subject of a further agreement between the EU and the United States in the context of transfers of passenger name record (PNR) data to the US Department of Homeland Security in connection with its anti-terrorism activities. The basis for the agreement lay in a decision by the United States that it would refuse to allow aircraft to enter its airspace unless information concerning all passengers had previously been made available to its authorities. Such data would invariably be classed as personal data under the Data Protection Directive and, insofar as it could relate to dietary requirements or the need for medical assistance, could be classed as sensitive personal data. Such transfers would not be sanctioned under the Directive.

Following extensive political negotiations, two Commission decisions were published in May 2004: the first declaring that an agreement had been reached on the transfer of PNR data and describing its terms; and the second declaring that in the light of undertakings provided by the Department of Homeland Security:

> For the purposes of Article 25(2) of Directive 95/46/EC, the United States' Bureau of Customs and Border Protection (hereinafter referred to as CBP) is considered to ensure an adequate level of protection for PNR data transferred from the Community concerning flights to or from the United States, in accordance with the Undertakings set out in the Annex.[42]

Promulgation of the decisions was controversial within Europe. The Article 29 Working Party had issued a number of critical opinions, although recognising that 'ultimately political judgements will be needed'.[43] Parliament had also expressed opposition, and upon the decisions being adopted, raised proceedings before the European Court of Justice, seeking the annulment of both measures. In June 2006, the Court handed down its judgment in *Parliament v Council*.[44] This declared the decision to be invalid on the grounds that it had been adopted under an inappropriate article of the Treaty of Rome. The treaty justification for the measure was stated to lie in Article 95, which refers to the functioning of the internal market, an argument which was accepted by the court. In respect of the decision relating to the finding of adequacy, this was grounded in Article 25(6) of the Data Protection Directive but it was held that the subject matter of the decision was outside the Directive's scope, Article 3(2) declaring that the measure did not extend to processing:

> in the course of an activity which falls outside the scope of Community law, such as those provided for by Titles V and VI of the Treaty on European Union and in any case to processing operations concerning public security, defence, State security (including the

---

[41] FAQ 13.   [42] Art. 1.

[43] Opinion 4/2003. 'On the Level of Protection ensured in the United States for the Transfer of Passengers' Data', available from <http://ec.europa.eu/justice_home/fsj/privacy/docs/wpdocs/2003/wp78_en.pdf>.

[44] Joined Cases C-317/04 and C-318/04.

economic well-being of the State when the processing operation relates to State security matters) and the activities of the State in areas of criminal law.

Again, the finding was that the decision should be annulled on the grounds of a lack of legislative competence.

Although the Court found in favour of the Parliament, it ruled that 'it appears justified, for reasons of legal certainty and in order to protect the persons concerned, to preserve the effect of the decision on adequacy' for the period of time that would have been required were the EU to have given notice of termination. This continued the validity of the agreement until the end of September 2006. A further short-term agreement was reached in October 2006 to cover the period up until July 2007. On 23 July 2007, a further agreement between the European Union and the United States on the processing and transfer of Passenger Name Record (PNR) data by air carriers to the US Department of Homeland Security (DHS) (2007 PNR Agreement),[45] was signed. This indicated that:

> For the application of this Agreement, DHS is deemed to ensure an adequate level of protection for PNR data transferred from the European Union.

On the same day, Council Decision 2007/551/CFSP/JHA[46] was adopted. Based now on Articles 24 and 38 of the Treaty of Rome, this provided that the terms of the Agreement were to enter into force.

As with previous agreements, provision is made for the US authorities to access a range of items of passenger data relating to identity and itinerary, together with information as to frequent-flier status and details of the method of payment, including details of any credit cards used. As originally agreed, this data would be collected on what is referred to as a 'pull system', whereby the US authorities are enabled to access the airline's computer systems and collect the required information. This approach has been the cause of criticism within Europe and the 2007 agreement provides that the:

> DHS will immediately transition to a push system for the transmission of data by such air carriers no later than 1 January 2008 for all such air carriers that have implemented such a system that complies with DHS's technical requirements. For those air carriers that do not implement such a system, the current systems shall remain in effect until the carriers have implemented a system that complies with DHS's technical requirements. Accordingly, DHS will electronically access the PNR from air carriers' reservation systems located within the territory of the Member States of the European Union until there is a satisfactory system in place allowing for the transmission of such data by the air carriers.

The 2007 agreement seems likely to be no less controversial than its predecessors. It has been subjected to perhaps unprecedented criticism by the Article 29 Working Party. Although the Working Party was not consulted prior to the conclusion of the agreement, in an Opinion published in August 2007,[47] it expressed dissatisfaction:

> that the opportunity to have adopted a more balanced approach based upon real need has been missed. While there has been much comment on the new agreement, the Working Party would have wished for a different outcome of the EU–US negotiations and feels that the new agreement does not strike the right balance to uphold the fundamental rights of citizens as regards data protection.

---

[45] OJ 2007 L204/18.   [46] OJ 2007 L204/16.

[47] Opinion 5/2007 on the follow-up agreement between the European Union and the United States of America on the processing and transfer of passenger name record (PNR) data by air carriers to the United States Department of Homeland Security concluded in July 2007, available from <http://ec.europa.eu/justice_home/fsj/privacy/docs/wpdocs/2007/wp138_en.pdf>.

It concluded that:

> the new PNR agreement contains some minor improvements in comparison with the previous accord but it is clearly disappointed at the inadequate data protection standard of the new PNR agreement. The new agreement does not even preserve the level of privacy protection of the previous agreement which was already considered weak by the Working Party in its previous opinions.

> The new PNR agreement as analysed in this opinion does not compare favourably with accepted data protection standards, such as those of Convention 108 and of the Directive. It will cause understandable concern for all transatlantic travellers who are worried about their privacy rights.

It may be noted that a less extensive agreement[48] on the transfer of PNR data to the Canadian Authorities received a positive Opinion from the Article 29 Working Party.[49]

Transfers when an adequate level of protection is not provided

Even allowing for the inclusion of those organisations from the United States, which are party to 'Safe Harbor', only a very small number of countries have been determined to provide an adequate level of protection. Alternative mechanisms require to be found therefore to legitimise data transfers with the rest of the world, whilst ensuring that the interests of European data subjects are safeguarded. Having laid down a prohibition against data transfers in Article 25, the Directive's Article 26 is headed 'Derogations' and proceeds to lay down a number of situations in which Member States must permit transfers and a further set of situations in which the Member States may authorise transfers. In respect of the first situation, it is provided that transfers are to be permitted when:

(a) the data subject has given his consent unambiguously to the proposed transfer; or

(b) the transfer is necessary for the performance of a contract between the data subject and the controller or the implementation of pre-contractual measures taken in response to the data subject's request; or

(c) the transfer is necessary for the conclusion or performance of a contract concluded in the interest of the data subject between the controller and a third party; or

(d) the transfer is necessary or legally required on important public interest grounds, or for the establishment, exercise or defence of legal claims; or

(e) the transfer is necessary in order to protect the vital interests of the data subject; or

(f) the transfer is made from a register which according to laws or regulations is intended to provide information to the public and which is open to consultation either by the public in general or by any person who can demonstrate legitimate interest to the extent that the conditions laid down in law for consultation are fulfilled in the particular case.[50]

In the main, the Act's wording follows that of the Data Protection Directive, but there is a divergence in respect of the exception relating to subject consent. Whilst the Directive requires unambiguous consent, the Act refers merely to the fact that 'the data subject has given his consent to the transfer'.[51] The Act also confers regulatory power on the Secretary

---

[48] OJ 2006 L 91/49.   [49] Opinion 1 of 2005, available from OJ 2005 L 82/14.   [50] Art. 26(1).
[51] The nature of these provisions is similar to those of the Sch. 2 conditions legitimising the processing of personal data.

of State to define more closely the circumstances under which transfers may, or may not, take place 'for reasons of substantial public interest'.[52]

Substantial guidance concerning the interpretation of the Article 26(1) exceptions has been provided by the Article 29 Working Party in its 'Working Document on a Common Interpretation of Article 26(1)'.[53] This confirms that the provisions of Article 26(1) constitute exceptions from the general principle that data can be transferred only under conditions that will ensure adequacy. As exceptions, they are to be construed narrowly. Referring to the possibilities for providing adequate protection listed in Article 26(2), the Working Party comments:

> The Working Party would find it regrettable that a multinational company or a public authority would plan to make significant transfers of data to a third country without providing an appropriate framework for the transfer, when it has the practical means of providing such protection.

Particularly relevant in this context are the use of contractual provisions and, a more recent development, the concept of adopting binding corporate rules.

The role of contract

The Data Protection Directive provides that:

> a Member State may authorize a transfer or a set of transfers or personal data to a third country which does not ensure an adequate level of protection—where the controller adduces adequate safeguards with respect to the protection of the privacy and fundamental rights and freedoms of individuals and as regards the exercise of the corresponding rights; such safeguards may in particular result from appropriate contractual clauses.[54]

Any exercise of this power must be reported to the Commission and the other Member States. If any party so informed objects 'on justified measures involving the protection of the privacy and the fundamental rights and freedoms of individuals', a proposal for action may be tabled before the Committee by the Commission and, if approved, will require the Member State involved to take necessary measures to conform.[55]

In implementing this provision, the Data Protection Act 1998 provides in Schedule 4 that transfers will be acceptable when they are:

- made on terms which are of a kind approved by the Commissioner as ensuring adequate safeguards for the rights and freedoms of data subjects[56]

- authorized by the Commissioner as being made in such a manner as to ensure adequate safeguards for the rights and freedoms of data subjects.[57]

Although the Act provides[58] for notification of approvals to be transmitted to the Commission, this has not happened to any extent. In its first report on the implementation of the Data Protection Directive,[59] the Commission comments:

> National authorities are supposed to notify the Commission when they authorise transfers under Article 26 (2) of the Directive. Since the Directive came into operation in 1998, the Commission has received only a very limited number of such notifications. Although there are other legal transfer routes apart from Article 26 (2), this number is derisory by

---

[52] Sch. 4, para. 4(2).
[53] WP114, available from <http://ec.europa.eu/justice_home/fsj/privacy/docs/wpdocs/2005/wp114_en.pdf>.
[54] Directive 95/46/EC, Art. 26(2).   [55] Art. 26(3).
[56] Sch. 4, para. 8.   [57] Sch. 4, para. 9.
[58] s. 54(7).   [59] COM/2003/0265 final, available from <http://eur-lex.europa.eu/LexUriServ/LexUriServ.do?uri=CELEX:52003DC0265:EN:NOT>.

comparison with what might reasonably be expected. Combined with other evidence pointing in the same direction, this suggests that many unauthorised and possibly illegal transfers are being made to destinations or recipients not guaranteeing adequate protection. Yet there is little or no sign of enforcement actions by the supervisory authorities.

In spite of a Commission Notice sent to the Member States in 2003 urging more extensive notification, matters do not seem to have changed significantly. In 2006, a Commission Staff Working Document noted that:

> the number of notifications received by the Commission services pursuant to Article 26 (3) of the Directive over the last four years is extremely limited: only 78 notifications from seven Member States (the Netherlands (34), Spain (20), Germany (14), Finland (5), Portugal (2), Austria (2) and Belgium (1)). In addition, most of these notifications concern the use of standard contractual clauses which, as outlined above, are not covered by the notifying obligation.
>
> Since the Directive entered into force in October 1998, the Commission has not received any notifications from the United Kingdom, France, Italy, Ireland, Greece, Sweden or Luxembourg. None of the new ten Member States has yet notified the use of contractual clauses or other adequate safeguards to the Commission.[60]

Authorisation may be given under the above provisions on an individual basis, but may also make reference to the controller's adherence to model contractual terms and conditions. There appears to be a general acceptance that the volume of transborder data flows is such that it is undesirable for decisions as to acceptability to require to be made in the context of individual transfers, and that more general provisions should be laid down.

The Article 29 Working Party produced a report in April 1998, outlining its 'preliminary views on the use of contractual terms in the context of transfers of personal data to third countries'.[61] This document identified a number of elements that must be found in any relevant contract. The contract must provide for observance of the data protection principles. Whilst it was recognised that no system could provide a total assurance of compliance, it would be required that the provisions should provide a reasonable level of assurance, should provide support and assistance for data subjects, and appropriate forms of redress.

Subsequent to the report of the Working Party, proposals for decisions on two sets of contracts, one for transfers between two data controllers and one for transfers between European data controllers and external data processors, were brought forward by the Commission. These were the subject of further Article 29 Working Party opinions in 2001;[62] two decisions were adopted by the Commission in 2001 and 2002, and Decision 2001/497/EC on Standard Contractual Clauses for the transfer of personal data to controllers in third countries was adopted in June 2001.[63] This required Member States to accept transfers conducted under its terms (ie using the standard form contract within the decision) as satisfying the requirements of adequacy.[64] Decision 2002/16/EC[65] contained standard contract terms relevant to the situation where an EU-based data controller wishes to transfer data to a processor established in a third country.

The annex to both decisions lays out a set of standard terms. Beyond customisation with the identifying details of the parties, these may not be changed or amended in any way whatsoever. This has been regarded in some quarters as an overly prescriptive approach but

---

[60] SEC (2006) 95, available from <http://ec.europa.eu/justice_home/fsj/privacy/docs/modelcontracts/sec_2006_95_en.pdf>.

[61] WP 9, available from <http://ec.europa.eu/justice_home/fsj/privacy/docs/wpdocs/1998/wp9_en.pdf>.

[62] Opinion 1/2001 and 7/2001, available from <http://ec.europa.eu/justice_home/fsj/privacy/workinggroup/wpdocs/2001_en.htm>.

[63] OJ 2001 L 181/19.   [64] Art. 1.   [65] OJ 2002 L6/52.

in common with any legal documents, it may be virtually impossible to know whether any change might have major or minor implications.

Clause 2 provides for identification of the parties and the nature of the transfer, and Appendix 1 provides a form in which these details may be provided. Clause 3 provides that third parties are to be able to enforce the contract—possibly assisted by a consumer protection agency. The possibility of third-party enforcement of contractual obligations had long been a stumbling block for the use of such contracts under English law. The Contracts (Rights of Third Parties) Act 1999 now provides a mechanism for such enforcement.

The model contract lays down in some detail the nature and extent of the obligations which are to be accepted by the data exporter and importer. The former is to warrant that the data has been processed in accordance with any relevant European data protection law up until the time the export takes place. If the data constitutes sensitive personal data, the subject is to be informed, before the transfer, of the fact that the legal system of the importer might not guarantee an adequate level of protection. Copies of the contract clauses are to be made available to data subjects and the exporter is to respond to any reasonable requests from its supervisory agency or from a data subject concerning the processing to be carried out on the data.

For the importing controller, it is required that an undertaking be given that the controller has no knowledge that any provisions of its domestic law will prevent fulfilment of obligations accepted under the contract. The processing is to be carried out in accordance with a set of mandatory data protection principles specified in the model contract. These effectively provide for measures equivalent to those found in the Directive (and also the Article 29 Working Party's WP12 on assessing adequacy), regarding matters such as limitations on the purpose of processing, the accuracy and up-to-date nature of data, the availability of subject access, etc. The importer undertakes to cooperate with requests for information from data subjects and relevant European supervisory agencies and also to submit its facilities for audit by the data exporter or a professionally qualified inspection agency selected by the exporter.

One of the most contentious provisions in the model contract is Clause 6, which provides that the parties are to accept joint and several liability for any breaches of the contract. The effect of this is that a data subject could choose to take action, either against the contracting parties jointly or hold either party solely liable. Given the problems of raising legal proceedings in a foreign jurisdiction or against a foreign party, the consequence might be that the data exporter may well be targeted by an aggrieved data subject as the sole object of any claim for compensation, even though any culpability might lie with the data importer.

The initial model contracts were criticised by some business interests as being cumbersome, inflexible, and out of touch with business needs. Recital 10 of the decision states that:

> The Commission will also consider in the future whether standard contractual clauses submitted by business organisations or other interested parties offer adequate safeguards in accordance with Directive 95/46/EC.

A new set of standard contractual clauses for data transfers was proposed by seven international business associations: the American Chamber of Commerce to the European Union in Brussels (AmCham EU), the Confederation of British Industry (CBI), the European Information and Communications Technology Association (EICTA), the Federation of European Direct and Interactive Marketing (FEDMA), the International Chamber of Commerce (ICC), the International Communication Round Table (ICRT), and the Japan Business Council in Europe (JBCE).

Following negotiations between these associations and the Commission Working Party, a new set of model contracts was approved by the Commission by Decision 2004/915. These sit alongside the initial contracts, with businesses being offered a choice between the two formulations. Welcoming the new decision the then Single Market Commissioner, Charlie McCreevy, was quoted as saying:

> This is a good example of regulating in cooperation with business. The business community has shown a serious commitment towards data protection and the Commission has carefully listened to business needs. That is good for EU citizens, whose privacy is better protected, and for our companies, whose competitiveness is reinforced.

Commenting on an earlier draft of the terms,[66] the Article 29 Working Party was perhaps less enthusiastic, although still broadly supportive of the initiative:

> The Working Party has doubts that the current proposals satisfy these conditions fully. It also has doubts that these clauses are easier to use by economic operators. The same business associations that criticised the Commission's standard contractual clauses in 2001 as 'unworkable' do not seem to have found better wording for many clauses and when the proposals deviate from Decision 497/2001/CE, the result is not necessarily clearer but rather more uncertain in legal terms.

In a set of frequently asked questions on the Model Contracts, the Commission suggests that:

> Both sets of clauses provide for a similar level of data protection, in other words, individuals are similarly protected by both sets on the basis of the same (adequate) data protection standards and principles. Differences between both sets are mainly of a technical nature (for example, the conditions under which a data protection authority may carry out an audit in the data importer's premises) or related to the differences in the system of liability already explained above.

Perhaps the major variation between the contracts is in respect of the issue of liability. The 2004 contracts state that:

(a) Each party shall be liable to the other parties for damages it causes by any breach of these clauses . . . Each party shall be liable to data subjects for damages it causes by any breach of third party rights under these clauses. This does not affect the liability of the data exporter under its data protection law.

(b) . . . In cases involving allegations of breach by the data importer, the data subject must first request the data exporter to take appropriate action to enforce his rights against the data importer; if the data exporter does not take such action within a reasonable period (which under normal circumstances would be one month), the data subject may then enforce his rights against the data importer directly. A data subject is entitled to proceed directly against a data exporter that has failed to use reasonable efforts to determine that the data importer is able to satisfy its legal obligations under these clauses (the data exporter shall have the burden to prove that it took reasonable efforts).

Although certainly more favourable towards the business parties involved, it is difficult to see that the provision affords the same level of protection to data subjects as that provided for under the 2001 contract.

Binding corporate rules

Whilst the conclusion of contracts, whether using the Commission's model contracts or a formulation devised by the parties themselves may provide an appropriate solution to the

---

[66] Opinion 8/2003, available from <http://ec.europa.eu/justice_home/fsj/privacy/docs/wpdocs/2003/wp84_en.pdf>.

requirements of many data controllers, difficulties have been identified in the situation where multinational organisations operate in a wide range of countries and are required to exchange personal data between the legal entities operating in the different countries. A contractual solution here might create a spaghetti forest of agreements between all possible permutations of national legal entities. Although it is possible under the contractual approach to have a single master agreement which is signed by a range of parties, this approach, with a requirement that details of all transfers be recorded, would be difficult to apply in what may well be an organisation subject to continual change and development.

In response to this situation, the Article 29 Working Party has developed the concept of binding corporate rules as an alternative mechanism for demonstrating that data will receive an adequate level of protection. Working Paper 74, applying Article 26(2) of the EU Data Protection Directive to Binding Corporate Rules for International Data Transfers,[67] was published in 2003 and lays down the basic principles which should be found in such rules. The Working Paper is supplemented by a Checklist published in 2004[68] and Recommendation 1 of 2007 containing a 'Standard Application for Approval of Binding Corporate Rules for the Transfer of Personal Data'.[69] As with all methods for ensuring adequacy, the notion of binding corporate rules seeks to ensure that processing takes place under conditions broadly equivalent to those laid down in the data protection principles. In terms of procedural aspects, the requirement is that one member of the undertaking should be given powers and responsibilities to ensure that the rules are observed throughout the organisation. This member must be located in the EU and will be responsible for seeking approval of the rules from a relevant supervisory agency. In many cases, multinational corporations will be operating in a wide range of EU States, and the Working Paper suggests that supervisory agencies should make use of the cooperation procedures established under Article 28 of the Data Protection Directive to enable a request for approval to be made to only one supervisory agency and, if granted, to be valid throughout all Member States.

Conclusions

The activities described indicate perhaps how complex is the task of applying national or regional rules regarding data protection in a situation where processing may take place anywhere on the planet. In February 2007, it was widely reported that Google, the world's most widely used search engine, was calling upon the UN to intervene to help protect the privacy of web users.[70]

Given much recent controversy concerning aspects of Google's own practices, including its data retention policy and the publication on 'Google Street View'[71] of images of individuals taken without their knowledge or consent, this may seem a classic instance of a poacher turning gamekeeper. As the discussions concerning the concept of binding corporate rules indicate, organisations operating on a global basis may find it easier to work on the basis of consistent global standards, even though these may place restrictions on their ability to process data in an unrestricted manner. To date, the UN's involvement in the data/privacy protection field has been somewhat peripheral. The Google plea for activity was also addressed to the OECD and certainly this agency has been much more active in

---

[67] Available from <http://ec.europa.eu/justice_home/fsj/privacy/docs/wpdocs/2003/wp74_en.pdf>.
[68] Available from <http://ec.europa.eu/justice_home/fsj/privacy/docs/wpdocs/2004/wp101_en.pdf>.
[69] Available from <http://ec.europa.eu/justice_home/fsj/privacy/workinggroup/wpdocs/2007_en.htm>.
[70] See, eg, <http://www.guardian.co.uk/technology/2007/sep/14/news.google>.
[71] <http://maps.google.com/help/maps/streetview/>.

the field. In a Ministerial Declaration on the Protection of Privacy on Global Networks on this, the ministers reaffirmed:

> their commitment to the protection of privacy on global networks in order to ensure the respect of important rights, build confidence in global networks, and to prevent unnecessary restrictions on transborder flows of personal data.
>
> They will work to build bridges between the different approaches adopted by Member countries to ensure privacy protection on global networks based on the OECD Guidelines.[72]

In June 2007, the OECD adopted a Recommendation on Cross-border Co-operation in the Enforcement of Laws Protecting Privacy.[73] In its introductory sections, the Recommendation indicates why action was considered necessary:

> When personal information moves across borders it may put at increased risk the ability of individuals to exercise privacy rights to protect themselves from the unlawful use or disclosure of that information. At the same time, the authorities charged with enforcing privacy laws may find that they are unable to pursue complaints or conduct investigations relating to the activities of organisations outside their borders. Their efforts to work together in the cross-border context may also be hampered by insufficient preventative or remedial powers, inconsistent legal regimes, and practical obstacles like resource constraints. In this context, a consensus has emerged on the need to promote closer co-operation among privacy law enforcement authorities to help them exchange information and carry out investigations with their foreign counterparts.

The Recommendation continues to indicate that Member States should act to ensure that 'Privacy Enforcement Authorities' are both empowered and obliged to cooperate with other national authorities. It is suggested that a national point of contact should be established in each Member State to facilitate cross-border requests for assistance.

Initially, international transfers generally took the form of couriering or posting packages containing disks or tapes. In the modern networked world, online transfers are the norm. With modern forms of electronic communications, national or even supranational boundaries are of limited significance and the European Union's attempt to control the flow of data has drawn comparison with the early English King Canute's attempt to order the incoming tide to retreat. The Canute legend, of course, is susceptible of at least two explanations. One refers to the folly of a monarch who believed that he could control the forces of nature and was surprised when he got his feet wet. A second, and more complex explanation, sees the exercise as a considered attempt to demonstrate to over-deferential subjects the limits of what human authority can and cannot do. In this second case, any folly lies more with those who seek to ascribe human agencies with almighty powers and are disappointed when perfection proves to be an unattainable goal. The fact that data protection legislation cannot prevent all forms of malpractice is no reason for not attempting to prevent some. Fear of the consequences of data havens was a motivating force behind much data protection legislation. Where the European model might perhaps be criticised is in substituting the notion of a European data protection haven. The tale is sometimes told of a discussion between proponents of Rolls Royce motor cars and those of Ford (or any other mass-produced models). The former can point to the quality of build, the levels of comfort, refinement, and reliability. Whilst conceding these points, the opposing case may be that mass-produced cars offer acceptable (adequate) levels of comfort, refinement, and reliability, with the additional fact that they can be afforded by most of the population. If some reduction in standards is the price to be paid for global acceptance of the importance of the need for data protection, the price may be one that is well worth paying.

---

[72] Available from <http://www.oecd.org/internet/ieconomy/1840065.pdf>.
[73] Available from <http://www.oecd.org/dataoecd/43/28/38770483.pdf>.

PART II

Computer-Related Crime

INTRODUCTION

I recall viewing (too) many years ago a BBC television series called 'Connections'. It sought to explain how apparently unrelated developments were in fact linked. Fascinating! I don't think it featured in that programme but, in the 1960s, the United Kingdom embarked on a major motorway-building programme. Also in the 1960s there was a substantial increase in the number of burglaries in rural villages. What was the connection?

Essentially city-based burglars realised that by using the new motorways they could travel sixty or seventy miles in an hour rather than twenty or thirty. They could expand the geographical range of their operations and realised that householders living in small villages would be likely to be less security-conscious than their urban counterparts.

It does appear to be a phenomenon of history that criminals have proved to be early and skilled adopters of new forms of technology. The computer has proved to be no exception to this rule. As the scope of the technology has expanded so has the range of criminal conduct. As with many aspects of our subject, terminology has tended to evolve. Initially we talked about computer crime (or computer-related crime). Today the talk is more in terms of e-crime or perhaps cybercrime. I'm not sure that any label is better than the others although, showing my age, I tend to refer to computer crime. Rather than worrying about terminology it is, I think, more important to focus on particular forms of behaviour and consider how these may be challenged by particular forms of criminal law. Following the theme of connections, it does seem that as computer technologies have evolved, so new criminal (or potentially criminal) outlets have developed.

Computer fraud

The Office for National Statistics publishes figures relating to almost every aspect of life. Its work relating to the scale of criminal activity tends to attract headline attention. For the first time in 2016 the attempt was made to assess the scale of computer (cyber) fraud. The results were somewhat surprising.

Based on Experimental Statistics from new fraud and computer misuse questions that were added to the Crime Survey for England and Wales from October 2015, adults aged sixteen and over experienced an estimated 5.8 million fraud and computer misuse incidents in the twelve months prior to interview; 3.8 million of these were fraud incidents and 2.0 million were classed as computer misuse incidents.[1]

This can be contrasted with statistics in the same report indicating that there were around 620,000 instances of what might be regarded as 'traditional' fraud offences. See Figure 9.1 below.

The scale of cyber fraud and the discrepancy in the number of reported instances seems difficult to accept although perhaps explicable when we consider the volume of phishing and scam emails that arrive in our email each year. Each would class as an 'incident' according to the classification scheme although very few people might actually fall victim to the scam. Similar considerations may apply to violations of the Computer Misuse Act and here it is likely that a reasonably prudent computer user would make use of anti-virus software that will prevent any damage being caused to the contents of their device.

Beyond uncertainties as to statistics, issues of loss, fraud, and the involvement of law enforcement agencies are all somewhat problematic issues. Following changes to English law introduced in the Fraud Act of 2006, there appears to be reluctance on the part of law enforcement agencies to accept crime reports from individuals and to require that issues be raised instead with a bank or other financial institution. The police will accept complaints only from (or at the request of) such a body and concerns have been expressed that instances may not be reported thereby skewing statistics as to the scale of the problem. The organisation 'Action Fraud'[2] has been established to serve as a single point to collate reports of fraud from members of the public although in some respects this does seem to serve the purpose of deflecting incidents of fraud away from the attention of the police, rather than promoting investigation of such conduct. Its website states that:

> After a report has been made to Action Fraud, it will be sent for assessment by the National Fraud Intelligence Bureau (NFIB). The NFIB's systems assess reports of fraud and cyber crime from across the UK, helping to build a national picture of where fraud and cyber crime is taking place and how. Experts review the data from these reports to decide whether there is enough information to send to a police force for investigation.

Fraud & cyber-offences shown as a proportion of overall crime

1.21m Criminal damage
0.37m Bicycle theft
0.88m Vehicle theft
3.70m Theft
1.27m Violence
0.15m Robbery
0.67m Household theft
0.70m Domestic burglary

Fraud and Computer Misue 5.77
Bank & credit card fraud 2.47m
Non investment fraud 1.04m
Advance fee fraud 0.11m
Other fraud 0.14m
Computer viruses 1.36m
Hacking emails & social media 0.65m

Figure 9.1 Fraud and cyber-offences shown as a proportion of overall crime

---

[1] Attention should be given also to the report published in September 2016 by Financial Fraud Action UK, see <https://www.financialfraudaction.org.uk/>. The members of this organisation include all of the major banks in the United Kingdom.

[2] <http://www.actionfraud.police.uk/>.

The NFIB aims to send you an update in writing around 28 working days after you have made your fraud report, to advise you what action has been taken on your report, for example if it has been sent to a police force for investigation.[3]

Questions have also arisen about the manner in which individuals are treated where there are disputes concerning the use or misuse of credit or debit cards that are protected by PIN numbers. The Financial Services and Market Rules (Payment Services Regulations) 2009 state that a consumer is to be held liable for fraudulent use of a card (above a limit of £50) only where gross negligence can be established. There has been a long-standing debate concerning the security of this system of protection. Banks have argued successfully before the courts, admittedly at only the county court level, that cards, at least when using the current Chip and PIN level of security, can be used only if the PIN had been disclosed by the holder. Other techniques can, of course, also be employed. Cameras can be placed by ATM machines to capture PIN numbers with the cards subsequently being stolen. So-called 'shoulder surfing' can be as effective with the criminal looking over the user's shoulder to observe what numbers are being pressed.

Media depictions of computer fraudsters and computer criminals generally tend to depict some form of computer genius. Reality is often rather more down to earth and, in many cases, the techniques are fairly basic. In respect of the Santander and Barclays attacks the device used is known as a keyboard video mouse (KVM). This gadget, which fit into the back of a machine, can cost as little as £10 and is widely available in computer stores or online.

It is, however, testimony to the ease with which money can be transferred electronically that such a simple and cheap device could be capable of facilitating the theft of sums of money far beyond the dreams of most traditional bank robbers.

Computer hacking

Much the same story might be told in respect of the next generation of computer crimes. From around the 1970s, telephone networks began to automate their operations and we also saw the introduction of the first networked services such as Compuserve and AOL. Inevitably we also saw the rise of hacking. Initially often referred to as 'phreaking', proponents sought to manipulate the dialling codes used by telephone networks to obtain free calls. The technology is now obsolete, but the early networks relied upon audio signals transmitted at specific frequencies to handle traffic. Sometimes the original hacking technologies were basic. One phreaker discovered that a toy whistle distributed as a gift in a box of breakfast cereals—aimed at the children's market—mimicked precisely the frequencies of major US telecommunications networks. Effectively, sending a series of musical notes down a telephone line would allow free access to the network.

With the emergence of computer networks around forty years ago we saw the emergence of computer hacking. One of the most famous (or notorious) groups in the field is the Chaos Computer Club which was formed in Germany in 1981. Perhaps anticipating recent leaks of government information, its manifesto pronounced it to be 'a galactic community of life forms, independent of age, sex, race or societal orientation, which strives across borders for freedom of information . . .'.

---

[3] Assessing the economic value of intangible assets is a difficult and largely subjective report. See this report <https://hbr.org/2016/09/do-you-know-what-your-companys-data-is-worth> from the *Harvard Business Review*.

To a greater extent in the 1980s than today, there was a range of views about the ethical and legal acceptability of hacking. Reference was sometimes made to the light and to the dark sides of the practice. Light-side, or good, hackers were interested solely in the technical challenge of obtaining access to computer systems and, it was argued, might be able to alert operators to vulnerabilities in their systems. This form of question of whether such conduct should be criminalised has been at the core of much of the debate in the field. It was estimated as long ago as 2011 that losses due to computer espionage cost the United Kingdom about £7 billion in 2011. But generally, as was explained by Professor Glanville Williams:

> It is absurd and disgraceful that we should still be making do without any legislation specifically designed to discourage this modern form of commercial piracy. Abstracting or divulging an official secret is an offence under the Official Secrets Act 1911, sections 1 and 2; but Leviathan is not much concerned to protect the secret and immensely valuable know-how of its subjects.[4]

Some thirty years on, that remains very much the legal reality in the physical world. As we will discuss, the online world has been regulated in different ways but the fundamental point remains significant. Discounting any peripheral offences that might be involved, if I am legitimately in a building, walk into an unlocked office, and photograph papers left lying on a desk, I will not have committed any offence. Put simply, the argument with computer crime legislation is whether any different result should pertain if I access data on a computer that has effectively been left unlocked? Just as is increasingly the case with house insurance policies, the question 'what is an effective lock?' raises other issues!

A point which continually arises in the field is 'what is a computer?' Most smartphones have apps which allow individuals to identify where friends or partners are at any point in time. Consent to being tracked will invariably need to be given in the phone's settings but this is a simple procedure. You might consider the following report which related to the Apple iPhone 'Find myFriends' app:

> The lovely thing about this app is that you can follow people only if they're happy to you to have you follow them. In this particular case, the poster—with the handle 'ThomasMetz'—claims that he had suspicions about the happiness of his marriage. He had a few suspicions about his wife's loyalty and activities. So he allegedly installed the app without happening to mention it.
>
> In his words: 'I got my wife a new 4S and loaded up find my friends without her knowing. She told me she was at her friends [sic] house in the east village. I've had suspicions about her meeting this guy who lives uptown. Lo and behold, Find my Friends has her right there.'[5]

Effectively such applications cause the target phone to transmit location data on request. Is this hacking? It appears that the technology is also used by parents to keep track of their children's movements—or to monitor a (typically) older person suffering from some form of memory loss. Again, is this hacking and what might be the issues of ownership and/or consent?

The notion and fear of computer hacking remains very prevalent today and a whole new topic is developing with notions of cyberterrorism and cyberwarfare. I'll say more about this later but that conduct essentially relates to the third main strand of computer crime involving attempts to modify or delete programs or data held on a computer.

The conduct is sometimes related to hacking and as such would represent what is referred to as the dark side of the practice. Essentially unauthorised access is a precursor to conduct that damages the intangible elements of a computer system. The distinction between tangible and

---

[4] *Textbook of Criminal Law*, 2nd edn (London, 1983), p. 739.
[5] <http://news.cnet.com/8301-17852_3-20121104-71/apples-new-find-my-friends-app-finds-wife-cheating/>.

intangible damage has occupied courts and legislatures for a good number of years. We might consider an analogy whereby somebody sprays paint onto the walls of a building. Leaving aside any issues of the aesthetic value of the finished work, it would generally be assumed that the structure has been damaged although it would not be the case that it is any more likely to fall down than it was before the incident. If data is corrupted on some form of computer storage device, there will be no direct physical evidence of the fact and the object will continue to be usable. You might think of a situation where all the contents of a computer are moved to its recycle bin and deleted. Discounting the use of very expensive data recovery services, the material has gone. The impact on the owner may be devastating but there is still a perfectly serviceable computer.

The story of how the law has come to deal with these issues is a fascinating one. In many countries, including the United Kingdom, we have seen the enactment of specific computer-crime statutes. Given the all-pervasive nature of computer applications today, it is arguable that there is the need to adjust general principles of criminal law to cope with the realities of the computer age rather than treating the device as an isolated creature.

From cybercrime to cyberwarfare and cyberterrorism

In its early stages, attention regarding unlawful activities involving computers focused on the activities of what might be regarded as traditional criminals. Over the past decade, paralleling developments in the real world, there has been increasing emphasis on the use of computer systems as a weapon either by terrorists or, and perhaps the other side of the coin, as a form of warfare by states. In its own turn, the distinction between cyberwarfare and cyberterrorism may be tenuous. Conduct is generally classified in the eyes of the beholder. As in the real world, the distinction between criminal conduct and terrorism may be difficult to define and in some respects the focus of discussion relates more to the scale and impact of conduct rather than the nature or motives of the perpetrators. Especially in the era of privatised utilities, attacks on private companies pose as substantial a threat to society as attacks on government installations.

In 2010 the UK government published its National Security Strategy. As developed by the National Security Council, this sought to identify the risks facing the country and place them into three tiers of severity. The threats in tier one were defined as being 'of highest priority for UK national security looking ahead, taking account of both likelihood and impact' and encompassed:

- international terrorism affecting the United Kingdom or its interests, including a chemical, biological, radiological, or nuclear attack by terrorists; and/or a significant increase in the levels of terrorism relating to Northern Ireland
- hostile attacks upon UK cyberspace by other states and large-scale cybercrime
- a major accident or natural hazard which requires a national response, such as severe coastal flooding affecting three or more regions of the United Kingdom, or an influenza pandemic
- an international military crisis between states, drawing in the United Kingdom, and its allies as well as other states and non-state actors.

A budget of £650 million (over a four-year period) was allocated to improve the country's 'cyberdefences'. This resulted in the adoption in November 2011 by the Cabinet Office of a National Cybercrime Strategy. This referred to the increasing importance of the Internet in all aspects of life and noted at paragraph 2.2 that:

> The digital architecture on which we now rely was built to be efficient and interoperable. When the internet first started to grow, security was less of a consideration. However, as we put more

of our lives online, this matters more and more. People want to be confident that the networks that support our national security, our economic prosperity, and our own private lives as individuals are safe and resilient.

Concerns about security have been growing for some time. In the global environment there is obvious need for international cooperation and within the EU, the European Network and Information Security Agency (ENISA) was established in 2004. The European Commission commented:

> ENISA is the EU's response to these cyber security issues of the European Union. As such, it is the 'pace-setter' for Information Security in Europe, and a centre of expertise.
> The objective is to make ENISA's web site the European 'hub' for exchange of information, best practices and knowledge in the field of Information Security.[6]

ENISA was established under Regulation (EC) No. 460/2004 of the European Parliament and of the Council.[7] Recital 1 of the Regulation states that:

> Communication networks and information systems have become an essential factor in economic and societal development. Computing and networking are now becoming ubiquitous utilities in the same way as electricity or water supply already are. The security of communication networks and information systems, in particular their availability, is therefore of increasing concern to society not least because of the possibility of problems in key information systems, due to system complexity, accidents, mistakes and attacks, that may have consequences for the physical infrastructures which deliver services critical to the well-being of EU citizens.

Within the United Kingdom the Centre for the Protection of the National Infrastructure (CPNI)[8] was established in 2007 following from the merger of the National Infrastructure Security Co-ordination Centre (NISCC) and a part of MI5 (the United Kingdom's Security Service), the National Security Advice Centre (NSAC). The National Infrastructure has been defined as encompassing:

> those facilities, systems, sites and networks necessary for the functioning of the country and the delivery of the essential services upon which daily life in the UK depends.[9]

It is categorised into nine sectors:

- communications
- emergency services
- energy
- financial services
- food
- government
- health
- transport
- water

The CPNI note that:

> The UK is facing an ongoing, persistent threat of cyber attack from other states, terrorists and criminals operating in cyberspace.

[6] <http://www.enisa.europa.eu/about-enisa>.
[7] <http://eur-lex.europa.eu/LexUriServ/LexUriServ.do?uri=CELEX:32004R0460:EN:HTML>.
[8] <http://www.cpni.gov.uk/>.   [9] <http://www.cpni.gov.uk/about/cni/>.

They go on to explain that:

> Cyberspace lies at the heart of modern society; it impacts our personal lives, our businesses and our essential services. Cyber security embraces both the public and the private sector and spans a broad range of issues related to national security, whether through terrorism, crime or industrial espionage.
>
> E-crime, or cyber crime, whether relating to theft, hacking or denial of service to vital systems, has become a fact of life. The risk of industrial cyber espionage, in which one company makes active attacks on another, through cyberspace, to acquire high value information is also very real.[10]

Terrorists are identified as a potential threat but increasingly, states are seeking to utilise cyberwarfare strategies as an alternative to more traditional military actions. As *The Guardian* commented in July 2011:

> Hostile foreign states have used cyberwarfare to attack and map the networks that are part of the country's critical national infrastructure, the government has admitted.
>
> Though officials refused to say what had been hit, the systems that provide the UK with its gas, water, and electricity supplies are all likely to have been targeted, raising the stakes in the battle to stop foreign powers, criminals and hackers from stealing information that could lead to services being disrupted or brought to a standstill.

The counterside of cyberterrorism is the attempt by states to use cyber-based activities as a weapon in their own right. It has, for example, been reported that British intelligence agents hacked into an al-Qaeda online magazine and replaced bomb-making instructions with a recipe for cupcakes. In 2010, Iran's nuclear programme was severely disrupted by the so-called Stuxnet virus. The virus apparently infected computers which controlled the operation of centrifuges which play an essential role in processing nuclear material to make it suitable for use for military purposes. The centrifuges were reprogrammed to spin at excessive speed resulting in major physical damage to their components. This is considered to be one of, if not the, most sophisticated and extensive viruses and the first which specifically targeted infrastructure. It has been widely reported that the virus was created by the US and Israeli security services.

---

[10] <http://www.cpni.gov.uk/threats/other-threats/>.

9

National and international responses to computer-related crime

INTRODUCTION

In considering the application of the criminal law to instances of computer-related conduct, a variety of issues arise. In the early days of computer-related conduct, any criminal charge was required to be brought under traditional legal headings. Incidents where damage was caused to the contents of a computer, either directly or by causing it to be infected by a computer virus, were successfully prosecuted as a species of criminal damage under the Criminal Damage Act 1971.[1]

Starting in the 1980s, a trend began for the adoption of computer-specific statutes. Perhaps the first was the US Computer Fraud and Abuse Act, enacted in 1984. Within the United Kingdom, the Law Commissions published consultative papers and reports in the 1980s.[2] Although the initial reports identified a case for the introduction of reform, considerable additional impetus came with the failure of the prosecution in the case of *R v Gold*.[3] The defendant in this case, together with another accused, had obtained password details, through the simple expediency of watching closely as an engineer typed in these details at a computer exhibition. He was then able to access an online database without paying the charges which would normally be levied in respect of such usage. The most relevant criminal offence would appear to have been that of obtaining services by deception. As will be discussed in more detail later, there was considerable uncertainty as to whether this offence could be committed when the 'victim' was a machine, and in the particular case the decision was taken to bring the prosecution under the terms of the Forgery and Counterfeiting Act 1981. The Act provides that:

> A person is guilty of forgery if he makes a false instrument, with the intention that he or another shall use it to induce somebody to accept it as genuine, and by reason of so accepting it to do or not do some act to his own or any other person's prejudice.[4]

---

[1] See, eg, *R v Whitely* (1991) Cr App Rep 25. In this case, the appellant had obtained unauthorised access to a number of computer systems and caused significant amounts of data to be deleted. Upholding his conviction on a charge of criminal damage, the Court of Appeal accepted that no physical damage had been caused to any element of the network but held that '[w]hat the Act requires to be proved is that tangible property has been damaged, not necessarily that the damage itself is tangible. There can be no doubt that the magnetic particles upon the metal discs were a part of the discs and if the appellant was proved to have intentionally and without lawful excuse altered the particles in such a way as to cause an impairment of the value or usefulness of the disc to the owner, there would be damage within the meaning of Section 1 [of the Criminal Damage Act 1971]' (p. 28).

[2] The Law Commission published a consultation paper, *Computer Misuse*, in 1988 (No. 110) and a report of the same title in 1989 (No. 186). Slightly earlier, the Scottish Law Commission had published a consultative memorandum, *Computer Crime* in 1986 (No. 68) and a report in 1987 (No. 106).

[3] [1988] 1 AC 1063.   [4] s. 1.

The problems identified earlier relating to the possibility, or impossibility, of deceiving a machine are overcome in this statute, with section 10 providing that attempts to induce a machine to accept the instrument are to be equated with attempts so to induce a person.

The defendants were convicted at trial but their appeals were accepted unanimously, initially by the Court of Appeal and subsequently by the House of Lords. Delivering his judgment in the Court of Appeal, the Lord Chief Justice concluded:

> We have accordingly come to the conclusion that the language of the Act was not intended to apply to the situation which was shown to exist in this case . . . It is a conclusion which we reach without regret. The Procrustean attempt to force these facts into the language of an Act not designed to fit them produced grave difficulties for both judge and jury which we would not wish to see repeated. The appellants' conduct amounted in essence . . . to dishonestly obtaining access to the relevant Prestel data bank by a trick. That is not a criminal offence. If it is thought desirable to do so that is a matter for the legislature rather than the courts. We express no view on the matter.[5]

Rightly or wrongly, the decision was widely seen as conferring a form of legal immunity on hackers. When the government failed to include proposals for legislation in its legislative programme for the following parliamentary session, a Bill was introduced as a private member's measure and, receiving a good measure of governmental support, received the Royal Assent in 1990 as the Computer Misuse Act. This remains the cornerstone of UK law in the field.

Traditionally, criminal law has been seen as the province of national authorities. As developments in technology gathered pace, it became increasingly apparent that national legislation might be of limited effectiveness. Rather, as was the concern in the field of data protection, the existence of computer crime havens might threaten the effectiveness of national computer crime statutes. Beginning with the Council of Europe Cybercrime Convention, which was opened for signature in 2001,[6] there have been a number of international initiatives with the European Union also becoming increasingly active in the field. As well as making provision for harmonising substantive criminal offences, there have been moves to enhance cooperation between law enforcement agencies at a procedural level.

The Council of Europe Cybercrime Convention

The Council of Europe Convention is a substantial document. Its drafting was a lengthy process, occupying some four years and more than fifty meetings of the Committee of Experts on Crime in Cyberspace. The Convention contains a mix of substantive and procedural aspects. In a manner similar to that adopted in the Council's Data Protection Convention, the instrument specifies attributes which must be found in the national laws of its signatory states. It will then be a matter for each state to implement the provisions in domestic law. Although many aspects of the Convention are rather technical and non-contentious, procedural provisions relating to interception and retention of communications data did cause more controversy. The civil rights organisation, 'Treatywatch', for example, commented that:

> The Cybercrime Treaty is an international agreement created for the ostensible purpose of helping police cooperate on crimes that take place on the Internet. Unfortunately, the treaty, which was drafted with very little public input, requires signatory nations to cooperate with

---

[5] [1987] 3 WLR 803 at 809–10.
[6] The United Kingdom signed the Convention in 2001 but did not complete ratification until 2011.

foreign dictatorships and give invasive new surveillance powers to law enforcement. It also lacks protections for privacy or other civil liberties, and applies far more broadly than to just the Internet.[7]

Although concluded under the auspices of the Council of Europe, the Convention (as is also the case with the data protection convention) is open for signature and ratification by non-Member States. To date, forty-five countries have signed the Convention, including the non-Member States of Australia, Canada, the Dominican Republic, Japan, the United States, and South Africa. To date thirty-six European states and four non-European (all signatories apart from South Africa) have ratified it and it is becoming a model for legislation in the sector.

OECD Guidelines for the Security of Information Systems

Also active in the field of computer crime has been the Organisation for Economic Co-operation and Development (OECD). As far back as 1986, the organisation published a report on *Computer-Related Crime: Analysis of Legal Policy*. This identified a range of actions relating to computers which it was suggested should attract criminal sanctions.

In 1992, the Council of the OECD adopted a Recommendation Concerning Guidelines for the Security of Information Systems. These guidelines were replaced by a further set of Guidelines 'For the Security of Information Systems and Networks'.[8] Addressed to all players in the sector, the Guidelines recognise that:

> Participants depend upon interconnected local and global information systems and networks and should understand their responsibility for the security of those information systems and networks. They should be accountable in a manner appropriate to their individual roles. Participants should review their own policies, practices, measures, and procedures regularly and assess whether these are appropriate to their environment.

Recognition that all parties share responsibility for developing and maintaining a culture of security perhaps highlights the close existence between concepts of data protection and computer crime. Many of the Guidelines are aimed primarily at computer users, including advice in matters such as ensuring that virus-checking software is installed and up to date and that any security patches issued by software developers are implemented.

An Implementation Plan for the Guidelines was published in 2003.[9] This recommended that governments should be:

- enacting a comprehensive set of substantive criminal, procedural, and mutual assistance legal measures to combat cybercrime and ensure cross-borders cooperation, which should be at least as comprehensive as, and consistent with, the Council of Europe Convention on Cybercrime
- identifying national cybercrime units and international high-technology assistance points of contact and creating such capabilities to the extent they do not already exist
- establishing institutions that exchange threat and vulnerability assessments, such as national CERTs (Computer Emergency Response Teams)
- developing closer cooperation between government and business in the fields of information security and fighting cybercrime.

---

[7] <http://www.treatywatch.org/>.
[8] Available from <http://www.oecd.org/dataoecd/16/22/15582260.pdf>.
[9] Available from <http://www.oecd.org/dataoecd/23/11/31670189.pdf>.

The Guidelines were further supplemented in 2005 with the publication by the Working Party on Information Security and Privacy of a report on *The Promotion of a Culture of Security for Information Systems and Networks in OECD Countries*. This includes a comprehensive account of national measures intended to implement the Guidelines.

EU initiatives

Within Europe, the EU has limited legislative competence in the criminal field and although it has been active in respect of Internet content, this has primarily taken the form of encouraging the development of schemes to categorise the contents of websites and of filtering mechanisms which can be used to restrict the range of sites which may be accessed from a particular computer. Typically, parents would be able to restrict their children's access to sites which displayed sexual or violent material. The EU has also adopted a Directive on combating the sexual abuse and sexual exploitation of children and child pornography.[10] A more general Directive on Attacks against Information Systems was adopted in August 2013.[11] These measures replace the 2004 Framework Decision on Attacks against Information Systems.[12] In a Communication published in February 2013[13] entitled 'An Open, Safe and Secure Cyberspace', the Commission outlined its legislative priorities indicating that:

> Information and communications technology has become the backbone of our economic growth and is a critical resource which all economic sectors rely on. It now underpins the complex systems which keep our economies running in key sectors such as finance, health, energy and transport; while many business models are built on the uninterrupted availability of the Internet and the smooth functioning of information systems.

A number of action lines were identified as having a high priority:

- achieving cyber resilience
- drastically reducing cybercrime
- developing cyberdefence policy and capabilities related to the Common Security and Defence Policy (CSDP)
- developing the industrial and technological resources for cybersecurity
- establishing a coherent international cyberspace policy for the European Union and promote core EU values.

In respect of substantive legal measures, the Directives referred to constitute the main EU legislation. Also to be noted, however, is the establishment of the European Union Agency for Network and Information Security (ENISA)[14] in 2004. The legal basis for ENISA is now found in the Regulation 'Concerning the European Union Agency for Network and Information Security (ENISA) and Repealing Regulation (EC) No 460/2004'.[15] The Recitals to the Regulation state that the goal of the agency, which is based in Heraklion in Greece, is to contribute:

> to the goals of ensuring a high level of network and information security within the Union and developing a culture of network and information security for the benefit of citizens, consumers, enterprises and public administrations.

---

[10] Directive 2011/92/EC, OJ 2011 L335/1.
[11] Directive 2013/40/EC, OJ 2013 L218/8.
[12] COM (2002) 173 final.
[13] JOIN (2013) 1 final.
[14] <http://www.enisa.europa.eu/>.
[15] Regulation 526/2013, OJ 2013 L165/41.

Effectively, ENISA is intended to be a source of information and advice for all parts of the EU as to emerging threats in the fields of cybercrime and security and as to techniques and procedures through which they may be countered.

At a perhaps more practical level, the European Cybercrime Centre (EC3)[16] has been established since January 2013 as a component of the European Police Agency, Europol. It is indicated that:

> The Centre will be the focal point in the EU's fight against cybercrime, contributing to faster reactions in the event of online crimes. It will support Member States and the European Union's institutions in building operational and analytical capacity for investigations and cooperation with international partners.
>
> . . .
>
> The purpose of EC3 Strategy & Prevention is to make the citizens and businesses of the EU safer through increased insight, knowledge and awareness raising. The EC3 analyses large amounts of data from a variety of sources—both crime data and open sources—to understand how cybercriminals, child sex offenders and fraudsters think and operate. What we learn not only helps law enforcement target its operations more effectively: it also informs changes in policy and legislation and, most important of all, is the basis for our advice to citizens and businesses on how to protect themselves from online threats.[17]

Conclusions

The topic of computer crime has occupied much legislative time around the world. In some respects, the early instances of computer viruses such as the 'I Love You' version, which infected millions of computers globally, served to provide a wake-up call for many governments, who had to come to terms with the existence of gaps in the coverage of national laws.[18] It did not take the Philippine authorities long to enact computer misuse legislation. The widespread adoption of the Council of Europe Convention on Cybercrime—certainly compared with the adoption of its data protection Convention outwith the ranks of the Council's Member States—indicates perhaps that this initiative has struck a chord. The provisions of this Convention, together with the manner in which these are implemented in the United Kingdom, will be considered in more detail in the following chapters.

---

[16] <http://www.europol.europa.eu/ec3>.

[17] <https://www.europol.europa.eu/ec3/strategy>.

[18] Dating from 2000, 'I Love You' was perhaps the first computer virus to attract widespread attention. The name relates to the subject matter of a message sent to millions of users which invited them to click on an attachment, with dire consequences for their computers' health. A useful account of the virus can be found at <http://news.bbc.co.uk/1/hi/uk/736080.stm>.

10

Substantive criminal law provisions

INTRODUCTION

As discussed in the previous chapter, the Council of Europe's Convention on Cybercrime has become accepted as the leading international instrument in the field. Its provisions, which are largely replicated in the EU's Directives, will be used in this chapter to indicate the major headings under which computer-related conduct might be prosecuted and to analyse the effectiveness of UK legislation in the field. In its provisions, the Convention defines four categories of conduct which it requires to be the subject of criminal offences:

- offences against the confidentiality, integrity, and availability of computer data and systems—this essentially refers to computer hacking and to attempts to impair the operation of computer systems through interception of communications, the promulgation of viruses or the launching of denial of service attacks

- computer-related offences—this category relates essentially to issues of computer fraud, whether through targeting computers directly or engaging in conduct intended to obtain personal data with a view to securing financial advantage, something generally referred to as identity fraud

- content-related offences—as defined in the Convention, this relates to conduct involving the production, dissemination, or possession of child pornography

- offences related to infringements of copyright and related rights.

The first three of these will be considered, respectively, in this and the following two chapters, whilst the fourth will be examined later when considering the general operation of intellectual property law. The Convention and EU legislation also contain extensive procedural provisions.

Offences against the confidentiality, integrity, and availability of computer data and systems

Under this heading, the Convention sets out the parameters of offences relating to illegal access, often involving hacking, illegal interception of data in the course of its transmission over a communications network, and also the concept of data and system interference, which may typically result from the promulgation of viruses or the use of denial-of-service attacks. The provisions of sections 1, 2, and 3 of the Computer Misuse Act, as amended by the Police and Justice Act of 2006, provide the major UK input in this regard.

Illegal access

Article 2 of the Convention requires that:

Each Party shall adopt such legislative and other measures as may be necessary to establish as criminal offences under its domestic law, when committed intentionally, the access to the whole or any part of a computer system without right. A Party may require that the offence be committed by infringing security measures, with the intent of obtaining computer data or other dishonest intent, or in relation to a computer system that is connected to another computer system.

Article 3 of the European Directive provides that:

Member States shall take the necessary measures to ensure that, when committed intentionally, the access without right, to the whole or to any part of an information system, is punishable as a criminal offence where committed by infringing a security measure, at least for cases which are not minor.

There are differences between the two approaches although the EU measures provide a minimal set of conditions. Member States may choose to adopt more punitive provisions.

The Council of Europe formulation confers considerable discretion upon signatory states, an approach that is repeated throughout its provisions. Largely, no doubt because it is dealing with provisions of criminal law which tend to be guarded jealously by national legislatures, the Cybercrime Convention provides for a much lower degree of harmonisation than was achieved by the Council's earlier Data Protection Convention. Article 2 provides an excellent example of the approach. There are three elements in its definition which allow states the option how to proceed. The core element of the offence is that conduct be carried out intentionally, something that will be discussed later, but there are also options for states to require the overcoming of security measures, the presence of dishonest intent, or—what might be referred to as the essence of hacking—the use of one computer to connect to and access data on another computer as pre-requisites for the commission of an offence.

The issue of whether criminality should be dependent upon access having been obtained through overcoming security devices has been debated extensively. Adopting such an approach would be compatible with legal provisions in respect of many other areas of activity. If a person obtains entry to premises by overcoming some security system—such as a lock on the door—an offence will generally be committed at that moment in time. If, however, the door has been left open by the property owner, the mere act of entering premises will not normally be unlawful unless and until the individual engages in further aggravating conduct such as damaging or removing objects. Although the Scottish Law Commission in its *Report on Computer Crime* had proposed that commission of an unauthorised access offence should be contingent upon an intention either to secure a benefit for the perpetrator or to cause loss to the computer owner, the Law Commission argued that the mere fact of obtaining unauthorised access should suffice:

because of the possibility that any attempted entrant may have had password access to important levels of authority, sometimes to a level which has enabled him to delete records of his activities from the system, any successful unauthorised access must be taken very seriously. Substantial costs are therefore incurred in (i) taking security steps against unauthorised entry . . . and (ii) investigating any case, however trivial, where unauthorised activity does in fact occur.[1]

Significantly, however, the Law Commission recommended that the offence should be regarded as a relatively minor one, attracting a maximum penalty of three months' imprisonment. As enacted, the Computer Misuse Act provided for a maximum sentence of six months' imprisonment, a period which was increased to two years with the entry into force of the Police and Justice Act of 2006.[2]

---

[1] Law Commission No. 186 at para. 1.29.

[2] In cases where the prosecution is on a summary basis, the maximum sentence is twelve months' imprisonment in England and Wales, but only six months' for Scotland.

Although in terms of its penalties, the unauthorised access offence (generally referred to as the 'basic offence') is the least significant of the Computer Misuse Act's provisions, its linkage with other provisions makes it in many ways the most critical element of the legislation. The offence is defined in section 1 of the Computer Misuse Act 1990, which, as amended by section 35 of the Police and Justice Act 2006, provides that:

1. A person is guilty of an offence if—

    (a) he causes a computer to perform any function with intent to secure access to any program or data held in any computer or to enable any such access to be secured;

    (b) the access he intends to secure or to enable to be secured, is unauthorised; and

    (c) he knows at the time when he causes the computer to perform the function that that is the case.

In common with other statutes in the field, no attempt is made to define the word 'computer'. This may lead to problems given the increasingly ubiquitous presence of microprocessors. Many modern appliances such as washing machines and motor cars make extensive use of these to control their functioning. In such a situation, it might be argued that a person who, without receiving the owner's permission, switched on a washing machine would be guilty of the unauthorised access offence. Again, a car thief might also face prosecution under section 1 of the Computer Misuse Act. Such a prospect was identified in Parliament, where the prospect was welcomed by at least one MP who, in opposing proposals to amend the offence to restrict its scope, argued:

> This is a computer misuse Bill. It seeks to tackle unauthorised access to computers which may well include electronic locks . . . Someone breaking into a car using an electronic key to operate the lock may not be caught under the present legislation if a policeman puts his hand on his shoulder before he gets in and tries to drive away. We are attempting to make it an offence for people to gain unauthorised access to an electronic system. The clause is properly drafted.[3]

Although the scope of the offence is broad, a number of conditions require to be established to secure a conviction. Three elements call for detailed consideration. The concept of access raises a number of issues and the scope of the definitions are extremely broad. Next comes the question of whether access is authorised. Finally, it must be established by the prosecution that an accused knew that access was being sought without authority.

Obtaining or enabling access to computers or data

The key step in the commission of the offence will consist of causing a computer 'to perform any function with intent to secure access to any program or data held in any computer'. A variety of elements from this definition call for further discussion and comment.

The Act provides that access will be secured to a program or data when the user, by causing the computer to operate in any manner:

(a) alters or erases the program or data;

(b) copies or moves it to any storage medium other than that in which it is held or to a different location in the storage medium in which it is held;

(c) uses it; or

(d) has it output from the computer in which it is held (whether by having it displayed or in any other manner).[4]

---

[3] HC Official Report, SC C (Computer Misuse Bill), col. 9, 14 March 1990.   [4] s. 17(1).

Although these provisions are somewhat tortuous (and are themselves subject to further definition in the Act), most actions whereby a user makes contact with a computer system will come within its ambit. The simple act of switching on a computer will cause start-up programs to function and cause various messages to be displayed on the screen.

The popular image of a computer hacker is of someone who accesses computer systems by making a connection from their own computer. This perception caused considerable problems in the first prosecution brought under the Computer Misuse Act 1990 and resulted in the accused being acquitted of charges under the Act on the direction of the judge. The case was referred to the Court of Appeal by the Attorney General, where it is reported as *A-G's Reference (No. 1 of 1991).*[5] The defendant in this case had been employed as a sales assistant by a wholesale locksmith. He left their employ, but subsequently returned to the premises indicating the intention to purchase an item of equipment. Details of sales transactions were entered into a computer terminal. The defendant was familiar with the use of the system and, taking advantage of a moment when the terminal was left unattended, entered a code into the system. The effect of this was to instruct the computer to give a 70 per cent discount on the sale. The invoice which was subsequently generated charged the sum of £204.76 instead of the normal price of £710.96. Upon these facts coming to light, the defendant was arrested and charged with an offence under the Computer Misuse Act 1990. At trial, the judge dismissed the charge, holding that the phrase in section 1(1)(a) referring to obtaining access to 'any program or data held in any computer' required that one computer should be used to obtain access to a program or data held on another computer.

Given evidence from many computer crime surveys that most instances of computer misuse are perpetrated by 'insiders', such a restriction would severely limit the application of the statute. The Attorney General, acting under the authority of the Criminal Justice Act 1972,[6] sought the opinion of the Court of Appeal on the question whether:

> In order for a person to commit an offence under Section 1(1) of the Computer Misuse Act 1990 does the computer which the person causes to perform any function with the required intent have to be a different computer from the one into which he intends to secure unauthorised access to any program or data held therein?

Delivering the judgment of the court, the Lord Chief Justice answered this question in the negative. There were, he ruled:

> no grounds whatsoever for implying or importing the word 'other' between 'any' and 'computer', or excepting the computer which is actually used by the offender from the phrase 'any computer'.[7]

Such a view, which is undoubtedly correct but a misunderstanding of the scope of the Act's provisions, has been a recurring theme over the years and perhaps indicates a lack of precision in the drafting of the offences.

As originally enacted, the Computer Misuse Act criminalised only the direct attempt to obtain access to a computer. The European Union Framework Decision (now replaced by the 2012 Directive) required that Member States also criminalise conduct which is intended to aid and abet those committing offences. It provides in Article 7 that:

> Member States shall take the necessary measures to ensure that the intentional production, sale, procurement for use, import, distribution or otherwise making available, of one of the following tools, without right and with the intention that it be used to commit any of the

---

[5] [1992] 3 WLR 432.   [6] s. 36.
[7] *A-G's Reference (No. 1 of 1991)* [1992] 3 WLR 432 at 437.

offences referred to in Articles 3 to 6, is punishable as a criminal offence, at least for cases which are not minor:

    (a) a computer programme, designed or adapted primarily for the purpose of committing any of the offences referred to in Articles 3 to 6;

    (b) a computer password, access code, or similar data by which the whole or any part of an information system is capable of being accessed.

The Police and Justice Act of 2006 adds a new section 3A to the Computer Misuse Act providing that:

    (1) A person is guilty of an offence if he makes, adapts, supplies or offers to supply any article intending it to be used to commit, or to assist in the commission of, an offence under section 1 or 3.

    (2) A person is guilty of an offence if he supplies or offers to supply any article believing that it is likely to be used to commit, or to assist in the commission of, an offence under section 1 or 3.

    (3) A person is guilty of an offence if he obtains any article with a view to its being supplied for use to commit, or to assist in the commission of, an offence under section 1 or 3.

    (4) In this section "article" includes any program or data held in electronic form.

This provision would have the effect of criminalisng websites which provided details of passwords that could then be used to obtain unauthorised access to other sites. Many tools, however, can be categorised as 'dual use' and the extent to which their creators or suppliers may be caught by the prohibition is unclear. Software packages are marketed that can, for example, generate enormous numbers of passwords. These can be used by network operators to check the effectiveness of their own security but can also be used by hackers seeking to obtain unauthorised access.

When is access unauthorised?

Access is held to be unauthorised when the user:

    (a) is not him or herself entitled to control access of the kind in question to the program or data; and

    (b) he or she does not have the consent to access of the kind in question to the program or data from any person who is so entitled.[8]

In many cases, the person entitled to control access will be the owner of the computer system itself. In other cases, a computer system may serve as a 'host', providing storage space and access facilities for programs or data controlled by other parties. In this situation, the question of who has the right to consent to access may be more complex. Most university computer systems provide illustrations of this form of activity. Here, the fact that a student is granted rights of access does not confer any entitlement to transfer these on to a third party.

In many cases, the initial act of making contact with a computer system will not suffice to demonstrate knowledge that access is unauthorised. Even though a hacker contacting computer systems at random (or making use of details supplied by a fellow enthusiast) may well suspect that their attentions may not be welcome, and may indeed be reckless as to whether this would be the case, it may be very difficult to establish that they had

---

[8] Computer Misuse Act 1990, s. 17(5).

actual knowledge that access was unauthorised at the point of initial contact. The dividing line between reckless and intentional conduct may well be crossed once contact is made. Typically, websites which intend to restrict access to authorised users will display a message on their home screen to the effect that 'Unauthorised access to this system is ILLEGAL under the provisions of the Computer Misuse Act 1990'. The mere presence of such a notice might be sufficient to justify the assumption that any further attempts to operate or access the contents of the system will be conducted in the knowledge that this is unauthorised. The installation of a security system, typically allocating authorised users with passwords and requiring these to be entered at the stage of initial contact, would undoubtedly reinforce this position.

Unauthorised use by authorised users

This is one of the most difficult aspects of the unauthorised access offence and the case law illustrates well the problems that have been faced in formulating laws to deal with technology. The Computer Misuse Act prohibits unauthorised access. In the case where an individual has no entitlement to access material, the application of the provision is relatively straightforward. Difficulties have, however, arisen in the situation where an individual is entitled to access information but uses this for an unauthorised purpose. An example might be taken from the case of *R v Thompson* discussed more fully in the following chapter, where a dishonest programmer used his access to his employer's computer to facilitate attempted theft. Similar, although perhaps less extreme, conduct was at issue in the case of *R v Bignell*.[9] Here, two police officers obtained access to data held on the police national computer in order to identify the owner of a number of motor vehicles. The information was sought for the officers' personal interest and was not connected with their duties as police officers. The conduct being discovered, they were charged under section 1 and convicted at trial. On appeal, although it was not contended that the use to which the data was put was authorised, the Divisional Court accepted submissions to the effect that:

> the primary purpose of the Computer Misuse Act was to protect the integrity of computer systems rather that the integrity of information stored on the computers . . . a person who causes a computer to perform a function to secure access to information held at a level to which the person was entitled to gain access does not commit an offence under S.1 even if he intends to secure access for an unauthorised purpose because it is only where the level of unauthorised access has been knowingly and intentionally exceeded that an offence is committed, provided the person knows of that unauthorised level of access.

The court held that no offence had been committed under the Computer Misuse Act, although it was suggested that charges might have been brought under the Data Protection Act 1984. As discussed more extensively elsewhere, under the provisions of this Act, any obtaining, holding, disclosure, or international transfer of data by a servant or agent of a data user which contravenes the terms of the latter's entry on the Register will render the individual concerned liable under both criminal and civil law.[10]

The decision in *Bignell*[11] was widely criticised and was reconsidered in the later case of *R v Bow Street Magistrates' Court, ex p Allison*.[12] This case concerned an application by the US authorities for the extradition of the applicant to face charges of, inter alia, securing unauthorised access to the American Express computer system with the intent to commit offences of theft and forgery. The issue before the court was whether the conduct alleged, had it taken place in the United Kingdom, would have constituted a breach of section 2

---

[9] *The Times*, 6 June 1997.   [10] s. 5(3).   [11] (1998) 1 Cr App Rep 1.
[12] [1999] 4 All ER 1. The decision of the Divisional Court is reported at [1999] QB 847.

of the Computer Misuse Act which established what is referred to as the ulterior intent offence. This provides that:

1. A person is guilty of an offence under this Section if he commits an offence under Section 1 above ('the unauthorised access offence') with intent—

   (a) to commit an offence to which this Section applies; or

   (b) to facilitate the commission of such an offence (whether by himself or by any other person).[13]

The offences referred to in the above passage are defined as being those for which the sentence is prescribed by law[14]—effectively the offence of murder or those for which a person with no previous criminal record might, upon conviction, be sentenced to a term of imprisonment of five years or more.[15] The maximum sentence for commission of the section 2 offence is itself a term of five years' imprisonment.

The declared intent behind the ulterior-intent offence was to bring forward in time the moment at which a serious criminal offence is committed. The issues will be discussed in more detail in the next chapter looking at computer fraud, but essentially general provisions of criminal law draw a distinction between conduct which is preparatory to the commission of an offence and that which is part (successful or not) of its perpetration. The Law Commission, in its report, identified a number of problems which might arise in the computer field creating circumstances where conduct might not constitute an attempt under the general provisions of criminal law, but which was felt to justify special treatment within the computer context.[16] One example cited concerned a hacker who secured access to a bank's computer system, the system being used for electronic fund transfers. In order to accomplish a transfer, a password would have to be transmitted. The Law Commission hypothesised that the hacker might attempt to transmit a large number of combinations in the hope of finding the correct one. In the event that the password was discovered, used, and a transfer of funds accomplished, the Law Commission was in no doubt that the offence of theft would be committed. The act of transmitting combinations of numbers and letters in the attempt to discover a valid password would not, it considered, be regarded as more than conduct preparatory to the commission of a crime. As such, it would not constitute a criminal attempt, especially in the event that further steps would be required in order to complete the transfer. Reference has previously been made to the speed at which vast sums of money may be transferred using the electronic fund transfer system. In terms of time, it seems clear that the gap between conduct preparatory of a crime and its perpetration may be very short where this form of conduct is at issue.

In *Allison*, the defendant had allegedly conspired with another party, Jean Ojomo, who had been employed by American Express. In the course of her work, she was instructed to access specific accounts but once online could access other account information. This was passed on to Allison, who was able to use it to encode credit cards, obtain personal identification numbers, and make withdrawals from automatic teller machines. Allison was later arrested in England in possession of forged cards, having been photographed using such a card to make a cash withdrawal. The conduct at issue, it was alleged, would have constituted a breach of sections 1, 2, and 3 of the Computer Misuse Act 1990.[17] Following the decision

---

[13] s. 2.   [14] s. 2(2)(a).   [15] s. 2(2)(b).

[16] Law Commission No. 186 (1989) at paras. 3.52–3.53.

[17] ss. 2 and 3 are considered later. Section 2 creates what is referred to as the 'ulterior intent' offence. This involves securing unauthorised access to programs of data with the intention of using the access to facilitate the commission of a further serious offence. Although extradition could only be authorised for a s. 2 offence, the penalties for breach of s. 1 being too low to warrant this process, it was necessary for the prosecution to establish commission of the unauthorised access offence as a prerequisite for liability under s. 2.

in *Bignell*,[18] it was held by the Divisional Court that the section 1 offence had not been committed and therefore there could be no question of a section 2 offence being committed.

The consequences of the Divisional Court's decisions in *Bignell*[19] and *Allison*[20] for the operation of the Computer Misuse Act 1990 were potentially significant. As stated above, most instances of computer fraud (and perhaps fraud in general) are committed by insiders. The decisions, therefore, were seen as conferring a degree of immunity upon such actors. An appeal was made in the case of *Allison* and resulted in a robust rejection by the House of Lords of the notion that the misuse of access rights could not incur criminal sanctions. Delivering the judgment of the House, Lord Hobhouse quoted from the provisions of section 17, which define the concept of access and authorisation. This provides that access is unauthorised if a person:

(a) is not himself entitled to control access of the kind in question to the program or data; and

(b) he does not have consent to access by him of the kind in question to the program or data from any person who is so entitled.

In both situations, it was held, account had to be taken of the use to which access was put rather than merely to the data which was accessed. The section, it was held:

> makes clear that the authority must relate not simply to the data or programme but also to the actual kind of access secured. Similarly, it is plain that it is not using the word 'control' in a physical sense of the ability to operate or manipulate the computer and that it is not derogating from the requirement that for access to be authorised it must be authorised to the relevant data or relevant programme or part of a programme. It does not introduce any concept that authority to access one piece of data should be treated as authority to access other pieces of data 'of the same kind' notwithstanding that the relevant person did not in fact have authority to access that piece of data. Section 1 [of the Computer Misuse Act 1990] refers to the intent to secure unauthorised access to any programme or data. These plain words leave no room for any suggestion that the relevant person may say: 'Yes, I know that I was not authorised to access that data but I was authorised to access other data of the same kind.'[21]

In terms which are reflective of the first decision under the Computer Misuse Act 1990, *A-G's Reference (No. 1 of 1991)*,[22] the Divisional Court was criticised for importing words into the statute. The Act, it was held was not concerned with access to 'kinds' of data. It looked rather at the entitlement to access particular programs or items of data. The decision of Kennedy J in the Divisional Court, it was held:

> treats the phrase 'entitlement to control' as if it related to the control of the computer as opposed to the entitlement to authorise operators to access to programs and data. He adopts the extraneous idea of an authorised level of access without considering whether, on the facts of the case, it corresponds to the relevant person's authority to access the data in fact accessed. He confines s. 1 of the Act to the 'hacking' of computer systems as opposed to the use of a computer to secure unauthorised access to programs or data. Upon a misreading of s. 17(5) [of the Computer Misuse Act 1990], he fails to give effect to the plain words of s.1. The meaning of the statute is clear and unambiguous.[23]

---

18 *R v Bignell* [1998] 1 Cr App Rep 1.
19 *R v Bignell* [1998] 1 Cr App Rep 1.
20 *R v Bow Street Magistrates' Court, ex p Allison* [1999] 4 All ER 1.
21 *R v Bow Street Magistrates' Court, ex p Allison* [1999] 4 All ER 1 at 7.
22 [1992] 3 WLR 432.
23 [1999] 4 All ER 1 at 9.

The decision in *Allison*[24] undoubtedly closed a significant loophole that had arisen with the Computer Misuse Act 1990. It is now clear that the statute is much more than an 'anti-hacking' measure and that misuse of facilities by authorised users will expose them to the risk of criminal prosecution.

Interception of communications

Article 3 of the Cybercrime Convention provides that Member States are to ensure that national laws prohibit the intentional interception:

> without right, made by technical means, of non-public transmissions of computer data to, from or within a computer system, including electromagnetic emissions from a computer system carrying such computer data. A Party may require that the offence be committed with dishonest intent, or in relation to a computer system that is connected to another computer system.

The provisions of the Regulation of Investigatory Powers Act 2000, provide in section 2 that an offence will be committed by a person who, without obtaining a warrant, intercepts any communication transmitted over a public or private communications system. Part 2 of the Act applies to surveillance and by section 27 provides that intrusive surveillance will be unlawful unless authorised under the legislation. Section 26 provides that:

> surveillance which—

> (a) is carried out by means of a surveillance device in relation to anything taking place on any residential premises or in any private vehicle, but

> (b) is carried out without that device being present on the premises or in the vehicle, is not intrusive unless the device is such that it consistently provides information of the same quality and detail as might be expected to be obtained from a device actually present on the premises or in the vehicle.

Attempts to identify the data being processed on a computer by detecting electromagnetic emissions could well fall foul of this provision.

In the above situation, it is likely that an offence would be committed under section 1 of the Computer Misuse Act, as the perpetrator will be causing equipment to perform a function in order to secure access to data on the victim's computer. Although there are no direct precedents, a not dissimilar scenario would see a party attempting to make unauthorised use of a wireless computer network. This appears to be a growing practice, although there appears little doubt that the conduct does constitute an offence under the Computer Misuse Act. In the first case of its kind, a party who accessed a wireless network from his laptop whilst sitting in a car outside the network owner's premises was fined £500.[25]

Data and system interference

The Council of Europe Convention contains two articles prohibiting respectively data and system interference. Data interference, which is the subject of Article 4, criminalises the intentional 'damaging, deletion, deterioration, alteration or suppression of computer data without right'. Article 5, which relates to system interference, criminalises the 'the serious

---

[24] *R v Bow Street Magistrates' Court, ex p Allison* [1999] 4 All ER 1.
[25] <http://news.bbc.co.uk/1/hi/technology/4721723.stm>.

hindering without right of the functioning of a computer system by inputting, transmitting, damaging, deleting, deteriorating, altering or suppressing computer data'.

There are close similarities between the offences. The concept of damage to data is one of the original forms of computer misuse and can be illustrated by reference to the dissemination of computer viruses. System interference is perhaps a more recent concept and would apply to incidents such as denial of service attacks—a topic that is attracting increasing media attention. These can take a range of forms and are generally referred to as either denial of service or distributed denial of service attacks. A typical approach may be to direct so much spurious traffic to an e-commerce website that bona fide customers are unable to access it. No physical damage will be caused and no data may be deleted but the economic impact may be substantial. Such tactics may be carried out using a single computer—in an example discussed later, an individual used an email-generating package running on his PC to send many thousands of copies of an email to his former employer. Distributed attacks are somewhat more sophisticated and involve the use of a network of computers. In many instances, this will involve the perpetrators taking over control of machines belonging to unsuspecting individuals. Such networks, generally referred to as botnets, can be established by infecting the computers with malicious software or malware. The magazine *PC World* reported, in 2009 for example:

> As fireworks boomed on the Fourth of July, thousands of compromised computers attacked U.S. government Web sites. A botnet of more than 200,000 computers, infected with a strain of 2004's MyDoom virus, attempted to deny legitimate access to sites such as those of the Federal Trade Commission and the White House.[26]

As with the Internet itself, networks of infected computers do not respect national borders, something which renders difficult the work of law enforcement agencies in seeking to counter and prevent attacks. In 2013 it was reported by the *Financial Times* that:

> A vast network of hijacked computers responsible for more than $500 billion in bank fraud has been taken offline by an assault involving Microsoft and the American Federal Bureau of Investigation.[27]

About 1,400 botnets have been created by the Citadel malware, which first emerged in early 2012. Microsoft said the Citadel kit could be bought from underground web forums for about $2,400. It added that more than 5 million people had been affected by the malware in as many as ninety countries, including the United States and Australia. In this case it is reported that the malware has been used to commit frauds estimated at $500 million.[28]

Damage to data

Anyone possessing a degree of familiarity with computers and their method of operation will be only too well aware how fragile is the hold on electronic life of any piece of data. To the risks of accidental damage must be added those of deliberate sabotage.

The vulnerability of computer users to such events is not questioned. Once again, our concern must be with the legal consequences that may follow from such behaviour. The basic scenario involves a party altering or deleting data held on a computer system, such action taking place without the consent of the system owner. Within this, a wide range of activities can be identified. At the most basic level, the perpetrator may use 'delete' or 'reformat' commands on a computer keyboard or even bring a magnet into close proximity

---

[26] <http://www.pcworld.com/article/170546/how_to_clean_bots.html>.
[27] <http://www.ft.com/cms/s/0/50448d3a-ce50–11e2–8313–00144feab7de.html#ixzz2lBZmELrP>.
[28] <http://www.ft.com/cms/s/0/50448d3a-ce50–11e2–8313–00144feab7de.html#axzz2lBZTGul2>.

to a computer storage device. Amendment of data may be made for a variety of motives. In some cases, such as that at issue in *R v Thompson*, amendment of data may be a component of a scheme of fraud. Other actions may be driven by the intent to cause disruption to the computer owner's activities. This might involve the manipulation of computer programs through, for example, the insertion of logic bombs, which cause a computer to function in a manner desired by the perpetrator rather than its owner, whilst an ever-expanding range of computer viruses present a continual threat to the well-being of computer owners. A more recent trend involves the use of 'ransomware'. This is a form of malware that will cause the data of the victim computer to be encrypted with the threat made that it will remain unintellible unless the perpetrator is paid—often by means of Bitcoins.[29]

As enacted, section 3 of the Computer Misuse Act provided that it would be a criminal offence—punishable by a maximum sentence of ten years' imprisonment—to knowingly perform an unauthorised act in respect of the contents of any computer. The concept of an unauthorised act encompasses both the addition of data or its alteration or erasure. A modification will be regarded as unauthorised if the person causing it is not authorised so to act or does not possess the consent of a person who is so entitled.[30] Again, the possibility of different categories of rights and privileges attaching to different users must be borne in mind. Typically, an employee or a student may be entitled to use the facilities of a computer system but will not be entitled to delete any portions or to add any programs.

The effect of the unauthorised act must be:

(a) to impair the operation of any computer;

(b) to prevent or hinder access to any program or data held in any computer;

(c) to impair the operation of any such program or the reliability of any such data; or

(d) to enable any of the things mentioned in paragraphs (a) to (c) above to be done.[31]

The 1990 Act provided that, as with the unauthorised access offence, the prosecution would have to demonstrate that an accused person had acted intentionally. The 2006 modifications reduce the burden somewhat in requiring that conduct may be either intentional or reckless as to whether impairment will be caused.

At the most basic level of activity, this provision would apply in the situation where a user intentionally causes the deletion of programs or data held on a computer. The manner in which this is accomplished will be immaterial. As indicated above, at the simplest level, the user may operate delete functions so as to remove programs or data.[32] In the first prosecution brought under this provision of the Computer Misuse Act 1990, the accused had installed a security package on a computer belonging to a firm which he claimed owed some £2,000 in fees. The effect of the installation was to prevent the computer being used unless a password was entered. As this was not disclosed, the computer was effectively rendered unusable for several days, with resultant losses estimated at some £36,000. The accused was convicted and fined £1,650.[33]

---

[29] Bitcoins and other forms of virtual currency are discussed in more detail in Chapter 23.

[30] Computer Misuse Act 1990, s. 17.

[31] s. 3(2).

[32] The use of such commands may well remove details of the programs or data from any directories. The program or data will not be removed at that stage, the effect of the command being to render it liable to being overwritten as further programs or data are added to the computer. Such conduct will constitute the unauthorised modification offence, even though the 'damage' may be recoverable.

[33] *R v Whitaker* (1993) Scunthorpe Magistrates' Court. Details of this and a range of other prosecutions under the Computer Misuse Act 1990 are reported in R. Battcock, 'Prosecutions under the Computer Misuse Act', *Computers and Law* 6 (1996), p. 22.

The offence may also be committed when data is added to a computer system. One example of this, that will be discussed later, occurs when a computer is infected with a virus. The offence will also be committed where logic bombs or other programs are added to the computer system with the intent that these will operate so as to cause inconvenience to the computer user. In one instance, an IT manager added a program to his employer's system which had the effect of encrypting incoming data. The data would automatically be decrypted when it was subsequently accessed. The manager left his employment following a disagreement and some time later the decryption function ceased to operate. Once again, the effect was to render the computer unusable. Despite claims that the encryption function was intended as a security device and that the failure of the decryption facility was an unforeseen error, the manager was convicted of an offence under the Computer Misuse Act 1990.[34]

A further case brought under the legislation concerned a contract for the supply of bespoke software. The customer was late in making payment for the software and shortly afterwards the software stopped working. It transpired that the supplier, anticipating possible problems with payment, had inserted a timelock function. Unless removed by the supplier upon receipt of payment, the software would stop working from a specified date. This conduct resulted in prosecution and conviction under the unauthorised modification offence.[35]

The issues raised in this case are undoubtedly less clear-cut than in a number of the other prosecutions brought under the Computer Misuse Act. It was argued that the use of such timelocks was a legitimate response to the failure of the customer to meet the contractual obligation to pay for the software. A further point which does not appear to have been raised was whether the supplier would retain sufficient intellectual property rights in the software to be entitled to control its continued use. It could also be argued that the action would have been lawful had notice been given to the customer of the fact that the software would stop working if payment was not made timeously.

It may be that the drafting of the offence is sufficiently broad to make the mere act of unauthorised use illegal. An example might concern an employee who types a private letter using their employer's computer. As section 3(5) of the Computer Misuse Act states that the fact whether a modification is permanent or temporary is immaterial, it would not even appear that there is a necessity for the text of the letter to be stored on the computer. In the event that a portion of text is stored on a computer's hard disk, utilising only a minuscule fraction of the disk's storage capacity, any degree of impairment of the computer's capabilities will be similarly minute. The Act, however, does not require that the degree of impairment be substantial or significant. Such conditions would add further levels of complexity and uncertainty to the task of defining the scope of the legislation. It is to be recognised, however, that the act of making an unauthorised act constitutes only one element of the offence and that the prosecution is required, additionally, to establish that the party responsible intended to impair the operation of the computer or was reckless as to whether impairment was caused.[36] In addition to proscribing acts impairing the operation of a computer, the unauthorised act offence may be committed when data held on a computer is modified in a fashion which may affect its reliability. A possible scenario might involve an individual giving false information with a view to causing the modification of an unfavourable entry on a credit reference agency's files. This might render unreliable the data held on the computer and, as such, may constitute an offence under section 3.

---

[34] Battcock, 'Prosecutions under the Computer Misuse Act', p. 22.
[35] Battcock, 'Prosecutions under the Computer Misuse Act', p. 22.
[36] s. 2(2).

Taking the concept of an unauthorised modification as a whole, it would seem clear that the offence might be committed by a person who creates a computer virus and sends it out into the world with the intention that it will infect other computers. The Computer Misuse Act provides in this respect that:

1. The intent need not be directed at—

    (a) any particular computer;

    (b) any particular program or data or a program or data of any particular kind; or

    (c) any particular modification or a modification of any particular kind.[37]

A virus creator will therefore cause the modification of any computer which is infected, even though they may not be directly responsible for the infection of any particular machine, this being brought about by an unsuspecting (or even reckless) authorised user. To this extent, the phrase 'to cause' must be interpreted in two senses: in respect of the act which causes the effect and also of the act which is proximately responsible for its occurrence.

One of the early and extensively publicised cases brought under the Computer Misuse Act involved the prosecution of Christopher Pile. Using the pseudonym 'Black Baron', the accused was reported as having told detectives that 'he had wanted to create a British virus which would match the worst of those from overseas'. A number of viruses were created by Pile and concealed in seemingly innocuous programs which he published on the Internet; from there they would infect any computer onto which they were downloaded. It was estimated that the effects of the virus cost companies in the region of £500,000 and Pile secured the dubious distinction of being the first virus writer convicted under the Act, being sentenced to a term of eighteen months' imprisonment.[38]

Denial-of-service attacks

Whilst there was no doubt that the original section 3 offence was an effective tool against those disseminating viruses, conduct involving denial-of-service attacks was widely perceived as more problematic. The All Party Internet Group in its report on the Computer Misuse Act[39] reported that:

> Almost every respondent from industry told us that the CMA is not adequate for dealing with DoS and DDoS (Distributed Denial of Service) attacks, though very few gave any detailed analysis of why they believed this to be so. We understand that this widespread opinion is based on some 2002 advice by the Crown Prosecution Service (CPS) that s 3 might not stretch to including all DoS activity.
>
> In contrast the Government, many academic lawyers and also, we understand, the NHTCU (National High Technology Crime Unit), believe that s 3 is sufficiently broad to cover DoS attacks. In April 2003 the Internet Crime Forum (ICF) Legal Subgroup pointed out that s 3 did not require unauthorised access, merely unauthorised 'modification of the contents of any computer'. They expressed the opinion that the test applied would be whether the attack had rendered unreliable the data stored on a computer or impaired its operation.[40]

The revised wording introduced by the Police and Justice Act by referring to conduct intended to impair or enable the impairment of the operation of any computer is intended

---

[37] s. 3(3).   [38] M2 Presswire, 24 March 1997.

[39] Formerly available from <http://www.apcomms.org.uk/apig/archive/activities-2004/computer-misuse-inquiry/CMAReportFinalVersion1.pdf>.

[40] paras. 60–1.

to make it clear that denial-of-service attacks are unlawful. In a manner similar to the applicability of the offence of criminal damage, as the 2006 Act was proceeding through Parliament, the Divisional Court declared unequivocally in the case of *DPP v Lennon*[41] that denial-of-service attacks were caught by the original offence. The respondent in the case had admitted downloading a mail-bombing program called Avalanche from the Internet and using this to bombard his former employers with emails. The program has been promoted in the following terms:

> Avalanche is a Windows 3.x and Windows 95/NT based mail-bombing program that was developed by *H-Master*. Unlike the other bombers, Avalanche comes with a number of configuration files that permits the attacker to customize, create, and select random mail headers and messages. Using a sophisticated GUI, the bomber can select the number of mail messages to send or can force the program to send messages continuously until explicitly stopped. For anonymity, Avalanche *'features'* fake mail headers with several built-in anonymous SMTP servers. Avalanche is distributed with over 20 pages of documentation consisting of a detailed user's guide, a *Tips for Bombing* tutorial, and an *Addon Implementation Guide*. The Addon support functionality is a unique feature of Avalanche, which permits the bomber to add new attacks and functionality to the tool without recompiling the source code. Also similar to KaBoom and Up Yours, Avalanche can be used to subscribe Internet citizens to numerous mailing lists without their knowledge.[42]

Over the course of a weekend, around 5 million emails were sent, the majority of which purported to come from the company's human resources manager who had been responsible for dismissing the respondent. Charges were brought under section 3 of the 1990 Act but the trial judge expressed the view that:

1. Section 3 was intended to deal with the sending of malicious material such as viruses, worms and Trojan horses which corrupt or change data, but not the sending of emails;

2. as D&G's servers were configured to receive emails, each modification occurring on the receipt of an email sent by Mr Lennon was unauthorized.[43]

It appears that the report of the case is in error on this point and that the judge was in fact holding that each modification was authorised. Accordingly, he held that there was no case to answer. The prosecutor appealed against this ruling and the Divisional Court was unequivocally of the view that denial-of-service attacks were covered by section 3. Delivering the leading judgment, Mr Justice Jack held that although a party with an email address must give some consent to receipt of emails and for any consequential addition of data to the computer system involved, this:

> plainly does not cover emails which are not sent for the purpose of communication with the owner, but are sent for the purpose of interrupting the proper operation and use of his system. That was the plain intent of Mr Lennon in using the Avalanche program. The difference can be demonstrated in this way. If Mr Lennon had telephoned Ms Rhodes and requested consent to send her an email raising a point about the termination of his employment, she would have been puzzled as to why he bothered to ask and said that of course he might. If he had asked if he might send the half million emails he did send, he would have got a quite different answer. In short the purpose of Mr Lennon in sending the half million emails was an unauthorised purpose and the use made of D&G's email facility was an unauthorised use.

---

[41] [2006] EWHC 1201 (Admin).
[42] <http://www.thecepblog.com/papers/html/bomb/node21.html>.
[43] para. 7.

Accordingly, the case was remitted back for trial with the suggestion that:

> One test which the District Judge might consider applying is the answer which Mr Lennon would have expected had he asked D&G whether he might start Avalanche—a point I have referred to in paragraph 9 above. I mention that because it seems to me that it points to the reality of the situation, something which, I consider, has been rather missed in this case thus far.

The respondent was subsequently convicted and sentenced to a two-month period of electronic curfew.

Misuse of devices

As indicated in the *Lennon* case, a wide range of devices may be used in connection with criminal conduct aimed at computers. A market also exists for trading in user names and passwords. Article 6 of the Cybercrime Convention seeks to deter such activities by providing that:

> Each Party shall adopt such legislative and other measures as may be necessary to establish as criminal offences under its domestic law, when committed intentionally and without right:
>
>   (a) the production, sale, procurement for use, import, distribution or otherwise making available of:
>
>   (i) a device, including a computer program, designed or adapted primarily for the purpose of committing any of the offences established in accordance with the above Articles 2 through 5;
>
>   (ii) a computer password, access code, or similar data by which the whole or any part of a computer system is capable of being accessed,
>
> with intent that it be used for the purpose of committing any of the offences established in Articles 2 through 5; and
>
>   (b) the possession of an item referred to in paragraphs a.i or ii above, with intent that it be used for the purpose of committing any of the offences established in Articles 2 through 5. A Party may require by law that a number of such items be possessed before criminal liability attaches.

The Police and Justice Act 2006 adds a new section 3A to the Computer Misuse Act, providing that:

1. A person is guilty of an offence if he makes, adapts, supplies or offers to supply any article intending it to be used to commit, or to assist in the commission of, an offence under Section 1 or 3.
2. A person is guilty of an offence if he supplies or offers to supply any article believing that it is likely to be used to commit, or to assist in the commission of, an offence under Section 1 or 3.
3. A person is guilty of an offence if he obtains any article with a view to its being supplied for use to commit, or to assist in the commission of, an offence under Section 1 or 3.
4. In this Section 'article' includes any program or data held in electronic form.

In summary proceedings, the offence attracts a maximum penalty of twelve months' imprisonment (six in Scotland) or two years' following conviction on indictment.

Although there has been general support for the principles behind the measure, the manner of its implementation was subjected to extensive criticism in Parliament. The perceived problem lay in the fact that those developing and supplying tools used legitimately for checking computer security know that there is a very strong likelihood that the devices will also prove attractive to those whose intentions are more malign. The UK approach is perhaps somewhat stricter than that required by the Convention, which refers to articles 'primarily' used for criminal purposes. It is suggested, however, that liability will (or should) arise only in the event that a developer or distributor supplies articles, knowing that it is likely that the particular acquirer will use them for criminal purposes.

Malicious communications

Considerable publicity has been given to the use of social media sites to disseminate communications which might be regarded as threatening to other people. The case of *Chambers v DPP*[44] is a significant authority. In this case the appellant had been annoyed when a flight from his local airport to take him to visit his girlfriend was cancelled because of bad weather. He posted a message via his Twitter account:

> Crap! Robin Hood Airport is closed. You've got a week and a bit to get your shit together otherwise I am blowing the airport sky high!!

The message came to the attention of airport employees who reported the posting to the police. The appellant was subsequently charged with and convicted of an offence under section 127 of the Communications Act 2003. This provides that an offence is committed by a person who uses a public communications network to send (or causes to be sent) 'a message or other matter that is grossly offensive or of an indecent, obscene or menacing character'. It is also unlawful under the provision if the message is intended to cause 'annoyance, inconvenience or needless anxiety to another' either by virtue of its contents or by reason of the frequency with which communications are sent. The offence can be punished by a term of imprisonment of up to six months.

The appellant's defence was that the post was intended as a joke. This view received some support in the initial police report on the case which noted that:

> Male detained re making threats to Doncaster Robin Hood Airport. The male in question has been bailed and his phone/computer has been seized—there is no evidence at this stage to suggest that there is anything other than a foolish comment posted on 'Twitter' as a joke for only his close friends to see.

The Crown Court, however, ruled that the message was of such a nature as to be considered 'menacing' per se. Some emphasis was put on the fact that the message had been seen by security services at the airport and reported to the police. It subsequently transpired that this was due less to genuine apprehension on their part than to a legal obligation to report any possible threat, however trivial it might appear, and convicted the appellant on the basis that he must either have intended the message to be regarded in this way or, at the least, been aware that it might have been so regarded by a recipient.

The High Court, overturning the conviction, disagreed with the approach adopted by the Crown Court. The key element of its decision was the finding that the message could not properly be regarded as menacing. Such a conclusion had to be reached after a thorough consideration of all the circumstances of the case. The High Court commented:

> Before concluding that a message is criminal on the basis that it represents a menace, its precise terms, and any inferences to be drawn from its precise terms, need to be examined in the context in and the means by which the message was sent.

[44] [2012] EWHC 2157.

Whilst recognising the high level of concern relating to the possibility of terrorist attacks, the message, it was ruled, did not contain any menace. Whilst criminals and terrorists can behave in as stupid a manner as anyone else, it would be an incredibly stupid individual who posted a genuine threat on Twitter under his own name.

> Much more significantly, although it purports to address 'you', meaning those responsible for the airport, it was not sent to anyone at the airport or anyone responsible for airport security, or indeed any form of public security. The grievance addressed by the message is that the airport is closed when the writer wants it to be open. The language and punctuation are inconsistent with the writer intending it to be or to be taken as a serious warning [paragraph 31].

Having determined that the message was not of a menacing nature, the appellant's conviction was quashed. The court went on, however to give some consideration to the issue of mens rea. It pointed out that the statutory formulation referring to a person sending (or causing to be sent) a malicious message, referred exclusively to the state of mind of the sender. If it could be established that the message was intended 'as a joke, even if a poor joke in bad taste, it is unlikely that the mens rea required before conviction for the offence of sending a message of a menacing character will be established' (at paragraph 38).

Revenge pornography

Much attention is paid to these topics and there has been recent legislation concerning these activities—although as is common in the field of computer crime—there is a strong argument that established principles of the general criminal law might be successfully invoked against conduct. Attempting to define a topic is always a difficult task, but reference is generally made to the topic of revenge pornography. Generally perpetrated by an unhappy ex-partner, this tends to involve posting intimate images in a public forum—normally an Internet site—order to cause distress or to damage reputation. An alternative form of conduct is to send images to family members or possibly to a new partner of the subject.

The Criminal Justice and Courts Act of 2015 established a new offence relating to the unwarranted dissemination of sexual images. Section 33 is the key provision and states that:

> It is an offence for a person to disclose a private sexual photograph or film if the disclosure is made—
>
> (a) without the consent of an individual who appears in the photograph or film, and
>
> (b) with the intention of causing that individual distress.

The maximum penalty provided under the Act is a term of imprisonment of up to two years and a fine.

Section 34 continues to provide definitions of the conduct that might constitute disclosure and the nature of photographs. These are compatible with notions of emailing copies of files or placing material on a website. Section 35 provides:

> (2) A photograph or film is 'private' if it shows something that is not of a kind ordinarily seen in public.
>
> (3) A photograph or film is 'sexual' if—
>
> (a) it shows all or part of an individual's exposed genitals or pubic area,
>
> (b) it shows something that a reasonable person would consider to be sexual because of its nature, or
>
> (c) its content, taken as a whole, is such that a reasonable person would consider it to be sexual.

As with many statutory definitions, this does raise as many questions as it provides answers. A further complication which is referred to in the provision relates to the creation of what are sometimes referred to as pseudo photographs. With digital photographs it is a fairly simple matter to manipulate images so that, for example, the head of a person may realistically be placed on the image of the naked body of another person. This will be unlawful under the Act.

It was reported in 2016 that more than 200 prosecutions had been brought under the statute in England and Wales.[45] Looking ahead, the near ubiquitous availability of high quality camera features in smart phones will almost certainly make the issues involved increasingly significant. A range of scenarios can be identified ranging from the surreptitious taking of photographs by an accused person to the consensual recording of images or, as attracts much publicity, the practice of 'sexting'.

Another practice which has attracted prominence with the increasing use of the Internet is that of 'trolling'. Again definitions are elusive but the essence is that false comments are posted—typically on social media websites—with the intention that they will cause distress to another person. The activity can create consequences in a number of contexts and reference has been made above to the potential implications in the area of defamation. The principal statute that is applicable in this context is the Malicious Communications Act 1998. This has been amended on a number of occasions and in its present form states that an offence will be committed by:

(1) Any person who sends to another person—

    (a) a letter, electronic communication or article of any description which conveys—

        (i) a message which is indecent or grossly offensive;

        (ii) a threat; or

        (iii) information which is false and known or believed to be false by the sender; or

    (b) any article or electronic communication which is, in whole or part, of an indecent or grossly offensive nature, is guilty of an offence if his purpose, or one of his purposes, in sending it is that it should, so far as falling within paragraph (a) or (b) above, cause distress or anxiety to the recipient or to any other person to whom he intends that it or its contents or nature should be communicated.

Again, the maximum penalty for the commission of the offence is a two-year term of imprisonment and a fine.

Also relevant in this context are provisions in the Communications Act 2003 that state that it is an offence to send 'by means of a public electronic communications network' a message or other material that is 'grossly offensive or of an indecent, obscene or menacing character'.[46] In 2015, more than 1,200 people were convicted of offences under this provision. It is perhaps testimony to the increasing use of the Internet that this figure is greater by a factor of almost ten than was the case in 2004. Between the two statutes it has been estimated that five people a day are convicted of offences.[47]

Finally to be considered in this context is the Protection from Harassment Act 1997. This Act provides in section 1 that an offence will be committed by a person who pursues a course of harassment. In determining what forms of conduct will constitute harassment, the Act

---

[45] For details of prosecutions that have been brought under the legislation see <http://www.cps.gov.uk/news/latest_news/prosecutors_being_advised_to_learn_from_revenge_porn_cases/>.

[46] s. 127.

[47] <http://www.telegraph.co.uk/news/uknews/law-and-order/11627180/Five-internet-trolls-a-day-convicted-in-UK-as-figures-show-ten-fold-increase.html>.

provides that it is to be determined by reference to 'a reasonable person in possession of the same information would think the course of conduct amounted to harassment of the other' (person). A 'course of harassment' requires that conduct occur on at least two occasions.

In most cases, the penalty for the offence of harassment is a sentence of up to six months' imprisonment (section 2). Where the conduct conveys a threat of violence this increases to a maximum term of five months' imprisonment (section 4). In addition to the initial criminal offence, the Act provides in section 3 that a victim may seek a civil court order prohibiting continuance of the conduct. Any breach of such an order can be punishable by up to five years' imprisonment. An interesting example of the use to which the Act can be put is seen in the case of *AMP and Persons Unknown*.[48] The background to the case perhaps illustrates much of the sexual conduct that receives extensive media publicity. The claimant had used her mobile phone to take sexually explicit photos of herself. As the case report puts it, these were 'taken for the personal use of her boyfriend at the time', a practice perhaps more generally referred to as 'sexting'.

The phone was lost or stolen and sometime later the woman received social media messages from a person with the threat that the photos would be published on the Internet unless the woman added him as a 'friend' on Facebook. A name was given but the actual sender was never identified. The 'request' was ignored and sometime later copies of the photos were uploaded to a website hosted from Sweden. The claimant succeeded in getting them removed from this site but they reappeared on file-sharing sites using bit-torrent uploading and downloading technologies. Proceedings were instigated before the High Court seeking an order prohibiting anyone within the court's jurisdiction from uploading or downloading the materials or identifying the claimant.

After hearing legal argument for the claimant (for obvious reasons the unknown defendants were not represented) the court held that an order should be made on two grounds. First the act of taking and disseminating photographs from a mobile phone infringed the claimant's right to privacy under Article 8 of the European Convention on Human Rights (ECHR). Not surprisingly, it was held that in balancing Article 8 rights which the right to receive and impart information guaranteed under Article 10, the privacy rights easily prevailed. More significantly for the present discussion, it was held also that the conduct would constitute harassment as prohibited under the Protection from Harassment Act 1997.

In another case brought under the Act, *Dowson v Chief Constable of Northumbria Police*,[49] six elements were set out as being relevant to the question whether conduct might amount to harassment:

1. There must be conduct which occurs on at least two occasions,

2. which is targeted at the claimant,

3. which is calculated in an objective sense to cause alarm or distress, and

4. which is objectively judged to be oppressive and unacceptable.

5. What is oppressive and unacceptable may depend on the social or working context in which the conduct occurs.

6. A line is to be drawn between conduct which is unattractive and unreasonable, and conduct which has been described in various ways: 'torment' of the victim, 'of an order which would sustain criminal liability' [at paragraph 142].

Applying these criteria, the judge held that:

> In this case . . . I consider that, on the current evidence, there has been conduct on at least two occasions; the conduct was targeted at the Claimant; it was calculated, in an objective

---

[48] [2011] EWHC 3454.   [49] [2010] EWHC 2621(QB).

sense, to cause alarm or distress; objectively judged it would be oppressive and unacceptable in the context in which it occurred and, in my judgment would cross the line and be conduct which amounts to harassment, alarm or distress.

Conclusions

Nearly twenty years of computer crime legislation has seen perhaps more than its share of ups and downs. Although a number of judgments limiting the scope of the Computer Misuse Act 1990 have been overturned by the higher courts, it is tempting to recall the words of the Law Commission, arguing that 'There is recurrent (and understandable) difficulty in explaining to judges, magistrates and juries how the facts fit in with the present law of criminal damage', and reflect that perhaps rather little has changed.

11

Computer fraud and forgery

INTRODUCTION

As indicated in the previous chapter, computer fraud was probably the first form of computer-related conduct to attract the attention of the criminal law. The concept of fraud has, of course, featured in the criminal law for many centuries and in the case where the perpetrator seeks to secure direct and unmerited financial gain at the expense of another person the fact that a computer is involved makes no significant impact. If a person obtains a debit card and PIN number and withdraws money from a cash machine without the consent of the account holder an offence is committed. One area where there may be issues, especially with global financial networks, concerns the questions of when and where an offence is committed? Many attempts at fraud are reported to originate in countries such as Nigeria or Russia.

Beyond jurisdictional problems, a more complex legal situation arises where advantage gained takes the form of avoiding charges that would otherwise have to be paid. A simple example from the non-computer world might be the attempt to make a train journey without purchasing a ticket.

As discussed previously in the context of the case of *R v Gold*, problems have been identified in cases where a perpetrator interacts only with a machine. Traditionally, English law offences were based on the notion that the perpetrator had made a false pretence. The Theft Act 1968 introduced the new notion of obtaining goods or services by deception. The change was justified on the ground that it focused attention on the impact of the conduct on the victim. This is perhaps a questionable approach in any event. In the train example given above it is perhaps hard to see a train-operating company as a human victim. It does, of course, also raise the metaphysical point whether a machine can be deceived.

Along with the notion of computer fraud we have another well-established criminal offence, that of forgery. In previous eras we had forged banknotes and coins. Today we may have forged (or cloned) debit and credit cards. As with fraud, in many cases there will be no doubt that an offence has been committed but evidential and jurisdictional difficulties in securing a conviction.

As with other aspects of the topic, the provisions of the Council of Europe's Cybercrime Convention have significantly influenced UK law in the field. Title 2 is headed Computer-related Offences and within it Articles 7 and 8 require the criminalisation of computer-related forgery and computer-related fraud, providing that:

> Each Party shall adopt such legislative and other measures as may be necessary to establish as criminal offences under its domestic law, when committed intentionally and without right, the input, alteration, deletion, or suppression of computer data, resulting in inauthentic data with the intent that it be considered or acted upon for legal purposes as if it were authentic, regardless whether or not the data is directly readable and intelligible. A Party may require an intent to defraud, or similar dishonest intent, before criminal liability attaches.

Each Party shall adopt such legislative and other measures as may be necessary to establish as criminal offences under its domestic law, when committed intentionally and without right, the causing of a loss of property to another person by:

(a) any input, alteration, deletion or suppression of computer data,

(b) any interference with the functioning of a computer system,

with fraudulent or dishonest intent of procuring, without right, an economic benefit for oneself or for another person.

Computer-related forgery

Although its application proved somewhat disastrous in the case of *R v Gold*,[1] there is no doubt that the provisions of the Forgery and Counterfeiting Act 1981 could successfully be applied to most instances of computer-related forgery. Perhaps the leading authority on the point is the case *of R v Governor of Brixton Prison and Anor, ex p Levin*.[2] This case concerned extradition proceedings, following a partially successful attempt by a number of computer hackers based in Russia to access customer account details on computers belonging to Citibank in the United States and to transfer balances to accounts controlled by members of the conspiracy. Although the balances were transferred and some sums of money withdrawn, the conduct was discovered. Some of the conspirators were arrested in the United States and the applicant was arrested by the UK authorities when he arrived at Stansted Airport, reportedly en route to a computer exhibition in London. The United States applied for him to be extradited to stand trial there. In line with normal provisions of extradition law, this request could be granted only if the conduct alleged would consititute an offence in the place where the individual was being held—England. Attention focused on the provisions of the Forgery and Counterfeiting Act 1981. Section 1 of the Act provides that:

A person is guilty of forgery if he makes a false instrument, with the intention to induce somebody to accept it as genuine to his own or any other person's prejudice.

As in *R v Gold*, the issue before the court concerned the identity of the false instrument. The applicant's conduct had caused modifications to be made to the data held on computer storage devices within Citibank. That constituted an instrument and in response to the issue of whether it should be classed as 'false', the court ruled that:

We consider the disk embraces the information stored as well as the medium on which it is stored, just as a document consists both of the paper and the printing upon it. Thus by entering false instructions onto the disk it was in our opinion falsified.[3]

Repelling arguments advanced by counsel for the applicant that the House of Lords decision in *R v Gold* indicated that such a disk could not be an instrument, the court referred to Lord Brandon's judgment in the House of Lords and his approval of the comments of the Law Commission, whose *Report on Forgery and Counterfeit Currency*[4] stated that a forged document contained two messages: one as to the nature of the document, and the second relating to the words intended to be acted upon. In the present case it was concluded, unlike

---

[1] [1988] 1 AC 1063.   [2] [1997] QB 65.   [3] [1997] QB 65 at 79.
[4] Law Commission No. 55, 1973.

the situation in *R v Gold* where data was held in the victim computer only momentarily, the data:

> were inserted onto the disk with the purpose that they should be recorded, stored and acted upon. The instructions purported to be authorised instructions given by Bank Artha Graha to Citibank. They were not authorised and in our view the disk with the instructions recorded and stored on it amounted to a false instrument.[5]

Computer-related fraud

Fraud is a somewhat complex area of the law and is capable of encompassing a wide range of forms of conduct. The simplest, in many respects, is where a perpetrator seeks to obtain money belonging to someone else by means of some form of trick or unauthorised conduct. In respect of this form of conduct, there will be little doubt concerning its criminality of conduct. Both Law Commissions, for example, expressed the view that 'when a computer is manipulated in order dishonestly to obtain money or other property, a charge of theft or attempted theft will generally lie'.[6]

If there is little doubt concerning the fact that once another person's property has been obtained, an offence will be committed, one matter which assumes some significance is the question of when the offence is committed. In this respect, the case of *R v Thompson*[7] furnishes a helpful illustration.

Thompson was employed as a computer programmer by a bank in Kuwait. Details of customers' accounts were maintained on the bank's computer system and, in the course of his work, Thompson was able to obtain information about these. Having identified five target accounts, Thompson opened an equal number of accounts in his own name at various branches of the bank. In what might be regarded as a classic form of computer fraud, he compiled a program which instructed the computer to transfer sums from these accounts to accounts which he had opened with the bank. In an effort to reduce further the risks of detection, the program did not come into effect until Thompson had left the bank's employ to return to England. The program was also intended to erase itself and all records of the transactions once this task had been accomplished. Although the law report does not go into detail on this matter, the fact that Thompson stood trial for his actions might indicate that this part of the scheme was not successful.

On his arrival in England, Thompson opened a number of accounts with English banks and wrote to the manager of the Kuwaiti bank, instructing him to arrange for the transfer of the balances from Kuwait to his new English accounts. This was done. Subsequently, his conduct was discovered and charges of obtaining property by deception were brought against him and a conviction secured at trial. An appeal was lodged on the basis that the English courts had no jurisdiction in the matter, as any offence would have been committed in Kuwait.

This plea did not commend itself to the Court of Appeal, which held that the offence was committed at the moment when the Kuwaiti manager read and acted upon Thompson's letter. At this stage, Thompson was subject to the jurisdiction of the English courts. Delivering the judgment of the court, May LJ stated:

> Discard for the moment the modern sophistication of computers and programmes [*sic*] and consider the old days when bank books were kept in manuscript in large ledgers. In

---

[5] [1997] QB 65 at 80.   [6] Law Commission Working Paper No. 110 (1988), para. 3.4.
[7] [1984] 3 All ER 565.

effect all that was done by the appellant through the modern computer in the present case was to take a pen and debit each of the five accounts in the ledger with the relevant sums and then credit each of his own five savings accounts in the ledger with corresponding amounts. On the face of it his savings accounts would then have appeared to have in them substantially more than in truth they did have, as the result of his forgeries; but we do not think that by those forgeries any bank clerk in the days before computers would in law have thus brought into being a chose in action capable of being stolen or of being obtained by deception.[8]

The conclusion that no offence involving theft or the fraudulent obtaining of property had been committed at the stage of making the false entry on the computer does not entail that no offence would have been involved. Thompson's conduct, had it taken place in the United Kingdom, might have constituted forgery under the terms of the Forgery and Counterfeiting Act. It is also likely that, following the decision in *Allison*, discussed in the previous chapter, and in *Levin*, discussed earlier in this one, the appellant would have committed offences under sections 1, 2, and 3 of the Computer Misuse Act, with the section 3 offence now attracting a maximum jail term of ten years. More recent reform has come with the enactment of the Fraud Act 2006, following the Law Commission's *Report on Fraud* published in 2002.[9]

Deception of a machine

In part, this issue can be seen as having arisen through a well-meaning, though perhaps short-sighted, incident of law reform. Under the provisions of the Larceny Act 1916,[10] fraud related conduct involving interaction with a machine was prosecuted on the ground of obtaining services by means of a false pretence. This remains the basis of liability in Scots law, and, in its Consultative Memorandum,[11] the Scottish Law Commission expressed the view that in determining whether this offence has been committed, attention should be paid to the conduct of the perpetrator. If the intention is to obtain services dishonestly, the offence will be committed and the fact of whether the conduct operates upon a human or a machine is irrelevant.

In England, the *Eighth Report of the Criminal Law Revision Committee* recommended a shift from false pretence to deception, on the basis that the word deception:

> has the advantage of directing attention to the effect that the offender deliberately produced on the mind of the person deceived, whereas 'false pretence' makes one think of what exactly the offender did in order to deceive.[12]

This report was published in 1966, long before the problems of the computer had fully penetrated general legal consciousness. Its recommendations were adopted in the Theft Act 1968, which defined the concept of 'deception' as involving:

> any deception (whether deliberate or reckless) by words or conduct as to fact or as to law, including a deception as to the present intentions of the person using the deception or any other person.[13]

---

[8] *R v Thompson* [1984] 3 All ER 565 at 569. The decision in *Thompson* has been strongly criticised by T. Smith in *Property Offences* (London, 1994), paras. 325–6, on the basis that if the transaction in Kuwait had been a nullity, its transfer to the United Kingdom could not become the theft of a 'chose in action'.

[9] Law Commission No. 276.   [10] s. 32(1).

[11] Scottish Law Commission Consultative Memorandum No. 68 (1986), para. 3.9.

[12] 'Theft and Related Offences', Cmnd 2977 (1966), para. 87.   [13] s. 15(4).

Although the point was never definitively settled, it was widely assumed that only a human being could be the victim of deception. In the case of *Davies v Flackett*,[14] a motorist was charged with obtaining car-parking services by deception. The car park in question had an automatic barrier control at its exit. Upon a motorist inserting payment of 5p into a machine, the barrier would be raised, allowing exit. The appellant approached the exit barrier, only to discover passengers from the preceding car forcibly lifting the barrier to allow that car to leave. Considerately, they remained holding the barrier and invited the appellant to follow. This conduct was observed by the police, who proved less charitably disposed, charging the appellant (and presumably the other actors in the drama) with dishonestly obtaining a pecuniary advantage by deception, contrary to section 16 of the Theft Act 1968. The charge against the appellant was dismissed by the justices on the basis that a machine had no mind and therefore could not constitute the victim of a deception. The prosecution appealed, seeking the opinion of the Divisional Court on the question of whether 'an act of deception directed towards a machine in the absence of any human agent is sufficient to support a prima facie case in the preferred information'.[15]

The Divisional Court agreed with the justices that the defendant should be acquitted, but expressed the view that the major flaw in the charge lay in the absence of any evidence that the defendant intended to evade payment. The evidence, it was held, indicated that the defendant had intended to pay when he entered the car park and remained of this intention until the very last moment, when the opportunity to avoid payment was presented to him. The question whether a machine could be deceived was treated very much as a subsidiary question, and differing views were expressed by the judges. Bridge J indicated doubt that this might be the case, commenting 'even if it is possible for a deception to be practised so as to establish that ingredient of the offence under Section 16 [of the Theft Act 1968] without there being a human mind to deceive (though for myself I doubt it)',[16] whilst Acker J, after holding that the case was not properly to be regarded as one involving deception of a machine, stated:

> Nothing which I say expressing my agreement that this appeal should be dismissed in any way suggests that an offence cannot be committed where there is any mishandling of a machine, and thereby an advantage is incurred.[17]

Rather like a ticking time bomb, the comments in *Davies* were to lie dormant for a period of years but ultimately produced explosive results when, rather than seeking a definitive ruling on the point, the decision was taken to bring the prosecution in the case of *R v Gold*[18] under the terms of the Forgery and Counterfeiting Act 1981. The acquittal of the Prestel hackers gave considerable impetus to the move to introduce computer-specific legislation.

In 2002, the Law Commission published a *Report on Fraud*.[19] This gave extensive attention to the question of whether a machine might constitute the victim in a scheme of deception. Initially, it was commented that:

> A machine has no mind, so it cannot believe a proposition to be true or false, and therefore cannot be deceived. A person who dishonestly obtains a benefit by giving false information to a computer or machine is not guilty of any deception offence. Where the benefit obtained is property, he or she will normally be guilty of theft, but where it is something other than property (such as a service), there may be no offence at all.[20]

---

[14] [1973] RTR 8.   [15] [1973] RTR 8 at 10.   [16] *Davies v Flackett* [1973] RTR 8 at 11.
[17] [1973] RTR 8 at 11.   [18] [1988] 1 AC 1063.   [19] Law Commission No. 276.
[20] Law Commission No. 276, para. 3.34.

Although consideration was given to the possibility that reform should provide that a machine could be deceived, it was concluded that this form of conduct should be criminalised under a new offence of dishonestly obtaining services. This offence will be considered later. In respect of the general law of fraud, it was proposed that there should be a shift from reliance upon the concept of deception to revert to a focus on the behaviour and intentions of the perpetrator. Accepting the Law Commission's recommendations, the Fraud Act 2006 was adopted. This provides in section 2 that:

(1) A person is in breach of this Section if he—

    (a) dishonestly makes a false representation, and

    (b) intends, by making the representation—

        (i) to make a gain for himself or another, or

        (ii) to cause loss to another or to expose another to a risk of loss.

(2) A representation is false if—

    (a) it is untrue or misleading, and

    (b) the person making it knows that it is, or might be, untrue or misleading.

The Law Commission had considered that this provision would have been sufficient to deal with the situation where a person's contact was only (or largely) with a machine. An example might be where a party obtains a credit card and PIN number belonging to someone else and uses this to obtain goods, either over the Internet or by using a chip and PIN machine in a shop. The government argued, however, that:

> We do not want law enforcers to face unreasonably technical choices in making charges and we consider therefore that the Bill should make it clear that a false representation should be an offence whether made to a machine or to a person. This is done by making amendments to provide expressly that representations may be implied and that a representation may be regarded as being made where it or anything implying it is submitted to any system or device, the aim being to clarify, for example, that the entering of a number into a chip-and-pin machine is a representation.[21]

Accordingly, a further subsection was introduced, providing that:

(5) For the purposes of this Section a representation may be regarded as made if it (or anything implying it) is submitted in any form to any system or device designed to receive, convey or respond to communications (with or without human intervention).

In line with developments in the field of computer crime generally, further provision is made to criminalise various forms of dealings in respect of materials that may be used to facilitate a scheme of fraud. Section 6 of the Act provides that possession of an article for use in the commission of a fraud will itself constitute an offence, whilst section 7 provides that:

(1) A person is guilty of an offence if he makes, adapts, supplies or offers to supply any article—

    (a) knowing that it is designed or adapted for use in the course of or in connection with fraud, or

    (b) intending it to be used to commit, or assist in the commission of, fraud.

---

[21] HL Official Report, vol. 679, col. 1106, 14 March 2006.

By section 8, it is provided that "'article" includes any program or data held in electronic form'. Lists of passwords or PIN numbers would come within the scope of this definition.

The dishonest obtaining of services

Money is not the only thing of value in the world. Increasingly, information may be the most significant asset of many businesses. It has long been the case that where information is linked to some tangible object, the informational content may be taken into account in determining the gravity of any offence. In terms of physical components—paper and ink—there will be virtually no difference between a £5 and a £50 note, but theft of the latter will be a more serious matter than theft of the former. It is well established, however, that information taken in isolation will not constitute property which may serve as the subject matter for an offence of theft.

A vast market exists for the provision of electronic information services. In the legal field, information services such as 'Lexis' and 'Westlaw' offer their wares to the legal world—at a price. In a typical scenario, a person wishing to make use of an information service will enter into an agreement with the service provider, and be provided with a password or other identifier, allowing access to all or part of the contents of the database in return for an agreement to make specified payments.

In the event that a party manages to secure unauthorised access to such a database, either by dishonestly obtaining password details or by finding a way to bypass the security system, information will be obtained without proper payment being made. The provisions of section 2 of the Fraud Act described above will not be applicable to the situation where services are involved as it is provided that the terms 'gain' and 'loss' 'extend only to gain or loss in money or other property'.[22] Services cannot come within the scope of this definition.

Recognising that it is more and more common for services to be supplied in situations where a party's only contact is with a computer or some other form of machine, the Law Commission recommended the establishment of a new offence involving the dishonest obtaining of services. Whilst falling short of providing that information could constitute the subject matter of theft, the offence is described as being 'theft-like' in nature. It was accordingly recommended that:

> Any person who by any dishonest act obtains services in respect of which payment is required, with intent to avoid payment, should be guilty of an offence of obtaining services dishonestly.[23]

Acting upon this recommendation, the Fraud Act provides in section 11 that:

(1) A person is guilty of an offence under this Section if he obtains services for himself or another—

(a) by a dishonest act, and

(b) in breach of Subsection 2.

(2) A person obtains services in breach of this Subsection if—

(a) they are made available on the basis that payment has been, is being or will be made for or in respect of them,

(b) he obtains them without any payment having been made for or in respect of them or without payment having been made in full, and

---

[22] s. 5.   [23] Law Commission Report 276, para. 8.13.

    (c) when he obtains them, he knows—

        (i)   that they are being made available on the basis described in paragraph (a), or

        (ii) that they might be,

    but intends that payment will not be made, or will not be made in full.

In line with general practice, the Act does not provide a definition of the term 'dishonest'. The case of *Ghosh*[24] laid down a two-stage test which is generally accepted as identifying the most appropriate criteria. First, it has to be determined whether conduct would be regarded as dishonest 'according to the ordinary standards of reasonable and honest people'. If that question is answered in the affirmative, it then has to be determined whether the defendant must also have realised that the conduct was dishonest. Although such questions will be a matter for the jury in any particular case, it is difficult to imagine that conduct of the kind at issue in *R v Gold*,[25] involving the surreptitious acquisition and use of a password, would not be classed as dishonest.

Conclusions

In many respects, although of obvious practical importance, issues of computer fraud raise relatively few issues of legal significance. Taking someone else's money without justification will always constitute some form of criminal offence, the exact nature of which will vary, dependent upon the nature of the conduct. The situation has been more difficult when the conduct involves evading the charges which would normally be levied in return for the provision of a service. The provisions of the Fraud Act 2006 should serve to close a loophole which had existed in English law since the move in the 1960s to reliance upon the notion of deception as the basis for this form of offence.

---

[24] [1982] QB 1053.   [25] [1988] 1 AC 1063.

12

Virtual criminality

INTRODUCTION

Previous chapters in Part II have considered how traditional crimes such as fraud and criminal damage might be committed in an online environment. In essence, the conduct at issue involves attempting either to secure pecuniary advantage or to cause some form of pecuniary loss to the victim.

Issues such as computer fraud and damage to data can be regarded, perhaps, as the first steps in the legal response to computer-related conduct. The Internet has become much more pervasive and is impacting on almost every aspect of our lives. Talk today is of the 'Internet of Things' in which previously mundane devices such as fridges will have Internet connectivity to enable them to interact with online retailers' systems to automatically re-order food as stock levels drop. More relevant to the aims of the present chapter, the Internet is impacting on the qualitative (and quantitative) aspects of our lives in a major fashion. OFCOM data indicates that the average UK citizen spends around thirty-five hours a month on line.[1] The growth in the use of social networking sites over the past decade has been phenomenal.

Change seems to be an inevitable element of the online world. Perhaps five years ago much of the discussion was centred on notions of virtual worlds. Probably the best known site was 'Second Life'[2] which created much publicity. Many organisations rushed to develop a virtual presence in this environment. Today its impact seems much reduced whilst sites such as Facebook and Twitter have come to dominate the market—for now. Essentially all social networking sites are about communications and interaction. As in the real world, relationships can be good or bad. There is much talk today of cyber stalking or cyber bullying. In some respects these are difficult issues to discuss from a legal perspective. Many aspects of the law remain rooted in the physical world. Bullying may (not always) leave physical scars. How can this concept be transferred to an online environment where the parties do not come into any form of physical conduct?

A very high-profile aspect of the topic relates to the use of the Internet to disseminate offensive material. This is a very broad notion and in itself illustrates one of the key legislative challenges in the sector. The Council of Europe's Cybercrime Convention has a section entitled 'Content Related Offences'. In spite of the use of the plural in its heading, the section refers only to conduct relating to child pornography. The clue to the result perhaps lies in the additional Protocol to the Convention 'concerning the criminalisation of acts of a racist and xenophobic nature committed through computer systems'.[3] The need for the Protocol arose because even a group of developed countries could not agree on any form of audio or visual content that should be criminalised other than child pornography. We will consider aspects of that conduct

[1] <http://stakeholders.ofcom.org.uk/binaries/research/cmr/cmr13/UK_4.pdf>.
[2] <http://secondlife.com/>.   [3] <http://conventions.coe.int/Treaty/en/Treaties/Html/189.htm>.

later, but essentially the attempt to extend the scope of the Convention was defeated by the refusal of the United States to sign up to provisions that might well be struck down by its courts as breaching constitutional guarantees to freedom of expression—however distasteful those expressions might be. The compromise solution was to restrict the Convention to the most minimalistic level and to include other conduct in an additional Protocol—to which the United Kingdom is also not a signatory.

Internet pornography

From its earliest days, the Internet has been used for the display and transfer of pornographic and other forms of unsavoury material. Its status as a communication channel largely outside existing schemes of broadcasting and publishing regulation has made it attractive to those whose activities operate on or beyond the edges of legality. The amount of pornographic materials is a source of some contention. One widely cited source from 2010 suggested that 37 per cent of the Internet was made up of pornographic material. Intuitively, this figure does seem excessive and even the original authors have indicated that they would no longer rely on it.[4] Other estimates put the figure as low as 4 per cent. As with estimates of computer crime generally, the most accurate assessment is that nobody knows. In this context also there is great uncertainty what content is unlawful with definitions varying widely between different countries.

A number of instances of successful prosecutions will be described later. Problems may, however, arise in two areas. First, there is the problem of defining or categorising the Internet. Different forms of regulation have tended to apply to different storage media and means of delivery. In part, this has been dictated by the accessibility of material to members of the public. A television broadcast, for example, is more accessible than a film in a cinema and is subject to more stringent regulation. Likewise, a greater degree of tolerance has tended to be given to printed works than to photographic materials. As has and will be discussed, the Internet does not fall easily into existing categories of communications media. A second problem may prove even less soluble. The Internet is a global network. Material may be placed on a server anywhere in the world and accessed anywhere else. In theory, this means that the Internet is perhaps the most heavily regulated sphere of activity in existence, as any country may claim jurisdiction in respect of material accessible from its territory. Claiming jurisdiction is very different from being able to enforce it in any meaningful manner. If material is lawful in the country from which it originates, there may be little that any other jurisdiction can do to regulate it. In a report on the work of the United Kingdom's Internet Watch Foundation, it was suggested that of 453 reports made concerning the presence of pornographic material, in only sixty-seven cases was the material held on a United Kingdom-based server. The bulk of the material was held in the United States with, rather more surprisingly, Japan constituting the second largest host country.

Concern at the possibilities for misuse inherent in the Internet has spawned a number of international, governmental, and industry-based initiatives. In January 1999, the European Commission adopted an 'Action Plan on Promoting Safe Use of the Internet'.[5] This claims as its objective:

> promoting safer use of the Internet and of encouraging, at European level, an environment favourable to the development of the Internet industry.[6]

---

[4] <http://www.bbc.co.uk/news/technology-23030090>.

[5] Decision 276/1999, available from <http://eur-lex.europa.eu/LexUriServ/LexUriServ.do?uri=OJ:L:1999:0
33:0001:0011:EN:PDF>.   [6] Art. 2.

In order to attain this, provision was made for funding to be provided to encourage work to be conducted in the Member States, under the guidance of the Commission, in specific fields. Particular reference was made to:

- the promotion of industry self-regulation and content-monitoring schemes (for example, dealing with content such as child pornography or content which incites hatred on grounds of race, sex, religion, nationality or ethnic origin);

- encouraging industry to provide filtering tools and rating systems, which allow parents or teachers to select content appropriate for children in their care while allowing adults to decide what legal content they wish to access, and which take account of linguistic and cultural diversity;

- increasing awareness of services provided by industry among users, in particular parents, teachers, and children, so that they can better understand and take advantage of the opportunities of the Internet;

- support actions such as assessment of legal implications; and

- activities fostering international cooperation in the areas enumerated above.[7]

The 'Safer Internet Programme' was originally scheduled to run for a three-year period between 2004 and 2007, with some €38 million of funding. This was extended for a further two years, and a further extension with a budget of €55 million was established for the period 2009–13. Work continues under the heading 'Better Internet for Kids'.

Much of the EU-funded work has concerned matters such as the development of net filters and the promotion of industry self-regulation. Within the United Kingdom, the Internet Watch Foundation was established by a number of the largest Internet Service Providers (ISPs) in 1996.[8] In part, this was a response by the industry to suggestions made by the Metropolitan Police that prosecutions might be brought against ISPs unless the industry took steps to regulate material accessible through its servers. As a number of recent cases have demonstrated, possession of material classed as child pornography is unlawful, whilst ISPs could also be classed as publishers and subject to prosecution under statutes such as the Obscene Publications Act 1964.

The Internet Watch Foundation's activities can be divided into two categories. It seeks to encourage the use of systems of content rating. A number of systems exist, such as PICS (Platform for Internet Content Selection) and RSACi, devised by the Recreational Software Advisory Council.[9] The Foundation also acts to report instances of potentially illegal material to the appropriate ISP and law enforcement agencies. To date, its efforts in seeking to prevent prosecutions being brought against service providers appear to have been successful, although it has been stressed by law enforcement agencies that no guarantee of immunity has been given. Implementation of the EU's Directive on Certain Legal Aspects of Information Society Services, in Particular Electronic Commerce, in the Internal Market[10] might reduce the liabilities of ISPs as a matter of law. Discussed in more detail later in the book, this provides in Article 12 that service providers will not be liable (other than to an injunction regarding future behaviour) where the provider:

(a) does not initiate the transmission;

(b) does not select the receiver of the transmission; and

(c) does not select or modify the information contained in the transmission.

---

[7] Art. 3.   [8] <http://www.iwf.org.uk/>.
[9] For information on rating schemes and a demonstration of their use, see <http://www.icra.org/>.
[10] Directive 2000/31/EC (the Electronic Commerce Directive).

The Internet and child pornography

Whilst initial concern tended to relate to pornography per se, with relatively conservative countries such as the United Kingdom fearing that national controls might be overwhelmed, attention has tended to become more and more focused on the specific topic of the use of the Internet as a vehicle for disseminating paedophilic material. Incidents such as 'Operation Ore', where the UK police forces are engaged in an ongoing investigation of several thousand UK citizens whose credit cards were used to pay for access to paedophilic sites based in the United States,[11] mean that the topic is seldom out of the news. It is perhaps testimony to the extent of public concerns that the Council of Europe's Convention on Cybercrime contains only one provision in its Title 3 Section headed 'Content Related Offences'. This provides that:

1. Each Party shall adopt such legislative and other measures as may be necessary to establish as criminal offences under its domestic law, when committed intentionally and without right, the following conduct:

    (a) producing child pornography for the purpose of its distribution through a computer system;

    (b) offering or making available child pornography through a computer system;

    (c) distributing or transmitting child pornography through a computer system;

    (d) procuring child pornography through a computer system for oneself or for another;

    (e) possessing child pornography in a computer system or on a computer-data storage medium.

2. For the purpose of paragraph 1 above 'child pornography' shall include pornographic material that visually depicts:

    (a) a minor engaged in sexually explicit conduct;

    (b) a person appearing to be a minor engaged in sexually explicit conduct;

    (c) realistic images representing a minor engaged in sexually explicit conduct.

3. For the purpose of paragraph 2 above, the term 'minor' shall include all persons under 18 years of age. A Party may, however, require a lower age-limit, which shall be not less than 16 years.

4. Each Party may reserve the right not to apply, in whole or in part, paragraph 1(d) and 1(e), and 2(b) and 2(c).[12]

The inclusion of this provision in what is intended to be a template for computer crime legislation at a global level highlights the point that there is near-universal legislative condemnation of child pornography. The Convention on Cybercrime provides no definitions of any of the terms used in Article 9. The explanatory memorandum accompanying the

---

[11] An indication of the global scale of pornographic activity can be taken from the fact that the US Postal Inspection Service, a federal agency charged with investigating online paedophile activity, seized records of credit card payments by some 250,000 persons, of whom around 7,000 were resident in the United Kingdom. More than two years after the details were passed to the UK authorities, although 1,230 individuals have been convicted of offences (only one prosecution having been unsuccessful) with the longest sentence being that of twelve years' imprisonment, 1,300 cases are still under investigation: <http://news.bbc.co.uk/1/hi/uk/3625603.stm>. The organiser of the original website was sentenced to 1,335 years' imprisonment in the United States!   [12] Art. 9.

Convention is rather more explicit, although even here, elements of uncertainty persist. It is provided, for example, that:

> The term 'pornographic material' in paragraph 2 is governed by national standards pertaining to the classification of materials as obscene, inconsistent with public morals or similarly corrupt. Therefore, material having an artistic, medical, scientific or similar merit may be considered not to be pornographic. The visual depiction includes data stored on computer diskette or on other electronic means of storage, which are capable of conversion into a visual image.

It is noteworthy that although there is absolute condemnation of those involved in the production, sale, or distribution of material, the Convention on Cybercrime leaves it open to signatory states to determine whether and to what extent the acts of obtaining or possessing material should be considered unlawful. Even in this context, international consensus is limited.

For the United Kingdom, the provisions of the Convention on Cybercrime do no more than restate existing legal provisions. The Protection of Children Act 1978 established a number of offences involving the making of photographic images of children.

Following the report of the Bryon Review, *Safer Children in a Digital World* in 2008,[13] a range of offences were established under the Coroners and Justice Act 2009 with the statute providing that it will be an offence for a person to be in possession of what is referred to as a 'prohibited image' of a child.[14] This is defined in terms of an image showing any form of sexual activity either involving a child or being carried out in the presence of a child.[15] The term 'image' includes:

(a) a moving or still image (produced by any means); or

(b) data (stored by any means) which is capable of conversion into an image within paragraph (a).

It is further provided that the term is not to include a photograph or pseudo-photograph. Effectively, it will apply to computer-generated images or to data which can be viewed on a computer.

Photographs and pseudo-photographs

In the Criminal Justice and Public Order Act 1994,[16] provisions were included to extend the ambit of the Criminal Justice Act 1988[17] and the Protection of Children Act 1978[18] to prohibit the possession or distribution of what are referred to as 'pseudo-photographs', where what appears to be an indecent image of a child is made up of a collage of images, modified by the use of computer painting packages, none of the elements of which is indecent in itself. It is provided that an offence will be committed where:

> If the impression created by a pseudo-photograph is that the person shown is a child, the pseudo-photograph shall be treated for all the purposes of this Act as showing a child and so shall a pseudo-photograph where the predominant image conveyed is that the person shown is a child notwithstanding that some of the physical characteristics shown are those of an adult.[19]

---

[13] <http://www.dcsf.gov.uk/byronreview/>.   [14] s. 62(1).   [15] s. 62(4)–(7).   [16] s. 84.
[17] s. 160.   [18] s. 1.   [19] Protection of Children Act 1978, s. 7(7).

The definition of a photograph extends to 'data stored on a computer disc or by other electronic means'.[20] Although this will certainly cover the situation where images are held on a computer disk on a permanent basis, the case of *R v Gold*[21] discussed earlier may be relevant as suggesting that a more transitory storage will not suffice. Given the development of communications technologies, possession of data or software is becoming of less importance than the knowledge that it can be accessed whenever desired.

Under the terms of the Protection of Children Act 1978, an offence is committed by a person who distributes such a photograph or who has 'in his possession such photographs or pseudo-photographs with a view to their being distributed or shown by others'.[22] The fact that possession may be a basis for conviction should give service providers cause for concern. A defence is provided that an accused 'had not himself seen the photographs or pseudo-photographs and did not know, nor had any cause to suspect, them to be indecent'.[23] In the situation where users of a service are responsible for loading images, the service provider may be able to make use of this defence. As with other areas of potential liability, it is unclear to what extent a service provider may be entitled to turn a blind eye to activities on the system. The phrase 'nor have any cause to suspect' might impose a higher standard in this area than is the case with liability for defamatory statements or conduct constituting a breach of copyright.

An indication of the conduct which would now be prosecuted under the Criminal Justice and Public Order Act 1994 can be seen in the case of *R v Fellows*.[24] The appellant, who was at the time employed by Birmingham University, had, without its knowledge or consent, compiled a large database of pornographic images of children. The database was maintained on an Internet-linked computer belonging to the university. The conduct in question occurred before the entry into force of the provisions of the 1994 Act. Given these changes to the law, it is now significant in only two respects. First, it appears to have been the first case in which the word 'Internet' appears in the judgment of an English court. Secondly, it provides an indication of the judicial response to the situation where new technology enables forms of behaviour which could not have been foreseen when statutory provisions were enacted.

Under the Protection of Children Act 1978, an offence is committed by a person possessing an indecent photograph of a child.[25] It is provided that 'references to a photograph . . . include the negative as well as the positive'.[26] The question before the Court of Appeal in *R v Fellows*[27] was whether images stored on a computer disk could be classed as photographs.

Answering this question in the affirmative, two issues addressed by the Court of Appeal call for comment. First, whether graphical files held on a computer fell within the statutory definition of a copy of a photograph for the purposes of the Protection of Children Act 1978, and, secondly, whether a computer hard disk containing these files could be classed as an 'article' for the purposes of the Obscene Publications Act 1959.

Although aspects of the noun 'photograph' are defined in Protection of Children Act 1978—for example, that 'references to a photograph include the positive as well as the negative version'—there is no general definition. In the Copyright Act 1956, 'photograph' was defined as 'any product of photography or of any process akin to photography'.[28] The trial judge and Evans LJ both made reference to dictionary definitions of the term as 'a picture or other image obtained by the chemical action of light or other radiation on specially

---

[20] Protection of Children Act 1978, s. 7(4)(b).
[21] [1988] AC 1063.   [22] s. 1(1).   [23] s. 1(4)(b).   [24] [1997] 2 All ER 548.
[25] s. 1(1)(c).   [26] s. 7(4).   [27] [1997] 2 All ER 548.   [28] s. 48.

sensitised material such as film or glass'.[29] On this basis, the data stored on the computer's hard disk could not be classed as a photograph. The statutory prohibitions, however, extended to 'a copy of a photograph'. The computerised images had been produced by scanning 'conventional' photographs and it was held that nothing in the 1978 Act required that the copy of a photograph should itself be a photograph.[30] Given the copyright status of a photograph as an artistic work and the broad definitions of copying applying to such works, there can be little ground to challenge such a finding.

Although this approach sufficed in the particular case, many cameras now record images directly onto disk rather than film. The contents of the disk may then be transferred directly to a computer and the image viewed on screen. There need never be any 'traditional' photograph to act as an original. In such a situation, it may be doubted whether even the most purposive interpretation of the Protection of Children Act 1978 could have sustained a conviction.

The Copyright, Designs and Patents Act 1988 adopted a new definition of photograph as 'a recording of light or other radiation on any medium on which an image is produced or from which an image may by any means be produced, and which is not part of a film'.[31] This marks a significant move away from the dictionary definition referred to earlier. In 1994, the Criminal Justice and Public Order Act 1994 adopted a different approach, providing that references to a photograph should include 'data stored on a computer disc or by other electronic means which is capable of conversion into a photograph'.[32] Juxtaposition of the two definitions can produce a sense of giddiness, but this aspect of changing technology does justify the need for reform of the Protection of Children Act 1978's provisions. Indeed, as is seen by the introduction of the new concept of a 'pseudo-photograph' in the 1994 Act, it may be queried whether the concept of a photograph remains apposite in the digital age. On this point, there is obiter comment by Evans LJ suggesting that the definition 'seems to us to be concerned with images created by computer processes rather than the storage and transmission by computers of images created originally by photography'.[33] Such a view appears unduly restrictive, and leaves open to question whether it would cover the situation where an original photograph was manipulated electronically so as to change the nature of the image.

Both the Obscene Publications Act 1959 and the Protection of Children Act 1978 were enacted before the impact of computers had permeated the legislature's consciousness. The Court of Appeal's judgment indicates that, providing basic concepts are robust, a purposive interpretation can maintain the relevance of statutory formulations so long as electronic activities retain a connection with tangible acts or items.[34] More substantial problems occur when electronic signals constitute the original record rather than a reproduction of a physical object. Here, law reform will often be required. It is somewhat ironic, however, that in a number of cases concerned with computer-oriented statutes, the purposive interpretative techniques adopted in the present case appear to have been replaced by a much more literal and restrictive approach.

Multimedia products

A further case concerned with the application of obscenity law to computer-related material is that of *Meechie v Multi-Media Marketing*.[35] The defendant company established

---

[29] *R v Fellows* [1997] 2 All ER 548 at 556.   [30] [1997] 2 All ER 548 at 557.   [31] s. 4(2).
[32] s. 84(4).   [33] *R v Fellows* [1997] 2 All ER 548 at 557–8.   [34] *R v Fellows* [1997] 2 All ER 548.
[35] (1995) 94 LGR 474.

a club, 'The Interactive Girls Club', described as being an 'organisation dedicated to the production of erotic computer entertainment for broad-minded adults'. One product presented users with a short game. Successful completion of this would cause the display of a series of erotic images. A knowledgeable user would have been able to isolate the game element, moving directly to the erotic display.

Under the provisions of the Video Recordings Act 1984, introduced to control the distribution of so-called 'video nasties', it is an offence to supply video recordings which have not been issued with a classification certificate. No certificate had been sought or issued for the particular game and charges were brought under sections 9 and 10 of the Act, alleging, respectively, supply and possession with a view to the supply of infringing recordings.

These charges were dismissed before the magistrates, who held that the product in question did not come within the scope of the legislation. Section 1 of the Video Recordings Act 1984 defines a 'video work' as:

> any series of visual images (with or without sound)—
>
> (a) produced electronically by the use of information contained on any disc or magnetic tape; and
>
> (b) shown as a moving picture.

Although it was accepted that the disk in question satisfied the requirements of section 1(2)(a) of the Video Recordings Act 1984, it was held that the images did not constitute a 'moving picture' by reason both of their brevity and of the staccato nature of the presentation, which appeared more akin to a series of still images. It was further held by the magistrates that the work in question was excluded from the legislation by the provisions of section 2, which provides that a video game is not to be subject to the classification requirements.

Both of these findings were reversed by the Divisional Court.[36] In a finding which may be contrasted with the dicta of the House of Lords in *R v Gold*[37] to the effect that the term 'recording' required storage for a more than transient period of time, it was held that the short duration of the images in no way prevented their being regarded as a 'moving picture'. A significant development arising from the advent of fast and powerful personal computers has been the linkage between text, sound, and graphics. In the present case, this relates to a computer game and picture sequences, but the same could be said of most multimedia products. It would appear arguable following the decision of the Divisional Court that many multimedia products could also be classed as video recordings, and hence be required to seek classification under the regulatory schema. Although there may be an argument in favour of such an approach, it would be difficult to explain to average computer users that their multimedia encyclopaedias are in reality video recordings.

The exemptions under the legislation apply to computer games and to works 'designed to inform, educate or instruct'. In the present case,[38] the court was able to separate the picture sequences from the game-playing element and so remove the former from the scope of the exemption. It must be likely that in the future there will be instances where video images are integrated more fully with the elements of a game, thereby making the classification more difficult. This will almost inevitably be the case with multimedia products. The court's dicta, which must be seen as affording a very restricted scope to the exemption, may make

---

[36] *Meechie v Multi-Media Marketing* (1995) 94 LGR 474. [37] [1988] AC 1063.
[38] *Meechie v Multi-Media Marketing* (1995) 94 LGR 474.

this of limited significance, and it would be arguable that many examples of multimedia products dealing with medical or artistic topics would be taken outside its scope.

A further point which may be a cause for future difficulty concerns the definition of a moving picture. Although the finding of the court to the effect that the duration of a recording is of minimal significance in determining whether it is to be classed as a 'moving picture', there cannot have been many traditional recordings with a running time of less than thirty seconds. In the present case,[39] the images could be analogised to a more traditional cinematographic recording. In other computer-related products, the duration of individual picture sequences may be very much shorter. Even more problematically, a user may be afforded the opportunity to select particular aspects of an image for expansion or, perhaps, to manipulate the form of the still image. Such activities may present the impression of movement, but it is not clear how they should be regarded for the purpose of the legislation.

Jurisdictional issues

A further, and perhaps more significant, issue concerns the difficulty of applying localised concepts of obscenity, which are dictated by cultural, religious, and societal values in the global environment of the Internet. Attempts by Nottingham County Council to prevent publication on the Internet of a copy of a summary of a report into the handling by social work officials of a case of alleged Satanic abuse illustrate graphically the near impossibility of such an endeavour.[40] Following publication of a copy of the report on a United Kingdom-based website, the Council obtained a High Court injunction preventing publication of the report on the basis that its reproduction infringed its copyright. It was stated that the order extended to any hypertext links to other sites maintaining copies of the report. Although the order was observed within the United Kingdom, by the time it was issued, copies of the report were also to be found on a number of other websites around the world. A letter from Nottinghamshire's County Solicitor to the operator of a US website threatening legal proceedings unless its copy was removed drew a somewhat stinging response. Admitting to the presence of a copy of a report, it was pointed out that the Council:

> ignore the fact that I and my website are located in Cleveland, Ohio, in the United States of America, a locus where the writs of the courts of the United Kingdom have never run.

Numerous other instances could be cited of the failure of attempts to impose national controls. In the so-called *Homulka* case in Canada, a husband and wife were accused of committing a horrendous double murder and were to be the subject of separate trials—the wife tendering a plea of 'guilty' to the charge of manslaughter. An order was made prohibiting the publication in Canada of any report of the hearings involving the wife until the husband's trial had been concluded. Once again, the ban was of some effect where traditional media were concerned, but served to prompt the establishment of a number of Usenet newsgroups, which carried full details of the case.

Other developments in the United States raise a further issue which is of wider significance. The individual states retain the power to determine what constitutes obscene material. This has raised questions of whether the operators of online services may be subjected to the most restrictive laws of the range of jurisdictions where the service is made available.

---

[39] *Meechie v Multi-Media Marketing* (1995) 94 LGR 474.

[40] For a comprehensive collection of material on the case, see <http://www.users.globalnet.co.uk/~dlheb/jetrepor.htm>.

Whilst this may be the case in the situation where a service provider has a physical point of presence in a particular locality, in other instances, a perceived danger is that there might be a 'race to the bottom' as countries compete to attract online business by offering a minimum set of regulatory requirements.

Against this argument, however, the case of *United States v Thomas*[41] illustrates that parties located within one jurisdiction but offering services or facilities over the Internet may find themselves subject to the most restrictive legal regime reached by their activities. In this case, the defendants operated a computer bulletin board allowing subscribers to download pornographic images (which appear to have been placed on the system in breach of copyright in the original pictures). Subscribers, who were required to submit a written application giving details of name and address, could also order videos which would be delivered by post. Under US law, a federal statute provides that an offence is committed by a person who:

> knowingly transports in interstate or foreign commerce for the purpose of sale or distribution, or knowingly travels in interstate commerce, or uses a facility or means of interstate commerce for the purpose of transporting obscene material in interstate or foreign commerce, any obscene, lewd, lascivious, or filthy book, pamphlet, picture, film, paper, letter, writing, print, silhouette, drawing, figure, image, cast, photograph, recording, electrical transcription or other article capable of producing sound or any other matter of indecent or immoral character.[42]

The interpretation of this provision may vary between states, the Supreme Court having accepted that the determination of whether material is obscene is to be made having regard to 'contemporary community standards'. The material in question was considered lawful in California.

Following a number of complaints, a postal inspector in Tennessee subscribed to the bulletin board under an assumed name. In return for a fee of $55, he was able to download a number of images. The defendants were charged and convicted before the Tennessee courts of breach of the federal statute cited above. Appealing against conviction, it was argued that material had not been transported by the defendants. Alternatively, it was contended that the trial court had erred in applying Tennessee standards of morality. Both arguments are clearly significant in the context of World Wide Web activities.

The argument against transportation is essentially a simple one. The material in question remained on the defendants' bulletin board. All that was transmitted was a series of intangible electrical impulses, whilst the terms of the statute related to tangible objects. This argument was rejected by the Court of Appeal:

> Defendants focus on the means by which the GIF files were transferred rather than the fact that the transmissions began with computer-generated images in California and ended with computer-generated images in Tennessee. The manner in which the images moved does not affect their ability to be viewed on a computer screen in Tennessee or their ability to be printed in hard copy in that distant location.[43]

A similar approach would appear to apply in the United Kingdom. In July 1999, an individual pleaded guilty to several specimen charges of publishing obscene materials contrary to the provisions of the Obscene Publications Act 1959.[44] The pornographic materials in question were stored on computers in the United States but could be accessed by customers in the United Kingdom (or anywhere else in the world) upon payment of a fee of around £20 per month.

---

[41] 1997 United States App LEXIS 12998.   [42] Title 18 USC 1465.
[43] *United States v Thomas*, 1997 United States App LEXIS 12998.
[44] *R v Graham Waddon* (1999, Southwark Crown Court, unreported).

Two contentions were critical to the defendant's case. First, it was argued that publication of the material took place in the United States. This argument was dismissed, with the judge ruling that publication took place whenever the images were downloaded onto a computer in the United Kingdom.[45] A further claim related to evidential requirements. As will be discussed in Chapter 13, the Police and Criminal Evidence Act 1984 requires that evidence be led indicating that a computer whose output is relied upon was operating properly at the relevant time. It was argued that this would have obliged the prosecution to lead information relating to the operation of the servers in the United States. Once again, the judge ruled against the defence, holding that the requirement was limited to demonstrating the reliability of the computer used to access the materials in the United Kingdom.

Although of limited precedential value, the case, coupled with the US decision in *Thomas*,[46] provides useful evidence that the 'lowest common denominator' standard will not always prevail. The prosecutions, however, could only succeed because the defendants were or could be brought within the court's jurisdiction. Where service provider and user are located in different jurisdictions, enforcement will become much more problematic. Invariably, extradition will only be sanctioned by national authorities where the conduct complained of would constitute an offence if committed on its own territory. If the service providers had been resident in the United States and had not made the mistake of entering the United Kingdom, it is unlikely that any prosecution could have been brought. In the Press Association report of the case, it was noted that:

> Vice Officers are increasingly finding that porn sites siphon subscription money through companies based in countries such as Costa Rica to avoid the attentions of authorities in Britain and the States. And while Internet Service Providers in Britain shut down sites after they are contacted by the police, Scotland Yard's appeals to American companies have fallen on deaf ears in a country where adult porn, however base, remains legal in some states.[47]

With the development of Internet banking, it is a relatively simple matter for accounts to be opened and maintained in offshore locations. Location is becoming an irrelevant consideration for e-commerce and in this, as in many other fields of activity, the prospects for effective national control are limited. As has been seen with Operation Ore, however, where the US authorities passed on details of credit card payments to their UK counterparts, there is evidence that international cooperation is increasing in this respect.

Where next for the criminal law?

Historically, the criminal law has been founded on notions of offences against the person and against property. Although in some civil law countries defamation, which might be loosely defined as causing injury to a victim's feelings, the common law has generally restricted in scope to conduct that causes actual or anticipated physical harm to a person.

A constant theme throughout this book has been that we live more and more (and increasingly significant) aspects of our lives in an online context. Actions occurring online can impact very significantly on our physical existence. A number of cases have been reported where, so-called, cyber bullying has resulted in the victim attempting suicide.

---

[45] See also the ruling in the defamation case of *Godfrey v Demon* [1999] EMLR 542.
[46] *United States v Thomas*, 1997 United States App LEXIS 12998.
[47] *Press Association Newsfile*, 30 July 1999.

In some instances there is little doubt that criminal offences will be associated with conduct. In one case that was reported in 2013,[48] a teenager had emailed explicit photos of himself in the belief that he was communicating with a fellow teenager of the opposite sex. He then received demands for payment of money failing which the photos would be passed on to family and friends. He committed suicide by jumping off the Forth bridge.

The demand for money in such circumstances must be regarded as a classic form of blackmail and the perpetrator could have faced prosecution on this basis. One complicating factor, of course, is that in the Internet era, that individual could be located anywhere in the world.

What raises more complex legal issues is that it appears that the victim had posted details of the threat on a social networking website based in Latvia 'ask.fm'. The website allows users to post questions and other users to respond anonymously. In this instance (and also in a number of other reported cases) advice on the question 'what should the poster do?' included the suggestion that the individual should kill himself. Unsavoury behaviour but is it criminal? In the 1970s the American TV show MASH was massively popular. A dark comedy set in the horrors of the Korean war, its theme tune contained the lines:

> Suicide is painless, it brings on many changes
>
> ...
>
> The game of life is hard to play, I'm going to lose it anyway.

Doubtless many other examples could be found in popular music but it is inconceivable that the lyricist, Michael Altman, could be held liable for the death of anyone who committed suicide after listening to the song.

What might be the difference? The obvious answer is the sense of intimate contact that we can experience on social networking sites. It can bring many advantages but there are also dangers. There is, I feel, a tendency in some quarters to expect too much of the Internet and, indeed of the criminal law. We do hear much of cyber bullying and the cases referred to above might be seen as examples. Bullying, however, has been a feature of life probably since the dawn of humanity. It is incredibly difficult to prevent in spite of a paper mountain of anti-bullying policies adopted by schools and similar institutions. In part problems may lie in the sense of intimacy when there is remoteness. In a heated argument I may tell an adversary to 'go jump in the river'. Matters might seem different if the other person was standing on the parapet of a bridge and I was to shout the same phrase.[49] As has been quoted in at least one report,[50] it is unlikely that even in such a case an offence would have been committed. It can be argued that the law should be changed in this regard, but the Internet is not the only culprit.

Conclusions

From media coverage, it is tempting to believe that Internet pornography poses massive challenges to the law. This is perhaps misleading. What has become clear over the past two decades is that it is difficult for nation states to enforce their own policies regarding what is or is not acceptable. There is no doubt that a computer user in the United Kingdom

---

[48] <http://www.bbc.co.uk/news/uk-scotland-edinburgh-east-fife-23712000>.

[49] This report <http://www.dailymail.co.uk/news/article-2205519/Crowd-encourage-suicidal-man-jump-50ft-building-post-video-YouTube.html> illustrates a juxtaposition between the virtual and physical worlds.

[50] <http://www.telegraph.co.uk/news/uknews/3108987/Suicide-teenager-urged-to-jump-by-baying-crowd.html>.

can readily access material which could not lawfully be purchased over (or under) the counter in a shop. There is very little that law enforcement agencies can do in this situation. Matters assume a different perspective when there is a commonality of approach between the jurisdiction where material is hosted and where it is accessed. In this, as in many other respects, the Council of Europe Convention on Cybercrime is a significant, albeit limited, development.

13

Detecting and prosecuting computer crime

INTRODUCTION

The preceding chapters have considered a variety of forms of conduct that may affect adversely the interests of computer users. Assuming that the fact of damage may be established, a variety of practical and legal problems may face the task of establishing the identity of the wrongdoer and obtaining sufficient evidence to support a criminal conviction. Issues of jurisdiction will also be of considerable significance in the situation where access is obtained to a computer system by means of some telecommunications link. In this situation, it is very possible that the perpetrator may be located in one jurisdiction and the victim in another. As was stated in the *Explanatory Report to the Council of Europe's Convention on Cybercrime*:

> One of the major challenges in combating crime in the networked environment is the difficulty in identifying the perpetrator and assessing the extent and impact of the criminal act. A further problem is caused by the volatility of electronic data, which may be altered, moved or deleted in seconds. For example, a user who is in control of the data may use the computer system to erase the data that is the subject of a criminal investigation, thereby destroying the evidence. Speed and, sometimes, secrecy are often vital for the success of an investigation.[1]

The Convention contains extensive provisions relating to procedural matters concerned with the detection of computer-related crime and elements of international cooperation. Also relevant at a more general level is the UN Convention against Transnational Organized Crime and its Protocols,[2] which was opened for signature in 2000 and entered into force in 2003, whilst at the political level extensive work has been carried out under the auspices of the G8, which established the 'Lyon Group of Senior Experts on Transnational Organized Crime'.[3]

Within the EU, the establishment of Europol[4] provides a basis for cooperation between law enforcement agencies and the 2013 Directive on Attacks against Information Systems[5] also contains some provisions relating to procedural aspects. Proposals are under consideration which would strengthen both the Directive and the role of Europol and an agreement was reached in June 2010 for the establishment of a Europol Cybercrime Task Force. In the United Kingdom the Office of Cyber Security and Information Assurance was established in

---

[1] para. 133.   [2] Available from <http://www.unodc.org/unodc/en/treaties/CTOC/index.html>.
[3] For a useful account of the G8's work, see <http://www.g8.utoronto.ca/adhoc/crime99.htm>.
[4] <http://www.europol.europa.eu/>.
[5] Directive 2013/40, OJ 2013 L 208/8. The Directive requires to be implemented in the Member States by 4 September 2015.

2009 to provide 'strategic direction' and to coordinate actions across government departments to tackle what is described as an 'ongoing, persistent threat from other states, terrorists and criminals operating in cyberspace'.[6] Also active in the field is the Centre for the Protection of the National Infrastructure (CPNI)[7] which is established as an expert agency to offer advice on protecting vital assets such as transport and power networks against criminal and terrorist threats. Its remit includes cyber security.

Interception of communications

In the situation where the conduct occurs entirely on the premises of the victim, as in the case of *A-G's Reference (No. 1 of 1991)*,[8] no particular problems may be anticipated in the acquisition of evidence. All matters will be within the control of the computer user and, assuming their willingness to cooperate, there are no legal problems facing the acquisition of evidence.

Greater difficulties arise where access is obtained remotely. The cases of *R v Gold*[9] and *R v Whiteley*[10] might be taken as illustrative of such situations. In both instances, intruders obtained access to computer systems from their own homes. Certainly, in such a situation, it is open to the victim to make available to the police and prosecution authorities any evidence within their control. This might include details of the time at which access was obtained to the computer system and details of activities undertaken in respect of the system.

In other cases, as has received massive publicity with the revelations about electronic eavesdropping by the National Security Agency (NSA) and Government Communication's Headquarters (GCHQ), communications may be intercepted in the course of their transmission over a public (or private) communications network. The Cybercrime Convention provides that:

> Each Party shall adopt such legislative and other measures as may be necessary, in relation to a range of serious offences to be determined by domestic law, to empower its competent authorities to:
>
> (a) collect or record through the application of technical means on the territory of that Party, and
>
> (b) compel a service provider, within its existing technical capability:
>
>   i. to collect or record through the application of technical means on the territory of that Party, or
>
>   ii. to co-operate and assist the competent authorities in the collection or recording of, content data, in real-time, of specified communications in its territory transmitted by means of a computer system.

The Regulation of Investigatory Powers Act 2000 (potentially to be replaced by the Investigatory Powers Act 2016) is the major UK statute setting out the circumstances under which a range of communications data might legitimately be intercepted. The original statute has been criticised in some quarters as being out of date and certainly the electronic

---

[6] <http://www.cabinetoffice.gov.uk/content/cyber-security>.   [7] <http://www.cpni.gov.uk/>.

[8] [1992] 3 WLR 432. In this case the accused was alleged to have physically accessed a computer on his former employer's premises and inputted data.   [9][1988] 1 AC 1063.

[10] (1991) 93 Cr App Rep 25.

communications world today is very different from the time the legislation was adopted. The 2000 Act replaced the Interception of Communications Act 1985, which itself marked a somewhat belated attempt to bring the United Kingdom's laws into conformity with the requirements of the European Convention on Human Rights (ECHR). The provisions of the earlier statute had been designed to regulate situations where voice-telephony messages were intercepted in the course of their transmission over a telecommunications network. This statute had certainly been overtaken by developments in technology. A particular factor has been the explosion in data communications and the switch from traditional circuit-based telecommunications to the packet-switching system that forms the backbone of the Internet. Unlike traditional messages, that are transmitted and require to be intercepted in real time, the use of packet-switching techniques, by which messages are split into a large number of segments, each of which may find its way to its destination by a different route, it will only be at this final stage that the whole message will be reassembled. Interception in the course of transmission will be almost impossible. With the increasing use of packet-switching techniques for voice data, similar problems are going to arise increasingly with attempts to intercept voice traffic. More positively for the authorities, copies of messages will normally be held on equipment belonging to an Internet Service Provider (ISP), even after they have been read by the designated recipient.[11] Such factors render easier the task of discovering the contents of email messages. Against this, however, the emergence of systems of cryptography as a tool which can be used by the average person means that interception of a message may reveal no useful or usable information.

Interception of content and communications data

The Regulation of Investigatory Powers Act provides mechanisms for authorising two distinct forms of data content and communications. The former effectively involves the attempt to discover the actual messages exchanged between suspects. In a previous era of telecommunications technology it was colloquially referred to as 'telephone tapping'. This has been regarded as a very intrusive form of surveillance and has been subject to substantial legal and procedural requirements—although it is not clear these have been complied with in the light of the ongoing NSA and GCHQ revelations. The 2015 Report of the Office of Interceptions Commissioner,[12] an independent official with the remit to oversee the operation of the legislation, indicates that in that year 3,059 warrants were issued throughout the United Kingdom.[13]

In many instances, the actual content of communications will be of limited interest or significance. Law enforcement and national security agencies may be more concerned with who is talking with whom, at what times, and how often. This is referred to as communications data. A total of 570,135 requests were made for access to communications data in the same period.

Interception of content

The Regulation of Investigatory Powers Act 2000 retains the basic structure introduced by the Interception of Communications Act 1985 whereby warrants for the interception of

---

[11] See also the provisions about data retention, discussed in Chapter 7, which will require ISPs and others involved in the provision of electronic communications services to retain selected items of data for periods of twelve months.

[12] <http://www.iocco-uk.info/docs/2012%20Annual%20Report%20of%20the%20Interception%20of%20Communications%20Commissioner%20WEB.pdf>.

[13] See <http://www.iocco-uk.info/docs/56850%20HC%20255%20ICCO%20Web%20only.pdf>.

content[14] must be authorised by the Secretary of State in situations where it is considered to be necessary:

  (a) in the interests of national security;

  (b) for the purpose of preventing or detecting serious crime;

  (c) for the purpose of safeguarding the economic well-being of the United Kingdom; or

  (d) for giving effect to international mutual assistance agreements in connection with the prevention or detection of serious crime.[15]

Financing interception

Until the 1980s interception was carried out on an administrative basis between the police and the then Post Office. With the emergence of competition in the sector, different issues arise. Maintaining a capability to intercept communications is a potentially expensive undertaking for network providers and beyond appealing to a sense of civic responsibility—not always present in corporate life—the question arises how interception is to be financed. In this respect the Act provides that:

  1. The Secretary of State may by order provide for the imposition by him on persons who—

     (a) are providing public postal services or public telecommunications services; or

     (b) are proposing to do so

of such obligations as it appears to him reasonable to impose for the purpose of securing that it is and remains practicable for requirements to provide assistance in relation to interception warrants to be imposed and complied with.[16]

Such obligations are only to be imposed following a system of statutory consultation[17] and are subject to parliamentary approval.[18] It is provided that grants are to be given to ISPs to cover additional costs incurred in providing the interception capabilities required under the Act.[19]

These provisions were the subject of extensive parliamentary debate and controversy. Concerns were expressed that the requirement to maintain an interceptory capacity in systems would create a ready-made opening for hackers. Additionally, concerns were raised that the cost implications of introducing such facilities would impose a substantial burden upon United Kingdom-based ISPs and would therefore conflict with the government's oft-stated intention of making the country the world's most e-commerce-friendly environment. Against this, the argument was put by the government that obligations to

---

[14] The term interception is defined in s. 2:

   a person intercepts a communication in the course of its transmission by means of a telecommunication system if, and only if, he—

   (a) so modifies or interferes with the system, or its operation,

   (b) so monitors transmissions made by means of the system, or

   (c) so monitors transmissions made by wireless telegraphy to or from apparatus comprised in the system,

   as to make some or all of the contents of the communication available, while being transmitted, to a person other than the sender or intended recipient of the communication.

[15] s. 5.   [16] s. 12.   [17] s. 12(9).   [18] s. 12(2).   [19] s. 14.

provide for interception of communications have traditionally been imposed upon telecommunications companies and that ISPs are licensed under the same regime. Whilst correct, it may be noted that there are very significantly more small and medium-sized ISPs than there are telecommunications companies. It was suggested in Committee[20] that such providers would be compensated for marginal costs incurred in providing the necessary facilities. Implementing the provisions of the Regulation of Investigatory Powers Act 2000, the Regulation of Investigatory Powers (Maintenance of Interception Capability) Order 2002[21] applies to companies that provide a public telecommunications service to more than 10,000 customers. This will include mobile phone companies and ISPs. Such companies may be required by the Secretary of State to maintain a capability to intercept communications at a level permitting the simultaneous interception and transmission to law enforcement agencies of transmissions in a ratio of 1 for every 10,000 users. Responses are to be provided within one working day of receipt of a request for interception.

Communications data

More discussion surrounded the provisions of Chapter 2 of the Regulation of Investigatory Powers Act 2000, which provides for law enforcement agencies to seek access to communications data. Such access may be sought under less restrictive conditions than those required to authorise interception of communications. With modern communications systems, especially mobile networks, data of the kind at issue might be used to track the movements of subscribers, whilst the detailed records of calls made and received could allow a detailed picture to be developed concerning the activities and relationships of individuals. The Regulation of Investigatory Powers (Acquisition and Disclosure of Communications Data: Code of Practice) Order 2007 approves such a code, which specifies the procedures under which a request for access may be made.

The final provision of the Regulation of Investigatory Powers Act 2000 which should be commented on in the context of information technology law concerns its provisions regarding encryption. The use of encryption is widely seen as providing a weapon to criminals to enable their plans to be communicated with minimal risk that, even if the communication is intercepted, its content could be deciphered. Various suggestions have been made by law enforcement agencies as to how the use of encryption might be regulated. The Act provides that where encrypted material has been intercepted in accordance with its provisions and there are reasonable grounds to believe:

(a) that a key to the protected information is in the possession of any person;

(b) that the imposition of a disclosure requirement in respect of the protected information is—

    i. necessary on grounds falling within Subsection (3); or

    ii. necessary for the purpose of securing the effective exercise or proper performance by any public authority of any statutory power or statutory duty;

(c) that the imposition of such a requirement is proportionate to what is sought to be achieved by its imposition; and

---

[20] HC Official Report, SC F (Regulation of Investigatory Powers Bill), 28 March 2000 (morning).
[21] SI 2002/1931.

(d) that it is not reasonably practicable for the person with the appropriate permission to obtain possession of the protected information in an intelligible form without the giving of a notice under this Section,

the person with that permission may, by notice to the person whom he believes to have possession of the key, require a disclosure requirement in respect of the protected information.[22]

Notices under this heading may be served, either on the owner of the key or on any third party who holds a copy. As an alternative to disclosing the cryptographic key, a copy of the information in decrypted format may be supplied.[23] A deliberate failure to comply with such a notice will constitute an offence.[24] A code of practice for the investigation of protected electronic information was approved by Parliament in October 2007,[25] specifying the procedures and circumstances under which these powers might be invoked.

It remains debatable how effective, or indeed how intrusive, the provisions of the Regulation of Investigatory Powers Act 2000 have been. There is no doubt that there is concern at the extent to which new communications technologies are threatening the effectiveness of traditional forms of law enforcement. As was said by the Minister of State at the Home Office in Committee:

> I should emphasise what the Home Secretary stated on Second Reading: we expect law enforcement to suffer as a result of the development of new technologies. That is a fact of life. That applies not only to encryption, which has been widely discussed, but to more fundamental developments in communications technology. We are trying to preserve as much as we can of valuable intelligence, while always focusing on the key purposes set out in clause 5 and remaining consistent with our e-commerce objectives. We should not adopt—and the Hon. Gentleman is not proposing—a philosophy of despair, of saying that we can do nothing about the matter or make any progress. However, we acknowledge that law enforcement will suffer from the development of new technology. Communications will be missed. We cannot establish a system that is totally rigid.[26]

The challenge for any new legislation in this field is to provide for effective systems of crime prevention and detection without affecting adversely the rights of the vast majority of totally innocent individuals. It does seem clear that as more and more personal information is recorded in electronic format, so the balance will have to be struck between protecting personal privacy and making use of what can be a valuable intelligence resource for law enforcement agencies.

The Investigatory Powers Act

The Regulation of Investigatory Powers Act was enacted in 2000 essentially as a reaction to the perceived deficiencies of existing laws relating to the interception of communications in the emerging era of mobile phones. The measure was controversial at the time of its enactment and that has remained the case. At one level—and largely outside the scope of the present work—concerns have been voiced regarding what have been seen as extensive use of physical surveillance techniques by local authorities in cases such as fly tipping and the attempt by a parent to get a child admitted to a school on the basis of a false claim

---

[22] s. 49.   [23] s. 50(1).   [24] s. 53.

[25] Available from <https://www.gov.uk/government/publications/code-of-practice-for-investigation-of-protected-electronic-information>.

[26] HC Official Report SC F (Regulation of Investigatory Powers Bill), 28 March 2000 (morning).

of residence in a particular locality. Reprehensible conduct perhaps, but maybe not sufficiently bad to be placed at a significant level on the spectrum of criminal activity.

A further criticism of the legislation takes a different direction with the argument
that in the communications field it has become out of date and of limited effectiveness.
What is probably the best known 'over the top' communications service, Skype, began
its operations in 2003, three years after the interception law was enacted. The technologies involved in such activities—involving the separation of communications into small
packages that potentially will be sent to their destination by a myriad of routes and reassembled only at the end point, means that the traditional notion of telephone tapping
involving listening in to telephone calls in real time in the course of their transmission
has become infeasible. A range of other factors have also come into play, including the
widespread use of encryption technology either by individual users or through features
incorporated in smart phones and applications such as messaging services.[27] Reference
should also be made to the expansion of cloud computing services that allow users to
share information without making use of what might be regarded as traditional forms of
communications. The sharing of links on a cloud service allows access to data without
actually sending the data to the recipient. The topic of data retention has also become
of increasing significance and will be discussed further. We might also take account of
the seemingly increasing use of bulk interception of communications data conducted
by national security agencies. At the moment in the United Kingdom, this is authorised
under section 94 of the Telecommunications Act 1984 although in a manner that is very
obscure in its nature. Headed 'Directions in the Interest of National Security etc', the section provides that:

(1) The Secretary of State may, after consultation with a person to whom this section
applies, give to that person such directions of a general character as appear to the
Secretary of State to be necessary in the interests of national security or relations
with the government of a country or territory outside the United Kingdom.

(2) If it appears to the Secretary of State to be necessary to do so in the interests of
national security or relations with the government of a country or territory outside the United Kingdom, he may, after consultation with a person to whom this
section applies, give to that person a direction requiring him (according to the
circumstances of the case) to do, or not to do, a particular thing specified in the
direction.

In general, legislation has developed in a rather unstructured manner, as have arrangements
for the oversight of the exercise of powers conferred by the law. There is a Parliamentary
Committee on Interception and Surveillance[28] and an Independent Reviewer of Terrorism[29]
as well as an Interception of Communications Commissioner[30] and the Information
Commissioner[31] whose remit extends over the wider field of data protection legislation.
Divide and rule has long been an element of government strategy although one of the key
elements in the new legislation is the appointment of an Investigatory Commissioner who
will take on the duties performed by the existing agencies.

In 2013 proposals were tabled by the then government for reform of the law but
these were withdrawn following opposition from its then coalition partners. They have

---

[27] Reference might be made to the recent controversy (and legal proceedings) between Apple and the US
law enforcement agencies concerning access to the contents of messages stored on a iPhone belonging to an
individual involved in a multiple killing.   [28] <http://isc.independent.gov.uk/>.
  [29] <https://terrorismlegislationreviewer.independent.gov.uk/category/reports/>.
  [30] <http://www.iocco-uk.info/>.   [31] <https://ico.org.uk/>.

now been reintroduced in the Investigatory Powers Bill which was initially presented to Parliament in November 2015 in draft form. A definitive Bill was tabled in March 2016 and the schedule envisaged by the government is that it should be enacted by December 2016.

As an opening comment it might be noted that the new measure is significantly larger than its precursor. The 2000 Act accounted for 113 pages on the statute book whilst the new measure weighs in more than double the size at 257 pages. Even allowing for consolidation of provisions across a range of statutes, this does represent a significant increase in terms of size and also of the complexity of the legislation.

Scope of the legislation

As indicated, the Act covers a wide range of forms of activity. Key provisions relate to the issuance of warrants relating to:

- the interception of communications (telephone tapping and seeking access to the content of sites accessed on the Internet or of email communications)
- access to communications and location data
- bulk interception warrants.

There are also further provisions relating to:

- data retention requirements
- the use of technologies that are designed to interfere with the operation of communications technologies such as mobile phones.

Some of these elements represent updating of existing law whilst others, principally concerned with the disruption of telecommunications and provisions for bulk interception, do mark a new development in the field.

Interception of communications

The ability to intercept communications has been a long-standing interest of governments. Initially this applied to postal communications and has extended into the era of electronic communications. In many respects, the monitoring of individual communications is a rather blunt weapon. A range of human rights instruments such as the ECHR place considerable emphasis on the right of individuals to engage in communications without the risk that they are being monitored by the state. Article 6 is one of the best known provisions in the Convention and states that:

1. Everyone has the right to respect for his private and family life, his home and his correspondence.
2. There shall be no interference by a public authority with the exercise of this right except such as is in accordance with the law and is necessary in a democratic society in the interests of national security, public safety or the economic wellbeing of the country, for the prevention of disorder or crime, for the protection of health or morals, or for the protection of the rights and freedoms of others.

As always, the sting is in the detail and the provisions in paragraph 2 of the article are of key importance. Historically in the United Kingdom (as in many other countries) telecommunications services were provided by the state and interception of communications was largely a matter for inter-departmental understanding. Such a *laissez faire* approach was declared to be incompatible with the requirements of the ECHR in the case of *Malone v United Kingdom*.[32] In this case the informal inter-departmental agreements that had operated in the country were declared to be incompatible with the Convention's requirements that interception should be 'in accordance with the law'. The Interception of Communications Act 1985 provided an initial response to this ruling and the Regulation of Investigatory Powers Act 2000 took legislative matters a stage further, although there does remain uncertainty as to whether UK law complies with the other requirement of the ECHR that interception should be 'necessary' in the context of the specific justifications identified. This adjective has been problematic for the United Kingdom in a number of contexts with governments mistakenly tending to equate the concept of necessity with that of desirability or utility.

A key feature of all the legislative instruments referred to is that interception of communications is unlawful unless it is appropriately authorised. This leads on to the further question of what forms of authorisation are required. Developments in telecommunications technology have made the question significantly more complex. In previous eras we would talk about interception of communications in terms of telephone tapping or the surreptitious opening and reading of postal communications. In the era of mobile phones and the Internet a much wider range of information is potentially available. In some respects the contents of communications are less significant than the identification of who is talking to whom, from where, and at what times. In a significant number of criminal cases, information relating to Google searches forms a significant element of the prosecution's evidence.[33]

If interception is unlawful unless authorised, consideration needs to be given to the issue of oversight. Who is to be empowered to authorise interception, and here the policy decision has tended to relate to whether responsibility should lie with a police officer, a government minister, or a member of the judiciary? As with many questions there is no simple or single answer. As indicated above, the concept of interception has become more complex.

The Bill contains extensive provisions in this regard. A request to intercept the contents of communications to and from identified individuals is required to be made to a Secretary of State. If approved by this government minister (and the requirement is that it should be personally approved) it requires also to be approved by a Judicial Commissioner who will be a senior member of the judiciary. In the event of conflict between these parties, a further appeal may be made to the Investigatory Powers Commissioner, a new appointment established under the legislation who will replace the trio of existing agencies identified above.

Location and communications data

In the age of land-line (fixed) telephones, location was not an issue of any real significance. A phone would be used where it was installed and that location would be a matter of record. Mobile phones have changed the situation dramatically and location data provides a source of data that can be of considerable value to law enforcement agencies. Location data, which is emitted whenever a mobile phone is switched on, can track its movements to a considerable degree of accuracy—in urban areas to within a few metres. At a simple level, apps used on smart phones allow users to track the location of their friends with their consent. Apps are also widely available that allow for more surreptitious monitoring although the legality of these is very debatable.

As well as location data we have the concept of communications data. This is a controversial topic that has relevance both to telephone usage and to Internet access and which

---

[32] <http://www.worldlii.org/eu/cases/ECHR/1984/10.html>.

[33] See, eg, the case reported at < http://www.valuewalk.com/2014/08/florida-man-asks-siri-how-to-dispose-of-a-dead-body/> and also <http://www.bbc.co.uk/news/uk-england-bristol-15368208>.

applies in relation to both fixed and mobile phones. The definition of communications data and its relationship with that of content data is complex with the Bill providing that:

'Communications data', in relation to a telecommunications operator, telecommunications service or telecommunication system, means entity data or events data—

(a) which is (or is to be or is capable of being) held or obtained by, or on behalf of, a telecommunications operator and—

(i) is about an entity to which a telecommunications service is provided and relates to the provision of the service,

(ii) is comprised in, included as part of, attached to or logically associated with a communication (whether by the sender or otherwise) for the purposes of a telecommunication system by means of which the communication is being or may be transmitted, or

(iii) does not fall within sub-paragraph (i) or (ii) but does relate to the use of a telecommunications service or a telecommunication system,

(b) which is available directly from a telecommunication system and falls within sub-paragraph (i), (ii) or (iii) of paragraph (a), or 5

(c) which—

(i) is (or is to be or is capable of being) held or obtained by, or on behalf of, a telecommunications operator,

(ii) is about the architecture of a telecommunication system, and

(iii) is not about a specific person,

but does not include the content of a communication.

The Bill continues to provide that:

(6) The content of a communication is the elements of the communication, and any data attached to or logically associated with the communication, which reveal anything of what might reasonably be expected to be the meaning of the communication but—

(a) anything in the context of web browsing which identifies the telecommunications service concerned is not content, and

(b) any meaning arising from the fact of the communication or from any data relating to the transmission of the communication is to be disregarded.

In the context of traditional voice based telecommunications, this is a relatively straightforward distinction. Communications data encompasses the numbers called and calling and the time and duration of the calls but does not extend to the words exchanged. Matters become more complex when we consider data relating to Internet access. An example might see a device associated with a particular IP address accessing a website associated with another IP address. The mere fact of access to a website will constitute communications data but depending on the scale of the site might indicate also the contents that have been accessed. There has been considerable debate on how substantial the level of detail relating to Internet access might be before it extends beyond communications data. In some respects the distinction is more important at the procedural rather than the practical level. Law enforcement agencies have long been able to seek access to the contents of communications but this has required to approval of a judge whereas approval for access to location and communications data can be given by a senior police officer. These powers have been used very extensively. The most recent statistics indicate that more than

517,000 such authorisations were given in 2014. This compares with around 3,058 warrants authorising the interception of communications.[34]

A controversial aspect of UK law relating to interception of communications has been that evidence obtained as a result of lawful interception of communications is not admissible or usable in the course of legal proceedings. The Bill provides that:

> No evidence may be adduced, question asked, assertion or disclosure made or other thing done in, for the purposes of or in connection with any legal proceedings or Inquiries Act proceedings which (in any manner)—
>
> (a) discloses, in circumstances from which its origin in interception-related conduct may be inferred, any of the content of an intercepted 35 communication or any related communications data, or
>
> (b) tends to suggest that any interception-related conduct has or may have occurred or may be going to occur.

Essentially, evidence obtained through the interception of communications may not be relied on (or questioned) directly in the course of criminal proceedings. The rationale behind this policy is explained clearly in a 2009 report, 'Intercept as Evidence'[35] presented to Parliament by the Home Office. This explained that:

> Sensitive intercept material, techniques and capabilities must be protected to avoid terrorists and other serious criminals evading detection and frustrating the investigation of their activities. Most targets have a rudimentary understanding of interception capabilities based on observation of police work and court proceedings, but it will be very imprecise. If terrorists and other criminals develop a more accurate understanding of the techniques and capabilities deployed against them, the task of protecting the public and national security will be considerably harder.

In 2014, the Information Tribunal—the major body responsible for determining the legitimacy of requests by individuals or organisations for access to official information under freedom of information legislation—ruled that a request for access to the legal advice underpinning this report should be made available.[36] To date this does not appear to have happened and the Bill largely continues existing practice in the area. Subject to some exceptions laid down in Schedule 3, it is provided that:

> (1) No evidence may be adduced, question asked, assertion or disclosure made or other thing done in, for the purposes of or in connection with any legal proceedings or Inquiries Act proceedings which (in any manner)—
>
> (a) discloses, in circumstances from which its origin in interception-related conduct may be inferred—
>
> (i) any content of an intercepted communication, or
>
> (ii) any secondary data obtained from a communication, or
>
> (b) tends to suggest that any interception-related conduct has or may have occurred or may be going to occur.

Any person breaching this provision is declared to be guilty of a criminal offence that may be punished by a term of imprisonment of twelve months.

---

[34] <http://www.theguardian.com/world/2015/nov/04/investigatory-powers-bill-the-key-points>.

[35] <https://www.gov.uk/government/uploads/system/uploads/attachment_data/file/228715/7760.pdf>.

[36] <http://www.informationtribunal.gov.uk/DBFiles/Decision/i1690/Bingham%20Centre%20EA.2014.0097%20%20Final%209Dec15.pdf>.

Interference with communications

Whilst much of the legislative focus is intended to ensure that defects in equipment design or manufacture do not inadvertently cause interference with other equipment, a further aspect concerns the use of technologies specifically designed to restrict or prevent mobile phone use. Such technologies might be attractive to, for example, theatres or train operating companies wishing to prevent mobile use that might interrupt performances or to enforce noise restrictions in 'quiet coaches'. Especially within the context of what is often referred to as cyber warfare, attention is being paid to the value of being able to disrupt electronic communications.[37] It has also been reported that:

> Thousands of people in the UK are using 'GPS jammers' that plug into car cigarette lighters and can stop tracking systems used to detect stolen cars, monitor vehicle use or stop drivers working overlong hours, according to new findings from experts.[38]

Guidance issued by OFCOM[39] has indicated that use of any such devices is likely to constitute a contravention of the Wireless Telegraphy Act 2006. This provides in section 8 that it is unlawful to use wireless telegraphy devices except in accordance with authorisations given by OFCOM and that these may only be given where devices are not likely to 'involve undue interference with wireless telegraphy'.[40] In addition to this specific provision, OFCOM has commented that the use of jamming devices is unlikely to meet the requirements of the Electromagnetic Compatibility Directive[41] as they are likely to cause interference with items of wireless equipment other than mobile phones and have effect in areas other than those in which they are intended to be effective.

One exception currently applies to the general prohibition in the form of the Prisons (Interference with Wireless Telegraphy) Act 2012. This provides that the Secretary of State may authorise prison governors (or the heads of similar institutions) to 'interfere with wireless telegraphy' inside the institution with the aim of preventing or detecting the use within those premises of any 'device capable of transmitting or receiving images, sounds or information by electronic communications (including a mobile telephone)'.[42] The intention is to allow prison authorities legally to take steps to block mobile phone reception and thereby the use by inmates of mobile phones within the premises.

The Investigatory Powers Bill takes matters rather further. It extends the range of institutions where jamming will be permitted to encompass psychiatric hospitals and immigration detention centres.

Bulk interception and acquisition orders

The concept of bulk interception orders is one of the most controversial aspects of the legislative proposals. It is essentially linked to the capability of intelligence agencies to intercept and filter massive amounts of communications data and was very much at the heart of the allegations made by the US whistleblower, Edward Snowden. The major UK security agency active in this area is the GCHQ which historically has worked closely with US security agencies such as the NSA. A review of existing UK practice was commissioned by the government from the Royal United Services Institute for Defence and Security Studies and

---

[37] See, eg, <http://www.ibtimes.co.uk/uk-special-forces-target-isis-communications-black-ops-electronic-warfare-1560137>. This describes how British aircrews attempted to jam ISIS communications, effectively by transmitting signals on the frequencies typically used and preventing their use.

[38] <http://www.guardian.co.uk/technology/2013/feb/13/gps-jammers-uk-roads-risks>.

[39] <http://stakeholders.ofcom.org.uk/enforcement/spectrum-enforcement/jammers/>.

[40] s. 8(5).   [41] Directive EC89/336 as amended.   [42] s. 1.

published in 2015.[43] This indicated that there was no evidence of abuse on the part of security services but that the legal regulatory regime should be clarified. It was arguable that the conduct could be legitimised under a range of existing legal provisions—in particular section 20 of the Regulation of Investigatory Powers Act, but that these should be brought together and specific reference made to forms of conduct.

Bulk interception orders may be sought only in respect of international communications. The explanatory notes to the Investigatory Powers Bill[44] explain that:

> A bulk warrant is sought for the interception of communications. The primary objective of the warrant is to obtain the communications of persons believed to be outside the UK, which are likely to be of national security interest and may be selected for examination subsequently. Due to the nature of internet-based communications, it is inevitable that some communications between persons in the UK will also be intercepted. In order to select for examination the content of those communications, a targeted examination warrant must be sought. This will need to be authorised personally by the Secretary of State and approved by a judicial commissioner.

Effectively, under the authorisation of a bulk interception warrant, security agencies will be able to collect large amounts of communications data and filter out those communications from outside the United Kingdom that appear likely to be of relevance to their work. These can be subjected to more detailed analysis but communications to and from the United Kingdom may only be scrutinised under the terms of a specific or targeted warrant.

Search warrants

A significant mechanism for obtaining evidence relating to criminal conduct is for law enforcement agencies to enter premises and search their contents under the authority of a search warrant. In the field of computer-related crime, a number of statutes establish the legal regime for the grant of warrants.

The Computer Misuse Act provides procedures for the grant of search warrants in cases where a breach of the section 1 unauthorised access offence is suspected. Section 14 provides that:

(1) Where a circuit judge or a District Judge (Magistrates' Courts) is satisfied by information on oath given by a constable that there are reasonable grounds for believing—

  (a) that an offence under section 1 above has been or is about to be committed in any premises; and

  (b) that evidence that such an offence has been or is about to be committed is in those premises;

he may issue a warrant authorising a constable to enter and search the premises, using such reasonable force as is necessary.

. . .

(4) In executing a warrant issued under this section a constable may seize an article if he reasonably believes that it is evidence that an offence under section 1 above has been or is about to be committed.

---

[43] <https://rusi.org/sites/default/files/20150714_whr_2–15_a_democratic_licence_to_operate.pdf>.
[44] <http://www.publications.parliament.uk/pa/bills/cbill/2016–2017/0002/en/17002en06.htm>.

Also relevant, and perhaps increasingly so, are the provisions of the Copyright, Designs and Patents Act 1988 in respect of activities suspected of constituting criminal infringement of copyright. Section 109 of the Act provides for the grant of a warrant under terms very similar to those laid down in the Computer Misuse Act.

The most general provisions relating to the grant of search warrants are contained in the Police and Criminal Evidence Act 1984[45] and, in respect of the basic unauthorised access offence, in the Computer Misuse Act 1990 itself. The provisions of the Copyright, Designs and Patents Act 1988[46] may also be relevant in respect of cases where software piracy is suspected.

The offences under sections 2 and 3 of the Computer Misuse Act 1990 are classed as serious arrestable offences for the purposes of the 1984 Act.[47] In this event, an application may be made for a search warrant to a justice of the peace who, if satisfied that a serious arrestable offence has been committed and that evidence relevant to the case is likely to be found on specified premises, may issue a search warrant.[48] Such a warrant will, with the exception of specified material,[49] empower the seizure of any item of property which is reasonably considered to relate to the offence under investigation. In addition, it is provided that where information is contained in a computer, the constable exercising the warrant may require that a printout be taken of that information if it is considered 'necessary to do so in order to prevent it being concealed, lost, tampered with or destroyed'.[50]

In the United States, seizure of computers and software was at issue in the celebrated *Steve Jackson* case, where the prolonged detention of the equipment was held by the courts to violate the constitutional guarantees of free speech.[51] Although the submission of the Association of Chief Police Officers suggests that innocent service providers should not be penalised for the actions of their users, there have been suggestions that extensive use has been made of the power of search and seizure. Under the provisions of the Police and Criminal Evidence Act 1984, it is provided that: 'Nothing may be retained . . . if a photograph or copy would be sufficient for that purpose.'[52] One barrister has been quoted as saying that more extensive and prolonged seizures have been justified on the basis that the equipment itself is needed as evidence at the trial.[53]

In respect of the basic offence, the Law Commission's recommendation was that there should be no provision for the issuing of a search warrant. In parliamentary debate, the case was argued that such a facility would be needed if there were to be any realistic possibility of the Computer Misuse Act 1990, section 1 offence being enforced. Particular reference was made to the situation where premises were subject to multiple entry. Although search warrants are not generally made available in respect of summary offences, the Minister of State accepted that:

> the basic hacking offence . . . is not untypically committed in a private house, remote from public gaze and with no one else present. I am not saying that this is a unique offence, but I cannot immediately think of many others that are committed in private houses to which the police have no access and that do not involve some party other than the offender.[54]

An amendment was accordingly made to the Bill, providing that a search warrant might be issued by a circuit judge where there are 'reasonable grounds for believing' that a Computer Misuse Act 1990, section 1 offence has been or is about to be committed in the premises

---

[45] As amended by the Criminal Justice and Police Act 2001.   [46] s. 9.   [47] s. 116.
[48] s. 8. In certain cases, as prescribed in s. 17, a search may take place without a warrant.
[49] s. 14.   [50] s. 19(4).
[51] *Steve Jackson Games Inc v United States Secret Service*, 816 F Supp 432 (1993); affirmed 36 F 3d 457 (1994).
[52] s. 22(4).
[53] Alistair Kelman, quoted in 'Privacy: The Strong Arm of the Law', *The Guardian*, 22 September 1994.
[54] HC Official Report, SC C (Computer Misuse Bill), col. 65, 28 March 1990.

identified in the application.[55] This provision does not extend to Scotland, it being stated in Parliament that equivalent powers already existed in Scotland, where applications for a warrant would be made to a Sheriff.

Computer evidence

The extent to which computer evidence might be admitted in criminal cases has been a somewhat contentious issue. The law of evidence is a somewhat complex and substantial branch of the legal system. Specific provision for computer-generated evidence was made in the Police and Criminal Evidence Act of 1984. As seems so often to have been the case, the attempt to introduce technologically specific legislation was not a conspicuous success. Section 68 of the Act provided that:

(1) In any proceedings, a statement in a document produced by a computer shall not be admissible as evidence of any fact stated therein unless it is shown—

    (a) that there are no reasonable grounds for believing that the statement is inaccurate because of improper use of the computer;

    (b) that at all material times the computer was operating properly, or if not, that any respect in which it was not operating properly or was out of operation was not such as to affect the production of the document or the accuracy of its contents.

It is a general requirement that when evidence is led that is generated by a machine there may be a challenge by the other party to its accuracy and reliability. This provision placed the onus on the prosecution to establish that a computer was operating properly. As every computer user knows, the machines are not infallible and where a defect has occurred it may, as happened in the case of *St Albans District Council v ICL*,[56] be impossible subsequently to replicate the combination of hardware, software, and user input that caused the problem. One of the best-known publishing misprints in history occurred in a copy of the Bible published in 1631 which informed its readers that the Commandments instructed that 'Thou shalt commit adultery'. In the era of computerised typesetting it might be difficult to establish—to the criminal standard of proof—that the blame lay with a human finger rather than a glitch in the software. Although not generally used in word-processing software most of us have probably sent text messages without realising that predictive spell checking has altered the meaning of our message.

Ultimately the Youth Justice and Criminal Evidence Act 1999 repealed[57] section 69 of the 1984 Act. The effect is to place computer-generated evidence in the same position as any other form of evidence. It may be admitted and the presumption will be that it is valid unless and until evidence to the contrary is led.

A further issue that may arise in respect of computer-generated evidence relates to the 'hearsay' rule. It is a general precept of the law of evidence that it must relate to actual knowledge rather than what a witness (whether human or a machine) has been told by someone else. The Criminal Justice Act 2003 provides that:

(1) Where a representation of any fact—

    (a) is made otherwise than by a person, but

    (b) depends for its accuracy on information supplied (directly or indirectly) by a person,

---

[55] s. 14.   [56] [1996] 4 All ER 481.   [57] s. 60.

the representation is not admissible in criminal proceedings as evidence of the fact unless it is proved that the information was accurate.

> (2) Subsection (1) does not affect the operation of the presumption that a mechanical device has been properly set or calibrated.

This could conceivably have been a very heavy standard of proof although the decision of the House of Lords in the case of *R v Shephard*[58] went some way to minimising the requirements. In this case the defendant was accused of stealing goods from a shop. Evidence was given by a store detective who had examined computerised till receipts corresponding to the time of the alleged theft. These indicated, it was stated, that no combination of the goods found in the defendant's possession had been purchased. Counsel for the defendant argued that section 69 required that evidence be given by someone with specialised knowledge of the working of the computer system. The House of Lords disagreed, holding that what was required was that evidence be given by someone who was familiar with the function that the computer was required to perform and could indicate that there was nothing in the nature of particular output to give cause to doubt its accuracy.

Jurisdictional issues

A practical problem relating to the prosecution of computer crime has previously been identified, in as much as the perpetrator of the conduct and the victim computer may be located within different jurisdictions. This is not, of course, an issue which is peculiar to instances of computer crime, but may occur in respect of many instances of fraud. A very simple example might see a person resident in Liverpool ordering goods from a mail-order firm based in Edinburgh tendering in payment a cheque which is known to be worthless.

In both England and Scotland, the status of the law relating to jurisdiction is widely regarded as being unclear. The Law Commission has called for urgent reform in the area, arguing that:

> International fraud is a serious problem . . . It is essential that persons who commit frauds related to this country should not be able to avoid the jurisdiction of this country's courts simply on outdated or technical ground, or because of the form in which they cloak the substance of their fraud.[59]

The Scottish Law Commission indicated that the approach of the Scottish courts has been to claim jurisdiction in the event that the 'main act' of the offence occurred within Scotland.[60] Until recently, the view has been taken that the 'main act' occurs when the fraud produces its result. In the example given, this would happen in Edinburgh when the goods were posted to the customer. A somewhat different approach is evident in the recent case of *Laird v HM Advocate*.[61] This concerned a complex case of fraud in which individuals resident in Scotland fraudulently induced other parties to enter into a contract for the sale of a quantity of steel, the steel to be supplied from England. In this situation, the application of the 'main act' test would appear to dictate that the Scottish courts would not be entitled to claim jurisdiction. In the event, criminal proceedings were instituted and convictions secured in Scotland. An appeal against conviction based on the lack of jurisdiction was rejected by the High Court. Two main points can be identified in the decision of the Lord

---

[58] [1993] AC 380.
[59] *Jurisdiction over Fraud Offences with a Foreign Element* (1989), Law Commission No. 180, para. 2.7.
[60] Scottish Law Consultative Memorandum No. 68 (1986), para. 7.1.e.   [61] 1984 SCCR 469.

Justice Clerk (Wheatley). First, it was suggested, where a 'continuous crime' is involved there may be dual jurisdiction within both countries concerned. In terms of the circumstances under which the Scottish courts might claim jurisdiction, he commented:

> where a crime is of such a nature that it has to originate with the forming of a fraudulent scheme, and that thereafter various steps have to be taken to bring that fraudulent plan to fruition, if some of these subsequent steps take place in one jurisdiction and some in another, then if the totality of the events in one country plays a material part in the operation and fulfilment of the fraudulent scheme as a whole there should be jurisdiction in that country.[62]

The concept of joint jurisdiction is one which the Scottish Law Commission recommended should be adopted in respect of any new statutory offences which might result from their deliberations. In similar vein, the Law Commission recommended that the English courts should enjoy jurisdiction when either the perpetrator or the victim computer was located within England.[63] This approach has been adopted in the Computer Misuse Act 1990, although the enabling provisions are somewhat tortuous. Separate provision is made for Scotland, England and Wales, and Northern Ireland.

The basis for any court to claim jurisdiction will be the existence of a 'significant link' with the country in question.[64] In this respect, the provisions relating to jurisdiction can be divided into two categories with the Computer Misuse Act 1990, section 1 and section 3 offences being considered together. In respect of these, a domestic court will have jurisdiction if either the accused person was located in the territory at the time the conduct complained of occurred or the computer to which access was obtained or whose data or programs were modified was so located.

The provisions relating to Computer Misuse Act 1990, section 2 offences are considerably more complicated. Under these, a domestic court may claim jurisdiction in three circumstances:[65]

1. All aspects of the conduct take place in that country.

2. The further offence referred to in section 2 is intended to take place in that country, regardless of whether the 'significant link' required for the establishment of the unauthorised access component of the offence can be established. Effectively, this means that the victim computer will be located in the territory.

3. The 'significant link' requirement can be satisfied in respect of the domestic country and the further offence will be committed (either wholly or in part) in a country (or countries) which recognises such conduct as constituting an offence. In this event, it will also be necessary for the further conduct to satisfy the section 2 requirements of seriousness.

Extradition

The basis for the United Kingdom's laws relating to extradition is currently found in the Extradition Act of 2003, which replaced a series of statutes dating back to the Extradition Act of 1870. The Explanatory Notes to the 2003 Act[66] state that:

> Crime, particularly serious crime, is becoming increasingly international in nature and criminals can flee justice by crossing borders with increasing ease. Improved judicial

---

[62] 1984 SCCR 469 at 472.   [63] Law Commission Report No. 186 (1989), para. 4.2.   [64] s. 5.

[65] See s. 7 (adding a new s. 1(1A) to the Criminal Law Act 1977 for England and Wales, s. 13 for Scotland, and s. 16 for Northern Ireland).

[66] Available from <http://www.uk-legislation.hmso.gov.uk/acts/en2003/2003en41.htm>.

co-operation between nations is needed to tackle this development. The reform of the United Kingdom's extradition law is designed to contribute to that process.[67]

As was commented by the then Home Secretary, in a foreword to the Home Office document presenting the Extradition Bill, the existing extradition laws:

> date from an age when suspicion and distrust characterised relationships between European nations and the courts saw their role as to protect those fleeing from despotic regimes.[68]

For the purposes of the Act, the world is effectively divided into two categories. Within the EU, the Act gives effect to the Framework Decision on the European Arrest Warrant,[69] creating a fast-track extradition arrangement with Member States of the EU and Gibraltar (Category 1). It includes in Article 3 a list of offences which will be covered. This includes 'computer related crime', albeit subject to a requirement that the offence should carry a penalty of twelve months' imprisonment. For the remainder of the world, power is conferred upon the Secretary of State to place countries in a Category 2 list; the Extradition Act 2003 (Designation of Part 2 Territories) Order 2003[70] gives initial effect to this power. The basic criterion for extradition is that the accused is charged with commission of an 'extradition offence'. This occurs when, inter alia:

> the conduct would constitute an offence under the law of the relevant part of the United Kingdom punishable with imprisonment or another form of detention for a term of 12 months or a greater punishment if it occurred in that part of the United Kingdom.[71]

With the extension of the Act's penalties in the Police and Justice Act 2006, this will now encompass conduct which could be prosecuted under section 1, 2, or 3 of the Computer Misuse Act were it to have occurred in the United Kingdom.

---

[67] para. 6.
[68] <http://www.cejiss.org/assets/pdf/articles/vol3–1/Bures-European_Arrest_Warrant.pdf>.
[69] OJ 2002 L 190/1.   [70] SI 2003/3334.   [71] s. 137.

PART III

Intellectual Property Issues

INTRODUCTION

Formal systems of intellectual property law date back around 700 years. In that sense they can certainly count as well-established areas of law. We tend to class intellectual property rights into three categories: patents, copyright, and trade marks. There are also a number of *sui generis* rights although these tend to be linked to the major topics—especially copyright.

Initially some branches of the law, particularly that of copyright, were highly contentious and copyright played an important role in the political and religious struggles of the Middle Ages, as the emergence of the printing press and the feasibility of making multiple copies of political and religious tracts threatened existing authorities.

From around the eighteenth century, the topic largely disappeared from the legal mainstream. I recall my own legal education in the 1970s where our entire exposure to intellectual property law was a half lecture in a course on property law that concentrated otherwise on rights in lands and buildings.

We live in changed days and, in our information-based societies, issues of rights in respect of information have assumed critical economic importance and intellectual property law is very much back in the legal mainstream. We have seen numerous examples of companies being purchased by competitors not because of the value of their physical assets but because of the perceived value of their intellectual property. In 2012 Google paid more than $12.5 billion for the technology company Motorola, in large part because of the 17,000 IT-related patents that the company owned.

This section will consider initially the law of patents, then copyright, before looking at more recent systems such as design rights, a notion that was at the core of a major UK dispute between Apple and Samsung concerning the question of whether Samsung's Galaxy tablet computer had copied Apple's iPad design. It was eventually held the Galaxy did not infringe Apple's design rights although perhaps the sting in the tale was the trial judge's comment that the Galaxy was 'not as cool' as its rival. Intellectual property law, on the other hand, is certainly a hot topic today.

PATENTS

Probably the oldest form of intellectual property right is the notion of a patent. Dating back to the fourteenth century, this effectively confers a monopoly on its owner in respect of the product or process specified. Patents may be awarded in respect of inventions but the difficult question is 'what is an invention?' Did Einstein, for example, 'invent' the theory of relativity? Essentially the answer is 'no'. It was simply a theory. Patents used to be referred to as an industrial (rather than intellectual) property law and this perhaps gives an indication as to its key features. You might get a patent for something that works. A term very frequently used by the courts is that it should produce a technical effect. We can think of devices such as the telephone that made its inventor, Alexander Graham Bell and his successors, massive fortunes, largely because the inventor was able to secure effective patent protection.

A perhaps pivotal move in the patent system came with its application to pharmaceutical products. Pharmaceutical companies invest billions of pounds each year in trying to develop new drugs and have been very successful in securing patent protection in many cases. But we have to ask where is the element of invention—or a technical effect? It is more an issue of discovering—often after massive investment in skill, effort, and money—that a particular chemical compound produces beneficial results in treating a particular condition.

A feature of pharmaceutical products, which is shared with software and other digital products, is that they can be very expensive to develop but once the formula is established the end-product can be reproduced easily and cheaply. To give one example, one of the most effective drugs for treating patients with AIDS cost $15,000 a year as supplied by the original developer. A pharmaceutical company in India was able to sell a copy for less than $300. The AIDS example has been massively controversial, but the reason why the original developer was able to claim such a high price (which they would, of course, argue was necessary to recoup their research and development costs) was because they had secured a patent and thereby a monopoly over the sale of the drug. It might be, and is, argued that without this level of protection companies would be unwilling to engage in research and development activities.

The process of innovation is a very complex, lengthy and it has been estimated that:

- Only one in 5,000–10,000 compounds tested eventually reach consumers.
- Only two out of every ten compounds that enter clinical testing reach the market.
- Only three out of ten drugs that reach the market ever earn back enough money to match or exceed the average R&D cost of getting them to the marketplace.[1]

There has been significant progress in making drugs legally available to Third World patients at costs which reflect those of production rather than including R&D costs. One difficulty that these efforts face is the ever-increasing impact of globalisation. In previous eras it was quite feasible for companies to separate markets. It was generally the case, for example, that an Indian edition of a textbook could be sold for a much lower price than that charged in the UK market with little chance that these copies would find their way back to the UK market and undercut the publisher's price. With global transport networks and especially in the case of digital works with the emergence of the Internet and e-commerce, the possibility of segregating markets is much diminished. Whether this is for good or for bad is an interesting question.

As with pharmaceutical products, software appears also to suffer from a high attrition rate with some 70 per cent of projects being reported as failing to deliver the expected benefits. For

---

[1] <http://www.innovation.org/documents/File/Pharmaceutical_Patents.pdf>.

both pharmaceutical products and software therefore the legal protection conferred by the patent system is highly valued as a means for protecting investment in those projects that do prove to be successful. I'm not aware of statistics for standard software packages but the failure of these is likely to result in the disappearance of the company from the market place. As individuals live longer, companies do seem to be suffering from a reduction in life expectancy. It has been reported that:

> The average lifespan of a company listed in the S&P 500 index of leading US companies has decreased by more than 50 years in the last century, from 67 years in the 1920s to just 15 years today, according to Professor Richard Foster from Yale University.[2]

I have seen statistics[3] indicating that the failure rate for information-related companies is higher than in any other sector of the economy. Only 37 per cent of start-up companies, it is reported, are still in operation four years later. The second sector most prone to failure is transport and utilities with a 45 per cent survival rate.

The key criterion for the award of a patent is that the product is novel and involves an inventive step. This means that the concept and implementation of the product would not be an obvious step. There is the famous saying attributed to Henry Ford to the effect that customers could have their car in any colour so long as it was black. It seems unlikely that the idea of a white car would be patentable because it would be such an obvious and technically trivial task to substitute one colour for another.

We will consider patents and their application in the software context in more detail in the following chapters. What should be emphasised at this introductory stage is the strength of the protection afforded. A patent is effectively a monopoly. Returning to the telephone, the name Alexander Graham Bell is universally known. That of Elisha Grey, the American electrical engineer, less so. Grey also invented a telephone and applied for patent protection. The official version of history is that Bell's application arrived at the US Patent Office a matter of hours before Grey's. Other versions tell a tale of skullduggery and switching of files, with the insinuation being that Grey submitted first and was effectively cheated of the patent. Regardless which version is correct, the undeniable fact is that Bell is famous and Grey (who happily went on to achieve success in other fields, eg, as the father of the modern music synthesiser) is essentially a footnote in history.

As we will discuss, the application of the patent system to software has been controversial. One of the major complaints is that patents have been awarded for technologies that are not truly novel. In such a fast-moving field, it is nigh on impossible for any patent examiner to be fully aware of what is referred to generally as the 'state of the art'. In one sense, any patent is valid only until it is challenged but we might also consider the perhaps less authoritative legal maxim that possession is nine points of the law. In the United States, and it seems to a much lesser extent in the rest of the world, we are seeing the emergence of what are referred to as patent trolls. Named after mythical and rapacious Norwegian monsters, the essence of a troll is that it buys up patents with no intention of exploiting them for its own purpose but as a bargaining tool to be used to persuade other companies to take out (at cost) a licence to use the technology. Such techniques are widely frowned upon although, in the light of the acquisitions of other companies by organisations such as Google, Microsoft, and Apple on account of their patent portfolios, it is perhaps unfair to see this as just a small-company phenomenon. Especially

---

[2] <http://www.bbc.co.uk/news/business-16611040>.
[3] <http://www.statisticbrain.com/startup-failure-by-industry/>.

from the United States we are seeing a seemingly endless series of disputes, often referred to as 'patent wars'. Few if any have reached the stage of definitive legal rulings and this is perhaps one of the key issues. It is difficult to separate hype from reality.

COPYRIGHT

Whilst the application of the patent system to software is debatable (and contentious), that of copyright has been less so. It is fair to say that every piece of software will qualify for copyright protection. Issues of its proper scope and the techniques that can be used to enforce copyright, however, have been and remain very contentious. In previous generations, copyright infringement on a commercial scale required significant investment in terms of equipment. You might think of this book. Producing unauthorised (pirate) copies is not cheap. A person could photocopy every page of this book but the cost of that would almost certainly exceed the cover price of the book and the quality of the reproduction would be very much lower than the original. It can be done and I am aware of one pirated copy of a previous edition of this book but it needs printing presses and binding facilities. What the Internet and peer-to-peer websites have done is to put mass copying capabilities into the hands of billions of Internet users. But how did we get here?

Copyright essentially originated in the fifteenth and sixteenth centuries in conjunction with the invention (or at least its appearance in Europe) of the printing press by Gutenburg in the fifteenth century. It does not appear that this invention was ever awarded a patent: not because the basic technology had been applied by the Chinese centuries before and was therefore part of the state of the art, but because at that time the award of patents was very much at the discretion of the monarch (government) and the potential availability of multiple copies of seditious works was a cause for great concern to governments. By not awarding a patent, dissemination of the techniques for manufacturing printing presses en masse was thereby inhibited.

In England, after a period of alternating between censorship and the freedom of the press, the compromise was reached whereby a private corporation, 'The Stationers' Company' was appointed as guardian of the technology. Books could, upon pain of civil and criminal penalties, be published only with its permission. Essentially the industry was asked to police itself and there are clear parallels with current developments whereby Internet Service Providers (ISPs) are being asked to shoulder responsibility for the online activities of their customers.

The Statute of Anne, variously dated to 1709 or 1710, is generally regarded as the world's first copyright statute although it essentially codified common law doctrine in many respects. Originally copyright was restricted to literary works, but as technologies have developed it has been extended to cover a range of other works including photographs, films, and radio and television broadcasts. From 1985 and the Copyright (Computer Programs) (Amendment) Act, it has been specifically provided that computer programs (software) are protected under the category of literary works.

The classification of software as a literary work was undoubtedly influenced by the technology of the time. Programs were essentially functional and essentially text-based. Whether the same approach would be taken today is an interesting question. Software is typically much, much more graphically intensive and certainly a modern computer game resembles a cinema film far more than it does a book. The latest edition of the popular computer game 'Grand Theft Auto' is reported to have cost £170 million to develop, a figure that would make it one of the most expensive films in history—yet also one of the most profitable. Many 'traditional' films, of course, also make extensive use of computer animation and it is, I think, fair to say that traditional boundaries between forms of work are becoming blurred. A term that is generally used is 'convergence' and there will be more discussion of that in the coming chapters.

Whilst there is no doubt that essentially every piece of software will benefit from copyright protection there is uncertainty how extensive the protection is. There is no doubt that the act of copying software without the consent of the copyright owner—often referred to as piracy—is unlawful. What is less clear is the extent to which a rival may lawfully reproduce what used to be referred to as the 'look and feel' of an original program. In cases where copyright infringement is alleged, a court will generally ask two questions: has the alleged copyist had access to the original work and are the two pieces of work substantially similar? The on-screen appearance and functionality of one program can be reproduced in another without the second party having any knowledge of the underlying code and it is debatable today whether copyright in software is effective against anything other than direct copying. It is certainly possible that artistic copyright might be claimed in an on-screen image such as the well-known computer game character 'SuperMario' although this perhaps belongs more in the area of trade mark law.

OTHER FORMS OF INTELLECTUAL PROPERTY RIGHT

Intellectual property law has many strands and it is often the case, especially with games, that aspects of characters will be protected by trade mark law. This allows for the protection of names, images, and other attributes. A popular series of computer games features the cartoon character 'SuperMario' and this is protected by a substantial number of trade marks. Also relevant in this context is the common law notion of 'passing off' which resembles in some respects the civil law doctrine of unfair competition. At a more hardware-related level, the law of registered (and unregistered) design rights has been at issue in high-profile disputes between, for example, Apple and Samsung.

If copyright and patents can be seen as overlapping to some extent, the role of trade mark law is significantly different. The role of a trade mark is to serve to distinguish the goods or services offered by one party from those of anyone else. The current UK law concerning trade marks is to be found in the Trade Marks Act 1994, which seeks to implement the EU Directive to approximate the laws of the Member States relating to trade marks.[4] Also relevant is the common law doctrine of 'passing off'. As the name suggests, this operates to prevent a party using names or other indicators which are likely to mislead third parties as to the true identity of the person with whom they are dealing. Typically, the impression will be given that a person is connected with some well-known and regarded organisation.

A trade mark may consist of anything which may be recorded in graphical format. Traditionally, marks have tended to take the forms of names or logos, but the scope is increasing, with sounds and even smells forming the subject matter of trade mark applications. For the present purpose, attention can be restricted to the use of names. Given the increasing commercialisation of the Internet, organisations frequently seek the registration of a domain name which creates an obvious link with their real-life activities. The software company Microsoft, for example, can be found at <http://microsoft.com>. In many cases indeed, firms have obtained trade mark registration for their domain name as such. Amazon.com, for example, is a registered trade mark in the United States.

---

[4] Directive 89/104/EEC (the Trade Mark Directive), OJ 1998 L 40/1.

Also relevant in an information technology context is the concept of design rights. The regime is in some respects analogous to the patent system in that eligibility for protection is dependent upon meeting criteria of novelty. Especially as the scope of copyright protection has narrowed, attention has been paid to the role that design right might play in protecting aspects of the look and feel of IT products.

As will be discussed in the following chapters, the task of fitting software and software-related applications into traditional forms of intellectual property law has not been a simple one. In some areas, the attempt has been made to develop new, specialised forms of protection. The two main areas in which this has been attempted have been in the fields of database and semiconductor chip design protection. In both areas, the impetus for reform in the United Kingdom has lain in EU Directives. Whilst providing specialised or *sui generis* forms of protection, both regimes draw heavily on the principles and policies of copyright law.

CONCLUSIONS

In our fast-changing societies, it is tempting to conclude that history has few lessons to teach us. Much depends, perhaps, on whether we see change as evolutionary or revolutionary. Prior to considering where and how intellectual property should develop, it is perhaps useful to look back to consider how and why the systems developed. The first intellectual property statutes were motivated very much by economic and trade considerations. In the English patent system, for example, invention took second place to the need to overcome by force of law the obstacles placed by local tradesmen against those seeking to apply techniques and technologies established in other countries but novel in England.

A similar trend can be mapped in respect of the copyright system. Essentially a product of the invention of the printing press, this seeks to protect a range of interests. The world's first copyright statute was the United Kingdom's Statute of Anne, enacted in 1709. The date of the Act's passage is significant. Although the notion of copyright had been developed under the English common law, it had not featured significantly in Scots law. Under the Act of Union between Scotland and England in 1707, an eighteenth-century equivalent of the European Single Market was established, with Scottish producers enjoying access to the economically stronger English market. Scots law was retained under the Act of Union and Scottish publishers discovered a useful source of income by producing what today would be regarded as 'pirate' copies of leading English literary works. One of the motives of the Statute of Anne was to introduce copyright notions into Scots law and prevent what was seen as a form of unfair competition.

Matters have not, perhaps, changed greatly over the past three centuries. In 1707, a relatively poor country saw little benefit in systems of intellectual property law and some advantage in their absence. Its richer, more powerful neighbour used economic and political muscle to cause the introduction of intellectual property laws. Today, it is not self-evidently to the benefit of the developing world to enforce intellectual property rights, which primarily benefit First World owners. The price of entry to the World Trade Organization (WTO) and access to First World market under the General Agreement on Tariffs and Trade (GATT) and General Agreement on Trade and Services (GATS) treaties is, however, that they accept the WTO Protocol on Trade Related Aspects of Intellectual Property Rights (TRIPS). This obliges signatories to recognise intellectual property rights and to provide enforcement mechanisms in the event rights are not observed. This obligation has been the cause of considerable controversy, most notably perhaps in relation to the production and distribution of anti-AIDS drugs, which are invariably protected by patent rights.

Perhaps surprisingly, almost no empirical evidence exists whether the patent system is effective in either economic terms or in ensuring that information regarding technical innovations enters into the public domain. Some studies have suggested that small and medium-sized enterprises make little or no use of patent specifications as a source of information regarding developments in their field of activity. In cases such as DNA research, it may be argued whether the publication of details of an end-product adds anything to the sum of human knowledge and, as such, whether the award of a patent adequately advances the aims of the patent system. A recent study conducted for the Commission on *The Economic Impact of Patentability of Computer Programs*[5] considered the literature on the economics of the patent system before concluding:

> The economics literature does not show that the balance of positive and negative effects lies with the negative. All it says is that there are grounds for supposing that the negative forces are stronger relative to the positive forces in this area than in some others and that any move to strengthen IP protection in the software industry cannot claim to rest on solid economic evidence.

In fields such as software and with projects such as the mapping of the human genome, it may be questioned how far the award of patents serves the end of encouraging further innovation. As in the example cited involving Elisha Grey and Alexander Graham Bell, different people may be working independently on the same idea simultaneously. It may be a matter of chance who stumbles on a practical method of implementation first. It may be questioned whether the interests of society in the development of technology are likely to be best served by the grant of a monopoly to one person or whether the existence of at least one competitor might have served as a spur to more rapid developments.

[5] Study Contract ETD/99/B5-3000/E/106, available from <http://ec.europa.eu/internal_market/indprop/docs/comp/study_en.pdf>.

14

Key elements of the patent system

INTRODUCTION

The history of the patent system has been a convoluted and complex one and the concept featured in some of the major political upheavals in the late Middle Ages, testimony to the fact that the element of monopoly conferred upon the holder of a patent has at least the potential to provide very significant economic benefits. This chapter will consider in general terms the nature and manner of operation of the patent system, whilst the following chapter will focus upon the somewhat complex manner in which the system has operated in respect of so-called software-related inventions.

As adopted in England, the purpose of the patent system was somewhat different from the modern regime. In the early Middle Ages, each town would have its guilds of craftsmen, who would guard access to the various trades jealously. Only a member of the appropriate guild could, for example, act as a butcher or carpenter. One of the major weaknesses of such an approach was that the guilds stifled innovation. Recognising that the country was lagging behind its Continental rivals in terms of technology, the practice began whereby the sovereign would encourage foreigners to come to England, bringing with them their advanced technical skills. To overcome the objections of the craft guilds, letters patent would be issued. Signed with the royal seal, these would command any citizen to refrain from interfering with the bearer in the exercise of the technical skills referred to in the letter. The first recorded English patent of this kind was issued in 1449 to a Flemish glazier, John of Utyman who came to the country to install stained glass windows in Eton College. The technology covered by the patent was new to the country rather than new in itself.

In the sixteenth and seventeenth centuries the system fell increasingly into disrepute and was all too often used to boost the royal revenues by conferring a monopoly in respect of basic commodities in return for payment (a bribe). In 1623 the Statute of Monopolies rendered illegal all monopolies except those:

> for the term of 14 years or under hereafter to be made of the sole working or making of any manner of new manufactures within this Realm to the true and first inventor ... [monopolies should not be] contrary to the law nor mischievous to the State by raising prices of commodities at home or hurt of trade.[1]

It was almost another hundred years, however, before it was settled that in return for the award of a patent, the inventor was required to specify details of the manner in which the invention functioned. An examination of patent applications was made with a view to establishing novelty. It is now clear that the presence of an inventive step is a pre-requisite for any award and that a balance has to be struck whereby in return for putting details of the manner in which the invention functions into the public arena, the inventor is to receive a temporary monopoly in respect of its exploitation. An oft-quoted description of the modern system explains that:

> The basic theory of the patent system is simple and reasonable. It is desirable in the public interest that industrial techniques should be improved. In order to encourage improvement, and to encourage the disclosure of improvements in preference to their use in secret, any person devising an improvement in a manufactured article, or in machinery or methods for making it, may upon disclosure of the improvement at the Patent Office demand to be given a monopoly in the use for a period of years. After that period it passes into the public domain; and the temporary monopoly is not objectionable, for if it had not been for the inventor who devised and disclosed the improvement nobody would have been able to use it at that or any other time, since nobody would have known about it.[2]

The United Kingdom's patent system is now found primarily in the Patents Act 1977. This statute was enacted in part to reform and update the UK law relating to patents but also in order to bring domestic law into conformity with the provisions of the European Patent Convention, opened for signature in 1973, which, as will be discussed later, provides for a measure of harmonisation in matters of substance and procedure amongst signatory states.

Whilst there is no doubt that inventiveness is a key requirement of the patent system, what has been more debatable has been the application of the system to software-related inventions—innovations where novelty resides primarily or exclusively in software components. Concern has tended to focus on two elements: first, whether software developments fit conceptually into the industrial heartland of the system and, secondly, whether the library and related resources exist to allow claim to novelty to be adequately assessed. This remains the most problematic aspect of the subject and will be discussed in more detail later.

Patents in the international arena

Until recent times, patent systems tended to be restricted to the developed world. The advent of the WTO has resulted in many more countries introducing systems of patent protection. Although there is some element of harmonisation, this is at a lower level than provided for under the Berne Copyright Convention, which provides for almost worldwide protection to be conferred automatically on literary, dramatic, and musical works. A UK patent will be valid within the United Kingdom and of no effect in Japan or the United States, and vice versa. A person wishing to secure widespread patent protection for an invention will have to undergo the time-consuming and expensive process of seeking to obtain a patent from each country where protection is desired.

The oldest international instrument which seeks to ease the task of inventors in securing patent protection on a multi-jurisdictional level is the Paris Convention (an instrument signed by ninety-six states, including all of the major industrial states).[3] This provides that the submission of an application for patent protection in one signatory state will serve to establish priority for the applicant in the event that equivalent applications are submitted in other signatory states within twelve months.[4] Although such a facility is of considerable value for inventors, the practical problems involved in obtaining patent protection

---

[2] T. A. Blanco White, *Patents for Inventions* (London, 1983), p. 1. For a good description of the history of the UK patent system, see the Patent Office website at <http://www.ipo.gov.uk/types/patent/p-about.htm>.

[3] The Convention was first opened for signature on 20 March 1883, with the most recent revision occurring in Stockholm in 1968. [4] Art. 4.

on anything like a worldwide basis are immense, and a number of subsequent agreements have sought to ease the task facing applicants.

The Patent Co-operation Treaty

The Patent Co-operation Treaty, which was opened for signature in 1970, prescribes basic features which are to be found in the national laws of signatory states. Under the provisions of the Patent Co-operation Treaty, an application may be directed to the patent authorities in any state and will indicate those countries within which patent protection is sought.[5] The national authority will then transmit the application to an International Searching Authority (defined as national patent offices of Austria, Australia, Japan, Russia, Sweden, and the United States, together with the European Patent Office).[6] The procedure to be adopted subsequently will depend upon the extent to which the state in question adheres to the Treaty. At the most basic level, the International Searching Authority will carry out a prior art search and submit reports to the designated national authorities.[7] Signatory states are given the option to adhere to a more significant regime which will permit the searching authority to conduct a preliminary examination.[8] Once again, reports will be sent to the designated national authorities. The Patent Co-operation Treaty does not contain any specific prohibition against the award of patents for computer programs,[9] but does state that an International Searching Authority is not to be obliged to conduct a search of the prior art in respect of a computer program 'to the extent that the International Searching Authority is not equipped to search prior art concerning such programs'.

The operation of the Patent Co-operation Treaty serves to eliminate a measure of the duplication of searches and examinations which would otherwise face an international applicant. Ultimately, however, the decision as to whether to grant or refuse a particular application is one for the national authorities.

The European Patent Convention

More extensive rationalisation of the patent system has been carried out within Europe with the adoption of the European Patent Convention. This Convention was opened for signature in 1973, and has been ratified by all of the EU States and also by a number of non-Member States such as Norway, Switzerland, and Turkey. The Convention establishes the European Patent Office (located in Munich) and the concept of a European Patent. The title, however, is something of a misnomer. An applicant is required to specify those countries in which it is intended that the patent will apply and, assuming the application is successful, the end-product will be the award of a basket of national patents. Effectively, the role of the Convention and the European Patent Office is to centralise the process for the award of national patents, with the costs to applicants rising in line with the number of countries in which protection is sought. As the European Commission has commented, one consequence of this process has been that 'the additional costs of protection for each designated country are prompting businesses to be selective in their choice of countries, with effects that run counter to the aims of the single market'.[10]

Applications for patent protection may be addressed to the European Patent Office. Once again, the applicant must indicate those countries to which they wish the patent to

---

[5] Art. 3.   [6] Art. 12.   [7] Art. 15.   [8] Art. 31.
[9] Art. 33 provides that the subject matter of a patent may be anything that can be made or used.
[10] Green Paper, *Community Patent and the Patent System in Europe* (1997), available from <http://europa. eu/documents/comm/green_papers/pdf/com97_314_en.pdf>.

extend.[11] Subsequently, all the examining procedures will be conducted by the European Patent Office, which will then also proceed to make the decision on whether to grant the patent. Although some differences of procedure and style can be identified between the practice of the UK Patent Office and its European counterparts, the principles which will be applied are virtually identical. The UK law relating to patents is to be found today in the Patents Act 1977. This statute was introduced in part to update domestic law, but principally to enable the United Kingdom to ratify the European Patent Convention. The Act provides that judicial notice is to be taken of decisions of the European Patent Office authorities and, as will be discussed later, decisions made within the European Patent Office have proved extremely influential in the domestic system. In one of the leading UK cases, the view was strongly expressed that:

> It would be absurd if, on the issue of patentability, a patent application should suffer a dif-
> ferent fate according to whether it was made in the United Kingdom under the Act or was
> made in Munich for a European Parliament (United Kingdom) under the Convention.[12]

As will be discussed later, the absurd has become very close to becoming the rule.

The unitary patent

For many years the European Union has sought to establish a patent system that would mean that a single patent could be issued covering all of the Member States. One of the major obstacles has been the linguistic one. Under the European Patent Office system a translation of the patent documents must be provided by the applicant for every country to which the patent extends. Translation costs are high and an Impact Assessment published by the European Commission[13] in 2011 noted that:

> Direct and indirect translation costs can add up to about 40% of the overall costs of pat-
> enting in Europe. It has been estimated that a European patent validated in 13 countries
> is more than ten times more expensive than a patent in the US or Japan . . . Specialised
> translators are needed to translate the technical text contained in patents. On average, EUR
> 85 is charged per page. The number of pages to be translated depends on the specific patent:
> a patent of typical length contains 15 pages of description, 4 pages of claims and 1 page of
> drawings.

Additionally, it was suggested, fees of up to €600 per country might have to be paid to national agents to facilitate the filing of translations with national patent offices. As a result, it was argued in a statement by Commissioner Barnier:

> The figures speak for themselves. In the United States, in 2011, 224 000 patents were granted,
> in China 172 000 while here in Europe only 62 000 European patents were delivered. One of
> the reasons for this difference is without a doubt the prohibitive cost and the complexity of
> obtaining patent protection throughout the single market.[14]

Commenting on the prolonged gestation period for the EU system he noted 'Since the 1960s, this project has been put forward, with successive failures. When I took up office, I said that I would not be the first Commissioner to work on the file but that I hoped to be the last.'

---

[11] Art. 79.   [12] Per Nicholls J in *Gale's Application* [1991] RPC 305.
[13] SEC(2011) 482 final. Available from <http://ec.europa.eu/internal_market/indprop/docs/patent/sec2011–482-final_en.pdf>.
[14] <http://europa.eu/rapid/press-release_MEMO-12–971_en.htm?locale=en>.

The new European regime was expected to enter into force in 2017 but, as with many aspects of IT law, it has been caught up in the fallout from Brexit. Entry into force is dependent upon ratification by France, Germany, and the United Kingdom. The first two countries have done this but it seems unlikely that the United Kingdom will follow suit. The consequence is that the regulatory package which is based on two Regulations, one detailing the mechanics of the system[15] and the other concerning the arrangements for translation will require to be re-negotiated by the remaining Member States.[16] In terms of substance there is no change from the provisions of the European Patent Convention. Applications will continue to be made to the European Patent Office and applications will require to be submitted only in English, French, and German[17] but any patent awarded will be valid in the twenty-five participating EU states.

The major structural change will be the introduction of a Unified Patent Court as part of the EU's institutions. The Court will consist of an appellate body which will be based in Luxembourg and a Court of First Instance which will be based in Paris with branches in London and Munich. The Court of First Instance will deal with cases alleging infringement in specific sectors. London was intended to deal with issues involving pharmaceutical products (leases have been entered into for the necessary office premises) and Munich with mechanical engineering. All other cases, which will include those concerning software-related patents will be determined in Paris. All cases concerned with the validity of patents will also be dealt with in Paris.

For cases at first instance, a panel of three judges will sit. Two will be legally qualified and one technically qualified (in respect of the nature of the patent under scrutiny). The Court of Appeal will sit as a panel of five, with three legally and two technically qualified judges.

Intellectual property in the GATS and WTO

Introduced shortly after the end of the Second World War, the General Agreement on Tariffs and Trade (GATT) has provided a legal mechanism to regulate and promote international trade. Reform to the system in the 1990s brought services into the international agreement for the first time through the adoption of the General Agreement on Trade in Services (GATS) and also introduced provisions relating to intellectual property rights. The Trade-Related Aspects of Intellectual Property Rights (TRIPS) Protocol[18] to the GATS requires signatories to make patents:

> available for any inventions, whether products or processes, in all fields of technology, provided that they are new, involve an inventive step and are capable of industrial application . . . patents shall be available and patent rights enjoyable without discrimination as to the place of invention, the field of technology and whether products are imported or locally produced.[19]

This provision was included at the behest of the developed world, and was prompted by concern that companies were suffering losses through audio, software, and video piracy in developing countries, with little legal recourse because concepts of intellectual property

---

[15] Regulation (EU) No. 1257/2012 of the European Parliament and of the Council of 17 December 2012 implementing enhanced cooperation in the area of the creation of unitary patent protection, OJ 2012 L 361/1.

[16] Council Regulation (EU) No. 1260/2012 of 17 December 2012 implementing enhanced cooperation in the area of the creation of unitary patent protection with regard to the applicable translation arrangements, OJ 2012 L361/89.

[17] Provision is made for small and medium-sized enterprises to be reimbursed for translation costs.

[18] Adopted in 1994, entering into force on 1 January 1995. The text of TRIPS is available from <http://www.wto.org/english/docs_e/legal_e/27-trips.pdf>.

[19] Art. 27.

law were not recognised by national laws. Effectively, TRIPS requires these states to introduce intellectual property statutes as the price for benefiting from the free trade provisions
of the GATS. Although not technically binding on either the EU or the European Patent
Office, there is no doubt that its provisions requiring that patents be made available 'for any
inventions' have proved highly influential in an ongoing debate concerning the patentabilty
of software-related inventions.

Requirements for patentability

A patent may be awarded in respect of an invention. The invention may relate either to a
new product or to a novel process. The Patents Act 1977 does not define the word 'invention', but it does specify attributes that any invention must possess. These require that:

  (a) the invention is new;

  (b) it involves an inventive step;

  (c) it is capable of industrial exploitation; and

  (d) the grant of a patent for it is not excluded.[20]

As will be discussed extensively in the next chapter, the categories of excluded subject matter are of great significance in the case of software-related inventions. Initially, however,
attention will be paid to the positive attributes which must be possessed in order for a
product or a process to be considered patentable.

Novelty

The question of novelty against patentability is assessed against the existing state of human
knowledge. Account will be taken of any material within the public domain which might
indicate that the concept of the claimed invention did not originate with the particular
applicant. It is not necessary that all the details of the alleged invention should have previously appeared in a single document. The test which will be applied is sometimes referred
to as the 'mosaic' test. The analogy might also be drawn with a jigsaw puzzle. This consists
of a number of pieces. Once completed, the subject matter will be readily identifiable, as
will the manner in which the constituent pieces fit together. Such a result might not have
been apparent to someone who merely saw a pile of unassembled pieces.

An indication of the complexity of the task of determining whether a claimed invention
is novel or whether key elements have been anticipated in earlier products or publications
can be taken from the case of *Quantel Ltd v Spaceward Microsystems Ltd*.[21] This concerned
a challenge to the validity of a patent awarded in respect of a computer-based device permitting the production of graphical images for display on television screens. The end-prod-
ucts of the system can be viewed every day in the captions and graphical montages which
appear on almost all television programmes.

A competing product having been placed on the market, proceedings were instituted
alleging breach of patent. In defending this action, the defenders alleged, inter alia, that
the patent had been incorrectly awarded to a development that was not novel. A variety of
material was presented in support of this contention, including a thesis submitted by an
American student and deposited in the library of Cornell University. Although the validity
of the patent was ultimately upheld by the court, when account is taken of the number of

---

[20] s. 1(1).   [21] [1990] RPC 83.

such works produced each year and the very limited publicity afforded to them, the incident demonstrates the magnitude of the task of determining whether an alleged invention is truly novel. The case also provides an excellent illustration of the fact that the grant of a patent may be only the first step for the inventor, who may be faced with a challenge to its validity in the course of any subsequent legal proceedings.

A further aspect of novelty concerns the question of whether details of the alleged invention might previously have been brought into the public domain by the applicant. Any significant disclosure of the features of an invention prior to the submission of an application for a patent will lead to its rejection. The Patent Office advises inventors:

> If you are thinking of applying for a patent you should not publicly disclose the invention before you file an application because this could be counted as prior publication of your invention. Any type of disclosure (whether by word of mouth, demonstration, advertisement or article in a journal), by the applicant or anyone acting for them, could prevent the applicant from getting a patent. It could also be a reason for having the patent revoked if one was obtained. It is essential that the applicant only makes any disclosure under conditions of strict confidence.[22]

Inventive step

The application of this test is as much a matter of art as of science and is linked to a considerable extent with the criteria of novelty. The Patents Act 1977 states that an invention:

> shall be taken to involve an inventive step if it is not obvious to a person skilled in the art, having regard to any matter which forms part of the state of the art.[23]

It is very much a question of fact whether the advance involved in a particular invention would have been 'obvious'. Again, the attempt has to be made to apply the test without engaging in the use of hindsight, but by reference to the state of the art at the time the invention was made.

An excellent example of a situation where the requirement of an inventive step was not satisfied can be seen in the case of *Genentech Inc's Patent*.[24] A research programme conducted by Genentech resulted in the identification and mapping of elements of DNA (one of the basic building blocks of life). The research furthered the knowledge of this basic structure and could be used as the basis for the production of anti-coagulant drugs. Genentech sought to patent the results of its efforts, the application ultimately failing when the Court of Appeal held that the work did not involve an inventive step. Mustill LJ referred to Genentech's activities in the following way:

> [T]hey won the race. The goal was known and others were trying to reach it. Genentech got there first.[25]

Whilst the achievement of a goal (equivalent, perhaps, to setting a new world record in a sporting event) would constitute evidence of novelty, if the target was widely known, winning the race might tell no more than that the winner was richer or more determined or luckier than others working in the same area. To this extent, therefore, the expenditure of time and effort in making a breakthrough will not, of itself, be conclusive evidence of the existence of an inventive step.[26]

---

[22] <http://www.ipo.gov.uk/types/patent/p-applying/p-apply/p-cda.htm>.   [23] s. 3.
[24] [1989] RPC 147.   [25] [1989] RPC 147 at 251.   [26] [1989] RPC 147 at 278.

Such arguments are of considerable relevance in the information technology field, where vast sums of money are being expended by large research units throughout the world, all pursuing the goal of faster, more powerful computing devices. A distinction can be drawn between this situation, where the goal can be expressed only in abstract terms, and that applying in *Genentech*,[27] where the target of the research was much more precisely defined. Even on this restricted analysis, the situation appears a little inequitable. The achievement of the goal of running a mile in less than three minutes might not be inventive, but would certainly be meritorious and deserving of recognition. The problem will be encountered in a number of areas and the traditional precepts of intellectual property may not fit well with developments in information technology, yet the effect of denying access to intellectual property rights is to deny any form of legal recognition and protection for the work in question.

Also at issue in the *Genentech*[28] litigation was the identification of the notional persons 'skilled in the art'—those persons to whom the making of the steps leading to the claimed invention would have been 'obvious'. It was recognised that, in respect of advanced areas of technology, the collected knowledge of a team of researchers might be the relevant factor rather than the knowledge possessed by any particular individual. The question also arises of whether the person or persons 'skilled in the art' should themselves be credited with possessing any inventive qualities. In the case of *Valensi v British Radio Corpn Ltd*,[29] it was stated that:

> the hypothetical addressee is not a person of exceptional skill and knowledge, that he is not to be expected to exercise any invention nor any prolonged research, inquiry or experiment. He must, however, be prepared to display a reasonable degree of skill and common knowledge of the art in making trials and to correct obvious errors in the specification if a means of correcting them can readily be found.[30]

A more expansive view of the abilities of the skilled person was adopted by Mustill LJ in *Genentech*. In a comment which is especially relevant in relation to developments in information technology, he held that:

> Where the art by its nature involves intellectual gifts and ingenuity of approach, it would, I believe, be wrong to assume that the hypothetical person is devoid of those gifts.[31]

Capacity for industrial application

The final requirement which must be satisfied in order for a patent application to proceed is that the invention involved should be capable of industrial application. This requirement is, in many respects, at the heart of the patent system. However novel an idea might be, it will be of little practical benefit if it cannot usefully be applied. Application may take two forms, with the subject matter of the patent application referring to a product or a process (sometimes referred to as apparatus and means). In many instances, applications will combine the two elements. A helpful illustration is provided in Laddie J's judgment in the case of *Fujitsu Ltd's Application*:[32]

> it may be useful to consider what the position would be in a case where someone had invented a new way of mowing grass which involved designing a new type of motor with micro sensors and blade adjustment motors on it, the sensors being used to determine both

---

[27] *Genentech Inc's Patent* [1989] RPC 147.   [28] *Genentech Inc's Patent* [1989] RPC 147.
[29] [1973] RPC 337.   [30] [1973] RPC 337 at 377.
[31] *Genentech Inc's Patent* [1989] RPC 147 at 280.   [32] [1996] RPC 511.

the softness of the grass to be cut and the height of it above the ground and then produced an output which operated the motors so as to adjust the height of the cut, the angle of the blades and the speed at which they rotated . . . considerations of novelty aside, such a device would be patentable and, so it seems to me, would be the mowing method itself.

In a software context, the claim may often be that the equipment operating in accordance with the program's instructions constitutes a novel product, whilst the algorithmic steps prescribed by the implementing programs represent a novel process. Virtually any product will be capable of being sold or otherwise disposed of and, in this respect, will satisfy the applicability test. With a process, slightly different considerations will apply. If the end result of the application of the process will be a product, it is likely that the process will be considered capable of industrial application. An illustration of the kind of development which will be excluded from patent protection can be found in the provisions of the Patents Act 1977, which states that:

an invention of a method of treatment of the human or animal body by surgery or therapy or of diagnosis practised on the human or animal body shall not be taken to be capable of industrial application.[33]

Thus, the intangible concept is not patentable. In the event, however, that new surgical tools or equipment are invented to facilitate the application of the new techniques, these will, assuming the other statutory criteria are complied with, be regarded as patentable.

Matters excluded from patent protection

In addition to defining the elements that must be found in an invention, the Patents Act 1977 lists a number of features which will not qualify for the grant of a patent. Section 1(2) (which mirrors Article 52 of the European Patent Convention) provides that patents are not to be awarded for:

(a) a discovery, scientific theory or mathematical method;

(b) a literary, dramatic, musical, or artistic work or any other aesthetic creation whatsoever;

(c) a scheme, rule or method for performing a mental act, playing a game or doing business, or a program for a computer; or

(d) the presentation of information.

Given the appearance of the phrase 'a program for a computer' in this listing, it may appear surprising that the topic should be of any significance in a text on information technology law. Matters, however, are not so straightforward. After reciting the list of prohibited subject matter, both the Patents Act 1977 and the European Patent Convention continue:

but the foregoing provision shall prevent anything from being treated as an invention for the purposes of this Act only to the extent that a patent or an application for a patent relates to that thing *as such* [emphasis added].

In his judgment in *Fujitsu Ltd's Application*,[34] which was subsequently affirmed by the Court of Appeal,[35] Mr Justice Laddie analysed the rationale behind a number of the statutory exceptions. The prohibition against the grant of a patent to a discovery illustrates

---

[33] s. 4(2).   [34] [1996] RPC 511.   [35] *The Times*, 14 March 1997.

perfectly the problems inherent in this area. The obvious objection to awarding a patent for a discovery, for example, of a new mineral, is that there is no discernible inventive step. However, as was pointed out in the judgment:

> most inventions are based on what would be regarded by many people as discoveries. Large numbers of highly successful and important patents in the pharmaceutical field have been and continue to be based upon the discovery of new strains of micro-organisms which exist naturally in the wild.[36]

Recognising this fact, the statutory prohibition against the grant of a patent is restricted to the case where the application relates to the discovery 'as such'.[37]

In principle, such an approach must be correct. Its practical application has proved more difficult, with particular problems surrounding the treatment of what are frequently referred to as 'software-related inventions'. In part, the problem may lie with the fact that both the Patents Act 1977 and the European Patent Convention were enacted in the 1970s. At that time, it was considered that computer programs could be separated from the hardware components and should be excluded from the patent system. Both the report of the Banks Committee in the United Kingdom and the initial Guidelines for Examiners produced by the European Patent Office make this point clearly. Over the last twenty-odd years, the nature of computer programs has changed and expanded, and the division between software and hardware has become a matter of choice as much as one of technology.

To complicate matters further, as the relevance of an obvious prohibition has declined, so it has also become apparent that software-related inventions are vulnerable to challenge under a range of the statutory exceptions. Applications have been rejected on the basis that they relate to a mathematical method, a method of doing business, the presentation of information, and a method for performing a mental act, all of which are excluded from the award of a patent. It is difficult to think of any other form of technology whose nature and range of application is sufficiently chameleon as to bring it within so many of the statutory prohibitions. Not unnaturally, those seeking patent protection for software-related inventions have sought to lay as much emphasis as possible on the task performed by the invention, and as little as possible on the contribution made by computer programs. The criterion applied by both the European Patent Office and the UK authorities is to require that the claimed invention produced a 'technical contribution' to the state of the art (also referred to as a 'technical effect' or 'technical application'). The next question, of course, is whether the mere presence of a technical contribution can outweigh the explicit prohibition against patentability.

Patenting software

Notwithstanding the present prohibitions, there is no doubt that software-related inventions can be patented. In the United Kingdom, approximately one hundred patent applications in their name are published each year. In proceedings before the European Patent Office, this figure rises to one hundred per month.[38] The report of the Parliamentary Office of Science and Technology on *Patents, Research and Technology*[39] indicates that 'in the last ten years the EPO has granted around 10,000 patents for software-related inventions, and

---

[36] [1996] RPC 511 at 523.   [37] Patents Act 1977, s. 1(2).

[38] European Commission Press Release, Proposal for a Directive on the patentability of computer-implemented inventions—frequently asked questions.   [39] March 1996.

has refused only one hundred applications'.[40] In 2003, it was estimated that up to 30,000 software patents had been issued by the European Patent Office;[41] although, in part because the existence of the statutory prohibitions requires that software-related inventions be catalogued by reference to their field of application rather than the software component, any calculation is a somewhat subjective assessment. It seems certain that the number of software patents will have increased significantly since 2003 but no definitive evidence is available. Even more substantial figures are quoted for the number of patents awarded in the United States, and there is no doubt that patents have a significant role to play in the field of information technology.

The process of obtaining and enforcing a patent

The application

The act of making an invention will confer no rights upon an inventor. A person wishing to secure protection is required to make an application for a patent and to pursue this through all the stages of the patent procedure.[42] The key components of the process are described in the following paragraphs.

Specification and statement of claim

The key elements of any patent application are the provision of a specification and a statement of claim(s).[43] The specification consists, essentially, of a description of the invention. It will describe the state of the technical art in the field and indicate the improvements which the invention makes and the manner in which this is accomplished. The specification should be formulated in such a manner as to permit the product to be made or the process operated by 'a person skilled in the art'.

The specification serves to indicate what may be regarded as the inventor's opinion regarding the optimum embodiment of its principles. Beyond this, claims for protection may be made regarding the functioning of the product or process—effectively, what the invention does. The drafting of these claims is critical to the success of a patent. Any claim alleging infringement of a patent will relate to the claims rather than to the specification. If the claims are drawn too broadly, a patent application may be rejected on the grounds that the applicant is seeking protection, either for matters which have not been disclosed in the specification or for matters which are not novel or inventive. If the claims are drawn more narrowly, the patent may well be awarded, but prove worthless, as competitors evade its scope by making minor changes to the design of the invention. In many cases, an applicant will submit a considerable number of claims, commencing with extremely broad references to the technology at issue, with subsequent claims narrowing down the level of protection, ending with a claim to protection for the invention 'substantially as described'.

An example of a failure in this regard has been reported concerning the patents granted to what has become the market-leading telephone modem. Modems play a vital role in the transfer of data between computers.[44] Just as with human telephone conversations, a basic requirement of data transmissions is the ability to identify when a communication has

---

[40] p. 31. The Follow-up to the Green Paper on the Community Patent refers to the existence of 13,000 patents in Europe.   [41] <http://eupat.ffii.org/>.
[42] Where an invention is made in the course of employment, the employer will be regarded as the inventor for the purpose of making a patent application.   [43] s. 14(2).
[44] *The Guardian*, 9 February 1989.

been completed and thereupon terminate the connection. This is referred to as the escape sequence. A particular sequence had been developed in which the initiating modem would transmit three + signs. Such a transmission would be most unlikely to occur in the course of a message and would signal to a compatible receiving modem that the communication had concluded. In this, as in many other areas of the intellectual property field, the question of compatibility is critical. Although it was not selected at random, the 3+s message possessed no unique qualities. The commercial success of the modem produced consumer demand for modems which transmitted and recognised this sequence. In laying claim to a patent for the modem design, the developers failed to claim in respect of the specific escape sequence. This proved a costly error. The resulting patent protection certainly prevented competitors from copying the specific design features of the modem, but the same effect, that of transmitting and receiving data communications, could readily be achieved using alternative and non-infringing means. Having done this, the absence of a claim in respect of the escape sequence left competitors free to utilise this, thereby acquiring compatibility with the market-leading product to their own commercial advantage.

The lodging of an application with the Patent Office serves to initiate the procedures leading to the grant of a patent. Until the Patent Act 1902, although substantial procedural requirements had to be observed, a patent would be awarded without the invention being subjected to any form of scrutiny. From 1902, increasingly stringent procedures have been introduced, whereby an application will be examined with a view to making a determination on whether it complies with the statutory criteria. Under the Patents Act 1977, a two-stage process operates, with applications being subjected to preliminary and substantive examinations.

Preliminary examination

The first purpose of the preliminary examination is to ensure that the application complies with all the formal requirements of the legislation.[45] If this is the case, the examiner will turn to consider the merits of the application. At the stage of the preliminary examination, the examiner's main task is to identify those documents and information sources which it is considered are likely to prove of assistance in applying the criteria of novelty and inventiveness. Having identified relevant documents, the examiner is to scrutinise the documents to such extent as is considered will serve a purpose in determining the application.[46] The results of the preliminary investigation are to be reported to the Comptroller of Patents and to the applicant.[47]

This initial report will be non-judgmental. It may indicate grounds for objecting to or refusing the grant of a patent. In such circumstances, it might become apparent to an applicant that the chances of the application being granted are minimal and the decision taken to withdraw the application.

Publication of the application

Unless notice of withdrawal is given, details of the specification and claims will be published 'as soon as possible' after the expiry of eighteen months from the date of application.[48] In most cases, an applicant will receive the report of the preliminary examination before the application is due to be published. Whilst publication will have no detrimental effect in the event that the patent is ultimately granted, if the application is unsuccessful, the consequence will be that the inventor will have disclosed information to

---

[45] Patents Act 1977, s. 17(2).   [46] s. 17(4)–(5).   [47] s. 17(2).   [48] Patents Act 1977, s. 16.

the public without securing the benefit of any in return. Equally seriously, publication may adversely affect the prospects of any modified application which the inventor might wish to make. Under the present US system, no details of an application are published until the patent is ultimately awarded. Although this may seem fairer to the applicant, problems have been encountered with what are referred to as 'submarine patents'. Even assuming a relatively straightforward application, it will be quite normal for the process to take two to three years. With more complex cases, perhaps including modification of the original application, this period may increase to ten years, or even longer. The essence of a submarine patent is that, originally describing what has been described as 'science fiction technology', it lurks unseen in the patent office awaiting the widespread application of the technology by third parties (perhaps being modified better to describe their applications). At this time, the patent surfaces with claims of patent infringement being fired at any users.

Substantive examination

In the event that the applicant wishes the process to continue, a request must be made for a substantive examination.[49] It is at this stage that the examiner will make a full study of whether the claimed invention is novel, involves an inventive step, is capable of industrial application, and does not fall within one of the prohibited categories. The request for a substantive examination must be made within six months of the date of publication.[50]

Although, as has been said, the determination of whether an invention is novel has to be made by reference to any material in the public domain, it would be unreasonable to expect patent examiners to be aware of every book or article deposited in any library anywhere in the world. The basic tool for examiners will be the collections of patents previously awarded in the world's major patent offices.

It is at the stage of the substantive examination that a decision will be made regarding the patentability or otherwise of the invention. The examiner will make a report to the Comptroller of Patents. In the event that this report makes objection to aspects of the application, the applicant must be afforded the opportunity to make observations or to amend the application so as to take account of the examiner's objections. In the event of the applicant's failure adequately so to do, the Comptroller may refuse the application.[51]

Third-party involvement

The Patents Act 1977 contains no provisions for the formal involvement of third parties in the processes leading to the grant or refusal of a patent. It is provided, however, that in any interval between publication of the application and the decision on grant, a third party may submit written observations to the Comptroller, who must take these into account in reaching a decision.[52]

Award of a patent

In the event that a patent is awarded, the Comptroller is required to cause a notice to this effect to be published in the *Official Journal (Patents)*. The maximum term of validity of a patent is twenty years, commencing from the date when the application is first submitted.[53] It should be noted, however, that a patent is not awarded for such a period. Protection will

---

[49] Patents Act 1977, s. 18(1).   [50] Patents Rules 1995, SI 1995/2093, r. 33.

[51] Patents Act 1977, s. 18(3).   [52] s. 21.   [53] s. 20.

be awarded for an initial period of four years; thereafter annual applications will require to be made (accompanied by a fee) to retain the patent's validity. Only a small percentage of patents remain in force for the full twenty-year period, the average lifespan of a patent being in the region of eight years.[54] By this time, it will have become apparent either that the patent has been overtaken by newer technologies or that the invention is of limited practical utility.

Infringement of patents

The definition of infringement is of critical importance. Under the terms of the Patents Act 1977, infringement may be either direct or indirect. Direct infringement occurs when a party, without the consent, express or implied, of the proprietor of the patent 'makes, disposes or offers to dispose of, uses, keeps, or imports' a product constituting the subject matter of the patent. Similar prohibitions apply in the event that the patent covers a process.[55]

Indirect infringement occurs where a party supplies or offers to supply any equipment which constitutes an essential part of the invention in the knowledge (or having reasonable grounds to believe) that infringement will result.[56]

The question of whether a subsequent product infringes the provisions of a patent is essentially one of fact. It will seldom be the case that the subsequent product is an exact copy of a patented object. In the event that any infringement is innocent, with the product being the result of the competitor's own researches, it is unlikely that every detail of the original will be replicated. Should the subsequent producer have been aware of and seek to evade the provisions of the patent, it is again likely that differences of detail will be introduced in an effort to conceal the fact of infringement.

In the event that products are not identical, the task for the court is to examine the patent specification and statement of claim in order to identify the essential features or integers possessed by the patented product. These are then compared with those of the competing product. If the latter replicates the essential elements, infringement may be established even though the product may differ in other respects. An example of the operation of this principle can be seen in the case of *Beecham Group Ltd v Bristol Laboratories Ltd*.[57] Here, the plaintiffs held a patent for a pharmaceutical product possessing a particular chemical structure. The defendant company produced a product possessing a slightly different structure, but the evidence established that the latter product became converted to the patented product upon being absorbed into the bloodstream. In these circumstances, it was held that there was a patent infringement.

In the case of *Catnic Components Ltd v Hill and Smith Ltd*,[58] the plaintiffs had been granted a patent in respect of a design of lintel. The patent made specific reference to the fact that the support member was to be vertical. The defendants subsequently produced a lintel possessing most of the features of the original design, but with the change that the support was angled slightly from the vertical. The alteration made the design slightly less effective, although the difference was of no practical significance. It was held that the similarity between the two designs was sufficient for infringement to be established.

The fact that the addition of further integers increases the efficiency of the product will not necessarily defeat a claim of infringement. As was stated by Bower LJ in the case of

---

[54] For an excellent analysis of the lifespan of patents, see J. Phillips and A. Firth, *An Introduction to Intellectual Property Law*, 3rd edn (London, 2001).

[55] Patents Act 1977, s. 60(1).   [56] s. 60(2).   [57] [1978] RPC 153.   [58] [1982] RPC 183.

Wenham Gas Co Ltd v Champion Gas Lamp Co Ltd,[59] 'the superadding of ingenuity to a robbery does not make the operation justifiable'. More difficult issues may arise in the event that the subsequent product substitutes or modifies some of the essential integers of the patented product. Here, the determination of whether there is any infringement will be strongly influenced by any expert evidence presented by the parties. If it can be established that it would have been obvious to the mythical 'workman, skilled in the art', presented with details of the modification at the date of publication of the patent, that the substitution of one feature for another would not have had a significant effect on the operation of the patented invention, infringement may be established.

Remedies for infringement of a patent

Four basic forms of remedy might be available to the holder of a patent. At the initial stage of legal proceedings, an injunction may be sought to prevent the defendant continuing with the alleged infringement. When the dispute comes to trial, three further remedies may be applicable. An order may be sought requiring the delivery up to the patentee of any infringing copies. In terms of financial compensation, the patentee may seek either an accounting of profits from the infringer or an award for losses suffered.

Revocation of a patent

A patent may be revoked by the court or the Comptroller on the application of any person if it is established:

1. that the invention is not a patentable invention;

2. that the patent was granted to a person or persons who were not the only persons qualified to obtain such a grant. Such an action may only be brought by a person or persons who would have been entitled to be granted the patent or to have shared in such a grant. The action must be brought within two years from the date of the patent grant unless it is established that the patent holder was aware that he or she was not entitled to the proprietorship of the patent;

3. the specification does not disclose the invention sufficiently clearly and completely for it to be performed by a person reasonably skilled in the art;

4. the matter disclosed in the patent specification is more extensive than that disclosed in the patent application; or

5. the protection conferred under the patent has been extended by an amendment which should not have been allowed.[60]

Although it is possible that a challenge to the validity of a patent may be brought in isolation, it will more commonly be raised as an issue in the course of proceedings by the patent holder alleging infringement. Effectively, therefore, the trial may provide the forum for reconsideration of the question of whether the application for patent protection should be granted.

This possibility is particularly relevant in the information technology sector, where substantial criticism has been made of the abilities of patent offices to identify all materials relevant to determinations of novelty and inventiveness. To this extent, acquisition of a patent may mark only the first stage in a continuing battle to establish its validity and enforce its terms.

---

[59] [1891] 9 RPC 49.   [60] Patents Act 1977, s. 72.

Conclusions

The processes for obtaining a patent are frequently lengthy and expensive. Although the UK Patent Office introduced a 'fast track' process in 1995, which aimed to make a decision on the patentability of an application within twelve months,[61] the patent process will normally occupy a period in excess of two years. Fees must be paid at all stages of the patent process.[62] In addition, the complexity of the processes may compel applications to make use of the services of patent agents—something which is recommended by the Patent Office.

Faced with these factors, coupled with the requirement in the European and UK systems that details of an invention be published prior to the decision being taken on whether to award a patent, it might be queried where the value of the patent system lies for those working in the software field. Given the pace of technical development, it will certainly be the case that, for many applications, the technology will be rendered obsolete before the patent is awarded. The US case of *Microsoft v Stac* provides perhaps the best example of the value of the patent system.[63]

At issue in the case was a patent describing novel techniques for the practice of data compression. As the name suggests, this technique is used to reduce the amount of storage space necessary to hold data. A recent application of compression technology can be seen with the MP3 system. MP3 is an audio compression format that enables audio files to be stored and transferred on a computer with a relatively small file size. Typically, three minutes of music recorded in digital format would require some 30MB of storage space. Use of the MP3 mathematical techniques, which are themselves patented in the United States[64] and the source of potential litigation, reduces the space required to about 3MB. Such a reduction makes it feasible to place musical tracks on, and download from, the Internet.

In the particular case, Stac held two US patents for a compression system which was sold under the name 'Stacker'. Interestingly, especially given the controversy which has existed concerning the eligibility of software-related inventions for patentability within the United Kingdom, one of the patents was originally issued in the United Kingdom to a British company, Ferranti, and was subsequently assigned to Stac. Microsoft wished to incorporate a compression system in a new version of its operating system. Negotiations followed with Stac but these proved unsuccessful, largely because Microsoft was unwilling to offer any payment for the use of the Stac system.[65] When the new version of the operating system appeared on the market, it did contain a compression system. It transpired that it was based on the Stac system. Microsoft's claim was that this had been used initially, but it had subsequently devised its own code. In copyright law, as will be discussed later,[66] this claim may well have succeeded and might at least have resulted in extensive litigation. As the techniques were protected by patents, all that Stac had to establish was that Microsoft had used these. In a jury trial, Stac was awarded $120 million in compensation.[67]

The litigation brought by Stac marked—at least until the anti-trust litigation brought by the US authorities—the most significant legal finding against Microsoft. As such, it is eloquent testimony to the strength of a patent. Software patents have been, and remain,

---

[61] <http://www.ipo.gov.uk/press-release-20070404.htm>.

[62] For current details, see <http://www.ipo.gov.uk/types/patent/p-formsfees.htm>.

[63] For details of the case, see <http://www.msversus.org/archive/stac.html>.

[64] See <http://www.mp3.com/news/095.html>.

[65] For details of Stac's claim, see <http://en.swpat.org/wiki/I4i_v._Microsoft_(2009,_USA)>.

[66] See discussion of *Computer Associates v Altai*, 982 F 2d 693 (1992).

[67] Ultimately, the two companies signed a cross-licensing agreement. Stac received $43 million in cash from Microsoft and Microsoft invested $39.9 million in non-voting Stac stock (about 15 per cent of the company's shares)—a total payout of $83 million.

an extremely controversial subject, especially in the United States. Objections appear to be based on a number of grounds. The system, it is argued, is inequitable in the situation where different people are working independently in the same field. The first one to obtain a patent is then in a position to stop others exploiting their own work. As can be seen from the example of Alexander Graham Bell and Elisha Grey cited earlier, this is not a new phenomenon. A further ground of objection is founded in the perception that the inability of the Patent Offices to make comprehensive searches in the field has resulted in the award of patents in respect of technology which is not truly novel or inventive. This is a more difficult ground to assess. It may be noted that examination is a relatively novel feature of the patent system. Until the twentieth century, the system was effectively one of registration. The fact that a patent is granted is not conclusive evidence of its validity. It may be challenged at any time. Against this, it should be stated that the onus of proving a patent to be invalid lies with the challenger, and patent litigation can be prolonged and expensive. These issues will be considered in more detail in the following chapter, which will consider the manner in which patent law has evolved in relation to patents for software-related inventions.

15
Patents

INTRODUCTION
AN OPENING QUESTION

In 2012 Google bought the IT company Motorola for $12.5 billion. Less than two years later it sold its physical assets to the Chinese manufacturing company Lenovo for $2 billion. Had Google made a stupid business decision?

AN ANSWER

Google did not want Motorola's factories and manufacturing equipment. It does not manufacture anything. Even its branded 'Chromebooks' are made by other companies. Motorola had a portfolio of around 17,000 patents and Google retained these after selling the physical assets. If you want an example of the value of intellectual property today, you need look no further. In similar vein, it is reported[1] that Microsoft makes much more profit from licensing its patented technology for use in Android phones than it does from sales of its own mobile phone operating system.

As indicated above, the United Kingdom's patent system is based primarily on the Patents Act 1977. This statute was enacted in part to reform and update the UK law relating to patents but also in order to bring domestic law into conformity with the provisions of the European Patent Convention, opened for signature in 1973, which, as will be discussed later, provides for a measure of harmonisation in matters of substance and procedure amongst signatory states.

Whilst there is no doubt that inventiveness is a key requirement of the patent system, what has been more debatable has been its application to software-related inventions—innovations where novelty resides primarily or exclusively in software components. Concern has tended to focus on two elements: first, whether software developments fit conceptually into the industrial nature of the system, and, second, whether the library and related resources exist to allow claims of novelty to be adequately assessed with the consequence being that patents of dubious validity might be issued. This remains the most problematic aspect of the subject and will be discussed in more detail below. There is always the possibility that patents may be revoked by the courts. A survey of cases before the English courts concludes that:

> About 43% of all court cases are filed alleging the infringement of a patent whereas around 31% of cases seek the revocation of a patent. Only about half of all cases proceed to final

---

[1] See, eg, <http://www.zdnet.com/article/microsoft-is-making-2bn-a-year-on-android-licensing-five-times-more-than-windows-phone/>.

judgment. Among those cases that ended with a judgment, we find that the by far the most likely outcome is the revocation of a patent—regardless of whether the case was filed as an infringement or revocation action.[2]

The quest for a technical contribution

Although the term 'technical contribution' (or technical effect) does not appear in either the Patents Act 1977 or the European Patent Convention, it achieved pivotal significance in the field of software related inventions since being introduced in Guidelines for Examiners drawn up by the EPO. In the original Guidelines it was stated:

> If the contribution to the known art resides solely in a computer program then the subject matter is not patentable in whatever form it might be presented in those claims. For example, a claim to a computer characterised by having the particular program stored in its memory or to a process for operating a computer under control of the program would be as objectionable as a claim to the program per se or the program when recorded on magnetic tape.[3]

By 1985 in view of the increasing importance of computer programs, it was considered desirable to offer more precise guidance, both to inventors and to the examiners in the EPO. To this extent, new Guidelines[4] were promulgated which seek to make it clear that the essential prerequisite for the grant of a patent is the making of a 'technical' invention, that is, a requirement that there be some tangible end product. Thus, although the revised Guidelines provided that:

> A computer program claimed by itself or as a record on a carrier is unpatentable irrespective of its content. The situation is not normally changed when the computer program is loaded into a known computer[5]

it was recognised also that inventions in which a computer program constitutes an essential element might qualify for patent protection, subject to the application of the Convention's general rules. The Guidelines continued:

> If, however, the subject matter as claimed makes a technical contribution to the known art, patentability should not be denied merely on the ground that a computer program is involved in its implementation. This means, for example, that program controlled machines and program controlled manufacturing and control processes should normally be regarded as a patentable subject matter. It follows also that, where the claimed subject matter is concerned only with the program controlled internal working of a known computer, the subject matter could be patentable if it produced a technical effect.

The aim of the new approach, it was stated, was to produce a workable system from the standpoint of the EPO (particularly in relation to the search and examination requirements) whilst 'responding to the reasonable desires of industry for a somewhat more liberal line than that adopted in the past'.

The first significant case following from the adoption of the new EPO Guidelines was the decision of the EPO Technical Board of Appeal in the case of Vicom/Computer-Related Inventions in July 1986.[6] This ruling has been of pivotal importance, being cited in virtually every subsequent EPO and UK decision.

---

[2] Patent Litigation in the UK. Christian Helmers and Luke McDonagh. Available from <https://www.lse.ac.uk/collections/law/wps/WPS2012-12_Mcdonagh.pdf>.

[3] OJ 1/1978.

[4] The current guidelines were published in 2007 and are available from <http://www.european-patent-office.org/legal/gui_lines/index.htm>.

[5] para. 22.   [6] *Vicom Systems Inc's Application* [1987] 2 EPOR 74.

The Vicom application[7] sought a patent for the use of a computer for image-processing purposes. Data representing the image in the form of electrical signals, would be processed by the computer so as to enhance the quality of the image as displayed on a monitor. It was accepted by the applicant that the process could be operated using a standard computer. The application was initially rejected by the examiner in the EPO on two grounds, first that it sought protection for a computer program and, second, that it related to a mathematical method. The electrical signal, it was argued, could be represented in mathematical terms, likewise the processed signal.

Appealing against this refusal, the applicants claimed that their invention made a novel technical contribution resulting from the novel manner in which data was processed. This, it was argued, produced a direct technical benefit as it allowed data to be processed more speedily than had hitherto been possible. The invention, it was argued:

> made a new and valuable contribution to the stock of human knowledge and patent protection for this contribution cannot be denied merely on the basis that the manner in which the invention is defined would appear to bring it within the exclusions of Article 52(3) EPC.[8]

Acting on a suggestion from the examiner, amended claims relating both to the apparatus required and the methods of processing utilized were submitted for consideration by the Board of Appeal. This held that the claims referred to patentable subject matter. In respect of the program objection it was held that:

> Generally, claims which can be considered as being directed to a computer set up to operate in accordance with a specified program (whether by means of hardware or software) for controlling or carrying out a technical process cannot be regarded as relating to a computer program . . .

Thus an invention that would be patentable in accordance with conventional patentability criteria should not be excluded from protection by the mere fact that for its implementation modern technical means in the form of a computer program are used. Decisive is what technical contribution the invention as defined in the claim when considered as a whole makes to the known art.[9]

It was further recognised that whilst a mathematical method could not be protected directly, different considerations arose when the formula was applied:

> [I]f a mathematical method is used in a technical process, that process is carried out on a physical entity ... by some technical means implementing the method and provides as its end result a certain change in that entity. The technical means might include a computer comprising suitable hardware or an appropriately programmed general purpose computer.[10]

What was required was that the mathematical method should be applied within a specific technical context which, being capable of industrial application, would qualify for patent protection. In this event, the mathematical methods could freely be used by third parties for any purpose other than the specified form of image processing. Such an approach overcomes one of the major concerns which has been expressed by opponents of software patents—especially in the United States—that a patent could be infringed by a party working out calculations with pen and paper.

---

[7] *Vicom Systems Inc's Application* [1987] 2 EPOR 74.
[8] *Vicom Systems Inc's Application* [1987] 2 EPOR 74 at 77–8.
[9] At 80–1.   [10] At 79.

In respect of the claims relating to the apparatus, it was conceded that the process could be conducted using conventional computing equipment. The Board of Appeal held, however, that:

> a claim directed to a technical process which process is carried out under the control of a program (be this implemented in hardware or in software), cannot be regarded as relating to a computer program as such within the meaning of Article 52(3) EPC [European Patent Convention], as it is the application of the program for determining the sequence of steps in the process for which in effect protection is sought. Consequently, such a claim is allowable under Article 52(2)(c) and (3) EPC.

As technology has developed it is frequently open to developers to determine whether applications should be implemented by dedicated hardware or through software running on multi-purpose computers. A simple example can be seen with satellite navigation systems. Initially, these tended to be marketed as stand alone devices but with the emergence of smart phones it is increasingly common for users to download a software application and use their phone as a navigation device. Commenting on this technical possibility, the Board of Appeal stated:

> In arriving at this conclusion, the Board has additionally considered that making a distinction between embodiments of the same invention carried out in hardware or in software is inappropriate as it can fairly be said that the choice between these two possibilities is not of an essential nature but is based on technical and economical considerations which bear no relationship to the inventive concept as such.

Generally speaking, an invention which would be patentable in accordance with conventional patentability criteria should not be excluded from protection by the mere fact that for its implementation modern technical means in the form of a computer program are used. Decisive is what technical contribution the invention as defined in the claim when considered as a whole makes to the known art.[11]

A number of significant features can be identified from the decision in *Vicom*.[12] The applicants' argument might well be noted that they had made 'a new and valuable contribution to the stock of human knowledge'. Protecting such work is at the core of the patent system. In terms of the decision of the Board of Appeal, there is recognition that what an invention does is more important than the manner in which it is achieved. As was stated in the decision, and as is increasingly the case, the distinction between hardware and software implementation of a concept is a matter of choice.

Software-related inventions returned to the EPO Board of Appeal in 1987 in the case of *Koch and Sterzel*.[13] Here, a patent had been awarded in respect of a 'diagnostic X-ray system operative in response to control signals from a stored program digital computer to generate an X-ray beam and to produce an image of the object through which the X-ray beam passes'.[14] The validity of the patent was challenged by two competitor companies, which argued that its subject matter differed from the state of the art only through the involvement of a novel computer program. The decision in *Vicom*,[15] it was suggested, was erroneous in that an application should not be accepted where the elements of novelty and inventiveness lay only in prohibited subject matter—in this case a computer program. Support for this contention was found in a decision of the German courts, to the effect that:

> a teaching is not technical if in its essence it states a rule that can be carried out without employing controllable natural forces other than human brainpower, even if the use of

---

[11] At 79.   [12] *Vicom Systems Inc's Application* [1987] 2 EPOR 74.   [13] [1988] EPOR 72.
[14] EP0001640.   [15] *Vicom Systems Inc's Application* [1987] 2 EPOR 74.

technical means appears expedient or indeed the only sensible and hence the necessary procedure, and even if reference is made to these technical means in the claims or description.[16]

We will return to this concept in discussing the impact of the prohibition against patenting schemes or rules for performing a mental act. In *Koch and Sterzel*, the Board of Appeal rejected the German approach, holding that:

> an invention must be assessed as a whole. If it makes use of both technical and non-technical means, the use of non-technical means does not detract from the technical character of the overall teaching. The European Patent Convention does not ask that a patentable invention be exclusively or largely of a technical nature; in other words, it does not prohibit the patenting of inventions consisting of a mix of technical and non-technical elements.[17]

The alternative approach, it was suggested, could result in a situation where technical aspects of an invention, which were themselves novel and inventive, would be denied patent protection because they were connected with non-technical aspects such as computer programs.

The question of where novelty is required to reside was a key issue in the next authority to be considered, the UK case of *Merrill Lynch's Application*.[18]

Just as *Vicom*[19] constitutes a landmark decision under the European Patent Convention, so the decision in *Merrill Lynch's Application*[20] has played a similar role in UK patent law.

The factual content of this case was very similar to that at issue in International *Business Machines Corpn's Application*.[21] Merrill Lynch had developed what was referred to as 'a data processing system for making a trading market in securities and for executing orders for securities transactions'. The application of computerised trading systems in stocks and shares has proved controversial in a number of areas. Some of the blame for the 'crash' of stock exchanges in times of financial crisis has been apportioned to the operation of systems whereby a fall in share prices automatically triggers the sale of shares which produces a further drop in prices, more selling, and a continuation of a downward spiral. Such considerations were not at issue in the present case, which was concerned solely with the question of whether a patent might be awarded in respect of one such system.

The patent sought by Merrill Lynch related to a business system that:

> retrieves and stores the best current bid and asked prices; qualifies customers' buy/sell orders for execution; executes the orders; and reports the trade particulars to customers and to national stock price reporting systems. The system apparatus also determines and monitors stock inventory and profit for the market maker.[22]

The specification went on to state that the programs involved could be implemented on a wide range of data-processing equipment. Effectively, what the application was claiming was that a general-purpose computer could operate the computer programs to produce novel effects.

The application was rejected within the Patent Office on the basis that the subject matter of the alleged invention fell within the prohibition of section 1(2) of the Patents Act 1977. The principal patent examiner held that the effect of this section was such that it would prevent the award of a patent in the situation where the program was incorporated in some other object (the computer) but where the novelty and inventive step resided in the elements of the program rather than in any of the other attributes of the subject matter.

---

[16] [1988] EPOR 72 at 74.   [17] [1988] EPOR 72 at 74.
[18] [1989] RPC 561, reported at first instance at [1988] RPC 1.
[19] [1989] RPC 561, reported at first instance at [1988] RPC 1.
[20] [1989] RPC 561, reported at first instance at [1988] RPC 1.
[21] [1980] FSR 564.   [22] *Merrill Lynch's Application* [1989] RPC 561 at 569.

This reasoning, which was upheld by Falconer J in the Patents Court, was challenged before the Court of Appeal. The critical issue concerned the interpretation of the concluding passage of section 1(2) of the Patents Act 1977, stating that the prohibitions against patentability extended only 'to the extent that a patent or application for a patent relates to that thing as such'. It was the applicant's contention that the claim related to apparatus operating in accordance with the requirements of the program and, therefore, was for more than the program as such.

Subsequent to the decision of Falconer J at first instance,[23] the Court of Appeal delivered its judgment in the case of *Genentech Inc's Patent*,[24] which also took account of the decision of the EPO Board of Appeal in the case of *Vicom's Application*.[25] Although the subject matter of this case concerned developments in genetic engineering, the issue of the extent of the prohibition against patentability was also discussed, in this case in the context of a discovery.

As described previously, Genentech had identified elements of DNA and obtained patents for applications based upon this research. These patents were revoked by order of Whitford J sitting in the Patents Court on the ground that, inter alia, the identification of the make-up of the DNA was in the nature of a discovery. Having made the discovery, its application was obvious. The only novelty, therefore, lay in the act of discovery. As discoveries cannot be patented, the patent was invalid.

This interpretation of the legislation was rejected by the Court of Appeal. Although the decision to revoke the patent was upheld on other grounds, it was acknowledged that many developments in the pharmaceutical field could be regarded in the same light. Once it is discovered, for example, that a particular drug has a beneficial effect on stomach ulcers, its application is very obvious. Dillon LJ commented:

> Such a conclusion, when applied to a discovery, would seem to mean that the application of the discovery is only patentable if the application is itself novel and not obvious, altogether apart from the novelty of the discovery. That would have a very drastic effect on the patenting of new drugs and medicinal or microbiological processes.[26]

The Court of Appeal in *Genentech*[27] was referred to the decision of Falconer J in *Merrill Lynch*.[28] Indicating their disagreement with the reasoning applied (although concurring with the ultimate result of the case), the court held that so long as the subject matter of the application as a whole satisfied the requirements for patentability, it would not matter that the requisite novelty and inventiveness resided in non-qualifying elements. Effectively, the test concerns what the invention does, as opposed to the manner in which this is accomplished.

Applying the reasoning of the *Genentech* decision[29] and that of the EPOs Technical Board of Appeal in *Vicom*,[30] the Court of Appeal affirmed that an invention could be patentable where the novel or inventive elements lay entirely in a computer program. However, the decision of the Patent Office to refuse Merrill Lynch's application was upheld on another ground. Even though the incorporation of the program in the computer equipment might serve to take it outwith the prohibition against the grant of patents for computer programs, attention had to be paid to the nature of the resulting application. In the present case, the result:

> whatever the technical advance may be, is simply the production of a trading system. It is a data processing system for doing a specific business, that is to say making a trading market

---

[23] *Merrill Lynch's Application* [1988] RPC 1.   [24] [1989] RPC 147.
[25] *Vicom Systems Inc's Application* [1987] 2 EPOR 74.
[26] *Genentech Inc's Patent* [1989] RPC 147 at 239–40.
[27] *Genentech Inc's Patent* [1989] RPC 147 at 239–40.
[28] *Merrill Lynch's Application* [1988] RPC 1.   [29] *Genentech Inc's Patent* [1989] RPC 147.
[30] *Vicom Systems Inc's Application* [1987] 2 EPOR 74.

in securities. The end result, therefore, is simply 'a method . . . of doing business', and is excluded by section 1(2)(c) [of the Patents Act 1977] . . . A data processing system operating to produce a novel technical result would normally be patentable. But it cannot, it seems to me, be patentable if the result itself is a prohibited item under section 1(2). In the present case it is such a prohibited item.[31]

It might be noted that Merrill Lynch subsequently obtained a patent for broadly the same application from the US Patent Office.[32] The case demonstrates that, not only must the invention produce some technical contribution—in itself no easy thing to define—but the end product must not constitute prohibited subject matter. In cases such as *Koch and Stertzel*,[33] where the programs control the operation of some product, this test is fairly easily established. In the situation where the effects are either internal or affect information— echoing back to the debate in *Slee and Harris*[34] on whether information can constitute a product—the prognosis for the grant of a patent is much less favourable.

This requirement was clearly expressed in the United Kingdom in the case of *Aerotel v Telco*, the outcome of which might perhaps be seen as declaring a measure of conditional independence from the internal disagreements within the EPO.

The facts in *Aerotel* can be relatively briefly stated. Aerotel had developed and sought a patent for a method for making telephone calls from phones without using cash. A user would deposit funds with the provider in advance and establish a credit balance. Upon dialling a particular code, the call would be routed to a special exchange. Upon entering a PIN number, the user would have calls connected up to the level of his credit. Although it is not specified in the report, the system could be used by indirect telephone service providers who might, especially for international calls, purchase capacity from BT and sell this on to customers. As with mobile phones, the pay as you go approach would obviate the need for complex contractual and billing procedures.

Aerotel were awarded a patent for the system and subsequently sued a competitor for infringement. The other party counter-claimed, alleging that the patent was invalid as relating to nothing more than a program for a computer. Although the case was settled, Aerotel appealed to the Court of Appeal, seeking reinstatement of the patent.

Delivering the judgment of the court, Lord Justice Jacob provided an extensive survey of the development of the law relating to software-related patents. The approaches adopted within the United Kingdom and before the EPO were summarised succinctly:

(1) The contribution approach

Ask whether the inventive step resides only in the contribution of excluded matter—if yes, Article 52(2) applies.

This approach was supported by Falconer J in Merrill Lynch but expressly rejected by this Court.

(2) The technical effect approach

Ask whether the invention as defined in the claim makes a technical contribution to the known art—if no, Article 52(2) applies. A possible clarification (at least by way of exclusion) of this approach is to add the rider that novel or inventive purely excluded matter does not count as a 'technical contribution'.

This is the approach (with the rider) adopted by this Court in Merrill Lynch. It has been followed in the subsequent decisions of this Court, Gale and *Fujitsu*.

---

[31] *Merrill Lynch's Application* [1989] RPC 561 at 569.
[32] This patent survived a challenge in the US courts.   [33] [1988] EPOR 72.
[34] *Slee and Harris's Application* [1966] RPC 194.

The approach (without the rider as an express caution) was that first adopted by the EPO Boards of Appeal, see Vicom, IBM/Text processing and IBM/Data processor network.

(3) The 'any hardware' approach

Ask whether the claim involves the use of or is to a piece of physical hardware, however mundane (whether a computer or a pencil and paper). If yes, Article 52(2) does not apply. This approach was adopted in three cases, Pensions Benefits, Hitachi, and Microsoft/Data transfer (the 'trio'). It was specifically rejected by this Court in Gale.

However, there are variants of the 'any hardware' approach:

(3)(i)   Where a claim is to a method which consists of an excluded category, it is excluded by Article 52(2) even if hardware is used to carry out the method. But a claim to the apparatus itself, being 'concrete' is not so excluded. The apparatus claim is nonetheless bad for obviousness because the notional skilled man must be taken to know about the improved, excluded, method.

This is the Pensions Benefits approach.

(3)(ii) A claim to hardware necessarily is not caught by Article 52(2). A claim to a method of using that hardware is likewise not excluded even if that method as such is excluded matter. Either type of claim is nonetheless bad for obviousness for the same reason as above.

This is Hitachi, expressly disagreeing with Pensions Benefits about method claims.

(3)(iii) Simply ask whether there is a claim to something 'concrete' e.g. an apparatus. If yes, Article 52(2) does not apply. Then examine for patentability on conventional grounds—do not treat the notional skilled man as knowing about any improved excluded method.

This is Microsoft/Data Transfer.[35]

Faced with such a baffling range of authorities, it was considered that, although it was a requirement to place great weight on decisions of the EPO Board of Appeal, the contradictory nature of the jurisprudence made it impossible to do so. Rather than relying on EPO authority, reference was made to the decisions of the Court of Appeal in *Gale, MerrillLynch,* and *Fujitsu's Applications.*[36] These, it was held, adopted the technical effect approach, with the additional qualification or rider that novelty could not lie only in the otherwise excluded subject matter.

Turning to the manner in which this principle should be applied, Lord Justice Jacob accepted a submission by counsel for the Commissioner of Patents which required the decision maker to:

1. Properly construe the claim.

This is a basic step for any patent application and requires identification of the nature and scope of the subject matter of the patent and the extent of the monopoly which is sought.

2. Identify the actual contribution.

This involves an assessment of the problem which the applicant claims to have solved, the manner in which the invention works and the advantages which it claims to offer

---

[35] [2006] EWCA Civ 1371 at para. 26.   [36] [2006] EWCA Civ 1371.

over existing technologies. Lord Justice Jacob summarised the requirement in the following terms '[w]hat has the inventor really added to human knowledge?'

3. Ask whether it falls solely within the excluded subject matter.

    This relates to the provision in the Act and Convention that inventions containing excluded subject matter are ineligible for patent protection only to the extent that they contain nothing more than excluded subject matter.

4. Check whether the actual or alleged contribution is actually technical in nature.

    In many cases, it was suggested, the answer to this question would be obvious from that of the previous one.[37]

The four-stage test, it was stated, was a reformulation of the approach followed by the Court of Appeal in Fujitsu.

Applying these tests, the Aerotel Application, it was held, was patentable. The system specified was novel in itself and not merely because of its application to the handling of telephone calls. This meant that it satisfied the second and third criteria. The system required the use of hardware components and so was technical in nature.

Following the decision in *Aerotel*, the Patent Office stated that the case:

> must be treated as a definitive statement of how the law on patentable subject matter is now to be applied in the United Kingdom. It should therefore rarely be necessary to refer back to previous United Kingdom or EPO case law.

In the subsequent case of *IGT v Commisioner of Patents*,[38] the *Aerotel* approach was adopted, albeit with comment to the effect that:

> The Court of Appeal has recently developed the approach which the courts should adopt to the correct interpretation of Article 52(2) and (3). Whether or not the application of the Article is now more or less straightforward, or clear, than it was before is perhaps a matter on which minds may differ.

In the case of *Symbian v Commissioner of Patents*,[39] the applicant sought a patent for what was claimed to be a better method for accessing data held on a computing device. As with all inventions in this field, the technologies are daunting but the key argument was that a computing device would 'avoid the difficulties and potential unreliability, and therefore the malfunctioning, of the prior art' and would have 'application to a wide range of electrical devices including any form of computer, various forms of cameras and communication devices such as mobile phones . . . and other products which combine communications, image recording and computer functionality within a single device.'[40]

The application was rejected in the Patent Office with the examiner ruling that as the effect was to make the computing device work more efficiently, this did not constitute a technical effect as required under the *Aerotel* test. This decision was overturned by Mr Justice Patten in the High Court[41] whose decision was upheld by the Court of Appeal. Reference was made to a 2007 decision of the EPO Board of Appeal, *Gameaccount Ltd*,[42] which it was suggested adopted an approach more in line with the *Aerotel* approach than older EPO decisions.

As in previous decisions, the Court surveyed extensively the jurisprudence of the English and European courts. The Court of Appeal was, it was held, bound by its own previous decisions unless there was evidence that a contrary and consistent line of

---

[37] [2006] EWCA Civ 1371 at para. 40.   [38] [2007] EWHC 1341 Pat.   [39] [2008] EWCA Civ 1066.
[40] At para. 3.   [41] [2008] EWHC 518 (Pat).   [42] T 1543/06.

jurisprudence had been developed before the EPO.[43] This was not, it was held, the case here. Whilst recognising, as has indeed been described throughout this chapter, that the inclusion of software within the patent system was 'rather imprecise and arbitrary',[44] the Court was clear that it should follow the *Aerotel* tests. Applying these tests, it was held that:

> not only will a computer containing the instructions in question 'be a better computer', … it can also be said that the instructions 'solve a "technical" problem lying with the computer itself'. Indeed, the effect of the instant alleged invention is not merely within the computer programmed with the relevant instructions. The beneficial consequences of those instructions will feed into the cameras and other devices and products, which… include such computer systems.[45]

Following the decision in *Symbian* a request was made by the President of the EPO that an enlarged Board of Appeal should consider four questions relating to the Board of Appeal practice and jurisprudence in respect of the patentability of software-related inventions.[46] The enlarged Board surveyed the EPO jurisprudence but ultimately came to the conclusion that the referral was inadmissible as in the opinion of the enlarged Board, there was no fundamental inconsistency within the jurisprudence.

Patents and the Internet

We have seen above that software-related inventions are potentially patentable. The precise criteria that are to be applied to determine such applications are not at all clear and, as was stated above, there is something of an arms race in progress between different patent offices. We have discussed the principles of patent law and some of the key issues relating to their application within a software context, but what do the figures tell us?

In 2012—quite a long time ago in technology terms—it was estimated that around 250,000 US patents had been issued (around one in six of active patents in all areas of technology) that might impact upon smartphones.[47] Numbers are likely to be significantly lower, but still substantial, within Europe. In 2014, the EPO received around 274,000 applications (for all fields of technology) and granted around 64,600 patents.[48] This might be compared with the situation in the United States where 615,000 applications were received and 300,000 patents awarded.[49] On the basis of this raw data, one might extrapolate a European figure of around 50,000 smartphone related patents. A further point to be considered is the discrepancy between the European regime, where the number of grants is around a third of the number of applications received, and the US system where the ratio is around one to two. This might suggest a difference in the level and severity of scrutiny afforded to applications in the two Patent Offices. There does seem to be a developing view in the United States that software-related patents have been granted following inadequate scrutiny regarding issues of novelty and inventiveness and a number of granted patents have subsequently been revoked.

---

[43] See *Actavis UK Ltd v Merck & Co Inc* [2008] EWCA Civ 444.   [44] At para. 26.   [45] At para. 54.

[46] Case No. G 0003/08. The text of the opinion is available from <http://www.epo.org/topics/issues/computer-implemented-inventions/referral.html>.

[47] <https://www.techdirt.com/blog/innovation/articles/20121017/10480520734/there-are-250000-active-patents-that-impact-smartphones-representing-one-six-active-patents-today.shtml>.

[48] <http://www.epo.org/about-us/annual-reports-statistics/statistics.html>.

[49] <http://www.uspto.gov/web/offices/ac/ido/oeip/taf/us_stat.htm>.

Who gets patents?

It is perhaps instructive to look at some data from the European and US Patent Offices. Data from 2014 from the EPO indicates which companies were awarded the highest number of patents. At the top of the list is Phillips, followed by Samsung, LG, Huawei, Siemens, Qualcomm, and Bosch. Microsoft enters the list at number 14.[50]

Indicating the increasingly global trends within the patent system, you will note that most of the companies involved are non-European. What is perhaps surprising and indicative of differences in approach between the European and US patent authorities is to consider comparative data from the latter office and identify names that are missing in a European context. Companies such as Apple, Google, and Microsoft feature prominently in the US data but the first two would not appear in a list of the top twenty-five European patent filers. Certainly these companies have applied for European patents but you might look at the case of *HTC Europe Co Ltd v Apple Inc.*[51] Here the Court of Appeal held an Apple patent to be invalid. The patent related to the technique used in iPhones and iPads whereby the user would make a swiping move across the screen in order to unlock it. Similar decisions have been delivered in a number of other European countries[52] and it appears that the patent remains valid only within the United States. Even in this jurisdiction, it does appear that claims for patents are being regarded rather more sceptically, in large part following the decision of the Supreme Court in the case of *Alice Corporation Pty Ltd v CLS Bank International et al.*[53]

Perhaps showing the existence of the phenomenon of globalisation, it will be seen that the majority of applications come from companies based in non-European countries.

The software patent wars

Most software patents relate to relatively trivial elements, but the potential for conflict and litigation is very clear. Reference is often made to the smart phone patent wars, where it does seem at times that most players are suing most other players. A particularly high profile dispute has been between Apple and Samsung. In 2014 Apple obtained a court judgment in the United States affirming that Samsung had infringed its patents and awarding it some $120 million in damages.[54] Whether it will ever receive the money is perhaps open to doubt. You might enjoy this site[55] although it does, I fear, fall into the category of an urban myth discussed in more detail below.

It is, of course, easier to initiate litigation than to conclude it in the courts. Very few of the actions in this area have reached the stage of a definitive court ruling. In most cases, parties make a commercial decision to negotiate a settlement that not infrequently involves some form of cross licensing agreement. One issue that has been significant in the United States and might possibly be crossing the Atlantic to land on the shores of the United Kingdom and Europe concerns the activities of what are referred to as patent trolls.

---

[50] <http://documents.epo.org/projects/babylon/eponet.nsf/0/4C30F69F33211B6EC1257F6A0049308F/$File/at_a_glance_en.pdf>.

[51] [2013] EWCA Civ 451.

[52] See <http://ipkitten.blogspot.co.uk/2015/09/apples-european-slide-to-unlock-patent.html>.

[53] <http://www.supremecourt.gov/opinions/13pdf/13-298_7lh8.pdf>.

[54] To put the sum into perspective, Samsung's profits in 2015 were in the region of $5 billion. A good portion of this related to sales of semiconductor chips to Apple.

[55] See <http://www.snopes.com/politics/satire/samsung.asp>.

Patent trolls

The notion of a troll comes from Norse mythology, in which the troll is a fearsome monster with the rather nasty habit of eating human beings. You have doubtless seen the term used in a number of Internet-related contexts. It often refers to people who post deliberately inflammatory postings on websites. In the patent context, the term troll is reserved for entities, sometimes less pejoratively referred to as non-practising entities, that seek to compile a substantial portfolio of patents, not with the intention of practising the technologies described therein, but to use the patents to persuade/intimidate other companies to enter into—and pay for—licencing agreements to allow them to continue to use the technologies without the threat of litigation for patent infringement.

In the past, patent trolls have been seen as operating primarily in the United States but there are signs that the United Kingdom may be becoming the new location of choice for such activities.[56] You might look at the case of *Unwired Planet International v Huawei Technologies, Samsung and Google.*[57] The claimant in this case had purchased a portfolio of IT-related patents from the Swedish telecommunications company Ericsson and was seeking to institute infringement proceedings against the defendants. The case is ongoing and it does appear that Unwired does have some limited research background in its own right although the bulk of its portfolio is represented by patents purchased from their original inventors.

Standard essential patents

The Internet, as with any other communications medium, can function only if and to the extent that devices can interact with each other. This can create an uneasy relationship with the precepts of intellectual property law. The most wonderful form of communication technology will be worth little if nobody can communicate with it. Its inventor can certainly maintain a monopoly over the use of patented technology, but this may be a very bad decision in economic terms. If technology becomes incorporated into a communications standard its value may well increase but there may be the issue whether the increased value is due to the inherent value of the technology or its locations within the standard environment. Although it was more concerned with copyright rather than patent law, relevant literature relates the disputes between the European Commission and Microsoft relating to the latter's handling of intellectual property rights issues.[58] A position of market strength in one sector can fairly readily be extended into other connected but not intrinsically connected areas of activity.

There is now a well-developed standardisation process covering many aspects of commercial activity. Within Europe particular reference can be made to the work carried out by the European Telecommunications Standards Institute (ETSI).[59] As shown below,[60] there are more European standards than formal legislative instruments.

LEGISLATION TOTAL	40163
SECONDARY LEGISLATION	34707
Regulations	11547
Directives	1842
Decisions	18545

---

[56] See <http://techrights.org/2015/10/05/patent-trolls-in-london/>.   [57] [2015] EWHC 1029 (Pat).
[58] See <http://ec.europa.eu/competition/sectors/ICT/microsoft/>.   [59] <http://www.etsi.org/>.
[60] Taken from <http://en.euabc.com/word/2152>.

Other acts	2773
INTERNATIONAL AGREEMENTS	5456
Agreements with non-member states or international organisations	1721
Acts of bodies created by international agreements	3700
Other acts	35
NON-BINDING ACTS	16917
Recommendations	1599
Communications	15136
White papers	36
Green papers	146
VERDICTS FROM THE EU COURT OF JUSTICE	15023
STANDARDS TOTAL	62397
CEN (European Committee for Standardization)	14163
CENELEC (European Committee for Electrotechnical Standardization)	6519
ETSI (European Telecommunications Standards Institute)	36932
CODEX ALIMENTARIUS (WHO&FAO food standards system)	4783
GRAND TOTAL	134500

Standards organisations such as ETSI have been seeking to develop policies to smooth the relationship between the rights of intellectual property owners and their involvement in the standardisation process. The concept of standard essential patents (SEPs) is integral to this. Essentially, if a standard relates to proprietary technology, the owner of intellectual property rights is obliged to license them to any other party upon fair, reasonable, and non-discriminatory (FRAND) terms. Determining what terms meet this requirement has not proved to be an easy task. On 24 April 2015, a judicial decision was issued by the High Court of Justice in the case of *Unwired Planet International v Huawei Technologies, Samsung and Google*.[61] From a legal perspective, the case offers the prospect of establishing a useful precedent in respect of the relationship between standards and intellectual property rights.

This is a significant case, albeit one that is still at a relatively early stage in what may be protracted legal proceedings, which raises important issues about patent licensing and its application in the situation where technologies protected by patents relate to technologies that form an essential part of product standards—generally referred to as standard essential patents or SEPs, as noted earlier.[62]

The case originates from the field of telecommunications. In this area of activity, ETSI has adopted a wide range of standards covering technologies such as 3 and 4G telephony. ETSI has a membership of more than 800 companies and organisations[63] and is the pre-eminent European standards association in the telecommunications sector. Under EU Regulation 1025/2012[64] (which consolidates a raft of other legislative instruments dating back to 1989) ETSI, along with the European Committee for Standardisation

---

[61] [2015] EWHC 1029 (Pat).

[62] The legal status of standard essential payments has also been considered by the European Court of Justice. See Judgment in Case C-170/13 *Huawei Technologies Co. Ltd v ZTE Corp., ZTE Deutschland GmbH*.

[63] <http://www.etsi.org/about/who-we-are>.   [64] OF L316/12.

(CEN) and the European Committee for Electrotechnical Standardisation (Cenelec), may be requested to develop standards in specified fields in order to support European legislation. As is stated by ETSI:

> [W]e produce Harmonised Standards (European Standards (ENs) with a special status). By adhering to these standards, manufacturers and service providers can claim 'presumption of conformity' with the essential requirements of a directive (by self-declaration) rather than having to go through costly type approval processes in different Members States. Manufacturers can also then use the well recognized CE marking for their products. This helps ensure the free movement of goods within the Single European Market and enables enterprises in the EU to be more competitive.[65]

Effectively, conformity with standards is equated to conformity with formal legal requirements.

Not surprisingly given the numbers involved, many techniques and technologies are covered by patents and ETSI, in common with other standard making organisations has adopted the concept of SEP. As it states:

> When it is not possible on technical grounds to make or operate equipment or methods which comply with a standard without infringing an IPR, i.e. without using technologies that are covered by one or more IPR, we describe that IPR as 'essential'.

The relationship between standards and intellectual property rights is a complex one, with considerations of copyright law also impinging on the equation.

There are clear benefits to a patent owner in having their protected technology incorporated into a standard. Anyone wishing to develop a product compatible with, for example, 3G telephony, will have to reach a financial agreement with relevant patent owners in order to lawfully make use of the technology. This places a powerful, perhaps excessive, weapon in the hands of the patent owner and the spectre of anti-competition law looms large in the field. Along with other standard making organisations, ETSI seeks to strike a balance between the interests of patent owners and the wider community wishing to make equipment complying with its standards.

The key notion is that if patented technology is to be incorporated in a standard (and there are normally alternative ways of implementing the basic technologies) the patent holder is required to undertake that its use will be licensed to any other undertaking upon FRAND terms. Essentially this means that a standard offer has to be made to anyone wishing to use the technology. It is further provided that if the owner of intellectual property rights disposes of their rights to a third party that equivalent obligations are to be contractually imposed on them.[66]

So far, so simple; but what is a standard offer and what terms can it legitimately contain? Standard making activities play vital roles both in protecting consumer interests and in securing interoperability between products from different manufacturers. This is especially important in a field such as telecommunications where it is largely due to the existence of international standards that we can enjoy near global connectivity. In spite of their practical importance, the legal status of standards and standard making activities remains uncertain in general with particular uncertainties surrounding the nature and extent of FRAND obligations. As was noted in the judgment:

> As far as the researches of the legal teams in this case have revealed, there are no decisions anywhere dealing with the legal status of this ETSI FRAND obligation.[67]

---

[65] <http://www.etsi.org/about/what-we-are/role-in-europe>.   [66] <http://wwww.etsi-ipr-policy.pdf>.
[67] para. 21.

The claimant in *Unwired* had acquired a number of patents from the Swedish telecommunications company, Ericsson. These were classed as SEPs in a number of ETSI standards relating to mobile telephony. It was alleged that the defendants made use of the technologies but had not taken out licences so to do. It was not disputed that Unwired had made two offers to license the technologies but for the defendants it was claimed that these had been linked to their accepting unconnected obligations. In competition law terminology, one agreement was tied to the party accepting other unrelated obligations. It was also denied that the patents in question were either valid or essential to the implementation of the ETSI standard. These questions will require to be resolved at a later stage in what may be protracted legal proceedings. At the present stage, attention is focused on the extent of the requirements relating to the offer of FRAND terms. Essentially the claimants were arguing that judgment should be given in their favour at this stage on the basis that there was no realistic prospect that Unwired could sustain the argument that they had offered FRAND terms at a full trial.

Perhaps not surprisingly given the burden of proof placed on a party seeking summary judgment in advance of a full hearing on the facts, the judge, Mr Justice Birss, declined to accede to the request. Amongst a range of more technically procedural issues he stated:

> The submission that the April 2014 proposal (offering a licence for standard essential and non-essential patents) cannot have been compliant with Unwired Planet's ETSI obligations seems to me to be Huawei's best point. However, I have decided that it would be wrong to rule out the possibility that the conclusion might be different once all the facts are found at trial.[68]

Essentially the issues were considered to be much more nuanced and complex than was being suggested by the defendants and the request for summary judgment was premature.

Many patent cases are initiated in the ICT field and a high percentage end up being settled out of court. It is impossible to predict what will happen in the case of the present action. Following a series of five technical (described as conventional patent hearings) concerning the validity of the patents at issue, the key standards/intellectual property case was scheduled to come before the court towards the end of 2016 with a provisional schedule of a thirteen-week hearing.

Assuming the timetable is adhered to, we might be looking at a High Court decision on the substantive merits of the case sometime in 2017. From a legal perspective, the case does offer the prospect of establishing a useful precedent in respect of the relationship between standards and intellectual property rights. The notion of interconnection is an integral part of the wired world, and will become more so as society moves towards the 'Internet of things'. Monopolistic rights conferred by patents sit uneasily with the distributive nature of the Internet.

Conclusions

There is an old story about a traveller seeking directions from a local resident. There follows a series of 'take the first road on the right and then the third on the left … or maybe the second on the left and then the fifth on the right …' followed by the conclusion 'actually if I was you, I wouldn't be starting from here in the first place'. This is perhaps a comment that might be made regarding the patent system, but as with road directions, we are where we are and have to make the best of it. This chapter has focused on developments within

---

[68] para. 59.

Europe and the at times convoluted attempts by the patent authorities and the courts to bypass the bald prohibition in the European Patent Convention against the award of a grant for a program for a computer. The European Patent Convention sought to take account of technological developments. US patent law dates back to the early 1950s with the key provision being that:

> Whoever invents or discovers any new and useful process, machine, manufacture, or composition of matter, or any new and useful improvement thereof, may obtain a patent therefor.[69]

---

[69] 35 US Code S101.

16

Copyright protection

INTRODUCTION

Although there appears globally to be an increasing willingness to bring software-related inventions within the ambit of the patent system, only a small proportion of computer programs will display the necessary degree of novelty and inventiveness to qualify for that form of protection. Virtually every program, however, will obtain a measure of protection under the law of copyright. In addition to software being protected by copyright, information recorded in electronic format such as email messages, multimedia packages, and web pages will also be protected by copyright.

It is difficult to open a newspaper or view a news website without seeing reports of Internet piracy and legal attempts to limit its scope. Copyright is a hot topic today.

Copyright basics

The essence of copyright can be deduced from the name itself. The owner of copyright in a work possesses the right to copy and, by inference, the right to prevent others from copying. Until the invention of moveable-type printing by Gutenberg in 1450, the issue of copying was of little legal importance. The beginning of mass publishing of literary works brought with it new forms of regulation and control, although these were concerned initially with issues of censorship rather than with the allocation and protection of rights in information. In England, use of the new technology was controlled by a requirement that printing be restricted to authorised printers and that the publication of individual books be licensed by the Crown. This scheme continued until 1695. With its abolition, petitions were presented to Parliament at the behest of the Stationers' Company, which had enjoyed an effective monopoly of publishing but which would now be subjected to competition. Responding to these representations, the first copyright Act, the Statute of Anne, was enacted in 1709. This Act (very short and simply, albeit archaically, worded), granted the author (or assignee) the exclusive right to reproduce the work. In respect of existing works, this right would subsist for twenty-one years, with new works being protected for up to twenty-eight years, subject to these being registered with the Stationers' Company. The registration scheme was a comparatively short-lived component of the UK copyright regime, although it continues to be a feature of the US system.

The copyright system has developed over the centuries, largely following changes in recording technology. As it became possible to record different forms of work in permanent form, so copyright law has tended to be extended to regulate the sector. In 1734, engravings became the first form of artistic work to be protected under the terms of the Engraving Copyright Act. In 1814, sculptures were brought within the copyright system by the Sculpture Copyright Act, and the Dramatic Copyright Act 1833 extended protection still further to encompass the public performance of musical and dramatic compositions. The Fine Art Copyright Act 1862 marked a significant recognition of the intervention of technology, with protection being extended to photographs. Study of the various copyright statutes enacted in the twentieth century indicates a steady expansion in the range of subject matter covered, normally following close on the heels of technological developments. In the Copyright Act 1911, reference is made to:

> any record, perforated roll, cinematography film or other contrivance by which the work may be mechanically performed or delivered.[1]

The Copyright Act 1956 extended protection to television and radio broadcasts made by the BBC or the Independent Television Authority.[2] During the 1980s, albeit motivated as much by the desire to introduce significant criminal sanctions as by uncertainty on whether the subject matter was protected under existing provisions of copyright law, the Copyright (Computer Software) (Amendment) Act 1985 brought this subject matter unequivocally within the ambit of copyright law.[3] The current UK copyright law is to be found principally in the Copyright, Designs and Patents Act 1988. As was the case with the Patents Act 1977, a variety of motives prompted the introduction of the new legislation. The previous statute, the Copyright Act 1956, had been subjected to piecemeal amendment and the need was identified for a consolidating piece of legislation, coupled with a measure of reform to take account of specific problems which had been encountered concerning the extent to which protection might be extended towards functional works such as the design of product components. These problems were manifested in the decision of the House of Lords in the case of *British Leyland Motor Corpn Ltd v Armstrong Patents Co Ltd*,[4] in which it was held that a motor-car manufacturer could not rely upon copyright law to prevent competitors from producing spare parts, such as exhaust systems which owners might wish to purchase when the original components required to be replaced. An IT-related area where the issue remains topical relates to the market for replacement ink cartridges and toner for printers. Finally, reform of the United Kingdom's copyright system, in the shape of the introduction of a system of 'moral rights', was required to permit ratification of the 1971 and 1979 revisions to the Berne Convention. In contrast to the situation with patent law where protection is offered on a national basis, the Berne Convention, which has been signed by all the world's major countries, provides for the recognition of copyright in all signatory states.

Although the Copyright, Designs and Patents Act 1988 remains the major statute in the copyright field, further reform has been introduced pursuant to the requirements of the European Directive on the Legal Protection of Computer Programs.[5] Effect has been given to the Directive's requirements by the Copyright (Computer Programs) Regulations 1992,[6] which make a number of amendments to the text of the 1988 Act. A further European Directive, 'On the Legal Protection of Databases', introducing a *sui generis* form of protection for the contents of electronic databases, was adopted in 1996 and required to be adopted within the Member States by 1 January 1998.[7] The Copyright and Rights in Databases Regulations implemented the Directive within the United Kingdom.[8] Further changes to domestic law have also been made by the Copyright and Related Rights Regulations 2003[9] in order to satisfy the requirements of the Directive 'On the Harmonisation of Certain Aspects of Copyright and Related Rights in the Information Society'.[10] Also relevant are the provisions of the 2004 Directive on the Enforcement of Intellectual Property Rights (the Enforcement Directive).[11] This was implemented in the United Kingdom by the Intellectual

---

[1] s. 1(2)(d).   [2] s. 14.   [3] s. 1.   [4] [1986] AC 577.
[5] Directive 91/250/EC, OJ 1991 L 122/42.
[6] SI 1992/3233. Despite their title, these regulations were introduced under the authority of the European Communities Act 1972, as opposed to the Copyright, Designs and Patents Act 1998.
[7] Directive 96/9/EC, OJ 1996 L 77/20.   [8] SI 1997/3032.   [9] SI 2003/2498.
[10] Directive 2001/29/EC, OJ 2001 L 167/10.   [11] 2004/48/EC, OJ L195/16

Property (Enforcement etc.) Regulations of 2006.[12] As has been noted repeatedly, it is unclear what the impact of Brexit will be on the continuing validity of these instruments.

This chapter will initially outline the key features of the copyright system and will continue to analyse the manner in which these have been applied within a software context. In many respects, the development of copyright protection for software displays almost a mirror image of the situation described in the previous chapter in respect of patents. Starting with a denial of patentability, the application of the patent system has grown over time. With copyright, early cases accepted a very high level of protection but with the passage of time this has been steadily weakened.

Obtaining copyright

In contrast to the patent system, the copyright regime is noteworthy for a near complete lack of procedural formalities. The substantive requirements will be considered in more detail later, but at the outset it may be stated that protection begins at the moment that a work is recorded in some material form. Copyright lasts during the lifetime of the author and continues for a period of up to seventy years after the author's death. During this time, civil and criminal penalties may be imposed upon a party who, without the consent of the copyright owner, reproduces all or a substantial part of the work or engages in one or more of a list of other prohibited acts.

Forms of protected work

The Copyright, Designs and Patents Act provides that:

1. Copyright is a property right which subsists in accordance with this Part in the following descriptions of work—

    (a)   original literary, dramatic, musical or artistic works,

    (b)   sound recordings, films, broadcasts or cable programmes, and

    (c)   the typographical arrangement of published editions.[13]

Although the Act refers to copyright constituting a 'property right', it is accepted that it is a specialised and limited right, the scope of which is to be found exclusively in the copyright legislation.[14] Although it is commonplace to talk about software theft and, indeed, the leading organisation set up to protect the interests of copyright owners is referred to as the Federation Against Software Theft (FAST),[15] dealings in copyright material cannot be the subject of a charge of theft—although the legislation does provide significant criminal penalties for incidents of breach of copyright.

The provisions relating to copyright in typographical arrangements does not require further consideration in this book. All of the other headings can impact upon software, however, although, as will be discussed later, the most significant category has been that of a literary work.

---

[12] SI 2006/1028.
[13] s. 1.
[14] See *CBS Songs Ltd and Ors v Amstrad Consumer Electronics Plc and Anor* [1988] AC 1013.
[15] <http://www.fast.org.uk/>.

The requirement of originality

The Act provides that only 'original' works are to be protected. Semantically, the word might be equated with the requirement of novelty applying under the patents regime. In reality, the requirement of originality has been construed as requiring only that the work is that of the author—that is, it has not been copied from any other source. In *University of London Press Ltd v University Tutorial Press Ltd*,[16] Petersen J held that:

> The word 'original' does not mean that the work must be an expression of original or inventive thought. Copyright Acts are not concerned with the originality of ideas, but with the expression of thought, and, in the case of 'literary work', with the expression of thought in print or writing. The originality which is required relates to the expression of the thought. But the Act does not require that the expression must be in an original or novel form but that the work must not be copied from another work—that it should originate from the author.[17]

Under the United Kingdom's copyright system, the most crass and unedifying piece of prose (or the most error-ridden computer program) is as entitled to the benefit of copyright protection as the most illustrious example of the species (although it may fare less well in the marketplace). In the case of *Shetland Times v Willis*,[18] it was accepted without debate that the headlines of newspaper reports could qualify for protection, with the case of *Exxon Corpn v Exxon Insurance Consultants International Ltd*[19] providing a very rare illustration of a situation in which the requirement of originality was not met. Here, it was held that copyright could not subsist in the single word, Exxon, albeit that it had been selected after lengthy and expensive public research to find a name to replace the well-known brand Esso. This was a requirement of US anti-trust litigation, although the name Esso continues to be used in the United Kingdom.

This approach is to be contrasted with that had applied in Germany, where the application of strict qualitative criteria resulted, prior to the EC Directive 'On the Legal Protection of Computer Programs',[20] in an estimated 95 per cent of computer programs being denied protection on the ground that they were not original. The Directive would appear to endorse the UK position on the legal protection of computer programs, stating in its Preamble that 'no tests as to the qualitative or aesthetic merits of the program should be applied' and providing subsequently that:

> A computer program shall be protected if it is the author's own intellectual creation. No other criteria shall be applied to determine its eligibility for protection.[21]

The phrase 'intellectual creation' is more reflective of the civil law's system of authors' rights than the common law notion of copyright, and it might prove sufficiently vague to allow a measure of discretion in this area. It remains uncertain, therefore, whether the Directive on the Legal Protection of Computer Programs will secure its objective of eliminating 'differences in the legal protection of computer programs offered by the laws of the Member States (which) have direct and negative effects on the functioning of the common market as regards computer programs'.[22]

[16] [1916] 2 Ch. 601.
[17] At 608–9.
[18] (1997) SC 316.
[19] [1982] Ch. 119.
[20] Directive 91/250/EC.
[21] Art. 1(3).
[22] Directive 91/250/EC, Preamble.

Ownership of copyright

The author of a work will, subject to one exception, be the first owner of any copyright which may subsist in it.[23] Where a work is the product of two or more authors, any copyright arising will be the joint property of the authors.[24] The criterion for determining the existence of joint authorship is whether the individual contributions of the authors can be distinguished.[25] In this case, each author will possess individual copyright in his or her portion of the work. This may be a matter of some significance in the software field, where in the case of a program intended for use in a specific area of business, production may require both programming skills and knowledge of the subject area. Unless suitable contractual arrangements are negotiated, the result could be the existence of two separate copyrights, each useless without the other.

Employee-created works

The exception to the principle that the author is the first owner of copyright in a work applies where the work is created in the course of the author's employment. In this event, copyright will, subject to any contractual provision to the contrary, vest in the employer.[26] This approach marks a change from the position under previous copyright statutes, where the employer's rights in respect of employee-created works were limited in the situation where the work was created for publication in a newspaper, magazine, or other periodical.[27] Although the employer would possess copyright in the publication containing the work, all other rights in respect of it would remain with the author. Thus, the inclusion of the work in a database would require the author's permission. Today, many newspapers make copies of previous issues available in the form of an electronic database. Under the provision described above, the consent of the author of every piece of information appearing in the database would have been required. Responding to lobbying on the part of media interests, the Copyright, Designs and Patents Act 1988 eschews any exceptions to the general rule conferring unrestricted copyright on the employer.

Computer-generated works

Computers are frequently used to assist in the production of a work. In many instances, this will not affect copyright in the work at all. This book, for example, was typed on an Apple MacBook™ computer, using Microsoft Word™ software. In this, and in many other situations, the computer is merely a tool and the author of the text acquires full copyright in the completed work—which is then assigned to the publisher. In *Express Newspapers plc v Liverpool Daily Post and Echo plc*,[28] another case determined at interlocutory level, the plaintiff ran a competition 'Millionaire of the Month' in its newspaper. A number of other national newspapers operated similar competitions. In each case, the key feature was that competitors would have to check the newspaper each day to see whether numbers allocated to them matched winning numbers. The defendant republished all the winning numbers with the obvious intention that readers could participate in the competitions run by other publishers without having to purchase copies of the newspaper. In defence to an action

---

[23] Copyright, Designs and Patents Act 1988, s. 11(1).
[24] s. 10(3).
[25] s. 10(1).
[26] Copyright, Designs and Patents Act 1988, s. 11(2).
[27] Copyright Act 1956, s. 4(2).
[28] [1985] 1 WLR 1089.

alleging copyright infringement, the defendant claimed that as the numbers were selected by a computer program, they were not entitled to protection. Dismissing this defence, Whitford J (as he then was) held that a great deal of skill and labour had been required to develop the computer program (not least to ensure that too many winning numbers were not selected). As with the word-processing example cited above, the computer was no more than a tool giving effect to the intentions of its human controller.

In other instances, the role of the computer may move beyond that of recording a user's work and may serve to embellish the creation. An example concerns the practice of digital sampling. Other applications in the musical field might concern the use of electronic synthesisers. Without delving into the technical details concerning the manner in which these products function, it is sufficient to note that the involvement of the computer is at a qualitatively greater level than that occurring in word-processing applications.

A further situation which may raise questions of the ownership of copyright might apply where a database or expert system program is acquired. The program will require the addition of data by the user and the combination of the program and the user-supplied data will produce a new product in the form of the processed output. Again, this finished product will owe a considerable amount to the underlying program.

The Copyright, Designs and Patents Act 1988 contains a provision which appears to be unique in copyright statutes. It introduces a specific category of computer-generated work and provides:

> In the case of a literary, dramatic, musical or artistic work which is computer-generated, the author shall be taken to be the person by whom the arrangements necessary for the creation of the work are undertaken.[29]

The concept of a computer-generated work is defined as one where 'the work is generated by computer in circumstances such that there is no human author of the work'.[30]

It is unclear when this provision might be applicable. Few, if any, works will be created by a computer in the absence of any human involvement. In circumstances such as those identified here, human involvement will be required. The question which may have to be determined by a court in the event of any dispute is whether the input of any of the parties is sufficiently substantial to qualify them for sole ownership of copyright (as will almost certainly be the case with a piece of text produced on a word processor) or whether there might be joint ownership of copyright. In many instances, the enabling computer programs may be sold under the terms of a contract which prescribes the use to which a completed work may be put. Typically, the purchaser of the program will be entitled to use it for his or her own purposes but prohibited from selling or disposing of any work thereby created without the further agreement of the supplier.

In determining whether there is no human author of a work, two issues may be relevant. The first would be whether there is no human involvement of any kind in the production of the work. It is difficult to conceive of situations where the computer will act entirely on its own initiative. Once the possibility of some human intervention is accepted, the statutory provision might appear otiose. The general criterion for a literary or other work to be protected requires that it be the author's 'original' work. Although the requirement of originality has limited application in the general field, the concept of computer-generated works can have meaning only if this is interpreted so as to exclude a human computer operator from qualifying for authorship where they make no intellectual contribution to the work. An example of such a situation might be where a computer program operates to produce a drawing on a completely random basis, with the operator's only contribution being to

---

[29] s. 9(3).   [30] s. 178.

initiate its operation. In this case, the operator, or a person who instructed that person to carry out the task, will become the owner of the computer-generated work.

The duration of copyright will depend upon the particular form of the work. In the case of a literary, dramatic, or musical work, copyright will subsist during the lifetime of the author and for a period of seventy years after the author's death.[31] In the event that the work is computer-generated, copyright will last for fifty years from the end of the calendar year in which the work is produced.[32] The same period of protection extends to films, sound recordings, and broadcasts,[33] whilst a shorter period of twenty-five years is applicable to the typographical arrangements of a published work.[34]

The lifespan of copyright is clearly much greater than that of a patent, although it must be doubted whether a period of protection which, depending upon the age and longevity of the author, may subsist for a century or longer is of any practical significance in the information technology field. Given the pace of technological development, it is unlikely that any piece of software will retain commercial value for more than a few years, although, as the publicity surrounding the Millennium Bug evidenced, many programs have enjoyed a longer lifespan than originally expected. Even in the case of the author's own word-processing package, the copyright notice refers to versions of the program dating back to 1983, although it is not clear how much original code remains.

Infringement of copyright

As discussed in the preceding chapters, the award of a patent serves to confer upon the successful applicant a monopoly in respect of the exploitation of its subject matter. Although judicial references have been made to copyright conferring a monopoly—in the case of *Green v Broadcasting Council of New Zealand*,[35] Lord Bridge, delivering the judgment of the Privy Council, stated that '[t]he protection which copyright gives creates a monopoly'—it is generally accepted that the copyright owner possesses only the exclusive right to perform certain acts in respect of the work. These comprise the rights:

- to copy the work or any substantial part of it[36]
- to issue copies of the work to the public[37]
- to perform, show, or play the work in public[38]
- to broadcast the work or include it in a cable programme service[39]
- to make an adaptation of the work or do any of the above in relation to an adaptation.[40]

The nature of copying

The act of copying is defined as involving the reproduction of the work, or a substantial part of the work in any material form.[41] This is to include 'storing the work in any medium by

---

[31] Copyright, Designs and Patents Act 1988, s. 12(1). The only exception to this rule applies in favour of the work, *Peter Pan*. Copyright in this work was bequeathed upon the author's death to the Great Ormond Street Children's Hospital, with the revenue accruing from royalty payments, etc constituting a significant portion of the hospital's income. The author, J. M. Barrie having died in 1937, copyright would normally have expired at the end of 1987. In what may be a unique provision, s. 301 and Sch. 6 of the Act provide, not inappropriately given the nature of the work's main character, that elements of the copyright in Peter Pan will never die.

[32] s. 12(3).   [33] s. 13.   [34] s. 15.   [35] [1989] 2 All ER 1056.

[36] Copyright, Designs and Patents Act 1988, s. 16(1)(a).   [37] s. 16(1)(b).

[38] s. 16(1)(c).   [39] s. 16(1)(d).   [40] s. 16(1)(e).   [41] s. 17(2).

electronic means'.[42] Thus, for example, the use of some form of scanning device to transform text into electronic format will constitute an infringement of copyright in the original text.

A popular saying is to the effect that if enough monkeys are given enough typewriters, eventually one monkey will hit the keys in such an order as to reproduce the works of Shakespeare. Discounting the inconvenient fact that the works of Shakespeare are out of copyright, and the considerable uncertainty as to whether a monkey could own copyright, the end-product would not infringe copyright for the reason that it represents an independent composition.

The question of whether one work infringes copyright in an earlier work is determined on the basis of objective criteria. It is not necessary that the act should have been deliberate. A number of cases have been brought in which the allegation has been made (and sometimes established) that a musical work was derived from an earlier composition which might well have been heard by the second composer, who retained a subconscious memory of the melody. The fact that the copying or plagiarism was unintentional will not serve as a defence. The key factors which will have to be established by a party alleging copyright infringement are that the alleged copyist would have had access to the work and that there are substantial similarities between the works which are not explicable by factors other than copying.

In situations where two or more people are working on the same topic, for example, a history of the Second World War, it is likely that similarities will exist between the finished works. In a non-fictional work, the ending must be the same and there is likely to be consensus regarding the key events of the conflict. Greater levels of similarity may raise suspicions that one author has relied too heavily on the work of the other.

In the United States' copyright system, a distinction is drawn between ideas—which are not protected by copyright—and particular forms of expression. In similar manner, the European Directive on the Legal Protection of Software provides that:

> Protection in accordance with this Directive shall apply to the expression in any form of a computer program. Ideas and principles which underlie any element of a computer program, including those which underlie its interfaces, are not protected by copyright under this Directive.[43]

Often referred to as the 'idea/expression dichotomy' this element has featured in many cases concerned with copyright infringement in software. Generally, however, although providing a useful sound bite, the idea/expression dichotomy can offer only limited assistance in determining whether copyright infringement has occurred.

How temporary is temporary?

One of the aspects of digital technology is that every act of use tends to require elements of copying. Copyright law gives rights owners a wide range of rights but in the analogue world there has been a distinction between what might be classed as active and passive acts of infringement. A party making an infringing copy of a work will commit an unlawful act but a person who reads or views such an article will not be considered guilty. As with many aspects of life, the Internet and digital technologies challenge established practice. The vulnerabilities of copyright owners have been well documented. It is also the case that users' rights are not clear-cut.

Consideration was given to the question when temporary acts of reproduction might constitute copyright infringement in the case of *Public Relations Consultants Association v*

---

[42] s. 17(3).   [43] Art. 1(2).

The Newspaper Licensing Agency Ltd and Ors.[44] As was explained in the leading judgment of the case, every act of viewing a page on the Internet causes a copy of the contents to be stored in the cache memory of the browser. At issue was the question of whether such temporary reproductions breached the rights of copyright owners.

The particular dispute concerned the business of the appellants who offered its customers a service whereby they would be notified of any Internet publications of interest to them. Typically, a company might want to be notified of any media mention of its activities or those of its competitor. The appellants had obtained a licence from the relevant copyright owners to provide this service. Initially customers would be sent an email giving hypertext links to the relevant materials. It was accepted by all parties that emails constituted a form of permanent storage and that customers would also be required to obtain a licence. A subsequent development which constituted the genesis of the litigation saw customers able to access the data on the appellant's website. The key question for the Supreme Court was whether the customers would be required to obtain a licence for use of material in this format? It was recognised, however that the issue had wider implications. As was stated:

> The issue has reached this court because it affects the operation of a service which is being made available on a commercial basis. But the same question potentially affects millions of non-commercial users of the internet who may, no doubt unwittingly, be incurring civil liability by viewing copyright material on the internet without the authority of the rights owner, for example because it has been unlawfully uploaded by a third party. Similar issues arise when viewers watch a broadcast on a digital television or a subscription television programme via a set-top box.[45]

Central to the dispute was the Directive on Copyright in the Information Society (Directive 2001/29/EC). This proclaims the intention to secure a 'high level of protection for copyright' but also to secure a harmonised approach across the Union towards the implementation of Article 9(2) of the Berne Convention which states that:

> It shall be a matter for legislation in the countries of the Union to permit the reproduction of such works in certain special cases, provided that such reproduction does not conflict with a normal exploitation of the work and does not unreasonably prejudice the legitimate interests of the author.

The balance between the legitimate interests of rights owners and users has proved to be very difficult to define. The Copyright in the Information Society Directive establishes in Article 5.1 a list of permitted activities. These encompass:

1. Temporary acts of reproduction referred to in Article 2, which are transient or incidental [and] an integral and essential part of a technological process and whose sole purpose is to enable:

   (a) a transmission in a network between third parties by an intermediary, or

   (b) a lawful use of a work or other subject-matter to be made, and which have no independent economic significance, shall be exempted from the reproduction right provided for in Article 2.

These exceptions are stated to be subject to the provisions of Article 5(5) which requires that activities must not conflict with a normal exploitation of the work or other subject matter and should not unreasonably prejudice the legitimate interests of the right holder.

---

[44] [2013] UKSC 18.

[45] *Public Relations Consultants Association v The Newspaper Licensing Agency Ltd and Ors* [2013] UKSC 18 at para. 4.

These requirements were paraphrased by the Court of Justice for the European Union (CJEU) in the case of *Infopaq International A/S v Danske Dagblades Forening* as requiring that:

The act is temporary;

it is transient or incidental;

it is an integral and essential part of a technological process;

the sole purpose of that process is to enable a transmission in a network between third parties by an intermediary of a lawful use of a work or protected subject-matter; and

the act has no independent economic significance.[46]

The Supreme Court understands these criteria as cumulative rather than individual in nature:

They are overlapping and repetitive, and each of them colours the meaning of the others. They have to be read together so as to achieve the combined purpose of all of them.[47]

In the present case, the Supreme Court made extensive reference to further cases before the CJEU.[48] Its judgment provides a useful summary and compilation of the CJEU's reasoning within the field.

In many ways at the heart of the debate was the submission by counsel for the copyright owners that Article 5(1) of the Information Society Directive applied only to acts committed in the course of transmitting Internet content to end-users. It did not, it was suggested, confer any rights on end-users themselves. The Supreme Court rejected this contention. Delivering its leading judgment, Lord Sumption stated:

In my opinion, this is an impossible contention. In the first place, it is clear from the Directive's recitals, and in particular from recital 33, that it was intended that the exception should 'include acts which enable browsing as well as acts of caching to take place.' Browsing is not part of the process of transmission. It is the use of an internet browser by an end-user to view web pages. It is by its very nature an end-user function.[49]

He continued:

Once it is accepted that part of the purpose of article 5.1 is to authorise the making of copies to enable the end-user to view copyright material on the internet, the various conditions laid down by that article must be construed so far as possible in a manner consistent with that purpose. It must, if the exception is to be coherent, apply to the ordinary technical processes associated with internet browsing.[50]

The ordinary technical purposes, it was held, included the use of caches to store records of sites visited by users. Although it was recognised that the extent and duration of the data held in caches could be influenced by actions of users, this did not impact significantly on the provisions of Article 5(1) of the Information Society Directive. Lord Sumption continued:

All that article 5.1 of the Directive achieves is to treat the viewing of copyright material on the internet in the same way as its viewing in physical form, notwithstanding that the

---

[46] Case 5/08 at para. 54. Available from <http://curia.europa.eu/juris/liste.jsf?&num=C-5/08>.

[47] *Public Relations Consultants Association v The Newspaper Licensing Agency Ltd and Ors* [2013] UKSC 18 at para. 11.

[48] In particular Case C-5/08 *Infopaq International A/S v Danske Dagblades Forening ('Infopaq I')* [2010] FSR 495; Case C-403/08 *Football Association Premier League Ltd v QC Leisure and ors*; Case C-429/08 *Karen Murphy v Media Protection Services Ltd* (2012) 1CMLR 769; and Case C302–10 *Infopaq International A/S v Danske Dagblades Forening.*

[49] *Public Relations Consultants Association v The Newspaper Licensing Agency Ltd and Ors* [2013] UKSC 18 at para. 27.   [50] para. 28.

technical processes involved incidentally include the making of temporary copies within the electronic equipment employed . . . if it is an infringement merely to view copyright material, without downloading or printing out, then those who browse the internet are likely unintentionally to incur civil liability, at least in principle, by merely coming upon a web-page containing copyright material in the course of browsing. This seems an unacceptable result, which would make infringers of many millions of ordinary users of the internet across the EU who use browsers and search engines for private as well as commercial purposes.[51]

It may not come as a surprise that the Supreme Court was very much in favour of ruling in a manner that legitimised normal Internet browsing activities. The need for a pan-European harmonised approach to these important questions was recognised and the Supreme Court decided that the CJEU should be asked to rule on the question whether:

> having regard in particular to the fact that a copy of protected material may in the ordinary course of internet usage remain in the cache for a period of time after the browsing session which has generated that copy is completed until it is overlaid by other material, and a screen copy will remain on screen until the browsing session is terminated by the user.[52]

This case is of interest at several levels. It provides a clear description and summation of the evolving jurisprudence of the CJEU in the field. More importantly, it provides a signpost as to the direction that the law should take in balancing the interests of right owners and those of the public who may wish to access the works. It is too early to say that we have a definitive ruling but based on its past precedents it would be surprising if the CJEU were to rule other than in accordance with the suggestions of the Supreme Court. It is perhaps unfortunate that more than a decade after the enactment of the Copyright in the Information Society Directive we are still awaiting a definite answer to the question of what activities are legitimate for Internet users. The Supreme Court ruling does seem to suggest a viable way forward and it is to be hoped that the decision of the CJEU will be delivered in the not too distant future.

Communication to the public

One of the key elements of copyright is the exclusive right to determine whether and to what extent a work is to be communicated to the public. This can encompass a range of issues and has, in the Internet context, been the subject of a significant amount of litigation before the European Court, essentially concerned with the legality of hypertext linking. The key issue is whether the use of such a link interferes with the right holder's control over the range of dissemination of the work.

In many instances, of course, a right holder will be keen to encourage linkage. Matters are not always so straightforward. One of the major cases is *Nils Svensson, Sten Sjögren, Madelaine Sahlman, Pia Gadd v Retriever Sverige AB*.[53] In some respects this is a classic exposition of the issues. A company published a website with news stories and another website provided its customers with links to these. Was this lawful? The original site was open to any member of the public who wished to use it. The European Court was quite clear.

> Article 3(1) of Directive 2001/29/EC of the European Parliament and of the Council of 22 May 2001 on the harmonisation of certain aspects of copyright and related rights in the information society, must be interpreted as meaning that the provision on a website

---

[51] para. 36.   [52] para. 38.
[53] Case 466/12.

of clickable links to works freely available on another website does not constitute an 'act of communication to the public', . . .

It also ruled that this would be the case even if the nature of linking was such as to give the impression that material was coming from the originating website.

Matters can become more complex in situations where the right owner either does not wish others to access the material or wishes to impose conditions. The case of *Ryanair Ltd v PR Aviation BV*,[54] for example, concerned a practice that many travellers will be familiar with known as web scraping. This can be contrasted with other forms of comparison websites whose business model is based on establishing a commission-based relationship with providers. Essentially web scraping sites seek to aggregate data from a range of publicly available sites—without there being any contractual relationship with the site owner—and to present this to users.[55] The case concerned the leading European airline, Ryanair. Obviously such a company will want customers to book flights with it and almost invariably (sometimes almost exclusively) will provide a website to enable this to be done. The defendant in the case was a Dutch site that provided facilities for consumers to compare prices offered by a range of airlines and, on payment of a commission fee, to make a booking via its own website. In effect, the site was providing users with a portal to effectively bypass the original website. Ryanair objected to this practice on a range of grounds. In common with many other transport websites, the company would charge commission on what were effectively adverts offering extra facilities such as car hire or hotel bookings. It might also afford customers the opportunity to request additional services such as assistance with boarding.

An initial issue concerned the question whether the site would be eligible for protection under the Database Directive. This claim was dismissed by the Court, and attention was focused on the site's terms and conditions of use. These provided in part that:

2. Exclusive distribution. This website and the Ryanair call centre are the exclusive distributors of Ryanair services. Ryanair.com is the only website authorised to sell Ryanair flights. Ryanair does not authorise other websites to sell its flights, whether on their own or as part of a package. . . .

3. Permitted use. You are not permitted to use this website other than for the following, private, non-commercial purposes: (i) viewing this website; (ii) making bookings; (iii) reviewing/changing bookings; (iv) checking arrival/departure information; (v) performing online check-in; (vi) transferring to other websites through links provided on this website; and (vii) making use of other facilities that may be provided on the website.

The use of automated systems or software to extract data from this website or www.bookryanair.com for commercial purposes, ('screen scraping') is prohibited unless the third party has directly concluded a written licence agreement with Ryanair in which permits it access to Ryanair's price, flight and timetable information for the sole purpose of price comparison.

The Court ruled that this provision was, subject to the provisions of national law, enforceable. The finding raises a number of interesting issues. It does highlight the limitations on the scope and application of the Database Directive, but more generally, it indicates the connection between contract and intellectual property law. In essence, Ryanair won the case because of its contractual terms. In some respects it is a strange conclusion. The airline could not be protected under intellectual property law but secured protection under contract law. The interaction between the two areas of the law is an important one.

---

[54] Case 30/14.
[55] For a good description of the technology see <http://www.bbc.co.uk/news/technology-23988890>.

The most recent case to come before the court is *GS Media BV v Sanoma Media Netherlands BV, Playboy Enterprises International Inc. and Britt Geertruida Dekke*[56] decided in September 2016. The background to the case was described by the court in the following terms:

> 6.   At the request of Sanoma, which is the publisher of *Playboy* magazine, on 13 and 14 October 2011 the photographer, Mr C. Hermès, took the photos at issue (of Ms Dekke), which were to be published in the December 2011 edition of that magazine. In that context, Mr Hermès granted Sanoma authorisation, on an exclusive basis, to publish those photos. He also granted Sanoma authorisation to exercise the rights and powers arising from his copyright.

GS media is a Dutch-based website whose *raison d'être* was described as being the publication of 'news, scandalous revelations and investigative journalism with lighthearted items and wacky nonsense'. Its publishers received an email from a pseudonymous party providing a link to a data storage system in Australia which hosted the pictures. It placed this link on its own website (which received around 200,000 visits a day) in spite of receiving a request to the contrary from the right owner. Proceedings were raised before the courts in Holland where the Court of Appeal stayed proceedings and sought a preliminary ruling on a range of questions. The following points were key:

> 1.   (a)   If anyone other than the copyright holder refers by means of a hyperlink on a website controlled by him to a website which is managed by a third party and is accessible to the general internet public, on which the work has been made available without the consent of the rightholder, does that constitute a 'communication to the public' within the meaning of Article 3(1) of Directive 2001/29?
>
>   (b)   Does it make any difference if the work was also not previously communicated, with the rightholder's consent, to the public in some other way?
>
>   (c)   Is it important whether the 'hyperlinker' is or ought to be aware of the lack of consent by the rightholder for the placement of the work on the third party's website mentioned in 1(a) above and, as the case may be, of the fact that the work has also not previously been communicated, with the rightholder's consent, to the public in some other way?

In answering these, the court considered a range of previous rulings. An early authority was that of *Football Association Premier League Ltd and Others v QC Leisure and Others and Karen Murphy v Media Protection Services Ltd.*[57] This case attracted a good deal of publicity in the United Kingdom at the time. It focused on the actions of a public house owner who obtained (legitimately) a satellite decoder for a Greek television channel that (again legitimately) broadcast English Premier League football matches. This was used to show football matches in the pub and incurred significantly lower charges than would have been incurred through taking out a subscription with BSkyB who had purchased the rights to broadcast the matches in the United Kingdom.

There are a number of interesting aspects to the case. The right owners—the English Premier League had sought to disseminate rights globally taking account of the costs that specific markets might be willing to accept. The sums paid by the Greek broadcaster were lower, and undoubtedly rightly so, because its domestic market was smaller than in the United Kingdom and perhaps less intrinsically interested in English football. Such segmentation of the market has long been practised by right owners but yet again the Internet

---

[56] Case C160/15.   [57] Joined cases 403/08 and 429/08.

(and satellite technology) changes matters. There is also a demonstration of the law of unintended consequences and you might look at the decision of the Court of Appeal following the European Court's ruling.[58]

The Copyright in the Information Society Directive gives Member States a significant margin of appreciation as to how extensive the level of copyright protection should be. The UK government had indicated the intention to maintain the highest possible level of protection but, as the Court of Appeal held, it had made a significant mistake in implementing the Directive. As was stated:

> It is also clear that, at the time the 2003 Regulations were made and the CDPA was amended to give effect to them, the Government did not appreciate that 'the communication to the public of the work' in the amended section 20 included the 'showing or playing in public of a broadcast' within section 72(1). In the language of Mr Mellor's oral submissions, the Government did not understand that the act of receiving a broadcast and showing it on a television to a public audience that had not paid for admission fell within the restricted act of communication to the public.[59]

It appears that to err is human, but to really mess things up requires governmental involvement.

Returning to *GS Media*, the European Court ruled that the Copyright in the Information Society Directive:

> [I]t is undisputed that GS Media operates the GeenStijl website and that it provided the hyperlinks to the files containing the photos at issue, hosted on the Filefactory website, for profit. It is also undisputed that Sanoma had not authorised the publication of those photos on the internet. Moreover, it appears to follow from the presentation of the facts, as they result from the order for reference, that GS Media was aware of that latter fact and that it cannot therefore rebut the presumption that the posting of those links occurred in full knowledge of the illegal nature of that publication. In those circumstances, it appears that, subject to the checks to be made by the referring court, by posting those links, GS Media effected a 'communication to the public', within the meaning of Article 3(1) of Directive 2001/29, and it is unnecessary to assess in that context the other circumstances referred to by that court, referred to in paragraph 26 of the present judgment.

The Directive, it was held:

> must be interpreted as meaning that, in order to establish whether the fact of posting, on a website, hyperlinks to protected works, which are freely available on another website without the consent of the copyright holder, constitutes a 'communication to the public' within the meaning of that provision, it is to be determined whether those links are provided without the pursuit of financial gain by a person who did not know or could not reasonably have known the illegal nature of the publication of those works on that other website or whether, on the contrary, those links are provided for such a purpose, a situation in which that knowledge must be presumed.[60]

In some respects the decision raises questions rather than providing answers. There is a range of factors that have to be taken into account including the existence of a profit motive. As we will see in the e-commerce context, this is not always easy to determine. A website will often be provided free of charge to an end user but the provider will be looking to make a profit from advertising revenue.

---

[58] [2–12] EWCA Civ 1708.
[59] At para. 50.
[60] At paras. 54–5.

The legitimacy of private copying

Unlike many European legal systems, English law has historically been reluctant to confer legitimacy on the reproduction of copyright protected materials for private purposes. In the digital era, this issue has assumed considerable significance. Many users will own a plethora of devices capable of using copyright materials. A music file may be played on an in house music system, a car system, a laptop computer, and a smartphone. The list of devices could doubtless be extended. Although a user's perception may not always be legally accurate, there is undoubted strength in the argument that if an item has been lawfully acquired, it should be capable of being lawfully used in whatever manner the customer might think fit.

Acting in large part on the basis of the Hargreaves Report on the Intellectual Property System referred to in a previous issue of the journal, the decision was taken by the government to liberalise the law relating to private copying. The Copyright and Rights in Performance (Personal Copies for Private Use) Regulations 2014[61] were made on 26 August 2014 and came into force on 1 October 2014. The Regulations introduced a new section 28B to the Copyright, Designs and Patents Act 1988. This provides that:

(1) The making of a copy of a work, other than a computer program, by an individual does not infringe copyright in the work provided that the copy—

    (a)   is a copy of—

        (i)   the individual's own copy of the work, or

        (ii)   a personal copy of the work made by the individual,

    (b)   is made for the individual's private use, and

    (c)   is made for ends which are neither directly nor indirectly commercial.

Directive 2001/29 on the harmonisation of certain aspects of copyright and related rights in the information society[62] provides the legislative basis for the legitimacy of private copying. It provides, however, private copying may be legitimised only

    (b) in respect of reproductions on any medium made by a natural person for private use and for ends that are neither directly nor indirectly commercial, on condition that the rightholders receive fair compensation.[63]

Recital 35 to the Directive elaborates:

In certain cases of exceptions or limitations, rightholders should receive fair compensation to compensate them adequately for the use made of their protected works or other subject-matter. When determining the form, detailed arrangements and possible level of such fair compensation, account should be taken of the particular circumstances of each case. When evaluating these circumstances, a valuable criterion would be the possible harm to the rightholders resulting from the act in question. In cases where rightholders have already received payment in some other form, for instance as part of a licence fee, no specific or separate payment may be due. The level of fair compensation should take full account of the degree of use of technological protection measures referred to in this Directive. In certain situations where the prejudice to the rightholder would be minimal, no obligation for payment may arise.

The UK Regulations made no provision for compensation to right holders and this formed the basis of a challenge to their validity in the case of *R v Secretary of State for Business*.[64] Following the production of a regulatory impact assessment, based in large part on research

---

[61] SI 2014/2361.   [62] OJ 2001, L167/10.   [63] Art. 5.   [64] [2015] EWHC 1723 (Admin).

carried out by the Intellectual Property Office, the government took the view that allowing private copying without making any arrangements for compensation would cause minimal loss to right holders. A key rationale was the belief that given the existing scale of private copying, right holders had factored, or 'priced in', costs when determining the price at which copies would be sold. This formed the basis for what proved to be a successful legal challenge.

The court ruled that the government's rationale for introducing the Regulations was fundamentally flawed. The EU legislation under which it was introduced provided that a no-compensation regime would be lawful only if there was evidence to support the view that it would not result in more than minimal losses to right holders. As was stated:

> In the present case the legal issue is whether pricing-in will lead to 'minimal or zero' harm since if it does not then, in law, a compensation scheme *must* in law be introduced. The legal issue guides the exercise: The evidence accepted by the Secretary of State must be sufficient to enable a reasonable inference to be drawn from it that this *de minimis* threshold has been met.[65]

After analysing the evidence forming the basis for the Secretary of State's conclusion that the new provision would result in zero or minimal harm, the court concluded that this did not support the inference that he had made. It was noted that no attempt had been made to determine what quantitative or qualitative thresholds might apply in defining levels of loss that could be classed as *de minimis*. On this basis the conclusion was that the legal justification for the Regulations had not been established and they would accordingly be declared null and void.

In some respects the impact of the decision may be limited. It was accepted by all parties in the action that it is virtually impossible to prevent private copying of protected materials. Increasingly, the focus of actions by right holders is targeted more at relatively high profile intermediaries such as Internet Service Providers (ISPs) with the courts being asked to order them to take steps to prevent customers accessing sites associated with copyright infringement. It is possible also that the government may seek to repeat its evidence-gathering and assessment exercise to better equip it to make a reasoned determination whether the reintroduction of the measure would cause minimal economic harm to right holders, although at the moment this appears to be an unlikely prospect. The defects identified in the judgment are susceptible of being remedied. It is possible also that, following the model of some other Member States, a system of compensation might be provided to right holders. For the moment, however, the United Kingdom remains in the situation where there is a legal prohibition against private copying which is almost universally accepted to be unenforceable.

Fair and unfair use of an earlier work

Beyond those situations in which it may be apparent that a protected work has been copied, translated, or adapted, situations may arise in which it is clear that the work has been used in the course of producing another work, but where the conduct cannot equivocally be regarded as involving any of the acts prohibited in the legislation. In a variety of cases concerned with literary works, the courts have adopted a broad view as to the scope of copyright protection, extending it to conduct which is regarded as involving the inequitable exploitation of the work of another—what might in everyday language be referred to as 'plagiarism'.

In the case of *Harman Pictures NV v Osborne*,[66] the plaintiff owned the screen rights in respect of a book dealing with the Charge of the Light Brigade. Negotiations had taken place

---

[65] At para. 237.   [66] [1967] 2 All ER 324.

with a view to the defendants acquiring the rights. The negotiations came to nothing, but some time later, the defendants indicated their intention to produce a film on the same theme. The screenplay for the film was written by the first defendant. The plaintiff sought an injunction to prevent the film's distribution, alleging that the screenplay infringed its copyright.

Comparison of the screenplay with the book revealed points both of similarity and dissimilarity. The defendant did not deny having knowledge of the plaintiff's work, but argued that their screenplay had been based upon a much wider variety of sources.

> Whilst accepting that it was permissible for a later author to make use of an existing work, it was held that this could not be utilised as a substitute for the expenditure of independent effort. As was stated by Sir William Page Wood V-C in the case of *Jarrold v Houlston*:[67] I take the illegitimate use, as opposed to the legitimate use, of another person's work on subject matters of this description to be this: If, knowing that a person whose work is protected by copyright has, with considerable labour, compiled from various sources a work in itself not original, but which he has digested and arranged, instead of taking the pains of searching into all the common sources and obtaining your subject matter from them, you avail yourself of the labour of your predecessor, adopt his arrangements, adopt moreover the very questions he has asked or adopt them with but a slight degree of colourable variation, and thus save yourself pains and labour by availing yourself of the pains and labour which he has employed, that I take to be an illegitimate use.

In the present case, the issue was whether the defendant had worked independently to:

> produce a script which from the nature of things has much in common with the book, or did he proceed the other way round and use the book as a basis, taking his selection of incidents and quotations therefrom, albeit omitting a number and making some alterations and additions by reference to the common sources and by some reference to other sources?[68]

Considering these matters, Goff J determined that the similarities between the two works were sufficient to justify the grant of an interlocutory injunction, with terms preventing the defendants from 'exhibiting, releasing or distributing any film of or based on [the screenplay]'.[69]

The question of the use which can be made of an earlier work was again at issue in the case of *Elanco Products Ltd v Mandops Agricultural Specialists Ltd*.[70] Elanco had invented and secured patent protection for an herbicidal product. During the currency of the patent's validity, both the plaintiff and independent research institutions had made extensive studies of the herbicide's application. Some of the information derived from these studies was incorporated in the form of instructions which were supplied with the product.

Upon the expiry of the patent, the defendant commenced production and marketing of the herbicide. Initially, they produced an accompanying instructional leaflet that was a virtual copy of the plaintiff's. The plaintiff objected to this action, alleging that it infringed copyright in its compilation of instructions, and the leaflet was withdrawn. A revised version was produced which also brought objections. When a third version was still considered objectionable, the plaintiff sought an injunction. Although the final version of the defendant's leaflet used terminology different from that of the plaintiff's, it was alleged that it remained based upon their material, thereby constituting an infringement of their copyright.

Holding in favour of the plaintiff, Goff LJ agreed that there was an arguable case of copyright infringement:

> It may well be that if the respondents had in fact at the start simply looked at the available information . . . and from that decided what they would put in their literature and how they

---

[67] (1857) 3 K&J 708 at 716–17.
[68] *Harman Pictures NV v Osborne* [1967] 2 All ER 324 at 334.   [69] At 337.
[70] [1980] RPC 213.

would express it, the appellants would at least have had considerable difficulty in bringing home any charge of infringement, even, having regard to the evidence, if the results had been extremely similar and the selection of items had been the same. But they chose, on the evidence as it stands at the moment, to proceed by making a simple . . . copy, and then they proceeded to revise it. It may well be that the result produced that way is an infringement.[71]

Concurring, Buckley LJ ruled:

As I understand the law in this case, the defendants were fully entitled to make use of any information, of a technical or any other kind which was in the public domain, for the purpose of compiling their label and their trade literature, but they were not entitled to copy the plaintiffs' label or trade literature thereby making use of the plaintiffs' skill and judgement and saving themselves the trouble, and very possibly the cost, of assembling their own information, either from their own researches or from sources available in documents in the public domain, and thereby making their own selection of information to put into that literature and producing their own label and trade literature.[72]

In one significant respect, the decision in *Elanco*[73] must be approached with a measure of caution. The fact that the defendant had originally produced a near total copy of the plaintiff's work must have cast a shadow over its subsequent conduct. One aspect of the case would, however, appear apposite in a software context. As is the case with much software, the literary works were functional in nature. Unlike the situation where works are created with a view to the reader's entertainment, their purpose was to provide instruction. In the situation where a user has become familiar with the instructions issued by one producer, the use of semantic variations may result in unnecessary confusion. Whereas diversity of expression may be a valuable attribute in literature, its virtues are less obvious in a more technical arena.[74]

Other rights belonging to the copyright owner

As it was introduced, copyright protected only against literal copying of a work. As it has evolved, more extensive rights have been conferred on the right holder and a number of these are relevant in the IT context.

Communication to the public

One of the key elements of copyright is the exclusive right to communicate the work to the public. This can encompass a range of issues and has, in the Internet context, been the subject of a significant amount of litigation before the European Court, essentially concerned with the legality of hypertext linking. The key issue is whether the use of such a link interferes with the right holder's control over the range of dissemination of the work.

In many instances, of course, a right holder will be keen to encourage linkage. Matters are not always so straightforward. One of the major cases is *Nils Svensson, Sten Sjögren,*

---

[71] At 228.   [72] At 231.

[73] *Elanco Products Ltd v Mandops Agricultural Specialists Ltd* [1980] RPC 213.

[74] Some recognition of the different status of product instructions can be seen in the case of *Wormell v RHM Agriculture (East) Ltd* [1987] 3 All ER 75. Once again, a pesticide product was at issue, with the purchaser alleging that its failure to eradicate weeds rendered it unmerchantable in terms of s. 14 of the Sale of Goods Act 1979. Although this action failed, the court accepted that the adequacy or otherwise of instructions constituted a relevant factor in determining questions of merchantability. This approach may be contrasted with the general refusal of the courts to consider claims that the quality of a written work is unacceptably low quality.

Madelaine Sahlman, Pia Gadd v Retriever Sverige AB.[75] In some respects this is a classic exposition of the issues. As noted earlier, in this case, a company published a website with news stories and another website provided its customers with links to these. Was this lawful? The original site was open to any member of the public who wished to use it. The European Court was quite clear.

> Article 3(1) of Directive 2001/29/EC of the European Parliament and of the Council of 22 May 2001 on the harmonisation of certain aspects of copyright and related rights in the information society, must be interpreted as meaning that the provision on a website of clickable links to works freely available on another website does not constitute an 'act of communication to the public', . . .

It also ruled that this would be the case even if the nature of linking was such as to give the impression that material was coming from the originating website.

Matters can become more complex in situations where the right owner either does not wish others to access the material or wishes to impose conditions.

To perform, show, or play the work in public

The acts of performing or showing the protected work in public are reserved to the copyright owner. The issue of what is a public performance is not defined in the legislation. It would seem clear, however, that the operation of a computer game program within, for example, a public house or an amusement arcade would constitute an infringing act if committed without the consent of the copyright owner.

To broadcast the work or include it in a cable programme service

Although this may appear unlikely to be of great application in a software context, the case of *Shetland Times v Willis*[76] provides some authority for the proposition that a website is to be classed as a cable programme service, with individual pages being classed as cable programmes. The Act defines a cable programme service as:

> a service which consists wholly or mainly in sending visual images, sounds or other information by means of a telecommunications system, otherwise than by wireless telegraphy, for reception—
>
> (a) at two or more places (whether for simultaneous reception or at different times in response to requests by different users), or
>
> (b) for presentation to members of the public[77]

with any item included in such a service being classed as a cable programme. The case concerned two websites, the *Shetland Times*, which was the electronic form of an established newspaper, and the *Shetland News*, which existed only in electronic form. The *Shetland News* website copied headlines from the *Shetland Times* site (something which in itself was held to be a breach of copyright) and placed hypertext links allowing users to go to the appropriate section of the *Shetland Times* website. The case did not proceed to the stage of a full hearing, the judge accepting that there was a prima facie case that the *Shetland News* was in breach of the *Shetland Times'* rights in this regard.

---

[75] Case 466/12.

[76] (1997) SC 316.

[77] Copyright, Designs and Patents Act 1988, s. 7. The Copyright and Related Rights Regulations 2003, SI 2003/2498 repealed the specific definition of a cable programme service and subsumed its scope into the general definition of broadcasting.

To make an adaptation of the work

In respect of computer programs, it is provided that adaptation 'means an arrangement or altered version of the program or a translation of it'.[78] Producing, for example, a version of a program originally designed to run under Microsoft Windows to operate on Apple computers will, in the absence of authorisation from the copyright owner, constitute unlawful adaptation.

The development of software copyright

Questions about the eligibility of computer programs for copyright protection began to emerge in the 1960s. Prior to this time, hardware and software tended to be supplied by the same party and generally equipment was rented by the customer (often with the manufacturer supplying staff to maintain the machine), rather than bought. In such an environment, there was little interest in issues of ownership of intellectual property rights. In 1969, prompted by anti-trust investigations by the US competition authorities, IBM, then the dominant player in the computer market, announced that it was to separate its hardware and software operations. This has been seen as a pivotal move in the development of a distinct software industry and today there is little doubt that companies such as Microsoft and Google are more significant players than hardware producers. Indeed, IBM itself has sold off most of its hardware production businesses and is focusing on consulting and re-engineering services.

Once a distinct market began to develop in software, issues of legal protection were not far behind. One of the striking features of software is that it can be massively expensive to develop but can be reproduced quickly and at very low cost. Although there were debates in the 1970s and 1980s as to whether computer programs were a proper subject for protection under the copyright system, the fact that the underlying source code was written in a form of English meant that there was—at least from the perspective of the UK system, which imposes almost no qualitative requirements for the grant of copyright—little dispute that software should be protected as a form of literary work. The Copyright, Designs and Patents Act 1988, the EC Directive on the Legal Protection of Computer Programs,[79] the Berne and World Intellectual Property Organization (WIPO) Copyright Conventions, and the World Trade Organization's Agreement on Trade Related Aspects of Intellectual Property Rights (TRIPS) now all provide that computer programs are to be protected on this basis.

As enacted, the Copyright, Designs and Patents Act 1988 provided simply that the term 'literary work':

> means any work, other than a dramatic or musical work, which is written, spoken or sung, and accordingly includes—
>
> (a) a table or compilation; and
>
> (b) a computer program.[80]

In common with many other aspects of the subject, the term 'computer program' is not defined in the legislation. This may have been a matter of limited importance in 1988, but is becoming more significant in our digital age. A computer program may be developed which will itself cause images to be displayed on screen. Many computer games will fall into this category and the technique is increasingly used to create or enhance images in feature

---

[78] Copyright, Designs and Patents Act 1988, s. 21(4).   [79] Directive 91/250/EC.   [80] s. 3(1).

films. Star Wars films rely very heavily on computer generated images, whilst the film *Toy Story 2* is reported to be the first production that exists entirely in digital format. No actors were involved, with all the images being produced within a computer environment. Copies of the film are recorded on computer storage media and projected directly from this. As will be discussed in more detail later, in such instances, it is difficult to tell where the computer program ends and the film begins.

In the course of producing a computer program, a good deal of other material may be developed. The process may begin with a general formulation of the intended purpose of the program. Subsequently, a detailed specification may be written down, describing all the functions and manner of operation to be provided in the completed work. This may take the form of a flow chart depicting the structure and sequence of the operations to be carried out. Drawings may also be made depicting various aspects of the screen displays to be produced.

It is almost certain that such preparatory works would have been protected under the original formulation of the Copyright, Designs and Patents Act 1988. As will be discussed at various stages later, the United Kingdom requires a very low degree of originality or literary merit in order to award copyright protection, and there is little doubt that even a few scribbles on a piece of paper would be protected. The situation was less clear in other EU Member States, and the Directive on the Legal Protection of Computer Programs made special provision for the protection of such materials.[81] In implementing the measure, the Copyright (Computer Programs) Regulations 1992[82] added a new section 3(1)(c) to the 1988 Act, referring to:

> (c) preparatory design material for a computer program.

In some respects, the amendment may create more problems than it solves. Where the preparatory work is in the form of lines of code and written descriptions of the intended functions, there will be no problem in offering protection on this basis. The preparatory material may also take the form of flow charts or drawings of possible screen displays. In the Copyright, Designs and Patents Act 1988, the term 'artistic work' is defined as including 'any painting, drawing, map, chart or plan'.[83] Whilst it may be that artistic copyright will continue to exist in these elements, the rationale for protecting plans and drawings as something which they clearly are not appears somewhat obscure.

Applying copyright principles to software

In discussing the extent to which activities relating to software might contravene copyright law, three categories of potential infringement can be considered. The first two relate to what is called literal copying of software. In the first instance, this involves the making of a direct copy of software. This may be done for commercial gain, and will be discussed under the heading of software piracy. Also involving direct reproduction is the act of using software. Every time a program is used, a copy of its contents is required to be taken from its storage location on the computer to the machine's active processing memory. This creates problems for the relationship between copyright owner and user, and has led in part to the emergence of software licences. These documents, which are an almost inevitable companion to mass-produced software packages, typically confer use rights, but at the expense of seeking to oblige the user to accept other provisions limiting or excluding liabilities in the event that the software fails to operate in a satisfactory manner and thereby causes some form of injury or damage to the user. Although the Copyright, Designs and Patents Act

---

[81] Directive 91/250/EC, Art. 1(1).   [82] SI 1992/3233.   [83] s. 4(2).

1988 as enacted was silent on all questions concerned with users' rights other than the somewhat nebulous concept of fair dealing, implementation of the EC Directive on the Legal Protection of Computer Programs[84] has brought about significant changes. Although the extent of some of the rights remains unclear, lawful users of software acquire a number of entitlements, ranging from a right to use software to the ability to reverse engineer and decompile, albeit in limited circumstances.

The third category of infringement raises the most interesting legal issues. It concerns the situation whereby two programs exhibit similarities at the level of screen displays but not at the level of code. Although the phrase has rather fallen out of legal favour, the argument might be put in terms that one program has copied the 'look and feel' of another. This topic might also be considered at two levels. In the first—and more common—case, the alleged infringer will have had some access to the original program's code. Typically, a programmer will have worked on the development of one package, moved to another employer and been involved with the development of a competing program. In the second category, the parties will act much more at arm's length, with the only access obtained by the alleged infringer being to the working copy of the program.

Software piracy

The term 'software piracy' encompasses a range of forms of conduct. The Business Software Alliance (BSA), an organisation which includes most of the major Western software producers amongst its membership, has identified a range of forms of conduct:

- *multiple installation*

  This is where you install more copies of a software program than you have licences. For example, if you buy ten single-user licences for a product yet install it onto twenty machines, you are using ten illegal copies.

- *end-user piracy*

  Similar to multiple installation, this involves an end user (or company employee) copying programs illegally or using unlicensed software in the workplace.

- *client/server piracy*

  This occurs when a program is run off a server (rather than from individual PCs) and is accessed by more end users than the company has bought licences for.

- *online piracy*

  This happens when software is downloaded from the web and installed but not paid for. There are other types of software piracy (grey software, counterfeit software, etc.).[85]

Essentially, any conduct which can be considered an infringement of copyright will come within these definitions. As the term 'piracy' would suggest, there is little doubt that the conduct at issue is unlawful. A considerable number of studies have sought to assess the scale of the problem. Most have been conducted by or on behalf of organisations such as the BSA. The fourteenth piracy study conducted by the BSA and IDA was published in May 2010[86] and gives statistics up to 2009.

The study indicated that the global piracy rate in 2009 was around 43 per cent indicating a reversal of a trend found in previous studies showing a reduction in the level of privacy. This, it is suggested, is due to a sharp increase in the number of personal computers

---

[84] Directive 91/250/EC.   [85] <http://www.bsa.org/uk/types>.
[86] <http://www.bsa.org/idcstudy.aspx>.

in regions associated with a high level of piracy. The 'distinction' of topping the piracy charts falls to Zimbabwe, with a 92 per cent rate. Other significant offenders are China and Nigeria, with 77 and 82 per cent rates. At the other end of the spectrum, the United States posts a rate of 19 per cent, the United Kingdom stands only slightly higher at 26 per cent, with Western Europe generally averaging at 32 per cent.

In economic terms, the total loss is estimated at $39.5 billion. Given the scale of software use within North America and Europe, it is not surprising that the regions with the highest financial losses were North America and Western Europe, although a worrying trend identified is that the biggest increases in software use is now coming from areas which have much higher piracy. A further estimate of the impact of piracy can be taken from a further study produced for the BSA by Price Waterhouse in 1998.[87] This calculated that:

> Reducing software piracy rates by realistic levels from the 1996 Western European average of 43 per cent for PC business software to the corresponding U.S. average of 27 per cent, and equivalent reductions in other software categories would generate as many as 258,651 more job and $13.9bn additional tax revenues by the year 2001, in addition to forecast market growth.

User rights in respect of software

Whilst the application of provisions of copyright law to software-based products is less contentious than is the case with the application of the patent system, the principles of the copyright system were designed for application in the literary and artistic fields. Information technology products operate in the practical arena, and it may be argued that fundamental concepts such as reproduction or adaptation require to be applied in a modified form in such circumstances. Two particular difficulties can be identified.

The essence of copyright is that it prohibits the copying of a work without the consent of the copyright owner. In the case of most works, this does not impinge upon a third party's normal use of the work. The purchaser of a book can read it without requiring to make any form of copy. Likewise, a television broadcast can be watched and an audio cassette listened to without the need for any form of copying. Software (and indeed other digital products, such as CDs) operates in a different manner. Any form of use requires that the contents of the work be copied from a storage location to be processed within the equipment. Normal use requires copying, a fact which creates complications, not just in the field of copyright but also—through the widespread use of software licences—in the area of liability. A further complication relates from the fact that today we tend to own multiple (and mobile) computing devices whilst many software licences remain based on the notion that permission is given for use on a single device. Nobody would suggest that a person who purchases a copy of this book to read at home would need to purchase a further copy to read on a train and another to read at work.

Fair dealing

Much is written and spoken about concerning the right of a user to copy a work to such an extent as is justified under the heading of 'fair dealing' for the purposes of research or private study.[88] Few of these expressions receive any form of definition in the legislation. The concept of fair dealing will undoubtedly permit a degree of copying of a protected work,

---

[87] Available from <http://globalstudy.bsa.org/2011/downloads/study_pdf/2011_BSA_Piracy_Study-Standard.pdf>.

[88] Copyright, Designs and Patents Act 1988, s. 29.

but the supplementary question 'how much?' cannot definitively be answered. At one time, the UK publishing industry suggested that the copying of up to 10 per cent of a book might be regarded as fair dealing. This was, however, an informal indication which was subsequently withdrawn. It would not appear that the extent of copying permitted under this heading has been at issue in any case.

Whilst the concept of private study is not one which will be of great practical significance in the software field, that of research is potentially much more so. It is to be noted that the word 'research' precedes the phrase 'private study' in the Copyright, Designs and Patents Act 1988. It would appear to follow, therefore, that its application is not restricted to the area of individual research, but will extend into the commercial sphere.

In the case of a traditional literary work, such as a book or article, the acts which encompass fair dealing can readily be identified. Clearly, researchers must be able to read the work and to quote small portions of it in any work which they themselves might compile. In the course of this task, they may copy portions of the work, perhaps by means of a photocopier, although infringement may occur equally well if the work is copied by hand. It must be accepted that the concept of fair dealing in a literary work cannot extend to the making of a copy of the complete work. Different considerations may apply in respect of software.

Two arguments can be put forward in support of such a proposition. First, whilst it is a very simple task to copy portions of a book—indeed it is much easier to copy a part than the whole—the reverse is the case with respect to a computer program. A second argument operates at a utilitarian level. The user of a book would generally be considered as having no legitimate need to take a second copy of the work in case the original suffers damage. This view would be justified on the basis that although the cosmetic appearance of a book may easily be harmed, for example through the spillage of a cup of coffee, the damage will seldom be such as to prevent its continued use. Software is a much more fragile creation and, terminal damage may easily result. In such an event, the making of a back-up copy might appear a reasonable precaution.

In concluding the examination of the fair dealing exception, the point must be stressed that any of the actions referred to above will be sanctioned only to the extent that they are carried out in connection with research. It is specifically provided that decompilation of a program will not be permitted under the fair use provisions.[89] Assuming that a copy of software may legitimately be made for research purposes, its status will change in the event that the research ends and the copy is put to operational use.

A use right for software?

Reference has previously been made to the fact that copying or adapting a protected work constitutes an infringement of copyright. This raises one significant issue in relation to software. Whenever a computer program is operated, the process requires that its contents be copied from the storage disk upon which it normally resides into the hardware's memory. The act of using software in its normal manner is capable, therefore, of constituting a breach of copyright.

Prior to 1992, this was arguably the case, although it is submitted that a persuasive case could have been made out for implying at least a basic use right. Substantial precedent exists for such judicial creativity under patent law, where it has been held that the purchaser of a patented product may exercise all the normal rights of an owner, including the right to resell, unless specific notice has been given of restrictions.[90] With most software products,

---

[89] Copyright, Designs and Patents Act 1988, s. 29(4).
[90] See, eg, *National Phonograph Co of Australia v Menck* (1911) 28 RPC 229.

the response of producers to the uncertain state of the law was to seek to incorporate the terms of a licence into the contract with the end-user. The status of software licences will be considered in more detail in the context of liability issues. Essentially, the licence would grant permission for the use of software in specified circumstances, but would frequently couple this with clauses limiting or excluding liability in the event the performance of the software was defective. In 1992, the provisions of the Copyright Designs and Patents Act 1988 were amended in order to implement the provisions of the EC Directive on the Legal Protection of Computer Programs.[91] The Copyright (Computer Programs) Regulations 1992[92] add a new section 50C to the 1988 Act, providing that:

> It is not an infringement of copyright for a lawful user of a copy of a computer program to copy or adapt it, providing that the copying or adapting—
>
> (a) is necessary for his lawful use; and
>
> (b) is not prohibited under any term or condition of an agreement regarding the circumstances under which his use is lawful.

In the European Commission's explanatory memorandum to the 1989 proposal for the Directive, it was argued that it was not clear:

> whether the practice of so-called, 'shrink wrap licensing' where use conditions are attached to a product which is, to all intents and purposes 'sold' to the user, constitutes a valid licence in all circumstances and in all jurisdictions.
>
> It is therefore proposed that . . . [w]here 'sale', in the normal sense of the word occurs, certain rights to use the program must be taken to pass to the purchaser along with the physical copy of the program.[93]

whilst the Preamble to the Directive on the Legal Protection of Computer Programs[94] states that:

> Whereas the exclusive rights of the author to prevent the unauthorized reproduction of the work have to be subject to a limited exception in the case of a computer program to allow the reproduction technically necessary for the use of the program by the lawful acquirer.
>
> Whereas this means that the acts of loading and running necessary for the use of a copy of a program which has been lawfully acquired . . . may not be prohibited by contract.

It may be queried how far the text of the Directive implements this. Article 4 makes it clear that the copyright owner retains the right to authorise:

> [the] permanent or temporary reproduction of a computer program by any means and in any form, in part or in whole. Insofar as loading, displaying, running, transmission or storage of the computer program necessitates such reproduction, such acts shall be subject to authorization by the rightholder.

Article 5 provides for an exception to this provision, stating that:

> In the absence of specific contractual provisions, the acts referred to in Article 4 . . . shall not require authorization by the rightholder where they are necessary for the use of the computer program by the lawful acquirer in accordance with its intended purpose.

In implementing the Directive on the Legal Protection of Computer Programs,[95] the UK government substituted the term 'lawful user'[96] for the original 'lawful acquirer'. Another

---

[91] Directive 91/250/EC.   [92] SI 1992/3233.

[93] COM (88) 816 final—SYN 183, paras. 3.4–3.5.

[94] Directive 91/250/EC.   [95] Directive 91/250/EC.

[96] Copyright, Designs and Patents Act 1988, s. 50A.

change was to substitute reference to 'lawful use'[97] for the Directive's 'intended use'. These changes undoubtedly complicate matters. The concept of 'lawful use', in particular, is defined as applying where a person has '(whether under a licence to do any act restricted by the copyright in the program or otherwise) . . . a right to use the program'.[98] This formulation relates to the status of the user as much as to the nature of the application, thereby producing a somewhat circular effect. Although there seems no doubt that the Directive sought to confer a use right, it is less clear whether the United Kingdom implementing legislation secures this and it is possible that the issue may some day have to be resolved before the courts.

Although a basic use right will now be implied, difficulties may arise in a number of areas. Increasingly, computers are being networked. The communications facilities provided by such a development means that one copy of a program may be used by a considerable number of different people. Depending upon the nature of the program and the network, use may be either simultaneous or successive. A further difficulty arises in the situation where a household accessed multiple computing devices. In this case, the user may well wish to use the same software (perhaps a word-processing program) on both computers. In these situations, the need and justification for licences will continue.

Error correction

It is received wisdom that every computer program contains errors or 'bugs'. In accordance with the requirements of the EC Directive on the Legal Protection of Computer Programs,[99] it is provided that an authorised user may copy or adapt a program 'for the purpose of correcting errors in it'.[100] This provision might appear to give a user carte blanche to copy a program in the quest to discover errors. An alternative, and perhaps preferable, view is that the right will extend only in respect of particular errors which have been discovered by the user in the course of running the program in a normal manner.

Even on this basis, uncertainties remain as to the extent of the user's rights. Computer programs are not like other literary works. A typing or grammatical error occurring in a book may be corrected without the act having any impact upon the remainder of the work. The relationship between the various elements of a computer program is much more complex. If an error is discovered in the course of running a program, its cause may lie almost anywhere in the program. If the source of a particular error is detected and a correction made, it cannot be certain that the effects of the change will not manifest themselves in an unexpected and undesirable fashion elsewhere in the program. There is, indeed, a school of thought in software engineering that suggests that when errors are detected, rather than amending the program, operating procedures should be changed to avoid the conditions which it is known cause the specific error to occur.

Back-up copies

Computer programs are frequently supplied, and invariably held, on some storage device, such as a disk or tape. Such storage media are notoriously fragile and it is all too possible that their contents might be accidentally corrupted or erased. In such circumstances, it might not appear unreasonable for a user to seek to take a second, or back-up, copy of the work, with the intention that this will be stored in a safe location and brought into use in the event that the original copy of the software is destroyed.

---

[97] s. 50A. [98] s. 50A(2). [99] Directive 91/250/EC.
[100] Copyright, Designs and Patents Act 1988, s. 50C(2).

As enacted, the UK Copyright, Designs and Patents Act 1988 (in contrast to several other copyright statutes) made no mention of the possibility that a user might make a back-up copy of a program which had been lawfully acquired. Although, once again, it is possible to argue that such a term must be implied into any relevant contract, the argument is more tenuous than that relating to the implication of a basic use right.

Implementation of the provisions of the Directive on the Legal Protection of Computer Programs[101] has brought about a measure of reform with the Copyright, Designs and Patents Act 1988 providing that a back-up copy may be made by a user where this is 'necessary . . . for the purposes of his lawful use'.[102] It is unclear how useful this provision might be. The making of a back-up copy will invariably be a wise precaution, but it is difficult to envisage any situation where the presence of a second copy is 'necessary' for the functioning of the original.

Some small measure of consolation may be offered to a user by the fact that the copyright owner may not validly restrict or exclude the operation of the provisions regarding the making of back-up copies.[103] It is doubted, however, whether the new provisions will alter significantly either the law or the practice in this area.

Caching

Perhaps the most controversial section of the Directive is contained in Article 5, which provides an exception from the prohibitions against reproduction where data is stored, or cached, on a temporary basis as part of normal Internet activities. The essence of caching is that an ISP, faced with what are likely to be numerous requests for access to a particular web page, will maintain a copy on its own machines rather than having to send each request off in search of the original page. Caching raises a number of technical and logistical issues. Popular websites such as the BBC news pages, will be updated on a minute-by-minute basis and there may be issues of how current a cached copy might be. Apart from these issues, the main legal problem relates to the fact that copyright law prohibits reproduction of material without the consent of the right owner. The Directive permits:

> 1. Temporary acts of reproduction . . . which are transient or incidental [and] an integral and essential part of a technological process and whose sole purpose is to enable:
>
>   (a) a transmission in a network between third parties by an intermediary, or
>
>   (b) a lawful use of a work or other subject-matter to be made, and which have no independent economic significance, shall be exempted from the reproduction right provided for in Article 2.

Recital 33 indicates the intent behind this provision:

> The exclusive right of reproduction should be subject to an exception to allow certain acts of temporary reproduction, which are transient or incidental reproductions, forming an integral and essential part of a technological process and carried out for the sole purpose of enabling either efficient transmission in a network between third parties by an intermediary, or a lawful use of a work or other subject-matter to be made.

A range of situations might be envisaged in which this provision will be applicable. The act of viewing information on a web page will involve the making of a temporary copy of that

---

[101] Directive 91/250/EC.

[102] Copyright, Designs and Patents Act 1988, s. 50A(1).

[103] Copyright, Designs and Patents Act 1988, s. 296A(1)(b).

data on the user's own equipment. The nature of the Internet, again, will mean that transient copies of email messages will be made at various stages of the message's journey from sender to recipient. Such copying clearly falls within the criteria of 'integral' and 'essential' used in Article 5 and poses no legal difficulty. The practice of caching, which is specifically referred to in the Recital, raises more difficult issues, and the inclusion of the phrase 'an integral and essential part' might be seen as robbing the provision of much of its meaning. The problem that may be faced under the Directive's provisions is that although the use of caching may be advantageous, it cannot be considered essential. The Internet could function without it although access speeds might be somewhat slower.

Copy protection and digital rights management

The use of copy-protection devices was a feature of many early software products. A wide range of techniques were utilised in the attempt to ensure that only an authorised user could make use of software. In some cases, anti-copying techniques would have been embedded in the software itself, in other cases physical devices were used. The absence of a uniform approach between producers meant that there was almost invariably a non-protected version of software available on the market and, given that the use of such devices normally made software more difficult to use, market forces compelled most producers to abandon such tactics.

Following a period when protection devices almost disappeared from the market, with devices such as digital video disks (DVDs) there are signs that the technique is returning to favour, although again there are questions as to how effective these might be. Here, manufacturers of disks embed a code corresponding to the region of the world in which the disk is marketed. DVD players are also coded in a similar manner, so the effect is intended to be that only disks marketed in one region can be played on equipment marketed in that area. A variety of techniques can be used to overcome this form of protection and the Directive sets out to provide legal sanctions against such acts. Article 6 provides that right holders be provided with legal remedies against those seeking to avoid or 'circumvent' 'effective' technical protection measures which utilise 'an access control or protection process, such as encryption, scrambling or other transformation of the work or other subject-matter or a copy control mechanism'.

Section 296 of the Copyright, Designs and Patents Act 1988 already provided a copyright holder who publishes work in a copy-protected electronic format with a right of action against a person who:

(a) makes, imports, sells or lets for hire, offers or exposes for sale or hire, or advertises for sale or hire, any device or means specifically designed or adapted to circumvent the form of copy-protection employed, or

(b) publishes information intended to enable or assist persons to circumvent that form of copy-protection

This provision with its limitation to devices 'specifically designed or adapted' is rather more restrictive than the Directive's provisions, which refer to an article's primary purpose.[104] Accordingly, whilst retaining the original formula in respect of computer programs (which are outside the scope of the Directive) the Regulations introduce a number of somewhat complex provisions—new sections 296ZA (circumvention of technological measures),

---

[104] Albeit, in a slightly different context, see the discussion of *CBS Songs Ltd v Amstrad Consumer Electronics plc* later, where the fact that a twin cassette deck had some legitimate uses provided a defence to a claim of copyright infringement, even though it might be argued that most purchasers would use the equipment for unlawful purposes.

296ZD (rights and remedies in respect of devices and services designed to circumvent technological measures), and 296ZE (remedy where effective technological measures prevent permitted acts).[105]

With traditional forms of literary work, it is customary to embed copyright details into the printed text. Where work is distributed in electronic format, the use of rights-management information would see details identifying copyright owners being embedded in the work, and a facility included to record the use made of the work. This would facilitate the tasks of establishing copyright and the extent of any infringing use of the work. As the Directive's Recitals indicate:

> (55) Technological development will facilitate the distribution of works, notably on networks, and this will entail the need for rightholders to identify better the work or other subject-matter, the author or any other rightholder.

We will return to this issue in more detail later. The Directive provides in Article 7 that:

> Member States shall provide for adequate legal protection against any person performing without authority any of the following acts:
>
> (a) the removal or alteration of any electronic rights-management information; or
>
> (b) the distribution, importation for distribution, broadcasting, communication or making available to the public, of copies of works or other subject matter protected under this Directive[106] or under [the Database Directive][107] from which electronic rights-management information has been removed or altered without authority, if such person knows, or has reasonable grounds to know, that by so doing he is inducing, enabling or facilitating an infringement of any copyright or any rights related to copyright as provided by law, or of the *sui generis* right provided for in [the Database Directive].

In order to implement this provision, the regulations add a further new section (296ZG) to the Copyright, Designs and Patents Act 1988. This provides that an offence will be committed by:

> a person (D) who knowingly and without authority, removes or alters electronic rights management information which—
>
> (a) is associated with a copy of a copyright work, or
>
> (b) appears in connection with the communication to the public of a copyright work, and
>
> (c) where D knows, or has reason to believe, that by so doing he is inducing, enabling, facilitating or concealing an infringement of copyright.[108]

Offences will also be committed by parties concerned with the importation, distribution, or communication to the public of copies from which electronic rights information has been removed.

Reverse engineering and decompilation

When software is supplied to a customer, it will be in a form known as object or machine-readable code. If this were to be viewed by a user, it would appear as a series (a very long

---

[105] SI 2003/2498, Reg. 24.   [106] Directive on Copyright in the Information Society, Directive 2001/29/EC.
[107] Directive on the Legal Protection of Databases, Directive 96/9/EC, OJ 1996 L 77/20 (the Databases Directive).   [108] SI 2003/2498, Reg. 25.

series) of zeros and ones. Obtaining sight of these digits will give little indication as to the manner in which the program is structured. Although it is possible for a program to be written in object code, much more programmer-friendly techniques are available and almost universally utilised. A number of what are referred to as 'high level' languages exist—examples are BASIC and FORTRAN. These allow programmers to write their instructions in a language which more closely resembles English, although the functional nature of computer programs limits the variations in expression which are a hallmark of more traditional literary works.

Most users, of course, will be concerned only with what a program does rather than the manner in which this is accomplished. Some, however, may have different motives. The practice of reverse engineering has a lengthy history in more traditional industries and, typically, involves the purchase and dismantling of the products of a competitor. In the computer context, reverse engineering may involve the study of the operation of a computer program in order to discover its specifications. This is essentially a process of testing and observation and might involve pressing various keys or combinations of keys in order to discover their effects. The technique known as decompilation may be used as part of this process. Normally involving the use of other computer programs to analyse the object code, the technique seeks to reproduce the original source code.

The two leading English authorities on the topic of reverse engineering point are *LB (Plastics) Ltd v Swish Products Ltd*[109] and *British Leyland Motor Corpn v Armstrong Patents Co Ltd*.[110] Although in the *LB Plastics* case, the alleged infringers had obtained a degree of access to the product drawings, in neither case was it argued that these had been reproduced directly. Instead, the case was based on the contention that by reproducing the finished object, respectively furniture drawers and a vehicle exhaust system, the provisions of section 48(1) of the Copyright Act 1956 had been breached. This provided inter alia: 'that copyright in a two-dimensional work, the product drawings, will be infringed by converting these into a three-dimensional form'.[111]

In *LB (Plastics)*,[112] the plaintiff designed and produced a drawer system. The key feature was that the drawers could be supplied to customers (generally, furniture manufacturers) in what was referred to as 'knock-down' form. This offered considerable benefits at the transportation and storage stages, whilst the design facilitated swift and easy assembly of the drawers by the final producer. The concept proved commercially successful and some time later, the defendant introduced a similar range of products. It was alleged that this was achieved by copying one of the plaintiff's drawers.

In the High Court, Whitford J accepted that the resulting product infringed the plaintiff's copyright in two of the original product drawings. Although this ruling was reversed by the Court of Appeal, which held that an insufficient causal link existed between the drawings in question and the defendant's product, it was reinstated by the House of Lords.[113] A significant factor underpinning the judgment would appear to have been the recognition that although the defendant was required by commercial dictates to ensure that their drawers were functionally compatible with those produced by the plaintiff, this could have been attained in ways which required less in the way of replication of the original design.

The decision in *LB Plastics* was approved in the subsequent case of *British Leyland Motor Corpn v Armstrong Patents*.[114] Here, the plaintiff manufactured motor vehicles. The multitude of parts which make up each vehicle were produced in accordance with detailed designs drawn up by the plaintiffs. The defendant specialised in the manufacture of spare parts, in the particular case an exhaust system, which would be offered for

---

[109] [1979] RPC 551.   [110] [1986] RPC 279.
[111] Copyright Act 1956, s. 48(1).   [112] *LB (Plastics) Ltd v Swish Products Ltd* [1979] RPC 551.
[113] *LB (Plastics) Ltd v Swish Products Ltd* [1979] RPC 551.   [114] [1986] RPC 279.

sale to motor-vehicle owners. In order to allow the replacement systems to be fitted to the plaintiff's vehicles, their design required to be virtually identical to that of the original component. This was achieved by taking an example of the plaintiff's exhaust system and examining its shape and dimensions.

The plaintiff's exhaust system was not itself eligible for copyright protection; neither was protection available under the law of patents or of registered designs.[115] The court's attention was directed, therefore, to the question of whether copyright subsisted in the original engineering designs and, if so, whether the defendant's conduct constituted an infringement.[116] Holding in favour of the plaintiff on the issue of copyright infringement, the court (Lord Griffiths dissenting on the basis that, although the majority's opinion was in line with precedent, the case was one which justified the application of the 1966 Practice Direction) held that the defendant's conduct amounted to indirect copying of the designs, constituting a breach of section 48(1) of the Copyright Act 1956. This provides that the conversion of a two-dimensional work into one of three dimensions will constitute reproduction.

A further relevant case on this point is that of *Plix Products Ltd v Frank M Winstone*,[117] a case heard before the High Court of New Zealand, whose decision was upheld on appeal to the Privy Council. This case concerned the design of containers for the transport of kiwi fruits. During the 1960s and 1970s, the plaintiff designed and produced a number of containers which offered significant advantages in respect of the safe storage and transportation of the fruit. The New Zealand kiwi fruit industry is subject to tight regulation, with the New Zealand Kiwi Fruit Authority having power to prescribe, inter alia, standards of packing. This power was exercised, with the standards being based on the plaintiff's designs. The defendants wished to penetrate this potentially lucrative market. Being aware of the potential intellectual property pitfalls, they sought to avoid infringement by engaging a designer who had no knowledge of the plaintiff's product. The designer was given the Fruit Authority's standards, together with samples of kiwi fruit and instructed to produce an appropriate design. Strict instructions were given that the project was not to be discussed with any other party and that no examination should be made of any existing product. Effectively, therefore, the designer was given a set of written specifications and instructed to begin work on a clean sheet of paper. Perhaps not surprisingly, the end result was a series of designs which, when put into production, resulted in a container extremely similar in appearance to the plaintiff's.

Holding that the plaintiff's copyright had been infringed, the High Court of New Zealand ruled that copyright in an artistic design could be infringed by a party who had been provided with a written or verbal description of the work in the event that the description provided was sufficiently detailed to convey the form (expression) of the work, as opposed to outlining the concept.[118] An illustration of the latter situation can be taken from the case of *Gleeson and Gleeson Shirt Co Ltd v H R Denne Ltd*.[119] Here, the plaintiff had designed a

---

[115] The Copyright, Designs and Patents Act 1988 introduced the concept of a design right which will apply to drawings such as those at issue in *British Leyland Motor Corpn v Armstrong Patents* [1986] RPC 279. This right will substitute for copyright but, significantly, does not extend to any aspects of the design which enable the finished article to be 'connected to, or placed in or around or against, another article so that either article may perform its function' (s. 213(3)).

[116] The plaintiff's action ultimately failed on a second ground, the House of Lords holding that its claim to copyright was defeated by the right of a purchaser of their vehicle to obtain spare parts as economically as possible. The relationship between the provisions of intellectual property and competition law is assuming some significance in EU law. Recent dicta would suggest that, whilst a refusal to grant competitors licences in respect of the use of intellectual property rights will not constitute an abuse of Art. 102 of the Treaty on the Functioning of the European Union (TFEU) (formerly Art. 82 of the Treaty of Rome), any element of discrimination may render the conduct an abuse of a dominant position.

[117] [1986] FSR 63.   [118] *Plix Products Ltd v Frank M Winstone* [1986] FSR 63.   [119] [1975] RPC 471.

novel form of clerical shirt. The design proved commercially successful. A competing firm was asked by one of its clients whether it could produce a similar product. To this end, a general description of the shirt was given to one of its employees who had previously produced shirts containing similar features (although not in a single specimen). The resulting product was alleged to infringe the plaintiff's copyright in the artistic designs relating to its shirt. Dismissing this claim, it was held that the instructions given related only to the underlying ideas and that the application of the employee's own skill and knowledge had resulted in the creation of an independent piece of work. A second factor which appeared to influence the Court of Appeal in reaching this conclusion was the fact that the drawings upon which the plaintiff's copyright was founded were more in the nature of sketches than designs intended to serve as the blueprint for production. To this extent, the notion of an 'idea' and its distinction from 'expression' becomes blurred. As was stated in *Plix Products*:

> There are in fact two kinds of 'ideas' involved in the making of any work which is susceptible of being the subject of copyright. In the first place there is the general idea or basic concept of the work. This idea is formed (or implanted) in the mind of the author. He sets out to write a poem or a novel about unrequited love or to draw a dog listening to a gramophone . . . Then there is a second phase—a second kind of 'idea'. The author of the work will scarcely be able to transform the basic concept into a concrete form—i.e. 'express' the idea—without furnishing it with details of form and shape. The novelist will think of characters, dialogue, details of plot and so forth. All these modes of expression have their genesis in the author's mind—these too are 'ideas'. When these ideas . . . are reduced to concrete form, the forms they take are where the copyright resides.[120]

Even so, the distinction between protected and unprotected aspects of a work remains obscure. A significant factor relates to what might be termed the 'added value' element introduced by the author. Where the idea is expressed in simplistic or general terms (as with the sketches in *Gleeson*), a considerable degree of reproduction may be considered legitimate. In the event, however, that the expression is 'ornate, complex or detailed', the would-be plagiariser must beware, as 'the only product he can then make without infringing may bear little resemblance to the copyright work'.[121]

Although the cases of reverse engineering are of considerable relevance to the present topic, one major point of distinction may be identified. It will be recalled that the legislation specifically provides that computer programs are to be protected as a species of literary work. Although no criterion of literary merit is applied, the protection must extend to a particular combination of letters and numbers. As stated, in the situation where access is obtained to these, it is arguable that a claim for breach of copyright will succeed, even though the literary aspects of the second work bear little resemblance to the original. Where there is no question of access, merely the assertion that the operation of the second program replicates the 'look and feel' of the original, and where there is little evidence of literal similarity, it is difficult to argue that the traditional reverse engineering cases referred to earlier have any applicability. In each case, the cornerstone of the copyright owner's claim has been that, albeit indirectly, protected drawings have been reproduced. In the event that the operation of a computer program is studied and the attempt made to replicate its functions, there may be no substantial similarity between the two sets of code which make up the programs.

A closer analogy with computer software may be found with the case of *Green v Broadcasting Corpn of New Zealand*.[122] The plaintiff, Green, had been author, producer, and presenter of a popular British television show, *Opportunity Knocks*. The show operated

---

[120] [1986] FSR 63 at 93.   [121] [1986] FSR 63 at 94.   [122] [1989] RPC 469.

according to a specific format and considerable use was made of catchphrases. Some years later, a programme with the same title was produced in New Zealand, making use of the same formats and catchphrases. With the interpolation of a new presenter, the programme, it might be stated, mimicked the 'look and feel' of the original. Upon discovering this, Mr Green instituted proceedings alleging, inter alia, that the later programme infringed his copyright in the original production. This action was rejected in the High Court of New Zealand, which held that, in the absence of evidence that scripts for the programmes had been reduced to writing, details of the dialogue could not be regarded as protected. An alternative head of claim concerned the dramatic format of the original programme, the various items which were included, and the order in which they appeared. This claim was also rejected, the court referring to the views of a US commentator to the effect that:

> Formats are thus an unusual sort of literary creation. Unlike books, they are not meant for reading. Unlike plays, they are not capable of being performed. Unlike synopses, their use entails more than the expansion of a story outline into a script. Their unique function is to provide the unifying element which makes a series attractive—if not addictive—to its viewer.[123]

With minimal substitution of terminology, these sentences would seem to describe exactly the nature and role of many items of computer software. Whilst the case would not provide authority for the proposition that the reproduction of every aspect of a user interface will be sanctioned, it does suggest that a considerable degree of commonality may be permitted.

Reverse engineering and computer programs

Computer programs can be divided into two broad categories—operating systems and application programs. An operating system—the best-known examples are perhaps Microsoft Windows or its Apple equivalent OSX—contains the basic instructions necessary for a computer to operate. A very simple analogy might be made with a railway system. The gauge of the track and the height and width of tunnels and bridges might be regarded as equivalent to an operating system. They set down basic parameters which must be respected by anyone wishing to build a train to operate on the system. If the track gauge is 4ft 8ins, no matter how technologically advanced an engine might be, it will be quite useless if its wheels are set seven feet apart. In the computer field, programs such as word-processing and spreadsheet packages constitute the equivalents of railway engines. They work with the operating system to perform specific applications and must respect its particular requirements.

A producer intending to develop an applications package for use on a particular operating system must be aware of its functional requirements. In most instances, the information necessary will be made available by the producer of the operating system, whose own commercial interests will be best served by the widest possible availability of applications to run on the system. In the event that the information is not readily available—or that it is suspected that only partial information has been made available—the attempt may be made to reverse engineer the operating system.

A second occasion for the use of reverse engineering occurs at the level of applications packages. Programs such as word processors and spreadsheets store data in a particular format. In the case of basic text, a widely used standard exists—ASCII (American Standard Code for Information Interchange). The text of most word-processed documents is a much

---

[123] R. Meadow, 'Television Formats: The Search for Protection', *Californian Law Review* 58 (1970), p. 1169 at 1170.

more complex creature. Particular fonts, type size, and line spacing will be used. Portions of the text may be printed in italics or may be emboldened or underlined. These matters are not standardised. A producer intent on developing a new word-processing program may wish to discover the codes used by rival producers so that conversion facilities may be built into the new product. From a commercial perspective, existing users are more likely to change to a new program if they can still use documents created using their existing program.

The final form of reverse engineering is the most controversial. Here, the object of the reverse engineering is to discover information about the user interface of an applications package, which may then be used as the basis for the attempt to produce a substantially similar package. In early court cases on the point in the United States, it was often asserted that the intent was to reproduce the 'look and feel' of the original package.

Given that a lawful user cannot be prevented from using a program for its normal purpose, some aspects of reverse engineering must be considered legitimate. A user who operates the program in a normal fashion in order to study its various aspects will not infringe copyright. Subject to strict conditions, a user will also be given the right to attempt to decompile a program's object code when this is done in order to produce a further program which will be interoperable with the copyright owner's. This would apply with respect to the first and second forms of reverse engineering discussed earlier. The right cannot be excluded by contract, but will apply only where the information required has not been made 'readily available' by the copyright owner. The term 'readily available' appears imprecise, and indeed was a key issue in anti-trust action brought by the European Commission against Microsoft. It would not seem to require that the information be supplied free of charge. The levying of excessive charges would obviously be incompatible with the provision, but the question will arise of what level is to be so considered. In most cases where interchange information is used, for example in the word-processing programs referred to earlier, it would appear that this is done under the terms of cross-licensing agreements between the parties involved.

A second issue raises more technical questions. Producers of operating systems will normally find it in their own commercial interest to make the information available to those who wish to produce applications to run on the system. In some cases, the producer of an operating system will also produce applications packages. The best-known example is Microsoft. Although sufficient information concerning its operating systems is made available to other producers, the systems have a number of what are referred to as 'undocumented calls' and it is frequently asserted that these are used by Microsoft's own applications packages. The situation might be compared with producing a road map of the British Isles which omitted all reference to motorways. A motorist who relied totally on the map would certainly be able find a route between Glasgow and London, although the journey might take considerably longer than one making use of the motorway network. Returning to the computer context, it may be queried whether the provision of incomplete information will resurrect the decompilation right. Against this, it may be noted that the legislation makes no mention of the quality of the interconnection which is to be enabled. If comparison is made with the patent system, which requires that an inventor disclose details of the manner in which the invention functions, the duty here is to disclose an effective manner of performing the invention, and not necessarily the optimum method. Any claim relating to the sufficiency of disclosure above and beyond that necessary to achieve interoperability might more reasonably lie under the heading of competition law.

The activities carried out in reliance on the decompilation right are to be restricted to the minimum necessary to obtain the information.[124] Again, this may be a difficult matter

---

[124] Copyright, Designs and Patents Act 1998, s. 50B(3)(b).

to determine. It might be that the user can determine which elements are essential to their legitimate goals only after the entire program has been decompiled. A further restriction imposed upon the user provides that information derived from the decompilation may not be passed on to any third party, except where this is done in order to produce the new interoperable program.[125]

The final restriction concerns the format of the finished program. This, it is provided, is not to be substantially similar in its expression to the original.[126] This is not to be implied as meaning that the program may not compete with the original. The producer of a word-processing program may decompile existing programs to discover details of their format so as to permit the new program to accept text files produced using the earlier program. What is not permitted is the production of a program which infringes copyright in the original. The question of how far copyright extends to the appearance and manner of functioning of computer programs is discussed in the next section.

Literal and non-literal copying

The question of when a basic idea is refined sufficiently to become a protected work is one of the most difficult issues in the field of copyright law. In the United States, what is invariably referred to as the 'idea/expression dichotomy' has assumed statutory form, with the US Code providing that:

> In no case does copyright protection for an original work of authorship extend to any idea, procedure, process, system, method of operation, concept, principle or discovery, regardless of the form in which it is described, explained, illustrated or embodied in such work.[127]

The EC Directive on the Legal Protection of Computer Programs[128] applies this principle in the specific context of computer programs, providing that:

> protection . . . shall apply to the expression in any form of a computer program. Ideas and principles which underlie any element of a computer program . . . are not protected by copyright.[129]

For the United Kingdom, although Lord Hailsham indicated in *LB (Plastics) Ltd v Swish Products Ltd* that 'it is trite law that there is no copyright in ideas', he continued, 'But, of course, as the late Professor Joad used to observe, it all depends on what you mean by "ideas".'[130] The notion of a formal separation between ideas and expressions is found nowhere in UK copyright law. Indeed, although the United Kingdom has incorporated most aspects of the Directive into national law—even where, as in the case of the application of protection to preparatory material, it is arguable that no specific provisions were required—no attempt was made to include this formulation in the implementing regulations.

The main justification for refusing protection to an idea lies in the belief that ideas as such are too intangible, too ethereal, to be protected. It is only when a thought or an idea is committed to paper or some other form of recording device, or even spoken in a public forum, that any evidence becomes available of the existence of what might be a protected interest. Even where this occurs, policy considerations operate to limit the scope of protection. Many legal journals (and academic CVs) would be much thinner if the first person to conceive of the notion of writing a learned article on the idea/expression dichotomy in copyright law had been granted a monopoly concerning the subject. The approach adopted

---

[125] s. 50B(3)(c).   [126] s. 50B(4).   [127] Title 17 USC at 102(b) (1982).
[128] Directive 91/250/EC.   [129] Art. 1(2).   [130] [1979] RPC 551 at 629.

under the law, both of patent and of copyright, has been to regard ideas as an unprotected step along the road to the protection of some concrete or practical manifestation of the concept. The grant of a patent requires a description of a practical application of the idea, whilst copyright law serves to protect a particular sequence of letters, words, figures, or symbols which constitute the application or expression of the underlying idea.

A second area of difficulty concerns the extent of the protection offered under copyright. There is no doubt that direct or literal copying of the work will constitute infringement. A less certain matter concerns the extent of the protection in respect of what is sometimes referred to as 'non-literal copying'. As discussed in more detail in the following sections, in the 1980s and early 1990s, this was regarded as the most critical issue in intellectual property law. From a high-water point of perceived protection around 1990, the effect of subsequent decisions in the United Kingdom and the United States has been to reduce the scope of protection. The increasing use of graphical interfaces and the application of text and graphic-rich applications such as multimedia products and, indeed, the Internet has brought with it a switch in emphasis from indirect protection of the underlying code to direct protection of the end-product. Given the ease with which material held in electronic format may be copied, attention has also tended to switch from the exercise of the exclusive rights which are pivotal to the copyright regime, to the issue of how copyright may be managed in the interests of both owners and users. An indication of the scale of the issue and the problems can be taken from a WIPO estimate presented to the European Commission's Legal Advisory Board that some 90 per cent of the costs incurred in producing a multimedia product made up of existing materials were related to the management of the intellectual property interests involved.

From a legal perspective, there is no doubt that the complete reproduction of software packages will constitute infringement of copyright. In other cases, elements of an earlier work may be reproduced. A typical scenario will see an employee changing jobs and subsequently producing software which incorporates routines from earlier works, the copyright in which will, of course, vest in the original employer. The issues involved here essentially concern the questions of whether a substantial amount of the previous work has been reproduced and whether any similarities can be explained by reasons other than that of deliberate copying. Particularly in the case of computer programs, a variety of producers may be operating in the same field. In such a situation, and especially given the technical constraints which may operate, close similarities between two works may occur in the absence of deliberate copying or plagiarism. Similarities in the educational background of different programmers might also result in the production of substantially similar portions of program.

The rise and fall of look-and-feel protection

With the emergence of the PC, the possibilities for copyright infringement increased dramatically. As has been discussed earlier, in the situation where one party makes a complete or literal copy of a program, there is no doubt that infringement has occurred. A more difficult issue arises where there is an element of independent creative activity on the part of the second producer.

Starting in the late 1970s, a number of cases of this nature were raised in courts in the United Kingdom and the United States. The disputes can reasonably be placed into two categories. In the first, a person or persons would have been employed to work on the development of a particular computer program. The employment would come to an end and the individual, either in his or her own right or as an employee of another company, would be involved in the development of a similar program. The program might well be written in a different computer language, providing limited evidence of literal similarities, and would often incorporate additional features or refinements not found in the original. The contention on the part of the original copyright owner would be that a substantial part of the original program had been copied into the new version.

A second category of case involves parties acting very much at arm's length. The alleged infringer will have had the opportunity to see a copy of the original program in operation and will have set out to create from scratch a competing product which will replicate all or part of the on-screen appearance of the original.

The computerised pharmacist

In the first category of disputes, there is no doubt that the individual responsible for the development of the allegedly infringing product will have had access to all significant elements of the original program. The English case of *Richardson v Flanders*,[131] which was the first case concerned with software copyright to reach the stage of trial in the High Court, might be considered as a typical example of the species.

At issue in this case was a computer program designed for use by pharmacists. The program, which was developed to run on the then popular BBC microcomputers, performed a number of tasks. Principally, when the computer was attached to a printer it would automate and simplify the task of preparing dosage instructions to be supplied with medicines. The program's other major function was to assist in stock-keeping by keeping a record of the drugs dispensed. The program was marketed by the plaintiff, who had also performed a significant amount of work on the original program. Subsequently, the first defendant was employed to work on the project. It was accepted that all relevant copyrights in the work belonged to the plaintiff.

The program achieved considerable commercial success. Relationships between the plaintiff and the defendant were not so happy. The defendant resigned from his position, although he continued to perform some work for the plaintiff as an independent contractor for a further period of time. With the advent of the IBM PC, one of the plaintiff's major customers expressed interest in a version of the program capable of running on this machine and which could be sold on the Irish market. Following discussions, the plaintiff decided not to proceed with the project but suggested that the defendant might be willing to perform the work. The program was completed and was sold in Ireland. The defendant subsequently contacted the plaintiff offering him the rights to market the product in the United Kingdom. These discussions proved fruitless and the defendant proceeded to market a modified version of the program in the United Kingdom. At that stage, the plaintiff initiated proceedings alleging that the new product infringed copyright in his original program.

Because of the fact that the programs had been developed to run on different computers, examination of the code used would have revealed few evidences of similarities. The programs did perform the same functions and had very similar appearances when operating on their respective hardware.

In the absence of any relevant UK precedent, the judge placed considerable reliance on US authority, notably the case of *Computer Associates v Altai*.[132] The court, it was held, should conduct a four-stage test designed to answer the questions.[133] This would seek to answer the following questions:

1. whether the plaintiff's work was protected by copyright
2. whether similarities existed between the plaintiff's and the defendant's programs

---

[131] [1993] FSR 497.   [132] 982 F 2d 693 (1992).   [133] *Richardson v Flanders* [1993] FSR 497.

3. whether these were caused by copying or whether other explanations were possible

4. in the event that copying was established, whether the elements copied constituted a significant part of the original work.

Given what has been said regarding the willingness of UK courts to confer copyright protection on a work, it is not at all surprising that the first question could be answered quickly and definitively in the affirmative. Consideration of the other issues was a more difficult task.

Examining the operation of the original program, the judge identified thirteen aspects of the functioning of the original program leading to the printing of the label for a drug container. This program also offered a stock-control function and some seventeen other features allowing a pharmacist to customise the program in accordance with any particular requirements. When the same analysis was applied to the revised program, seventeen points of similarity were identified between the two programs which would require further investigation to determine whether they were the product of copying.

These similarities were identified from an examination of the screen displays and key sequences. The judge did not attempt to compare the underlying codes. Although an expert witness for the plaintiff had presented an analysis of alleged similarities between the source codes of the two programs, the judge indicated that he found this 'extremely difficult to understand'. Counsel for the plaintiff failed to pursue an invitation to attempt further explanation, and the analysis formed no part of the final decision.

One obvious cause of similarities, that of deliberate copying, was rejected by the judge. It was accepted, however, that the defendant must have retained considerable knowledge of the plaintiff's program and that if similarities resulted from the unconscious use of this material, infringement might be established.

Examining the similarities between the two programs, most were considered explicable by reasons other than copying. The two programs, for example, presented dates in a similar format. Conventions for the presentation of dates are well established and the fact that two works utilise a similar format is more likely to be caused through adherence to such conventions rather than by copying.

In a second aspect, the original program had presented the pharmacist with the option of placing a date other than the current date on a label. This feature was reproduced in the revised program. Although the judge held that it was likely that this had been copied from the original, he held that, given there were a very limited number of ways in which the idea could be expressed, the fact that the two programs utilised very similar approaches did not establish infringement.

In total, six of the seventeen similarities identified by the judge were considered explicable by reasons other than copying. The remaining eleven items it was considered, with varying degrees of conviction, might have been copied from the original program. Eight of these, however, referred to matters which in the opinion of the judge did not amount to a substantial part of the program. One element found in both programs gave users an indication that their instructions have been accepted. In both programs, the message 'operation successful' would appear on the screen and the computer would emanate a double-beep sound. This aspect of the original program, it was held, 'lacks originality and cannot have required any significant skill or effort to devise it'.

Ultimately, infringement was established in respect of only three of the points of similarity, comprising editing and amendment functions and the use of dose codes. The similarities in respect of the editing function were perhaps especially noticeable as it operated in the same idiosyncratic (and probably erroneous) manner in both programs. The dose code facility allowed the user to abbreviate certain instructions regarding the dosage and the manner in which the medication was to be taken. Thus, in both programs, use of the abbreviation AC (*ante cibum*) would cause the instruction 'before food' to be printed on the label. Although a number of the abbreviations were held to be obvious, the fact that eighty-four out of ninety-one codes found in the original program were reproduced in an identical format in the later version, with only minor changes in another five, was held to raise an inference of copying.

Although copyright infringement was ultimately established, the plaintiff's victory was heavily qualified.[134] The copying was described as constituting 'a fairly minor infringement in a few limited respects and certainly not . . . slavish copying'. Although some of the processes adopted clearly differ from those in *Computer Associates*,[135] the effect of the judgment is similar in recognising that for functional works, external forces may well be the cause of similarities, thereby excusing conduct that might otherwise appear to constitute a breach of copyright.

Agricultural software

Allegations of copyright were again before the High Court in the case of *Ibcos Computers v Barclays Mercantile Highland Finance*.[136] Again, there was a background of the major defendant having worked for the plaintiff on the development of a software product intended for use by agricultural dealers, which was marketed under the name ADS. On leaving its employment, he developed a further and competing product which was marketed under the name of Unicorn. The plaintiff alleged that sufficient features of this were copied from the original to constitute an infringement of copyright.

In determining the criteria which would be applied in answering the question of whether infringement had occurred,[137] Jacob J was somewhat critical of the extensive references to the US decision in *Computer Associates*,[138] and warned against 'overcitation of United States authority based on a statute different from ours'. The approach to be adopted was for the court to determine whether there was a sufficient degree of similarity between the two works which, coupled with evidence of access to the original work, would establish an inference of copying. The onus would then switch to the defendant to establish that the similarities were explicable by causes other than copying. Evidence that 'functional necessity' served to narrow the range of options open to the defendant would be relevant. Trivial items may well provide the most eloquent testimony. As was said in *Bilhofer v Dixon*:

> It is the resemblances in inessentials, the small, redundant, even mistaken elements of the copyright work which carry the greatest weight. This is because they are the least likely to have been the result of independent design.[139]

In *Ibcos*, evidence was presented that the same words were misspelled in the same manner, the same headings were used in the two programs, and both shared the same bit of code which served no useful purpose for the functioning of the program. Beyond this, there were considerable similarities at the level of the code itself. In respect of one element of the programs, it was held that:

> there are 22 identical variables, 8 identical labels, 1 identical remark, 31 identical code lines and one identical redundant variable. This to my mind plainly indicates copying and enough in itself to constitute a significant part.[140]

---

[134] *Richardson v Flanders* [1993] FSR 497.
[135] *Computer Associates v Altai*, 982 F 2d 693 (1992).   [136] [1994] FSR 275.
[137] *Ibcos Computers v Barclays Mercantile Highland Finance* [1994] FSR 275.
[138] *Computer Associates v Altai*, 982 F 2d 693 (1992).   [139] [1990] FSR 105 at 123.
[140] *Ibcos Computers v Barclays Mercantile Highland Finance* [1994] FSR 275 at 308.

The court recognised in *Ibcos* that copyright protection must extend beyond the literal aspects of the program code to aspects of 'program structure' and 'design features'. In the case of the former element, it was held that copyright subsisted in the compilation of individual programs which made up the ADS system. Although some differences existed between ADS and Unicorn, it was held that the defendant had taken 'as his starting point the ADS set and that set remains substantially in Unicorn'. Although the two programs had a different visual appearance and it was recognised that 'Unicorn is undoubtedly to the user a much friendlier program than ADS was at the time', the defendant, it was held, had taken 'shortcuts by starting with ADS and making considerable additions and modifications'.

Financial markets

A further significant decision was delivered by the High Court in April 1999, in the case of *Cantor Fitzgerald International v Tradition United Kingdom Ltd*.[141] Both companies involved in the case operated in the financial services market. The plaintiff had developed a computer package which was used in the course of its bond-broking activities. Much of the work in respect of this had been carried out by its Managing Director, a Mr Howard, and a team of programmers appointed by him. The Managing Director was dismissed in 1991. He subsequently secured employment with the defendant, in large part because of his suggestion that he could develop a similar system for it. On taking up employment, he secured the recruitment of three other members of the plaintiff's programming team.

The defendant obtained computers of the same type as those used by the plaintiff, and the employees (who were also defendants in the litigation) began work. In a period of less than three months, a working system was produced. Action alleging copyright infringement and breach of confidence was initiated by the plaintiffs, who argued that it would have been impossible for the programs involved to have been written from scratch in the time available.

Initially, the programmers denied that they had had access to any of the plaintiff's other source code. When the process of discovery highlighted evidence suggesting copying of certain modules, the truth emerged that the programmers had taken a copy of the plaintiff's source code with them. The defendant dropped its initial denial of any copyright infringement and the case proceeded on the basis of how extensive the copying had been.

Expert witnesses were appointed by both parties. The witness for the plaintiff was subjected to severe criticism by the trial judge, Pumphrey J, who opined that the witness had held back relevant information and had acted as an advocate for the plaintiff rather than as an objective and impartial expert. The defendant's witness, on the other hand, was regarded as 'an admirable expert'. His conclusions were perhaps surprising, and were summarised by the judge:

> The Tradition system comprises some 77,000 lines of source code divided into some 363 'modules'. A total of 2,952 lines of code are admitted to have been copied, of which some are repeated copies of a single block of code. In addition Dr McKenzie has identified some 1,964 lines of code which he says are questionable, although he says that the majority of the questionable code was probably not copied. This means that if the admissions are exhaustive, the copied code represents 2 per cent of the system by number of lines. If all the questionable code is included as well, the figure is about 3.3 per cent.[142]

---

141 [2000] RPC 95.
142 *Cantor Fitzgerald International v Tradition United Kingdom Ltd* [2000] RPC 95 at 102.

Faced with this report, the plaintiff restricted its claim of copying to thirty-five of the systems modules. The question, therefore, was whether what was copied constituted a substantial part of the original program. It also made two claims alleging breach of confidence in respect of the techniques used for developing programs of the kind at issue and also in respect of the code itself, arguing that if the programmers had used their access to the plaintiff's code to 'increase their confidence' in the accuracy of their new work, that would of itself constitute misuse of confidential information regardless of whether the code was subsequently copied.

Initial reference was made to the decision of Jacob J in *Ibcos Computers v Barclays Mercantile Highland Finance*,[143] laying down the steps to be followed in deciding an action for infringement of copyright:

1. What are the work or works in which the plaintiff claims copyright?
2. Is each such work 'original'?
3. Was there copying from that work?
4. If there was copying has a substantial portion of that work been reproduced?

The situation in *Cantor*[144] was in many respects more complex than in *Ibcos*. Although the start point may have been the same, it was more questionable whether the end-product could be regarded as the product of copying of a substantial part of the original programs and, indeed, of whether what had been copied satisfied the criterion of originality required for copyright to come into existence. Pumphrey J expressed some doubt as to whether the application of criteria developed in a literary context was a proper approach when dealing with a functional product such as software:

> A program expressed in a computer language must not contain errors of syntax (or it will not compile) and it must contain no semantic errors. Computers do not have the capacity to deduce what the author meant when they encounter errors in the kind of software with which this action is concerned. If the software contains semantic errors it will produce the wrong answer or no answer at all: it may merely fail to run. The only opportunity that the programmer gets to express himself in a more relaxed way is provided by the comments in the code, which are for the benefit of the human reader and are ignored when the code comes to be compiled.[145]

It might be suggested from this that every line of code in a program should be considered essential for its operation and, therefore, that any copying would involve reproduction of a substantial part of the original. The Australian case of *Autodesk v Dyson*[146] was cited as authority for this proposition. For the United Kingdom, however, the court was not willing to follow such a line of argument. Whilst it was accepted that every line of a program was essential in order for it to function, the view of the court was that the determination of whether a substantial part of the work had been copied required to be made by reference to qualitative rather than to quantitative criteria:

> In the general case it is well established that a substantial part of the author's skill and labour may reside in the plot of a novel or play; and to take that plot without taking any particular part of the particular manner of its expression may be sufficient to amount to copyright infringement.[147]

---

[143] [1994] FSR 275.
[144] [2000] RPC 95 at 102.
[145] [2000] RPC 95 at 130.
[146] [1992] RPC 575.
[147] *Cantor Fitzgerald International v Tradition United Kingdom Ltd* [2000] RPC 95 at 134.

For software, it was suggested:

> It seems to be generally accepted that the 'architecture' of a computer program is capable of
> protection if a substantial part of the programmer's skill, labour and judgment went into it.
> In this context, 'architecture' is a vague and ambiguous term.[148]

Two possible meanings were identified for the term, the first relating to the overall description of the system at a high level of abstraction. It could also mean, as was at issue, the overall program structure. Here, functions which it was agreed between the parties were essential elements of the particular software package were grouped into programs, with copyright being recognised in the 'compilation of the programs'.

In spite of the somewhat reprehensible nature of the programmer's work in *Cantor*[149] (which included documenting plans to alter code so as to disguise the fact that it had originated in the plaintiff's program), only a very limited degree of copyright infringement was established. The defendant had accepted liability for the points of similarity identified by its expert witness and in all other respects the finding of the court was that there was no infringement. Similarities were considered either to relate to insubstantial pieces of work or to be explicable by reasons other than copying.

The judgment in respect of the claims of breach of copyright follows what appears to be a general trend to limit the scope of copyright protection to little more than direct or literal copying. As such, it might appear to leave a copyright owner with limited protection. The alternative claim relating to breach of confidence fared better. Although it was held that the techniques used in the development of the original programs were not sufficiently novel or unusual to be regarded as trade secrets and entitled to protection on this basis, it was found, albeit without any detailed explanation, that the use of the original code as an aide-memoire constituted breach of confidence.

Arm's length reproduction

In all of the cases cited here there had been some prior relationship between the parties which had given the alleged copyist access to the underlying source code of the original software packages. This eliminates any issue of whether the alleged copyist had had access to the protected work. Although there was a history of dealings between the parties, the High Court decision in *Navitaire Inc v easyJet Airline Company and Bulletproof Technologies Inc*[150] provided the first occasion where a copyright infringement case arose from a situation where the alleged infringers had enjoyed no significant access to the source code of the original program, but had based their work upon analysis of the operation of the program. The claimant, Navitaire had developed a computerised reservation system, 'OpenRes', designed for use in the airline environment. The defendant, easyJet, one of the United Kingdom's biggest airlines, had licensed this program for use in the course of its operations. After a period of time, it decided to develop its own system and employed the second defendant, a California-based software development company, to develop the programs which were completed and put into use under the name of 'eRes'. It was common ground between the parties that 'easyJet wanted a new system that was substantially indistinguishable from the OpenRes system, as easyJet used it, in respect of its "user interface"'. The claimant alleged that 'eRes' infringed its copyright in 'OpenRes'.

---

[148] [2000] RPC 95 at 134.
[149] [2000] RPC 95.
[150] [2004] EWHC 1725 (Ch).

The infringement proceedings were prolonged and complex. In the final analysis, although some small elements of infringement were established, the great preponderance of the judgment was in favour of easyJet. The judge, Mr Justice Pumphrey commented:

> I consider that the better approach is to take the view that it is not possible to infringe the copyright that subsists either in the source code for a parser or in the source code for a parser generator by observing the behaviour of the final program and constructing another program to do the same thing. In expressing this view, I am verging on drawing a distinction between the 'idea' of the program and its 'expression'.

Such an approach had not previously been a feature of UK copyright law but support was taken from the provisions of Article 1(2) of the European Software Protection Directive stating that:

> Protection in accordance with this Directive shall apply to the expression in any form of a computer program. Ideas and principles which underlie any element of a computer program, including those which underlie its interfaces, are not protected by copyright under this Directive.

Much legal ink and judicial time has been spent on discussion of the question of when an unprotected idea becomes sufficiently detailed and specific to be classed as a protected form of expression. Counsel for the claimant placed reliance upon a number of authorities concerned with the topic of non-literal copying. In the case of *Harman Pictures v Osborne*,[151] for example, the owner of copyright in a book about the Crimean War was successful in a claim of copyright infringement against the producers of a film which depicted the same incidents as those described in the book. In all the cases cited, the critical difference from the present case was that the alleged infringer had enjoyed access to the copyright work.

Computer programs, it was suggested by the judge, could not easily be analogised with other forms of work. The difficulty, it was stated, was that, unlike any other form of literary work, there was limited linkage between the letters and words used in the original code and the end-product as displayed and operating on a computer screen. Two completely different sets of code could produce virtually identically functioning computer programs, even though the creator of the second had not had any form of access to the code of the first program.[152]

In the final analysis, the decision was reached that:

> Navitaire's computer program invites input in a manner excluded from copyright protection, outputs its results in a form excluded from copyright protection and creates a record of a reservation in the name of a particular passenger on a particular flight. What is left when the interface aspects of the case are disregarded is the business function of carrying out the transaction and creating the record, because none of the code was read or copied by the defendants. It is right that those responsible for devising OpenRes envisaged this as the end result for their program: but that is not relevant skill and labour. In my judgment, this claim for non-textual copying should fail.

Such a conclusion, it was stated, was not reached with any form of regret. It was the stated policy of the European Software Directive that computer languages and the ideas underlying computer programs should not qualify for copyright protection. It would be wrong for these exclusions to be circumvented by seeking to identify some overall function behind

---

[151] [1967] 1 WLR 723.
[152] para. 125.

the program when this was a direct consequence of the operation of the unprotected elements. Additionally, it was held:

> As a matter of policy also, it seems to me that to permit the 'business logic' of a program to attract protection through the literary copyright afforded to the program itself is an unjustifiable extension of copyright protection into a field where I am far from satisfied that it is appropriate.[153]

Initially, it was indicated that an appeal would be lodged against this decision. The parties, however, reached an out-of-court settlement. Similar issues did reach the Court of Appeal in the subsequent case of *Nova Productions Ltd v Mazooma Games Ltd and Ors*.[154] The appellant in this case was a software game developer who had produced a computer game, based upon the game of pool, for use in arcade machines. A player would be presented with the image of balls on a pool table and using an electronic cue would attempt to strike the cue ball in such a manner as to cause it to knock one of the object balls into a pocket. Cash prizes would be paid depending upon the player's degree of success. The various defendants were responsible for the development of another game of pool and its use in arcade gaming machines. Although it was not alleged that the defendants had had any form of access to the original code, it was argued that they had seen the original and appropriated elements of its manner of operation sufficient to constitute infringement of copyright. These claims were rejected in the High Court, where the judge held that no features had been copied from the original game. Although a number had been 'inspired' or 'affected' by the study of the original this was not sufficient to establish breach of copyright. An appeal was lodged with the Court of Appeal with an initial request, which was rejected, that a number of questions be referred to the European Court of Justice for a preliminary ruling.[155]

Delivering the judgment of the court, Lord Justice Jacob reviewed the law relating to the protection of computer programs. In similar manner to his comments on the Patents Act and the European Patent Convention cited earlier, he lamented the fact that the drafts of the statutory instrument which implemented the Software Directive into the United Kingdom had strayed from its exact wording thereby adding additional levels of complexity to the task of interpreting its meaning. In particular, although not of major importance to the case, the UK Regulations appeared to treat computer programs and their preparatory materials as the objects of two different forms of copyright, whereas the Directive envisaged only a single copyright in the program, including any preparatory materials.[156]

The key question related to whether what had been taken (if anything) was restricted to unprotected ideas or whether it formed elements of the expression of the software. For the appellant, it was suggested that elements of its game, such as the feature where the appearance of the cue 'pulsed' in proportion to the level of force which the player intended to put into a shot, was sufficiently detailed to merit protection. This claim was rejected. Although the original program may have been inventive, this was a criterion which was applicable in patent law rather than copyright. The claim for infringement of the program as a literary work failed on the ground that what was found to have inspired some aspects of the defendants' game was just too general to amount to a substantial part of the claimant's game.[157]

Although the issue was not analysed in great detail, it was also stated that the appeal would fail through the application of the principles laid down in *Navitaire v easyJet*. This, it was stated, was a stronger case, 'yet the claimants lost'.[158] The judge in *Navitaire*, it was held, 'was quite right to say that merely making a program which will emulate another but

---

[153] paras. 129–30.   [154] [2007] EWCA Civ 219.
[155] [2006] EWCA Civ 1044.   [156] para. 28.
[157] para. 44.   [158] para. 46.

which in no way involves copying the program code or any of the program's graphics is legitimate'.[159]

Lord Justice Jacob's concluding remarks perhaps mark the final nail in the coffin of look-and-feel protection for software although a referral has been made to the European Court of Justice in the recent case of *SAS Institute v World Programming Ltd*.[160] Noting that it was agreed by all parties that the case had significance for the whole computer games industry, he acknowledged that counsel for the claimant had suggested that if the trial judge's decision was upheld, the consequence would be that computer games would be denied any effective form of protection in respect of conduct involving anything other than literal reproduction of the program code. Whilst this might be the case, consideration had to be given to the original nature and purpose of copyright and the concept of a balance being struck between protecting the work of an author and encouraging the creative works of others. The famous scientist, Sir Isaac Newton, once wrote, 'If I have seen further, it is because I stood on the shoulders of giants'.[161] In like manner, Lord Justice Jacob recognised that almost all literary work was derivative to some extent and acknowledged the importance of the fact that copyright law should not stifle the creation of new works, concluding:

> If protection for such general ideas as are relied on here were conferred by the law, copyright would become an instrument of oppression rather than the incentive for creation which it is intended to be. Protection would have moved to cover works merely inspired by others, to ideas themselves.[162]

Computer programs as visual works

In addition to protecting literary works, copyright has steadily been extended to cover other forms of recorded work, closely following developments in technology. The 1988 Act provides that:

> Copyright is a property right which subsists in accordance with this Part in the following descriptions of work—
>
> (a) original literary, dramatic, musical or artistic works,
>
> (b) sound recordings, films, broadcasts or cable programmes.

In the early days of computers, very little was provided in the way of visual content. The first computers were effectively calculating machines with no form of visual display unit. Even when these became commonplace, and even with the move to applications such as word processing, the small amounts of memory and limited processing capacity of computers meant that there was little interest in the aesthetic appearance of a computer program. The world today, of course, is very different with many computer games utilising sophisticated graphics.

Two issues are of relevance in this context: first, the question of whether an image generated through the operation of a computer program might be classed as an artistic work and, secondly, whether moving images might be classed as films.

---

[159] para. 52.   [160] [2010] EWHC 3012 (Ch).

[161] Letter to Robert Hooke (a rival scientist), 15 February 1676, cited in the *Concise Oxford Dictionary of Quotations*.

[162] [2006] EWCA Civ 1044 at para. 55. In *SAS Institute v World Programming Ltd* [2010] EWHC 1829 (Ch) a referral was made to the European Court of Justice seeking a preliminary ruling on a number of questions concerning the extent of protection conferred under the Directive. The judge, Mr Justice Arnold, did indicate on a number of occasions that whilst making the reference, he was not persuaded that the previous decisions were in error.

The issue of artistic copyright in software was discussed by the Court of Appeal in the case of *Nova Productions Ltd v Mazooma Games Ltd and Ors*.[163] The facts of the case have been described earlier. The games, although not identical, shared a number of elements and it was the claimant's contention, inter alia, that the defendants' games infringed its artistic copyright in 'Pocket Money'. The case hinged upon the subset of artistic work referred to as 'graphic works',[164] and centred upon the individual screen frames. It was accepted that comparison of individual frames did not demonstrate any substantial degree of similarity but it was argued that 'there was in effect a further kind of artistic work, something beyond individual freeze-frame graphics'.[165] What the defendants had done, it was argued, was to 'create a "dynamic reposing" of the original game, changing some of the level of details but retaining 'an essential artistic element of the original'.[166] At trial, the judge was prepared to accept that this was an arguable point, although he went on to hold that there had been no infringement in the particular case. Delivering the judgment of the Court of Appeal, Lord Justice Jacob disagreed:

> 'Graphic work' is defined as including all the types of thing specified in s. 4(2) which all have this in common, namely that they are static, non-moving. A series of drawings is a series of graphic works, not a single graphic work in itself. No-one would say that the copyright in a single drawing of Felix the Cat is infringed by a drawing of Donald Duck. A series of cartoon frames showing Felix running over a cliff edge into space, looking down and only then falling would not be infringed by a similar set of frames depicting Donald doing the same thing. That is in effect what is alleged here.
>
> This reasoning is supported by the fact that Parliament has specifically created copyright in moving images by way of copyright in films. If (the claimant's argument was accepted), the series of still images which provides the illusion of movement would itself create a further kind of copyright work protecting moving images. It is unlikely that Parliament intended this.[167]

There would be no doubt that reproduction of the individual frames would have constituted infringement.

To date, there have not been any cases involving the claim that a computer program is classed as a film. Many modern films make very extensive use of computer-generated images, to the extent that some characters, such as Gollum in the *Lord of the Rings*, are entirely computer-generated.[168] There appears to be little doubt that the programs responsible would qualify for protection as a film. Films, of course, enjoy copyright protection in their own right and there might be little benefit in bringing a claim for infringement on the basis of the software rather than the end-product. Discounting the concept of piracy, whereby all of a work is copied and passed off as an original, there is limited value for a later party to slavishly copy elements of an earlier work of entertainment. Copying the appearance and actions of the character of Gollum from the *Lord of the Rings* and inserting this in a film on a different topic would not be likely to increase the appeal of the later film; rather the reverse as audiences who had seen Gollum would prefer to view a novel character. Different considerations apply with software products which are functional in nature and a user who has acquired familiarity with one form of interface will not unnaturally want to be able easily to transfer skills to another package produced by a different developer.

---

[163] [2007] EWCA Civ 219.

[164] s. 4(1).   [165] para. 13.

[166] para. 13.

[167] paras. 16–17.

[168] For an account of developments in the field see <http://en.wikipedia.org/wiki/Computer-generated_imagery>.

New directions in UK copyright law

It is sometimes a feature of the UK legislative process that changes to one area of legislation are quietly introduced within a statute primarily directed at other areas of activity. This has been the case with the enactment of the Enterprise and Regulatory Reform Act 2013, a measure that makes some significant changes to UK copyright law. In large part the provisions relate to topics that were dropped from the Digital Economy Bill (now Act) 2010 in order to enable it to complete its parliamentary passage before the legislature was dissolved prior to the 2010 general election.

In common with many other statutes, the copyright provisions in the Enterprise and Regulatory Reform Act establish a framework which may be filled in by Regulations to be introduced by government ministers. This has been the cause of some controversy as, given that secondary legislation is subject to a significantly reduced level of parliamentary scrutiny than is the case with primary legislation, a potentially broad discretion has been given to the government concerning the definition of the final legal regime.

A further reform was introduced in the Legal Deposit Libraries (Non-Print Work) Regulations 2013. For many years, the law (most recently in the form of the Legal Deposit Library Act 2003) has required that a copy of every published printed material is to be supplied by the publisher to the British Library. A number of other, so-called deposit libraries in England, Scotland, and Ireland are entitled to request a copy (free of charge) of every printed work. In reality requests are made as a matter of course. The 2013 Regulations extend this provision to cover works such as blogs and even Twitter postings published in electronic form. As we rely more and more on electronic communications, Internet-based activity is no longer of merely ethereal significance. The British Library has commented:

> If you want a picture of what life is like today in the UK you have to look at the web . . .

> We have already lost a lot of material, particularly around events such as the 7/7 London bombings or the 2008 financial crisis.

> That material has fallen into the digital black hole of the 21st century because we haven't been able to capture it.

> Most of that material has already been lost or taken down. The social media reaction has gone.[169]

Orphan works

The emergence of the Internet has seen a massive increase in the amount of data in existence. It is estimated that more data has been created in the past few years than in the whole of previous human history. More data is available online than has ever been the case in printed form.

The proliferation of data and the new publications opportunities established by the Internet create many issues for copyright law. A particular issue addressed by the new Act is that it is not always easy for a party wishing to use data to discover who the copyright owner is in order to seek their permission to reuse the work in another publication. A simple example can be seen in the search engine Google Images which will generally link to images but often give limited information as to who owns the copyright in them. At a further level, given the length and uncertain duration of copyright protection—the life of an author and up to seventy years after death—there are many literary works for which it will be difficult to trace the owner of copyright. Although much remains to be defined, that

---

[169] <http://www.huffingtonpost.co.uk/2013/04/05/british-library-to-harvest-web_n_3018784.html>.

Act provides that the Secretary of State may by Regulations provide for the grant of licences in respect of works that qualify as orphan works under the Regulations.

These Regulations may specify a person or a description of persons authorised to grant licences, or provide for a person designated therein to specify a person or a description of persons authorised to grant licences.

In order for a work to qualify as an orphan work, it is a requirement that the owner of copyright in it has not been found after a diligent search made in accordance with the regulations. In such a case, provision may be made for the granting of licences to do, or authorise the doing of, any act restricted by copyright that would otherwise require the consent of the missing owner. Any such licences must be formulated so as:

- to have effect as if granted by the missing owner
- not to give exclusive rights
- not to be granted to a person authorised to grant licences.

The Regulations may apply to a work although it is not known whether copyright subsists in it, and references to a missing owner and a right or interest of a missing owner are to be read as including references to a supposed owner and a supposed right or interest.

Perhaps surprisingly, the Act does not define the concept of 'orphan works' but the term is generally interpreted to refer to works where the copyright owner cannot be identified. There is also, of course, the question of who should be allowed to grant licences for orphan works. The Act provides that anybody may approach the Secretary of State (the government minister responsible for operating the legislation). It was originally envisaged that the power to grant licences would be conferred upon the Copyright Licensing Association which is the major body acting on behalf of authors in respect of granting licences in respect of the use of works. Ultimately, however, it was determined that the role should be performed by the Intellectual Property Office.

There is much, perhaps too much, that remains uncertain concerning the scope of the new provisions. The general approach is to be commended. The Internet offers significant new opportunities to disseminate data. Books that may have been out of print for decades may enjoy a new lease of life when published electronically—although a cynical author might suggest that it is difficult to think of many examples. We have seen in recent years the emergence of, and litigation surrounding, the attempts by Google to digitise copies of as many books as it can get its electronic scanners close to. The issues are important and perhaps the major point that will almost certainly arise concerns the treatment that should be given to a long-forgotten work—by a long-forgotten author and possibly deceased—that becomes a major commercial success thanks to the Internet.

Harvesting the Internet

As mentioned earlier, the British Library has started to compile a record of the contents of the Internet, or at least those parts which are published in the United Kingdom. Given the global nature of the Internet this may not always be an easy issue to determine. The Regulations provide that:

(a) it is made available to the public from a website with a domain name which relates to the United Kingdom or to a place within the United Kingdom; or

(b) it is made available to the public by a person and any of that person's activities relating to the creation or the publication of the work take place within the United Kingdom.[170]

---

[170] Reg. 18.

The sum of £3 million (around €3.6 million) has been invested in the project. Two techniques may be utilised. Agreement may be reached between the Library and major content providers (such as online newspapers) for the latter to provide copies of works. The Regulations mandate also the use of web harvesters, defined in Regulation 2 as 'a computer program which is used to search the Internet in order to request delivery of online work on behalf of a deposit library'. The software will search all publicly available websites within the.uk country domain. The initial search is estimated to take three months.

Preservation of its cultural heritage has long been seen as an important task for any country. Extension of existing library holdings to include works available only in electronic form is to be welcomed at least in principle. There are, however, concerns about some elements of the project. Collecting and preserving for posterity copies of individuals' Facebook pages and Twitter postings does raise concerns about the protection of personal privacy. Much has been written and said about the problems individuals have had of restricting access to their social networking publications—particularly if their circumstances have changed.

Conclusions

In many respects, developments in the field of software copyright provide a mirror image to the situation with software patents. In the latter case, at least at the level of decisions in the European Patent Office and even more so in the United States, there has been a move from an initial denial of patentability to a much more liberal approach. With copyright, whilst there has never been any significant doubt that software is eligible for protection, recent judicial decisions have significantly limited the scope of protection so that it will extend to little more than direct copying. As cases such as *Navitaire v easyJet* illustrate, a complex balancing act often requires to be performed, considering the interests of software developers, users, and in many instances, end-consumers.

Whilst copyright may no longer extend to cover the 'look and feel' of a program, there is no doubt that it does prohibit direct copying of the underlying code. Although at first sight unobjectionable, this does create problems for users. Unlike any other form of literary work, use of software requires copying. In this respect, software, which in the case of application packages such as word-processing or spreadsheet programs is effectively a tool, sits rather uneasily in the context of a form of protection designed for literary or artistic works. As the *Gowers Report* on the future of intellectual property law points out, for a user to burn the contents of a CD which he or she has bought onto an MP3 player constitutes a breach of copyright. Few users, it may be assumed, are aware of this and it may be doubted whether (m)any of those who do, care. A situation where conduct which almost everyone would regard as acceptable is in breach of the law can serve only to bring the law into discredit. Conversely, of course, software, given its digital format, is massively vulnerable to large-scale copying at little or no cost to the copyist. There is a need to rethink some of the basic tenets of copyright law and the following chapter will consider the provisions of the rather grandly named 'Copyright in the Information Society' Directive.

Several decades of European integration have produced a massive body of legislation that the United Kingdom has sought diligently to incorporate into domestic law. The result has not always been successful. One of the country's most prominent intellectual property judges, Mr Justice Arnold delivered the Herchel Smith intellectual property lecture in 2014 at the University of London[171] and commented in the following terms regarding events in the copyright field following the last significant piece of domestic legislation—the

---

[171] <http://www.elgaronline.com/view/journals/qmjip/5–2/qmjip.2015.02.01.xml>.

Copyright, Designs and Patents Act of 1988. Perhaps not surprisingly given the amount of technological developments in the near three decades since the Act received Royal Assent, he noted that:

> the 1988 Act has been amended a quite extraordinary number of times. By my count, there have been no less than 80 amending Acts and statutory instruments to date. Some of these amendments have been required to implement the European Directives. Others have been the result of purely domestic initiatives, such as those I have described. Amendments have repeatedly been made to earlier amendments. To call the result a patchwork quilt would be an insult to the art of quilting. A closer analogy would be an obsessively re-used palimpsest.[172]
>
> . . . .
>
> [T]he Act as it presently stands is considerably longer than the Act as originally enacted, considerably more complicated, cannot be understood in isolation from the EU Directives and the implementing regulations and lacks coherence. As a result, the law is inaccessible to creators, exploiters and users of copyright works, which is to say, everyone in the UK.

This, perhaps, is an all too common (and justified) criticism of the state of intellectual property law today. Comparison might be drawn between the famous Statute of Anne that introduced the statutory concept of copyright law in less than a dozen pages and the many hundreds of pages that now relate to the concept.

In one respect Brexit may assist the process of reforming and simplifying the statute book, especially in the copyright field. There has always been tension between the common and civil law approaches to copyright law and many of the measures that have been adopted at the European level have involved complicated and often unsatisfactory compromises. The European Commission is on the cusp of publishing proposals for a major reform of the EU copyright regime and it may be that Brexit will facilitate reformation both in the United Kingdom and the rest of the EU. Even if there should be differences of approach, it is arguable whether the much vaunted 'digital single market' has had significant impact, largely because of linguistic issues. The issues that form key components of it, such as licensing and the treatment of orphan works, can easily be dealt with at a domestic level. There is a real need to reform and simplify copyright legislation. To some extent the United Kingdom's hands will be tied by the need to comply with the provisions of the Berne Convention, but there is no doubt that Mr Justice Arnold's criticisms are merited. We can perhaps never go back to the simplicity of the Statute of Anne but a situation where few, if any of us, would claim to understand the totality of the legislation cannot be sustainable. Certainly there are options for the way forward, and few would argue that the current state of intellectual property law in the EU is satisfactory.

---

[172] The word 'palimpsest' is generally taken to refer to an old-fashioned manuscript that has had its original text partially erased and new text added but in a manner that allows traces of the original to be discerned.

17

Enforcement issues

INTRODUCTION

This chapter will look at some of the issues associated with enforcement of copyright considering the extent to which intermediaries such as Internet Service Providers (ISPs) might be held liable for infringing acts committed by their users. Increasingly also, attention is being paid to the possibility that rights owners might proceed against the (possibly tens of thousands) of users whose actions infringe their rights. In many cases this will require the cooperation of ISPs and a major component of the Digital Economy Act was concerned with the manner in which this process might be managed.

The Directive on Copyright in the Information Society

As has been noted in the context of data protection, law-making in the European Union can be a lengthy process. A Green Paper entitled *Copyright and Related Rights in the Information Society* was published by the Commission in July 1995 but it was not until 2001 that the Directive on the Harmonisation of Certain Aspects of Copyright and Related Rights in the Information Society was finally adopted and implemented in the United Kingdom in 2003 by the Copyright and Related Rights Regulations.[1]

The Explanatory Memorandum to the original proposal[2] identified discrepancies in the level of protection offered within the Member States, not so much at the level of fundamental principle, but in respect of detailed implementation and the provision of exceptions. Thus, all Member States accept that a right holder possesses the exclusive right to reproduce material, but differ in respect of issues such as whether a temporary reproduction will constitute infringement. Variations occur also in respect of concepts such as fair dealing and the provision of special regimes for the educational sector. Again, some states make provision for a levy to be imposed upon the sales of recording media. The proceeds of this will be distributed between right holders with users being granted a right in return to make copies of works for private purposes.

Beyond the issue of reproduction, significant issues concern the extent of rights to distribute a work or to communicate its contents to the public. With the development of 'on demand' services for the delivery of digital information in the form of audio or video material, lacunae exist between provisions relating to private communications and broadcasting. The Directive on Copyright in the Information Society[3] sets out to make provision for these matters and to harmonise existing national provisions, keeping in line with the provisions

---

[1] SI 2003/2498.

[2] European Commission, Explanatory Memorandum on the Proposal for a Directive on the Harmonisation of Certain Aspects of Copyright and Related Rights in the Information Society, Brussels, 10 December 1997.

[3] Directive 2001/29/EC.

of the Berne Convention and the 1996 World Intellectual Property Organization (WIPO) Treaty on Copyright and Performances and Phonograms. In essence, the Directive is evolutionary rather than revolutionary in its contents. As Recital 5 indicates:

> Technological development has multiplied and diversified the vectors for creation, production and exploitation. While no new concepts for the protection of intellectual property are needed, the current law on copyright and related rights should be adapted and supplemented to respond adequately to economic realities such as new forms of exploitation.

Reflecting this approach, the initial articles of the Directive do little more than confirm existing principles of copyright law. Article 2 provides authors, performers, producers, and broadcasters with the exclusive right to prohibit direct or indirect, temporary or permanent reproduction of the protected work by any means or in any form. Article 3 provides for similar exclusive rights in respect of the communication of all or part of a work to the public by wire or wireless means. It is specifically provided that the provision is to extend to the situation where the works are communicated in such a way that 'members of the public may access them from a place and at a time individually chosen by them', for example over the Internet. Article 4 provides for authors to enjoy the exclusive right to control the distribution of works to the public by sale or otherwise.

Even though the United Kingdom does not legitimise domestic copying,[4] a measure of tolerance is shown by the fact that the criminal penalties applicable in the event of copying for commercial purposes do not extend where copying is carried out for social and domestic purposes. Such an approach can be justified in the context of analogue copying. It would be a rare student who has not infringed copyright at some stage through over-zealous use of a photocopier. Most readers will be familiar with the limitations of this copying technology. A photocopy of an article in a journal or a chapter of a book will invariably be of lower quality than the original. Slight movement of the page as the copy is being made will cause blurring of lines, the size of the book being copied and the paper being used in the photocopier may differ, again with adverse consequences for the appearance of the copy. Problems will be exacerbated if a photocopy is itself copied and by the time the process is repeated over a few generations of copies, the final version will be virtually indecipherable. Similar factors will apply when a cassette copy is made of a musical recording or television or film production. In general, with equipment normally available to the domestic copyist, the copying process is a laborious one and the results inferior in quality to the original work.

Where information is recorded in digital format, the task of the copier is very much easier. A copy of a digital work will be identical in terms of quality to the original, and the same result will apply no matter how many generations of copies are produced. The speed with which copies may be made is also generally increased, whilst the emergence of the Internet makes it possible for a program to be placed on a website and copied by tens or even hundreds of thousands of users around the world. The popular encryption program PGP was released to the world in this manner in order to pre-empt attempts by the US authorities to prevent its distribution. Not even the might of the United States could put the technological genie back in that particular bottle. Today, much debate focuses on the availability of copyright protected material over the Internet through the medium of file sharing websites. As will be discussed later, one legal response to the problem has been to seek to impose liability on commercial third parties whose equipment or facilities are regarded as facilitating the infringing acts of private individuals. The question arises also as to what should be the level of liability imposed on the individual's concerned?

---

[4] Save in the case of use of a video recorder to record a television broadcast 'solely' in order to allow it to be viewed at a more convenient time (Copyright, Designs and Patents Act 1988, s. 70).

Regulation 26 of the Copyright and Related Rights Regulations 2003[5] provides for an extension of the scope of criminal offences. Previously, an offence was committed only when a copyright infringer acted in the course of a business. The Copyright, Designs and Patents Act 1988 is now amended to provide that:

> (2A) A person who infringes copyright in a work by communicating the work to the public—
>
> (a) in the course of a business, or
>
> (b) otherwise than in the course of a business to such an extent as to affect prejudicially the owner of the copyright, commits an offence if he knows or has reason to believe that, by doing so, he is infringing copyright in that work.[6]

As the *Gowers Report* comments, however:

> The fact that the letter of the law is rarely enforced only adds to the public sense of illegitimacy surrounding copyright law. Yet copyright is essential for protecting the investment that UK creative industries make in artists, performers and designers. If uses such as transferring music from CDs to an MP3 player for personal use are seen to be illegal, it becomes more difficult to justify sanctions against copyright infringement that genuinely cost industry sales, such as from freely downloading music and films using the Internet.[7]

A problem facing right holders seeking to take action against individuals is to identify those concerned. As has been discussed in the context of privacy, true anonymity is an elusive commodity where the Internet is concerned. It is feasible for right holders to acquire the details of the Internet Protocol (IP) addresses used by computers which are identified as uploading or downloading copyright-protected material. IP addresses are allocated to end-users by ISPs and these organisations are in a position to match names with IP addresses.

Attempts by aggrieved parties to seek court orders, commonly known as *Norwich Pharmacal* orders after the House of Lords' decision in the case of that name, have been a feature of a number of actions in the field of defamation and the principles described in that chapter of this book will also be relevant in the copyright field. Specific, albeit controversial, legislative action has now been adopted in the form of the Digital Economy Act 2010 and this chapter will continue to give consideration to the scope of this statute.

Copyright enforcement

Enforcement of copyright

The European Intellectual Property Enforcement Directive[8] provides in Article 3 that:

> Member States shall provide for the measures, procedures and remedies necessary to ensure the enforcement of the intellectual property rights covered by this Directive. Those measures, procedures and remedies shall be fair and equitable and shall not be unnecessarily complicated or costly, or entail unreasonable time-limits or unwarranted delays.

The UK regime provides for a range of civil and criminal remedies in the event of an infringement of copyright. Section 96 of the 1988 Act provides that:

> (1) An infringement of copyright is actionable by the copyright owner.
>
> (2) In an action for infringement of copyright all such relief by way of damages, injunctions, accounts or otherwise is available to the plaintiff as is available in respect of the infringement of any other property right.

---

[5] SI 2003/2498.   [6] s. 107.   [7] para. 327.   [8] Directive 2004/48/EC. OJ 2004, L 195/16.

To the extent that rights and remedies are generic, consideration in this section can be relatively brief. The Act provides in section 97(1) that an award of damages may be made by a court, except in cases where the infringer did not know or have any reason to believe that infringement was taking place. The normal measure of damages in civil cases takes account of losses suffered by the innocent party and attempts to put them in the position they would have been in the absence of the infringing conduct. In exceptional circumstances the Act continues to provide that:

> (2) The court may in an action for infringement of copyright having regard to all the circumstances, and in particular to—
>
>   (a) the flagrancy of the infringement, and
>
>   (b) any benefit accruing to the defendant by reason of the infringement,
>
>   award such additional damages as the justice of the case may require.

This provision has not been widely utilised but relevant cases are those of *Nottinghamshire Healthcare NHS Trust v News Group Newspapers Ltd*[9] and *Absolute Lofts South West London Ltd v Artisan Home Improvements Ltd and Anor*.[10] Both cases concerned issues of copyright in photographs and in both additional damages were awarded to reflect the nature of the conduct. In the first case, after engaging in an extensive survey of the background to the provision, Mr Justice Pumphrey commented:

> It seems to me to follow that carelessness sufficiently serious to amount to an attitude of 'couldn't care less' is in my judgment capable of aggravating infringement and of founding an award of damages under s 97(2). Recklessness can be equated to deliberation for this purpose.

Accounting of profits

As discussed in the context of patent law, an alternative for a claimant to seeking an award of damages may be to require the defendant to account for profits made as a consequence of unlawful activity. The making of such an award is at the discretion of the court. For an example of a recent authority on this point reference might be made to the decision of the High Court in the case of *Twentieth Century Fox Film Corporation v David Harris*.[11] This case is the latest, and possibly, the last stage in proceedings involving a file sharing website called Newzbin. We will consider the details of the original litigation below, but subsequent to the initial proceedings it was discovered that the defendant in this case was the controlling mind behind the site and, as was found by the court, had conspired to syphon off its financial assets beyond the reach of the claimants who had successfully sought damages for copyright infringement. The court had little hesitation in ordering the defendant to account for the profits that had been made as a result of his involvement with the site.

Delivery up

Again as is the case with patent law, provision is made for the court to make, at its discretion, an order for the delivery up of any infringing copies of a work. It provides in section 99 that:

> (1) Where a person—
>
>   (a) has an infringing copy of a work in his possession, custody or control in the course of a business, or

---

[9] [2002] EWHC 409 (Ch).   [10] [2015] EWHC 2608 (IPEC).   [11] [2014] EWHC 1568 (Ch).

(b)   has in his possession, custody or control an article specifically designed or adapted for making copies of a particular copyright work, knowing or having reason to believe that it has been or is to be used to make infringing copies,

the owner of the copyright in the work may apply to the court for an order that the infringing copy or article be delivered up to him or to such other person as the court may direct.

This provision draws comparison with the terms of the world's first copyright statute; the Statute of Anne of 1709. This stated that any offender against copyright in a literary work

shall forfeit such book or books, and all and every sheet or sheets, being part of such book or books, to the proprietor or proprietors of the copy thereof, who shall forthwith damask, and make waste paper of them; and further, That every such offender or offenders shall forfeit one penny for every sheet which shall be found in his, her, or their custody, either printed or printing, published, or exposed to sale, contrary to the true intent and meaning of this act; the one moiety thereof to the Queen's most excellent majesty, her heirs and successors, and the other moiety thereof to any person or persons that shall sue for the same.

An interesting amalgam of civil and criminal penalties! The 1988 Act makes separate provision for criminal liability. These will be considered below but first we will consider the extent to which third parties may be held responsible for acts of infringement committed by others.

Follow the money

In terms of the question of whether infringement of copyright has occurred, there is little doubt that the individual responsible for copying a work in electronic format will incur liability where this act is done without the authority of the copyright owner. An individual who downloads a copy of a software program or the text of an article from a bulletin board or other form of online service will infringe copyright. A constant thread in discussions of audio, video, or software piracy has concerned the impossibility, and, indeed, the desirability, of bringing proceedings against thousands if not millions of individual infringers. Much attention has been paid to the possibility of holding liable those parties who provide the equipment or facilities used for infringing acts. As the European Commission has commented, IP policy is increasingly oriented in the direction of following 'the money'. Especially in the context of Internet-based copyright infringement where millions of individuals may download relatively limited amounts of material it may not be feasible or cost effective for a copyright owner to take action against them—although you might look at the decision in the case of *Media CAT v Adams and Ors*[12] where letters threatening legal proceedings were sent by a firm of solicitors to substantial numbers of individuals who were alleged to have downloaded unlawful copies of pornographic films. The approach did not meet with judicial approval.

Blocking orders

A recent trend in intellectual property litigation has been for copyright owners to seek court orders requiring that ISPs take technical measures to prevent (or at least hinder) their customers' access to websites implicated in facilitating copyright infringement. The basis for these actions has lain primary in Section 97A of the Act. This provides that:

1.   The High Court . . . shall have power to grant an injunction against a service provider, where that service provider has actual knowledge of another person using their service to infringe copyright.

[12] [2011] EWPCC 6.

2. In determining whether a service provider has actual knowledge for the purpose of this section, a court shall take into account all matters which appear to it in the particular circumstances to be relevant and, amongst other things, shall have regard to—

    whether a service provider has received a notice . . . and the extent to which any notice includes—

    (i)   the full name and address of the sender of the notice;

    (ii) details of the infringement in question.

The first case brought under this provision was *Twentieth Century Film Corporation v BT*[13] which was decided in 2010 and in the following years orders have been made restricting access to more than 500 websites by the courts[14] in the course of around 120 actions. Although BT was technically the defendant in the action, the proceedings were non-contentious in their nature. Effectively BT's position was that 'we do not object to blocking access but we want the court to tell us to do it'. The real target of the action was a file-sharing website, Newzbin. This company had been the defendant in previous cases before the courts. Operating as a form of online members' club with users being required to pay subscription fees in return for access, it provided access to information and technology which could (and by all the evidence was) used by members to make unlawful copies of copyright protected works. In 2010 a High Court ruling[15] held that it was liable jointly with users for their acts of copyright infringement on the basis that the site owners knew full well what activities were going on.

The initial High Court ruling effectively put the original Newzbin out of business. Websites are not geographically dependent however and in a short period of time Newzbin2 was established and commenced operations. Further proceedings were commenced in which a range of copyright owners requested that the High Court order BT, which was the UK's largest ISP, to use the same technical methods that were applied to block access to sites identified as containing child pornography to block access from the United Kingdom to Newzbin.

Three questions were identified by Mr Justice Arnold as being of critical importance in determining whether an order should be made under section 97A. First, what must the service provider have 'actual knowledge' of? Second, in what manner may a service provider be given 'actual knowledge' of something that it did not know before? Third, if some actual knowledge should be proved, what might be the scope of any injunction that would be granted?

The first question has been important in a number of cases. The issue and debate has centred in the past on the question of whether a party such as an ISP might, out of fear of being joined as a defendant in litigation, act too readily and hastily when presented with a complaint. In defamation cases the concern has been that an ISP might block access to a posting which is allegedly defamatory thereby setting up a clear conflict with the rights of freedom of expression guaranteed under Article 10 of the European Convention on Human Rights (ECHR).

Matters are perhaps a little simpler in the copyright context where issues of infringement may be more clear cut and where there is less of an issue regarding freedom of expression. In respect of the manner in which notice might be given, there was little disagreement between the parties. As the judge concluded:

It is clear from section 97A(2) that, in considering whether a service provider has actual knowledge, it is relevant to consider whether the service provider has been given notice of

---

[13] [2011] EWHC 1981 (Ch).

[14] You can find a good deal of information about these procedures from this link <http://ipkitten.blogspot.my/2015/07/500-and-counting-websites-blocked-by.html>.

[15] [2010] EWHC 608 (Ch).

the infringement. There was little dispute between counsel in the end that a service provider may be given actual knowledge of infringement by receipt of a sufficiently detailed notice and a reasonable opportunity to investigate the position.

In the course of the proceedings BT expressly accepted that it had actual knowledge (was aware of) of the previous litigation against Newzbin. This was held to be sufficient. As the judge commented:

> In my judgment it follows that BT has actual knowledge of other persons using its service to infringe copyright: it knows that the users and operators of Newbin2 infringe copyright on a large scale, and in particular infringe the copyrights of the Studios in large numbers of their films and television programmes, it knows that the users of Newzbin2 include BT subscribers, and it knows that those users use its service to receive infringing copies of copyright works made available to them by Newzbin2. . . . that knowledge satisfies the requirements of section 97A(1).

Twentieth Century Fox v Sky UK and BT (and Ors)

The issue how far intermediaries might be held responsible for preventing acts of copyright infringement being committed by their customers has been litigated frequently and discussed in previous case notes. The present case[16] concerned in part the attempt by copyright owners to obtain court orders requiring ISPs to take steps to block access by their customers to web streaming and bit torrent websites. This was non contentious and dealt with on a documents only basis with no requirement being imposed for an oral hearing of the issues. More judicial concern was expressed relating to applications seeking orders to block access to sites whose operations made use of a different form of technology, referred to as 'Popcorn Time type sites'. As Mr Justice Birss commented:

> The Popcorn Time type sites raise new and different issues from those considered hitherto. Indeed, as became obvious at the hearing, it was not always clear to all members of the legal team representing the claimants how the Popcorn Time sites operate.[17]

Essentially the difference in technology appears to lie in the fact that contrasting with bit torrent and web streaming sites there is a greater element of separation between the developers and suppliers of Popcorn type systems and end-users. They are also easier to use. As the judge commented:

> In evidence at the hearing was an article about Popcorn Time which appeared on the Bloomberg news website on 25th February 2015. The headline was 'This Torrenting App is too good to be legal'. The article describes that the application made its debut in March 2014 and describes it as the 'kinder, gentler face of piracy online'. The article also states that Popcorn Time has made BitTorrent far more user-friendly and less obviously sketchy. Apparently as many people in the Netherlands searched Google for 'Popcorn Time' as they did for well known lawful streaming services.[18]

In practice, a user will download the basic Popcorn application from a Popcorn website, in the same way as any other piece of software might be downloaded. The application provides a catalogue of available files, inbuilt BitTorrent capability and the ability to download materials. It appears that it is possible that the application can then be used without any further reference to the Popcorn website. But, and there is always a but, an application such as this

---

[16] [2015] EWHC 1082(Ch).
[17] para. 15.   [18] para. 23.

benefits enormously if its catalogue content can be updated to incorporate newly released materials. This is generally done. As the judgment notes:

> The content available using the Popcorn Time applications is constantly updated. That is because in addition to their links with peers and torrent catalogue sites, the Popcorn Time applications maintain links with a website which they use as a source of update information ('a SUI website'). That link is made so that the indexes held by the application are updated, so that new content is made available to users and so that the Popcorn Time application itself can be updated.[19]

If the updating facility on the SUI website was inextricably linked to the Popcorn website, it would have been difficult to distinguish Popcorn from other forms of file sharing technology that had previously been the subject of blocking orders from the courts. It was accepted before the court however that such a linkage could not always be established. An analogy might perhaps be drawn with the situation where the user of a word processing program downloads printer drivers from the website of the printer manufacturer. Responsibility for the drivers would be quite distinct from responsibility for the word processing application.

It is generally accepted that suppliers are not responsible for the use to which their products are put, at least in the situation where there is a strong likelihood that the use will be lawful. A word processor user may use the application to type out material in breach of copyright law, but it is inconceivable that the application provider would be held liable for this. Most applications are capable of being put to lawful or non-lawful purposes. The judge was rather skeptical regarding Popcorn type applications.

> It is manifest that the Popcorn Time application is used in order to watch pirated content on the internet and indeed it is also manifest that that is its purpose. No-one really uses Popcorn Time in order to watch lawfully available content. One can therefore entirely sympathise with the claimants in seeking to block its operation and use.[20]

Sympathy is one thing, application of legal requirements may be another. Blocking orders in the form of injunctions issued against ISPs require that 'actual knowledge' of infringing conduct be evidenced.[21] Most computer applications—as with other tools—can be used for lawful or for unlawful purposes. In most cases, it is unreasonable to hold a manufacturer liable for the use that may be made of a product. In copyright terms, as was stated:

> There are four matters which need to be established for the court to have jurisdiction . . . to make the (blocking) order sought: (1) that the ISPs are service providers, (2) that the users and/or operators of the target websites infringe copyright, (3) that users and/or the operators of the target websites use the services of the ISPs to do that, and (4) that the ISPs have actual knowledge of this.[22]

The first three points were considered easily proved. The last was critical. In itself, it contains a number of elements. In previous cases involving earlier forms of technology there had been a conclusion that the service provider had been so closely involved in the infringing conduct as to be taken as committing the tort of purporting to authorise infringing conduct. In the case of Popcorn technology, however, the conclusion was different:

> The difference with the Popcorn Time system is that now it is the application itself running on the user's computer which presents to the user catalogued and indexed connections to the sources of the copies. If a PTAS site is purely the source from which the Popcorn Time application software is downloaded and the application itself, once operational on the user's computer, never connects back to the PTAS site then can the reasoning employed in the earlier cases apply? I do not believe it can.

---

[19] para. 22.   [20] para. 24.   [21] Copyright, Designs and Patents Act 1988, s. 97A.   [22] para. 25.

Again, in some earlier case, the providers of the streaming software had themselves been taken to communicate copyright works to the public, thus effectively acting as a form of broadcaster. Again the degree of separation between the application provider and the end-user was such as to prevent any such finding:

> If a PTAS site is purely the source from which the Popcorn Time application software is downloaded and the application itself, once operational on the user's computer, never connects back to the PTAS site then can the reasoning employed in the earlier cases apply? I do not believe it can. I cannot see how the operator of the PTAS website commits an act of communicating copyright works to the public. The PTAS site simply does not communicate any copyright works to anybody. There is no transmission (or retransmission) of the copyright work at all.[23]

Although the role of SUI sites in updating lists of available files was more entwined with the activities of the end-user, even here the degree of linkage was not considered to be sufficient.

Ultimately, however, the claimants succeeded on a final ground of argument—albeit the one upon which they had placed most weight. The providers of the Popcorn application, it was ruled, acted as joint tortfeasors with the end-users. As was stated:

> The issue I have to decide is whether the suppliers of the Popcorn Time applications are jointly liable with the operators of the host websites. In my judgment they are. The Popcorn Time application is the key means which procures and induces the user to access the host website and therefore causes the infringing communications to occur. The suppliers of Popcorn Time plainly know and intend that to be the case. They provide the software and provide the information to keep the indexes up to date. I find that the suppliers of Popcorn Time have a common design with the operators of the host websites to secure the communication to the public of the claimants' protected works, thereby infringing copyright.[24]

Accordingly, an order was made requiring the defendant ISPs to use specified technological methods to block access by their customers to sites offering to supply the Popcorn application.

In some respects this decision confirms a judicial approach that has been developed in a significant number of earlier cases. It also demonstrates the difficulties in attempting to balance static legal principles with technology that is evolving at speed. Certainly blocking orders were made in the case but on more limited grounds than has been the case with previous judgments. The difference between lawful and unlawful conduct is becoming more blurred and it is not inconceivable that some well-worded disclaimers might serve to confer immunity on application providers in future cases.

Blocking orders and trade marks

The case of *Cartier and Ors v British Sky Broadcasting and Ors* raises a number of interesting issues concerned with blocking orders. In some respects this case follows the well-trodden copyright path. The principal claimants are a world-renowned producer of expensive watches whilst the respondents were acting in the context of their activities as ISPs. The claimants were concerned that a number of websites were offering counterfeit copies of their goods for sale in breach of their trade mark rights and asked the court to require that the respondents make use of technical measures to prevent their subscribers from accessing these sites. Such a course of action has been a reasonably prominent feature in the copyright field but this is the first case to be based on trade mark rights. It raises a number

---

[23] para. 38.   [24] para. 55.

of interesting issues both in respect of the application in itself and also in respect of the relationship between UK and European law in the aftermath of the 2016 referendum (Brexit). The case was initially dealt with in the Chancery Division of the High Court of England[25] whose decision was subsequently affirmed by the Court of Appeal.[26]

As stated in paragraph one of the High Court judgment:

> The Claimants (collectively, 'Richemont') are the owners of a large number of United Kingdom Registered Trade Marks for CARTIER, MONTBLANC, IWC and other brands ('the Trade Marks'). The Defendants ('Sky', 'BT', 'EE', 'TalkTalk' and 'Virgin', collectively 'the ISPs') are the five main retail internet service providers in the United Kingdom. Between them, they have a market share of some 95 per cent of UK broadband users. By this application Richemont seek orders requiring the ISPs to block, or at least impede, access by their respective subscribers to six websites which advertise and sell counterfeit goods ('the Target Websites').[27]

The Court of Appeal found that the right holders are entitled to blocking orders against intermediaries (here, the ISPs) also in cases of trade mark infringement. Further, the Court of Appeal ruled that the costs involved in blocking access should fall on the ISPs.

The initial High Court decision was handed down by Mr Justice Arnold. He identified a number of questions that were critical to the case of issuing a website blocking order:

- Did the court have the power (*jurisdiction*) to make a blocking order of the kind sought?
- If the court did have jurisdiction, what conditions would have to be satisfied in order to justify the making of an award?
- Were these conditions satisfied in the present case?
- Assuming the conditions were satisfied, would the making of a blocking order be an appropriate and proportionate response?

In part the issues relate to questions of domestic law but also, and likely to be very significant in the coming years, relate to the extent to which elements of EU law have become inextricably linked with those of domestic law.

As indicated above, for a number of years the English courts have issued orders requiring ISPs to apply technical measures in order to block access by their customers to websites containing copyright infringing material.[28] These cases have been brought under the authority of section 97A of the Copyright, Designs and Patents Act 1988, a provision that was introduced in the course of implementing the requirements of the European Directive on Copyright in the Information Society.[29] The Copyright Directive requires in Article 8 that:

> 3. Member States shall ensure that rightholders are in a position to apply for an injunction against intermediaries whose services are used by a third party to infringe a copyright or related right.

In implementing it, section 97A of the Copyright, Designs and Patents Act 1988 provides in part that:

> (1) The High Court (in Scotland, the Court of Session) shall have power to grant an injunction against a service provider, where that service provider has actual knowledge of another person using their service to infringe copyright.

---

[25] *Cartier and Ors v British Sky Broadcasting and Ors* [2014] EWHC 3354 (Ch). A further action ([2016] EWHC 339 (Ch)) was brought relating to a different range of websites but effectively this has been subsumed into the original action and will be governed by the decision of the Court of Appeal in that case.

[26] *Cartier and Ors v British Sky Broadcasting and Ors* [2016] EWCA Civ 658.

[27] *Cartier and Ors v British Sky Broadcasting and Ors* [2016] EWCA Civ 658 at para. 1.

[28] See, eg, *Twentieth Century Fox Film Corp v British Telecommunications plc* [2011] EWHC 1981 (Ch).

[29] Directive 2001/29/EC of 22 May 2001.

The present case was somewhat different. It was again concerned with a request from right owners that ISPs be required to block access to websites, but on this occasion the allegation was that the sites in question were offering counterfeit goods for sale in infringement of the claimants' trade mark rights. It marks the first occasion on which such a claim has been made in the United Kingdom.

Legal basis

The key question that had to be determined was what would be the legal basis for such a ruling. There is no equivalent in the United Kingdom's trade mark legislation to section 97A. The 2004 Directive[30] on the Enforcement of Intellectual Property Rights does however provide in Article 11 that Member States:

> shall ensure that, where a judicial decision is taken finding an infringement of an intellectual property right, the judicial authorities may issue against the infringer an injunction aimed at prohibiting the continuation of the infringement. Where provided for by national law, non-compliance with an injunction shall, where appropriate, be subject to a recurring penalty payment, with a view to ensuring compliance. Member States shall also ensure that rightholders are in a position to apply for an injunction against intermediaries whose services are used by a third party to infringe an intellectual property right, without prejudice to Article 8(3) of Directive 2001/29/EC.

Duration of injunctions

A crucial issue is whether such injunctions can be permanent or merely temporary in their nature? No steps were taken by the UK government specifically to implement the third sentence of Article 11 within a trade mark context on the basis that existing law was sufficient to ensure compliance. This approach was criticised by Mr Justice Arnold who commented in the High Court decision that its consultation exercise on how the Directive should be implemented was significantly flawed:

> [T]his is very confused, for a number of reasons. . . . the consultation paper states that the court is only able to issue an interim injunction against a person against whom a cause of action exists, but does not suggest that a copyright or trade mark owner would have a cause of action against an intermediary which was not itself infringing the relevant right. Thirdly, the consultation paper notes that Article 8(3) of the Information Society Directive was implemented by section 97A of the 1988 Act, but offers no explanation as to why, if section 97A was required in cases involving copyright and related rights, no similar provision is required in cases involving other intellectual property rights [at paragraph 118].

In the event, Justice Arnold based his decision very much on an analysis of the domestic legislation that preceded the Enforcement Directive. Section 37(1) of the Senior Courts Act 1981 provides that:

> The High Court may by order (whether interlocutory or final) grant an injunction . . . in all cases in which it appears to be just and convenient to do so.

This, he held, enabled him to award an injunction requiring the ISPs to seek to block access to the sites in question in accordance with what were considered to be established precepts of English law.

Such a response was, he held, a proportionate response to the risk of losses faced by the right holders and he granted the right holders the order that they sought, albeit with a sunset clause providing that it would expire after two years unless renewed by the court.

---

[30] Directive 2004/48/EC of 29 April 2004.

Cost issues

It is often said that money is the root of all evil, and issues who is to meet the costs associated with implementing blocking orders have featured prominently in much of the litigation and relate very much to the question of proportionality raised above. When orders have been made in respect of copyright infringement (under section 97A of the Copyright, Designs and Patents Act) the courts have tended to require that costs be met by the ISPs involved. This has largely been justified on pragmatic grounds based essentially on the fact that the blocking technology is essentially in place (it was originally developed to block access to pornographic websites) and the cost implications for the ISPs involved would be limited. As actions have proliferated and now expanded into the trade mark field, cost issues are becoming more significant.

Upholding the judgment of Mr Justice Arnold, Lord Justice Kitchen in the Court of Appeal ruled that the costs involved in blocking access should fall on the ISPs. Summarising the trial judge's findings in the following terms:

> First, rightholders had over the preceding three years used their resources to seek relief only against the most egregious infringers. Secondly, it was nevertheless manifest that granting website blocking orders in respect of infringements of trade marks would increase the costs burden on the ISPs. Thirdly, it was possible that a large number of applications for such orders would be made. In that regard, Richemont had identified nearly 240,000 potentially infringing websites of which 46,000 had been confirmed as infringing. Fourthly, the costs of preparing applications for website blocking orders and the costs of monitoring the effectiveness of such orders would impose a constraint upon the rightholders but it was difficult to predict how effective this would be. Fifthly, the implementation costs incurred by ISPs were presently small compared to the operating costs of the ISPs' internet access businesses, but were likely to increase. It was difficult to say by how much, however. Sixthly, the EU legislators had decided that it was economically more efficient to require intermediaries to take action to prevent infringements occurring using their services than it was to require rightholders to take action directly against infringers. Seventhly, the ISPs could either absorb the costs themselves or pass them on to their customers.

Lord Justice Kitchen endorsed the conclusion that had been reached.

Significantly, however, whilst agreeing that the blocking order should be made, Lord Justice Briggs who also heard the case on appeal dissented on the issue of costs. He noted that:

> So, I would have allowed this appeal to the extent of imposing upon the applicant for a trademark blocking order the specific cost incurred by the respondent ISP in complying with that order, but not the cost of designing and installing the software with which to do so whenever ordered. It is, according to the evidence, a modest cost but one which in principle the rightsholder ought to defray as the price of obtaining valuable injunctive relief for the better exploitation of its intellectual property. I consider that, while there may be exceptional cases justifying a different order, the judge was wrong in principle in concluding that the ISP ought usually to pay the costs of implementation.[31]

This is an issue that is likely to become of increasing importance in the years to come as the number of requests for the grant of blocking orders is likely to increase. In the present case it was indicated that some 239,000 websites had been identified as potentially infringing, with significant evidence of infringement already obtained in respect of 46,000 of these. It is easy to see how the cost implications of blocking orders could start to escalate. At the moment, as was stated in the judgments, actions have tended to be raised

---

[31] para. 211.

only in respect of websites that operate in flagrant breach of IP law. Many rather more reputable sites will also host infringing materials—reference might be made to the case of *L'Oreal v eBay*.[32]

Norwich Pharmacal orders and threats of litigation

Enforcement measures have been a source of considerable controversy in the intellectual property field. As discussed elsewhere, one of the features of the Internet is that it gives individuals access to technology to make copies of a work on a large scale. The Copyright, Designs and Patents Act 1988 (as amended by the Copyright and Related Rights Regulations 2003)[33] moves away from the traditional legislative approach which limited criminal liability to instances where copyright infringement was carried out with a view to commercial gain to focus on the impact that conduct has on the right owner. Section 107 provides:

> A person who infringes copyright in a work by communicating the work to the public—
>
> (a) in the course of a business, or
>
> (b) otherwise than in the course of a business to such an extent as to affect prejudicially the owner of the copyright,
>
> commits an offence if he knows or has reason to believe that, by doing so, he is infringing copyright in that work.

In addition to facing prosecution under copyright legislation (with a maximum penalty of three months' imprisonment) there have been a number of high-profile prosecutions against the administrators of alleged file-sharing websites on a charge of conspiracy (with other users of the site) to defraud (copyright owners). In one case heard at Newcastle Crown Court, the administrator of a file-sharing website that had reportedly received an income of £300,000 per annum from advertising was sentenced to a four-year term of imprisonment. As a report[34] on the case indicates:

> At its peak the site attracted more than 400,000 visitors a day and was ranked as one of the top 500 websites in the world.

Beyond those who facilitate copying on a large scale there is no doubt that an individual who makes a single infringing copy of a work will be liable to an action for damages. There has been some increased emphasis on such activities. The case of *Media CAT v Adams and Ors*[35] provides an example of conduct that appears to have occurred in a number of countries. In this case, lawyers claiming to act on behalf of copyright societies had obtained (largely through the use of *Norwich Pharmacal* orders) lists of names and addresses of thousands of individuals who had been allocated IP addresses that were suspected of having been used to commit copyright infringement—in the particular case by downloading copies of pornographic movies. Letters were sent to tens of thousands of individuals threatening to commence legal proceedings for infringement of copyright unless a specified sum (£495) was offered by way of settlement.

The approach of seeking to act against persons alleged to have downloaded pornographic material appears to have been a common feature of these campaigns on an international basis—perhaps relying on an embarrassment factor to persuade recipients of the letters to make payment. The procedural aspects of the case were complex and involved a number

---

[32] [2009] EWHC 1094 (Ch).   [33] SI 2003/2498.

[34] <http://www.out-law.com/en/articles/2012/august/website-operator-jailed-for-four-years-for-conspiring-to-defraud-copyright-owners/>.

[35] [2011] EWPCC 6.

of hearings and judgments. Essentially when some individuals rejected the 'offer' and legal proceedings were initiated the claimants faced with extensive and generally adverse publicity sought to discontinue proceedings. This led to Mr Justice Birss sitting in the Patents County Court to delve deeply into the background to the litigation. The end result was that the cases were dropped, the law firm involved became bankrupt, and the solicitor with prime responsibility was struck off the register of solicitors.

It might be a brave claimant who will try to pursue similar tactics in the future. One of the major issues debated concerned the difficulty in identifying with any degree of certainly the particular individual responsible for online conduct. This will be considered in more detail later, but with households having multiple devices connected to the Internet and the near ubiquitous presence of wireless connections outside a work environment it can be very difficult to establish with any degree of precision which person in a multi-occupancy household engaged in any particular form of conduct.

Conclusions

Copyright was born in turbulent times, when the invention of the printing press served as a catalyst for radical political and religious reforms. Although the nature of the controversies may have changed, with disputes predominantly between copyright owners and users, the role of the state as an enforcement agency through the application of criminal law sanctions remains significant and, certainly, the scope and extent of copyright protection and enforcement remain matters of considerable controversy.

In general, it may be stated that the approach in the Statute of Anne 1709 is more consistent with the attempt to balance competing interests rather than to confer exclusive rights. It seeks specifically to promote learning. Over the centuries, the range of works protected by copyright has expanded steadily, as has the protection afforded to copyright owners and the extent of their remedies. Less and less emphasis is placed on the educative goals of the system or on the rights of those who seek to use the protected works.

Whilst the basic notion that a work should not be copied for commercial gain remains valid, the application of copyright law is hindered by the fact that digital technology operates in a different manner than its analogue equivalent. Although one motive behind statutes such as the United States Digital Millennium Copyright Act and the Directive on Copyright in the Information Society[36] is to confer a measure of legal immunity on users and ISPs, it is difficult to see why a user's freedom to act in a reasonable manner should depend upon exceptional provisions.

The problem may not be one only for users. Another aspect of digital technology is that it puts extensive copying facilities in the hands of private individuals. The existence of systems such as Napster and MP3 provides eloquent testimony to this. In the Council of Europe's Cybercrime Convention, when providing for the imposition of criminal sanctions for various forms of copyright infringement, the instrument eschews the traditional formula that copying take place for commercial purposes with the requirement that copying take place on a commercial scale. This undoubtedly reflects the fact that a single individual with an Internet connection can, without seeking to secure any direct financial gain, cause significant loss to copyright owners.

Whilst there will always be those users who wish to obtain something for nothing, a perception of imbalance between the rights afforded to producers and users can only encourage disregard of the law. It may be that just as software companies have reduced levels of piracy

---

[36] Directive 2001/29/EC.

in part through offering added value in the form of upgrades and customer support services to legitimate users of software packages, so the wider information industries might have to make use of similar techniques. The purchaser of a music CD might, for example, qualify for reduced price admission or preferential access to concerts performed by the artist(s) involved.

At a more legalistic level, in the English case of *R v Gold*,[37] the House of Lords had to consider the question of whether the transitory holding of data in part of the memory of a computer system satisfied a requirement that data be 'recorded or stored'. Holding that this was not the case, the court ruled that the process required 'a degree of continuance'. It may be that the implementation of a similar approach could resolve at least some of the issues arising in respect of digital information. In general terms, there needs to be recognition that whilst an author or other inventor may choose to keep a work out of the public domain, once the decision has been taken to make it available, rights have to be balanced against those of other parties, especially those who invest time or money in order to use the work. As is often noted in the context of human rights law, rights are accompanied by responsibilities. It is difficult either in law or in practice to see that these are currently in balance in the intellectual property field.

Unlike many European legal systems, English law has historically been reluctant to confer legitimacy on the reproduction of copyright protected materials for private purposes. In the digital era, this issue has assumed considerable significance. Many users will own a plethora of devices capable of using copyright materials. A music file may be played on an in house music system, a car system, a laptop computer, and a smartphone. The list of devices could doubtless be extended. Although a user's perception may not always be legally accurate, there is undoubted strength in the argument that if an item has been lawfully acquired, it should be capable of being lawfully used in whatever manner the customer might think fit.

Acting in large part on the basis of the Hargreaves Report on the Intellectual Property System, the decision was taken by the government to liberalise the law relating to private copying. The Copyright and Rights in Performance (Personal Copies for Private Use) Regulations 2014[38] were made on 26 August 2014 and came into force on 1 October 2014. The Regulations introduced a new section 28B to the Copyright, Designs and Patents Act 1988. This provides that:

(1) The making of a copy of a work, other than a computer program, by an individual does not infringe copyright in the work provided that the copy—

    (a)   is a copy of—

        (i)   the individual's own copy of the work, or

        (ii) a personal copy of the work made by the individual,

    (b)   is made for the individual's private use, and

    (c)   is made for ends which are neither directly nor indirectly commercial.

Directive 2001/29 on the harmonisation of certain aspects of copyright and related rights in the information society[39] provides the legislative basis for the legitimacy of private copying. It provides, however, private copying may be legitimised only:

    (b)   in respect of reproductions on any medium made by a natural person for private use and for ends that are neither directly nor indirectly commercial, on condition that the rightholders receive fair compensation.[40]

Recital 35 to the Directive elaborates:

In certain cases of exceptions or limitations, rightholders should receive fair compensation to compensate them adequately for the use made of their protected works or other

---

[37] [1988] 1 AC 1063.   [38] SI 2014/2361.   [39] OJ 2001, L167/10.   [40] Art. 5.

subject-matter. When determining the form, detailed arrangements and possible level of such fair compensation, account should be taken of the particular circumstances of each case. When evaluating these circumstances, a valuable criterion would be the possible harm to the rightholders resulting from the act in question. In cases where rightholders have already received payment in some other form, for instance as part of a licence fee, no specific or separate payment may be due. The level of fair compensation should take full account of the degree of use of technological protection measures referred to in this Directive. In certain situations where the prejudice to the rightholder would be minimal, no obligation for payment may arise.

The UK Regulations made no provision for compensation to right holders. Following the production of a regulatory impact assessment, based in large part on research carried out by the Intellectual Property Office, the government took the view that allowing private copying without any arrangements for compensation would cause minimal loss to right holders. A key rationale was the belief that given the existing scale of private copying, right holders had factored, or 'priced in', costs when determining the price at which copies would be sold. This formed the basis for what proved to be a successful legal challenge.

The court ruled that the government's rationale for introducing the Regulations was fundamentally flawed. The EU legislation under which it was introduced provided that a no-compensation regime would be lawful only if there was evidence to support the view that it would not result in more than minimal losses to right holders. As was stated:

> In the present case the legal issue is whether pricing-in will lead to 'minimal or zero' harm since if it does not then, in law, a compensation scheme *must* in law be introduced. The legal issue guides the exercise: The evidence accepted by the Secretary of State must be sufficient to enable a reasonable inference to be drawn from it that this *de minimis* threshold has been met.[41]

After analysing the evidence forming the basis for the Secretary of State's conclusion that the new provision would result in zero or minimal harm, the court concluded that this did not support the inference that he had made. It was noted that no attempt had been made to determine what quantitative or qualitative thresholds might apply in defining levels of loss that could be classed as *de minimis*. On this basis the conclusion was that the legal justification for the regulations had not been established and they would accordingly be declared null and void.

In some respects the impact of the decision may be limited. It was accepted by all parties in the action that it is virtually impossible to prevent private copying of protected materials. Increasingly, the focus of actions by right holders is targeted more at relatively high profile intermediaries such as ISPs with the courts being asked to order them to take steps to prevent customers accessing sites associated with copyright infringement. It is possible also that the government may seek to repeat its evidence gathering and assessment exercise to better equip it to make a reasoned determination whether the reintroduction of the measure would cause minimal economic harm to right holders. The defects identified in the judgment are susceptible of being remedied. It is possible also that, following the model of some other Member States, a system of compensation might be provided to right holders. For the moment, however, the United Kingdom remains in the situation where there is a legal prohibition against private copying which is almost universally accepted to be unenforceable.

---

[41] para. 237.

18

Protection of databases

INTRODUCTION

UK law has long protected compilations of information under copyright law, with very (very) limited exceptions.[1] Most other jurisdictions have adopted a more restrictive policy although where effort and money has been expended in producing compilations of information such as directories or catalogues, protection may well be offered under the law of unfair competition. Rather like privacy, this is not a concept that is recognised as such in the United Kingdom although as with privacy, similar results may be obtained through the operation of a number of other legal principles.

The 1980s and 1990s saw the beginnings of markets in electronic databases. The capability of computers to store and process large amounts of data opened up new commercial markets. The United States was quick to exploit these possibilities and companies based there acquired a major share of the global database market.

Within Europe a perceived discrepancy in the legal protection was afforded to databases across the Member States. As the Commission noted:

> While droit d'auteur Member States protected only 'original' databases that required an element of 'intellectual creation', the common law Member States also protected 'non-original' databases involving considerable skill, labour or judgment in gathering together and/or checking a compilation ('sweat of the brow' copyright).
>
> In practice, the higher standard of 'originality' that applied in droit d'auteur countries had the effect of protecting fewer databases by copyright (protection was limited to so called 'original' databases).[2]

The solution adopted took the form of the EC Directive of 11 March 1996 on The Legal Protection of Databases.[3] This is implemented in the United Kingdom by the Copyright and Rights in Databases Regulations 1997.[4]

The Database Directive creates a new form of intellectual property right—the database right. Its scope and extent will be considered in this chapter but at the outset a note of scepticism may be sounded. Both before and after the implementation of the Directive, United Kingdom-based companies have consistently produced more databases than any other Member State (around double the number produced by the next largest country, Germany). It is almost certainly the case that linguistic issues are a greater factor in market access and success than legal

---

[1] In the case of *Exxon Corpn v Exxon Insurance Consultants International Ltd* [1982] Ch. 119 the High Court held that the single word 'Exxon' was not protected by copyright. This is perhaps the only case in which protection has been denied. In the Scottish case of *Shetland Times Ltd v Jonathan Wills and Anor* (1997) FSR the court had no difficulty in accepting that the headlines of newspaper stories were protected by copyright.

[2] First evaluation of Directive 96/9/EC on the legal protection of databases. Available from <http://ec.europa.eu/internal_market/copyright/docs/databases/evaluation_report_en.pdf>.

[3] Directive 96/9/EC, OJ 1996 L 77/20 (the Database Directive).

[4] SI 1997/3032.

factors. More generally, as the Commission noted in 2005, the concept of a *sui generis* database right (which is not found in any other major country) may have proved counter-productive:

> According to the Gale Directory of Databases, the number of EU-based database 'entries' was 3095 in 2004 as compared to 3092 in 1998 when the first Member States had implemented the 'sui generis' protection into national laws.
>
> It is noteworthy that the number of database 'entries' dropped just as most of the EU-15 had implemented the Directive into national laws in 2001. In 2001, there were 4085 EU-based 'entries' while in 2004 there were only 3095.[5]

Not the most impressive track record and there is no later evidence of improvement.

What is a database?

The concept of a database is one which does not receive specific mention in the United Kingdom's copyright legislation. The term tends to be used with specific reference to computers; the *Concise Oxford Dictionary* defines it as a '[l]arge body of information stored in a computer which can process it and from which particular bits of information can be retrieved as required'. The initial draft of the EC's Database Directive adopted a similar approach, limiting its application to:

> a collection of work or materials arranged, stored and accessed by electronic means, and the electronic materials necessary for the operation of the data base such as its thesaurus, index or system for obtaining and presenting information.[6]

Although there might be pragmatic reasons for limiting the scope of legislation, there is no reason in principle why more traditional forms of data storage, such as a card-index file, should not also be classed as a database. In the final version of the Database Directive,[7] and in the Copyright and Rights in Databases Regulations 1997, which implement the provisions of the Directive for the United Kingdom, a broader definition applies, referring to:

> a collection of independent works, data or other materials which:
>
> (a) are arranged in a systematic or methodical way; and
>
> (b) are individually accessible by electronic or other means.[8]

The Preamble to the Database Directive expands on this definition somewhat, stating that:

> Whereas the term 'database' should be understood to include literary, artistic, musical or other collections of works or collections of other material such as texts, sound, images, numbers, facts, and data; whereas it should cover collections of independent works, data or other materials which are systematically or methodically arranged and can be individually accessed; whereas this means that a recording or an audio-visual, cinematographic, literary or musical work as such does not fall within the scope of this Directive.[9]

Examples of databases

Starting with non-automated systems, a paper telephone directory can be classed as a database. Here, data in the form of names, addresses, and telephone numbers are arranged in alphabetical order, and may be retrieved by users through opening the directory at the

---

[5] First evaluation of Directive 96/9/EC on the legal protection of databases.
[6] COM (92) 393 final, Art. 1.   [7] Directive 96/9/EC.
[8] SI 1997/3032, Reg. 3.   [9] Directive 96/9/EC, Recital 17.

appropriate page. Card-index systems, such as those catalogue systems which used to occupy significant areas of floor space within libraries, also function in a similar manner. On the basis of the definition cited earlier, one might even class the contents of the library itself as a database.

With the dawning of the digital revolution and the ability to record and store any form of information in electronic format, the range and commercial value of databases has increased dramatically. Introducing the proposed regulations in Parliament, the Minister of State stated that:

> The database sector is a major United Kingdom industry. Estimates of the size of the UK database market range up to £10 billion but even that may be an underestimate. It is growing at more than 11% a year. About 350 firms are believed to be active in the sector, 30 of which are large suppliers and the rest small and medium-sized enterprises. UK suppliers have a share of the wider European Union market which has been put at more than 50%.[10]

Many electronic databases are accessible on an online basis. Most lawyers will, for example, be familiar with the 'Lexis' database. Located in Dayton, Ohio, this represents the world's largest collection of case law and statutory material. The parallel 'Nexis' service provides access to electronic copies of the contents of a vast range of newspapers and journals. Also on the market is a wide range of CDs. Such capacity devices typically have a storage capacity of around 650MB of data. A 500-page book would occupy somewhere in the region of 2.5MB. A single CD could, therefore, contain the text of some 300 volumes, although this figure would drop if pictures and illustrations were to be embedded in the text.

Databases and new technology

Traditionally, one of the basic requirements for a functional database has been that its contents are stored in accordance with a predetermined structure. A similar requirement applies to many automated databases, where data is stored in predetermined fields. With developments in retrieval software and what are referred to as relational databases, it is less and less necessary for information to be stored in accordance with a predetermined structure. In general, the tendency is to allow users maximum flexibility in using a database rather than requiring searches to be formulated in accordance with predetermined structures. Once again, the telephone directory may provide an apposite example. With a paper directory, a user can search effectively only by means of the structure devised by the publisher—effectively in alphabetical order by reference to subscribers' surnames. CD directories typically allow searches by reference to any item of data—or to a combination of items. Reverse searching is a popular feature which allows names to be identified from telephone numbers or a listing produced of all subscribers resident in a particular street.[11]

Where a database comprises an amalgam of data and retrieval software, it will be necessary for the software to compile indexes of words used in the data, such indexes being used in subsequent acts of retrieval. Such a system is likely to come within the definition. More problematic issues will arise where the retrieval software is separate from the data being searched. The *www*, for example, consists of tens of millions of individual items of data controlled by millions of users. It is difficult to think of a less structured network than the *www*, yet search engines such as Google provide increasingly sophisticated searching facilities. Whilst it must be likely that many items on the *www* will qualify for copyright

---

[10] Fourth Standing Committee on Delegated Legislation, 3 December 1997.

[11] See, eg, BT's online directory at <http://www.bt.com/phonenetuk/> and the more extensive service at <http://www.192.com/>.

protection in their own right, others may not, for example, law reports or copies of statutes from countries which regard such materials as being in the public domain. It may be that the list of materials identified by a search engine as meeting the user's request will itself constitute a database. In this instance, there might be a further issue, discussed later—who is to be considered owner of any resulting database right?

Traditional forms of protection for databases

The rationale behind the Database Directive lies in the belief that 'databases are at present not sufficiently protected in all Member States by existing legislation'.[12] This may certainly have been the case in some other Member States, notably Germany, which have required strict qualitative criteria for the award of copyright, but it is less applicable in a UK context. The basis for the legal protection of databases lies in the copyright system. As we have seen, section 3 of the Copyright, Designs and Patents Act 1988 defines a literary work so as to include 'a table or compilation'. Although there is little precedent on the point, there seems little doubt that a database would fall within the latter category.

Copyright in respect of the contents of a database may arise in two ways. First of all, the individual pieces of work located therein may qualify for copyright protection in their own right. An example might be of a database consisting of a collection of poems. Each poem, it may be assumed, will be protected by copyright. Additionally, the database may qualify for protection in its own right, a matter which may acquire particular importance if portions of the subject material are not so protected, for example, because the author has been dead for more than seventy years or, in the case of collections of factual material, because the nature of the data excludes copyright protection. The names of individual companies, for example, will be unlikely to be protected by copyright, but a compilation such as the FTSE 100 will enjoy protection as a compilation. Again, as was at issue in the case of *Ladbroke (Football) Ltd v William Hill (Football) Ltd*,[13] although the names of individual football teams will not be protected by copyright, a compiled fixture list will be eligible for protection.

Discounting the issue of whether the contents of a database might qualify for protection in their own right, the issue arises whether the degree of effort which accompanies the compilation of a database is sufficient to qualify for such a grant? Traditionally, a major element of the task facing the compiler of a database has been to determine the order in which the material is to appear and subsequently give effect to this concept. Using modern technology, text can be scanned and converted into digital format. Whereas traditional compilations such as directories will require to be carefully structured to make it easy for users to find particular items of information, the utilisation of appropriate software will mean that the entire contents of a database may be scanned with reference to a particular word or phrase. In such a case, there is less need for the database compiler to expend effort in arranging the layout of the database.

It is also one of the features of many computerised services that they seek to take advantage of the processing and storage capabilities of computers in order to present a comprehensive collection of materials. The goal of a legal database such as Lexis is to provide a transcript of every High Court decision delivered in the English courts. Similarly, the website of the Scottish Courts Administration[14] provides the text of every High Court and Court of Session judgment. This is to be contrasted with the more traditional law reports, which contain only a comparatively small number of decisions, and where some skill and

---

[12] Recital 1.
[13] [1964] 1 WLR 273.
[14] <http://www.scotcourts.gov.uk/>.

labour will be expended by the publishers to determine which cases are of sufficient importance to warrant a place in a particular volume.

The 'sweat of the brow' doctrine

In the event that a database seeks to provide a comprehensive coverage of its chosen subject area, it may be difficult to evidence any originality in the selection process. It is here that a significant divergence exists between the UK approach and that adopted in almost every other copyright system. As has been stated, the UK system imposes minimal qualitative requirements relating to originality. In the case of a compilation, the traditional justification for extending protection has been the effort that has gone into selecting the works to be incorporated therein—what has been referred to in the United States as the 'sweat of the brow' doctrine. This approach is well illustrated in the case of *Waterlow Publishers v Rose*.[15] The plaintiff, under contract to the Law Society, had published listings, arranged geographically, of English solicitors and barristers in a publication known as the *Solicitors' Diary and Directory*. A listing of all solicitors was supplied to the plaintiff by the Law Society, and this was used to send out forms seeking further information about areas of specific expertise.

Prior to 1984, a company owned by the defendant had been contracted to print copies of the directory. Following a takeover of the plaintiff, this work was transferred to another firm. The defendant thereupon determined to publish a similar work, the *Lawyers' Diary*, which would compete with the plaintiff's publication. The defendant's manner of work was to commence with the *Solicitors' Diary*, which constituted the only comprehensive public listing of the names and addresses of solicitors. A copy of the entry in the *Solicitors' Diary* would be sent out to the individuals concerned and they would be asked to reply, either confirming the accuracy of the information or making any changes that were felt desirable. The plaintiff alleged that this method of work meant that the resultant publication infringed its copyright.

In deciding the case, the court had to consider, first, the question of whether copyright subsisted in the compilation of names, addresses, and other information published in the *Solicitors' Diary* and, secondly, whether the defendant's conduct constituted infringement. Although it was recognised that the nature of compilations was such that it might be difficult to identify a single person as author, the fact that the plaintiff was identified as publisher established a presumption that copyright was owned by it. Regarding the issue of infringement, the Court of Appeal held that:

> Mr Rose argued that he only used the existing directory to get in touch with the solicitors and that his work was then based upon the forms returned to him . . . There were something like 50,000 forms and the names and addresses to which they were sent were all obtained from the Solicitors' Diary 1984 . . . In my judgement that goes beyond lawful use of an existing publication and amounted to an infringement of the plaintiff's copyright.[16]

The effect of this and of similar decisions is that extensive copyright protection is afforded to databases compiled in the United Kingdom. A similar approach had been followed in the United States, until the landmark Supreme Court case of *Feist Publications Inc v Rural Telephone Service Co Inc*[17] signalled a significant change of direction.

The case concerned the extent of copyright protection in a telephone directory. The respondent, Rural, was a telephone service provider which was required under the terms of its operating licence to publish a directory of its subscribers. A substantial number of similar service providers operated in the United States, each publishing directories covering a small

[15] [1995] FSR 207.
[16] *Waterlow Publishers v Rose* [1995] FSR 207 at 221.
[17] 111 S Ct 1282 (1991).

geographical area. The appellant, Feist, was a publishing company which specialised in publishing directories which covered a wider geographical area than that of a typical small-scale provider such as Rural. It entered into negotiations seeking licences to publish from eleven different telephone utilities. Only Rural refused permission.

Despite Rural's refusal, Feist went ahead with the publication, extracting the necessary information from Rural's directory. Although it added some items of information and attempted to verify other items independently, 1,309 entries in the Feist directory were identical to their Rural counterparts. More damningly, four of these were fictitious entries inserted by Rural in order to provide a means of detecting unauthorised copying.

Rural's action alleging copyright infringement succeeded before the lower courts. The Supreme Court took a different view.[18] Infringement, it was held, could occur only when what was copied was protected under the copyright regime. Although the level of original-ity required as the basis for protection was low, there was 'a narrow category of works in which the creative spark is utterly lacking or so trivial as to be virtually non-existent'. Rural's telephone directory, it was held, fell into this category. Its selection of listing 'could not be more obvious'. Rural, it was held, 'expended sufficient effort to make the . . . directory use-ful, but insufficient creativity to make it original'.

The decision in *Feist* produced considerable comment and controversy within the United States and prompted a significant tightening up of the criteria for the award of copyright generally. Certain aspects of the court's reasoning are potentially significant for the UK system. In particular, the court explicitly rejected the notion that the expenditure of effort, the 'sweat of the brow', could suffice for the grant of copyright. Even so, the court makes it clear that only a modicum of creativity is required. Although copyright does not subsist in an alphabetical listing of subscribers, subsequent cases have held that 'yellow pages'-type listings, where subscribers are grouped according to the nature of their business or profes-sion, will attract protection.

A further illustration of the new US approach can be found in the case of *ProCD v Zeidenberg*.[19] As was stated in the case report:

> Plaintiff spent millions of dollars creating a comprehensive, national directory of residential and business listings. Plaintiff compiled over 95,000,000 residential and commercial list-ings from approximately 3,000 publicly available telephone books. The listings include full names, street addresses, telephone numbers, zip codes and industry or 'SIC' codes where appropriate. Plaintiff sells these listings on CD-ROM discs under the trademark 'Select Phone TM', as well as under other trade names and trademarks.[20]

The plaintiff's pricing strategy was to sell copies of the CD at a low price for consumer use, but to levy higher rates for those seeking to make commercial use of the product. The defendant purchased a copy of the consumer CD, which retailed for less than $100. Using its own retrieval software, it placed a copy of the plaintiff's listings on an Internet site, from where it allowed users to extract up to 1,000 listings free of charge. More extensive access, typically for commercial purposes, could be obtained at a cost less than that charged by the plaintiff. The site was soon attracting up to 20,000 visitors a day and, fearing significant adverse effects on sales of its CD, the plaintiff sought an injunction preventing its continued operation. Although at first instance the injunction was refused, the Court of Appeals even-tually found in favour of the plaintiff on the ground that the defendant was bound by the terms of a licence accompanying the CD which prohibited its use for commercial purposes; it was common ground that no copyright subsisted in the data itself.

---

[18] *Feist Publications Inc v Rural Telephone Service Co Inc* 111 S Ct 1282 (1991).
[19] 86 F 3d 1447 (1996).
[20] 86 F 3d 1447 (1996) at 1447.

More recently, litigation was initiated by the legal database supplier, Lexis, against an Internet-based company, Jurisline. In the United States, Lexis markets compilations of law reports in CD format. Jurisline admitted copying the contents of these CDs and placing the material on a website. Access to the site is free of charge, with the intention being that the site's costs will be met by advertising. As in the *ProCD* case,[21] the CDs in question are supplied subject to the terms of a licence which restricts the use to which the materials may be put. It appears, however, that the terms of the licence are not made accessible to the user until after the CD is purchased. An additional argument advanced on behalf of Jurisline is to the effect that Law Reports in the United States are regarded as being in the public domain so that:

> the limitations built into Lexis' licensing agreement attempt to control an 'essential facility' in violation of federal antitrust law.
>
> Lexis may not use a contract to take public domain material such as court opinions—which are explicitly not covered by the federal copyright law—and create a level of protection that is tantamount to a federal copyright.[22]

The litigation was settled prior to trial but the case does serve to indicate the complexity of some of the issues involved. Whilst there is little scope for originality in the production of a comprehensive collection of law reports, denial of protection for the efforts and investment required to gather the material together might dissuade commercial publishers from making the initial effort. Such a decision would deny copyists their raw material, but would also produce the same effect for the public.

As indicated in *ProCD*,[23] one of the consequences of the *Feist*[24] decision has been the emergence of a new market in the United States for CD and Internet-based compilations of telephone directories. Selling for a few dollars, these will contain hundreds of millions of names and numbers, often providing additional facilities such as a reverse-search option allowing a person's address to be identified from a telephone number. In the United Kingdom, BT has continued to assert copyright in telephone directories and has threatened copyright actions against parties planning to introduce competing products. This situation has now changed, not through the operation of copyright law but as a result of the actions of the Director General of Telecommunications, who inserted a clause in BT's licence requiring it to make directory information available to third parties.

A major goal of the Database Directive[25] is to eliminate obstacles to the creation of a single market by harmonising the level of protection afforded to databases. Although not explicitly stated in the Preamble, there was undoubtedly the feeling that the United Kingdom's 50 per cent share of the EU database market was due in part to the fact that strong legal protection provided an incentive for database producers to locate their businesses in the United Kingdom. An alternative explanation might refer to the advantages of working in the English language and the larger market available to such databases.

The database regime

The provisions of the Database Directive can be grouped into three categories. First, it makes provision regarding the application of copyright to the contents of databases. Secondly, it provides for the extent of and exceptions to such copyrights. Finally, a new *sui generis* right is established to benefit some databases that are excluded from the copyright regime.

---

[21] *ProCD v Zeidenberg*, 86 F 3d 1447 (1996).
[22] Cited in D. Wise, 'Lexis Battles Web Upstart', *New York Law Journal*, 8 February 2000.
[23] 86 F 3d 1447 (1996).   [24] 111 S Ct 1282 (1991).   [25] Directive 96/9/EC.

Copyright and databases

Article 1 of the Database Directive[26] provides that:

> databases which, by reason of the selection or arrangement of their contents, constitute the author's own intellectual creation shall be protected as such by copyright.

The key phrase in this provision refers to work being 'the author's own intellectual creation'. This term is not defined further. In the implementing UK Regulations, it is provided that:

> For the purposes of this Part, a literary work consisting of a database is original if, and only if, by reason of the selection or arrangements of the contents of the database the database constitutes the author's own intellectual creation.[27]

The formula that work will be protected when it is the author's 'own intellectual creation' is also used in the EC Directive on the Legal Protection of Computer Programs,[28] which provides that these are to be protected as literary works. When the Directive was implemented into UK law, this phrase was not included. Introducing the Regulations in Parliament, however, the Minister of State commented that:

> Some people felt that no amendment of the [Copyright, Designs and Patents Act 1988] was needed to introduce the test and that the current test for the originality of literary works was enough.
>
> The government do not share that view. The Directive is clear. It requires copyright protection for databases 'which by reason of selection or arrangement of their contents, constitute the author's own intellectual creations'.
>
> This is intended to exclude so-called sweat of the brow databases—that is, ones that involve time, money or effort but no intellectual creation, such as the white pages telephone directory.[29]

Assuming this view is correct, it gives rise to the suggestion that the United Kingdom has failed to implement the Database Directive[30] adequately. If the view is incorrect, the effect of the Regulations has been to introduce unnecessary complexity into copyright law. Prior to implementation of the Directive, section 3(1) of the Copyright, Designs and Patents Act 1988 provided that the term 'literary work' was to encompass:

> any work, other than a dramatic or musical work, which is written, spoken or sung, and accordingly includes:
>
> (a) a table or compilation;
>
> (b) a computer program; and
>
> (c) preparatory design material for a computer program.[31]

This is now amended to read:

> any work, other than a dramatic or musical work, which is written, spoken or sung, and accordingly includes:
>
> (a) a table or compilation other than a database;
>
> (b) a computer program;

---

[26] Directive 96/9/EC.

[27] SI 1997/3032, Reg. 6 introducing a new s. 3A(2) into the Copyright, Designs and Patents Act 1988.

[28] Directive 91/250/EC, OJ 1991 L122/42 (the Software Protection Directive).

[29] Fourth Standing Committee on Delegated Legislation, 3 December 1997.

[30] Directive 96/9/EC.

[31] s. 3, as amended by the Copyright (Computer Programs) Regulations 1992, SI 1992/3233.

(c) preparatory design material for a computer program; and

(d) a database.[32]

For the purposes of this Part of the Act, a literary work consisting of a database is original if, and only if, by reason of the selection or arrangements of the contents of the database the database constitutes the author's own intellectual creation.[33]

Given that databases were hitherto regarded as a form of compilation, this approach might not be considered entirely satisfactory, and it is unclear where the division between the two categories lies. The Preamble to the Database Directive recites that:

> as a rule, the compilation of several recordings of musical performances on a CD does not come within the scope of this Directive, both because as a compilation, it does not meet the requirements for copyright protection and because it does not represent a substantial enough investment to be eligible under the *sui generis* right.[34]

Under previous UK law, there is little doubt that such a work would benefit from protection as a compilation. The question discussed later in this chapter is whether implementation of the Directive will alter this situation.

Licensing and databases

In the first draft of the Database Directive,[35] provision was made for database owners to be required to grant licences to users in certain circumstances:

> If the works or materials contained in a database which is made publicly available cannot be independently created, collected or obtained from any other source, the right to extract and re-utilize, in whole or substantial part, works or materials from that database for commercial purposes shall be licensed on fair and non-discriminatory terms.[36]

It was also provided that licences should require to be issued:

> if the database is made publicly available by a public body which is either established to assemble or disclose information pursuant to legislation or is under a general duty to do so.[37]

At least in respect of the first category, compulsory licences would only be available in very limited circumstances. It might be commented, in particular, that in most cases where only one party could obtain data, this might fall into the category of confidential information or be regarded as a trade secret, and would certainly not be made available to the public. In the event, the proposal was dropped following objections from Parliament, although it is provided that the issue is to be kept under review by the Commission, which had to report to the Council and Parliament within the first three years of the Database Directive's[38] operation, indicating whether the operation of the new regime:

> has led to abuse of a dominant position or other interference with free competition which would justify appropriate measures being taken including the establishment of non-voluntary licensing arrangements.[39]

Extensive provisions are made in the Copyright, Designs and Patents Act 1988[40] for the handling of licensing agreements between copyright owners and those wishing to make use of their materials. The Copyright Tribunal is established to determine disputes as to the

---

[32] Copyright, Designs and Patents Act 1988, s. 3(1).

[33] SI 1997/3032, Reg. 6, introducing a new s. 3A into the Copyright, Designs and Patents Act 1988.

[34] Directive 96/9/EC, Recital 19.   [35] Directive 96/9/EC.

[36] COM (92) 393 final, Art. 8(1).   [37] Art. 8(2).   [38] Directive 96/9/EC.

[39] COM (92) 393 final, Art. 16(3).   [40] See Chs. VII and VIII.

nature and extent of such schemes. The Regulations extend the scope of the statutory provisions and of the Tribunal's jurisdiction to matters relating to database licences.[41]

Other copyright changes

A number of other changes were made to the provisions of the Copyright, Designs and Patents Act 1988. In order to implement the provisions of the Software Protection Directive,[42] amendments were made by the Copyright (Computer Programs) Regulations 1992,[43] which had the effect of allowing the lawful user of a program to perform acts which might otherwise be restricted by copyright. In particular, this would sanction such copying of the program as was necessary for its use. Similar considerations will apply with electronic databases (whether online or held on disk) and the regulations add equivalent authorising provisions to the 1988 Act. Any attempt contractually to restrict or exclude the operation of these rights is now declared void.[44]

The database right

Implementation of the Database Directive[45] will have the effect of removing the protection of copyright from certain databases. Balancing this, a new database right is created which will arise when:

> there has been a substantial investment in obtaining, verifying or presenting the contents of the database.[46]

The maker of the database will be the first owner of the database right except in the case where the work is created by an employee, in which event the employer will own the right.[47]

It is not clear how much investment will be required to justify application of the adjective 'substantial'. The Database Directive's[48] assertion that a musical compilation will not require substantial investment has been cited earlier. Dependent upon the popularity of the music involved, it may be, however, that a high price will need to be paid to obtain the necessary copyright licences.

The database right is not presently found in any international agreements, although the World Intellectual Property Organization (WIPO) has proposed a draft treaty which would establish such a right. Pending the adoption of this instrument (which has been the subject of considerable hostility from certain quarters in the United States, where it is seen as marking a retreat from the principles of free access to data enshrined in the *Feist*[49] decision), protection is limited to individuals or undertakings who are nationals of, or incorporated in a state within, the European Economic Area (EEA).[50] Assuming that the effect of the changes to the Copyright, Designs and Patents Act 1988 discussed earlier do have the effect of taking databases outwith the scope of copyright protection, the effect will be to reduce the level of protection afforded to databases owned by non-EEA nationals or undertakings, without conferring the compensatory benefit of the new database right. To this extent,

---

[41] SI 1997/3032, Reg. 25.
[42] Directive 91/250/EC.
[43] SI 1992/3233.
[44] Reg. 9, inserting a new s. 50D into the Copyright, Designs and Patents Act 1988.
[45] Directive 96/9/EC.
[46] SI 1997/3032, Reg. 13.
[47] Reg. 14.
[48] Directive 91/250/EC.
[49] *Feist Publications Inc v Rural Telephone Service Co Inc*, 111 S Ct 1282 (1991).
[50] SI 1997/3032, Reg. 18.

non-EEA database owners may be significant losers under the new regime. This may cause difficulties where databases are maintained on the WWW. Implementation of the Database Directive[51] in the United Kingdom might have the effect of removing some such databases from the copyright regime, but where the database is controlled by a non-EEA national, the compensatory database right will not be available. The effect of the new regime will be, therefore, to reduce the level of protection afforded within the United Kingdom to, for example, United States-based database providers.

It is immaterial for the existence of this right, which is stated to be a 'property right', whether the database or its contents are protected by the law of copyright. The right will be infringed by a person who:

> without the consent of the owner . . . extracts or reutilises all or a substantial part of the contents of the database.[52]

This may take the form either of a single act or of a number of smaller extractions. Where conduct by a lawful user would not infringe the database right, it is provided that any term or condition which seeks to restrict this will be null and void. The traditional copyright exemption permitting such use as comes under the heading of fair dealing is restated in modified form for the new right. This provides that:

> Database right in a database which has been made available to the public in any manner is not infringed by fair dealing with a substantial part of the database for the purposes of illustration for teaching or research, other than teaching or research for a commercial purpose, provided that the source is indicated.[53]

Infringement of the database right will expose the perpetrator to actions for damages, injunctions, or accounting of profits as specified in section 96 of the Copyright, Designs and Patents Act 1988.[54] Significantly, however, although the Database Directive[55] confers considerable discretion on Member States as to the nature of the rights and remedies adopted in respect of the new right, the 1988 Act's provisions relating to criminal penalties do not extend to infringements of the database. Also unavailable are the rights of seizure of infringing copies and the right to demand delivery up. It may be that such rights are of limited relevance to online databases but, as has been discussed, the right extends to a wide range of electronic and manual products.

Duration of the right

The right will come into existence when a database is made available to the public and will subsist for a period of fifteen years. It is provided, however, that:

> Any substantial change to the contents of a database, including a substantial change resulting from the accumulation of successive additions, deletions or alterations, which would result in the database being considered to be a substantial new investment shall qualify the database resulting from that investment for its own term of protection.[56]

The application of this provision should be non-problematic where databases (perhaps a telephone directory) are issued on an annual basis. Its application to online databases may be more contentious, and the provision cited above was amended from earlier proposals to

---

[51] Directive 96/9/EC.
[52] SI 1997/3032, Reg. 16.
[53] Directive 96/9/EC, Art. 9, as implemented by SI 1997/3032, Reg. 20.
[54] SI 1997/3032, Reg. 23.
[55] Directive 96/9/EC.
[56] Directive 96/9/EC, Art. 10(3), as implemented by SI 1997/3032, Reg. 17.

try to cover the situation where a database was subject to continual minor amendment. The example might be taken of an online database of law reports such as Lexis. In most areas, cases are stored for a period of fifty years. If reports are added on a daily basis, each day will see a database which is very slightly different from the earlier one. On a rough-and-ready calculation, the change from one day to another will be in the region of 0.0001 per cent of the total database. This can surely not be considered substantial. As additions accumulate and are accompanied, perhaps, by changes to the structure of the database itself, it must be likely that the criteria will be satisfied before the expiry of the fifteen-year period. Assuming continuing development of the database, it will obtain perpetual protection.

In practice, it must be likely that the issue of whether the contents of a database remain protected by the database right will be significant only when legal proceedings are brought alleging infringement. A database might, for example, be made available to the public in the year 2000 and subjected to continual minor amendments. In 2020, the database owner might institute proceedings against a third party, alleging breach of the database right. In this event, evidence could be submitted to the court of the state of the database in 2000 compared with its 2015 incarnation. In the event this indicated substantial additional investment, the court would have to conclude that a new period of protection began in 2015 and that infringement had occurred.

The database right in the courts

The extent of the database right was at issue before the English Courts in the case of *British Horseracing Board Ltd, the Jockey Club and Weatherbys Group Ltd v William Hill Organization Ltd.*[57] The claimant in this case is the body responsible for the operation of the horse-racing industry in the United Kingdom. The defendants are a major firm of bookmakers. As part of its activities, the claimants compiled and maintained databases of horses and jockeys scheduled to participate in horse races. The databases were extremely large and subject to a process of continual updating. It was estimated that some 800,000 entries were added or revised each year. The cost of the work was put at some £4 million annually.

The database had been used by the defendant and other betting operators for a number of years. No complaint had been made regarding this. As with so many other aspects of life, the emergence of the Internet—in the particular case as a medium for betting—changed circumstances. William Hill published information concerning horses and riders competing in particular races taken from the database on its website, only for the claimants to allege that this constituted unauthorised extraction and reutilisation of a substantial part of the database. Each day's use of the data, it was argued constituted extraction and reutilisation of a substantial part of the database. Alternatively, it was argued that even if the individual extracts were not to be considered substantial, the totality of the defendant's practices amounted to repeated and systematic extraction or reutilisation of insubstantial elements of the database, a practice which was prohibited by Article 7(5) of the Database Directive.

For the defendant, it was argued that a distinction had to be drawn between the protected elements of the database, a concept which was described as its 'database-ness', and the underlying information which was not protected. Factual information such as the names of horses and riders and the races in which they were registered to compete could not be the subject of protection under the Directive.

---

[57] [2001] 2 CMLR 12.

Expanding upon the definition of the concept, it was suggested that:

> Since no right is created in the works, data or other materials, the 'database-ness' of a database must lie in the fact that the independent materials are arranged in a systematic or methodical way, and are individually accessible . . . the acts amounting to infringement of a database must in some way take unfair advantage of this 'database-ness'. Any acts which do not make any use of the arrangement of the contents of the database, nor take advantage of the way in which the maker has rendered the contents individually accessible, cannot infringe the database right.[58]

This is perhaps the crux of the debate. Whilst early database software packages required that great attention be paid to the structure and layout of the database, modern techniques permit searching to be carried out independently of structure. The idea that a predetermined structure was necessary for the establishment of protection was rejected by Mr Justice Laddie, who ruled that there was nothing in the Directive to support the existence of a concept of 'databases-ness' which, he held, converged two distinct concepts:

> the feature of form which have to exist before a database will be recognised as existing and the features of content or investment which are protected once a database is held to exist. Thus a database consists of a collection of data brought together in a systematic or methodical way so as to be individually accessible by electronic or other means.

The form of the database, might be protected by copyright rather than the database right. As regards the contents of the database, he stated, it was made clear in the Recitals to the Directive that a user was not entitled to take the contents and rearrange them. As was provided in Recital 40:

> the object of this *sui generis* right is to ensure protection of any investment in obtaining, verifying or presenting the contents of a database for the limited duration of the right; whereas such investment may consist in the deployment of financial resources and/or the expending of time, effort and energy.

In the particular case, the claimant had expended considerable effort in taking details of horses and riders from its existing database, placing them in the context of a specific race, and verifying the accuracy of the resulting lists of horses and riders. The essential reason why the defendant's conduct infringed the database right was not that they had copied details of horses and riders but that they had relied upon the investment made by the claimant to ensure that the data was accurate.

The claimants also succeeded in their second contention that the defendant's conduct amounted to repeated and systematic extraction and/or reutilisation of insubstantial parts of the database. For the defendants, it was argued that there was not one single database but that as it was continually updated, there was in effect a whole series of works. Each act of extraction and reutilisation had to be considered as occurring in respect of a novel database. The judge was not convinced. The Directive, it was held:

> has to be construed to make sense . . . There is nothing in the Directive which suggests that it was not to apply to dynamic databases in just the same way as it applies to ones which are built and modified in discrete, well defined steps. Many of the most valuable databases are those which are under constant revision . . .

The claimant's database, it was ruled, was a single database which was constantly being refined. This, of course, raises the spectre of continuous protection for databases. If protection were to begin anew each time new items of data were included, the consequence would

---

[58] [2001] 2 CMLR 12 at para. 45.

be that for at least some forms of database—and the one at issue in the present case would furnish a prime example—protection might be eternal, at least for so long as the database was maintained:

> In my view the BHB Database is a single database which is in a constant state of refinement. It seems to have been so regarded by all the witnesses. An attempt to split it into a series of discrete databases, besides being impossible to do, would not reflect reality. Its contents change with time and without any obvious break. So too, the term of protection changes. As new data are added, so the database's term of protection is constantly being renewed. However, an unlicensed third party who takes only older data from it only faces a database right which runs from the date when all of that older data was present in the database at the same time. This does not render Article 10(3) meaningless. First, it emphasises that the term keeps being renewed as the database is renewed. Secondly, it makes clear that if someone takes an existing database and adds significantly to it, he obtains protection for the database incorporating his additions. This would be so even if the new author is not the same as the author of the original database . . . [59]

Repeated references in the judgment make it clear that the purpose of the new right is to protect investment rather than creativity. In determining whether a substantial part of the database had been extracted, account was to be taken of qualitative and quantitative aspects. No hard-and-fast rule could or should be laid down for the task of balancing quantitative and qualitative aspects. As was stated:

> No useful purpose would be served by trying to assess this issue first on a quantitative basis and then, separately, on a qualitative basis. They should be looked at together.

The importance of the information to the alleged infringer is not irrelevant. In some cases, of which this is an example, 'the significance of the information to the alleged infringer may throw light on whether it is an important or significant part of the database'.[60]

Following the decision in the High Court, the defendants appealed to the Court of Appeal which stayed proceedings[61] in order to request the European Court of Justice to issue a preliminary ruling on a set of eleven questions relating to the scope of the Database Directive. The court delivered its opinion in November 2004.[62] Largely disregarding the opinion of the Advocate General, the court adopted a very restrictive view as to the scope of the database right.

Initial consideration was given to the second and third questions posed by the Court of Appeal. These asked:

(2) What is meant by 'obtaining' in Article 7(1) of the Directive? In particular, are the facts and matters (at issue in the case) capable of amounting to such obtaining?

(3) Is 'verification' in Article 7(1) of the Directive limited to ensuring from time to time that information contained in a database is or remains correct?

The court referred to the Directive's Recitals which referred to the intention to promote investment in systems which contribute to the development of the information market. A distinction was drawn between the expenditure of resources to compile and verify existing material which it compiled into a new database, and the use of resources for the creation and verification of new materials. In the present case, the activity fell into the latter category.

---

[59] *British Horseracing Board Ltd, the Jockey Club and Weatherbys Group Ltd v William Hill Organization Ltd* [2001] 2 CMLR 12 at 244.

[60] At 235.

[61] [2001] EWCA Civ 1268.

[62] [2004] EUECJ C-203/02.

The court was also asked to consider where the distinction should lie between substantial and insubstantial acts of reproduction and when repeated acts of extraction could be taken to unreasonably prejudice the rights of the database owner as laid down in Article 7(5) of the Directive. Again, the court's interpretation was restrictive. The prohibition against repeated acts of extraction, it was held, applied only where the end result would be the recreation of the whole or a substantial part of the database. Although William Hill's acts were systematic and repeated, there was not, it was held, any

> possibility that, through the cumulative effects of its acts, William Hill might reconstitute and make available to the public the whole or a substantial part of the contents of the BHB database.

Following the decision of the European Court of Justice, the Court of Appeal overturned the ruling of the High Court,[63] albeit with a measure of reluctance, Lord Justice Clarke commenting:

> I am conscious that in doing so I have agreed to allow an appeal against a decision which I was inclined to think was correct when the case was last before the Court of Appeal in July 2001.[64]

The claimant's case, it was stated, rested on the approach that the Directive covered all aspects of the process of compiling the databases. The European Court ruling, however, in the words of Lord Justice Jacobs,

> implicitly rejected that approach. It focussed on the final database—that which is eventually published. What marks that out from anything that has gone before is the BHB's stamp of authority on it. Only the BHB can provide such an official list. Only from that list can you know the accepted declared entries. Only the BHB can provide such a list. No one else could go through a similar process to produce the official list.
>
> . . . So if one asks whether the BHB published database is one consisting of 'existing independent materials' the answer is no. The database contains unique information—the official list of riders and runners. The nature of the information changes with the stamp of official approval. It becomes something different from a mere database of existing material.[65]

The Directive, it was held, did not protect the claimant's database.

Football fixture lists

The decision in the *BHB* case constituted a blow to the scope of the database right. The extent of this was again at issue in the High Court in the case of *Football Dataco Ltd and Ors v Brittens Pools and Ors.*[66] At issue in the case were rights in respect of fixture lists prepared for the major football associations in England and Scotland. The defendants, it was claimed, were making unauthorised use of the fixture lists in breach of the database right. It was also claimed that their conduct infringed the claimant's copyright in the fixture lists.

Extensive evidence was provided as to the manner in which the fixture lists were compiled, a process which it was claimed was 'a mixture of art and science'.[67] A range of factors had to be taken into account to ensure, for example, that two clubs in the same city would not play at home at the same time. Clashes with other large-scale events were also to be avoided so that, for example, Chelsea would not be scheduled to play at home during the period of the Notting Hill Carnival which is held close to their stadium. It was accepted by the judge, Mr Justice Floyd, that the process involved significant skill and labour. The work, he concluded,

---

[63] [2005] EWCA Civ 863.
[64] para. 37.
[65] paras. 129–30.
[66] [2010] EWHC 841 (Ch).
[67] para. 15.

is not mere 'sweat of the brow', by which I mean the application of rigid criteria to the processing of data. It is quite unlike the compiling of a telephone directory, in that at each stage there is scope for the application of judgment and skill. Unlike a 'sweat of the brow' compilation, there are some solutions which will simply not work, and others which will be better.[68]

Following the decision in *Football League Ltd v Littlewoods Pools*[69] in 1959, it had been accepted that fixture lists were protected by copyright as a literary work under domestic law. The question arose whether the introduction of the database right had altered the situation. It was recalled that one of the aims of the Directive was to eliminate discrepancies in the level of protection across the Member States. A broadly similar case to the present had been referred by other national courts to the European Court of Justice as *Fixtures Marketing v Oy Weikus AB and Ors.*[70] Giving a preliminary ruling, the European Court of Justice gave consideration to the scope of Article 7 of the Directive, which provides that:

> Member States shall provide for a right for the maker of a database which shows that there has been qualitatively or quantitatively a substantial investment in either the obtaining, verification or presentation of the contents to prevent extraction and/or re-utilization of the whole or a substantial part, evaluated qualitatively and/or quantitatively, of the contents of that database.

The Court ruled that fixture lists were not protected under Article 7. Echoing its judgment in the *BHB* case it held that in determining whether there was investment in obtaining the contents of a database, account had to be taken only of the effort expended in obtaining the data used to make up the database and did not extend to effort spent in manipulating existing data. With fixture lists, whether involving horse races or football matches, the data was there and there could not, therefore, be a claim to database protection.

This conclusion was followed in the present case. Unlike in the *BHB* case, however, there was a secondary and successful claim under copyright law. There was, it was accepted, no element of individual identifiability in the work. Unlike, for example, crosswords where regular users can identify the individual styles of the problem setters, no one looking at a particular sequence of fixtures would be able to identify a particular creator. This, it was held, was not required and the true test was whether sufficient judgment and discretion was required to reach the threshold for protection under database copyright. The work involved here satisfied the test and the fixture lists were deemed to be protected under copyright.

How much is too much?

The Database Directive and the *sui generis* right it establishes has not featured extensively before the courts in the United Kingdom. The decision in the leading case of *British Horse Racing Board v William Hill* was widely seen as limiting the value of the right although the decision in *Dataco* demonstrated the continuing application of the more general database copyright. In the case of *Beechwood House Publishing v Guardian Products Ltd and Precision Direct Marketing Ltd,*[71] heard before Judge Birss QC in the Patents County Court, there was no dispute that the claimants owned the database right but the court had to consider a range of issues relating to the acquisition and extent of the database right.

The facts of the case are relatively straightforward. The claimant company publishes a database listing contact details of a large number of health professionals working in GP practices. The database was first created in 1994 and was subject to a continuing process of updating. In 1997, another party, Bespoke Database Organisation Ltd, purchased a licence for a single use of that part of the database (then referred to as edition 5) which listed nurses

---

[68] para. 43.
[69] [1959] 1 Ch 637.
[70] Case C-46/02.
[71] <http://www.bailii.org/ew/cases/EWPCC/2011/22.html>.

working in medical practices. At that time there were 8,363 nurses identified on the database. In breach of contractual obligations the data was not deleted after its single use (for a mailing exercise) but a copy was retained and formed part of a larger database which was eventually sold to the second defendants in 2006 and used in 2007 to conduct a mailing to practice nurses on behalf of the first defendants (both companies were owned by the same person although legally they were distinct entities). It was accepted that at that stage 6,901 of the practice nurse details were identical (others may have been modified over the years to reflect changes in personnel). The database was used to send a mailing to, inter alia, 6,000 practice nurses. Of these, 4,783 records were identical to those found in the original 1997 database.

As with many database producers, the claimants had seeded their database with a small number of false entries, in one case using the name and address of its managing director. Such tactics can assist in proving infringement. It would be possible for another party to compile a database covering the same subject-matter—all of the data is in the public domain—and produce an identical product through their own work. It would be implausible beyond belief, however, that independent work could produce the same false entries. In the event, a copy of the mailing arrived at a seeded address and the parties were on their way to the courts.

The copying was not an issue but the case focused on the question whether what had been taken represented a substantial part of the original database. There was also a claim by the defendants that the data which originated from 1997 was out of date and possessed no commercial value.

In respect of the issue of substantiality, the Database Directive requires that there should be extraction and or reutilisation of a substantial part of a protected database. The Directive provides:

> 'substantial', in relation to any investment, extraction or re-utilisation, means substantial in terms of quantity or quality or a combination of both.

It will be seen that there are a number of elements here. A database will be protected only if there has been substantial investment in its creation and the database right will be infringed only if what is extracted or reutilised represents a substantial part of the work.

Counsel for the defendants pleaded first that there had been no evidence led to show that the claimants had made a substantial investment in the database. This claim was rejected. Evidence submitted to the court by the claimant had indicated that in 2009 maintaining the database cost the claimant around £110,000 per annum. This was largely made up of staff time spent telephoning around 11,500 GP practices to confirm or update the details associated with them. Although there was no direct evidence regarding costs incurred in 1997, the figures were considered to be scaleable. The judge ruled:

> 37. . . . if one wanted numbers for edition 5, a simple pro-rata calculation would give them. Edition 5 was 43,000 records, whereas in 2009 evidence, the database was about 150,000 odd records. Thus edition 5 is about 30% of the size of the database today.
>
> 38. Accordingly, considering the number of phone calls made per year, the figures are as follows: Instead of 52,000 phone calls per year, pro-rata about 15000 phone calls per year will have been made at the relevant time. Thus 8,000 practice nurses in edition 5 will represent 8/43rds of the total, which is just under 3,000 phone calls per year. 6,000 records would represent about 2,200 phone calls per year. The lowest number of all, 4,783 identical records present in the mailing list, would correspond to about 1,800 phone calls. One can do the same with the figures for the man weeks' worth of telephone research. 80 man weeks today . . . pro-rata would represent about 24 man weeks at the time of edition 5 and 6,000 practice nurses from edition 5 would represent 3 man weeks per year for telephone research.

This, it was ruled, was sufficient evidence to justify a conclusion that there had been substantial investment in the original database.

On the question of whether what had been extracted or reutilised was a substantial part of the original database, reference was made to the decision of the European Court of Justice in the *BHB* case:

27. How does one assess what is substantial? The answer is provided by *The British Horseracing Board v. William Hill* . . . :

. . .

(71) The expression substantial part, evaluated qualitatively, of the contents of a database refers to the scale of the investment in the obtaining, verification, or presentation of the contents of the subject of the act of extraction and/or reutilisation, regardless of whether that subject represents a quantitatively substantial part of the general contents of the protected database. A quantitatively negligible part of the contents of a database may in fact represent, in terms of obtaining, verification, or presentation, significant human, technical, or financial investment.

. . .

44. In terms of the quantitative question, we are comparing 6,000 records out of 43,000 records, i.e. about 14%. Even if one considers the 4,783 identical records, the fraction is about 11% . . . In my judgment . . . 'quantitatively substantial' cannot require the numerical majority of the records. It must refer to a part having substance. In terms of volume, 11 or 14% of the data must be at the lower end of what could be regarded as quantitatively substantial. It seems to me, however, that even 11% represents a significant part of the volume of the database whose creation required substantial resources . . .

45. Alternatively, regardless of my conclusion from a quantitative point of view, I find that the 6,000 records or the 4,783 identical records are qualitatively a substantial part of the edition 5 database. It seems to me that the scale of the investment that these records represent, (as I have found, thousands of phone calls and staff working for weeks to compile and validate the data) is a significant human and financial investment. On that basis, regardless of whether the volume is or is not quantitatively substantial, it is qualitatively a substantial part of edition 5.

A further claim made on behalf of the defendants was that the passage of time between the compilation of the 1997 database and the use made of its contents by the defendants in 2007 meant that the data was likely to be inaccurate (the defendants suggested that only 20 per cent of the records would remain completely accurate) and of no commercial value.

The obvious retort to this argument is clearly along the lines that if the data was inaccurate why did the defendants use it? This point was made by the judge, but at a more legalistic level he ruled that:

The fact that the commercial value of what was taken may be low when it was taken ten years later, cannot be relevant. The point may or may not be relevant to quantum, but, in my judgment, it cannot be relevant to substantiality. The database rights last for 15 years. It seems to me that if the part extracted would have represented a substantial part in 1997, when it was current data, it would still be a substantial part of that 1997 database 10 years later. It does not stop being substantial just because time has passed and the world has moved on.

Conclusions

Since the US Supreme Court moved away from the 'sweat of the brow' doctrine in its decision in *Feist*,[72] the United Kingdom (and to an extent, Commonwealth jurisdictions) have been isolated in terms of the extent of copyright protection. Copyright has been held to

[72] *Feist Publications Inc v Rural Telephone Service Co Inc*, 111 S Ct 1282 (1991).

extend to subjects such as a football fixture list, whilst the threat of copyright litigation was used by BT during the latter years of the twentieth century to deter parties who were planning to publish competing telephone directories in CD format. There is perhaps little doubt that the British Horse Racing Board could have succeeded in an action for copyright infringement under the old UK regime. The fact that the case was litigated to the extent that it was may be indicative of a point made by Mr Justice Laddie:

> These propositions dovetail with a more general point, namely that database right is to be construed so as to be narrower than the protection which used to be afforded to compilations under English copyright law.[73]

Given the increasing economic importance of the informational content of databases, this is a rather paradoxical conclusion. As has been the case in other areas, there is a degree of tension between the common and civil law legal traditions. It is arguable that if the United Kingdom afforded too much protection to works possessing little or no literary worth, other Member States afforded too little protection. The result, in the form of the Database Directive, has been a compromise. Only time will tell whether the compromise will be a successful one. In 2005, the Commission published a review of the working of the Database Directive.[74] This accepted that the scope of the *sui generis* right had been 'severely curtailed' by the decision of the Court of Justice in *William Hill* and similar cases. The basic purpose of the Directive was to promote the development of the European database market and the evaluation aimed to determine:

> whether the European database industry's rate of growth increased after the introduction of the new right; whether the beneficiaries of the new right produced more databases than they would have produced in the absence of this right; and whether the scope of the right was drafted in a way that targets those areas where Europe needs to encourage innovation.[75]

The evidence for the success of the Directive was limited. Although a majority of those expressing views felt that databases were more strongly protected under the Directive than previously (presumably excluding the United Kingdom), the report stated:

> The economic impact of the '*sui generis*' right on database production is unproven. Introduced to stimulate the production of databases in Europe, the new instrument has had no proven impact on the production of databases. Data taken from the GDD (Gale Directory of Databases) . . . show that the EU database production in 2004 has fallen back to pre-Directive levels: the number of EU-based database 'entries' into the GDD was 3095 in 2004 as compared to 3092 in 1998. In 2001, there were 4085 EU-based 'entries' while in 2004 there were only 3095.[76]

Views were sought on four options for change. These involved: the repeal of the Directive, the repeal of the *sui generis* right, the modification of the *sui generis* right, or the maintenance of the status quo. Fifty-five comments were received, with the Commission reporting in 2006 that:

> 8 contributions support Option 1, 3 contributions support Option 2, 26 support Option 3 and 26 support Option 4.[77]

Eleven years on, there has been no indication from the Commission that anything other than maintenance of the status quo is under active consideration.

---

[73] *British Horseracing Board Ltd, the Jockey Club and Weatherbys Group Ltd v William Hill Organization Ltd* [2001] 2 CMLR 12 at 232.

[74] Available from <http://ec.europa.eu/internal_market/copyright/docs/databases/evaluation_report_en.pdf>.

[75] At Section 1.2.   [76] At Section 1.4.

[77] <http://ec.europa.eu/internal_market/copyright/prot-databases/prot-databases_en.htm>.

19

Design rights

INTRODUCTION

Whilst the patent system can offer protection in respect of the manner in which an object functions, the system of registered designs protects elements of its appearance. In some respects the regime can be seen as similar to the copyright system. Section 17(3) of the Copyright, Designs and Patents Act 1988 provides that copyright is infringed by a person who makes 'a copy in three dimensions of a two-dimensional work [or] . . . a copy in two dimensions of a three-dimensional work'. The limitation of copyright protection is that it extends only to end-works that satisfy the statutory requirements relating to artistic creativity. Section 51 of the 1988 Act provides that:

> It is not an infringement of any copyright in a design document or model recording or embodying a design for anything other than an artistic work or a typeface to make an article to the design or to copy an article made to the design.

Especially with the heavy involvement of systems of computer-assisted design in modern manufacturing it will be doubtful whether many designs will qualify for copyright protection. The system of design rights provides potential protection in such a situation.

The development of design right and key legislative instruments

Two forms of design right are available in the United Kingdom: registered and unregistered design rights. The former is the older concept and can trace its origins back several centuries. Initially applicable to designs intended to be imprinted on linen, the system was extended to other forms of product by the Copyright and Design Act of 1839. This offered protection for 'the ornamentation and for the shape and configuration of any article of manufacture'.[1]

There has been a close linkage between the administration of the system of registered designs and that of patents. The Registered Designs Act of 1949 provides that applications for the grant of a registered design are to be submitted to the Comptroller General of Patents, Designs and Trademarks.[2] The 1949 Act is still in force although its provisions have been amended substantially by the Copyright, Designs and Patents Act 1988 and by the Registered Designs Regulations 2001[3] which was introduced in order to implement the European Directive 987/71 on the legal protection of designs.[4] A further minor change was made by the Regulatory Reform (Registered Designs) Order 2006.[5]

Also relevant is Council Regulation (EC) No. 6/2002 of 12 December 2001 on Community Design.[6] This Regulation establishes the notion of a 'registered Community

---

[1] <http://www.ipo.gov.uk/types/design/d-about/d-whatis/d-history.htm>.   [2] s. 44.
[3] SI 2001/3949.   [4] OJ 1998 L289/28.   [5] SI 2006/1974.   [6] OJ 2002 L3/1.

design' which may be awarded by the Office for Harmonisation in the Internal Market—the same office that is responsible for the Community Trademark. The provisions of the Regulation will be considered in more detail later within the context of litigation between Apple and Samsung concerning the question of whether the design of Samsung's Galaxy tablet computer infringed Apple's design right in respect of its iPad.

The notion of unregistered design right was introduced to the United Kingdom in the Copyright, Designs and Patents Act 1988. This was brought about in large part because of a confused trail of judicial precedent concerning the relationship between registered designs and copyright which culminated in the decision of the House of Lords in the case of *British Leyland v Armstrong Patents*.[7] The case concerned the design of exhaust systems for cars produced by British Leyland. As with many other elements of motor vehicles, exhaust systems require to be replaced at periodic intervals and a number of third-party companies, including the defendant sought to produce replacement systems which could be purchased by car owners rather than obtaining these from the original manufacturer. We see the same situation arising in many areas of economic activity; a significant example today is the acquisition by customers of replacement ink supplies for printers and copiers.[8] The designs did not qualify for registered design protection because their shape and dimensions were dictated by the design of the original vehicle but the House of Lords ruled that they were entitled to protection under the law of copyright.[9] The somewhat paradoxical result was that a design which could not qualify for registered design right (which then gave protection for a maximum period of fifty-five years) would benefit from the (at that time) copyright protection of life plus fifty years.

The 1988 Act amended the copyright definition of artistic works to reduce the scope of protection for industrial designs. Section 51 provides that:

> It is not an infringement of any copyright in a design document or model recording or embodying a design for anything other than an artistic work or a typeface to make an article to the design or to copy an article made to the design.

As a form of compensation for industrial designers the maximum duration of registered design protection was extended from fifteen to twenty-five years and a new form of right—the unregistered design right—was introduced.

---

[7] [1986] RPC 279.

[8] See *Canon v Green Cartridge* [1997] UKPC 19 where the Privy Council held that a Hong Kong manufacturer who manufactured printer cartridges designed to be compatible with the appellant's laser printers had infringed copyright. The decision in British Leyland was distinguished on the basis that printer cartridges require to be replaced on a more regular basis than do motor-vehicle spare parts such as exhaust systems. The Privy Council cited data relating to the cost of running a printer that suggested that:

> The aftermarket (as it is called) in cartridges contributes a significant part to the plaintiff's profits. The defendant's business plan, prepared when it decided to enter the market in 1990, analysed the lifetime cost of one of the plaintiff's typical desktop laser printers as follows. The initial cost was US$1,700. During a projected life of 5 years or 200,000 copies, the owner would need about 62 cartridges at $120 each, involving a further expenditure of $7,500 [paragraph 4].

[9] In some respects the decision was a pyrrhic victory for British Leyland as the House of Lords proceeded to rule that the company must be considered to have impliedly given customers a licence to obtain replacement parts for their vehicles and, by implication to permit third-party manufacturers to produce and market such components. The issue of whether this approach is compatible with human rights legislation has been doubted. Copyright is stated to be a 'property right' and the first protocol to the European Convention on Human Rights (ECHR) provides that:

> Every natural or legal person is entitled to the peaceful enjoyment of his possessions. No one shall be deprived of his possessions except in the public interest and subject to the conditions provided for by law and by the general principles of international law [Art. 1].

It is difficult to see how a requirement to grant a licence can be compatible with this provision and the Privy Council in *Canon v Green Cartridge* explicitly refused to adopt their Lordships' dicta on this point.

Registered design right protection

Within the United Kingdom, the 1949 Act (as amended) sanctions the registration and protection of designs that relate to 'the appearance of the whole or a part of a product resulting from the features of, in particular, the lines, contours, colours, shape, texture or materials of the product or its ornamentation'.[10] The term 'product' is defined to encompass 'any industrial or handicraft item other than a computer program; and, in particular, includes packaging, get-up, graphic symbols, typographic type-faces and parts intended to be assembled into a complex product'.[11] A 'complex product' is any product 'which is composed of at least two replaceable component parts permitting disassembly and reassembly of the product'.[12]

A product will be eligible for registration if it satisfies the criteria that it is 'new and has individual character'.[13] Novelty is established if the design has not been previously published within the European Economic Area.[14] The concept of 'individual character' refers to the fact that:

> a design has individual character if the overall impression it produces on the informed user differs from the overall impression produced on such a user by any design which has been made available to the public before the relevant date.[15]

This requirement has been contentious in the IT field and will be considered in more detail later. Design rights are not available in respect of any 'features of appearance of a product which are solely dictated by the product's technical function'.[16]

Applications for registration are to be made to the Intellectual Property Office. Unlike the patent system where the onus of establishing issues of eligibility rests with the applicant, in cases where an application is made for a registered design right it is provided that an application shall not be refused unless the Registrar can show due cause.[17] The grounds upon which the Registrar may refuse an application are limited and effectively refer designs which may offend public morality or which seek to make unauthorised use of protected symbols such as national flags or symbols relating to the Olympic Games (introduced in the context of the London 2012 Games).

At the stage of dealing with an application for registration, the possibility for examination is limited. The details of the application will be made public and the Intellectual Property Office indicates that a decision should be reached within a month of the receipt of the application. As with patents, it is more likely that the validity of the award will be challenged in the context of subsequent legal proceedings brought by a party claiming that the design is not truly eligible for protection.

A successful application gives a monopoly right to use of the design for a period of up to twenty-five years. As with the patent system this represents the maximum period of protection. An award will be granted for an initial period of five years and this may be renewed at similar intervals up to the maximum period of protection.

Unregistered design right

As its title would indicate, the Copyright, Designs and Patents Act provides the statutory basis for design right. In similar manner to the provisions relating to copyright and to patents it provides that:

> Design right is a property right which subsists in accordance with this Part in an original design.[18]

---

[10] Reg. 2 of the Design Right Regulations 2001.   [11] Reg. 2.   [12] Reg. 2.   [13] Reg. 2.
[14] Reg. 2.   [15] Reg. 2.
[16] Reg. 2. See also the discussion of the case of *British Leyland v Armstrong Patents* at Chapter 20.
[17] Reg. 4.   [18] s. 213.

By comparison, design right confers automatic protection for the internal or external shape or configuration of an original design, namely its three-dimensional shape. Design right allows you to stop anyone from copying the shape or configuration of the article, but does not give protection for any of the two-dimensional aspects, for example surface patterns. Protection is limited to the United Kingdom, and lasts either ten years after the first marketing of articles that use the design, or fifteen years after creation of the design—whichever is earlier. For the last five years of that period the design is subject to a licence of right. This means that anyone is entitled to a licence to make and sell products copying the design commencing from the date when the design is first made available to the public.

As with copyright, design right comes into existence with its creation with no procedural requirements. In addition to the general design right there is a system of registered design right.

Design rights in tablet computers

Recent years and months have seen a plethora of intellectual property lawsuits between technology companies as each tries to use its portfolio of intellectual property rights to secure a competitive advantage over its rivals. Most of these cases have led either to a settlement between the parties or have yet to reach the higher levels of the judicial exception. The case of *Samsung Electronics (UK) Ltd v Apple Inc* is a notable precedent with the English Court of Appeal delivering final rulings in October and November 2012.

In 2004 Apple (under the name of, inter alia, Steve Jobs) was granted a Community Registered Design[19] in respect of features of what we now know as tablet computers. The first iPad was introduced in 2010 and a number of other manufacturers, including Samsung sought to market competing products.

Apple's response to the emergence of competition from Samsung was to claim that the design of its Galaxy tablet infringed its design right. In the present litigation, Samsung's lawyers reached the court first and sought an order to the effect that it had not infringed Apple's design right. An additional claim was that the design right should not have been granted and should be declared invalid. Proceedings to that effect had been initiated by Samsung before the Office of Harmonisation for the Internal Market (OHIM) which is responsible for the administration of the system of Community Design Rights.

In parallel with the English litigation, actions alleging infringement were brought before the German, Dutch, and Spanish courts. In all jurisdictions, Apple lost its case although it did secure an injunction against Samsung's sale of its tablet computers under German unfair competition law. As was stated, however, in the English High Court:

> It was not disputed that Apple has the right to start full infringement proceedings in those countries and that the preliminary decisions are not binding. This action is the first substantive hearing in the Community of the issue of infringement.[20]

Six (or, by the time proceedings came to court, eight) years is a long time in the development of computer technology and the court made it clear that the issue was not whether Samsung's Galaxy Tablet copied Apple's iPad (that might be the subject for a future copyright case). The question was a narrower one of whether the Galaxy design infringed Apple's 2004 design right.

---

[19] No. 00018,1607–0001.
[20] [2012] EWHC 1882 (Pat) at para. 6.

Article 3 of the European Regulation provides that:

'design' means the appearance of the whole or a part of a product resulting from the features of, in particular, the lines, contours, colours, shape, texture and/or materials of the product itself and/or its ornamentation;

Under Article 4, designs might be protected to the extent that they are 'new and (have) individual character'. These terms are defined further in Articles 5 and 6 respectively:

A design shall be considered to be new if no identical design has been made available to the public.

A design shall be considered to have individual character if the overall impression it produces on the informed user differs from the overall impression produced on such a user by any design which has been made available to the public.

The scope of Community design right protection is defined in Article 10:

The scope of the protection conferred by a Community design shall include any design which does not produce on the informed user a different overall impression.

Effectively a later design will infringe if an 'informed user'—a criterion analogous to the patent system's 'person skilled in the art'—regards it as equivalent. Apple, as is well known, were early market leaders in the field of tablet computers. Samsung and other manufacturers were seeking to compete in the market.

Judge Birss gave detailed consideration to the features in Apple's design right specification compared to those found in the Samsung product. In respect of the Apple design he concluded:

The extreme simplicity of the Apple design is striking. Overall it has undecorated flat surfaces with a plate of glass on the front all the way out to a very thin rim and a blank back. There is a crisp edge around the rim and a combination of curves, both at the corners and the sides. The design looks like an object the informed user would want to pick up and hold. It is an understated, smooth and simple product. It is a *cool* design.[21]

The adjective 'cool' is not one which is frequently found in judicial decisions. It appears again in the judge's final conclusion:

The informed user's overall impression of each of the Samsung Galaxy Tablets is the following. From the front they belong to the family which includes the Apple design; but the Samsung products are very thin, almost insubstantial members of that family with unusual details on the back. They do not have the same understated and extreme simplicity which is possessed by the Apple design. They are not as *cool*. The overall impression produced is different.[22]

An uncool product clearly could not infringe a 'cool' design and the judge found in favour of Samsung.

The next stage was to consider the question of remedies. A declaration of non-infringement was non-controversial but Samsung sought more. It asked for an injunction restraining Apple from continuing to argue that the Samsung design infringed its right. The judge rejected this but did accept a further and rather unusual request that Apple should arrange (and pay) for the publication of a notice in a number of UK publications (including the *Financial Times* and *Guardian* newspapers) and on its own website to the effect that:

On 9th July 2012 the High Court of Justice of England & Wales ruled that Samsung Electronic (UK) Limited's Galaxy Tablet Computers, namely the Galaxy Tab 10.1, Tab 8.9

---

[21] para. 182, emphasis added.   [22] para. 190, emphasis added.

and Tab 7.7 do not infringe Apple's registered design No. 00181607-0001. A copy of the full judgment of the High Court is available via the following link: [2012] EWHC 1882 (Pat).

The ruling went into considerable detail concerning the prominence to be given to the notice. It was to appear not later than page 6 of the newspapers and for the website was to appear on the home page 'in a font size no smaller than Arial 11pt'. There should also be a hyperlink to the judgment both of which should remain displayed for a period of six months.

Apple subsequently brought an appeal to the Court of Appeal both on the substantive aspects of the judgment and regarding the nature of the remedy proposed. In July 2012, the Court of Appeal agreed to postpone the publication requirement pending its final deliberations.[23] This came with the publication of a judgment in October 2012.[24] In essence this confirmed the decision of Judge Birss in the High Court. In the intervening period, however, a German court had delivered an interim judgment which contradicted the findings of the English High Court and found in favour of Apple. This attracted the wrath of Lord Justice Jacob in the Court of Appeal and it is appropriate to quote this section of the judgment at some length as it has wide significance for the operation of intellectual property law within the European Union:

56. Firstly I cannot understand on what basis the Court thought it had jurisdiction to grant interim relief . . .

57. . . . It is true that Samsung applied for declarations of non-infringement on the same day, 8th September 2011 in Spain, the Netherlands and England and Wales and there could be (but I think rather overtaken by events given that the trial and appeal are over here) a dispute about which case started first in point of time. After all there is now a Community-wide decision on the point, now affirmed on appeal. One would think that ought to put an end to all other litigation about it.

58. Secondly I cannot see any basis for an interim injunction. The UK court had already granted a final declaration . . .

. . .

61. Finally I regret to say that I find the Oberlandesgericht's reasoning on the merits sparse in the extreme . . .

62. What the Oberlandesgericht did not do was to consider Judge Birss's decision in detail. It gave only meagre reasons for saying 'The Court cannot concur with the interpretation of the High Court'. I regret that. In Grimme v Scott [2010] EWCA Civ 1110, this Court said:

'Broadly we think the principle in our courts—and indeed that in the courts of other member states—should be to try to follow the reasoning of an important decision in another country. Only if the court of one state is convinced that the reasoning of a court in another member state is erroneous should it depart from a point that has been authoritatively decided there. Increasingly that has become the practice in a number of countries, particularly in the important patent countries of France, Germany, Holland and England and Wales. Nowadays we refer to each other's decisions with a frequency which would have been hardly imaginable even twenty years ago. And we do try to be consistent where possible.'

'The Judges of the patent courts of the various countries of Europe have thereby been able to create some degree of uniformity even though the European Commission and the politicians continue to struggle on the long, long road which one day will give Europe a common patent court.'

63. That principle was not followed by the Oberlandesgericht. If courts around Europe simply say they do not agree with each other and give inconsistent decisions, Europe will be the poorer.

---

[23] [2012] EWCA Civ 1223.   [24] [2012] EWCA Civ 1339.

Different legal systems and courts have different traditions but the basic thrust of the argument seems to be irrefutable. If the notion of a single market is to have any meaning, there does need to be a high degree of cooperation between national courts.

A final element to the case relates to the requirement that Apple publish information about the litigation. In an interim hearing before the Court of Appeal in July 2012, the judges agreed to postpone the implementation of this part of the ruling until the full hearing in October. At this time Lord Justice Jacobs indicated that he would, in isolation, have concluded that the 'massive publicity of HHJ Birss's "not as *cool*" judgment had made it unnecessary' (at paragraph 82, emphasis added). He continued:

> 83.   But I have come to the firm conclusion that such an order is necessary now. The decision of the Oberlandesgericht received much publicity. What was the ordinary consumer, or the marketing department of a potential Samsung customer to make of it? On the one hand, the media said Samsung had won, on the other the media were saying that Apple had a German Europe-wide injunction. Real commercial uncertainty was thereby created. A consumer might well think 'I had better not buy a Samsung—maybe it's illegal and if I buy one it may not be supported'. A customer (and I include its legal department) might well wonder whether, if it bought Samsung's 7.7 it might be in trouble before the German courts. Safest thing to do either way is not to buy.

Although it was recognised that the decision of the Court of Appeal would also attract publicity, the court was critical of Apple's behaviour in the months between the High Court ruling and the appeal proceedings. It had given extensive publicity to the interdict issued by the German court and had taken steps to have it enforced. Ultimately, Apple undertook before the Court of Appeal that it would take steps to have the German interdict withdrawn. Nonetheless, the court ruled that the publicity requirements should be upheld. The purpose, it was stated, was not to expose Apple to 'public humiliation' but to recognise that Apple's conduct in Germany had prompted a fall in Samsung's market share in the UK tablet market from 10 per cent to 1 per cent.

That should have been the end of the matter but the parties were to return to the Court of Appeal in November 2012[25] with Samsung claiming that Apple had failed to comply with the publicity order. It had delayed unreasonably the publication of adverts in newspapers and journals. In respect of its web page (Apple.com/uk), whilst this did provide a link (in the most minimalist way compatible with compliance with the Court order) to a copy of the judgment, it followed this by several paragraphs of text which gave a partial and prejudiced summary of the judgment. These sections began:

> In the ruling, the judge made several important points comparing the designs of the Apple and Samsung products:
>   'The extreme simplicity of the Apple design is striking. Overall it has undecorated flat surfaces with a plate of glass on the front all the way out to a very thin rim and a blank back. There is a crisp edge around the rim and a combination of curves, both at the corners and the sides. The design looks like an object the informed user would want to pick up and hold. It is an understated, smooth and simple product. It is a *cool* design' [paragraph 11, emphasis added].

The Court of Appeal was singularly unimpressed. Apple, it was held, had engaged in misleading and deceptive practices. Statements were either factually inaccurate or were taken out of context in such a way as to render them misleading. It must publish the order as issued by the court without modification or addition.

---

25   [2012] EWCA Civ 1430.

Conclusions

The *Apple v Samsung* litigation shows some of the difficulties that exist in trying to apply EU-wide rights (the Community Design Right) when enforcement remains the province of national courts. Whilst it is apparent that English courts are increasingly citing decisions from other jurisdictions and the practice is presumably reciprocated, linguistic differences must be an issue and it does seem that the results may differ across national borders.

Although it has occupied a fair amount of judicial time in the United Kingdom—and in other EU Member States, it is not apparent what has been the point of the exercise. In many respects the case can be seen as a skirmish within a wider Internet Protocol (IP) war but it is not clear if there can ever be winners and losers, at least in the legal sense. In the present case, Samsung won but its market share in the United Kingdom it has plummeted. The case was, perhaps, on a relatively obscure branch of IP law and there is a massive gap between public (and journalistic) perceptions of the outcome and the rather narrower legal findings. Apple had registered a design in 2004. The iPad it eventually put onto the market was certainly not identical to that design. A major fact was that developments in processing power and designs meant that the 2010 production model could be thinner and lighter than anything that could have been produced in 2004. It was not alleged (at least in this case), that Samsung had copied the iPad.

Samsung won the case but, aided by Apple's publicity machinery, one may suspect that the message most non-legal people will take from the litigation, is that the Galaxy is not as 'cool' as the iPad!

It is always dangerous to try to take too many messages from a single case. What we can see, perhaps, is how fluid IP law is. We have seen the expansion of the topic of software patents and the decline of the relevance of copyright law—at least at the level of non-literal copying. The battleground continually changes and what we have in the design-right litigation is something that sounds a bit like copyright, but is not. It is something that sounds a bit like patent litigation, but is not. At the end of the day, property is about money, and what we see in the intellectual property sphere are disputes between commercial undertakings all of whom are seeking to secure some form of financial advantage.

20

Trade mark and domain-name issues

INTRODUCTION

Along with patents and copyright, the system of trade marks constitute a key component of the system of intellectual property rights. In the United Kingdom, the system originated in the Trade Marks Registration Act 1875. The present law is to be found in the Trade Marks Act 1994, which was introduced in order to enable the United Kingdom to comply with its obligations under the 1988 EC Directive to Approximate the Laws of the Member States Relating to Trade Marks.[1] The 1993 Council Regulation on the Community Trade Mark[2] established a Community Trade Mark to operate in parallel with national systems. At the international level, the Madrid Agreement Concerning the International Registration of Marks provides for a system of international registration of trade marks.[3]

As defined in the Trade Marks Act 1994, a trade mark is:

> any sign capable of being represented graphically which is capable of distinguishing goods or services of one undertaking from those of other undertakings.
>
> A trade mark may in particular, consist of words (including personal names), designs, letters, numerals or the sale of goods or their packaging.[4]

Details of trade marks are recorded in the Register of Trade Marks, a document which is open to public inspection.

The scope of this definition is broader than might initially appear to be the case. In our digital age, virtually everything is capable of being represented in graphical form. The process of 'sampling', for example, would allow any sound to be depicted in graphical format. A trade mark has been awarded for the distinctive sound of the telephone which features in advertising for the Direct Line Insurance company. In similar vein, the Chanel No. 5 perfume smell has been trade marked under the description:

> The scent of aldehydic-floral fragrance product, with an aldehydic top note from aldehydes, bergamot, lemon and neroli; an elegant floral middle note, from jasmine, rose, lily of the valley, orris and ylang-ylang; and a sensual feminine base note from sandal, cedar, vanilla, amber, civet and musk. The scent also being known by the written brand name No 5.

This latter description illustrates a difficulty with the system. Although the description may identify the ingredients used, it makes no reference to the relative proportions of the ingredients or to the manner of manufacture. It would be possible to perform a chromatographic analysis and

---

[1] Directive 89/104/EC, OJ 1989 L 40/1 (the European Trade Mark Directive).

[2] Regulation 40/94/EC, OJ 1994 L 11/1. Although dated '94' the Regulation was adopted on 20 December 1993.

[3] The text of the Agreement is available from <http://www.wipo.int/madrid/en/legal_texts/trtdocs_wo015.html>.   [4] s. 1(1).

provide a much more detailed and specific description of the product. This might also prove useful to would-be counterfeiters. In the particular instance cited, inspection of the Register of Trade Marks would be of little assistance to anyone wishing to determine whether a product infringed the Chanel trade mark. This could only be determined by an inspection of samples of the perfumes involved. What is protected may not be apparent from scrutiny of the register.

In terms of their manner of issuance, trade marks fall somewhere between patents and copyright. Registration of the trade mark (in the United Kingdom, responsibility for the system vests in the Patent Office) is an essential requirement. This distinguishes the system from the copyright regime, where the right arises as soon as work is recorded in some manner. Although there are provisions relating to what form of marks may or may not be used, these require-ments fall short of the exacting requirements of novelty and inventiveness applied under the patent system. The Register of Trade Marks is divided into forty-two categories and an appli-cant will be required to specify those in respect of which he or she would wish the trade mark to apply. A sliding scale of fees will apply, depending on the number of categories applied for.

Once accepted for registration, a trade mark will be valid indefinitely. The first trade mark was issued in 1876 in respect of the red triangle symbol found on containers of Bass beer and remains valid to this day. The two main threats to trade mark owners are that the mark will fall into disuse or, at the other end of the spectrum, will become so widely used on account of the proprietor's failure or inability to take action against infringers that it takes on a generic mean-ing rather than 'distinguishing goods or services of one undertaking from those of other under-takings'. The word 'aspirin', for example, was once a registered trade mark (and remains so in France) owned by the German Bayer company. The trade mark rights in the United Kingdom were lost in the First World War, and the term may now be used to describe any painkiller containing the drug aspirin.

At the international level, the Madrid Agreement Concerning the International Registra-tion of Marks provides for a system of international registration of trade marks. The Agree-ment provides that the owner of a trade mark in one signatory state may request the national authority to present an application for international registration to the International Bureau of the World Intellectual Property Organization (WIPO), indicating those countries in which recognition of the mark is sought. In turn, the International Bureau notifies each state referred to which must give notice of a refusal to accept the trade mark, generally within a period of twelve months. The effectiveness of the international system is limited by the fact that many significant countries, including the United States, are not signatory to its various constituent agreements and protocols.[5]

Effect of trade marks

As with other forms of intellectual property, trade marks constitute 'property rights', con-ferring upon the proprietor the exclusive right to certain forms of use of the mark.[6] A trade mark will be infringed in two main situations:

1. where an identical or similar mark is used in respect of goods or services which are identical or similar to those forming the subject of the trade mark and where there is a consequential likelihood of confusion on the part of the public

---

[5] The text of the Agreement (as amended on a number of occasions), is available from <http://www.wipo.int/madrid/en/legal_texts/trtdocs_wo015.html>.

[6] Trade Marks Act 1994, s. 2.

2. where the identical or similar mark is used and the goods or services are not identical or similar to those forming the subject of the trade mark but where the trade mark has a reputation in the United Kingdom and where its reproduction 'takes unfair advantage of, or is detrimental to the distinctive character or repute of the trade mark'.[7]

In the first situation, dispute is likely to centre upon the issue of whether an allegedly infringing mark is sufficiently similar to confuse members of the public. Thus the name 'OXOT' has been held to infringe the trade mark 'OXO'. In most cases, the fact that the mark is used in respect of different categories of goods or services will defeat a claim of infringement. Where the trade mark has widespread recognition, infringement may occur when the use of the name (or a similar name) is regarded as seeking to benefit unfairly from association with the brand name or is likely to reduce its standing. In one US case, use of the name 'Dogiva' for dog biscuits was held actionable on the first of these grounds by the proprietors of the trade mark 'Godiva', representing the well-known Belgian chocolates.

Passing off

By no means every name or indication of origin can be protected under the law of trade marks. Although US practice appears to be somewhat more liberal, in the United Kingdom popular names and geographic indicators cannot be protected as trade marks as these are considered insufficiently descriptive of the origin of goods or services. Thus, a name such as McDonald cannot be protected by trade mark, although, as is the case with regard to the well-known fast-food supplier of that name, trade marks encompass almost every other aspect of the business, from the 'Golden Arches' symbol through styles of writing and design to the names of individual dishes, for example 'BigMac'. On occasion, in deciding on the eligibility of a name submitted for trade mark registration, the Patent Office has had recourse to documents such as telephone directories in order to determine whether a name is in common usage.

A trader finding that it is unable to register its name as a trade mark will not be deprived of legal protection. The doctrine of 'passing off' is a common law creation located in the law of tort and is based on the premise that 'nobody has any right to represent his goods as the goods of somebody else'. The action is effectively one of unfair competition and will lie where a competitor markets goods or services in such a manner that the public are likely to be confused as to their origins. In the case of *Erven Warnink v Townend*,[8] Lord Diplock identified five requirements for a successful action:

(1) a misrepresentation

(2) made by a trader in the course of trade,

(3) to prospective customers of his or ultimate consumers of goods or services supplied by him,

(4) which is calculated to injure the business or goodwill of another trader (in the sense that this is a reasonably foreseeable consequence) and

(5) which causes actual damage to a business or goodwill of the trader by whom the action is brought or . . . will probably do so.

Although the doctrine of passing off is limited to use of a name in a manner which will harm commercial interests, recent decisions under the Internet domain-name dispute resolution procedures indicate that protection may extend to private interests in respect of the practice sometimes described as 'cybersquatting'.

---

[7] s. 10.   [8] [1979] FSR 39.

Trade marks and information technology

As with many other forms of products and services, information technology products are likely to seek the protection of trade mark law. Many product names are trade marked—the names Apple and Microsoft, for example, are both registered trade marks, together with symbols such as the famous Apple logo. In these situations, the application of trade mark law raises no novel issues.

With the emergence and increasing commercialisation of the Internet, many businesses have sought to establish a presence in cyberspace. Typically, they will seek to register a domain name which incorporates their real-life identity. British Airways, for example, can be found at <http://www.britishairways.com>. In some cases, businesses which exist wholly or primarily on the Internet have sought to register aspects of the domain-name structure as a trade mark, an example being Amazon.com, where the.com element is part of the registered mark. The UK Patent Office has published notices on 'Practice on Trade Marks Incorporating the Word Net'[9] and on 'Registration of Internet Domain Names as Trade Marks'.[10] The notices indicate that in deciding whether a mark should be registered, elements such as http, www, .com, and .co.uk are to be discounted in determining the eligibility of the mark. The term will then fall to be judged on normal criteria. Initially, applicants should show that the mark is distinctive of their business or that goods or services have been supplied under the name in such a manner as to show factual distinctiveness.

Where novel issues have arisen is in the relationship between trade mark rights and the allocation of Internet domain names. As the systems of allocating domain names developed, the responsible agencies adopted a first come, first served policy. As the commercial attractiveness of the WWW has increased, so more and more commercial organisations have sought to develop a presence. The impact of a web presence will obviously be enhanced by use of the organisation's trading name, something which may well be protected by trade marks. What many have discovered is that, whether by accident or design, the name is already in use. In such instances, consideration may well be given to the possibility of raising an action alleging infringement of the trade mark. Unfortunately, the application of trade mark law to the operation of the Internet is not without its difficulties.

Problems are exacerbated by a number of features of the system of Internet domain names. In many instances, the names of undertakings may be shared by many individuals. There are in excess of 2,000 Macdonalds listed in the Glasgow telephone directory alone. Although the existence of sub-domains such as .co and .ltd means that the same name might be used in these various sectors, there may not be enough sub-domains to go around. Even where domain names identical to a trade mark have been obtained by another commercial undertaking, there may be no question of infringement when this undertaking's activities are conducted in different sectors. Again, domain names cannot incorporate a distinctive type font or style of presentation of a name or identifying badges or signs.

Additional problems exist in respect of the generic top-level domain names such as .com. These may be obtained by anyone from anywhere in the world. This global system sits uneasily with the trade mark system which, albeit with mechanisms for international cooperation, is still based on the notion of national rights. It may well be the case that the same trade mark is owned by different persons or undertakings in different states. An example is Budweiser beer. Although this has been the subject of a dispute between United States- and Czech-based brewers, for historical reasons, the name has been used by two distinct parties.

---

[9] Available from <http://www.ipo.gov.uk/tmmanual-chap3-add.pdf>.
[10] Available from <http://www.ipo.gov.uk/types/tm/t-about/t-whatis/t-domain.htm>.

In considering the relationship between trade marks (and other legal rights such as passing off) and domain names, consideration will first be given to a number of cases which have been brought before the courts in the United Kingdom. Following this, reference will be made to the dispute resolution procedure adopted by Internet regulatory agencies.

Internet-related trade mark disputes

Most of the disputes which have reached the courts have concerned the question of whether use or possession of a domain name including a trade mark constitutes infringement. Two situations might arise, the first concerned with cases of domain-name hijacking as discussed earlier, and the second with the more problematic case of honest concurrent usage.

Domain-name hijacking

As indicated, domain registries have operated (and to a considerable extent, continue to do so) on the basis of accepting the first application for registration of a particular domain name. This has been open to exploitation by street- (or Internet-) wise users, who have sought to register large numbers of popular names. Names such as Macdonalds, Hertz, and Rolex were issued to applicants with no connection with the well-known firms. The practice of seeking a domain name corresponding with a well-known organisation is generally referred to as 'domain-name hijacking'. As the commercial usage of the Internet has increased, so the benefits of obtaining a domain name which is readily identifiable with the owner's business has become recognised. It is reported that one domain name (pizza.com) has been sold for no less than £1.3 million,[11] with a number of firms conducting online auctions for the sale of attractive domain names.[12]

In the case of a number of the names mentioned above, the return of these to their 'rightful' owners has been accompanied by the making of payments to charity. Other 'hijackers' have acted from less altruistic motives. The first Internet-related dispute to come before an English court provides an illustration. In *Harrods v Lawrie*,[13] the plaintiff successfully asked the High Court to order the defendant to give up all claim to the domain names Harrods.com and Harrods.co.uk. It was noted that the defendant had also registered the names ladbrokes.com and cadburys.com. A spokesman for Harrods suggested:

> There can be only two purposes in him registering the name. One is to demand money from us to relinquish it, and the other to stop us using it. Either purpose is, we think, illegal and we believe that the existing laws of this country should be sufficient to establish that a company may protect its name and reputation on the Internet.

The decision in this case was handed down in the absence of the defendant and is of very limited precedential value. A non-Internet-related case which may be of relevance in illustrating the issues involved is that of *Glaxo plc v Glaxowellcome Ltd*.[14] Here, a merger had been proposed between two pharmaceutical companies, Glaxo and Wellcome. The news was announced in a press release on 23 January 1995, which stated that the new company would trade under the name Glaxo-Wellcome plc. The following day, one of the defendants, who acted as a company registration agent registered a company under the name Glaxowellcome Ltd. The defendants' normal business was to create 'shell' companies which

---

[11] <http://news.bbc.co.uk/1/hi/7331042.stm>.
[12] See, eg, <http://www.domdeal.com/>.
[13] *Daily Telegraph*, 14 January 1997.
[14] [1996] FSR 388.

would be sold for a fee of £1,000. The plaintiffs discovered the details of the registration which would have prevented their own use of the name. The defendants refused to sell the rights in the name for their standard fee, but indicated 'without prejudice' that this might be arranged for a fee of £100,000. The plaintiffs alleged that the defendants were guilty of the tort of 'passing off' and sought an order requiring the defendants to change the name of their company to something 'which did not contain the names "Glaxo" or "Wellcome" or any other confusingly similar words'.

This order was granted in the High Court, Lightman J holding that the plaintiffs were not obliged to follow the statutory procedures for challenging the registration of a company name with the Registrar of Companies, proceedings which could well be lengthy. The court, he stated:

> will not countenance any such pre-emptive strike of registering companies with names where others have the goodwill in those names, and the registering party then demanding a price for changing the names. It is an abuse of the system of registration of companies' names[15]

and granted an injunction 'specifically requiring the company and subscribers to take all such steps as lie within their power to change or facilitate the change of name'.

A more significant and directly relevant decision is that of the Court of Appeal in *British Telecommunications plc, Virgin Enterprises Ltd, J Sainsbury plc, Marks & Spencer plc and Ladbroke Group plc v One in a Million*.[16] The defendant, One in a Million, together with four other companies, acted as dealers in Internet domain names. Included in the names registered by them were:

ladbrokes.com	bt.org
sainsbury.com	virgin.org
sainsburys.com	marksandspencer.co.uk
j-sainsbury.com	britishtelecom.co.uk
marksandspencer.com	britishtelecom.net
cellnet.net	britishtelecom.com

The plaintiff companies alleged that the defendant's conduct constituted both threats to engage in and completed acts of passing off and trade mark infringement. Judgment was granted in their favour in the High Court, with the judge accepting that the defendant's conduct demonstrated a consistent and deliberate pattern of registering domain names which were either identical or confusingly similar to names and marks owned and used by other persons. In the absence of any evidence justifying acquisition of the names, the plaintiffs were awarded a permanent injunction.[17]

The defendants lodged an appeal but the Court of Appeal upheld the initial judgment in all respects. In respect of the allegation that the defendant had engaged in passing off, it was argued that the mere act of registering names was not sufficient. Although the defendant had in the past registered and sold domain names, there had been no attempt to offer the present names for sale—perhaps because the plaintiffs were so quick to seek an injunction. For the defence, it was argued that until some attempt was made to use or sell the names,

---

[15] *Glaxo plc v Glaxowellcome Ltd* [1996] FSR 388 at 391.
[16] [1999] FSR 1. The decision at first instance is reported at [1998] FSR 265.
[17] [1998] FSR 265 at 273.

there could be no element of threatened trade mark infringement or risk of deception to the public. This contention was rejected. Delivering the judgment of the court, Lord Justice Walker identified the criteria that should be applied by a court in deciding whether to grant relief:

> The court should consider the similarity of the names, the intention of the defendant, the type of trade and all the surrounding circumstances . . . If, taking all the circumstances into account the court should conclude that the name was produced to enable passing-off, is adapted to be used for passing-off and, if used, is likely to be fraudulently used, an injunction will be appropriate.[18]

The judge proceeded to examine the activities of the defendant in some detail. As indicated, a considerable number of instances were identified when names of well-known companies had been registered and subsequently offered for sale. British Telecommunications had been offered the domain bt.org for about £5,000. This had itself resulted in threats of legal action by BT, which culminated in the defendants agreeing to the transfer of the domain name. Burger King was also reported to have been offered the domain burgerking.org for a 'mere' £25,000. After considering a number of similar cases where he considered there was an express or implicit threat to sell the domain names to a third party, Walker LJ described the defendants' conduct as evidencing 'systematic registration' of well-known brands names with the intention of 'extracting money from the owners of the brands'.

In respect of a number of the domain names, the defendant argued that there could be other legitimate holders of the name:

> [T]here are people called Sainsbury and Ladbroke and companies, other than Virgin Enterprises Ltd, who have as part of their name the word Virgin and also people or firms whose initials would be BT.[19]

Even the defendant had to concede that this argument could not apply in respect of the name marksandspencer.co.uk. The court was also unimpressed with the arguments relating to the other companies. Once again, the pattern of the defendants' behaviour was damning.

A number of the plaintiffs also brought action alleging trade mark infringement. Section 10(4) of the Trade Marks Act 1994 defines what constitutes use of a trade mark:

> For the purposes of this section, a person uses a sign if, in particular, he—
>
> (a) affixes it to goods or the packaging thereof;
>
> (b) offers or exposes goods for sale, puts them on the market or stocks them for those purposes under the sign, or offers or supplies them under the sign, or offers or supplies services under the sign;
>
> (c) imports or exports goods under the sign; or
>
> (d) uses the sign on business papers or in advertising.

In *One in a Million*, Walker LJ took the view that the use was in connection with the defendant's business of supplying services. Counsel for the defendant argued that in order to constitute infringement there had to

> be a trade mark use in relation to goods or services, in the sense that it had to denote origin. He also submitted that the use had to be confusing use.[20]

---

[18] *British Telecommunications plc, Virgin Enterprises Ltd, J Sainsbury plc, Marks & Spencer plc and Ladbroke Group plc v One in a Million* [1999] FSR 1 at 8.

[19] At 23.

[20] At 25.

These issues are potentially significant in the Internet context. In the present case, the defendant's conduct again told against them, it being held that:

> I am not satisfied that Section 10(3) [of the Trade Marks Act 1994] does require the use to be trade mark use nor that it must be confusing use, but I am prepared to assume that it does. Upon that basis I am of the view that threats to infringe have been established . . . The domain names were registered to take advantage of the distinctive character and reputation of the marks. That is unfair and detrimental.[21]

The issue of 'trade mark use' and the possibility of confusion were discussed in more detail in the Scottish case of *Bravado Merchandising Services Ltd v Mainstream Publishing (Edinburgh) Ltd*.[22] An author had written a book about the pop group, 'Wet Wet Wet'. The group had trade marked its name in categories relating to printed matter. The book's title was *A Sweet Little Mystery—Wet Wet Wet—The Inside Story*. It was alleged that this constituted trade mark infringement.

Delivering judgment, Lord McCluskey made frequent reference to the criterion of whether the name was used 'in a trade mark sense'. He pointed out that:

> a travel writer who wrote an article about a fortnight's hill walking in the Lake District might well, if he had been unlucky enough, give it the title 'Wet Wet Wet'.

Such usage would be descriptive of the topic and would not constitute use in a trade mark sense. In the present case, however:

> The repeated reference to 'Wet' has nothing to do with moisture or political timidity. On the contrary, the use of 'Wet Wet Wet' is avowedly and obviously a use of the name which the group has registered. Accordingly, even if the use is appropriate to indicate the subject matter of the book on whose cover it appears that use does not thereby cease to be used in a trade mark sense.[23]

If use of a trade mark as the title of a book constitutes trade mark use, there can be little doubt that use as a domain name would be similarly regarded. Lord McCluskey went on, however, to consider the defence provided by section 11(2) of the Trade Marks Act 1994. This sanctions:

> the use of indications concerning the . . . intended purpose of goods or services . . . provided the use is in accordance with honest practice in industrial or commercial matters.

In the present case, the use of the trade mark was to indicate the subject matter of the book. The judge commented that:

> In the course of the discussion, as I noted earlier, such names as Ford, Disney and Guinness were discussed. It would be a bizarre result of trade marks legislation, the primary purpose of which is to 'guarantee the trade mark as an indication of origin', if it could be used to prevent publishers from using the protected name in the title of a book about the company or product. If that had been the intention of Parliament, I would have expected it to be made plain.[24]

Accordingly, the claim of trade mark infringement was dismissed. It is perhaps unlikely that a defendant such as One in a Million could satisfy the Trade Marks Act 1994, section 11(2) defence, but the issue may be more open in the case where a site contains material about a trade mark owner. If the author's book could legitimately use the group's name as its title,

---

[21] At 25.
[22] [1996] FSR 205.
[23] *Bravado Merchandising Services Ltd v Mainstream Publishing (Edinburgh) Ltd* [1996] FSR 205 at 213.
[24] At 216.

the same might be said of a website containing information or comment about the group. On the same basis, someone establishing a website to discuss the current US anti-trust litigation involving Microsoft might well wish to include reference to the company in the domain name.

Honest concurrent use

In the cases discussed so far, there appears little doubt that the parties seeking to register the domain names were acting, at the least, in bad faith and without possessing any colourable title to use of the name. Other circumstances may be less clear-cut, with two or more parties possessing rights in respect of a name. The problem may arise in a number of ways. With forty-two categories of goods and services in the Trade Mark Register, the same name may have been allocated to a number of persons. The existence of many national trade mark regimes is likely to result in further duplication, whilst in the case of trade marks which can be used as human surnames, tens of thousands of persons may have an entitlement to the name.

A number of actions have reached the courts involving disputes between parties as to the right to a particular Internet domain name. Many of the disputes have also involved the organisations responsible for the administration of the system of domain names and these have devised a bewildering range of policies in the attempt to limit their exposure in trade mark disputes. If a name is retained following a challenge from a trade mark owner, there is the possibility that the registered owner may regard them as jointly liable with the name holder. If the name is withdrawn following a complaint, an action may be brought by the registered owner alleging breach of contract. The case of *Pitman Training Ltd v Nominet United Kingdom*[25] is illustrative of the situations that are likely to arise.

The Pitman publishing company was established in 1849 and expanded to cover a range of publishing and training activities. In 1985, the various divisions of the business were sold, the publishing business being acquired by Pearsons, the second defendant in the present case, and the training business by the plaintiff. An agreement was reached at that time providing for the continued use of the Pitman name by the new owners.

In February 1996, a request was submitted to Nominet United Kingdom, the organisation which administers much of the .uk domain-name system, by an Internet Service Provider (ISP), Netnames, acting on behalf of the publishing company and seeking registration of the names 'pitman.co.uk' and 'pitman.com'. The application was accepted. Although the publishers had plans to establish a website and reference to its new domain names was used in some of their advertising, it does not appear that any significant use was made of the Internet.

In March 1996, another ISP acting on behalf of the plaintiff, Pitman Training, made a totally independent request for the allocation of the domain name 'pitman.co.uk'. Under the allocation rules operated by Nominet, a system of 'first come, first served' applied. Under this provision, the plaintiff's request should have been rejected. Owing to some administrative mishap, however, the request was accepted and the original registration was removed and reallocated to the plaintiff, who promptly made extensive use of the name, sending out significant mailings and publishing adverts inviting email responses to the 'pitman.co.uk' address. From a commercial perspective, the exercise was not successful. Only two replies had been received by the date of the trial.

It was not until December 1996 that the second defendant discovered that its domain name had been withdrawn. It made a complaint to its ISP, requiring reinstatement of its

---

[25] [1997] FSR 797.

name. Prolonged negotiations followed, involving all of the parties to the case but without an acceptable solution being reached. Finally, on 4 April 1997, Nominet, applying its 'first come, first served' rule, indicated that the domain name would be removed from the plaintiff and reallocated it to the second defendant. Matters then switched to the High Court.

On 11 April, a consent order was made restraining Nominet from transferring the domain name pending a full hearing or further order. In May 1997, the matter returned to the High Court, where the Vice-Chancellor held that the injunction should be withdrawn on the basis that the plaintiff had not demonstrated a reasonable prospect of succeeding in its action. As was stated:

> It is trite law and, of course, common ground that interlocutory relief in an action can only be granted in support of some viable cause of action. If a plaintiff cannot show a reasonably arguable cause of action against a defendant the plaintiff cannot obtain any interlocutory relief against that defendant however convenient the grant of that relief might appear to be.[26]

In terms of intellectual property, the plaintiff's main ground of action was that the defendant had committed the tort of passing off. This contention was not accepted by the judge. The name Pitman had been used for publishing for almost 150 years. The agreement at the time of the break-up of the original company provided for its continued use in this context. Indeed, it was suggested, given the terms of the agreement, if any party was guilty of passing off it was more likely to be the plaintiff. He concluded:

> That there may be some confusion experienced by some members of the public is undoubtedly so. But that confusion results from the use by both companies, PTC and Pitman Publishing, of the style Pitman for their respective trading purposes. No viable passing off claim against Pitman Publishing arising out of the future or past use by Pitman Publishing of the 'pitman.co.uk' domain name has, in my judgment, been shown.[27]

In many respects, it may be considered that the problems of trying to apply national trade mark law in the context of the Internet are intractable. Final reference may be made to the case of *Prince plc v Prince Sports Group*.[28] The plaintiff was a UK company providing a range of computer consultancy and training services. The defendant was a major United States-based sports goods manufacturer which possessed US and UK trade marks in respect of the use of the name Prince for sports goods.

In 1995, the plaintiff applied for and was awarded an Internet domain name as Prince.com. In 1997, the defendant became aware of this fact and its attorneys wrote a letter to the plaintiff, indicating that a failure on its part to relinquish rights in the name would constitute trade mark infringement and impliedly threatening legal proceedings:

> Dear Sirs:
>
> We represent Prince Sports Group, Inc, with respect to trademark and other intellectual property matters. Prince is the owner of the famous PRINCE trademark, which has been used in connection with tennis rackets, squash rackets, other sporting items and clothing for at least the past 20 years in the United States. Prince is the owner of several US registrations for the PRINCE mark, many of which are incontestable, e.g., Registration Nos 1,049,720; 1,074,654; 1,111,008; 1,103,956; 1,233,680; 1,284,452; 1,290,202; and 1,290,217. Our client has also registered the PRINCE mark in many other countries throughout the world, including the United Kingdom.
>
> Through extensive sales and advertising under the PRINCE mark and the excellent quality of our client's products, the PRINCE mark has become an asset of immeasurable goodwill and value to our client.

---

[26] *Pitman Training Ltd v Nominet United Kingdom* [1997] FSR 797 at 806.   [27] At 807.
[28] [1998] FSR 22.

It has come to our client's attention that you have registered 'PRINCE.COM' as a domain name with Network Solutions Inc, (NSI) thereby preventing our client from registering its house mark and trade name as a domain name. We are writing to advise you that your company's use and registration of PRINCE as a domain name constitutes infringement and dilution of our client's trademark rights in PRINCE, as well as unfair competition, under the Lanham Act, 15 USC 1051 *et seq.*

This matter can be amicably resolved by an assignment of the PRINCE.COM domain name to Prince Sports Group, Inc, in accordance with the procedures of NSI and an agreement not to use PRINCE as part of any new domain name you may select. While we are willing to wait for your orderly transition to a new domain name, we must have your immediate written agreement to assign the PRINCE.COM domain name to Prince Sports to avoid litigation.

We look forward to hearing from you or your attorneys in the very near future.[29]

The plaintiff considered that the letter related to proceedings in the United Kingdom. Under UK trade mark law, an unjustified threat to institute infringement proceedings is actionable, section 21 of the Trade Marks Act 1994 providing that:

1. Where a person threatens another with proceedings for infringement of a registered trade mark other than—

    (a) the application of the mark to goods or their packaging;

    (b) the importation of goods to which, or to the packaging of which, the mark has been applied; or

    (c) the supply of services under the mark any person aggrieved may bring proceedings for relief under this section.

2. The relief which may be applied for is any of the following—

    (a) a declaration that the threats are unjustifiable;

    (b) an injunction against the continuance of the threats; or

    (c) damages in respect of any loss he has sustained by the threats.

The plaintiff sought all three remedies as well as a further declaration that its own conduct did not constitute trade mark infringement. It achieved significant but not total success. Although the plaintiff's letter made extensive reference to US trade marks and to provisions of US law, it was considered that it could also reasonably be understood as relating to proceedings in the United Kingdom. The threat of action did not come under the headings in section 24(1) of the Trade Marks Act 1994. Although the plaintiff's business involved the supply of services, the threat of action was general in its terms. The court therefore awarded the remedies under section 24(2)(a) and (b). It rejected the request for a more extensive declaration of non-infringement, holding that such a determination was not appropriate for interim proceedings. As regards damages, the court was of the view that the plaintiff had not suffered any financial loss sufficient to sustain a claim for damages.

Reverse domain-name hijacking

Whilst there is little doubt that the attempt wrongfully to utilise a trade mark or similar identifier as a domain name will be struck down, the practice referred to as reverse domain-name hijacking has acquired some publicity, albeit without any significant legal authority. The practice has been defined by the Internet Corporation for Assigned Names

---

[29] *Prince plc v Prince Sports Group* [1998] FSR 21 at 24–5.

and Numbers (ICANN) as the attempt to use procedures 'in bad faith to attempt to deprive a registered domain-name holder of a domain name'.[30] An example of the application of this doctrine can be seen in a dispute between the Driver and Vehicle Licensing Agency (DVLA) in the United Kingdom and a United States-based company, DVL Automation. Although it owned the domain name DVLA.gov.uk, the DVLA objected to the registration of the domain DVLA.com by the US company and instituted arbitration procedures before WIPO under the Uniform Dispute Resolution Rules (discussed in more detail later). It was argued that:

> Ignoring the '.com' domain name extension, is identical to the Complainant's famous DVLA name and trademarks. There is no difference between the Respondent's chosen domain name and the Complainant's trade name and trademarks. The impression given to web users is that the Respondent's domain name and the Complainant's marks are one and the same, that is, that any associated goods or services are sponsored by, endorsed by, or affiliated with the Complainant.

It was further argued that as the respondent traded under the name DVL Automation it would have a legitimate interest in the name DVL.com but not DVLA.com. It was also asserted that the respondent had no trade mark registered in the name DVLA and no legitimate interest in its use. These arguments were unequivocally rejected by the arbiter:

> The Complainant claims that the Respondent cannot have a legitimate interest in the domain name since it does not have a trademark in 'DVLA'. However, the Policy does not require, and has never required, that the Respondent have a registered mark for it to have a legitimate interest in a domain name. Alternatively the Complainant argues that the Respondent's trading name is 'DVL Automation' rather than 'DVLA', and therefore there is 'no reason why the Respondent should have any interest in a domain name incorporating "DVLA"'. It is hard to know how to respond to this sort of assertion, except to say that if this were the standard by which a Respondent's legitimate interest was assessed then almost no Respondent could ever hope to retain its domain name. It is an unsupportable statement, on a par with the Complainant's assertion that the Respondent has no legitimate interest in the domain name 'since the Respondent trades as DVL Automation and not as DVLA.'
>
> The Complainant's final assertion, that there 'is no evidence that the Respondent is making a legitimate non-commercial or fair use of the Domain Name' is dangerously close to an outright lie. The Complaint specifically discloses that the Complainant has seen the website at 'dvla.com', which the Respondent is using for its clearly bona fide business purposes, and which is utterly removed from vehicle licensing or any other usage which might be characterized as illegitimate. The Respondent is a registered company, doing business at a domain name which has an obvious connection with its company name. The Complainant notes as much in its Complaint, and yet it maintains this position. It cannot do so in good faith.

The conclusion was damning:

> I consider that the Complainant has brought this action in bad faith . . . the Complaint discloses that the Complainant is aware of the business and corporate status of the Respondent, and has examined the website available at the domain name. The domain name was registered over 6 years ago, and is being used for a legitimate business.

The DVLA case is in some respects a typical example of the issues which have arisen when a party seeks to stretch the level of protection conferred by trade marks. An alternative

---

[30] <http://www.icann.org/dndr/udrp/uniform-rules.htm>.

form of the practice has occurred in several cases where the target of the complaint is what is generally referred to as a.sucks website. These are typically established by dissatisfied customers of an organisation and, prefixed with the name of a company, provide a forum for the ventilation of complaints against the company. The basic purpose of trade mark law is to prevent confusion in the minds of the public about the origin of goods or services and increasingly of a website. Perhaps reflecting the early and evolving nature of the cases, decisions have been contradictory and, as with the DVLA case, have been brought in the course of dispute resolution procedures established by ICANN or by national domain-name registries. Consideration will next be given to the manner in which these procedures have been operated.

The Uniform Dispute Resolution Rules

A feature of early disputes concerned with rights relating to domain names was the attempt by domain-name registries such as Network Solutions and Nominet to devise policies designed to render them immune from legal action. In many respects, the agencies were put in difficult legal positions. In the *Pitman* case[31] discussed earlier, for example, the domain-name registry, Nominet, was threatened with legal action by one party unless the name was reassigned and with action by the other in the event that it was reassigned. A classic example of a 'no win' situation.

With the emergence of ICANN as the coordinating body for the system of domain names, a new approach has been adopted to the problem of trying to resolve domain-name disputes without invoking national courts. Any organisation wishing to act as a registry in respect of the generic domain names is obliged to conduct business according to the 'Uniform Domain Name Dispute Resolution Policy'.[32] This requires applicants for domain names to submit to mandatory dispute resolution procedures before approved dispute resolution service providers in the event of any claim that:

(i) your domain name is identical or confusingly similar to a trademark or service mark in which the complainant has rights;

(ii) you have no rights or legitimate interests in respect of the domain name; and

(iii) your domain name has been registered and is being used in bad faith.

The onus is on a complainant to establish all of these heads of claim.[33]

Originally, four organisations were recognised as offering dispute resolution services under the ICANN rules:

1. the Asian Domain Name Dispute Resolution Centre[34]

2. International Institute for Conflict Prevention and Resolution (CPR)

3. the National Arbitration Forum

4. WIPO.[35]

The CPR Institute and the National Arbitration Forum—which described itself as the 'largest provider of domain name dispute resolution in North America'—are no longer active in the field. Throughout, the major player has been the WIPO, which as of 2007 had received almost 12,000 complaints concerning the use of domain names.

---

[31] *Pitman Training Ltd v Nominet United Kingdom* [1997] FSR 797.
[32] Available from <http://www.icann.org/udrp/udrp.htm>.
[33] Uniform Dispute Resolution Rules, r. 4a.
[34] <https://www.adndrc.org>.   [35] <http://arbiter.wipo.int/domains/>.

An early decision of the WIPO dispute resolution panel in the case of *Jeanette Winterson v Mark Hogarth* illustrates how these requirements might be applied. In this case, the complainant, a well-known author, objected to the registration by the respondent, a Cambridge University academic, of the domain names:

jeanettewinterson.com

jeanettewinterson.net

jeanettewinterson.org[36]

In circumstances similar to those at issue in the *One in a Million* case,[37] the registrant had registered a range of domains, making use of the names of well-known authors. Contact had been made with a number of these; in the case of one, Joanna Trollope, a letter was sent to her literary agent indicating the intent to auction the names to third parties, but giving the author a right of 'first refusal' to acquire the names for a fee of 3 per cent of her 1999 gross book sales. Similar communications were made to the complainant.

In answer to complaints, the respondent wrote to the effect that:

> The Complainant also contends that the Respondent has no rights to or legitimate interests in respect of the domain names in issue, that the Complainant has not consented to use of the Mark by the Respondent and that the Respondent has registered and is using the domain names in bad faith.

The respondent stated that:

> he registered the domain names in issue in the belief that JEANETTE WINTERSON was not a trade mark or a service mark and that the domain names in issue were registered with a view to developing a website devoted to the work of the Complainant.

It was held by the panel that the Uniform Domain Name Dispute Resolution Policy required that a complainant establish all three grounds specified—namely, use of an identical or confusingly similar mark, in breach of a trade or service mark in which the respondent has no rights, and in circumstances evidencing bad faith.

It is clear that the name used is effectively identical to the complainant's name. More significant was the finding of the panel in respect of the next ground. Here, it was ruled that:

> The Rules do *not* require that the Complainant's trademark be registered by a government authority or agency for such a right to exist.

The complainant being resident in England, it was ruled, English law had to be applied to determine the extent of rights. The doctrine of passing off, it was held could also be invoked:

> 6.11   There are a number of English cases dealing with passing-off the names of well-known individuals and personalities, which all—as may be expected—turn on the facts. These include, the Uncle MAC case [*McCulloch v Lewis A May (Produce Distributors) Ltd* [1947] 2 All ER 845]; the KOJAK case [*Taverner Rutledge v Trexpalm* (1975) FSR 479]; the WOMBLES case [*Wombles Ltd v Wombles Skips Ltd* [1977] RPC 99]; the ABBA case [*Lyngstad v Anabas Products* [1977] FSR 62]; and the Teenage Mutant Ninja Turtles case [*Mirage Studios v Counter Feat Clothing Co Ltd* [1991] FSR 145]. The case for decision here does not concern whether or not passing-off has occurred *but* whether the Complainant (Jeanette Winterson) has rights in her name sufficient to constitute a trade mark for the purposes of para. 4a of the Policy.

[36]   A copy of the decision can be obtained from <http://arbiter.wipo.int/domains/decisions/index.html>.

[37]   *British Telecommunications plc, Virgin Enterprises Ltd, J Sainsbury plc, Marks & Spencer plc and Ladbroke Group plc v One in a Million* [1999] FSR 1.

6.12 In the Panel's view, *trademarks* where used in para. 4a of the Policy is not to be construed by reference to the criteria of registrability under English law [the ELVIS
PRESLEY case] but more broadly in terms of the distinctive features of a person's
activities, in other words, akin to the common law right to prevent unauthorised use
of a name. Thus, applying English law the Complainant clearly would have a cause
of action to prevent unauthorized use of the Mark JEANETTE WINTERSON in
passing-off.

The other tests being satisfied, the panel ordered that the registrations should be transferred to the complainant.

The decision in this case appears in line with the authorities cited. The complainant
was a well-known and successful author and the effect of the registrations complained
of would satisfy the criteria for the award of a remedy by the English courts. The English
courts have never, however, accepted that any general right to personality exists which can
be infringed by use of a name or other indications of identity.[38] It must remain an open
question whether any action would lie against registrations such as those reported to have
been made in the name of the recent Prime Minister Tony Blair's youngest son ('leoblair.
com' and 'leoblair.co.uk').

Some time after the development of dispute resolution schemes for WWW sites within
the generic top-level domains, a similar scheme was adopted to deal with disputes within
the.uk top-level domain. Operated by the domain-name registry Nominet, a panel of
around thirty experts act as adjudicators with individual cases being heard by a single person.[39] The basis for any complaint is that there has been 'abusive registration of a domain
name'. This encompasses a domain name which either:

i. was registered or otherwise acquired in a manner which, at the time when the
registration or acquisition took place, took unfair advantage of or was unfairly
detrimental to the Complainant's Rights; or

ii. has been used in a manner which took unfair advantage of or was unfairly detrimental to the Complainant's Rights.[40]

Beyond substituting the perhaps more pejorative term 'abusive registration' for the ICANN
criterion of 'bad faith', the substance of the policy is broadly similar.

The first decision under the new procedure was delivered in 2001. The pharmaceutical
company, Eli Lilly, was successful in its application to have rights in the domain xigris.ci.uk
transferred to it. Eli Lilly had obtained a European Community Trade Mark in the name
Xigris in 1999. The domain name had been registered by an ex-employee in June 2001.
No representations were made by the employee in response to Eli Lilly's complaint and,
although there was no evidence available as to the purpose for which the registration might
have been made, the expert held that the circumstances surrounding the case were such
that a prima facie case of abuse had been made out and that, in the absence of any attempt
at explanation, the request for transfer should be granted.[41]

In total, more than 6,000 disputes have been referred to the UK dispute resolution service,
although around 25 per cent of these have been declared invalid on procedural grounds
and did not therefore proceed to any form of dispute resolution. Following receipt of a valid
complaint, the first step in the process is to attempt mediation and more than half of the
cases are resolved at this stage. In 2014, the last year for which statistics are currently available,

---

[38] See discussion in W. Cornish and D. Llewelyn, *Intellectual Property: Patents, Copyrights, Trademarks and
Allied Rights* (London, 2007), paras. 16.33–16.34.

[39] <http://www.nominet.org.uk/disputes/drs/>.

[40] <http://www.nominet.org.uk/disputes/when-use-drs/policy-and-procedure/drs-policy>.

[41] DRS 0001 (2001).

726 complaints were made regarding domain names although only around 250 continued to the level of formal dispute resolution procedures.[42] Historically, in almost 80 per cent of cases that have advanced to the level of formal proceedings, the decision has been in favour of the complainant. Appeals may be made against the decision of an individual expert. These will be heard before a panel of three experts. To date, twenty appeals have been made, half being determined in favour of the appellant and half sustaining the original decision. The roll-call of complainants includes some of the best-known names in the United Kingdom's commercial and public life, featuring organisations such as Harrods, Vodaphone, Barclays Bank, Nokia, the Royal Marines, and Interflora. It appears almost to be the case that an incident of cybersquatting is an integral consequence of commercial success.

Trade marks and Internet search engines

During the initial days of the Internet there was substantial litigation concerning the use of trade marks as a component of an Internet domain name. Thanks to the adoption of ICANN's domain-name dispute resolution policy and its national equivalents, these issues have largely disappeared from the law courts. As one source of litigation has dried up, however, others have surfaced in respect of the use of trade marks to influence the manner in which search engines present users with the results of search requests and also the responsibility of online market places such as eBay where counterfeit goods are offered for sale on their virtual premises.

The workings of search engines are complex and different engines utilise different algorithms to determine the order in which results are presented. This raises some interesting legal issues and the case of *Interflora v Marks and Spencer*[43] illustrates well some of the problems in the field.

The claimant Interflora is the accepted market leader in the sector consisting of the remote delivery of flowers. In the United Kingdom it delivers some 3.2 million flower orders every year accounting for about 18 per cent of the total market for cut flowers (around 65 per cent is represented by direct sales in supermarkets and other retailers). When Interflora was established in 1908, customers would visit a local outlet and a telephone or telegraph order would be placed with the franchisee closest to the recipient's address. As with many other businesses much of the activity is now carried out online and more than half of orders are now placed that way.

Interflora is essentially a network operation involving cooperation between thousands of independent florist companies. It has some 40,000 members in 140 countries. Traditionally, members have been small operators with only one or two sales outlets. More recently Interflora has entered into marketing agreements with some larger suppliers including the major UK supermarket chain Sainsbury's. As was noted in court:

> From 1995 to about 2000 IBU had a relationship with Sainsbury's that involved co-branded Sainsbury's/Interflora leaflets being placed in selected Sainsbury's stores. These invited customers to place an order with Interflora via a dedicated telephone number. Calls on that number were answered 'Interflora Sainsbury's'.

Essentially, the operation was a virtual one. Orders placed via the Sainsbury promotion would be passed on for fulfilment by local Interflora members and the flowers delivered would carry only the Interflora branding. A further and continuing relationship exists

---

[42] <http://nominet-prod.s3.amazonaws.com/wp-content/uploads/2015/10/Nominet_domain_disputes_2014.pdf>.
[43] [2013] EWHC 1291.

between Interflora and the Cooperative funeral care service under which the availability of Interflora funeral wreaths is advertised on the Cooperative website.

The Interflora brand is widely recognised and, as was noted in court, the term is widely used in web searches by users wishing to arrange for the delivery of flowers:

> According to a United Kingdom newsletter . . . in February 2008 **interflora** was the most searched for term in the flower sector and accounted for one in five visits to the top 25 flower websites, followed by the generic term "flowers". At that time M & S was not listed in the top 10 flower delivery websites. **Interflora** was searched for 30 times more frequently than 'marks and spencer flowers'.

The name 'Interflora' is protected under trade mark law and there was no suggestion that the trade mark is not fully valid. Search engines such as Google earn almost all of their income from advertising and a major component of this income comes from companies who are willing to pay in return for their goods or services being given a high ranking in what have been referred to at various times as 'sponsored links' or 'Ads' (advertisements).

A company wishing to advertise in this manner will seek to register a number of words with Google. When a user types the word the relevant sponsored link box will appear. Many companies make extensive use of this service. In respect of the first defendant, evidence was given to the effect that:

> Over time, M & S has built up a large number of keywords it bids on. As at 21 December 2012, there were approximately 4.2 million keywords spread across 80,556 ad groups, 2,659 campaigns and 32 accounts. The vast majority of these keywords are generic terms, such as 'suits'. Many of them are selected on exact match, but M & S also use phrase match, broad match and negative matching. Mr Lemon's evidence was that about 92.5% of M & S's keyword advertising budget was now spent on generic terms, about 5% supporting M & S's own brands and about 2.5% on competitive brand bidding.[44]

Google UK (unlike many of its other European affiliates) allows advertisers to pay to register third-party trade marks as search terms. More than one company may register the same terms and indeed a sort of auction can occur whereby the company that offers the highest payment will receive the highest ranking in the sponsored links. A user entering a search request will receive on the first results page a list of sponsored links clearly marked as such within a shaded box. This will be followed by a ranking of results in accordance with the normal operation of the search engine's algorithms. Payment by the advertiser to Google is triggered when a user clicks on the sponsored link and is taken to the relevant home page.

The claimants alleged that the actions of Marks and Spencer constituted unlawful use of their trade mark. Following an initial hearing before the High Court in 2009,[45] a number of questions relating to the scope and extent of trade mark law were referred to the European Court of Justice[46] which delivered its ruling in 2011.[47] Following a series of domestic procedural issues, the case returned to the High Court which delivered its ruling in May 2013.

Initial consideration was given to Article 16 of the Trade Related Aspects of Intellectual Property Rights Agreement which provides that:

> The owner of a registered trademark shall have the exclusive right to prevent all third parties not having the owner's consent from using in the course of trade identical or similar signs for goods or services which are identical or similar to those in respect of which the trademark is registered where such use would result in a likelihood of confusion. In case of the use of an identical sign for identical goods or services, a likelihood of confusion shall be presumed . . .

---

[44] para. 133.   [45] [2009] EWHC 1095 (Ch).
[46] [2010] EWHC 925 (Ch).   [47] [2013] EWHC 1291 (Ch).

Whilst Article 5 of the European Trademark Directive states that:

> The registered trade mark shall confer on the proprietor exclusive rights therein. The proprietor shall be entitled to prevent all third parties not having his consent from using in the course of trade:
>
> (a) any sign which is identical with the trade mark in relation to goods or services which are identical with those for which the trade mark is registered;
>
> (b) any sign where, because of its identity with, or similarity to, the trade mark and the identity or similarity of goods or services covered by the trade mark and the sign, there exists a likelihood of confusion on the part of the public, which includes the likelihood of association between the sign and the trade mark.

In a classic case of trade mark infringement the infringer will place names or logos belonging to the right holder on what are effectively counterfeit goods. The situation in the present case is somewhat different in that there was no visible use by the defendants of the Interflora trade mark. As Mr Justice Arnold noted:

> The case law of the CJEU establishes that the proprietor of a trade mark can only succeed in a claim under Article 5(1)(a) of the Directive . . . if six conditions are satisfied: (i) there must be use of a sign by a third party within the relevant territory; (ii) the use must be in the course of trade; (iii) it must be without the consent of the proprietor of the trade mark; (iv) it must be of a sign which is identical to the trade mark; (v) it must be in relation to goods or services which are identical to those for which the trade mark is registered; and (vi) it must affect or be liable to affect the functions of the trade mark.

It was accepted that the first five conditions had been established by the claimants and the discussion focused on the final condition: had the defendants' conduct affected the functioning of the Interflora trade mark? In order to determine this it was necessary to consider other authorities, in particular the decision of the European Court in the further trade mark case of *L'Oreal and Ors v eBay and Ors*,[48] following a further reference made by Mr Justice Arnold in July 2009.[49]

In this case a series of ten questions were referred to the European Court concerning the legality under trade mark law of the offering for sale on eBay of a range of cosmetic products in respect of which trade mark rights were unquestionably owned by L'Oreal. Some of the questions referred to the conduct of the sellers but probably the major issues of principle related to the extent to which eBay, which provided the online marketplace for sales, would be liable in its own right for trade mark infringement on the part of its users or whether it might benefit from the protection of the defence provided under the E-Commerce Directive to the effect that it acted merely as a host for material provided by its users. This states that:

> 1. Where an information society service is provided that consists of the storage of information provided by a recipient of the service, Member States shall ensure that the service provider is not liable for the information stored at the request of a recipient of the service, on condition that:
>
>   (a) the provider does not have actual knowledge of illegal activity or information and, as regards claims for damages, is not aware of facts or circumstances from which the illegal activity or information is apparent; or
>
>   (b) the provider, upon obtaining such knowledge or awareness, acts expeditiously to remove or to disable access to the information.

---

[48] Case C-324/09.   [49] [2009] EWHC 1094.

Although there is to be no liability in damages (or under criminal law), the Directive makes it clear that there is to be no immunity from the grant of a court order 'requiring the service provider to terminate or prevent an infringement' (injunctive relief).

In respect of the liability of the individual sellers the Court made the important observation that trade mark rights can be enforced only against a party who acts in the course of trade—'in the context of a commercial activity'. The emergence of sites such as eBay does undoubtedly create some issues in determining whether sellers are acting in the course of a business. In the real world the status of a seller may be readily apparent from the nature of the premises used for transactions. This is less apparent on sites such as eBay and the distinction between private sellers, those acting in the course of a hobby, and outright commercial sellers is not always easy to make.

As with most aspects of life, the operations of eBay are not entirely simple and straightforward and a number of issues are discussed. Three are of particular importance. Does the fact that eBay processes its user's data in order, for example, to allow online auctions to be conducted take it outside the scope of the 'hosting' defence? Secondly, assuming the defence is potentially available, what level of awareness might be ascribed to eBay regarding the presence of materials on its site in circumstances that would suffice to take it outside its protection? Finally, the Court considered the nature of the injunctive relief which might be available against eBay to claimants such as those in the present case.

In common with many aspects of the legislation, the E-Commerce Directive offers little guidance as to the scope of the activity of hosting, although Recital 42 of the Directive indicates that:

> The exemptions from liability established in this Directive cover only cases where the activity of the information society service provider is limited to the technical process of operating and giving access to a communication network over which information made available by third parties is transmitted or temporarily stored, for the sole purpose of making the transmission more efficient; this activity is of a mere technical, automatic and passive nature, which implies that the information society service provider has neither knowledge of nor control over the information which is transmitted or stored.

There is no doubt that eBay acts as more than a passive host in respect of its customers' data. The Court provides a synopsis of its *modus operandi* in paragraphs 28–30 of its judgment:

> eBay operates an electronic marketplace on which are displayed listings of goods offered for sale by persons who have registered for that purpose with eBay and have created a seller's account with it. eBay charges a percentage fee on completed transactions.
>
> eBay enables prospective buyers to bid for items offered by sellers. It also allows items to be sold without an auction, and thus for a fixed price, by means of a system known as 'Buy It Now'. Sellers can also set up online shops on eBay sites. An online shop lists all the items offered for sale by one seller at a given time.
>
> Sellers and buyers must accept eBay's online-market user agreement. One of the terms of that agreement is a prohibition on selling counterfeit items and on infringing trade marks.

In spite of this, the Court ruled that:

> the mere fact that the operator of an online marketplace stores offers for sale on its server, sets the terms of its service, is remunerated for that service and provides general information to its customers cannot have the effect of denying it the exemptions from liability provided for by Directive 2000/31.

This, however, is not the end of the matter. The issue of when eBay might be assumed to be aware of illegal actions by its users is of great significance. In the case of ordinary (typically non-commercial users), the Court ruled that:

> In situations in which that provider has confined itself to a merely technical and auto-matic processing of data and in which, as a consequence, the rule stated in Article 14(1) of Directive 2000/31 applies to it, it may none the less only be exempt, under paragraph 1, from any liability for unlawful data that it has stored on condition that it has not had 'actual knowledge of illegal activity or information' and, as regards claims for damages, has not been 'aware of facts or circumstances from which the illegal activity or information is appar-ent' or that, having obtained such knowledge or awareness, it has acted expeditiously to remove, or disable access to, the information.

For ordinary users the Court indicated that to benefit from the exemption a site owner would have to publish contact details in a sufficiently prominent manner to facilitate the making of complaints by right owners. This is itself a requirement of the E-Commerce Directive.

All users, however, are not the same and in some cases eBay will seek to develop a closer relationship with commercial sellers. eBay's documentation refers to the concept of 'power sellers' who have generated significant sales over a period of time. The site also embodies the concepts of anchor sites. As the Court noted:

> In some cases eBay assists sellers in order to enhance their offers for sale, to set up online shops, to promote and increase their sales. It also advertises some of the products sold on its marketplace using search engine operators such as Google to trigger the display of advertisements.

In such a situation a higher degree of responsibility would lie with eBay. In words perhaps analogous to Mr Justice Arnold's comments in the High Court suggesting that eBay should stand behind its sellers as an insurer in the event of any claim of infringement of intellectual property rights, the European Court ruled that:

> Where . . . the operator has provided assistance which entails, in particular, optimising the presentation of the offers for sale in question or promoting those offers, it must be con-sidered not to have taken a neutral position between the customer-seller concerned and potential buyers but to have played an active role of such a kind as to give it knowledge of, or control over, the data relating to those offers for sale. It cannot then rely, in the case of those data, on the exemption from liability referred to in Article 14(1) of Directive 2000/31.

The European Court considered the extent to which right owners might be entitled to seek injunctive relief against information society service providers. Although not explicitly stated in the E-Commerce Directive, such remedies are certainly not excluded as is the case with other forms of civil and criminal liability.

The key issue which the Court was asked to address concerned the range of parties against whom injunctive relief might be sought and, quite recently in the United Kingdom in the light of the recent controversy about super-injunctions, the breadth of the coverage of injunctions. In this context the European Court's pronouncements have also to take account of the provisions of the Copyright Enforcement Directive.[50] Under this, Member States are required to ensure 'that rightholders are in a position to apply for an injunction against intermediaries whose services are used by a third party to infringe an intellectual property right . . .'

---

[50] Directive 2004/48/EC of 29 April 2004 on the enforcement of intellectual property rights. OJ 2004 L 195/16.

A key issue for the Court was to determine whether:

that provision requires the Member States to ensure that the operator of an online market-place may, regardless of any liability of its own in relation to the facts at issue, be ordered to take, in addition to measures aimed at bringing to an end infringements of intellectual property rights brought about by users of its services, measures aimed at preventing further infringements of that kind.

It was argued on behalf of eBay that an injunction could only be issued to prevent the continuance of 'specific and clearly identified infringements'. The Court, following the opinion of the Advocate General, rejected such a restrictive interpretation holding that the objectives of the Enforcement Directive required the possibility that an injunction might

order an online service provider, such as a provider making an online marketplace available to internet users, to take measures that contribute not only to bringing to an end infringements committed through that marketplace, but also to preventing further infringements.

Whilst the E-Commerce Directive specifically excludes the imposition of any general or specific duty on the part of an Information Society Service Provider to monitor activities by its users, the grant of injunctive relief must be available not only for past actions but also to prevent 'further infringements of that kind. Those injunctions must be effective, proportionate, dissuasive and must not create barriers to legitimate trade.'

The key issue is that of proportionality. Here the words of the Advocate General are worth repeating:

The requirement of proportionality would in my opinion exclude an injunction against the intermediary to prevent any further infringements of a trade mark. However, I do not see anything in Directive 2004/48 which would prohibit injunctions against the intermediary requiring not only the prevention of the continuation of a specific act of infringement but also the prevention of repetition of the same or a similar infringement in the future, if such injunctions are available under national law. What is crucial, of course, is that the intermediary can know with certainty what is required from him, and that the injunction does not impose impossible, disproportionate or illegal duties like a general obligation of monitoring.

An appropriate limit for the scope of injunctions may be that of a double requirement of identity. This means that the infringing third party should be the same . . . and that the trade mark infringed should be the same in the cases concerned. Hence, an injunction could be given against an intermediary to prevent the continuation or repetition of an infringement of a certain trade mark by a certain user. Such an injunction could be followed by an information society service provider by simply closing the client account of the user in question.

Issues relating to trade marks and the Internet have been before the European Court on a number of occasions. In cases such as *L'Oreal* the focus has been on the appearance of counterfeit items on sites such as eBay and the extent to which intermediaries such as eBay should be held liable. The present case is somewhat different in that it related to the question of whether the defendants' conduct was lawful or unlawful.

Following initial proceedings before the High Court, Mr Justice Arnold referred four questions to the European Court for a preliminary ruling. As seems to be commonly the case, the Court conflated these into a single issue, whether the use of a trade mark for the purpose of what is generally referred to as comparative advertising could constitute infringement. As was stated at paragraph 43 of the judgment:

It is therefore appropriate to provide the referring court with guidance on interpretation in relation to the trade mark's function of indicating origin, its advertising function and its 'investment' function.

The Court continued:

> 51. In carrying out its examination of the facts, the referring court may choose to assess, first, whether the reasonably well-informed and reasonably observant internet user is deemed to be aware, on the basis of general knowledge of the market, that M & S's flower-delivery service is not part of the Interflora network but is, on the contrary, in competition with it and, second, should it become apparent that that is not generally known, whether M & S's advertisement enabled that internet user to tell that the service concerned does not belong to the Interflora network.

> 52. In particular, the referring court may take into account that, in the present case, the commercial network of the trade mark proprietor is composed of a large number of retailers which vary greatly in terms of size and commercial profile. The Court considers that, in such circumstances, it may be particularly difficult for the reasonably well-informed and reasonably observant internet user to determine, in the absence of any indication from the advertiser, whether or not the advertiser— whose advertisement is displayed in response to a search using that trade mark as a search term—is part of that network.

The European Court ruling is perhaps somewhat less Delphic in its pronouncements than is often the case and it did send a fairly clear signal to the High Court.

After presenting an extensive analysis both of the jurisprudence of the European Court and cases from the national courts of other Member States, Mr Justice Arnold ruled in favour of Interflora. The early European jurisprudence, he indicated laid emphasis on whether informed consumers might be misled by the use made of the trade mark. Most of the cases to date have concerned comparative advertising regarding prices—with, for example, one shop claiming that it was offering an item for sale at a lower price than a named (and trade marked) competitor. The requirement is that care has to be taken to ensure that like is being compared to like. In the present case the key question to be answered was whether a reasonably informed consumer might gain the false impression from seeing the Marks and Spencer sponsored link after entering the word 'Interflora' as a search term that there was a commercial connection between the two undertakings? Mr Justice Arnold answered the question in the affirmative. The reasonably informed consumer would, he ruled, have been aware that Interflora was the trade mark for a network of independent flower suppliers. Reference was made to further guidance supplied by the European Court in its preliminary ruling. This was to the effect that:

> The function of indicating the origin of the mark is adversely affected if the ad does not enable normally informed and reasonably attentive internet users, or enables them only with difficulty, to ascertain whether the goods or services referred to by the ad originate from the proprietor of the trade mark or an undertaking economically connected to it or, on the contrary, originate from a third party [paragraph 84].

It continued at paragraph 89:

> In the case where a third party's ad suggests that there is an economic link between that third party and the proprietor of the trade mark, the conclusion must be that there is an adverse effect on the function of indicating origin.

Effectively, Mr Justice Arnold ruled, the Court was saying that if the theoretical possibility of confusion was established, the onus of proof lay with the defendant to establish that this had not occurred. Whilst comparative advertising was not per se unlawful and indeed had been supported by the European Court as a means for promoting competition, in the particular case Marks and Spencer had not led any evidence to challenge Interflora's contention that consumers had been misled and that there had been an adverse effect on the functioning of its trade mark.

This is an interesting case but, as with all interesting cases, it perhaps creates more questions than answers. There have been many cases of trade mark owners losing their protection because they have allowed the mark to become a generic term. 'Hoover' is perhaps the classic case where the trade mark became widely used to refer to vacuum cleaners. With any form of intellectual property right there is a fine line between legitimate and excessive use of the right. Comparative advertising and the attempt to persuade a consumer to modify their initial preference are well established. 'Are you sure that you want to buy a BMW? Maybe an Audi would be a better purchase?' As e-commerce expands, these issues are going to arise increasingly in an Internet context.

The situation with Interflora is somewhat unusual in that the organisation is made up of a network, mainly of very small members but with linkages to much larger organisations. There were certainly grounds for the judge to conclude that informed users might be misled whether Marks and Spencer were associated with Interflora. One might be inclined to differ with his conclusion, but the judge is the sole determinant on questions of fact and it seems very unlikely that his decision can be challenged on this ground.

There is perhaps a final twist to the tale. In March 2013, at almost the same time as the High Court ruled in favour of Interflora it was reported that Google had imposed sanctions on Interflora in respect of alleged attempts by them to manipulate their search rankings in ways prohibited under Google's own rules. According to one report in March 2013:

> Interflora, the popular online florist, had been kicked into the long grass by Google for breaching the search engine's rules, or Webmaster Guidelines as it calls them, has triggered a fair bit of talk across the search engine optimisation (SEO) and marketing community.[51]

The timing was bad for Interflora coming in the period just before Mothers' Day which is one of the busiest times for floral deliveries. The effect of Google's action was effectively to blacklist the company so that searches for the name 'Interflora' would not provide any links to its services. There is no suggestion that the blacklisting (which was for only a limited period of time and has now been removed) was linked in any way to the court case. It is perhaps, however, another piece of evidence to suggest that law and Internet technology are uneasy companions.

Conclusions

With the emergence of global and national dispute resolution procedures, trade mark disputes involving the use of domain names appear to have largely vanished from the legal system. Although most disputes are settled, statistics from the dispute resolution organisations do show that the majority of decisions reached are in favour of the complainant. Given the nature of many of the incidents above which involve blatant hijacking of the name of a business, this rate is not in itself a source of surprise. What may be a greater cause for concern is the fact that the law applied in a number of instances appears to be almost, but not quite, trade mark law. In one sense, disputes are being hijacked from the courts to tribunals which are strongly supported by commercial pressures. The approach, especially concerning the allocation of generic domain names, may represent a way forward for dispute resolution in what is an increasingly globalised society, but great care needs to be taken to ensure that it acquires a considerable measure of legitimacy and is not seen as the captive of particular interest groups.

---

[51] <http://blogs.independent.co.uk/2013/03/01/interflora-suffers-seo-setback-as-mothers-day-approaches/>.

21

Internet regulation and domain names

INTRODUCTION

The communications sector has always been subject to regulation and the Internet is no exception. In some respects, it may be argued that the Internet is the most heavily regulated electronic communications network in the world in that activities carried out over it are subject, in theory if not always in practice, to a regulation in every country in which its contents might be accessed. When it comes, however, to the issue of regulation of the overall network, specific legal provisions are more limited. Reference to the Internet is entirely lacking in the Communications Act 2003, which provides the basis for the regulation of electronic communications networks and services and, indeed, when the legislation was before Parliament, government ministers were at pains on numerous occasions to point out that the measure was not intended to regulate the Internet. The Digital Economy Act 2010 does contain some provisions relating to Internet regulation but only at a relatively minor level in connection with the operation of domain-name registries. Section 1 of the Act adds a new section 134C to the Communications Act 2003 requiring the Office of Communications to prepare, at the request of the Secretary of State, a report relating to the allocation of domain names and as to any potential misuses of the system.

At a functional level Internet access involves two major factors: Internet (generally referred to as IP) addresses, which are a functional equivalent to telephone numbers, and domain names. The former element raises a number of technical issues but is generally non-contentious. As will be discussed in more detail later, systems of domain names—which effectively serve as an alias for IP numbers—are much more controversial and raise major issues how the Internet should be regulated.

Beyond names and numbers, an issue of current discussion is the notion of 'net neutrality'. The underlying theory is simple. Access to the Internet should be available to all content providers on equal terms. The scope of the concept, however, is rather more limited. All Internet users will be aware that the speed of Internet access is dictated in part by technical factors— much is written and spoken about the broadband divide where urban networks are generally capable of carrying traffic at much higher speeds than their rural counterparts. Again, most Internet Service Providers (ISPs) will limit customers' access speeds depending on the amount that they pay for the service. Effectively, therefore, net neutrality is limited to networks with the key concept being that some content providers should not be able to pay in order for their traffic to obtain priority over that from other providers. Adoption of such a policy has been advocated by the European Commission although there appears to be disagreement between the Member States as to whether this approach is justified. An alternative approach is to suggest that the market should be left to its own devices. One ISP might, for example, target its services at users who essentially want access to textual material and restrict the speed of video downloads. Other ISPs may adopt the opposite approach.

The emergence of Internet regulation

Who governs the Internet?

The notion of Internet governance has been defined in the following (rather general) terms:

> Internet governance is a broad term used in many different contexts. It applies to activities as diverse as the coordination of technical standards, the operation of critical infrastructure, development, regulation, legislation, and more.[1]

One of the notable features of the Internet is its openness. Like any organisation, however, the Internet does need structures and agencies to ensure its efficient operation. The relationship between these agencies and more established bodies such as the ITU in the telecommunications sector and, indeed, with national governments has not always been an easy one with a range of contentious issues involving technical competence and democratic legitimacy.

In seeking to identify and assess agencies concerned with Internet governance we might identify three categories of actors:

- Agencies with powers to make decisions affecting the operation of the Internet/*www*
- Agencies that seek to influence Internet policy
- Inter-governmental actions relating to Internet governance.

One of the longest established agencies is the Internet Society. Its website http://www.internetsociety.org/ indicates that it:

> is a global cause-driven organization governed by a diverse Board of Trustees that is dedicated to ensuring that the Internet stays open, transparent and defined by you.
>
> We are the world's trusted independent source of leadership for Internet policy, technology standards, and future development. More than simply advancing technology, we work to ensure the Internet continues to grow and evolve as a platform for innovation, economic development, and social progress for people around the world.
>
> . . . We establish and promote principles that are intended to persuade governments to make decisions that are right for their citizens and each nation's future. Everything we do is based on ensuring that a healthy, sustainable Internet is available to everyone –today and for the next billion users.

In diagrammatic form (see Figure 21.1), it describes its role as follows:

All very commendable, but there are two criticisms that have been made about the Internet Society and, indeed, of most organisations working in the field. Who votes for the Trustees? Again, a comment that is widely applied is that organisations are rather United States-centred. Given the extent of US involvement in the development of the Internet, this is perhaps not surprising. We can perhaps see a parallel with postage stamps. The United Kingdom was the first country in the world to introduce this system and remains the only country not to print its name on stamps. The issue is perhaps more problematic in the context of inter-governmental discussions about Internet governance. The United States has strong constitutional provisions guaranteeing the freedom of expression, even

[1] <http://www.internetsociety.org/sites/default/files/ISOC framework for IG assessments—D Souter—final_0.pdf>.

How We Work

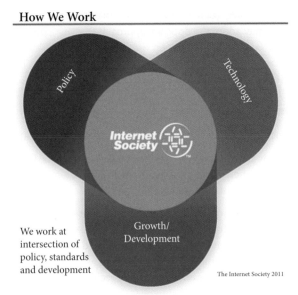

Figure 21.1 The Internet Society's role

in respect of materials that many people would find objectionable. Other countries exert more stringent controls. There are arguments for and against both approaches, but seeking to find consensus in the case of a global network such as the Internet is proving a difficult task.

Other key agencies involved in Internet governance are the Internet Engineering Task Force (IETF) and the Internet Assigned Numbers Agency (IANA). Essentially the IETF is a technocratic organisation. Its work has resulted in the promulgation of many technical standards, generally referred to as RFCs (requests for comments). In some respects, the nomenclature is indicative of the manner in which the Internet has developed. The legal status of standards is an interesting topic, perhaps fortunately outside the scope of this course. There is a range of standard-making bodies at both a national and international level. In some cases, especially perhaps within the European Union, conformity with standards is equated to compliance with legal obligations relating to product quality. Making requests for comments is indicative of a collaborative rather than commanding mentality although then end product may be much the same.

The latter is now subsumed within the Internet Corporation for Assigned Names and Numbers (ICANN) an organisation that will be considered further below. Its major role is to allocate the IP numbers that are critical to the functioning of the Internet. Although we are familiar with the system of domain names—which will be considered in more detail below—it is important to keep in mind that at the technical level the Internet functions on the basis of numbers, namely, Internet Protocol (IP) numbers. An analogy might be made with mobile phones. Most of us rely on contact lists when making calls. It has been reported that more than half of mobile phone users in the United Kingdom cannot recall their partner's phone number when asked.[2] They do tend to remember the person's name!

From an efficiency standpoint numbers have advantages over names. Names may often be duplicated so that there are, for example, towns called Glasgow in Jamaica, South Africa,

---

[2] <http://www.telegraph.co.uk/technology/news/7885227/Most-people-cannot-remember-partners-mobile-phone-number.html>.

and Zimbabwe. In the United States, there are Glasgows in Alabama, Minnesota, Delaware, Iowa, California, Georgia, Illinois, Missouri, Ohio, Oregon, West Virginia, Kentucky, Missouri, Montana, North Carolina, Virginia, and Pennsylvania.[3] There is, however, only one city of Glasgow with the telephone dialling code of 44 (0)141.

The system of IP numbers enable any user to connect to the Internet. There are no social or political controls over the making of a connection and cost implications are minimal. All computers linked to the Internet are allocated a unique identifier known as an IP number. The most widely used system at the moment is referred to as IPv4 and allocates numbers of 32 binary digits in length (normally in the region of eight or nine decimal numbers) to each connection. Just as Oftel required to insert an extra '1' into all UK telephone numbers in 1994 in order to secure what appears to be temporary relief from a shortage of available numbers, so has the exponential rate of growth in Internet usage, compounded by the increasing availability of Internet access via mobile phones, led to the introduction of a new numbering system known as IP V6. The associated increase in number length to 128-bit numbers is calculated to provide capacity for some 340 billion, billion, billion, billion computers. Even at the Internet's (and mobile phone networks') current rates of expansion, this should be sufficient for the foreseeable future, although take-up of the new system remains slow and some respected commentators have issued warnings that the Internet may be entering 'turbulent times'.[4]

The Internet of things

It is estimated that around 40 per cent of the world's population has an Internet connection today.[5] Statistics are often misleading, but to put matters in perspective it has been estimated that almost 90 per cent of households in the world have a television receiver.[6] Television has been operational for around seventy years whilst the Internet as a mass media has existed for only a third of that time. In 1995, less than 1 per cent of the world was online. The number of Internet users increased tenfold from 1999 to 2013. A billion users were connected in 2005, 2 billion in 2010, and 3 billion in 2014. Figure 21.2 shows the number of global internet users per year since 1993.

One issue that many of us will be familiar with is that we no longer use a single device for Internet access. We have desktop computers, laptops, tablets, and smartphones. In addition to the number of connected individuals, with the emergence of the, so-called, 'Internet of Things', Internet connectivity is being incorporated into an increasing number of devices. It has been estimated that the average household in the United Kingdom has around 7.5 Internet connected devices.[7] We have already referred fairly extensively to the growth in the number of smartphones, but you might look at 'Regulation (EU) 2015/758 of the European Parliament and of the Council of 29 April 2015 concerning type-approval requirements for the deployment of the eCall in-vehicle system based on the 112 service'.[8] From 2018 e-call technology will require to be fitted to all new motor vehicles allowing them to

> automatically call emergency services in case of a serious crash. The 'eCall' system automatically dials 112—Europe's single emergency number—in the event of a serious accident.

---

[3] <http://bmcphee.com/glasgow_places.htm>.

[4] See, eg, <http://www.guardian.co.uk/technology/2010/nov/11/google-vint-cerf-internet>.

[5] <http://www.internetlivestats.com/watch/internet-users/>.

[6] <http://vrworld.com/2011/01/26/digital-divide-global-household-penetration-rates-for-technology/>.

[7] <http://www.theguardian.com/technology/2015/apr/09/online-all-the-time-average-british-household-owns-74-internet-devices>.

[8] OJ 2015 L 133/77.

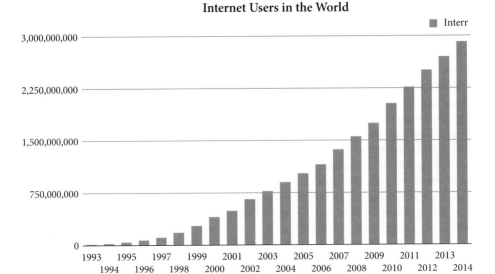

Figure 21.2 Internet users in the world

It communicates the vehicle's location to emergency services, even if the driver is unconscious or unable to make a phone call. It is estimated that it could save up to 2,500 lives a year.[9]

Around 2.5 million new cars are sold in the United Kingdom alone each year. The figure for the European Union as a whole is around 12 million. Under the new regime each new car will have Internet connectivity built in. Many domestic appliances have (or shortly will have) Internet connectivity. A fridge might , for example, be able to monitor its contents and place orders automatically with an online delivery service if stocks run low.[10] One prominent aspect of the topic is the emergence of what are referred to as 'wearables'. Smart watches are becoming more common, as are health and fitness monitoring applications. The demand for Internet access is growing massively and with it the demand for IP addresses.

From IPv4 to 6

For most of the last two decades, the Internet relied on a numbering system called IPv4. Any numbering system can be considered as similar to a scheme of telephone numbers. The more digits that are utilised, the more possible unique permutations will exist. With IPv4 some 4.3 billion addresses are possible and effectively they have been used up. We are now seeing a migration to a new numbering system, IPv6, which uses larger number strings and capable of allocating 340 undecillion unique addresses. That equates to 340 trillion, trillion, trillion possible IP addresses. Even with the massive increase in devices requiring connectivity, associated with the Internet of things, this will hopefully provide enough numbers to keep the Internet world going for a few years to come. As we will discuss below, names are a rather more scarce resource.

---

[9] <http://telematicswire.net/european-commission-makes-ecall-mandatory-in-cars-from-2015/>.
[10] This article <http://www.telegraph.co.uk/technology/ces/11340738/10-technologies-that-will-make-the-Internet-of-Things-a-reality.html?image=3> gives an interesting account of emerging technologies.

ICANN

Undoubtedly the most significant player in the field of Internet governance is the Internet Corporation for Assigned Names and Numbers (ICANN). It is often stated that the person who controls access to files and records is the most powerful individual in any organisation or, indeed, country. The same can be said of the Internet. In order to function as a global communications network, global cooperation is needed and the key question is who is to perform this role?

ICANN is the effective coordinator for the allocation of IP numbers (through the activities of IANA) but rather more contentiously manages the system of domain names. These roles are pivotal to the operation of the Internet. Reference has been made above to the massive range of IP numbers available under IPv6. Even so, allocation of numbers needs to be controlled. It appears to be the case that if you gather twenty-three people in a room, there is more than a 50 per cent chance that two will share the same birthday.[11] If a random selection policy was to be permitted with IP addresses, the same phenomenon would be likely to apply. Perhaps more significantly, the potential would be there for communications to be directed to the wrong address.

Internet operations are based on the operation of a relatively small number of what are called root servers. You might think of them as a (very) large scale equivalent of a telephone directory. IP numbers are allocated to Internet Service Providers (ISPs) by ICANN (IANA). You might think of an analogy in terms of the manner in which telephone numbers are allocated. Subscribers to a particular mobile network will tend to be allocated a number following a particular opening sequence—in the United Kingdom in the region between 071 and 079. You can imagine the complications that might follow if two people had the same telephone number and the issues are much the same in the Internet context.

Domain names raise different issues. It is perhaps important to stress that in technical terms the Internet functions by reference to numbers (IP addresses). If you open your web browser and type in '212.58.246.92' you will arrive at the BBC website. As suggested above, few of us are good at remembering such large numbers. Typing an address such as www.bbc.co.uk in a web browser initiates a process of trying to match the name with the appropriate IP number. Initially, the attempt will be made by the ISP's own equipment. If it fails to make a match, the query will be passed on to more comprehensive name servers, a process known as domain name resolution. The definitive tables of names and numbers are maintained on what are referred to as root servers. There are thirteen of these machines. Ten are located in the United States, with the remaining three being in England, Japan, and Sweden.[12] The key root server is maintained by Network Solutions, with the other servers downloading information about new domains from this server on a daily basis. Although many ISPs will maintain their own domain name server, the information on this will invariably have been copied, perhaps with a delay of a few days, from the root servers. In order to be accessible to the Internet world, therefore, it is imperative that a user be issued with an IP number and that the registered name and domain be accepted by the Network Solutions root server.

Whilst, as discussed above, with the emergence of IPv6, the supply of IP numbers is virtually inexhaustible, words are in rather shorter supply. A typical directory might contain in the region of 200,000 words. At the level of personal names, large numbers of individuals co-exist happily under the same identifiers. The Glasgow telephone directory, for example, lists some twenty pages of McDonalds. Because each domain name has to be mapped with

---

[11] See <http://www.theguardian.com/notesandqueries/query/0,5753,-22978,00.html>.

[12] You can find a good deal of information about the role of root servers at this site <http://www.root-servers.org/>.

a specific IP number, the Internet is not nearly as flexible. Although, as will be discussed below, the domain name structure offers a range of categories based both on national origin and nature of activity, the issue of allocation of, and rights to, particular domain names remains one of the most problematic aspects of the Internet and its regulation.

There are, by reasonable estimates,[13] close to a billion websites. A good number of these will be inactive. It is easier to obtain a web address than to maintain it, and cost implications are very small. Against this element of diminution in actual numbers of websites, there appears also to be increasing use of social media websites such as Facebook to provide an entry point to the Internet community rather than relying on a stand alone website. A long running problem has been that the supply of memorable domain names is limited.

As indicated in the introduction to this chapter, domain names, which are mapped against the appropriate IP address, are commercially significant. People will remember names to a greater extent than is the case with numbers.[14,15] From the inception of the commercial Internet, demand for names has always tended to exceed supply.

Domain names and URLs

We are all familiar with the system of Internet addresses that we probably access every day. The full address is referred to as a Uniform Resource Locator, more commonly abbreviated to URL. Its purpose is to allow a user to be directed to a desired Internet location. The element of the URL that we will all be familiar is the component www. This conveys the message that a user is looking for a location that constitutes part of the World Wide Web. You will also be familiar with terms such as 'http' (hypertext text transfer protocol) or 'https' (secure hypertext text transfer protocol). The latter is frequently associated with e-commerce websites that may require the transfer of financial identifiers such as credit card numbers and indicated that transfer of data to and from the site will be encrypted. Modern Internet browsers tend to do away with the need to type prefixes such as http or www although these will appear in the address bar when a site is accessed. The tell-tale sign that a site is using encryption is that the letters 'https' will appear in green in your browser. These components of the URL have no legal significance—at least in the intellectual property sector and we need not give them further consideration. Our prime focus will be on the individual identifiers that relate a site to a particular undertaking.

The nature of domain names

The notion of domain names was first introduced in 1985.[16] A domain name will begin with an individual identifier, typically a name or names associated with an organisation. The University of London, for example is abbreviated to 'Lon' whilst the University of Oxford becomes 'Ox'. In both cases, this is followed by a full stop (dot) and then the domain ac (academic) and after another dot, the UK country code. Generally academic institutions have tended to co-exist without many legal disputes over rights to a geographic name or

---

[13] <http://www.theatlantic.com/technology/archive/2015/09/how-many-websites-are-there/408151/>.

[14] See this report explaining why PIN's typically have four digits <http://news.bbc.co.uk/1/hi/business/6230194.stm>.

[15] It is suggested that more than 50 per cent of people cannot remember their partner's mobile phone number. See <http://www.telegraph.co.uk/technology/news/7885227/Most-people-cannot-remember-partners-mobile-phone-number.html>. Around a third of people, it is also reported, do not know their own landline number.

[16] For a brief account of the origins of the domain name system see <http://www.domainavenue.com/faq_history.htm>.

abbreviation.[17] The increasing number of private colleges has raised some new issues and you might look at this case <http://www.wipo.int/amc/en/domains/decisions/html/2001/d2001-0975.html>. It was brought under the WIPO domain name dispute resolution procedure (more on that later) and involved the successful attempt by the University of Oxford to have rights in the domain oxford-online.com transferred to it by a private entity.[18]

Top level global (or generic) domain names

Initially a range of what we now refer to as generic (non-country specific) domain names were introduced.[19] These comprised the following domains:

.com

.org

.net

.int

.edu

.gov

.mil

Although most of the names were available to any eligible entity in any country, the last three domains were, and are, reserved for use by United States-based organisations. As introduced, the system was administered by the National Science Foundation, the US organisation that was responsible for funding many of the initial stages of the Internet. Domain names could be sought and were awarded by the US National Science Foundation (NSF) free of charge. In 1993, the NSF awarded a contract to a commercial firm, Network Solutions, under which it had the exclusive right to administer a number of domains, including and most significantly that of .com. Initially the practice of allocating names free of charge was continued but in 1995 the NSF sanctioned the imposition of charges by Network Solutions—a portion of which was to be passed on to the NSF to be used to fund further research into Internet technology.

The role of Network Solutions was internationally contentious being seen in some quarters as an attempt to secure US dominance over an Internet that was starting to become a significant commercial player with the beginnings of what we now refer to as e-commerce. A particular complaint was that in the case of domain name disputes, it gave greater weight to US marks than those issued in other countries.

A brief history of Internet governance

Following international pressure, the Internet International Ad Hoc Committee (IAHC) was established in 1996 'at the initiative of the Internet Society, and at the request of the Internet Assigned Numbers Authority', with the remit to

---

[17] In part this may be because eligibility for allocation of a name in the .ac.uk domain is tightly controlled by the Joint Information Systems Committee (JISC) a public sector, not for profit organisation (See <https://www.jisc.ac.uk/about> which exerts strict controls over eligibility for award of a domain name. You might look at its current policy and proposals for change at <https://www.jisc.ac.uk/sites/default/files/ac.uk_eligibility_policy_for_consultation.pdf>.

[18] The University of Oxford appears to have been quite zealous in protecting its domain (and variants on it). You might search under 'Oxford' on the WIPO search engine at <http://www.wipo.int/amc/en/domains/search/>.

[19] See here for a report on the first domain names registered <http://www.computerweekly.com/news/1280090622/The-first-ever-20-domain-names-registered>.

resolve a difficult and long-standing set of challenges in the Domain Name System, namely enhancing its use while attempting to juggle such concerns as administrative fairness, operational robustness and protection of intellectual property.

The IAHC recommended that administration of the .com domain should be removed from the sole control of Network Solutions and made available to a number of competing registries. It also recommended an expansion in the number of generic domains. At the conclusion of its work, the IAHC put forward for signature by the various interest groups a Generic Top Level Domain Memorandum of Understanding. (gTLD-MoU). The Memorandum, which is published in the name of the 'Internet Community' endorsed the final report of the IAHC, which recommended expansion of the number of generic top level domains and the adoption of a set of six principles:

the Internet Top Level Domain (TLD) name space is a public resource and is subject to the public trust;

any administration, use and/or evolution of the Internet TLD space is a public policy issue and should be carried out in the interests and service of the public;

related public policy needs to balance and represent the interests of the current and future stakeholders in the Internet name space;

the current and future Internet name space stakeholders can benefit most from a self-regulatory and market-oriented approach to Internet domain name registration services;

registration services for the gTLD name space should provide for global distribution of registrars;

a policy shall be implemented that a second-level domain name in any of the CORE-gTLDs which is identical or closely similar to an alphanumeric string that, for the purposes of this policy, is deemed to be internationally known, and for which demonstrable property rights exist, may be held or used only by, or with the authorization of, the owner of such demonstrable intellectual property rights. Appropriate consideration shall be given to possible use of such a second-level domain name by a third party that, for the purposes of this policy, is deemed to have sufficient rights.[20]

In 1997, the United States adopted a 'Framework for Global Electronic Commerce'.[21] Even though dated it remains a significant document in the field. Internally for the United States and paralleling developments globally, it marked a shift in governmental responsibility for Internet matters from the Department of Defence (the major funder of the NSF) to the Department of Commerce.

The IAHC had attracted contributions from around the world. In January 1998, however, the US Department of Commerce published a Green Paper, *A Proposal to Improve Technical Management of Internet Names and Addresses*.[22] This proposal studiously avoided making any reference to the work of the IAHC and the Global Memorandum of Association. It received a lukewarm response from the EU, which commented that the Paper appeared to be seeking to retain US dominance over the Internet. A further US White Paper, *Management of Internet Names and Addresses*,[23] published in June 1998, moved much closer to the proposals of the IAHC and the terms of the Global Memorandum and drew the speedy response from the Commission that it

can now confirm that the EU should act to participate fully in the process of organization and management of the Internet that has been launched by the US White Paper.[24]

---

[20] Section 2, available from <http://www.gtld-mou.org/gTLD-MoU.html>.
[21] <http://clinton4.nara.gov/WH/New/Commerce/read.html>.
[22] Available from <http://www.ntia.doc.gov/ntiahome/domainname/dnsdrft.htm>.
[23] Available from <http://www.ntia.doc.gov/ntiahome/domainname/6_5_98dns.htm>.
[24] <http://www.ispo.cec.be/eif/dns/com98476.html>.

Ultimately, agreement was reached that yet another new body be set up, the Internet Corporation for Assigned Names and Numbers (ICANN).[25] This was established in October 1998 and is described as:

> a non-profit, private sector corporation formed by a broad coalition of the Internet's business, technical, and academic communities. ICANN has been designated by the U.S. government to serve as the global consensus entity to which the U.S. government is transferring the responsibility for coordinating four key functions for the Internet: the management of the domain name system, the allocation of IP address space, the assignment of protocol parameters, and the management of the root server system.[26]

Following this quite precise job description, there is something of a reversion to platitude in the document with the comment that:

> ICANN is dedicated to preserve the operational stability of the Internet; to promote competition; to achieve broad representation of the global Internet community; and to coordinate policy through private-sector, bottom-up, consensus-based means.

The remit of ICANN extends across quite a range of technical and policy issues. This can be a somewhat uneasy juxtaposition and is perhaps at the heart of some of the controversies that tend to attend its actions. In terms of its legal status, ICANN is stated to be a 'not for profit public benefit corporation' registered under the law of California. ICANN may operate on a not for profit basis but, as we will see, its income from domain name registrations is substantial.

Effectively, ICANN has taken over the domain name role coordinating role previously played by IANA which remains in existence but as a component of ICANN. Initially this took place by means of a Memorandum of Understanding[27] and subsequently by a contract with the US Department of Commerce.[28] The agreement removed the monopoly of Network Solutions in respect of the .com domain. Whilst the first part of the process was carried out smoothly, negotiations with Network Solutions were more difficult, with legal action being threatened by Network Solutions on more than one occasion. Agreement was eventually reached in November 1999 and at the time of writing, more than thirty organisations were accredited to act as registries for the .com domain.[29] In order to qualify to act as a registry,[30] an organisation must provide evidence of both financial and technical stability.

Since the establishment of ICANN, the number of top level domains has increased steadily. In the early years of the present century, ICANN carried out two application rounds for new gTLDs. In 2000 it introduced the domains .aero, .biz, .coop, .info, .museum, .name and .pro; and in 2004, .asia, .cat, .jobs, .mobi, .tel, and .travel. As most Internet users will be aware, take up of these has been limited with most commercial users seeking to locate themselves within the better known .com domain. A contentious addition in 2010 was the .xxx which is available for sites offering online adult services (pornography). Depending on perspectives it was seen as enticing children to view unsuitable material or as keeping such material within defined boundaries.

To an extent these changes represented mere tinkering with a system that was struggling to cope with the demands being placed on it. The intention was that an increase in domains might allow different organisations to register their business name as an Internet domain

---

[25] <https://www.icann.org/>.

[26] <http://www.icann.org/general/fact-sheet.htm>.

[27] Available from <http://www.icann.org/general/icann-mou-25nov98.htm>.

[28] See <http://www.icann.org/general/iana-contract-09feb00.htm>.

[29] For an up-to-date list see <http://www.icann.org/registrars/accredited-list.html>.

[30] For full details of the accreditation process, see <http://www.icann.org/registrars/accreditation.htm>.

name. In practice, large companies wishing to avoid dilution of their trade mark rights tended to register under every conceivably applicable domain. You might look at this site <https://who.is/>. It is the definitive list of the owners of Internet domain names. If you take a company such as Starbucks as an example, you will find that it owns a wide range of top level domains although if you type the name of most of these into your browser, you will find that the page is not operational. Effectively, ownership of the domain is a mechanism to stop anyone else using the name. In fairness, keep in mind the threat to trade mark owners of allowing their mark to be diluted. In this, as in many other areas, there is an uneasy relationship between the goals of the domain name structure and the provisions and requirements of trade mark law.

In addition to the problems identified above, the structure of the domain system was also limited in that it would recognise only characters written in the Roman alphabet. Given that the largest volume of Internet traffic today is carried within the Asia-Pacific region, the exclusion of Chinese, Arabic, (and also, indeed, Cyrillic) characters was a major limitation. Following lengthy discussions there have been more major changes in the generic domain structure and, as discussed below, some have followed through to the level of country specific domains.

The future of ICANN and Internet governance

At the time of its establishment, ICANN was seen in some quarters as providing a blueprint for a more democratic form of Internet regulation. Provision was made for a number of its directors to be elected by those Internet users. In the hard light of experience, these hopes were unrealistic and the work of ICANN has been subject to considerable criticism.

At a basic level, ICANN was established by unilateral action on the part of the US government, albeit with the tacit support of the European Commission. As Internet penetration has increased in other areas of the world, this narrow focus has been a cause for complaint. ICANN's role is in respect of the generic domain name codes but in more recent times country-level codes have begun to assume greater importance and the relationship between ICANN and the agencies responsible for the administration of country codes has at times been difficult.

In autumn 2002, the initial contract between the US Department of Commerce expired. It was extended for a further year[31] but on condition that ICANN introduced substantial reforms to its procedures and on the understanding that its progress would be closely monitored. In an accompanying statement,[32] the Department expressed concern that:

> ICANN has been troubled by internal and external difficulties that have slowed its completion of the transition tasks and hampered its ability to garner the full support and confidence of the global Internet community.

It continued:

> ICANN's reputation in the Internet community has suffered. In particular, ICANN has been criticized for over-reaching, arbitrariness, and lack of transparency in its decision making. Concerns have been raised about ICANN's lack of accountability and that it is inserting itself too much into the pricing and nature of services offered by, and business practices of, domain name companies. Some consider ICANN too slow to act on various issues, especially the roll-out of new gTLDs. There has also been growing concern that ICANN's structure, processes, and inability to make progress on other key DNS issues have undermined its

---

[31] <http://www.ntia.doc.gov/ntiahome/domainname/agreements/Amend5_09192002.htm>.
[32] <http://www.ntia.doc.gov/ntiahome/domainname/agreements/docstatement_09192002>.

effectiveness and legitimacy. Not surprisingly, many in the Internet community have called for ICANN to review its mission, structure, and processes for efficacy and appropriateness in light of the needs of today's Internet.

Extensive reforms have been put in place by ICANN but the future of the organisation remains uncertain. Given the importance of the Internet for all aspects of modern life, it cannot be considered satisfactory that a central coordinating body should continue in existence on a year-by-year basis and longer-term resolution is required. It may be that for the longer term, an agency similar to the International Telecommunications Union should assume responsibility for the technical aspects of the work. Although the Union's structures might themselves be criticised as providing excessive weight to governmental interests in an era of increasing private sector involvement in the communications sector, its deliberations do bring together public and private sector interests.

Second (country) level domains

In addition to the system of global or generic domain names—which we will return to shortly—there exist also what are referred to as country code domain names. Based on ISO standard 3166, these consist of a two-letter denominator for every country in the world. There are around 250 two-letter country-code TLDs (ccTLDs), which identify a country or territory. The United Kingdom, for example, is referred to as .uk, France as .fr, and Germany as .de. There is a designator .eu that relates to the European Union.

Many countries have established their own systems of domain names. The situation with regard to the national domains is rather complex, with a mix of public and private sector organisations playing the role of domain name registry. In the United Kingdom, this role is played by a non-profit-making company Nominet.[33] As with much of the Internet, the legal basis for its actions is unclear, it being stated that:

> Nominet UK derives its authority from the Internet industry in the UK and is recognised as the UK registry by the Internet Assigned Numbers Authority (IANA) in the USA.

In many countries the national domain structure mirrors that of the traditional generic domain structure. A commercial organisation in the United Kingdom, for example might seek to register a name under the domain .co.uk. Some studies have shown that Internet users have a preference for country specific domain names as indication of a point of geographic location for the undertaking that they may wish to ideal with. It should be noted, however that there is no requirement that a company be established or operate in a particular country in order to register a domain name in that location.

One country domain name with an interesting tale is that of Tuvalu. Tuvalu is a collection of nine, small coral atolls in the Pacific Ocean close to Fiji. It is classed as a 'Least Developed Country', with a population of about 10,000 and a GDP of $11 million. Its only export is copra. It has one computer connected to the Internet. It also 'possesses' the ISO code of TV and, in 1998, entered into a deal worth $50 million with a Canadian company to licensing rights to the domain .tv. The company planned to sell domain names to television companies wishing to establish a web presence. Sadly for the Tuvaluans, the deal fell through when the company failed to make payments, although it has recently been announced that a similar, albeit less valuable, agreement has been concluded.

Other locations which have proved popular 'homes' for websites are Tonga, whose ISO code is .to, and Italy, with the designator .it, clearly a designator which has attraction to the

---

[33] <http://www.nic.uk/>.

IT industry. One country that may be of particular interest to the academic community is Ascension Island. This is a small territory located in the South Atlantic Ocean. It is a British overseas territory and importantly for the present discussion has the ISO designator ac and the country domain .ac. This is promoted quite extensively as a suitable domain for bodies involved in the educational sector. You might look at this website <https://www.nic.ac/> and perhaps note some of the disclaimers applied. Only the most cynical commentator could cast doubt on their sincerity.

Ascension Island is somewhat unusual (although certainly not unique) in its domain used in isolation. In most countries, there is a further indicator of the nature of the activity associated with the owner of a domain name. In the United Kingdom, domain names may be registered in the following categories:

Name	Intended usage
ac.uk	Academic
co.uk	Commercial
gov.uk	Governmental
ltd.uk	Limited liability companies
mod.uk	Ministry of Defence
net.uk	Internet networks
nhs.uk	National Health Service
plc.uk	Public limited companies
police.uk	Police
sch.uk	Schools

Although many organisations operating at an international level may seek to obtain a generic domain name there are some advantages in having one associated with a particular country. There is some evidence to suggest that consumers are happier to deal with a small or medium sized company if its Internet domain suggests that it has a physical presence in the country. As has been discussed above, this may be illusionary. A second benefit may apply at a more legalistic level. Under the European Union's e-commerce legislation a commercial supplier is subject to the law of a consumer if its directs commercial activities at that country. This is relatively easy to establish when a business conducts all activities from a physical location. It is more difficult when all that the consumer can interact with is a website. The issue of geographic location on the Internet is becoming accepted as a matter of considerable significance.

The new(ish) top level domain policy

Following a prolonged discussion process, ICANN introduced a new domain policy in 2012. This marks some significant changes from the traditional system of generic top level domain names and has resulted in a major expansion in the number of domains. We will consider the new system in more detail below but essentially rather than having to work within the constraints of a domain such as .com, anyone can apply to act as domain name registrar for any term in any language or form of script such as Chinese or Cyrillic. At the time of writing there are now than 500 generic top level domains and the number is increasing month by month. We will consider the procedure for applying for such domains in more detail below.

A number of categories of names have proved popular in the new system. Geographic indicators have been sought after and, for example, we now have .London and .Paris domains. Another popular sector relate to forms of activity. There are now the domains such as .soccer and .hockey. You can find an up to date list of accepted domains at this site

<http://newgtlds.icann.org/en/program-status/delegated-strings>. Perhaps most significantly and contentiously, a number of major companies have obtained domains in their own name. We now have top level domains .Apple, .Toshiba, and .Canon to give just three examples. You will identify the trade mark issues that might arise from such registrations. In all the above cases, the domain is registered to the company that owns these rights. Another application was rejected, in this case the online retailer Amazon had sought to register its name as a top level domain. This was rejected following objections from South American countries that the company was seeking to register a name in respect of regions that fell within their own geographic territories. You will find a report on this case at this website <http://www.theregister.co.uk/2013/07/18/amazon_loses_dot_amazon_vote/>.

Consideration of the new system has to take place at two levels. First we have to consider the procedures for allocating domain names and then what may happen if there is a dispute about who should be able to use a particular domain name? The second has been a major issue with the original domains such as .COM and issues raised there remain very relevant in the context of the new system.

Applying to act as a domain name registry

Managing the allocation and operation of domain names is a complex technical process involving matching names with IP addresses and ensuring that there are no conflicts. One of the concerns expressed has been that poor quality registries might threaten the stability of the Internet. This has been an oft-stated concern within the telecommunications sector with concerns that the connection of unauthorised equipment to networks might threaten their stability. Experience has indicated that concerns are rather exaggerated and that networks are more robust than pessimists might suggest. The suspicion may be that the same will apply in relation to the Internet which was, at least in part, designed to ensure the resilience of telecommunications in the aftermath of a nuclear attack.

The basis for the activities of domain name registries lies in a contract that they are required to enter into with ICANN. The contract has been modified from time to time with the current version being adopted in 2013. You can find a copy of the contract at this site <https://www.icann.org/resources/pages/approved-with-specs-2013-09-17-en?routing_type=path>. There are now many hundreds of domain name registries around the world. You can find a listing of the accredited domain registers at this site <https://www.icann.org/registrar-reports/accreditation-qualified-list.html>.

It is open to domain name registries to enter into sub-contracts with domain name resellers. A wide range of organisations may offer to supply domain names. Once again, this will take place subject to the terms of a contract between the domain name reseller and the relevant registry.

The new top level domain application process

In 2012 ICANN invited applications from those wishing to operate new top level domain names. More than 1,900 applications were received. ICANN has published an Applicant's Guidebook which explains the process in detail. Much of the content is concerned with establishing that the applicant has the technical capability to run a registry but there are also significant legal elements.[34]

Running a domain name registry can be a profitable business. A domain such as .london[35] might be attractive to many local businesses. In order for a geographic domain

---

[34] See <http://newgtlds.icann.org/en/applicants/agb>.
[35] <http://domains.london/about/>.

to be considered for registration an application must be accompanied by documentation of support or at least of non-objection from the relevant governments or public authorities:

The Handbook specifies rigorous criteria relating to the technical and ethical standards required of a potential applicant. A history of domain name abuse, for example would be a very bad indicator. The entire process has not been without its critics. One of the longest established players in the domain name registry field, Verisign, published a report in 2013 that was highly critical of the process.[36]

The evaluation process

Anyone seeking to obtain a domain under the new system has to pay an initial evaluation fee of $185,000 has to be paid. Clearly applying to register a domain is not something to be undertaken lightly. There is no guarantee that the application will be accepted and the costs of establishing, promoting, and maintaining a domain also have to be factored in. The Guidebook itself is 338 pages long. It contains ninety-four pages of advice and an application form of 244 pages. There is a fairly complex and lengthy evaluation process in respect of applications. ICANN indicate in the FAQs associated with the process that:

> The shortest path for a successful application is to pass Administrative Check (lasting 2 months), Initial Evaluation (lasting 5 months) and then a move to Pre-delegation (lasting approximately 2 months) without any third party objections being filed. In this case the evaluation process could take as little as 9 months to complete. On the other hand if an application does not pass Initial Evaluation and elects Extended Evaluation and/or is in the Dispute Resolution or String Contention stages then the evaluation process could take up to 20 months to complete (or longer in the event that unforeseen circumstances arise).[37]

According to statistics published by ICANN[38] as of the end of September 2016, 1,930 applications had been submitted to register one of the new domains. If you recall that the application fee is $185,000 it is clear that we are talking about rather significant sums of money. Of these, 1,188 have been approved, 583 have been withdrawn and forty-one applications have either been rejected or the applicant informed that the application will not proceed. A further 120 applications remain in the evaluation process.

Domain auctions

The point has been made on a number of occasions in this chapter that some names are likely to be attractive to Internet users and to domain registries. A number of applications may be made in respect of the same domain. Assuming there are no trade mark issues, the end result will be an auction of the rights to administer the domain.[39] Some large sums of money are involved. The domain most in demand so far has been .app where the winning bidder paid more than $25 million for the right to the domain.[40] You might note the important caveat from ICANN to the effect that winning an auction does not mean the domain will be awarded. To date this does not seem to have occurred.

---

[36] See <https://investor.verisign.com/secfiling.cfm?filingid=1014473–13–12> and a rather shorter summary at <http://zodiacregistry.com/chehade.html?lang=en>.

[37] <https://newgtlds.icann.org/en/applicants/global-support/faqs/faqs-en>.

[38] <https://newgtlds.icann.org/en/program-status/statistics>.

[39] You can find information about the auctions that have been conducted at this site <https://gtldresult.icann.org/application-result/applicationstatus/auctionresults>.

[40] You can find information about this auction at <https://gtldresult.icann.org/application-result/applicationstatus/applicationdetails:downloadauctionreport/13?t:ac=1343>.

Trade mark issues and the new domains

If you look at some of the new domains, such as .Canon and .Toshiba it is clear that there are trademark issues involved.[41] It is also very relevant in respect of disputes under the established systems of domain names. ICANN has established what is referred to as the 'Trademark Clearing House'. This is referred to as 'a global repository for trademark data'.[42] It offers an opportunity for the owners of trade marks and similar intellectual property rights to register this details. These will be made available to domain name registries. When a new domain begins to prepare for operation there is also to be what is described as a 'Sunrise' period. Around three months in length, this gives trade mark owners a period of priority to seek to register within the domain before it is made available for public applications.

Large organisations may well be able to monitor domain name developments on a continuing basis but this is certainly not a trivial or non-time consuming task. In perhaps a majority of cases a trade mark owner will only become aware of the fact that a name is being used as, or as part of, a domain name after the event has occurred. Throughout Internet history disputes regarding rights to possess a particular domain name have been common. Initially these tended to be ventilated before courts of law, but for the past decade have essentially been the province of alternative systems of dispute resolution sponsored by ICANN. It has established what is referred to as the Uniform Domain Name Dispute Resolution Policy. A requirement to adopt and to adhere to this is incorporated into all of the contracts that ICANN enters into with domain registries.

The Uniform Dispute Resolution Rules

A feature of early disputes concerned with rights relating to domain names was the attempt by domain name registries to devise policies designed to render them immune from legal action. In many respects, the agencies were put in difficult legal positions. A claimant would typically assert rights in a domain name held by someone else and threaten to sue the registry if the name was not transferred to them. The existing name holder would threaten to sue the registry if the name was removed. A classic example of a 'no win' situation for the registry. There were also disputes between parties themselves concerning the use of a domain name. Although such disputes have now largely disappeared from the court system you might look at the decision of the Court of Appeal in *British Telecommunications plc, Virgin Enterprises Ltd, J Sainsbury plc, Marks & Spencer plc and Ladbroke Group plc v One in a Million*[43] discussed above. Here the claimants, who are all well-known UK companies, succeeded in claims of trade mark infringement and passing off against the defendant who had registered their trading names as domain names. Such cases are now of little more than historical significance. With the emergence of ICANN as the coordinating body for the system of domain names, a new approach has been adopted to the problem of trying to resolve domain name disputes without invoking national courts. Any organisation wishing to act as a registry in respect of the generic domain names is obliged to conduct business according to the 'Uniform Domain Name Dispute Resolution Policy'.[44] Adherence to the policy is also contractually binding upon anyone applying for a domain name.[45]

---

[41] See this report from WIPO, albeit one that was written at a fairly early stage of the consultation process leading to the establishment of the new system <http://www.wipo.int/amc/en/domains/reports/newgtld-ip/>.

[42] <https://newgtlds.icann.org/en/about/trademark-clearinghouse/faqs/>.

[43] [1999] FSR 1. The decision at first instance is reported at [1998] FSR 265.

[44] The latest version of the rules can be found at <https://www.icann.org/resources/pages/udrp-rules-2015–03–11-en>.

[45] The policy and related documents relating to its application can be found at <https://www.icann.org/resources/pages/help/dndr/udrp-en>.

The policy requires applicants for domain names to submit to mandatory dispute resolution procedures before approved dispute resolution service providers in the event of any claim that:

(i)   your domain name is identical or confusingly similar to a trademark or service mark in which the complainant has rights;

(ii) you have no rights or legitimate interests in respect of the domain name; and

(iii) your domain name has been registered and is being used in bad faith.

The onus is on a complainant to establish all of these heads of claim.[46]

Originally, four organisations were authorised by ICANN to offer dispute resolution services under its rules:

- The Asian Domain Name Dispute Resolution Centre[47]
- CPR Institute for Dispute Resolution[48]
- The National Arbitration Forum[49]
- The World Intellectual Property Organisation.[50]

The CPR Institute is no longer active in the field but there are new players in the form of:

- The Czech Arbitration Court Arbitration Centre for Internet Disputes[51]
- The Arab Centre for Domain Name Dispute Resolution.[52]

To date, these have been relatively small players in the field. The largest dispute resolution fora have been the National Arbitration Forum which had heard 23,000 cases by 2015.[53] The major player has been the World Intellectual Property Organisation (WIPO) which had by 2015 determined more than 30,000 cases. You might look at this page[54] to get an indication of the scale and range of activities. WIPO has been criticised in some quarters as giving excessive weight to the interests of intellectual property owners. Given its nature this would not be surprising. We are told on its website that:[55]

> WIPO is the global forum for intellectual property services, policy, information and cooperation. We are a self-funding agency of the United Nations, with 188 member states.
>
> Our mission is to lead the development of a balanced and effective international intellectual property (IP) system that enables innovation and creativity for the benefit of all. Our mandate, governing bodies and procedures are set out in the WIPO Convention, which established WIPO in 1967.

WIPO's remit is to promote and develop intellectual property rights and trade marks are clearly an important component of these. It is perhaps worth noting that in around 86 per cent of cases, WIPO proceedings have resulted in the transfer of a domain name to a complainant whilst under the UK system that operates on the basis of very similar rules, the figure is around 55 per cent. As has been stated before, statistics can be misleading, but there does appear to be quite a significant discrepancy here.

---

[46] Uniform Dispute Resolution Rules, r. 4a.
[47] <http://www.adndrc.org/adndrc/index.html>.
[48] <http://www.cpradr.org/ICANN_Menu.htm>.
[49] <http://www.arbforum.com/domains/>.
[50] <http://arbiter.wipo.int/domains/>.
[51] <http://www.adr.eu/index.php>.
[52] <http://acdr.aipmas.org/default.aspx?lang=en>.
[53] See <http://www.adrforum.com/news>.
[54] <http://www.wipo.int/amc/en/domains/statistics/>.
[55] <http://www.wipo.int/about-wipo/en/>.

Consideration will be given below to a few of the decisions made under the WIPO and then the uk dispute resolution procedures.

Rationale and content of the domain resolution rules

The background to the rules can be stated briefly. As has been stated on more than one occasion above, demand for names generally exceeds supply. There has to be a mechanism to determine who is entitled to use a name in the Internet context.

Disputes fall into a range of categories. The common factor is that there is a dispute over who has the right to a name. In the majority of cases proceedings arise after a name has been allocated to a user only for another party to claim that they have a better claim to it—typically but not universally based on trademark rights. In many instances—as in the *British Telecommunications plc, Virgin Enterprises Ltd, J Sainsbury plc, Marks & Spencer plc and Ladbroke Group plc v One in a Million* case referred to previously—this arises where names have been registered by a party who has no entitlement to them but who is willing to sell them to their 'rightful' owners at a price. Such tactics were fairly common in the early days of the commercial Internet where even large companies were frequently unaware of the benefits that an Internet presence could bring to their business and discovered too late that a more entrepreneurial character had registered their name as a domain name. Such a situation is much, much less likely to occur today.

An example of an action brought in this context was a dispute heard before the WIPO panel involving the mark ABTA.[56] Generally associated with the Association of British Travel Agents who own trade marks in the acronym, the domain name ABTA.net was registered by a hotelier. In the event, the WIPO panel found for ABTA on a range of grounds, including use of a mark 'identical or confusingly similar' to a trade mark. The Panel also found in favour of ABTA on the bad faith issue. Key elements here were that the name was not being used and that the holder had not evidenced any plans to make use of the name. 'The concept of a domain name being used in bath faith', it was held, 'is not limited to positive action: inaction is within the concept'.

Dot.sucks

This is another form of dispute that is difficult to place into any precise legal category. The notion refers to sites that are set up to criticise products or services supplied by a particular supplier. Without in any way endorsing its content, this site[57] is what might be considered a traditional example of the genre. You might well immediately think of 'defamation' and may have seen the notice on the site 'MANAGED AND EDITED FROM SOMEWHERE IN CENTRAL EUROPE'. The legal protection afforded by such a notice may be limited in its effect, but it does illustrate the practical difficulties that right owners may face in seeking to enforce their intellectual property rights and also in seeking to defend the reputation of their business.

There is now a specific .sucks domain under the new top level regime.[58] The wording on the front page of this registry identifies it as a forum that companies might use to obtain consumer feedback, whether positive or negative, regarding their goods and services. This perhaps is not the use to which the concept has been used and a good number of sites have

---

[56] <http://arbiter.wipo.int/domains/decisions/html/d2000–0086.html>.
[57] <http://arnoldclark.150m.com/>.
[58] <https://www.registry.sucks/>.

been registered with a company name followed by sucks to enable aggrieved customers to post complaints about it. A report in the *Wall Street Journal* reports on criticisms made in the US Congress:

> [B]rands are being coerced into paying $2,000 or more to buy domains ending in .sucks, to prevent critics from seizing the addresses as a platform. Trademark holders are 'being shaken down,' U.S. Rep. Bob Goodlatte, a Virginia Republican, said at a House Judiciary Committee hearing last week.

The .sucks domain is controlled by Vox Populi, which proposed it, as one of 628 new domains created since 2012 in a broad expansion of the Internet naming system. Its suggested price of $2,499 for an address is much higher than other new domains, such as .support and .lawyer, where addresses generally cost less than $100.[59]

Again, as was mentioned above, we might have the situation where large companies—the report mentions Apple, Goole, Microsoft, and Yahoo—purchase domains to stop others making use of them. At the time of writing, search requests for all of the sites referred were met with the response that the site was not available.

The creation of the .sucks domain has created a good deal of controversy as can be seen from any search engine request using the term.[60] In some respects the term 'sucks'—which is essentially American in nature—is excessively pejorative in nature and if used by someone other than the undertaking operating under the name could be seen as defamatory in nature in many legal systems. Equally, however, the Internet has value in providing a mechanism for allowing users to express grievances concerning the nature of products—'Microsoft Office lost a day's work' or this site[61] '10 Reasons Why I Hate Microsoft Windows'. The balance is not an easy one to strike and the spectre of defamation lurks around some sites of this nature. As well as defamation, you might also consider trade mark issues. Using a trade mark as part of a domain name may incur liability especially if the effect is likely to be to cause damage to the commercial interests of the right owner.

Arbitration decisions

Reference has been made above to the arbitration activities of agencies such as WIPO and the National Arbitration Forum. These agencies have dealt with some 50,000 disputes. This is undoubtedly a large number, but it does have to be placed in the context of a situation where there are currently around 1 billion[62] websites in the world. As we all know, websites come and go and the number of sites that have been in existence since WIPO and other agencies began work in 1999 must be significantly higher. Even taking the figure of 1 billion, a count of 50,000 disputes reaching the stage of formal arbitration proceedings equates to one dispute for every 20,000 website. This does, of course, discount disputes raised in respect of country level domain names, but it is important to keep matters in perspective.

Arbitration decisions differ from traditional court proceedings in that there is no notion of precedent or judicial hierarchy. Throughout this book there have been references to decisions of the High Court of England and Wales which might be followed, those of the Court of Appeal that carry significantly more weight and the utterances of the Supreme Court that are effectively definitive statements of the law and must be followed by lower courts in any subsequent cases raising the same point of law. In respect of domain names, there are

---

[59] <http://blogs.wsj.com/digits/2015/05/19/new-domain-sparks-icann-debate/>.
[60] See, eg, <http://marketingland.com/controversial-sucks-domain-almost-here-121505>.
[61] <http://www.marksanborn.net/software/10-reasons-why-i-hate-microsoft-windows/>.
[62] See <http://www.internetlivestats.com/total-number-of-websites/>.

some 50,000 arbitration decisions, many raising interesting issues but with no guarantee than any decision would be replicated in a future dispute.

That is perhaps a weakness in the system of arbitration. In its favour, it provides a relatively low cost[63] opportunity to have disputes resolved. Most proceedings will be conducted on the basis of paperwork with no need for an oral hearing. It should be noted, although it does not appear to have happened in practice, that decisions of arbitration panels can subsequently be reviewed by the courts, albeit upon rather limited grounds.

National dispute resolution procedures

Paralleling the development of dispute resolution schemes for sites within the generic top level domains, a similar scheme was adopted to deal with disputes within the .uk top level domain.[64] Operated by the domain name registry, Nominet, a panel of around thirty experts act as adjudicators,[65] with individual cases being heard by a single person. The basis for any complaint is that there was 'abusive registration of a domain name'. This encompasses a domain name that, as stated by Nominet, either:

  i. was registered or otherwise acquired in a manner which, at the time when the registration or acquisition took place, took unfair advantage of or was unfairly detrimental to the Complainant's Rights; OR

  ii. has been used in a manner which took unfair advantage of or was unfairly detrimental to the Complainant's Rights.[66]

Beyond substituting the perhaps more pejorative term 'abusive registration' for the ICANN criterion of 'bad faith', the substance of the policy is broadly similar.

The first decision under the new procedure was delivered in 2001. The pharmaceutical company, Eli Lilly, was successful in its application to have rights in the domain name, xigris.ci.uk transferred to it. Eli Lilly had obtained a European Community Trade Mark in the name Xigris in 1999. The domain name had been registered by an ex-employee in June 2001. No representations were made by the employee in response to Eli Lilley's complaint and although there was no evidence available as to the purpose for which the registration might have been made, the expert held that the circumstances surrounding the case were such that a prima facie case of abuse had been made out and that in the absence of any attempt at explanation, the request for transfer should be granted.[67]

By the end of 2016 around 17,000 disputes had been referred to the UK dispute resolution service, although around 25 per cent of these have been declared invalid on procedural grounds and did not therefore proceed to any form of dispute resolution. Following receipt of a valid complaint, the first step in the process is to attempt mediation and more than half of the cases are resolved at this stage.

Appeals may be made against the decision of an individual expert. These will be heard before a panel of three experts. To date, fifty-five appeals have been made. The roll-call

---

[63] The UK domain agency, Nominet estimates savings of around £15,000 in legal costs for each decision that it disposes of compared with formal legal proceedings. See <http://www.nominet.uk/wp-content/uploads/2015/10/Nominet_domain_disputes_2014.pdf>.

[64] For information about the Nominet dispute resolution service see <http://www.nominet.uk/domains/resolving-uk-domain-disputes-and-complaints/>.

[65] You can find details of the arbiters and their professional backgrounds at <http://www.nominet.uk/wp-content/uploads/2015/08/DRS-Experts-List.pdf>.

[66] You can find the full policy at <http://www.nominet.uk/wp-content/uploads/2015/11/DRS_Policy.pdf>.

[67] The full text of the decision can be obtained from <http://www.nic.uk/DisputeResolution/Decisions/EliLillyAndCompany-v-DavidClayton.html>.

of complainants includes some of the best-known names in the United Kingdom's commercial and public life, featuring organisations such as Harrods, Vodafone, Barclays Bank, Nokia, the Royal Marines, and Interflora. It appears almost to be the case that an incident of cybersquatting is an integral consequence of commercial success.

Conclusions

Domain name disputes seem likely to remain a prominent feature on the Internet landscape. The precise nature and form of a domain name is becoming less important. As you are doubtless aware from your own experiences, we tend to use search engines more to locate domains but there remains the potential for consumer confusion. One of the instances cited in the 2014 Nominet report is the not uncommon example of a site bearing a name similar to that of an official government website. The difference is that whilst the official site offers its services free of charge, the alternative site charges for in effect acting as an intermediary. A change of a couple of letters—or as more increasingly be the case—of domain may be confusing for users. In some instances the interface between trade mark law and domain names may provide a legal remedy. In other instances, however, trade marks may not be applicable. In the example cited above, there was undoubtedly confusion between the driving licence and registration services offered by the official Driver and Vehicle Licencing Agency (DVLA) and a commercial organisation <dvla-driving-licence.co.uk> offering to provide assistance to users applying for a licence in exchange for a fairly substantial fee. If you type <dvla-driving-licence.co.uk> into your web browser, you will see that the official agency succeeded in having rights to the domain transferred to it. The practice does continue in other areas. UK citizens can (at least for now) obtain free of charge what is known as an E 111 card. This provides evidence of their entitlement to obtain medical treatment in other Member States of the European Union on the same basis as citizens of those states. Type 'E 111' into your browser and, certainly at the time of writing, you will see prominently displayed references to a site offering (for a fee) to check and submit an application for a card. A user may well mistake this site for the official one and pay charges that are not necessary in order to obtain the document. Again a difficulty is that the name 'E 111' is not protected by trade mark. The proliferation of domain names may make this kind of situation more common and problematic.

Historically only a small number of top level domains have been available for registration by users, .com being the most well-known example. As discussed above, demand for domain names exceeds supply and in the attempt to alleviate the problem ICANN introduced a new domain policy.

Following a prolonged discussion process, ICANN introduced its new domain policy in 2012. The first domains were allocated towards the end of 2014. This constitutes a very significant change from the traditional system of generic top level domain names and has resulted in a major expansion in the number of domains.

A number of categories of identifiers have proved popular in the new system. Geographic indicators have been sought after and, for example, we now have .london and .paris domains. Another popular sector relates to forms of activity. There are now the domains such as .soccer and .hockey. Perhaps most significantly and contentiously, a number of major companies have obtained domains in their own name.

Consideration of the new system has to take place at two levels. First we have to consider the procedures for allocating domain names and then what may happen if there is a dispute about who should be able to use a particular domain name? The second has been a major issue with the original domains such as .COM and issues raised there remain very relevant in the context of the new system.

Managing the allocation and operation of domain names is a complex technical process involving matching names with IP addresses and ensuring that there are no conflicts. One of the concerns expressed has been that poor quality registries might threaten the stability of the Internet. This has been an oft-stated concern within the telecommunications sector with concerns that the connection of unauthorised equipment to networks might threaten their stability. Experience has indicated that concerns are rather exaggerated and that networks are more robust than pessimists might suggest. The suspicion may be that the same will apply in relation to the Internet which was, at least in part, designed to ensure the resilience of telecommunications in the aftermath of a nuclear attack.

The basis for the activities of domain name registries lies in a contract that they are required to enter into with ICANN. The contract has been modified from time to time with the current version being adopted in 2013.[68] You can find a copy of the contract at this website. There are now many hundreds of domain name registries around the world.[69]

It is open to domain name registries to enter into sub-contracts with domain name resellers. A wide range of organisations offer to supply and register domain names. Once again, this will take place subject to the terms of a contract between the domain name reseller and the relevant registry.

Is the new domain policy working? Many questions are difficult to answer. The following passage from the *Telegraph* newspaper illustrates some of the issues:

> Of the more than 325m web addresses registered worldwide, around 24m are made up of the thousands of new top level domains. On the face of it, this is respectable, considering that the first ones went online less than three years ago.
>
> But numbers fail to tell the whole story: few major websites have adopted the new domain names, to the extent that many web users are unaware they exist. There has been little reason for most businesses to attempt a risky switch, and many of the new domains have been snapped up not for use, but by opportunists wishing either to sell their patch of the web at an inflated price at some point or for more malevolent aims.
>
> Internet crooks, using the almost-endless number of new web addresses, have used them to masquerade as legitimate companies in order to defraud idle browsers and steal their details. These impersonators have also been able to spread misinformation by appearing to be reliable sources: last year, shares in Twitter rose by 8pc after 'Bloomberg.markets', a fake website, reported that the social network was being bought by Google.[70]

Most individuals like to stick with what they know. The 'old' domain .COM remains a dominant player and it will take a lot to shift it from that position.

---

[68] <https://www.icann.org/resources/pages/approved-with-specs-2013–09–17-en?routing_type=path>.

[69] See <https://www.icann.org/registrar-reports/accreditation-qualified-list.html> for a listing of registries.

[70] <http://www.telegraph.co.uk/technology/2016/08/29/the-webs-domain-name-revolution-has-been-a-missed-opportunity/>.

PART IV

E-Commerce

INTRODUCTION

It is difficult today to open a newspaper or view a website without seeing some story relating to e-commerce. Lauded in some quarters, it is vilified in others as contributing (along with out-of-town superstores) to the demise of the traditional High Street. This book will focus on the legal implications of e-commerce but it is useful to take some time at the outset to set the scene.

The notion of transactions occurring between sellers and buyers located hundreds of miles apart is not at all novel. With the development of efficient railway and postal networks in the nineteenth century we saw the emergence of catalogue or mail order selling. Usage of the electric telegraph (and postal networks) in the nineteenth century had societal impacts similar to those brought about by the Internet and modern notions of e-commerce. Although statistics are scarce, it does appear that catalogue selling in the late nineteenth and early to mid-twentieth centuries accounted for levels of sales comparable to those reported today for consumer e-commerce transactions.

It is always tempting to look at the past through rose-tinted spectacles, but whilst the traditional High Street would provide butchers and bakers (perhaps not so many candle-stick makers) the range of goods available to shoppers was rather limited and catalogues provided access to items that would otherwise be difficult to obtain or provided competition to what would otherwise have been monopolistic suppliers. At a personal level, I grew up in the 1960s in a medium-sized town in Scotland (about 20,000 people) and recall that there was only one shop that sold electrical appliances such as TVs and washing machines.

The catalogue selling industry was particularly prominent in the United States with the catalogue issued by the Sears corporation acquiring almost mythical status. In an era where people living in rural areas had very limited access to retail facilities, catalogue selling provided an opportunity to access current designs for clothing and household objects.

Moving on, the modern notion of e-commerce dates back to the 1960s when businesses began to set up arrangements with customers and suppliers for the electronic ordering and supply of goods. The initial arrangements, generally known as electronic data interchange (EDI) agreements, were closed networks. Only the contracting parties could operate under their provisions. A very simplistic example might see a contract between a supermarket and a producer of baked beans. When the supermarket's check-out systems recorded the sale of a can of beans, it would place an order with the producer for the delivery of another can. The essential legal feature is that a valid contract can be created without any direct human involvement. Today we are starting to hear a great deal about machine-to-machine communications and EDI systems are one of the pioneers in the field.

More recently there have been moves to open up supply contracts between public and private sector organisations establishing web portals that invite tenders for the supply of goods and, increasingly, services. The Government Procurement Service (GPS) is an executive office of the Cabinet Office with a remit to encourage widespread participation by small and medium enterprises in public procurement and to centralise procurement across the sector. This might be, for example, by concluding a model contract for the supply of paper clips that might be utilised by any public sector body and obviate the need for each department and agency to conduct its own procurement exercise. The GPS website indicates that its procurement contracts cover energy, travel, fleet, office solutions, communications services, print, professional services, ICT, e-commerce, and property and facilities management.

In the late 1990s the United Kingdom (and many other developed countries) experienced what was referred to as the dot com boom. Like many booms it was followed by the dot com crash around the beginning of this millennium. The reasons were many and various but a major factor was that physical delivery networks struggled to cope with orders resulting in a loss of consumer confidence as presents intended to be opened on Christmas Day failed to materialise until the New Year. Recent years have seen a resurgence within the sector.

The latest statistics from the Office for National Statistics indicate a continuing growth in e-commerce. It now accounts for around 19 per cent of all sales. It should be noted, however, that around 14 per cent of sales (around two-thirds of e-commerce transactions) fall into the category of EDI and represent sales between businesses or similar organisations. So-called B–C (business to consumer) transactions, that attract the main share of media publicity concerning e-commerce, make up a minority share in terms of value.

In the context of B–C e-commerce sales, OFCOM's Communications Market report published in August 2013 indicated that '(a)verage weekly internet retail sales grew 10.3 per cent year on year to May 2013, up from £528m to £582m'. Perhaps not surprisingly, sales peaked in the December 2012 where sales amounted to £847 million, itself an increase of nearly 18 per cent on the figures for December 2011. A particular growth sector, especially in the developing world, is in mobile commerce, where transactions are concluded using a mobile phone. In the United Kingdom, mobile advertising revenue increased nearly twentyfold in the period 2008–12 (from £29 million to £526 million). Research suggests that quite a high percentage of mobile browsing of e-commerce sites stops at the payments page, perhaps because the prospect of keying in long credit card numbers on a mobile phone screen is challenging. Some systems have been introduced to simplify the process such as 'Pingit'. Operated by Barclays Bank, it allows users to enter a pre-arranged five-digit code to authorise transactions.

A more recent category of e-commerce sees transactions between consumers (C–C) on electronic marketplaces such as eBay. According to OFCOM more than half of the United Kingdom's online population visited eBay on an average month. Sites such as eBay facilitate sales between consumers, effectively operating as a giant street market or car-boot saleroom. Within the United Kingdom eBay sales have reached around £1 billion a year with a profit of around £250 million. Although it is increasingly common for businesses to use eBay and similar sites as a portal for their online sales a substantial portion of eBay sales are between consumers.

The legal dimension

We will discuss legal issues in significantly more detail in the following chapters but it may be helpful at this stage to give an overview of the key topics. One will be very familiar to anyone who has read this far in the book. We live in a global society with globalised businesses. Perhaps not a purely legal issue, but there has been considerable publicity about the ability of online businesses (and multinational companies generally) to minimise their exposure to national taxes. It is reported, for example, that eBay paid UK taxes of £1.2 million in 2010 on the back of profits of around £250 million. That represents a tax rate of 0.48 per cent. The distinction between tax avoidance (legal) and tax evasion (unlawful) is hard to draw but it is, I think, fair comment that national states are struggling to regulate companies operating in cyberspace.

As indicated, distance selling is not a new phenomenon. Purchasing goods or services on this basis does mean that it is difficult for the customer to examine them prior to concluding a contract. There are some moves towards the use of 3D holograms and augmented reality technologies to allow, for example, a customer to get a sense of how a particular clothing outfit might look when superimposed on their own image. Even with such technologies it is difficult to recreate fully the look and feel of objects. One of the ways that distance-selling legislation has developed has been to provide consumers with a period within which they can cancel the contract if they discover that goods or services do not meet their expectations.

What we see in this respect is perhaps another area where the law is struggling to come to terms with technology and also good business practice. Just as in the real world some companies—Marks and Spencer comes to mind—have improved consumer confidence and brand awareness by offering returns policies that are more generous than required by law, so some Internet retailers have secured recognition for their returns policy. The retailer Amazon typically scores highly in consumer surveys in this respect.

Services such as airline tickets raise some complex issues. There is not the same question of whether the customer will like the way an item of clothing looks or feels on them. I may simply book a flight from Glasgow to London on 24 March 2017. Obviously there may be legal issues after the flight if it is heavily delayed or my baggage is lost but I know from personal experience that online booking is not always an infallible process. It does appear that most airline booking systems are different. It is all too easy, and I write from personal experience, to make a booking for the wrong date. How and whether this can be corrected is uncertain as a matter of law. Some airlines allow online bookers a period, typically twenty-four hours, to correct any mistakes free of charge. Others do not!

One of the inconveniences for most of us wishing to acquire goods or services is that we have to pay for them! Payment mechanisms play a vital role in driving e-commerce. We have established systems such as credit and debit cards but they are predicated on formal banking systems. Especially in the developing world, relatively few people have bank accounts and there have been significant developments—now reaching to the developed world in respect of transferring funds using mobile phones. Especially with the growth in the number of people using 'smart phones', now more than half of the UK population, mobile commerce and payment is becoming a major issue.

I've mentioned eBay and one of the most profitable parts of the company is its payment system 'PayPal'. There are more than 20 million UK PayPal accounts. PayPal is registered as a bank in Luxembourg so at one level the comment might be that a third of the United Kingdom's population has an offshore bank account. On another level we might consider the appropriate level of regulation for what is often referred to as microfinance. Again this is a concept which is established in developing countries—with a Nobel Peace Prize being awarded to its 'inventor', Mohammad Yunus, in 2006. As is so often the case, authoritative statistics are lacking but it appears that the average PayPal account balance is around £30. Whilst a failure of the system might be annoying, the consequences would not compare to the worst-case scenarios arising from the banking crisis of 2007–8 when, we have been told, the British Prime Minister considered putting the army on the streets to prevent a breakdown of law and order should banks have closed their doors and cash machines stopped dispensing money.

The global reach of the Internet raises other issues, not least that of jurisdiction and choice of law. International commerce has, of course been in existence for many millennia but has tended to be specialised in its nature. When I studied my law degree, commercial law was studied under the name Mercantile Law which itself traces its origins to the body of rules devised by merchants to regulate international transactions. Until the emergence of the Internet, consumer international trade was essentially limited to the purchase of tacky souvenirs from Majorca or Benidorm. Everyone would accept that caveat emptor was the rule of the day and if the goods fell apart on their return to the United Kingdom, matters would be written off to experience. If consumers purchased more expensive items such as the holiday itself, it would generally be done by means of a contract with some United Kingdom-based intermediary, typically a travel agent. One of the features of the Internet is that intermediaries play a much diminished role in consumer life and increasingly we contract directly with foreign suppliers. The question arises, of course, what happens when things go wrong? Three issues will be of critical importance. Which legal system will govern the transaction, which country's courts will have jurisdiction to try any case, and what are the procedures and possibilities for enforcing any judgment in another country? From the consumers' standpoint, if we are based in the United Kingdom and have a complaint about the service provided by a Greek hotel we would clearly want to bring a case before the domestic courts. Equally of course, the Greek hotel will almost certainly want to have the case heard in Greece. One of the key factors for the courts in making a decision will be whether the Greek hotel actively solicited business from the United Kingdom. If it has a website in English, the answer may well be yes; if the site is only in the Greek language, the conclusion will probably be different.

Yet again, there are lots of questions, and in many cases we are waiting for definitive answers. In the age of the Internet it is difficult to think of anything that we cannot buy online. It is largely outside the scope of this book but electronic conveyancing means that we can buy and sell houses without using a single piece of paper. One of the major issues in this kind of situation is how we can replicate electronically traditional requirements that documents be signed. Cryptography and notions of digital signatures provides a major part of the answer.

With electronic commerce, many of the issues that we have considered in previous sections arise again. We are seeing global markets. Online delivery of items such as software, MP3 files, and e-books makes location entirely irrelevant. Improvements in logistic delivery systems, themselves largely a by-product of e-commerce, make the transfer of physical objects such as books and laptop computers a much simpler and cheaper prospect than was the case a decade ago. One of the issues that has arisen concerns individuals using the Internet to order goods from a foreign supplier. Traditionally, individuals travelling abroad have been allowed to bring goods to a certain value into the United Kingdom without being liable to pay import taxes or VAT (duty-free allowance). How can this translate into an e-commerce context? Some specific issues have arisen in the context of the Channel Islands. Connected in some respects with the United Kingdom which has responsibility for their defence and foreign affairs, in other respects they are independent and are not considered part of the European Union. Significantly, the Channel Islands do not have a system of VAT. This encouraged many e-commerce operators to set up a warehouse in the Channel Islands to fulfil orders from UK customers, effectively being able to undercut domestic suppliers by 20 per cent (the rate of VAT at the time of writing this book). The loophole—if it was one—has now been closed but it illustrates both the legal issues that can arise and also the practicalities (or impracticalities) for customs forces to examine millions of individual letters and packages arriving in the United Kingdom.

22

International and European initiatives in e-commerce

INTRODUCTION

The growth of e-commerce has been one of the most notable developments of the Internet age. Following a stutter at the time of the so-called dot com crash around the turn of the century, the sector has resumed what appears to be a remorseless rise. Any statistics are perhaps of fleeting value but the following data may indicate the qualitative and quantitative scale of e-commerce in today's Britain. Seventy per cent of UK households and 62 per cent of the population, it is estimated by the Office of National Statistics, make use of the Internet for buying goods or services. The value of online sales was estimated to be £4.4 billion in June 2010 with increases in value of more than 20 per cent in the past year. By 2012 around 10 per cent of all national expenditure took place online. Significantly in societal terms, a third of individuals have indicated that when shopping for goods or services which can be obtained either online or in the High Street, they would actively prefer to deal online. Perhaps marking a return to earlier days when, especially in more rural areas, catalogue shopping was a popular activity, online sales figures in fields such as clothing are increasing faster than the average with 2010 figures marking a 32 per cent increase on the previous year.

Although in the e-commerce sector it is frequently difficult to distinguish hype from reality, there is no doubt that an increasing range of contracts will be concluded using some form of electronic communication. In many cases concerned with services, delivery, and perhaps performance, will also take place within an electronic environment.

In the context of traditional business activities, it is often stated that the three attributes most critical to commercial success are 'location, location, and location'. It is regarded as one of the hallmarks of e-commerce that issues of location, at least at the physical level, are of no significance. Paradoxically, however, when consideration is given to legal issues, location returns very much to the forefront. The most important questions concern the determination of when and where a contract is made and which laws and tax regimes will govern the transaction.

International initiatives

Given the international nature of the topic, it is not surprising that many of the activities in the field of e-commerce have been initiated by international organisations. The UN Commission on International Trade Law (UNCITRAL) adopted a model law on e-commerce in 1996 whilst, in December 1999, the Organisation for Economic

Co-operation and Development (OECD) agreed Guidelines on Electronic Commerce.[1] The goal of the guidelines, it is stated,

> is that consumers shopping on-line should enjoy transparent and effective protection that is not less than the level of protection that they have in other areas of commerce. Among other things, they stress the importance of transparency and information disclosure.

The model law and the guidelines have no binding force. In focusing on regulatory activity, attention must concentrate on the activities of the EU and of national legislatures. EU involvement in the field of e-commerce can be traced primarily to a Commission Communication, 'A European Initiative in Electronic Commerce', published in April 1997.[2] Itself building on earlier information society initiatives, this outlined a programme for regulatory action across a range of topics. In what might be considered chronological order, action was required in order to ensure that organisations were enabled to establish electronic businesses in any of the Member States, that legal barriers to electronic trade should be removed, and that provision should be made for the manner in which contracts should be negotiated and concluded. Finally, legislation might be required in the field of electronic payments.

The mechanics of e-commerce constitute one aspect of the regulatory task. It was also recognised that other more general principles would require to be applied in the context of commercial applications. Issues such as data protection arise whenever personal data is transmitted and received. Again, as will be discussed in the following chapter, the use of cryptographic techniques as a means for enhancing security, both to preserve privacy and to enhance consumer and business confidence in the integrity of electronic communications, raises significant and controversial regulatory questions.

Although it is tempting to regard e-commerce as a new phenomenon, this is to neglect a significant existing market sector—that dealing with mail-order or catalogue selling. Especially in the United States, there is a substantial tradition of sales being conducted on this basis—dating back to the Wild West days beloved of cyberspace analogists. Given the federal nature of the US Constitution, such sales also occurred across state boundaries. The oft-cited Uniform Commercial Code was first promulgated in 1940 to provide means to overcome jurisdictional and substantive problems arising when a supplier located in one jurisdiction contracted with a customer in another. Subject to some variations, it provides a common body of rules applicable throughout the fifty states. Recent (and highly controversial) developments in the United States have resulted in proposals to amend the venerable provisions of the Uniform Commercial Code to take account of the special nature of software sales.[3] Most initiatives seeking to amend the Code are the joint product of two bodies, the American Law Institute (ALI) and the National Conference of Commissioners on Uniform State Laws (NCCUSL). Originally, it was proposed to table an amendment to Article 2 of the Code. This provision deals with the law relating to the sale of goods. During 1999, a division occurred between the two drafting bodies, with the ALI taking the view that the proposal as drafted was too heavily weighted in favour of the interests of software developers and suppliers. The NCCUSL proceeded with the proposal, which was changed into a stand-alone statute, the Uniform Computer Information Transactions Act. The measure has been passed to the fifty states, although it has been enacted in only two (Maryland and Virginia).

---

[1] Available from <http://www.oecd.org/dataoecd/18/13/34023235.pdf>.

[2] Available from <http://www.cordis.lu/esprit/src/ecomcom.htm>.

[3] For an extensive range of materials and comments on the proposed new law, see <http://www.2bguide.com/legart.html>.

Key legal instruments

A number of measures adopted or proposed by the EU are relevant to any discussion of e-commerce. Three are of particular relevance. The Distance Selling Directive[4] and substantive law elements of the Electronic Commerce Directive[5] will be discussed in the present chapter. The Electronic Commerce Directive also contains provisions relating to the legal recognition of electronic contracts in cases where national laws require that contracts be concluded in a particular form. These matters, which are also covered in the Directive on 'A Community Framework for Electronic Signatures'[6] will be discussed in the next chapter.

The Distance Selling Directive

The market for distance selling through catalogues is a well-established one, especially in remote areas where retail outlets are few and far between. The sector is particularly well established in the United States, and it is anticipated that businesses with experience of these forms of transactions will be well placed to benefit from the move to e-commerce. Over the past decade, the telephone, email and the *www* have been used to solicit consumer contracts. One of the most important European legal instruments is the Directive on the Protection of Consumers in Respect of Distance Contracts.[7] The Directive applies to all forms of distance selling, but contains some provisions relating specifically to the use of electronic communications. A number of these have been supplemented by the terms of the Electronic Commerce Directive.[8] The Distance Selling Directive was required to be implemented within the Member States by June 2000. The Preamble makes its rationale clear:

> Whereas the introduction of new technologies is increasing the number of ways for consumers to obtain information about offers anywhere in the Community and to place orders; whereas some Member States have already taken different or diverging measures to protect consumers in respect of distance selling, which has had a detrimental effect on competition between businesses in the internal market; whereas it is therefore necessary to introduce at Community level a minimum set of common rules in this area.[9]

The Distance Selling Directive defines the term 'distance contract' as:

> Any contract concerning goods or services concluded between a supplier and a consumer under an organized distance sales or service-provision scheme run by the supplier, who, for the purpose of the contract, makes exclusive use of one or more means of distance communication up to and including the moment at which the contract is concluded.[10]

Annex 1 contains an illustrative list of communication technologies. In addition to traditional categories, such as letters and press advertisements, reference is made to the use of systems of videotext, email, and facsimile transmission.

The Distance Selling Directive's provisions begin to operate at the stage where the consumer's entry into a contract is solicited, the principal requirement here being that promotional techniques must pay due regard to the consumer's privacy, conform to the 'principles of good faith', and provide 'clear and unambiguous information' regarding the nature of any product or service, its price, and the identity of its supplier.[11] In the case of telephone

---

[4] Directive 97/7/EC.   [5] Directive 2000/31/EC.
[6] Directive 99/93/EC, OJ 2000 L 13/12.
[7] Directive 97/7/EC, OJ 1997 L 144 (the Distance Selling Directive). A further proposal for a Directive concerns the distance selling of financial services, COM (98) 468 final of 14 October 1998.
[8] Directive 2000/31/EC.   [9] Recital 4.
[10] Directive 97/7/EC, Art. 2(1).   [11] Art. 4(2).

communication, the supplier is obliged to make its identity, and the fact that the call is commercial in nature, clear at the commencement of a call.[12]

The Distance Selling Directive also provides that two forms of technology, automated calling systems and fax machines, may be used only with the prior consent of the consumer— what might be referred to as an 'opt in' system.[13] Automated calling systems involve the use of a computer system to call numbers and on answering, play a pre-recorded message to the recipient. Such technologies are effectively prohibited in the United Kingdom as their use would require a licence from OFTEL, which has indicated objections to the practice. In the case of other forms of communication, it is provided that these are to be made only when the consumer has not indicated a clear objection to receipt of solicitations.[14] The operation of an 'opt out' system would be compatible with this requirement.

The rationale behind the selection of specific prohibited technologies is not clear. Recital 17 of the Distance Selling Directive[15] asserts that the consumer's right to privacy should extend to 'freedom from certain particularly intrusive means of communication'. It is difficult to argue, however, that a pre-recorded telephone message is intrinsically more intrusive than other forms of telephone canvassing. Unsolicited faxes also are unlikely to be seen as invasive of privacy, and perhaps a more persuasive basis for restricting these lies in the fact that the recipient of a fax incurs cost in terms of the paper and ink used for its reproduction. This was, perhaps, more of a factor with previous generations of fax machines, which required the use of special (and expensive) paper.

Assuming that discussions between supplier and consumer extend beyond the initial contact, there is a clear need to ensure that the latter is made aware of the terms and conditions associated with a particular contract. The Distance Selling Directive provides for two approaches, the first of which is outwith the scope of the present study, requiring the grant of a 'cooling off' period following the conclusion of the contract.[16] More relevant are provisions requiring that the consumer be given information as to terms. Article 4 specifies the items of information which must be given. These relate primarily to the identity of the supplier, the nature and cost of the goods or services, and any arrangements for delivery. These are relatively easily satisfied in traditional mail order or catalogue sales, but in respect of electronic communications, Recital 13 states that:

> Whereas information disseminated by certain electronic technologies is often ephemeral in nature insofar as it is not received on a permanent medium; whereas the consumer must therefore receive written notice in good time of the information necessary for proper performance of the contract.

Whilst the comment regarding the transient nature of information displayed on a website, for example, is basically true, the text of an email message can be as locatable as any written message. It would seem somewhat Luddite were a party engaging in e-commerce to be required to supply confirmation details on paper. The Distance Selling Directive requires that confirmation be supplied in writing or:

> in another durable medium available and accessible to him.[17]

It may be that the transmission of an email which may be stored on the consumer's computer would satisfy this requirement. This is the view which has been adopted by the then Department of Trade and Industry, which commented in its second consultation paper:

> We consider that confirmation by electronic mail would meet the definition of confirmation in 'another durable medium available and accessible to [the consumer]', where the order has

---

[12] Art. 4(3).   [13] Directive 97/7/EC, Art. 10(1).   [14] Art. 10(2).
[15] Directive 97/7/EC.   [16] Art. 6.   [17] Art. 5.

been made by means of e-mail. We have not however specified this in the Draft Regulations since the Directive is not specific on the point, and only a court can determine the meaning of the wording.[18]

The Electronic Commerce Directive and Regulations

A proposal for a Directive on 'Legal Aspects of Electronic Commerce' was introduced in November 1998.[19] The proposal was debated in the European Parliament[20] and following its comments, an amended proposal was introduced in September 1999,[21] becoming law on its adoption by the Council of Ministers in May 2000.[22] It is implemented in the United Kingdom by the Electronic Commerce (EC Directive) Regulations 2002,[23] which follow very closely the wording and format of the Directive. Following a lengthy period when the measures were not at issue before the courts, there have recently been a number of cases concerning aspects of the legislation. These will be considered later but in many respects it might be doubted whether the Directive would have been adopted in the same form had the law-makers been able to predict the ways in which technology would develop.

The Directive was drafted at a relatively early stage of the development of the Internet at a time where the majority of domestic users were accessing services via dial-up or narrowband connections. In 2000 the UK telecommunications regulator OFTEL, estimated that less than 1 per cent of UK domestic users had broadband connections. Although the bulk of the Directive's provisions which relate to consumers' rights in respect of contracts concluded or performed over the Internet are technologically neutral and have stood the passage of time quite well, the specific provisions dealing with the liability of intermediaries have been relatively seldom tested in the courts and when this has occurred their application in the modern Internet context has been difficult.

The scope of the measure is broad-ranging. It applies to what are referred to as 'Information Society Services' which are supplied by 'Information Society Service Providers'. Although the E-Commerce Directive refers to information society services, the definition of these is to be found in Directive 98/48/EC which relates to issues of standardisation within the EU. This provides that the term encompasses:

> any service normally provided for remuneration, at a distance, by electronic means and at the individual request of a recipient of services.

For the purposes of this definition:

> 'at a distance' means that the service is provided without the parties being simultaneously present,

> 'by electronic means' means that the service is sent initially and received at its destination by means of electronic equipment for the processing (including digital compression) and storage of data, and entirely transmitted, conveyed and received by wire, by radio, by optical means or by other electromagnetic means,

> 'at the individual request of a recipient of services' means that the service is provided through the transmission of data on individual request.

The rationale for the requirement that services should be provided with a view to some remuneration is explained in the Recitals to the Directive. Recital 19 states:

> Whereas, under Article 60 of the Treaty as interpreted by the case-law of the Court of Justice, 'services' means those normally provided for remuneration; whereas that characteristic is

---

[18] para. 3.9.   [19] OJ 1999 C 30.

[20] Material relating to all stages of the Directive's passage can be found at <http://ec.europa.eu/internal_market/e-commerce/directive_en.htm#preparatory>.

[21] COM (99) 427 final.   [22] Directive 2000/31/EC, OJ 2000 L 178/1.   [23] SI 2002/2013.

absent in the case of activities which a State carries out without economic consideration in the context of its duties in particular in the social, cultural, educational and judicial fields;

Effectively, the European Union has limited legislative competence in the situations where services are provided other than for commercial purposes. If a service is provided without there being any intention to make some form of profit, the Electronic Commerce Directive and the implementing UK Regulations can have no application. Given the high rate of failure among e-commerce operations, it is clear that the quest for profit need not be successful but the aspiration must be present.

The Recitals to the Electronic Commerce Directive envisage the possibility that commercial benefit for the service provider might not come about in a direct manner:

> (18) Information society services span a wide range of economic activities which take place online; these activities can, in particular, consist of selling goods online; activities such as the delivery of goods as such or the provision of services off-line are not covered; information society services are not solely restricted to services giving rise to online contracting but also, in so far as they represent an economic activity, extend to services which are not remunerated by those who receive them, such as those offering online information or commercial communications, or those providing tools allowing for search, access and retrieval of data; information society services also include services consisting of the transmission of information via a communication network, in providing access to a communication network or in hosting information provided by a recipient of the service.

In the case of search engines such as Google, for example, although the service is provided free of charge to end-users, the service provider seeks (and obtains) significant profit from selling advertising services to other providers. As stated above, however, if there is no commercial motive underpinning the provision of services, the legislation does not apply. In the case of *Metropolitan International Schools Ltd v Designtechnica Corporation and Google UK and Google Inc*,[24] a case concerned in part with the liability of a search engine provider for defamatory comments accessible via links provided by it, the judge, Mr Justice Eady, quoted from the leading textbook on the topic, *Gatley on Libel and Slander* (11th edn) at paragraph 6.28, to the effect that:

> Many internet service providers charge no fee to users and derive their revenue from advertising or commission on telephone charges but the remuneration presumably does not have to be provided by the user so the vast majority will be covered, though a business organisation operating an internal network would not.

He concluded:

> Although the matter is by no means free from doubt, it would appear on balance that the provisions of the 2002 Regulations are apt to cover those providing search engine services.

Defences provided to Information Service Providers

One of the key purposes of the E-Commerce Directive is to harmonise the level of liability applying across the EU Member States and to provide reassurance to those acting or contemplating entering into the sector that they will not be subject to excessive levels of liability greater than those applying to more traditional operators. Three specific defences are provided in the legislation applying where the Information Society Service Provider acts only in the capacity of hosting material generated by its customers, holds data merely for

---

[24] [2009] EWHC 1765 (QB).

caching purposes to facilitate access and onward transmission, or provides a 'mere conduit' through which customers data flows.

The provisions of the caching and hosting defences have been considered in more detail in Chapter 17 in the context of Internet Service Provider (ISP) liability for copyright infringement. The 'mere conduit' defence has been perhaps the most contentious provision of the legislation and has been at issue in a number of cases brought against website administrators whose facilities have been, it was alleged, used to perpetrate acts of copyright infringement. Analogies are frequently drawn with the operation of postal or telecommunications networks where the network provider will have no knowledge of the contents of messages sent using its facilities. The Directive provides in Article 12 that:

1. Where an information society service is provided that consists of the transmission in a communication network of information provided by a recipient of the service, or the provision of access to a communication network, Member States shall ensure that the service provider is not liable for the information transmitted, on condition that the provider:

    (a) does not initiate the transmission;

    (b) does not select the receiver of the transmission; and

    (c) does not select or modify the information contained in the transmission.

2. The acts of transmission and of provision of access referred to in paragraph 1 include the automatic, intermediate and transient storage of the information transmitted in so far as this takes place for the sole purpose of carrying out the transmission in the communication network, and provided that the information is not stored for any period longer than is reasonably necessary for the transmission.

3. This Article shall not affect the possibility for a court or administrative authority, in accordance with Member States' legal systems, of requiring the service provider to terminate or prevent an infringement.

The Electronic Commerce (EC Directive) Regulations provide similarly:

(1) Where an information society service is provided which consists of the transmission in a communication network of information provided by a recipient of the service or the provision of access to a communication network, the service provider (if he otherwise would) shall not be liable for damages or for any other pecuniary remedy or for any criminal sanction as a result of that transmission where the service provider—

    (a) did not initiate the transmission;

    (b) did not select the receiver of the transmission; and

    (c) did not select or modify the information contained in the transmission.

(2) The acts of transmission and of provision of access referred to in paragraph (1) include the automatic, intermediate and transient storage of the information transmitted where:

    (a) this takes place for the sole purpose of carrying out the transmission in the communication network, and

    (b) the information is not stored for any period longer than is reasonably necessary for the transmission.

There do not appear to be any significant variations between the two sets of provisions.

The operation of these terms has been discussed in two English cases in the context of actions for defamation. In the case of *Bunt v Tilley and Ors*,[25] the claimant alleged that a number

---

[25] [2006] EWHC 407.

of statements posted on websites were defamatory of him. Among the defendants were three ISPs—AOL, Tiscali, and BT—who had provided services to three individual defendants who were the authors of the postings. Although the point was somewhat peripheral to the main argument which concerned the nature of the definition of a publisher of defamatory information as laid down in the Defamation Act 1996, the court appeared to accept the proposition that ISPs should be regarded as playing a role analogous to that of the operators of a telephone network in that they had no actual knowledge or control over the contents of communications.

The issue was discussed more extensively in the case of *Metropolitan International Schools Ltd v Designtechnica Corporation and Google UK and Google Inc.*[26] In this case, the claimant alleged that the second and third defendants, who operated the well-known search engine Google.com and provided access from within the UK domain-name system (Google.co.uk), made available links to a website operated by the first defendant which contained material which was defamatory in nature. Evidence was led as to the scale of Google's operations with the search engine indexing around 39 billion publicly available web pages. The index was compiled entirely automatically. Search requests were also met entirely by automatic means with no element of human intervention.

The second and third defendants applied to have the action dismissed on a number of grounds, including, most relevantly, that Google could benefit from the 'mere conduit' defence. In this context the judge, Mr Justice Eady (who delivered also the judgment in *Bunt v Tilley*) held that:

> When a search is carried out by a web user via the Google search engine it is clear, from what I have said already about its function, that there is no human input from the Third Defendant. None of its officers or employees takes any part in the search. It is performed automatically in accordance with computer programmes.
>
> When a snippet is thrown up on the user's screen in response to his search, it points him in the direction of an entry somewhere on the Web that corresponds, to a greater or lesser extent, to the search terms he has typed in. It is for him to access or not, as he chooses. It is fundamentally important to have in mind that the Third Defendant has no role to play in formulating the search terms. Accordingly, it could not prevent the snippet appearing in response to the user's request unless it has taken some positive step in advance. There being no input from the Third Defendant, therefore, on the scenario I have so far posited, it cannot be characterised as a publisher at common law. It has not authorised or caused the snippet to appear on the user's screen in any meaningful sense. It has merely, by the provision of its search service, played the role of a facilitator.
>
> Analogies are not always helpful, but there will often be resorted to when the common law has to be applied to new and unfamiliar concepts. Here, an analogy may be drawn with a search carried out in a large conventional library. If a scholar wishes to check for references to his research topic, he may well consult the library catalogue. On doing so, he may find that there are some potentially relevant books on one of the shelves and make his way there to see whether he can make use of the content. It is hardly realistic to attribute responsibility for the content of those books to the compiler(s) of the catalogue. On the other hand, if the compilers have made an effort to be more informative, by quoting brief snippets from the book, the position may be different. Suppose the catalogue records that a particular book contains allegations of corruption against a living politician, or perhaps it goes further and spells out a particular activity, such as 'flipping' homes to avoid capital gains tax, then there could be legal liability on the part of the compiler under the 'repetition rule': see e.g. *Gatley on Libel and Slander* (11th edn) at paras 11.4 and 32.8.

It was noted that in a number of jurisdictions specific legislative provision had been made to confer immunity on the operators of search engines. In some jurisdictions this took

---

[26] [2009] EWHC 1765 (QB).

place in connection with the 'mere conduit' defence and in others in relation to a further defence provided in the directive relating to 'hosting' of material. The possibility of adopting a similar approach for the United Kingdom was discussed in a Consultation Paper published by the then Department of Trade and Industry in 2005 but the matter was not progressed. In the event, the judge did not feel it necessary to give a definitive ruling on the application of the defence as it was found that Google had not published the material under the terms of the Defamation Act 1996.

To date, therefore, there has been no English authority directly concerned with the application of the 'mere conduit' defence either generally or in the specific context of intellectual property rights. A recent Swedish authority appears to have been involved with similar issues. In the so-called 'Pirates Bay' case the Stockholm District Court tried a number of defendants who were responsible for the operation of a website, 'The Pirates Bay'. This website provided a facility for users to upload and download torrent files but an important distinction lies in the fact that on the basis of the findings of the Swedish court, the Pirates Bay website provided storage facilities for its users to upload and download material. The case therefore proceeded on the basis of other provisions of the E-Commerce Directive relating to the caching and hosting of material.

One of the defence claims was to the effect that the service provided only a search-engine facility and that there was no knowledge of the contents of files exchanged between users. This was rejected by the court which ruled that it must have been obvious to the defendants that the site contained torrent files which infringed copyright and that they took no active steps to remove these. The conclusion reached by the court was that even if it could not be said that there was precise knowledge of each infringing file, there was a general culture of indifference towards copyright infringement which was sufficient to remove the immunity from liability offered under the E-Commerce Directive.

Substantive provisions in the Directive

When and where is a contract made?

In order for a contract to be concluded, there must be an unconditional offer and acceptance. In many instances, of course, there may be several iterations of offer and counter-offer before the parties reach agreement on all important matters concerned with the contract.

In the situation where a customer purchases goods in a shop, there is little problem in determining the question where a contract is made. The question when the contract is concluded is a little more problematic. In the situation where goods are displayed in retail premises, it is normally the case that the display constitutes an invitation to treat. An offer to purchase will be made by the customer, which may be accepted (or rejected) by the seller. There are sound reasons for such an approach, not least due to the possibility that goods might be out of stock or that the wrong price tag may have been placed on an item by mistake (or through the action of some third party). In practical terms, it can be said that a contract will typically be concluded when the customer's offer of payment is accepted by the seller.

Subject to any other mechanism agreed between the parties, it is generally the case that acceptance becomes effective when it is communicated to the offeror. Clearly, in the case of a face-to-face transaction, this occurs at the point where the acceptor indicates—whether by words or actions—that the offer is acceptable. Matters become rather more complex when the parties to the transaction are at a distance. Here, two sets of rules have been developed, depending on the nature of the communications technology employed. The rule relating to postal contracts form a well-established feature of the legal system. Here, it is provided that the contract is deemed to have been concluded at the moment the acceptance is placed into the postal system. The main rationale for such an approach is that once the message has been posted, it moves out of the control of the sender. The effect of this is, of course, that a contract will be concluded before the offeror is aware of the fact of acceptance. It is also the case that having been posted, an acceptance cannot be withdrawn, even though this may have been brought to the attention of the offeror prior to delivery of the acceptance.

The postal rule is to be contrasted with another rule relating to the use of forms of technology which might be classed as involving 'instantaneous communication'. In *Entores Ltd v Miles Far East Corpn*,[27] the question at issue was where a contract made following communications by telex should be regarded as having been concluded. The plaintiffs, who were located in London, had made an offer which had been accepted by the defendants in Amsterdam. Holding that the contract was made when the acceptance was received by the plaintiffs in London, Parker LJ held that where

> parties are in each other's presence or, though separated in space, communication between them is in effect instantaneous, there is no need for any such rule of convenience. To hold otherwise would leave no room for the operation of the general rule that notification of the acceptance must be received. An acceptor could say: 'I spoke the words of acceptance in your presence, albeit softly, and you did not hear me'; or 'I telephoned to you and accepted, and it matters not that the telephone went dead and you did not get my message' . . . So far as Telex messages are concerned, though the despatch and receipt of a message is not completely instantaneous, the parties are to all intents and purposes in each other's presence just as if they were in telephonic communication, and I can see no reason for departing from the general rule that there is no binding contract until notice of the acceptance was received by the offeror.[28]

This view was endorsed by the House of Lords in the case of *Brinkibon Ltd v Stahag Stahl und Stahlwarenhandel GMBH*,[29] although it was recognised by Lord Wilberforce that the result might have to be reviewed in the event that it could be established that there was

> some error or default at the recipient's end which prevents receipt at the time contemplated and believed in by the sender . . . No universal rule can cover all such cases; they must be resolved by reference to the intentions of the parties, by sound business practice and in some cases a judgement where the risks should lie.[30]

In the context of the present work, the key question is whether emails and other forms of message transmitted over the Internet will be classed as coming under the postal rule, or whether the provisions relating to instantaneous communications will apply. Although the issue of determining when an email contract is concluded might appear to be of the 'number of angels on a pinhead' category, this is not always the case, especially when—as in the *Entores*[31] and *Brinkibon*[32] cases—transactions possess an international dimension. In such cases, the questions will arise of which law will govern the transaction and which courts will have jurisdiction in the event of a dispute. In the event that a contract is silent on the point, the location where a contract is concluded will be a major factor in determining the choice-of-law question.

In terms of speed of transmission, email might generally be equated with fax or telex transmission. In the event of problems or congestion on the networks, messages may be delayed by hours or even days and, in terms of the nature of transmission, the more accurate parallel may be with the postal system. An email message will be passed on from point

---

[27] [1955] 2 All ER 493.   [28] [1955] 2 All ER 493 at 498.

[29] [1982] 1 All ER 293.   [30] [1982] 1 All ER 293 at 296.

[31] *Entores Ltd v Miles Far East Corpn* [1955] 2 All ER 493.

[32] *Brinkibon Ltd v Stahag Stahl and Stahlwarenhandel GMBH* [1982] 1 All ER 293.

to point across the network, with its contents being copied and forwarded a number of times before being delivered to the ultimate recipient. There is no single direct link or connection between sender and receiver.

The Electronic Commerce Directive provides a somewhat complex mechanism for determining the moment at which a contract is concluded. It is stated that:

> Member States shall lay down in their legislation that, save where otherwise agreed by professional persons, in cases where a recipient, in accepting a service provider's offer, is required to give his consent through technological means, such as clicking on an icon, the contract is concluded when the recipient of the service has received from the service provider, electronically, an acknowledgment of receipt of the recipient's acceptance.[33]

Such an approach posed problems for the UK system which, as stated earlier, sees offers emanating from the customer rather than the supplier. There appears also to be an element of unnecessary complication by adding the requirement of acknowledgement of receipt of acceptance as a condition for the conclusion of a contract. The original proposal was even more prolonged, stating that the contract would not be concluded until acknowledgement was made of receipt of the acknowledgement! Receipt of acceptance would seem quite sufficient for this legal purpose. An alternative, and perhaps preferable, approach is advocated by the International Chamber of Commerce, whose draft Uniform Rules for Electronic Trade and Settlement propose that:

> An electronic offer and/or acceptance becomes effective when it enters the information system of the recipient in a form capable of being processed by that system.[34]

Albeit intended primarily for business-to-business contracts rather than the EU's consumer contract focus, this approach seems to achieve the legal requirements in a rather simpler fashion. Simplest of all, however, would be the UK approach, which would allow the seller to combine acceptance of the customer's offer with acknowledgement of the terms of the transaction.

A further obligation is proposed in the EC Electronic Commerce Directive. Member States are required to ensure that national laws require that:

> the service provider shall make available to the recipient of the service appropriate means that are effective and accessible allowing him to identify and correct handling errors and accidental transactions before the conclusion of the contract. Contract terms and general conditions provided to the consumer must be made available in a way that allows him to store and reproduce them.[35]

Whilst the provision is well meaning, it is difficult to identify how the result might be achieved. The provisions relating to the moment of formation of contract discussed earlier require that 'the service provider is obliged to immediately send the acknowledgement of receipt'. We can assume that in most cases this will be transmitted automatically. This affords very little time for the customer to identify and seek to correct any mistakes which have been made.

An alternative approach would be to provide consumers with a 'cooling off' period within which a contract might be terminated. The Distance Selling Directive provides for a seven-day period, beginning with the date upon which goods supplied under the contract were received by the consumer.[36] The provision does not, however, apply to contracts for the provision of services where 'performance has begun with the consumer's agreement, before the end of the seven-day working period'. This will exclude contracts for the electronic delivery

---

[33] Directive 2000/31/EC, Art. 11.   [34] Art. 2.1.1.
[35] Directive 2000/31/EC, Art. 11(2).   [36] Directive 97/7/EC, Art. 6.

of software. Exemption is also provided in respect of contracts 'for the supply of audio or video recordings or computer software which were unsealed by the consumer'. The legitimate concern in all these cases is that the consumer would have the ability to copy the material before returning the originals to the supplier and seeking a refund of the purchase price.

Choice-of-law issues

As has been stated frequently, location is irrelevant in e-commerce. It is also the case that the largest body of sites offering to supply goods or services is in the United States. A consumer located in the United Kingdom and wishing to engage in e-commerce is almost inevitably going to have to deal with United States-based companies. International trade, which hitherto has been almost exclusively the preserve of large commercial operators, is assuming a significant consumer dimension.

In any situation where buyer and seller are located in different jurisdictions, two key legal issues will arise. The first is to determine which legal system will govern the transaction and the second to determine which courts will be competent to hear disputes arising from the transaction. In many instances, it will be the case that the parties make explicit contractual provision for both matters. In a contract between parties in Scotland and France, for example, it might be provided that French law will govern the transaction but that disputes may be raised in the French or the Scottish courts, the latter being required to decide the case according to the relevant principles of French law.

In general, parties have (subject to the legal systems chosen having some connection with the subject matter of the contract) complete freedom to determine choice-of-law issues. Different rules apply where consumers are involved. Problems also arise where the parties fail to make explicit provision for issues of jurisdiction. In this case, the matter may fall to be decided by the courts.

As discussed in the context of contract formation, the question of when and where a contract is concluded is a major factor in determining which legal system is to govern the transaction. Where transactions are conducted over the Internet, the question is not always easy to answer. The global top level domain name.com gives no indication where a business is located. Even where the name uses a country code such as .de or .uk there is no guarantee that the undertaking is established in that country. It is relatively common practice, based in part upon security concerns, to keep web servers geographically separate from the physical undertaking. A website might, for example, have an address in the German (.de) domain. Its owner, however, might be a United Kingdom-registered company.

The question of whether an Internet-based business can be regarded as having a 'branch, agency or establishment' in all the countries from which its facilities may be accessed is uncertain. The OECD has pointed out in the context of tax harmonisation that the notion of permanent establishment, which is of major importance in determining whether an undertaking is liable to national taxes, may not be appropriate for e-commerce.

Within Europe, the Brussels[37] and Rome[38] Conventions make special provision for consumer contracts. The latter provides that a supplier with a 'branch, agency or establishment' in the consumer's country of residence is to be considered as domiciled there. Further, consumers may choose to bring actions in either their country of domicile or that of the supplier, whilst actions against the consumer may be brought only in the consumer's country of domicile.

The Brussels Convention builds on the Rome Convention's provisions and provides that an international contract may not deprive the consumer of 'mandatory rights' operating in the consumer's country of domicile. The scope of mandatory rights is not clear-cut but,

---

[37] C 189 of 28 July 1990.   [38] OJ 1980 L 266/1.

given the emphasis placed on the human rights dimension in many international instruments dealing with data protection, it is argued that any attempt contractually to deprive consumers of rights conferred under the Council of Europe Convention and the EC Electronic Commerce Directive[39] would be declared ineffective on this basis.

More recent developments may complicate matters. The Electronic Commerce Directive provides that transactions entered into by electronic means should be regulated by the law of the state in which the supplier is established. This approach is justified on the basis of supporting the development of the new industries, Recital 22 stating that:

> in order to effectively guarantee freedom to provide services and legal certainty for suppliers and recipients of services, such Information Society services should only be subject to the law of the Member State in which the service provider is established.

At the same time, however, the Commission has adopted, by the Regulation on Jurisdiction and the Recognition and Enforcement of Judgments in Civil and Commercial Matters,[40] amendments to the Brussels and Rome Conventions which have the effect of subjecting all consumer contracts to the law of the consumer's domicile.[41] This approach is justified on the basis that the consumer is regarded as the weaker party in any contract with a business organisation.

There appears to be an inescapable conflict between choice-of-law provisions designed to favour the development of e-commerce by making more predictable the nature of the liabilities incurred by service providers, and giving priority to the interests of consumers by maximising their access to local courts and tribunals. The Explanatory Memorandum to the draft Regulation stated that:

> The Commission has noted that the wording of Article 15 has given rise to certain anxieties among part of the industry looking to develop electronic commerce. These concerns relate primarily to the fact that companies engaging in electronic commerce will have to contend with potential litigation in every Member State, or will have to specify that their products or services are not intended for consumers domiciled in certain Member States.

The intention was announced to review the operation of Article 15 two years after the Regulation's entry into force. In the shorter term, public hearings on the subject were announced and were held in Brussels in November 1999. The hearings attracted an audience of several hundred persons and produced several hundred pages of comments and suggestions. No consensus was—or perhaps could be—reached and the position remains one where different Commission Directorates appear to be promoting different policies.

Alternative dispute resolution

One palliative for jurisdictional problems is to try to obviate the need for formal legal proceedings. Two provisions in the Electronic Commerce Directive[42] seek to facilitate this. Article 16 requires Member States and the Commission to encourage the drawing up at Community level of codes of conduct designed to contribute to the implementation of the substantive provisions of the Directive. Such codes, which will be examined by the Commission to ensure their compatibility with Community law, might provide a valuable unifying force throughout the EU. Article 17 obliges Member States to

> ensure that, in the event of disagreement between an Information Society service provider and its recipient, their legislation allows the effective use of out of court schemes for dispute settlement, including appropriate electronic means.

---

[39] Directive 2000/31/EC.   [40] Regulation 44/2001/EC, OJ 2001 L 12/1.
[41] Art. 15.   [42] Directive 2000/31/EC.

Although a number of online dispute resolution services have been established, these have mainly been in the United States and do not appear to have attracted significant custom. In the United Kingdom, the 'Which Web Trader' scheme operated by the Consumers Association was introduced in 1999 and required participating traders to observe a code of practice. The scheme closed on the ground that it was not economically viable in 2003.[43]

In 1998, the Commission adopted a 'Communication on the out-of-court settlement of consumer disputes'.[44] A Commission Working Document on the creation of a European Extra-Judicial Network (EEJ-NET)[45] was published in March 2000. This notes that:

> The continuing expansion of economic activity within of [sic] the internal market inevitably means that consumers' activities are not only confined to their own country. Greater cross border consumption has arisen due to an increase in consumer travel and the emergence of new distance selling technologies like the Internet. This increase in cross border consumption, especially with the ever-increasing expansion of electronic commerce and the introduction of the Euro, is invariably likely to lead to an increase in cross border disputes. It is, therefore, necessary and desirable to create a network of general application which will cover any kind of dispute over goods and services.

The Commission is now proposing the establishment of a network of National 'Clearing Houses'. These organisations will give consumers wishing to pursue complaints against suppliers located in their jurisdiction information about available facilities for dispute resolution. The Clearing Houses will also assist their own national consumers who are in dispute with a supplier in another Member State by liaising with the relevant Clearing House to provide information about dispute resolution procedures. A further Green Paper on alternative dispute resolution in civil and criminal law was published by the Commission in 2002.[46]

Conclusions

The scope of the Electronic Commerce Directive[47] is broad-ranging and is generally non-controversial. Even matters such as the procedure for concluding a contract may cause theoretical rather than practical problems. The major criticism that might be made of the EU's activity in the field of e-commerce is that initiatives are dispersed across a range of measures. As well as complicating the task of determining what the law is in a particular respect, there is the potential for internal conflict, as has been discussed in relation to the issue of choice of law.

Perhaps the key message which can be taken from the initiatives discussed in this chapter is that in most cases, the application of traditional legal provisions will be quite adequate in order to regulate e-commerce. The key issue is perhaps the negative one that legal requirements should not impede the operation of e-commerce. This issue primarily arises in the context of formal or procedural requirements that a contract be concluded or evidenced in writing.

---

[43] <http://www.out-law.com/page-3223>.
[44] COM (98) 198 Final.
[45] Available from <http://europa.eu/legislation_summaries/consumers/protection_of_consumers/l32031_en.htm>.
[46] COM (2002) 196 Final.
[47] Directive 2000/31/EC.

23

Electronic money

INTRODUCTION

We are fast moving towards, indeed it is fair to say we live in, societies where paper, or as is emerging,[1] plastic currency notes and coins are being used less and less. There is much talk of a 'cashless society'. Recent estimates indicate that retail transactions made using credit or debit cards account for almost 80 per cent of all sales.[2] The advent of contactless cards—that may also be linked to smart phones—allows for the very speedy payment of small transactions (currently a limit of £30 applies to their usage) and makes their use much more attractive than previously for transactions such as the purchase of a cup of coffee or a newspaper. In many situations such as e-commerce it is effectively impossible to pay for transactions with cash and even in the physical world, businesses such as twenty-four-hour garages are often reluctant to accept cash late at night.

The use of established systems of credit and debit cards to finance transactions raises few issues at domestic level although as discussed elsewhere, this has been contentious in the context of international e-commerce where there have been questions whether credit institutions are obliged to compensate consumers in respect of transactions with businesses located outside the United Kingdom. Increasing use is also being made of other forms of electronic payment mechanisms where the linkage with traditional banking institutions is more limited.

Generally referred to as electronic or e-money, applications may be either hardware- or software-based. E-money can be software- or hardware-based. Store gift cards are an example of the former category as would be a transport card such as London Transport's 'Oyster card' whilst e-money stored on an account in the Internet, such as PayPal, is software-based e-money. The gift card market in the United Kingdom has been valued at some £5 billion per annum.[3] In some cases, stores offer their own gift card facility—Amazon for example—but most of the serried ranks of cards displayed in supermarkets and other retail outlets are produced by third-party e-money issuers under contract to the particular retailer.[4] As has been extensively publicised, individuals holding such cards may be financially vulnerable in the event that the company promoting the card becomes insolvent.

Two more recent developments also merit consideration. Linked in some respect to the notion of e-money has been the introduction of systems of virtual currencies[5] of which Bitcoins is perhaps the best known and most controversial example. In essence, virtual currencies offer an

---

[1] See <http://www.bbc.co.uk/news/business-24029785>.

[2] <http://www.theukcardsassociation.org.uk/wm_documents/UK%20Card%20Payments%202015%20 Summary.pdf>.

[3] <http://www.ukgcva.co.uk/>. A perhaps unpublicized benefit to retailers is that it is estimated that some £250 million worth of gift cards are not redeemed each year (see <http://www.bbc.co.uk/news/uk-17644528>).

[4] See, eg, <http://www.svmeurope.co.uk/Products/GiftCardecodes.aspx>.

[5] For an explanation of the technologies involved <https://www.imf.org/external/pubs/ft/sdn/2016/ sdn1603.pdf>.

alternative to traditional financial systems. The value of any currency depends in part on its legal status and also on its acceptance in the market. An example can be seen in the situation in the United Kingdom where the legally approved currency is issued by the Bank of England but where banknotes issued by banks in Scotland and Northern Ireland are generally accepted as equivalent in terms of their face value—essentially because the banks that issue the notes are perceived as financially reliable. As with all currencies, relative values may rise and fall. The case has been widely recorded of an individual who invested $27 in Bitcoins around the time the system was established in 2009 and found in 2013 that they were worth nearly $900,000.[6] More recently, following raids by US law enforcement agencies against organisations suspected of using Bitcoins to facilitate money laundering, their value has declined with reference to other established currencies.

A further evolving trend, particularly since the global banking crisis and the reduction of credit facilities available from these institutions, has been the practice of 'peer to peer' lending. Essentially responding to a climate of low interest rates for savers and the lack of traditional credit, a number of firms have established themselves as facilitators between the parties. In some respects the model follows the well-publicised system of micro-finance for the developing world that earned its inventor the Nobel Peace prize.

E-money

Considerable attention has been given over the past decade as to how the issuance and use of such forms of electronic money should be regulated. Whilst the interests of consumers require that operators be regulated, there is a general recognition that the application of the full panoply of regulation associated with traditional banking and credit card operations may be excessive in the context of what are often fairly small scale operations and where the consumers level of exposure is generally quite limited.

National and European legislation

Initial sector-specific legislation was introduced by the European Union in the form of the Directive on the taking up, pursuit of, and prudential supervision of the business of electronic money institutions.[7] In the United Kingdom, the Financial Services and Markets Act 2000 designated the issue of e-money as a 'regulated activity'[8] and particular provision to implement the Directive was made in the Electronic Money (Miscellaneous Amendments) Regulations 2002.[9]

The 2000 Directive was criticised in many quarters[10] as being too demanding of small e-money providers and a simplified and revised version was adopted in the 2009 Directive of the same name.[11] This required to be implemented in the Member States by May 2011. For the United Kingdom, this took the form of the Electronic Money Regulations 2011.[12]

---

[6] <http://www.theguardian.com/technology/2013/oct/29/bitcoin-forgotten-currency-norway-oslo-home>. The headline figure is a little misleading. Any attempt to realize the value of all the Bitcoins would have had the effect of depressing the value of the currency very significantly.

[7] Directive 2000/46/EC L275/39.

[8] s. 19. More detailed provision was made in the Financial Services and Markets Act 2000 (Regulated Activities) Order 2001, SI 2001/544.

[9] SI 2002/765.

[10] See the 2005 Evaluation Report on the Working of the Directive, available from <http://ec.europa.eu/internal_market/payments/docs/emoney/evaluation_en.pdf>.

[11] Directive 2009/110/EC, OJ 2009 L 267/7.

[12] SI 2011/99.

A range of forms of electronic money can be identified with the major variants relating to identified e-money and anonymous e-money (also known as digital cash). Identified e-money contains information revealing the identity of the person who originally withdrew the money from the bank. Also, in much the same manner as credit cards, identified e-money enables the bank to track the money as it moves through the economy. Anonymous e-money works just like real paper cash. Once anonymous e-money is withdrawn from an account, it can be spent or given away without leaving a transaction trail.

The nature of e-money

The term 'electronic money' is defined as electronically (including magnetically) stored monetary value as represented by a claim on the electronic money issuer which is issued on receipt of funds for the purpose of making payment transactions and is accepted by a person other than the electronic money issuer; 'electronic money' does not, however, include:

(1) monetary value stored on instruments that can be used to acquire goods or services only in or on the electronic money issuer's premises or under a commercial agreement with the electronic money issuer, either within a limited network of service providers or for a limited range of goods or services; or

(2) monetary value that is used to make payment transactions executed by means of any telecommunication, digital or IT device, where the goods or services purchased are delivered to and are to be used through a telecommunication, digital or IT device, provided that the telecommunication, digital or IT operator does not act only as an intermediary between the payment service user and the supplier of the goods and services.[13]

The last paragraph above was drafted to remove uncertainties as to whether mobile phone service providers might be caught under the legislation in respect of pre-paid customers. The first paragraph does perhaps create a loophole in respect of gift cards. Where these can, as is usually the case, be used only in one store, the safeguards introduced by the e-money Directives and Regulations will not apply—as has been seen in a number of business failures in the United Kingdom where consumers have been left with gift cards of limited or no value.

In some instances electronic money will be associated with traditional financial service providers and will be regulated in the same manner. A number of other players, sometimes quite small in size, are entering the market. The best known is perhaps PayPal which provides payment mechanisms for services such as eBay. Their modus operandi is for customers to transfer funds to them which they may then use to purchase goods or services on-line with PayPal acting as an intermediary to transfer payment to the seller. An alternative model sees the use of stored credit on payment cards. A well-known example is the Oyster card which is extensively used for public transport services in the London area. Here customers make payment to the provider and in return have credit stored on their card which can be used.

E-money issuers and small e-money issuers

Anyone issuing e-money requires to be authorised by the Financial Conduct Authority (the successor to the Financial Services Authority). The authority is required to maintain a

---

[13] Reg. 2(1).

register[14] of authorised electronic money institutions and small electronic money institutions. Small electronic money institutions are defined as organisations which do not have more than €5 million worth of e-money in circulation at any time.

In addition to commercial electronic money issuers it is specifically provided that the Authority may include on the register any EEA-authorised electronic money institutions; the Post Office Limited; the Bank of England, the European Central Bank and the national central banks of EEA states other than the United Kingdom, when not acting in their capacity as a monetary authority or other public authority or government departments and local authorities when acting in their capacity as public authorities; where such persons issue electronic money.

Criteria for admission to the register

The Regulations specify detailed criteria that must be satisfied for an application for authorisation as an e-money issuer (or registration as a small e-money issuer) to be accepted. Essentially evidence must be submitted relating both to the financial stability of the organisation and its suitability (in respect in particular of the lack of criminal convictions or insolvency incidents amongst the directors and senior management).[15] An authorisation will lapse if e-money is not issued within twelve months of its grant.

Safeguarding arrangements

The Regulations make extensive provision both regarding the capital requirements that must be satisfied by a prospective e-money issuer and also as to the internal financial procedures that must be put in place, effectively to ring fence money received in order to obtain e-money from other aspects of the provider's business.

Passport rights

The Directive and the Regulations make extensive reference to so-called 'passport rights'. This refers to the ability of a company which has been authorised as an electronic money issuer in one EU country to commence operations in other states. One of the most high profile examples is PayPal which began its European life with authorisation from the United Kingdom and expanded to other states on the basis of this. It is now regulated under Luxembourg law.

Virtual currency

The notion of a currency other than one issued by banks under legislative authority is not new. In many respects notions of currency and money have become conflated but it is perhaps fair to suggest that money is anything that can be used to purchase goods or services. It may be represented in terms of a value related to currencies but this is not always an accurate reflection of intention.

An early but relatively recent example of an alternative form of currency could be the system of 'Green Shield' stamps that were issued by many businesses from the 1950s. Customers would receive stamps (similar in appearance to postal stamps) in quantities dependent on the value of their purchase. These could be redeemed for other goods. The Trading Stamps Act 1964[16] required that all such stamps display a cash amount for which

---

[14] The Register is accessible at <http://www.fsa.gov.uk/register/2EMD/2EMD_MasterRegister.html>.
[15] Regs. 6 and 13.
[16] Now repealed by the repealed by the Regulatory Reform (Trading Stamps) Order 2005 SI 2005/871.

they could be exchanged. This tended to be set at a derisory level so that perhaps 1,000 stamps (equivalent to around £50 of purchases) would be needed to exchange for around one penny in cash.

Trading stamps have effectively disappeared from the market place[17] and been replaced by loyalty cards but they do provide an early (and the notion of trading stamps dates back in some respects to the nineteenth century) example of an alternative form of currency, albeit one linked to an established financial system.

More modern examples of alternative currencies might be seen in the frequent flier schemes operated by many airlines. There is a secondary market for air miles. A quick search on a system such as eBay will show many offers to sell air miles. Air miles have value although it is difficult to quantify these. Flights booked with air miles tend to require the customer to pay taxes and (unspecified) charges. These charges can be so high that it is not uncommon to find that a flight booked with air miles is actually more expensive than one bought for cash. The system is effectively a closed one, however, in that the miles can be redeemed only with the airline or with nominated partners.

Moving into the Internet era we start to see the emergence of virtual currencies.[18] Perhaps more popular a decade ago than today we saw the development of alternative online worlds. The site Second Life was a prominent example which sought to replicate many of the attributes of the real world. Users could but virtual property and furnish it with assets. In part Second Life works on the basis of traditional currencies but users can also purchase what are referred to as Linden Dollars—a virtual currency that could be used to buy and sell assets with other users. The site's terms and conditions state that:

> 4.5 'Linden Dollars' are virtual tokens that we license. Each Linden Dollar is a virtual token representing contractual permission from Linden Lab to access features of the Service. Linden Dollars are available for Purchase or distribution at Linden Lab's discretion, and are not redeemable for monetary value from Linden Lab.
>
> …
>
> You acknowledge that Linden Dollars are not real currency or any type of financial instrument and are not redeemable for any sum of money from Linden Lab at any time. You agree that Linden Lab has the right to manage, regulate, control, and/or modify the license rights underlying such Linden Dollars as it sees fit and that Linden Lab will have no liability to you based on its exercise of this right. Linden Lab makes no guarantee as to the nature, quality or value of the features of the Service that will be accessible through the use of Linden Dollars, or the availability or supply of Linden Dollars

Although as with air miles Linden dollars can be bought or sold on sites such as eBay and there are some procedures for them to be converted back into physical currencies, they have primary value only in the context of Second Life—just as air miles can ultimately be redeemed only in the context of the airline's programme.

Systems such as Bitcoin mark another stage in the development of virtual currencies and attempts to tie the virtual more closely to the physical financial world. Bitcoin's origins can be traced to a research paper published in 2009 by an author writing (apparently) under the pseudonym Sakoshi Nakomato. The paper,[19] entitled 'Bitcoin: A Peer-to-Peer Electronic Cash System' described a system of virtual currency based upon the application of cryptography. Bitcoins are created ('mined') by individuals using dedicated software to identify

---

[17] Green Shield stamps had set up a chain of shops where customers could redeem their stamps. The name has disappeared but the stores continue, having been re-branded in 1973 as Argos.

[18] For an interesting study on the nature of virtual currencies see the Research Paper published by the Bank of Canada at <http://www.bankofcanada.ca/wp-content/uploads/2013/11/wp2013–38.pdf>.

[19] <http://bitcoin.org/bitcoin.pdf>.

appropriate cryptographic identifiers and can be bought by users via currency exchange sites. As its website states:

> Bitcoins have value because they are useful as a form of money. Bitcoin has the characteristics of money (durability, portability, fungibility, scarcity, divisibility, and recognizability) based on the properties of mathematics rather than relying on physical properties (like gold and silver) or trust in central authorities (like fiat currencies). In short, Bitcoin is backed by mathematics. With these attributes, all that is required for a form of money to hold value is trust and adoption. In the case of Bitcoin, this can be measured by its growing base of users, merchants, and startups. As with all currency, bitcoin's value comes only and directly from people willing to accept them as payment.[20]

Bitcoins provide an alternative to established forms of currency transfer. As the original paper indicated, it operates on a peer-to-peer, or user-to-user, basis and thereby eliminates many of the transaction costs associated with other forms of fund transfers. As a paper published by the European Central Bank indicates:

> Users have several incentives to use Bitcoins. Firstly, transactions are anonymous, as accounts are not registered and Bitcoins are sent directly from one computer to another. Also, users have the possibility of generating multiple Bitcoin addresses to differentiate or isolate transactions. Secondly, transactions are carried out faster and more cheaply than with traditional means of payment. Transactions fees, if any, are very low and no bank account fee is charged.[21]

Because of the mathematics involved in the mining of Bitcoins, it is stated that there cannot be more than 21 million in existence. The value of the currency is established in relation to physical currencies. One of the notable features of the system is that there have been extensive fluctuations in conversion rates. These are often associated with external events. One of the concerns that has been raised about the virtual currency is that it is susceptible to being used by criminals—as, of course, is any other form of currency. In October 2013 the website, 'Silk Road' was implicated in drug dealing and was shut down by the FBI. Bitcoins valued at some $3.6 million were seized from its operator. It had been estimated that 5 per cent of Bitcoins usage was related to that site. In the immediate aftermath of the FBI action, the value of the currency plummeted but very quickly recovered. The incident is interesting. Publicity linking the virtual currency with criminal conduct caused its value to drop but a perception that the problem had been eliminated created a sense of respectability—although it now appears that the website in question has reappeared in much the same form.

The future of virtual currencies remains unclear. With respect to Bitcoin, some states such as Germany and Austria are seeking to bring them within the general taxation system. Thailand has attempted to prohibit use of the currency.[22] The problems within the Eurozone and also currency crisis in countries such as Argentina indicate the limitations of national states. It may be that systems such as Bitcoin will come and go but there is perhaps an argument that a Bank of Google might carry as much credibility as the Bank of England.

Peer-to-peer lending

A recent development has seen a number of companies providing, so-called peer-to-peer lending facilities. It is reported that at least one major retail bank is considering entering the market which, at the latest estimate, provides around £380 million of credit annually. In

---

[20] <http://bitcoin.org/en/faq>.
[21] <http://www.ecb.europa.eu/pub/pdf/other/virtualcurrencyschemes201210en.pdf>.
[22] <http://www.telegraph.co.uk/finance/currency/10210022/Bitcoins-banned-in-Thailand.html>.

large part, peer-to-peer lending is a product of the Internet age and also of the credit shortage resulting from the banking crisis which continues to affect most countries.

In essence the scheme is simple. The companies involved act as on-line intermediaries between individuals who want to invest money and companies (and in some cases individuals) who wish to borrow money. The company will carry out credit checks on potential borrowers and will award a credit rating. This will determine the rate of interest that will be charged for any loan. Investors can determine how much they wish to invest and identify the companies they wish to lend to. The amount will generally start at a small sum, around £20 and the advice is normally that loans should be spread across as wide a range of borrowers as possible. The peer-to-peer company will receive and transfer the money (via a ring fenced account with a High Street bank) and take responsibility for seeking to obtain repayment in due course.

The peer-to-peer system is claimed to offer benefits to all concerned. Even allowing for the perhaps inevitable bad debts, it is claimed that the average investor will receive a return of around 6 per cent, significantly more than can be obtained from most other forms of investment. Borrowers receive access to credit which would otherwise be unobtainable and, even where other sources might be available, pay a relatively low rate of interest. The peer-to-peer facilitating company receives a commission on all transactions.

A considerable measure of government support has been given to the system. In December 2012, the Department for Business, Industry and Skills announced public funding of £55 million to match an equivalent amount from private sector sources would be made available to a number of peer-to-peer companies.[23]

At the moment there is limited regulation of the sector. The Office of Fair Trading is the United Kingdom's major consumer protection agency and is responsible for issuing licences to organisations involved in the credit field. Any peer-to-peer company will require to obtain a licence although this is in respect of a relatively minor field of debt administration. Effectively this requires that they demonstrate only that they have appropriate procedures in place to manage repayment of loans.

Concerns have been expressed about the basic structure of the industry with the *Financial Times* commenting that the 'hands off' nature of the peer-to-peer company's involvement raises echoes of one of the major causes of the financial crisis; that institutions sought to offload responsibility for the repayment of loans and so had no incentive to act responsibly.[24] Whilst this is currently a relatively minor risk, it could become more significant as the sector expands, perhaps paradoxically with financial support from the public sector.

In 2013, the Financial Conduct Authority was established as a new agency to take over responsibilities for the financial services sector from the Office of Fair Trading and the Financial Services Authority. The latter agency had been widely criticised for a failure to exercise appropriate regulatory oversight at the time of the banking crisis. In a consultation paper published in March 2013, views were sought on how future regulation might evolve. Specific reference was made to peer-to-peer lending with the proposal made that such lending should be considered a 'bespoke regulated credit activity' with enhanced protection provided to both borrowers and lenders. The consultation paper commented:

> We envisage the lending aspect of a peer-to-peer platform's activities being treated as an investment activity and that lenders providing the finance should be appropriately protected regardless of the status of the borrower (for example whether the borrower is a consumer, sole trader, partnership or company).

[23] <http://news.bis.gov.uk/Press-Releases/Small-businesses-offered-110-million-of-new-finance-684c2.aspx>.

[24] <http://www.ft.com/cms/s/0/04d6bdce-f2ee-11e2-802f-00144feabdc0.html#axzz2b5NoOzSb>.

... Among the rules that we are considering applying primarily to protect consumer borrowers are:

- a requirement for the platform to provide borrowers with adequate explanations of the key features of the credit agreement (including identifying the key risks) before the agreement is made;

- a requirement for the platform to assess the creditworthiness of borrowers before the credit agreement is made;

In seeking to implement these recommendations, a statutory instrument was laid before Parliament. The Financial Services and Markets Act 2000 (Regulated Activities) (Amendment) (No. 2) Order 2013 makes a number of significant changes to existing regulation. It introduces the concept of 'Operating an Electronic System in Relation to Lending'.

Crowd funding

As well as spending money that we have, most of us need also on occasion to make use of credit facilities, perhaps to buy a house, or a washing machine. One of the lasting effects of the banking crisis that befell the global economy in the first decade of this century has been a significant reduction in the funding that is available for consumers or businesses from traditional banking sources. The problem has been particularly acute in the business sector where, especially for new companies, there may be a significant degree of risk associated with lending and little available in the way of security for the loan. Lack of access to funding has been identified as a major problem facing new businesses. Even when money is forthcoming the cost may be high. In one case in Scotland, a newly formed football club applied for a loan and was required to pay an annual interest rate of 30 per cent even though it was able to offer property based security for the loan.[25] This was at a time when central bank lending rates were at very low levels—0.25 per cent in the case of the European Central Bank and 0.5 per cent for the Bank of England. A recent European Commission Communication notes that:

> Access to finance is one of the most pressing problems for SMEs who report a deterioration in public financial support (-13%), access to loans (-11%), trade credit (-4%) and the willingness of investors to invest in equity (-1%).[26]

There is nothing that nature abhors more than a vacuum and alternative financial mechanisms have come into play. This section will consider the role of what is normally referred to as 'crowd funding' whereby, generally using an intermediary, a number of individuals make funding available to another person or business. It may be that a thousand individuals each make £10 available to a debtor. As with many areas of business activity, it is because of the processing capabilities of modern IT systems that such distributed forms of lending can emerge. The Commission Communication cited above gives an indication of the scale and potential of the activity:

> In 2012 about €735 million was raised for all forms of crowdfunding in Europe and the predicted figure for 2013 is around €1 billion. This figure is rather marginal compared to retail bank lending to non-financial institutions (€6 trillion in 2011), but it is promising compared to the financing provided by business angels (visible market segment estimated at €660 million in 2010) or venture capitalists in seed, start-up, later and growth stages (€7 billion

---

[25] The case has been widely reported. See, eg, <http://www.scotsman.com/sport/football/spfl-lower-divisions/1-5m-loans-for-rangers-are-part-of-the-plan-1-3317447>.

[26] 'Unleashing the Potential of Crowdfunding in the European Commission'. COM (2014) final.

in 2012). Crowdfunding is an important source of finance to some half a million European projects each year that otherwise may not obtain the necessary funds to be realised.[27]

The United Kingdom is reported to be the third largest operator in the crowdfunding market, after the United States and China.[28]

The crowdfunding system had its origins as a mechanism for providing aid to individuals in the developing world where donors might make small loans available to potential entrepreneurs. Although the hope would be that the loan would be repaid, the transaction was more in the way of a gift as any repayments would normally be reinvested in other burgeoning businesses. One of the leading operators in the field is Kiva[29] which was established in 2005 as a non-profit making organisation providing micro finance[30] to individuals and small businesses. Potential donors visiting its website can see requests for finance—one reasonably typical example was from a person looking to raise $700 to buy a dairy cow to help provide milk for her family and an income stream from the sale of surplus milk—and offer any sum from $25 upwards.[31]

Loans are administered through 'field partners' who are located in the country where the loan is received. They are responsible for collecting repayments and Kiva claim a repayment rate of 97.2 per cent.[32] Somewhat controversially,[33] although Kiva does not charge any interest on loans, field partners can and do charge sometimes very high rates of interest—equivalent almost to the 'Payday' loan companies that are proliferating in the United Kingdom. It appears also that the individuals represented on the website as applying for loans have already been granted the finance sought. Effectively, although donors may think that they are financing a particular person, the reality is that they are contributing to a wider pool. It is made clear to potential investors that, in spite of the high level of repayments cited above, there is no legal protection for their investments. As will be discussed in more detail below, this is one of the major issues in respect of more commercial crowd funding activities.

Notions of collective funding have been available for many years. The system of credit unions dates back to the nineteenth century, being pioneered in the United Kingdom and Germany, and it is currently estimated that there are more than 40,000 unions in almost eighty countries around the world.[34] The model is for individuals (members) to pool their savings in the Union and for funds to be distributed by way of loans to other members. Effectively it has been a form of mutual support between individuals living in a particular town—or perhaps working for a particular employer. As with the Kiva model described above, the intent was to provide finance to people who would not otherwise have access to traditional (reputable) lenders.

Crowd funding can certainly involve the provision of loans with a view to repayment. A range of other models also exist. Generally referred to as crowd sponsorship, funders may receive rewards or products in return for funding. A number of films and theatre productions are seeking funding on this basis with individual funders being offered priority

---

[27] 'Unleashing the Potential of Crowdfunding in the European Commission'. COM (2014) final.

[28] <http://www.ft.com/cms/s/0/9c7a4896-aac5-11e3-9fd6-00144feab7de.html#axzz31glzuXM4>.

[29] <http://www.kiva.org>.

[30] Microfinance is a term generally used to describe the provision financial services to low-income individuals or to those who do not have access to typical banking services. The concept was devised by Dr Mohammad Yunus who was awarded the Nobel Peace Prize for his work in 2008.

[31] Originally operating in developing countries, Kiva has now extended its operations to eighty-two countries including the United States. See <https://www.kiva.org/lend/kiva-u-s>.

[32] <http://www.kiva.org>. Other crowd funding operators report similar statistics.

[33] See <http://philanthropyaction.com/nc/a_mostly_comprehensive_guide_to_the_kiva_and_donor_illusion_debate/ which provides a series of links relating to micro-financing>.

[34] <http://www.abcul.org/credit-unions/history-world-facts>.

access to tickets and the opportunity to meet the actors involved. Funding may also be sought in order to bring a product to the marketplace. One of the major companies in the field is Kickstarter whose website[35] promotes a range of product concepts seeking funding. Anyone providing funding of a specified amount is offered a copy of the product when (or if) it reaches the marketplace. An example might be seen in a proposed product called a 'bedjet'. Essentially this is a fan that is claimed to heat or chill a bed in three minutes.[36] Anyone offering $329 in funding was promised a copy. In the event an insufficient number of investors expressed interest and unfortunately (or not) the world is still awaiting the bedjet.

Other crowd funding schemes offer the prospect of some form of financial return (other than a specified rate of interest). Investors may, for example, be promised a share in the future profits of a company in much the same manner as shareholders have traditionally received dividends.

Depending on the particular kind of funding model utilised, a range of legal issues may arise. The Commission Communication indicates that:

> The main issues EU legislation addresses with regards to all types of crowdfunding include anti-money laundering, advertising, consumer protection and—where relevant—intellectual property protection.[37]

Intellectual property issues are likely to arise when an inventor is seeking funding for a novel product and potential investors seek disclosure of the underlying technology in order to assist in determining whether to risk their funds.

There is also, of course a raft of domestic and European legislation concerning the financial services sector and this may well impact on crowd funding activities. Some states including Germany, the Netherlands, Belgium, and the United Kingdom have begun to introduce specific regulatory controls in the sector. In the United Kingdom, the lead is being taken by the Financial Conduct Authority which was established in April 2014 to replace the Financial Services Authority (which was seen as having been ineffective in the UK and global banking crisis) and also the Office of Fair Trading which previously had been the main agency responsible for consumer protection issues.

The Financial Conduct Authority is responsible for issuing licences to organisations involved in the credit field. Any peer-to-peer company will be required to obtain a licence although this is in respect of a relatively minor field of debt administration. Effectively this requires that they demonstrate only that they have appropriate procedures in place to manage repayment of loans.

Concerns have been expressed about the basic structure of the industry with the *Financial Times* commenting that:

> the 'hands off' nature of the peer to peer company's involvement raises echoes of one of the major causes of the financial crisis; that institutions sought to offload responsibility for the repayment of loans and so had no incentive to act responsibly. Whilst this is currently a relatively minor risk, it could become more significant as the sector expands, perhaps paradoxically with financial support from the public sector.[38]

In a consultation paper published in March 2013, views were sought on how future regulation might evolve. Specific reference was made to peer-to-peer lending with the proposal

---

[35] <https://www.kickstarter.com/>.
[36] The product is described at <http://www.theguardian.com/technology/2013/dec/13/crowdfund-this-bedjet-kickstarter>.
[37] <http://eur-lex.europa.eu/legal-content/EN/TXT/?uri=CELEX%3A52014DC0172>.
[38] < http://www.ft.com/cms/s/0/04d6bdce-f2ee-11e2-802f-00144feabdc0.html#axzz2b5NoOzSb>.

made that peer-to-peer lending should be considered a 'bespoke regulated credit activity' with enhanced protection provided to both borrowers and lenders. The consultation paper commented:

> We envisage the lending aspect of a peer-to-peer platform's activities being treated as an investment activity and that lenders providing the finance should be appropriately protected regardless of the status of the borrower (for example whether the borrower is a consumer, sole trader, partnership or company).
>
> . . . Among the rules that we are considering applying primarily to protect consumer borrowers are:
>
> - a requirement for the platform to provide borrowers with adequate explanations of the key features of the credit agreement (including identifying the key risks) before the agreement is made;
>
> - a requirement for the platform to assess the creditworthiness of borrowers before the credit agreement is made and to make this information available to potential lenders.[39]

These principles have been implemented in the Financial Services and Markets Act 2000 (Regulated Activities) (Amendment) (No. 2) Order 2013. Having come into effect on the first of April 2014 the Order introduces the concept of 'Operating an Electronic System In Relation to Lending' and will apply in respect of loans where no individual will lend more than £25,000 (around €30,000).[40] The principles set out in the Order are defined further in the Crowdfunding and the Promotion of Non-Readily Realisable Securities Instrument 2014[41] which was adopted by the Financial Conduct Authority in March 2014.

A further governmental move may also increase the appeal of peer-to-peer lending. Whilst in most cases individuals are required to pay tax on interest received from savings, there exists a system referred to as ISA (Individual Savings Accounts) under which interest in respect of approved accounts can be received tax-free. It was indicated in the 2014 Budget that peer-to-peer lending systems would fall under the ISA umbrella. Typically these are offering returns in the region of 6–8 per cent per annum—at a time when savers are lucky to receive 2 per cent from more established institutions.

The major risk with peer-to-peer lending is that of default, especially since the schemes are not included in the financial guarantee arrangements under which the government guarantees the safety of bank and similar savings accounts. The issue of risk has been a significant factor in formulating rules for investment-based crowd funding schemes where it is recognised that there is a very significant risk that a newly established company will fail in the marketplace. It is estimated that anything up to 75 per cent of companies will cease trading in their first year. The Financial Conduct Authority rules now provide that investment opportunities in this area can be promoted only to 'sophisticated investors' or to individuals who establish that no more than 10 per cent of their investable income will be committed to this form of activity. It remains to be seen how easy it will be to interpret and apply these criteria.

The Internet has transformed many aspects of business activity. It is no surprise that the financial services sector should be impacted. A number of very difficult issues are emerging. Much has been written and promoted about the rate of return that crowd investors might obtain. Provisions such as those described above seeking to restrict access to opportunities to 'sophisticated investors' are inevitably controversial. On one level this can be seen as

---

[39] Financial Services Authority. Consultation Paper CP13/7 at paras. 8.19–20.

[40] For information about the new rules see <http://www.fca.org.uk/your-fca/documents/policy-statements/ps14-04>.

[41] Available from <http://www.fca.org.uk/static/documents/policy-statements/ps14-04.pdf>.

limiting access to potentially lucrative investment opportunities to 'ordinary' individuals whereas 'sophisticated' investors receive preferential treatment. One recent example from the United Kingdom concerns the part privatisation of the Royal Mail. A number of investment brokers were given preferential access to shares with, apparently, an unwritten understanding that they would not immediately resell the shares. The share value soared and it transpired that a number of these firms had sold their shares at a very significant profit.

That is one side of the coin. It is also, of course, the case that a basic function of consumer protection law is to protect consumers from their own impetuousness and indeed naivety. There is the old adage that if a deal looks too good to be true, it almost certainly is!

Only time will tell whether crowd funding will become a major player in the financial services sector or whether it will remain a niche activity. Certainly, savers have done badly out of traditional bank accounts in recent years with interest rates well below the rate of inflation. A lack of 'reputable' credit sources has also forced many borrowers into the hands of payday lenders and their high interest rates. What might be seen as an updating of the credit union model may provide a way forward—perhaps using social networking as an alternative to the geographical proximity that characterises the older credit unions.

Conclusions

The Bible tells us that money is the root of all kinds of evil.[42] Possibly true, but most people would find it difficult to survive without the commodity in our personal or business lives.

Towards the end of 2016, there was extensive publicity concerning the decision of the Indian government to render invalid a number of large denomination bank notes. The suspicion was that they were frequently utilised by persons seeking to evade taxation. We hear much about the 'black (or shadow) economy'. One study by the bank of England[43] has suggested that half of the United Kingdom's banknotes are used to fund the black economy. Almost at the end of this book, we return to a topic that we began with. Paying in cash provides a very considerable degree of anonymity with regard to our transactions. There are of course risks to those holding large amounts of cash—not least those of theft. In many respects we are moving towards a cashless economy driven in large part by the processing and communication capabilities of IT systems. Electronic money is, of course, vulnerable to criminal activity. In November 2016, the Tesco bank suffered a major hacking attack and several million pounds was taken from its customers' accounts. In such cases, loss falls ultimately on the bank but in the more general situation, the use of electronic money does come at a price for the anonymity of consumers.

---

[42] 1 Timothy 6:10.
[43] <http://www.bankofengland.co.uk/publications/Pages/quarterlybulletin/2015/q3prerelease_1.aspx>.

24

Contractual liability for defective software

INTRODUCTION

Software is the driving force of the information society. By any standards, the sector is a major contributor to national economies and employment and it should be borne in mind that these figures relate to only one part of the information technology industry. The traditional notion of a computer is that it consists of a monitor, processing unit, keyboard, and sundry peripherals such as the ubiquitous mouse. Most people will recognise such a device when they see one. It is less easy to recognise a motor car or video recorder as a computer, yet a modern motor car is in many respects a sophisticated computer system, to the extent it has been calculated that the 'chip cost of a new car is now greater than the metal cost'.[1] A vast range of objects, from domestic appliances to nuclear power stations, is dependent on microprocessors. In many cases, these are, quite literally, built into a structure. Worldwide, it is estimated that there are some 20 billion embedded chips in use, a fact which caused great concern in the context of the Millennium Bug. It has been reported that:

> All buildings built between 1984 (the year when building services started to computerise) and 1996/7 (the period when most new buildings were fitted with systems that were millennium compliant) are likely to be affected by the millennium bug. Bovis Construction Group, one of the biggest building contractors has written to the owners of 870 buildings it has built since 1984 warning them integral systems ranging from ventilation and heating to intruder alarms and connections to the electricity supply network may fail. This is because many building systems use microchips to identify dates for switching machinery on and off and to alert maintenance staff of the need for servicing.[2]

As the importance of software increases, so does the level of societal vulnerability in the event of any failure. In purely economic terms, losses are potentially massive. Although it is tempting to take the example of the Millennium Bug as a case where the degree of risk was exaggerated, even what might be regarded as a false alarm proved an extremely costly exercise. The British Bankers Association estimated that UK banks spent £1 billion checking and repairing systems. British Telecom budgeted for expenditure of £300 million. Worldwide, costs were estimated at some £400 billion. To put these figures into perspective, these figures exceed the total financial cost of the Vietnam War.[3]

Matters could, of course, have been significantly worse in the event of extensive problems materialising. One estimate suggested that the effect of the bug would cause 8 per cent of Western European companies to fail. The prospect of global recession was frequently raised in

---

[1] <http://www.scl.org/members/emagazine/vol9/iss3/vol9-iss3-peter-cochrane-art.htm>.
[2] Cited in evidence to the House of Commons Select Committee on Science and Technology.
[3] *Sunday Times*, 10 August 1997. The cost of the Vietnam War has been estimated at some £370 billion.

reports. Additionally, as indicated, the application of information technology in a vast range of applications conjured up the spectre of hospital patients dying because of failures of medical devices; trains, planes, and automobiles crashing; massive power cuts; and shortage of food and drink due to failures in retailers' distribution systems. Fortunately, the predictions of computer doom proved unfounded, but the incident may have served a useful, albeit expensive, purpose in bringing home the extent of our society's dependence on information technology. What the incident also achieved was to highlight the fact that where losses arise through the improper operation of systems and equipment, considerations of legal liability will not be far behind.

To date, comparatively few cases concerned specifically with issues of software quality have reached the stage of court proceedings. A variety of explanations may be proposed for this state of affairs. Although parties may not wish to litigate when the answer is certain, excessive uncertainty as to the very basis upon which a court may decide will itself inhibit litigation. Some of the most basic questions concerning the application of provisions of contractual and non-contractual liability in the information technology field admit of no easy or certain solution. With one exception, all of the cases which have reached the stage of High Court proceedings have concerned relatively high-value contracts for software which has either been developed under the terms of a specific contract (bespoke software) for one or a small number of clients or has been modified extensively to suit the needs of a particular customer (customised software). To date, there have been no cases concerned with the extent of the liabilities which will apply to mass-produced or standard software packages such as word-processing or spreadsheet programs. A further factor complicating such cases is the invariable presence of a software licence. The role of these documents in respect of intellectual property issues has been discussed previously. In respect of liability considerations, the terms of the licence inevitably seek to limit or exclude the producer's liabilities in the event that the performance of the software does not match the user's expectations.

Forms of liability

Two main strands of liability run through the field of private law. The law of contract confers rights and imposes duties upon contracting parties. Whilst the nature and extent of these may be determined in large part by the expressed wishes of the parties, these may be constrained by the provisions of statutes such as the Sale of Goods Act 1979 and the Unfair Contract Terms Act 1977. It is, of course, a basic tenet of the common law that contractual rights can be enforced only by those who are a party to the contract. In the situation where no contract exists, attention must turn to non-contractual remedies. Until recently, the basis of these has rested in the law of tort/delict. The prerequisite for a successful action in tort is evidence of negligence on the part of the defendant (absent exceptional circumstances where strict liability has attached to this party's actions). The passage of the Consumer Protection Act 1987 has radically transformed the non-contractual position. Based on the provisions of an EC Directive on the Approximation of the Laws, Regulations and Administrative Provisions of the Member States Concerning Liability for Defective Products,[4] this serves to impose a strict liability regime, whereby the producer of a product is held liable for personal injury or damage to non-commercial property resulting from the presence of a defect within the product, irrespective of any fault on their part.

---

[4] Council Directive 85/374/EEC, OJ 1985 L 210/29.

The nature of software defects

Prior to considering issues of legal liability, it might be helpful to attempt a brief analysis of the nature of the differences which exist between software and the tangible products with which society and the law are more familiar. Defects in a traditional product such as a motor car may originate in one of two ways. Design defects relate to some failure at the design stage, with the consequence that the failure node will be exhibited in every species of the product. A more commonplace form of defect is introduced during the production stage. It might be, for example, as happened in the case of *Smedleys v Breed*,[5] that a caterpillar found its way into a can of peas somewhere within the canning process. Such defects will be restricted to one or to a limited number of examples of the product. In the *Smedleys* case, for example, only four caterpillars or other foreign bodies had been reported from an annual production of 3.5 million cans.

If a party is trying to establish that a product fails to comply with relevant quality requirements, the task is almost invariably simpler where defects arise in production. In most cases, what a claimant will seek to establish is that compared with other examples of a product, the one at issue is of inferior quality. The case might be put, for example, that 3,499,996 cans of peas did not contain foreign bodies. The four that did should, therefore, be considered exceptional (or exceptionally bad). Evidential burdens are more extensive when all examples of the product exhibit the same properties. A prime example is in the pharmaceutical field, where adverse reactions to a product are generally caused because of the properties of the drug, rather than through contamination of a particular tablet or bottle of medicine.

Where software is concerned, the nature of the digital copying process is such that there can be a high degree of confidence that every copy of software will be identical. If particular copies are corrupted, the likelihood is that they will not work at all, so that any defect becomes apparent before any damage is caused. If a customer should wish to establish that a copy of a word-processing program which has been purchased is not of satisfactory quality, argument will have to proceed by reference to word-processing programs produced by other producers and to general standards. Although the task can be accomplished, it is a significantly more onerous burden than that faced by a person claiming the existence of a production defect.

A more general difference may be identified at the level of the testing which may be carried out in respect of a product. With a product such as a motor car, it is possible to test every component so as to provide definitive information about its properties. Often, however, testing entails destruction of the item involved and, even where this is not the case, it will seldom be commercially feasible to test every specimen of the product. In production, it is possible that some components will be of inferior quality to those tested. Only a portion of products will possess any particular defect and these may not be the ones which are selected for inspection. The conclusion from this analysis is that it is possible to test one item exhaustively, but that the results have limited applicability regarding other items of the same type.

The situation is radically different where software is concerned. It is impossible to test even the simplest program in an exhaustive fashion. This is because of the myriad possibilities for interaction (whether desired or not) between the various elements of the program. In the world of popular science, much publicity has been given in recent years to what is known as the chaos theory. This suggests that every event influences every other event; that the beating of a butterfly's wings has an impact upon the development of a hurricane. On

---

[5] [1974] AC 839.

such an analysis, totally accurate weather forecasting will never be practicable because of the impossibility of taking account of all the variables affecting the climate. The theory's hypothesis is reality in a software context. Although software can and should be tested, it has to be accepted that every piece of software will contain errors which may not materialise until a particular and perhaps unrepeatable set of circumstances occurs. It is commonplace for software to be placed on the market in the knowledge that it contains errors. Early users, in effect, act as unpaid testers. As faults are reported to the producer, fixes will be developed and incorporated into new versions of the software.[6]

Especially where software is used in safety-critical functions, it is sometimes advocated that where an error is discovered, it is preferable to devise procedures to prevent the circumstances recurring than to attempt to modify the software. The argument is that any change to the software may have unanticipated consequences, resulting in another error manifesting itself at some time in the future. The cause of a massive failure which paralysed sections of the US telecommunications system in 1991 was ultimately traced to changes which had been made in the call-routing software.[7] The software contained several million lines of code. Three apparently insignificant lines were changed and chaos ensued. By way of contrast, the operators of London's Docklands Light Railway, whose trains are driven under computer control, took the decision that they would not make any changes to the software after it had passed its acceptance tests. The result was that for several years, trains stopped on an open stretch of line, paused for a few seconds and then continued with their journey. It had been intended to build a station at the site. After the software was accepted, the plans were abandoned, but the trains remained ignorant of this fact.

Forms of software

As indicated, software is supplied in a variety of situations and under a range of conditions. Viewed across the spectrum, at one end we can identify bespoke or made-to-measure software products. The cost of these may run into many millions of pounds, with the essential feature being that the supplier agrees to design and develop software to suit the needs of a particular customer, or a comparatively small number of identified customers. The software will be supplied under the terms of a written agreement negotiated between the parties. Perhaps not surprisingly, given the costs involved, almost all of the software-related disputes which have reached the courts have been concerned with such forms of contract.

At the far end of the software spectrum are standard software packages. In this category, identical copies will be supplied to users—perhaps tens or even hundreds of thousands in number—often via a substantial distribution chain and at a cost ranging from tens to thousands of pounds. There will seldom be any written agreement negotiated in advance between the parties, with the producer attempting to introduce a set of terms and conditions through the device of a licence. As will be discussed later, the validity of software licences is open to challenge on a number of grounds.

A final and more nebulous category of software is referred to as having been 'customised'. This involves the supplier modifying existing software, developed either by themselves or by a third party, better to suit the requirements of a particular customer. The degree of customisation may vary from making very minor adjustments to a single package

---

[6] See the discussion in the case of *Saphena v Allied Collection Agencies* [1995] FSR 616.

[7] Most of the examples of software failure cited in this chapter have been culled from the columns of comp. risks, an Internet-based newsgroup which chronicles the failures of safety-critical systems and the risks they pose to the public.

to developing a unique system based on a combination of a number of existing packages. With developments in 'object oriented engineering' it may be expected that the range of customised products will increase substantially as developers base their operations on a 'pick-and-mix' philosophy.

The legal status of software and software contracts

Throughout this book, use has been made of terms such as 'software industry' and of software being 'produced'. Such terms are in common use. The pages on the Microsoft website describing its software packages are titled 'products',[8] whilst the Price Waterhouse study discussed in the context of copyright law is titled *The Contribution of the Packaged Software Industry to the European Economies*. The fact that terms are in popular usage does not, of course, mean that their legal interpretation will be the same, and over the years, much legal ink has been spilled in discussion of the question of whether contracts for the supply of software should be regarded as a species of goods or as a form of services.

Much of the discussion regarding status has focused on two decisions of the Court of Appeal. In *Lee v Griffin*,[9] the Court of Appeal was faced with a contract under which a dentist undertook to make a set of dentures for a patient. A dispute subsequently arising, the court was faced with the question of the contract's proper categorisation. Holding the contract to be one of sale, the court held that the essential test was whether anything that could be the subject matter of a sale had come into existence. In the event, for example, that an attorney was engaged to draw up a deed for a client, it was held that the contract would be one for services. In other situations, however:

> I do not think that the test to apply to these cases is whether the value of the work exceeds that of the materials used in its execution; for, if a sculptor were employed to execute a work of art, greatly as his skill and labour, assuming it to be of the highest description, might exceed the value of the marble on which he worked, the contract would in my opinion, nevertheless be a contract for the sale of a chattel.[10]

On this basis, it would appear that the supply of software on some storage device such as a disk or CD would be classed as involving goods. The increasingly common situation where software is supplied electronically, typically being downloaded from a website, could not, of course, come within the definition.

The distinction between goods and services was again at issue before the Court of Appeal in the case of *Robinson v Graves*.[11] The contract here was one whereby an artist agreed to paint a portrait of his client's wife. On the basis of the situation hypothesised in *Lee v Griffin*,[12] it would appear that such a transaction should be regarded as one of sale. In the event, however, it was held that it should be regarded as one for services. In reaching this conclusion, the court sought to identify the prime purpose of the contract. In the oft-quoted words of Greer LJ:

> If the substance of the contract . . . is that skill and labour have to be exercised for the production of the article and . . . it is only ancillary to that that there will pass from the artist to his client or customer some materials in addition to the skill involved in the production of the portrait, that does not make any difference to the result, because the substance of the contract is the skill and experience of the artist in producing the picture.[13]

---

[8] <http://www.microsoft.com/en/us/default.aspx>.
[9] (1861) 1 B&S 272.
[10] At 278.
[11] [1935] 1 KB 579.
[12] (1861) 1 B&S 272.   [13] [1935] 1 KB 579 at 587.

Although the court in *Robinson*[14] did not overrule, or even distinguish, the earlier authority, it must be doubted how far the two approaches can truly be considered compatible. It
would appear that the decision in *Robinson* has been the more influential in recent years
but, even so, its application in a software context has not been without its difficulties.
Whilst it would seem to suggest that contracts for the development of bespoke software
should be regarded as services, standard software exhibits many of the attributes associated
with goods.

In the final analysis, the precise categorisation of software contracts may be a matter of limited practical significance. In most of the cases which have come before the
courts, the dispute has centred on the interpretation of a specific contract between the
parties. The court's task is to determine what the contract said, rather than concern itself
unduly with categorisations. Even where no detailed contract exists, there is little difference between the relevant statutory provisions. The Sale of Goods Act 1979 implies terms
relating to title, description, and quality. The Supply of Goods and Services Act 1982
implies requirements that the supplier should exercise reasonable skill and care and that
any goods ultimately supplied will comply with identical requirements relating to title,
description, and quality as those required under the Sale of Goods Act 1979. Faced with
this convergence between the statutory provisions, it is not surprising that Staughton LJ,
delivering judgment in the case of *Saphena Computing Ltd v Allied Collection Agencies
Ltd*, was able to state:

> It was, we are told, common ground that the law governing these contracts was precisely
> the same whether they were contracts for the sale of goods or for the supply of services. It is
> therefore unnecessary to consider into which category they might come.[15]

In the case of *St Albans District Council v ICL*,[16] the Court of Appeal was braver—or more
foolhardy. Here, Sir Iain Glidewell posed the question, 'Is software goods?' He continued:

> If a disc carrying the program is transferred, by way of sale or hire, and the program is
> in some way defective, so that it will not instruct or enable the computer to achieve the
> intended purpose, is this a defect in the disc? Put more precisely, would the seller or hirer of
> the disc be in breach of the terms of quality or fitness implied by s. 14 of the Sale of Goods
> Act [1979].[17]

There was, he recognised, no English or indeed any common law precedent on this point.
An analogy was drawn, however, with another form of informational product:

> Suppose I buy an instruction manual on the maintenance and repair of a particular make
> of car. The instructions are wrong in an important respect. Anybody who follows them is
> likely to cause serious damage to the engine of his car. In my view the instructions are an
> integral part of the manual. The manual including the instructions, whether in a book or a
> video cassette, would in my opinion be 'goods' within the meaning of the Sale of Goods Act
> and the defective instructions would result in breach of the implied terms.
>
> If this is correct, I can see no logical reason why it should not also be correct in relation
> to a computer disc onto which a program designed and intended to instruct or enable a
> computer to achieve particular functions has been encoded. If the disc is sold or hired by
> the computer manufacturer, but the program is defective, in my opinion there would prima
> facie be a breach of the terms as to quality and fitness for purpose implied by the Sale of
> Goods Act.[18]

---

[14] *Robinson v Graves* [1935] 1 KB 579.
[15] [1995] FSR 616 at 652.
[16] [1996] 4 All ER 481. Reported at first instance at [1995] FSR 686.
[17] At 492.　　[18] At 493.

As will be discussed, this statement will have implications for all of those involved in the information market. In the case of *Wormell v RHM Agriculture Ltd*,[19] the Court of Appeal recognised that where instructions for use were supplied along with a product, the sufficiency and adequacy of these should be taken into account in considering questions of the product's merchantability. *St Albans District Council v ICL*[20] appears, however, to be the first occasion in which instructions per se were subjected to the qualitative requirements of the Sale of Goods Act 1979. It remains uncertain, however, how extensive liability will be. The analogy drawn with a motor instruction book may be appropriate. In the circumstances described, where following the instructions will result in serious damage, there could be little argument that the book is not fit for its purpose. The decision becomes much closer if the complaint is that the book describes an inefficient method for performing work. Another problematic case might be where an instruction is so obviously wrong that no reasonable person would follow it. Equivalents in a software context might be inefficient methods of saving word-processed documents or defects which require a user to 'work around' them. Further cases will be required before we can attempt a plausible answer to the question of what these qualitative requirements mean in a software context.

There is, of course, the increasing possibility that software might be downloaded over the Internet so that no tangible objects change hands. Indeed, in the present case, the practice for installing software was that an ICL engineer would visit, load the software from disk, and retain the disk. In such cases, there could be no transfer of goods. In such situations, it was indicated, in determining the extent of the parties' obligations:

> The answer must be sought in the Common Law. The terms implied by the Sale of Goods Act . . . were originally evolved by the Courts of Common Law and have since by analogy been implied by the courts into other types of contract.
>
> . . .
>
> In the absence of any express term as to quality or fitness for purpose, or of any term to the contrary, such a contract is subject to an implied term that the program will be reasonably fit for, i.e. reasonably capable of achieving the intended purpose.[21]

Given the existence of a specific contract between the parties, these comments must be regarded as *obiter dicta* rather than as binding precedent. They do appear, however, to be in line with a judicial trend to imply requirements that software be fit for its purpose into contracts unless the terms make clear provision to the contrary. Any ambiguities will be interpreted *contra proferentem*, with the case of *Salvage Association v CAP Financial Services*[22] providing a good illustration of how restrictive this doctrine may be. The key issue, therefore, must be to determine what concepts, such as fitness and the newly introduced requirement that goods be of 'satisfactory quality', might mean in an informational context.

Implied terms in software contracts

The Sale of Goods Act 1979 provides for three conditions to be implied into a contract of sale. Although there is room for argument whether software is generally sold by virtue of the fact that intellectual property rights will remain with the original owner, the Supply of Goods and Services Act 1982 provides that the implied terms will extend to any other

---

[19] [1987] 3 All ER 75.   [20] [1996] 4 All ER 481.
[21] *St Albans District Council v ICL* [1996] 4 All ER 481 at 494.
[22] (9 July 1993, unreported), CA. The case is reported at first instance at [1995] FSR 654.

contract for the supply of goods. Although interpretative problems may remain in the situation discussed in the previous section, where software is supplied over the Internet, for example, the categorisation of contracts as forms of sale or rental or loan is of no significance. Reference throughout this section will be to the provisions of the Sale of Goods Act 1979, as amended by the Sale and Supply of Goods Act 1994. Reference is made also to the Consumer Rights Act 2015 although this has not been at issue before the courts at the time of writing.

One of the cornerstones of English commercial law has been the doctrine of *caveat emptor* ('let the buyer beware'). Traditionally, no provisions relating to the quality of goods has been implied into contracts of sale. In previous eras, this approach was not as inequitable as it might appear in the twenty-first century. Goods were simple in nature and composition, and it was a feasible task for a buyer to make an assessment of their condition and suitability. As goods became more sophisticated, it became increasingly difficult for an inexpert customer to examine them. Even if a potential buyer wanted to do this, the reaction of the seller of a computer could well be predicted in the event that a customer was to produce a screwdriver and seek to disassemble the equipment. The notion of the implied term has been developed, first by the courts and now enshrined in statute, as a means for protecting the interests of the consumer. In general law, of course, an implied term is overridden by any contrary express agreement made between the parties. Often such an express term will seek to reduce or exclude the liability of the seller in the event that the performance of the goods is inadequate. Again, the first attempts to control these contractual tactics were made by the courts, with Parliament intervening in 1977 with the passage of the Unfair Contract Terms Act 1977. The following sections will consider the extent of the obligations implied by law into contracts for the supply of software. Attention will then be paid to the extent to which these might validly or lawfully be reduced by the application of devices such as licences or contractual terms.

Title in software

By virtue of section 12 of the Sale of Goods Act 1979, a seller must guarantee that he or she possesses the right to sell the goods and that full title to the goods will be transferred to the buyer, except for such limitations as are brought to the buyer's attention prior to the contract of sale. In terms of the usage of the goods, it is provided that the buyer is to enjoy 'quiet possession'. This entails that the buyer's freedom to deal with the goods in such manner as might be desired is not to be restricted by virtue of any rights retained by the seller or by some third party. In many cases concerned with software, the sale will be made by a retailer, with the producer retaining ownership of copyright in the work and remaining an interested third party.

The major limitations imposed upon the buyer's freedom to deal with software are found in the copyright legislation. As has been seen, the mere use of software might constitute a breach of copyright. The buyer's right under section 12 of the Sale of Goods Act 1979 is always subject to the caveat that the use proposed is lawful. The terms of the European Directive on the Legal Protection of Computer Programs[23] might have implications for the operation of section 12. Under the Directive, a number of forms of behaviour concerned with software, for example modification for the purpose of error correction, will be permitted unless the terms of a contract or licence provide otherwise. Where the copyright owner intends to exercise this option and seeks to do so by means of a licence document whose contents are not disclosed to the buyer until after the contract of sale is concluded, the failure to give prior notice might place the seller in breach of section 12.

---

[23] Directive 91/250/EC, OJ 1991 L 122/42.

Description

Section 13 of the Sale of Goods Act 1979 provides that where a sale is by description, there is to be an implied condition that the goods will correspond with this description. In the course of many contracts of sale, a variety of claims may be made concerning the attributes of the product involved. Not all such elements will be incorporated into the final contract. Many laudatory phrases, typically used in promotional materials, will be regarded as too general. A claim that a product is 'user-friendly' might, for example, be regarded as insufficiently precise to be considered as a description, although in such cases it may be that an action will lie on the ground of misrepresentation.

Claims of compatibility with other products, typically that a piece of software will operate on a specified piece of hardware, might be regarded as descriptive. Equally, lists of the features possessed by a product will be considered as part of its description, although even here the matter may not be beyond doubt. In the case of a popular laser printer, for example, the product specification made reference to a printing speed of four pages per minute. The statement appears true, but what is not made clear is that the printer can only print four copies of the same page in any given minute. The printing process requires that data regarding the contents of any page be transmitted from the computer to the printer. This process takes some time, with the result that the speed for printing a multi-page document slows to little more than a single page per minute. One factor which is relevant throughout all the discussion of liability is the absence of clearly defined industry standards and conventions. In the absence of these in respect of speed of printing or many other attributes concerned with the functioning of information technology systems, it may be difficult to establish liability in respect of claims that are accurate but potentially misleading.

Quality

The Sale of Goods Act 1979 requirements relating to product quality are so well known that little exposition is required. Two partially overlapping conditions will be implied into a contract of sale. Goods must be of satisfactory quality and reasonably fit for any particular purpose for which they are supplied.[24] The requirement that goods supplied be of satisfactory quality was introduced in 1995 in substitution for the concept of merchantable quality. The notion of merchantable quality can be traced back to the Middle Ages. It assumed statutory form for the first time in the Sale of Goods Act 1893 and was retained in the Sale of Goods Act 1979. The latter statute also introduced a new definition, providing that goods would be of merchantable quality if they are:

> as fit for the purpose or purposes for which goods of that kind are commonly bought as it was reasonable to expect having regard to any description applied to them, the price (if relevant) and all the other relevant circumstances.[25]

The law relating to sale of goods was the subject of a report by the Law Commissions in 1987.[26] This expressed concerns at the suitability of the venerable concept of merchantability to deal with the complexities inherent in many modern products. Beyond the issue of whether the terminology itself was not unduly archaic, the notion of a general requirement of fitness for purpose (as opposed to the more specific instantiation in the second implied term) was developed in an era of comparatively simple products, which would either work

[24] s. 14.   [25] s. 14(6).
[26] A Joint Report was published: Law Commission No. 160, Scots Law Commission No. 104, Cm. 137.

or fail to work. With a modern product, such as a motor car or a software product, the manner or quality of performance is of at least as much importance.

Acting on the Law Commissions' recommendations, the requirement that goods be of satisfactory quality was substituted in the Sale and Supply of Goods Act 1994. The definition of the new requirement retains echoes of its predecessor. It is now provided that:

> goods are of satisfactory quality if they meet the standard that a reasonable person would regard as satisfactory, taking account of any description of the goods, the price (if relevant) and all the other relevant circumstances.[27]

The statute goes on, however, to list a number of specific factors which are to be taken into account in determining whether goods are of satisfactory quality:

> [T]he following (among others) are in appropriate cases aspects of the quality of goods:
>
> (a) fitness for all the purposes for which goods of the kind in question are commonly supplied;
>
> (b) appearance and finish;
>
> (c) freedom from minor defects;
>
> (d) safety; and
>
> (e) durability.

A number of points from this new definition may be of considerable significance in a software context. Problems have arisen in the past where an object is fit for only some of its normal purposes.[28] An integrated spreadsheet/word-processing/database package, for example, might perform satisfactorily in two modes but be unworkable in the third. A design package may be satisfactory for external designs but unsuited for internal design. It is now clearly stated that products must be fit for all the purposes for which they are commonly supplied. Products of the kind mentioned above will fail to meet the statutory requirement. Producers will be well advised to give greater care to the descriptions of their products and, at the risk of blunting their marketing strategy, make clear any design limitations applying to the product.

A number of the other features of the definition of satisfactory quality will also be relevant in a computer context. The criteria relating to appearance and finish might be invoked in respect of the user interface and screen displays of a software product. Perhaps the biggest source of problems may arise with the specific mention of 'freedom from minor defects'. Given that all software products contain defects, this may be of considerable significance. It must be stressed, however, that the Sale of Goods Act 1979 does not require that goods be perfect. The standard relates to the expectations of a 'reasonable person'. The major impact may lie in the fact that the specific mention of minor defects may be expected to draw a court's attention to this aspect of an allegedly defective product. Assessment of software products causes particular difficulties. With most products, defects are likely to be introduced at the production stage. If a complaint relates to the allegedly defective performance of a television set, the item at issue can normally be compared with other examples of the same model produced by the same manufacturer. Given the fact that all copies of a software product are likely to be identical, the only basis for comparison will be with the products of competitors. This creates problems in comparing like with like.

The decision as to whether a product is satisfactory is a factual one. A variety of factors may be taken into account. The question of price is one which is of considerable weight in many cases. In *Rogers v Parish*, Mustill LJ stated that '[t]he buyer was entitled to value for

---

[27] Sale of Goods Act 1979, s. 14.
[28] *Aswan Engineering v Lupdine* [1987] 1 WLR 1.

his money'.[29] In the vast majority of cases, one might reasonably expect that a more expensive product will be of better quality than a lower-priced alternative. This approach may break down to some extent in the context of software. The physical components make up such a small part of the value of a package that it is unlikely that any significant variation might be expected here. The point can also be made that it is easier and cheaper to emulate than to innovate. On this basis, and ignoring possible intellectual property complications, it might not be unreasonable to expect a lower-priced derivative package to attain a similar level of quality to that of the original. The speed of development in the entire information technology field also makes difficult the task of determining issues of quality and value for money. A product which might have been regarded as of acceptable quality if sold for £500 on 1 January might be regarded much less favourably if sold for the same amount (or even at a lower price) on the following 31 December.

Further problems may arise in determining the proper purpose of an item of software. Difficulties may be exacerbated by a lack of customer knowledge, as epitomised in the first reported software dispute, *MacKenzie Patten v British Olivetti*.[30] In this case, the plaintiff, a small firm of solicitors, entered into an agreement for the supply of a computer in the apparent belief that this would be able to access court schedules held on a computer at the Old Bailey. This was notwithstanding the fact that neither computer possessed any form of communications capability. It is also the case, of course, that design limitations are not as apparent in software products as may normally be the case. Under the provisions of the Sale of Goods Act 1979, a customer wishing to receive the benefit of the fitness-for-purpose condition is obliged to inform the seller if it is intended to put the product to some unusual purpose. No specific mention need be made if the product is intended to be put to its normal use. 'Normal' in this sense may be interpreted in two ways. First, consideration must be given to the normal uses of a product of the type in question. Thus, a screwdriver is to be used to insert and remove screws. Use as a crowbar would not be classed as normal. A second element might relate to the scale of the intended use. Most products might be intended for a specific sector of a market. A low-cost and low-powered electric drill might be suitable for occasional use in domestic circumstances, but would not be fit for intensive use by a professional builder or joiner. With most products of this kind, design limitations will be apparent. A customer putting a product to excessive use might not receive the court's sympathy in the event of a claim that the product was not fit for its purpose. With software products, design limitations will be much less transparent. A disk retailing at £10,000 will look no different from a blank disk worth a few pence. The development of cheap personal computers has led to the marketing of 'cut-down' versions of computer programs originally designed for the commercial market. Intended for domestic use, these may be marketed on the back of the original but may lack some of its features and capabilities. This may render the program unfit for use at a commercial level of activity. The limitations will not be as apparent as with the electric drill, and sellers may be faced with a dilemma. If they do not make them clear to potential buyers, they may run the risk that a naïve and inexperienced business user may purchase the product and find it unsuitable, whilst drawing excessive attention to the limitations of the product might not be advisable in marketing terms.

Remedies for breach of the implied terms

In the event of a breach of any of the implied terms, the buyer's claim may be to reject the goods supplied as failing to conform with the contractual requirements. It follows that if the goods are validly rejected, the buyer will be released from any obligation to pay for

---

[29] [1987] 2 All ER 232 at 237.   [30] (1985) 48 MLR 344.

them. If the seller's breach of contract has resulted in the buyer suffering any further loss, the rejection of the goods may be accompanied by a claim for damages.

The right to reject will be lost where the buyer's conduct indicates acceptance of the goods. The Sale of Goods Act 1979 provides that the buyer is to be given a reasonable opportunity of examining them. This may occur before or after the sale.[31] One factor which may arise in software contracts, given the near certainty that every copy of a particular package will be identical, concerns the problem of whether the opportunity to examine a copy in the seller's premises will debar the right of rejection, even though a different copy is supplied to the customer.

The Sale of Goods Act 1979 provides further that the right to reject will cease when the buyer does any act which is inconsistent with the seller's continuing ownership or by the lapse of a 'reasonable time'.[32] In respect of the first of these elements, it might be queried whether the act of completing and returning a licence agreement accompanying the software might be regarded as an act inconsistent with the seller's ownership. In the case of many popular software programs, the disks are contained in an envelope inside the packaging. The envelope bears a legend to the effect that opening it signifies acceptance of a licence agreement. The validity of such techniques will be explored in more detail later, but the buyer may be put in the position whereby taking the steps that are physically necessary to use the software might involve an act which is inconsistent with the seller's title. Given that the buyer's right to use the software will otherwise be severely restricted, such a view would appear harsh but by no means illogical.

More difficult still is the question of what will be considered a reasonable time to examine the goods. In the case of *Bernstein v Pamsons Motors (Golders Green) Ltd*,[33] a new motor car was sold to the plaintiff. Some three weeks after delivery, the car suffered a major and potentially dangerous breakdown on a motorway. Examination revealed that a blob of sealing compound had somehow found its way into the vehicle's lubrication system during the course of manufacture. During the course of the engine's short life, the object floated around the system until the occasion when it caused an obstruction, blocking the flow of oil, to the severe detriment of the engine.

Under the terms of the Sale of Goods Act 1979, goods are accepted when the buyer retains them beyond a reasonable length of time without intimating any complaint to the seller. In this case, it was held that the passage of three weeks sufficed to prevent the buyer from rejecting the vehicle. A purchaser, it was held, was entitled to such time as was required to make a general examination of the goods. Although this time would vary depending upon the complexity of the goods, no account would be taken of the nature of the particular defect in question.

The implications of this case for software purchasers are not positive. Although particular defects may not manifest themselves for a considerable period of time, it seems unlikely that a general examination of software, of the kind sanctioned in *Bernstein*, would occupy a substantial period of time. It must be stressed, however, that the fact that the right to reject is lost does not imply that the buyer possesses no remedies. In the event that goods are unmerchantable or are not fit for their purpose, a remedy will remain in damages. The situation at issue in *Bernstein* is again relevant in a software context. The engine of the motor car suffered significant damage in the incident. The seller was willing to repair those components which had identifiably been affected. The customer, however, expressed the fear that the stresses incurred during the incident might have affected other components, rendering them more likely to fail in the future. This fear served to reduce significantly the customer's confidence in the vehicle. Although the judge accepted that the vehicle was not

---

[31] s. 34(1).   [32] s. 35(1).   [33] [1987] 2 All ER 220.

of merchantable quality and an award of damages was made, it is arguable that this provided an inadequate remedy. In the software context, it might be argued that a customer who discovered significant defects in a software product might justifiably fear that efforts on the supplier's part to correct these might create further problems or, alternatively, that other defects might be lying in wait. The fact that software is not susceptible of exhaustive testing, coupled with its intangible nature, makes the issue of customer confidence a significant one.

The fact that a buyer no longer possesses the right to reject goods for non-conformity with contractual obligations does not mean that no remedies are available. An action for damages will always be competent. In respect of the product itself, the measure of damages will reflect the difference between the value of the goods as supplied and the cost of acquiring goods which will conform with the contractual obligations. The implications of this may be significant. An example might be taken of a seller who, having been informed of the buyer's requirements, supplies a system for £4,000. In the event that the system proved not to be fit for that purpose and evidence indicated that a sum of £10,000 might be required in order to meet the requirements, the measure of damages would reflect this difference. This may not be an unlikely scenario in the information technology field. One of the criticisms made in the inquiry into the failures of the London Ambulance Service's computer system was that the cost of the system was approximately half of that which might have been expected for such a significant project.

Software quality and the courts

Having outlined the general principles applicable in any contractual action relating to the quality of goods supplied, attention will be paid in the remainder of this chapter to the approach adopted by the courts in the limited number of cases which have reached the High Court or Court of Appeal. Initially, examination will be made of the application of the quality requirements. It is a feature of software contracts that the attempt is normally made to limit or even to exclude liabilities which would normally arise under the application of the law of contract. Such provisions are subject to judicial scrutiny under the provisions of the Unfair Contract Terms Act 1977. In respect both of quality requirements and of the validity of exclusion clauses, a variety of judicial approaches can be identified and even nearly twenty years after the first case reached the Court of Appeal, it remains difficult to lay down precise guidelines concerning the nature and extent of liability. In some respects, the situation may be characterised as similar to that applying in respect of the categorisation of contracts as involving goods and services where two precedents exist rather uneasily in the cases of *Lee v Griffin*[34] and *Robinson v Graves*.[35]

Questions of time

The inclusion of the word 'reasonable' or 'reasonably' in the statutory requirement indicates that a customer may not be entitled to expect perfection. This may be relevant in two respects. The first concerns the condition in which the goods are delivered, and the second, the broader question of the level of quality ultimately attained by the product. In the case of *Eurodynamic Systems v General Automation Ltd*,[36] the High Court was faced with a dispute concerning, inter alia, the quality of an operating system for a computer. Steyn J stated that:

> The expert evidence convincingly showed that it is regarded as acceptable practice to supply computer programmes [*sic*] (including system software) that contain errors and bugs. The

---

[34] (1861) 1 B&S 272.   [35] [1935] 1 KB 579.   [36] (6 September 1988, unreported), QBD.

basis of the practice is that, pursuant to his support obligation (free or chargeable as the case may be), the supplier will correct errors and bugs that prevent the product from being properly used. Not every bug or error in a computer programme can therefore be categorised as a breach of contract.

It is not, of course, only with software that a product may originally be supplied suffering from minor defects. Although the continued presence of these after the supplier has been offered the opportunity of repair will eventually lead to a finding that the product is not of satisfactory quality, the courts have tended to require that this opportunity be given. In the Scottish case of *Millars of Falkirk Ltd v Turpie*,[37] a new car was sold to the defendant. Immediately upon taking delivery, he discovered an oil leak emanating from the power-assisted steering unit. Upon being notified, the sellers attempted to repair the defect. This attempt proving unsuccessful, the defendant refused to pay for the vehicle and purported to reject it. Holding that he was not entitled so to do, the Court of Session ruled that although the car as supplied was not of merchantable quality, the seller must be granted a reasonable opportunity to repair the defect. 'Many new cars', it was stated, 'have on delivery to a purchaser, some defects, and it was not exceptional that a car should come from the manufacturer in the condition of the defendant's new car on delivery.'[38] As the buyer had failed to allow this, the breach of contract was on his part.

Given the received wisdom that all software contains defects, it would appear that a customer will have to extend reasonable tolerance towards their supplier if or when minor defects manifest themselves. This is well illustrated by the case of *Saphena Computing v Allied Collection Agencies Ltd*,[39] the first software dispute to reach the Court of Appeal. The appellant, Saphena Computing, was a small firm specialising in the supply of third-party hardware and software, either produced or customised by itself. The respondent was engaged in the business of debt collection. Under an initial contract between the parties, it was agreed that Saphena would supply a quantity of software. The software was ordered in January 1985 and installed between February and April. Despite initial teething problems, it was functioning satisfactorily by May 1985. In August 1985, a second contract was made for the supply of further software. It was intended that this would upgrade the defendant's system. Upon installation of the system, a degree of modification was required as a result of difficulties in attaining compatibility with the existing system and through changes in the defendant's requirements.

Although attempts were made to remedy the problems, it was common ground between the parties that the system was not operating in a satisfactory manner by February 1986. On 11 February, a telephone conversation took place between representatives of the parties. In the course of this, it was agreed that the relationship should be terminated. Unfortunately, untangling the legal consequences was to prove no simple matter, and when the dispute went to trial, proceedings before the High Court lasted for seventeen days.

Subsequent to the termination of the contract, another programmer was contracted to work on the system. In the course of this work, the source code of the programs produced by the plaintiff was copied. Responding to this action, the plaintiff instituted proceedings alleging breach of copyright in its programs. It was further claimed that the defendant had acted wrongfully in terminating the contract and that the plaintiff was entitled to the price of the goods or services supplied under the contract. This latter contention was challenged by the defendant, who counterclaimed for damages, alleging that the software supplied was not to be considered fit for its purpose. The plaintiff succeeding in all significant aspects of its claim, the defendant appealed to the Court of Appeal which unanimously

[37] 1976 SLT (Notes) 66.   [38] At 67.   [39] [1995] FSR 616.

affirmed the findings of the lower court. In particular, it was held, there was an implied term as to the fitness for the purpose for which the software was required. It had to be reasonably fit for such purposes as had been notified to the supplier before the orders were placed or were notified subsequently and accepted by the supplier. These obligations had not been fulfilled by the supplier at 11 February when the relationship was terminated. Although the software was usable at this stage, it was not entirely fit for the defendant's purposes. There remained faults which required correction. However, the defendant was not entitled, at that stage, to terminate the agreement on this basis. Software, it was held by Staughton LJ:

> is not a commodity which is delivered once, only once, and once and for all, but one which will necessarily be accompanied by a degree of testing and modification.[40]

Thus, it would not be a breach of contract to deliver software in the first instance with a defect in it. In this respect, software must be distinguished from other products, in that the concept of delivery is a much more fluid one. In part, this is due to the necessary interaction between supplier and customer:

> Just as no software developer can reasonably expect a buyer to tell him what is required without a process of feedback and reassessment, so no buyer should expect a supplier to get his programs right first time.[41]

The eradication of defects may be a lengthy and laborious process. In the absence of specific provisions relating to acceptance tests and procedures, it is debatable as to how long the buyer must allow this process to continue. Certainly, the message from *Saphena* would indicate that the buyer must exercise caution and restraint before seeking to terminate a contractual relationship. In this instance, the effect of termination was that:

> the defendant thereby agreed to accept the software in the condition in which it then was and, by agreement, put it out of the plaintiff's power to render the software fit for its purpose. The original agreements were thereby varied by deleting the fitness term.[42]

In the event, the plaintiff was held entitled to payment of a reasonable sum in respect of its work on the software and was freed from the requirement to conduct any further work on the system. The defendant's counterclaim for damages in respect of losses caused by the alleged unfitness of the software was dismissed.

The final question before the court concerned the extent of the defendant's right to seek to rectify the defects. To effect this process, would require access to the programs' source code. Although the plaintiff's contractual conditions made it clear that the source code remained its property, in view of the circumstances under which the agreement had been cancelled, the court held that the defendant must be allowed such access to this as would enable it to cure the defects in the software. Insofar as the defendant had gone beyond this by copying portions of the code, it was acting in breach of copyright.

The principal lesson which might be taken from the *Saphena* case[43] is that there is need for precision in the drafting of contractual provisions. In this case, the court had to find its way through a number of written agreements, coupled with evidence of verbal negotiations and promises which were considered to have also constituted part of the agreement. In spite of these factors, the parties do not appear to have addressed the basic question of what level of quality was to be expected, how conformity with this was to be established, and what periods of time would be appropriate for testing and the rectification of errors.

---

[40] *Saphena Computing v Allied Collection Agencies Ltd* [1995] FSR 616 at 652.
[41] At 652.   [42] At 618.   [43] At 652.

Problems with the Community Charge

Although it was held in *Saphena* that the customer could not expect software to work perfectly from the moment it was supplied, the next case to be considered, *St Albans District Council v ICL*,[44] illustrates that this cannot provide a defence in a situation where software proves incapable of meeting its basic purposes.

The background to the case began with the introduction of a new form of local taxation, the Community Charge. This tax, more commonly known as the poll tax, proved one of the less popular forms of taxation in recent British history. In fiscal terms, the tax is no longer operative but, thanks to the litigation in *St Albans*, it has made a significant contribution to information technology law. The case was concerned with the acceptability of hardware and software supplied to the plaintiff for the purpose of administering the operation of the tax. The case is undoubtedly the most significant precedent in the field of information technology law and deserves detailed consideration.

The key element of the poll tax was that, subject to a very limited number of exceptions, all those aged eighteen or above living in a local government district were required to pay an identical sum. No account was taken of a taxpayer's income, so that a person earning £100,000 would pay the same as a person earning £10,000. In administrative terms, this approach simplified the task of the local authorities. Effectively, all that was required was to calculate the income required, the number of persons liable to pay the tax, and divide the one by the other.

If ever a task could be seen as made for the computer, this was surely it, and apparently without exception, local authorities invested heavily in IT systems to administer the tax. Many of the authorities, St Albans included, entered into contracts with the computer supplier ICL, who promoted an IT system referred to as 'The ICL Solution'. At the time the contract was signed, the elements of the system required to cope with the specific demands of the Community Charge had not been completed or tested. This fact was promoted as a positive benefit to the authority. The developers would use a seventy-strong development team to produce the necessary software and by entering into the contract, the Council would be able 'to input into the development process in order to be sure that this product meets your specific requirements'.[45]

The contract, valued at some £1.3 million, was concluded subject to ICL's standard terms and conditions, which excluded all liability for consequential loss and limited liability for other losses to a maximum of £100,000. The system was delivered to the council timeously but, as envisaged in the contract, the software required was to be delivered and installed in stages as various elements were completed and in line with legislative requirements relating to the introduction of the new tax. Initial elements were to be completed in autumn 1988, with the full system being operable by February 1990.

One of the first tasks which needed to be conducted by local authorities was to calculate the number of persons in their area liable to pay the tax. Many local authorities were politically opposed to the new system, and in order to prevent them delaying its introduction, the legislation provided a rigid timetable for the various actions required, with penalties being imposed upon recalcitrant authorities. St Albans Council was, therefore, faced with the requirement to complete its count by a certain date. Once the figure had been calculated, the legislation provided that it could not be altered.

The calculation was carried out using the ICL system in early December 1989 and a figure of 97,384.7 was produced. Unfortunately, the version of the software used had a bug and, for some unknown reason, a new release which would have cured the problem was

---

[44] [1996] 4 All ER 481. Reported at first instance at [1995] FSR 686.
[45] At 483.

not installed on the Council's computers prior to the calculation. The correct figure, it was subsequently discovered, was almost 3,000 lower at 94,418.7. The financial effects were significant. The council was effectively caught in a double-edged trap. Their income was reduced because the 3,000 phantom taxpayers would clearly not produce any income. To compound matters, part of the Community Charge income was destined to be transferred to the larger Hertfordshire County Council and this figure was also calculated on the basis that St Albans' taxpaying population was greater than it actually was. When the accounts were finally completed, it was calculated that the loss to St Albans was over £1.3 million.[46]

Although the defendant did not dispute the fact that the software involved in the calculation had been defective, it argued that its obligation was merely to supply a system which would be fully operative at the end of February 1990. Until then, as was recognised in the contract, the system would be in the course of development. Save where it could be shown that the supplier had acted negligently, it was argued, the case of *Saphena v Allied Collection Agencies*[47] provided authority for the proposition that 'the plaintiffs had impliedly agreed to accept the software supplied, bugs and all'. This contention was rejected, with Nourse LJ stating in the Court of Appeal that:

> Parties who respectively agree to supply and acquire a system recognising that it is still in the course of development cannot be taken, merely by virtue of that recognition, to intend that the supplier shall be at liberty to supply software which cannot perform the function expected of it at the stage of development at which it is supplied.[48]

In the particular case, it was of critical importance that the system should have been able to provide an accurate population count in December 1989.

The defendant's arguments relating to the protection conferred by its exclusion clause will be considered in more detail later. Although it might be argued that the defect in *St Albans* was considerably more serious than the failures in *Saphena*, the tenor of the judgment does seem to be much more 'user-friendly' than was the case in the earlier judgment.

Water privatisation

ICL was also the defendant in the case of *South West Water Services Ltd v International Computers Ltd*.[49] Once again, the origins of the case lay in politics, on this occasion the privatisation of the English water companies. Following the establishment of the Office of the Water Regulator, a formula was devised which would limit the ability of the companies to increase charges to customers. The intention was that the companies would only be able to maintain their profits through efficiency gains. The plaintiff identified its billing system as a candidate for such savings. The introduction of a new IT system, it was considered, would allow forty-six employees to be made redundant.

A prolonged contractual process then followed, although, as was the case in *St Albans*,[50] external factors, in the form of scheduled reviews to be conducted by the Regulator, imposed immutable deadlines for the accomplishment of a working system and its associated cost savings. One false start ensued, with a contract being entered into with a major supplier who quickly discovered that the project could not be completed on time. The contract was cancelled by South West Water (SWW).

---

[46] In the event, ICL was held liable for only some two-thirds of the amount, it being held that the remainder could be recouped from taxpayers by increasing the rate of tax in the next financial year.

[47] [1995] FSR 616.

[48] *St Albans District Council v ICL* [1996] 4 All ER 481 at 487.

[49] [1999] Masons CLR 400.

[50] *St Albans District Council v ICL* [1996] 4 All ER 481.

A new call for tenders was initiated on the basis of a User Requirements Specification (URS) drawn up by SWW. The defendant entered into negotiations on the basis of customising a package (Custima) developed by a third party, Creative Computer Systems (CCS), in which it held a 30 per cent stake. The Custima package would require to be customised to meet the user's requirements. The extent of customisation required was at the heart of the subsequent legal dispute. In his findings of fact, the judge held that:

> In my view the problem started here. Although SWW never agreed with ICL or CCSL any specification other than in conformity with the URS, ICL proceeded on the basis that in the end it would be able to persuade SWW that it did not need to provide what was specified in the URS.[51]

Essentially, it would appear, the supplier was very keen to obtain the contract, not least because with the existence of a considerable number of privatised utilities, it saw prospects of a lucrative market in selling further versions of the system. The customer's specifications were seen as being unnecessarily rigorous and it was hoped that it could be persuaded to accept a more realistic approach, one which would involve significantly less work in customising the Custima software.

Following extensive discussions, a contract was awarded to ICL in September 1994, with the completed system being scheduled for delivery on 31 October 1995. The contract was costed at some £3.6 million. Expert evidence before the court was of the view that the timetable was a tight one. Progress was poor, with several deadlines for delivery of component parts being missed. Even though a delay in completion until the end of March 1996 was agreed between the parties, by early in that month it was clear that the timetable would not be met and the customer served notice terminating the contract. An action was brought seeking recovery of sums paid under the contract plus compensation for additional losses. The claims were based on allegations both of misrepresentation and of breach of contract. These contentions were rejected by the supplier, who argued that its entry into the contract had followed misrepresentations from the customer regarding the amount of work that would be required in order to customise the software to suit its needs. It was also contended that exclusion clauses in the contract served to limit the extent of its liability.

In the event, the customer succeeded on all counts. A key factor in the failure of the contract was identified as lying in the lack of a properly structured agreement between ICL and CCS. The need for what was described as a 'seamless relationship' between these parties had been identified as critical by the customer. In its absence, there could be no guarantee that the effort required to customise the software would be forthcoming. It was argued on behalf of ICL that there could be no representation as, at the time relevant statements were made, there had been the intention to conclude such a contract. The judge disagreed, holding that there was no evidence to support such an assertion. Records of discussions between ICL and CCS indicated clearly that the latter would not have been willing to enter into a contract on the basis of the arrangements proposed by ICL. Even if the representation had originally been made in the belief it was warranted, there was ample evidence to show that ICL must have been aware before the conclusion of the contract that it did not continue to be valid.

In respect of ICL's claim that the customer had misled them as to the amount of work required, the judge was not able to accept that the evidence supported this. In any event, it was clear that:

> Not only were ICL not misled but ICL were in fact the experts whose duty it was to evaluate the project and use their skill, with the assistance from (CCS) in making proposals as to how the project was to be carried out.[52]

---

[51] [1999] Masons CLR 400 at 402.   [52] At 402.

Whilst this falls short of imposing duties to advise, counsel, or warn customers regarding the merits and suitability of their wares, it does suggest that suppliers cannot, as was indicated in this case, remain silent concerning what are considered to be unrealistic expectations on the part of the customer in the belief that it could subsequently be persuaded to adopt a more realistic view as to its requirements.

The Monday software package

In *SAM Business Systems Ltd v Hedley & Co*,[53] the claimant supplied the defendants, a small firm of stockbrokers, with a software package called Interset. The software was intended to replace an existing system called ANTAR, which it was feared (perhaps wrongly) was not 'year 2000 compliant'. Following some negotiations, the contract was signed in October 1999 and it was estimated that a period of twelve weeks would be required to install the software and transfer the defendant's processing operations from its old system.

In pre-contractual negotiations, the customer alleged, the sellers stated that the system would cost no more than £180,000, with a money-back guarantee in the event it failed to work in a satisfactory manner. Although no particular figures were specified in any of the contractual documents, the case proceeded on the basis that this was the appropriate figure relating to the supply and installation of the software and some items of associated hardware. The licence for supply and use of the software was costed at £116,000. Half of this sum was to be paid at the time the contract was entered into, with two further payments to be made when the software was installed and finally when it had been accepted. Under the terms of the contract, the customer was given a period of thirty days to test the software to ensure conformity with specification. In the event that defects were discovered, these were to be reported. If they were not rectified within ninety days, the customer would have the option to reject the software and obtain a refund of all sums paid. This, it was stated, represented the full extent of the supplier's liability.

The migration to the new system proved an unhappy experience for all concerned. The salient facts will be considered in more detail but in February 2001, some seventeen months later, the defendants decided to abandon their efforts to make the new system work and had decided instead to outsource their processing operations to another company. By this stage, the defendants had paid a total of £183,000, reflecting payments in respect of the licence, the purchase of some items of hardware, and a sum of approximately £14,000 in respect of a separate maintenance contract. The final licence installment had not been paid. Further negotiations took place between the parties, but in June 2001, the claimant commenced proceedings claiming some £310,000 partly in respect of the outstanding licence fee but principally for what was described as 'post-installation maintenance'. A total of 785 hours of work was alleged to have been expended in this manner. The defendant counterclaimed, seeking nearly £790,000, reflecting a total refund of all sums paid for Interset, plus damages reflecting 'increased cost of working, write-offs, fines and additional charges, mitigation costs, and loss of profits'.

As has been typical in cases involving liability for software, the judgment can be split into two components concerning the questions of whether the software supplied complied with contractual and legal requirements relating to quality and, in the event that the answer to this question was in the negative, whether clauses limiting or excluding the supplier's liability complied with the requirements of unfair contract terms legislation. In respect of the quality requirements, the court accepted that terms must be implied into the contract to the effect that the software would be developed and installed with 'all professional skill and

[53] [2002] EWHC 2733 (TCC), [2003] 1 All ER (Comm) 465.

care' and that it would be 'reasonably fit' for the purposes required by the customer and, more specifically, would perform in such a way as to allow the customer to meet its own obligations as required by the Financial Services Authority.[54]

From the early stages, the attempts to introduce Interset proved difficult and doubtless frustrating for both parties. The judgment charts a familiar if depressing path through the detritus of a failed commercial relationship lasting for some eighteen months. The software was supplied timeously but errors continually manifested themselves, to the extent that the defendant was warned by the financial services regulator for failing to comply with its requirements regarding record keeping and accounting and was also fined by the Inland Revenue for late payment of stamp duty taxes arising from transactions. Although the suppliers acknowledged that there were some bugs in the software which required to be corrected, it was also argued that the defendant's staff were largely to blame for failures. The system did mark a substantial change from the defendant's existing package which operated under the DOS operating system, making use solely of keystrokes for command and control purposes. Interset operated under Microsoft Windows and provided the now ubiquitous graphical user interface. As was concluded by the judge:

> what was being presented to Hedleys was a system with a very high degree of automation, a system that was going to be operable by ordinary people, and not technically qualified people.[55]

This was to be a matter of some importance, as one of the claimant's chief arguments was to the effect that the system had been installed and was working effectively in a considerable number of other business environments. A prime cause of any failure to operate in a satisfactory manner for the defendant was allegedly 'because the staff at Hedley's were not trained for the work or were otherwise incompetent'. Although it was acknowledged that the staff's IT knowledge was limited and somewhat dated to the extent that they were not familiar with the use of a mouse,[56] it was accepted that they were committed to attempting to make the new system work. It was the supplier's responsibility to provide training and blame for failures in this respect was placed upon the trainer supplied by them, whose evidence left the judge rather unimpressed. He commented that she 'gave her evidence in a curiously deadpan manner. Perhaps it was due to nervousness, but if she taught in that manner I can understand that she might have difficulty in communicating computer skills'.[57]

The fact that Interset was used successfully elsewhere was considered to be a matter of limited significance:

> I am no more impressed by it than if I were told by a garage that there were 1,000 other cars of the same type as the one I had bought where there was no complaint of the defect that I was complaining of so why should I be complaining of a defect? We have all heard of Monday cars, so maybe this was a Monday software programme.[58]

Given that it is received wisdom that all copies of software are identical, this is at first sight a rather puzzling comment. Certainly, there should be few if any instances of what can be classed as production defects in copies of software. Linked with the issue of training, however, indication can be seen of some of the complex interactions which impact upon the user's ability to use software effectively. Many of the applications of Interset software

---

[54] [2002] EWHC 2733 (TCC), [2003] 1 All ER (Comm) 465 at [50].
[55] At [21].
[56] *SAM Business Systems Ltd v Hedley & Co* [2002] EWHC 2733 (TCC), [2003] 1 All ER (Comm) 465 at [5].
[57] [2002] EWHC 2733 (TCC) at [83].
[58] *SAM Business Systems Ltd v Hedley & Co* [2002] EWHC 2733 (TCC), [2003] 1 All ER (Comm) 465 at [103].

were in larger organisations. At the time of the case, the evidence was that only one other stockbroking firm was using the system and in general it appears that most users had staff with greater IT skills than those possessed by the defendant's.

A litany of complaints is reported in the judgment[59] and the claimant expended very significant amounts of staff time in seeking either to rectify problems or establish work-around procedures to allow operators to avoid undesirable results. The decision of the Court of Appeal in the case of *Saphena v Allied Collection Agencies*[60] was cited as authority for the proposition 'that in a bespoke system bugs were inevitable'. The later decision of the court in the case of *St Albans District Council v ICL* was also referred to, Lord Justice Nourse here ruling that:

> Parties who respectively agree to supply and acquire a system recognising that it is still in the course of development cannot be taken, merely by virtue of that recognition, to intend that the supplier shall be at liberty to supply software which cannot perform the function expected of it at the stage of the development at which it is supplied.[61]

The systems involved in both *Saphena*[62] and *St Albans*[63] were referred to as 'bespoke' systems and therefore distinguishable from the customised system supplied to the present defendant. This is perhaps putting matters too strongly. In *Saphena*, the supplier's business was described as consisting of providing 'hardware obtained from others, and software comprising some standard items and others specially written'. In *St Albans*, the tax collection system at issue had also been supplied to a number of other local authorities. Where a better distinction perhaps lay was in the state of development of the system. In *St Albans*, the software was being developed in parallel with the enactment of the legislation establishing the tax which it was designed to help collect. Upgrades and revisions were continually being supplied to the users and, indeed, the fluid nature of the software posed serious problems in trying to replicate and explain the nature of the error which gave rise to the litigation. Interset, however, had been promoted as a 'developed system'. Such a system, it was held, should not have any bugs in it. This is perhaps a counsel of perfection but the judge did accept that if defects were speedily rectified without cost to the customer there may well be no liability on the part of the supplier. This seems an eminently correct ruling, although as was recognised in the judgment:

> SAM, like some others in the computer industry seem to be set in the mindset that when there is a 'bug' the customer must pay for putting it right. Bugs in computer programmes are still inevitable, but they are defects and it is the supplier who has the responsibility for putting them right at the supplier's expense.[64]

In line with these arguments, the sums claimed by the claimant in respect of the time and effort incurred in seeking to modify the software was rejected. The defendant was held to have been entitled to take the view that the software contract had not been completed in a satisfactory manner and the claimant's claim for additional payments was rejected. However, from its perspective, it was unfortunately also necessary to consider the effectiveness of the claimant's exclusion clauses, which effectively limited its liability to providing a refund of sums paid in the situation that the customer followed the contractual procedures regarding rejection. As will be discussed later, the defendant failed in this task, rendering victory in respect of the claim of defectiveness pyrrhic.

---

[59]   *SAM Business Systems Ltd v Hedley & Co* [2002] EWHC 2733 (TCC), [2003] 1 All ER (Comm) 465 at [103].
[60]   [1995] FSR 616.
[61]   [1996] 4 All ER 481 at 487.
[62]   *Saphena Computing v Allied Collection Agencies Ltd* [1995] FSR 616.
[63]   *St Albans District Council v ICL* [1996] 4 All ER 481 at 487.
[64]   *SAM Business Systems v Hedley* [2002] EWHC 2733 (TCC) at [19].

The dog with an MBA

It is sometimes said that 'whilst to err is human, to really foul it up requires a computer'. The recent English case of *BSkyB v EDS and Ors*[65] perhaps provides evidence suggesting that the age of human frailty is not yet past.

As with many software disputes, the case began with lofty aspirations. BSkyB (better known as Sky) is the United Kingdom's leading satellite TV broadcaster. The market for providing access to television (and increasingly also telephone and Internet services) is a competitive one and the efficient handling of customer enquiries, requests, and complaints is vitally important. In many respects, customer retention has become a more important issue than customer acquisition and the case report makes extensive reference to the phenomenon known as 'consumer churn'—the proportion of customers who switch suppliers in any given year and the desirability of reducing this as much as possible. Sky decided that a solution lay in the development of a new customer-relationship management system to create a 'world class customer experience' and, following a competitive tender process, the contract was awarded to a consortium including the lead defendant in the present case. The value of the contract was initially £47 million and it was provided that the new system should be developed and made operational within a nine-month period.

As with many software projects, initial optimism soon faded and it was recognised that the original schedule and costings were unsustainable. The agreement was modified between the parties but it took an additional four years of work before the new system was functioning in an acceptable manner and the costs had risen to £265 million. Inevitably, perhaps, the lawyers were not far behind with Sky instituting legal proceedings seeking damages of around £709 million in respect of losses which it claimed to have suffered in its business activities because of the late completion of the contract. In large part this was on the basis that customers who should have received a 'world class customer service' had incurred a poorer experience and had as a consequence taken their custom elsewhere. In logistical terms the case is undoubtedly massive. The trial occupied 109 days of court time with legal costs estimated at around £70 million. The judgment which was handed down in December 2009 ran to almost 500 pages.

Whilst the case is likely to go down as one of the most expensive in legal history, its legal dimensions are perhaps less significant. The agreement between the parties provided, as is fairly standard procedure, for limitations on liability in respect of any contractual breaches. There was no doubt that the clauses had been validly incorporated into the agreement which, if effective, would have limited EDS's liability to around £30 million. The contract had a further provision—generally referred to as an 'entire agreement' clause. Again, this is commonplace in commercial contracts. In a case such as the present one, there will have been extensive negotiations and discussions between the parties prior to the conclusion of the contract. The effect of the clause is to affirm that every matter related to the contract is contained in the final agreement and that prior statements—referred to as representations—were to be disregarded.

At this stage, things might appear bleak for Sky. Its basic argument was that it had been led into concluding the contract on the basis of false representations made by an employee of EDS. In most cases, this would have been covered by the 'entire agreement' clause but the argument put forward on behalf of Sky was that these had been made not by accident or even through negligence but as part of a deliberate policy of deceit. As such, the statements would be classed as fraudulent misrepresentations. For perhaps obvious reasons, it was held, a party who has procured the making of a contract through fraud cannot rely on any contractual clauses limiting the extent of liability.

---

[65] [2010] EWHC 86 (TCC).

Essentially the case turned upon the judge's assessment of the character of the key witness for EDS. This individual claimed to have been awarded the degree of MBA (Master of Business Administration) from an institution, Concordia College, located on the Caribbean island of St John. The nature of this qualification was tested extensively in court. The witness claimed that he had attended lectures and seminars at the institution over a period of many months. Unfortunately, the evidence established that the 'college' did not actually have any teaching premises. It was effectively what is referred to as a 'degree mill'—an organisation that will offer a purported degree certificate to an individual subject to no other criterion than an ability to pay for it. Although the witness presented what appeared to be a transcript of his class marks and a (glowing) letter of recommendation from the college principal, counsel for Sky was able to demonstrate to the court that an application made on behalf of his dog produced an MBA, an identically worded letter of recommendation, and a rather better set of class marks.

It is not uncommon for individuals to exaggerate the nature and extent of their qualifications. A considerable number of well-known individuals have been caught claiming to possess qualifications of doubtful value. It is an old maxim that if a person finds himself in a hole, the first thing to do is stop digging. This the witness signally failed to do. More and more elaborate tales regarding the degree were presented in the witness box only to be demonstrated to be false. Ultimately, the judge concluded regarding the witness:

> This is not a case where there was merely a lie as to the MBA degree. Such a lie might have had a limited effect on credibility and might be explicable on the basis that (the witness) wished to bolster his academic qualifications and was embarrassed about the way he did it. However his dishonesty did not stop at that. He then gave perjured evidence about the MBA, including repeatedly giving dishonest answers about the circumstances in which he gained his MBA . . . In doing so, he gave his evidence with the same confident manner which he adopted in relation to his other evidence about his involvement in the Sky CRM Project. He therefore demonstrated an astounding ability to be dishonest, making up a whole story about being in St John, working there and studying at Concordia College. EDS properly distance themselves from his evidence and realistically accept that his evidence should be treated with caution.
>
> . . . In my judgment, (the witness's) credibility was completely destroyed by his perjured evidence over a prolonged period. It is simply not possible to distinguish between evidence which he gave on this aspect and on other aspects of the case. My general approach to his evidence has therefore to be that I cannot rely on the truth of his evidence unless it is supported by other evidence or there is some other reason to accept it, such as it being inherently liable to be true.[66]

Essentially, it was argued that the witness had engaged in a course of deliberately deceitful behaviour, including the forging of emails designed to conceal a mistake in financial calculations made by the witness. Counter-evidence existed in respect of the allegations but, given the comments quoted above, it is not surprising that the judge concluded that:

> Having come to the conclusion that I have about his conduct in relation to the Concordia MBA and the evidence that he gave in court, I have no hesitation in finding that (the witness) simply created the 12 July email to cover his error in the hope that he could convince everyone that he had spotted the error at the time and dealt with it.

In English civil cases, the decision has to be made by a judge on the basis of an assessment of the balance of probabilities. Where the credibility of a witness has been destroyed in one context, it must be at least damaged in others and in a number of instances throughout the case the judge accepted the evidence of witnesses for Sky as being more likely to be accurate.

[66] paras. 194–5.

The legal victory for Sky was by no means complete. Save for the issue of fraud, the judge held that the contractual provisions and limitation clauses were effective in protecting EDS against the full financial consequences of its failure to meet its contractual requirements. Nonetheless, although the final award of damages remains to be fixed it appears to be generally accepted that the award will be in the region of £200 million. Initially it was indicated that an appeal would be lodged against the decision at first instance. Perhaps driven in part by changes in ownership of EDS, this was not pursued and an agreed damages payment was fixed at just over £300 million.

Exclusion or limitation of liability

In the previous sections in this chapter, consideration was given to the nature and extent of the liabilities which may arise pursuant to the production, supply, and use of software. Although the argument that software should be treated in the same manner as any other product is a weighty one, it must also be conceded that software producers may be exposed to a greater degree of risk than their more traditional counterparts. First, if one copy of a software product exhibits defects, it must be extremely likely that all copies will be so tainted. With manufactured products generally, most defects are introduced at the production stage and affect only a portion of the products in question. A finding that one copy of a software package is unmerchantable might, by way of contrast, leave its producer liable to every purchaser. A further problem is that many losses resulting from software defects will be economic in nature. Such losses may not only be extensive but are also extremely difficult to quantify and, accordingly, to insure against. A spreadsheet program, for example, may be used for domestic accounting purposes, where the degree of financial exposure in the event of error may be minimal, or in the course of preparing a multi-million pound construction contract, where any error might threaten the financial viability of a contracting party.

Few would argue that the state of the law relating to software liability is satisfactory. Uncertainty feeds upon uncertainty and perception appears more significant than reality. The producer's fear that it may be exposed to crippling legal actions has resulted in an almost universal practice of seeking to exclude some and place limits on the extent of their liabilities in respect of other forms of loss resulting from the operation (or non-operation) of their software. The validity of such clauses[67] has been at issue in most of the disputes which have reached the courts.

An initial point to note is that in order to be effective, a clause must be incorporated into the contract. The rules relating to this are to be found in common law rather than statute, and require that reasonable steps be taken to bring the existence of the clause to the notice of the other contracting party. This may be accomplished in a number of ways, with a major factor being whether the software is supplied pursuant to a written contract signed by both parties. In such cases, there will generally be little doubt that the exclusion clause forms part of the contract, and discussion will focus on the effect of the provisions of the Unfair Contract Terms Act 1977 and the Unfair Terms in Consumer Contracts Regulations 1999.[68]

More difficult issues arise when software (typically standard) is supplied through less structured channels. Such software is typically supplied subject to what is generally referred to as a 'shrink-wrap licence'. The term appears to date from early forms of consumer software, mainly computer games. These were typically supplied on an audio cassette, with

---

[67] In this section, the term 'exclusion clause' will be used to refer both to clauses which seek to exclude and to those which limit the extent of liability. Most terms under discussion fall into the latter category.

[68] SI 1999/2083.

the terms of a very basic licence printed on the cellophane wrapping of the cassette. Today, licences tend to be printed on substantial booklets (often making separate provisions to accommodate the legal requirements of a range of countries in which the software is sold) included inside packaging. The validity of these is subject to some debate.

Enforceability of shrink-wrap licences

Many contracts, of course, are made other than by means of a signed document; a typical example might relate to the purchase of a piece of standard software from a shop. In this situation, the legal requirement will be that reasonable steps should be taken to bring the existence of any contractual provisions to the notice of the other party prior to the conclusion of the agreement.[69] It is not required that he or she should be aware of all of the details or of the legal implications arising from the contract. An example can be taken from a railway ticket. The ticket will contain reference to the carrier's conditions of carriage but will not itself contain details of these. The presence on the ticket of a notice referring the customer to the conditions will suffice to incorporate them into the contract. Returning to the software context, the display of a clause on the outside of the packaging (or perhaps on a notice displayed in the seller's premises) will serve to give the customer notice of its existence. It is increasingly the case that software is supplied over the Internet. The practice has implications in respect of a number of areas of the law, not least concerning the tax liabilities associated with online software transactions. From a licensing perspective, use of the Internet may simplify the supplier's task of establishing customer awareness of and agreement to the licence terms. It is a simple matter to cause either a set of the terms or at least reference to their existence to be displayed, with the customer required to 'click' on a button marked 'I accept' before the transaction can proceed.

Assuming that the terms of the licence—including its provisions restricting liability—become incorporated into the contract, attention must again turn to the effect of the Unfair Contract Terms Act 1977 and the Unfair Terms in Consumer Contracts Regulations 1999.[70] To date, all litigation concerned with the effectiveness of exclusion or limitation clauses in software contracts has occurred in the context of commercial transactions. The increasing use of software within the home must increase the importance of the consumer sector and initially, therefore, consideration will be given to the potential application of the legislation in this regard.

Consumer contracts

Somewhat confusingly, different definitions of the term 'consumer' are found in the Unfair Contract Terms Act 1977 and 1999 Regulations. The Act provides that a person deals as a consumer if:

(a) he neither makes the contract in the course of a business nor holds himself out as doing so; and

(b) the other party does make the contract in the course of a business.[71]

Additionally, where goods are supplied under the contract, these must be of a kind ordinarily used for private use or consumption. It would seem that computer games must satisfy

---

[69] See *Thornton v Shoe Lane Parking Ltd* [1971] 2 QB 163, where the display of exclusion clauses inside a car park was held to be ineffective, the contract having been concluded at the point when the customer entered into the premises.

[70] SI 1999/2083.   [71] s. 12(1).

this requirement. Although the status of other forms of software, such as word-processing or accounting packages or Internet access software, may at one stage have been debatable, it would seem that they are now sufficiently widely used to be classed as consumer products. This issue may not arise under the Regulations, which make no reference to the nature of goods, requiring only that they be obtained for non-business purposes.[72]

In respect of statutory requirements relating to title, description, or quality, the Unfair Contract Terms Act 1977 provides that exclusion or limitation will not be permitted.[73] In the case of consumer contracts falling under the ambit of the Sale of Goods Act 1979, the prohibition is even more extensive. Here, the Consumer Protection from Unfair Trading Regulations[74] (previously the Consumer Transactions (Restrictions on Statements) Order 1976)[75] provides that any attempt at restriction or exclusion will constitute a criminal offence. An offence will also be committed when any form of guarantee is offered other than those provided for in the Sale of Goods Act 1979, unless it is made clear that this is offered in addition to, rather than in substitution for, the consumer's rights under the legislation. It appears common practice amongst the suppliers of computer games to display notices restricting the buyer's rights to the supply of a replacement game in the event that the original is defective. In the event that the contract is regarded as one involving the sale or supply of goods, the display of such notices will render the supplier involved liable to criminal prosecution.

In terms of their scope, the 1999 Regulations are broader,[76] applying to any term in a non-negotiated contract for goods or services other than those defining the main subject matter or relating to the adequacy of the price. Such terms will not be binding on the consumer if they are determined to be unfair. An unfair term is one which:

> contrary to the requirements of good faith causes a significant imbalance in the parties' rights and obligations under the contract to the imbalance of the consumer.[77]

This is a somewhat nebulous criterion. Schedule 2 to the Regulations contains an 'indicative and non-exclusive list of the terms which might be considered unfair'. These include clauses purporting to limit the legal rights of consumers in the event of unsatisfactory performance. A further illustration stigmatises clauses

> making an agreement binding on the consumer whereas provision of services by the supplier or seller is subject to a condition whose realisation depends on his own will alone.

It might be that this provision could be invoked in the event that a software producer seeks to link a right to use software to the acceptance of restrictive terms within a licence.

A further aspect of the 1999 Regulations[78] may be of considerable significance. Although many forms of exclusion clause have long been regarded as of dubious quality, the difficulties facing individual litigants have prevented these being challenged before the courts. The Regulations establish a role for the Director General of Fair Trading providing that the Director is to consider any complaint that a contract term is unfair and may then seek an injunction preventing the continued use of the term (or any similar term) in consumer contracts.[79]

Non-consumer contracts

In the case of non-consumer contracts for supply of goods, as well as any contracts where standard form contracts are used, limitation or exclusion clauses will be valid only insofar as they satisfy the statutory requirement of reasonableness.[80] The Unfair Contract Terms

---

[72] s. 2.   [73] s. 6.   [74] SI 2008/1277.   [75] SI 1976/1813.   [76] SI 1999/2083.
[77] Unfair Contract Terms Act 1977, s. 4(1).
[78] SI 1999/2083.   [79] Reg. 10.   [80] s. 8.

Act 1977 lists a number of factors that are to be taken into account in deciding any such question.[81] These include the strength of the parties' respective bargaining positions, the practice of the trade or profession involved, and whether the customer was given the option of contracting on terms which did not seek to exclude liability.

The term 'standard form contract' is not defined in the Unfair Contract Terms Act 1977. In the Scottish case of *McCrone v Boots Farm Sales*,[82] it was held that a standard form contract existed where a party invariably sought to do business on terms which did not differ to any material extent. It was immaterial whether these were reduced to writing or were, at least in part, agreed orally. Such an approach has been upheld in subsequent cases, with the courts being willing to overlook minor variations where it can be shown that a party will generally do business only on the basis of a substantially identical set of terms and conditions.

The definition of standard form contracts in a software context was considered in the case of *Salvage Association v CAP Financial Services Ltd*.[83] At issue here was a contract for the computerisation of the plaintiff's accounting system. The project proved unsuccessful, and, after a number of broken completion dates, the plaintiff terminated its agreement with the defendant and sought damages. Much of the dispute centred on the applicability and enforceability of clauses limiting the defendant's liability in the event of breach of contract. In respect of the question of whether the clauses were to be classed as standard form contracts, Thayne Forbes J analysed the history of the contract, pointing to the fact that extensive negotiations had taken place between the parties prior to its conclusion. Although the terms of the agreement 'closely followed CAP's standard terms of contract', this fact was not to be taken to mean that the contract was one of a standard form. Six factors were identified as relevant to the determination:

(i) the degree to which the 'standard terms' are considered by the other party as part of the process of agreeing the terms of the contract;

(ii) the degree to which the 'standard terms' are imposed on the other party by the party putting them forward;

(iii) the relative bargaining power of the parties;

(iv) the degree to which the party putting forward the 'standard terms' is prepared to entertain negotiations with regard to the terms of the contract generally and the 'standard terms' in particular;

(v) the extent and nature of any agreed alterations to the 'standard terms' made as a result of the negotiations between the parties; and

(vi) the extent and duration of the negotiations.

Applying these criteria he concluded that:

> In this case SA had considered the various drafts of the contract that had been sent by CAP and had taken legal and other advice on all the proposed terms in order to decide what alterations it wished to make. To the extent that SA sought changes and additions to the draft terms, CAP largely agreed them. I am satisfied that the terms of the second contract were not imposed on SA by CAP, but were fully negotiable between parties of equal bargaining power and that CAP was prepared to engage in a meaningful process of negotiation with SA as to those terms. The process of negotiation between the parties took place over a considerable period of time.

---

[81] s. 11 for England and Wales, s. 24 for Scotland, and Sch. 2 applying throughout the United Kingdom.

[82] 1981 SLT 103.

[83] (9 July 1993, unreported), CA. The case is reported at first instance at [1995] FSR 654.

The contract was not, therefore, a standard form contract, although, as will be discussed, its terms were struck down on the basis that they constituted an unreasonable attempt to evade liability for negligence.

A different conclusion was reached in *St Albans District Council v ICL*.[84] Here, the Council published a call for tenders, negotiated—albeit fairly incompetently—with a number of potential suppliers, engaged in further negotiations with ICL, and concluded a contract, one clause of which stated that it was subject to ICL's standard terms and conditions. As was stated by Nourse LJ in the Court of Appeal:

> Scott Baker J [the judge at first instance] dealt with this question as one of fact, finding that the defendant's general conditions remained effectively untouched in the negotiations and that the plaintiffs accordingly dealt on the defendant's written standard terms for the purposes of s 3(1) (see [1995] FSR 686 at 706). I respectfully agree with him.

A similar decision was reached in *South West Water v ICL*.[85] Once again, the customer had initially argued that the agreement should be made on the basis of its own standard terms and conditions. The defendant countered by submitting a contract governing a previous agreement between the parties. This was subject to some negotiation, but it was agreed that the limitation clauses in the contract were taken from ICL's standard terms. Considering the nature of the agreement, Toulmin J made reference to the leading textbook, *Chitty on Contracts*. This stated that:

> Since in any event, no two contracts are likely to be completely identical, but will at least differ as to subject-matter and price, the question arises whether variations or omissions from or additions to standard terms thereby render them 'non-standard' and they do not whether all the terms become standard terms.[86]

Referring to the decision in *St Albans*,[87] it was held that the contract was a standard form contract.

In some respects, the conclusion may be seen as a surprising one. A water authority is a substantial party and the decision makes several references to the fact that discussions between the parties were extensive. Evidence from ICL concerning one meeting was to the effect that:

> It was a take it or leave it session. They [SWW] were very hard negotiators but we took the decision to proceed as it was too good a long term opportunity to walk away from.

Perhaps the most significant factor was the fact that the contract signed between the parties was silent on what was described as the 'very obvious circumstance' of what should happen in the event of a total failure to deliver a workable system. The judge concluded:

> The reason it was not covered is because the parties used a standard ICL contract which was only slightly adapted. Those standard ICL terms were not appropriate where substantial development work was required to adapt the basic system, as in this case.[88]

The requirement of reasonableness

In determining whether clauses limiting or excluding liability can be considered fair and reasonable, the Unfair Contract Terms Act 1977 provides initially that regard is to be had to 'the circumstances which were or ought reasonably to have been, known to or in

---

[84] [1996] 4 All ER 481.   [85] [1999] Masons CLR 400.
[86] J. Chitty, *Chitty on Contracts*, 27th edn (London, 1994), para. 14–056.
[87] *St Albans District Council v ICL* [1996] 4 All ER 481.
[88] *South West Water v ICL* [1999] Masons CLR 400.

the contemplation of the parties when the contract was made'.[89] It provides further that account is to be taken of:

(a) the resources which he could expect to be available to him for the purpose of meeting the liability should it arise; and

(b) how far it was open to him to cover himself by insurance.

Schedule 2 to the Act continues to provide a set of 'Guidelines' to be taken into account. These include:

- the strength of the parties' respective bargaining positions
- the general practice of a particular trade or profession
- whether the goods are made, processed, or adapted to the special order of the customer.

In the case of *Photo Production Ltd v Securicor Transport Ltd*, Lord Wilberforce stated with reference to the Unfair Contract Terms Act 1977:

> [I]n commercial matters generally, when the parties are not of unequal bargaining power, and when risks are normally borne by insurance, not only is the case for judicial intervention undemonstrated, but there is everything to be said, and this seems to have been Parliament's intention, for leaving the parties free to apportion the risks as they think fit and for respecting their decisions.[90]

In *Salvage Association v CAP Financial Services Ltd*,[91] it was accepted that the parties were of equal bargaining power. There had been genuine negotiations and the plaintiff had at all relevant times the realistic option of giving its business to another producer. A number of factors, however, operated to justify a finding that the limitation clause was unfair. First, reference was made to the discrepancy between the contractual limit of £25,000 and the defendant's general acceptance of liability up to £1 million. Additionally, whilst the losses claimed by the plaintiff were covered under an insurance policy taken out by the defendant, albeit one which was subject to a £500,000 excess, it was accepted by the court that the plaintiff would have been unable to obtain insurance cover against losses of the kind incurred at other than a prohibitive price.

The decision of the Court of Appeal in *St Albans District Council v ICL*[92] provides further evidence of a judicial willingness to scrutinise the terms of contracts entered into by large organisations. Following the introduction of the Community Charge legislation, the plaintiff, in common with all other local authorities, was under considerable pressure to introduce new computer systems capable of coping with the administrative demands of the new tax. After an initial call for tenders, the choice of supplier was effectively between the defendant and IBM. Assessing various elements of the competing bids, including the terms and conditions associated with each, the decision was made to accept the defendant's tender and Council officers were instructed to negotiate with ICL to secure the best possible deal.

The negotiations do not appear to have been conducted by the Council with great expertise. Following submission of a draft contract based upon a Council official's previous employment with London Transport, everything proceeded on the basis of ICL's standard terms and conditions (again, out of date in respect of the level of liability accepted). As the deadline for the introduction of the new tax approached, the Council was under some pressure to conclude the agreement. When concerns were raised concerning the limitation on liability clause, the defendant's response was to indicate that

---

[89] s. 11.   [90] [1980] AC 827 at 843.

[91] (9 July 1993, unreported), CA.   [92] [1996] 4 All ER 481.

unless the contract was concluded by the following Monday, there could be no guarantee that the system would be delivered in time for the introduction of the tax, a consequence which could have dire financial consequences for the authority. A letter from the defendant stated:

> With regard to ICL's contractual terms and conditions . . . our offer is based on these standard terms and conditions, and given the tight time-scale, I would advise you to make use of them.
>
> These standard ICL conditions are accepted by over 250 local authorities, and in no way detracts from the business partnerships.[93]

The plaintiff promptly signed the contract. Given these circumstances, it is not surprising that the court held that the contract was a standard form contract and that it did not satisfy the statutory criterion of reasonableness. In reaching this decision, the Court of Appeal approved the judgment of Scott Baker J at first instance, where he identified as determining factors, the points that:

(1) the parties were of unequal bargaining power;

(2) the defendants have not justified the figure of £100,000, which was small, both in relation to the potential risk and the actual loss;

(3) the defendants were insured; and

(4) the practical consequences.

> I make the following observations on the fourth point, which follows on in a sense from the third. On whom is it better that a loss of this size should fall, a local authority or an international computer company. The latter is well able to insure (and in this case was insured) and pass on the premium cost to the customers. If the loss is to fall the other way it will ultimately be borne by the local population either by increased taxation or reduced services. I do not think it unreasonable that he who stands to make the profit (ICL) should carry the risk.[94]

The decisions of the Court of Appeal in the cases of *St Albans District Council v ICL*[95] and *South West Water v ICL*[96] cast significant doubt on the effectiveness of contractual provisions whereby software suppliers sought to limit the extent of their liabilities in the event that software failed to operate in a proper manner. A further decision of the court in the case of *Watford Electronics Ltd v Sanderson CFL Ltd*[97] may signal a less interventionist policy on the part of the judiciary. Albeit of less precedential value, the decision of the High Court in *SAM Business Systems Ltd v Hedley & Co*,[98] discussed earlier, also provides useful guidance concerning the application of the statutory criteria.

In *Watford Electronics v Sanderson CFL Ltd*,[99] the supplier, Sanderson, undertook to provide an integrated software system to control all aspects of the customer's business. Unfortunately, the project was not completed to the satisfaction of the customer and legal proceedings were initiated seeking damages of some £5.5 million. At trial, the judge found that the supplier was in breach of its obligations to supply a system of reasonable quality. The supplier's conditions of contract limited its liability to the cost of any defective goods supplied. The bulk of the customer's claim related to losses of profit resulting from the

---

[93] *St Albans District Council v ICL* [1995] FSR 686 at 695.

[94] At 711.

[95] At 711.

[96] [1999] Masons CLR 400.

[97] [2001] EWCA Civ 317, [2001] 1 All ER (Comm) 696.

[98] [2002] EWHC 2733 (TCC), [2003] 1 All ER (Comm) 465.

[99] [2001] EWCA Civ 317, [2001] 1 All ER (Comm) 696.

failure of the system to operate in a satisfactory manner. The trial judge ruled that this clause was invalid under the provisions of the Unfair Contract Terms Act 1977, which provide that exclusion clauses found in standard form contracts will be valid only insofar as they can be considered fair and reasonable. The present clause, it was held, could not be so regarded.

The Court of Appeal took a different view. The customer, it was held, was an experienced and established business. There had been extensive negotiations between the parties. It was noted that the customer used a very similar form of exclusion clause in contracts with its own customers. The conclusion reached was that:

> Where experienced businessmen representing substantial companies of equal bargaining power negotiate an agreement, they may be taken to have had regard to the matters known to them. They should, in my view be taken to be the best judge of the commercial fairness of the agreement which they have made; including the fairness of each of the terms in that agreement. They should be taken to be the best judge on the question whether the terms of the agreement are reasonable.[100]

The exclusion clause was therefore upheld and the supplier's appeal was upheld.

The judgments in *Watford v Sanderson* do not refer to the decisions in *St Albans*[101] and *South West Water*[102] and the tone does differ markedly. It may be noted that especially in the *St Albans* case, negotiations between the parties appear to have been conducted in a rather ineffective manner. Owing to an error, indeed, the contract limited liability to a sum less than that which the supplier would normally have accepted. External factors also placed the customer under considerable pressure to conclude the agreement. It may be that in these circumstances, the present court would also have declared the exclusion clause to be unfair. *Watford v Sanderson* does indicate, however, that where it appears that genuine negotiations have taken place and where it is clear that the customer has freely determined to enter into a contract in awareness of the nature and significance of exclusion clauses, the courts will be slow to interfere.

A similar approach was taken by the High Court in the case of *SAM Business Systems Ltd v Hedley & Co*[103] discussed earlier. Here, the contract provided in part that the customer would have a period of thirty days following installation in which to test the software and report defects. It was only if defects continued for more than ninety days from the date of installation that the contract provided for the customer's right to initiate proceedings for rejection. This, effectively obtaining a refund of the purchase price, was stated to be the sole remedy available to the customer. The customer in the present case had suffered a significant loss of business and, whilst the computer system cost around £185,000, it sought damages of almost £800,000. The supplier sought to rely upon the contractual limitation provisions but the customer contended that these were not fair and reasonable.

Given that the terms were part of the supplier's written terms of business there was little doubt that the Unfair Contract Terms Act 1977 should apply. The judgment gives extensive and helpful consideration to the extent to which the various criteria identified as components of the requirement of reasonableness may be relevant in cases such as the present. A key factor to be taken into account was whether it would have been feasible for the customer to have obtained similar software without the accompaniment of exclusion clauses. The evidence before the court was to the effect that '[t]he only way to get the software they needed was by contracting on terms that made rigorous exclusions of liability because

---

[100] At [55]–[56].
[101] *St Albans District Council v ICL* [1995] FSR 686 at 695.
[102] *South West Water v ICL* [1999] Masons CLR 400.
[103] [2002] EWHC 2733 (TCC), [2003] 1 All ER (Comm) 465.

those were the terms on which all suppliers were contracting'.[104] The fact that similar terms were commonplace in the field is a relevant factor in determining issues of reasonableness.

Ultimately, considering the contract as a whole, the judge concluded that its terms were fair and reasonable. The customer was buying under constraints of time as the year 2000 was fast approaching and its existing system was not capable of coping with the change to the third millennium as required by its sector regulator, the Financial Services Authority. To a considerable extent, it was accepted, the customer was the cause of its own misfortunes. Whilst an attempt totally to exclude liability would have been considered unreasonable, in the circumstances of the case, the judge concluded:

> Not forgetting my duty to look at each term individually, it is important to look at each in relation to the whole contract. Before contract, SAM says, 'We think our system is marvellous and will do everything you need, but if you are not satisfied you can ask for your money back' . . . Having regard to the enormous potential liabilities, that seems to me to be a reasonable arrangement in the circumstances existing between the two parties.[105]

The end result of the litigation might be considered as a draw. The supplier was not able to recover additional costs incurred in seeking to place the software into a satisfactory state and the customer was similarly unsuccessful in securing reimbursement of losses caused through the failure of the software to operate in a satisfactory manner.

Towards fair dealing obligations in contractual relationships?

The doctrine of *caveat emptor* has historically driven much of English commercial law. It epitomises the pragmatic, unsentimental way in which the common law has approached commercial relationships. If parties do not take steps to protect their own interests, they should not look to the law to do their job for them.

To an extent and as discussed above, the rigours of the doctrine have been softened by the development of the notion of implied terms. In contracts for the sale of goods, for example, terms of conformity with description, fitness for purpose, and satisfactory quality will be implied into contracts. An implied term can generally be excluded by a contrary specific provision but this is expressly prohibited in the case of consumer contracts and with the emergence of unfair contract terms legislation can also be difficult to achieve in commercial contracts.

In spite of these developments, a conceptual difference exists between what has been described as 'continental (civil law) paternalism and Anglo-Saxon (common law) individualism'. Whilst civil law systems—and the hybrid system that is Scots law—impose obligations of fair dealing on contracting parties, there has been resistance to this in England. The decision of the High Court in the case of *Yam Seng Pte Ltd v International Trade Corp Ltd*[106] suggests that times and views may be changing.

The case centred on a contract for the supply and distribution of male toiletry products to be manufactured by the defendant and displaying the joint brand names of Nike and Manchester United Football Club. The intention was that the claimant would distribute these for sale in duty free outlets in airports in the Middle and Far East. Provision was also made in the contract for the claimant to distribute the products in the domestic Chinese market.

Although the contract was between two companies, both were in effect the vehicles of individuals and the relationship between these people was critical. As is often the case with human relationships matters began well—including invitations to attend Manchester United football games—but ended in acrimony. The key problem was that scheduled

---

[104] At [70].   [105] At [71]–[72].   [106] [2013] EWHC 111 (QB).

delivery dates for supplies of the products were missed. The claimant, who had been working with duty free airport outlets for many years claimed that he had expended effort and utilised goodwill to ensure that space was made available to feature the goods only to find that no stocks were available. At a different level, the claimant discovered (in part through being presumably inadvertently copied into an email sent to the defendant) that the products were available for sale at mainland stores in Singapore at prices lower than had been agreed for airport sales—in spite of what were felt to be clear undertakings to the contrary from the defendant. This prompted a response:

> I am led to believe that your email of January this year, where you had confirmed the price of $65 (the minimum price to be charged on the mainland) to me, was deliberately misinforming me, and I was not told the truth.[107]

After around a year of increasingly ill-tempered email correspondence between the parties the claimant indicated that it considered that the contract had been terminated by reason of the defendant's breach and sought substantial damages. Where, however, was the breach? A variety of grounds were advanced, but of relevance to the present discussion, the most interesting was the argument that there was an implied obligation in the contract that the parties would act in good faith towards each other. In this respect the case broke new ground. As the judge noted:

> The subject of whether English law does or should recognise a general duty to perform contracts in good faith is one on which a large body of academic literature exists. However, I not am aware of any decision of an English court, and none was cited to me, in which the question has been considered in any depth.[108]

In general, it was held, parties to a contract were not obliged to point out facts that could be to their disadvantage. A person selling a used car is not obliged to point out cosmetic defects on the vehicle. Surveying the situation in a range of civil law and indeed other common law systems such as Australia and Canada the judge recognised that:

> In refusing, however, if indeed it does refuse, to recognise any such general obligation of good faith, this jurisdiction would appear to be swimming against the tide.

The key phrase in the above passage is 'if indeed it does refuse' and a detailed analysis was conducted with particular emphasis given to the role of implied terms.

Implied terms are a perhaps unusual feature of English law. In some instances they are mandated by statute. In the motor car example given above, sale of goods legislation incorporates (implies) into any contract of sale the requirement that goods should be of satisfactory quality and reasonably fit for purpose. In more general cases, the courts are willing to imply a term when it is so obvious that no reasonable parties would feel it necessary to make specific provision for it. More relevant to the present case, a term may be implied when it is necessary to give business efficacy to the contract and does not conflict with any express contractual term. A simple example (which might also fall under the category of obviousness) might see a contract made between two parties resident in England which specifies that a payment of '50 pounds' is to be made. It would certainly be implied that this related to British pounds rather than Egyptian pounds or that of any other country using this name for their currency.

Considering whether an implied term of good faith was necessary in the case of this contract to ensure business efficacy, the court examined a range of case law and noted that:

> The modern case law on the construction of contracts has emphasised that contracts, like all human communications, are made against a background of unstated shared understandings which inform their meaning.[109]

---

[107] para. 74.   [108] para. 120.   [109] para. 133.

In considering what might constitute the relevant background, it was ruled that this would include

> not only matters of fact known to the parties but also shared values and norms of behaviour. Some of these are norms that command general social acceptance; others may be specific to a particular trade or commercial activity; others may be more specific still, arising from features of the particular contractual relationship. Many such norms are naturally taken for granted by the parties when making any contract without being spelt out in the document recording their agreement.[110]

Indeed, it was suggested, the act of seeking to incorporate a contractual provision relating to honesty, might have the undesirable effect of damaging trust between the parties, 'the requirement that parties will behave honestly is so obvious that it goes without saying. Such a requirement is also necessary to give business efficacy to commercial transactions.'[111] The judge continued:

> While it seems unlikely that any duty to disclose information in performance of the contract would be implied where the contract involves a simple exchange, many contracts do not fit this model and involve a longer term relationship between the parties which they make a substantial commitment. Such 'relational' contracts, as they are sometimes called, may require a high degree of communication, cooperation and predictable performance based on mutual trust and confidence and involve expectations of loyalty which are not legislated for in the express terms of the contract but are implicit in the parties' understanding and necessary to give business efficacy to the arrangements.[112]

After analysing and rejecting a variety of reasons why the law might reject the application of a doctrine of good faith, it was concluded that:

> In the light of these points, I respectfully suggest that the traditional English hostility towards a doctrine of good faith in the performance of contracts, to the extent that it still persists, is misplaced.[113]

Applying this principle to the present case it was held that the defendant had been in breach of contract and was liable to compensate the claimant for losses caused by this.

It is perhaps important not to read too much into a single judgment by a trial judge. The fact, however, that it has not been appealed does lend some further weight to its findings. The scope for applying an implied term of good faith is also limited. It will not apply to a single transaction such as a contract for the sale of a motor car. Here, it would seem that the application of the general implied terms relating to quality (and to title and description) will be quite adequate. The value of the implied term will lie in more complex contracts that require to be performed over a considerable period of time. Software development and/or maintenance contracts might well fall into this category. It would be unusually gifted lawyers who could draft such contracts in terms that would unequivocally cover any eventuality that might arise. Assuming that the present decision is followed and even developed in future cases, it could assist in closing what has often proved to be a significant lacuna in English law.

The Consumer Rights Act 2015

Increasingly over the past decades, the law has come to draw a distinction between sales between two parties acting in the course of their business and consumer transactions where the seller is acting in the course of business and the consumer is not. In the former case,

---

[110] para. 134.   [111] para. 137.   [112] para. 142.   [113] para. 153.

although statutory warranties relating to quality are provided for, the parties, as will be discussed below, have considerable freedom to frame the terms of their own contract and to agree to waive warranties that might otherwise arise. In respect of consumer contracts, exclusion of warranties is prohibited but in this case there can be dispute what the statutory warranties mean in practice, for what length of time they might apply and what remedies may be available at the request of either the customer or the supplier.

The adoption of the Consumer Rights Act 2015—which applies only to consumer contracts may prompt an increase in litigation in respect of standard software although these are likely to be resolved at a low level of the judicial hierarchy.

Background to the Consumer Rights Act 2015

The Consumer Rights Act 2015 is one of the first measures adopted under new UK legislative processes that allow for a measure to be scrutinised over two Parliamentary sessions as opposed to the more traditional single session (normally equivalent to around a calendar year). Apart from its rather lengthy Parliamentary process, the Act is the product of fairly extensive consultative exercises in the United Kingdom and is also heavily influenced by European legislation. Domestically, the Act was adopted following a Consultation Paper and Report published by the Law Commissions[114] and specifically in the current context an extensive report commissioned by the Department for Business, Innovation and Skills that considered the uncertain state of the current law relating to digital products and made recommendations for reform.[115] The 2015 legislation amends a number of existing UK consumer protection statutes such as the Sale of Goods Act 1979, the Supply of Goods and Services Act 1982, and the Unfair Contract Terms Act 1977 to restrict their application to business contracts. It also repeals a number of items of secondary legislation, bringing many of their provisions within its own scope. The Act also implements a raft of European consumer protection measures. Given the length of time afforded to the measure it is rather disappointing that it adopts quite a conservative approach, albeit with some attempt to include digital technologies in the legislation. We can perhaps also finally put to rest the long and rather sterile debate about whether software and other digital items should be classed as goods or as a form of services. We are now to talk about digital products and the criteria applicable to these are to be applied.

The 2015 Act is the first UK statute that makes specific reference to digital products—or digital content—although the definition of this is rather broad with section 2, mirroring the provisions of the Consumer Rights Directive,[116] defining the concept as relating to 'data which are produced and supplied in digital form'. This is rather akin to defining a book as a product that is supplied on paper. Accurate, but perhaps not terribly helpful in determining the qualitative standards that must be met. The Explanatory Notes[117] accompanying the Act state that:

> Digital content may be supplied on a tangible medium (in which case special rules apply) for example a DVD or software, on a computer or not, for example an e-book or music download. The creation of a category of digital content in this Act does not affect the treatment of digital content in any other legislation.

Copyright law would constitute a prime example of the situation referred to in the final sentence quoted above.

[114] The Law Commission No. 292/The Scottish Law Commission No. 199, 2005.
[115] Consumer rights in digital products, BIS, 2010. Available from <https://www.gov.uk/government/uploads/system/uploads/attachment_data/file/31837/10–1125-consumer-rights-in-digital-products.pdf>.
[116] Directive 2011/83/EC.
[117] <http://www.legislation.gov.uk/ukpga/2015/15/notes>.

In terms of qualitative requirements, a key provision is found in section 34 of the Act. This provides that:

> Every contract to supply digital content is to be treated as including a term that the quality of the digital content is satisfactory.
>
> The quality of digital content is satisfactory if it meets the standard that a reasonable person would consider satisfactory, taking account of—
>
> (a) any description of the digital content,
>
> (b) the price mentioned in section 33(1) or (2)(b) (if relevant), and
>
> (c) all the other relevant circumstances (see subsection (5)).
>
> The quality of digital content includes its state and condition; and the following aspects (among others) are in appropriate cases aspects of the quality of digital content—
>
> (a) fitness for all the purposes for which digital content of that kind is usually supplied;
>
> (b) freedom from minor defects;
>
> (c) safety;
>
> (d) durability.
>
> The term mentioned in subsection (1) does not cover anything which makes the quality of the digital content unsatisfactory—
>
> (a) which is specifically drawn to the consumer's attention before the contract is made,
>
> (b) where the consumer examines the digital content before the contract is made, which that examination ought to reveal, or
>
> (c) where the consumer examines a trial version before the contract is made, which would have been apparent on a reasonable examination of the trial version.
>
> The relevant circumstances mentioned in subsection (2)(c) include any public statement about the specific characteristics of the digital content made by the trader, the producer or any representative of the trader or the producer.

The Act states further that these warranties may not be excluded by the terms of any contract between the supplier and the consumer.[118]

The concept of satisfactory quality has been at the core of UK law since the Sale of Goods Act 1979 substituted it for the venerable but rather vague notion of 'merchantable quality' that had previously featured in the law. There is perhaps a good deal of room for argument concerning the scope of a number of these concepts, especially when trying to apply them within a digital context. We might reasonably expect less of free software than products that are charged for, but the concept of what constitutes free software is a nebulous one and one that causes some controversy, especially in the mobile context where many 'free' apps make provision for 'in app' purchases. It is not always clear what software costs.[119] Although Guidelines have been published by the United Kingdom's consumer protection authorities,[120] these are somewhat limited in their scope.

Again, a number of terms in the provision have limited application, especially within the software context. It is impossible to conceive how a consumer might inspect digital products. Apart from a lack of opportunity or expertise, products are delivered in the form of object code which does not reveal the underlying source code. How can an invisible

---

[118] s. 47.

[119] See <http://www.macworld.co.uk/feature/iosapps/7-most-expensive-in-app-purchases-3525619/>.

[120] See <http://webarchive.nationalarchives.gov.uk/20140402142426/>, <http://www.oft.gov.uk/OFTwork/consumer-enforcement/consumer-enforcement-current/childrens-online-games/>.

component be inspected? It is also common practice for a consumer to be allowed a free trial of software for a limited period of time. The question what limitations should have been discovered could be an interesting one, especially in the context where a trial copy intentionally has limited functionality.

In keeping with the traditional approach towards warranties, section 35 goes on to require that digital content shall be fit for any particular person for which it is supplied and by section 36, to comply with any specific description that might be attached to it. Again these are features historically found in the law of sale of goods. Their application in a digital product context may be more limited but do perhaps highlight an issue that can arise with software in particular. Most products are intended for limited purposes that should be apparent to even an unskilled customer. A customer wanting to purchase a hammer to put a picture nail into a wall would be unlikely to buy a sledge hammer—and very unlikely to have any legal redress in respect of damage to the wall that might result. Software is often a more versatile tool and can be used for a variety of purposes[121] that pose a wide range of physical and financial risks.

Further issues relate to the remedies that may be available in the event that a digital product does not perform in a satisfactory manner. The legislation seeks to apply the same principles as those applicable to other products. This is not always an easy task. With most products there can be an issue when defects arose. Were they present at the time of sale or were they introduced, possibly as the result of consumer misuse, subsequently? We expect physical products to deteriorate over time but the same cannot be said of digital products—except in respect of the storage medium in which they are held.

Questions of time

Traditionally, the consumer's right has been limited to reject the product within a reasonable time after its acquisition. Effectively this amounts to returning the product and receiving a refund of the purchase price. One problem that is not addressed in the Act is how a digital product might be returned to the supplier, especially when it is supplied online? The 2015 Act places emphasis on remedies in rather different directions although there do remain questions as to how appropriate these may be within a digital context.

As a starting point there is the statutory assumption that if a defect appears in a product within six months of its acquisition, the defect is presumed to have been present at that time.[122] The onus of proving otherwise lies with the supplier. This is a very consumer friendly provision in respect of tangible products but does sit rather uneasily with the reality of digital products. A good number of potential problem areas might be identified.

In the early days of the PC age, a consumer might buy a disk containing a copy of software and that would effectively mark the conclusion of the contract. Especially in the online context, this is no longer the case and it is an unusual digital product that is not subject to frequent—and perhaps excessively obtrusive—updates. In an oft quoted comment from a leading case, it was stated that software is not a

> commodity which is delivered once, only once, and once and for all, but one which will necessarily be accompanied by a degree of testing and modification.[123]

It may, of course be the case that an update will introduce new defects into a digital product. This is a problem that is becoming increasingly difficult as updates seek to deal with

[121] See, eg, <http://www.theatlantic.com/technology/archive/2014/10/behold-the-awesome-power-of-the-spreadsheet/381604/> and also <http://www.eusprig.org/horror-stories.htm>.
[122] See s. 42(9).
[123] *Saphena Computing v Allied Collection Agencies Ltd* [1995] FSR 616 at 652.

a wide range of versions of products. A recent problem concerned an update that Apple made available for devices (iPhones and iPads) that had the effect of locking some users of older iPhones out of their devices.[124] Given the close linkage between Apple hardware and software (and indeed the degree of control that Apple exerts over third-party applications made available in its App Store) the example is perhaps an unusual one, but does illustrate the uncertainties that might arise in the field. When might the six-month period referred to above start and terminate? There is a very plausible argument that a consumer purchasing a device such as an iPhone will never receive a definitive copy of the associated software. A further question relates to the scenario—as appears to have happened in this case— where hardware/software has functioned in a satisfactory manner until disrupted by an update to the software. Can a digital product be considered satisfactory in the state in which it is initially supplied but subsequently be classed as unsatisfactory due to deficiencies in the upgrades supplied to consumers? The Consumer Rights Act provides in section 40 that:

> Where under a contract a trader supplies digital content to a consumer subject to the right of the trader or a third party to modify the digital content, the following provisions apply in relation to the digital content as modified as they apply in relation to the digital content as supplied under the contract—
>
> (a) section 34 (quality);
>
> (b) section 35 (fitness for a particular purpose);
>
> (c) section 36 (description).
>
> Subsection (1)(c) does not prevent the trader from improving the features of, or adding new features to, the digital content, as long as—
>
> (a) the digital content continues to match the description of it given by the trader to the consumer, and
>
> (b) the digital content continues to conform to the information provided by the trader as mentioned in subsection (3) of section 36, subject to any change to that information that has been agreed in accordance with subsection (4) of that section.
>
> A claim on the grounds that digital content does not conform to a term described in any of the sections listed in subsection (1) as applied by that subsection is to be treated as arising at the time when the digital content was supplied under the contract and not the time when it is modified.

Legislation cannot ever be completely precise, but this provision is extremely vague and its meaning will not become clearer unless and until we have a good number of court decisions. It illustrates perhaps the difficulty in seeking to apply traditional (analogue) legal concepts in a digital context. The intention is good, but as any user will be aware, upgrades comprise an amalgam of bug fixes, 'improvements', and new features. It does appear from the last paragraph above that the supplier is to be held liable for breach of the warranties of satisfactory quality, fitness for purpose, or conformity with description in respect of the digital product as originally supplied. There would seem to be little legal incentive to supply upgrades. This provision has, however, to be read in conjunction with sections 42 to 44 which lay down the remedies that might be available in the event that a digital product is not of the required quality.

Under previous consumer law, the consumer had no right to require that a supplier seek to repair an item, although a refusal to do so would be a significant factor to be taken into account by a court in determining whether a demand to reject goods and receive a

---

[124] See <http://www.bbc.co.uk/news/technology-35898788>.

refund of the purchase price was reasonable. This served to create difficult situations. If the consumer acted hastily in seeking to return goods and receive a refund, the claim might fail on the ground that the supplier had not been given the opportunity to repair the defect. If the consumer allowed the supplier too long or too many attempts to cure faults, an attempt to reject good might be declared invalid on the ground of excessive delay. The Consumer Rights Act seeks to establish a different set of priorities providing in section 42 that:

> If the digital content does not conform to the contract, the consumer's rights (and the provisions about them and when they are available) are—
>
> (a) the right to repair or replacement . . .;
>
> (b) the right to a price reduction (up to a full refund).

Damages may also be sought in respect of any additional losses caused through the improper operation of the product and section 42 specifies a number of other specific remedies that may be sought and awarded at the discretion of the court.

The remedy of replacement will perhaps be of most relevance in the situation where a digital product is supplied in or on some tangible device and where that device is damaged in some way—a DVD might have a scratch that prevents the media it holds from playing properly.

The right to require repair is also likely to apply where damage is restricted to some tangible item. Reference has been made above to the common practice whereby suppliers will issue upgrades to software. The Act does not impose any requirement on consumers to ensure that they keep software up to date and, again as stated above, questions relating to the compliance with statutory standards of digital products are to be determined by reference to its condition at the time it was supplied. It is for the consumer to determine whether to require repair or replacement and the supplier must accede to such a request unless this is either impossible or would involve disproportionate cost. An example of the former situation would be where the supplier acts as an intermediary between the original creator of the digital product and the consumer—a retail outlet selling proprietary computer games would be an example—and where modification to the content would infringe the copyright of the original developer. Issues of disproportionate cost may arise where a consumer has specific requirements that a digital product does not satisfy. If the product—and almost all products supplied to consumers will fall into this category—is supplied to large numbers of other consumers, repairing (modifying) for a single consumer is unlikely to be a feasible option. The Act provides here that:

> Either of those remedies is disproportionate compared to the other if it imposes costs on the trader which, compared to those imposed by the other, are unreasonable, taking into account—
>
> (a) the value which the digital content would have if it conformed to the contract,
>
> (b) the significance of the lack of conformity, and
>
> (c) whether the other remedy could be effected without significant inconvenience to the consumer.

> Any question as to what is a reasonable time or significant inconvenience is to be determined taking account of—
>
> (a) the nature of the digital content, and
>
> (b) the purpose for which the digital content was obtained or accessed.[125]

---

[125] s. 43(4).

As is the case with many of the elements of the Act, whilst the decision to bring digital products into the mainstream of the law is to be welcomed, traditional models and remedies are not always ideally suited for the digital era and this provision raises more questions than answers. In most instances it would seem that the remedy of seeking a refund of the purchase price would be the appropriate remedy although, as mentioned earlier, the determination whether a digital product has been returned might be a difficult one.

Further questions may arise in the situation where the failure of one component may cause damage to other elements of a consumer's products. A simple example might see virus detection software failing to identify a virus that continues to infect and damage digital content on the consumer's computer. The Act states in section 46 that a claim for compensation will be appropriate in the event that:

(a) a trader supplies digital content to a consumer under a contract,

(b) the digital content causes damage to a device or to other digital content,

(c) the device or digital content that is damaged belongs to the consumer, and

(d) the damage is of a kind that would not have occurred if the trader had exercised reasonable care and skill.

This is a rather strange provision. In the example that was given above of a virus or piece of malware that damages data on a computer or prevents the user from accessing it, there will invariably be the question of who owns the data? If software should be infected or damaged we have to keep in mind that consumers do not buy software but acquire merely a licence to use it with ownership remaining with the original developer. If a virus overcomes a detection program and attacks a proprietary program on a computer, it is difficult to see that the consumer would have any remedy under this provision.

Exclusion of liability

In line with the general provisions of consumer protection law, strict limits apply concerning the extent to which the rights provided under the Act can be restricted or excluded. Section 47 of the Act provides that:

A term of a contract to supply digital content is not binding on the consumer to the extent that it would exclude or restrict the trader's liability arising under any of these provisions—

(a) section 34 (digital content to be of satisfactory quality),

(b) section 35 (digital content to be fit for particular purpose),

(c) section 36 (digital content to be as described),

(d) section 37 (other pre-contract information included in contract), or

(e) section 41 (trader's right to supply digital content).

(2) That also means that a term of a contract to supply digital content is not binding on the consumer to the extent that it would—

(a) exclude or restrict a right or remedy in respect of a liability under a provision listed in subsection (1),

(b) make such a right or remedy or its enforcement subject to a restrictive or onerous condition,

(c) allow a trader to put a person at a disadvantage as a result of pursuing such a right or remedy, or

(d) exclude or restrict rules of evidence or procedure.

It will be interesting to see how these provisions work in practice. The Consumer Rights Act is based closely upon provisions of European law. It is to be commended for its attempt to make specific provision for the increasingly important digital sector. That said, it is not clear how well traditional legal concepts fit into a digital environment. Software does not age and deteriorate physically in the manner that an object such as a motor car does. Equally, however, the pace of change in the sector is such that a product that represented the state of the art in 2016 might well be functionally obsolete in 2018. The seemingly ever increasing frequency of software updates will also make the process of determining issues of satisfactory quality a difficult one. Finally, as referred to above, issues of ownership are much more complex in respect of digital than physical products. This is, of course, an issue that has implications far beyond the concept of software quality.

Conclusions

In any situation where finances are involved, litigation is never too far removed. It is perhaps surprising that there has been so little litigation in the software field. Those cases we have had do illustrate some of the issues that arise in the field. It can be difficult, if not impossible, to replicate the situations that caused faults to materialise.

Some long standing issues are perhaps now resolved. Although only at the level of a High Court ruling, the case of *The Software Incubator Ltd v Computer Associates UK Ltd*[126] makes extensive reference to the status of software:

> In common parlance, and without wishing to state the obvious, I believe that as a piece of sophisticated, commercial non-bespoke software, it would be regarded, at the very least as a 'product'. It would not be regarded, nor is it, a 'service'. Like other pieces of software, it is 'commodified' i.e. it is capable of transfer and commercial exploitation. Moreover, so far as 'tangibility' is concerned, while software itself is intangible and its method of delivery may be electronic, it can only operate in a tangible environment i.e. (a) being loaded onto a hard disk or server or some other permanent storage system, somewhere, and (b) when it runs, it will be run on a computer, tablet, reader mobile phone (depending on the software) and so on. In that sense it is akin to digital music. As Professor Clark of University College Dublin put it in an article called 'The Legal Status of Software' in March 2016, 'Digital content . . . possesses a functional equivalence to goods.'

This does seem to be undeniably correct, although as indicated above, the near universal practice of updating software on a regular (perhaps too regular) basis does mark a point of divergence from more traditional products that are supplied on a single occasion.

---

[126] [2016] EWHC 1587 (QB).

Index